FIRST TRILOGY

SHADER

AGAINST THE UNWEAVING

SHADER

FIRST TRILOGY
AGAINST THE UNWEAVING
D.P. PRIOR

ISBN-13: 978-1497413832

ISBN-10: 1497413834

D.P. PRIOR

"Prior has a talent
for characterization"
(Readers Favorite)

BOOK ONE

SHADER

SWORD OF THE ARCHON

SHADER

BOOK ONE
SWORD OF THE ARCHON
D.P. PRIOR

Fourth Edition, 2013

ACKNOWLEDGEMENTS

I'D LIKE TO thank my editor, Harry Dewulf for the excellent comments about language and his attention to the minutiae.

Paula Kautt has been invaluable for her suggestions, demanding clarification and pointing out inconsistencies, and also for proofreading the story.

I'm extremely grateful to Valmore Daniels for a crucial re-edit after the text was changed to US English, and for formatting, and cover design.

Theo Prior, as always, has been my sounding board and has listened patiently to each successive revision read aloud. He also provided the inspiration for a number of new characters and plot developments on those long walks to the comic store in Naperville. If that's not enough, he also produced the map of Sahul—which is no mean feat at nine years of age.

Thanks are also due to Mike Nash for the iconic image of Shader on the cover, and for the map of *The Nousian Theocracy*.

Finally thanks must go to the people who read my stuff and take the time to feedback: John Jarrold, for his comments on the original story, Tony Prior, Ian Prior, David Dalglish, C.S. Marks, Moses Siregar III, Ray Nicholson, Dallas Dredske, and M.R. Mathias.

Norga

Sarmatia

Verusia

Britannia

Gallia Graecia

Latia

Quilonia

Ashanta

Numosia

Make

The Anglish Isles

Sahul

Rujala

The Nousian

According to the terms of Aeternam A

The Great West
Nazca
evar
New Ithaka
Theocracy
greement: Year of the Reckoning 24
W
E
S

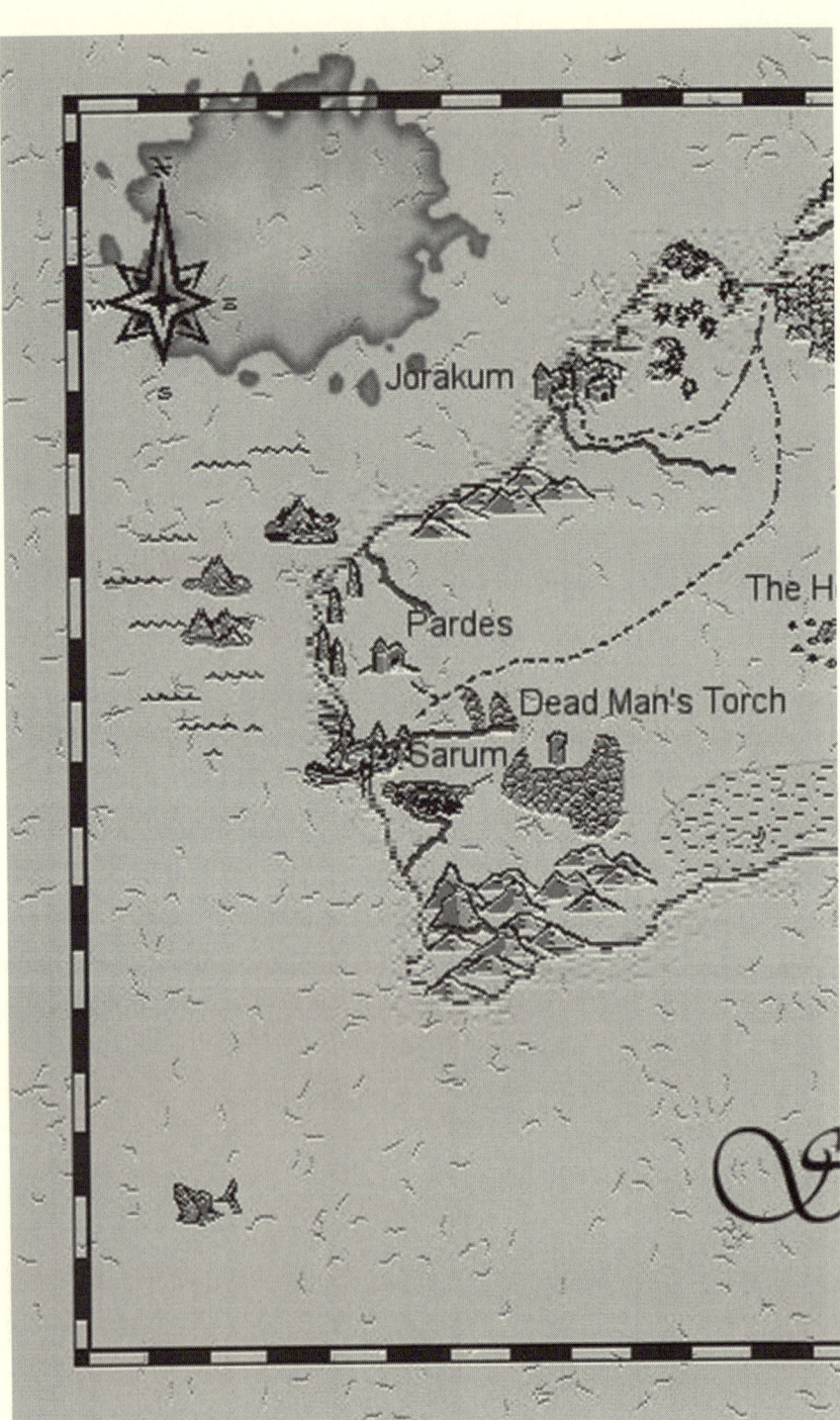

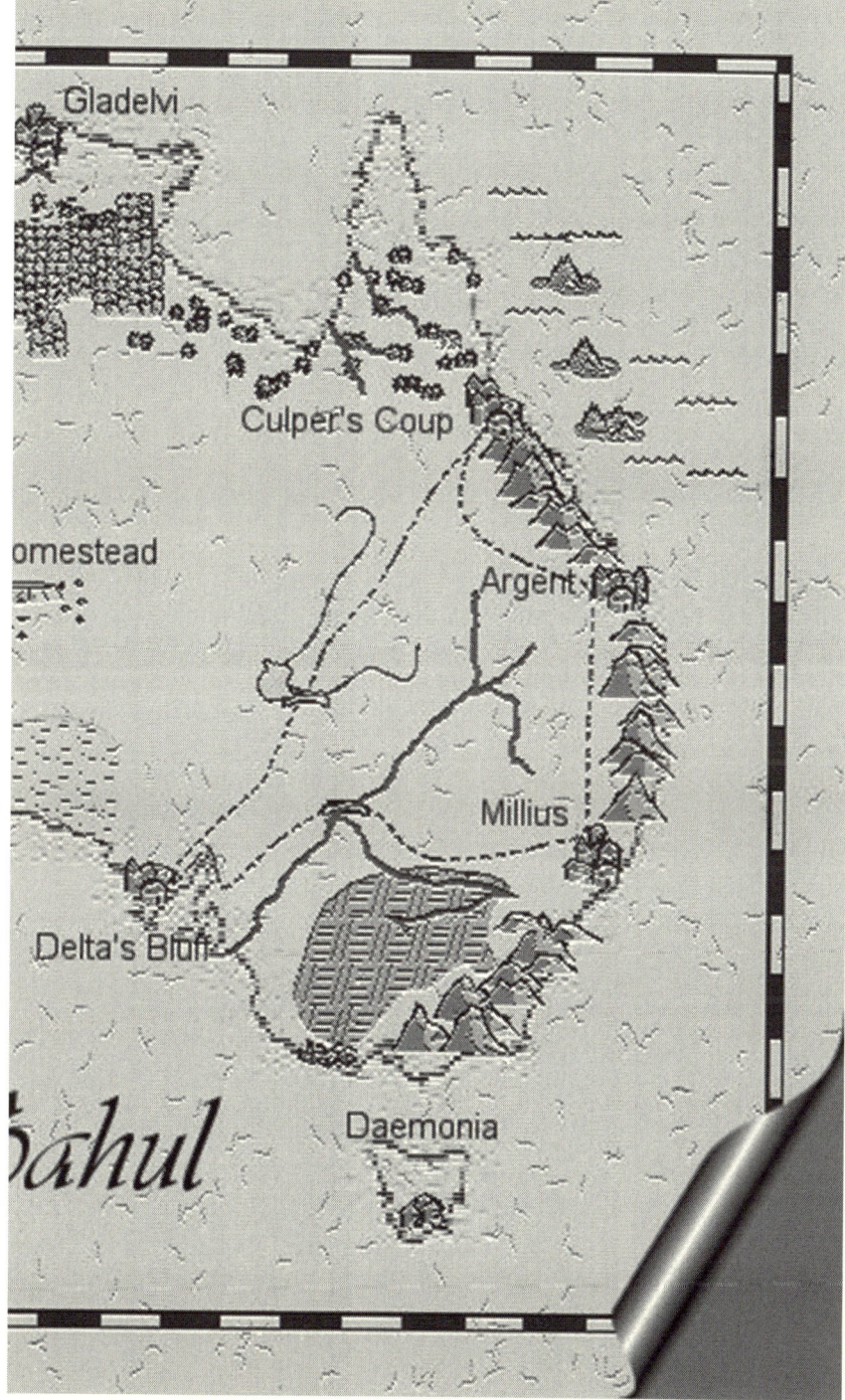

THE KNIGHT

City of Aeterna, Latia

Year of the Reckoning: 908

The crowd jeered. All the way around the Colosseum, people stood from their bleachers, turning their thumbs down and booing. You'd have thought it was an Ancient-world mob, baying for the death of a gladiator. For a moment, Deacon Shader thought it was aimed at him. He'd only just stepped into the arena; only just drawn his sword. But as he tilted his hat to get the sun out of his eyes, he saw just what they were jeering at. Or rather who.

Sonas the Strangler, they called him, on account of his shovel-sized hands. Word was, he wasn't so bad when you got to know him, but on the battlefield, he was an axe-wielding demon. It was an odd choice of weapon for an Elect knight, and Sonas was the only man not to bring a sword to the tournament. Made you wonder what he aimed to do if he won; if he'd have any use for the prize: the mythical Sword of the Archon.

Sonas raised his axe in one hand, and gave the crowd the finger with the other. The jeering went up a notch, and it went up again when Sonas jabbed the same finger across the arena at Shader, then drew it across his throat.

"Great," Shader muttered under his breath. The first round, and he had to come up against the Strangler.

But just the admission of the challenge settled his nerves. Same as on the field, calm descended the moment a threat presented itself. The sword in his hand seemed suddenly lighter, and he stepped across the arena on the balls of his feet.

Sonas trudged rather than stepped. Lumbered like an ox. But there was no denying his menace. He must have been more than seven foot tall, bull-necked, and with a mass of knotted muscle. Whereas Shader had kept his long coat on, in spite of the heat, Sonas was stripped to the waist. He looked more like a barbarian than a knight of the Templum, and the chipped and dark-mottled blade of his battle axe did nothing to shatter the illusion.

A thousand men, they say he'd killed. In Verusia, he'd been hailed a hero for making a stand against a horde of undead. But none of that mattered to Shader. He'd won honors in Verusia, too. He'd led the Seventh Horse on the decisive cavalry charge that had broken the Verusian line and won the day for the Templum.

Halfway to the center, and Sonas began to jog. A dozen more feet, and he was running. Half a dozen more, and it was a full-on charge.

Shader took a wide stance, twirled his blade once, sucked in a breath.

Sonas roared as his axe came up. A gasp ran through the crowd.

Shader darted under the axe's arc and scored a line of red across the giant's chest.

On the battlefield, Sonas would have been dead. In the arena, he was supposed to have yielded, but when he swore and made a scything riposte, Shader had the feeling the rules no longer mattered.

Air whistled past Shader's head, and the axe missed him by a hair's breadth. His hat fell to the ground.

He flicked a look at the black-robed Exempti watching from the clerical enclosure; glimpsed the white robe of the Ipsissimus, supreme ruler of the Templum, in among them. Surely one of them would say something, call for the fight to be stopped.

Sonas swung again, but Shader swayed out of the way. He skipped back, circled to the right, and forced himself to focus. Rules or no rules, he'd be a bloody spatter on the ground if that axe caught him napping. If it was a real fight the giant wanted, then so be it.

Sonas set his feet square, tracked Shader's movements with his piggy eyes. His face was more scar than skin; his forehead a granite slab sticking out from the tangle of his wild hair. No one could have looked less like an Elect knight. If he'd been under Shader's command in the Seventh Horse…

Before he could finish the thought, he realized just how absurd the idea was. Sonas in the Seventh Horse. There wasn't a horse big enough to hold his weight.

Say one thing for the Strangler, though: he wasn't as stupid as he looked. Rather than lunging in for a third hack, he stood his ground, waiting for Shader to make a move.

This time, when the crowd jeered, Shader knew it was for him. He'd been thrown at first by the ferocity of the giant's attacks. He hadn't expected more than a few thrusts and parries of a sword, a display of skill and speed, and the yielding of his opponent. Because he knew they would yield. He'd been preparing for this tournament since a boy, and there was no way he was going to lose.

He aimed a thrust at Sonas's midriff, but as the axe came down to block, turned his wrist and sliced toward the throat. Sonas stumbled out of the way, but something entered his eyes. Shader had seen the same thing a hundred times before: the bewilderment that he could move so swiftly; the realization that he couldn't be beaten.

Sonas responded with rage. He kicked sand in Shader's eyes and thundered in with an elbow. As Shader backed out of the way, blinking to clear his vision, he felt rather than heard the axe come down. He threw himself to one side, rolled and came up with his sword held out. The axe head bit into the ground and stuck there. Sonas swore, and swung a haymaker. Shader blocked with the flat of his blade, but a hook came in from the other side, struck his temple and sent him reeling to the deck. Sonas's boot came down on his sword hand, forced him to release the hilt.

Shader saw double, but on instinct, kicked out, hit something, and heard it crack. Sonas hopped back swearing. Shader rose, swaying, and reached down for his sword. Dizziness swamped him, and he staggered and almost fell.

Sonas yanked his axe free from the ground and fixed him with a glare.

"No more messing," the giant said, finding Shader with that finger again. "Dead meat." He tried to take a step, but his leg buckled, and he went down on one knee.

Shader shook his head to clear it; backed away until he could see properly. It was some punch Sonas had caught him with. His guts came up into his throat. He fought down the urge to vomit.

Sonas pushed himself up on his axe. He used it as a crutch to half-lurch, half-hop toward Shader. There were two of him, until Shader squinted, and the images merged into one.

Sonas teetered as he swung, and Shader stepped around him, pressed the tip of his sword to the giant's belly.

"Do you yield?" he asked, his voice an icy rasp.

Sonas growled and took another swipe. Shader blocked two-handed, then smacked the giant in the face with the flat. Sonas spat out a tooth and went for a wild chop. Shader dodged, and punched him in the jaw. He winced at the impact; damned near broke his fist.

Dropping his axe, Sonas tried to grapple him, but Shader bobbed and weaved beneath the giant's grasping hands, then cracked him on the nose with the pommel of his sword.

Sonas grunted and fell back, blood streaming down his face. This time, Shader didn't give any quarter. He followed up with blow after blow to the giant's face—fist, pommel, fist. Sonas's attempts to block grew slower and slower. In desperation, he lunged, but Shader stepped around it, and stuck his leg out. The giant went sprawling into the sand, and air whuffed from his lungs. In an instant, Shader pinned him with a sword in the back; not enough to harm him, but an incentive to stay down. Sonas tried to rise. Shader pressed harder. Blood trickled around the point. Harder still, and the Strangler shrieked in frustration.

"All right, I yield. I shogging yield, OK?"

Cheers went up from the bleachers.

"Bravo!" someone shouted.

Shader caught the glimpse of a bald head above a white toga.

Aristodeus. So, the philosopher had come to Aeterna for the tournament, after all. Shader's boyhood tutor. The man who had first sown the seed that he might one day win the Archon's sword.

He looked again, but the philosopher was nowhere to be seen amid the chanting crowd. Typical. Always coming and going like a summer cloud back home in Britannia.

One round down, five more to go before he had a crack at the final. It might be the only chance he'd get at fulfilling his boyhood dream. The tournament only came round when there was a vacancy: when the previous Keeper of the Sword of the Archon had died. When a new man was needed for the job. Problem was, Shader didn't want the position. He'd already made his decision to leave the Elect when he'd left Aeterna for Sahul three summer's ago. He was only back now to prove himself. Prove himself, then put it all to rest. He was done with the life of a knight. He was done with fighting.

The subsequent rounds were easier than the first. Sonas had been something of a legend, a monster more than a knight. And Shader was warier now, suspecting others might disregard the rules same as the giant had; that they might favor victory by any means over the spirit of the contest. He was taking no chances. Two opponents yielded in less than a minute. The next spent more time on the back foot than launching any attacks of his own. Aristodeus had always taught Shader a good defense would only get you so far, and he was proven right. After a canny defensive fight, the knight missed a block and Shader didn't miss his opportunity. The fourth was a good swordsman, but nowhere near fast enough; and the fifth could have been great, if he'd thought less about the possibility of losing and kept focused on the whirl and glitter of blades.

In between bouts, he watched the dragoon Galen batter his way to victory after victory. The man had skill, it was true, but it was brute force and an iron determination that won the day in each and every round. He was a middle ground between Sonas and Shader, it seemed. Brutally strong, but a passable swordsman with a good eye. He might prove harder to beat.

Predictably, Galen reached the final, and then Exemtpus Cane stood up from the Divine enclosure and announced a recess. Time for the combatants to eat and sleep before the outcome was decided in the morning.

13

***

On and on, he ran through burning streets. Torrents of lava rose in scalding walls to either side. Geysers of flame spouted high into a sky thick with acrid smoke. His skin bubbled and blistered; his lungs were clogged with fumes. Behind him, there was such screeching, as if all the souls of the damned were on his heels. He pushed himself faster and faster, screaming at the leering horrors shambling from every twist and turn of the fiery maze.

Keep running! He told himself. *Keep running.*

***

Shader woke with a start and flung the bedclothes back as if they were on fire. Sweat drenched the sheets beneath him, and his throat felt like he'd swallowed sand. Lots of sand. He must have been yelling in his sleep again. It was starting to become a problem.

He propped himself up on one elbow and groaned. Every muscle in his body protested, shouted at him to lie back down and stay there for a week. He screwed his eyes up against the stark light lancing through the louvered shutters. With a jolt of panic that he'd missed the final bout of the tournament, he stood, wincing at the cramp in his calves, and hobbled over to the window.

Throwing wide the shutters, he blinked against the blaze of the sun. Bit by bit, the skyline of Aeterna came into focus, an infinite panoply of domes and spires, columns and arches indistinguishable from those that had been reduced to rubble during the Reckoning. Every brick, every mosaic, every statue had been painstakingly restored, to the greater glory of Nous.

Down below, the piazza was awash with color, as the red-robed Exempti processed from Luminary Tajen's Basilica on the way to the Colosseum. There was still time, then, but not as much as he'd have liked.

The preliminaries had taken it out of him. Not that he'd received more than a scratch, and the pounding head Sonas had given him. But the footwork, the thrust, parry, slice took its toll on a body—and it wasn't as if he was a young man anymore.

The dream still hovered on the edge of his consciousness. He'd been in the Abyss, he was certain of it. Same as he'd been night after night since setting sail for the Holy City of Aeterna. And each time, before the flames surrounded him, before the demons came, he'd been back in his childhood home in Britannia. His birthday. The day the philosopher Aristodeus had come to tutor him.

He'd been seven when the old man had first told him he might one day win the Sword of the Archon, and here he was now, thirty years on, finally within a bout of achieving just that. And for what? To make up for his failures in Sahul on the other side of the world?

He strapped on his sword belt and slipped his father's longsword half out of the scabbard. It was nicked in a dozen places and badly in need of sharpening, but there hardly seemed much point. One more fight, and it could go back into retirement, same as it had when he finally left the Seventh Horse to become a monk. He slammed it back in its scabbard.

He'd always known what this was about, really. Prove to himself he could win the Archon's sword. Prove he was the best of the best, and then give it all up for Nous. That is, if the monks at Pardes would have him back. He'd have plenty of time to think about that on the return voyage to Sahul. Plenty of time to lick his wounds if he lost, or to temper his pride if he won.

Somewhere outside, a dog barked, and the ruined face of the bulldog he'd had as a boy drifted up behind his eyes, tongue lolling, flanked by ropes of blood. Poor old Nub.

Shader had all but forgotten about the dog until the dreams had started. Even now, when he thought about it, he still burned with rage toward Brent Carvin, the boy who'd bashed the dog's head in with a rock. That was the other memorable thing about his seventh birthday. Chances are, if he saw Carvin again—saw him as a man—he'd cut him into pieces before he could stop himself.

He gave a wry smile at that. It would make for one hell of a confession. Still, if he'd read the looks right between his mother and father all those years ago, someone had paid for Nub's death. Jarl Shader wouldn't have been able to help himself. It was all about justice, in his book. He would never have gone after the boy, but Brent's father would have been fair game.

Shader poured himself a glass of tepid water from the pitcher on the nightstand and plonked himself down on the bed to drink it. Every sip soothed his throat and cleared the cobwebs from his mind.

He caught himself staring at the Monas on the far wall. It was a symbol he'd seen every day of his life—hell, it was even on his surcoat, embroidered in red—and yet he still wondered how it came to represent Nous, the son of Ain the Unknowable.

It was vaguely man-shaped: a cross for a torso, with stick arms and wavy legs. The head was a circle with a single eye at its center, and the whole was topped with a crown in the shape of a crescent moon. He knew the meaning of each aspect inside out, but something about the Monas had always niggled away at him. He couldn't say what it was, only that it felt... wrong.

He scoffed at that. There was nothing wrong with the Monas. Nothing wrong with Nous and his holy Templum. The problem was with him. Always had been. Jarl Shader had got it right all those years ago when he'd refused the faith, knowing he could never give up what he was. You can't serve both Nous and the sword, he used to say; and he never made a secret about of his view that the knights of the Templum Elect were a contradiction steeped in hypocrisy.

Shader shook his head and finished off the water. He'd given it his best shot, fought the holy wars in the black forests of Verusia, sent hundreds of Nous's enemies back to the Abyss that spawned them, and yet he'd never once felt like he was doing Nous's will.

A knock at the door saved him from wallowing deeper in a past he'd sooner have forgotten. He set down the glass and pulled his hair back into a ponytail as he stood.

"Come," he called as he took his greatcoat from its hook and shrugged it on.

The door opened a crack, and then, as if gaining confidence, a few inches. A hand appeared on the jamb, followed by a broad face flanked by ears an elephant would have been envious of.

"Magister!" Shader said. "I wondered if you'd come."

"No need for you to call me that any longer," Adeptus Ludo said, rounding the edge of the door. "It's been more years than I care to remember since you had to endure my classes." He straightened his black and purple cassock and beamed.

Shader had forgotten just how huge the man was. Even with his stooped posture, the result of decades of study, his old theology master towered above him, and Shader was a tall man by any measure.

Ludo raised his bushy brows high above his spectacles. "Widow's peak. I knew it! You hide it well under that hat of yours, Brother."

Shader smiled and took the hat from its peg, tugging the brim low. "Keeps the sun out of my eyes. Every little advantage..."

Ludo came all the way in and shut the door behind him. "You'll need all the help you can get against my man Galen."

"Galen's yours?"

"My warden, assigned by His Divinity, and I must say, I'm glad of it. Oh, it's a new

15

thing they brought in since you left. Dangerous times to be a priest, my friend. The hand of Sahul reaches further with every passing year."

"You don't believe that," Shader said. "The Templum's always needed an enemy outside of Nousia. Keeps the masses from focusing too closely on the politics at home."

Ludo's eyes sparkled through his lenses, and he gave his characteristic finger wag. "Haven't changed, I see. Still don't trust authority. I had wondered if the campaign in Verusia might have fixed that."

Shader puffed out his cheeks, hoping to find a different topic. Verusia had changed a hell of a lot for him, but if anything, it had made his mistrust of authority even stronger. Too many men had died needlessly. And how they had died at the hands of the Liche Lord's minions.

Ludo must have sensed his unease. He clapped a shovel-like hand on Shader's shoulder and looked him in the eye.

"Good luck with the final, old friend, and I really mean that. I'll be rooting for Galen—it's a loyalty thing, I suppose—but you will always be my favorite. You were my only student in Nous knows how many years to challenge Berdini's paradox." Ludo's eyes strayed to the sword at Shader's hip. "And yet here you are, still caught up in it yourself. Oh, that reminds me. How are things in Sahul? How is the famed Gray Abbot? I can't imagine he's thrilled you're here and fighting once more."

"His idea," Shader said, leading Ludo to the door and opening it for him.

The Gray Abbot thought a loss at the tournament would better prepare Shader for a life of humble prayer. But whatever happened, he was insistent Shader made a choice. He shared Jarl Shader's view of fighting for Nous, in spite of what the Templum preached when they needed new recruits for the the Elect.

"He's backing you to win?" Ludo asked. "That would be a turn up for the books."

Shader shook his head and gave a polite laugh. "I don't think so."

As he closed the door, the thought struck him that Ludo might have had a point. Maybe the Gray Abbot was secretly hoping Shader would win the Sword of the Archon and get back his taste for action. Maybe he was hoping Shader simply wouldn't come back.

THE SWORD

City of Aeterna, Latia

The whole world was reduced to a point between the eyes of his opponent. The roaring of the crowd kept beat with the pounding of blood in his ears. His sword danced without time lag between thought and action.

Shader was bordering on ecstasy as he eased into another purple patch. They were becoming commonplace.

Galen's eyes flicked to the right as he feigned a thrust, turned his wrist, and struck at Shader's unprotected left—just as he was meant to.

Shader parried and touched the tip of his blade to Galen's chin. The big man fell back, wiping the blood from his dimple and muttering beneath his mustache. First nick he'd had, Shader reckoned.

He waited, sword loose at his side, as Galen tugged his uniform straight and puffed out his chest. The red jacket of the Templum Dragoons could get a whole lot redder yet, if the bluff old sod didn't yield.

Galen frowned, raised his saber, and eyed Shader like he meant to hack the head from his shoulders.

The attack was sudden—a flurry of jabs, an eviscerating slash, a butcher's hack, all deftly blocked or slicing air.

"Stay still, you ruddy blackguard!"

The crowd laughed. Galen scowled. Shader lifted his blade in salute.

Scratching his whiskers, Galen began to circle him, thin strands of hair standing to attention over his great pink head.

Shader had to give him credit: he was no coward, and no mean fighter, too. He'd bashed aside the competition with a combination of skill and brute force. Good qualities for a swordsman. The kind that led to fame. But he was horribly outclassed.

Galen bellowed and charged. Shader swayed aside and scratched the back of his thighs as he passed. Could have hamstringed the idiot, but that would have been as far from the spirit of the tournament as what Sonas the Strangler had done in the first round.

Galen spun and swiped, kicking, stabbing, spitting his frustration. Shader gave ground, rode out the storm, and then broke off, resuming the *en garde* stance.

Galen sucked in air, mopped sweat from his brow, and advanced. Shader stamped his lead foot, half-stepped, and then jump-lunged, jabbing him below an epaulet. Galen roared. His saber arced down, and Shader ducked, coming up straight into the path of a fist. His sword thrust on instinct and exited through the back of Galen's hand. The big man yelped and then squealed as the blade tore free.

"Sorry." Shader put up his sword and took a step toward him.

Galen screamed and hacked with all his might. Shader deflected the blow, but numbness shot through his arm. He switched the sword to his left hand, the blade twirling and glittering, sliding between Galen's basket-hilt and fingers to send his saber clattering to the floor. Shader pressed the point of his sword into Galen's nostril.

"Yield."

Galen went rigid, scarcely daring to breathe. His eyes strayed from Shader's blade to his own.

"Don't," Shader said.

The big man's chest heaved, threatening to pop the polished buttons from his jacket and rip the brocading. He pulled his head carefully away from the tip of Shader's sword, probed with a finger inside his nostril to gauge the damage. Blood pooled from his pierced hand, dripped down to spatter his boots.

"Do you yield?"

The crowd had gone deathly quiet.

Galen scanned the Colosseum, face flushing as he acknowledged his supporters.

"Yes, I bloody yield!" He snatched up his saber and stormed from the arena.

Shader spotted a dash of purple hurrying through the crowd and smiled. Adeptus Ludo scurried down the concourse, one hand flapping, the other holding his spectacles on his nose as he chased after Galen.

Shaking his head with a mixture of amusement and affection, Shader bowed to the crowd, only now becoming aware of their sheer numbers. They filled tier upon tier of bleachers set between fluted columns and gaping arches. The applause fuddled his thoughts, burying them like an avalanche. He swayed as the sky lurched, stumbled, and would have fallen had strong hands not steadied him.

"A disorienting feeling—giving up the focus of combat for the baying of the mob." A clipped voice, measured and familiar. Ignatius Grymm.

The grand master led him by the shoulder toward the clerical enclosure, ramrod straight, one hand resting on the pommel of his dress-sword.

Ignatius was everything the Elect were created to be: immaculate, efficient, and utterly obedient to the Ipsissimus. The old knight genuflected, bald patch an island amid iron-gray hair as clipped as his voice. He lifted one arm to receive the benediction, sunlight glinting from mailed sleeves, the Monas symbol bleeding from his surcoat like a mortal wound.

"Who do you present to the First of the Servants of Ain?" Exemptus Cane asked, trembling with infirmity, clutching tight to the handle of his stick. A thin line of spittle glistened in the crease of his chin.

"I present," Ignatius declaimed for the entire crowd to hear, "Deacon Shader, former Captain of the Seventh Horse, leader of the charge that broke the Verusian line at Trajinot, and now Keeper"—he turned to take in the Colosseum—"of the Archon's sword."

Give a blade a legendary name, Shader thought, and men would do anything to win it. Men like Galen. Men like all the others he'd beaten on his way to the final. If the Archon wasn't just a myth, the last thing he'd need was a sword, and it wasn't very likely he'd approve of such a brutal display in order to claim it. The Templum was many things to many people, but for Shader it was consistent only in one: the paradox of a brotherhood of love, born from the ashes of the Old World, and enforced by the legions.

Exemptus Cane nodded, licking his lips, wet and rheumy eyes sliding to appraise Shader.

"Are you consecrated?"

"I am, Your Eminence." Had the senile old fool forgotten that he'd been the one doing the anointing? That was the sad truth about the Templum, Shader thought: all that talk about the uniqueness of each and every Nousian, but in reality, they were just bums on seats.

"Good, good." The exemptus seemed to have run out of things to say, his tongue clicking as he looked over his shoulder at the supreme ruler of the Nousian Theocracy.

Ipsissimus Theodore was seated like a god, white robes perfectly contiguous with the gleaming throne, a huge leather-bound Liber open on his lap, giving the impression he continually meditated upon the scriptures; that he was, in fact, their human embodiment. He was a small man, gaunt and deathly pale. A white biretta was perched perilously too far to one side of his head. Bright eyes stabbed at Shader from sunken sockets. Eyes full of vitality and the rumor of a quick mind.

The Ipsissimus lifted his hand, and Shader knelt to kiss his ring. A glint of gold caught his eye: a Monas hanging from a heavy chain. An amber stone sparkled within the head—a single all-seeing eye.

"You accept the Sword of the Archon?" The Ipsissimus's voice was thin and rasping. He gave a delicate cough, the merest hint of a wince.

"If that is your will, Divinity."

The Ipsissimus nodded to Exemptus Cane, who wagged his stick at the priest standing to the right of the throne. The man stepped forward, holding out a velvet cushion, upon which was a covering of white linen.

The Ipsissimus whisked away the cloth to reveal a dull blade: a double-edged shortsword with a tapered tip for thrusting, a knobbed hilt, and ridges for the grip. He passed the sword to Shader. Etchings on the blade shimmered in the sun's rays.

Hands shaking, Shader mouthed the words as he read them: "*Vade in pace.*" He glanced at the Ipsissimus.

"Go in peace. Beautiful irony, don't you think?" He gave a little wave of his hand, and Shader backed away.

Vade in pace. Shader could almost hear Adeptus Ludo's voice drilling the point home: "Imperative sense. A command, not a noun." Some things you never forget, no matter how dull and pointless. Maybe it had all been in preparation for understanding the Ipsissimus's jokes.

"Show the crowd," Ignatius whispered in his ear.

Walking back to the center of the arena, Shader held the sword aloft. The cheers were deafening, like cascading water. The sword seemed to like it, odd as it sounded. He shifted his grip on the handle, momentarily shocked. He was certain the thing had trembled. No, more than that: the sword was purring.

***

"Gladius," Ignatius said, filling Shader's glass. "A weapon of the finest pedigree; old before even the time of the Ancients."

Shader spun the sword on the tabletop, light from the oil lamps dancing along the blade and picking out the inscription. It read like an invitation to return to Sahul, to put away the trappings of the Elect once and for all and rejoin the contemplative life at Pardes.

He wondered what the Ipsissimus would think of that. Leaving the consecrated knighthood was not exactly encouraged, and the Keeper of the Archon's Sword setting foot outside the city of Aeterna—that didn't bear thinking about.

"Our illustrious founders used them." Ignatius waved a hand around. "Aeterna was built on the strength of weapons like this. Quick, efficient stabs between a wall of advancing shields. Whole empires swept aside. Brutal men. Clever men. Ruthless."

The grand master was obviously quite taken with them, which wasn't exactly a surprise.

"It's yours, if you want it."

Ignatius spluttered into his wine and nearly choked. "You can't give it away. You swore to serve."

"I did?"

"You accepted, remember. Just as Erlstein did, and Baladin before him."

An unbroken line of champions serving unto death; bound to the heart of the Templum, the last guardians against an imaginary threat. If the Technocrat, Sektis Gandaw, who'd once lorded it over the Old World, was still a menace, you had to ask, what was keeping him?

"You know I didn't come back for this."

Ignatius frowned and set down his glass. "Then why? Surely you knew no one could beat you, least of all that oaf, Galen."

Shader laughed. "He was pretty good. He'd have given you a run for your money."

"If I had no arms, perhaps—" Ignatius picked up his wine. "—and was blind, and sitting on a field chair." His expression became suddenly serious. "Still torn?"

Shader let out a long sigh. Ignatius couldn't possibly know about the conflict that had sent him running for cover back to the abbey: the disarming feelings he'd felt for Rhiannon ever since he'd found her mauled by mawgs on the edge of Oakendale.

He'd been under no illusions about her. She was your typical Sahulian lass—coarse and feisty, and more than a match for the men. But her appearance had never quite fitted her manner. She was wan and willowy, the sheen of her long black hair off-setting her milky skin. Not at all the bronzed look you'd expect of a farmer's daughter from Western Sahul. Her eyes were a little too deep-set, her lips slightly curled, sneering at the absurdity of things.

Shader had been fascinated by her; reckoned he knew her better than she knew herself. Thought she was one step through the veil between the world and the eternal paradise of Araboth. He had to laugh now, though. Distance put a different hue on things. The otherworldly appearance could just as easily have been consumption, and the sneering was most likely aimed at him. He suspected, not for the first time, that Rhiannon Kwane was an enigma of his own making.

He studied his glass for a moment, twisting the stem on the table. "Am I really sworn? The Gray Abbot's expecting me back."

"If I were caught between two masters, I know which one I'd be obeying," Ignatius said.

"The one all in white, with the biggest army in Nousia to back him?"

Ignatius' brows knitted, and he leaned across the table.

"Sorry, Grand Master." Shader lowered his eyes and flinched.

The silence hung heavy between them. The waiting was excruciating. Couldn't he just get on with it? The usual dressing down for irreverence? The speech about faith and duty?

Ignatius seemed to catch his thoughts and chuckled. "What would be the point?" He sat back and clasped his hands behind his head. "Even when you were under my command, you never took a blind bit of notice of anything I said."

"That's not—"

"Deacon, I've known you a long time. I consider you my friend. You don't need me to tell you the right thing to do. Think about it. All that training, all that prayer; the battles—don't forget the battles. How else can Ain test us in the world? You've proven yourself a hundred times over. Except to one person." Ignatius rocked forward and touched his palm to Shader's chest.

"But Verusia..." Shader pinched the bridge of his nose.

"I know." Ignatius' voice had softened. "I was there. The things we saw in those forests would have corroded the faith of lesser men, but not you. Ain's blood, Deacon, you led the charge that won the day."

Shader shook his head, bit the tip of his thumb. "It's not just—"

"Faith, my friend. Faith. It's all you need. Ain loves you. All He asks is that you do your duty. No more than that."

***

The docks were deserted. Dark as pitch, and silent, but for the lapping of waves on the jetties, the creaking of yards.

Shader pulled his coat tighter, tugged down the brim of his hat, and ducked into the salty wind.

"Perfick time for slipping away." An old man hobbled from the boathouse, wheezing and hacking up phlegm. His shaggy hat was pulled low, and a thick cloak was draped around his shoulders.

"Perfect time for sleeping," Shader said, hoping he'd take the hint.

The old man coughed into his hand, hunkered down by the door. "Sleep's for the dead. Ample time for that when I gets to the Abyss."

Shader reached into his pocket, jangled some coins. "What's it going to cost for you to keep your mouth shut?"

The old man gave an innocent look. "About what? Unless you mean a knight of the Elect, Keeper of the Archon's sword, slinking off in the dark, looking for a ship to take him to the other side of the world, maybe even as far as Sahul."

"Who are you?" A chill crept beneath Shader's skin. No one but the Gray Abbot knew of his plans, and he'd not set foot outside of Sahul in decades. Although, Ignatius knew, of course. Knew Shader was thinking of returning to the abbey, but probably didn't expect him to go through with it.

"Bonds between lovers outweigh oaths to hierophants. That's just the way of things. Human nature in a nutshell."

Between lovers? Was he referring to—?

Shader's hand instinctively went to the hilt of his longsword.

"I'd use the other one, if I was you. It's got a much keener edge."

"If you insist." There was a soft rasp as Shader drew the gladius. "Now, cut the acting. You with the Judiciary? Where are the others?"

The old man chuckled. He pulled his hat off and straightened up, the cloak falling away.

"Aristodeus!"

Moonlight bounced from the philosopher's bald head, etched deep grooves in his face. He rubbed his white beard between thumb and forefinger, as he always did when pleased with himself.

"How the Abyss did you find me?"

"Oh, the advantages of age and wisdom. Mind you, who says I was looking for you? I do have other things to attend to, you know. Always hopping about like one of those kangaroos you have in Sahul. Here one minute, goodness knows where the next. Must admit, though, I was hoping you'd head back. Well, actually, I knew you would."

"I promised the Gray Abbot."

Aristodeus stuck out his bottom lip. "Yes, the noviliate. Round two, eh?" He threw a few shadow punches, bobbing and weaving.

"I'm serious. No more fighting. I'm done."

"I don't doubt it," Aristodeus said. "Good idea, if you ask me. Prove yourself the best, and then pack it all in for a life of prayer. The sort of thing I'd have done myself, only you know my thoughts on Nousians."

Shader knew them only too well. The philosopher always seemed to move in Nousian circles, though, teaching, advising, debating. He'd even schooled Shader to enter the Templum all those years ago, back home in Britannia. Ever since Shader was a child, he'd had Aristodeus to guide him, first as a tutor hired by his father, and then as a friend. He'd missed the old man's advice since he'd left for Sahul.

"It would be good to have some company," Shader said. "Six weeks at sea's enough to rot your soul, if all you have to talk to are drunken sailors and the ship's cat."

"I'm afraid I must disappoint. Business with the Templum." Aristodeus raised his eyes along with his hands.

"Good. Then you can return the sword
for me."

The philosopher leaned in for a theatrical whisper. "Don't suppose they'll notice if you keep it. I won't say anything, if you don't."

Shader knew they'd have his blood if they found out what he was doing. A knight of the Elect—no matter how former—reneging on his duties to the Ipsissimus. That would be the kind of excuse they needed to bring back the stake. If the Templum Judiciary wasn't already on his tail, it would be come morning. With any luck, he'd be halfway to Rujala by then, and well on the fringes of Nousian territory.

"Sword and man are bonded." Aristodeus adopted that look of grim seriousness he saved for making his strongest points. "It is a matter beyond ceremony and the tinpot power of Ipsissimi. Unlike so much that is to be found in the Templum, the Sword of the Archon is a lot more than just smoke and mirrors. A whole lot more."

Shader's eyes narrowed. The disparagement of religion was nothing new. Aristodeus had always considered himself above such superstitious nonsense. Nevertheless, he'd still indulged Shader's mother by arranging for the boy to join the knights of the Elect in Aeterna.

And now Shader was leaving once more. Leaving the heartland of the Templum. Leaving the life of the Elect. It was a mantle that had never fit right, no matter how hard he tried. Maybe it was his father's attitude, rubbing off on him.

Aristodeus was watching him with that pretend questioning raise of the eyebrows that said he was reading you like a book.

"The sword is yours, my friend. Take it with you to Sahul. Shove it under your bed at the abbey. Shove it anywhere you like. But take it. It is… necessary."

The flesh on Shader's back began to crawl. The wind whipped up, spraying salt water in his face. He sheathed the gladius and put one hand on his hat to stop it blowing away.

"Don't worry about the Ipsissimus," Aristodeus said, heading off down the gangway. "He'll be mad for a while, but it will pass. All the best with the novitiate."

Shader turned and started out along the jetty.

"Oh," called Aristodeus over his shoulder. "Give my love to Rhiannon."

Shader spun. "How do you…?"

But the old man was gone.

THE AURA PLACIDA

At sea, between Latia and Numosia

The ship lurched, and Shader was tipped back into the passageway, clutching the doorframe with rigid fingers. His stomach heaved again, even though it was beyond empty. With a desperate surge, he rebounded through the doorway and stumbled onto the deck.

The clouds were thinning, and the rain had slowed to a spit. The storm head was roiling off the stern, back toward Latia. The tail end of the gale bloated the square sails on the main-mast and set them snapping. The yards groaned and creaked as he slipped and skidded his way below them and bent into the wind to climb the steps to the forecastle.

Captain Amidio Podesta was leaning on the prow railings, black hair streaming like wet seaweed behind him, his gaudy finery looking like the cheap rags they really were, all sodden, clinging, drooping about his stout frame.

He seemed to sense Shader's approach, even above the din of the passing storm, turning and cramming his tricorn tightly onto his head. The man had an unnatural link with the ship that alerted him to every shift of the sea, every step upon the deck.

"You see, I told you." Podesta gave a gap-toothed grin, his usually sleek mustache dangling limply, jowls hidden by a braided trident beard. "Some storms you run before, eh? And others,"—he flicked his hand after the dark mass fleeing from the aft—"you take head on. It's just like the great Nicolau Rama said, eh? A ship has a bowsprit for two reasons." He rubbed affectionately at the base of the pole projecting from the prow, loops of rope hanging carelessly, jibs creased and furled along the length. "An anchor for the forestays." He indicated the standing rigging in front of the closest mast, where a couple of mangy sailors still hung like spiders challenging the wind to dislodge them. "Everyone knows that, uh?"

Shader only knew because Captain Diaz had bored him senseless with endless nautical lessons on the voyage from Sahul. Diaz's point had been that every able-bodied passenger needed to be a sailor, just in case. The sea was a capricious beast with no mercy. When the crisis came, as it would, either you stood up and did your part, or you went down with the ship along with everyone else.

Podesta frowned, forcing his chin into his neck and giving Shader a look that was at once confused and worried, like the one a father might give a child who had not grasped the most elementary point about playing with fire. "You don't want the foremast falling into the main, uh? You understand? Good, good. Two points, he says, and the second you will like, you being a pious man."

There was no hint of mockery. Indeed, Podesta gave the slightest of bows and touched his fingertips together.

"It is like"—the captain swept his arm along the line of the bowsprit thrusting out over the waves—"the point of a spear piercing a wall of shields, uh? You understand these things, no?"

Shader did, but quite how Podesta knew that he did was beyond him.

"It is like the horn of a charging unicorn. It is like…" And here he paused, gazing into the gray distance. "… a needlepoint of love piercing the heart of Ain. You like, eh? You see, us Quilonians are not so ignorant as you think."

They might have punched their way through the storm, but the carrack still reared and fell heavily in the troughs, and off of the starboard side, white horses frothed and spat.

Podesta followed Shader's gaze and slapped him on the shoulder.

"The Narala Reef, my friend. We are closer to Numosia than Latia now, you know. Didn't I tell you I knew a fast route? Faster than that charlatan Diaz, eh? And the *Aura Placida*"—he swept a hand out to encompass the ship—"might not be as swift as Diaz's caravel, but she is bigger, no? And she has comfort, strength, and soul." He thumped his chest and stuck his chin out, as if the superiority of his vessel were plain to see.

Shader agreed about the comfort. The *Dolphin* had indeed been fast, but her quarters were cramped, and she'd had scant space for cargo. Diaz had taken the long route to Aeterna, skirting the coast of Britannia and sailing through the channel between Quilonia and Gallia. They'd not landed at Britannia, and Shader couldn't say he minded. The feel of the place had altered since his father's death, and he suspected he now saw it as it really was. The dappled sunlight piercing the leaves of Friston Forest, the scent of fresh-cut grass, the comforting presence of the Downs: the world seen through a child's eyes. But when Jarl had rotted, when the wasting had transformed him from a titan into a repugnant sack of meat and shit, the child had died with him. There was a joke in Aeterna that Shader had been the butt of as he rose through the ranks: Britannia was the bowel of Nousia, the cesspit of the Templum's empire. The Latians had made no attempt to conceal their scorn for Shader's heritage. Britannia, for them, had more in common with the barbaric forests of Verusia than with Nousian culture.

"No," Podesta continued to blather on, as he stared out to sea, "your friend Diaz would not have the guts to take this route. He'd never navigate the reef, and even if he did, he lacks the stomach for the Anglesh Isles."

Podesta's route would take them past the mawg homeland. Shader was in no hurry to reacquaint himself with the beasts that had fallen upon the Abbey of Pardes, showing up his contemplative dream for what it was. He'd been the only one with the skills to oppose them; the only one to track them down as they rampaged south to Oakendale.

Podesta pulled a metal flask from his boot and unscrewed it. "Don't you worry, my friend. The *Aura Placida* will look after us, and my crew are as ferocious as any mawg, eh?"

Shader doubted that, although they looked a hard bunch: the sort of men who'd stick you for a bronze dupondii.

Podesta caught him observing the sailors spilling over the deck, shouting to each other and striking up a shanty that seemed to be composed mainly of expletives.

"They're good boys, eh?" Podesta rubbed his beard and frowned. "If you know how to treat them. Rum?"

Shader declined, and looked away as the captain took a swig and wiped his mouth with the back of his hand.

"Looks like you need something to put the color back in your cheeks, eh? The worst of the rough is past us now. Go and see Sabas. Tell him you need melted cheese and bread. Say the captain sent you."

***

The *Aura Placida* bobbed contentedly, the calls of sailors, the creaking of yards a muffled reminder of the world outside the galley.

The salty scent of grilled cheese set Shader's stomach rumbling, his tongue moistening his lips. Sabas set the plate before him with meaty black hands and lowered his bulk onto a stool, watching Shader intently as he sniffed the bread base and lifted it to his mouth. It was an effort not to wolf it down to fill the void in his guts. Under the expectant eyes of the chef, Shader nibbled a corner, savored its tanginess, and made appreciative grunts as he swallowed.

"You like how we eat in Numosia? Cheese of the goat and sourdough." Sabas opened his hands, thick lips chewing the words languidly rolling from his mouth with a lisp. "A touch of mustard from Verusia"—he gave Shader a sideways look with wide eyes—"and a sprinkling of black pepper. How do you think I got so fat?" He slapped his paunch, double-chin rippling as he gave a deep belly-laugh. "Oh, Mr. Sabas," he rumbled like a passing storm, "you one big blubbery man."

A red-faced lad stuck his head through the door, more acne than skin, hair a greasy mop of ginger. His eyes darted over his shoulder and then at Shader's plate.

"Got any spare, Chef?" he whined, rubbing his stomach. "I'm 'alf starved."

Sabas slapped a big hand down on the table, belly rolling with mirth.

"Ah, Elpidio. Always hungry. You sit down, and don't you breathe none. Maybe you won't be missed."

The youth slid through the crack of the door and crept to a stool, offering Shader a nervous smile.

"Elpidio is like a son to me," the black man said as he sliced some bread and started to top it with shavings of cheese. "Ain't that right, boy? You been eating that grub I send you? You sure don't look like it."

Elpidio's eyes didn't lift from the table. He fiddled with a fork.

"It eat it, right enough. When it don't get took from me."

"Cleto?" Sabas closed the lid of the pan and thrust it into the flames.

"Uh huh."

"Don't you go messing with that fork, boy. That's a clean one. Don't want to wash it for no good reason."

"Sorry, Chef."

Sabas dropped onto the stool beside him and lowered his head to look up at the lad.

"Don't go being sorry now. Everything all right?"

Shader took a bite of cheesy bread and chewed vigorously. "Who's Cleto?"

"Nothing I can't handle. Ain't that so, boy?"

Elpidio nodded, face breaking into a smile. "That's right, Chef. Is it done yet?"

Sabas rolled his eyes and went to check on the pan.

Elpidio's gaze flicked to Shader and then back down at the table. "You a priest?"

"No. Not yet, in any case."

"What, a soldier, then?"

"You ask a lot of questions, Elpidio." Shader took another bite and poured himself some water from the jug.

"It's just the lads. They been wondering. Say you're a bloody Nousian, and you wear that symbol thing on your tunic, but Cleto says you brought a sword on board."

Shader swallowed and set his bread down. "There's a lot of Nousians outside Quilonia. Pretty much the rest of the world, save for Sahul and parts of Numosia." Sabas grunted at that. "Not forgetting Verusia, of course."

Elpidio lifted his head, eyes wide, mouth rounded like a guppy's, then looked back down at his fingers drumming on the tabletop.

Sabas set some cheese-bread before him, and he snatched it up and tore a great bite out

25

of it, spitting crumbs as he spoke.

"Lads ain't got no time for Nousians, begging your pardon. Reckon we'll stick to our own ways."

Besides Verusia, which was under the rule of the Liche Lord, Quilonia was the only northern land to resist Templum protection.

"Do you Quilonians still vote for your leaders?" The idea had always struck Shader as bizarre: entrusting the governance of a country to the whims of an uneducated mob. No sense in it. No continuity. Not to mention that a canny would-be tyrant could easily hoodwink the masses into electing him. It was one small step from freedom to dictatorship.

"Don't know about that. No interest in politics."

Just as Shader thought. If that was the general attitude, then he'd much rather stick with the Ipsissimal succession. At least that way, there was order, everyone knowing their place in the grand scheme of things.

"Elpidio's a country boy," Sabas said. "From a hard-working family, ain't that right, son?"

"Vintners." The lad grinned proudly in mid-chew.

"As good a trade as any. What made you leave?" Shader asked.

"You ask a lot of questions, too." Elpidio pushed his plate away and stood. "Some of us have work to do. Thanks for the food, Chef." Without meeting Shader's gaze, he stalked from the galley.

Sabas leaned forward on the table, big fingers interlaced. He kept his voice to a low rumble.

"The vines were burned to the ground. His folks and sister killed. The boy was in town at the time, delivering wine. Captain was a customer. Took the news real bad and went after the folk that did it. Killed them all real bad, too, no messing. Good man, the captain, but a hard one. Has the crew's respect, and with these dogs, that's saying something."

Shader started as light spilled through the open door, and Captain Podesta poked his head in.

"Nousians value people over profit," he said. "Regrettably, in Quilonia, it's the other way round. Elpidio's family had the misfortune of being too successful. Shame for the boy. Shame for my wine rack, eh? Down to my last dozen, but I'm willing to open one, if you'd care to join me."

"Maybe some other time." Shader lifted the prayer-cord from his belt, picking at a largish knot. He'd been meditating on that one for days, and almost had it.

"I see," Podesta said. "Prayer ahead of wine. Very good, eh, Sabas? A holy man on board bodes well for our voyage."

Funny, Shader thought. One of the oldest stories in the Liber, involving a very big fish, made it seem like the worst possible luck.

RUJALA

Port of Rujala, Numosia

Rujala spewed from the Numosian coast in a slurry of rotting seaweed. A wall of roughly-mortared boulders hemmed the bay and sprawled across the harbor mouth parallel with the shore. Timber jetties bristled with doggers, barks, dories, and dugouts unloading their catches or preparing to set out to sea. A high-prowed galleon loomed above them, white sails furled upon three massive masts, bowsprit jabbing at the harbor village like an accusation.

Shader squinted at the crumbling buildings standing back from the shoreline, crowds of dark-skinned Numosians teeming around them, voices a muffled wall of sound punctuated by the talking of drums.

The crew of the *Aura Placida* were throwing their packs to the jetty and jostling to be the first to join the rancid carnival beyond the life of the ship. Coins were counted, and swiftly thrust from sight, curses exchanged, and backs slapped as they moved off like rats after refuse.

"Want me to bring you one back?" Sabas's face was all teeth and jowls as he waddled backward down the jetty, waving up at Shader. "Numosian whores have the biggest buttocks." He shook his cheeks and blew air through pursed lips. "And their boobies…" He cupped his own sizeable breasts. "Oh, I can't wait."

"Same as the *Dolphin*, uh?" Captain Podesta leaned on the rail beside Shader, smiling at his men like a doting father.

"Oh, no. That was worse."

Podesta's crew might have been coarse and hard men, but Diaz's had been killers, the whole lot of them. The absolute dregs of the world; the scum of virtually every country he'd heard of. All drunkards, gamblers, cutthroats, and libertines. The *Dolphin* had been the only ship leaving Sahul for Nousia at the time. Shader probably would have foregone the tournament had he known she was a privateer.

A trio of white-cloaked soldiers were pushing their way through the throng, chainmail shirts dazzling in the breaking sunshine. Their hands never left the hilts of their longswords, and each bore a kite shield emblazoned with a complex red knot.

"Ahoy there, gentlemen," Podesta called down to them. "It brings joy to my heart to see Nousian law and order in this pit of depravity. You want to come aboard, uh?"

The soldiers stopped at the foot of the gangplank and touched their foreheads. The man in the middle took a stiff step forward and clicked the heels of his polished boots together.

"You are the captain of this vessel?"

"Indeed I am. Captain Amidio Podesta, at your service, and"—he produced a letter from his inside pocket with a flourish—"in the employ of His Divinity."

Shader's eyes flicked to Podesta and back to the soldiers. If he was bluffing, it was a dangerous game. Pretending to a Templum commission could well get them arrested. The last thing Shader needed was to have the sword come to light. Ipsissimus Theodore might be a moderate, but the desertion of his newly appointed Keeper might be just what was needed to sway him to the tougher stance advocated by Exemptus Silvanus and the traditionalists.

The lead soldier came closer, and Podesta leaned over the side to hand him the document.

"What are you doing?" Shader whispered, but Podesta's eyes never left the soldier's, his face fixed in a broad grin, bloodshot eyes twinkling.

"All in order, Captain." The soldier handed back the letter. "We're with the *Pleroma*." He indicated the galleon, as if there were any possibility of doubting where they had come from. I'm Lieutenant Scorm, serving under Captain Harkyl. I'm obliged to ask, Captain, whether you've had sight of a caravel flying the flag of Sahul."

"Not this far north, surely?" Podesta looked flummoxed.

"Six days we've been following reports of it. If there's any truth in the matter, captain's a devil of a navigator. Not seen hide nor hair of it, yet we have it on good information she's been spotted in Nousian waters."

"Sounds like she's given you quite the runabout, eh?"

"The men are calling her the *Ghost*."

"That's sailors for you," Podesta said. "I'm sorry to disappoint. We've seen nothing."

"Thank you for your time, Captain. Ain be with you."

Podesta's arm draped over Shader's shoulder as he watched the soldiers march back down the jetty.

"Bad times coming, eh, my friend? Hagalle is getting bolder, I think."

Shader doubted that. The emperor scarcely had control of his own lands. He wasn't likely to ruffle the Templum's feathers. "Probably a hoax. Either that, or mistaken identity."

"Stranger things have happened." Podesta raised his eyebrows in a manner that suggested agreement, or a private joke.

"Seems you have friends in high places, Captain."

Podesta patted his jacket pocket and opened his mouth in mock astonishment. "Even men as blessed as His Divinity sometimes require the services of simple sailors of fortune. Our business is in Gladelvi, but you will disembark before that, and so need not worry yourself further, eh?"

The Emperor Hagalle was famously suspicious of the Nousian community at Gladelvi in the north of Sahul. In fact, he had a reputation for paranoia regarding supposed Aeternam plots. Shader wondered if he'd been too hasty a judge, and if Hagalle had a point after all.

"Now," Podesta said, making a sweeping gesture toward his cabin, "I am too old for wenching, and I've no desire for another case of the pox. You, my friend, are too holy to succumb to the temptations of the flesh, am I right? In which case, I insist that you join me in a bottle of Quilonian red, and who knows, we may even get Elpidio to pour it for us. After all, it's his family label; a brand soon to pass through my bladder into the pisspot of history."

***

The flickering of the hanging lantern lent a stuttering animation to Podesta's bow scraping across the strings of his battered violin.

The screeching and grating softened to a muted melody behind Shader's muddied thoughts as he lolled in the captain's chair, vaguely aware he was smiling, the pleasant warmth of wine prickling at his skin.

Elpidio's head was on the table, one hand idly squeezing the wax of a guttering candle, the other tapping out a rhythm with a spoon. Three empty bottles of the family label stood among the orange-smeared bowls and crusts of bread left over from their meal.

Shaking the grogginess from his head, Shader rolled himself out of the chair and took a stumbling step toward the walnut bookcase, running his fingers along the perfectly planed edges while squinting at the spines of the books. You could tell a lot about a man from his library, but in Podesta's case, the clues were somewhat conflicting: Nicolau Rama's *Science of the Navigators*, and *Carracks, Caravels, and Galleons*; DuMelo's *Roots of Quilonian Democracy: A Graecian Legacy*; Cuello's *Wonders of the Ancients*, a somewhat speculative work Shader had read in Aeterna.

Cuello claimed that the Templum jealously guarded the scientific secrets of the Ancients, from time to time opening its archives to keep ahead of its dwindling rivals. If Sahul produced chainmail, it would manufacture plate; if Quilonia had carracks, it would make Galleons. The Templum had never denied holding the repository of Ancient knowledge, but it had always spelled out the dangers of releasing it. The world was not ready for such power; the Ancients had proven that, and they had been duly punished.

Cuello countered that the Ancients' science had not been solely destructive. They had developed cures for many diseases, answers to famine, feats of construction that had enriched people's lives. He accused the Templum of depriving the world of the good along with the bad, an accusation that had neither been affirmed nor denied.

Podesta set down his violin, took a swig from his empty wine glass, frowned, and banged it on the table, until Elpidio took the hint and got up to open another bottle.

"Interesting man, Cuello, no? Makes you wonder how he knows such things, eh?"

Podesta swayed from his stool and thumbed along the spines until he found what he was looking for.

"LaRoche's *Fall of Otto Blightey*. You heard of him? The holy man turned devil. Burned at the stake by the religious authorities of his day."

"Every Nousian has."

"Not just a myth, eh?" Podesta tapped the side of his nose with a finger. Lamplight glinted from his eyes; threw wavering shadows across his face.

"Oh, Blightey's real enough," Shader conceded. He knew from bitter experience in the forests of Verusia. "But don't tell anyone I told you." He imitated Podesta's nose tapping. "You're not meant to know about the dark secret at the heart of the Templum."

Podesta shot a look at Elpidio, who was struggling with the corkscrew. "You all right, boy?"

"Course."

The captain leaned toward Shader. "What makes a man so, eh? Born bad? Bad choices? Bad friends? Maybe just bad chroniclers. You know, the victors writing history."

Shader rolled his head from side to side. It was hard to think with all the wine flooding his brain.

Aristodeus had said something similar about the Templum's bogeyman. In the times before the Reckoning, Blightey had been an exemplary contemplative, largely recognized as the holiest man of his generation.

"Some people say he was the conscience of the world." Hard to believe, having seen what Blightey was capable of at Trajinot.

"A conscience, eh? Good thing we have the Templum to separate out right from wrong, uh? What a mess the world would be in, if we were free to act as we pleased; free to choose our leaders and think our own thoughts."

Elpidio popped the cork from the bottle and filled Podesta's glass. "We are free in Quilonia. Don't see why anyone else puts up with it. Don't know why we don't just get rid of the bloody Templum."

And replace it with what? Mob rule and the elevation of wealth above people? There were always freethinkers praising the Quilonian model, but Shader felt they were only freethinkers because the Templum taught them to be so.

"Elpidio, my boy," Podesta said, "there is a simple reason these things will never come to pass: power."

"But we've got the best navy, the hardest soldiers."

"Blah, blah, blah. Doesn't every country say that? Clear the table, and I'll show you." Podesta reached up to a shelf and pulled down a rolled chart.

Elpidio stacked the bowls, but before he could collect the wine bottles, Podesta swept them to the floor with a loud crash. Shader helped him unfurl the map and hold down the edges.

"This—" Podesta put an arm around Elpidio's neck, drawing him close. "—is the whole sphere of the Earth. Flattened out, of course, but you get my meaning, uh?"

"I know what a map is."

Podesta pointed to a large land mass south of Gallia. "This is Quilonia."

The lad smiled, clearly missing the point.

"And this is Nousia." Podesta stabbed at points all over the surface of the map: "Britannia, Gallia, Latia, Graecia in the middle. The Great West, too." He traced the outline of the huge continent. "And most of Numosia."—The sprawling land south of Latia.

Elpidio's face fell.

"Little Quilonia is like a lamb hemmed in by wolves, you see?"

That's hardly how the Templum would have put it, and neither would Shader. Without the glue of Nousia binding the nations together, there would be nothing but petty rivalry and war. You only needed to look at Quilonia's internal wrangling to see that.

"Whose is this?" Elpidio pointed to a cluster of islands in the far south.

"The big one is Sahul, bigger than Quilonia and even more independent. This"— Podesta indicated a smaller island to the east—"is New Ithaka, Sahul's bitterest enemy; and these, to the west, are the Anglesh Isles. We will pass between them on our way to Sahul, and if we are lucky,"—he gave a look of feigned horror—"we'll not be eaten by the mawgs."

"Mawgs?" Elpidio said. "Thought you knew a safe route, Captain."

Podesta let go of the boy's neck and plonked himself on a stool. Wine dripped onto the map as he took a gulp, looked up at the ceiling, and sighed.

"We will be quite safe, my boy." He caught Shader's eyes, and gave a good impression of a sober look. "The mawgs only raid west, off of Ashanta, these days; ever since Governor Gen built up the Sarum fleet."

"You ever seen a mawg, Captain?"

"Oh, yes, Elpidio."

"Me, too," Shader said, seating himself once more.

Podesta shot Shader a look that was part surprise, part respect.

"Tracked a large band of them from Pardes." The catalyst that led him to abandon the abbey. You could hardly be a contemplative, and then grab a sword at the first sign of trouble.

"They were sniffing around the abbey for days, as if they were looking for something. Then they seemed to pick up another trail and headed south. The Gray Abbot was worried about what they were doing on Sahulian soil and, knowing my background, sent me after them."

He'd protested, but that was one of the drawbacks with vows of obedience. No matter how much he tried to be a better man, he'd never been able to outrun the shadows of the past. The problem was, once the incursion was dealt with, the Gray Abbot resumed his criticism of violence; made Shader seem a failure for doing as he'd been told.

"I came upon them outside the village of Oakendale." He could still feel the jolt along his arm as his sword thudded into a leathery carapace, the beast falling on top of Rhiannon, snarling and aroused.

He'd learnt quickly where to aim: a soft patch beneath the jaw, where the blade had slid in effortlessly, the mawg's black blood spilling on the half-naked woman beneath.

"You fought them?" Podesta sat bolt upright, staring straight at him, beads of sweat glistening on his brow.

"Killed them." He'd been particularly adept at it.

Shader lowered his eyes to his wine glass, let the images play across his mind: mawgs engorged on the flesh of the villagers, victims stripped to the bone—right down to the marrow. Row upon row of needle-sharp teeth; feral eyes and spraying blood as he hacked into them. Images of slaughter. There was no point trying to suppress them. Once the seed was planted, they took on a life of their own. He doubted he'd sleep much tonight, and the wine only seemed to make the flashbacks stronger.

"What were they like?" Elpidio asked in a voice hushed with awe.

Podesta scratched at his flaking scalp and drew in a deep breath. "Scabrous monsters, all bunched up and knotted. Fur like a wolf's; scaly hide. Unnatural. Trust me, boy, not something you want to see, eh, my friend?"

Shader continued to stare into his wine. Podesta raised an eyebrow and went on.

"I ran into them, too, a long time ago. I was about your age at the time, Elpidio. It was off the southern coast of Sahul, when I crewed on the *Crucible*. We were hunting sharks—the big ones that can take a man and eat him whole. The Ashantans pay a fortune for their fins. Make them into soup.

"A mist came up with the dawn, so the captain had us stay put in case we ran into the reef. I was scrubbing the deck—"

Elpidio frowned at that.

"Oh, I've not always been a captain, my boy, so there's hope for you yet, uh? The men started muttering and staring out into the fog, so I gets to my feet and I see this great black ship coming at us out of the gloom. A galleon, by the size of her, fully square-rigged and with a bowsprit set too low in the water. Wasn't till she hit us that we realized why: big iron ram that cut through our hull and snagged us firm."

Podesta's eyes seemed focused elsewhere as he blindly poured another drink, most of it running down his fingers and onto the map.

Shader was watching him now, pulled in by the rasping timbre of his voice, his stillness upon the stool.

"Captain sent me below, and I went, but not before I saw one. Gray it was, all shaggy but for its torso, which was like a molded breastplate, ridged and leathery. The legs were bent backward, ending in claws like a bird's. They had three long fingers, and opposing thumbs that scraped the deck as they loped toward us. Their eyes were like the crescent moon, but the color of piss. Their mouths, though, that was the worst of it."

Shader grunted his assent. He'd seen what they could do to flesh, muscle, bone; seen how even if you smashed a sword into their teeth, another row slid forward to replace them.

"They are like the teeth of a plant," Podesta continued. "You know, the ones that eat insects." He shivered and gulped down his wine.

"I lingered too long on deck. You should always follow the captain's orders promptly, eh? Got this scar from a claw." He stuck his boot on the table and rolled up his trouser-leg, twisting the knee to afford them a view of his hamstring. Three puckered white lines crossed the flesh.

"I was lucky. The mawg slipped on blood, and I made it to the hatch. I guess the man behind me wasn't so lucky." Podesta winced. "Not judging by his screams, and the ripping, crunching sound that followed me below."

"How did you beat them?" Shader reached for the bottle and poured himself another.

Podesta sat staring into space, his mustache quivering, the skin beneath his left eye twitching.

"We didn't."

Elpidio's mouth dropped open. "But…"

"The screaming went on for hours. I found a space in the hold, hid under some nets, and held my breath. I heard men hitting the water. Must have leapt from the decks to get away from the mawgs, but then they started screaming, too. Expect the sharks got them. Doesn't bear thinking about, eh? Trapped between mawgs and sharks. Reckon I'd take my chances with the mawgs. Especially with our friend Mr. Shader, here, to protect us."

"But the crew…" Elpidio's voice was growing shrill. "Why didn't they fight back?"

"They did." Podesta eyed Shader. "But it takes an exceptional fighter to take down a mawg, eh, my friend?"

Shader sipped his wine and mumbled, "Maybe."

The mawgs had been ferocious, rabid even, and that had been their weakness. Creatures of rage and instinct in the heat of battle. He'd always found an enraged enemy the easiest to conquer. It was the cold ones you had to watch. They'd been powerful, true enough, and terrifying in a way that would have paralyzed most men. Not Shader, though. When it came to danger, he'd always been blissfully at ease. The difficulties only came when he wasn't fighting.

Podesta shrugged and rubbed at the wine stains on the map.

"I hid below for days, long after the screaming had stopped. Don't tell the crew, but I pissed myself. Shit myself, even, and just lay there in my own mess. When the coastal patrol found me, they put a sack over my head so I couldn't see the remains of my crewmates on deck. The mawgs hadn't even taken the ship. Just ate everyone on board and left. Like sharks, they are: eating and disgorging, so they can kill and eat some more. Evil shoggers."

Shader set down his glass. His head was swimming, the room starting to shift around him.

"You still think we're taking the best route? Diaz's might've been longer, but it was a damned sight safer."

"Trust me, my friend. I know the Anglesh Isles like the back of my hand; and even if we did see a reaver, the *Aura Placida* isn't an old wreck like the *Crucible*. She can outrun any mawg ship, and besides, if they catch us, our crew is mostly Quilonian." He slapped Elpidio on the back so hard, the boy almost threw up. "None tougher, eh, my boy?"

"Well, gentlemen, I'm about ready for bed."

Shader pushed his way out of the chair and fell face down on the table, the map creasing up beneath him, and his wine glass shattering on the floor. He groaned and felt bile rising in his throat, swallowed it back down, and tried to stand. He lurched and spread his arms to steady himself.

"Have we put back out to sea?"

"I fear it is the strength of Quilonia." Podesta scrutinized the label on the wine. "Why do you suppose it is, my friend, that you Nousians forego so many of the pleasures of the world, yet make alcohol your bedfellow?"

Shader swooned and would have fallen, if Elpidio hadn't caught him.

"I never drink." Not strictly true, but near enough for it not to warrant confession.

"Ah, a virgin of the vine. Then I am impressed. We'll make a sailor of you yet, eh? Elpidio, would you show our guest to his cabin, there's a good lad."

The deck was a pitching blur, Shader's feet disconnected and tripping over each other. He anchored himself on Elpidio's shoulder, fighting down the urge to vomit.

A door bashed against his head as Elpidio bundled him through an opening, sounds of clashing and banging following in their wake. The lad went in front as they stumbled down below to the cool dark and bounced from wall to wall of the corridor until they reached Shader's cabin door.

"You shouldn't leave it open," Elpidio said as he shouldered his way through, half carrying Shader. "Some of the lads ain't too honest."

Shader didn't care right at that moment. He didn't even mind the clothes and books strewn around the base of the bed, the scabbarded Sword of the Archon poking out from under them. He shook off Elpidio's grip and took a lunging step toward the bed.

There was a rush of movement behind, the smell of old sweat, and then a hand clamped over his mouth, another holding a blade to his throat.

"Cleto!" Elpidio said.

"Shit on you, boy. What you have to come in for?" A hard voice, more growled than spoken, spit spraying into the back of Shader's neck.

"Captain'll kill you. Stealing ain't allowed."

"Captain ain't gonna know till it's too late. Chuck me that sword, boy, and be quick about it."

Elpidio edged into the room, eyes never leaving Shader's.

"It's all right, Elpidio," Shader tried to say, but it came out as a series of grunts.

"Who the shog asked you?"

Cleto wrenched Shader's head back, nicked his throat with the blade. There was no pain—just a tickle as blood oozed down his skin.

"Way I see it," Cleto said, breath hot and rancid on Shader's cheek, "I got myself a bit of a quandary. See, I meant to be gone before you'd done with your private party. Now I got to ask myself whether to chance leaving you alive while I head for shore, or whether it's easier to kill the pair of you."

Elpidio picked up the sword by the scabbard and held it out to Cleto.

"Here, boy. Closer." Cleto let go of Shader's mouth and reached for the hilt. "Don't you move, or I'll slit you like a pig."

Shader's heart was pounding, his muddle-headedness starting to lift. He tried to think of anything but the blade slicing across his throat; tried to let his body go limp. Was this how it was to end? His journey from Elect knight to a monk of Pardes cut short by too much drink and a cowardly piece of scum he could have beaten without thinking, face to face.

The hilt of the gladius was a blur between his eyes as Cleto's fingers curled around it.

"Shit!" Cleto's hand recoiled as if burned. "Shogging thing's alive!"

Shader crashed his elbow into Cleto's ribs, twisted under him, and threw him down hard, keeping a grip on the knife arm. Cleto let out a rush of air and tried to rise, but Shader straightened his elbow and folded back the hand so that he dropped the knife and screamed.

"My arm! You're breaking my shogging arm!"

Captain Podesta appeared in the doorway, cutlass drawn, and looking like he'd never touched a drop of wine.

"You really need to work on your vocabulary, Cleto."

"Captain! I can explain."

Podesta sheathed his cutlass and crouched down beside him.

33

Cleto tried to get up, but squealed as Shader gave his wrist a sharp tweak. Sweat streaked his pockmarked face and glistened from the sharp stubble covering his chin.

"You are new, Cleto, so I will not feed you to the sharks this time. It is, however, advisable for a crewman to learn something of his captain before he boards a ship. I am known for my gusto, my wit, and my good humor, am I not, Elpidio?"

"Sir."

"But Captain Amidio Podesta is not a man to be crossed. My crew may be as hard as nails; they may laugh and joke and call me a drunken old sot; but none of them that know me would break the rules of this ship. Am I clear?"

"Clear," Cleto whimpered.

"Good. Fetch me some rope, boy."

"Rope?" Cleto's voice had a tremulous quality now.

"Oh, we'll forego the hanging this time, but you will need to be kept in the brig until we can organize a flogging. I find that men rarely learn lessons without a good dose of pain. Wouldn't you agree, Mr. Shader?"

All Shader could think about was running Cleto through with the sword. Hardly the Nousian way, but nevertheless... "Sounds fair."

Cleto twisted his neck so that he could glare at Shader with murderous eyes. He had a face lined from permanent scowling, a broken nose, and yellow teeth. His bald head was scarred and cratered, crusted with scabs amid a downy dusting of hair. As Shader studied the face, keen not to forget it, Cleto forced a smile that was more of a leer.

Some men don't learn, even with pain, Shader thought. But it was Podesta's ship, and what he said went. Obedience aboard the *Aura Placida* didn't seem quite as negotiable as that in Pardes.

THE ASSASSIN

Village of Broken Bridge, Sahul

The last of the punters left the Griffin Tavern, and the lights went off inside. Shadrak waited till the stragglers passed into the darkness beyond the pale glow of the lantern above the door. Till the slurred voices and scuffing footfalls grew muffled, then still. Till the barkeep came out and locked up, before heading home.

He stepped out from the shadows of a porch across the road, confident he'd not been seen. Then, just as they'd planned, he slipped down the alley beside the tavern and in through the the back door.

True to his word, Bovis Rayn had arranged for the door to be left open. And true to his word, he was waiting inside, alone.

Shadrak wouldn't have expected anything less from a Nousian. All that bullshit about love and peace got up his nose, but at least they kept their promises.

Bovis was seated at a table beside the dying fire. He'd been reading, by the looks of it. There was a leather-bound book open before him. Charred logs smoldered in the hearth, from where someone had hastily smothered the flames with sand. All perfectly to plan: shut up shop, and clear the place as quick as you can. Last thing Shadrak wanted was to hang around this dump any longer than he had to.

He wouldn't have been there at all, if imperial thugs hadn't rousted him from his bed. Someone had betrayed him; let on where he lived; and as soon as he was done in Broken Bridge, he'd be straight back to Sarum to make enquiries. That, and he'd hunt down the scuts that came for him and make sure they never did it again.

Bovis couldn't hide the surprise on his face when he saw Shadrak enter. He'd obviously been expecting someone taller; someone with blood in their complexion, and eyes any color but the most unsettling pink.

Give him his due, he tried to disguise his shock, the way he slowly closed his book and made a good show of talking like Shadrak wasn't some kind of freak.

"You made it, then." Bovis gestured for Shadrak to take the chair opposite. He dropped the book into his coat pocket. It was a Nousian Liber, Shadrak was sure of it. "That's good. Good you've taken the first step."

But the first step to what? That was the question. Bovis thought he had a convert, an assassin sick to death of all the killing, needing help to flee the guild. Shadrak almost had to feel sorry for him.

"Thank you," Shadrak said, making sure there was a quaver in his voice. "Thank you for coming."

He was a hard man to entice to a meeting, Bovis Rayn. It seemed he still had his business connections, in spite of his change of career. Some of them were minders, watching his back. You could hardly blame him. Being a preacher of Nous in Sahul was as good as painting a target on your back. But it was a right pain in the arse when you wanted to get close enough to take him out.

Bovis was dressed the same way he would have been when he was a rancher—a very successful rancher, who'd had contracts with Duke Farian in Jorakum. Shadrak always did his homework. You could never be too prepared; never know too much about your target.

Word was, at one time or another, Bovis Rayn had supplied horses to the elite among the emperor's cavalry. He obviously didn't know when he was onto a good thing. The stupid scut went and found Nous; sold his business for a pittance, and gave what little profit he made to the poor.

Had to feel sorry for his wife, the sour-faced cow. She hadn't signed up for a life of holy poverty, but that's what she'd gotten, just the same.

"You are quite safe, Shadrak," Bovis said. "No one else knows you're here, not even my wife."

Shadrak nodded his gratitude. He knew he'd get no trouble from the preacher. Word got around: Bovis Rayn was as good as they got; a Nousian to put the Templum to shame. Shog, they were already calling him a luminary. Not in public, because that would have been taking their lives in their hands. The Templum's religion was outlawed throughout Sahul. A few pockets of devotees survived, but the reasons were mostly political. Once there was a change of the guard in Sarum and up north in Gladelvi, they'd be sent scurrying back to Aeterna. Those that didn't have their throats slit.

"What is it?" Bovis said. His eyes flitted about the darkened room, as if he'd sensed something.

He hadn't. There was no one there. Shadrak would have known if there was, and they'd already be dead.

"What's on you mind?" Bovis went on. "Second thoughts?"

Shadrak hadn't anticipated them having a conversation. Time was a wasting.

His fingers found the cheese-cutter Albert the poisoner had lent him. They dug deeper in his pocket, till he felt the resin Albert had prepared. "Just a few flakes, crumbled into a drink," the poisoner had said. "And remember, don't lick your fingers."

"This is hard for me," Shadrak said. He lowered his eyes, made it look like he was embarrassed.

Bovis leaned across the table, tentatively put a hand on Shadrak's arm.

That would have got him a knife in the balls, any other time, but here, in the Griffin, here, when so much was at stake, Shadrak didn't have the luxury of improvising. It had to be a tidy job, with a confusion of clues to keep the local authorities guessing. That's how the imperials wanted it, and anything less, Shadrak might never see his most cherished possession again. For they'd taken the urn bearing Kadee's ashes. Even dead, his foster mother was his greatest vulnerability; the only way shoggers like that could get to him.

"Go on, Shadrak. Nous already knows everything you've done. He only wants to hear you say it to one of his own. Only wants you to ask his forgiveness."

"But..." Shadrak made it look like he was choking up; wiped away an imaginary tear.

"You've had a hard life, Shadrak. I know that. I can see it in your eyes."

Probably, he could see their bloody hue. He should have taken that for a portent of what was to come.

Shadrak cleared his throat; angled a look at the bar.

"You need a drink?" Bovis said. The ghost of a frown crossed his face, but then he softened it with a nod and a smile. "I understand. Beer, or something stronger?"

"Water. Water will be fine," Shadrak said. He never liked to drink on the job. "I'll get it. You've already done too much."

He got up and went over to the bar; squinted through the near dark at the pumps and bottles.

"On the left," Bovis said. "Nigel has a barrel of spring water for the rare punters, like myself, who don't drink."

Shadrak filled two glasses. Bovis was looking off into the dark, rubbing his nose and mouth, no doubt planning his strategy for evangelization.

Shadrak took out the resin and rubbed it between his thumb and fingers, getting a good quantity in Bovis's glass. The good thing about having a perfect memory was, he wasn't likely to forget whose was whose.

He carried them back to the table and pushed one toward Bovis.

"Cheers," Shadrak said, as he sat and took a sip.

Shadrak, Kadee's ghost said in his mind. *Fellah, this isn't right.*

Not now, Kadee. Can't you see I'm working.

She'd never done that before: bothered him on the job. But afterward, she could be a pain in the arse. Still, he'd rather that than never hear from her. Rather be mad as shog and hearing voices, than lose all sense of her presence.

"Yes, yes, cheers." Bovis took a drink, licked his lips, and finished the whole glass. "Hadn't realized I was so thirsty. Thanks, Brother."

Brother? If only you knew. Presumptuous little scut.

"Forgive me for asking," Bovis said, "but I was just wondering how an assassin of the Sicarii got to hear the word of Nous. You're based in the city, right? In Sarum? It had to be Mater Ioana, or one of the other priests at the Templum of the Knot."

Shadrak gave a sheepish smile.

"I knew it," Bovis said. "It's a wonder they're still there. Between you and me, I think Governor Gen tolerates them. If true, that's quite a sacrifice. Imagine what the emperor will do if he finds out."

Imagine. That would be a job worth taking. Shadrak could probably retire on the money.

"But I digress," Bovis said. "It matters not how you came to be here. It just matters that you are here, and ready to give yourself to Nous. I think you know what happens next."

Shadrak wished there were more light. He couldn't see if the poison was taking effect yet. Albert said it was a quick one; but of course, Albert could have been lying. You never knew with the poisoner.

"What is it?" Bovis said. "You need more light? Of course. It's helpful to see the confessor's face; see how you are not judged; how Nous loves you."

Bovis made a trip to the bar, then over to the remnants of the fire, where he stooped. He returned with a guttering candle. It cast his face in eerie shadow, but it was better than nothing.

Shadrak tried not to squint as he looked again for signs. There. Was that the skin starting to mottle?

Shadrak, Kadee chided. *It's not too late to stop this.*

Yes, it is—if Albert were to be believed. *Way too late.*

"So," Bovis said, settling back down in his chair. He coughed into his hand. Dark drool seeped from the corner of his mouth. He coughed again. "Sorry. Water's not so good. Goes stagnant, if it's left in the barrel too long. Now, where do you want to start?"

There was no way Shadrak was carrying on with the charade. Tell his secrets to a shogwit like Bovis Rayn? Confess his sins? He didn't have till the shogging unweaving of all the worlds. He wanted this over and done with half an hour ago.

"What's that?" he said, glancing over Bovis's shoulder.

Bovis turned, and Shadrak sprang, wrapping the cheese-cutter round his throat.

The shogger was quick, though, and lashed out with an elbow. Shadrak swayed aside from it, but lost his grip. He hadn't expected this: resistance from a shogging pacifist.

Bovis got his hands under the cheese wire. He thrashed wildly; turned the table over. Shadrak spun clear, whipped out his thunder-shot. As his hand came up firing, Bovis bashed his arm, and the shot went wide. Glass shattered. Before Shadrak could fire again, Bovis threw himself on top of him. The thunder-shot went off, and Shadrak grunted. Felt like a hammer blow to his guts, and hot wetness splashed the front of his jerkin.

He threw out a palm, caught Bovis in the nose and cracked his head back. Bovis squealed, hand flying to his face.

Shadrak raised the thunder-shot again, and this time he didn't miss.

Bang.

A dark hole appeared in Bovis's forehead. He teetered for a moment, then dropped like a sack of shit.

Shadrak winced at the pain in his chest. He covered the wound with a hand as he bent to check Bovis for a pulse. Then he picked up the cheese-cutter and lurched toward the back door, every breath sending shards of glass in between his ribs. Let the authorities make of the mess what they could, but he wouldn't be here when they found Bovis's body.

He stepped into the street and pulled up sharp; thought he could hear someone weeping. Had he been made? Had someone spied on what he'd done? Had the boom of the thunder-shot been heard outside?

Quick as it came, the sound passed, and he realized it was in his own head. It was a weeping he'd heard as a child, whenever he did something she didn't approve of.

Because there was no doubting who it was. This comforting haunting was starting to become a liability. Last thing he needed was a conscience. Last thing he needed was to upset Kadee each time he killed a scut.

THE LICHE

City of Sarum, Sahul

Ernst Cadman flipped open his pocket watch and squinted at the digital display. It was a testament to the craftsmanship of the Ancients the thing still worked after all these centuries. To anyone else, it would have appeared magic, dark sorcery; but Cadman had been there before the Reckoning that had ended the old world, and he recalled a time when a watch like his would have been considered "retro."

It took a moment for his sleep-dulled mind to register that he wasn't wearing his pince-nez. His bedroom was blacker than he'd known it. He couldn't even see his hand in front of his face. Couldn't see the pocket watch now, either—which seemed a little odd.

He reached out and patted the hard wood of his nightstand with tremulous fingers. Precisely four reassuring dull taps, not the sharp raps he'd feared. Not that it was a reasonable fear, he told himself. He'd worn the illusion of fatness for so long now, it had the familiarity of an old coat, the comfort some children glean from a favorite blanket. He brushed against the frames of his pince-nez, felt them skid away from him, but managed to snag them before they could fall.

He fumbled and squeezed them into place on the bridge of his nose, and saw clearly that the time was 3:33 a.m. and 55 seconds precisely. He gulped—more out of habit than necessity. The two number fives danced around his mind, taunting, warning, predicting.

Just my rotten luck. Cadman grimaced, his mind already permutating to make them into anything but what they really were. 5+5=10, the ritual began. And 1+0=1, which is 4 less than 5, but added to 5 makes 9. That was where he needed to stop, he reminded himself. 9 was a good number—it was 3x3, after all. But if you added it to the original 5... He groaned. That made 14, and 1+4...

How the deuce can I see the watch when I can't even see my own sausages? Cadman wiggled his fingers in front of his eyes. It struck him as odd, too, that the pince-nez had made a difference. It was a matter of illumination, not of focus, and he'd never really needed them for that. Like so much about him, they were merely for show, and not a little comfort.

Gosh, it's cold. Not that that was anything new. Even Sahul's scorching summers had done nothing for the chills. But it was a darned sight colder than normal. Freezing, even. He expected to see his breath misting before him—well more of a death-rattle than actual breath—but couldn't see anything in the pitch blackness. It was becoming rather worrisome. He tugged at the end of his mustache, as if it could ward off evil. The evil of the Void.

Cadman began to run the numbers through his mind, adding, subtracting, dividing, as the panic began to rise. If only he could get to the curtains without tripping over and breaking his neck. He tugged aside the blankets and rolled his great bulk to the edge of the bed.

"Cadman."

—A voice like the rustling of paper.

He froze, black heart thumping against his ribs and threatening to shatter the illusion of flesh. *Someone's in the room. Someone's in the room. Someone's—*

"Cadman."

The blackness darkened at the foot of the bed.

It was all Cadman could do to turn his head. His hands clenched the covers, ready to tug them back over his face. A sliver of shadow curled toward him, as if it were going to stroke his cheek.

Cadman drew back, pulled the blankets up to his nose.

Tentacles sprouted from the heavy dark, bobbing and undulating, poking and retracting. A series of pustules erupted from the central mass, lumps of twisting blackness that could have been heads, lolling, nodding, shaking. It was still too dark to see any more than the outline of black on black, and Cadman was grateful for that.

He opened his mouth to speak, but no words came out. Both hands were on his mustache, and the number seven raced around his mind. *Damn those fives. Curse them. Now look what they've done.*

"I come in answer to your call."—A Cheyne-Stoking rasp from one of the heads.

"I bring what you seek."—A malign susurrus from another.

Call? Seek? "I called no one. Please go away." *Unless…*

"You read books of knowledge." The first voice rippled and crunched.

Blightey's grimoire? Indecipherable poppycock. All sigils and wards, pious sounding words and a bunch of warnings meant to frighten the ignorant. He shouldn't have read it again—nor any of the other works of his one-time master, the Liche Lord of Verusia. But when you'd lived as long as Cadman, you had to refresh your memory by rote—every last bit of it. Systematically. Some might even say slavishly. It didn't pay to forget.

"I came to Otto Blightey, as I now come to you," one of the heads said. "I offer knowledge of things that can ease your suffering."

"What do you know of my suffering?" The fear was turning to anger now, as he'd hoped it would. Seven was great for that. A strong number. Very resolute.

"Every time you feed your needs, I feel it." A voice thick with pity, as if it considered him less than the smokers of narcotics whose every waking moment was consumed with the desire for more.

Which is not so far from the truth. Perhaps, if there were another way. It was all very well clinging onto existence, but there had to be more dignified ways of doing it. Ways that didn't involve guzzling down the gory remains of prostitutes and beggars. All these centuries, he'd been nothing more than a parasite, but what choice did he have? It was either that or… He squeezed his eyes shut. He never liked to think about oblivion.

"What are you? What can you offer me?" Almost immediately, Cadman wished he hadn't asked. He'd learnt all he could stomach of the dark paths from Blightey back in Verusia. There was a limit to how far he was willing to go. He knew Blightey had taken things much further—he'd seen the fruits of it in the mutilated victims, the impaled corpses outside the castle walls: white and rigid, the stench of feces and putrescence. Some of them had continued to gurgle and gasp around the stakes protruding from their mouths for hours. Days, even. If that's what knowledge of the Abyss did to a man, Cadman wanted none of it. It's why he'd fled. Why he'd come to this accursed backwater on the other side of the world. Well, it was one of the reasons.

Another head plopped from the black mass and swayed toward him on a sinuous neck. "You know of Eingana?"

"The serpent goddess of the Dreamers?" A giant snake worshipped by the indigenous people of Sahul.

The black mass gurgled and hissed, its appendages lashing the floor, dark heads rolling. "The mother of life, they say." There was a note of irony in the voice this time. "Keeps the creatures of the Dreaming in being by the slenderest of threads."

"Ah, the *funiculus umbilicalis*. I'm not entirely ignorant of Sahulian mythology." Always paid to study the native culture. Might make all the difference in a tight spot. You could never be too careful. "Cords of her own flesh, invisibly sustaining all life in the world of the Dreaming. Once severed, so the Dreamers believe, the creature ceases to be." Cadman shuddered. Such a graphic description of the precariousness of existence. Every moment a tightrope walk over the Void. "Correct me if I'm wrong, but isn't she also the bringer of death?"

The creature roiled toward him, tentacles rearing and coiling like vipers in heat. "All things have two natures," one of the heads hissed. "You of all people should know that."

Cadman felt it could see through him, through his corpulent disguise and right down to the bone. He backed up against the headboard, dragging the covers with him.

"I know what you fear." Another head spoke now, its voice soft and empathetic. "I, too, have endured on the threshold of existence, the Dweller of the space between dreams and the Abyss. I, who have seen so much, felt so much. I can help you."

The Dweller? The firstborn of the Father of Lies? The spawn of the Demiurgos, lord of the Abyss?

"Why?" *What's in it for you?* Nothing good ever came free.

"Because we are fellow sufferers. Because what I have I would share with you."

That didn't sound at all appealing, judging by the look of the thing. "You would have me become like you?"

All the heads laughed in unison, a loathsome cacophony that rattled the windows. "There can be no others like me. My creation was... unique. What I offer is the knowledge to endure; the fullness of the life of Eingana."

"And that's yours to give?"

The tentacles settled to the floor, the heads turning as one to glare at him with eyes blacker than the darkness.

"It is yours to take."

"It is?"

"When the Dreamer Huntsman used the Statue of Eingana to bring about the Reckoning, it was split into five pieces and hidden from the world."

"So I heard," Cadman said. "Huntsman didn't want it falling into the hands of the Technocrat. Can't say I blame him."

"Indeed. With the statue's power, Sektis Gandaw would have the means of unweaving all the worlds."

"It's a hobby," Cadman said. He immediately regretted it, when the Dweller hissed and shook its loathsome body.

"One of the pieces has surfaced."

"Oh?" *And that's my concern, why?*

"Even now, it is on the way to Sarum, to the office of Governor Gen."

"Really?" The governor's office was only two floors up from Cadman's at Arnbrook House, where he functioned as the doctor in charge of public health.

"Jarmin the Nousian, the Anchorite of Gladelvi, has been invited for a private audience with Governor Gen. For centuries, he has been in possession of one of the pieces of the statue. It is why he has lived so long."

Is it now?

"It's what the statue does," the Dweller said. "What Eingana does: bequeathes life. Bestows immortality."

Cadman licked his lips. His black heart thudded about his ribcage. Immortality. A clean immortality, without the need for blood. It was… tempting.

But taking a piece of the statue from this Jarmin would involve action, and action never came without risks.

Quick as a flash, he made up his mind not to get involved. Better the devil you knew. Better a life of anonymity, tucked away amid the populace of Sarum and none of them any the wiser. So what if he needed to feast every now and again. At least he endured. At least that way he continued to stave off the Void.

"I've survived this long without your help, thank you very much. If it's all the same to you, I'd prefer to keep things just as they are."

The demon surged toward him, limbs flailing and agitated. "You cannot refuse," hissed one of the heads. "It is your destiny. You will not refuse."

Cadman pressed his back into the headboard, wishing he could pass right through it, through the wall, and out into the street beyond.

The Dweller squelched over the foot of the bed, tentacles bashing against the floor.

"You will not refuse." Thud, crash, bang. "You cannot refuse." Thud, crash, bang…

***

Thud, crash, bang.

Cadman sat bolt upright in bed, patting his face to make sure it was still there. Cheeks and jowls, bushy mustache, great mop of hair. All present and correct.

"Hold on," he called out to whoever was knocking at the door.

What time is it? He snatched up his pocket watch from the nightstand and flipped open the lid. *3:34 and 16 seconds. Who the hell's bashing at my door at this infernal hour?*

Dirty light from the street lanterns spilled through a gap in the curtains. He rolled out of bed, eyes adjusting to the gloom, and found his pince-nez atop the book he'd been reading himself to sleep with: Otto Blightey's *Voices from the Abyss*. He shoved it onto the floor. Damned nonsense had fired his imagination.

The knocking from downstairs grew louder and more urgent.

"All right, I'm coming. Give me a chance, would you."

He lumbered across the room and threw on his dressing gown. Shuffling out onto the landing, he turned up the gas lamp he always left burning at night. A dangerous business, but better than the darkness.

Someone was still hammering at the door, as if all the demons of the Abyss were coming for them. Cadman skipped nimbly down the stairs, feet clattering on the tiles by the door.

Oh dear.

He took a peek at his reflection in the entrance hall mirror. More of a skull than a head—just the merest strips of parchment-thin flesh clinging to mottled bone. His hands were rotten, black with mildew. Skeletal fingers cracked and groaned, joints barely articulated by decaying ligaments. He frowned at his bony toes; tapped them on the floor.

Careless, Cadman. Very careless. Caution, caution, and caution again.

He watched the fleshiness re-form in the mirror—great rolls of fat dripping from his jaw, waistline ballooning beneath the dressing gown, fingers swelling until they resembled bloated slugs.

Another flurry of thumps, and the door rattled like the lid of a restless sinner's coffin.

"One moment!" *Uncouth bloody Sahulians. No manners. Absolutely none whatsoever.*

You wouldn't have had to put up with that sort of thing back home in Britannia. If only he could go back. If only it were safe to. But while Blightey still lived—if you could call it living—Sahul was a far safer bet. At least there was half a world of ocean between them.

Cadman stroked his rapidly returning mustache.

Better. Now then, let's see what this racket's all about.

He pulled back the three heavy bolts, twisted the key in the uppermost lock, fumbled in his dressing gown pocket for the big key for the deadlock, and then inched open the door until it caught on the chain.

A small, pallid hand flopped through the gap. Blood stained the fingers.

Oh, my giddy aunt! Cadman took a step back.

"Open up," a voice wheezed from the other side. "I'm a Sicarii."

An assassin. Another one of Master Frayn's paid killers. This is getting beyond a joke. The fifth in as many weeks.

Cadman entertained the idea of slamming the door on the hand and crushing it until it either fell off or withdrew. Not really an option, despite the appeal. It didn't pay to upset the Sicarii.

"Name?" he demanded.

"Shadrak." There was pain in the voice. Labored breathing.

"Bear with me a jiffy." Cadman waddled into his study and snatched up the list Master Frayn had made for him—in the unlikely event that any of his cutthroats should require discreet medical attention. *Unlikely, my foot.* If Cadman had done what any other self-respecting doctor would have, and charged them through the nose for his services, he'd have been a rich man by now. But he'd never been one for the pursuit of money. It always brought too much attention.

He ambled back to the door and peered through the gap. His visitor was surprisingly small for a hit-man. Exceedingly small. Couldn't have been an inch over three feet. He was dressed like all the others in dark leather, a billowing black cloak trailing over his shoulders. His face was as white as his hand—and it wasn't just from loss of blood. He was clutching at his chest, a misty look passing across the most unnerving eyes: pink irises and pinprick pupils. Eyes that flitted this way and that, as if expecting danger from every direction. *Something we may well have in common.* Even his stubbly hair and neat box-beard were white.

"You're not on the list."

"Frayn gave you a list?" When he spoke, there was a flash of pearly teeth. *Quite the perfectionist, aren't we?* "Course I ain't on it. I'm Shadrak... the Unseen."

But not any longer, I fear. "That hardly makes me want to let you in. If your reputation depends on invisibility and anonymity, what will you do once I've sewn you up?" He started to close the door, gently enough to let the fellow get his fingers out of the way, but the albino wedged a boot into the opening instead.

"Open the shogging door, or I'll put a hole in your fat head." The hand returned, clutching a pistol.

Now there's a surprise. I've not seen anything like that for a while. Not since the Reckoning, and that was a very long time ago. Nine hundred and eight years, four months, and sixteen days, to be precise.

"You sure you know what that thing is?" Cadman stepped back from the door.

"Know what it does."

Yes, quite. Of course you do.

"Don't worry, Doc." A pink eye pressed into the crack, took everything in. "I won't do you; you're far too useful to Master Frayn, and I reckon I can trust you with my little secret, don't you?"

Cadman didn't miss the threat. He never missed a threat—even when he was told he'd got it wrong. Oh, there were some fine actors out there, but he could always smell a rat. He had a knack for it.

He slid back the chain and opened the door. Shadrak stumbled into the hallway, pitched to his knees and moaned, a trickle of blood dripping through the fingers covering his chest wound and spattering the tiles.

"Follow me." *If you can. Hopefully, the little runt will drop dead before he can bleed all over the carpet as well.*

He led Shadrak along the corridor and opened the surgery door for him. All beautifully white and clinical. Pristine. Sturdy shutters locked against prying eyes; shelves of gleaming instruments, all perfectly stowed in their alphabetized trays. Not a speck of dust to be seen. *Immaculate.* The midget might as well have been in a sewer, for all the appreciation he showed.

Cadman beckoned him to sit on the edge of the treatment table, then flicked the switch on the angle-lamp, one of his few surviving Old World artifacts. Shadrak cocked his head but said nothing as the lamp hummed and flickered to life, casting its stark glow over the table.

"Don't make 'em like they used to, eh?" Never hurt to talk in the patient's vernacular. Always paid to put them at ease. "Regenerating plasma cells. Keep it powered till doomsday. Seems you have some knowledge of the Ancients' technology yourself." Cadman nodded at the gun. "Might I ask where you came by such a relic?"

Shadrak winced as he holstered it, then fell back on the table. "No."

Thought as much. "I'm something of a collector, but alas, technology's not all it's cracked up to be. It's fine one minute,"—he grabbed some latex gloves from the vacuum store and snapped them on—"and the next, it's useless junk. Now, tell me,"—he lifted Shadrak's hand away from the chest wound—"what seems to be the problem? Ah..." He pressed down on the edges of the puncture, causing the assassin to whimper, and bright blood to gush over the gloves. "Bullet wound. You really shouldn't play with such dangerous toys."

"Wasn't... playing," Shadrak croaked. "On a job. Bastard grappled me. Thunder-shot went off."

"Nasty." Cadman shoved a gauze square over the hole. "Press on this, would you." He scurried around the table and rolled Shadrak groaning onto his side. "No exit wound, which means a spot of digging in the dark."

At least it had missed the lung, otherwise the midget would most likely be spewing blood. *As long as there's no cavitation or fragmentation, he should be all right. Assuming the shock doesn't kill him, which would be a crying shame.*

Cadman pulled over his trolley and ripped open some packets. Supplies were getting low. Soon he'd be reduced to the same barbaric butchery as his competitors, unless a miracle happened, and the Templum opened its archives. All that knowledge shut up for the supposed good of the world, to prevent a return to the evils of the past. It hadn't been that bad, Cadman mused. It all depended whose side you were on.

Pinching a wad of gauze with some forceps, he dunked it in saline and swabbed the wound. Shadrak gave a pathetic cry, tears welling from his pink eyes.

"Stings a bit, I'm afraid. Would you like something for the pain?"

"Just get on with it," the assassin growled through clenched teeth.

"As you wish." Cadman angled the light so that it shone directly on the wound. He pushed his pince-nez further down his nose and squinted over the top. "A touch of laudanum? A tincture of lignocaine? No? Suit yourself." *Don't say I didn't warn you.*

He picked up some shiny tweezers and stabbed them into the hole. Shadrak screamed and thrashed about on the table. Cadman forced him down with a meaty hand and continued to push and twist with the tweezers until he touched something hard. Shadrak had gone still, his jaw slack, a snail's trail of dribble oozing down one side of his chin.

"Nighty night." Cadman patted his cheek, and then reached behind to grab his magnifying glass from the trolley.

Peering through the lens, he could see nothing but blood washing over the tweezers. Sometimes he wished he had a third hand, so that he could rinse away the gore and see what he was doing.

The aperture widened as he forced the tweezers against soft flesh. For an instant, he glimpsed the dark shell of the bullet, before the blood rushed back in. With one last push, he had it, whipped it out clean as a whistle, and dropped it clattering onto the trolley. He swabbed around the wound with iodine, leaving yellow stains on the skin, and began to stitch it up with a curved needle.

Shadrak shuddered, his chest rising and falling erratically.

Breaking off the thread, Cadman bent to inspect his work, dabbing at the seepage with a cotton wool ball and allowing himself a satisfied nod.

Splendid job, Cadman. Splendid.

He took down an antibiotic solution from its box on the shelf, drew it up with a syringe, and injected it into Shadrak's vein.

That was all he could do for now. Either he'd live or he'd die. It was all the same to Cadman.

*****

A cock crew way off in the suburbs, causing Cadman to look up from his book. Something about the sound always startled and reassured him at the same time: an intrusion upon his peace, and the death of the night and all its terrors.

He'd given up on Blighley's grimoire. There was only so much mumbo jumbo he could take, and what he'd read had unsettled his sleep. It was bad enough surrendering to the little death, as he called it, without being frightened out of his wits by nightmares from the Abyss.

He patted his breast pocket and plucked out his cigarette case, all shiny silver and engraved with his initials. A parting gift from Mama before he'd set off for Verusia. He frowned and thought of some numbers to drive away the memories. Sixes and sevens mostly, with the odd nine thrown in for good measure.

He lit a cigarette with his ancient Zippo and relaxed against the leather backrest of his chair, chunky legs stretched out beneath the desk.

He spent a moment eyeing the faded sepia pictures in their tarnished frames. What had happened to the proud young man in the gown and mortarboard, clutching a scroll? The boy all in white with the cricket bat, kneeling at the front of the team? He knew where the others were—his teammates, his family, his friends.

Dust and ashes, like I should be. Back to the elements or lost in the Void.

Why did he go through this ritual every morning, clinging onto the memories of the dead?

Because I must remember. Because that's all I am; all that stands between the last wispy threads of my being and oblivion.

He took a long drag on the cigarette, imagining the smoke burning his lungs. They'd long since rotted, along with the rest of him, now no more than emphysemic sacks that made every breath a dying gasp. His chin slumped against his chest. All that remained was a crumbling skeleton housing a shriveled heart and the blackened embers of his spirit, if that's what you could call it. "Will" was a better word, he fancied. The will to endure at all costs.

He puffed out his illusory cheeks and turned his attention back to the book: *Meditations on Plenitude* by Alphonse LaRoche. Funny how it came round so quickly. It seemed only yesterday he'd read the pre-Nousian classic, and yet, judging by the hundreds of completed books he'd returned to their precise locations on the shelves, it must have been a century. The eternal ritual, cycling through the entire library, re-reading every word in an effort to preserve more memories than the mind could hold.

It would probably take another century to wade through LaRoche's turgid prose and metaphysical balderdash. It never got any easier, but it was one of those arduous tasks one simply had to get on with. He just wished the man hadn't written so much.

LaRoche had been writing up until the Reckoning, a sort of last champion of the old superstition that passed for religion until Sektis Gandaw's technocracy had all but eradicated it. *Bloody good job, too,* Cadman thought, although the human capacity for self-deception didn't die easily.

LaRoche had sat out the cataclysm at his Abbey of Pardes in Sahul. His name had vanished over the years, but Cadman had read that he'd reinvented himself as the mysterious Gray Abbot. He'd reputedly helped the Templum drive the Liche Lord, Otto Blightey, back into Verusia, seventy years after the Liche Lord had steered its rebirth from the ashes of the Old World.

Blightey had a way of upsetting his allies, it had to be said. Apparently, he'd gotten his claws on some ancient artifact that belonged to the Ipsissimus. It wasn't the first time he'd clashed with the religious authorities, either. The first time, they'd burned him for it.

A rustling noise followed by a clash roused him from his brown-study.

A bit early for the morning post, surely.

Cadman squeezed out of his chair and plodded down the hallway.

Someone had shoved a piece of paper through his letterbox.

Bloody junk mail. Of all the things that had to survive the Reckoning. If Governor Gen didn't put a stop to the damned Merchants' Guild and their intrusive activities soon, Cadman would be voting for the other side come next election.

His knees clicked as he stooped to pick it up: a creased and stained flyer announcing some sorry sounding recital at an even sorrier sounding pub out beyond the black stump, as the locals would no doubt say. He was about to screw it up, when a word caught his eye: "Eingana".

Ash dropped off the cigarette hanging limply from his lips as he read the flyer more carefully:

The Epic of The Reckoning
by Elias Wolf

Venue: The Griffin, Broken Bridge

Hear how the world of the Ancients was destroyed by beasts from the Dreaming. Relive the death of Sektis Gandaw's machines at the hands of the shaman Huntsman wielding the magic of the serpent goddess, Eingana.

Performance starts at sundown.

No formal dress required.

Broken Bridge... Broken Bridge... Now where the deuce is that? And Elias Wolf... I'd swear on Mama's grave I've heard that name before? Cadman flicked the flyer with one fat finger and hurried back toward his study—and straight into Shadrak.

"Awake so soon?"

"I heal quick."

Cadman didn't doubt it. There was something about the assassin's appearance that nagged at his overburdened mind. It was in there somewhere; just needed to be dredged up from the depths, filtered out from all the dross and scum of the centuries.

"What do I owe you?"

More than you can afford.

Cadman tried not to sneer as Shadrak searched through a pouch for some loose change. He was adorned with pouches, replete with them, all the way around his belt, and two strapped over his shoulders, running alongside the twin baldrics with their gleaming blades and razor stars. The pistol was holstered at one hip, a stiletto sheathed at the other. All kitted out for killing, and looking just the part with his deathly complexion and eyes like diluted blood.

"Do you know a place called Broken Bridge?" Cadman made a show of scrutinizing the flyer.

"Shithole twenty miles south. Why?" Shadrak gave him a look that could have been mistaken for nonchalance by anyone other than Cadman.

"You've been there?"

"What's it to you?"

"Quite, quite." Twenty miles might not have seemed far, but to Cadman, that was the end of the Earth. He'd not left Sarum in decades, and got into a panic if he had to go further than the city center. Travel was not something he did anymore, if he could help it; and that created something of a dilemma.

"May I see the wound?" He took a step toward Shadrak, but stopped when he caught the look in the midget's eye.

"Told you I heal quick. Just needed you to get the…"

"Bullet."

"Whatever. To get the bullet out."

It came to Cadman like an aneurysm. "Homunculus!"

"What?"

He was sure that was the word. He'd come across it in one of Blightey's books. The little folk, denizens of Aethir, wasn't it? The world of the Dreaming. He would have loved to ask questions, but doubted Shadrak would be very forthcoming.

"Just thinking aloud. Put the purse away; there are other ways to settle a debt. Do you have any urgent engagements?"

He could see Shadrak didn't like it. His eyes were darting all over the place, fingers stroking the tops of pouches.

"What you got in mind?"

"Oh, nothing too strenuous. Wouldn't want to impede your recovery." Actually, the albino already looked fully healed, and that wasn't natural. Whatever Shadrak was, Cadman very much doubted he was human. "How do you fancy a trip to Broken Bridge tonight?"

"Who d'you want dead?"

Now there's a thought. "No one." *At least, not right now.* "Think of it as more of a reconnaissance; information gathering." Cadman handed him the flyer. "Go to this recital, and come back with everything you can glean about Eingana."

"That it?"

"That'll pay for your treatment. If it leads to any more work, I'm sure I could rustle up a denarius or two."

Shadrak's pink eyes widened at that.

Avaricious barbarian. Just like the rest of these Sahulian cow-herders and sheep-shaggers: despising everything about Nousia, except for the value of its currency.

"Excellent," Cadman said. "Every last detail about Eingana, remember. I don't want you to miss a jot."

THE EPIC OF THE RECKONING

Village of Broken Bridge, Sahul

The wavering glow of the oil lamps, the crackling fire in the hearth, the smell of pipe-smoke and beer all added to the mood as the bard sang his epic to the accompaniment of a guitar.

Shadrak couldn't think of a better place than the Griffin for the story of the Reckoning. Couldn't think of anywhere better to unwind from the bustle of the city, either, despite what'd he'd done in this very room last night. He could almost smell the blood rising from the jarra wood floors, some of it his, most Bovis Rayn's.

Still, he reckoned the rough-hewn tables, the long bar carved out of the trunk of a colossal karri tree, had soaked up more than a little blood over the years. The Griffin had probably seen its fair share of spilled beer, puke, and tears, too, in the eight centuries or so it had been standing.

His eyes were drawn to a flash of color out of place. Someone had thrown a rug over a patch of floor by the hearth. Probably hadn't had time to get the stain up. On the mantelpiece, the framed Charter of the Sahulian League had a hole in the glass, fracture lines making a jagged jigsaw. The shot that missed. Waste of shogging ammo.

It was hard to believe the founding fathers had forged their alliances here more than three hundred years ago. The spear of Ishgar, the first Sahulian emperor, had been propped in a corner, its haft speckled with red. The wall where it had hung was still discolored, but at least it now looked like damp rather than blood. Ishgar was probably turning in his grave. He'd celebrated his victory over the Eastern Lords here at the Griffin, back when the port city of Sarum up the road was still the capital of Western Sahul.

Shadrak looked away, tried to focus on the performance. If it hadn't been for the spellbinding pull of his music, the straggly-haired bard would have looked a right plonker in his patchwork trousers and rabbit-skin coat. Most of the onlookers appeared too rapt, or too pissed, to notice. As for Elias Wolf, he appeared totally consumed in his song, lost in the story of history's passage to the present.

Shadrak felt drawn to the bard's fingers, plucking away at the strings. The words swirled around him like the cries of distant birds spiraling on the thermals. He swooned and felt the room pitch; drifted helpless before the wave of images and sounds that washed over him.

The Griffin gave way to an ocean of red dust, as he began to see through the eyes of Elias's protagonist, the mythical Dreamer shaman who had instigated the fall of the Ancients.

***

The Homestead burst from the desert like a blister; an island mountain bathed in the blood of the fleeing sun.

It was during the red light at the close of the day that Adoni always heard the whispering and saw movement in the Dreaming. He'd been told that he writhed like a snake and foamed at the mouth when he had the visions. Jirra said that he pissed himself, and he made sure that Ekala knew. That's why she was no longer Adoni's one-day-mate; why she no longer held his hand.

"You ready, boy?" The Wapar Man picked between his teeth with a curling thumbnail. His black skin was streaked with white, like the bleached bones of the dead who'd been taken by the bush. Crystals glinted from ropey hair, and bones pierced his lips.

Adoni turned to look at the Barraiya People spread out behind, a hundred eyes staring his spirit down. The children stood at the front, parents' hands on their shoulders. He caught Jirra smirking, but the others may as well have worn masks. Ekala's eyes shone brighter than the rest, but there was no expression on her face, not even repulsion. Looking up at the Wapar Man, he nodded.

The Wapar Man jabbed a long finger at a man in the crowd, weaved it through the air and pointed at another. The two men stepped forward, sweat streaking through the dust on their skin. The Wapar Man studied them and made little growling noises deep in his throat. He shook his gourd rattle, and the men took hold of Adoni by the shoulders, spears upright in their free hands.

"Don't look back," the Wapar Man called as they walked him toward a fissure in the sandstone. "All is Dreaming now. Listen for the gods. Maybe they take you."

They hadn't taken the last boy. Adoni remembered the Wapar Man leaning into the opening then pulling back, covering his nose and mouth. That's what always happened, Adoni's father told him. The last person the gods had taken was the Wapar Man himself, and no one could remember when that was.

Something stabbed at the back of his neck. He thought it might be a fingernail.

"See through the dark." The Wapar Man's breath was on his cheek. "You come to the core of the Dreaming."

—The maggot-ridden heart of Eingana, the serpent goddess; mother of all life.

Adoni nodded and sucked in a deep breath.

The Wapar Man leaned across him to draw a line in the sand with his staff. "You cross back over this line without the blessing of the gods,"—the Wapar Man made a sharp clicking noise—"the sinew will snap. Understand?"

"I will fall from Eingana?"

"You will die."

He felt the Wapar Man withdraw.

The hands holding him were hot and slick, stiff with anticipation. The men on either side tensed and then threw him forward into the opening.

***

Shadrak winced and pulled the stiletto out of his thigh, wiping the blood on his cloak before sheathing it. Pain seemed to do the trick, though; cut through the fug.

Shogging bard was still playing his guitar and droning on; thumbing an alternating bass like a heartbeat, fingers picking a beguiling melody. His singing was low and sonorous, voice carrying effortlessly to every corner of the bar. More sorcery, no doubt.

Shadrak stroked the weapons in his baldrics. Shogger's rabbit-skin coat was thick enough to offer some protection against a blade or club, but the neck was exposed. Best options would be either a head-shot or a razor star to the jugular. If killing had been his mission.

Shadrak felt the tug of the music once more, and scratched at the skin of his forearm. The wound in his thigh was already healing, no more than a dull ache. The chest wound from last night was barely even noticeable. Some of that was down to that fat bastard, Cadman, but most of it was down to nature. Shadrak had always been a quick healer.

The story had washed over him, drenched him with emotions he could do without. His foster mother, Kadee, had been a Dreamer. The only person he'd ever given a shog about. But she'd gone the same way everyone went, sooner or later: back to the mud; no more than a memory, and a chiding voice at the back of his mind.

The shogging music had made him passive. The part of his mind that always remained alert, watching, assessing, had slept. Except for the tiniest spark that had screeched its silent warning, told him what to do to bring himself back. He focused it now on the bard's techniques. If he could work it out, expose the illusion, the charm would lose its hold on him. If he was right, he'd be free to glean information, rather than wallow in sentiment.

The words: that was where he'd start. Separate them out, analyze their meaning, root out any mention of Eingana. He'd always had an analytical mind; always been able to outthink his opponents, observe their behavior, and predict their movements. Principle was the same.

The bassline thumped beneath his skull.

Di dum, di dum, di dum.

Shadrak's vision started to blur. Images danced before his drooping eyelids.

Di dum, di dum.

He shook his head and fixed his eyes on the posters plastering the wall behind the bard—line drawings of angular people, all cylinders and squares; a pointed tube soaring skyward with smoke spewing from its tail; symbols, slogans:

"NO MORE GLOBAL-TECH!"

"IT'S YOUR GARDEN, MAN!"

"SEKTIS GANDAW, GLOBAL-TECH WHORE!"

Shadrak slapped himself on the cheek, trying to drive the grogginess from his head. What was the bard saying?

Listen to the words. That was the way to break the spell.

"Adoni's breathing became fast and shallow, and he felt as though the walls and ceiling were moving in to crush him."

Di dum, di dum, di dum, di dum.

Shadrak reached for the stiletto, sluggish fingers coiling around the hilt.

"Sticks, or something else, cracked beneath his feet, and he occasionally stumbled over small rocks."

Di dum, di dum, di dum.

Shadrak tried to focus on the nook beside the fireplace, the table with its vacant stools. Saw Bovis Rayn sitting there after closing, a Nousian Liber before him. The idiot was smiling, thinking no doubt he'd made a convert, and never realizing he'd made a mistake.

Di dum, di dum.

Bovis had lent a fatherly ear, promised confidentiality. Said he was tight with the landlord, could meet him there after hours. No one would see them coming or going. He'd still been beaming with sickening benevolence, just before his skin mottled and black drool trickled from his mouth.

Di dum.

Shadrak tried to summon the feeling of tightening the cord around his throat, splitting the skin and half severing the head. Wasn't how it happened, but that had been the plan—keep them guessing; save himself some—what was it Cadman had called them? Bullets. He was sure Albert's toxin would've done the trick by itself. Hadn't earned his reputation as the guild's master poisoner for no good reason, but it never paid to take chances.

Di dum, di dum.

Bovis flung the table over. They wrestled. Thunder-shot went off. Glass cracked.

Di dum.

Fired again—Shadrak swooned at the remembered pain.

Di.

Hit Bovis in the nose with the heel of his hand.

Dum.

Leveled the thunder-shot at the shogger's head...

Numbness seeped into Shadrak's fingers. His arm hung limp. He bit down on his bottom lip, tasted salty blood. If he could just focus on the words...

***

Adoni could see nothing. He shuffled sideways along the passage, face scraping against stone. Every footfall was marked with a crunch or a snap; occasionally a squelch. The air grew thinner the deeper he went. It was clogged with dust and the stench of something rotten.

He slipped and fell, jarring his ankle. Steadying himself with his hand against the wall, Adoni tested the ground with his toes, found a ledge, and gingerly lowered his foot. He stepped down and repeated the action, each time descending, turning, and twisting deeper into the darkness.

The passageway widened and leveled off. His heart was racing, as he could no longer feel the wall. Stumbling forward, fingers stroking the rocky surface to his right, Adoni became aware of the faintest of glows at an unknowable distance.

He took a faltering step toward the light. Fixing his eyes on it, scarcely daring to blink in case it vanished, he crept further into the gloom. He calmed himself by mumbling the name of Eingana and drawing in the stale air with long, deep breaths.

The glow came from a niche in the far wall. It spilled amber radiance upon a bowl and cup set on the floor.

Adoni crouched down, the light revealing a carpet of bones studded with empty-eyed skulls staring at him like messengers from the Void. Grubs wriggled in the bowl. He snatched up a handful and crammed them into his mouth, savoring their moist meatiness.

Picking up the cup, his nostrils flared at the pungent odor that burned all the way to his brain. He touched his lips to the fluid, which was sweet and thick like honey. Draining the cup, he fell back on his haunches and started to twitch and shake, warmth coursing through his veins, effusing from his skin and radiating outward.

A reddish sheen washed across the floor and painted the walls and ceiling of a cave pocked with holes and scarred with fissures.

"Would it like to see more?" a voice grated from somewhere to his left.

Startled, Adoni dared not breathe.

"Is it hungry? Does it thirst?" asked another voice, reedy and croaking.

Adoni had the heart of a startled brolga. He shot looks all around, but saw no one.

"Would it like to see more?" repeated the first voice.

"Yes," Adoni whispered.

51

He shielded his eyes as the amber glow from the niche flared, catching dust motes in its beams.

"Many have come here."—The grating voice again, this time from behind. "We have spoken to all. Most screamed, tried to flee, but others outside stopped them leaving. Many lost their minds and attacked us with rocks and lengths of bone. How is it that you talk instead?"

Adoni turned around and froze.

Before him stood a gigantic naked man with a brown muscular body and the head of a crocodile. Tawny eyes with slits for pupils fixed him with a hungry stare.

There was a rush of movement to his right, and Adoni spun to face another man-like creature, this one dwarfish, with a bloated belly and the head of a toad. Its long tongue darted out. Adoni threw his hands up and recoiled.

With one eye on Crocodile-head, the other on Toad, Adoni said, "I do not know. Maybe I am too scared to scream."

Crocodile-head nodded.

Toad sucked his tongue back in and squatted down, thighs bulging, ready to spring. "Funny fellah, you are. Too scared to scream!"

Crocodile-head eyed Toad for a second. "This one is different. He has power, like the Wapar Man."

"What is your name?" asked Toad, his eyes popping.

"I am called Adoni."

"Sunset," Toad said. The creatures looked at each other.

"Sahul gave it to my father on the dream quest."

"End of the day." Toad's tongue snapped out at an invisible fly. "Last of the light. Blood light. Sahul has not spoken to you? Given you a soul name?"

"No."

"Come with us," said Crocodile-head, plucking a glowing sack from the niche.

A section of the wall dissolved, revealing a rough-hewn stairwell wending its way into the depths of the earth.

With Crocodile-head before him and Toad behind, Adoni descended into the darkness, guided by the amber glow from the sack.

They headed down for an eternity. Adoni's knees burned, and his heart rattled like the Wapar Man's gourd. Finally, they came to a vast cavern with scores of tributary tunnels. Cobwebs thick with dust drooped from the ceiling a hundred feet above, many still holding their victims: large bats, the occasional human, and mottled skeletons with legs like an emu's, dangling arms, and wolfish skulls.

A shadow moved across one of the larger tunnels, sending a twinge through Adoni's guts. At a gesture from Crocodile-head, he crept closer, and away from the illumination offered by the sack.

Something massive waited in the mouth of the corridor.

"Welcome, my child," a voice sounded in his head.

He went to it willingly, heart leaping with joy. Something brushed against him, tugged him toward a bulbous body. Silky strands stuck to his flesh as he was twirled and wrapped. Rows of eyes glinted; mandibles clicked, dripping fluid into his mouth. It burned as he swallowed, but it tasted good.

"What do you hear?" The mandibles moved in time with the voice.

Only Adoni's head protruded from the cocoon; he had lost all sensation below the neck. For the first time he could remember, he felt at peace. He closed his eyes and drifted.

"What do you hear?" the voice asked again.

"Whispering. A word spoken over and over. A name."

"Sahul's gift to you. What is the name?"
"Huntsman."

***

Stab, drip, drip. Stab, drip, drip…

Shadrak hardly felt a thing as he plunged the dagger repeatedly into his thigh. But it had been enough. Enough to bring him back round again.

He scanned the captive audience, shaking his head at the white-cloaked knights listening like awe-struck kids. None of them was above twenty years of age, to his mind. Probably most were younger. What the shog was wrong with them, wearing the red Monas of Nous. If they did that in the city, they'd be hanging from a gibbet, or brutally stabbed to death and slung in the river by his brother Sicarii.

He switched his attention to a black-haired bitch sitting by herself, obviously bored out of her mind, and drinking like a fish. Drowning her sorrows, by the look on her miserable face. She ought to try smiling, because there was a good-looking bird beneath the gloom. Not that she'd have given Shadrak a second look. Women generally didn't do that.

He turned away, but not quite fast enough, and she saw he'd been watching.

There was a loud thud, and when he looked back, she was slumped over the table in a pool of her own vomit, the half empty pitcher beside her head.

It looked like she'd chundered in the beer, disgusting cow.

She shook her head and pushed her chair back with a sound like nails on a chalkboard that cut across the music. Not that anyone noticed. They were still spellbound. It was only the pain from stabbing himself in the leg that kept Shadrak free to observe, at one step removed from the bard's beguilement.

Bouncing from person to person, and with no one seeming to mind, the black-haired bint stumbled out of the door and let it slam behind her.

Shadrak watched her go, and then glared at one of the boy-knights. Had the lad just moved his head? Had the scut been watching him?

Blood was pooling on the floor beneath Shadrak's chair as he continued to make rhythmic stabbing motions with his hand. He watched it in rapt fascination, like it wasn't his own. The blood blurred in and out of vision, took on the appearance of desert—the ocher dust plains of central Sahul.

His heart sounded like a muffled drum beat in his ears, keeping time with the rise and fall of his dagger.

Stab, drip, drip. Stab, drip, drip…

***

Huntsman's knees clicked as he crouched at the base of the Homestead and held out a hand.

Jirra shuffled closer, skin daubed white, gray hair framing a face like fruit that had been left too long in the sun. When had he grown so old? When had the rest of them, even Ekala? Only Huntsman had avoided the ravages of time. Even the Wapar Man had succumbed to old age, in the end.

Jirra handed the bundle to Huntsman and stepped back among the Barraiya People, all streaked with white, arms smeared with their own blood, looking like ghouls of the desert.

Ekala was watching him with rheumy eyes, one hand on her daughter Cardinia's shoulder, the other hugging her granddaughter close.

Huntsman peeled back the paper-bark securing the bundle, and held out the contents for all to see: the ocher-stained bones of the Wapar Man.

"See what is left of our Kadji." He lifted the skull, and the people covered their eyes to protect their souls. "See what is left of our Clever Man." He moved the skull through the air, causing the people to bow and moan. "Walu the Sun Woman has taken his flesh, and now we must give his bones to the Homestead."

Huntsman turned his back on them, and stooped to place the Wapar Man's skull in the opening. Something grabbed it and whisked it away inside the rock. He pushed the rest of the Wapar Man's remains inside, nodding as they were snatched. Shaking off the last dust of his Kadji, Huntsman waved the paper-bark before the people and let it fall to the ground.

"The Wapar Man has gone to the gods of the Dreaming. May he watch over the Barraiya People. May he—"

The droning of a thousand bees filled his ears, punctuated by a thwop, thwop, thwop, and the roar of a waterfall.

Huntsman stared to the north, where black dots spewed into the sky. Birds, maybe; but he'd never seen so many.

The people turned to follow his gaze, looking from the sky to Huntsman, as if they expected him to know what was happening. He was the Clever Man now. He was the Kadji. The Wapar Man would have known what to do; but Huntsman could only stand and watch as the shapes drew nearer, silver glinting in the failing sun.

"Kutji spirits!" Jirra cried, and looked to Huntsman. "The Clever Man knows what to do. He will steal their power, make it his own."

Huntsman stared blankly at Jirra, and his hands began to shake. Even if they had been Kutji, he wouldn't have known what to do; the Wapar Man had never shown him.

Jirra blew air through his lips and turned away, then the people began to scatter.

Huntsman pressed himself against the face of the Homestead, fingers fumbling inside the sack hanging at his hip.

The flying things fanned out, great metal beasts with flashing blades, and wings as wide as twenty men. Thunder rolled, and smoke spewed from their maws, striking the earth and bathing the people in flames.

A group turned back, sprinting toward him, hands outstretched, as if he could save them.

Huntsman's fingers tightened around the object in the sack, stroked along its curves. His heart was pounding, his thoughts racing.

Was this the time?

Should he open the sack, after all these years?

"You will know when the time comes," the Great Spider had said. "Do not uncover it until then. *He* must not find it. Keep it hidden."

A blast ripped into the runners, spraying him with their blood. One woman kept stumbling forward, screaming his name, hands reaching for him.

Ekala.

Huntsman took a faltering step toward her, and then ducked as a shadow closed in from above, and a deafening roar filled his ears. There was a staccato peal of thunder, a whimper, and a dull thud. When he lifted his hands from his eyes, Ekala lay sprawled out before him, blood pooling from a score of wounds.

The earth shook, and flames licked at the sky. Clusters of Barraiya People swarmed toward the Homestead, for there was no other cover in the bush. A flock of metal birds swooped above them, dropping silver eggs the size of boulders. Upon striking the ground, the eggs split open, the metal within warping and twisting, sprouting legs, arms, and domed heads, each with a single glaring eye.

Huntsman started to climb, fingers and toes searching out holds in the sandstone. He glanced over his shoulder at the Barraiya People huddling together with no hope of escape, but swiftly turned away before the metal men were upon them.

He struggled on toward the summit, tears stinging his eyes, the death-cries of his people carried on the breeze.

Forcing himself to the flat surface of the Homestead, Huntsman opened the sack. Amber rays burst from it, drawing the metal beasts like moths to the flame. The summit began to explode as he reached inside and pulled out the contents.

"Eingana," he whispered at the radiant amber statue of a serpent poised to strike, eyes aflame, and fangs like lightning. "The power of life and death," the Great Spider had told him. "Mother of the Dreaming."

Blast after blast pounded all around, showering him with rock, and throwing up twisting plumes of smoke.

Huntsman settled into the waking-sleep, his mind awash with all manner of terrible beings that flew, scuttled, crawled, and slithered. The creatures of the Dreaming writhed and reproduced endlessly, until his mind was full to bursting.

His left hand reached for the knife in his belt. His body grew incandescent with the power streaming from the statue. Taking hold of the bone hilt, he raised the blade, and plunged it through his heart.

CHILDHOOD SWEETHEARTS

Village of Broken Bridge, Sahul

Gaston Rayn squinted and looked up from the page. A moth fluttered into the lantern twirling above the porch, fizzed and popped, then went still. He rocked back in his chair, flicked the hair out of his face, and scratched his itching scalp.

Time for the annual trip to the barber's, he reckoned. Long hair was a bloody pain in the summer. Shame, though. Always was when he had his locks trimmed, Mom used to say, back when they were still talking. She'd told him the girls would love his long blond hair, and she'd been right. Dad used to say he looked like a... But that was before he'd met Soror Agna; before he became a preacher. Doubtful he'd say it now, even if he still thought it. Wouldn't be saying anything ever again. Not after last night.

Gaston blinked back the tears. He hadn't let them fall yet, and wasn't about to start now. Weren't exactly on speaking terms when the ol' man was alive. Dying wasn't gonna change that any.

Girls. Mom hadn't been wrong there. They'd flocked to him right enough—all but the one that really mattered. Not that he wanted their attention these days. Bad for the soul, Shader had said. Not that he was one to talk. Nothing like the lure of the flesh to lead a man from Ain. That, and fighting, if Dad had his way. Never approved of the White Order. Said he was disappointed...

Gaston reclined in the easy chair, wrenched his focus back to the open book in his lap.

The muffled music from the Griffin drifted beneath the chatter of the cicadas. Barek would be there, along with Elgin and Sol. He smiled at that. They'd all been farm boys, until Shader offered them a new life. Called it the true resurrection, the renewing power of Nous. Dad said pretty much the same thing, only he reckoned Shader had it all wrong. Can't serve Nous and live by the sword, he used to say. Try telling that to the Templum Elect. Try telling it to the Ipsissimus.

He supposed Justin would be there, too, no doubt white-anting Gaston and blowing his own trumpet. He'd have to be dealt with, sooner or later. A cut or two during a duel should shut him up. Justin was a decent swordsman, but Gaston knew he was better.

Flipping the book over, he stifled a yawn, and forced himself to read. Shader had lent it to him; said it was required reading for the Elect. Training in fortitude, he'd called it. Hundreds of pages of mind-numbing theology, most of it written before the Reckoning. Alphonse LaRoche might have been the last great Pater of the Old Faith, but he was still a boring bastard.

He'd finished the chapter where the Aeonic Triad, the Archon, Eingana, and the Demiurgos fell through the Void from the Supernal Realm. Children of Nous, according to LaRoche. Shader said it was a metaphor, and Gaston was just starting to grasp what that meant. Children of Nous and grandchildren of Ain. That was the part he couldn't get his head around. If Ain was nothing—or rather, "no thing", as LaRoche claimed—how could he have a child? Shader had tried to explain it using the analogy of a mirror: Ain's boundless love overflowing into a perfect self-image. Gaston's head started hurting whenever he thought about it. Nothing reflected is still nothing, as far as he could tell.

Maybe the book would get easier the further he got into it. He frowned at the title of the next chapter and doubted that would be the case: "The Rape of Eingana." Bound to be uplifting, that one.

He looked up as the gate banged shut. Someone was stumbling up the garden path, hands held wide, clutching two bottles of wine. Gaston closed the book and smiled.

"Elias lost his touch, Rhiannon? Didn't reckon to see you again so soon. Must've been all of ten hours." He'd not expected to see her ever again, truth be told. She'd already said her goodbyes this morning, ahead of moving to Sarum to join the novitiate. There were stains on her dress, and her hair was matted at the ends.

"Music lost its power after the second pitcher." She stepped into the light of the lantern, her face sharp with shadows, big grin stretching her lips.

Gaston caught a whiff of beer and something else—vomit, perhaps.

"Everyone else in the Griffin's stiff as corpses." She put her hand over her mouth. "Oh, shit, I'm sorry. I didn't think."

It felt like she'd sliced a knife up his chest. Gaston forced his best "no worries" smile before the tip plunged deeper. "Those for sharing?" He wasn't supposed to be drinking, not now he was the leader.

"That's the idea. Wanna go inside? Flaming gnats are eating me alive."

Gaston rocked out of the chair and opened the door for her. He lit a couple of candles as she settled onto the couch, kicking off her shoes.

"Make yourself at home."

"Ah, you know me, Gaston."

He certainly did. He'd known her since childhood. They'd been inseparable, until he'd tried to kiss her. She'd forgiven him, but things had never been the same since. She seemed all right now, though. Maybe she could tell he'd changed. Changed herself, too, he reckoned. Must have, if the Templum of the Knot had accepted her.

"What you reading?"

"Oh, some theological crap Shader lent me."

Her face dropped at that. It was no secret there'd been something between her and Shader. She'd denied it to him, but Gaston could tell. He'd seen the way Shader behaved around her—almost boyish. Always giggling, making jokes.

"What did he say before he left?"

Gaston shrugged. "Said he had doubts. About the Order, mostly. Said he'd always had trouble marrying the sword and the Monas and didn't feel good about leading the rest of us down that path."

"So why'd he start it?"

"Mawgs, I guess. Someone needed to do something to make sure they didn't come back."

Rhiannon winced, probably remembering. She'd been an inch away from being torn apart, devoured, and disgorged. If it hadn't been for Shader…

"What I don't get is," Rhiannon said, "if it's over,—the White Order—why are the boys still dressed in their uniforms?"

Shader had told Gaston to disband it, but the lads had objected. Couldn't say he blamed them. All that training, all that discipline, and for what? Just so they could go back to being farmers scraping a living from the harsh soil of Sahul?

"No, it's not over. Don't reckon I share his conflicts. Sometimes you can dig too

57

deeply into this stuff." He slung the book on the floor. "Better to keep it simple. Clear rules, hard discipline."

"Your dad, Gaston…"

"Was a bloody heretic. Would've told the Ipsissimus and all the Exempti they were wrong, if he had half the—"

"No, not that. I mean, about last night."

"What about it?"

She shifted on the couch, looked him in the eye, serious all of a sudden. "You ready to talk now?"

Gaston sucked on his top lip, wished he had a drink in his hand.

"Nothing to say. The ol' man practically disowned me, and Mom went along with it, like she always does. He made his choices, and I made mine. Reckon that's an end to the matter."

"Your choice, mate, but if you ever want to—Shog me!" Rhiannon glanced at the bottles still in her hands. "I'm bloody sober."

"Well, that can't be good. You'll have way too much time for that when you get to Sarum."

He grabbed the bottles from her and wandered into the kitchen to open them. Rhiannon followed him, still a little unsteady, despite what she said.

"What happened between us, Gaston, is it OK now?"

"Forgotten," he said. "I was wrong, and you set me straight."

"Same thing happened with Shader."

Gaston felt his cheek twitching and set to work on the cork. "That why he left?"

Rhiannon sighed. "Maybe."

Couldn't take the rejection? Or the shame of people knowing he wasn't quite so holy after all? Made a certain kind of sense.

"Shog Shader." Gaston poured some wine and offered it to Rhiannon.

"Shog him." She grinned, raising the glass. There was no answering sparkle in her eyes, though.

She threw back her head and downed the wine.

Gaston poured himself one, spilling some in his hurry to catch up with Rhiannon, red veins trickling across the table and dripping to the floor. He knocked his back and poured them both another, opened the second bottle and tucked it under his arm as they returned to the living room.

"Bit flaming spartan, isn't it?" Rhiannon was frowning at the bare walls, giant shadows sprawling across them, animated by the flickering candles.

"Guess I don't need much." Gaston gulped down some wine. "Keeps me focused on the inside."

Rhiannon nodded vacantly, took a sip, and faced him. Gaston couldn't be sure in the gloom, but he thought she'd been crying.

"Gaston, are we still mates?"

He took a step toward her, but she held up a hand, shut her eyes.

"Can I still talk to you? Tell you everything?"

Gaston sat on the edge of the couch, leaving space for her to do the same. She hesitated, and then dropped down beside him, head pressed into the cushions. She reached out, missed his hand, and then found it, gave it a pat. A giggle escaped her, and she hiccuped.

"Drink something." Gaston topped her up.

"Gaston." She turned her bleary eyes on him, doing her best to look sincere, lips slightly parted, pupils dilated. "Huntsman came to see me."

The Dreamers' witch doctor? No one had seen him for years. "What the heck did he want?"

Gaston finished the wine in his glass and gave himself a refill. Rhiannon seemed to be slowing down, but he was just getting started. He felt an urge to brush her face with his fingers; managed to resist. It made him think of the last time, when she'd given him a black eye. He'd stayed home until it had gone, scared someone would see.

"He asked me to turn down Shader."

Dump him? Did that mean...?

Rhiannon was studying his face, her eyes black in the dim light. "Sha... Deacon proposed to me." She spluttered out laughter and snot, wiped her face, and sobbed, all in an instant.

"But..."

"I know. He's consecrated. Vows in Aeterna, and more vows at Pardes. We went through all that. In spite of it all, he wanted me."

More than Nous? More than the Elect? What did that say about the White Order? Where did that leave him and Barek, Justin, Elgin and the others? Rhiannon seemed to know what he was thinking.

"He loved you, Gaston. Loved you all. He would have stayed, too, if I'd said yes. Oh, rules would have had to be changed, but what the shog? Rules are meant to be broken."

"What's that got to do with Huntsman?"

"Destiny." Rhiannon rolled her eyes. "Matters beyond my puny mind and selfish desires."

"He said that?"

"Not exactly, but that's what he meant. Even reminded me about going into the novitiate, though how the heck he knew about that, I'll never know."

"You told him where to go, right?"

Rhiannon lowered her head and stared into her glass. "He told me things. Things about powers that were older than the Reckoning." She sniffed and took a sip.

Gaston did the same, starting to feel the warmth prickling beneath his skin, the easing of self-consciousness.

"Remember those stories Elias used to tell?" Rhiannon said. "The Archon, the Demiurgos, and Eingana?"

"Falling from the Void? Eingana is raped by her brother, the Demiurgos; has some weird baby..."

"The Cynocephalus."

"That's it. Dog-headed ape, or some shit. You listened to this?"

"And a whole crock more." She shuffled closer to him and rested her hand on his knee. "There are powers behind everything, Huntsman said. Even the Templum. Shader is caught up in it. Wouldn't say how, but he said he had a role to play, and that I'd prevent him fulfilling his destiny."

"What did Shader say about it?"

"I didn't tell him."

So, she just dumped him, like she dumped me. Bet she didn't give him a shiner, though.

Gaston emptied his glass and looked at Rhiannon's face. She didn't look away, like he'd expected. There was wine on her lips, and her tongue rolled across them. The candlelight picked out her teeth, unnaturally white, it seemed to him.

He leaned in to steady her glass before she spilled it, risked a touch of her hand. When she didn't pull away, he grew bolder, stroking her fingers, her wrist, her forearm. He sucked in a gulp of air, head dizzy with the scent of her. The puke smell was still there, but it was tinged with something sweet and musky. He felt a swelling in his groin, brought his knees up, so she'd not notice. His fingers were in her hair, lifting it away from her neck. He slid his face in closer, felt her breath on his skin. Their cheeks brushed, and he shuddered. He pressed his lips to hers, seeking an opening with his tongue.

"What the—?"

Her fist cracked into his nose. White-hot needles lanced into his brain. His hands flew to his face, glass shattering on the floor, wine splashing.

Rhiannon reached out, eyes wide, mouth open. "Gaston, I'm sorry. I... I—"

He punched her square in her jaw, sent her sprawling. She tried to wriggle backwards, but he caught her ankle. Her other foot kicked him in the chin, jolted his head back, blurred his vision. He threw his weight on top of her and hit her again—this time in the mouth. She gasped and sobbed, spitting out blood. Gaston cursed himself for an idiot. His knuckles had ripped on her teeth. Should have hit her in the eye; see how she liked that. She screamed and clawed at his face.

"Shogging bitch," he snarled, thumping her again, splitting the skin around her eye before starting to throttle her. She was gonna get it this time, shogging whore. Make up for what she did to him before.

Pressing down on her neck with one hand, he stuck the other between her legs, tugged at cloth, felt something tear, forced an opening. She screamed again and struggled furiously. He threw his head back and crashed it into her face. There was a sound like the splitting of a melon, and she went limp.

Ripping away her skirt, he tugged open his pants and entered her. She moaned something, head lolling to one side, blood running from her nose.

He began to grunt, cursing and spitting. Shog his dad. Shog Shader. Shog her. All the rage bubbled up his spine and hit his brain. He shuddered, groaned, and flopped on top of her.

"Shogging bitch," he growled. "Filthy, shogging, filthy..." He stared open-mouthed at her rag doll body, all ripped and ruined.

He started to whimper, delicately rubbing her face, dabbing away the blood.

"I-It wasn't me. Rhiannon. It w-wasn't me," he said, over and over, stammering like he always used to.

She stirred and started to slide from under him. He raised himself on one arm and let her. She rolled to the floor and waited there a moment, panting on her knees.

"R-R-Rhiannon. It wasn't—"

"Shog... you... scut."

He winced, fumbled with his pants; pushed his back into the couch so he could pull them up.

"Listen t-t-to me. The wine. You h-h-hit me first. I was in s-shock." What if she told someone? She wouldn't even need to. Ain, what had he done to her face? "N-N-Not me, n-not me, not me."

Rhiannon stood, wrapping the remains of her clothes about her.

"Don't g-go. Please wait. Someone will see."

She stumbled toward the door.

Gaston leapt up and got in front of her, palms raised. "W-Wait, Rhiannon. P-P-Please. I c-can—ooooph!"

Her knee caught him in the nuts, doubling him up. Air blasted from his lungs.

The door clicked open and slammed.

Gaston fell on his arse, clutching his balls, gasping for breath.

He noticed the book Shader had lent him, tossed carelessly on the floor: LaRoche's *Foundations of Holiness*, lying there like an accusation.

"Shog you!" Gaston kicked the book, crying out as he felt a sharp pain in his groin.

Moaning, he rolled onto his side and sobbed like a baby.

"Dad... You can't be... Dad!"

WHERE NOUSIA ENDS

Port Sarum, Sahul

The stars looked different in Sahul, fell in different patterns—pinpricks in the pall of night; a thousand openings onto a silvery hereafter.

Shader uncrossed his legs, rubbing and patting them to encourage the blood to flow. He rolled to his knees and sat back on his haunches.

"Ain't you finished yet?" Elpidio stomped up the steps to the aftcastle. "Captain says we're nearly there."

Shader closed the Liber and returned it to his coat pocket. "He's got better eyes than me, then."

"You can see the moon, can't you?"

It hardly needed pointing out, but Elpidio did so all the same: a sickle-blade of silver low down on the horizon.

"You can navigate by the moon?"

Elpidio leaned over the prow, resting his chin in his hands. "Captain can. Guess anyone could with a chart and a thingy."

"A sextant. You forget already, eh?" Podesta climbed up to join them. "What are you doing kneeling? I'm not the Ipsissimus, you know."

Shader stood, grimacing as the blood pooled toward his feet. "I thought we were running blind to avoid the mawgs. Didn't realize you knew where we were heading."

Podesta put his hands on Elpidio's shoulders and stared out into the blackness. "There's a monster of a reef just north of here. Dreamers call it the Makara. Running blind would likely leave us hulled. Don't want to be swimming for it in these waters, eh, boy? Sharks here are as big as horses. I'll let you into a secret. The reason the mawgs never catch us is that they can't navigate by night. That's why we can take the Anglesh route. It's good, eh? All you need is a sextant,"—he clapped Elpidio on the head—"some charts, and an almanac. Easy. I should show you, eh?"

"What's that?" Elpidio pointed at the black outlines of what appeared to be a forest on the sea.

"Port Sarum. It seems Hagalle has been busy, eh? That's a lot of masts, and most of 'em galleons, or my name's not Amidio Podesta. Maybe he's going to invade Ashanta, uh?"

"Doesn't have the strength," Shader said. "He's more likely to use them to ferry his troops round the coast to give the Eastern Lords a bit of a reminder."

Podesta smacked his lips. "Maybe. It would be easier than a march across the interior. That's a lot of new ships to just sit there, eh?"

***

The *Aura Placida* slipped into the harbor, gentle waves sloshing against the prow, sailors nattering in the rigging, smoking on the deck.

Shader lifted his eyes from his prayer cord as the first hints of crimson appeared on the horizon, and the skyline of Sarum started to emerge: jutting towers and arched bridges, the benign glow of lamplight from the sprawl of awakening houses.

Far to the north, he could see the abbey's bell-tower: Pardes, stark and lonely, hunched in among the limestone monoliths of the "petrified forest". He wondered if the Gray Abbot knew the ship was in. Wondered how he'd respond to Shader's triumph in Aeterna. Would he even see it as a triumph?

"Now what do you make of that, my friend?" Podesta sprang up the steps and clapped him on the shoulder.

They were passing alongside a smaller vessel with a shallow keel and four masts.

"Isn't that the *Dolphin*?" The ship that had taken Shader to Aeterna. But what was it doing back in Sarum on the other side of the world?

"Must have left Latia just after we did." Podesta shook his head. "Impossible Diaz should have gotten here first."

"She's a fast ship."

"Not that fast." Podesta clicked his fingers. "He must have taken our route. The spineless bastard finally struck up the nerve to try the Anglesh Isles, eh?"

Shader couldn't imagine Captain Diaz taking unnecessary risks. He was a calculating man, hard and unscrupulous, but he'd never chance running into mawgs. The flesh-eaters put the fear of Ain into the man. Unless…

"Someone must be paying him big money, eh?" Podesta said. "Maybe the Templum?"

The *Dolphin* retreated from view as they found their berth, and Podesta gave orders for the lowering of the gangplank.

Shader retrieved his coat and hat from his cabin, said a quick prayer of thanks to Nous, and headed for dry land.

"Good luck, my friend," Podesta called from the forecastle.

Shader made a visor of his hand and squinted up at the captain's silhouette against the rising sun. "Not staying in Sarum?"

"Maybe a day or two. Our business in Gladelvi…" He touched a finger to his lips. "The Templum contract I told you about."

He hadn't exactly said much. He'd made it sound like it was no one else's concern.

Podesta must have read the frown on Shader's face, as he added, "Medicines, supplies. You know the sort of thing. Just don't tell the Emperor Hagalle, eh?"

A crewman bumped into Shader and muttered a curse. With a will of its own, Shader's hand flew to the hilt of the gladius.

—Cleto.

Blood crisscrossed the back of his shirt, evidence of a recent flogging. He sneered, as if to say, "Go on, then," but then put his head down and moved off.

As Shader waved goodbye to Podesta, he caught sight of the lad, Elpidio, staring down from the crow's-nest at Sarum, as if it were a fairy-tale castle.

Shader had been the same the first time he'd seen it four years ago, when he'd marveled at the cloud-piercing towers left over from the fall of the Old World.

The black chef, Sabas, lumbered from the galley and gave him a meaty grin, and then Shader was off down the gangplank and back on Sahulian soil for the first time in three months.

***

Shader stamped red sand from his boots, pulled his broad-brimmed hat off, and held it to his chest. Squinting at the pink and purple sky, he ran his fingers through sweat-drenched hair.

Dawn broke in a matter of heartbeats in Sahul, the sun always in a hurry to scorch everything in sight without mercy.

Tugging off his coat, he began to fold it, but then caught sight of something moving in the hazy distance: a dark smudge, shimmering in the heat, heedless of the sun, just as he'd been when he'd first arrived in Sahul.

The figure came into focus the way a sharp slap could shake the grog of drunkenness from you. A tall hat, sunlight glinting from a buckle at the front. Long black coat—not dissimilar to Shader's, and totally unsuited to the Sahulian summer.

The man stopped twenty yards from him, one hand on the hilt of a rapier, the other clutching a heavy book. He tilted the hat to show his face—a lean face with sunken eyes and a triangle of a beard flecked with gray.

"Deacon Shader?"

Shader dropped his coat, letting the man see the swords scabbarded at his hips, the hint of mail beneath his surcoat. He flipped his hat back into place, pulling down the brim to keep the sun from his eyes.

"Yes, I see that you are." The words were quietly spoken, precise and measured. "The *stolen* gladius more than gives it away."

Stolen? It shouldn't have surprised Shader the Templum saw it that way. The sword was intended for its Keeper. He should have left it behind; would have done, if not for Aristodeus telling him to keep it.

"I have had more trouble finding you than I would have liked, but I am not one to *complain*. Do what must be done, *Ain* willing."

"You followed me all the way from Aeterna?" Apparently, the Ipsissimus's anger hadn't abated as quickly as Aristodeus had thought.

"Bardol Shin. *Investigator* Shin of the Templum Judiciary. You know, of course, why I have come."

Shin's expression remained neutral. He didn't even show the slightest discomfort at the rivulets of sweat running down his face from beneath his hat.

"The Ipsissimus noticed his new Keeper was missing? Sent you to bring me home?"

No trace of a smile. He may have sighed, but if he did, it must have been a small one. There was the slightest shrug of his shoulders, the minutest ruffle of his coat.

"His Divinity has *absolute* trust in the Judiciary. I doubt he is even aware of my mission. Anything he needs to know will be conveyed to him by Exemptus Silvanus, and in your case, I'm sure His Divinity would have *much* sympathy."

Unlike Silvanus. The Prefect of the Judiciary was a notorious conservative, utterly puritanical and widely favored to be the next Ipsissimus. With the backing of his henchmen in the Judiciary, Shader couldn't see it being any other way.

"I have been at sea for *six* weeks. Six weeks with the scum of the earth. Privateers, I'll warrant, under a certain Captain *Diaz*." Shin enunciated the name with great precision, as if he were dredging it from a carefully organized mental archive. "You are familiar with the name?"

"I think you know the answer to that." How could Shader forget the outward bound trip to Aeterna on board the *Dolphin*? "That how you found me?"

"Diaz said he had never heard of you. He was *lying*, of course. I can always smell a rat. He seemed to have a plan to get me drunk, but the trouble with such *scheming* is that—"

"You don't drink."

"Precisely."

"You're not likely to go down well in Sahul, then."

Shin took a step closer. "Going down *well* in Sahul is hardly top of my list of desires. I am a simple man, Shader. A simple *family* man. All I desire is to do Ain's will; but as he speaks only through his most *reverent* servants, I am bound to do the exemptus's. You will not, I take it, return without a fight?"

"And land myself in the Judiciary's dungeons? Hardly proportionate to the crime of wanting to be left alone."

Shin bent over from the waist to lay his book on the ground. "If you wanted to be left alone, you should not have taken *solemn* vows. There is no place in Nousia for lapsed *consecrated* knights."

"Then perhaps you've not noticed: Sahul isn't part of Nousia."

Shin may have wrinkled his nose at that, but it was such a small reaction as to be almost indiscernible. "It is the *people* who make the kingdom."

There was the faintest of rasps as he drew his rapier.

Shader's blades leapt clear of their scabbards, his father's longsword and the Sword of the Archon.

"I have been to the abbey, you know." Shin made a couple of practice lunges and held the blade vertically in front of his face. "The Gray Abbot was as tight-lipped as I would have expected, but a certain Frater *Elphus* was most instructive. He said you had not been cut out for monastic life. Said you had once caused a spot of *bother* in the city. He also mentioned your exploits in the village of *Oakendale*." Again the careful pronunciation, as if he'd committed the name to memory, along with Ain knows how many others, all filed away for some undisclosed day of retribution. "Establishing an order of religious knights, even if only a poor *parody* of the Elect, is about as serious a crime as you can commit. Besides *reneging* on your vows, that is. I am afraid they will have to be dealt with, once I have *finished* with you."

"You might want to examine your conscience, Investigator. Thought I detected a note of pride there."

Shin frowned—just for a moment. "Confidence in one's *divinely* bestowed abilities is not the same thing as pride. If Ain has blessed me with the finest *fencing* skills in Nousia, who am I to deny it?"

"Such a pity we're in Sahul."

Shader sprang to the attack, longsword thrusting, gladius arcing in a vicious swing.

Shin spun away from the onslaught with the grace of a dancer, the tip of his rapier darting for Shader's unprotected heart. With a turn of the wrist, the longsword parried it, and slid down its length to the basket-guard. Shin snatched the blade away and skipped back in a tight semicircle.

"Good eyes, I will grant you. Sharp reflexes, too. I see the rumors among your *confreres* were not exaggerated."

Shin was good himself. More than good. Shader could tell from his poise, his balance, that he was a master swordsman, and he was swift as a striking serpent with it.

"I am a little surprised you showed no recognition of my name." Shin circled him, sword point lowered. "I have quite the *reputation* back home."

"With the ladies? Or for being the life and soul of the party?"

One of Shin's cheeks began to twitch, and his eyes narrowed. Shader tracked them, scarcely daring to blink. There! The tiniest glance to the left gave the game away.

Shin lunged with bewildering speed. Shader swayed out of the way and felt the hot spray of blood on his forearm as the gladius found its mark in the investigator's throat. Shin's eyes bulged, his lips moving, nothing but pink froth coming out. The rapier dropped to the ground, his knees buckled, and he fell on top of it.

Shader picked up Shin's Liber and opened it upon his corpse. He wiped the gladius on

Shin's coat, and sheathed both swords.

The investigator should have caught up with him in Aeterna, spared himself six weeks aboard the Dolphin. Ain knows what that would have done for his soul.

Shader knelt beside his body and thumbed through the pages until he came to the Liturgy for the Dead.

A single drop of rain spat upon the page before he'd mouthed the first word of prayer. The sun vanished behind a smudge of cloud that had crept in from the ocean unnoticed. That was Sahulian weather for you.

Shader picked up his coat as the rain pattered on the Liber and splashed ripples in the blood pooling upon the thirsty ground.

RHIANNON'S HOUSE

Village of Oakendale, Sahul

Elias Wolf pulled on the reins, and the cart rolled to a halt before the Kwane household. A line of White Order knights stood at the edge of the garden, glaring at him like he was the enemy.

He glanced at Rhiannon still sleeping in the back among the instruments and books, head resting on a sack of weed.

She'd come to him during the night, a sorry, sodden mess, stumbling through the rain. He'd assumed she'd been smoking the gear he'd given her; assumed she was shit-faced on booze. He'd been right about the latter, but it was far worse than that. Gaston had raped her. The shogging little scut had shown himself a phony and a hypocrite, just like the rest of the douche bags in the Templum.

Her face was a mass of yellow and black, one eye a puffy slit. Brownish blood was crusted in streaks beneath her nose, and there were angry welts around her neck. Her breathing was shallow and ragged, mouth slightly open, teeth stained red.

He considered waking her, then thought better of it. She didn't need this, after all she'd been through.

By the looks of things, Gaston had already gotten to her folks, and there was nothing but trouble waiting.

Elias jumped down from the cart, moving alongside Hector and giving the shire horse a reassuring pat. He felt his face flush with anger, and his hand tightened around the Statue of Eingana in his pocket.

The shield wall parted, and Gaston strode toward him, Yeffrik and Jessy Kwane trailing behind, little Sammy just visible sitting on the doorstep.

Gaston's nose was purple and swollen. His long blond hair was tied back, giving away center-stage to his arse of a face. Elias had never realized what a small chin he had. Almost no chin at all. He was dressed like the rest of the knights in the white surcoat and red Monas that Shader had paid for with other people's money. The chainmail, too, no doubt brought in from Jorakum at considerable expense—all in the name of religion. Though where they'd got the money for it was anyone's guess. The council certainly wouldn't have forked out that much, even if they could have.

"You see." Gaston waited for Rhiannon's folks to come alongside. "Screwing the bard." He spat the words and narrowed his eyes at Elias. "And this is what I get for trying to stop her." He jabbed a finger at his misshapen nose.

Yeffrik looked like a man who'd been told the Earth went round the sun, having always believed the opposite. He hunched his massive shoulders and bit his lip. "Elias?"

"What? No. It was him. Look at her!" He backed away to the cart. "Just look at what this holy little shit did. To your daughter!"

Jessy tugged on Yeffrik's sleeve. "See, I told you we should've had Sheriff Halligan come over."

"What would be the point?" Elias said. Halligan hated his guts. Had done ever since he busted Elias for possession of pituri. Bastard confiscated the whole stash, too. And besides, what could a lone sheriff do against so many armed men?

"Halligan's scared shitless of these thugs. Didn't I say this would happen if Shader got his way and started training the local boys? Fascist. The bloke with the most swords always rules the roost, and right now," —he glared at Gaston—"that's everyone's favorite son of a preacher man."

Rhiannon mumbled something and pushed herself up on one arm. "Dad?" she rasped, turning her head to look through her good eye.

Yeffrik's jaw dropped, and he stiffened, fists clenched, arms shaking.

Jessy brushed past him and covered her mouth with her hands.

"Mom." Rhiannon started to sob.

Elias looked along the line of knights, shields locked together like they were expecting to meet a charge.

He recognized Barek, sandy hair poking from beneath a basinet, blinking rapidly and licking his lips. Elgin Fallow was beside him, looking like the playground bully, desperate for someone to thump. Justin Salace was there, too, a thin smile upon his lips; and Solomon Jonas, staring blankly ahead, as if none of this were happening.

There were twenty, at least, all local lads he'd once told tales to or taught music. Most were friends of Rhiannon's. She really needed to make better choices.

"Who… did… this?" Yeffrik finally found the words.

"She attacked me." Gaston had a hand on the hilt of his sword. "I was trying to help."

"And you hit her?" Jessy's face twisted into a snarl.

"That wasn't me!" Gaston glared at Elias. "It was him!"

"Now wait a minute." Elias looked from Rhiannon to Yeffrik to Jessy. "Surely you don't believe him?"

Rhiannon was panting hard, shaking her head, as if she couldn't understand something. "What the shog are you talking about?" She pointed straight between Gaston's eyes. "It was this piece of shit!"

"Lies!" Gaston had his sword half drawn as Yeffrik's fist crunched into his nose, splitting it like a ripe melon.

Gaston went down hard, Rhiannon's dad kneeling astride him, clubbing away at his face.

Justin shoulder-charged Yeffrik, sent him sprawling to the dirt. Yeffrik tried to rise, but Gaston was up in a flash with his sword, and ran him through the chest.

Rhiannon screamed, and Elias began to shake.

Jessy ran toward her husband, but Justin caught her and flung her to the ground. She got straight back up, but Elgin smashed his pommel into her head. Her eyes rolled, and her legs folded under her. With a sickening thud, she went down, blood trickling from her lips.

A door slammed, but Elias couldn't see the house as the shield wall came toward him. He tripped over the step of the cart, trying to scramble up. Rhiannon's screaming shredded his thoughts. He was vaguely aware of the Statue of Eingana cutting into his fingers where he gripped it so tightly.

Gaston lunged at him, sword aimed at his face. Elias tumbled out of the way, the statue starting to singe his skin.

More screaming—not Rhiannon, this time, but a muffled wailing from a dark place. Something thrashed and cowered behind his vision: a shaggy ape with the head of a dog. Shapes spilled from its eyes, hideous, contorted, all teeth and talons, boiling flesh, and lashing limbs. The images swelled until his mind burst, spewing them forth.

Shrill cries tore through him as the knights blocked their ears and clawed at their eyes. Shields clattered to the ground, swords clashing on top of them. White knights, swaying knights, screaming knights; froth bubbling from gaping mouths; eyes like saucers staring at invisible horrors.

Elias climbed into the driver's seat, dropped the statue beside him, and cracked the reins.

Hector lurched forward, swatting a knight aside with his great head.

Elias turned the cart toward the road and leaned forward to slap the horse into a run.

As they rolled onto the gravel, he cast a look over his shoulder. The knights were all down, writhing on the ground next to the bodies of Yeffrik and Jessy. Rhiannon hung half over the side of the cart, wailing and sobbing.

Elias caught a glimpse of a small boy running for the woods behind the house—Sammy, Rhiannon's little brother. He should stop; go back. The boy was only five.

But the cart kept on moving, and the house swiftly fell away from them.

Last thing he saw was knights climbing to their feet, Gaston yelling orders and slashing the air with his sword.

THE ANCHORITE

City of Sarum, Sahul

Cadman frowned at the blood smeared across his cellar wall, while still keeping count of the blows at the back of his mind. Thirteen lashes of the cat-o'-nine-tails, and already Jarmin the Anchorite of Gladelvi was blathering for all he was worth.

The midget, Shadrak, drew back his arm for another crack of the whip, and then paused to peel a strip of skin from one of the barbs. His white face was speckled with Jarmin's blood, pink eyes glinting with rather too much enjoyment for Cadman's liking.

Do a thing with gusto, by all means, but please let's not debase ourselves.

The irony wasn't lost on him. He'd been debasing himself for centuries, but there was a world of difference between need and gratuitousness.

"Please," Jarmin sobbed, the martyr well and truly beaten out of him. "Please. I've told you all I know."

"Yet you haven't said what you are doing in Sarum, visiting our beloved governor. Nor have you told us how you got here so quickly, on foot, all the way from Gladevli. What's that, fourteen, fifteen hundred miles? You haven't revealed why it is people say you've been around for generations and haven't changed a jot." *Though, by the looks of him, the wizened old coot, he should already have one foot in the grave.*

"You do realize, Governor Gen will be finished if word of your visit reaches Jorakum. Hagalle will have his guts for garters. So, do be a good chap, and tell me, what brings the most notorious Nousian in Sahul to town? The prospect of a conversion?" Zara Gen had, when all was said and done, been uncharacteristically tolerant of the Nousian priests at the Templum of the Knot. Elsewhere, the Sicarii would have been sent in to show them just how much they were wanted.

"Shogging herb trade, if you ask me," Shadrak said. "Know what I mean?"

Cadman raised a hand to tell him to take a rest.

The midget threw the whip aside and helped himself to a bottle of Shiraz, pushing the cork in with a slender knife.

Only five bottles left on the rack. Cadman winced. Not that he minded Shadrak taking the wine—he'd long since lost the ability to taste anything, and alcohol hadn't affected him for donkey's years. It was the nuisance of having to get away from the number five that was so unsettling. Either they'd have to drink another bottle, or go out and buy some more.

Grinding his teeth with the annoyance of it all, Cadman turned back to Jarmin, who was suspended by his wrists, toes just about reaching the floor. He was naked, not because Cadman took any pleasure from seeing him that way, but because he'd learned long ago—in Wolfmalen Castle in Verusia—that nakedness deprived a man of any number of defenses, not the least his dignity.

"How does it work?" Cadman held up the piece of amber they'd taken from Jarmin. It was a little shorter than his finger, and half as thick. One end tapered to a point. He was sure the thing was vibrating.

"I promised not to use it." Jarmin's head dropped. He must have known that was the wrong answer by now.

"I gave no such promise." Cadman tried to sound amiable. The fat face and big mustache had always made that easier, he found. People seemed to trust him.

Shadrak set down the bottle a little harder than necessary and twirled the knife on the tip of his finger.

Jarmin's eyes flitted from the blade to Cadman, the anticipation of what was to come clearly evident on his face.

"What if I close my eyes?" Cadman did so. "And focus my will through the… fang, would you call it?" Because he was certain that's what it was: a piece of the serpent statue of Eingana the Dweller had spoken of in his dreams. The demon had said Jarmin was coming; that he had a piece of the statue on him; and for a denizen of the Abyss, the Dweller had proven true to his word.

Then, synchronicity of all synchronicities, the morning after his dream, someone shoved the flyer through his door, informing him of the bard's performance of the Epic of the Reckoning. Something was going on. Something Cadman should have steered well clear of; but at the same time, he had to know. Had to know what was in it for him. Had to know if the Dweller's promise of a clean immortality could be true.

Cadman shut out all other thoughts and gave it his best shot, reaching with his mind into the amber fang.

Nothing happened.

"Hmm. Disappointing. I don't know about you, Jarmin, but I'm getting rather tired of this. How about you, Shadrak?"

"Bored as shog." The assassin took a step toward Jarmin. "Want me to cut an eye out?"

Jarmin squealed like a girl, and yellow piss sprayed down his leg, pooling on the stone floor.

Cadman turned his nose up and let out an enormous sigh. "Shadrak here enjoyed a performance at Broken Bridge last night. All about the Statue of Eingana, it was."

Shadrak pressed his face right up to Jarmin's, and slowly moved the tip of his knife toward an eye.

Jarmin began to shake and whimper. "Please. Please."

"Shadrak tells me there are five pieces of the Statue of Eingana. Two eyes, two fangs, and the body." *Five blasted pieces. Or could you count the body as separate? Still led to four and one, in any case.* "Nod, if you agree."

Jarmin nodded frantically.

"Good. Now we're getting somewhere. The Dreamer, Huntsman, gave a fang to you, which you've done a good job of guarding, up until now." Cadman flipped the amber into the air and caught it in a chubby hand. "Who has the other pieces?"

Jarmin squeezed his eyes shut, face all puckered up like a sphincter, knees knocking together.

"One name, then. That's all it'll take, and then you can go free."

Jarmin looked up, blinking in disbelief. "I can go? You won't kill me?"

"Why would I? We're not animals, you know. Give me what I want, and I will be more than happy. Your death would be of no benefit to me, and Shadrak here has probably had a surfeit of killing."

Actually, he's probably working out how to do away with both of us once we're

70

finished.

Cadman shot a glance at the shadows gathered in the alcove by the entrance and tried not to betray that he saw one move. *Faithful old Callixus, doing his duty.* Well, faithful probably wasn't the right word. *Compelled, then.*

Jarmin took a deep breath, tongue moistening his lips.

"The Gray Abbot has an eye."

"Really? Now who'd have thought it? The eye of a Dreamer goddess and one of her fangs entrusted to two of the Templum's holiest luminaries."

"Can I go now?"

"Indeed." Cadman held up the amber fang between thumb and forefinger. "Before you do, though, I wonder if you'd mind witnessing this. You see, I think I've worked out how to use it. Visualization. Am I right?"

Cadman closed his eyes and tightened his grip on the fang. He formed a picture of Jarmin's flesh being ripped apart, felt the amber throb, and heard a sound like the pulping of ripe fruit. Something warm and wet splashed his face, and he opened his eyes.

A bloody mess hung from the ceiling. Shadrak was peering at it with more curiosity than disgust.

The fang felt hot in Cadman's hand. He uncurled his fingers and frowned.

The amber had dulled considerably, and veins of green and brown had spread across the surface. Somewhere in the distance, a bird cried out.

Cadman suddenly felt uneasy, like he'd been caught with his hand in the cookie jar. He cocked his head to one side and listened, but heard nothing else.

Silly, Cadman, you paranoid old sod.

He caught Shadrak watching him and gave a shrug.

"Might take a bit of practice, eh?" He thrust the fang into his jacket pocket. "So, the Gray Abbot. I don't suppose you fancy a trip to Pardes?"

"Reckon I've paid my debt. There's plenty of work back at the guild, and besides, I've got a score to settle with my previous employers."

Cadman chewed the end of his mustache. He'd not been expecting that.

"I take it you're all right about me knowing who you are." He felt a rush of trepidation. "You being Shadrak the Unseen and all that."

"If you can keep your mouth shut, you've nothing to fear from me."

"Quite. Quite. And thank you. What are you doing?"

Shadrak pried open the grille on the cellar floor and lowered himself into the hole it had covered.

"You're not going down there?"

"Best way to see the city."

"What about the wine?"

"You finish it."

Shadrak slid the grille back into place and dropped from sight.

A shadow detached itself from the wall and drifted to Cadman's side.

"Thank you, Callixus, but it seems you weren't needed after all."

The wraith hovered over him, adding its chillness to the cold he already felt.

Cadman scrabbled about in his pocket for a cigarette. "Can you make the journey to Pardes?"

"You want me to kill the Gray Abbot?" There was a hint of reluctance in the wraith's voice. He was, after all, a former grand master of the Elect, and didn't take to murder all that easily.

"Only if you must. Bring me his piece of the Statue of Eingana. Who knows, with two segments, I may have double the power."

Then again, he might just be getting deeper into something than he ought to.

71

What on earth was he doing? He thought about the tentacled nightmare that had invaded his bedroom and shattered the illusion of safety.

The cat's out of the bag, Cadman. Either you see this through, or get as far away from here as possible.

But anywhere that wasn't Sahul was that much closer to Verusia, and the last thing he needed was to come to the attention of his old master, Otto Blightey.

Outside in the street, someone screamed.

Cadman shrugged. It wasn't anything unusual. He'd chosen to live amid the depravity of the suburbs so as not to draw attention. In the main, he'd been left well alone, save for Frayn and his accident-prone assassins.

He climbed the cellar steps, starting to feel that sinking feeling of unreality that told him it was time to eat. He didn't relish the idea, exactly. The thought of ripping into raw chunks of scabby prostitute was hardly a match for the gourmet cuisine he'd enjoyed in his day. It was sad, really. Sad that it had come to this. Still, you had to make the most of it. You could at least be civilized about it, whatever the ghouls dragged to his table.

He made his way to the dining room and pulled out a chair. He was about to send out a mental command to the scavengers he had out patrolling the slums in search of sustenance, when there was another scream from outside. Then another. Pretty soon, you could have been forgiven for thinking you were in the Abyss, hearing the unrelieved torment of the damned.

He crossed to the window and peeked out through the blinds.

People were dropping like flies. Not dead. At least, not yet. But they were writhing on the ground in pools of their own vomit, and those that weren't had their hands over their mouths and noses and were backing away as quick as they could.

Something throbbed in his jacket pocket, and he reached inside to pluck out Jarmin's amber fang. The brown veins it had acquired were pulsing, and it was wreathed in a corona of filth.

Oh dear, Cadman thought as the screams went on and on. *Did I do that?*

THE ORPHAN

Village of Oakendale, Sahul

One of the knights heard something and held back. The others pressed on, a staggered line sweeping through the trees with the subtlety of stampeding cattle.

Huntsman scuttled along the branch and lowered himself by a silken thread. He hung above the knight's sandy hair, watched him turn in response to a sniffle from the undergrowth.

Huntsman swung back and forth then sprang as the knight set off toward the sound. He landed lightly on the back of a white tunic that covered silver mail. The knight ducked under branches, crashed through ferns with no recognition that he had a passenger.

A boy scampered out of a thicket, mud-stained and miserable, squealing like a spitted pig. It was Sammy Kwane, Rhiannon's little brother. Huntsman knew them both from their visits to the bard's house, where they came for stories and lessons in music. Elias Wolf was one of the custodians of Eingana, and Huntsman kept a close eye on him.

The knight lunged at Sammy, caught hold of his shirt and ripped it away, sending him sprawling on his face.

"Stay away, stay away!" the boy cried, crawling on hands and knees.

"Sammy, it's me, Barek." The knight held up his hands and inched forward.

Huntsman dropped to the forest floor, spindly legs retracting, flesh boiling, twisting, growing, until he stood as a man behind the knight.

Barek's hand went to his sword, and he turned, gaping like a pituri chewer.

Huntsman curled his lips back to show the stubs of his teeth, rolled his eyes up into their lids, and hooked his fingers like the fangs of a death adder.

"Barek!" Huntsman sprayed him with spittle. The knight staggered back with his arm across his face, but Huntsman advanced, sticking out his jaw, hissing, and flicking his tongue. "I have your name, white fellah." He clenched his fists and ground them together.

Barek tripped and fell on top of the boy. He rolled away and backed toward the nearest trunk.

"I'm not going to harm him!" His body shuddered, and froth spilled from his mouth.

"First your name, then your breath; last your heart." Huntsman started to pull his fists apart, stretching Eingana's invisible sinew, tauter, tauter, tauter…

"Please!" Barek shrieked. "I've done nothing. Do it to Gaston!"

Sammy looked from Huntsman to the knight, head shaking, tears cutting trails through the dirt on his face. He frowned at Barek, winced, and tapped his temples, as if he couldn't understand something.

In that instant, Huntsman's focus shifted, and the knight fled through the trees.

"Mommy!" Sammy wailed. "Mommy!"

Huntsman stepped toward him, but the boy screamed.

"Shh!" Huntsman said. "Bad men will hear you."

Sammy screamed even louder, eyes and nose streaming, limbs shaking.

Huntsman scooped out some maban dust from his medicine bag and blew it in the child's face. Sammy gasped, inhaled the powdered crystal, stiffened, and dropped like a stone.

Huntsman lifted the boy to his shoulder, scented the air, and slipped into the undergrowth.

He carried the child beyond the forest and deep into the bush, along trails that would have been invisible to any but a Dreamer.

The knights wouldn't follow him into the open, where there was no shade from the blazing torch of Walu the Sun-Woman.

He set the boy down on the ocher earth, covering him with the cloak of feathers.

Huntsman balanced on one leg like a brolga and stilled his breathing until he could feel the heartbeat of Sahul. It throbbed beneath his sole, pulsed through his veins, pounded in his head, and brought him emptiness. Slowly, the web began to spread out from his calm center, strands of ghostly light creeping to the horizon, sensing, feeling, vibrating.

The questing threads recoiled from the north, where they touched the dead earth around the Sarum. That was nothing unusual; but as he sent them on into the city, Huntsman felt the web sicken, like a fish in stagnant water.

Breaking the link with Sahul, he let the strands fade and sat upon the earth. There was badness at the heart of Sarum, a poisoning of the breath of Eingana. Her power seeped into the city, but it was not pure. Something warped it, turned it against its nature. Someone had used a fragment of her statue. Used and abused it; twisted it to ends it was never intended for.

Sammy groaned and pushed the cloak away. A bull ant danced upon the back of his hand. The boy sat up to peer closely at it, muttering and cocking his head.

Huntsman pressed a finger to his lips and wondered. He'd intended to take the child to Rhiannon to atone in part for what he'd put her through. All for the greater good, Aristodeus had said, but Huntsman was no longer sure the philosopher had Sahul's best interests at heart. He was a pale-skin, after all, and that seldom boded well for the land.

He'd said a battle was coming; the end of the Dreaming. The Unweaving of all things.

Huntsman shook his head. Aristodeus said it had happened before; said he'd been there. Last time, he'd failed in some way, and all was nearly lost. But this time, he claimed he was prepared. Huntsman had believed him and gone to Rhiannon, told her to reject Deacon Shader and free him for the destiny Aristodeus had planned.

Watching the boy with the ant gave Huntsman another idea. Perhaps Sahul was trying to tell him something. Perhaps she had plans of her own.

"What does it tell you?" He crouched over the boy.

"Monsters underground." The boy smacked his lips and pointed to the north. "Heading for the city."

"What kind of monsters?"

Sammy jumped up and blew the ant away. He thrust his hips back and stooped, letting his arms dangle, knuckles scraping the ground. Baring his teeth, he opened his mouth wide in a snarl.

It was a good impression; one Huntsman recognized. "Mawgs are coming?"

The boy nodded, a look of remembered horror passing across his face. Mawgs had come to his village before; come to Oakendale to feast, until Deacon Shader had driven them off.

"Statue must be drawing them," Huntsman thought aloud. "Some fool has been using it."

Sammy's eyes filled with tears, and he began to shake. "Mommy? Daddy?"

Huntsman raised his hand to strike him; drew it back down. Sahul had spoken to the child, he was certain of it, but now grief had claimed him once more. Patience of the crocodile—that is what was needed. Let the boy grieve. Sahul had marked him. She would not let him go.

"Come, Sammy." Huntsman's mind was made up, and he turned his face to the north. "We will go to Sarum and help Eingana." And maybe find Rhiannon; return her little brother. If that's what Sahul wanted.

Sammy didn't complain about the heat, or the endless trudging through the red dust. The desert was occasionally broken by a tuft of spiky weed or a skeletal gum tree. The tears dried as quickly as they had come. Huntsman knew the child had retreated into the Dreaming, where the horror of his losses would not be felt.

He glanced at the boy, noting the empty stare, the silent determination that would see him walk with no particular destination until the heat and the miles finally claimed him. He recognized the symptoms, for they were common among his people, who would wander the bush in pursuit of answers, wisdom, or death. He had undertaken such a journey himself, before the Wapar Man had finally caught up with him and taken him to the Homestead.

The midday sun was scorching, and even Huntsman's enchantments could not keep them from its life-sapping heat. Scanning the hazy horizon, he spotted a lone and leafless tree in the distance.

The Sun-Woman's torch harried them until he settled his ward beneath its skeletal limbs, his feathered cloak draped from the branches for shade.

"Why did they kill Mommy and Daddy?" Sammy asked, stretching out beneath the shelter.

Huntsman had asked himself similar questions about the slaughter of his people before the Reckoning.

"Hearts of people have two seeds," he explained, picking up two small stones and holding them before the boy. "First is bright with life. If it grows, it overflows with light and love, so that they take root in others. This is way of things, to join together. Two beasts become one..." Huntsman tailed off and cleared his throat. "Second seed is not from Sahul."

Sammy looked at him blankly.

Huntsman thought for a moment. He was not used to children. He tried again.

"Everyone has a seed of good and a seed of evil. Life is a fight between these seeds. If evil seed grows stronger than good, people do bad things, things that hurt others."

"So, it was the seeds that killed Mommy and Daddy, not the men?"

"No," Huntsman said carefully. "Seeds open different paths. It is task of folk to choose between paths; between Sahul and Deceiver."

"Deceiver?"

"Father of Lies, white folk call him. Demiurgos. He is brother of Eingana, frozen in ice at heart of Abyss."

Sammy's forehead wrinkled up like an old man's. "I know about him. Soror Agna—my sister's friend—she told me. So, good seeds come from Sahul, and bad ones come from the Demi... Demiur... Abyss?"

Huntsman laughed. "Barraiya People see signs everywhere." He swept his arm out to encompass all the land they could see. "Signs from Sahul, like ants talking to children."

Sammy's face lit up at that.

"And evil signs, like Kutji spirits. It is why we have Kadjis to guide us, help us to make right choices."

75

"How?"

It was a good question. Huntsman bit his thumbnail off, spat it to the red dust.

"With some things, choices are difficult." He spoke now almost to himself. "Strands of good and evil grow twisted, like vines and creepers. Become knotted. Each choice has its own dangers."

Sammy looked even more perplexed.

"Some choices," Huntsman continued, "are easy. Anything that brings harm cannot come from good seed. By hurting your mother and father, men chose bad path."

Sammy nodded his understanding. "But what if a person hurts another to stop them doing bad things to someone else?"

Huntsman ruffled the boy's hair. "Then you must follow voice of your heart, wise little fellah, for there, paths have become so tangled, it is hard for mind to unravel."

"So, Gaston, Justin, and Elgin weren't really our friends? They are bad? All those knights are evil?"

"What they do makes them so."

"Can they become good again?"

Huntsman did not answer, and looked away into the sprawling red desert. His thoughts were troubled by the statue, and whatever was warping its power, sending waves of sickness through the web around Sarum.

Can evil become good? He stroked the boy's hair, smiling as Sammy closed his eyes, his breathing deepening. Can a poisoned stream regain its purity? Can a thing once changed become what it was before?

He settled down beside the boy, spirit drifting in the timelessness of the Dreaming.

He saw himself atop the Homestead, plunging the blade into his chest; felt once more the fire of the statue burning away his flesh, re-forming him as something both more and less than human.

What did he care for good and evil, for life and death? All these things had ceased to concern him since the moment of the Reckoning. He was one with the Dreaming, bound to Sahul in the spirit. If the land lived, nothing else mattered. Nothing except the statue, for it contained the essence of Eingana, mother of the Dreaming.

In Huntsman's hands, it had destroyed the power of the Ancients and their Technocrat; but before that, long before the birth of the boy named Adoni, Sektis Gandaw had found a way to enslave Eingana in the Dreaming and turn her power to his own ends.

A gust of wind brought him back from his musings. A storm head was rolling in from the north, and the temperature had dropped. He'd need to wake the boy, and soon; find him better shelter.

He lifted a hand to shake Sammy, but hesitated as the thought struck him: What if the mawgs finally found a piece? What if they returned it to their master? Was this the coming crisis that Aristodeus had foretold? After all, he had spoken of the Unweaving of all things.

THE PRODIGAL

Soulsong Estuary, Sahul

Shader's coat grew sodden and heavy, his hat lank and misshapen. Clay slurped at his boots. The rain falling in sheets pocked the track with puddles. Clouds smothered the sky with a roiling black blanket, and wind buffeted the grass-trees, their leaves fanning and flapping, anchored by stunted trunks.

Splash, slurp, splash. Splash, slurp, splash: steps like the beating of a diseased heart. The sound took hold like a mantra, drawing him to the still center within, where the storm was muffled and remote.

The waters of the Soulsong were swollen and dangerous, yet there were tents pitched along the bank, hunched figures running between them, shouts merging with the howling wind. Swinging lanterns cast their eerie glow across the precarious village, half a dozen hemming the platform of a swaying watchtower. To the northeast, Shader could make out the dark outline of Sarum, the spires of its Old World buildings stabbing the sky in retaliation for the downpour.

A burly spearman struggled toward him, cloak snapping like a lateen. Rain pattered against his helm, streamed down the nose-guard and soaked into his beard.

"Corporal Farley, Fifth Regiment, Imperial. Where you heading?"

"Business at the abbey," Shader shouted above the squall.

"Best tell them to stay away from Sarum. Plague's hit. Only got out by the skin of our teeth. There are people dropping in the street."

"I'll let them know." Not that it was necessary. No one had left Pardes for a very long time. No one, that is, besides Shader.

"Hit like a flash flood." Another soldier approached, a captain judging by his epaulets. "Janks. Captain Janks. Lucky to get out, we was. But our orders now are to stop anyone else from doing the same."

When Shader frowned, and looked him up and down for any sign of illness, the captain said, "We never came into contact with it. Started in the suburbs, they say. Reckon its the sanitation. Off to the abbey, is it? What business could be so urgent it can't wait till this shogging storm passes?"

"I was gonna ask him that," Farley said, ramming the haft of his spear into the mud and doing his best to stand up straight.

The blast of a horn had everyone turning. Soldiers, bent double against the gusting winds, scurried from their tents, and ran along the bank in the direction of the ocean.

"What is it?" Shader asked Captain Janks, who was wrapping his cloak about himself like a shroud as he headed after the others.

"Mawgs, most likely. Shoggers are getting cocky again. Been driving 'em off all the way down the coast."

"Mind if I join you?" The chill of anticipation ran up and down Shader's spine, fueled by flashing images of Oakendale's dead, steaming pools of gore staining the streets.

"You know what you're asking?"

Shader pulled back his coat to reveal the hilt of his longsword. "I know evil and how to deal with it."

"Right you are." Janks slapped him on the shoulder. "Don't suppose another pair of hands is gonna hurt any."

They ducked into the wind to catch up with the group of soldiers gathering at the base of the lookout tower.

Janks cupped his hands and threw his head back. "What is it? Mawgs?"

"No, sir!" the horn-blower yelled back, pointing to the west. "There's a boat coming up the river."

Even as he spoke, it drifted into sight, prow low in the water, lone mast supporting a patchwork sail. Mist partially obscured the view, but as the craft approached, Shader spotted a stout figure at the helm. Devilish horns glinted in the lamplight spilling from the mast. As it drew nearer, though, he saw that it was a helmed human, dwarfish and powerfully built, with a great mane of gray hair and a long braided beard. He wore a dark habit beneath a pale cloak embroidered with a red cross. The wind tore at his garments, revealing glimpses of banded armor underneath. The dwarf held a war hammer aloft, the boat seemingly steering itself.

"Shog me," Janks said. "It's the Fallen."

Resounding murmurs came from the soldiers. Shader shrugged and shook his head.

"Maldark the Fallen." The captain's voice quavered. "It's said he's sailed the waterways of Sahul since the Reckoning."

"Shall we stop him, sir?" Corporal Farley asked.

"I'm not sure that we could." Janks turned to watch the boat float silently past, heading for Sarum.

"What's he doing here?" Shader thought aloud.

"Who knows?" The captain continued to stare after the boat. "Bit of a coincidence, don't you think, that the Fallen arrives right on the heels of the plague?"

"Sorcery?" Shader's fingers curled around the hilt of the gladius.

"Maybe. Maybe not. But one thing's for sure: wherever the Fallen's seen, death's not far behind. Stand down, everyone!" Janks called over the wind. To Shader, he said, "You need a tent for the night?"

"I'll press on to the abbey."

"Suit yourself. Tell me one thing, though, "before you do. You a Nousian?"

Shader felt his face tighten, his mind racing for the right response. The captain was watching him, as if he already knew the answer.

"Don't worry. We've got no orders on that account. Reckon the Sicarii get paid more than enough for that job. You'll get no trouble from me." Janks leaned in closer. "Haven't the stomach for it. I'm curious, mind, as to what business a fighting man has at the abbey."

"As am I, Captain. As am I."

Shader shook Janks's hand and set off along the bank. He headed west, until he came to a wooden bridge, crossed the Soulsong Estuary, and entered the shelter of Darling Wood. A path through the trees opened onto a scree slope ascending to the lone spire of Pardes.

***

Shader paused before the wrought-iron gates of the abbey. Aeterna seemed suddenly even more remote than the other side of the world. It was as if he had never left Pardes, as if the time at Oakendale, the weeks of travel, and the tournament had been a tantalizing dream.

"You will live and die here," Frater Trellian had told him when he'd first arrived as a postulant. "Pardes is your tomb. Here, you will be buried with Nous."

The romance of sharing the death of the Son of Ain had carried him through the first few months, but deep down he'd always known it was a temporary arrangement. Simplicity and contemplation drew him like a moth to the flame, but he'd recoiled from the burn.

Lifting the latch with tremulous fingers, he pushed through the gate and closed it behind him. One last trip, he'd told the Gray Abbot; a final expiation, then he could accept the cold hand of Nous. The tournament was supposed to end his life of action, lay to rest the striving for excellence. Reach the heights, and then abandon the old life. No regrets, no wondering what he might have achieved.

His feet scuffed against the cobbles wending toward the abbey doors. He walked the way of the luminary one dragging footfall at a time. Hesitant steps. Deliberate. Gallows steps.

THE TEMPLUM OF THE KNOT

City of Sarum, Sahul

Elias drove the cart through the southern suburbs of Sarum, the scarf wrapped about his face offering scant protection from the plague. The storm had finally given way to clear skies, and the sun's heat was already halfway to drying his clothes.

He was starting to wish he hadn't used the statue to break through the cordon of imperial troops quarantining the city. Just a gentle use, mind; enough to convince the guards to let them pass. Seemed he was already getting attuned to it, same as he did with any other instrument. Problem was, this time he'd felt a presence, a shadow squatting at the back of his mind. He thought he'd heard something, too: the cry of a bird—but not of any bird he recognized.

Perhaps he should have listened. Huntsman had warned him never to use the statue all those centuries ago, when Elias had gone searching for the stories of the Dreamers.

He plucked a harmonica from his pocket, gave it a good blow to clear the holes. Tunes were the only way he could relax sometimes; put himself under the influence, just like the punters, stupid bloody lemons. He hit a lilting melody.

Rhiannon was sleeping fitfully once more, head rocking with each turn of the cartwheels.

Hector clomped down streets of shabby single-story houses and boarded-up shops with signs faded by the sun, paint all cracked and peeling. Rotting food clogged the gutters, where crows pecked voraciously, and scavenging rats grew ever more daring.

The few people Elias saw were furtive, heads wrapped in scarves. Some of them watched the passing cart with forlorn eyes, and others tipped their hats or bowed their heads. A few even approached—too quickly for Elias's liking—motioning for him to stop. Shifty looking ne'er do wells, as far as he was concerned. There was as much chance of him stopping as there was of him skinny-dipping in shark-infested waters.

The only other traffic he saw was the death-carts that made their way slowly from door to door. The imperial troops hadn't been joking. Plague had come to Sarum, and it was taking a serious toll.

Turning into Teledor, a couple of blocks from the city center, Elias was surprised to find more activity.

People bustled around a scrappy improvised market, haggling over meager portions of food or the dubious wares of a mountebank in a death's head mask and black robe.

The people here had abandoned the vain protection of scarves over mouths and noses, and went about their business with fatalistic indifference. Famine seemed their chief concern, a threat against which they still had the power to act.

Passing a row of two-story buildings marked as the property of the Teledor

Agriculturalists' Guild, Elias could now see the immense spires and lofty towers of Sarum's central district. There were a dozen such structures, each impossibly high and immeasurably ancient. It was the architecture of his day, like the high-rises back home in old England, or the skyscrapers of cities like New York in what was now the great West. Some were constructed of smallish, uniform red bricks, but the majority were of metal and glass that reflected the brilliant sky, but cast doleful shadows on the city beneath.

"Sammy!" Rhiannon cried out as they passed onto Wharf Way. "Elias, stop. We left Sammy behind."

Elias kept his eyes on the road, shook his head gently. He'd been dreading her waking. All the while she was asleep, he could bury his head in the sand, pretend that it hadn't happened.

"It was too late." He hated the sniveling tone, but it's all he had. "Had to get you away. You know how it was. They'd have... you know... You saw what they did."

He heard her clambering up from the back, felt her hand on his shoulder, and then she was beside him on the seat, face pressed up close—too close. "We can't just leave him."

"I know. But what can we do?" He should have done it already. Should have gone back soon as he realized. Nothing but a spineless chicken—that's what he'd been all these centuries; why he never went anywhere. You'd have thought being ageless would have made you fearless, but he'd always found it had the opposite effect. It was odd how brave mortality made people. Everything hanging in the balance, death hiding around every corner, but you kind of got used to it. It had been so liberating, in a morbid sort of way.

"Turn around. Take me back."

Elias shook his head more vigorously now. "No, no, no. Can't do that. There's guards around the city. Imperial troops. No one gets in or out. I'm sorry, Rhiannon. There's nothing we can do. Just pray—" Now there was a thought. "Just pray he's all right. They won't hurt a child." Well, he hoped not, anyway. "Someone will—"

"How'd we get in?"

"What?"

"How'd we get in, if the city's guarded? No one gets in or out, you said."

Bugger. He couldn't tell her about his use of the statue, how he'd made the guards turn a blind eye. She wouldn't understand. She'd insist he used it again. But she hadn't felt what he'd felt. If he wasn't a coward before, he certainly was now, after feeling that presence, hearing that sound. Sammy would be all right. Made no sense for the knights to harm him.

"I talked my way in. Told them a sob story about you being on your last legs, and me—"

"Then talk our way out." She turned his face to look at her.

Elias blinked back the tears, pulled away. "Can't. Said they'd let us in on condition we didn't change our minds. We go back, they'll fill us with arrows."

Rhiannon closed her eyes and seemed to be holding her breath. For a moment, he thought she was going to explode, shove him off the cart, and head back herself. But then her shoulders sagged and she looked at him with her good eye. "I don't know what to do, Elias." She put her face in her hands. "I just don't—"

"I know," Elias said. He wanted to pat her on the knee, thought better of it. "Me neither."

They headed toward the jetty and the glistening waters of the Soulsong River, which wound its way through the city before meeting the ocean to the west.

Rhiannon leaned into Elias, let her head rest on his shoulder, and was soon dozing once more.

Hector turned onto the Esplanade, right onto Ishgar Terrace, and then left onto the cobblestoned Domus Tyalae, at the end of which sat the Templum of the Knot.

The templum was basically a squat rectangle of clay-brick construction, with a bowed roof and a crumbling transept of age-worn stone protruding from either side. To the rear, a narrow corridor ran off at an angle, connecting it to a long gray building that looked like it had been recently added on. Shrubs skirted the edges of the templum, and a manicured lawn of brown grass fronted it like a badly frayed rug.

"What you about?" An old man in a mud-stained white habit reared up from behind a wheelbarrow, garden shears in hand. "We're full to bursting with the sick, and Mater Ioana's not in, if that's what you're thinking. Out tending folk in the streets, she is."

Elias gently lowered Rhiannon's sleepy head from his shoulder and cocked his finger, like one of those things they had back before the Reckoning... Gun, that was the word.

The man was hunched with age, but still stocky and strong. His oily gray hair was slicked back over a gnomic face, worn and ruddied, most likely from years of manual work outdoors.

"A fine Nousian welcome to you, too, Frater..."

"Hugues."

"Frater Hugues," Elias continued amiably. "I can see the emperor has nothing to fear from your mission. With charm like yours, the Nousian menace will be extinct within a year or two."

"Now you just watch it," spluttered Hugues. "I've half a mind to call the militia."

"I suspect you have half a mind for a lot of things," Elias said, leaping lightly from the cart. "That's the trouble with you religious types. Half a mind on the spirit, the other on the flesh. Know what I mean?"

"You're a very rude man," huffed Hugues, turning on his heel and trudging toward the templum.

Elias trotted beside him, hoping to sound insufferably cheerful. "It's not that I'm saying religion is a bad thing. Far from it. It's the application to real life that's the problem. Take, as an example, the summing up of the Eleven Holy Admonishments by none other than Nous himself. Number one: Love Ain with all your heart and follow all his precepts—terminology's a bit quaint, but what do you expect? Number two:—and check out the paradox, or is it a mystery, aha!—Do whatever you bloody well like, so long as you're always hospitable. OK, so I'm paraphrasing, but that's it in a nutshell. The core of Nousian teaching, and yet you can't even get that right. Not so much as a 'How you going, young geezer?', which would be stretching it, in view of my age, admittedly. Not so much as a, 'What can I do you for, me ol' mate?' And not even the merest tad of concern for my friend here, who's just been beaten and raped by some holy bleeding twat not too dissimilar to—"

Frater Hugues slapped him in the face. A heavy slap. Quite jolting, actually.

"More of a navvy than a luminary," Elias said, putting his hands to his head and blinking away the stars. "Fair do's, though."

"Forgive me, Brother." Hugues fussed around him like a terrified mother who'd just dropped her baby on its head. "You went on so. Are you sure you're all right?"

"Leave him, Hugues."

A woman in white hurried from the templum doorway. A slim, very prim ol' girl in her late fifties, by the looks of her. She wore enormous glasses that covered most of her face; peered through them with bulging fish eyes. "I'll see to our guests."

"Right you are, Velda." Hugues looked warily one more time at Elias before shuffling off round the back of the building.

"Thank you, Soror." Elias gave his most theatrical bow. "Your arrival was—"

"Oh, my poor dear, what has happened to you?" Velda walked straight past him to the cart, and climbed into the tray to examine Rhiannon.

"She was beaten and raped by..."

"Hush, young man."

Elias was a little gobsmacked. He ran his fingers through his hair, and stood by like a naughty child who'd been told off for picking his nose.

Velda held Rhiannon's head against her breast and cradled her like a mother.

Rhiannon stirred and opened her eyes. She let out a sigh and sat up.

"Soror? We're at the templum, then?"

"You are indeed," Velda said. "Fret no longer." She cast a swift glance at Elias. "You will be safe here."

"This is Elias Wolf..."

"Who, this?" Velda's fish eyes grew as big as her lenses. "Isn't that a lovely name? What is it you do, Elias?"

This was the point Elias would normally dance a little jig and then give his deepest bow. If he had a hat on, he'd invariably roll it up his arm and flip it back into place. "Bard," he mumbled, without even a shuffle of his shoes.

"A bard? How splendid. Perhaps you'll sing for us later. Ah, Pater Cadris."

An immensely fat priest emerged from the templum, fussing at the strands of hair meticulously combed across his barren pate.

"Hugues said there was trouble," he declaimed with the pomposity of a bad orator.

"Not trouble, Cadris, just friends in need." Velda climbed out of the cart and helped Rhiannon down. "Make yourself useful, and tether this gentleman's horse, if you please."

Cadris paused a moment, as if he were going to protest, but then straightened his robe and waddled over to take Hector's reins. As he led the horse and cart off toward a lean-to at the edge of the templum grounds, he appeared to be muttering under his breath.

"Pater Cadris is our scholar," Velda explained as the trio made their way into the templum. "Such a gifted writer."

The interior would have been very difficult to reconcile with the usual idea of a templum, although Elias had only ever seen the shells of ancient ecclesial buildings until now. The nave was a makeshift infirmary, with coughing, sweating, blood-soaked people lying on pews or pallets on the floor. The whole place stank like an abattoir.

"There are fifty-six patients," Velda pointed out as she led Rhiannon and Elias down the center aisle. "A small token of the plague's victims, but it's the best we can do."

They looked like writhing hunks of bad meat, bodies weeping putrescence, the air thick with the stench of decay.

Elias found his hand covering his nose and pulled it away. Could have been construed as a bit rude, that, so he held his breath instead.

An elderly priestess with a head like a mottled skull tufted with gray, and twisted spectacles low on her nose, was hobbling about ministering to the sick and dying.

"Soror Agna!" Rhiannon cried, rushing to embrace the woman.

Elias wagged his fingers in greeting, having met Agna on a couple of occasions when she'd visited Rhiannon in Oakendale.

Agna held Rhiannon out at arm's length and examined her bruising.

"Oh, my sweet girl, what's happened?"

Rhiannon lowered her head and began to shake. Agna looked up at Velda, who merely nodded her assent. Agna then led Rhiannon across the sanctuary and through the sacristy door.

"Do you know," Velda said, "it never occurred to me that this could be Agna's Rhiannon. I must be getting soft in the head. We've been preparing for her arrival, but I never expected her to turn up in such a state, the poor dear."

"Rhiannon's had this thing about joining the Templum since she was a teenager," Elias said. "Soror Agna used to make the journey to Oakendale every couple of months to speak with her."

"Yes, yes, the pre-novitiate. Agna spoke of her often. There have been no other candidates, mind."

"The emperor's none too keen on Nousians. I imagine the people either share his views, or are too scared to go against them. You must be feeling a bit isolated these days. Since the missionaries at Jorakum packed up and scurried on back to Aeterna, and that nasty business at Delta's Bluff, there's been just you and the Pardes community."

"And Gladelvi." Velda puckered her lips. "I must see to the sick. If you pop outside, Pater Cadris will find you a room."

Elias gratefully left the mephitic stench of the templum, passing the skulking Frater Hugues in the narthex. He found fat Cadris just leaving Hector under the lean-to, the cart parked in the shade of a copse of black wattles.

"That is a most fine specimen. The equestrian beast, I mean. Robust and strong as a…"

"As a horse, Pater?" offered Elias.

"As strong as a titan, I was about to say. I see you have some books in your cart."

"And a few instruments. It's all part of the trade, you know."

"Quite, quite," sniffed Cadris.

"Soror Velda said to—"

"A room. Quite, quite. Come along." And with that, Cadris lumbered toward the gray stone house behind the templum, beckoning over his shoulder for Elias to follow.

THE MAZE

Beneath the City of Sarum, Sahul

Shadrak stretched to loosen his muscles, dug his fists into his back until it popped. Even the smell of other people's shit could be relaxing, if it's what you were used to.

He set off through brick tunnels that were oozing with sludge, covering his face against the stench with his cloak. He guessed that's what they meant by familiarity breeding contempt. Might feel like home, but it stank worse than a cat's arse.

Reaching one of the marks he'd carved into the concrete floor, he dropped to his hands and knees and felt around. A small rectangle of concrete shimmered and dissolved, revealing a metal panel studded with buttons. He pressed a combination of numbers and stood back as a circle opened in the floor. Silver gleamed down below.

Dropping through the hole, he landed with a clang. Couldn't have been anywhere better. Here, he could skulk unnoticed. Here he was unseen, far beneath Sarum's foundations.

Sinuous steel corridors angled away in each direction, leading to oval chambers via doors that slid open at the touch of a button. Some rooms contained cages of various sizes, many holding the skeletal remains of animals, and some of humans. Shadrak had also found chambers in which chairs like hollowed-out eggs rose from the floor around plinths of lights and mirrors; and some in which pallets of a malleable substance slid from walls, illuminated by soft violet light from an invisible source.

He'd first discovered the Maze as a child—literally fell into it as he fled from a pair of corpse-sucking ghouls. He'd been searching through the bins behind the Green Man and disturbed their meal—some tart fool enough to work the backstreets at night. Perhaps, like Shadrak, she hadn't had much choice. Food was hard to come by back then, especially with Kadee rotting away in bed and Shadrak too young and too freakish to work. One of the hatches leading down from the sewers had been left open. Took him days to figure out the codes to get back out again.

Cold blue lights sprang to life, sharply illuminating another metallic corridor with numerous tributaries. Each had an arched lintel engraved with an identifying numeral.

He made a quick calculation and checked it against his mental map. He might have been a devil-eyed midget, but at least he'd been blessed with a perfect memory, and that was the key to his success. Not only did it furnish him with all the twists and turns of the Maze, the openings to the city above, which he could creep from unseen and scurry back into like a rat, but it also ensured he never forgot a face.

Shadrak stiffened as he heard movement up ahead, a barely audible footfall, and the merest rustle. Something made a hushing noise.

More than one, then.

The light from the blue ovals on the ceiling meant there were no shadows to hide in, so he loosened his cloak and reached for the blades in his baldric.

He lay prone, peeking from the hood as three mawgs came into view, sniffing the air, bat-like ears twitching. Dark fur shrouded their faces, and slitty yellow eyes glared above jutting snouts. Daggers wouldn't do much good against their torsos. They were all knotted and gnarled, rashes of fist-sized warts and carbuncles sprouting from scaly carapaces. The legs were sinewy, bent backward like a bird's, ending in curved talons and spiky spurs. Hook-like fingers with opposable thumbs scraped along the floor at the end of drooping arms.

The largest of the mawgs curled its black lips, revealing a mouth like a fly-trapping plant's, row upon row of spiny teeth all the way to the back of its throat. They had the scent of him, nostrils flaring, eyes ravenous.

The big mawg growled at the others, and they kept back while it crouched over Shadrak's cloak, reaching out with two clawed fingers.

Stab.

Shadrak saw it at the last minute—a soft patch crying out to be punctured. He felt the blade bite. Hot blood, thick and oily, splashed over his hand.

The other two mawgs looked stunned by the sudden seizure that gripped their leader, who then collapsed, stiletto jutting from its groin.

Shadrak sprang from beneath his cloak and hurled daggers at them both. One mawg howled and dropped, a knife through its eye. The other, a blade piercing its throat, charged.

Shadrak threw himself into a backward flip, simultaneously pulling the thunder-shot from its holster.

The mawg leapt, jaws wide, teeth bristling.

Its head exploded the instant before thunder boomed and echoed down the corridor.

One shot. Good. More than good: perfect.

Shadrak crouched down to examine the creatures. Ammunition was hard to come by in the Maze. Six rounds left, and then he'd need to search for another cartridge to slot into the grip.

Mawgs beneath Sarum would go down like a Nousian at the emperor's table. According to the guild, they'd recently butchered their way through Gladelvi in the north, within hours of Jarmin the Anchorite leaving to visit Governor Gen. Maybe the mawgs were following the stench of his sandals. Maybe they hated Nousians as much as Hagalle did. Or maybe it had something to do with that piece of amber Cadman had taken from Jarmin. Only other option was that it was a coincidence, but that didn't sit right with Shadrak. Everything happened for a reason. It was all cause and effect.

It was hard to believe this was anything but a recce, the vanguard of thousands of mawgs swarming toward the city, merciless as locusts in a crop of sugarcane.

The Sicarii weren't gonna like it. Bad for business. How could an assassin make a living, if the people were already dead, their clothes, flesh, and even bones devoured? Better to leave now, cross the desert into Barraiya lands, and then head for Millius, or take a ship to New Ithaka. If the mawgs had found a way into the city, Sarum was finished.

Shadrak crept to the next intersection, feeling inside a pouch for an exploding globe, in case there were any more mawgs up ahead. As he ducked into the left-hand corridor, blue lights blinked on in succession, receding into the distance.

He set off at a jog, clanging footfalls echoing throughout the Maze.

You should tell someone, Kadee's voice nagged at the back of his mind. *Give them a chance.*

"Not my problem," he said out loud, taking a right turn and stopping to check the number etched into the lintel.

People will die. Thousands of people. Children, too.

"And?"

You are my boy, Shadrak. Eingana's gift to me. The hope of the Dreaming.

All nonsense. An old woman's fancy. Her deathbed comfort. He'd wanted to believe it once; believe that he was special, that his deformity had a purpose, his life a direction and meaning.

Kadee had been a little crazy from smoking pituri, but if anyone else had said it, he'd have gutted them. She'd sworn Shadrak had been brought to her by one of her gods of the Dreaming. As a child, he'd accepted it all without question, but life had taught him some hard lessons, chief among them that fantasy was the twin of despair.

Kadee was an oddity among the Dreamers, choosing to live in squalor on the fringes of Sarum, disowned by her people, ignored by the city-folk. She'd always said she did it for him, for the gods, for the Dreaming; but since she'd gone, it seemed more likely she'd done it all for nothing.

Shog Sarum. It deserved to be destroyed, its people reduced to piles of stinking mawg puke.

He reached a junction and squinted at the lintel. The numbers danced a blurry jig. His head pounded with the effort of focusing.

"Leave me alone," he said through gritted teeth to the face forming in his mind.

Kadee's brown eyes shone with the love she'd always shown him, her special one. The hint of a smile touched her lips, and she gave the slightest of nods before retreating like the sun behind a cloud.

Shadrak felt the warmth of her presence, felt himself smiling and shook his head. She'd done it again. He could never refuse her in life, and in death she was just as persuasive.

Turning back the way he'd come, he started to retrace his steps, all the while working out what to tell the guild, and what he could safely leave out.

Later, he thought, half-expecting Kadee to object to the delay. If he was staying, he still had the little matter of imperial goons coming to his house with the contract to kill Bovis Rayn. Couldn't have people knowing where he lived, and it was about time he paid them a return visit. And more than that, he needed to get Kadee's ashes back.

It begged the question, though, how they'd found him in the first place; why they'd not gone through the guild.

Or maybe they had. Maybe the guild had gone to them, in which case, someone was trying to expose him, weaken his position. All part of the constant in-fighting that weeded out the weak from the strong. There was no honor among assassins, which was a good thing. At least when he found out who it was that had betrayed him, there'd be no need to give a warning.

THE DARK

Abbey of Pardes, Sahul

The light from a guttering candle danced across Rhiannon's flesh. Her face flickered between paleness and shadow, like a ghost on the threshold of the Void.

Her grip on Shader's wrists was tight, but not painful; her thighs hot and slick with sweat. Shader strained toward her lips, but she resisted, tongue brushing her teeth.

His hands slid down her back, pulling her closer. She bent down, crushing her breasts against his chest, nuzzling her face into his neck, licking, sucking, biting. Shader sighed, one hand cupping a breast, the other squeezing her buttock in time to their thrusting.

Sweet pain ripped through his throat. Warm blood oozed and trickled. Rhiannon lapped at it like a dog, gulping it down and hissing with satisfaction. Her nails raked at his chest, tearing out clumps of hair and flesh. She pressed down harder with her hips; silenced his protests with salty, wet lips.

Her tongue coiled around his, knotting, wrenching. He gagged and rolled on top, pushing her shoulders into the bed. Her hands latched onto his buttocks, rooting him in her. Her tongue grew more insistent, pulling his face toward her wide open maw, fangs dripping with saliva.

He arched away, striking out with the flat of his hand. She gurgled and sighed, humping her hips against his. He hit her again, this time with a fist, battering her head from side to side until the tongue let go.

"Ain's teeth!" Shader rolled from the bed and snatched up the gladius. "Back to the Abyss, demon!"

She held her breasts, offering them to him, eyes wide and innocent, black hair tumbling about her shoulders.

"Back, succubus! Get out!"

She purred and crawled toward him, tongue running around her lips.

Shader screamed.

The gladius punched through her face and exited the back of her head.

***

"Frater?" Tap, tap, tap. "Frater, are you all right?"

Shader sat up, staring straight at the gilt Monas on the wall of his cell. He rubbed the sleep from his eyes and tried to get his bearings.

Tap, tap, tap. "Frater Deacon?"

"I'm fine. A bad dream, that's all."

He waited until the footsteps retreated down the corridor before standing.

Reaching beneath the bed, he pulled out his swords, strapping them to his waist and frowning at the Monas before heading to the refectory.

Frater Elphus paused in his reading, but failed to meet Shader's eyes as he entered.

All the brothers noted, each in their own way, his carrying of weapons.

The Gray Abbot simply played with his porridge. His ashen hair fell in ringlets over his charcoal scapular. The robe beneath was the color of slate. His hands were pallid, his face pasty and textured like bark. The impression was of a statue carved from different strata of rock. That would have been enough to earn him his name, but it was the eyes that were the real clincher: beads of glistening hoarfrost.

"Investigator Shin sends his greetings." Shader leaned across the lectern until his face almost touched Elphus's. "Said he found you a great help."

Elphus coughed and fussed with the pages, eyes darting from Shader to the Gray Abbot.

"May I continue?" Elphus asked, looking up from the lectern and rolling his eyes.

The Gray Abbot chastised him with a barely perceptible flick of his index finger, before returning it to the stroking of his upper lip.

The other monks continued with their breakfasts, clanking spoons against bowls and, it seemed to Shader, slurping their porridge with intentional noisiness.

Elphus resumed the reading through clenched teeth, as looks of mirth passed between the brothers.

***

Yesterday's rain had left a bright sheen on the trees and the grassy tufts poking through the sea of red sand around the abbey. As was the norm for Western Sahul, the weather had reverted swiftly to clear blue skies and a blazing sun.

From the parapet, Shader could just about make out the tallest spires of Sarum in the distance, the ground in between flat and featureless, save for the odd gum tree. The woods smudging the hills about the city were sparse compared with the forests of Britannia, or the Schwarzwald of Verusia.

It seemed that, even here, with its towers rendered so small by the distance, Sarum still cast a heavy shadow. Shader recalled how, during his time in the city, the sun had always been at least partially obscured by the buildings, no matter where it stood in the sky.

From the abbey, the shadow was of a different kind. He felt it more as a pull, like that of a rusted magnet drawing all manner of decayed and discarded matter toward it.

The cackling-warble of a kookaburra roused him from his reflection. Scanning the woodland to the east of Pardes, he was met with the spectacle of a host of brightly feathered lorikeets launching from the treetops as a murder of crows descended.

The sun hid behind a bank of cloud that surreptitiously crept in from the west, and Shader's ill humor immediately returned.

He went back inside through a trapdoor in the roof and made his way down the spiraling stairs. Darkness followed him, a black pall settling over the abbey.

Hurrying to a window, he glanced outside, and was astounded to see that night had fallen, where only moments ago he'd stood in the brightness that follows dawn.

The temperature plummeted. A chill wind whistled from nowhere, rattling doors and windows. Instinctively, reassuringly, Shader's left hand closed around the hilt of the gladius, and he found himself first walking, then running back to the refectory.

***

Shader burst through the door, longsword in one hand, gladius in the other.

Frater Elphus shot him a withering stare, then continued to drone on with the reading.

The refectory was steeped in shadow, but the monks didn't seem to notice the blackness outside the windows. They barely registered Shader's entrance, though the Gray Abbot might have glanced his way. For once, it seemed, they were actually listening to Elphus, lost in the meditative reflection of *lectio divina*.

There was a pooling of the newly descended darkness upon the refectory table. A small vortex of misty black thread formed from the cloud smothering the abbey.

A gasp went up from the brothers, and all eyes were suddenly fixed upon the burgeoning center, as it sucked in the fog and, like a potter's wheel, gave it form.

The figure that coalesced from the shadow grew tall and sprouted skeletal limbs. A mildewed skull twisted into place, jaws opening to unleash a rancid rush of air in the face of the Gray Abbot.

The abbot tried to rise, clutching at the amber-eyed Monas around his neck. As he brought the symbol up, the figure took on more clarity: a surcoat of faded white, a rusty mail hauberk, and a time-blackened helm that formed around the skull. Pinpricks of ember smoldered through the eye-slit.

The Gray Abbot trembled as he said, "Callixus!"

—The grand master of the Lost, the Elect knights who'd been sent to Sahul, never to return.

Shader could only watch spellbound as the wraith snatched the Monas from the Gray Abbot's hand, snapping the chain and hissing in triumph.

"Ain preserve us!" the Gray Abbot said. "Callixus!"

Callixus drew a sword of shadow. Flames of fuligin licked about the blade.

The Gray Abbot screamed and turned to his confreres for help, but they were cowering on the floor, hands over their ears.

Shader tried to move, to do something, but his limbs refused to obey. Was it magic, or just fear, plain and simple?

Callixus faltered, the black sword wavering above the Gray Abbot's head. With agonizing slowness, he thrust it back in its scabbard. He closed his gauntleted fist around the abbot's Monas, raised it high, and screeched like a banshee.

The windows exploded, and the stench of decay washed over the room. Rotting fingers fumbled at the window frames, and corpses riddled with shards of glass began to clamber inside.

Frater Elphus was a thrash of limbs in Shader's peripheral vision. Pallid hands grabbed him from behind and dragged him screaming through the window.

Shader took a lurching step into the room, then another. Paralysis fell away from him like broken shackles.

"In the name of Nous!" He pointed the gladius at Callixus. "Everyone out!"

The monks crawled toward the doorway, moaning, whimpering.

Corpses caked in the red soil of Sahul shambled after them—disinterred bodies, in varying stages of decay, some bloated and livid, others no more than brittle bones held together by shredded ligaments.

Shader charged at the wraith, swung for its neck with his longsword—but struck only air. In the same fluid motion, he thrust with the gladius, skewering its belly.

Callixus emitted a shrill cry, as insects and larvae spilled from his wound. The vortex whipped up around him, and in an instant, he dissolved back into fog and shadow, and melted from the room.

The monks scrambled behind Shader, but the Gray Abbot remained rooted to the spot.

The corpse-creatures continued to lumber toward them, white eyes vacant, flayed limbs groping the air.

Shader threw himself among them, longsword arcing viciously to left and right, gladius stabbing and blocking.

Putrid bodies fell before him, and yet still they came, piling in, forcing him back through sheer weight of numbers.

Shader could no longer see the Gray Abbot. All he could do was hack and thrust like a madman, arms weakening, breath burning in his lungs as he sought a way through.

With a surge, the corpse-things slammed him against the wall, sending his swords clattering to the floor.

A mouth rank with decay clamped over his, fetid breath making him retch. Cold hands held him like iron. The corpse shuddered as it started to suck.

Shader's fists hammered pulpy flesh, splattering pus and gore. Ice crept through his veins. Mist fell over his eyes; but just as darkness threatened to engulf him, the cadaver pulled back, and flame erupted from its head.

It thrashed about in a macabre parody of a dance, before collapsing in a pile of smoking ash.

Shader scrabbled about for his swords, fingers stiff and numb.

The undead were swaying to a sonorous chant that came from somewhere behind them. A corridor opened through their ranks, and the Gray Abbot walked toward Shader incanting Aeternam words of prayer.

"...*sicut et nos dimittimus debitoribus nostris...*"

Flame licked dead flesh, flared to the ceiling, and left nothing but dust and ashes in its wake.

"*Et ne nos inducas in tentationem...*"

The Gray Abbot stopped before Shader, placed a hand on his shoulder, and sighed. "Thank you, Frater."

He had aged alarmingly.

Shader rose to his feet; gripped his arm. He met the Gray Abbot's gaze and recoiled. The face that had always been a well of peace and wisdom was now riddled with horror, set into a mask of despair.

THE WHITE ORDER

Vicinity of City of Sarum, Sahul

Gaston stood in the stirrups and looked back along the column of knights riding single file across the red dust, chainmail glinting, surcoats the virgin white of Nous. Fifty of the best recruits from across the villages. The most accomplished. The most zealous.

They rode well. He nodded his approval. No more slouching in the saddle; no more idle talk. If he didn't know better, he'd have thought them veterans, professional soldiers, and not the impoverished farm boys he'd grown up with.

His father would have objected; wanted things done his way, same as ever. But he would have been wrong. Berdini's paradox would have shown him that, if he'd ever looked into it: the justification for Nousian warfare. Even Shader never really got it. But Gaston did.

He was sure that was why Aristodeus had come to him—because Shader had let the side down. Because Gaston was Bovis Rayn's son. Because he had zeal for Nous, *and* he knew how to swing a blade.

Finding the old man sitting in his darkened living room had been such a shock that, at first, he'd thought Sheriff Halligan had grown some balls and come to arrest him for what he'd done to Rhiannon. To her family. Before Gaston could turn about and flee, Aristodeus had laughed—like he knew what had happened. Knew and didn't care.

"The sheriff won't trouble you, Gaston," he'd said. "Oh, he was going to. He'd even started putting together a posse to confront you. But he's a reasonable man, and an agreement has been reached. I'm sure the same can be said of you. I'm sure you're a reasonable man, too."

Gaston hadn't liked the philosopher's tone. It was amiable enough, but there was something jarring: an implied threat, and a smug certainty that he had Gaston under his thumb.

Assemble the White Order.

The words were still clear in his mind; the pounding of his heart just as strong.

The Templum of the Knot is in danger. The priests need you. Shader needs you.

Gaston objected that he couldn't face Shader. Not now. Not after what he'd done.

Atonement, Gaston. Atonement and forgiveness. Everything is possible for Nous.

Gaston wasn't so sure. His stomach still tightened when he let the memories surface. His eyes still filled with tears, and he still wanted to hurt himself—only that wasn't the Nousian way.

There had been one more reason to lead the White Order to Sarum, though. Bovis Rayn had been poisoned and half garroted, but Aristodeus said it was the hole in the head that gave it away. The philosopher had a contact in the Sicarii, a guild master he'd first met while visiting the Emperor Hagalle, whom he claimed was a former pupil. The hole in the head, his contact said, was caused by a weapon of the Ancients, and was the calling card of an albino midget known as Shadrak the Unseen.

And Gaston meant to find him.

"We're within a mile of the suburbs," Barek Thomas said, riding up alongside, his horse lathered with white sweat. "Imperial troops are stationed along the river between us and the city. They're letting no one in or out."

"Is there a way around?"

"None that I could see. Think they know we're coming?"

Gaston shook his head, wincing at the pain from his swollen nose. The stitches were pulling something terrible. Should have got someone other than Justin to sew him up.

"How would they know?" The thing was, whether they knew or not, imperial troops would only react one way to Nousian knights approaching Sarum. It was one thing to play at being Templum Elect in the villages, but out here, the lads would be seen as the enemy; as an incursion onto Sahulian soil by the forces of the Ipsissimus.

Barek shrugged. "Well, maybe there's something else going on. Mawgs, perhaps."

"How did they appear? Ready for battle?"

"Don't think so. Most were still sleeping, the rest setting fires for breakfast."

Gaston was only half-listening. Aristodeus's voice was foremost in his mind, firm, sure, and prophetic.

The Templum needs you.

They couldn't turn back now. Strong leaders are decisive, Shader always said. Fortune favors the brave.

"Move the column into a diamond."

"We're not going to attack?" Barek's mouth hung open. "Shouldn't we talk to—"

"Do it!"

Barek stiffened and rode back down the column, barking orders to the men.

"Surely he doesn't think we can just ride up and ask them nicely to let us in," Justin said, cantering up from behind.

"What do you think?" Gaston watched over his shoulder as Barek spoke to the men, grasping hands and patting backs.

A leader should gain the affection of his men, Shader had said; but where that wasn't possible, he should force their respect.

"I think what you think, man—boss, or whatever we're supposed to call you. Grand Master? General?"

"Gaston will do just fine." At least until he'd had a chance to earn a title. The last thing he needed was for the men to think him a pompous prat. He knew what these lads admired. Actions, not words, would win their loyalty. Fancy titles would gain him nothing but coarse Sahulian satire.

Gaston picked at his stitches, trying to think what Shader would have done. He shut his eyes and muttered a swift prayer to Ain. If this was the wrong path, surely there would be a sign, a pang of conscience, some sort of clarity.

The clop of approaching hooves snapped him back to alertness, and he became aware he was chewing his knuckles.

Barek drew up and saluted. "The men are in formation. We await your order."

Do you? Gaston couldn't bring himself to meet Barek's gaze. He swiveled in the saddle to take in the men and horses formed up in a tight rhombus, perfectly still, perfectly disciplined.

Were they ready? There was no way of telling. They'd had the training, they knew the drills. Shader had been an Elect cavalry captain. Said he'd taught them all he knew. What they had to learn next was something that only came with experience.

Gaston felt his heartbeat hammering away inside his ribcage, his doubts growing. Without further thought, he did what he always did when shitting himself: turned it into rage.

"Advance!" he bellowed, spurring the mare into a canter, and not even checking to see if the others were following.

Twenty yards, and he crested the rise. Another ten, and he was coming down the other side through dense forest. Barek had forgotten to mention that. It was the last thing they needed.

He glanced behind. The others were keeping pace, but already, their diamond formation was disintegrating into ragged clusters as the horses wove in and out of the trees.

If he turned back now, they'd think him a right clacker. Rather than that, Gaston kept up his pace, zigzagging through the forest with a skill that would inspire the others and spur them on.

He could see a break in the tree line up ahead; caught a glimpse of tents, the waft of smoke in the air. He started to slow, meaning to pull up at the edge of the clearing and wait for the others.

But then he caught sight of a man with his britches round his ankles, taking a piss against a trunk. A captain, judging by his epaulets.

The man looked up, shaking off the drops. His mouth fell open, more in confusion than fear.

And in that instant, Gaston charged.

The captain turned to run, but tripped over his britches. From the forest behind Gaston came the thunderous sound of hooves.

The captain tried to pull his sword free, but the scabbard was tangled between his legs.

Gaston leaned down as he passed and slashed his sword across the man's face. Blood slung in a crimson arc on the follow through, and a cry went up from the camp. Soldiers seated at cook fires scrabbled for their weapons.

Gaston veered his horse round, looked back to see Barek at the head of the sloppily re-formed diamond. Dust billowed into the air, and the ground shook.

The captain thrashed about in the dirt. He made it to his knees, a bloody gash where his eyes had been. He held his arms out in front of him and lunged to his feet, teetering and muttering with shock.

Justin's horse barreled into him, trampled him underfoot, and kept on galloping after Barek in the lead.

For a moment, Gaston sat astride his mare, staring down at the mangled body of the captain. This was wrong. It was all so wrong.

Horses passed him by on both sides; riders he knew. Riders he'd helped train. Knights he commanded.

It was too late now. He'd set things into motion, and a good leader followed through on his plans. It's what Shader would have done, wasn't it? And it's what Aristodeus would have expected.

He dug his heels into the horse's flanks and flowed in with the tide. His mind was made up, any indecision quelled by the tumult of hooves on hard-packed earth, the blood speckling his blade, the yells and screams up ahead, and the clangor of steel.

Gaston spurred his horse away from the main diamond and galloped toward the front.

All around the camp, imperial troops abandoned their breakfasts and ran for their weapons. Some were better prepared, and unleashed a score of arrows into the front riders.

A handful of knights dropped from their horses, and one of the beasts fell, its legs folding under it, a shaft lodged in its throat.

Gaston's mare swerved to avoid it, but the knight behind crashed into the fallen horse and was thrown headlong from the saddle. Chaos rolled through the following knights, and the charge faltered.

Up ahead, a swordsman ran at Barek, slashing wildly. Barek parried but clutched at his shoulder. Gripping with his knees, he rode on, knocking another man from his feet.

The five knights who had speared the charge with him were down, screaming, groaning, crying like babies. All about them, imperial troops closed in to finish them off.

Gaston rode to their aid, hacking about with a fury, but a spear grazed his horse. The mare whinnied in shock and lurched. Its knees buckled.

Gaston leapt from the saddle, and braced himself as a clutch of soldiers came at him. He snatched up a second sword, dropped by one of his lads—it might have been Harven Thrindy, but the face was off.

An arrow thrummed past his ear, struck the eye of one of the lads riding to his aid and exited the back of his head.

Cramp took hold of Gaston's guts. He turned away; thought he was gonna shit himself.

A blade came down, and he parried on instinct. He looked into the gleaming eyes of an imperial soldier, parried again, ducked a punch.

He swung his borrowed sword wildly, like he didn't have a clue. The soldier took confidence from that and sneered. That was enough to do it for Gaston. With a surge of rage that settled his nerves, he blocked a thrust, and hacked right through the shogger's neck.

Three more took his place, though, but now Gaston was ready.

He roared, and strode right for them, twin blades a silvery arc, clashing against steel, ripping through flesh. One went down, then another, clutching his guts. The third would have run, but half a dozen more came to his aid, and it was all Gaston could do to stay alive.

He was dimly aware of horses flashing past on either side. Divots of mud flew overhead. Screams reached his ears, but they sounded muffled to him.

A blade glanced off his mail. A shield slammed into him, knocking him back. With deft footwork, he righted himself and countered. Swords met his, over and over, but his eye was in now, and he wove a web of steel with his twin blades.

At first, his attackers faltered, but then one of them got brave and chanced a lunge. Gaston chopped down, and the man's arm fell wriggling to the dirt.

A horse reared up behind the imperials. Hooves smashed into a soldier's head, shattering bone and spraying blood.

As the others spun to face the new threat, Gaston cut into them mercilessly, felling two in quick succession. The remaining three turned back again.

The rider dropped from his saddle and dispatched one from the rear. Gaston brutally chopped through another's shoulder with one sword, and finished him with the other.

The last soldier tried to make a run for it, but a horse cannoned into him, and a blade came down to make sure he didn't get up.

It was Justin astride the horse, a fierce grin on his blood-flecked face.

Barek was the knight who'd dismounted to come to Gaston's aid.

He nodded at them both.

Barek was holding his arm. He'd somehow managed to kill his man using his left hand. It was something they'd all been working on, in emulation of Shader. But until now, Gaston was the only one who'd mastered it.

"You hurt?" he asked Barek.

"Sword arm's dead." Barek wrinkled his nose, gave the barest shrug. "But I'm good."

Gaston grinned. He knew it was wrong, but it felt good. Their first real fight, and they'd won. It didn't matter that they'd had the element of surprise, and more than their fair share of luck. The lads of the White Order had done him proud.

The rest of the knights were among the tents, running down the survivors.

A horn blast went up from the west, and, for a moment, the fighting ceased, then the few remaining soldiers sprinted in the direction of the sound.

"Leave them," Gaston shouted. "Let them go."

He walked over to his injured mare and remounted.

Barek sheathed his sword and found his own horse. With a foot in the stirrup, and his good hand clutching a fistful of mane, he half-pulled, half-rolled into the saddle.

"You did well, Barek." Gaston rode over and slapped him on the shoulder. "You too, Justin."

He wheeled the mare to face the Old Sarum Road. There was heat in his face, fire in his veins; fire that burned away all doubt about what they'd done here today; about what they were called to do.

***

The Old Sarum Road was little more than a dirt track through the bush. A few hundred yards along it, a volley of arrows hissed out from the scrubland, thudding into horses and riders. A shaft glanced from Gaston's armor as he beat his ailing mare into a gallop that took him beyond the range of the archers. The troop followed, another volley ripping into them and claiming three more riders.

Gaston slowed to a canter as the road merged with another, pockmarked and gray, with glinting studs of silver forming a broken line down its center.

The clopping of hooves announced their arrival to the tin-roofed shacks on the fringes of Sarum, but there was no sign of life. It was as if everyone had up and left. Either that, or the approach of the knights had frightened them, and they were all holed up indoors.

Gaston drew rein and watched the column pass, counting the survivors, and noting the injured. Thirty-nine knights, many carrying minor wounds. One—Tray Vogen from Broken Bridge—had the flight of an arrow jutting from his shoulder.

Despite the botched charge, Gaston was more than pleased with their performance. Their training had paid off against the imperial troops. Ain had favored his own. You had to see it as vindication.

The column of knights rode swiftly through the southern suburbs. Here, disheveled people with scarves over their mouths and noses scavenged among the refuse piling up on the roadside.

They crossed the Kaldus Bridge and came to the Arch of Foundation, marking the southern access to the city center.

The first and last time Gaston had seen it, he'd been a child, clutching his dad's hand. The memory was sharp as a dagger thrust. Seemed like it had been only yesterday. He could hear Dad's voice bubbling up from the depths, like it was muffled by fog: *This is not the way... Not the way.*

A ragged group of militiamen jogged toward them, spears leveled, shields reflecting the glare of the sun.

Gaston signaled his knights to stop. Barek and Justin rode alongside him as the militia formed up and locked shields.

A stocky man, red-faced and mustached, stepped forward, chainmail clinking, boots squeaking.

"Captain Harding, City Militia," he barked in a gruff voice, blinking ten to the dozen. "Will you stand down?"

Justin leaned over the pommel of his saddle. "Now, why would we do that?"

Gaston watched the shogger like a hawk. One wrong move, one wrong word, and they'd roll over this lot like they did the others.

Barek raised his hand, and the knights began to fan out across the street, hooves clattering sharply on stone.

"By order of Governor Gen..." Harding coughed to clear his throat. "By order—" he started again, but Gaston cut him off.

"What's happening here, Captain? Why do imperial troops surround Sarum?"

Harding spluttered, his blinking intensifying. "You don't know?"

"He doesn't know," Justin said. His look added, "So answer the shogging question."

"Plague," Harding said. "The city's under quarantine."

Gaston exchanged looks with Justin and Barek. Aristodeus never mentioned anything about plague. Was that the the threat to the priests? The threat to Shader? Because if it was, he didn't have a clue how the White Order was going to help. Suddenly, he didn't feel quite so buoyant as he had following the fight.

"How did you get past the cordon?" Harding said. His eyes roving the blood-spattered knights betrayed that he already knew.

"Captain," Gaston said. "There's no need for any more trouble. We're here to help. Can you take us to the Templum of the Knot?"

Harding mopped the sweat from his brow and sucked air through gritted teeth. He looked about at his men, as if gauging whether they had the strength to take on Gaston's knights. They clearly didn't, and Harding must have known it.

"I... uh... I need to speak with the governor. But first, we should get your men off the streets, tether your horses. People will be frightened, and they already have enough on their plates with the plague."

The militiamen led them deeper and deeper into Sarum, along roads flanked by ancient red-brick buildings, and past immense towers that cast cooling shadows across the city.

Finally, Harding stopped them before the iron gates of a walled enclosure, his men bringing up the rear.

"This used to be the imperial barracks. They left at the first sign of the plague. You'll find stabling for your horses and food for your men."

"You want to lock us in?" Gaston's fingers curled around the hilt of his sword. He wouldn't stand for it. No shogging city militiaman was going to stop him from... stop him from...

Ain, he was tired. No, not tired—confused. Dizzy with it.

Images erupted like pustules behind his eyes: severed limbs, gaping wounds; the captain fumbling around with his arms outstretched, face a mass of blood. What had they done? What had he done?

Harding opened the gates and stood aside. "It would avoid any further misunderstanding. You have my word Governor Gen will hear of this immediately. If your business is with the Templum of the Knot, you won't find him wholly unsympathetic. But the troops outside the city: that's another thing altogether. Not sure even the governor can protect you from the consequences of that."

Gaston shakily waved the knights through the gate. Once the last rider was within the enclosure, he turned to Harding. "Captain, have you heard of Shadrak, the Unseen?"

"Everyone has."

"Know where to find him?"

Harding looked from side to side before answering in a hushed voice. "Wouldn't want to if I could. You don't want to be worrying about the Sicarii. We've got enough problems with this blasted plague."

Gaston nodded and followed the others inside. He felt suddenly anxious and uncertain, a little fish in a big pond. Fear of contagion clamored for his attention, challenging his faith and begging the question: would Ain protect them?

As Harding turned the key in the lock, Rhiannon's face flashed to mind, scowling with contempt. Gaston swallowed down bile, clutched at his guts. Reeling in the saddle, he fought for control, and felt he'd received his answer. Why on earth would Ain look out for him?

THE GUILD

City of Sarum, Sahul

Shadrak dropped from the rooftop, rolled, and came up standing in the shadows cast by the Tower of Glass.

The monolith reached to the stars, its surface mirroring the night's blackness and rippling in the moonlight.

An old woman hacked and coughed as she tottered past, a heavy basket in each hand. Something about her reminded Shadrak of Kadee—the crook of her back, the chin tucked into her chest, eyes on the ground. He was half a step toward giving her a hand, when she coughed again, this time more violently, and blood spattered the ground. Shadrak pulled his hood tight over his nose and mouth and waited for her to pass.

Looking about to make sure he wasn't seen, he sprinted for the shadows cast by the lintel above the doors, which were smooth like the rest of the tower, meeting in the middle with a hairline crack.

Pulling on a soft leather glove, he flipped open the cover of a panel and pressed a sequence of buttons. There was a rush of air as the doors parted. He stepped across the threshold, removing the glove, careful not to touch the outside where it had been in contact with the buttons. He'd seen what happened to those who didn't take precautions; how the skin of their fingers blistered; how they coughed up shit and collapsed. He flung the glove into a cylindrical container in the entrance hall.

Soft light pulsed from long strips set into the ceiling, illuminating the marble stairs leading to the next floor. A red triangle shone above a recess housing a silver door that slid open as he approached.

Stepping into the cubicle, he pressed button number 75 and braced himself as the door shut, and the cubicle started to shudder. His stomach lurched, and he staggered, supporting himself with a hand on the rear wall. The light in the ceiling flickered, and a low drone raced toward a shrill whine before the cubicle juddered to a halt.

The door hissed open onto a corridor of windows that overlooked the sleeping city from a dizzying height. A covered cart was making its way along Weaver Street toward the monument of Gorkan the Great in the plaza, where the bodies of plague victims were starting to pile up.

Shadrak crept to the door at the far end, opened it enough to slip through, and slunk into the shadows.

A black-cloaked figure stood guard at the end of a passageway lined with doors. Shadrak approached, gliding on the balls of his feet, and pressed the tip of his finger into the guard's back.

The man squealed and raised his hands.

Shadrak gave him a friendly pat. "All right, Tony?"

The assassin turned and looked down at him. "You sneaky little sod. Scared the bleeding life out of me! Better go in; they're waiting."

The meeting room was a small amphitheater with banks of colored chairs that rotated upon narrow pedestals. Half the seats were occupied by black-cloaked Sicarii journeymen, all watching him as he entered.

The guild's four masters sat below them around a crescent-shaped table made of red glass.

The windows were shuttered to prevent any spill of the wavering light coming from strips of crystal set into the ceiling.

"Good of you to join us, Shadrak." Master Paldane smiled through thin lips, his good eye bloodshot and blinking, the other milky and blind.

"Don't leave the Maze much these days, Master."

"Except on imperial business," Master Grayling said. He was painfully thin, and a rash of blisters almost completely covered one side of his face. "Don't think we didn't hear about the visit you paid a certain Bovis Rayn."

"Weren't by choice," Shadrak said. "Someone broke my cover; told the shogging Imperials where I lived." *Someone in this room, most likely.*

Shadrak scanned the assembled assassins, many of whom looked away.

Only the poisoner, Albert, caught his gaze, piggy eyes flitting from him to the table as he deftly sliced some cheese with a garrote. Funny that, seeing as he lent Shadrak his cheese-cutter to strangle Bovis with.

He looked more like a fat restaurateur than a paid killer, dressed in a sharp black jacket and pressed trousers in the style of the Ancients.

His bald head was permanently glistening with sweat, which ran in rivulets to dampen the narrow band of hair at the base of his scalp. It would have been easy to assume it was nerves, but Shadrak suspected it was the effect of dosing himself with all manner of poisons in order to build an immunity.

Master Rabalath looked down his broken nose at Shadrak. "You should be more careful," he began, the other masters already nodding their agreement. "When people know where you live, it's hard to remain unseen. Whatever you might argue, the only way for a Sicarii to pick up a job is through us. Anything else gets... messy."

"If the emperor's men come to my house with a job," Shadrak said, "I have to assume it's because one of you scuts shopped me."

There was a rustle of cloaks around the amphitheater.

"Can't say I take too kindly to that." He made a show of scraping the dirt from beneath his fingernails.

"How's your old mom, Shadrak?" asked Master Frayn, the youngest of the masters, lean and muscular to the point of vanity, and sporting a thin, oiled mustache. "Must say, I found her rather charming, for a Dreamer."

Muffled giggles and exchanged whispers.

Kadee might not have been his real mother, but she was the best person Shadrak had known. Almost good enough to balance out his darker leanings. But not quite.

"Died last winter." Speaking the words made it so much more real. If he hadn't had his anger, he might have shown weakness. "Surprised you didn't know, intelligence being your strong point and all."

Frayn stiffened at the slight. A master out of touch was a master in danger of losing the respect of those below him; and the Sicarii were always jostling for position. It was positively encouraged.

Shadrak gave his most malignant grin to Frayn, at the same time imagining what it would feel like to rip that ridiculous mustache from his face along with the skin.

"Good of you to ask, though. Makes me feel tingly all over, knowing a master cares about my family. How's the little nipper coming on, Frayn? He must be, what, two? Three? No better part of the city to raise a child than Charinbrook, wouldn't you say?"

The blood drained from Frayn's face, and he glowered while tugging the ends of his mustache straight.

"But to answer your concerns, Master Rabalath, the emperor's men who paid me a visit won't be doing that again. Took the job, did the bastard, then did the scuts that hired me."

He'd retrieved Kadee's ashes, too, and made sure they couldn't be used against him again. After he'd spent some time alone with them, remembering, he'd scattered them on the banks of the Soulsong. Not as good as the Homestead, the most sacred site of the Dreamers, but it would have to do. Kadee would understand.

"Now, I'm guessing if anyone else knows where to find me, they must be in this room." He gave them all a good look, let them know he was memorizing their faces. "As to the matter of freelancing, I find the suggestion... insulting." He made sure the last word hung heavy in the air.

Albert cocked an eyebrow, but Shadrak tried to keep his face blank. If the guild found out the pair of them had been creaming off some lucrative contracts over the past few years, things could turn very nasty. He didn't doubt Albert had already prepared something suitably deadly, in case they were made: an airborne toxin, or a contact poison to be daubed on the seats of the latrines. But there were other Sicarii equally as dangerous, and you didn't get to be a master without knowing how to survive your colleagues while having them retired on the quiet.

"Glad to hear it," Rabalath said, to the nodded agreement of everyone in the room.

"So," Frayn said, back to his pompous-arsed self, "how's it going in your shitty little kingdom under the city?"

Shadrak stared at Frayn for an uncomfortably long time. The master's cheek twitched, and he began to fiddle with his mustache again.

"Found more Ancient-tech weapons?" Paldane sought to ease the tension.

"No." Shadrak wasn't about to tell them the truth about that. "Reckon mine's the only one. But to answer Master Frayn, I've spent hours beneath Arnbrook House. Seems the council are getting jittery about this plague."

"As are we all," Rabalath wheezed, coughing into a handkerchief like he was about to drop dead from it.

"Governor's been spending a lot of time with his public health advisor," Shadrak said. "Seems they're trying to reassure Jorakum; get this shogging quarantine lifted."

"That'll be my man, Cadman." Frayn sat back with his arms folded across his chest, looking at the other masters like a schoolboy who'd just come top of the class.

"No doubt Hagalle thinks the plague's punishment for all the missionaries he's shogged in the arse and sent scarpering back to Nousia," Grayling said. "Templum curse or some bollocks."

Frayn frowned and sat upright, stroking his chin and looking all business, as if he were commanding everyone's attention. As if he were head of the guild and not Rabalath. He opened his mouth to speak—

"Terribly sorry to interrupt," Albert said around a mouthful of cheese, "but perhaps it is we who should be worried. Hagalle may give the orders, but we're the ones who give the Nousians a good poking, aren't we Master Rabalath?"

If looks could kill, Albert would have been holding handfuls of his own guts, the way Frayn was glaring at him.

Rabalath gave a girlish laugh, but it was hard to tell whether it was from nerves, or some hidden shame.

"Good point, Albert," Paldane said with a fawning chuckle, obviously trying to keep in with the poisoner—and who could blame him? "Didn't you once secrete thorns dipped in scorpion venom in their robes? I heard you even mixed their incense with toxic resin, and wiped out the Nousian community at Delta's Bluff with a donation of mushroom soup."

The journeymen burst into laughter, and Albert nodded appreciatively, dabbing his lips with a patterned handkerchief.

"From what I see," Shadrak said, "Governor Gen don't exactly share Hagalle's penchant for whacking Nousians."

"The Templum of the Knot?" Paldane rubbed at his eye, then examined his finger.

Shadrak nodded. The community of Nousian priests sat slap bang in the center of Sarum, for shog's sake.

"Nauseating scuts," Grayling said, looking up, as if he expected applause.

"Yes, how come they're off limits?" Frayn turned to Rabalath, who simply shrugged and gave a superior flick of his head, as if Frayn were an annoying fly or a splatter of seagull shit.

"The reason I wanted this meeting,"—Shadrak cut through the crap—"was because I ran into mawgs under the city."

"How many?" Grayling asked, doing his best to look like he wasn't bricking it.

"Three. All dead now."

"But how—?"

"The Maze is big, Master Grayling, bigger than the city. No telling how many ways in and out there are. My problem is, that if I alert the council, they'll either commandeer it, or try to destroy it."

"Small loss." Frayn put his feet on the table. "If you hog all the entry codes, it's no use to the rest of us."

The idiots had tried for weeks to work out the panels. Problem was, they'd grown frustrated tapping out random numbers. None of them had the brains for it. Not like Shadrak. When he'd first stumbled upon the Maze and got locked in, he'd gone through all the combinations in sequence till he found the right one. He later spent weeks doing the same with the other panels, and wasn't about to share the knowledge with his rivals, no matter how much they claimed to be colleagues. He'd shown Albert how to access the outer doors when they'd started working together, but even he didn't need to know more than that.

"Nevertheless,"—Rabalath drummed his fingers on the table—"the less the council knows, the better. Let's see if we can't deal with the mawgs on the quiet. You never know, Governor Gen might even thank us one day."

"Mawgs ain't stupid, Master Rabalath," Shadrak said. "If there's more down there, they'll be wary now."

"And you can't deal with them by yourself?" Frayn was loving it. A big smirk crossed his weasely face.

Rabalath closed his eyes and steepled his fingers. "We can't let the city fall, otherwise who'd pay us?"

Some of the brown-nosers among the journeymen laughed.

"You will take a group of Sicarii, find out where the mawgs are coming from, and seal the tunnel," Rabalath concluded. It had ceased being a discussion.

Shadrak nodded. He didn't like it, but it had to be done. Otherwise he'd be floating down the Soulsong, along with Kadee's ashes. She'd never let him hear the end of it.

EVILS PAST AND PRESENT

Abbey of Pardes, Sahul

Shader found the Gray Abbot at prayer in his cell. He waited in silence, casting his gaze about the tiny room. It was bare but for a mattress, a wooden Monas, a carving of the Dark Mother of Ain, and a vast oil painting depicting fire breathing dragons swooping down upon towers of metal and glass.

"It was quite a spectacle," the Gray Abbot said, rising to stand before the painting. "Countless millions died that day, and those who survived had their culture, their homes and, most devastatingly, their technology destroyed."

"By dragons?" Shader moved closer to examine the beasts. Everyone knew the myth, but he'd taken huge parts of it with a pinch of salt.

"The dragons were just one dream of many. The human mind contains so much that is destructive. Why should the Cynocephalus be any different? Abandoned by his mother, terrified of his father. Not to mention the Liche Lord threatening to drink his soul, then stealing his magical armor so that he could wade through the black river at the heart of the Abyss.

"Huntsman's magic unleashed the power of nightmare that lay dormant in the Dreaming, the unconscious fears of the son of Eingana. The great civilizations of the Old World were powerless against it."

Shader had heard the story of the Reckoning many times before. Who had not? Its effects were felt by every nation on Earth, the potency Huntsman had invoked rippling out from Sahul like a colossal tsunami. How had the Dreamer harnessed such power? Prior to the Reckoning, there had been no magic—save the dark kind Blightey had dredged up from the Abyss. There had only been the accomplishments of the Ancients, which had long-since faded into myth themselves.

The Gray Abbot seemed to be following his thoughts.

"Huntsman merely applied the key to the lock. That is how he explained it to me."

The Gray Abbot gazed at the stars outside the window. "The statue, whatever it actually is, was entrusted to him by his ancestral gods beneath the Homestead rock. He didn't know how they had come by it, but it was ancient even then, over nine hundred years ago, and it had been unimaginably old when his gods first brought it to Earth."

"Brought it from where?" Shader was starting to lose interest, his thoughts caught up in this morning's attack and the snatching of the Gray Abbot's only cherished possession, the oak-carved Monas, with its polished amber eye.

"I don't think Huntsman really knew. He merely used to say the Dreaming. The power of the Statue of Eingana unsettled him in some way. When the statue divided itself following the Reckoning, he took great pains to find safe hiding places for each of the pieces. The body of a snake, two fangs, and two eyes. One fang was lost to him. He entrusted an eye to me."

Shader looked up, and the Gray Abbot nodded.

"I've also seen the other eye. I had a hand in restoring it to its rightful guardian. Oh, it was long before you were born, Frater. Our friend Otto Blightey again. I wonder, do they still tell horror stories about him in Aeterna?"

Shader nodded. He'd heard little else during the Verusian campaign: stories of cruel torture, forests of impaled bodies still gasping for days on end.

"He was close to the Ipsissimus," the Gray Abbot said. "Closer than anyone should be. He stole the Ipsissimal Monas with its amber eye and combined its power with forces drawn from the Abyss. Latia and its neighbors were devastated by plague. As for the other pieces, where they are and in whose keeping, I have no idea. Maybe even Huntsman no longer knows. It's possible that, after all these centuries, the segments could have exchanged hands many times."

Shader wondered at the Gray Abbot's fate now that he'd lost the power of the amber eye. He'd always appeared incredibly vital, but already he looked haggard, his cheeks sunken, eyes ringed with shadow.

"The creature that attacked you, Pater Abbot... You called it Callixus."

The Gray Abbot turned his face toward the statue of the Dark Mother, the Nousian pledge of triumph over evil. "Callixus was grand master more than five hundred years ago. I remember his arrival with the Elect as if it were only yesterday."

"The Lost."

The Gray Abbot turned back to Shader. In the moments he had faced away, he appeared to have aged again. His shoulders slumped, and he let out a long sigh.

"They came to aid the abbey. The emperor had left us at the mercy of the Anglesh mawgs, who terrorized much of what is now the shire of Oakendale. I suspect the creatures had been drawn by my piece of the statue. Huntsman warned me never to use it, but you know how men are. It took months for the Ipsissimus to send us aid, and when it finally arrived..."

He stared into space. Fresh wrinkles etched deep grooves into his face, and his eyes had darkened to pools of shadow.

"I met them from their ships at the Soulsong Estuary. Callixus, a fine warrior and humble with it, led his men toward Sarum, where they were to parley with the governor, pledge their swords to purging the mawgs from the Southwest, and then commence with the liberation of the lands around Pardes, which had lain virtually under siege throughout the winter.

"Governor Travos Gen was accommodating, even in the face of the emperor's hostility toward Nousian interference. The knights set up camp in one of the western suburbs, while Travos Gen arranged barracks for them in the inner city. Within two days, the entire force had vanished. There has never been a satisfactory explanation for their disappearance."

"I've heard all sorts of theories," Shader said, "but Aeterna has no official position. Another contingent was never sent. I believe I'm the only consecrated knight to enter Sahul since."

"Aeterna was shaken by the incident," the Gray Abbot said. "The Ipsissimus recommended our recall from Sahul. Most of the other missions took his advice, but we remained. We remained," he continued whimsically, "at the behest of Huntsman."

"Because of your piece of the statue?"

The Gray Abbot's hand went to his chest, as if he expected to find the Monas still there.

"Huntsman was not clear why it should stay in Sahul. He received feelings, intuitions, but ultimately I think he was as clueless as the rest of us. I once told him the whole business was akin to faith. Can't say he liked the idea very much. Has quite a temper, you know. When the Lost disappeared, Huntsman dealt with the mawgs himself. Storms of lightning, packs of rabid animals, swarms of insects—none of it terribly Nousian, of course, but it scared the living daylights out of the mawgs."

The Gray Abbot turned to look once more at the painting of gargantuan winged serpents spewing fire upon the civilization of the Ancients.

"Why should Callixus reappear now, after so many centuries?" Shader asked. "What does he want with the statue?"

"I have no idea." The Gray Abbot pinched the bridge of his nose, closed his eyes. "But I sense a trail of darkness, like a vein carrying corrupted blood back to the heart. And that heart is Sarum."

"Could it be Blightey?"

The Gray Abbot shook his head. "Blightey's not left Verusia for centuries. If he did, the Templum would know about it. No, I doubt even his reach extends to Sahul. This is something else."

He coughed and bent double. Shader took hold of his shoulders and guided him onto the edge of the bed.

"Time's catching up with me," the Gray Abbot rasped through snatches of breath. "Should have felt this a long time ago."

"You want me to go after Callixus?" Shader asked.

The Gray Abbot spat out phlegm and dabbed at his mouth with shaky fingers. "You feel the hand of Ain in this, or the promise of more bloodshed?"

"You think we should do nothing?"

The Gray Abbot raised a hand, shaking his head. "Forgive me, Frater. I'm hardly the one to judge. It's doubtful the path of peace is still open to us. Maybe it never was. Perhaps you were right all along."

Shader's stomach knotted. He felt as if one of the joists supporting reality had just been split. Suddenly, the world around him didn't feel natural. Either that, or there was something wrong with him; as if the world rejected him. He was like a man displaced; not belonging.

He shut his eyes and winced; held his breath until the sensation passed. When he opened his eyes again, the Gray Abbot was even more wizened and stooped with age.

"What's that supposed to mean?" Shader said, "Me being right all along?"

"I remember a novice I once sent into Sarum, a reformed man, humble to the point of obsession."

Shader knew where this was going and looked away.

"He was passing a tavern in one of the rougher districts of the city—the Mermaid, I believe—when he witnessed a bunch of wharfies setting upon a young man. Oh, the fellow was a merchant or some such, and probably deserved it. I heard later that he'd swindled one of the dockworkers out of his home."

"I never knew that," Shader said, his voice a whisper.

"It hardly matters," the Gray Abbot said. "Except to illustrate that things are often other than they seem. You saw a defenseless man being beaten to death, and despite your calling, you could not simply look on and let it happen."

Shader winced at the recollection. His first impulse had been to fight, but something had held him back: his love of the Gray Abbot; the example of his life.

"I pulled the merchant to his feet and told him to run. Stood in their way. Let them hit me instead."

The Gray Abbot sighed and put a hand on Shader's shoulder.

"The way of peace," he said. "Nonviolent resistance. I often asked myself afterward, while you were recovering at the Templum of the Knot, if your example had changed any of those involved. I wondered if they ever asked themselves why you didn't fight back, why you let them nearly kill you. I suppose even someone who's lived as long as I have can still be naive. I was proud of you, proud of the abbey, proud of Nousians."

"And then I went back," Shader said, hunching his shoulders. "I went back and did to them what they did to me. Only I didn't stop."

"You went back, and you did what was in your blood. Yes, I felt betrayed. Yes, I felt my faith corroded by that bitter reminder of human nature—not just yours, but all of ours. Mine, even. I was glad when you left. I needed no further evidence of what we really are. But when you returned, still intent on trying, I was forced to confront Nous's infinite mercy. I even dared to hope again."

"You thought that if I won the tournament—"

"—you'd excise the violence; become more than human: detached and otherworldly. I know it's an outmoded theology, but that's my flaw. Sometimes I wonder why Nous cares; if he cares. I know if I were him, Ain forbid, I'd have turned my back on this world eons ago."

Shader's eyes flicked back to the painting. The Ancients: brutal, efficient, and utterly dismissive of life. Their's was a culture of death. It had simply been about utility and power for them, and all the peace and love in the world had been seen as a disorder. It was only when the dragons had come, along with every other nightmare from the Dreaming—

"I'm not even clear about what's at stake," the Gray Abbot said. "It all depends on what Callixus plans for the statue, and, more importantly, I suspect, what the statue plans for itself. My fragment is only one of five. It's granted me long life, and enhanced my ability to heal. Besides that, I still know next to nothing about it."

"But you said you sensed an evil trail. Surely Callixus intends some mischief."

The Gray Abbot shuffled fully onto the mattress, leaned back against the wall. The energy leaving him was almost palpable. He seemed to be growing older by the minute. "I must take the blame for the conflict you experienced in Sarum, when I last sent you. I doubt much has changed since."

"I am ready, Pater Abbot. This evil has restored my purpose."

The Gray Abbot gave him a long, searching look. "Callixus was a good man, strong and firm in the faith."

"And I am not?"

"Maybe this is your calling, Frater Deacon. Set aside past failings, high expectations. Pray often, and trust only in Ain. A Monas has been stolen. Return it to me, and in so doing, let us hope you retrieve something of your own also. This is either Ain's work or the Demiurgos's. If you are strong in prayer, there's nothing to fear from the latter and everything to gain from the former."

THE SHAMAN AND THE IPSISSIMUS

City of Sarum, Sahul

Huntsman's stubbly legs probed at the base of the door, the hairs on his back sticking up, mandibles tasting the air. Flattening himself, he scuttled through the gap, feeling the floorboards for telltale vibrations, listening, watching, scenting. Besides the musk of disuse and the smell of rotting vegetables, there was nothing.

Drumming his limbs on the floor, he shuddered and split, wriggled and grew. The air about him shimmered, until he once more stood in the form of a man.

He felt his cheeks, touched both arms, and rocked from foot to foot. A wave of nausea passed from his stomach to his head. Grimacing, he shook himself and sucked in a gulp of stale air.

Satisfied the room was unoccupied, he opened the door, and Sammy entered, bleary-eyed and yawning.

Dust lay thick upon the hardwood floor, and swirled in moats, where light peeked through holes in the curtains. Sammy tugged them open and leaned his chin on the windowsill. Huntsman put his hands on the boy's shoulders and peered over his head.

A death-cart was being loaded with bodies from the house across the street by heavily cloaked and masked orderlies. An unmasked woman, robed in white, looked on. Vast towers dominated the distance, and buildings of brick, iron, and wood sprawled in every direction—scabs on the skin of Sahul.

"Why are there so many dead people in Sarum?" Sammy asked.

"Plague. But do not worry, little fellah; it does no harm to children."

He had intuited that much from the distressed cries of the statue—not audible cries, but sensations, ripples deep in the marrow he had felt since the Reckoning.

The polluting of Eingana's power by unnatural currents affected the soul before spreading to the body. Like the Kutji spirits, it fed on disorder and impurity. Where those things were not present, it could not take hold.

Sammy looked reassured, and sat himself on a wooden pallet strewn with stained blankets. He yawned widely, but refused to give in to sleep. Huntsman smiled at him, seating himself in a decrepit rocking chair by the door. The boy lay down his head and began to hum a tune, his eyelids growing heavier.

"Why is the red rock burning?" Sammy muttered.

Huntsman cast his eyes around the room. "What red…?"

And then he realized. The boy meant the Homestead. Sahul must still be talking to Sammy, showing him the events that scarred her past.

"Long time ago, little fellah. Do not worry now. Red rock is safe."

Sammy sat bolt upright. "No," he said. "Not safe. Monsters are coming. Metal monsters and fire. Lots of fire."

Huntsman rocked forward and forced a smile, hoping he could keep the pain of the past from his eyes. "I was there," he said in a soothing tone. "I made them go away. It will not happen again."

Sammy stared right through him, as if focused on something else. "You are wrong. It happened before, and it will happen again. He comes for them. He comes to start the Unweaving."

Huntsman felt an icy knot forming in the pit of his stomach. "Sahul tells you this?"

Sammy shook his head. "Not tells. It's what I see when my eyes are closed."

"Look now," Huntsman said. "Describe it to me."

Sammy shut his eyes, and his body immediately went rigid. "Dark. A cave. Under the red rock." He gasped and half-opened his eyes.

"What is it?"

"A man. A big black man. His head is... is..."

Huntsman leaned out of the chair to place his hands on Sammy's shoulders. "Head of a snake?"

The boy nodded.

"Do not be afraid. He is a friend. Sahul loves—"

"No," Sammy cried. "Not afraid of him. Afraid for him. The monsters are coming, all silver and fire."

Huntsman had the heart of a cornered rabbit. This was no memory of the events of the Reckoning. There had been no attack on the caves beneath the Homestead, and the snake-headed god, Mamba, had not been there.

"All dead," Sammy whispered, a single tear rolling down his cheek. "Snake-head, toad, crocodile..."

"Dead, how?" Huntsman asked, the chill creeping up his spine.

Sammy's eyes fixed on his. The boy wept freely now, his bottom lip trembling. "I saw a spider, too," he said. "A big one, all curled up and smoky."

Huntsman fell back in the chair, his heart thumping so hard he could hear it like a drum.

"He tried before." Sammy's voice was reedy and distant. "And now he tries again."

Huntsman was paralyzed with dread and foreboding. It was all he could do to breathe.

"Aristodeus had no ward against me," the unearthly voice continued. "He knows that now; knows what to do. But it is a trap within a trap."

"Eingana?" Huntsman threw himself out of the chair and started to shake Sammy.

"Sektis Gandaw has the scent. He has not forgiven my grandchildren. Help them, Huntsman. Help my grandchildren. Help me."

"Eingana? Goddess? Speak to me. Speak!"

"It goes beyond him. Beyond Sektis Gandaw. Beyond the end of all things." Sammy coughed and spluttered. His eyes rolled, and then he began to scream.

Huntsman pulled him into a hug, resting his head on the boy's shoulder, eyes brimming with tears.

Sammy went limp in his embrace. Huntsman settled him down on the bed and watched as the boy's breathing grew soft and regular. Covering Sammy with his cloak of feathers, Huntsman sat back in the rocking chair and turned his attention inward.

Earlier, he had sensed power from the body of the Statue of Eingana—the piece he had entrusted to the bard. It was close by. Closer than it should have been.

It seemed the bard was finally on the move. Soon, the mawgs would come for it, as they had come for the eye held by the Gray Abbot many lifetimes ago.

Most of the custodians had heeded his warnings not to use the power of Eingana, but the Gray Abbot had grown careless, and nearly brought about the destruction of his abbey. Huntsman thought he had learned his lesson, but then the Gray Abbot had used the power again, for some trifling matter, and the mawgs had returned. This time, the knight, Deacon Shader, had driven them off, but they'd marauded south to Oakendale, feasting on the white folk.

Huntsman couldn't help wondering if they'd scented the body of the statue even then, before Elias had used it. Perhaps the thought and energy the bard had put into the writing of his epic had been enough to attract them, without quite giving the location away.

And now Elias had succumbed to the temptation to draw upon the statue's power, even after the scolding Huntsman had given him following the performance at the Griffin. It was a dangerous thing, speaking about the statue. Sektis Gandaw had eyes and ears everywhere. The gods had warned Huntsman of this centuries ago.

Two of the pieces were missing: an eye and a fang. The fang had been taken from Jarmin the Anchorite during his visit to Sarum. Huntsman could feel its closeness. It was still somewhere in the city.

The second had been wrested from the Gray Abbot, and this time, there had been palpable distress from the piece. It had been taken by unnatural forces: forces abhorrent to Eingana.

Huntsman's eyes narrowed, and he clicked his tongue against the roof of his mouth. The pieces were together, he could feel that much, and something was using their power. Using it for purposes inimical to the nature of the statue. He could feel its revulsion, and already the results could be seen in the streets of Sarum.

He contemplated the now sleeping form of Sammy. The child had endured unbearable suffering, and yet had trusted Huntsman like a parent from the moment he had led him from the woods.

There was something about the boy. Sahul favored him, and Eingana spoke through him. Maybe it was to balance the demands that had been made on his sister, Rhiannon; or maybe Sahul was just being fickle. Huntsman wondered what the Wapar Man would have thought of a pale-skin speaking with ants. Would he have taught the boy the ways of the Dreaming?

Sammy's breathing softened into that of deep sleep, and Huntsman's thoughts returned to the present.

Three pieces of the Statue of Eingana were somewhere in the city, and another was still accounted for: the amber eye of the Ipsissimal Monas in Aeterna.

He'd kept track of their whereabouts for more days and nights than there were grains of sand in a desert. He sometimes lost the trail of a piece for a while, but he would always find it again.

The fifth piece, however, had always eluded him. Ever since the Reckoning, when the statue had divided itself, he had not been able to locate the other fang.

He had taken one eye to the first Ipsissimus, Thesarius, over nine hundred years ago. He could not explain why, but it was what the statue had wanted. The other three pieces he had scattered the length and breadth of Sahul. One of them, a fang, had changed hands often, sometimes warranting intervention from Huntsman. He had finally reclaimed it from Ogalvy of Makevar and entrusted it to the anchorite of Gladelvi, where it had remained safe for centuries—until Jarmin's visit to Sarum.

Huntsman was bound to the statue. Since the Reckoning, he had felt like its twin. If he took no action, the statue might be powerless to prevent itself falling into the wrong hands, and yet there was no guarantee that any action of his would not make matters worse. He must have done something right, he figured, for in more than nine hundred years, the statue had remained hidden from Sektis Gandaw, and life had been allowed to continue.

But the gods—Sammy had seen them all dead. He had spoken with the voice of

Eingana.

It is a trap within a trap.

What did he mean by that?

Help my children.

Whatever threatened them, Huntsman would stop it. He had to: they were his gods, his greatest love.

Rising from the rocking chair, he looked down at Sammy curled up beneath the cloak of feathers, snoring lightly. He could hear the rattling of the death-cart pulling away, and glanced out of the window.

The white-robed woman was kneeling beside a man who'd collapsed in the street. Behind the towers of the Ancients, Walu the Sun-Woman had entered the tunnels beneath the earth, painting herself with ocher that stained the clouds as she fled.

Matching his breathing to the rocking of the chair, Huntsman settled into the rhythm of the Dreaming and let his spirit soar free.

***

He found Ipsissimus Theodore kneeling before the Monas in his private chapel in Aeterna.

Twin candles cast long shadows on the walls and ceiling. Frankincense burned on the altar, rising like Huntsman's spirit, which drifted above the Ipsissimus.

"I am sorry for pain in your body," Huntsman said. "Others would have used statue's power by now."

Theodore turned toward Huntsman's spirit-form. "Don't fret about me, old friend. I'm ready for my rightful home."

"That is good. Many dream of forever, which statue can give. Eye of Eingana"—Huntsman indicated the pendant Theodore wore, the Monas with its amber eye—"can heal, yet you choose death."

"There are better things than to simply endure," Theodore said.

"Not all Ipsissimi were of same mind. Most used Eingana's power, caused much trouble, but even so, they are back in ground."

"Whereas you, without a piece of the statue, haven't aged a day in centuries." Theodore grew suddenly serious. "Sektis Gandaw seeks the eye, always has. It was you that told us, Huntsman. Told my predecessors. We Ipsissimi have all lived in fear of him coming in our lifetime. That's why I haven't used it. Nothing to do with bravery or holiness. The thing I never understood, though, was why you entrusted one of Eingana's eyes to the Templum."

"Was where it wished to be."

"A Dreamer goddess, seeking refuge in the heart of Nousia? I'd find it heartwarming, were she not in the form of a serpent."

Huntsman chuckled. "Snakes sacred to us. Eingana has power over life and death. She gave birth to a child, part ape, part dog. It is his dreams Barraiya People walk with."

"Yes, yes," Theodore said. "We've had this conversation before. The same stories run through our Liber, though the weighting is different. Children of Nous, the scriptures say: Eingana, the Archon, and the Demiurgos."

"Pah," Huntsman said. He didn't need to tell the Ipsissimus what he thought of Nous. There had been no Nous before he'd inaugurated the Reckoning. Something else, yes: the old faith that had been changed by the Liche Lord.

He drifted down to settle at the same level as Theodore, met his eyes, and said, "Two pieces of statue are missing."

A ripple ran through the Ipsissimus's white robe.

"My gods say it is not Sektis Gandaw," Huntsman continued, "but statue's power has been used. He will know of it. There has been a vision."

Theodore frowned at that, but gestured for Huntsman to go on.

"A boy has seen dark things. My gods burned beneath Homestead. Something is coming. I fear this. Maybe even Sektis Gandaw himself. Maybe Unweaving of all things."

"Can you find the pieces?"

"I have their scent, but others have it, too. Mawgs hunt beneath Sarum, and a Nousian seeks piece taken from Gray Abbot."

"One of the brothers?"

Huntsman shook his head. "One of your Elect."

"But I have no knights in Sahul. Unless... The Keeper of the Sword of the Archon! So, Deacon Shader went back to Pardes. I wonder if Silvanus's man, Investigator Shin, caught up with him."

Theodore rubbed his chin, stared at the Monas atop his altar. "Should I inform the Saphra Society?" He turned to Huntsman for an answer.

"No."

Theodore struggled up from his knees, stumbled, and reached out to steady himself on the altar. Huntsman instinctively tried to help him, but his spirit hand passed through the Ipsissimus's arm.

"And why is that?" Theodore asked.

"I do not know," Huntsman said. He only knew there was deception in that name: Saphra. Sahul told him so, and the gods confirmed it, though none of them could tell him why. "Aristodeus convinced your predecessors to found this Society."

"Yes, I know," Theodore said. "To protect the Monas. To keep safe the eye of Eingana. And now his former pupil, Shader, is its head, the Keeper of the Archon's sword. Only, I never got to reveal that to him." Theodore bit down on his lip, and a flash of something that could have been anger entered his eyes. "You think Aristodeus can't be trusted?"

"His judgment, maybe," Huntsman said. "Has head of an ox and feet of a sparrow."

"You mean, he's too big for his boots? That he lacks humility?"

"That, and more." Huntsman did not feel comfortable around the philosopher. He couldn't put his finger on it. There was just something wrong about him.

Theodore was watching him closely, no doubt trying to read his thoughts.

"Can't say I'm exactly fond of him, either. Oh, he's always been there, lending a hand, offering his pearls of wisdom. I can't think of an Ipsissimus who hasn't benefited from Aristodeus's counsel. But it was the same way with Otto Blightey, back in the beginning, when the Liche Lord guided our passage from the ashes of your Reckoning. Not that the Templum knew he was the Liche Lord back then," he hastily added. "So, if I'm not to alert the Saphra Society, what do you want me to do? You do want me to do something, don't you? Wait a minute... these two missing pieces: couldn't you use mine to locate them?"

Huntsman raised his palm. "Power would pass between all three. Sektis Gandaw is not blind." He found himself staring at the Monas hanging over the Ipsissimus's chest. It was glowing faintly. Theodore noticed it, too, and lifted it by its chain.

The room dissolved around Huntsman, until he and the Ipsissimus were standing upon the red earth of Sahul, looking up at the Homestead. Fire burst from the summit. Rock dust billowed into the air. And from high above came the sounds of battle: steel upon steel, yells and screams, the rattle and boom of weapons he'd never thought to hear again.

The vision passed in an instant.

Theodore was staring at him, concerned.

111

"What is it, my friend? What just happened?"

"Eingana wants you there," Huntsman said simply. He had no idea why. "Wants you in Sahul. Needs your aid at the Homestead."

Theodore turned away. Turned back again swiftly.

"Is this it? Is this what we've been dreading for so long?"

Huntsman shrugged. He didn't know. He only hoped not. All he could do was what he'd always done: follow the promptings of the statue, and assume Eingana knew what she was doing.

"It will take weeks," the Ipsissimus said. "Do we have that long?"

"There is no way of telling," Huntsman said. "All I know is that you must come. Come to Sahul. Bring many ships. Many men. I will speak with Sahul. She will obtain a favorable wind from the spirits of air and water."

"Oh?"

The Ipsissimus wouldn't have liked that. There was no place in his religion for such beings. But they were there, in every ocean, beneath every hill or mountain, in every spring or brook. It had always been that way, even before the time of the Reckoning. You only had to have eyes to see. The eyes of a Kadji.

Theodore was nodding, a look of grim determination on his face. It was a wonder he was taking it so well. A wonder he put up no argument against the idea. When was the last time he had left Aeterna? Had he ever left, since his election?

"I'll be there," Theodore said. When Huntsman opened his mouth to thank him, the Ipsissimus cut him off. "We've been friends a long time, Huntsman. Longer than most people live. You don't need to explain yourself to me. I know you are doing everything you can to keep Eingana safe,"—he let the Monas fall back against his chest—"but all your eggs in one basket? Are you sure?"

Huntsman hadn't thought of that. Didn't it increase the risk of Sektis Gandaw getting what he wanted, if all the pieces of the statue were gathered together in Sahul? All but the missing piece, and that could be anywhere.

The eye of the Monas around the Ipsissimus's neck glinted for an instant, and Huntsman had an idea.

Maybe Eingana wasn't just concerned about herself.

The vision of fire atop the tabletop mountain rose once more to mind; the same vision Sammy had seen at the behest of Sahul.

Maybe she was doing what any good mother would. Any good grandmother.

He glanced at the Ipsissimus, Supreme ruler of the Nousian Theocracy. The man with the greatest army the world could boast.

Maybe she was protecting the gods of the Dreaming in the caves beneath the Homestead.

Maybe she was protecting her grandchildren.

THE CHILD IN THE ROAD

Templum of the Knot, Sarum

Elias scratched his scalp as he rummaged about in the cart.

The templum made him feel uneasy; not just all that holier than thou stuff, but the festering patients in the nave. He couldn't stand all that phlegm and pus. It made him feel so… organic.

He had a feeling the serpent statue would protect him from the plague, and yet he couldn't stop checking his armpits for buboes, and he'd developed a cough he was sure was imaginary.

In the brief time he'd spent at the Templum of the Knot, he'd been largely on his own. Rhiannon had fallen in with her old tutor, Agna, and looked certain to be taking holy orders as soon as her bruises had healed. He'd briefly met the superior, Mater Ioana, an industrious woman, who seldom slept, and rarely rested from her forays into the city to help the sick and dying.

A strange grizzled man, less than five feet tall, and sporting a horned helm, accompanied Ioana on her journeys. He had the look of a Nousian about him, only his discolored white cloak sported a red cross rather than a Monas. It was a throwback to how things had been before the Reckoning; not the dwarf, the cross. Nothing ever changed. Same people, same bullshit, same insipid fantasies.

Elias introduced himself to the dwarf, but was met with a stony stare from fierce violet eyes. There was no hostility, merely a sense of shame, as if the dwarf carried a burden impossible to bear.

Fat Cadris told Elias the dwarf was called Maldark, but would say little more. There was no need. Elias knew the name from the songs of the Dreamers, and couldn't say he was pleased to make the acquaintance: Maldark the Unfaithful. Maldark the Doom of Aethir. Maldark the Fallen.

Soror Velda labored tirelessly in the makeshift infirmary, and was seldom available for a chat, which was a shame. She was a sane old bird—or at least as close as you could get to sanity among Nousians.

Besides the skulking Hugues, who always seemed to be pottering around just within earshot, there was only the sorry figure of Pater Limus, an elderly priest, rotund and white-bearded, who had fallen from a horse the previous winter.

Limus could just about recall his own name, and repeatedly apologized for not recalling anyone else's. He became muddled in conversation, and his long pauses in speech invariably resulted in a change of subject that was as frustrating as it was confusing.

Nevertheless, Limus was a wellspring of compassion, and there was something about him that Elias found authentic, to the extent that he could almost see some value in the

Nousian life, but only the way Limus lived it.

As the sun dipped below Sarum's great towers, Elias dug out his mandola, sat in the driving seat with his feet up, and began to strum. Hector chewed hay nonchalantly, soothed by his music.

His first trip to Sarum in half a century, and he couldn't say he was enjoying it. He'd never really liked it, even back before the Reckoning, but anything was preferable to the massacre he'd fled.

It had all been going so well. The Global Garden Festival was bigger than Woodstock—the mythology of which had shaped his childhood—and the message was finally starting to sink in. A bit too much for some, it seemed, as the tank-bots had rolled in, and gunships had roared overhead. He'd been lucky to survive, he guessed. A damned sight luckier than Morphic Free-Love, incinerated in the flames of the main stage. Sergeant Sunshine, too, arguably the greatest rock band since Zeppelin, shredded with shrapnel and dropping like crimson bird-shit on their gobsmacked fans.

The busking years in Sarum had paid the rent, but he'd never really settled until he went outback. He'd set up shop in Broken Bridge, performing at functions, and fanning the flames of Sahulian folk music, most of which was already dead and buried and needed re-inventing. It was easy enough to do; folk music was all much of a muchness, and no one knew the first thing about tradition in these parts.

Rhiannon had loved his lessons as a child, and she'd stuck by him as a woman, whereas the other locals shunned him as an eccentric. She was the closest thing he had to a friend. Blood almost. His daughter, even.

Bollocks! He thrashed the strings. He should have been able to protect her. Should have saved her family. If he'd used the statue sooner...

Even now, he could feel its warmth pulsing in his pocket.

"Don't look so worried, my friend," Limus said, limping toward him. "No point troubling yourself with past..." There was a pause as Limus sought the right words, and then gave up.

"Beautiful evening for music." He gestured toward the mandola.

Elias smiled, and began to pluck a melancholy ballad, while Limus settled himself on a bench a few yards from the cart. The old priest closed his eyes and swayed gently to the music.

As he finished the song, Elias swung his legs over the edge of the cart, leaving the mandola on the seat. His hand instinctively felt for the statue.

"There is no evil in what you carry." Limus sounded half asleep.

"What?"

"I sometimes sense these things. Forgive me. Since my accident, I can discern the thoughts of... What were you saying?" Limus rubbed at the shiny yellowish patch on his forehead—the scar tissue from his accident. "You are leaving us, Brother...?"

Elias sat beside him; looked off into the distance, not at anything in particular; just replaying scenes—Yeffrik, Jessy; a pang of guilt about little Sammy. Wishing he'd done more. Tearing up over Rhiannon. "Elias, Pater. The Bard of Broken Bridge."

"That's right. I won't remember, though."

"Yes," Elias said. "I'm leaving. Off some place new; never time to let the dust settle." Except he'd traveled nowhere for decades, and the thought of giving up his shack set his heart racing in a way that couldn't be good. Couldn't go back, though. Not just the risk, either. He'd never be able to live with himself; with all the reminders.

"You'll not stay with the girl?"

Elias thought for a moment before shaking his head. "No, Pater. She'll be safe, or she won't. Nothing I do will alter that."

"And that thing you carry?"

Elias took out the black statue and showed it to Limus. Its coils rippled with amber radiance, and Elias thought he could feel it breathing.

"It's a... Oh!" Limus shook his head in frustration.

"Snake?"

"Yes, that's right. One of the children of Nous. There were three, you know."

Elias smiled with good humor. "Nous had kids? Are you sure?" The poor sod was senile. "Way I heard it, they fell through the Void. The Aeonic Triad: the Archon, the Demiurgos, and their sister,"—he gave the statue an affectionate pat—"Eingana."

Limus appeared not to hear him. "Will you say goodbye to the others?"

"I'm no good with adieus; and besides, the perimeter guards probably won't let me out. I could be back before you can say, 'Neo-capitalist-monomaniac-tech-whore.'"

Elias vaulted into his cart and snatched up Hector's reins, squinting at something scuttling over the lip of the tray.

"What is it, Brother?" Limus asked.

"Nothing. Just an insect." *Or a spider. And a large one at that.*

Elias drove out onto the Domus Tyalae and turned into Ishgar Terrace.

A golden-haired child stood in the road, holding aloft a sliver of glowing amber.

"Sammy?"

The child turned and ran.

Elias lashed Hector in pursuit.

The boy headed left into Haldegon Road, the cart rattling after, tipping onto two wheels as it took the corner too quickly. Elias swung his weight to one side, and the cart crashed back level, bouncing along the cobbles.

It seemed, no matter how fast Hector went, the child maintained the same lead. He scampered right into a winding road, forcing Elias to swerve around a heavily laden death-cart.

Slowing Hector to take the bends, Elias reached an intersection with a branching signpost. The child waited on the right, midway between Draco Road and Wharf Way.

Suddenly, he dashed inside a boarded-up house on the other side of the street.

Elias pulled up outside, and leapt from the driving seat without straightening the cart in the road.

The door to the building was open, the entrance hall beyond unnaturally dark and thick with cobwebs.

His heart was pounding, his mind racing with reasons not to enter.

Had the child been holding a piece of the Statue of Eingana? One of the fangs? Why show him? Was it a trap? Course it was. Must've been. But what if there was a chance...?

He thought about Sammy fleeing from the house after seeing his parents murdered; cringed with shame at his failure to go back.

Gripping the statue tightly in his pocket, Elias stepped inside.

THE FALLEN

Vicinity of City of Sarum, Sahul

The waters of the Soulsong rippled red in the setting sun as Shader spotted the tents he'd passed on the way to the abbey.

Bare-chested soldiers were digging atop a low mound, while others bathed at the river's edge. Fiddling with the knots on his prayer-cord, Shader crossed the bridge toward them.

"Nousian!" bellowed a sentry on the other side.

The soldiers washing their wounds scrambled for weapons, blood still swirling on the surface of the river. The others ceased their digging for the dead strewn hacked and bloody around the camp, and glared at Shader with hard eyes.

He started to fasten the buttons on his coat, then realized it was too late for that. They'd already seen the Monas on his surcoat. No point denying what he was. The shame that he'd even considered it was already nagging at the back of his mind.

"What happened here?"

The sentry stepped back, drawing his sword.

"Put it away." Shader held up a hand. "I'm not your enemy."

Half a dozen soldiers ran up to the bridge with weapons ready. A single archer notched an arrow and took aim.

"Don't I know you?" said a burly man with a wiry ginger beard. "You spoke with Cap'n Janks when the Fallen passed."

"Is he here?"

"Buried, along with half our troop."

"Mawgs?" Even as he said it, Shader knew it hadn't been mawgs. The bodies were too intact; still recognizable as human.

"Cavalry," said the sentry he'd first approached, a scrawny youth who'd taken a gash across his cheek, just beneath the eye.

"Evil shogging bunch," Ginger-beard said. "Nousians by the look of 'em. Leader wore a white cloak with the same symbol you've got on your surcoat. Young, he was, with blond hair. Fought like a demon with two swords."

The chill of recognition touched Shader.

"Plowed right through us as we broke our fast," the sentry said. "Headed straight for Sarum. With any luck, the plague will get 'em."

"Why would they…?" It was obvious these men wouldn't know. They looked as bewildered as Shader felt. He tilted his hat back and met Ginger-beard's eyes. He tried to connect, reassure him, but it wasn't something he was good at.

Ginger-beard must have seen that look others had told Shader about. There was a shift in his demeanor, a widening of the pupils. He didn't want any more trouble. Might just as well have put his hands up and backed away.

"I've business there, too," Shader said, nodding in the direction of the city. "Will you let me pass?"

"What..." Ginger-beard cleared his throat. "What business?"

"Something was stolen from the abbey. I believe it's been taken to Sarum."

"You'll not get out again. Sure you want to chance it?"

"Don't see I have much choice."

The Gray Abbot was ailing fast. Without the amber eye set into his Monas, he'd be lucky to last out the week. And besides, Callixus needed to be dealt with. Evil like that couldn't be allowed to roam free.

Shader pulled the Liber from his coat pocket.

"But first, may I pray for your dead?"

The soldiers exchanged looks, muttering to one another. Ginger-beard fixed Shader with a sullen stare.

"Best save your breath. Don't reckon they'll listen."

***

Within the hour, Shader strode through the empty streets of Calphon, Sarum's northernmost suburb.

Calphon had been his route into the city the last time the Gray Abbot had sent him. That was when his belief in nonviolent resistance had been beaten out of him outside the pub. He could almost feel the fists hammering his face to pulp, the kicks smashing his ribs. He could still taste the vengeance, brutal and demonic, eating at his faith, until he'd assuaged it that night in the Mermaid.

The outer suburbs had altered little since the Reckoning: squat buildings, broad avenues, empty plazas. The wider roads were divided by islands and flanked by colossal metal posts topped with glass globes, some of which glowed orange in the gray dusk. Tawdry eateries, taverns, and stores lined the concourse leading to the central district, many of them shuttered, doors daubed with black snakes, the Sahulian symbol of death.

Shader headed for the one place in the city he knew well: the Templum of the Knot.

He walked for perhaps an hour along streets piled with shrouded bodies, passing masked figures lurking in doorways or scavenging like rats.

Just beyond the metal bridge spanning Wharf Way, Shader came to a crossroads. There was a hastily parked cart in Martyr's Street, lone horse stamping and snorting outside a looming wooden townhouse. The facade was in poor repair, flecks of greenish paint peeling from the timbers. A rusty lantern hung above the open doorway, swathed in cobwebs.

The cart was laden with books and musical instruments. A few hessian sacks had been placed toward the front, the fabric torn and spilling dried herbs, and what appeared to be powdered mushroom.

Shader stroked the flanks of the cart horse, rubbed its ears.

"Hector?"—Elias Wolf's horse. He'd recognize Hector anywhere, from his sheer size alone. Shader and Rhiannon had shared many a ride between Broken Bridge and Oakendale in the bard's cart after nights at the Griffin.

Nostrils flaring, eyes wide, the horse tried to move back from the building, but was restrained by its tether.

What was the Bard of Broken Bridge doing in Sarum? Shader had never known Elias Wolf to travel further than the woods outside the villages in his never-ending hunt for herbs and fungi.

Moving to the entrance, he became aware of a rhythmic whisper drifting down the hallway like a malignant prayer. He stepped inside, keeping close to the wall, clumps of spiderweb clinging to his coat. A tottering hatstand stood back from the door, a pile of scuffed and filthy shoes at its feet.

He inched his way along the narrow corridor. The walls were stained with damp, plaster hanging from the ceiling to reveal the slats of floorboards above. The air was thick with sulfur, and dust motes swirled in amber beams spilling from the cracks of a door at the far end.

As Shader crept closer, the susurrus took on more clarity: four words in a language that could have been Aeternam, but accented strangely, repeated without variation. Other sounds came from beyond the door: guttural growling, sharp hissing. A voice dripping with malice clamored above the urgent calling in his head.

"Leave clothes, human."

A mawg—grinding out words ill-suited to its thick tongue. As far as Shader could tell, it was a female.

"We find what we want in your meat."

Typical mawg. They'd maul their prey, ripping flesh and grinding bone, disgorging anything they couldn't digest. Once sated, the creatures would search through the regurgitated mess and pick out jewelry, coins, and anything else of value.

Another voice, quavering yet lyrical, sounded from the other side of the door: Elias's voice, swiftly cut off.

"Mouth! Be silent! Better. Yours puny magic to a vraajo."

Shader had encountered mawg vraajos during his liberation of Oakendale: sorcerers of awesome power, revered by their tribe as avatars, links to their dark and distant god, the Technocrat, Sektis Gandaw.

Fearing he might already be too late, Shader drew his swords and kicked the door open.

The first thing he saw was Elias Wolf shining like a small sun, amber effusing from his coat.

The bard was cowering at the center of a pack of mawgs, lumpy hides tufted with coarse hair, knuckles scraping the floor. A huge female towered above them, long black tussocks braided with gut; bare breasts, flaccid and empty, drooping to her midriff. Her snout was pierced with shards of bone and rusty iron rings.

The mawgs turned, snarling, to face Shader. The vraajo crouched and made quick, clutching movements with her hands.

Elias fumbled for something in his pocket, and then all eyes were back on him as he raised the statue of a snake above his head. It looked like the black serpent figurine he kept in his music room: "the ashtray of Eingana", he called it. Its jaws were always crammed full of weedsticks, and whatever else the bard had been smoking. But if it was the same statue, it was no longer black. It was bursting with amber radiance.

The vraajo let out a gasp and pointed with a clawed finger.

The mawgs pounced, but were met by a blast of light from the statue that slammed them back. At the same time, Shader heard a chilling caw that seemed to come from another place entirely. Elias must have heard it, too, for he thrust the statue back in his pocket and turned to flee.

The vraajo let out a curse, and Elias slipped, tumbling in a heap.

Baying like wolves, the other mawgs surged toward him.

Shader charged, his longsword glancing from the back of one creature, the gladius skewering another through the neck. For an instant, there was confusion enough to allow him to pull Elias to his feet and drag him toward the doorway.

The vraajo roared dark spells that blurred the entrance hall and filled it with gouts of flame.

Elias's clothes caught fire, but Shader was spared, not even feeling the heat. He lunged at the vraajo, striking air as she sped toward the ceiling in the form of a bat.

Elias threw himself to the floor, rolling to smother the flames. Shader took up a position between him and the mawgs.

Ducking beneath a vicious swipe from a claw, Shader spun on his heel and slammed the gladius into a mawg's belly. Sensing movement behind, he back-slashed with the longsword, which bounced from hide as tough as a cuirass.

Enraged, the creature grabbed his coat and yanked. Shader lost his footing and skidded toward it. In desperation, he rammed the gladius to the hilt in the mawg's chest. It released its grip, black blood bubbling over Shader's hand. He regained his feet, hacked down with the longsword, and clove the creature's skull. His left hand snaked out, ripping the gladius free.

A quick glance showed him Elias was still alive, eyes glazed with shock, clothes charred and smoldering.

Shader rolled beneath a bludgeoning arm, slicing into flesh and sinew with a backswing as he passed.

Something swooped down—the vraajo, suddenly reappearing behind the mass of mawgs, weaving her hands through the air and barking strange words.

Shader was thrown against the wall by a blow from behind. Another mawg raked at his shoulder, claws bursting the links on his chainmail and gouging the skin beneath.

Vision blurred with pain, he flailed lamely about with the longsword, the gladius thrusting and cutting with a mind of its own. He was tiring, his shoulder burning, as if acid, not blood, gushed from the wound. He had no idea how many he'd killed, but, undaunted, the others piled on top of him.

As he went down, he glimpsed another figure enter the room and pass unhindered through the flames.

The vraajo froze in mid-spell, and the mawgs fell away from Shader, turning to face the newcomer.

Panting for breath, Shader peered through the mass of fur and scales and saw a short, burly warrior in a white cloak, gray hair trailing beneath a horned helm. Eyes of violet lightning glared from his thickly bearded face. It was the dwarf he'd seen sailing down the estuary toward Sarum: the Fallen, Captain Janks had called him. Maldark.

Pushing back his cloak to reveal bands of iron armor underneath a brown habit, the dwarf raised a huge war hammer and brought it crashing down with a clap of thunder.

The mawgs broke and fled through the door opposite the one Shader had entered by.

The vraajo squatted down and ground her claws together, spitting and hissing. "Curses on you, Fallen. I'd suck the flesh from your bones, if that wasn't what you desired."

Darkness swirled about her, and then, in the form of a black rat, she scampered away.

A white-robed woman, thick-set and middle-aged, moved to stand beside the dwarf. Shader recognized her, too; knew her from the time he'd spent recovering at the Templum of the Knot.

"See," the dwarf said, "thou shouldst trust thy senses, Mater. Thou art graced."

Mater Ioana. What was she—?

Ioana frowned. "Did you not hear it?"

Maldark tapped the head of his hammer, faced her, and shrugged. "I am lacking in grace."

"Mater Ioana," Elias said. "How did you know?"

Shader approached the trio, swords trailing beside him, dripping black blood.

Ioana's eyes fell on him, even as she replied. "Something called me. A voice, in my head, and yet—"

"Whispering," Shader said. "Words I should have recognized."

Ioana pursed her lips and rolled her eyes—it was that old familiar expression that said she didn't fully understand, but she had an inkling. "Prayer," she said. "Prayer for deliverance. A cry for help, but to whom, and whose cry?" She shook her head, brows knitting in a frown. "Deacon Shader. I didn't expect to see you in Sarum again."

The dwarf cocked his head to one side and studied Shader. He covered his mouth with a beefy hand, tapping his cheek with one finger.

Shader switched his gaze to Elias.

"Something was stolen from the Gray Abbot—an amber eye set into a Monas."

Elias put his hand in his pocket. "One of the eyes of Eingana?"

Shader nodded and turned to Maldark. The dwarf was squinting at him, looked like he was going to say something, but gave way as Shader spoke first.

"Thank you... Maldark, isn't it? Maldark the Fallen?"

The dwarf sighed. "So 'tis said. I hath borne the epithet a long time."

Ioana placed a hand on his shoulder.

"A dwarf of the Dreaming," Elias said. "Or should I say, Aethir, the world dreamed by the Cynocephalus?" He circled Maldark, as if inspecting a prize bull, then dipped his head and raised his eyebrows for Shader's benefit. "Funny how much truth there is in myths."

"Not everything on Aethir was dreamed," Maldark said.

"Ah." Elias wagged a finger at him. "Sektis Gandaw. So, tell me, what creatures did he cross to make you lot?"

Maldark's violet eyes smoldered beneath heavy brows.

"Why were the mawgs afraid of you?" Shader asked.

"I know them of old. I was not the only one to arrive from Aethir."

"Come," Ioana said. "Let's go back to the templum. There is someone there, Frater Deacon, you should see. What about you, bard? Do you still wish to leave?"

"Plague gives me the creeps." Elias plonked himself down on the body of a mawg. "But mawgs scare the proverbial—Ugh!" He leapt back up and dusted himself down, stepping away from the corpse and wrinkling his nose. "Well, I think I've got a phobia. Call me a pusillanimous old codger, if you like, but the sooner I get out of the big smoke, the better."

"You plan to use statue to get past soldiers, like you did when you arrived?"

Where before there had only been cobwebs, a man in a feathered cloak now stood. A Dreamer, brown-skinned and impossibly wrinkled. He looked a thousand years old. "I warned you, music man, not to use its power."

Elias went white. "It won't happen again, Huntsman. I've got ways and means of my own, you know."

Huntsman. The Dreamer shaman who'd brought about the Reckoning. The man who'd entrusted the pieces of the Statue of Eingana to different guardians, the Gray Abbot had said. Is that what Elias was? A guardian of the statue? If he was, Shader wondered how good a judge of character the ancient Dreamer was.

Huntsman held out a hand to Elias, palm up. "It begins. Sektis Gandaw comes. Give statue to me."

"No!" Elias backed away, tripped over the dead mawg, and fell flat on his backside.

"Yes!" Huntsman commanded. There was a moment's resistance, and then Elias handed over the once more black serpent.

"You do not know me, Deacon Shader," Huntsman said, turning away from the bard, "but I know you. Take this. Eingana wills it."

A fist-sized lump formed in Shader's throat. "Why? Why me?"

Huntsman thrust his weazened face toward Shader. "It is what statue wants. Your friend said this would happen—bald meddler. He said statue would choose you. You carry Archon's sword."

"Aristodeus? But how—?"

The statue dropped into Shader's hand. The sibilant voice in his head returned for an instant.

Deo gratias. Deo...

Wasn't that one of the forbidden words, a blasphemy punishable in the Judiciary's dungeons?

Shader thrust the statue back, as if it were on fire, but Huntsman was nowhere to be seen.

Breathing deeply to calm his nerves, he turned the serpent over, running his fingers along the stony scales. Its mouth was agape, as if about to strike, but it had no fangs, just dustings of ash that spilled out onto Shader's coat. Above the mouth, there were only empty sockets for eyes.

Something moved in his peripheral vision, and Shader spun to see a large spider scuttling across the floor and squeezing through a crack.

"Great!" Elias said. "Ter-bloody-rific! Without the bleeding statue, I'm up shit creak. There's no way I can get past the imperial troops without it."

"Thought thou had ways and means of thine own," Maldark said.

"Ha shogging ha! Remind me to book you for the panto next Christmas—not that you bloody Philistines would have any idea what a panto was. Nor Christmas, for that matter. Come to think of it, you probably don't even know what a Philistine is, either."

"Thou wouldst be surprised at what I know." Maldark's voice had dropped to a whisper. His shoulders sagged, and some of the fire went from his eyes.

"Well, if you're not going now," Ioana said, "perhaps you could give us a lift back to the templum. All this excitement has quite worn me out, and I'm about ready for bed."

"And another thing," Elias said. "How come I'm the only one to get burnt?"

Shader wondered about that, too. Of the three, Elias was the only one not dressed in the white of Nous, though the dwarf's cross symbol could hardly be described as a Monas. *Divine protection? Not likely*, he thought.

"Perhaps there is evil in your heart," Ioana said, with a cheeky grin. "Or lack of faith."

"Not evil," Maldark said, drawing Ioana's gaze. "That cannot be the answer." The priestess seemed about to say something, closed her eyes briefly, and patted him on the arm.

"What's that supposed to mean?" Elias asked as Ioana led the dwarf from the room.

"Maybe the power was focused on you." Shader stood aside to let the bard go first. "Perhaps they saw you as the greatest threat."

"You think?" Elias said, cocking his head and rubbing his chin.

"Either that, or the mawgs thought you'd be more palatable toasted."

"Hilarious. No wonder you couldn't hack it as a knight, copped out of being a monk, and screwed up with Rhiannon. You missed your vocation, mate. Should've been a shogging comedian."

Shader glared, fingers tightening around the hilt of the longsword. Elias seemed oblivious, flouncing past as if a sword thrust in the back was the last thing on his mind.

Then the thought struck Shader like a bolt of lightning: Elias Wolf in Sarum. The knights of the White Order attacking the imperial troops outside. What was going on? A mass migration from Oakendale and Broken Bridge?

"Why are you here, Elias? You and the White Order."

"White..." The color left Elias's face. "The White Order, here? Oh, shog. Oh, shoggedy shog shog."

Shader grabbed him by the collars of his jacket and pulled him close.

"What's going on, Elias?"

"They followed me," the bard said. "They must have done. I mean, why else would Gaston bring them here?"

"What are you talking about?" Shader said. "Why would they follow you?" It was no secret the White Knights didn't approve of the bard. They considered him some sort of pagan. Shader only had himself to blame for that.

"I saw," Elias said. "Saw what they did... to Rhiannon's mom and dad. Gaston killed them. Him and the others. Cut them down outside their own home."

Shader let go and backed away, reeling.

Killed them? Killed Yeffrick and Jessy? "But why?" It made no sense.

"Started as an accident," Elias said. "Yeffrick took a swing at Gaston, after I told him."

"Told him what?"

Elias flinched at the scalding heat of Shader's tone.

"He raped her, Shader."

No. Sweet Nous, no.

"Gaston raped Rhiannon."

THE MEETING

Arnbrook House, Sarum

Sixty-five, sixty-six, sixty-seven, and break.

Cadman gave a slight shuffle, glancing about to make sure no one had noticed, and resumed his plod along the broad corridor that dominated the fourth floor of Arnbrook House like a clogged aorta. Council staff bustled this way and that, leaving him feeling like a rock in a fast-flowing stream, clerks and cleaners swirling around him, nodding and cow-towing with feigned deference.

Arnbrook House. He counted off the letters for the umpteenth time while still monitoring the number of his steps within a deeper stratum of his mind, and reaching for his cigarette case with the layer beneath consciousness. A-R-N... seventy, seventy-one...

He emerged from the gaggle of plebs into an antechamber, feeling somewhat like he had as a schoolboy summoned by the headmaster. A young chap slouched on a bench beside the grand oak doors, head in hands, blond locks tumbling about his shoulders and crying out to be trimmed. The lad was armored and wore a blood-speckled white surcoat bearing the Nousian Monas.

Curious. Though it does lend a certain credence to the rumors surrounding our beloved governor. Rumors that Zara Gen was a Templum sympathizer at best, and at worst, a traitor, guilty of high treason.

"Afternoon," Cadman said, touching his forelock in the absence of a hat to tip.

"G'day." The youth forced a smile. Looked like he'd been in the wars, poor chap. He had a puckered gash down the middle of his nose that looked like it had been sewn closed by an upholsterer.

Cadman bent closer to examine the stitches. *Good grief, what did they use, a knitting needle?*

"Ernst Cadman, public health advisor to Governor Gen. And you are?"

The door opened before the fellow could answer, and Lallia slid through the gap.

Officially, she was a clerk, but like all the low-paid council workers in Arnbrook House, she was basically a dogsbody. She looked a mess, to say the least, but that was nothing unusual. Her chestnut hair was bundled up on top of her head, presumably because she'd not had time to brush it; and her eyes were set in dark cavities.

"They're waiting."

Seventy-seven steps in all. Two sevens are fourteen and one plus four equals...

Cadman flipped the cog on his lighter and sucked on the cigarette. "Who's in there?"

"Everyone." Lallia rolled her eyes and opened the door a little wider.

"Everyone? Never a dull moment, eh?"

Lallia shoved the door back for him and held up a hand to the youth, who had risen from the bench. "Wait here."

Oh, the dominance of the woman! Where did Zara Gen find her?

"Governor Gen!" He gave a little bow as he entered the meeting room, one sweep of his eyes taking in the motley crew assembled around the table.

"Master Frayn." He acknowledged the black-clad Sicarii twirling his oiled mustache.

"Gentlemen." He nodded to a red-faced man in chainmail with a much more manly mustache than Frayn's, and to a stiff, important-looking weasel with a haughty demeanor, dressed in the yellow robes of an imperial herald.

He was already thoroughly familiar with the last person he turned to. "Dr. Stoofley." Cadman gave his most affable smile to the cachexic old idiot.

Stoofley inclined his ridiculously large head toward him and attempted a smile that was more of a snarl, tufts of cotton-fine hair sticking up on his liver-spotted pate. "Cadman," he said, before looking away, no doubt shutting his eyes and mentally shaking his head.

Lallia pulled out the chair next to Stoofley and gestured for Cadman to sit.

"Thank you, my dear," he said, before adding in a whisper, "Late night?"

"Dr. Cadman." Zara Gen was all business. "Thank you for coming so promptly."

Heads turned at that, but Cadman thought it best to take it in the positive sense in which it wasn't meant.

"Urgent matters require a hasty response. I only wish I could have made it sooner. I assume this meeting concerns the plague?"

Lallia seated herself beside Zara Gen and picked up a pad and pencil.

"Among other things," Frayn said, twanging his mustache with a flourish and doing his utmost to maintain eye contact.

"Quite." Zara Gen raised a finger. "But the plague is top of my list."

Frayn nodded rather too enthusiastically. "Absolutely, Governor. The plague is priority number one."

"Too bloody right," said the herald. "Some of us have messages to carry to a master who will not brook tardiness."

"Which is why you have been invited to our emergency meeting, Mr. Torpin. It's in all our interests to end this plague as soon as possible." Zara Gen turned to Cadman. "Doctor, this is Dan Torpin, herald to... I'm sorry, who was it again?"

"Duke Farian, second only to the emperor himself." Torpin touched his hand to his breast.

"Honored to meet you," Cadman said.

"Likewise, Doctor. Likewise."

Stoofley splayed his fingers in a gesture that looked part exasperation and part indignation. "If you'll excuse me, Governor, I fail to see why it is necessary to have two medical experts on this panel, when both Dr. Cadman and I are extremely busy with the sick and dying. I'm sure, if the doctor wants to return to his patients, I will be more than able to speak for both of us."

Zara Gen sighed and twiddled with his ponytail—a sure sign he was growing irritable, Cadman knew from experience.

"I appreciate your concern, Dr. Stoofley, but there are important differences in the way you two practice that might actually help in this instance."

Stoofley gave a sullen nod and picked up his pen, fanning the air and coughing delicately.

Cadman held up his cigarette. "My apologies, Doctor. Such a disgusting habit. I would put it out, only—"

"Here." Lallia pushed back her chair and came round the table to snatch the cigarette from him.

Cadman thought she was about to stub it out on the carpet, but instead, she sauntered over to a window and flicked it outside before returning to her seat with another roll of her eyes.

Obviously didn't find what she was looking for last night.

"Besides the plague, and Master Frayn's little matter," Zara Gen said, doing his best to avoid Frayn's look of affront that said his matter was anything but little, "are there any other issues you'd like to table?"

The ruddy-faced soldier gave a polite cough and leaned forward.

"Captain Harding?"

"Just one matter, Governor. A spot of bother at the Arch of Foundation. Ringleader's outside. Thought you should see him."

Zara Gen frowned and took a deep breath. "Thank you, Captain? Anything else? No? Good. Dr. Stoofley, perhaps you could fill everyone in on this blasted plague."

Stoofley coughed into his fist and knitted his brows, nodding sagaciously. He left a long enough pause to ensure all eyes were upon him, and just when Zara Gen seemed about to prompt him to get on with it, Stoofley spoke.

"Five hundred and twenty-seven dead..." He paused for effect. "And by my last reckoning, eight hundred and sixty-six in the infirmaries. Perhaps Dr. Cadman will correct me, if I'm misinformed."

Cadman beamed at him, reached for another cigarette, caught Lallia's glare, and dropped his hand to his lap. "I have absolute faith in your figures, Doctor."

Zara Gen put his head in his hands, but only long enough to realize he was doing it. Before the others had noticed, he was leaning forward intently, hawkish face thrust toward Stoofley. "Are we coping?"

Stoofley sat back and spread his hands. "As soon as the infirmaries fill up, they empty again, but not because patients are getting better. The death-carts are collecting night and day, and the grave pits are woefully inadequate."

"Excuse my ignorance," Cadman said in his most affable voice, "but shouldn't we be burning the bodies?"

"Correct me if I'm wrong,"—Stoofley gave an exaggerated sigh—"but I was under the impression there was a fire ban. The last thing the governor needs,"—he gave a sycophantic nod to Zara Gen—"is a bush fire. We're already stretched to the limit."

"Burn them," Zara Gen said.

"But—"

"Dr. Cadman,"—Zara Gen turned away from Stoofley—"what is your opinion of this plague?"

Magic, of course, and if I wasn't wasting my time at this tedious excuse for a meeting, I'd be well on my way to discovering a cure.

Not that he was unduly concerned about the victims. The wretches started along the path of decay the moment they were born. Accelerating the process was neither here nor there. But the matter of their dying by the hundreds was turning all eyes toward the source of the pollution—for that's what it was, not a bacillus.

They were like dead fish floating to the surface of a poisoned lake. Sooner or later, people would realize the only remedy lay in identifying the contaminant and removing it; and Cadman doubted whether they'd differentiate between the amber pieces of the Statue of Eingana and his own dark craft, which they amplified.

The side-effects of such a communion had at first been a curiosity, but had now rapidly become a worry.

"If Aeterna would open its archives, we'd have it beaten in no time." *That'll put the cat among the pigeons.*

"Absolute rubbish!" Stoofley was on his feet, as if he were going to walk out in protest at such idiocy.

"Sit down, Doctor!" Zara Gen said.

"But, Governor, must we go through this pointless discussion yet again?" Stoofley said. "It's utter nonsense. Unmitigated madness. There is not the slightest shred of evidence to support the idea that Aeterna has access to the secrets of the Ancients."

"The emperor believes the rumors." Dan Torpin interlaced his fingers on the tabletop, eyes widening in surprise that anyone could possibly be challenging Hagalle's judgment.

"I... Well, I mean," Stoofley spluttered.

"Do you mean to say the emperor has wasted the wealth of Sahul by building up the fleet?" Torpin said. "Is he responding to a threat that doesn't exist? Really, Dr. Stoofley, we must deal with this pestilence as quickly as possible, so that you can convey the news to him. Perhaps he'll even allow you to treat his paranoia, if that's what you think it is."

Stoofley resumed his seat, eyes darting around the table for any hint of support.

Master Frayn gave a condescending laugh and shook his head, turning to Zara Gen, as if he expected to see his response mirrored.

The governor ignored him, and used unwavering eye contact to ensure everyone knew it was Cadman he wanted to hear.

"I must say, gentlemen, I'm a little surprised," Cadman said. "It's no secret that I have one or two odds and ends of Aeterna-tech in my surgery. Why, Master Frayn here has seen it put to good use."

Frayn nodded absently and then sat up, a hard expression coming over his face.

"Governor," Cadman continued, "do you recall the coughing plague among the Barraiya Dreamers? Easily eradicated with a simple potion, and thus no need for a—what's the right word? Cull?"

"Excellent work, for which you've been more than rewarded." Zara Gen swished his ponytail. "But if the solution is as easy this time, why have you done nothing?"

Cadman spread his hands and sighed. "No more potion."

"This is hardly the same as the coughing plague," Stoofley said. "The symptoms are quite different: no fluid-filled lungs, no organ failure. I very much doubt the same formula would work in this case. It is my considered—"

Zara Gen waved Stoofley to silence. "Do we have the means of procuring the potion?"

Cadman stuck out his bottom lip and shook his head. "Without the right technology, the potion couldn't be analyzed. It's hard to say what constituted it." *Though I could hazard a guess.* "If only we had access to Aeterna's libraries, I'm sure we could build instruments with which to study the bacillus and manufacture a cure."

"If only!" Stoofley threw up his hands. "This is all rather spurious. Technology! Bacilluses! Utter rubbish."

"Actually, it's bacilli," Cadman said. "Don't they teach Aeternam at med-school anymore?"

Dan Torpin guffawed. "If they did, they'd soon have their tongues cut out, eh, Master Frayn?"

"Oh, yes." Frayn gave a self-satisfied smile.

"So," Zara Gen said, "unless we invade Nousia and commandeer the libraries of Aeterna, this idea of a curative potion is about as useful as fairy dust."

Cadman leaned forward and tapped his nose with his index finger. "Know thine enemy, Governor; that's the point I'm making. We may not have the potion, but we do know, from our dealings with the coughing plague, that the cure was aimed at a bacillus; a bacillus that spread through water droplets and other bodily fluids. What we need are masks, gloves, and fires to incinerate any materials that may have come into contact with the plague. We need to isolate the victims and cordon off the areas where there's been an outbreak. The people,"—*bless them*—"must be educated in hand hygiene, advised to avoid crowds, and made to wear masks or scarves at all times."

Zara Gen nodded at Lallia to make sure she was getting all this down. "And what if it doesn't work, Doctor? What do we do next?"

"We burn Sarum, street by street."

There was a hushed silence as they considered the enormity of what Cadman was suggesting.

The poor fools are so desperate, they'll believe anything.

"Shall we move on to other matters?" Zara Gen said. "Master Frayn?"

Frayn cracked his knuckles, and then hid his hands beneath the table at the looks he received. "My superiors asked me to raise the matter of the Templum of the Knot, Governor." Frayn's eyes flitted to Dan Torpin and back to Zara Gen.

Torpin was sitting bolt upright, apparently much more riveted by this turn of conversation than he'd been by the plague.

"They feel," Frayn said, "our imperially sanctioned work in this respect is being impeded."

"Do they now?" Zara Gen scratched underneath his ponytail.

"Actually," Torpin said, "this was one of the reasons for my visit."

"Was it, indeed?" Zara Gen said.

"Elsewhere, the Nousian threat has been rooted out," Torpin said. "The Sicarii have been given free-rein in all the major West Sahulian cities, and now, besides a smattering of hermits in the jungles outside Gladelvi, only the Pardes community and your lot remain."

"My lot?"

"Forgive me, Governor. The Templum of the Knot. My master, Duke Farian, has been commissioned by the emperor to bring this project to a close. His Grace is a little concerned about the tardiness of the Sicarii's work in Sarum. Upon my arrival,"—Torpin exchanged looks with Frayn—"I met with senior guildmembers and discovered that they were being hampered in their task by the City Militia."

Captain Harding's face grew a shade redder, but he continued to sit like a statue, as if none of this concerned him.

"There is a time for everything," Zara Gen said, "and it is my belief that the Templum of the Knot is best left alone right now." He raised a hand to silence Torpin's protests. "Dr. Stoofley, do the priests not operate an infirmary for victims of the plague?"

"They do, Governor, and a very good one, if I might say so."

"Is there anything unusual about their infirmary, Doctor?"

Cadman's attention pricked at that. He flipped a cigarette into his mouth and let it hang there unlit.

"Well, Governor," Stoofley said, "it's come to my attention that the priests tend the victims without any of the precautions my colleague Dr. Cadman just mentioned, and yet, unlike the nurses at our own hospitals, they do not grow sick."

Interesting.

"You think they have Aeterna-tech?" Zara Gen directed the question at Cadman.

"It's possible." Cadman shrugged. "But not very likely. Maybe they have better hand-washing skills, and encourage their patients to cover their mouths when coughing." *Or maybe there's a hint in all this about the nature of the affliction and its associated risk factors. Purity, after all, is not solely attained by ablutions.* "The victims,"—Cadman turned to Stoofley—"do they share any common factors?"

Stoofley rubbed his chin for a moment before replying. "The first victims were from the docks, but the plague quickly spread through Dalantle's whores. We assumed it had passed from the sailors and spread like the clap, only then it decimated the business district and some of the poorer suburbs. I can see the connection between sailors, whores, and the riffraff of Calphon, but that doesn't account for bankers and some of our most respected merchants."

"All very fascinating," Dan Torpin cut in, "but is this any reason to obstruct an imperial command?"

Zara Gen stood. "This is not a matter of obstruction, Mr. Torpin, and if I hear any further suggestions to the contrary, you'll be removed from this meeting. Is that understood?"

"You wouldn't dare!"

"Captain Harding," Zara Gen snapped.

Harding clapped a hand on Torpin's shoulder. "Is there going to be any more trouble?" he growled.

Torpin glowered and shook his head.

"Good," Zara Gen said. "Then perhaps we can move on. The Templum of the Knot, as far as I'm concerned, is providing an invaluable service during a time of crisis. Once the threat to Sarum has passed, we will, I'm sure, cooperate all the more diligently with the emperor's decrees. Next." He glanced at Lallia's notepad. "Something about the sewers, is it, Master Frayn?"

"One word, gentlemen," Frayn said, standing and making a pyramid of his fingers. "Mawgs."

Well, that was dramatic.

"One of my people encountered them in the sewers; a scouting party, most likely. All dead now."

Zara Gen's face was ashen. "Mawgs beneath Sarum? Captain Harding, how many men can we spare?"

"We've barely enough to man the watch; but in an emergency, we could reduce the patrols."

Zara Gen shook his head, deep furrows etched into his brow. "Not with the plague; the looting would be terrible. I will not stand for anarchy."

"Already in hand," Frayn said, folding himself smugly into his seat. "I've dispatched a team to deal with the threat."

"Good, Master Frayn, good," Zara Gen said. "How many?"

"Six. All good men."

Dan Torpin sucked in his cheeks. "Awfully charitable of the guild to help out in a time of crisis, Master Frayn. What's in it for you?"

Frayn gave a lopsided grin. His cheek had started to twitch beneath his right eye. "I'll be honest with you, Mr. Torpin: cash. If the city falls, the Sicarii might well survive, but who would be left to pay us? We'd have no choice but to move north. Much as Jorakum's a magnificent city, it's too darned humid. I couldn't see the lads taking to it without going troppo."

Troppo! The inventiveness of the Sahulian vernacular never ceases to amaze me. I really must start a dictionary of neologisms.

"Six men, you say?" Zara Gen pressed a finger to his lips. "Is that enough?"

"All depends on how many mawgs they find," Frayn said. "They're experienced men. Once they know what they're up against, they'll send word. I will personally keep you updated, Governor."

"Tell your colleagues, I'm in their debt. Yours too, Master. You have my thanks."

Frayn could barely keep the smile from his face. He sat back, folding his arms across his chest and doing his best to look nonchalant.

"Moving on," Zara Gen said, with another glance at Lallia's pad. He squinted and queried her with a look of bewilderment.

Lallia leaned in, perhaps a bit closer than was absolutely necessary, Cadman thought, and whispered in his ear.

"Ah, yes, Captain Harding. What's all this about trouble at the Arch?"

Harding stood to attention and addressed Zara Gen in a parade ground bark, cheeks reddening further by the second. "A troop of cavalry arrived from—"

"About time, too!" Torpin said, flinging himself back in his chair. "Help from Jorakum. I knew it!"

"From the villages," Harding pressed on. "They seem to have had a bit of a run-in with the imperial troops cordoning off the city."

"Cordoning off!" Torpin threw himself forward. "You make it sound like a quarantine!"

Zara Gen pulled his ponytail so hard, Cadman thought it might come off. "Well, it is, isn't it? What else would you call it?"

A ring o' roses?

"Merely a precaution," Torpin said through gritted teeth. "The emperor is trying to help."

"If you want my opinion," Cadman said, finally giving in and lighting his cigarette, to the accompaniment of glares from Lallia and coughs from Stoofley, "he's doing just the right thing: containing the plague until it either runs its course or starves when there's no more fodder left for it to feed on. I'd do the same, unless of course I had access to the medicines of the Ancients, or whatever it is that grants the priests immunity."

Zara Gen shot Cadman a furious look before turning back to Harding. "What kind of a run-in?"

"Their leader says they had to fight their way in. Lost a few men, but not nearly as many as the enemy."

"This is intolerable!" Torpin banged his fist on the table. "Enemy? You are talking about your emperor's loyal soldiers."

"A figure of speech, sir," Harding said. "I merely meant 'opposition'."

Zara Gen muttered something to Lallia, who stood and walked over to the door.

Torpin hadn't quite finished yet. "And you, Captain," he almost spat at Harding, "find it acceptable that so-called cavalry from the provinces attack imperial troops?"

"No, sir, I do not, but—"

"But what?"

"Well..." Harding looked at Zara Gen. "They're here. Thought perhaps we could use their help."

The door opened, and Lallia ushered inside the youth Cadman had passed on his way in.

"Governor," Harding said, "this is Gaston Rayn of Oakendale."

"Thank you, Captain. Oakendale, eh?" Zara Gen gestured for the young knight to take the seat beside Cadman. "Farmer?"

"My father used to be a rancher, but he gave that up to—"

"He's retired?"

"Dead. Killed by an assassin working for the emperor."

Torpin stood so violently that his chair crashed to the floor. "How dare you! Governor, I will not stand for this scurrilous outrage!"

"Then shut up and sit down!" Zara Gen's shout was as stunning as a sledgehammer to the head.

Lallia dropped her pencil and ducked under the table to find it. Cadman took a long drag on his cigarette and surreptitiously tapped the ash onto the carpet. Harding rather graciously righted Torpin's chair for him, and then they both re-seated themselves. Torpin's eyes were fixed on his fingers, and no doubt flaming with ire.

Master Frayn was back to twiddling his mustache, studying the lad as if he were trying to work out which one of his men had committed the murder.

"You say your name is Rayn? Your father was Bovis Rayn?" Zara Gen said.

The youth looked partway between shock and rage, neither hinting at much in the way of self-control. Cadman was starting to like him.

"You knew him?"

"Knew of him. Heard him speak once. A Nousian, as I see are you." Zara Gen flicked a look at the others around the table. "Made quite a name for himself. Perhaps a bit too much of a name. Tell me, Gaston—may I call you Gaston? What brings you to Sarum?"

"The Templum of the Knot. I must go to them."

Torpin looked up at that, but he didn't risk opening his mouth.

"For what purpose?" Zara Gen asked.

"I was told they're in danger. I was also told to look for my old master, Deacon Shader."

"The monk? I'd heard he'd gone back to Pardes after the beating. Terrible affair, that. You remember it, Captain Harding?"

Harding grunted beneath his mustache. "Don't suppose I'll forget it any time soon, Governor."

Gaston frowned and shook his head. "He left the abbey after that; came to Oakendale and drove the mawgs out. That's when he founded my Order."

"And then left you?" Torpin finally found the courage to speak. "Tell me, Mr. Rayn, was your master in contact with Aeterna? If I'm not very much mistaken, he's encouraged you to dress like the Templum Elect."

Yes, I was wondering about that. Uncannily like the surcoat Callixus wears, although without the cobwebs and the odor of decay.

"He returned to Aeterna for a tournament; I've not seen him since. Shader once served with the Elect. May do again, as far as I'm aware. He wanted us to be like them, only better."

"Better how?" Torpin asked. "Better at infiltrating Sahulian cities and paving the way for a Templum invasion? That's what the emperor's going to think."

Gaston turned to Cadman, who shrugged and puffed smoke in his face.

"Better spiritually," Gaston said with a cough. "Better morally." He hung his head as he said the last word, and that piqued Cadman's interest immeasurably more than anything that had been discussed so far.

Torpin's confidence was returning with irritating rapidity. "Governor, I propose that this man and his so-called Order be arrested on grounds of treason."

Zara Gen held up his hands. "Mr. Torpin—"

"I absolutely insist! Nousian knights attacking imperial troops and entering one of our cities! It's unthinkable. When the emperor hears of this, he'll want them all hanged."

At an almost imperceptible nod from Zara Gen, Master Frayn flowed from his chair and drifted around the table. Torpin showed no sign of having noticed.

"In fact, if we do nothing, he'll have *us* all hanged, or worse. Now, do I have to remind you—gurgh!"

Torpin was dragged over the back of his seat with Frayn's arm around his neck. In one fluid movement, Frayn flipped him on his front and snapped him in a wrist-lock.

"Captain?" Frayn invited Harding to take the other arm.

Zara Gen gave a curt nod, and the captain and the guildmaster escorted Torpin from the room.

"Told by whom?" Zara Gen said to Gaston. "You said you were told the Templum of the Knot was in danger, and that you were to look for Deacon Shader. Who told you this?"

There was a long pause, while Gaston stared dumbly. Eventually, in a slightly bewildered tone, he said, "Aristodeus."

Zara Gen exchanged a look with Captain Harding, who shrugged. Cadman shrugged, too.

"He's a philosopher," Gaston said. "Shader used to speak about him. Aristodeus taught him as a child."

"Hmm," Zara Gen said. "And now Shader's back in Sarum, and there's some undisclosed threat to the Templum of the Knot. I assume this Aristodeus didn't mean the plague."

"I don't know, Governor," Gaston said. He slumped down in his chair, suddenly looking very much a boy, and nowhere near the man he'd been striving to be when he entered the room.

"Lallia," Zara Gen said, "would you mind showing Dr. Stoofley to his carriage. I think our meeting has reached its natural end. Thank you for your input, Doctor, and let me assure you, I'll take your suggestions very seriously indeed."

"But—"

"Goodbye. Oh, and Lallia, please close the door behind you."

Zara Gen waited until their footsteps had faded before getting up to perch on the edge of the table. "The greatest attribute a politician can have is to be able to empty a room when things must be said in secret."

Gaston was wide-eyed and fidgety, but Cadman was intrigued. Slipping his hand under the table, he dropped his cigarette stub on the carpet and ground it underfoot.

"It may be that we can help each other." Zara Gen placed a hand on Gaston's shoulder. "I am keen that no harm should befall the Templum of the Knot." He raised a finger to prevent Cadman from asking the obvious question. "My reasons are my own, but as you will no doubt one day learn, Gaston, all reasons are political. I also have a militia very much depleted by the plague, and could use some extra manpower. In return, I'll protect you from Hagalle's people and give you quarters at the barracks. Does this sound acceptable to you? Good. Excellent.

"Dr. Cadman, if the priests are immune to this plague, I want to know why. Take Gaston to see them; talk with them, observe them, and give me something I can use. If we can end the plague, Gaston—and that's a big 'if'—you may have some bargaining power with Hagalle. Once the quarantine's lifted, he's bound to send more troops, and when he does, your best hope will be our account of your part in the saving of Sarum."

Zara Gen held the door open, but gestured for Cadman to wait. "One last thing, Gaston." The lad paused in the doorway, eyes like dinner plates, cheeks the color of a boiled lobster. "Do you always do what this philosopher asks?"

"Never met him before." Gaston looked like he couldn't wait to leave. Poor boy was utterly out of his depth. "I... I did something... He said coming here would help. Help bring me back to Nous."

Curiouser and curiouser... Starting to sound like my kind of person.

Zara Gen gave Cadman a quizzical look and received a shrug in return. "Thank you, Gaston." The governor almost squashed the lad against the jamb of the door as he shut him out of the room.

"Doctor." Zara Gen inclined his head so that he could whisper. "I recently received an unusual visitor to my office. Were you made aware?"

One, two, three.

"I see that you were." Zara Gen rubbed his chin and tutted. "Absolute discretion, I said, and yet virtually the whole staff of Arnbrook House seems to know my business. If Hagalle should find out about my meeting with Jarmin the Anchorite, my head will be on a spike at the top of the Tower of Glass. My people tell me Jarmin never made it out of the city. I suspect the Sicarii got him. Ain knows they'll probably come for me next, although Frayn's playing it close to his chest, if that's the case. Have you heard

131

anything?"

Cadman had stopped counting at three; stopped breathing, too. "As a medical man,"— he stood and opened the door a crack to make sure Gaston wasn't within earshot—"I can assure you that anything you say to me will be held in the strictest confidence. Regrettably, I've seen nor heard nothing of Jarmin since his little visit, and I only knew about *that* due to the indiscretion of one of the staff."

"Who?"

"Forgive me if I don't say." Cadman stared pointedly at the chair Lallia had recently occupied.

"Thank you, Doctor." Zara Gen pried Cadman's fingers from the door and held it open for him. "And good luck with the templum."

Cadman shuffled along the corridor to catch up with Gaston. The lad was frowning back toward Zara Gen's office.

"I'm starting to think I made a big mistake coming here."

Farm-boy in the big city? Whiskerless youth swimming with the sharks of Sahulian political life? Oh, you poor witless child, "mistake" doesn't even begin to cover it.

"Nonsense, Gaston. I'd say your arrival has been most fortuitous; a gift from Ain, you might say." *If you were a dumb savage with offal for a brain.* "Come, my carriage is outside. Let's take a look at these knights of yours, and then we'll pop over to the templum. Tell me," he said, putting an arm around Gaston's shoulder, "did your Mr. Shader ever speak about the legend of the Lost?"

"The Elect knights sent from Aeterna to aid the Abbey of Pardes centuries ago?"

"Quite, quite. I have a friend who has rather a passion for the subject. You really should meet him; I think he'll enjoy you immensely. But first, allow me to take a look at that nose of yours. Can't have you going around with stitches like that. People might think it's my handiwork."

KNOTS

Templum of the Knot, City of Sarum

R aped.
    Gaston had raped her.
    Rhiannon.
    The empty eyes of the Dark Mother of Ain were like tunnels onto the Void; invitations to take the final leap that either led to the Supernal Realm or oblivion. The statue stood out from the triptych altar-piece in the Lady chapel and provided the priests of the Templum of the Knot with a focal point for their meditations.

"Gaston lost it," Elias Wolf had told him on the way to the templum. His dad was murdered. Bovis Rayn had been killed by the Sicarii. People were saying it was Shadrak the Unseen.

Shader could have forgiven Gaston almost anything, after what he'd been through: all those months not even speaking to his father, all because the lad had remained loyal to Shader and the idea of the White Order.

Bovis hadn't approved. He'd have seen eye to eye with Jarl Shader, though they were on opposite sides of the fence.

Bovis had got Nous real good, given up his ranching business, and dedicated his life to preaching. That would have come to the attention of the imperial authorities. That would have led to a contract with the assassins' guild.

Then Shader had abandoned the lad. Promised him everything and left, the minute the going got tough. The minute Rhiannon had rejected him.

But that was what he couldn't forgive. He tightened his fist around the prayer cord. What Gaston had done to Rhiannon.

Elias said Rhiannon had been drunk at his performance at the Griffin. She'd left early and gone to see Gaston. Her intention, she told the bard, was to say goodbye to her childhood sweetheart before she left for the novitiate, because Rhiannon had her sights set on being a priestess. With Gaston's inner turmoil, and the two bottles of wine she'd brought with her, it was a seething cauldron of trouble waiting to happen.

But Gaston was still to blame.

Shader tried to focus on the knots of the prayer cord dangling between his knees, but his eyes seemed to have a life of their own.

Rows of votive candles glowed like marsh gas through the clouds of frankincense rising from a censer. Death-rattles and hacking coughs from the nave syncopated his thoughts and set him cursing under his breath. He saw a flash of white and looked up to see Soror Velda scurrying between the pallet-beds, no doubt offering false hope to the victims of the plague.

He should have gone straight to Rhiannon. Even now, he could have asked Velda to take him to her. But he wasn't ready. He didn't know what to say, and in a perverse sort of way, he thought she might blame him. Blame him for what his protégé had done.

His shoulder throbbed beneath the broken links of his chainmail. Blood stained the surcoat a deep crimson. He fumbled at the Gordian knot on the prayer cord, but he was too tired for impossible tasks, so he moved on to a simple dog-shank and tugged out a section of the line.

Almost immediately, his thoughts shifted to a cavernous stillness that swallowed awareness of everything but his rapt focus on the unweaving. That's where Ain was at one with his people: the place in which Shader had come to hear his voice.

"It could heal your shoulder, you know."

Shader resisted the impulse to sigh as Elias Wolf dropped down on the pew beside him.

"My statue—Eingana. Be right as rain in a jiffy, only he's bound to throw a fit if you use it. Huntsman, I mean."

Shader tied the prayer cord onto his belt and took the serpent statue from his pocket.

It had lost its glow and faded to a dull black. He ran his thumbs over the empty eye sockets and traced the indentations where the fangs should have been. The scent of stale tobacco reached his nostrils, and he bent to examine the serpent's mouth, scraping out burnt leaf and ash.

Elias gave a little cough. "On second thoughts, perhaps you're better off having the priests look at the cut. I got away with using it a couple of times, but then it started to give me the creeps. Like someone was watching."

Shader held the statue out in front of him and stared at it. "I feel nothing."

"Good," Elias said, clapping him on the back, and then snatching his hand away, as if he expected to get hit in return. "Then he's probably just after me, what with me being so famous and all. Suppose I'll just have to get a new hash tray."

"Who's after you?"

Elias stood and went to examine the Dark Mother. "Bit somber, don't you think? All that blackness and the empty-eye thing. If you ask me, I'd say she looked better in blue and white."

He rose on tiptoe and pirouetted, coming to face Shader with a little bow.

"Who's after me? I was being ironic—or is it sarcastic? But the vibe, well that's pure gothic, if you get my meaning; which of course you don't, coz no one's heard of a Goth or a Visigoth for centuries. Do you know how lonely it is being the only man alive to know anything about history? Real history, that is,"—he cocked a thumb at the Dark Mother—"not this fabricated balderdash that's been floating around since the Reckoning like a turd that won't flush down the toilet. Gah!" Elias slapped himself on the forehead. "Last man alive to have pooed in a flushing loo, too. Poo, loo, too. Like it! There's a song in there somewhere. Sorry, what was the question? Knight's move thinking, you see. Happens when I get scared. It's not every day you nearly get chewed up and regurgitated by mawgs; and me going round thinking I'm immortal and all that. Gaw, I'm such a kid at times."

Shader narrowed his eyes and fixed Elias with an unwavering stare. The bard's finger wagged back and forth like a pendulum, as if he were retracing his thoughts. After a moment, he tapped the side of his nose.

"Who's after me? The bleeding ghost of Sektis shogging Gandaw, no less, drawn by my reckless use of the ashtray of Eingana."

"Sektis Gandaw's dead. Has been since the Reckoning." Although death held no guarantee of permanence, thought Shader. Not if Callixus was anything to go by.

"That's why he's a ghost," Elias said. "Although, that's not what Huntsman wants us to believe, but then what would you expect from a geezer who thinks shoving crystals down your gullet is the road to eternal wisdom?"

"If not Gandaw, then who?" A chill began to claw its way up Shader's spine.

"Look to your mythology—or don't they call it that in Aeterna? What do they say? Theology?"

Shader sucked in a deep breath through gritted teeth. Elias held up his hands, as if to apologize, and went on.

"The Aeonic Triad fell through the Void. Surely you've heard that bit. What people fail to ask, though, is where they fell from?"

"The Supernal Realm," Shader said, as nonchalantly as he could.

"Right. Very good. Fine. So we can skip that bit, then. Why they fell is another matter for another story, but suffice it to say that they fell, and that they were three: the Archon, the Demiurgos, and their sister, Eingana.

"The Demiurgos fancies a bit of the ol'—well I don't want to say too much about that, what with you being a religious man, but you get my drift. He ravishes his sister and knocks her up.

"The Archon is mightily pissed about this—my guess is he was jealous, but that's not the official line. While the boys duke it out, metaphysically speaking, Eingana, slithers off among the stars and starts nesting down, only she can't give birth to her little bastard coz her... she lacks a big enough orifice.

"Back comes the Archon with a wickedly sharp sword, slices her open, and drags out a baby with the body of a baboon and the head of a dog. Mommy is not a happy snaky, and she's also rather scared that the Demiurgos is coming back for more, so she abandons the child and buggers off, dispersing herself all over the Earth and seeding all sorts of new life.

"The baby is traumatized, and literally does what the rest of us can only do figuratively: it creates its own womb to hide in."

"Aethir, the world of the Dreaming?"

"Ah, so you *were* listening back in Oakendale. Nice one. Makes my job easier. Anyway, the Cynocephalus—strange name for a baby, I know, but with a face like his, what do you expect? The Cynocephalus forms a whole new world around himself, a world populated with his own dreams. The trouble with being an abandoned child, though, is that your dreams are mostly nightmares.

"Meanwhile, Uncle Archon chases Uncle—or should I say Daddy?—Demiurgos back into the Void, hoping to annihilate him.

"Demi's tougher than he looks, though, and manages to sustain himself by a pure act of will. Thinking him trapped, the Archon goes off in search of his sister, but finds only her essence permeating the creatures of Earth. That's all the excuse he needs to start poking his nose into our business and encouraging all sorts of bizarre religious practices geared toward the higher morality of the Supernal Realm."

Shader was starting to wish he hadn't asked the question. That was the trouble with bards: they were always looking for a platform to perform.

Elias seemed to sense his impatience and rubbed his hands together.

"To cut a long story relatively short, if the statue really is anything to do with Eingana, and if someone really is looking for it—and I'll grant you, I've felt some weird shit when I've used it—then surely there are better candidates than Sektis 'snuffed it at the Reckoning' Gandaw to consider, no matter what Huntsman says."

"The Archon?" Shader's hand covered the hilt of his gladius.

"Maybe," Elias said, "but let's not forget the black sheep of the family. If there's a shadowy presence after the statue, my guess is, it's more likely to be the Demiurgos."

"Metaphysically speaking?"

"Naturally," Elias said. "Well, let's hope so, anyway."

Shader stood, towering over the little bard, and frowned down at him. "This isn't a game, Elias. You were one of Huntsman's guardians, like the Gray Abbot, yes?"

Elias shuffled uneasily, eyes locked to his feet. "Custodian's a better word. I lack the muscle for guardianship. But yes, Huntsman entrusted the body of the statue to me, for some bizarre reason, and I've not aged a day since."

Shader had been wondering about that. "The Gray Abbot aged as soon as his Monas was stolen."

"Suppose you're going to tell me I've gone gray?" Elias ran his hands through his lank hair.

"You don't look any different; perhaps because you're still close to the statue."

A look of mock horror crossed Elias's face. "You mean to say I have to follow you around everywhere or else I'll start decomposing? Course, the Gray Abbot was probably an old fart when he got his bit of statue. What do you reckon he was, eighty? Ninety?"

Shader moved toward the chancel with a hand to his ear. He could hear a sound like heavy rain beneath the coughing and groaning of the patients.

Pater Cadris was reading from the Liber to a young boy covered with purplish welts, and with eyes so red they seemed to be bleeding. Shader waved him to silence, and the fat priest rolled his eyes and closed the book.

Mater Ioana burst out of the sacristy, her shaven head glistening with sweat, her robes as grubby as a well-used floor-cloth.

"There are horses coming down the Domus Tyalae," she said. "And a black carriage."

Cadris stood up, jowls quivering, and waddled to her side. "Who is it?" he almost squealed.

Ignoring him, Ioana marched down the nave and opened the doors. Elias made to follow her, but Shader clamped a hand on his shoulder.

"One last thing. Who were the other guardians?"

"Huntsman wouldn't tell me. The Gray Abbot was a tad obvious—you can't stay in the top job in the same place for centuries without people gossiping. I mean, I ask you! I've heard whisperings over the years that one of the pieces—an eye reputedly—was taken to Aeterna and given to the Ipsissimus. I kind of want to believe that one—there's a beautiful irony to the hierophant of Nousian orthodoxy possessing the relic of a pagan goddess."

The clopping of hooves from outside was as loud as hail on a tin roof. Shader flicked a look toward the open door, but couldn't see past the backs of Ioana and Cadris.

"If I gave you the statue back, could you use it to locate the Gray Abbot's piece?"

Elias's face seemed suddenly drawn and haggard. He held Shader's gaze, as if he were trying to discern the seriousness of the proposition.

"Who stole the Abbot's Monas?" he asked in a low voice.

"A creature of darkness. A ghost of some sort. A wraith."

Elias swallowed and lowered his eyes. "I've been many things in my long life," he said, "but in every instance, I've had a single thread of continuity."

Shader frowned his incomprehension.

"I'm a bleeding coward. Last thing I need is the attention of the living dead. I told you I'd sensed some evil shit around the statue. You're welcome to it, mate. I'd sooner take my chances with ol' Father Time."

The thunderous noise from outside had subsided, and Shader could hear voices—Ioana's and another voice he thought he recognized.

"Shader," Elias said, "there's something I wanted to tell you."

"Later."

Shader strode toward the doors with Elias scurrying behind.

"It's about Rhiannon's brother, Sammy."

Shader's heart lurched. He'd completely forgotten about the boy.

"What—?"

But before he could say anything else, he was at the doors and could do little more than gawp in disbelief.

Fanned out around the templum portico there were getting on for forty armored horsemen wearing white surcoats emblazoned with the red Monas of Nousia.

It took a moment to register that these were the lads from Oakendale and not the Elect of Aeterna. He'd never seen so many together in one place, and his reaction was a mixture of pride and trepidation.

A gleaming black carriage was parked behind the knights, its lone driver hunched over the reins, a battered, very tall hat crammed low on his head, the brim obscuring his eyes.

The carriage door opened, and an immensely fat man stepped onto the driveway. He was dressed in a voluminous jacket of bottle-green velvet, a bulging waistcoat, pleated trousers, and polished brown leather shoes. The face was all cheeks and jowls, ruddy and mustached, and topped with a mop of wavy gray hair. Sunlight glinted from the frames of pince-nez perched on the bridge of his nose.

The fat man reached into his waistcoat and took out what looked like a golden locket attached to a chain. He flipped it open, glanced between the locket and the sun, shook his head, and tutted.

Shader was distracted by one of the knights speaking to Ioana: the voice he thought he'd recognized.

Gaston looked like a hero from legend, sat astride a white mare, leaning over the saddle pommel.

Only, he wasn't a hero. His appearance seemed a mockery, an insult to all that was decent and good.

It was the first time Shader had seen the lads in armor. None of them had been able to afford it during the training, and the council had refused funding, even when he played upon their fears of the mawgs returning. Armor cost more than the average house in Oakendale, and Shader had given up on the idea of ever procuring any, when Aristodeus showed up unexpectedly with a purse full of gold coins stamped with the head of the emperor. The first suits arrived the day Shader left.

There was a puckered scar along Gaston's nose, neatly stitched. His jaw dropped when he saw Shader, but when Elias came into view, he went pale.

"He's the one, Mater!" Elias said, pushing past and jabbing a finger at Gaston.

Shader met the eyes of Barek Thomas, who gave the slightest of nods.

Justin Salace walked his horse alongside Gaston's, glaring at Elias like he meant to kill him.

"What do you mean?" Ioana said, but something about her expression told Shader she already knew the answer.

"The one I told you about." Elias sounded like a schoolboy desperate to be believed. "The rapist."

Justin started to draw his sword, but Gaston placed a hand on his arm.

"I..." Gaston licked his lips.

Shader approached the mare. He felt his knees weaken, and had to hold onto the bridle for support. This was the lad he'd trained. The best of the best.

When his eyes snapped open, his vision was blurred by moisture. "Gaston? Is it true?"

Gaston's bottom lip was trembling, and he looked away.

"It's true, all right," Rhiannon said, emerging from the templum, arm in arm with Soror Agna.

She was dressed in a simple white robe, her satin hair braided in a thick plait. Black and yellow bruising surrounded one eye, and her jaw looked swollen.

"Rhiannon?" Shader's heart jumped into his throat. "I thought you... thought you were..."

"It's what I was trying to tell you," Elias said. "I brought her here after what he did to her."

Shader took a step toward Rhiannon, but she threw up an arm, as if he were going to hit her. Him, of all people!

Spinning on his heel, he grabbed Gaston's cloak and pulled him from the saddle.

Gaston squealed as he fell, but managed to twist and roll, the cloak coming away in Shader's hand.

Shader dropped it, drew the gladius, and advanced as Gaston scuttled away on his backside.

Ioana barked something to Cadris, who hurried inside.

"Deacon, don't," Rhiannon said, reaching for his arm.

He pulled away, more violently than he'd intended, and grabbed Gaston by the hair, pressing the shortsword against his throat.

"If I may..." The fat man lit a cigarette and drew on it three times in quick succession. "Dr. Cadman, Public Health Advisor to Governor Gen. My friend here and I are on Council business. If there are scores to be settled, then might I suggest they are resolved through the proper channels?"

Shader snarled and slammed Gaston's head into the ground.

Justin drew his sword, and the other knights followed suit.

Shader pulled his longsword from its scabbard and faced the mass of knights doubly armed.

Gaston regained his feet and snatched up his cloak. "I came to help," he cried, pushing his way back through the horses. "I'm sorry!" He started to run back down the Domus Tyalae.

"Boy!" Shader shouted after him, and Gaston turned. "Back here tomorrow. You and me. And bring your sword."

Gaston swallowed and nodded before walking away with as much dignity as he could muster.

"Now, the rest of you whelps do the same," Maldark growled, striding out of the templum with Cadris in tow.

"Who the shog do you think—?"

Justin's words were cut off by Maldark swinging his hammer overhead and slamming it into the ground. There was a terrific clap of thunder as rocks and dust flew into the air.

The lead horses reared, and Justin dropped his sword as he clung to the saddlebow in an effort to stay seated. When the dust settled, Rhiannon handed it back to him.

"Better do as he says."

Justin sheathed his sword and looked daggers at her. Nevertheless, he wheeled his horse and cantered down the Domus Tyalae.

The others followed in a cacophony of hooves clattering on cobbles, all except Gaston's abandoned white mare and Barek, who lingered as if he had something he wanted to say.

"What's going on, Barek? There are a lot of very pissed off soldiers outside the city." Shader grimaced at his own language and touched two fingers to his forehead.

"Things got out of hand," Barek said, shifting in the saddle. "Gaston ordered the charge. What else could we do?"

Shader caught the accusation; after all, he was the one who'd insisted upon absolute obedience along the chain of command. "But why assemble the Order? Why bring them here?"

"Gaston had a visitor—some old man who said he knew you. Bald bloke. Said you needed us. Said the Templum did, too. We were just trying to help."

Aristodeus. What was he up to now? Shader was starting to get sick of the philosopher popping up all over the place and setting things in motion. He'd always seen him as a friend and mentor, but there was a whole other side to Aristodeus starting to emerge, a side that had probably been there all along. It felt like a betrayal, like being raised by loving parents your whole life, only to discover you'd been adopted.

"And Rhiannon?" Shader shifted closer to Barek, kept his voice down. "What...? Why did Gaston...? How did this...?"

Barek closed his eyes, clenched his jaw. "He told us it was the bard. Took us to her parents to warn them. Elias brought her home, there was an argument... a fight." Barek opened his eyes, tears streaming down his cheeks. He tried addressing Rhiannon, but she wouldn't meet his gaze. "It wasn't meant to be like that. You have to believe me. Sammy... Rhiannon, I—"

She looked up at that. "What? What the shog have you done to him?"

"Nothing. I... Huntsman has him."

"Huntsman?"

"He just appeared, Rhiannon. I tried to..."

She took her head in her hands and began to sway. Agna hugged her close and scowled at Barek.

"Rhiannon, please..." Barek gave up and turned back to Shader. "What are you going to do? We need you, Deacon. Gaston's lost it. The men follow him, but only because he's the leader. They're just doing what you taught them. If you came back—"

"Go, Barek." Shader dismissed him with a wave. "You can't blame me for what's happened. This isn't what I trained you for. I expected better from you—you of all people."

"But—"

"Get out of here!"

Barek rode alongside Gaston's mare and leaned over to take its reins. He cast a final look over his shoulder before kicking his heels into his horse's flanks and trotting down the Domus Tyalae with the mare in tow.

The fat man—Cadman—trod his cigarette underfoot. "Boys," he said with an exaggerated sigh. "And yet Governor Gen thinks they could help."

"Zara Gen sent them?" Ioana said.

"Sent us all, actually. Years of research and medical practice, and I'm still just a dogsbody."

Shader returned his swords to their scabbards and tried to make eye contact with Rhiannon, but she turned her back on him and went inside with Agna.

He'd acted like an idiot, and yet, if Gaston came back, he'd do the same again. What did she expect him to do? Turn the other cheek? That was one bit of the Liber he couldn't subscribe to. He'd tried it before, but it had only delayed the inevitable.

"Are you really a doctor?" Cadris asked, his voice squeaking like a rusty hinge, fingers drumming on his belly.

"Many times over," Cadman said, whipping off his pince-nez and blowing on the lenses once, twice, three times. "And not just of medicine." He fished a polka-dot handkerchief from his pocket and gave the glass a good rub, lips moving almost imperceptibly—as if he were reciting a prayer... or counting.

Cadris threw his head back somewhat disdainfully and folded his arms over his chest. "Well, we're terribly impressed, but I have to say—"

"Cadris!" Ioana's voice cracked out like a whip. "Soror Velda's on her own with the patients."

"But Agna and Rhiannon are in—"

"What was it we were discussing over breakfast?"

"Yes, quite, but really, this does not—"

"Obedience, Pater. Obedience and humility."

Cadris's cheeks flushed, and he winced, before bowing his head and waddling inside.

Cadman returned his pince-nez to the bridge of his nose, shook out his handkerchief, and crammed it into his pocket.

"Mater, I'm so terribly sorry about all this bother. I should have come alone, but I foolishly thought I could kill two birds with one stone. Governor Gen felt the knights might come in handy—extra manpower, you know the sort of thing. They were more than a little keen, too. You heard what the lad said: apparently they came to Sarum to help you."

"With what, exactly?" Shader asked.

Cadman squinted at him, beady eyes scanning him from head to foot, one eyebrow rising. "Who can tell? Do you know, I'm finding this quite fascinating. Gaston told me all about you. Said you left the Elect in Aeterna before founding the White Order. Governor Gen has some interesting tales about you, as well. Seems you're something of a celebrity. I must say, it's an honor to meet you."

"Really?" Shader said. "Seems you know a lot more about me than I know about you."

The fat man plucked another cigarette from a silver case he kept in his breast pocket. "As I said, I'm Dr. Cadman. Ernst Cadman. Office of Public Health at Arnbrook House. I also run a little private practice out in the suburbs—services to the poor, that kind of thing. Which reminds me, Mater." Cadman beamed at Ioana. "How are you getting on with the plague? I hear great things about the care you provide: exemplary barrier nursing."

"I'm sorry?"

"Oh." Cadman took three short puffs on his cigarette. "I assumed that's why none of you were infected: you know, masks, gloves, stringent hand-washing. The governor thought you might like to share the secrets of your success, so that we can hold you up as an example to the hospitals and get this plague beaten."

Ioana frowned and stuck out her bottom lip. "This is no ordinary plague, Dr. Cadman."

Cadman slid his pince-nez further down his nose and raised his eyebrows. "Go on."

"The people who are infected... I don't wish to sound judgmental... and I'm not..."

Cadman was nodding. "But?"

"They are mostly people from the... the..."

"Less salubrious trades? Most degenerate areas?" Cadman said. "Interesting, isn't it? My esteemed colleague, Dr. Stoofley, made similar observations; only for him, the pattern of depravity broke down when it came to bankers and merchants getting ill. Maybe he doesn't bank where I do."

Elias sighed, muttered something under his breath, and slipped away toward his cart, where he made a fuss of Hector before climbing aboard and hunting through the instruments and sacks of herbs.

Maldark, had a sullen look on his face. He kept glaring at Cadman and then patting the head of his hammer.

The doctor noticed and tried to lead Ioana inside the templum.

"Mater," he said, shooting Shader a look that said this was a private conversation. "I wonder if you'd allow me to see your patients and have a word with the carers. Zara Gen is convinced you have some mystical immunity, and it is my intention to prove him wrong. Science is what we are about, is it not, Mater?"

Shader felt a warm glow from within his pocket as Cadman brushed past him. He slipped his fingers inside and withdrew them, as if bitten. The Statue of Eingana was gently throbbing.

Maldark was watching him, and gave the slightest of nods.

Cadman cast a furtive look over his shoulder before ushering Ioana inside the templum.

Turning his back on Cadman's driver, who'd remained as still as a corpse throughout, Shader took the statue from his pocket. The amber dweomer had returned, and the slightest of ripples ran along the serpent's scales.

"You felt it also?" Maldark touched the statue reverently with the tips of his fingers. He stared at it with a mixture of awe and affection.

Shader slipped it back in his pocket. "It seemed to react to our visitor."

Maldark rubbed at his beard and shut his eyes, as if he were trying to listen. His chest rose and fell, the iron bands of his armor grating, leather straps creaking. At that moment, he looked impossibly old to Shader, an animated fossil from a long-forgotten epoch.

"You're not taking that muck in the templum!"

Frater Hugues was beside Elias's cart, engaged in a tug of war with the bard, a hessian bag stretched taut between them and spilling black seeds to the ground.

Elias let go of his end, and Hugues fell flat on his back, the bag's contents emptying over his face. He tried to sit up, spitting out seeds, but Elias smashed a mandolin over his head, leapt from the cart, and scarpered toward the residences. Hugues shouted a stream of obscenities and ran in pursuit with the stiffest, most ungainly gait Shader had ever seen.

"A bacillus, Mater, a bacillus!" Cadman inveighed as they re-emerged. "There are no mysteries, except those waiting to be uncovered by science."

Ioana was no fool, and Shader could tell she was unconvinced by whatever the doctor was telling her.

"Ain forgive me for saying it," she said in a low voice, "but the victims are all cutpurses, whores, and drunkards. You name it, they've done it—even the youngsters."

Cadman snatched away his pince-nez and made a show of looking flustered. "Scum, every last one of them, though I admire your reluctance to call a spade a spade. Highly commendable, if you ask me. But a plague preying on immorality! As a man of science, I really must object."

"So, what's your theory?" Shader asked, straightening to his full height and narrowing his eyes.

Cadman fiddled with his mustache, crammed the pince-nez back in place, and patted his breast pocket three times; twice more, and then—pointedly—once again.

"Filthy people are drawn to filthy places, and filthy places are made by filthy people. Dalantle, Calphon, Edgebriar—rat-infested backwaters with the demography of a penal colony. Ninety percent of the dross of Sarum is crammed into those dumps in the most unsanitary conditions. The docks are just as bad—all those salty dogs and seaman's logs…"

"Dr. Cadman, if you please!" Ioana's voice had regained its stridency.

"Forgive me, Mater, but the point I'm making is that plague is spread through dirt and rodents, streets flowing with excreta—all the things you're going to find in those regions."

"And the bankers?" Maldark said. "How doest thou explain them?"

"Whores, thieves, assassins—all the sort of company kept by your typical financier; and if the bankers have the pox, well it's only a matter of time before the merchants come down with it. Mater, I'd like to share my observations with the governor and arrange for the hospitals to adopt your practices."

"What observations?" Ioana asked. "Which practices?"

"Oh, don't you worry," Cadman said, giving Shader a wide berth and raising his eyebrows. "Nice coat. Aeternam?"

"Britannish."

Cadman inclined his head, his eyes bulging above the pince-nez. "Ah, Britannia, Britannia. All that hope, all that glory wasted on the other side of the world. Alas, Mr. Shader, I fear I'll never see her shores again."

Cadman opened the door of his carriage and turned back. "Isn't it a bit hot for a coat, and a black one at that? Unless, of course, you're like me. Doesn't matter what the sun's doing, I'm always frozen to the bone. Well, cheerio everyone. And Mater, don't you worry. I have everything I need. You've all been most helpful. Together, we'll soon have this plague under control. Just a quick word in the governor's ear, and it will all come out right as rain. Right as rain, Mater. Good day."

The carriage shuddered and groaned as Cadman clambered inside and pulled the door to. "Tally-ho!"

The driver suddenly lurched upright, snapped the reins, and the twin black stallions surged forward.

Ioana came to stand beside Shader. "What was that all about?"

Shader shook his head as the driver turned the horses onto the Domus Tyalae, and the black carriage clattered into the distance.

"Something tells me there's more to Dr. Cadman than meets the eye."

Ioana threw up her hands and then shrugged. "Well whatever it is, I'm sure it can wait." She wandered back inside, leaving Shader alone with Maldark.

The dwarf leaned on the haft of his warhammer, staring in the direction the carriage had taken. "Eingana called me to Sarum," he muttered, so quietly that Shader thought he might be talking to himself. When Shader made no response, Maldark looked up at him.

"You think you've found the reason why?" Shader asked.

"Mayhap." Maldark shouldered his hammer and headed after Ioana.

Shader put his hand in his pocket and curled his fingers around the statue. It felt cold and lifeless once more.

Why had it reacted like that around Cadman? Was it afraid of him? Was it trying to communicate? Shader had the nagging feeling he'd come close to something important, something that prickled the hairs on the back of his neck.

He'd grown sensitive to the aura of evil during the campaign in Verusia, and it was something that hovered around Cadman like a cloud of malarial midges.

Not much he could do about that right now, he thought, and besides, there were other matters that needed taking care of.

In spite of what he'd told Barek, Shader had to deal with the White Order. Like it or not, he'd created them, trained them, and then abandoned them. The responsibility for everything they'd done was starting to settle like a mountain on his shoulders.

Then there was the duel with Gaston. He couldn't back down from it; he knew his own nature too well for that. Finally, there was the thing he dreaded most of all. It might not involve swords and heroic levels of guilt, but he'd rather have faced all the demons of the Abyss in its stead. Sooner or later, he was going to have to speak with Rhiannon.

ILLUSIONS SHATTERED

Arnbrook House, Sarum

A *cigarette, a cigarette, a cigarette.*

That was the biggest drawback occupying the Office of Public Health in Arnbrook House: it didn't matter how fine the stained paneling was if you couldn't have a smoke. Might give the wrong impression. Never mind how lush the carpet, the—Cadman couldn't quite settle on an adjective for the crystal chandelier suspended dangerously above his head like a big glittery Sword of Damocles. Gaudy, he decided just as the door inched open.

"Anything to drink, Doctor?" Lallia asked, peering through the gap and faking a smile.

Cadman knew she hated having to ask, but that, unfortunately, was her job, and he was loving every minute of it. "Tea, please, my dear. Britannish, if you have any, with a splash of milk and three sugars."

Lallia entered it all in her notepad, speaking without looking up. "That's a lot of sugar for the Public Health Advisor."

She might as well have called him a fat git, thought Cadman, pursing his lips and wondering if that was the correct Sahulian vernacular for the insult. "Yes, I suppose it is," he said with forced jollity. "Just don't let on about it."

He waved her away with a flick of his fingers, and the door closed with a resounding thud. He could get used to this: being waited on hand and foot, lounging in luxury, and only intruded upon by the odd sniffling politician trying to get treatment as a personal favor. It never worked. Cadman was almost religious about that. His job was advice and planning. The last thing he wanted was contact with ill people. The thought would have made his skin crawl—if he'd had any besides his illusory corpulence.

He could never understand why he'd gone into medicine all those centuries ago. The memory was so remote, it blurred with all the stories he'd confabulated about his past. A man needed something to build upon. There was nothing worse than a black hole at the core of your being.

Cadman rested his fleshy chin on the tips of his fingers as he contemplated the amber fang and eye on the desk before him. It seemed logical to suppose they were halves of pairs and that, if the legends of Eingana were true, they belonged to a serpent statue of sorts. Two eyes, two fangs, one body. Five pieces, in all. Cadman groaned. Not a good omen, and surely all the warning he needed to cease this folly while he still had the chance.

He picked up a piece in either hand and rolled them between his forefingers and thumbs, wondering how they joined to the body. Maybe a fixative was required, although, on closer scrutiny, he could detect no trace of gum or resin. They pulsed gently, like blood through an artery, and Cadman bent his ear to listen, thinking he could hear them hissing. Shaking his head to rid himself of the sensation, he gingerly touched the pieces together.

Warmth invaded his arms, passing through the phony flesh and heating his bones. He gasped and then sighed as it began to drive back the eternal cold. It was like… Cadman dug about for the memory. It was like settling into a hot bath.

Making fists around the amber, he stood and walked to the window. Closing his eyes, he sought out the missing parts of the statue, and to his surprise knew instantly that one was near—so close, indeed, that he felt he could merely extend a hand and pluck it from the air.

A face formed in his mind, gaunt and hard, scarred with furrows from hidden conflicts. Cadman recognized the chill blue eyes, the firm jaw dusted with dark stubble; long black hair tied behind the neck, the wedge of a widow's peak retreating from a high forehead. It was the face of a man in his fifties, although Cadman suspected he was considerably younger: he wouldn't have put him at anything much more than thirty-five. It was the face of Deacon Shader.

That's what self-flagellation and fasting will get you, Cadman thought, before reminding himself of his own misleading appearance.

A hard lump grew in his stomach, as it always did when he recalled what he really was. It wasn't real, of course, but it was uncomfortable all the same. Crossing his arms over his bulging belly, he shut his eyes and tried to imagine the softness of real flesh, the sensation of warm blood coursing through his veins. On a good day, he could almost feel it, but today was too full of worries to be considered good.

Cadman opened his eyes, finding it hard to keep them from the amber relics. They seemed to confirm what he'd sensed at the templum: Shader had a piece of the Statue of Eingana.

He'd detected something else, too: a residue of power, or perhaps another piece, more distant, better concealed. Maybe with three segments assembled, the fourth would reveal itself; but that would involve further action, and something told Cadman this Shader was not a man to be crossed.

Cadman.

He started at the whisper and threw his gaze around the office.

Ice clamped around the black spark that passed for his heart, radiating through his bones and snatching away the brief respite he'd had from the amber.

Close your eyes.

Fat chance of that! Cadman thought, backing away toward the desk.

"Where are you?" he said in a voice he hoped sounded more angry than scared. He bumped into the chair and collapsed into it.

Don't be afraid. Close your eyes.

His eyelids felt like they had lead weights hanging from them. They fluttered momentarily, and then shut like the final curtain at a theater.

A vignette of heroically attired actors sprang to mind, and lithe and dainty dancers—one might almost say skeletally thin—fanned out on the stage around them.

Before he could put a name to the scene, Cadman's focus shifted, affording him a glimpse of a shimmering portal, a celestial gateway to another world that evoked within him a tangle of buried desires, forgotten hungers: dreams, magic, the power to endure.

For a few seconds, he probed and tested the edge of the portal with ethereal hands, and then he was through.

His spirit eyes opened upon magnificent alien vistas beneath a heavy cobalt sky.

A snow-capped mountain range rolled away beneath him, forming a natural wall between a sprawling desert dotted with settlements and a churning cloud of smog that hung like a pall over the lands beyond.

He wafted through a murky forest, where the twin suns were thwarted by a thick canopy of leaves and writhing foliage. A colossal man wreathed in flame raged atop a smoking volcano, while dark goblins skulked through the trees below.

Cadman soared in the spirit, ever aware of the anchor of his earthly frame, his life force stretched between worlds like a frayed sinew.

He passed a magnificent city surrounded by impenetrable walls made from huge blocks of stone, seamlessly mortared. Spires and minarets glinted like fool's gold from within the ambit of the walls.

He saw villages among the trees, and coracles upon glimmering lakes. Armored legions marched across a septic wasteland strewn with bleached bones and bordered by an endless rotting marsh.

His gaze was drawn to a single black mountain sticking up from the white desert like a colossal dorsal fin. Silvery spheres spiraled about the summit, and one drew closer to investigate—all the prompting Cadman needed to glide away.

He flew deep into the heart of this new world, diving through the bubbling miasma of a steaming crevasse and into smoldering passages, where the whispers grew louder.

Something roiled and seethed in the shadows below, slick as oil and just as black. Tentacles quested through the darkness, and grimacing heads sprouted from a central brooding mass, teeth grinding, empty eyes reflecting the Abyss.

Cadman drifted to the floor of a cavern that seemed to be formed of coal.

"You have done well, Cadman. Soon the pupil will outgrow the master. Even Blightey never held such power." The voice had the quality of leaves rustling in the wind, the head that spoke the words bursting and then reabsorbed by the body.

Lies, Cadman told himself. *Don't believe a word of it. No more reckless action.*

But, on the other hand, imagine if he did grow more powerful than Blightey. No more hiding in anonymity in the rectum of the world. He could leave Sahul and return to Nousia. Maybe he could even set foot once more on the soil of Britannia.

"My master is pleased with your progress. It is his desire that you possess the entire statue," said another head, its neck twisted at a grotesque angle.

"Your master?"

The head gave a gurgling laugh. "I am the Dweller of Gehenna, Cadman. The Dweller on the threshold of the Abyss."

Between a rock and a hard place. Cadman groaned internally. On the one side, the sadistic Otto Blightey, sequestered in his castle in deepest Verusia; and on the other, the Demiurgos—the father of decay, despite, and dissipation. Ancient balderdash, he'd always thought, but falsification of the myth was proving much more difficult now Cadman was faced with the undulating demon from his nightmare; now that he held within his hands the power of the Demiurgos's sister. All he needed was for the Archon to show up in a blaze of light, and he'd swallow the whole Aeonic Triad myth hook, line, and sinker.

"You must think I'm really desperate, if you think I'm going to enter into some Mephistophelean pact with your hell-spawned master."

Now there was a play to fire the imagination, Cadman thought, recalling the terror he'd felt at the protagonist being dragged off kicking and screaming to a fiery pit. He was damned if he could remember what it was called…

A tremor passed through the Dweller, and it shuffled back with a sound like sifting sand.

"My master is not from hell, though he is acquainted with it. He is lord of his own creation, free from the evils of the Ancient of Days, the capricious god Blightey renamed Nous to hoodwink the survivors of the Reckoning. The Demiurgos seeks only to share his freedom with you."

"What freedom? I heard he was trapped in the bubble of his own imagination on the brink of the Void. Think I'll take my chances on my own, if you don't mind."

The Dweller oozed back further. "As you wish. I will trouble you no more. Everything is in motion now. Either you will prevail or—"

"Or what?" Cadman almost shrieked as the demon started to thrash and blister, its tentacles retracting into its body, heads popping and liquefying.

"You have made a gambit, Cadman. A flip of the coin between eternal perdurance and oblivion. The wheels have been turning since first we met, when you cowered beneath the covers on your bed. Since you elected to clutch at hope. Fate plays out inexorably, and who knows what she will bring? Whereas my master only deals in certainties."

The Dweller collapsed in on itself and splashed to the rough coal floor; an oily puddle that immediately began to shrink, until only a single drop remained.

"Wait!" Cadman cried, cursing himself for his rashness.

The drop shuddered and grew, spurting upward in a great torrent of goo that set like tar in the form of a naked youth with glistening skin, blacker than the shadows.

"I need more time," Cadman said.

The demon bowed and spread its arms. "Then you shall have it. By all means, go after the statue on your own. I wish you luck; but if you should need my help, know that it comes at a cost. Like you,"—the youth gave him a sickly-sweet smile that revealed serrated teeth carved from obsidian—"I need to feed. One life in return for one task; that is all I ask. We can discuss the finer details nearer the time."

Cadman tried to swallow, but there was a lump in his throat. An illusory one, but a lump nonetheless. "Then you'll wait?"

"Like an obedient dog." The Dweller dissolved into mist and shadows, leaving only empty space in its wake.

Cadman forced open the eyes of his earthly body and stared at the amber glow from the fang and the eye suffusing his bony hands.

"The illusion!" He thrust the pieces into his jacket pocket and raised his fingers to his face, feeling only the dry hardness of his skull, and cavities where once there had been eyes.

"Callixus!" he rasped, reaching out with his mind and feeling the wraith's sullen consciousness. "I need food. Quickly, bring it to me!"

Cadman jumped out of his chair as the door opened.

Lallia stood there suspended in time as she stared at him with the blankness of shock. Her hands let go the tray, which crashed to the carpet in a spray of china shrapnel and splashing tea.

Before she could find her voice, Cadman scuttled across the room, tugged her inside, and slammed the door.

"I know," he said, doing his best to sound nonchalant. "I know I look terrible." He locked the door and pocketed the key.

Lallia never once took her eyes off him. Her mouth hung open, and all the blood had drained from her face.

She swooned, and Cadman grabbed her with a skeletal hand, fearing she was about to faint. Lallia pulled away, and then vomited all over his jacket.

"Ugh!" Cadman leapt back, struggling out of the jacket and flinging it in the corner.

Yuk! Bodily fluids. I'd probably throw up myself, if I still could.

Still, he'd retained his illusory clothes, this time, which was something. He hadn't quite lost as much control as he'd feared.

"You're..." Lallia coughed up some more sick, wiping her mouth with the back of her hand. "You're a monster!"

Cadman tried to frown, but then realized he had no facial muscles with which to

146

express himself. "That might be putting it a bit harshly."

"Help!" Lallia screamed at the top of her voice.

Cadman slipped between her and the door, holding his hands behind his back. "Now look," he started, but Lallia wasn't listening.

A shadow detached itself from the opposite wall and drifted toward her. She stammered something and dropped like a stone as Callixus took on some semblance of solidity, red eyes smoldering through the slit of his great helm.

"I brought you these," he said, unrolling a cloth bundle and dropping fresh meat to the carpet: a pallid breast, a blood-drenched heart, and a succulent hunk of flesh that could only have come from a buttock. "Seems you won't be needing them, after all."

"What?" Cadman snapped, wondering how he was going to get the stains out of the carpet before his next appointment. "No, you imbecile, she's not for eating! She works here. She'll be missed." He crouched down to pick up the buttock flesh and tore out a strip with his teeth. "Where'd you get this?" he asked with his mouth full.

"The ghouls must have left them outside in the alley."

Cadman half expected to gag, but then gave a shrug. When you were a virtual cadaver with a burning hunger, one meal was as good as another—as long as the flesh was human.

"It is another mark against your soul, Doctor, using me thus."

Cadman spat out a gristly bit. "Just do as you're told. Trust me, Callixus, things can get a damn sight worse for you."

Lallia stirred and groaned. Cadman dropped the meat and helped her to sit. She was initially dazed, but as soon as she focused on him, the terror returned.

"This is not what it seems," he said, instantly regretting the cliché. "I'm still Dr. Cadman; it's just that I'm... How do I put this? I'm not very well."

Lallia looked like she was about to scream again. Cadman clamped a bony hand over her mouth.

"Shh!" he said, releasing the pressure a little when she nodded. "Now, I realize this is distressing. Believe me, I go through the same thing every morning when I wake up. I don't expect you to understand, but I would appreciate your discretion."

Lallia's eyes narrowed at that.

"Good," Cadman said. "That's better. Now, then, what's this going to cost me? I have money, antiques, the finest wines from Quilonia." He took his hand away from her mouth and leaned in closer. "I even have some very potent pills from Aeterna that would heighten your pleasure beyond your wildest dreams."

Lallia pushed herself to her feet and brushed the sick from her shirt. "I wouldn't be too sure. I have some pretty wild dreams."

Cadman's joints creaked as he moseyed over to the desk and rummaged about in the bottom drawer.

"Here," he said, tossing her a jar of tablets. "Take one half an hour before, and the earth will most definitely move."

"It better," Lallia said, thrusting the jar down her top and trying the door handle.

Cadman waved the key at her, crossed the room, and inserted it in the lock. "Absolute discretion," he said as Callixus drew alongside.

Lallia's eyes flicked from the wraith back to Cadman. "Deal," she said.

Cadman turned the key and let her go. "A plate, Callixus." He locked the door and strode back to the meat. "Next time, bring me a plate and utensils. I will not be reduced to licking my meals from the carpet like a dog."

Callixus hovered over him, eyes flaring, the black mist of his body rippling with what Cadman had learnt was nervous anticipation.

"You don't need to ask me today, Callixus," Cadman said, biting into the heart and

D.P. PRIOR

reforming the illusion of fleshiness. He rubbed his restored girth with some satisfaction. "I have decided to awaken the Lost."

"My Elect?" hissed Callixus with a rush of what sounded like excitement.

"The time is right," Cadman said, savoring a particularly moist morsel and wiping the blood from his mustache. "I know how long you've waited, but without the power of Eingana, I couldn't raise them. I intend to bring Gaston." The lad had been missing since his run-in with Shader at the templum. "Meet me at the tumulus after dark."

Callixus gave a shallow bow before walking straight through the wall.

Cadman retrieved the eye and the fang from his discarded jacket. They'd returned to a dull amber, cold and lifeless. He slipped them inside his waistcoat pocket and frowned down at the gore staining the carpet.

"Lallia!" he called, rushing over to the door, fumbling with the key and tearing it open. She should have been long gone by now, but Cadman knew she'd be eavesdropping.

"Yes," she said a little too eagerly, looking like she was about to knock on the door opposite.

"I wonder if you might be a dear and help me with this mess." Cadman beckoned her inside. "I'm such a butterfingers, I've dropped some specimens, and there's also the spillage from your little accident with the tea tray."

Lallia blanched when she saw the half-eaten flesh. Cadman moved to one side in case she was sick again, but she just grimaced and swallowed.

"It'll cost you more."

"Naturally," Cadman said. "I'll have a rummage around. I'm sure I've got something else just to your liking."

Filthy little trollop, he thought as he left her to it and went off to find Gaston Rayn.

THE MAWGS BENEATH

Beneath Sarum

The five assassins trailed Shadrak like ducklings following their mother on their first swim. Hard to believe these men were killers, a couple of them big names in their own narrow orbits.

He took them on a winding tour of the Maze, keeping them as far from the cluster of chambers at the hub as he could. It was bad enough bringing his fellow Sicarii to the tunnels at all, but there was no way he was going to share his greatest secrets.

Uniform passages of shimmering metal were splashed with blue light from the globes set into the ceiling that flickered on as they approached and winked out as they passed.

Shadrak held up a hand to halt the group. They'd arrived at another crossroads, and he needed to check the numerals above each of the four arches.

"Still know where we are?" Porius asked, looming over him, perspiration trickling from his bald head and running down the gullies of his face. "Only, I was hoping to be back by now. Wife's on her own with the girls."

Shadrak visualized his map, mentally ticking off the corridors they'd passed through. They were almost at the edges of the area he'd committed to memory, and there seemed no sign of the tunnels ending.

"Think you can find your way back? One less won't make no difference. I'm sure Master Rabalath will understand." He was renowned for his fatherly concern and compassion. Last bloke stupid enough to ignore an order had his guts pulled out and draped around his neck like a scarf.

Porius peered back down the stark passageway with nothing to distinguish it from the dozens they'd already navigated. Nothing but the numerals, that is, but they were meaningless without the legend Shadrak had discovered at the heart of the Maze, and he wasn't about to reveal that to anyone.

"Nah, reckon I'll see this through. Couldn't live with myself if I left you with this bunch."

Shadrak raised an eyebrow, cast a look over his shoulder at the rest of the group. "Thanks for that," he said without any trace of enthusiasm. "Makes me feel all warm and fuzzy."

Shadrak had always reckoned Porius utterly unsuited to the life of an assassin. He was a family man, devoted to his wife and daughters. He'd refused to be drawn on the reasons for his choice of profession. Maybe he'd fallen on hard times, or taken the law into his own hands, only to find there was no going back after what he'd done. Whatever the case, Porius wasn't your typical Sicarii.

He'd started his own bakery a few years back, and spent the early hours kneading dough and loading the oven. His Sicarii duties were conducted in the afternoon, and very rarely at night, when the children were sleeping.

He'd endured his fair share of crap from some of the other journeymen, who would every now and again challenge his position in the guild. When Master Rabalath told them to do something about it, if they didn't like it, the sensible ones let the matter drop. The others were never seen again, except maybe by fish. Porius wasn't scum, like the rest of them, but neither was he a pushover.

The other four were shoggers through and through.

Kilian and Julul were obviously green as snot, and yet cocksure little pricks with it. Shadrak must have missed their induction into the guild, which was a shame because he'd have probably black-balled them. Julul looked about as fit as a tub of lard, and was probably a virgin of the razor. Kilian was older, lean and lanky, with a spiteful look about him: a look that would one day get him killed, as he didn't look like he could back it up with anything more than a limp slap.

Kelvus and Deggin, on the other hand, had been around for years. Always worked as a pair; shared the same mannerisms and dress sense. They were your classic journeymen, garbed in black and brown, with heavily-laden baldrics crisscrossing their torsos.

Kelvus was supposed to be the more deadly, but Deggin was cunning as a shit-house rat. Alone, they were second-rate cutthroats; but together, they were a tricky couple of scuts. Shadrak couldn't exactly say he cared for them all that much. It was one thing to take pride in your work, but these two went about it with inhuman glee.

Even now, they spoke in hushed voices, flicking the occasional glance at their companions, no doubt sneering and plotting.

Albert once told Shadrak of his plans to poison them, following their part in the Marsden family massacre. Albert had secured the contract and coordinated the strike, only to have Kelvus and Deggin alert the watch while they disappeared with the takings.

There was no place for grievances in the Sicarii—guild members were meant to settle their own scores. Right now, Shadrak was wishing he hadn't persuaded Albert to stay his hand. Maybe then, Master Rabalath would have chosen him some better companions—perhaps even Albert himself. He might've been a poisonous, backstabbing bastard, but at least he was good at it.

"Left," Shadrak said, leading the way, and not bothering to see if the others were following.

He knew they would be. His brother assassins both feared and despised him, and not just due to his freakish looks. None of them, not even Rabalath, had been able to work him out. He always kept himself apart, and guarded his secrets jealously.

The masters were aware that he was often economical with his intelligence, and yet they put up with him out of the respect he'd brought the guild. Time and again, Shadrak had succeeded where even the most skilled of assassins had failed. He'd survived his fair share of plots, too—enough to make him something of a legend among his peers. Reputation had grown into mystique, and that made him virtually untouchable.

They stopped at yet another intersection.

"How the shog are we supposed to track them down here?" Kilian asked. "It all looks the same. No dirt, no footprints, no nothing."

"Hear that, Kelv? Boy's keen to catch himself some mawgs," Deggin said. "Reckon he'll be able to face 'em without pissing himself?"

Kilian glared, but wisely said nothing. Deggin gave him a knowing smile and chuckled.

"How come it's so clean now?" Julul said. "When we came in, the floor was covered in shit."

"Maybe the shit grew legs and a fat arse so it could follow us around asking stupid questions," Kelvus said, imitating a whining brat.

Julul's mouth hung open, his eyes flicking to the others, as if he expected them to say something—tell Kelvus off, perhaps, like in the nursery.

"Ah, don't worry, big boy," Deggin said, thumping him on the shoulder. "He's just kidding, ain't you Kelv?"

"Nope."

Kilian crouched down so that his face was level with Shadrak's. That nearly got him a knife in the eye for taking the piss, but fortunately for him, Shadrak recalled something Kadee had said about giving the benefit of the doubt. He wasn't comfortable with the idea, but he'd do it for her.

"This is a waste of time, Shadrak." Kilian spoke softly, as if he were trying to avoid giving offense. Even so, Shadrak couldn't help finding the tone patronizing, to the degree that he had half a mind to forget Kadee's Dreamer bullshit. "We could walk in circles for days, and still not see a single mawg."

"We're making a systematic search of the tunnels." Porius came to the rescue. "Takes time, lad, but it's the only way to get the job done."

"Why don't we split up?" Kelvus shuffled from foot to foot, thumbs rubbing against fingers, desperate for something to do.

"Because we'd waste even more time when I had to come and find you," Shadrak said. "Just remember, you're here because Rabalath sent you, not because you're of any use to me. You can either shut up and do as you're told, or shog off down the tunnels and starve to death. I'm good either way." Oh, he'd pay for that remark once they returned to the surface; you could be sure of it—unless, of course, he made the first move.

When they passed the passage where he'd killed the three mawgs, Shadrak could find no sign of the bodies, not even a trace of blood. Either more mawgs had come for their dead, or the Maze's army of minute cleaners—beads of liquid silver—had broken down the corpses like they did the sewage.

The group moved on to the right, where the corridor doubled back on itself, wending its way north of the city center.

The Maze was truly colossal, maybe even extending beyond the suburbs, and yet there was no indication of who'd built it, and why. It must have been very old, Shadrak reasoned—at least as old as Sarum's foundations; and shog knows when they were laid.

They continued their meandering path for what seemed an age, until Shadrak's nostrils flared at the smell of roasting meat, and he gestured for the others to stop. There was another odor, too, subtler and harder to identify.

"What is it?" Porius asked, moving to his side.

Mangy dogs—the merest ghost of a whiff, mingled with the sterile air of the tunnel. "I think we're getting clo—"

Before Shadrak could finish, Kilian and Julul pushed past and took a left turn.

"Wait!" Shadrak hissed, but they ignored him.

Kelvus followed suit, Deggin sauntering up from behind.

"Cacking yourself over a few mawgs, Shadrak? Surely not," Deggin said, walking backward as he passed, so that Shadrak could see the derision on his face. "Thought you said you killed three by yourself. That means that Kelvus could take six, and I'm good for four, at the very least. Porius could handle a couple, I reckon, and the boys, one each. How many do you suppose there could be?" Deggin spun away and swaggered round the corner.

Porius looked at Shadrak before shrugging and following the others.

Shadrak held back to check the ammunition in the thunder-shot. His fingers ran over the knives in his baldrics and the other assorted weapons he kept concealed on his person. Satisfied all was in order, he drew his cloak about him, pressed his back to the wall, and crept in pursuit.

The passageway opened onto a circular area about fifteen feet in diameter.

Kilian was ahead of the group, poking at a joint of sizzling meat suspended by a hook from the ceiling. The heat seemed to be coming from a glowing red cube on the floor.

"Dead end," Kilian said, picking off a piece of flesh and tasting it.

Julul swore, and then sat petulantly with his back against the wall.

"What's this?" Kelvus bent to examine the cube. "Aeterna-tech?"

"Buggered if I know," Deggin said, running his thumb along the edge of his knife. "I've heard of mawgs with weapons and the like from before the Reckoning. They say they got them from Sektis Gandaw, him that made them. Time for caution, I think."

"Bit late for that," Shadrak muttered under his breath, eyes flicking in every direction.

What Deggin said made sense, though. Sektis Gandaw was meant to have created the mawgs by joining wolves with humans and something reptilian, before his disappearance at the time of the Reckoning. Kadee had been obsessed with the legends, blaming the Technocrat for all the ills of her people, and preparing for his return. Wasted fears. A life tarnished by paranoia. For all her prophesying, Gandaw hadn't shown, and if he ever did now, Kadee wouldn't be around to see it.

Porius began to walk around the circular space, feeling its walls with the tips of his fingers, and delivering sharp raps with his knuckles.

Shadrak held his position in the corridor, watching the way they'd come, finger resting lightly on the trigger of the thunder-shot.

Something moved into sight about twenty yards down the passageway. Another shape joined it, and then another.

The five Sicarii were talking carelessly now, and hadn't noticed the hunched and shaggy shapes loping toward them.

Shadrak waited until the creatures were almost upon him before easing a glass globe from his pocket and hurling it. As it struck the floor, the glass shattered. There was a flash of light, a sickly smell, and then the thud of three bodies hitting the ground.

"What the shog—?" Kelvus began, but his words were cut off by a succession of hissing noises as sections of the wall around the circle slid upward.

Mawgs poured from the openings, rabid eyes blazing yellow, claws like daggers tearing into the assassins.

Porius went down first, throat ripped out, blood spraying all over.

Dozens of the creatures scrambled out from concealed alcoves, giving the Sicarii no time to defend themselves.

Shadrak fired into a gaping maw lined with row upon row of needle-sharp fangs. The creature staggered, and the mawgs behind dragged it to the floor, ripping at its flesh in a feeding frenzy.

More and more of the beasts swarmed into the circle, smothering the assassins.

Deggin was the last to scream, arms torn from their sockets, great gouts of blood gushing all over the gleaming walls.

Shadrak began to edge back along the corridor, wrapped in his cloak, but more mawgs cut off his retreat as they rounded the corner. At their head was a giant female, bare-breasted, hair braided and adorned with bones.

Shadrak raised the thunder-shot and fired, but a wall of green light flew up around the female, stopping the bullet in mid-flight.

Looking frantically about, Shadrak saw that the mawgs behind had finished with his companions and were stalking toward him, blood staining the fur of their faces, strips of flesh and sinew stuck in their teeth.

The female raised her arms, plucking at unseen forces above her head. Shimmering mist swirled about her hands, and the air reeked of sulfur. She threw back her head and barked strange words that set Shadrak's skin crawling.

He fired mindlessly into the mass of fur, thoughts racing, seeking an escape, probing for vulnerabilities, picking targets.

And then the mawgs were all over him, and he'd fired his last shot.

THE LOST

Fenrir Forest, near Sarum

The black carriage bumped and clattered through thick forest beneath a starless sky. It must have been Fenrir, north of the city, but it was hard to be sure in the dark. The evening had been overcast and damp, the never-ending drizzle sowing familiar seeds of melancholy in Gaston's heart, something he'd thought was supposed to end with his conversion to Nous.

It all seemed so pointless—the feud with his dad, the training with Shader, all the years of friendship with Rhiannon. Now Dad was back to the ground, and Mom wasn't even talking to him. Shader had left, like he didn't think Gaston was worth it; like he thought the White Order he'd founded was a complete and utter failure. And Rhiannon had... well, Gaston had... He couldn't bear to think about it.

What was it about him? Why did everyone turn against him, sooner or later? The answer was pretty plain, he reckoned. If there was broken link in the chain that needed fixing, it was him. Always had been.

Cadman, sat opposite him in the carriage, tapping rhythmically at his breast pocket and saying nothing to distract Gaston from his thoughts. He merely smiled whenever Gaston looked up. It was probably meant to be reassuring, but Gaston felt the hairs on the back of his neck prickling.

Much as he hated to admit it, Gaston felt the loss of Shader like an amputated limb. He had been elated in his company, studying the art of war alongside the Liber and finding it no paradox. If anything, it had been a remedy for his dad's insipid Nousianism.

By training his body to respond without the tardiness of thought, combat became, at its best, an expression of the bliss of spiritual unity; and by forming his mind through unpicking of the knots on the prayer cord, he'd left no room for morbid ruminations.

The perfection hadn't always lasted, but with the disciplines of weapons practice and prayer, he'd felt he was doing enough to claim the gift of salvation.

Up until the day Shader had left.

Made salvation seem a crock of shit, said his cynicism, if Shader had been willing to sacrifice it for the sake of a woman. Didn't matter that he'd changed his mind, gone running back to the abbey. Fact was, he hadn't fully believed.

Gaston usually fought off such thoughts with an increase in devotion and exercise. As head of the White Order, he couldn't afford to let his doubts reassert themselves, erode the faith that Nous was on their side; that he wouldn't abandon them.

But that threw up a whole bunch of other questions. If Nous looked after his own, why were the knights growing sick? When they'd returned from the templum, a few of them were already feverish, the first signs of swelling and discoloration visible on their skin. Was it lack of faith, or something else? Had Nous abandoned them, or had he never been there in the first place?

Here, in Cadman's carriage, the doubts seemed magnified, and the pervasive gloom outside had done nothing to bolster his defenses.

"Worried about the duel?" Cadman asked, peering over the top of his pince-nez.

Gaston's stomach twisted, and his heart deflated even further, if that were possible.

"What's to worry about?" He did his best to make it sound like he wasn't bothered. "Shader's older, slower, and unfocused. He taught me well, but I've outgrown him."

"That's the spirit." Cadman reached forward and patted him on the knee. "Time for the pupil to put the master in his place, eh?" A pensive expression came over Cadman's face, and he seemed to wince. Gaston shot him a questioning look, but Cadman just sighed. Then he threw his hands up and beamed as the carriage stopped dead.

"Come," Cadman said, opening the door and clambering down.

Gaston followed him outside, but could see little besides the outline of the driver sitting stoically beneath the dark covering of night, tall hat like a burned-out chimney.

Cadman led the way through gnarled and knotted trees, branches swaying, reaching, jabbing; leaves rustling, rain running off them like tears.

Pushing through thick gorse, they came to an enormous dome-shaped mound in the heart of the forest. Cadman wandered around its perimeter, bending down to examine patches of the grassy surface, poking and prodding.

"Eureka!" he said with a clap of his pudgy hands. "Driver!" he hollered through the trees. "Be a good chap and bring a spade." He beckoned for Gaston to come take a look.

It all appeared the same to Gaston. He put his hand over the area Cadman indicated, but the grass there was just as slick as the rest, the mud soft and loamy. He pushed a finger into the surface, got it as far as the second knuckle, and struck something hard. Cadman was breathing down his neck; put his head over Gaston's shoulder.

"That, my dear Gaston, is the way in."

It seemed like metal Gaston was touching. Vibrating metal that sent tiny shocks along his finger.

A branch snapped somewhere behind. Gaston almost swallowed his heart and spun away from the mound. Cadman put a hand on his arm and led him to one side. The driver was trudging toward them, a shovel over his shoulder.

"Here," Cadman said, pointing, before flipping open a metal case, counting the cigarettes inside, and returning it to his pocket.

The driver removed his hat and set it on the ground. Gaston gasped and tried to step back, but Cadman draped an arm around him and gave him a fatherly squeeze. The skin of the driver's face was waxy and pale, his scalp threaded with lank hair and pocked with hives and blisters. There was a wide cavity at the back of his skull, and through it, Gaston caught a glimpse of something moist and spongy. The man, or whatever he was, thrust the spade into the base of the mound and set to work.

Gaston saw a fleeting movement out of the corner of his eye. He shuddered and tried to focus on the driver, who was throwing up great clods of soil at an alarming rate.

Cadman released Gaston and tapped the cigarette case through his breast pocket, as if he were thinking of taking it out for a recount.

"What I am about to show you has remained hidden for countless years. Centuries, even. Remember the Lost?"

Gaston nodded, a chill crawling beneath his skin. Shader had told him the tale of the Elect knights sent to aid the Abbey of Pardes against the mawgs more than five hundred years ago.

"Well, now they've been found. Actually, they were never really lost at all; not in the sense of being misplaced like a favorite hat or a front door key."

"They ran into something evil and vanished from history," Gaston said.

"Not so, not so." Cadman produced a shiny metal device from his pocket and flipped open the top. His thumb pressed down, and there was an answering click. A feeble flame sparked up and died, sparked and died, sparked and died.

"Not really smoking weather." Cadman snapped the lid shut and gave a world-weary sigh. "It's like a Britannish summer: utterly miserable. Still, mustn't complain, eh?"

Gaston glimpsed another movement in his peripheral vision. He didn't dare look, but sensed an icy presence come to rest behind him.

Cadman's eyes darted fleetingly in that direction before he continued.

"Things are not always as they seem, Gaston. Take me, for example. How old would you say I am?"

Gaston shrugged. "Fifty? Sixty?"

"Twenty times that, at the very least," Cadman replied, his form withering, dissolving as he spoke. Flesh melted away, leaving leathery strips hanging from a mottled skeleton, and Cadman's fine clothes gave way to tattered robes dappled with mildew.

Gaston gagged and took a step back. Something cold touched his shoulder, and he turned to see ember eyes glaring at him from the slit of a great helm. Where the body should have been, a coil of black mist twisted like a corkscrew, coalescing into the form of a tall man in a yellowish-white surcoat above rusty mail, a faded red Monas just visible on the breast.

"Remain still," it hissed.

"You have nothing to fear from us, Gaston," the creature that had been Cadman said in a grating voice. "I wish only to show you how appearances can be deceptive. History, too, can deceive us, for it is seldom written without bias. The Lost did not fall prey to evil; they served it. Their mission to Sahul afforded them the opportunity to flee from that evil, but they underestimated the reach of the Ipsissimus's malevolence. Isn't that right, Callixus?"

The wraith paused before answering, and when it spoke, the words were carefully measured. "My knights and I were damned for failing to carry out the Ipsissimus's command. We were cursed to an eternity of undeath beneath this very barrow."

"Indeed," Cadman said. "You see, Gaston, we have the Lost to thank for the fact that Sahul isn't just another part of Nousia."

"The Ipsissimus sent the Elect to aid Pardes," Gaston said, "not to spearhead the conquest of Sahul."

His mind was reeling with the consequences of believing what he was hearing. Cadman had to be lying, otherwise, what did that say about Shader and the White Order? What did it say about Dad? Gaston himself? He winced as his mind replayed what he'd done to Rhiannon; the attack on the imperial troops outside Sarum. By their fruit you will recognize them, it said in the Liber.

"The Ipsissimus is the Father of Lies," Cadman said, jaw clacking, empty eye-sockets boring into Gaston, pleading for understanding; demanding it. "Why do you think the emperor fears the Templum so much? He knows what the Ipsissimus is planning."

"The emperor's a paranoid nut," Gaston said. "Everyone knows that."

"But where did that rumor start?" Cadman held up a bony finger. "Ask yourself, my dear Gaston, why it is that the priests of the Templum of the Knot suffer no ill effects from the plague, and yet even your own knights, who would no doubt be considered heretics by Aeterna, grow sick. And let's not forget your founder, the great and holy Deacon Shader, who would have discarded his vows for the flesh of a woman. Isn't that what you said? How deeply do you think he could have held his convictions? You will have noticed, too, that Shader bares no buboes, no putrid sores, no hacking cough. Where do you think this plague comes from? Could it be that Hagalle's not quite so paranoid, after all?"

"What is it you want?" Gaston asked, head pounding, thoughts breaking up like waves over rocks.

"I want to free you, Gaston, from the deceptions of the evil one."

"You... can... trust the Doctor," the wraith whispered, voice harsh with effort. "He... rescued me... from this tomb. He will awaken... awaken my knights." Callixus lost some of his substance, and the glare faded from his eyes.

"Callixus is right," Cadman said. "I have revealed this to you"—he indicated his decomposing body—"to show that I hold no secrets. This is as I am, afflicted by the Ipsissimus's curse. It was envy that drove him to treat me so, for I discovered that which his vile religion was impotent to bestow: immortality."

"You are immortal?" Gaston asked, thoughts racing with too many questions; hopes and fears mixing, separating, mixing again.

"Thanks to the Reckoning. I would have remained perfect of body also, were it not for the curse of that evil hierophant lurking at the heart of Nousia."

Cadman gripped Gaston's shoulders with skeletal fingers. "I can grant you this same gift of immortality, real eternal life and not just some poetic promise that will amount to nothing but decay and oblivion. All I ask in return is that you aid me in my work."

"What work?" Snatches of past conversations, the words of scripture, faces, feelings, regrets swirled around Gaston's mind in a whirlpool of confusion.

"I seek the power behind the Reckoning: the Statue of Eingana. Already, I have two of its components. The others, I fear, are in the hands of the servants of the evil one. Gaston, if we can reassemble the statue, we can dispel this curse of the Ipsissimus's and enjoy the true gift of immortality. This is what the ancient Paters meant by the resurrection of the body. This! Not the diluted half-truths offered by the creature who now sits on the throne of Aeterna."

"I don't know," Gaston said, reeling with everything he'd heard. He felt like the world had tipped on its axis; like he'd just been struck by lightning. "I need to think."

"And so you shall, my friend, for the choice must be yours. I will not sink to the methods of enticement employed by so-called Nousians. First, however, will you accompany us into this barrow, seeing as my driver has finished digging?"

The driver had opened up a hole in the side of the hill that was just about large enough for Cadman's skeletal frame to duck down and scuttle through. Gaston followed at a crouch, but Callixus's ghostly body merely glided through the mound as if it weren't there.

Once inside, there was more headroom, but it was black as the grave. They stood upon a hard, ungiving floor, the air dank and dusty. Gaston heard a click, and the patch of floor immediately in front of them was illuminated.

Cadman was holding a slender tube that shone with the glow of a hundred candles, revealing badly subsided flagstones with veins of silver glinting through the cracks. In response to Gaston's bemused look, he shrugged and aimed the light at the walls and ceiling.

"I'm surprised it still works. I've had it for an eternity. You just can't get craftsmanship like this anymore."

They were in a smooth-walled corridor with a peeling fresco of sigils and words in a script Gaston didn't recognize. Cadman looked as if he were about to explain, but then thought better of it and motioned Gaston further along the corridor until they reached an intersection. Ignoring the continuing tunnel and its off-shoots, Cadman took a couple of careful steps backward, muttered something under his breath, and then let out a hiss of satisfaction as the floor before him parted to reveal a spiraling metal stairwell.

"This is the way," he said with a joviality that would have better suited his fat form. "The ground level is for the uninvited—grave robbers, and worse. You wouldn't want to

157

be wandering around it by yourself, believe me. Pits and spikes, gas and darts. You name it, you'll find it. Whole level's a veritable death-trap."

"What is this place?" Gaston asked, shuddering at the thought of going down the stairs.

"Once a kind of ship," Cadman said. "But now a sort of warehouse, preserving that which I hold most dear. It's been somewhat redundant these past few centuries, but does make an excellent—what would you say, Callixus? Barracks? Tomb?"

Callixus didn't reply, but his spectral body rippled as they began the steep and winding descent.

The bare bones of Cadman's feet clattered and scraped on the narrow steps, followed by the resounding clang of Gaston's boots. Callixus made no sound, but drifted like a dark cloud, his fiery eyes glowing brighter with anticipation.

The further they went, the thicker the cobwebs grew, clogged with chips of masonry and the husks of tiny insects. Cadman's strange lantern illuminated only the three or four feet before him. To the rear, except for the burning coals of Callixus's eyes, Gaston could make out nothing but impenetrable darkness.

And so, he followed Cadman deeper and deeper beneath the earth, feeling every bit like a lamb led to the slaughter, but not really having much choice, the way he saw it. He shuddered to think what would become of him if he refused to go on; and besides, his curiosity was aroused. He needed to see this for himself; and he needed some time to think about all that Cadman had told him.

The stairwell wound downward forever. Gaston's knees ached, and his heart thumped, either from the effort, or his mounting fear.

Finally, they reached a tunnel of polished silver so shiny their reflections followed them along the walls, ceiling, and floor. They rounded a dogleg, and Cadman stopped, shining his glowing cylinder on a door-sized panel. He raised a bony hand to a rectangular protrusion and slid it across to reveal rows of numbered black studs. He tapped in a sequence and exhaled with relief as the metal door emitted a rush of air and rose.

It opened onto an immense black-metal cavern filled with gently swirling mist that was backlit by a bluish glow. Within the mist, wreathed in its tendrils, Gaston saw the shadowy forms of mounted knights, swords drawn, horses rearing or in mid-turn. He gasped as he took in the sheer size of the chamber and the army it housed. Ain, there had to be at least two hundred men and horses.

Cadman led him up close to a rider and shone his lantern on it. The armor was intact, but brittle and rusted, the once white cloak encrusted with age. The horse beneath the knight was little more than a skeleton held together by rotting ligaments.

Cadman reached up and gently pulled the rider toward him so that he could raise its visor. All that remained of the knight's face was a brownish skull with empty cavities, where once there had been eyes.

Gaston was startled by a low groan and turned to see that it had come from Callixus.

"Don't worry, my friend," Cadman said. "All will be well. With these pieces of the Statue of Eingana, I have enough power to raise the entire company. You must believe me when I say I would have done so before, but I lacked the means."

Callixus said nothing, so Cadman continued.

"It has been all I could do to maintain my fleshly form and stave off death these past few centuries. The residue of magic left in the wake of the Reckoning has greatly diminished. If I could have brought back your knights sooner, I would have."

Callixus nodded, but Gaston thought it was a sinister gesture, full of foreboding.

Cadman took two glowing amber pieces from his pocket. "You will excuse me," he said to Gaston, "but what I am about to do requires a great deal of concentration. It's not enough to simply will these things. The necromantic arts go somewhat against the natural bias of Eingana."

Cadman laid the pieces on the floor, produced a piece of chalk from his tattered garments, and began to draw complex symbols on the flagstones.

After some minutes, he stood and walked to the edge of the chamber, where he proceeded to draw a vast triangle about the knights. When he'd finished, he collected the pieces from the center and gestured Gaston and Callixus to the outside of the triangle.

Holding the amber pieces aloft, he began to chant in a low, sonorous voice that echoed about the walls to the accompaniment of a chilling sibilance.

Reddish light spread through the chamber, emanating from the eye sockets of the mounted skeletons. Slowly, painfully, it seemed, joints that couldn't have been used for centuries began to creak and move.

Gaston was transfixed, horribly fascinated by the jerky animation, the cracking of dry bones, the squeaking links of ancient armor.

A rumbling sound started up, and the entire chamber began to shake. The noise rose in pitch and volume, whining and growling, the floor pitching, walls shuddering. Within a matter of moments, the room stilled, and the noise whirred softly into silence.

Cadman walked to the center of the skeletal horses, the pieces of amber like molten lava in his hands. "Welcome back," he said, "my knights of the Lost."

The riders turned their helmeted heads toward Callixus, who merely nodded.

Cadman suddenly bent double and thrust the amber pieces into the tatters of his robe. He looked frantically from side to side, as if he expected to be struck at any moment. Slowly, vertebra by vertebra, he straightened up and sidled closer to Callixus, moving together with him through the ranks of the knights until he stood before the wall opposite the stairwell. He ran his hand over the surface and located a concealed panel. Thrusting it inward and twisting, he stood back as a crack appeared in the center of the wall and parted with a hiss to reveal a ramp leading down to the dark woodland beyond.

Gaston followed Cadman outside.

The burial mound had gone, replaced by an enormous black dome that jutted from the ground, its surface flecked with sparkling green, great piles of freshly dislodged earth around its base.

He was about to ask for an explanation, when a terrific clatter came from back within the dome.

Cadman pulled him to one side, claw-like fingers digging into Gaston's flesh.

Callixus emerged and drifted down the ramp, a deafening wall of sound following, as the knights of the Lost returned to the world of the living.

THE TECHNOCRAT

The Perfect Peak, World of Aethir

Sektis Gandaw's breath was a solar wind, streaming particles into empty space. Arterial fluids chilled, hardening flesh, slowing thoughts. The sloshing beats of his prosthetic heart grew further apart. He counted the seconds between them like a child anticipating the next peal of thunder. Red pulsed in his peripheral vision, no more than a hazy acknowledgement pushed to the extremities of awareness by the burgeoning silence.

He waited for the patterns of the Unweaving.

Perfectly on cue, light swirled from the metal vambrace on his forearm, settling into streams and arcs, circles and squares, all present and correct, as he knew they would be. Next came the polygons, dancing with numbers. Once they would have triggered a migraine; now they were a symphony rising to rapture. But even in ecstasy, the niggling continued. Without adequate power, all this was just a light show, an exercise in algebra, a set of calculations so vast it was like cramming the cosmos into his skull and trusting his head not to explode.

If only he'd not made the dwarves... The whirling display flickered, and daggers jabbed Gandaw's brain. If only he still had the energy of the so-called goddess, Eingana... There's been tantalizing glimpses of her power these past few days, and he'd sent mawgs to investigate. But so far, nothing.

Red light flashed; the hissing crackle of white noise.

"Sorry to disturb you, Technocrat." The grating voice of a homunculus, distorting through his aural implants.

Bloody Mephesch again. Was there no peace?

The shapes and numbers swirled into a maelstrom and then zipped back into the vambrace.

A ripple ran through Gandaw's tunic as the exoskeleton beneath reactivated, and a thousand pinpricks pierced his skin. His regenerated flesh was suffused with warmth, arteries thawed, and his mechanical heart resumed its bracing tattoo.

With a tap of a button on his vambrace, he stimulated the phosphorescence of the green veins that fractured the black scarolite walls. He stood and switched on the vambrace's com-screen, his plastic stool melting away into the floor.

"Mephesch, I'm trying to work."

The homunculus's face was pressed too close to the camera, just those inscrutable eyes set in sockets like calderas.

"Apologies, Technocrat. It's the lizard-man, Skeyr Magnus. He's found a way out. Taken the rest of them with him."

"Show me."

SWORD OF THE ARCHON

The image changed: a sentroid's aerial shot of the mountain's perfectly symmetrical peak. There was a rupture near the summit, through which scores of lizard-men were pouring. The display cut to another sentroid's camera, further back, showing the scarolite mountain stark against the bleached dust of the Dead Lands.

"There," Gandaw said. "That's him."

The sentroid moved in for the kill, Skeyr Magnus scampering away on reptilian legs that were never designed for speed.

Gandaw should have aborted the lizard-men long ago. They had shown themselves good for nothing. Another failed experiment—just like the dwarves.

"Wait," he spoke into the vambrace. "What's that on his hand?"

The sentroid zoomed in.

"Is that one of my gauntlets?"

Blue tongues of flame licked across the black glove on the lizard-man's right hand. Gandaw squinted in order to focus his optics. The projection gauntlet? Skeyr Magnus, nothing but an engineered brute, had a projection gauntlet?

"It's how they got out, Technocrat," Mephesch said through the aural implants. "Punched a hole in the top of the mountain. Nothing else could do that to scarolite."

"But the shields—"

"Only work—"

"—from the outside," Gandaw finished. "Then seal the breach and exterminate them in the Dead Lands."

A throng of lizard-men formed around Skeyr Magnus, moving in unison like a single organism.

Gandaw rubbed his chin, admiring his handiwork. Perhaps they hadn't been an unmitigated disaster, after all. They were maximizing their chances of survival by protecting the individual with the most power.

Blue fire streaked toward the sentroid's camera, and the screen went dark.

"Switching to another sentroid," Mephesch said.

Gandaw shook his head. What would be the point? The lizard-men were too close to the edge of the Dead Lands, the limits of the sentroids' range.

"Let them go. They'll never make it out of the Sour Marsh."

"Point taken," Mephesch said. "I'll mobilize a team to repair the breach, and I'll see to it that the gauntlet is replicated. Sorry for the interruption, Technocrat. I'll try not to disturb you again. There is, however, one more thing…"

Wasn't that always the way? Nothing happened for centuries, and then all of a sudden, there were two matters demanding his attention.

"Hold it till I get there. I'm coming down."

***

Gandaw stepped from the elevator into the cathedral cavern at the heart of the mountain. The intolerable escape of the lizard-men had already been rendered tolerable by chemicals. Just how he liked it: everything back to normal. Perfect homeostasis.

His gaze flicked across the screens that studded the walls. Images assailed him from every angle: long-shots, close ups, heat residues, and fractals, all beamed from a network of satellites so ancient as to be unsuspected by the people of Earth.

Each screen had a seat of molded plastic before it, and its own dedicated krych, eyes wired into the receivers, bat wings folded behind shriveled female bodies. Human bodies. Among the more successful of his early meldings.

He made an efficient sweep of the monitoring stations that spiraled up from the ground in concentric tiers to terminate in the single round eye of screen 55 on the ceiling,

161

trained perpetually on the Void.

A familiar knotting started in his stomach as he stared into the swirling black of the Void, feeling it tugging at the core of his being. Nothing but a singularity, he told himself as the biostat kicked in to relax him. Needles delivered their sedatives, and equilibrium was resumed as quickly as it had been lost.

Definitely a black hole, but that didn't account for the gaseous tendrils crisscrossing the Void like the webbing of a cosmic spider, the slenderest threads here and there touching Aethir's underground realm of Gehenna.

The superstitious called it the Abyss. His former master, Otto Blightey, had been trapped there once, and had reached across the stars with his prodigious will to request Gandaw's aid.

All that so-called magic, but in the end it had been science that had brought Blightey home; science that had found a foothold in the nebulous reality covering the mouth of the Void.

The homunculus, Mephesch, was running his checks, scurrying from station to station, testing the connections with the kryeh, all of whom remained taut with anticipation, staring blankly at the images in front of them.

They might as well have been carved out of the rock of the mountain, dead things crafted from the same scarolite ore Gandaw had created the dwarves to mine following his flight from Earth a millennium ago.

His optics zoomed in on Mephesch, dressed like Gandaw himself in a dull gray tunic, gray trousers, and black shoes that never needed polishing. The homunculus was barely three feet tall, craggy faced, with plastinated dark hair—again like Gandaw's, which never required cutting. Mephesch's eyes were like black pebbles peering mockingly from beneath ledge-like brows. Not Gandaw's design at all. The homunculi were more like fairy-tale gnomes than the evolutionary dead-end he'd first suspected.

He was certain the creature meant to betray him; it was in his nature. After all, the homunculi claimed to be the spawn of the Demiurgos, the entity reputedly trapped at the center of the Void.

Utter nonsense, of course, but the thing that really annoyed him was that, no matter how diligently he sifted through the life forms of Aethir and Earth, no matter how much he scrutinized and distilled the basic energies and elements of the cosmos, he could not account for the existence of the homunculi.

A kryeh let out a screeching caw.

Mephesch ran to its side, then turned to Gandaw with a wide-eyed look.

"Another surge from the statue?" Gandaw said.

Before Mephesch could answer, the kryeh cawed again, and this time, it didn't stop. It wrenched its head away from the console, ripping the electrodes from its eyeballs and spraying a fine mist of blood over the screen.

Its wings unfurled and thrashed against the railings. Wires tore free of its arms and stomach, but its ankles remained strapped to the chair.

Gandaw raised an eyebrow. It was all that was needed. Instantly, a sentroid descended from the apex, little more than a flying ball of steel with a battery of phase cannons studding its circumference.

As the kryeh flapped into the air, dragging the chair with it, the sentroid fired.

There was a burst of blue lightning, the smell of ozone, the sizzle of cooking flesh, and a crash as the chair hit the third tier. The charred remains of the kryeh puffed into the air, a sooty cloud that cascaded all the way to the bottom of the control room.

All this activity was making the kryeh excitable again, and if there was another thing he couldn't stand, it was deviation from the task in hand. The creatures were good, their senses as keen as he could get them, but they weren't perfect. No matter how much he manipulated the basic elements nature had bequeathed him, nothing was ever perfect. Never would be, until he stripped it bare and started again from first principles.

Mephesch pointed at the screen as a team of homunculi wheeled a replacement kryeh into position, wiring in the eyes.

The sentroid began to spiral down the chamber one tier at a time, vacuuming up the dust, careful not to let even a single speck remain.

"Sarum again," Mephesch said. "Just a blip from the statue, but it set the kryeh off nonetheless."

"Increase the sedative," Gandaw said.

Mephesch complied, tapping out a sequence on his vambrace. "That's three pieces now active."

"Three?" That only left two unaccounted for. "Still active? Can we get a lock?"

Mephesch shook his head. "Just brief flare-ups, all from the vicinity of Sarum."

"Did the mawgs find anything?"

"Not exactly," Mephesch said. "But they do want to talk to you."

"Talk to me? Mawgs? Are you wasting my—?"

"They captured a homunculus beneath Sarum."

"What?" He glared at Mephesch, even as needles pricked his skin and calmed his mounting ire.

"Nothing to do with me," Mephesch said. "I just thought you should know."

The only business homunculi had on Earth was when Gandaw sent them to harvest specimens, and he'd not done that for centuries. His last remaining plane ship had been stolen by the hybrid spawn of Eingana, and when he'd told the homunculi to make him another one, they'd claimed to have forgotten how.

There was no getting away from it; he needed to see this for himself.

With a command to his vambrace, a silver disk rose from the floor. He stepped onto it and let it carry him toward the top of the chamber. He got off at the uppermost walkway and lowered himself into his projector seat.

Relaxing back, he sent a mental coupling signal to his exoskeleton, and scores of microfilaments shot through the weave of his clothes to attach to the frame of the chair, leaving him festooned in a tangle of blinking lights. He closed his physical eyes and opened their virtual counterparts.

He threw up an arm as a cavernous maw thrust toward him, rows of thorny teeth extending all the way to the back of the throat. Needles pricked his skin, and calm was restored in an instant.

"Back away from the projector, you ignorant brute." He was pleased that his voice retained its coldness.

The picture shook as the mawg retreated, its yellow eyes coming into focus above a long snout rimmed with fur. It appeared to be a female, for what it was worth.

"Master," it growled, and offered a grotesque parody of a bow. "I vraajo of mawgs. My name is Varg—"

"Yes, yes." Gandaw cut across its fawning with a tone of extreme boredom. "I know what you are. What you call yourself is of no matter to me. Why have you contacted me?" *This had better be good.*

The mawg gestured to the mass of hunched and shaggy forms behind it. They parted, and two of the creatures dragged a diminutive figure into sight :a homunculus, no bigger than Mephesch, and yet the creature had milky white skin and pink eyes. It was dressed in black and brown leather and a dark cloak.

The homunculus looked directly into the screen, eyes widening as it focused on him. "What magic is this?"

"Science," Gandaw said in his most matter-of-fact voice. "There's no such thing as magic. I would have expected your kind to know that."

The homunculus looked him in the eye. "What's that supposed to mean?"

"Being what you are."

"Which is?"

"Interesting." Gandaw touched a finger to his lips. "Quickly, now. Where are you from?"

"What's it to you?"

The vraajo roared and stuck its snout in the homunculus's face.

"Sarum." The albino seemed to sag, and some of the insolence left his eyes.

"Originally?" Gandaw asked.

"Like I said, Sarum. I was born there. My mother was—"

"Impossible," Gandaw snapped, and instantly regretted it. More fluids flooded his veins, restoring equanimity. "Never mind. Vraajo, what are you doing with this creature?"

The vraajo's snout came back into view. "Found it under city, Master. Ate its friends. Kept this one to show you. Knew it shouldn't be here."

Not bad for a mindless brute, thought Gandaw. The mawg was right. He'd always known the homunculi were devious, but what did this new discovery mean? He didn't like mysteries; they were a side-effect of a flawed universe. "You'd better kill it."

Another channel opened, and Mephesch's voice crackled in his ear. "You might want to see this first."

Gandaw was incensed. "Are you listening in to my..."

He tailed off when the image of a tall man appeared in a window beside the homunculus and the shaman. He wore a tall broad-brimmed hat, which shrouded his eyes in shadow. The face was gaunt and angular above a white surcoat and long black overcoat.

"It's the same knight who drove our mawgs from Oakendale," Mephesch said. "I retrieved this from the satellite when I followed up on an echo from the statue. If I'm not mistaken, this man has a piece of the statue. It could even be the body."

The vraajo let out an excited yelp. "He does, he does. Seen him in the city house, we have. Came to aid music man who had serpent's body. Must have taken it from him."

"The signal is very faint," Mephesch continued, "but it's coming from the Templum of the Knot. The big surge that set the kryeh off has resulted in a flurry of activity around the council buildings, some of which is headed toward the templum."

"Show me," Gandaw said as needles jabbed him repeatedly.

Another window opened. Gandaw squinted to make sure he was seeing correctly. Hordes of what looked like freshly disinterred corpses were shambling about outside the building known as Arnbrook House.

The realization hit Gandaw like a block of ice in his stomach. "Someone is using Eingana's power to locate the other pieces."

"I agree," Mephesch said. "The strongest signal came from Arnbrook House, but it's moved, and I can't get a fix on it."

Gandaw didn't like this. All these centuries waiting like a spider for a fly to fall into its web, and now some outsider was going to beat him to the prize. "Vraajo, take your mawgs to the templum. We must get this piece before our rival does."

A chorus of whimpering sounded from the mass of mawgs around the vraajo. "Can't, Master. My people frightened."

"Nonsense," Gandaw said. "What is there to be—?"

"The Fallen."

"Maldark?" But that wasn't possible. The dwarf must have died centuries ago.

"I see him. See him with these two eyes. See him leave townhouse, go to the templum."

Gandaw's fist clenched and he grimaced as a hundred needles pierced his skin all at once.

Maldark the Fallen: the dwarf who had betrayed him and whisked away the Statue of Eingana before Gandaw could complete the Unweaving of all things.

"I'll go," the albino homunculus said.

"What?" Gandaw was on the brink of switching off the projector.

"I'll get the statue for you. I have some expertise in these matters. It's what I'm paid for."

"Paid for?" Gandaw didn't pay for things. People either did what they were told or...

The homunculus pressed his face right up to the screen. "I am Shadrak the Unseen. Tell your creatures to let me go, and I'll get your statue."

He was a homunculus. How could Gandaw trust such a creature?

He opened one physical eye and glanced at the newly replicated projection gauntlet, an orange light indicating it was partially charged—at least enough for a demonstration.

He thrust his hand into the gauntlet and made a fist.

Shadrak glanced up at the black form materializing above his head, eyes widening in terror as the fingers of a gigantic black hand curled around him.

"I see everything," Gandaw said, giving a squeeze. "If you betray me, I have the means to wring the life-essence from your body. You will be nothing more than a desiccated husk. Do I make myself clear? There will be nowhere you can hide from me. I have eyes and ears everywhere."

Shadrak nodded.

Gandaw was satisfied he'd got the message. He released his grip and tugged his hand from the gauntlet. Its giant counterpart dissolved from view.

"Bring the statue to the Anglesh Isles. I will instruct the mawgs there to expect you."

THE PENITENT

City of Sarum, Sahul

The knights had been dead, brittle with decay, rotted down to the bone from centuries locked in their unearthly tomb; and yet Cadman had raised them to some sort of new life.

They had moved—slowly and jerkily at first, but then with greater ease. Ain, they'd even ridden from the mound, or ship, or whatever it was. All under Cadman's power. But Gaston couldn't think of them as resurrected, not in the Nousian sense. Their bodies lacked the perfection and luminosity promised by the Paters.

Was this the immortality Cadman offered? A grisly parody of life, the animation of corpses directed by his will? Could the knights even think for themselves? Did they know who they were anymore? Did they remember their loved ones, long-since gone back to the ground? Callixus seemed sentient enough, and yet there was nothing much human about him. And Cadman himself, stripped of his illusion, was hardly more than a skeleton.

Gaston crossed his arms over his chest, shivering at the unnatural coldness that seemed to radiate from within. He felt like he was holding together a ripped and sodden paper sack in a desperate attempt to stop the last sorry scraps of faith from leaking out.

Unable to sleep, he wrapped his white cloak about his shoulders, fastened his sword belt, and left the spartan confines of the barracks.

The other buildings were in darkness as he emerged, the rest of the knights sleeping, apart from the sentries around the perimeter wall.

He passed the infirmary on his way to the stables, and heard the coughing and groaning of those who'd been infected by the plague. He still couldn't understand why they'd grown sick while the priests were immune. Did they not also serve Ain? Maybe Shader had been right all along: maybe Ain was a god of peace who would not tolerate violence in his name.

If that were the case, Gaston thought, allowing himself to indulge the anger that he'd been suppressing since Shader had buggered off to Aeterna, why had Shader passed on his own problems to the White Order? It seemed he understood the contradiction at the heart of his own vocation, but was powerless to do anything about it. That made him a victim, as far as Gaston was concerned, unworthy of teaching others.

If Gaston had learnt anything these past few days, it was that Shader had betrayed him—betrayed them all. With the right mentor, Gaston could have become a Friend of Ain, like his father had been. He could handle the devotions and the mortifications, and without Shader's influence, he could have avoided the conflict the dual roles of Nousian and knight had brought.

It was starting to look like Dad's advice had been right after all. If Gaston had listened to him and not Shader, things might have turned out differently.

He stopped himself there, before he followed the train of thought to its conclusion. His faith might be dwindling, but he still had his honor, and that told him it was unfair to blame Shader for the attack on the imperial troops; and not just them, either. As much as he wanted to shed the guilt of what he'd done to Rhiannon, he couldn't lay it on Shader. The man might have been a charlatan, but Gaston wouldn't make him a scapegoat. If there was one thing Bovis Rayn had taught his son, it was that he was responsible for his own actions, no excuses.

Reaching the stables, he saddled the white mare and rode for the main gate of the enclosure.

Darik Yonas, on sentry duty, snapped to attention.

"Master Rayn?"

Gaston wanted to sneer at the title, but Darik was a good lad and deserved better. Wasn't his fault if Gaston didn't deserve his respect.

"Can't sleep, Darik. I'm going to ride around the city for a while."

"I wouldn't advise it, sir." Darik peered beyond the gate. "I hear things out there in the dark."

Gaston could see nothing. The dark was as absolute and impenetrable as anything he might expect to find in the Void.

"If there's anything lurking out there,"—he patted the pommel of his sword—"then it's in for a surprise. Open the gate."

He rode out into the pitch blackness of Sarum, the clopping of the mare's hooves a challenge to the silent streets.

His eyes were drawn to the waning moon hanging like a fragment of bone amid clusters of glistening stars—pinpricks of silvery light from Araboth that illuminated his way along road after deserted road.

Once or twice, he stopped the horse, convinced something was following him. He couldn't be sure if he'd heard the padding of feet, or just the echo of his own progress.

He rode aimlessly, breathing in the night air, scarcely a thought in his head. Gradually, though, he began to recognize buildings and street names. Maybe it was just unconscious, or maybe the horse was merely retracing her steps, but Gaston suspected the hand of Ain was guiding him as he made his way inexorably toward the Templum of the Knot.

Dismounting at the entrance to the Domus Tyalae, he tethered the horse to a tree and continued on foot until he reached the templum.

Scouting the exterior, he came upon the residential block, but there was no light from within. He paused for a moment to consider whether to awaken the priests, but decided to come back in the morning. As he turned to leave, a figure emerged from the shadows.

"What art thou doing here, boy? Thought thou wouldst have learnt thy lesson earlier."

It was a gruff voice, deep and uncompromising. Gaston had heard it before, when he'd walked away from the confrontation with Shader, but he'd been too ashamed to turn around and look.

Squinting through the darkness, he could just about make out a thickset but short figure with a long, braided beard and eyes that glinted dangerously in the moonlight. The man was cloaked in white and leaning on an immense war hammer.

Gaston's fingers twitched above the pommel of his sword, his heartbeat thumping in his ears. He slowed his breathing, tried to relax his shoulders.

"I'm Gaston Rayn, Master of the White Order."—Darik's term, but it would have to do.

"I know who thou art, boy, but that was not my question. Why art thou skulking around the templum at this hour? Having second thoughts about the duel? Didst thou think to end it before it has started?"

"What?" Gaston half drew his sword, but the dwarf didn't flinch. "Are you calling me a cutthroat?" He knew he was overreacting, but he couldn't help it. "Do you really think I'd stoop to murder?" Isn't that what that bastard Shadrak had done to his dad? "Stick around till morning, mate, and then you'll see I don't need to sneak around at night to get the job done. Now, get out of my way. I need to see Mater Ioana."

Gaston tried to step past, but the dwarf moved to intercept him. His head only came up to Gaston's shoulders, but there was something about him that made Gaston pause. The dwarf looked rooted to the spot, an immovable object that might just as well have been carved from granite.

"I am Maldark, known as the Fallen. The only way thou shalt see Mater is through me."

"Shog off," Gaston said through gritted teeth, "or you're about to get a whole lot shorter." He drew his sword further from its scabbard, let the dwarf see the glint of steel.

Maldark stood his ground, completely unperturbed by Gaston's bluster.

Normally, people would back down when he raised his voice, and if they'd seen him in action with a sword, they'd think twice about confronting him.

Gaston felt his cheek twitching, and put his hand to his face to stop the dwarf from seeing.

Without warning, Maldark hefted the war-hammer to his shoulder, and Gaston stepped away.

"I'll take thee to her," Maldark said.

"Don't bother." Gaston turned to leave.

"I'll take thee to her now." Maldark slapped the hammer haft into his palm and glowered.

Gaston forced himself to relax. He was afraid of no man, but there was something about the dwarf that unnerved him, a self-assurance that didn't allow for any possibility of doubt. No boasting, no threats. Just a dreadful certainty that if Gaston didn't do as he was told, he'd have as much chance as a baby in a croc-infested creek. He lowered his head and nodded, letting the sword slip back into its scabbard.

Maldark led Gaston to the main door of the residences. "Wait here," he said, before going inside and shutting the door.

After a few moments, Gaston could hear the murmur of voices, and then saw the soft glow of candlelight dancing past the windows.

The door opened again, and Mater Ioana stood there in a white gown, her shaven head reflecting the yellow flame of the candle she carried. She studied him like a surgeon examining a wound, the barest suggestion of a frown tugging at the corner of her mouth.

"My, you have been in the wars, haven't you? You'd better come in. Can't have you staggering around with all that weight on your shoulders."

Gaston started to tremble, a wave of emotion welling up within him. He dared not speak, in case he lost control.

"Come along, Gaston." Ioana held the door open for him.

Maldark was lurking just inside, a sullen expression on his face. He made as if to follow them, but Ioana waved him away before leading Gaston along the main corridor, past six or seven closed doors, and into a small chamber at the end.

She touched her candle flame to the wicks of three votive lights, their warm, flickering glow revealing the blues and reds of the stained glass windows flanking a simple altar, and glinting from the surface of the gilt Monas that stood upon it.

She drew up a couple of chairs, but Gaston threw himself to his knees before the altar, tears already spilling down his cheeks. Tears of shame. Tears of release. He bowed his head, clamped his eyes shut, and began to sway.

"Mater, I have sinned."

Ioana said nothing, but Gaston could feel her eyes upon him. A hard lump was growing in his chest, forcing him to go on.

"I've d-d-done things..." He hated the quavering of his voice. "Shameful things. Broken... the Admonishments. D-Disgraced my Order."

"We are not required to be perfect," Ioana said. "Rules should guide, but never burden. Sometimes, things happen. Nous understands. He is closer to us than we are to ourselves."

Gaston shook his head, flaming coals threatening to burst out of his chest. "No, Mater." His voice was a grating squeak. "I've done evil things."

"Rhiannon?"

Gaston winced, as if she'd struck him. He screwed his face up tight, sniffed back the snot. "Mater, I... I..." He couldn't say the words. Hated himself for it. Hated his weakness.

He felt Ioana's hand on his shoulder. She gave it a gentle squeeze, let out a sigh that might have been sympathetic, might have been disapproval.

"What will you do, Gaston? How will you atone for it?"

"I c-c-can't. Never can. She won't... She won't let me. Can't let me."

Ioana cradled his head against her shoulder. "No, Gaston, she can't. At least not now."

"Then what? What can I do?"

"Be gentle with yourself, Gaston. Think of all that has happened—your father. I never met him, but Soror Agna says—"

"No," Gaston pulled away and stood. "No excuses. I d-d-didn't come here for that."

"Then what did you come here for?" Ioana lowered herself onto a chair and watched him with big attentive eyes.

"P-P-Penance, Mater. Please. I need a penance. Bind me to the service of Nous. I n-n-need to atone."

Ioana nodded, her eyes still on him, but seemingly distant, focused far away. A shadow passed over her face, her demeanor suddenly that of a frightened child, or an anxious parent. "We will talk about that in the morning. After this... this business with Deacon Shader."

If there was any "after", Gaston thought, almost hoping there wouldn't be.

"What else, Gaston?" Ioana's look was pleading. "Have you confessed everything? I sense there is something else, a stain on your soul. What's happened?"

"N-N-Nothing." Gaston's lips trembled as he spoke. "I'm ashamed, Mater. Ashamed of w-w-what I am. What I've d-d-done. Ashamed of my l-l-lack of faith."

He thought about telling her what he'd witnessed beneath the mound, what he'd discussed with Cadman, but he could barely think about it, never mind tell anyone. He prayed for the strength to confess it, to exorcise all that was troubling him, but each time he made the resolve, Rhiannon's swollen face rose before him like an accusing ghost, telling him he didn't deserve forgiveness. Telling him he was damned, whatever he did.

"There is remorse in your heart," Ioana said. "Whatever you have done, Ain already knows, just as he knows how sorry you are. He is the lord of forgiveness, Gaston. For Ain, all things are possible. To serve him, you only need to want to be a better person."

Gaston already knew all that—he'd been telling himself the same thing, but it wasn't helping. Maybe Ain could forgive him, but Rhiannon couldn't; and what if he couldn't forgive himself? Wouldn't he be damned anyway?

"Mater, tell me about the resurrection," Gaston suddenly blurted out. "What happens when we die?"

Ioana knelt beside him, her eyes closed in concentration. She gave a little sigh before she answered.

"Some parts of the Liber are much older than others," she said. "After the Reckoning,

169

different streams merged with the Old Faith, sometimes enriching it, but more often than not muddying the true meaning."

Gaston thought about what Cadman had said about the Ipsissimus being the Father of Lies. It was starting to sound like the Templum had fabricated great sections of the Liber to appeal to as many people as possible. That would certainly account for its rapid spread, the willingness of so many nations to accept Nousian control. But if there were a true thread running through the teachings, what kind of sick mind would bury it all in the name of temporal power?

"Resurrection is one of the most ancient teachings," Ioana continued, "and one of the purest. Ain has promised that, at the end of time, we will be restored to bodily life, just as Nous was when he appeared to the first luminaries and gave them the original Liber."

"But what will our bodies be like?" Gaston shuddered at the recollection of the animated corpses riding from their tomb. If that was resurrection…

"Tajen speaks of luminous bodies. The degree is dependent upon sanctity. Arcadine, I think it was, says that the resurrected will not have individual organs: all will be harmonized in the spirit."

"H-H-How does he know that?" Gaston searched her face for any hint of a lie. "How do we know any of it's true?"

Ioana shrugged.

It seemed to Gaston she was on shaky ground, though she was doing her best to sound confident. As far as Gaston knew, she might indeed be confident. That was the problem: he couldn't be sure of anything anymore.

"The words of the witnesses," Ioana said. "Faith."

Gaston groaned. It was like beating his head against a brick wall. Why were there no clear answers?

"Faith is accepting without proof," Ioana said. "There are no certainties, no guarantees. It's an attitude, an orientation."

Gaston was rocking from side to side. "B-B-But what if it's all lies?" What if the promises of Ain had as much substance as Shader's to the Order? What if there was no truth, no morality outside what people invented for themselves? If that were the case, then where was the harm in what Cadman was doing? And who could condemn Gaston for the things he'd done?

"What is it, Gaston? You can tell me."

Gaston went rigid and looked at the Monas on the altar through blurry eyes. "I've… seen things." His voice came out as a whisper.

Ioana rose from her chair, took hold of his face with both hands, and forced him to look at her. "What kind of things?"

"The living dead."

Ioana stepped back and rubbed the top of her head. She frowned, lost in thought for a minute, and then fixed Gaston with her gaze once more. "Does this concern your friend Dr. Cadman?"

Gaston nodded.

"What is he up to?"

"He has power over the dead. He promises me things."

"Resurrection?"

"Immortality. He says the Ipsissimus has c-c-cursed him. Says there's a w-w-way to lift the curse and wants my help."

Ioana sniffed contemptuously.

"H-How do I know that w-w-what Cadman says isn't true?" Gaston asked.

"What does your heart tell you?"

"In my h-h-heart there is only…" Gaston felt his face twisting into a grimace.

"Only what?"

He couldn't say anymore. If he did, he felt the admission would destroy him. Closer to the surface than it had ever been was the affliction that had clouded his life since he'd lost his dad to Nous, since his mom had followed him on the same insipid path. He tried, as he'd always tried, to evade the great emptiness opening up inside him, to distract himself from the terror of the Void. He looked at Ioana and forced a smile, but he knew by the worry on her face that she'd read his fear.

"Bow your head, Gaston," she said in a shaky voice. "Pray for Ain's forgiveness, and I'll grant you absolution."

"No." Gaston recoiled. "That's n-n-not what I want. I d-d-don't deserve it. Just a p-p-penance, Mater. A p-penance."

"As you wish," she said, her face suddenly gray and drawn. "You may stay with us tonight, and we'll work something out in the morning."

Gaston nodded, and then the realization hit him. "Shader's s-still here, isn't he?"

Ioana put her hand to her mouth. "I'm sorry, Gaston. I didn't think. But the offer still stands. You'll be quite safe. He'd never abuse our hospitality."

For a moment, Gaston considered doing what Maldark had accused him of. If there was no omniscient Ain watching over his every move, why shouldn't he just slit Shader's throat while he slept? Wasn't that the way of life? Wasn't that what Cadman was doing, making his own rules just so he could keep all the advantages and ensure his own survival in an uncaring world?

It was tempting, but Gaston couldn't be certain of anything right now. Either Ain existed or he didn't, but Gaston wasn't ready to chance it.

The one thing he knew for certain was that the dead could walk again, and that meant there was some possibility of continued existence after death.

Ain might not be watching over him, but you could bet your life on it that Bovis Rayn was.

171

MALICIDE

Templum of the Knot, Sarum

The refectory was rather a drab affair, the walls bare except for a coat of flaking magnolia and a couple of battered cupboards, the floor a jigsaw of cracked and filthy terracotta tiles. Rhiannon was hunched over a steaming cup of tea at one end of the karri-wood table, whilst Soror Agna fiddled with a dusty oil lamp she'd set upon the worktop. The basin was piled with dirty crockery, a sodden cloth draped over the side and smelling like rotten fruit. The failing sun peeked through smeared windows, its sickly light giving the left side of Rhiannon's face a jaundiced hue.

Shader lurked in the doorway, wishing Agna would leave Rhiannon alone for just one minute. As if sensing his thoughts, Agna turned her head, thick spectacles crooked on her sallow face and making one eye look bigger than the other.

"Oh," she said with a mixture of surprise and disdain.

Rhiannon looked up mid-sip, rolled her eyes and slurped. "What d'you want?" she asked, setting down the cup with a clatter.

Shader half-entered the refectory and stopped, feeling awkward and self-conscious—how he usually was around women, but never Rhiannon. She'd always made him feel … all right, whatever he did or said. She just took everything with a pinch of salt, accepted him for what he was, let him move on from his mistakes. And it was so natural, not like the priests in the confessionals trying to view you with the eyes of Ain and all the time letting slip a slight air of condescension, as if they thought you were something they'd just trodden in.

Agna stepped back from the lamp, raised her hands and looked like she was about to chastise it. Her shoulders touched her ears as she drew in a whistling breath through the gaps in her teeth, and then sagged as she gave an exaggerated sigh.

"Savages." She shook her head. "Can't even make a working lamp. That's one thing you can say for Aeterna: at least there they know how to make stuff. Heathen rubbish." She took a swipe at the lamp, stopping a hair's breadth from hitting it and giving it a flick with her finger. "Naughty light," she said in a voice like a little girl reprimanding a truculent doll. "Come in, come in." She waved Shader to a seat opposite Rhiannon. "I'm sure you two have lots to talk about." The tone was friendly, but the eyes were hard.

"Thank you," Shader said, sitting and offering Rhiannon a feeble smile.

"Can I get you some tea?" Agna asked.

"No thank you, Soror, I'm fine."

"Are you sure?"

"Yes, thank you."

"It's no bother."

"No, really, I'm fine."

Agna stuck out her bottom lip. "Oh, well, suit yourself." She patted Rhiannon on the head as she hobbled toward the door. "Shout if you need me. I'll be in the chapel."

She gave Shader a final look, nodded to herself with a decisive grunt, and then left them in peace.

"Rhiannon," Shader began, his mouth dry. "I—"

Rhiannon stood unexpectedly and went to a cupboard. "You acted like an arse. Want some bread?" She took down a loaf and tore off a chunk, cramming it into her mouth. She winced and touched a hand to her jaw. "Shog that hurts. Bloody cock-sucker."

"Rhiannon!" Shader stood and closed the door. "This is a—"

"A templum? Yeah, I know. I'm the one in the poxy robe. What, you don't like the swearing? Not Nousian enough for you? Least I don't go round with a couple of bloody swords strapped to my waist."

"Fair point," he conceded. "We are what we are, I suppose." He crossed the room and hovered at her shoulder.

"Lame," Rhiannon grunted, spraying him with crumbs.

Shader made a show of wiping them from his face, doing his best to look stern.

Rhiannon's lip showed the barest curl at the edge, and then she guffawed, bent double and clamped her hands over her mouth to stop the bread from spewing out. Shader chuckled, feeling some of the tension leave him, but when Rhiannon straightened up her face was streaming with tears. He felt an urge to hold her to him, to ease away her pain; to reconnect with whatever it was they'd lost; but as he leaned towards her she flinched.

"I'm sorry." He backed away. "I was only—"

"He stabbed him, Deacon." She held onto the edge of the table for support. "Gaston stabbed him ... Dad ... a sword in his chest."

Shader sat back down. "I know."

Rhiannon nodded and returned to her seat.

Shader put a hand over his eyes and tried to think, but nothing was making much sense. The idea sounded crazy: Gaston killed Yeffrik... with the sword Shader had given him?

"And Mom..." Rhiannon shook her head, chin trembling with the effort to hold back more tears; to stop her from breaking down completely.

"Someone hit her." Her voice was shrill, like a distraught child's. "Might've been Elgin. She fell. There was blood..." She indicated her mouth with her forefinger. "Gaston tried to blame Elias." She looked at Shader like she wanted to make sure he believed her. "Tried to blame him for what he did to me. Dad didn't believe him; went for him."

Shader slammed his fist against the table. The skin of his face was stretched taut, and his head was starting to pound.

"You mustn't fight him." Rhiannon put her hand on top of his. "We're Nousian, remember. Please tell me I haven't done this for nothing."

Shader almost scoffed at that. He might have been a Nousian, but he was no luminary. He doubted his anger could be contained by any impossible ideas of forgiveness. Gaston was going to die for this; more than that, he was going to suffer.

"Rapists don't deserve second chances," he said through gritted teeth. "And neither do murderers. He's not walking away from this."

"You can't kill him." Rhiannon gripped his hand so tightly her nails pierced the skin, drawing blood.

"It's what you do to evil." Shader pulled his hand away and licked at the scratch. "Luminary Berdini called it malicide."

Shader winced: he'd openly condemned Berdini's argument in Aeterna. It was the sort of justification of opposites that gave Nousianism a bad name; and it had played no small part in his decision to leave the Order.

The problem was, he now realized, Berdini's paradox was also his own: a man torn between peace and war, held together by a uniform and symbols that defined his behavior and provided the frame through which he viewed the world. It was no different to gazing at a painting and only seeing what the artist intended, the view truncated, forcing a singular perspective. Shader's frame was obviously rotting, he thought, the painting spilling beyond the edges to where everything was that much more uncertain.

"Bullcrap." Rhiannon glared at him. "Besides, there's no time for pissing around with Gaston shogging Rayn."

"Rhiannon!" Shader couldn't believe the language she was using, especially with her sitting there in the white robe of a postulant.

"Will you shut up about my swearing! I couldn't give a damn if these dried-up scuts hear me. My brother's missing, don't you see? My little Sammy!" The tears were flowing unchecked now, her eyes wide and pleading.

Shader stood, hands resting on the table. What was it Barek had said? Huntsman had him. Surely the Dreamer wouldn't have…

"I'll find a horse," he said. "Go look for them. You coming?"

Another voice answered: a male voice, deep and thickly accented. "No need. Boy is close by."

Shader started, and half drew the gladius, backing away from the table.

Rhiannon was staring at a large spider by her feet. It had a smooth, segmented body and long legs twisted forward like a crab's.

The air shimmered, and the spider began to grow, thrashing and warping, until it attained the stature and form of a man—a dusky-skinned man in a cloak of feathers, his nose pierced with bones.

"Huntsman!" Rhiannon said.

Shader slid the gladius all the way out of its scabbard.

The Dreamer made a claw of his left hand and held it before Shader's face, fixing him with an unblinking stare. His eyes swirled like yellowish whirlpools, and Shader felt a compulsion rising up from the depths of his mind and forcing him to re-sheathe the sword.

"It was not my wish to frighten you." Huntsman lowered his hand and perched on the edge of the table. "I follow you here." He swiveled his head to take in Rhiannon. "I came to say sorry, and to tell you boy is safe."

"Sammy?" Rhiannon shoved her chair back and stood. "Where is he?"

"Near," Huntsman said. "But not for long. There is somewhere I must take him."

Rhiannon came round the table at him. "You bring him here, right now!"

Huntsman didn't flinch. He merely eyed her calmly, as if he considered her something of a curiosity, but not interesting enough to hold his attention. He switched his gaze back to Shader. "Eingana is safe?"

Shader felt the statue in his pocket shudder in response.

Huntsman gave the slightest of nods then faced Rhiannon. "I am sorry you suffer for her sake. Know this, though: it was bald Clever Man, not Eingana, who told me you must not be joined."

"What?" Shader almost spat the word. "Aristodeus planned this?" He looked from Huntsman to Rhiannon, noting how she turned away. "You knew?"

"Only what he told me." She indicated Huntsman with a jab of her thumb. "But he never said anything about Aristodeus. He made me swear not to say a word about it. Said there was too much at stake. Otherwise, I'd have told you. You have to believe me, Deacon." She tugged at her robe. "This isn't… isn't what I…"

Shader clenched his fists, turning from side to side in the need to find something to hit. Suddenly, his hand snaked out and grabbed Huntsman by the throat.

"You did this, Dreamer. Why?"

Huntsman's hand came up, the fingers once more curling into a claw.

But Shader was ready. He slammed it to the table and held the wrist tight, all the while choking the Dreamer with his other hand.

Huntsman's eyes were bulging, and drool trickled from his mouth.

"Deacon!" Rhiannon placed a hand on his shoulder. "Deacon, stop. You'll kill him."

"Good! It's what he deserves. Interfering... bloody... savage!"

Rhiannon's grip grew firmer. "But Sammy. He knows where Sammy is."

Shader released Huntsman; shoved him so hard in the chest, his head cracked against the wall.

"Not my choice," Huntsman said hoarsely, rubbing his throat and gingerly probing the back of his head. "Bald fellah came; told me things no one should know. Said my people all die. Your folk, too. All people. An enemy comes, Deacon Shader. Enemy of my gods. He hunt them for many lifetimes. Them and grandmother of my gods, Eingana. Statue you now protect."

Shader was still lost in thoughts about Aristodeus. The more he heard about the philosopher, the more he realized he never knew him. Why keep Shader from Rhiannon? How did that benefit him? Did he see her as a distraction? An obstacle in the way of whatever he had planned? Surely it had nothing to do with sanctity, not if Aristodeus were concerned.

"Purity and focus," Huntsman said, guessing his thoughts. "Makes you his secret weapon. Thinks you are our best hope."

"Best hope for what?" Rhiannon asked, hands on her hips, breasts heaving with each intake of breath.

Shader looked away.

"Keeping back dark." Huntsman's pupils narrowed to slits.

"And you," Shader said. "What do you think?"

Huntsman pulled his cloak around him like a cocoon. "At first, I believe him. My gods have hidden in fear of this enemy for a long time. What they feel, I also feel, and bald one played upon this fear. He means well, but acts like a god. He tries to squeeze all worlds into his head, and one day, his head crack like a nut. Other powers there are. Powers he cannot control. Not even enemy control them. Not yet."

Rhiannon sat down, her eyes flicking between Shader and Huntsman. "What enemy?" she said. "Who is it?"

Huntsman pressed his fingertips together beneath his nose. "Sektis Gandaw."

Shader laughed. "The Technocrat of the Old World? I'd sooner believe his former master, Otto Blightey, had recovered from the bloody nose we gave him at Trajinot and was up to his old tricks again. Sektis Gandaw died at the Reckoning. You of all people should know that."

Huntsman's eyes lost their focus. "Disappeared, not died. I stopped him killing my people. Caused Reckoning, ended time of Ancients with power you now protect. Power he has always wanted. Power he would use to end all things."

Shader's heart was thumping, his breathing shallow and rapid.

"I had to do it," Huntsman continued. "My people... My..." He shook himself; brought his gaze back to Shader. "He will unweave all worlds. Become his own god. He fled Reckoning, but my gods knew where. It was once their home. Sektis Gandaw survives in Dreaming, but he has eyes and ears in this world."

"Aristodeus is using me to stop Sektis Gandaw?" Shader said, his scalp burning, head starting to throb.

Huntsman considered him for a moment. "Tried once himself, he says. Tried and failed. Now he tries through you, but this..." He waved a hand to take in Rhiannon. "...

not part of plan. Says he saw you slain. Saw all worlds lost. Must be pure, he say. Must have focus."

Shader felt a curtain of blackness fall over his vision. He swayed, heard the sound of a chair moving, and then felt Rhiannon's arms about him, holding him up.

"What if we tell him to go shog himself?" Rhiannon said. "What if we refuse?"

Huntsman ignored the question. "He walks through time, that one; speaks in riddles. I look for his spirit and see nothing. My gods say he lost in Abyss, but what they mean by this, I do not know."

Rhiannon guided Shader into a chair, where he sat with his head in his hands.

"He is right to want Gandaw stopped," Huntsman said, "but other powers, older and darker, play with him—play with us all. Eingana is goddess of higher place. My people believe she holds all in existence with a sinew of her flesh. She is mother of life and bringer of death. All depends on how power is used. Gandaw seeks statue. With it, he will unmake worlds, but even he is an insect compared to powers that move him."

"The Demiurgos?" Shader asked.

Huntsman shrugged. "Perhaps. It is more than I see. My gods teach us songs of children falling from darkness. Three children, they say: serpent, light, and shadow—Demiurgos who made Abyss from his own mind."

"Whose children?" Shader asked. "Nous's?" That's what the Liber said.

Huntsman sniffed. "Maybe some truth there. Maybe only half truth. Even my gods cannot see other side of darkness."

"This is bullshit," Rhiannon said. "Fairy stories we can do shog-all about. Just tell me where Sammy is, and bugger off back where you came from."

"You will see him soon," Huntsman said, and before she could react, he vanished, leaving a spider scuttling across the floor under the table.

Rhiannon tried to give chase, but the spider was too quick, disappearing through a crack in the wall.

"Great," Rhiannon said. "Shogging great! Now what do we do?"

Shader pushed himself to his feet, one hand clutching the pommel of the gladius. "What we can," he said, feeling all their actions now had a grim inevitability about them. "What we're best at."

"Which is?" Rhiannon asked, crossing her arms.

"In your case, it's masquerading as a Nousian."

She visibly flinched at his remark, and Shader knew he was being unfair, but couldn't bring himself to apologize.

He knew he should have said something about looking for Sammy; knew that's what she needed, but it was all too much to take in. All too much.

Rhiannon's face hardened, her eyes narrowing in a manner that told Shader she wouldn't be forgetting this any time soon. "And what about you?"

"I'll do what I always do," he said, heading for the door and pausing to look over his shoulder at her. "Cut down evil wherever I find it, starting in the morning with Gaston Rayn."

TROUBLE AT BREAKFAST

Templum of the Knot, Sarum

Gaston awoke before sunrise, threw his cloak over the clothes he'd slept in, buckled on his sword and wandered outside to sit by the templum porch. He leaned back and listened to the birds chirping excitedly as the first ribbons of pink and purple appeared on the horizon. Calm wrapped around him like a blanket following a restful sleep—the first he'd had in a very long while. Maybe he wasn't quite so alone as he'd believed. Maybe he could trust Ioana to guide him, see him through this bleak patch. Even the specter of his dad was feeling more like a comfort in the dawn light, and less like the horrors he'd seen beneath the mound.

Cadman's offer had sorely tempted him, but at the same time it had inflamed his conscience, almost given it the perspective of an outsider. And what he had seen with that conscience troubled him. It had been reckless to attack the soldiers outside Sarum, but what he'd done to Rhiannon felt a whole lot worse. She'd been his friend; she'd trusted him, and he'd betrayed that trust in the worst possible way. He was almost glad Shader was going to make him pay for it. Almost, but not quite, for nothing Shader did to him could make things right.

Gaston felt a wave of nausea, an uncomfortable tightening of his stomach. What if he lost the duel? What if he was killed before he could atone for what he'd done? Before he could complete his penance? The calm returned as swiftly as it had left. Ioana would know what to do; she was sure to speak with Shader, make him see sense. They were all Nousians. Shader would understand the need for redemption and stay his hand. Gaston crossed his legs and shook his head, laughing at himself for being such a clacker. There'd be no duel today. The more he thought about it, the more the whole thing sounded ridiculous.

He stared out at the reddening sky, not wanting to miss a moment. The problem with good moods was that they had a habit of slipping away like dreams on waking the second you took your mind off them. It felt like someone had swept a mountain of mold-blackened leaves away from the center of his skull, but they'd forgotten to take them outside. They were still there at the edges, putrefying, seeping back towards the center. Just like the dark cloud that had settled over his spirits since meeting Cadman. Gaston had been utterly convinced of the path he was following—his dad's path, but the way Shader lived it; the path of Nous. Now, after hearing Cadman's accusations against the Templum, after witnessing the grotesque awakening of the Lost, he felt he'd abandoned Ain. Worse, a nagging voice kept telling him that Ain didn't exist. He no longer knew whether to hate or embrace the Templum. Denounce its lies or beg forgiveness for his unbelief.

An elderly priest limped from the residences, covered his mouth with a hand as he coughed, and made his way to sit beside Gaston. The man was old before his time, the thinning hair of his head prematurely white, a thick beard framing his chin. The eyes were damp and rheumy, and a deep scar ran across his forehead, the skin around it yellowish and hard.

"G'day, Frater," the priest said, his voice thin and reedy.

"Morning, Pater ... uhm... I'm Gaston. Gaston Rayn."

The old man flapped his hands. "There's no need to give me your name, son. Don't suppose I shall remember it in a minute or two. Can't even recall my own. It'll come to me—most likely when one of the others calls me for breakfast. Is that a sword you're carrying, Frater?"

Gaston nodded, already feeling the shame creeping back.

"Not a new novice, then?" He leaned closer to examine the embroidery on Gaston's cloak. "You wear the holy Monas on a white cloak. Now let me see... An Order of fighting monks..."

"The Elect?"

"Yes, that's it. Surely they've not reached Sahul?"

"I'm with the White Order founded by the former Elect, Deacon Shader."

"I know the name." The priest looked rather pleased with himself. "In fact, I believe he is staying with us at the moment. So you're one of Shader's boys."

"Not any more."

"Does it cause you much confusion, serving both the Monas and the sword?"

Ordinarily Gaston would have snapped at such a question, but today he felt different, less certain. "There's an ancient argument," he began, watching the old man's face intently, "allowing combat that is judged to be just."

The priest's eyes glinted with either humor or mischief. Gaston continued, uncomfortably aware that he was quoting Shader. "As Nousians, we are commanded not to kill, but those who have rejected Ain for their own ends are the enemies of life."

"They are evil?" the priest asked, eyes widening.

Gaston's cheeks were burning. He licked his lips and tried to inject some confidence into his voice. Problem was, he sounded like a bullshitting pillock, even to himself. "In such cases, the act of killing is not so much homicide as malicide," he concluded, hoping he'd got the words the right way around.

The old man scratched his beard and frowned. "But you no longer believe this?"

"Used to, Pater, with all my heart. Acted as though it were true, as well. I've killed, and unjustly at that. Didn't think so at the time, but I know it now."

The old man's face softened and his eyes lost their glint. "Murder?"

"Nothing else you could call it. Told myself I killed those who opposed Ain's will, but now I haven't a clue what that is. Don't think I really knew then. It was my own will that was defied, my own vanity and anger that led to violence. Pater, is there any way back?"

"The path of redemption begins with the acknowledgement of guilt. If you are contrite, Ain's forgiveness is limitless."

"Pater Limus!" a shrill voice called from the residences. "Breakfast!"

Limus put a finger in his ear and gave it a good rub. "Coming! Will you join us, Frater...?"

"Gaston. Yes, Pater, thank you."

The pair made their way along the central corridor of the residential block, past the chapel in which Gaston had spoken with Ioana, and down a narrow passageway that opened onto the refectory.

Spoons clattered, knives scraped, chairs creaked, and priests mumbled and whispered, talking more with their hands than their mouths. Everyone looked up as they entered, touched their foreheads, and then returned their eyes to the table. Butter was spread and passed along, honey drizzled into bowls, the pages of Libers rustled as they were turned with sticky fingers. A frater with a weatherworn face, and a habit so muddy it might as well have been brown, roughly guided Limus to a chair as the others tucked into porridge and thick rounds of toast. Soror Agna glanced at Gaston as she carried a large tea pot over to the table and began pouring for everyone—even those who held up their hands to say no. Ioana gestured for him to sit beside her, but no sooner had his bum hit the chair than Rhiannon entered the refectory with Shader at her side. He still wore his mail beneath the white surcoat, like he always did. Probably slept in it. His overcoat hung open, and he clutched his hat to his chest. He flipped it deliberately onto his head the instant his cold blue eyes met Gaston's.

Gaston felt his lips quivering with shame or fear. He focused his gaze on Rhiannon, fighting an overwhelming urge to make public his confession and beg her forgiveness. He was halfway out of his seat when Shader drew his shortsword, grabbed him by the collar and dragged him across the table. Gaston was too stunned to react, and then it was too late as the tip of Shader's gladius was pressed against his throat.

"Deacon Shader!" Ioana surged to her feet. "This man is a guest in our house."

Beside her the dwarf, Maldark, stood and snatched up his hammer.

Shader tensed but didn't release his grip. "This man is a rapist and a killer. In the name of Ain I'm going to cut his throat right here!"

Rhiannon looked pale with shock and did nothing but stare at Gaston, open-mouthed.

Gaston had finally attuned to the situation and realized the danger he was in. "P-P-Please—"

"Shut it!" Shader said, heaving Gaston the rest of the way over the table and dumping him on the floor.

Gaston whimpered as Shader tugged his head back by the hair and pressed the blade firmer into his throat, forcing him towards the doorway.

There was the grating of a chair being pushed back and then Limus limped to intercept them.

"Get out of my way, Pater," Shader said, his voice full of ice and menace. "There's no need for anyone else to get hurt."

"You plan to murder the boy?"

"Execute. But the result's the same. Now get out of the way."

"I'm not good at remembering names," Limus went on as if he hadn't heard Shader. "You must be Ain's right hand, or perhaps even the Angel of Death. What is it we were just saying, Gaston?" Everyone glanced at Limus in astonishment. "Is your death to be by way of homicide or malicide?"

Shader's eyes narrowed as he pushed past the old priest. The chill blue had been swamped by a roiling gray that seemed utterly inhuman. Cold fear washed through Gaston's limbs and it was all he could do to stop from puking, or pissing himself, or worse.

There was a gasp from behind and Shader turned, taking Gaston with him. Maldark brought his huge hammer crashing down on the table, sending crockery flying and splashing white robes with tea. Soror Agna touched her fingers to her lips and then began to dab at the front of Ioana's robe with a handkerchief.

"Enough!" Maldark roared.

Shader paused long enough for Gaston to squirm free.

"I-I-It's true," Gaston directed the words at Ioana. "All true. This is what..." He flicked a look at Rhiannon, but she was trembling, staring at nothing. "...what I deserve."

Ioana's fingers were clenching and unclenching above the table. Her eyes never left Shader's, but her face was contorted as if she were struggling for the right thing to say. When she did speak, her gaze faltered. "This is not the way of Nous."

Shader raised the gladius and squinted at the keen edge of the blade. "Exactly what the monks of Pardes said when the mawgs came." He extended his arm and took aim at Ioana with the point of the sword. "Evil must be opposed, Mater. It's no good being Ain's hands and feet if you just stand by and do nothing."

Gaston found himself agreeing, but didn't like where this was leading. Perhaps there was another way. He tried to will Rhiannon to meet his gaze, but she continued to shake, eyes wide and unblinking.

Shader looked him up and down for a moment, sneering, before turning on his heel. "Outside!"

He led the way to the gravel surface in front of the templum. The sun had just risen to a cacophony of birdsong and the maniacal cackling of a kookaburra. Elias Wolf's cart was parked to the left of the Domus Tyalae, but Hector was under the lean-to at the edge of the templum grounds, head dipping into a feed sack. Gaston could just make out Elias's feet protruding from the end of the cart. Clearly the bard wasn't happy sleeping in the templum buildings. Either that, or he knew Gaston was staying and wanted to keep as far away from him as possible.

Rhiannon trailed Shader like a lost child and tugged at his sleeve. "Don't do this, Deacon. It's not what I want."

"Then what do you want?" he thundered, and then immediately turned his head away.

Rhiannon teetered back against the door, jaw slack, the blood draining from her face. But in an instant she pushed herself off the frame and grabbed Shader by the arm, the color flooding back until her cheeks looked ready to explode. "I don't know," she snarled. "But how the shog do you think butchering Gaston's gonna help? I can fight ... fight my own..." She sagged like a burst wineskin, ran her fingers through her hair.

Gaston slunk between them, averting his eyes, and moved towards the Domus Tyalae where he began to go through a series of thrusts and mock parries with his longsword. The priests and Maldark fanned out behind Rhiannon and Shader to stand in front of the porch.

"What is it you want me to do?" Shader asked more gently. Gaston strained so that he wouldn't miss a word. At least the focus had shifted from him, and that gave his courage room to trickle back.

"When you drove the mawgs from Oakendale," Rhiannon said, touching Shader's cheek and searching his eyes, "I thought you were so bloody holy. You fought with sadness, with regret. You took up the sword again just to protect others. It wasn't about pride or revenge. When did you become such a violent jerk? What happened to that man?"

"He never existed," Gaston said, ceasing his practice and turning to face Shader. If Shader was determined to go through with this, then Gaston saw no point holding back. He'd do what he was best at—belittle his opponent, anger him; who knows, maybe even the great Deacon Shader would prove fallible in some small way. He'd already shown he could lose control. All it took was one lapse. "Having second thoughts, Master Shader?" Gaston swished his blade through the air and walked through some basic stances. "Perhaps I should have practiced somewhere else."

Shader eyed him momentarily and then turned back to Rhiannon.

Gaston knew he wouldn't back down now—pride wouldn't let him. He brutally suppressed a wave of worry that rose from his stomach. Too late for that, he thought. Hope of any reprieve had vanished the moment he started goading Shader, though to be honest, there hadn't been much beforehand.

Rhiannon nodded at Shader and leaned close to whisper something in his ear. As she moved back to stand with the priests and Maldark, Shader sheathed the gladius and drew his longsword.

"Only the one sword today?" Gaston would have preferred him to have used two like he normally did. Shader was making concessions, and that made Gaston feel a pang of doubt.

"No point messing up two blades on scum like you, boy."

"Perhaps you'd like some time to warm up." Gaston was starting to despair of riling Shader, but he lost nothing in trying. "Loosen up those old joints?"

"I'm ready if you are." Shader twirled his sword, tongue wetting his lips.

THE DUEL

Templum of the Knot, Sarum

Elias's eyelids flickered open at the sound of voices. He pulled the dew-damp blankets aside and sat up in the cart, rubbing his eyes. Seeing Gaston he quickly ducked down again. Shader moved into view, sublimely poised, walking on the balls of his feet. They were both armed and not taking their eyes off each other. Chances of this being a passionate tango seemed a bit slim, so Elias guessed it must've started. His money was on Shader, but that was more from bias than any objective appraisal of their skills. He'd like nothing more than to see Gaston bleeding from a thousand cuts and force-fed his own stunted little prick. Not that Elias knew what Gaston's cock looked like, but you could always tell when someone was compensating. He rummaged around for his notebook and then settled back to watch the duel over the edge of the cart.

Gaston's attack was sudden and terrifying. Without warning, he leapt in with perfect balance, slashing and thrusting with dazzling speed. Elias's breath caught in his throat. Looked like he'd backed the wrong horse. He was certain it would all be over in a second.

Shader merely stepped back and to the left a little, his sword arm relaxed and moving in easy motions to parry Gaston's fury. Sunlight glinted from the blades, momentarily blinding both fighters. Gaston withdrew, breathing heavily, whilst Shader began to circle him. Elias nodded knowingly. The old dog was getting out of the sun's glare.

Gaston blinked repeatedly and shielded his eyes with his free hand. He moved in again, more cautiously this time, and began to probe Shader's defenses with a series of thrusts. Shader did likewise, the combat resembling a simple warm up exercise but increasing in tempo as their bodies limbered up and hand-eye coordination became more assured. Suddenly, Gaston feigned a wild slash to Shader's neck, but at the last moment dropped his elbow and lunged at his belly. Shader caught Gaston's blade on his own, spun on his heel and sent a vicious riposte across Gaston's face. Gaston swayed back, sword coming up in the nick of time to block, steel juddering, arm trembling with the force. He skipped away, twirling the blade in his hand and twitching his fingers, wincing all the while.

Elias had seen many duels, and had written poems to commemorate the more important ones. He could see that Shader was the more skilled swordsman, moving with greater economy, reading each of Gaston's moves; yet he had only launched one attack. Gaston, on the other hand, was relentlessly looking for openings, and sooner or later he would find one. Elias started to scrawl some notes, but Gaston attacked again, his sword a glittering blur in the sunlight. Again Shader parried easily, but this time his own sword snaked out in a tight arc causing Gaston to spin away and block the blow awkwardly.

Shader reversed his swing and jabbed the blade deftly at Gaston's midriff where it was again met with defensive steel. Shader pressed home his advantage and brought a vicious blow down on Gaston from above. Elias half closed his eyes, expecting to see splattered brains and shards of skull, but Gaston swept his own sword above his head with both hands, metal chinking, sparks flying. Even so, he was jolted backwards by the force of Shader's attack. He sought desperately to regain his balance, but Shader advanced with a combination of thrusts and slashes that caused Gaston to trip and tumble to the earth. Shader placed a booted foot on Gaston's sword arm, the tip of his longsword pressing into his throat.

A terrific clatter and rumble coming down the Domus Tyalae stole the moment. Elias stood up in his cart and watched as the sleek black carriage of Dr. Cadman pulled up in front of the templum. A man in scarlet robes, oiled black hair tied in a neat ponytail, climbed out of the carriage followed by the velvet clad bulk of Cadman. The driver sat motionless beneath a chimney-stack hat.

***

Shader swore under his breath, but secretly he was relieved. He stepped away, sheathing his sword. Would he have actually done it, pressed down on the hilt, driven the point all the way through Gaston's throat and out the back of his neck? Gaston was watching him with bloodshot eyes, every inch the frightened, stuttering kid he'd been when he'd first plucked up the courage to ask about the training. Could he have left him squirming there, pinned to the ground, blood frothing from his mouth? Shader shut his eyes, tried to summon happier images. A wave of remorse washed over him as he remembered the lad coming to him, face streaked with tears, after he'd run away from home. He'd fallen out with Bovis again, neither being able to stomach the other's take on Nousianism. Shader had held him while he sobbed himself dry, and then without a word they'd gone to the practice barn and fenced till their palms bled.

Shader opened his eyes. Gaston was still looking at him, lips quivering. He returned Gaston's sword and allowed him to scramble to his feet.

"Gaston, my boy," Cadman called out, opening his arms wide.

Gaston ran into his embrace, let the fat man stroke his hair and whisper in his ear. Shader took a step towards them, but then stopped and lowered his eyes. Part of him wanted to protect Gaston, punch Cadman right in his pudgy face. But it wasn't Cadman the lad needed protecting from, he acknowledged. The stinging truth of Rhiannon's words came home to haunt him: he was nothing but a violent jerk.

Mater Ioana approached the man in the scarlet robes. "Welcome to our templum, Governor," she said. "Even if it is a somewhat unexpected honor."

Zara Gen looked decidedly uncomfortable and could not meet Ioana's eyes. "In the name of the Emperor Hagalle," he announced to the group in front of the porch, "I am here to inform you of the dissolution of the Templum of the Knot. My men will soon arrive to search the premises…" He looked fleetingly at Cadman. "…and once they've confiscated anything suspicious, you will be escorted to Port Sarum, where you'll board ship for Nousia."

That didn't sound much like Hagalle's style, Shader thought. He'd have just sent the Sicarii. Zara Gen was lying, but he didn't exactly look comfortable about it.

"But you are … you have always been a friend to us, Zara Gen," Ioana said. "What's happened?"

Cadman stepped away from Gaston and pulled two pieces of amber from his pocket, one curved and pointed like the fang of a serpent, the other round and looking suspiciously like the eye of the Gray Abbot's Monas. "These! Relics of your esoteric sect that have brought pestilence upon us."

Shader touched the statue in his pocket and shot a quick glance at Elias, who was watching the scene intently.

"It would seem, Mater," Zara Gen said, "that the plague is generated by these pieces of amber, one of which was brought to Sarum by Jarmin the Anchorite." Zara Gen shut his eyes for a second, his face creased with tension. "And the other was found on the person of the Gray Abbot of Pardes."

"It was you who attacked Pardes?" Ioana asked, a trace of fear in her voice.

A confusion of emotions crossed Zara Gen's face, but he could not find the words to reply.

Cadman spoke instead. "My suspicions were aroused when it was observed that, of all the people in Sarum, only you priests were unaffected by the plague. Some swift enquiries revealed that the Gray Abbot was the ringleader of what increasingly looks like a Templum plot. My visit here yesterday showed me that there was nothing exceptional you were doing that would ward off contagion. Ipso facto, as they say in Aeterna, your protection from the plague must be altogether more … sinister."

"Don't look too poorly yourself," Hugues said, patting his stomach and coming to stand with Ioana.

"Not yet," Cadman said, "but who knows when my time will come?"

"You're no fool, Dr. Cadman," Ioana's eyes narrowed. "You know full well this is no ordinary contagion. There are occult forces involved."

"You have knowledge of the workings of the plague?" Zara Gen's hand went to his ponytail.

"I have started to sense something of its nature. It has more of the feel of pollution than disease."

"Pollution from what, Mater?" Zara Gen asked.

"Isn't it obvious?" Cadman said, holding up the eye and the fang. "My theory is that those closest to the power of the amber are immune to its negative effects. None from Pardes have grown ill, and it is my contention that another piece of this artifact lies somewhere within the Templum of the Knot."

"Perhaps you can explain, Doctor—" Shader eyed Cadman coolly. "—why the Abbey of Pardes was attacked by living corpses."

"Creatures that fled before your unsurpassed evil, Deacon Shader. I think we have all seen enough of that on display today." Cadman gestured towards Gaston. "Mater, I must say I'm surprised to see you permit such violence in front of your templum. Whatever would the Ipsissimus say?"

"Living corpses?" Maldark stepped alongside Shader, war-hammer grasped firmly in both hands. "Explain thyself, Doctor."

Zara Gen shot Cadman an uneasy glance.

"They were but men." Cadman shook his head. "I fear our friend Mr. Shader here is attempting the age old Nousian strategy of demonization. What would you say, Mater?"

"Zara Gen,"—Ioana ignored Cadman—"this is such a sudden turn of events. I know you must have your reasons, but I don't understand. Give us time to answer these charges, or at least to work out what to do."

Zara Gen's face creased with discomfort. "I'm sorry, Mater. We have to act now."

"But you can't just expect us to pack up and walk away."

Zara Gen turned and climbed back into the carriage.

"This is our home!"

Cadman draped his arm around Gaston and pulled him close to whisper in his ear. Gaston shook his head and tried to pull away. The fat man took a firmer grip, both hands on Gaston's shoulders, and fixed him with an intense gaze over the top of his pince-nez.

Shader strode towards them and barged into Cadman.

"Terribly sorry, Doctor," he said. "I hope you're not hurt."

Cadman made a show of dusting himself down and resituating his pince-nez on his nose. "No, no, I'm perfectly all right, Mr. Shader." He shot a questioning look at Gaston, who lowered his eyes. "No harm done, eh?"

Ioana held out a hand and Gaston took it. She pulled him into an embrace and glared daggers at Cadman, who ambled over to the carriage and then turned back to face them.

"Horses for courses, Mater," Cadman said, thrusting his hands in his pockets and puffing out his cheeks. And then a little more somberly, "Horses for courses. Well, Gaston, I'm here if you need me." And with that he clambered inside and the carriage clattered away down the Domus Tyalae.

Shader stiffened as Gaston broke away from Ioana and walked towards Rhiannon. Her fists were clenched and she kept looking from Agna to Shader. Gaston went down on one knee, looking like he was proposing, but with his head hung in shame. Shader's hands went to his hips, the skin of his face tightening until he thought it might split.

"I-I-I don't deserve to ever be f-f-forgiven for what I've done," Gaston said in a shaky voice. "B-B-But please let me t-t-try to make things right."

Rhiannon raised a hand as if to strike him. Her fingers were trembling, her breathing rapid and shallow.

Gaston flinched and stood, taking a quick step backwards. "I'll do whatever it t-t-takes. Just tell me what you n-n-need and—"

"Shog you!" Rhiannon shoved him in the chest and stormed into the templum, Soror Agna following close behind like a clucking old hen.

Gaston turned to Ioana, face flushed and eyes glistening with moisture. "Mater, you said Ain was merciful. Please, tell me what he wants from me."

"Maybe he wants you to sod off with your fat friend," Elias said, standing up in his cart and scribbling away at a notepad. "Actually..." He cocked his head as if he were listening and flung the notepad over his shoulder to land amongst the rest of the junk in the cart. "...that's exactly what he's saying right now. 'Piss off, Gaston, and everyone will feel a whole lot better.' Wow, what do you think of that? My first mystical colloquy! Praise Ain, I'm saved!"

"Shut up, Elias," Shader said, pointing a finger at him and holding it there until the bard threw his hands up and started to fuss around with his instruments.

Gaston opened his mouth to say something, but the din of scores of horses cantering down the Domus Tyalae averted everyone's attention. Shader frowned as he recognized Justin Salace riding at the head of the White Order.

The knights spread out around the front of the templum, nearly forty men, heavily armored and cloaked in pristine white. They each carried a light lance and wore a cavalry saber at the waist. Shader wondered where they'd come by such impressive armaments. He glanced over at Gaston who look dumbfounded.

"Justin," Gaston said stepping forward, "what's going on? Where'd you get this gear?"

"Thought you knew, man," Justin said. "It was delivered last night. Thought that's why you'd gone."

Gaston glanced at Shader, looking once more like the lost boy who'd fled the family home. He drew himself up straight and threw his voice so that it would reach all the knights. "Why'd you bring the Order here?"

"Governor Gen showed up first thing with Dr. Cadman," Justin said. "Told us all about this amber crap causing the plague. There's something wrong here, man." Justin glanced at the templum as if it were the entrance to the Abyss. "Magic, or some shit. Bad magic."

"You've been fed a bunch of lies, Justin," Shader said, stepping towards him.

"Master Shader." Justin acknowledged him with a curt nod, but continued to address Gaston. "Our orders are to search the templum and everyone here, then escort the priests to Port Sarum and see them off."

"You take orders only from me," Gaston said.

"I assumed it's what you'd have done, if you'd been there when the governor came. I thought we were pledged to his service, or have I got it wrong?"

There was something like belligerence creeping into Justin's tone. Shader scanned the other knights, trying to read their intentions. He hoped to catch sight of someone he could trust, thought he glimpsed Barek, but the lad's eyes were cast down.

"We'll ride back to the barracks," Gaston said, "then I'll discuss the matter with Governor Gen and Dr. Cadman."

"There's nothing to discuss," Justin said, looking to the knights around him. "The governor couldn't have been clearer. So come on, man, get your leader head back on and help us carry out his orders. You know it makes sense."

There was an expectant silence as all eyes turned upon Gaston. Shader crossed his arms over his chest and prayed, for Gaston's sake, the lad gave the right answer.

"We are Nousians first, Justin. I've promised to do whatever Ain wills, but I'm not too good at hearing what he has to say." Gaston cast a wry look in the direction of Elias's cart. "So I've decided to put myself, and the Order, under the authority of Mater Ioana."

Justin leaned over the bow of his saddle. "Then you're shogged, Gaston. Can't you see this ain't right? Our own lads grow sick and yet these priests are unaffected. Dr. Cadman is right: it's the work of the Father of Lies. Never much believed that stuff before, but now it's starting to make sense. The Demiurgos is prowling around us, man, looking for ways to deceive." Justin shot an accusing look at Shader.

Maldark hefted his hammer to his shoulder and moved to stand directly in front of Justin's horse. "Boy," he growled, "turn around and get thee hence, or I'll smite thee, so help me God."

God? Shader felt a thrill run up and down his spine. He didn't know whether to be outraged or intrigued, but now was not the time for either.

Justin snarled and started to draw his sword. Before the blade was even halfway clear of the scabbard, Maldark swung his hammer over his head and struck the ground. There was a crack like thunder, and stones flew up startling the horses. Justin struggled to keep his saddle, but still managed to bark a command to the knights: "Attack!"

As Maldark raised his hammer for another blow, Shader drew both his swords and stood alongside him.

"No!" Ioana shouted, the command in her voice so strong that the knights froze with indecision. "There will be no more fighting. Everyone inside."

The priests scurried into the templum with Gaston, Maldark, and Shader reluctantly following. Once they were all in the narthex, Hugues shut and bolted the doors.

"Will they break in?" Cadris was already beginning to perspire.

Ioana glared at him before moving to look from a window. "Looks like they're waiting for something," she said.

Shader glanced at Gaston, but then realized the lad probably knew as little as he did. What hold did Cadman have over the Order? And more worryingly, what had made Zara Gen, the only leader in Sahul with any sympathy for Nousians, change so dramatically?

CADMAN'S COUP

Arnbrook House, Sarum

Looks like we've lost Gaston to the Templum," Zara Gen said, settling himself into the broad leather chair behind his desk.

Cadman stroked his mustache idly for a moment before moving to the drinks cabinet.

"Master Rayn has his demons to lay to rest," he said with a pronounced note of cynicism. "Don't worry, Governor, he'll be back."

And if he wasn't, Cadman didn't really give a damn. Justin Salace might have been an opportunist little runt, but he was ideal for the task in hand.

"Can I get you something? Whiskey? Water?" *Which looks about all he's got in here, puritanical nincompoop. Not at all like Councilor Arkin.*

Zara Gen's brow furrowed, as if he didn't quite approve of Cadman helping himself. He sighed and leaned back in the chair.

"Whiskey—a small one, mind. Need to keep a clear head in these matters." He tugged on his ponytail and grimaced. "You're sure these pieces are to blame?"

Cadman unscrewed the cap on the whiskey and filled a glass before handing it to Zara Gen. "Sorry," he said. "Bit over-zealous with the pouring."

Zara Gen accepted it with sigh. "Don't suppose it'll hurt this once." He took a sip that turned into a glug and then waved the glass under Cadman's nose. "The pieces, Doctor."

Cadman topped him up and replaced the bottle.

"Ah, yes, the pieces. Well, you know the legends as well as I do." Actually Cadman doubted anyone did, after the amount of reading up he'd been doing, but that was the way to talk to politicians: make them feel superior, or at the very least, equal. "The Statue of Eingana is shrouded in superstition—Dreamer mumbo jumbo in the main, but it's generally supposed to be a force for good."

Zara Gen took another swig and leaned forward, eyebrows raised.

"However," Cadman said, pausing for effect, "like all such powers, it's something of a mixed blessing. In the right hands, Eingana is the bringer of life…"

"And in the wrong?" Zara Gen was getting his point.

"Absolutely, Governor. It's the combination of raw, atavistic power with the dubious morality of Aeterna that has led to our problem."

Zara Gen was making irritating noisy circles with his glass atop the desk, but Cadman did his best not to mention it, biting down on his bottom lip and counting to three.

"I'm not sure, Cadman. The priests have always been…" Zara Gen struggled for the right words.

"Wolves in sheep's clothing, Governor, just as the emperor's always said. Think how grateful Hagalle's going to be when he learns what you've done here: banishing the last

Nousians from Sarum, and confiscating the cause of the contagion. I see great things for you, Governor. A duchy, perhaps."

"I don't know about this." Zara Gen ripped off the black ribbon and shook his hair free. "I've known Mater Ioana for a long time; and Jarmin—well he was only in this very office a short while ago. We spoke at length, and I saw nothing to—"

"Governor," Cadman interrupted again.

Zara Gen's eyes narrowed, but he let it go.

Cadman raised a hand in apology, but continued anyway. "Doesn't it strike you as odd that the most prominent Nousian in the North just happens to pop in for a visit?"

"I invited him," Zara Gen said.

Cadman gave his most sympathetic sigh. "Yes, Governor, but think about what led to you making such a politically… sensitive move."

Zara Gen's face reddened, and he drummed his fingers on the desktop.

"Most out of character." Cadman whipped off his pince-nez and squeezed the bridge of his nose. "And I dare say it didn't go unnoticed in Jorakum. You know how the staff gossip. My point is, however, that soon after Jarmin departed, our itinerant holy knight, Deacon Shader, turned up in Pardes, where the Gray Abbot just happened to have a piece of the Statue of Eingana."

Zara Gen pushed his chair back and stood, his eyes suddenly keen and radiating clarity.

"Which you knew all about, Doctor. What was it Shader said you sent after it? Living corpses? No, Doctor, this doesn't feel right. If the Gray Abbot is as morally reprehensible as you claim the priests are, then why was there no ill-effect from his possession of a piece of the statue?"

"He's lived a very long time." Cadman was clutching at straws. He crammed the pince-nez back on his nose. "Who knows what—?'

"Oh, come on, Doctor! I may not have all your degrees, but I'm no idiot. I agree that the statue has a part in all this, but the Nousians? You're starting to sound like Hagalle. You're supposed to be a man of science. Where's the evidence to support your hypothesis? And, more to the point, just how long have you had those pieces?"

So, the governor's not as stupid as he looks. Oh, well, onwards with plan B.

Cadman took the eye and the fang from his pocket and rolled them about in his fingers. "You already know about my acquisition of the Gray Abbot's eye."

Cadman flicked it into the air and deftly caught it.

"The other piece, I have you to thank for. If you hadn't invited that odious hermit to your office, I might never have learnt of its whereabouts. Actually, I doubt I'd have ever given this whole silly business of Eingana a second thought."

Scarcely a moment had passed since when Cadman hadn't wondered if he'd been better off out of it; sticking to his life of anonymity and preying on the nauseating citizens of Sarum.

The blood had drained from Zara Gen's face. Cadman touched a hand to his cheek, thinking the illusion might have wavered again, but then he realized Zara Gen was probably shocked at the idea of being spied on.

"Thicker walls, Governor." Cadman gave the paneling a sharp rap. "Soundproofing. It was all the rage in my day, what with the paparazzi, the sellers of secrets, and jealous rivals. We even had little devices you could secrete in plant pots. If you'd been more cautious, I'd have been prevented from eavesdropping. As it is, your carelessness has led me to a place I'd rather not have come, and it's looking increasingly like there's no turning back."

Cadman sauntered to the door and locked it.

"Guards!" Zara Gen called out, rushing round the table and pushing past Cadman to take hold of the door knob. "Someone call Captain Harding!" He turned the key and pulled the door open.

A shadow blocked his way, causing him to back into the office, until he was pressed up against the desk.

The shadow drifted toward him, taking on more clarity, a full-faced great helm, translucent armor, and a diaphanous surcoat, yellow with age, but still bearing the red Monas of the Templum.

"What... What is...?" Zara Gen's teeth were chattering, and he clutched his arms across his chest.

"Governor, Callixus. Callixus, Governor Gen. Now do be a good chap and sit down before you fall down." Cadman waved Zara Gen back to his chair. "Splendid."

He whipped out his cigarette case, tapped it three times, and replaced it. Not the best time to smoke, he decided. Some jobsworth was bound to investigate the smell.

Walking straight through the ethereal form of Callixus, he went back to the drinks cabinet.

Callixus's eyes smoldered.

"Are the Lost in position?" Cadman asked, pouring himself a large whiskey. Wouldn't have the slightest effect, but ancient habits die hard.

"They have entered the city," the wraith said. "The imperial troops were no match for them."

"Good, good. Tell them to come straight here. A bit more terror and panic can't do us any harm, eh, Governor? I expect the good people of Sarum are quite getting used to it, what with the plague and all. Sterling stuff. Sterling."

In spite of his bravado, Cadman was worried. More worried than he'd been in centuries. It wasn't in his nature to take such bold action; and yet wasn't that the way life worked, throwing up opportunities for advancement, each acceptance bearing its own risks?

"What are the Lost?" Zara Gen had taken on the complexion of wax, and his knuckles looked almost arthritic from gripping the arms of his chair so tightly.

"'Who' would be more apposite, don't you think, Callixus? Governor, Governor, things have gotten ahead of themselves, as I knew they would. Action begets more action, I always say, and all action leads inexorably to climax, dispersal, and disintegration. I'm afraid it doesn't bode well for dear old Sarum, but what's a man to do when the entire cosmos is just waiting to take a swipe at him? Back in my day, we had something known as the Lost and Found—I expect you have something similar here at Arnbrook House, what with this being a thoroughly bureaucratic institution. What others have lost, I have found, and intend to put to good use. Let's see if this particular climax can't be twisted to a positive end." *More positive for some than others, if fate doesn't defecate in my celebratory champagne.*

"Don't worry, Governor, once I have the rest of the statue, I won't be sticking around here. You might even get out of this alive—if you stay put and do as you're told. Now, do be a dear and zip it, as they used to say."

Cadman touched the amber pieces together; watched them spark and glow. He closed his eyes and reached out into the streets of Sarum, hunting, probing.

"Now look here, Cadman, we're both reasonable men," Zara Gen said, breaking Cadman's concentration.

"Perhaps I didn't make myself clear, Governor. Shut up!"

Zara Gen shrank back into his chair as Cadman once more closed his eyes and sought out the dead of Sarum.

He didn't have far to look. The wisps of his questing soul were drawn to the fresh corpses of a death-cart a couple of blocks away.

Siphoning off the power of Eingana to enhance his own necromantic art, he breathed black life into the cadavers, and felt the first stirrings of undeath.

Casting his net wider, Cadman scoured the morgues and hospitals, animating all the dead flesh he could find, before passing over the cemeteries and revisiting the tumuli outside the city. He felt their groaning protests, these reluctant slaves drawn back from the grave. There were hundreds of them, all connected to his will by the merest sliver of awareness; not enough to think for themselves, but enough for mechanical movements and a burning hunger that would never be sated, no matter how many victims they feasted on.

"Good," Cadman said, pocketing the pieces of amber. "That went well. Now then—"

A distant caw sounded from deep in his mind. Cadman slapped the side of his head and pounded his ear like a swimmer trying to void water.

The caw was answered by another, louder and more urgent, and then another. Icy dread crept up his spine, adding to the cold that never left him.

Bugger. Now what have I done?

"Callixus." Cadman's voice was shaking. He coughed to clear his throat and turned to the wraith, who was hovering just a little too close for comfort. "Meet the Lost outside and take them to the templum. Justin will be expecting you." *Not that I don't trust the boy knights to get the job done, but you can never be too careful.* "Get rid of the priests, and then search every nook and cranny. If there is a piece of the statue there, I want it, do you understand?"

A ripple passed through Callixus's ghostly body. "What of Shader? He was able to harm me before."

"So the odds are even. The legends say you were the greatest of the Elect; surely, even in death, you can best a neurotic upstart who doesn't seem to know whether he's coming or going. Oh, and Callixus, send one of your men to me. Someone's going to need to keep an eye on the governor here."

Callixus's eyes narrowed to red slits, and then he dispersed in a puff of black smoke.

"There's still time to put an end to all this." Zara Gen was half out of his chair.

The sound of breaking glass came from somewhere downstairs.

"No, there's not. The game's afoot, Governor. If I were you, I'd sit very, very still. Do nothing, say nothing, and who knows, you might turn out to be the luckiest man alive."

Cadman headed for the door, but it opened just before he reached it.

A massive knight stood in the doorway, skeletal jaw hanging slack, one shriveled eyeball dangling from a thread across a bony cheek. The links on its rusty chainmail were broken here and there, leaving unsightly tears, like a moth-eaten rag. It wore the surcoat of the Elect, blackened with mildew, and carried a dented kite shield and jagged longsword.

That was quick.

"I am Abelard," the dead knight rasped, its jaw falling to one side and looking like it was about to drop off. "Marshal of the Elect, and second only to Callixus."

"A pleasure," Cadman said, holding out his hand and then withdrawing it, thinking Abelard's might come off. "You sound eminently qualified for the job. This"—he turned to Zara Gen—"is our beloved governor. Under no circumstances is he to leave this room. If he tries anything, kill him."

Judging by the petrified expression on his face, Zara Gen wasn't likely to try anything very much at all—although he was starting to look like he needed to relieve himself.

"On second thought,"—Cadman turned back to Abelard—"he may need the W.C. You'd better wait outside, or he'll never stop going, and I'd hate for him to run out of toilet paper. Right, I must leave you two to get acquainted." *I have business to discuss with a rather shady customer who's got more tentacles than an octopus.*

190

It was another step down the slippery slope, but what else could he do? The die was cast, the players assembled. Now it was up to him to ensure that the odds were stacked definitively in his favor.

THE SIEGE

Templum of the Knot, Sarum

Shader stared at the bolted double doors of the templum, back starting to ache from sitting hunched over on the pew for so long.

Confinement had never sat well with him. He'd always enjoyed the great open spaces of his father's lands in Britannia.

A hand clamped down on his shoulder.

Shader looked up to see Maldark following his gaze toward the doors.

"They're taking their time," the dwarf grumbled.

"Perhaps you frightened them off," Shader said.

"By God, I'd have taught them a thing or two, had it not been for Mater Ioana."

Shader raised an eyebrow at the use of the forbidden name. In Nousia, you could end up in the Judiciary's dungeons for less.

"I know, Maldark, and I expect you would have won."

"Or mayhap died trying," the dwarf mumbled beneath his beard. "Begging thy pardon, Shader, but something hath been troubling me. Methinks I hath seen thy face before. It is most familiar. Are you sure we hath not met at some other time?"

Shader shook his head. "I would have remembered."

Gaston moved to stand in front of the doors. His fingers played with the pommel of his sword, and his eyes never lingered long on any one thing or person.

"Why don't they attack?" He sounded like a child complaining about the rain forcing him to stay inside.

"Pray, thou tell us, boy." Maldark planted his hammer before him as he sat on a pew and rested his hands on the haft. "Art they not thy knights?"

Shader stood and wandered back into the nave, where Pater Limus tended the sick and dying who lay upon pallets, skin ruptured with pustules, thick froth fouling their chins. Limus uttered soft words of encouragement and offered them his smile, which appeared at once beatific and vacant.

Further back, in the chancel, Rhiannon and Soror Agna were engaged in animated yet hushed conversation. Rhiannon was flustered and tearful, her arms clamped over her chest as she rejected Agna's attempts to comfort her.

Ioana turned away from peering out of a window, climbed down from the pew she'd been standing on, and ambled over to Shader with Cadris clamoring behind for answers.

"Why have they chosen now to persecute us?" the fat priest asked. "Why do they just sit there? Are they going to attack?"

Ioana gritted her teeth. "Just get on with your work, Cadris. There are ill people to tend, and I'm starting to think it's because they're sick of your whining."

Cadris stopped, mouth hanging open, and then stomped over to the pallet-beds.

Frater Hugues took up Ioana's vigil at the window, a look of grim determination on his face.

"Tell me about this statue," Ioana said.

"The Gray Abbot told me it's the Statue of Eingana," Shader said. "The artifact used by Huntsman to end the time of the Ancients. After the Reckoning, it divided into five pieces, two of which are now in the hands of Dr. Cadman."

"He was convinced we were connected with it," Ioana said.

Shader pulled the black serpent from his pocket, running his fingers over the ridges of its scales and squinting at the slender veins of amber now barely visible on the surface. "I shouldn't have brought it here."

Ioana reached out a hand to the statue and quickly drew it back. "It's sentient."

Shader raised an eyebrow and studied it more intently. "I lack your intuition, Mater, but something tells me we would be wise to keep the statue from Dr. Cadman. I think that's why Huntsman entrusted it to me. The bard was being a bit too reckless."

"Sweet Nous!" Ioana said, looking around. "Where is Elias?"

"Hiding in his cart," Hugues said from the window. "I see him pop his head out from time to time. Poor fellow looks frantic." Hugues grinned maliciously.

Ioana returned her attention to the statue in Shader's hand. "What do you propose to do with it?"

Shader shrugged and put it back in his pocket. "Guard it as best I can," he said, "and find a way to retrieve the Gray Abbot's piece."

Ioana nodded, eyes focused inward as she thought things through. "Can Huntsman be trusted?"

"No idea," Shader said.

There were a thousand things the Dreamer wasn't telling them, but that wasn't any different to what Aristodeus had been doing all Shader's life. Could either of them be trusted? When you didn't even know the rules of the game, how could you know anything? Either you acted as you saw fit at the time, or you shut yourself away and did nothing, and that wasn't in Shader's nature.

He wandered over to the window to peer over Hugues's shoulder.

"Keeps poking his head out," Hugues said, pointing toward Elias's cart.

Elias was visible as a wriggling lump beneath the dirty blankets he covered his instruments with. Sure enough, his head appeared, and his eyes met Shader's. He was red-faced and grimacing. He withdrew a hand from his covers and pointed frantically at the area of his crotch, like he was desperate to relieve himself.

Hugues sniggered as Elias ducked back out of sight.

The knights had started to move, fanning out until they completely surrounded the templum and its outbuildings.

"Looks like they're getting ready for something," Hugues said, sounding every bit the battle-honed corporal.

Ioana gave him an enquiring look.

"The knights have us encircled," Shader explained. "It seems we are under siege."

"What does he mean 'under siege'?" squealed Cadris, scurrying over to Ioana.

"We must wait, Cadris," she said. "Trust in Ain."

"But what if they break in?"

"Then we smite them." Maldark patted his hammer.

Cadris gulped, rubbed at his glistening forehead, smoothed a few stray wisps of hair back in place, and went back to bustling around the patients.

Shader doubted they'd attack. They'd have done so already, if that were the plan.

He gazed out along the Domus Tyalae, scanning the trees flanking the road. They were waiting for something, he decided, but it didn't make much sense. They already had overwhelming numbers, and he doubted their inaction was due to cowardice.

He caught Gaston watching him and raised an eyebrow. Gaston immediately looked away.

"I-I-I'd have ordered the at-at-attack by now," he said, "but Justin's ob-ob-obviously following orders."

"Cadman's?" Shader asked, his voice harsher than he'd intended.

Gaston winced, staring at his boots. "C-C-Cadman's a very c-cautious man," he said. "He w-w-won't be taking any ch-chances. Whatever's coming, it's not gonna be n-n-nice."

Shader ground his teeth and shook his head. Images of rotting corpses smashing their way into the Abbey of Pardes danced behind his eyes.

"This Cadman..." Shader knew the answer even before he'd finished the question. "There's more to him than meets the eye, right?"

Gaston blanched, his cheek starting to twitch. He nodded, and finally met Shader's gaze with wide and pleading eyes.

"No, Gaston," Shader said, fixing him with a cold stare. "There's no forgiveness for what you've done. When the time comes, I'll fight beside you, but nothing more."

Rhiannon was watching them, her eyes narrow, mouth curled into a grimace. She looked like she was going to be sick.

"He pretends t-t-to be fat," Gaston said. "B-b-but really he's just a corpse, like the others. L-Like the Lost."

"The Lost? You mean Callixus?"

"There's m-m-more. C-Couple of h-h-hundred, at least. I s-s-saw them. Saw him bring them b-b-back."

"Where, Gaston? Where did this happen?"

"M-M-Mound outside the city. Deep in a f-f-forest. Fenrir, I think."

Shader curled his fingers around the hilt of the gladius. This Cadman was a liche. Had to be, with that sort of power over the dead. A liche like Blightey and the things that served him in Verusia.

He nodded grimly to himself and went back to stand with Maldark. The dwarf was twirling the haft of his hammer, the stone head grating against the floor.

"I am impatient for the battle to commence," he said. "It vexes me to just sit and wait."

Shader put a hand on his shoulder, thankful Maldark was with them. "I don't think this is going to be an ordinary battle."

Memories of Trajinot crept up from the dark recesses of his mind. When the aberrations had surged out of the trees, and the advance of the Seventh Horse had faltered, Shader had felt one overwhelming emotion: terror.

His stomach knotted as the corrosive onset of despair threatened once more to take hold. He'd done the only thing he knew how to do back in the Schwarzwald skirting Verusia, the thing he'd been trained for since birth. He'd charged, and seeing it as a sign of bravery, the Seventh Horse had charged with him.

Maldark looked at him with eyes that had seen their own share of horror, eyes that seemed heavy with a secret burden; and for an instant, something was communicated between them. There was no give in the dwarf, Shader realized. He'd never falter, and right now, he couldn't have wished for anything more.

THE SUMMONING

City of Sarum

Cadman stepped inside the carriage and rapped on the ceiling with his knuckles. The ever-silent driver cracked the reins, and they lurched away from Arnbrook House.

A scattering of militiamen had barricaded themselves in the alleyways leading off of Mercator Street, watching, but taking no action against the graveyard ghouls now prowling around the Council buildings.

Cadman rubbed at his fleshy chin and pondered.

He'd grown euphoric on the power of Eingana, and as far as he was concerned, there was nothing more dangerous. Euphoria bred carelessness, and carelessness led to mistakes. Not only that, but it was an almost indisputable law of life—sod's law, they used to say—that such rapturous feelings always preceded a calamitous crash. He needed to sober up, so to speak. Sober up and stop burying his head in the sand every time he heard those infernal caws and felt invisible eyes watching him. Sober up and take stock of the state of play. He'd had a good innings so far, but that usually meant time was running out until the opposition started padding up to bat.

Commanding the undead marauding in and around Arnbrook House was as effortless as the automatic counting that ground on of its own accord in a detached compartment of his brain. It had also become easier to maintain his corpulent form, and his appalling parasitic hunger had retreated into the background. He no longer felt compelled to send the ghouls—or Callixus—in search of sustenance; indeed, he was starting to feel repulsed by the practice of filching, as he'd termed his feeding habits centuries ago. It was a repugnance he'd not experienced since he'd first discovered his need for the warm lifeblood of humans to maintain his precarious hold on existence.

Had it been worth it, he wondered? All those decades of skulking unnoticed in the great population centers, barely daring to act, in case suspicions were aroused; suspicions that every so often gave rise to fear, anger, and retribution. Had mere endurance ever been enough?

Cadman shuddered at the thought of the alternative, and then smiled as he recalled the promise of the Dweller: not only immortality, but self-contained immortality. No more dependence on the lives of others. No more parasitism. No more filching.

Careful, Cadman, he admonished himself. *You're getting hooked again. Caution first, caution last, caution always.*

Ah, said an emboldened part of his mind that hadn't seen the light of day in decades. *But you're already in too deep. In for a penny, in for a pound, as they used to say back home, before the Templum graced us with denarii and aurei. Pretentious Romanophiles.*

Was he in too deep? Cadman had a vivid image of the carriage hurtling down a sheer slope, over the edge of a cliff, and shattering into pieces on a rock-strewn beach. Every action had its consequences, and he'd been far too active of late; ever since his dreams had been invaded by the Dweller.

I suppose I'm to blame for that, am I? said the old familiar voice in his head.

You didn't have to listen, said the resurgent one. *But now you've gone this far, there's no turning back. What's the worst that could happen?*

The carriage slowed to a halt outside Cadman's townhouse. It was an undistinguished three-story building nestled among a score of similar dwellings in a quiet and not particularly desirable backwater. He wrinkled his nose out of habitual disdain for the neighborhood, but he had to admit, it had served its purposes admirably.

Cadman waited while the driver clambered down and went to check for intruders. He flipped open his pocket watch and kept an eye on the front door once the driver had disappeared inside.

The curtains of the house next door parted slightly, and he caught sight of his nosey-old-hag-of-a-neighbor peering out at the carriage. She saw he'd noticed and dropped the curtains back in place, just as the driver re-emerged and nodded the all-clear.

Thirty-two seconds in all. The man was getting faster. Cadman only hoped he wasn't getting careless. He thrust the pocket watch back in his waistcoat, trying not to think about the sum of three and two.

He waited on the pavement as the carriage clattered away to whatever dark and neglected part of the city the driver kept it in. Cadman would really rather not know. The man, or whatever he was, had given his services in return for treatment for a cat. It must have been over fifty years ago when he'd entered the surgery, dressed from top to toe in black. He'd not spoken a word, merely held out the stinking mog and ignored Cadman's protestations that he was not a vet.

The animal had been dead for weeks by the look of it, but the man seemed incapable of accepting the fact. He'd stood with his arms crossed, sullen eyes staring from beneath a battered top hat. Despairing of ever getting the man out of his surgery, Cadman had engaged in a little necromancy. He'd been in agony for weeks afterward, but the cat had moved and hissed, and the fellow had seemed quite pleased. He'd offered no money, and Cadman didn't press the point, but the next day, he'd arrived outside in the black carriage and had dutifully come whenever Cadman had called ever since.

Cadman paused in the hallway to make doubly sure it was safe, looked in on the surgery to check nothing had been tampered with, and then lumbered up the stairs to the attic, where he would attempt to summon the Dweller.

He still felt torn about which path to take—withdrawing and hoping the whole affair died down, or pressing on in the acceptance that things had already gone too far.

He very much wanted to hide away, but the new voice in his mind was growing more insistent, and had started to convince him that inaction at this stage would nevertheless still constitute action, and most likely a fatal one at that.

The other voice, the one that had guided him successfully all these years, reminded him he had no real idea what he was dealing with. The Dweller had radiated such malevolence and power, and in spite of its praise, he'd felt condescended to, as if all the forces he'd learned to manipulate barely broke the surface of an ocean of mystery.

His initial plan had been to use Gaston's knights, backed up by Callixus and the Lost; but Callixus had been spooked by the presence of Deacon Shader. And there was something unsettling about the ferocious dwarf who had taken up residence in the templum. Better to make certain, he told himself. The Dweller would most likely annihilate the lot of them, and then Cadman would use the power of Eingana to send it back to the Abyss. And if that attracted unwanted attention, then so be it. After all, what were they going to do, caw him to death?

Probably a damned sight worse, said the cautious voice, before he squashed it with a metaphorical boot and ground it underfoot.

Cadman's experience in the mantic arts initially came from Blightey's occult practices, but he'd later learnt to exploit the residue of magic left over from the Reckoning.

He'd long ago discovered that, since Huntsman's use of the Statue of Eingana, the Earth had been permeated by a web of enchantment that was connected to the Dreaming, and was infinitely malleable to those with the knowledge. It had been child's play to Blightey. He'd been typically smug about it; said he was already more than intimate with what he sneeringly referred to as the Dreaming.

Cadman, on the other hand, had dedicated years to the study of the phenomena that followed the Reckoning: the horrific creatures of nightmare that had sprung up all around the world, the blossoming of arcane powers within the most unlikely of people. He'd researched all the traditions of magic in an attempt to control this new force, but had little success. Ultimately, it was a moving of the heart that gave him the key; or rather a desperate insistence on his own survival. Somehow, inexplicably, he had reached out with single-minded ambition, perfectly focused by his dread of annihilation, and literally forced the enchantment to do his bidding.

The cost had been great. His body suffered terribly, the joints swelling, bones warping, festering pustules bursting forth all over his skin; but nevertheless, he had endured.

He'd come to the belief that these horrific side-effects were due to his abuse of magical currents that were never intended to serve such individualistic ends, and certainly not intended to steal the life force from others in a perverse quest for immortality.

Cadman's entire experience was in the art of necromancy, not the summoning of demons, but he recalled having read much about such conjurations in some of the grimoires he'd been made to study back in Verusia.

Better safe than sorry, his old inner voice reassured him as he began to draw a chalk circle upon the bare wooden floor of the attic.

He painstakingly inscribed sigils in scripts that were termed angelic, often with accompanying words in a long-forgotten language, and lit candles at each of the cardinal points. He traced out a triangle to the north, the so-called triangle of manifestation into which the Dweller was to appear, and placed a brass censer within, lighting the charcoal and dropping on a few grains of sandalwood.

Although the summoning was to be effected purely by the focus of his will, channeled through the amber pieces, Cadman chose to recite the Goetic words of invocation Blightey had beaten into him, just in case they increased his control of the demon.

The air in the attic was thick with candle smoke and incense as he finally settled down within the circle, fang in one hand, eye in the other, and began to incant the barbarous names.

It was a shock how quickly his spirit made contact with the demon, which waited, just as it said it would.

The amber pieces blazed, growing hot to the touch, and suddenly, before he was ready, there was another presence in the room. Not just in the room, but within the circle.

Cadman opened his eyes and barely suppressed a gasp of horror. The Dweller had clearly not complied with the requirement that it manifest in the triangle, and now sat cross-legged only a few feet from him, a sleek miniature humanoid, perhaps three feet tall, its ebon skin glistening and rippling in the candlelight; cold eyes of gray fixing him with their malevolence.

"So glad you called," the demon said, slug-like tongue running across thorny teeth. It inclined its head to one side and touched the tips of its elongated fingers together.

"You will do my bidding?" Cadman asked.

"If we have a contract. One soul is all I ask."

"Good. Then you will eradicate all life within the Templum of the Knot and bring me the piece of the statue they are hiding. For your payment, take the soul of the one you find it on."

"I fully intend to." The demon's jaw opened impossibly wide, granting Cadman a view of a black throat lined with spikes. "But do understand, if I cannot take that soul, you must provide me with one bound to it in love; otherwise, I'll be feasting on yours."

That wouldn't be a very substantial meal.

Cadman's jowl wobbled, and he was surprised to find that his illusory body was sweating.

"Agreed."

He groaned inwardly as he made the pact, feeling his fate open up before him like a bottomless pit.

The glistening black figure began to grow and metamorphose, its fingers stretching into sinuous, writhing tentacles, its torso bubbling into a great churning mass, from which innumerable misshapen faces leered and gibbered.

The Dweller seethed and undulated, its form never static, heads, arms, claws sprouting from its amorphous body, bursting and reforming, bursting and reforming.

Cadman stood and moved to one side as the horror roiled past him and slithered down the stairs, its grotesque form swelling until, at last glance, it was twice the height of a man and just as wide.

Cadman held the eye and the fang tightly before thrusting them back into the pockets of his waistcoat.

It was done.

There was no going back now.

He'd played his hand and would have to wait and see what fate had in store for him.

A fist of ice closed about the shreds of his heart, causing him to bend double and clutch his chest. His fingers were bare bones, rapping against the ribs protruding from his tattered robes. He let out a rattling breath, the jaws of his skull clacking uncontrollably.

He took out the amber pieces and was about to draw upon their power to restore his flesh, but something told him not to. Not a voice this time, just a feeling deep in his bones, where the marrow had once been.

Too many risks, Cadman, said his old familiar voice.

Maybe, said the other, *but the alternative is to hunt for food, and you're hardly in a fit state.*

"Just a little then," Cadman said to himself, pocketing the fang and accessing the power of the eye—just enough to restore his corpulence.

He tilted his head and waited.

Nothing.

Not the slightest indication that anyone had noticed.

He tucked the eye away and trudged downstairs to his bedroom for a well-deserved nap. No sooner had the door closed behind him, than it struck him like a bolt of lightning: a single, solitary squawk that seemed to come from beyond the stars.

"Fiddlesticks!" Cadman said, opening the door and making his way down to the living room.

No chance of a nap now. Nothing for it but to endure another chapter of Alphonse bloody LaRoche, while swilling a humongous dose of totally ineffectual brandy.

He'd barely picked up the book and located the bottle, when he felt something tugging at the back of his mind. He approached the window, half-expecting the Dweller to come crashing through the glass at any moment, telling him it had already failed, telling him it needed his soul in payment.

He drew back the curtains a crack and dimly saw the shadowy figure of his driver standing on the roadside, waiting, so it seemed. Waiting for his passenger.

With a sigh, Cadman slung LaRoche across the room, knocked back the brandy, and headed to the front door.

Whatever had possessed him to make him think he could sleep this night? Whatever had made him think he could relax enough even to read?

Apparently, the driver knew him better than he knew himself.

There was nothing for it, then, Cadman thought. Nothing for it but to go see for himself what happened when the Dweller arrived at the templum.

THE COMING TERROR

Templum of the Knot, Sarum

They've got the bard!"

It was Hugues' voice.

Shader instinctively drew the gladius and joined him at the window, straining to see in the silvery moonlight. Gaston looked up, the ghost of a sneer crossing his face before he lowered his eyes to his boots. Maldark stood, hammer at the ready, apparently awaiting Shader's lead.

"Coming?" Shader asked as he strode to the doors and began to unbolt them.

"You can't go out there," Gaston said, rising from his pew.

"He's right," Cadris piped. "You're putting us all in danger. Mater?"

Ioana suddenly looked like the strength had leaked out of her. She blinked rapidly, holding a shaky hand up in front of Cadris, one finger raised and wagging slightly. She opened her mouth to say something, but it was another voice that spoke.

"Help him." All eyes turned toward the sacristy where Rhiannon stood clutching her arms across her chest, an expression like a mortal wound on her face. "Please, Deacon. Help him."

Shader watched her over his shoulder as he and Maldark took hold of a door handle each. Rhiannon gave him the slightest of nods, a hollow gesture that may have been gratitude.

Shader threw back his door and stepped outside with Maldark close behind. The knights of the White Order were stunned into inaction and Shader took full advantage, striding straight toward them and throwing his voice with authority. "Release the bard. Now!"

The knights turned to each other, lost in indecision. Shader knew he had them, knew if he pressed home his advantage…

Justin Salace rode forward, face twisted with rage. "You have no right—"

He never finished the sentence. Shader leapt at him and dragged him squealing from the saddle. Justin flailed about with his arms and legs but Shader cracked his head brutally against the stone of the driveway until he stopped moving. Shader stood and immediately pushed his way in amongst the mounted knights, none of whom moved to stop him. Maldark shadowed him, glowering malevolently. Shader could just see Elias's motley-clad form draped over the saddle of a horse passing round a bend in the Domus Tyalae. There was something about the horse… An old familiar terror washed over him, and his chest began to tighten. Breaking through the ring of the White Order, he started to give chase, but stopped. A new force emerged from the darkness beneath the trees to block his path.

"Nous!" he cursed, the blood freezing in his veins. "The Lost."

Scores of armored knights on fleshless horses spilled across the road. The riders wore corroded armor beneath the faded tatters of Nousian surcoats, their shields jagged-edged and corroded, their swords brown with age. A shadowy wraith drifted to their fore, its spectral form garbed similarly in full armor and a white surcoat, ghastly red eyes burning through the slit of its visor.

"Callixus."

The wraith grew a fraction more substantial. "Shader."

The knights of the White Order had regained their composure, a group of about twenty moving in behind Maldark and Shader to cut off any retreat. The others maintained their cordon around the templum. Shader glanced back toward the open doors from where Ioana watched, her face impassive.

Callixus followed his gaze. "Priestess," he hissed. "We are coming."

Shader took a step toward him, but Callixus instantly vanished in a wisp of black smoke. The skeletal steeds before Shader stamped and scraped their hooves, snorted soot and flame. The death-knights sitting astride them lifted their visors as one, jaws clacking in a macabre semblance of laughter. Shader stiffened, and would have panicked had it not been for a surge of warmth from the gladius. He drew his longsword and stood doubly armed before the assembled host. Maldark swung his hammer in a wide arc that drove back the White Order. "'Tis too late for the bard," he bellowed. "We must get back inside!"

"You go first," Shader said. "I'll be right behind."

"Aye," Maldark growled. "Let's get to it." He crunched his hammer into the head of a horse that got too close.

Shader lost sight of him as the dwarf barged his way into the throng, bashing left and right and bellowing at the top of his voice, "For God, for Aethir, for Arnoch!"

And then the Lost charged, shrieking a deathly battle cry. Shader moved to intercept the first knight, who slashed down at him with a rusty broadsword. He sidestepped with ease and decapitated the cadaver with a fierce backslash. The head spun to the ground and glared up at him, teeth still chattering. The skeletal horse twisted its neck and tried to bite him, its headless rider thrashing about blindly with the sword. Shoulder-charging the steed, Shader knocked it to the ground. Bones splintered, ligaments snapped, but both horse and rider continued to drag themselves toward him.

Shader danced away from the sluggish attacks of four more knights before weaving in among them, hacking this way and that with both blades.

He put down one after another, but the fallen still came at him, a grisly cluster of reaching and grasping limbs, scratching and clattering about the cobbled drive.

The undead continued to press forward, their movements slow, their attacks easy to counter, but sheer weight of numbers threatened to overwhelm him. He tried to back away in the direction of the templum, but tripped on something that proceeded to scurry up his leg. He brushed off the severed hand with the flat of the gladius and barely managed to parry a blow aimed at his head, a rusty blade shattering against his longsword.

Callixus materialized three ranks back, red eyes blazing, black sword pointing at Shader and urging the horde forward like a tidal wave. Unnatural winds fanned the death-knights' cloaks and added an eerie howl to the clash of steel.

Shader was beginning to slow, his footing growing unsteady. With a flurry of desperate blows, he broke through the line of the Lost and staggered toward Maldark and Rhiannon. As the three formed a defensive circle, Shader managed one brief, appalled glance at Rhiannon before blocking a strike from a rusty sword that disintegrated and showered them with iron.

"Too many," Rhiannon gasped. "And what the shog are they?"

Before Shader could answer, all three came under a concerted assault from front and back, and Shader was sent hurtling into Rhiannon by a fierce blow from a mace. He struggled to rise, but felt an agonizing pain in his chest. A rib or two had been crushed. Rhiannon wrenched him to his feet and turned back to deflect a saber aimed at her head. Shader caught a slash with the longsword, wincing as pain jolted along his arm. He cut the attacker down with the gladius, thinking he recognized the face, dropped the longsword and let his arm hang limp.

Rhiannon sagged against him, blood gushing from a shoulder wound. A horse reared to her left and then bore down upon her, a White Knight swinging his saber above his head. Shader tugged her out of the way and braced himself for the killing blow, but the knight twisted in agony as a sword lanced through his ribs. Behind him, Barek Thomas pulled his blade free, and spurred his gray gelding back amongst the White Order knights.

Rhiannon slipped in a pool of her own blood and Shader caught her, no longer caring about his own defense. Maldark fought on furiously, but was so closely surrounded by death-knights that he could barely swing his hammer. The end was very close.

And then Ioana was amongst them, holding aloft the wooden Monas that stood behind the altar, a look of absolute compassion and love on her face that seemed disarmingly incongruous. The knights of the White Order did not move against her; indeed, it seemed they had parted to let her through. The undead shrieked and hissed, but came no closer. Callixus floated to their fore, his eyes a molten fury, but even he didn't approach.

Barek rode back to the head of the White Order, and it was then that Shader realized he had somehow taken command during the fight and had allowed Ioana through. Not only that, but he had saved Rhiannon—saved Shader—at the expense of one of his own men.

"Into the templum," Ioana commanded.

Shader picked up his longsword and followed Rhiannon and Maldark back toward the entrance. Ioana brought up the rear, the death-knights keeping their distance from the Monas. Shader nodded to Barek as he passed, but the lad didn't seem able to meet his gaze as he ordered his remaining men to dismount. Ioana held back the undead long enough for the surviving White Knights to make their way into the templum, leaving their horses abandoned outside.

Agna set about staunching the bleeding from Rhiannon's shoulder, whilst Velda fussed over the worst of Maldark's many wounds. Shader lay heavily on the ground, wincing at the pain in his ribs. His fingers curled tightly around the statue in his pocket and he accepted its power without thinking. Suddenly his body was infused with blissful warmth and he sat up refreshed and painless. Cadris looked at him in amazement. Gaston raised an eyebrow then went to retrieve his sword from the floor beside Rhiannon.

A crow cawed from somewhere in the distance, or maybe Shader was imagining it. He shook his head and climbed to his feet, returning both swords to their scabbards.

The knights of the White Order crowded inside and looked about in bewilderment. Barek raised his arms for silence and tried to reassert some sort of discipline.

Ioana paused in the doorway to cast one last glance over the hellish cavalry milling around the porch. She backed into the templum, but as she did so she seemed to glimpse something behind the mass of undead. She slammed the doors and pressed herself against them, fighting for breath.

"Mater?" Shader took her hands and led her from the door as Maldark slid the bolts across.

Ioana merely waved toward the rear of the templum. Her fear was contagious, and soon everyone was edging back into the nave. Barek ordered some of the knights to help move the sick to the sacristy, whilst Gaston simply glowered at him. Shader took the statue from his pocket, determined to use its power on Rhiannon and Maldark, when suddenly a dreadful chill pervaded the templum and the doors began to warp and buckle.

THE DWELLER

Templum of the Knot, Sarum

Shadrak was lucky to be alive, he supposed, but at what cost?

According to his mental map, it should be just past the next intersection. He scanned the silver ceiling with its blue lights and found the symbols he was looking for. Running the palm of his hand over a section of the left wall, he was greeted by a sharp hiss. A panel slid open to reveal metal rungs set back a couple of feet behind the wall.

He hurried up the ladder and crawled into a crumbling and foul smelling tunnel that was lit only by moldy phosphorescence. There was a ledge a few feet above him, cold air spilling down and giving him pause. He became aware of the blood rushing in his ears, the rapid pounding in his ribcage. He flicked his eyes in every direction and held his breath as he listened.

Nothing.

As he reached for a handhold, Shadrak's arm trembled. His knees went slack and he felt the urge to turn about and run.

"I am Shadrak the Unseen," he whispered. "Killer, hunter, the knife in the dark."

He gripped a jutting rock and jabbed a foot into an indent, pulling himself upwards until he hung from the ledge. Swinging one leg over the edge, he rolled onto a flagstone floor.

There was an iron grill set into the low ceiling. Reaching up, Shadrak tugged until it came away in his hands and he dropped it clanging to the floor. He sprang, catching hold of the sides of the opening and pulling himself through.

If he was right, he should be in the crypt beneath the sanctuary.

From somewhere up above he heard a great chorus of screams and began to shake once more. He shut his eyes, fighting for calm. Was he losing it? He'd never felt anything like this before. He was like a child frightened of the dark. And so he did what he'd have done as a boy: focused on the one face that had brought him comfort, the one person he could always turn to.

Kadee's eyes gleamed their warmth from the brown skin of her face. Her gray hair was braided with strips of leather and sparkling quartz. Her mouth was moving silently and he strained to hear her speak, knowing all the while she'd never utter another word.

Shadrak's eyes opened and he gritted his teeth.

"Anger, not tears," he told himself, pulling up his hood and sprinting for the stone steps that led to a trap in the ceiling.

***

The doors lasted longer than Shader expected. The wood blistered and cracked, the frame smoldered, and the bolts screeched in protest.

Barek's lads dragged the pallet-beds with the patients still lying on them to the sanctuary and set up a protective ring around them. There can't have been many more than thirty knights left. Ioana forced a smile for their benefit, and Gaston approached them, head down, sword trailing behind, scraping the floor. Barek clapped him on the shoulder and made room for him.

The priests huddled in front of the altar, a few paces behind the knights. Shader and Maldark stood shoulder to shoulder halfway down the nave, eyes riveted to the straining and groaning doors. The surrounding wall shuddered and the doors buckled further, the wood warping to an alarming degree. Thin black tendrils slid beneath and around the sides of the frame, feeling their way to the center where they began to knot and intertwine. Within moments the doors were completely obscured by the writhing feelers, which suddenly tensed and then sagged as the doors finally gave way. The tendrils relaxed their hold, allowing the shards of the doors to clatter to the ground, and there in the doorway roiled a seething formless horror. Heads sprouted forth from a central mass of gelatinous blackness, eyes rolling, teeth grinding until they burst and reformed as legs, arms, or thick lengths of tentacle dripping with slime.

The abomination's bulk filled the entrance and radiated such terror that Shader's body sought to run, or collapse, until the warmth of the statue flowed once more and gave him the strength to stand firm. Maldark, likewise, withstood the fear that emanated from the beast and hefted his war-hammer with a look upon his face that was something between repulsion and anger.

Behind them, the cordon of knights turned away in panic. The priests scattered and sought the nearest exit. Even the plague victims upon their beds started to drag themselves toward the sacristy and the link corridor to the residences in order to get as far from the aberration as possible.

The creature roared—a loathsome gurgling susurration that immediately halted all activity as the priests, knights, and the sick screamed in absolute horror.

Shader's arms and legs were trembling as he fumbled with the gladius. The blade left its scabbard, bursting with golden fire that suffused throughout the templum. Strength and courage such as he had never known flooded his body.

The monster lurched forward and those still in the sanctuary fought and screamed in their desperation to get away. Shader put his free hand on Maldark's shoulder. The dwarf was shaking violently.

"Get the others out. I'll hold it here."

"'Tis the Dweller," Maldark said, his face ashen. "There is nothing thou canst do."

"I can give you time. Now go!"

Shader risked a look over his shoulder as Maldark backed away toward the sanctuary. Ioana was ushering the others into the link corridor when the flagstone behind the altar shifted and a head appeared from the crypt beneath. Shader caught a glimpse of a pallid face and pinkish eyes before a small man in a black cloak clambered up.

"Quickly," the albino shouted.

As fast as they could, the priests and knights began to lower the sick to the relative safety of the crypt. Gaston was staring at the newcomer, sword shaking and suddenly looking too heavy for him.

The Dweller roared again and surged forward.

"Deacon!" Rhiannon screamed, as the bubbling black mass bore down upon him.

"Get out!" Shader shot her a despairing look. "Everybody get out!"

The Dweller belched and emitted a noxious vapor that almost overpowered him. He lashed out with the gladius and an arc of fire followed the blade, searing into vile black flesh. The Dweller hissed and belched again, and this time Shader was blinded by a cloud of soot. Instinctively he clutched at the statue in his pocket and accepted its power. The blindness passed, but even as it did he was ensnared by countless tentacles that squeezed cruelly about his legs and torso, cutting into the flesh with serrated edges. As he hacked at the sinuous limbs, the gladius slicing and burning, Shader craned his neck and saw that the evacuation was almost complete. Only Ioana, Rhiannon, Maldark, and, surprisingly, Gaston remained.

Maldark took a step forward.

"Flee!" Shader bellowed as he cut his way free of the tentacles and leapt at the central mass hacking and slashing, a pattern of flame left in the wake of his sword. No matter how many times he cut and burned the demon, its oily flesh simply reformed. He drew the longsword and redoubled his efforts, but the mundane steel merely rebounded from the Dweller's hide. This was a fight Shader knew he couldn't win. All he could do was delay the inevitable.

Gaston ran toward him, eyes wide with fear, sword arm trembling. Maldark caught hold of Gaston's arm and spun him in the direction of the crypt, but not before Shader glimpsed the tears spilling down his face.

More tentacles fastened around Shader's boots and tugged him toward a cavernous maw. The gladius sliced through black flesh, affording Shader enough time to glance over his shoulder to see Maldark climbing down to the crypt, herding the others before him.

Shader launched a frantic attack in the hope of wounding the demon enough for him to make his own escape whilst it reformed. He hewed great gouges into the ever changing form and jumped backwards, batting aside a lashing tentacle with his longsword. He was about to turn and run when there was a sudden numbing sensation in his back. He stood motionless for a moment, blinking with shock, and then dropped to his knees as the Dweller surged over him.

***

Cadman watched Shadrak pull his stiletto from Shader's back and slip behind the altar as the demon smothered the fallen knight.

Backstabbing little runt. That could have been me. Could have been me. Could have been... Oh my giddy—

The Dweller exploded in a flash of amber and gold. The blast roared toward the shattered doors, smashing Cadman from his feet. Shreds of shadow shot past his face amidst a terrible screeching.

Callixus!

A black cloud descended over Cadman's eyes. He tried to fan it away, but his hands wouldn't move; suddenly felt he needed to breathe, but couldn't. *One, two, three. Oh cripes. Oh cripes, no!* The dark fog was inside his skull, eating away at what was left of his brain, rolling down to consume his innards. *Oblivion! Not me! Not meee!*

Cadman sat bolt upright. Someone was screaming. Someone was... *Oh, it's me.* He shook the fug from his head and tried to orientate himself. Misty black ribbons swirled beside him, coalescing into Callixus. Cadman followed the burning glare of the wraith's eyes, saw movement in the templum as the smoke began to clear.

Shadrak crept back to Shader's body, bent over the face as if listening for breath, then felt around the throat.

Probably as skilled at detecting death as I am.

Callixus drifted past Cadman's shoulder, heading down the nave. Shadrak glanced up, then hurriedly rummaged through Shader's pockets. He pulled out something dark and sinuous. Cadman squinted. That had to be the statue, the body of Eingana. It was still smoking, throwing off sparks of amber. Callixus drew his black blade, raised it to swing, but Shadrak managed to thrust the statue into a pouch and throw himself into a twisting backflip in one fluid motion. As Callixus struck air, the assassin darted behind the altar and seemed to be swallowed up by the ground.

Callixus started back down the aisle, eyes like twin red suns.

"No, you idiot!" Cadman's toes clattered on stone as he stormed toward him. Bloody illusion had gone again, and with it every last scrap of security. "The statue! Get the sodding statue!"

The wraith sped back to the altar and dispersed through the floor.

Cadman sagged and nearly fell. He lacked the strength to resume his fatness. Lacked the strength to go on. *What have you done, you stupid, stupid fool? Keep to the shadows, didn't I always say? Never do anything rash. Just lie low and endure.* But now someone else had the power of Eingana, and goodness only knew what that meant.

Cadman dragged himself as far as Shader's body, which was lying in a steadily growing pool of blood. He almost felt sorry for the knight. You had to admit, his final stand had been somewhat valiant. But what chance had he had against the Dweller, not to mention a knife in the back? *Comes to us all, in time.*

Cadman knelt down on creaking joints and closed Shader's eyes; didn't think he could stand back up again. Something glinted, and he felt the distinct thrum of power. It was coming from Shader's gladius. He reached for the hilt, but a jolt of pain shot up his arm.

Blasted thing zapped me!

He scowled at the sword, and he was sure it would have done the same to him, if it had eyes. Something about it made him feel extremely uncomfortable. Dirty, even.

He crawled away from it on his hands and knees, but stopped as he felt a different sensation.

Heat radiated from the pocket of his tattered robe, burning away the frost in his bones. Well, it couldn't hurt, could it? If Eingana wanted to help him in his weakness, who was he to refuse? Just a quick dribble of power and he'd be right as—

He started at a squawk and slipped in a patch of blood, landing on his bony arse. He looked every which way, heart slapping crazily at his ribcage like there was no tomorrow.

Nothing. There was nothing there.

"Caw."

There it was again, only this time closer, more urgent. He could almost feel something breathing down the back of his neck. The ice in Cadman's bones chilled a few hundred degrees, sent its necrotic fingers around his heart. The walls of the templum closed in around him, the roof starting to drop like the lid of a tomb.

Breathe, you silly old sod. Breathe.

Suddenly the emptiness of the Void was looking like an old friend in comparison to the mess he'd got himself into. Well, maybe that was overstating it. He winced at the tightening in his stomach—psychosomatic of course, like the ghosting the amputees had reported to him back on the front. Back when... Back...

Too many chances, blast it. Too many actions. *Didn't I always say it would come to this? In for a penny, in for a pound, then. Too late to back out now.*

His fingers closed around the amber pieces, absorbing their warmth, accepting their comfort. So what if some antediluvian bird cawed every time he used their power. It wasn't as if anything bad had happened. Just needed to act fast, that's what. Decide what to do with all that power and do it quick, before there were consequences.

The pieces throbbed in his hands, sent stabs of heat into his brain.

"Show me." Cadman pressed the eye and the fang together, amber radiating from their contact like a miniature sun. "Show me what to do!"

Blistering flames filled his skull, burning away the fog and indecision. Clear as day, he saw it all laid out in front of him. The Dweller oozing malice, returning to claim its due. A blast of amber so powerful it seemed to burn the world. A face so bloodless it could have been made of wax. The most unnatural eyes of electric blue locked onto him, scrutinizing him as if from the other end of a microscope. Banks of screens flickering between images, row upon row of bat-winged demons staring at them with sightless eyes. Something dark dropping from the sky—a monstrous black spider, legs curling around him. No, not legs, they were fingers. Not a spider, then. A hand, gripping, squeezing, crushing.

"What have I done?" Cadman sent the eye and the fang clattering to the floor. "What have I done?"

Too late, old boy. Far too late.

The amber glow cast long shadows about the templum and momentarily lit up Shader's dead face, formed a halo around his head like the Ancients' paintings of the Luminaries, or whatever they'd been called back then.

And then Shader was lost to the dark as Eingana's light faded and died. For the briefest of moments, Cadman was back in his cot, tiny hands grasping through the bars, tears streaming down his cheeks. "No, Mama. Please! Don't turn out the light!"

He picked up the amber pieces and shoved them deep in his pockets, turned and headed back outside like a diver striking for the surface.

In for a penny—

Shut up!

In for a—

"I said shut..." Cadman took a deep breath and finished in a whisper. "Shut up."

Outside, the knights of the Lost waited for him like his faithful children. Only they weren't. They hated him, just as much as Callixus hated him. Couldn't say he blamed them, either.

As he walked toward them they parted, revealing his black carriage at the end of the Domus Tyalae, the driver standing with the door open, chimney-stack hat held to his chest. He'd never done that before, and it quite put the frighteners on Cadman. He stepped inside and the driver shut the door behind him. For one very nasty moment, Cadman had the distinct feeling he was being taken to his own funeral.

As the carriage clattered away, he put his head out of the window. The driver's back was silhouetted against the silvery moon, creating the impression he was frozen in ice, like the Demiurgos at the heart of the Abyss.

He must have sensed Cadman watching, and twisted in the seat to look over his shoulder. Crimson flame flickered from his eyes and he began to chuckle. He turned back to face the road ahead, and the chuckle bubbled up into a full and throaty laugh.

The story continues in

Shader book 2:

Best Laid Plans

D.P. PRIOR

"Gritty and thought-provoking,
Shader is an absolute
triumph of fantasy."
(Journal of Always)

BOOK TWO

SHADER

BEST LAID PLANS

SHADER

BOOK TWO
BEST LAID PLANS
D.P. PRIOR

Third Edition, 2013

ACKNOWLEDGEMENTS

I'D LIKE TO thank my editor, Harry Dewulf for the excellent comments about language and his attention to the minutiae.

Paula Kautt has been invaluable for her suggestions, demanding clarification and pointing out inconsistencies, and also for proofreading the story.

I'm extremely grateful to Valmore Daniels for a crucial re-edit after the text was changed to US English, and for formatting, and cover design.

Theo Prior, as always, has been my sounding board and has listened patiently to each successive revision read aloud. He also provided the inspiration for a number of new characters and plot developments on those long walks to the comic store in Naperville. If that's not enough, he also produced the map of Sahul—which is no mean feat at nine years of age.

Thanks are also due to Mike Nash for the iconic image of Shader on the cover, and for the map of *The Nousian Theocracy*.

Finally thanks must go to the people who read my stuff and take the time to feedback: John Jarrold, for his comments on the original story, Tony Prior, Ian Prior, David Dalglish, C.S. Marks, Moses Siregar III, Ray Nicholson, Dallas Dredske, and M.R. Mathias.

Norga

Sarmatia

Verusia

Britannia

Gallia   Graecia
Latia
Quilonia

Ashanta

Numosia

Make

The Anglish Isles

Sahul

Rujala

The Nousian

According to the terms of Aeternam A

The Great West

Nazca

war

New Ithaka

Theocracy

Agreement: Year of the Reckoning 24

W   E

S

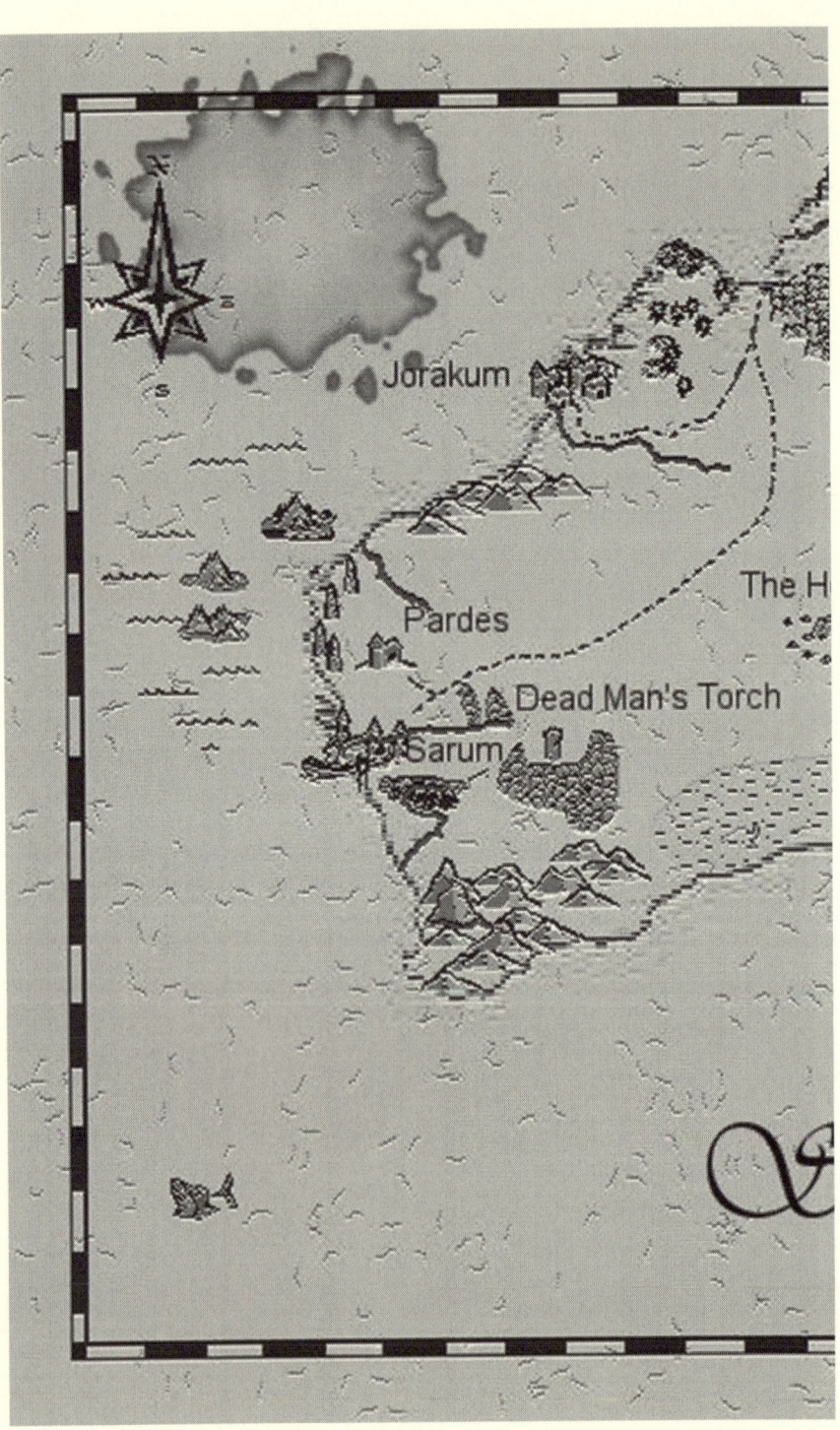

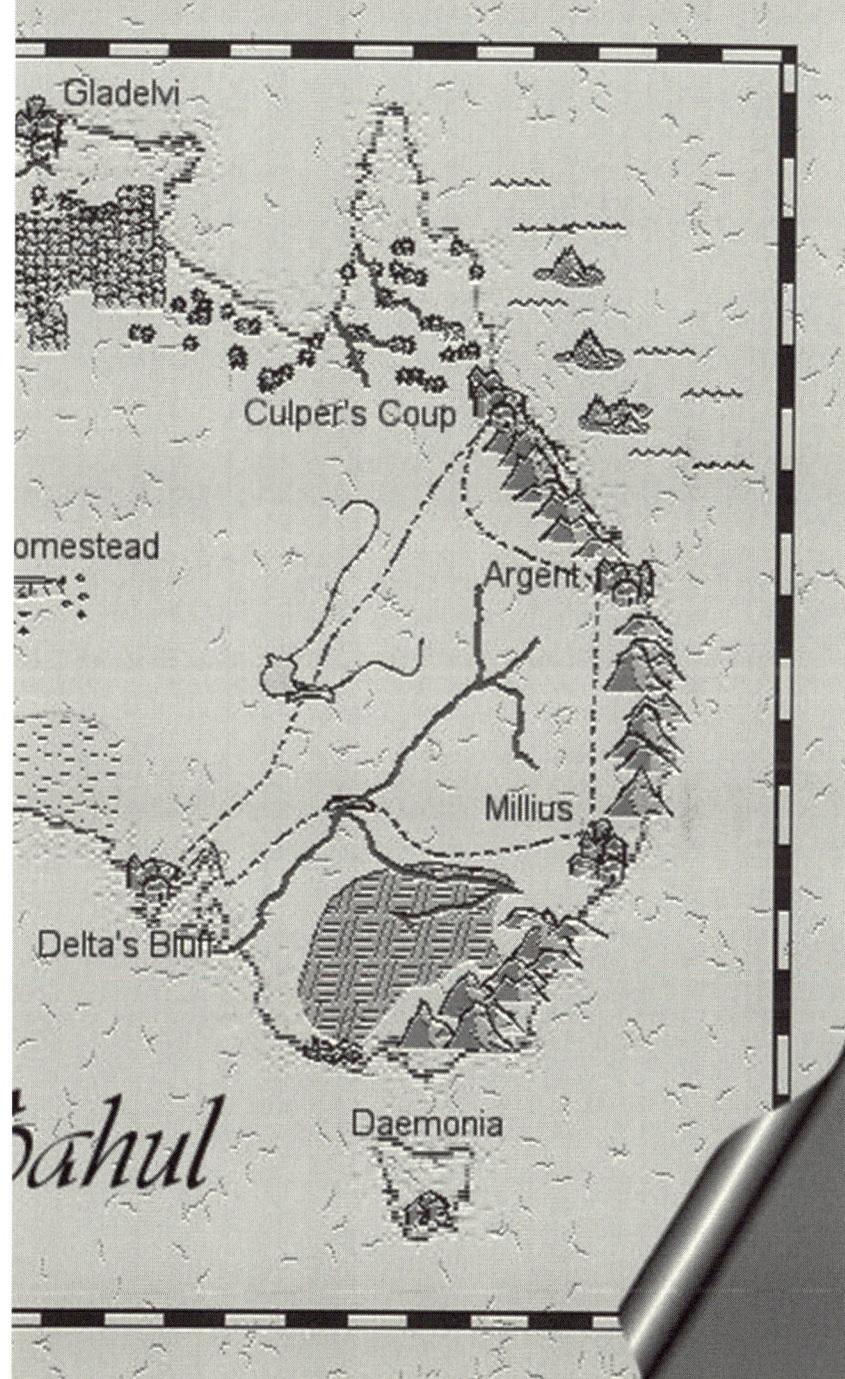

OCEAN'S EYE

MALDARK HELD FIRM to the mast of his boat, eyes narrowed against the spray and the squall. The yawl reared and plunged, wind punching the sail. A fierce gust whipped hair in his face, the boat lurching as wave after wave broke across the bow. There was a moment's calm, a gentle bobbing, and then stillness.

He held his breath, eyes fixed to the reflections of the twin suns rippling on the surface.

Mouthing a prayer, he wrung the moisture from his beard, tasted its saltiness. He flopped onto the bench, ran cold fingers through limp hair, and listened.

Nothing. He was almost disappointed.

Lying back, he stared up at the bloated clouds, blood pounding in his ears. He started to hum the tune always gnawing at the back of his mind: the lament of his fellow dwarves in the Abyss. A lament or an accusation, for had he not betrayed them, along with the hybrids and all the races of Aethir?

The oaken hull began to creak, quietly at first, and then with increasing strain. There was a scrape and a crash as his war-hammer slid across the deck to lodge beneath a bench. His hand snaked out catching his helmet by a horn as it rattled in pursuit. Jamming it on his head, Maldark scurried around the ship looking over the side. The keel was warping and buckling under tremendous force, the sea sucking greedily as violent eddies and swirls formed up ahead.

There was a sudden blast of wind, the ship heaving dangerously as it was wrenched against the swell. Ocean walls rose on either side, a frothing corridor of roaring water. Maldark clung to the mast as the boat sped along the channel toward a spinning black maelstrom.

"Lord?" he cried, eyes riveted to the whirling darkness up ahead. "Is it finally Thee?"

He prayed that it was; prayed for an end to the years of drifting on the seas, seeking atonement, but knowing there was none; hoping for a way to make things right, to put an end to Sektis Gandaw—still untouchable in his black mountain, still warping the creatures of Aethir and dreaming of the unweaving of all creation. How could Maldark have believed his lies?

The skin of his face was stretched taut, his back crushed against the mast. Shutting his eyes and fixing his mind on God's hallowed name, Maldark shrieked a plea for forgiveness as the ship fell into the dark and merciless eye of the vortex.

Oblivion did not come.

The bobbing of the boat told him that. His eyes opened upon mist rising from a slick black river that bubbled through a gorge of steaming rock.

Gehenna, he realized. The underworld connecting Aethir to the Abyss. He'd been here once before, when he'd removed the black axe, *Pax Nanorum*, from the world above lest his people fell for the deception. Power is the bait used by the Demiurgos, he'd explained at the time, and most of the dwarves had accepted his wisdom. Most, but not all. The safest solution had been to send it back from whence it came. But its curse had stayed with him, in spite of the precautions he'd taken, the briefness of the contact. He'd not aged a day since, and now he'd forgotten just how old he was. Impossibly old—even for a dwarf.

Vast stalactites dripped from the ceiling like an inverted forest, globs of oily liquid clinging to their tips, heavy and threatening to drop like poison from one of Sektis Gandaw's pipettes. Poison that altered rather than killed, forcing life along predetermined routes, twisting, changing. Metamorphosis, Gandaw had called it. Forced evolution. The terms had meant little to Maldark, but the effects of the process had been clear. New creatures, dark creatures; creatures molded to suit every purpose of their creator. Creatures to be discarded like soiled rags once their usefulness was at an end. Creatures like Maldark and the rest of his deluded race.

Muffled cries penetrated the fog, fading from the walls of the gorge and falling upon the oozing stream with the silence of death. Sulfurous fumes burned his nostrils, made him hack and rattle deep in his chest.

The boat was snatched by an invisible current and lurched toward the middle of the river. Maldark straightened the prow with the merest of thoughts, steering a course toward the cries. Funny how so natural an action could still make him think of the dwarves who'd made the boat, who'd made so many of the wonders of Aethir. His heart was heavy with the thought that he'd never see them again. He didn't deserve to.

A pitiful wail came from the shore, sending ice through his veins. The gloom was darker further back along the bank: empty spaces or shadows roiling in the mist, whispering to him, beseeching him, accusing him. One stocky wraith detached itself from the throng and drifted out over the black flow. Maldark's breath caught in his throat, and his heart thumped against his chest. He knew what it was even before the face emerged from the smog: a face etched with pain, eyes like the Void, and a beard matted with blood.

Maldark opened his arms, the tremors in his legs threatening to pitch him over the side. The dwarf came to his embrace, the chill of its touch driving all warmth from him. It was a communion of death, a condemnation, and a plea all in one. The air about the wraith shimmered, its eyes turning from black to gray, its beard transfigured into the white of virgin wool. It passed through the mast, wafting silently down the river and fading from view.

The boat continued on its way, going wherever the black river would take it. Maldark's ears were full of the calls of the dead walking over the acrid surface toward him. Arms wide like a father's for a child, he bade them come.

***

If time passed, he did not know how much, but he was sure he'd crossed over into the Abyss. It only seemed right. Perhaps God had finally given him what he deserved.

The boat drifted past scenes of fire and blood, and grotesque figures groaned or screamed from the banks. He lost count of how many wraiths he embraced—the ghosts of the dwarves he had led to their doom. Their pain seemed more pitiable the further he traveled, the deeper he went into the realm of the Demiurgos. Did his touch truly help them, free them from this hellish limbo, or had he been deceived?

They ceased to come as the gorge forked, the left-hand stream frothing with black foam as it coursed downwards into the dark. The waters to the right rushed toward a whirlpool shimmering with greenish light. With only an instant to make his choice, Maldark willed the rudder to take him to the right. He held onto the mast as the boat was caught in the maelstrom's grip and sent into a dizzying spiral. He shut his eyes and fought back the urge to vomit. There was a brief surge of pressure, a loud pop, and a blast of warm air.

The watery portal spat forth the little ship, spluttered momentarily, and then retracted through an infinitesimal point. The boat landed heavily on stone and Maldark was jolted against the mast.

The first thing he noticed was the color of the sky: gone was the familiar cobalt of Aethir to be replaced by a hazy azure, cloudless and shimmering with the intensity of a single alien sun. Maldark surveyed the damage to the keel and saw that it was minimal. Peering over the stern he looked upon this new and arid land from a great and vertiginous height. The horizon stretched out to infinity, the intervening terrain a ruddy desert spotted here and there with hardy shrubs and the occasional jutting monolith. The boat had come to rest atop a sprawling tabletop mountain.

Grabbing his war-hammer and clambering over the side of the ship, Maldark alighted on hard reddish rock and let his eyes run across its surface. A hundred yards to his right something glinted in the sun. He set off toward the light and saw that it came from a small crevice in the summit. Reaching into the gap, he pulled forth a slender shard of glowing amber, half an inch long, one end curving slightly toward a vicious point.

Maldark could hear the blood pumping in his ears. Recognition filled him with elation and dread. What was a piece of the Statue of Eingana doing here? A fang? Why had the statue been sundered? What trick of fate had merged his destiny with that of the supernal being he had betrayed?

Something about the fang's radiance spoke to him of distress. Empathically, the amber reached out and guided his next actions. Placing the shard upon the rocky surface, he raised the mighty war-hammer and brought it down with full force. There was a massive burst of light and a clap like thunder. Maldark was blasted from his feet, his hands clutching the hammer as if melted onto the haft. Rising shakily he looked to where the shard had been and saw only a blackened patch on the red rock. Raising the hammerhead to eye level, he saw that it exuded a soft amber glow for a few moments before fading back to gray.

How could one so unworthy be entrusted with so crucial an artifact? Was this some trick of the capricious Creator? Maldark looked up at the unfamiliar sun and wondered at the penance God had worked out for him now. Would he ever be rid of the stain of sin, of the atrocities he had committed? Never, he concluded, for how could one such as he ever be forgiven?

Gazing once more at the endless horizon, Maldark the Fallen resolved to pull the little ship by ropes across this vast and hostile landscape as if it were the physical counterpart of the sins that all the oceans of Aethir could never wash away.

A TRICKY VENGEANCE

908 Years Later

S HADRAK LEAPT THE last few steps and tumbled over the ledge clinging on by the tips of his fingers.

I know, I know, he told Kadee's face as it loomed in his mind and gave him a very disapproving look. *But what was I s'posed to do? My life or his, and that's a no-brainer, I reckon.* The poxy knight, Shader, was as dead as shog. Weren't no point fretting about it now. Sometimes Kadee's presence could be a right pain in the ass.

He felt an unnatural coldness blow over his fingers and tensed, ready to drop if necessary. After waiting a moment, he pulled his chin above the edge and risked a look. The wraith reached a dead end, pushed its hand through the wall and looked like it was going to disappear into the rock, but then it stopped, its great-helmed head swiveling, coal-fire eyes burning into Shadrak's. The spectral knight shot toward him like a sail catching the wind and Shadrak let go.

He landed with a clang on the metal floor of the Maze and reached for one of the glass globes in his pouch, but hands grabbed him from behind.

"Got you," said a blond-haired youth in an outfit similar to the one Shader had been wearing when Shadrak stabbed him. The lad had a strong grip on his arm.

A sandy-haired knight had a lock on his other wrist. Shadrak knew his face from that night at the Griffin when the bard had sung the tale of the Reckoning.

Careless, Shadrak. Very careless! But what could you expect in the situation?

A circle of armored youths sprang up around him, some of whom he also recognized from the Griffin. The blond one, though, hadn't been there. Shadrak was sure of that; but there was something familiar about his face.

"Don't I know you?" the sandy-haired knight said, his face creased with the effort of holding Shadrak still and wracking his brain for an answer to his own question. "You were in the pub when Elias performed his epic. What I want to know is…"

A shadow fell over the group as the wraith floated toward them.

The sandy-haired knight's eyes widened. "In the name of Nous!"

"Callixus," the blond one said. "Stay out of this. He's mine." He twisted Shadrak's arm behind his back and pressed his mouth close to his ear. "I know what you did, you stunted little bastard. And I have a little surprise for you. Remember the preach—"

"He has something that Dr. Cadman needs," hissed the wraith. "Give it to me and none of you will be harmed."

A grizzled warrior, not much taller than Shadrak, pushed through the cordon of knights, sparks crackling around the head of a war-hammer.

"Be gone, demon," the dwarf snarled, "or I'll give thee a taste of my hammer."

Callixus drew a black sword, the blade a shifting length of smoke as immaterial as his

220

body. As he drifted closer to the dwarf, Callixus and his sword grew more solid, the blade hardening into obsidian wreathed in black light. The dwarf raised his hammer to strike, but an old woman in a white robe stepped to his side. Her head was shaven, her face broad and stern. She held a small black book in her hands and proceeded to chant the words she read there.

"*Non timebo mala quoniam tu mecum es.*"

The wraith faltered and glanced at the book, the fire in his eyes dimming.

"Aeternam. It's been a long time since I heard it spoken."

The woman looked up from her reading. "It is still the language of the servants of Nous. His spirit can never be driven from you, brother, even in death. Go in peace. I will pray for you."

Callixus looked from her to Shadrak before ramming his sword back into its scabbard. "Mater, I have… I have done…"

"I know," the woman said. "It was you who attacked the Gray Abbot, wasn't it?"

The wraith lowered his head.

"And you led the forces that attacked the templum." The woman closed her book and studied the wraith with the sort of look Kadee would no doubt have given Shadrak, had she been alive: a look both sorrowful and compassionate. "You have been lost, brother, but Ain will find you. Don't despair. He will not forsake you. Now go to your master and tell him you found nothing down here. I know it's a lie, but Ain will forgive it."

Callixus wavered a moment more then rose into the air.

"I will do as you ask, Mater, but know this." He fixed Shadrak with a smoldering glare. "I will come for you, assassin. You are not as unseen as you like to think."

The wraith turned in midair and merged with the shadows.

The blond knight's grip slackened slightly. Shadrak glanced out of the corner of his eye. The lad was trembling. He looked up, hatred flaring from damp eyes, and at the same time Shadrak remembered where he'd seen the face before. Not the exact same face: the one he recalled was older, but the cheek bones, the chin and the nose, there was no mistaking where they'd come from.

"Like I was saying," the lad said through gritted teeth, "I've got a little surprise for you. I know who you are. Face like yours ain't exactly hard to spot." He released his grip so that he could draw his sword."

It was all Shadrak needed. He twisted his hips and spun round, crashing his fist into the sandy-haired knight's nose. The lad fell backward in a spray of blood. Shadrak barged through the ring of knights and sprinted down the tunnel, tripped and catapulted himself straight on top of a groaning, sweat-soaked woman lying on the floor. The corridor was littered with coughing and moaning people; there was no way past except by clambering over them. He glanced back and saw the knights with their swords drawn blocking his retreat. Up front, he could see a fat priest and three priestesses who'd been tending the sick. One of the women made a path for him, weaving in and out of the bodies on the floor. He recognized her from the Griffin, too—she'd been the drunkard who'd left early. Her black hair was tied back in a long ponytail, her face pale, the eyes set in dark circles. Blood stained her white robe around the shoulder, which was noticeably padded—no doubt bandaged over-zealously by an amateur.

"Stop him!" the blond lad yelled, pushing his way to the front of the knights.

The woman with the dark hair folded her arms across her chest and frowned at Shadrak. "Who the shog are you?"

An elderly priestess put a hand to her mouth, her eyes widening. "Rhiannon! Language!"

"Don't let him past," the blond lad said. "He's Shadrak the Unseen, the assassin who killed my dad."

Bovis shogging Rayn. Spineless Nousian bastard. Squealed like a pig when I shot him. Wonder if his son will do the same.

"Well, well, well," Shadrak said, drawing two knives from his baldric and flicking his cloak back from his shoulders. "Bovis Rayn had a son, and there's me thinking he was just some dried up Nousian turd."

The lad took a step forward, eyes narrowing, knuckles whitening from gripping the sword too tight.

Good, thought Shadrak. *Nice 'n' easy.*

"You got a name, boy?" Shadrak said, dropping into a crouch. "Or should I call you Squealer, after your dad."

"You and me," the lad said. "One on one."

Even better.

"OK, you've got me. Ready when you are."

"Gaston," said the sandy-haired youth from the pub. "Don't be a clacker. There's enough of us to bring him down without anyone getting hurt."

"Shut it, Barek," Gaston said. "This is between me and him."

"Gaston, you're being an arse," the black-haired woman said—the old girl had called her Rhiannon. "Listen to Barek."

Gaston licked his lips and took a careful step forward. "Don't think I can take him? I might not be as good as Shader, but at least I'm not the one lying dead in the templum with this shogger's knife in my back."

The old priestess appeared behind Gaston and put a restraining hand on his shoulder. "Gaston," she said. "This is not our way."

"Maybe not," Gaston said. "But it sure is mine."

The knight's attack was so fast that Shadrak had to sway backward to avoid being skewered. His heel touched something that caused him to stumble and Gaston took full advantage, lunging for his chest. Shadrak turned the blade with his left-hand dagger and made a feint with the right. Gaston's head snapped back out of reach, and Shadrak shot a quick glance at the obstructions behind. There was a narrow path between the patients, which he instantly committed to memory. As Gaston came at him with a combination of thrusts and slices, Shadrak danced away backward on the balls of his feet.

Gaston pressed forward like a man walking a tightrope, one arm outstretched for balance, the other tracking Shadrak with the tip of his sword. Shadrak threw a dagger, which Gaston batted aside to clatter against the metal walls. The second knife grazed Gaston's cheek as Shadrak continued to retreat, one step, two steps, and then back-flipped past the remaining bodies. The fat priest and the priestesses scurried out of the way.

Shadrak came to his feet at a crossroads, which afforded him more room to move. Gaston stepped past the last of the bodies and charged before he could draw another dagger. Shadrak ducked beneath a slash, spun on his heel, and kicked Gaston in the shin. The sword arced down, but clanged from the floor as Shadrak rolled away, springing to his feet with a sword-breaker in his right hand and a push-dagger in the left.

Gaston circled him warily now, reaching down to feel his shin with his free hand. Shadrak dropped his shoulders allowing his cloak to fall forward. The lad took the opportunity and stabbed toward his head, but the sword-breaker came up, catching Gaston's blade in its comb-like slots and holding it firm. Shadrak immediately stepped in and punched the push-dagger between Gaston's ribs. Could have finished the scut there, but Kadee distracted him and Shadrak pulled back.

Gaston clutched his side, blood dripping through his fingers. He glared at Shadrak and snarled, taking a two-handed grip on his sword and coming on with huge clubbing blows. Shadrak threw himself out of the way and rammed the push-dagger into Gaston's kidney.

The lad screamed and backslashed with the sword, but Shadrak jumped clear. Ignoring Kadee's pleading face, he was about to step in for the killing blow when Rhiannon came hurtling into him from out of nowhere. Shadrak's head cracked against the wall and he dropped his blades. Her fists were a hazy blur as she pounded his face and for a moment he couldn't react. Instinct took over and he sagged to the floor, rolling out of the way of a vicious kick. His hand slipped inside a pouch and took hold of a glass vial, which he shattered against the floor. There was a flash, and black smoke filled the corridor. Without wasting a single look back, Shadrak pelted down the left-hand tunnel, one hand patting his pocket to make sure he still had the Statue of Eingana.

MAMBA

I
T WAS DARK inside. Darker even than home when Mommy and Daddy turned off the lanterns and blew out the candles. Back then Sammy had cried himself to sleep. Sometimes Rhiannon had crept into bed beside him and snuggled him up. He missed the warmth of her body pressed against his back almost as much as he missed Mommy and Daddy. The world had grown much darker the day they'd been taken from him, but not as dark as it was beneath the Homestead.

He could hear Huntsman's breathing from somewhere behind, but he knew he'd get no comfort there. This was the place of testing, the place where Huntsman had found his power. The place where Sammy would find his, if he was worthy.

Something crunched beneath his feet, causing him to jump backward and whimper. With the next step, his foot came down on a hard object that rolled away. Sammy lost his balance and tumbled to a carpet of twigs, or shells, or something else. He felt the tears coming and started to sniff, but he refused to cry out. Huntsman had done it and so would he. If there was magic to be found under the tabletop mountain then Sammy was going to find it, no matter what.

"Sssssssss."

Sammy clamped a hand over his mouth and tried not to breathe. The sound had come from somewhere to his left, a hissing whisper that set his spine tingling. His eyes strained against the darkness, but he could see nothing. He waved his other hand in front of his face, but still there was only black. He listened, trying to screen out the pounding of his heart, hoping to hear Huntsman's breath, feel his presence.

Nothing.

Silence.

Darkness.

Sammy turned around, looking for the chink of light from the entrance, but even that had vanished around the bends in the tunnel that opened onto the cave. He started to panic. How could he get out? He had no idea which way he faced. He could spend forever scratching around in the blackness and still never retrace his steps.

"Sssamuel."

Two yellow pinpricks flared like twin suns in an otherwise starless night. They swayed and grew larger, slits of black cutting through their centers.

"Sssahul ssspoke of you. The boy who talksss with antsss. Huntsssman isss here with you?"

Sammy shielded his eyes as fire sprang up illuminating the Dreamer's face.

"I am," Huntsman said, a small blaze crackling on the palm of his hand. He held it out to the speaker, who stepped into the glow.

A scaly head took shape around the yellow eyes, and a long forked tongue tasted the air. At first, Sammy thought it was a giant snake, but then he realized the long wavy neck was sprouting from the body of a man—a huge black man, thickly muscled and naked but for a cloth covering his loins. Sammy scrabbled backward across a sea of bones, seeking the safety of the dark.

The snake-man raised a bulging arm, his palm facing Sammy.

"Ssstay, little one. No need to be afraid. I am Mamba."

Huntsman gave a slight bow and held out a hand to Sammy, who used it to pull himself to his feet and then hid behind the Dreamer.

"Mamba is friend, Sammy," Huntsman said. "A god of Barraiya People."

"Not a god," Mamba chuckled deep in the coils of his throat. "Sssimply an elder. You have a mother, Sssammy? A father?"

Sammy shook his head, a lump forming in his throat. He squeezed Huntsman's hand tighter, and the Dreamer stroked his hair.

Mamba rolled his head and blinked. "Ssso sssorry." He crouched down and peered at Sammy through the crook of Huntsman's arm. "But you have grandparentsss, yesss?"

Sammy nodded. He'd not seen Grandpa Piet and Nana Josie since they'd moved down south when he was four, and Granddad Tom and Granny Anwen weren't talking to Mom and Dad again. Sammy wondered if they even knew what had happened; if they cared.

Huntsman stood aside as the snake head pressed close to Sammy's face, its long tongue darting out and licking him on the nose.

"Ssso you know what it'sss like being a grandchild. My people are not godsss, really. But we are the grandchildren of Eingana, and many people think her a goddesss."

Huntsman's brows knit together and his lips curled back. He opened his mouth to speak, but then shook his head.

Sammy flinched as Mamba's tongue flicked out again, moistening the end of his nose. He tried to give a stern look, but a laugh slipped out instead. Mamba's tongue dabbed him on the ear and then an eyelid, and Sammy spluttered and gurgled before bursting into great peals of laughter.

Mamba laughed with him, poking at Sammy's ribs with his big black fingers. Huntsman was grinning from ear to ear and then roared with mirth as Sammy gave a big slobbering lick to the snake-man's face.

Mamba hoisted him into the air and twirled him around, Sammy squealing with joy. The snake-man let him go in midair. Sammy screamed, and then Mamba caught him and tucked him under a massive arm, patting him on the head.

"Sssseemsss all right for a white fellah." Mamba did a pretty good impression of Huntsman.

"He isss not bad," Huntsman jibed back. "Thisss here isss a very sssspecial boy."

Mamba put Sammy down and looked closely at him. Sammy lowered his eyes and snuggled in beside the snake-man, taking hold of his hand.

"We ssshould take him to sssee the othersss," Mamba said. "No other whitesss have come to the cavesss asss friendsss."

"Nor spoken with ants," Huntsman said.

Mamba gave Sammy's hand a gentle squeeze. "Want to meet my family?"

Sammy liked the big snake-man. He was friendly and funny. Maybe his family would be, too. "OK," he said.

Mamba crouched down and offered Sammy his back. "Jump up, little Sssammy. Old Uncle Mamba will carry you."

Sammy wrapped his arms around the scaly neck and clung on with his legs as Mamba straightened up.

"Down we go," the snake-man sang as he trudged into the dark. "Down, down, deep down."

"Down, down, deep down," Sammy joined in.

"Into spider's lair," Huntsman added, and then gave Sammy a big grin that said it was going to be all right.

ARABOTH

WARM BREEZE CARESSED him as he stepped lightly over a carpet of silken rose petals beneath a sapphire sky. He ate up the leagues with easy, effortless, strides, the fallen petals giving way to polychrome sands flanked by glistening silver pinnacles; a majestic shimmering city born from the very earth itself.

He paused for an age amid the glint of the silver monoliths, savoring the crispness of the air and rejoicing in his independence from its life-giving gases. Something beat within him, but it was no heart of flesh. No, it was a harmonious note, binding him together in unity with all that he gazed upon and much more.

He would have sat there forever, so content was he, but something called him onward like the whispering of a familiar lover. He learnt quickly. He now no longer strode the glorious landscape, but merely surveyed its horizon and found himself present at his chosen destination with the speed of thought. And yet there were no thoughts as such, merely an unselfconscious harmony that bore him along gently, as carefree as a sleeping babe.

A glade appeared in the distance, and in an instant, he stood beneath its trees. These were no ordinary trees. Instead, they rose to impossible heights and shone with the light of stars. Ripe and succulent fruit hung from laden branches and he savored the sight of their beauty, but did not eat of them; there was no need.

An old man with a white beard and sparkling eyes sat cross-legged beneath a tree. He wore a simple brown habit pulled in at the waist by a dark leather belt. His feet were shod in plain sandals and a begging bowl rested in his lap.

As the wanderer approached, the old man's form shimmered and transformed, the years falling away. His now naked body grew toned and muscular, his eyes sharp and as blue as the sky. A dazzling luminosity shone forth from his flesh causing the wanderer to shade his eyes until they adjusted to the brightness.

"Welcome, Frater." The man smiled. "I was called Jarmin, and I see no reason to dispense with that name."

"Jarmin?"

"Jarmin the Anchorite. I dwelt in the city of Gladelvi."

"And now?"

"And now," Jarmin chuckled a little at some secret joke, "I just dwell."

"What is this place?"

"This is the waiting room for the End of All Things; the forecourt of the Garden of Eternity."

"And I am?"

"You were called Deacon Shader, Frater." Jarmin's smile was radiant, full of compassion. "And if you like, you shall remain Deacon Shader."

"It is a name as good as any. May I sit here awhile."

"But of course," Jarmin said. "You may sit for all eternity if you wish."

As he settled himself beneath the tree, Shader became aware of his own nakedness and the perfect form and function of his body, which also glowed, although not with the intensity of Jarmin's.

"I am dead, then?"

"Slain by a knife in the back and a demon."

Shader frowned as thoughts began to form and disappear, like dolphins arcing their way through choppy seas. There was a captain, a lad with a sextant, a big black cook. The smell of grilled cheese wafted into recollection and was gone. "I don't remember."

"I don't recall the manner of my own passing, although Tajen tells me it was horrific."

"Tajen?"

"The luminary. You will meet him soon enough."

"Am I in Araboth?"

Jarmin furrowed his brows before he answered. "You are, as are all who are redeemed, but you are not yet as well."

Shader shook his head. It seemed as though a cloud had settled over his memories, smothered his thoughts.

"What you call Araboth lies at the end of time. By its nature, we are all already there, and yet, for those still connected to the temporal world, this presents a rather difficult paradox. When you die, your next recollection is of the end of time, and yet to those who mourn you, time continues on its journey through the eons. You cannot be both out of time and a decaying memory to those who still inhabit it."

"And so?"

"And so you are here—and there. At the end of time you will pass there, but the end of time is no time, and so you are there already; and not."

"And Ain?"

"Ah, there is the current dilemma. We are told that in death, we shall see Him face to face, but, wondrously harmonious as things are here, faith is not yet redundant. Tajen is the best one to talk to about such things. He calls this place the garden of Ain, which is but one step closer to our eternal home. Perhaps we could visit Tajen together. I know he will be intrigued by your presence here."

"Why is that?"

"Besides myself, you are the only person in countless generations to reach Araboth. Apparently, all is not as it should be in the temporal realm."

"What is wrong?"

"Tajen believes that Ain has been separated from the Earth."

"How can that be? Surely, for Ain to be Ain He must be all powerful."

"Whatever the truth of the matter, Ain's Spirit no longer infuses all life on Earth and has not done so for a very long time. There is a shadow across the Void that connects us to the Supernal Realm. It is something of a mystery, even here. And to think, the luminaries believed they had earned their rewards and would never again walk in the darkness! Which, of course, they don't at the end of time, but do here."

With an impish grin, Jarmin leapt to his feet, clapped Shader on the back, and took him, in the blink of an eye, to see the luminary.

GODS OF THE DREAMERS

MAMBA CARRIED SAMMY down the last of the rough stone steps that wound deep into the earth below the Homestead. Shapes waited for them in the shadows of an enormous cavern, black outlines beneath a gigantic natural arch: one squat and dwarfish; one tall and hulking; the third a sprawl of legs sticking from a massive bloated body.

The snake-man reached over his head and grasped Sammy under the arms, heaving him to the floor with an exaggerated grunt. Sammy would have laughed normally, if he'd not been so scared. He'd felt the strength in those hands; knew Mamba found him as light as a feather; could crush him as easily as snapping a twig. He seemed friendly enough, but what if that all changed now they were down here? The boys back home always acted differently once they got with their friends.

"So this is the ant-child?" the squat figure croaked.

Sammy winced at the firm grip of Huntsman's hands on his shoulders.

"He is called Samuel," the Dreamer said as the three shapes shifted from the shadows into the greenish glow coming from the walls of the cave.

Sammy swallowed and looked to Mamba for reassurance. The snake-man's mouth opened, baring his fangs. He may have been trying to smile. "Sssammy, this is Thindamura."

A hunched man only a little taller than Sammy flicked out an even longer tongue than Mamba's. Bulbous eyes rolled atop his toad-like head. "Thisss isss Baru." Mamba indicated the hulking muscular man who had the elongated snout and mottled amber eyes of a crocodile.

Baru opened his jaws and nodded, all the while watching Sammy hungrily. Sammy pushed back against Huntsman, but the Dreamer patted him softly on the shoulder. The jaws snapped together, rows of dagger-like teeth protruding like a warning.

"And thisss isss Murgah Muggui."

The mass with the many legs lurched forward and dragged itself into view. The body was gray and smooth, the head studded with glinting red eyes above clacking mandibles. The legs—there were eight of them—were twisted forward like a crab's.

"Welcome, Samuel," Murgah Muggui said in a soft, high voice that reminded Sammy of his mother's. "Sahul has spoken through your suffering, and you are blessed to have heard her. You are the first of your kind to have done so. Why have you brought him here, Kadji?"

Huntsman approached the great spider and planted a kiss on its head. "Ants told him mawgs were beneath Sarum. He is favored by Sahul. I will teach him."

Huntsman seated himself beneath the body of Murgah Muggui, who wrapped her front legs around him and brushed the top of his head with her mandibles.

"So you thought to test him in the dark?" she said. "No pale-skin has come here and lived."

Sammy followed Huntsman's gaze to the ceiling high above where thick webs clung to the skeletal remains of humans. He pressed up close against Mamba.

"He wasss ssstrong in the dark," Mamba said. "He did not sssuccumb to madnesss."

Baru loomed closer to Sammy and glared at him, his jaws clacking as he spoke. "And Eingana? Does she call him too?"

"He has not felt her power," Huntsman said. "But his movements are touched by her. He is known to music man and to Deacon Shader."

"He wanted to marry my sister," Sammy blurted out, "but she's gonna be a priestess."

Thindamura hopped behind Sammy and began to circle him, his tongue whipping out to snare a fly.

Huntsman closed his eyes and settled back in the spider's embrace. Murgah Muggui's eyes burned into Sammy.

"Your sister is a Nousian?"

"Uh huh," Sammy grunted while watching the toad-headed Thindamura stalking him.

"And you still want to train him, Huntsman?"

"I must," Huntsman said blearily. "I owe it to his sister. She sent Shader away at my bidding."

Mamba folded his bulging arms across his chest. "Yoursss or the philosssopher'sss?"

Sammy frowned, trying to work out what they were saying. Huntsman knew Rhiannon? He'd told her to send Shader away? So he was the one who'd made her unhappy. "What's a philosopher?" he asked.

Huntsman opened his eyes, but ignored Sammy's question. "Aristodeus's plan fails. All this sacrifice is for nothing. Eingana's power has been misused, and Sektis Gandaw has noticed."

"We, too, have sensed his eyes," Murgah Muggui said. "Everything is happening as it did before."

Thindamura leapt to a rock and perched there. "But this time we have Shader," he croaked.

"Plucked from his true time," Baru said. "But how will it change the outcome? Aristodeus said—"

"It is not for him to say." Murgah Muggui's legs unfurled from Huntsman, and she reared up. "Nothing like this has been tried before. In its way, what he's done is as unnatural as what Sektis Gandaw plans to do."

"It'sss the lesser of two evilsss," Mamba said. "Tinkering with time or sssubmitting to the unraveling of the universsse. What choice does he have?"

The great spider's eight red eyes turned back to Sammy, making him feel like a piece of meat at the market. "We must offer the boy to the Archon."

Mamba gripped Sammy's shoulders and held him tight.

"But I have taken him for Sahul," Huntsman said. "I will teach him about Eingana. This Archon is nothing to us. He is a white-man's god."

"He is Eingana's brother, Huntsman," Murgah Muggui said. "He aided her birthing of the Cynocephalus and made possible the Dreaming. He is the law opposing the deceptions of the Demiurgos. There is too much at stake, old friend. If Aristodeus is failing for the second time, we must appeal to a higher power."

A spray of webbing shot from the body of the spider and smothered Sammy's face. He tried to raise his arm, but Mamba held him firm. The web smelled of something sweet and sickly. His head grew suddenly heavy and dizziness overcame him. He felt himself falling, supported only by Mamba's arms, and as he drifted into blackness, he heard Murgah Muggui's voice like a distant echo. "If Sammy has a part in all this, the Archon will know. The boy must go to him."

TAJEN

DON'T BE DECEIVED, Deacon Shader. This is not Araboth." Tajen was a stocky man with a ruddy face. His wiry black hair had been cropped unevenly short, and his brown eyes brooded beneath thick brows. He was dressed in a grubby tunic of beige linen, and sandals so caked in dried mud that they appeared fossilized. The other six luminaries gathered around Shader were naked, clearly at ease with their finely proportioned physiques. They each exuded a soft glow in varying shades of white, rose, and gold.

A tall man, bronzed and bearded, clapped Shader on the shoulder. "Do not heed Tajen, Frater. He has ever been the pessimist."

Shader studied him for a moment, noting the tears in his flesh, holes that seemed to suppurate bright light. He knew that this must be Milo, who had been flayed alive in the forests of Verusia by his own prior, the notorious Otto Blightey.

Jarmin, now clothed in a brown habit, his body bent and wizened, sat stiffly in the shade of a silver monolith.

One of the luminaries, a beautiful youth with a golden radiance, shook his head and smiled benevolently. "You still resist the truth, Frater Jarmin."

"I rather suspect, Frater Narcus, that the truth is not dissimilar to a mirror in this land of limbo," Jarmin said.

"Tajen, Tajen," Milo said, raising his hands in mock dismay. "How quickly you have sullied the soul of our new brother. Where is your trust? How can we best help you?"

There was genuine concern in the big man's words and no hint of any concession that Tajen might be right. Indeed, Shader could see nothing but absolute, unquestioning harmony in all those assembled, with the exception of Tajen and Jarmin. Perhaps they were simply not ready yet. Maybe Araboth had its layers, different degrees of peace and luminosity, just as some of the Paters had speculated.

Milo turned his attention back to Shader. "Besides Frater Jarmin, you are the first to enter Araboth for centuries."

"No one else has come here? Then, why us?" Shader asked.

Milo spread his hands and let out a great sigh. "Humans never learn. They cannot easily let go their inner darkness. They are closed to Ain's gift of life. The longer human society endures the more evil it seems to become. Jarmin and you are rare exceptions of holiness."

"Poppycock!" Jarmin growled from beneath his rock.

Milo merely smiled benignly.

"But my father..." The memory of Jarl bobbed to the surface of Shader's mind, an island in an empty sea. "Was he rejected because he had no faith? What about all the priests? The Ipsissimi? Why are they not—?"

"Will you walk with me, Deacon Shader?" Tajen asked, his brow furrowed with concern.

Shader eyed him for a moment and then nodded. Something felt very wrong. If this was Araboth, why did he feel an old familiar knotting in his stomach? Whatever brief harmony he had first felt was already being dashed apart by waves of discord. It made no sense. What was he doing here when far better people had not made it?

"Be wary of the tempter," Milo said as the two set off. "Frater Tajen has fallen at the final hurdle, I think. If he does not drag you down, then perhaps you can help us bring him back to Ain."

Shader and Tajen walked in silence for an age. The sun never once shifted its position in the sky, which was alive with the majestic movement of brightly-colored birds and butterflies. Tajen kept his eyes on the ground; his presence was dull and leaden in comparison with the tranquil beauty that surrounded them.

"Would you stay here for all eternity?" Tajen finally asked, seating himself on a verdant hillock.

Shader sighed and lowered himself to the ground, running his hands through the grass and savoring its sweet scent. "It's certainly peaceful."

Tajen watched him closely until Shader felt compelled to speak again. "If not for you and Jarmin," he said carefully, "my contentment would be complete."

Tajen did not look offended. He nodded thoughtfully before dropping his gaze and idly drawing in the earth with his finger. "Have you no thought for those you so recently left behind?"

Lightning ripped through Shader's mind, dispersing the fog. He gasped for air, as if he were waking from being buried alive. He had completely forgotten Rhiannon, Maldark, the priests, and the White Order knights. Were they still trapped in the crypt beneath the templum? What if the Dweller had—?

"Ah, good!" Tajen clapped his hands and, for a moment, actually looked lively. "You feel some guilt."

"That's a good thing?"

"Milo and the others believe we need no longer be concerned with the world. The only thing that matters to them is eternal peace."

"Perhaps they are right," Shader said.

"If Ain is concerned for Creation," Tajen said, "for human life on Earth, then should not we be?"

It wasn't just Shader's memories that had returned. The jagged edge of his cynicism reasserted itself like a rusty blade. "How do we know that is what Ain is like?"

"Nous! That is how we know! That is why we are Nousians, is it not?" Tajen seemed more exasperated than angry. He had evidently had this conversation many times before. "These fools—" Tajen spoke more softly, his arm sweeping out to indicate the luminaries who were no longer visible. "—are witless ecstatics, little better than the smokers of opium. If sensual pleasure could be prolonged for eternity, they would take their rest and call it Araboth."

"But how do you know that isn't what Araboth is?"

"I don't know." Tajen sighed. "But I feel strongly the lack of concern for others, for the millions of humans still struggling, for the heaving and groaning of Creation. Ain cares; I have to believe that. I care, and I am not prepared to rest on my laurels until every last atom of Creation has been brought into Ain's loving embrace."

Shader stared at his fingers clenching around a tuft of grass. He pulled out a fistful of rose-scented sod and held it before his face. Heaviness settled throughout his new form, his heavenly body. He felt suddenly weary, like he'd returned to the fight after he'd thought the battle won.

"Here we are in such harmony," he said, letting the soil crumble between his fingers. "Our bodies are perfect. We can move anywhere at will, and in an instant. We cannot die.

Perhaps if we can cultivate this concern for others that you mention we will have good cause to feel content." He didn't believe a word of it. The illusion had already passed like the innocence of childhood.

"Union with Ain should make us more real, Deacon Shader. There is no depth of reality here. I once thought as the others do, but then I began to have the nagging feeling that something was missing. What I have said to you is as much as I am able to grasp. I feel disconnected from life here, marginalized from existence. If we remain here, then we may lie outside the world's salvation. Your arrival, and Jarmin's, has only made matters seem more urgent. Where are the others going after death? Why did you come here? What does this mean for the rest of us?"

"Then what must we do?"

"I wish I knew!" Tajen cried with a mixture of frustration and despair. "But there is something about you and Jarmin that reminds me of what we have lost. You must think, Deacon Shader, try to remember the circumstances of your life, and, more importantly, your death. Therein lies the way out of this limbo, I suspect."

IN THE SERVICE OF THE ARCHON

AMMY STOOD UPON an impossibly tall pillar amid a whirlwind of shifting colors and deafening roars. He teetered dangerously and should have fallen, but his body remained taut, his feet rooted to the summit as if they grew from it. He chanced a look downwards, but could see only a yawning hole of blackness, a clinging mist covering its mouth like a cobweb.

There was a tremendous crash and then searing jags of lightning blasted apart his thoughts. He was dead, he knew it. He wanted to cry out, but didn't know how. There was nothing; nothing but a churning in his stomach and fire behind the eyes. Something bubbled up from deep inside him—a jumble of white-hot letters that formed into words and shattered, formed and shattered. Somehow, he knew he was being asked a question. He couldn't hear it; couldn't read it in the dizzying patterns of letters, but he felt it pulsing in his veins, squeezing through his innards, and rippling beneath his skin. His answer, though he had no idea why, was an unspoken yes.

All was still.

Sammy felt the softness of a cushion beneath him. He was sitting on an armchair before an open fire. A thickly woven rug formed a rectangle atop polished wooden floorboards. Soft sunlight filtered through latticed windows flanked by velvet curtains. It was like a storybook room. Maybe he was dreaming. Maybe he'd dozed off while Mommy was reading to him. Maybe she'd be there if only he could wake up. But the heat from the fire felt far too real; the fabric of the chair was rough and sent up little puffs of dust when he patted it. He sneezed and then sniffed, wiping away a tear.

The room was a perfect square with white walls and dark-stained beams crossing the ceiling. There were no doors. He stood and went to the window so that he could peer outside. Twin suns hovered in infinite darkness, a tiny dot circling each. A third light appeared between the suns, a ball of flame streaking a long tail behind, its surface shimmering and changing until it became a face made of fire. There was a blinding flash of light. Sammy raised his hand to protect his eyes, staggered backward and fell into the chair. He rapidly blinked away the stars behind his eyelids and lowered his arm. A man in a brown hooded robe was drawing the curtains.

"Two suns light the heavens above the Void," the man said in a voice that crackled like paper being scrunched up. "An unusual sight for an Earth-boy, and even more so for a white one."

Sammy sank back into the chair and shut his eyes tight. If he tried hard enough he might find himself back at home.

"You are not dreaming, boy."

Sammy heard the man shuffling toward him and began to shake. Heat fell on his face, feeling like the time he'd gotten too close to the fire at the Winter Fest pig roast so he could watch the fat dripping and fizzing. Rhiannon had pulled him away by his ear; told him he'd be roasting on a spit if he did it again. He opened his eyes a crack and peeked at

D.P. PRIOR

a face of golden flame. He blinked against the glare, but couldn't look away. The blazing eyes made him keep looking, silently promising him a secret that seemed as necessary as breathing. Tears blurred his vision as the heat burned his skin and stung behind his eyes. Sammy began to whimper, his head rocking from side to side. Sweat soaked his clothes and streamed from his forehead. He shook so hard the chair began to clatter against the floor, scraping and twisting, jumping on the rug. His breathing grew quicker, high up in his chest. He felt his heart thumping, the blood rushing in his ears. His eyes widened, fixed upon the burning face, and he opened his mouth to scream; but the scream turned into a gasp as something unseen stabbed his heart. White-hot flames ripped through his innards, singeing, melting, blistering. A burning coal lodged in his throat, choking him. Steam seared his nostrils, and the tears streaming down his face sizzled and boiled.

The hooded man turned away, and the pain stopped. Sammy sagged in the chair. He was panting like a dog after water. He lifted his arms and saw no blisters. The skin was unharmed. His hands patted his chest. Nothing. No hole, no blade. He looked to make doubly sure. He was drenched in sweat, and the skin of his chest rippled like a beaten drum, but there was no blood—not like there had been with his dad.

"I am the Archon," the cowled figure said. He parted the curtains slightly so he could look out. "Come."

Sammy forced himself out of the chair and stood at the window. One of the suns appeared larger, as if it had drawn nearer. The dot circling it was now a ball of grayish-blue.

"Aethir," the Archon said. "The world of the Dreaming. Watch as it turns."

The Archon waved his fingers, and time seemed to speed up in response. The suns shifted across the dark, the planet turned on its axis, and blackness crept over its surface.

"Two sides to the Dreaming, boy. Light and darkness. You are now looking at Qlippoth, the dark side of Aethir. These are the nightmares of the Cynocephalus." Light spilled from the Archon's hood as he spoke. Sammy had no idea what he was talking about.

"Huntsman's people have a connection with Aethir. They worship the offspring of its creator, but the lord of Aethir is a pitiable creature, frightened of his own shadow." The Archon bowed his head as if remembering. When he looked up, he pointed to the smaller of the two suns, its own orbiting planet a black speck.

"This other world—" He took hold of Sammy's shoulders to grant him a better view. "—is known to its inhabitants as Thanatos."

Sammy felt the tug of the dark world. It drew his eyes, called to him. He felt himself reaching toward it.

"It does not belong here." The Archon's hands felt oddly cold as he pressed Sammy's head downwards to look upon the inky black hole beneath, its emptiness covered by the misty web he'd seen from the top of the pillar.

"And neither does the Abyss. My brother is the great deceiver. Where I brought with me the laws of our father, he brought nothing but despite and disorder. Even when I cast him back into the Void, he found a way to survive." The Archon's voice spat and popped like a bushfire. Wisps of smoke escaped from beneath his hood, and his fingers dug into Sammy's shoulders, spreading their peculiar chill. "Tell me, child, would you go there?" The Archon released his grip and lowered his voice. "Would you enter the Abyss if the fate of worlds depended on it?"

Sammy stared at the mist covering the Void and felt it pulling at him. He knew he should be scared, but he felt only calm. He started to imagine a tunnel through space connecting him with the Abyss and gawped as a spiraling green cone began to form in front of him.

The Archon touched his hand to it, and it disappeared. "Good," he said. "Now listen to

234

what I expect of you. I have granted you powers to rival even the greatest of the Dreamers. You will make the journey to the Abyss soon. Someone is trapped there." The Archon's hood rustled as he shook his head. "Without him, we may not be able to stop the coming crisis."

Something felt wrong. Sammy didn't like the way the Archon was telling him what to do. It wasn't as if he was his dad. "I'm with Huntsman," he said, hoping that would make things clear.

"Huntsman serves the children of the Cynocephalus," the Archon said.

Sammy stuck his bottom lip out, not understanding.

"Murgah Muggui, Baru and their kind. Children of the Cynocephalus and grandchildren of my sister, Eingana. They have pledged themselves to me so that together we may thwart the Unweaving."

"But... But what—?"

"Did Huntsman ever tell you about the Reckoning?"

Sammy shrugged. He'd mentioned it, but most of what Sammy knew came from listening to Elias. They'd taught about it at school, too: stuff about dragons and demons pouring from the sky and destroying the world of the Ancients.

"Huntsman saved your world from Sektis Gandaw, a scientist of the worst kind who saw the creation of the cosmos as imperfect and believed he could make a better one. His long and murky history began centuries ago when he was first contacted by the Liche Lord, Otto Blightey."

"The bogey man?" Sammy said, remembering stories Elias used to tell the kids about Jaspar Paris and Renna Cordelia, and an evil skull that drank souls.

"Sektis Gandaw's dark science developed out of Blightey's magic," the Archon said. "Both bear the mark of the Abyss."

Sammy was completely lost now. He screwed his face up into a frown. Rhiannon would have called it his "old man" look.

"The Unweaving is like seeing someone else's picture in the sand and raking over it in order to start your own," the Archon said. "Everything would end. In effect, it would never have started. Do you understand what that means?"

Sammy thought he did. "Sounds like a selfish clacker. Least that's what my sister would say."

The Archon chuckled. "A little more than selfish, I think, but that will do. He has been stopped twice before, but he is determined. There is so much you don't know: the relationship of the Supernal Realm to the Earth; the changes brought by the Abyss and Aethir; the closing of the Void; the mechanics of the Unweaving..."

Sammy's head hurt. He wanted the Archon to stop; needed him to stop. He bunched his hands into fists and struck himself on the temples.

The Archon turned toward him, flame erupting from beneath his cowl. "Too much for a child to comprehend," he said. "All you need to know is that Huntsman serves his so-called gods, and they serve me. You are his apprentice, and I have a task for you."

Sammy looked away from the Archon and back down at the wispy mesh of the Abyss. "I don't want to go there," he said in a weak voice, while an altogether different part of him wondered what it would be like, what secrets it held.

"What is happening now has happened before," the Archon said, coming to gaze at the darkness with Sammy. "Last time we failed. I trusted a philosopher named Aristodeus to bring down Sektis Gandaw, but he was not equal to the task. He succumbed to the deceptions of the Abyss, and it is there he now languishes."

"You want me to bring him back?" Sammy asked, feeling suddenly rather brave.

"No." The light spilling from the Archon's hood flared. "He has sunk too deep into the mire of the Abyss. Yet he has a new plan to avert the catastrophe. He has cheated time, changed things in the past to influence the future. Players have been assembled and the game has commenced, but now our greatest hope has fallen at the first hurdle." The Archon rested a hand atop Sammy's head. "Events are moving inexorably toward the Unweaving. Aristodeus's hubris may have led him deeper into deception."

"Then what do you want me to do?" Sammy asked.

The Archon began to break up into tongues of fire that swirled around Sammy's head. "Deacon Shader," a voice like a storm sounded from the flaming vortex. "The man who loves your sister."

Sammy stared into the fire, knowing he had only moments left and so much still to learn. "Deacon? What's he got to do with any of this?"

"Everything," said the voice of the Archon. "He was slain before his time and does not know the perils his soul now faces. I will go ahead of you. I cannot remain long in the Abyss, but I will leave a beacon there for you, something to guide you. Find him, child. Bring him back."

***

"The Archon hasss accepted him." Mamba's yellow eyes bored into Sammy's skull as he came to in the cavern beneath the Homestead.

A shadow alerted Sammy to the looming presence of Murgah Muggui. "What did he say to you?" she said, mandibles clacking with every syllable.

Sammy sat up and rubbed his pounding head. Ignoring the great spider, he sought out Huntsman.

"Who is Deacon Shader, really?" he asked, staring into Huntsman's eyes as if he could read the truth there.

"I do not understand," Huntsman said.

Sammy nodded. Huntsman wasn't lying. No matter. He knew who Shader was to Rhiannon, and that was more important to Sammy than all the confusing things he'd heard from the Archon. "He's lost," Sammy said, pushing himself to his feet.

The hybrids formed a circle around him: Murgah Muggui as massive and as solid as the Homestead itself; Baru glaring like he meant to bite, but with his arms folded across his chest and great head nodding; Thindamura crouched, bulbous eyes rolling and tongue flicking. Mamba's snake-head bobbed upon its long neck, the opening and closing of his mouth suggesting concern.

"His piece of statue?" Huntsman took a step toward Sammy and abruptly stopped.

Sammy smiled to let him know everything was OK, but then noticed how quiet the others had gone. They were rooted to the spot, staring at him like they'd seen a ghost.

Golden light danced on the tips of his fingers. He lifted a hand and watched the color change from gold to blue, then red and green. With a thought, the light faded, and he thrust his hands behind his back.

"I don't know about the statue," Sammy said. "But I know what I need to do."

He raised his hands and let brilliant green light burst from his fingertips. He turned his wrists, tugging the light into circles that pulsed before him, growing, deepening, swirling into a shimmering tunnel in the air.

"Hold me," he moaned, feeling his body give way.

Mamba's arms closed around him and lowered him to the floor beneath the mouth of the tunnel of light. Sammy let his eyes close and heard a sharp click as he drifted into the air. With a last look at his body lying on the floor of the cave, he allowed himself to be drawn into the tunnel.

THE WAY BACK

SHADER SAT BENEATH a gnarled oak in the forest of his youth. Soft sunlight edged the overhanging canopy of leaves with gold and filled him, body and soul, with warmth. He was clothed once more in a white tunic bearing the red Monas of the Elect; he wore sandals rather than boots, and he sported no weapons.

Luminary Tajen sat opposite him in the shade of a gigantic yew, his expression a mixture of dour brooding, frustration, and excitement. "See how Araboth reflects our innermost needs and desires," Tajen said, indicating the trees.

"It's a pleasant change from Sahul," Shader said. "I'd forgotten how comforting the sun could be. In Sahul, we avoid it at all costs. I once saw a man brought to the abbey after being found in the bush without shade or water. Skin was a mass of weeping blisters that burst at the slightest touch. Flesh practically dripped off the bone. The Gray Abbot did what he could, but the fellow was dead within hours, all dried up and shriveled like a mummy."

"The same sun," Tajen said, "only from a different perspective. Here in Araboth you see the one you love the most. I often found myself on hills like those of my homeland, or beside a great and tranquil river such as I had known in Aeterna."

"Ah, the Tiber," Shader said. "I imagine the view has changed a good deal since your time." The banks of the great river were flanked by vast buildings with intricate domes, sprawling colonnades, and high arches, inspired by the drawings of the pre-Ancient civilization that had flourished by its banks. Tajen would have known only the ruins of the Ancients' own city, functional and uniform, towering structures that kissed the sky and declared the triumph of humankind.

"It is my doom—" Tajen's voice was low, tinged with sorrow. "—that I cannot bask in the reflections of my soul like the others can. This is the Araboth Milo expected, but it is nothing like I ever imagined. It's pleasant enough, I admit, but it has the quality of a dream."

"How can we know which version is real?" Shader asked, suppressing the feeling that the earth was about to open up and swallow him.

"I am not a man who trusts the fulfillment of his own desires. Nous is my life and my master. I am content to follow where he leads."

"But how can you tell this isn't what he wants?"

For the first time since he'd settled in Oakendale—since he'd been with Rhiannon—Shader was almost at peace. So what if Araboth wasn't the promised land; it was good enough for him, and he was tired of trying to guess what Nous did and didn't want.

"Because I have never felt so removed from life." Tajen said, 'so disconnected from the world and its people. I feel safe here, but with that safety comes complacency. In one such as myself that is the recipe for despair. I'm not saying that Milo and the others are entirely wrong about this place. It may well be a taste of Araboth, but it is too closely allied to our expectations. Our journey is not yet complete, and I have a suspicion we have tarried here too long. It seems the more time passes, the deeper we grow enmeshed in delusion."

"You think something has gone wrong? Ain's salvation is thwarted?"

"Perhaps." Tajen studied Shader's eyes. "Although it makes no theological sense. How can an omnipotent god be thwarted? It may be that I am mistaken, that we are still on the path to salvation, and my own failings are limiting my experience of Ain."

"You don't sound convinced." Shader felt the heaviness of tension returning, settling upon his shoulders like a sodden coat. A chill breeze rustled the leaves of the forest, and cloud smothered the light of the sun. Shader felt an icy prickling at the nape of his neck.

"Something terrible has happened," Tajen said, cocking his head and shutting his eyes.

"What…?" Shader began but was arrested by Tajen's silencing hand.

The color drained from the luminary's face as the enormity of what he'd perceived dawned on him. "Death." His eyes snapped open, the pupils like two gaping holes onto the Void.

Almost immediately the sky blackened with thick clouds, and a shrill wind began to gust about the clearing. Screams sounded in the distance.

"Come," Tajen said, winking out of existence.

Shader followed, instinctively knowing the luminary's destination. They appeared in the darkness of an immense cavern. Stalactites glistened with droplets of a reddish liquid and spread an eerie haze throughout the interior. There was a dim glow coming from something on the ground, a dark and bloated shape looming over it. The other luminaries began to materialize, visibly shaken and gasping at the sight that greeted them. The lifeless body of Jarmin the Anchorite lay sprawled upon the rocky floor, his luminescence fading as the thing straddling him sucked and slurped at his mouth.

Jarmin's assailant was a pitch-black avalanche of blubber with squat arms and legs; a grotesque parody of a man jiggling with rolls of fat, its swollen face dripping cheeks that melted into the torso.

Shader took a step toward the monster, but froze as it raised its head and let out an anticipatory sigh, shifting its bulk to get a better look at him.

"So," it gurgled, "you followed me, little man. You realize you are mine. An agreement was reached."

"Agreement? What agreement?"

"Oh, of course, you weren't present. Nevertheless, a deal's a deal. If you have a grievance, address it to Dr. Cadman."

"Cadman?"

"What's up, honey, don't you recognize me? Don't you remember my touch?"

Shader stiffened at the memory of the demon's noxious belches, its tentacles cutting into his flesh, its undulating bulk smothering him.

"The Dweller." His voice quavered, and the demon closed in like a shark scenting blood. Shader scrabbled about for time. "Cadman sent you?"

"My lips are sealed." The Dweller gave a sickly grin. "You were promised to me, and believe me, it's better all round if you come quietly. By the way, how do you like my new look?" It lifted up the apron of flab covering its loins and wobbled it about. "Come on, my darling. Give us a hug."

The luminaries backed away and Shader felt hands tugging at him, but he shrugged them off. Ice formed in his veins as he watched the Dweller in fascinated horror. His guts churned in revulsion. He wanted so desperately to scream, to turn and run, but he was rooted to the spot as the creature lumbered toward him. The Dweller's tongue ran across its lips, thick ropes of drool oozing down its cheeks. It belched and held its belly, lifted the flab to reveal a flaccid maggot between its legs. With one hand, it began to rub there until the maggot starting to swell at an alarming rate.

The air shimmered, and a cowled figure appeared between Shader and the Dweller. It held out a shortsword with intricate letters etched into the blade. Shader recognized it instantly, as if it had cut through the fog of his amnesia.

"Archon," the Dweller snarled. "My master will trap you here."

Ignoring it, the cowled figure lifted its head toward Shader, bright light effusing from the hood and dazzling him.

"Take back my sword, Deacon Shader," the Archon said in a voice like the wind. "It learns from experience. It will prove stronger this time. Aid is on its way, drawn to the gladius. I cannot stay. This place is poison to…"

The gladius started to fall as the figure faded from view.

Snatching the hilt, Shader thrust the tip toward the Dweller, and golden light flared around the blade. The demon howled and dropped to its knees, frantically burrowing into the cave floor. Its fat backside wobbled and strained, and then squeezed into the hole with a plop. Earth and rock fell back behind it, covering its escape. Sounds of its underground digging thumped up through the cave floor for a few moments and then all was quiet.

Milo, Tajen, and Narcus crept forward and stood over the crumpled husk of Jarmin's body.

"How can this be?" Milo asked.

Tajen placed a hand on his shoulder, his eyes distant, frown-lines like gouges between his eyebrows. "Now do you see?" he said. "We have not arrived. We are still running the race."

The glow from Narcus's skin was noticeably dimmer. Fine tremors rippled through his limbs as he reached for Tajen's hand and pulled him close. "What is happening, Tajen? Where are we?"

"Besides Jarmin and Shader," Tajen said, "no soul has entered this so-called Araboth for centuries. As for that thing, that Dweller…"

Shader relaxed his grip on the sword and its light died. "I faced it on Earth, just before I came here," he said. "I suspect this is its natural abode."

"But why should it appear now?" asked Milo, his bronze tan dissolving in the sweat beading his skin.

Shader shrugged. "I remember it smothering me. There was a flash and then I was here with no idea of who I was. Something happened at the moment of my death."

Tajen knelt beside Jarmin's body. "What is it about you two that attracted the beast?"

Shader struggled to think as the luminary closed Jarmin's eyes. "It sensed something in me. Presumably, the same thing that drew it to Jarmin."

Take back my sword, the cowled man had said. The Dweller had referred to him as the Archon. More than ever, Shader was convinced he was dreaming, trapped in a nightmare of his own imaginings. The inklings of an explanation were starting to form in his mind. "I had a piece of an ancient artifact," he said to Tajen. "Is it possible Jarmin once possessed another?"

"What artifact?" demanded Tajen, turning from the corpse and standing. "Describe it to me."

Shader bent down and traced the outline of the serpent statue on the dust of the cave floor.

Tajen nodded. "Eingana, one of the three beings who fell from the Void. She who is forever pursued by her brother, the Demiurgos. Maybe that's what drew you here. Jarmin too. You'd both touched her power. It is like a scent, drawing the attention of the Demiurgos. But the demon…"

"I think it may have been wounded when it tried to consume me back in the templum," Shader said. "Perhaps the power of the sword and statue combined…" Shader tailed off.

Tajen's mouth was hanging open, as if he'd realized what he was saying. And then the penny dropped. Eingana, the Archon, and their brother, the Demiurgos. Shader had learnt something of the old myths from Aristodeus. Picture language, he'd called it. Metaphysics. If the Demiurgos existed, and if he'd drawn them here, then this could only be...

Shader met Tajen's eyes. The luminary stared blankly back at him, his mouth working, but no words coming out.

"What must we do?" Milo asked.

As if in answer, an aperture of green light appeared in the cave wall, and a young boy stepped out, freckled face streaked with grime, mousy hair matted and plastered to his scalp.

"Sammy!" Shader cried in disbelief.

"Quickly," the boy said. "Follow me."

Shader glanced at Tajen, who managed a shrug and a nod. "There is no other action open to us," the luminary said. "Act in faith and perhaps we shall all yet be saved."

The luminaries huddled together, their eyes flitting from Tajen to Shader and the boy. Shader didn't think it seemed right leaving them here, but Sammy continued to tug at him.

The cave began to tremble, a sound like an earthquake coming from the depths. Cracks ran across the floor, spewing forth rock-dust and acrid fumes. Distant laughter rumbled, and a voice echoed from the depths.

"I have your scent now. Run as fast as you can and despair."

The glow fell from the bodies of the luminaries. They looked to Shader more like the damned than the saved: hunched and twisted, flesh rough and gray like over-cooked meat. Tajen's eyes were wide and brimming with tears. He looked like a man who'd been proven right and wished he hadn't been.

"Go now, while you still can. We are not in Araboth." He took in his fellow luminaries who were babbling incoherently, their skin blistering and hanging from them in strips. "We are in the Abyss, the realm of the Demiurgos. We have all been deceived."

Reaching out a hand toward Tajen, Shader allowed Sammy to drag him away as the luminary's body erupted with buboes and pustules. Laughter reverberated around his skull. Nothing was real—maybe not even the luminaries, he realized with terrible clarity. Perhaps they'd been present because that's what he'd expected to see in Araboth. But how could he be sure? There was no point to any of this. No hope.

He lurched sideways, almost fell, but Sammy continued to pull him toward the aperture. Body limp, mind blank with despair, Shader stumbled and tripped, green light closing around him. The cackling ceased as if a door had been closed on it, leaving only silence in its wake.

THE LACUNAE

UNTSMAN'S SPIRIT HOVERED over the Void, feeling its pull and at the same time repelled by the ghostly web covering its mouth. He was reminded of the trapdoor spiders of Sahul lurking beneath their covers of soil and vegetation, trip lines set to warn of approaching prey. He felt the revulsion of the gods far away beneath the Homestead, their bodies pressed close to his in order to lend their strength to his spirit. He was gazing upon the abode of the dark god who had ravished Eingana and sired their father, the Cynocephalus. Huntsman shuddered, and a ripple passed through the light that formed his spirit-body. One touch of the misty strands and he would be trapped forever, and yet Sammy had been granted the power to enter the Abyss. The thought of the boy ensnared for eternity by the Demiurgos had led to his attempt to follow, but now he was close he knew there was little he could do other than watch and hope.

A tunnel of green light opened on the edge of the web, but a tendril of dark stuff lashed out and struck it, sending green sparks into the mist, where they were devoured. Two figures tumbled out and started to drift back toward the Abyss. Huntsman sped as close as he dared, the mist suddenly warm and inviting, promising to catch him and spare his spirit from oblivion. He could see Sammy now, hand in hand with Shader, struggling away from the Void like swimmers against the tide.

The Abyss bulged and shook, and for an instant, Huntsman could see the enormous face of a bald man with a white beard, eyes dark-ringed, lips curled into a grimace.

Aristodeus.

The Abyss sagged, and the philosopher's face was dragged back into its darkness, but not before he mouthed a silent word. The sword in Shader's hand blazed with the light of a thousand stars.

Sammy and Shader sped toward a rupture in the blackness before them.

"No," Huntsman called. "This way. You will be lost."

Sammy saw him and then looked past Huntsman to the Void, where splotches of inky blackness were hurled into space by the tendrils at the edge of the Abyss. The boy and the knight gaped with horror and then passed into the rupture.

The patches of Void stuff poured after them, holes in the darkness of space, pools of nothingness. Huntsman was about to follow when Aristodeus's voice sounded in his head. It was wracked with strain and torment.

"Fly, my friend. You can do nothing to help them. They are pursued by lacunae—the empty spaces. The Demiurgos is grasping the power of the Void."

"But what about you?" Huntsman said.

The voice grew fainter, as if walls had suddenly been thrown up around it. "I have done what I can—a word that should not be uttered. Would that it were enough. Do not concern yourself with me. I will prevail. It is Shader who needs you. Help him."

Silence fell, and Huntsman felt suddenly like a creator god surveying the bare matter of the cosmos and considering what he could make to drive back the darkness. His head began to hurt with the magnitude of the emptiness before him. Infinite blackness in every direction, the Void yawning even blacker below, and above there was just the glimmer of two distant stars, not the usual spray of lights that he could see from Sahul.

For an instant, golden light surged from the tear Sammy and Shader had passed into, but then even that died as the split closed like a healed wound. Huntsman offered a prayer to Sahul in the hope that she would draw them home, and then returned with a heavy heart to his body in the caves beneath the Homestead.

***

Shader could see Sammy was ailing fast. Every step took them into a new realm, each jarringly different and disorienting. They stood at a junction overlooking kaleidoscopic vistas that never settled long enough for the eyes to focus. They shouldn't have made it. The Abyss had them in its pull, but then came that word, soundless yet with the force of thunder, and the sword had responded. Shader both knew the word and didn't. It was familiar, but not yet. A memory waiting to be retrieved, or a glimpse of something to come. Somehow it was beyond speech, beyond his ability to decipher.

"Sammy, fix your gaze on me," Shader found himself shouting, and then realized that all was silent.

When the boy dragged his eyes away from the shifting landscapes Shader saw only fear and uncertainty; the sort of fear you'd expect from a child, and yet he could sense something different about Sammy, the unveiling of depths he'd hitherto not suspected.

"I'm sorry, Deacon," Sammy said, eyes flooding with tears. "I don't know the way."

Shader pulled the boy into a hug and Sammy nestled his head into his chest, trembling as he sobbed.

"No one could know the way in this," Shader said. "It took someone special to find me at all, and for that you will always have my thanks."

Sammy looked up, rubbing the tears away with the back of his hand. "I did OK?"

"More than OK." Shader lifted Sammy's chin and looked deep into his eyes. "It's good to have friends I can rely on."

Sammy smiled at that, but there was still the hint of a frown tugging at his face.

"Don't worry about your sister, Sammy. She's safe; she made it to the templum."

"Are you OK with her?" Sammy pulled away.

"Always," Shader said. It was more the case of was she OK with him? "Come. You got me out of the Abyss; the least I can do is get you home, right?"

"Right."

As they resumed their passage through the planes, Shader turned his attention to the fleeting skies of gold, purple, black, and crimson. He shivered at a blast of icy air that immediately gave way to searing heat and then muggy humidity. They were assailed by sleet and rain on the one step, lightning, snow, or calm on the next. Shader had just grown used to traveling without delay to wherever he imagined, but in this jumble of worlds, he had no idea where to go, and try as he might to visualize a destination back home, nothing happened. Perhaps the ability to travel instantaneously had been just another deception of the Demiurgos, no more real than Araboth.

The sword's light was the only constant in the chaos of worlds, and Shader held firmly to its hilt, following its pull like a diviner looking for water.

"We can rest a while, if you like," Shader said, placing a reassuring hand on the boy's shoulder.

Sammy slapped it away and sucked in his top lip. "We mustn't stop. The Archon says monsters are coming."

"The Archon?"

Sammy waved him to silence and led him into yet another world, this time atop a scorched volcano, the air thick with noxious fumes. One step more and they were submerged in viscous golden fluid; yet another and they stood in green fields beneath a mauve sky.

Suddenly, the air was rent with black holes, chaotic shapes of emptiness that appeared from nowhere and swarmed toward them. Shader dragged Sammy backward into a realm of metal bathed in silver light. The patches of nothingness swooped after them, closing in on Shader like flies drawn to sugar. He swiped at one with the gladius, but the sword refused to strike. Shader pushed Sammy behind him and swayed out of the way of a cluster of empty blobs.

"Don't let them touch you," Sammy cried. "The Archon says they are lacunae, the stuff of the Void."

Shader could imagine what that meant.

The lacunae quivered as one and then split, each shape becoming two holes in the fabric of the worlds. They raced toward Shader in a pincer movement, causing him to flee into another world, shoving Sammy before him.

They stood upon a narrow ledge over an infinite drop. Above them, fire filled the sky and a fierce wind was gusting. Sammy teetered on the edge, but Shader grabbed him and helped him to shuffle sideways into a forest made of tar. Cobalt skies broke through the oily foliage and dark mist swirled from a staff that had been thrust into the earth—centuries ago judging by the creepers and vines that wound about it.

The lacunae blinked into view one at a time and continued their relentless stalking of Shader. This time it was Sammy who pulled them into another world and Shader immediately realized their doom. They were backed up against a sheer cliff face with only the narrowest of passes before them. The lacunae slipped through the gaps between the worlds and began to merge, forming an impassable wall of emptiness. As they floated toward the pair, Shader stepped in front of Sammy, determined to charge the lacunae in the hope that his destruction would put an end to their pursuit. Before he could take a step, the gladius purred in his hand and white fire flared along the blade, streaking into the sky. The trail of flame bent and twisted as if searching for something and then arced behind Shader and struck the cliff. A green glow sprang up in answer, spiraling upon the rock until it formed an opening. A huge man emerged, black-skinned and with the head of a serpent. Shader raised the sword to strike, but Sammy pulled at his shoulder.

"No, don't. It's Mamba."

"Quick, Sssammy," the snake-man opened his arms and the boy leapt into his embrace. The green portal was already starting to close. "Ssso sssorry." He gave Shader a pitying look as he stepped back inside the aperture with the boy. "No time for a sssecond trip."

Shader nodded as the opening vanished. Steeling himself for the touch of oblivion, he turned to face the advancing wall of blackness.

"Focus, Shader," said a voice in his head that reminded him of the crunch of brown autumn leaves beneath the feet. "You'll get only one chance. This is the best I can do."

An image formed behind his eyes—a body lying in a pool of its own blood.

"Focus. Shut your eyes and concentrate on my sword with your whole being."

The wall of emptiness was so close now Shader could feel his skin crawling, the dread of annihilation twisting a knot in his stomach.

Gripping the sword with both hands, he raised it before his face and, taking a deep breath that was likely to be his last, closed his eyes. He felt the gladius throbbing, attuned himself to it, and let his awareness of all else fall beneath an obscuring cloud of darkness.

The roar of a million stars exploding tore him apart.

In an instant, it was over, and Shader was shocked to find he still held the sword. Even with his eyes closed, the blade's incandescence was blinding. He gasped for breath and blinked until his vision returned.

The dead body came into sharp focus at the end of a tunnel through the cliff face. It was armored beneath a black coat and a white surcoat with the red Nousian Monas. Blue fingers clutched a longsword in one hand, and a broad-brimmed hat lay crumpled beside the head. Black hair framed the gaunt face like a dark halo; the eyes were white and vacant. The body faded away, and the cliff grew once more solid and impassable. Shader glanced over his shoulder. The wall of nothingness was still there, a hair's breadth away.

Something yanked at his umbilicus, spinning him from the path of the lacunae. He felt the emptiness rushing toward his back, but then his spine arched violently and he was catapulted face first toward the cliff. He tensed before he struck, but there was no impact, only blackness as featureless as the Void itself. The terrible realization struck him that he'd missed his chance and the lacunae had struck him from existence.

THE RESURRECTION OF DEACON SHADER

*H*OLDING THE SWORD.
Still thinking.
I am.

Gray walls of mortared stone emerged from the darkness. Rows of pews stretched away from Shader down a long nave to the shattered wooden doors of the Templum of the Knot. He was suspended above the altar, the gladius still held firmly in both hands, but its light now spent. He craned his neck to see what was holding him in the air, but there was nothing.

And then he saw the body and the pool of viscous blood in which it lay. The skin was ashen, the black hair slick with gore, and the once white tunic stained crimson. In that instant, as he gazed with cold dread upon his own corpse, he knew that Tajen had been right: he'd not been dreaming—the gladius was proof of that; and he'd not been in Araboth, the realm of the dead, either. The doppelgänger sprawled on the templum floor was testimony that he'd been in two places at once. His flesh had bled out on Earth, while his soul was trapped on the brink of oblivion in the demesne of the Demiurgos.

Time stood still as Shader contemplated his spirit body. The flesh felt real enough, and yet it now levitated above the ground. It seemed possessed of boundless energy, its organs harmonized and orientated beyond the usual petty desires and instincts with which he was accustomed. It was a good feeling, exhilarating; but it no longer seemed real. The corpse below him was his anchor to reality, the bedrock of his humanity. It was so clear now; his struggle was not a war between the flesh and the spirit, it was a search for authenticity. For the first time, he knew what the Gray Abbot had meant when he'd quoted one of the ancient Paters: *The glory of Ain is a human fully alive.* Rhiannon had been wrong. No, Huntsman had been wrong. Aristodeus had been wrong. Shader felt his muscles tighten, even in the spirit. Rhiannon was no threat to his purity. If anything she was as essential to his being as the beating of his heart.

Fully alive: not one thing or the other, knight or monk. Just a man.

Nothing stirred beyond the wreckage of the doors. The templum was empty, leaving Shader to wonder at the outcome of the battle with the undead and the Dweller. He turned his attention back to the body on the floor and was about to check its pockets for the serpent statue when a cowled figure materialized in the air above the chancel.

"It has gone, Deacon Shader. Already taken."

Shader lowered his eyes. "I heard your voice in my head when I fled from the Abyss."

"My voice is often in your head, only you never cease your internal chatter long enough to hear it. So, you believe in me now, do you?"

The Archon? Shader had assumed he was just a Templum myth propagated to bolster the supernatural elements of the faith. "Well, I have your sword," he said, twirling the gladius in his hand, "and that seems real enough."

The Archon laughed—a sibilant rustling sound like a breeze through dried leaves. "You find it easier to accept magic than the existence of angels?"

"Is that what you are?"

"No," the Archon said. "But that is what I have been called for centuries. Tell me, what does it feel like to be a being of pure spirit?"

Shader looked from his spirit hands to the body of flesh lying on the floor like a wax effigy. "Incomplete," he said.

"Good. A man who finally knows his place." The Archon drifted down to stand before Shader and placed a hand on his head. The gladius quivered slightly and seemed to sigh.

"You must be whole again, Shader," the Archon said. "The Ipsissimus is coming for the final battle, and he will need you."

Shader pulled away, drifting further back into the sanctuary. "I'm out of favor in Aeterna. The Ipsissimus sent the Judiciary after me. He'd rather I was dead than dissenting."

The Archon turned, sparing Shader the blaze from his face. "I'm afraid your friend Aristodeus was insistent on you leaving with the sword. Things are desperate; more desperate than you could ever know. I've entrusted him with this move, despite his previous failure. If we lose again, I'm not sure fate would be so forgiving a second time."

"What...?"

The Archon held up a hand that appeared to be made from porcelain. "I go too far. I have already said too much. Forgive me, Deacon Shader, and grant me one thing." Light spilled from the edge of the hood as the Archon tilted his head to look at Shader. "Your faith."

Shader frowned. "That's something I have in short supply."

"Understandably," the Archon said. "These are the times of deception. My brother must be very pleased with his progress. Even the Templum is divided, and it is no small task to keep it on the path of light. Theodore is a good man, but he will not be Ipsissimus forever."

Shader nodded his understanding. Everyone knew that Exemptus Silvanus was his most likely successor. The Prefect of the Judiciary was a rigid traditionalist, a hard-liner. Shader had fallen under his influence during his formation in the Elect. *The Discipline*, they'd called him on account of the punishments he'd inflict for even the slightest deviation from his particular brand of orthodoxy.

"Tell me," the Archon said, interrupting his train of thought, "do you believe in resurrection?"

Shader was taken aback by the question and scrabbled about for an answer. "It's mentioned in the Liber."

"Not as much as it once was," the Archon said, white fire flaring from his cowl. "The Liber has been altered, but there is still gold to be found there if you know where to look."

"But—"

"Another time. Resurrection. What is it? A new life? The same life restored? The raising of a spiritual body?" The Archon flashed a look at Shader. "Or is it something altogether more subtle, intangible? What would happen, I wonder, if you were to touch your own flesh? Come, try it."

Shader floated down to his double and knelt. The sword shifted restlessly in his grip. He bent over the body and reached out a hand. As he made contact, he felt a sickening thud and found himself staring up at the ceiling. Something damp and sticky clung to his head. Reaching up he felt it was a lock of his own hair slick with congealed blood.

"How do you feel?" the Archon asked, looming over Shader. "Resurrected, or something else?"

"Heavy. My back hurts like the Abyss."

"Excellent. So there is no difference between how you were at the moment of your death and how you are now. You are still fully human."

Shader forced himself into a sitting position. The wound in his back began to seep more blood. He felt queasy and started to swoon. The Archon leaned in close and pressed down on it with his hand. Immediately, the flesh knitted together, the pain faded, and warmth flooded back into his once dead body. Sparing a quick glance at the oddly purring gladius, Shader hurriedly sheathed it and rose to his feet.

"What am I?" he asked. "Another animated corpse like those that serve Cadman?"

The Archon dipped his head for a moment before making his reply. "You are the same man risen, Shader, but you have seen things no one should see. I am not convinced that Aristodeus is right about you. You are the desperate plan of a desperate man, but it is the best we have. You may not have found your faith, but I will make you the gift of mine. Find your friends—they have fled this place; take counsel, and do not be swayed by power for that is the chief weapon of the Deceiver. Fulfil your task, Deacon Shader. It is a long road you must take. If it is the wrong one, then the error is Aristodeus's, but the guilt is mine for permitting it."

"But why me? Why can't you...?"

White fire consumed the Archon, coalescing into a ball of flame and winking out of existence. Shader was left staring at his boots, feeling leaden and exhausted. It took all his will to lift his eyes and scan the emptiness surrounding him, the wreckage of the doors through which the Dweller had forced its entrance.

Tajen's contorted face came unbidden to his mind, flesh peeling from his skull, the blank look of despair filling his eyes. Shader shook his head and the image dispersed like mist in the breeze. Clenching his jaw, he drew back his shoulders and set off down the nave. All he could think of was the urgent need to gain some distance from the desolation of the templum.

PLANS AND PREPARATIONS

S HADER MADE HIS way through the deserted streets of Sarum. Occasionally, he would glimpse a face peering at him through gaps in shutters, and once or twice he spotted dark clad vagabonds rifling the bodies of the dead. None approached him; he felt like a lion among hyenas.

He made for Arnbrook House with the intention of enquiring about the fate of his friends. Passing the stone Arch of Welcome that had stood as long as Sarum's ancient spires, he pressed himself flat against a wall as he was confronted with a gruesome sight that turned his stomach. Cadman's deathly troops had apparently found new recruits among the plague victims. A vast undead army now filled the square before the council offices, spilling into the adjoining streets. To the rear of the horde, he could see the horsemen of the Lost. In all there must have been a thousand rotting and animated corpses assembled, all waiting with the patience and stillness of the grave. Muttering a curse, he retraced his steps. If the others had survived, if they weren't among the numbers of the walking dead, they'd have found somewhere to hole up in the city. The priests would stick out like diamonds in dung. Somebody must have seen them.

In spite of the rule of undeath, the city had started to come back to some semblance of life now that the plague appeared to have relaxed its grip. Sarum's drawn and haggard populace began to creep forth from their dwellings, still wary at first of contact with one another, still frightened and grieving. Here and there, a market stall was erected where those with the foresight to store and preserve their wares now profited from the desperate hunger of their fellows. It was from such a stall that Shader learned that the priests were hiding in a dilapidated townhouse in Edgebriar. Apparently, a fat man in a white robe had come this morning to purchase rations.

Cadris screamed when he opened the door to Shader and then started blubbering about Nous and resurrection. Soror Agna almost genuflected, but opted instead for an open-mouthed look of astonishment. Ioana, when at last she came downstairs, looked for the wound in his back, noted its disappearance, and simply sniffed.

Once the initial shock of his arrival had passed, Shader was bustled up three flights of stairs and a flimsy ladder to the attic.

Gaston was sitting with his back against a joist. Soror Velda was stooped over him adjusting the bloodstained bandages that were wound about his torso. Her spectacles kept slipping down her nose, causing her to tut and shove them back up. Shader felt his mouth curling into a tired smile—it was like Sisyphus pushing his boulder up the hill only to have it roll back down again. The smile turned to a frown as he remembered it was Aristodeus who had told him the story. The philosopher claimed it came from his homeland of Graecia millennia before the Reckoning.

Maldark mooched beneath the eaves, his chin resting on the stone head of his war-hammer. His eyes widened slightly at the sight of Shader, and he almost smiled.

Rhiannon had an open Liber in her lap, her lips moving silently to the words of a prayer. Shader thought how drab the white clerical vestments made her look, and for a moment entertained the image of tearing the garments from her and unleashing her great raven tousles. The image startled him. It was the first indication that all was not pure and uncomplicated since his return to life. Rhiannon looked up abruptly, as if she'd read his thoughts. The color fled her face and her mouth hung open.

"You're dead," she said. "Gaston saw…"

Shader shook his head and moved to make way for the priests coming up the ladder behind him.

Gaston waved Velda away and pulled on his surcoat, leaving his armor heaped on the floor.

"I-I-I wasn't lying." He shot a look at Rhiannon before rising and to examine Shader. "It was Shadrak—the assassin who m-m-murdered my dad."

"The lad speaks sooth," Maldark said. "He pushed past me on the stairway to the crypt. Brave or foolish, 'tis hard to say, but in any case, he was too late."

"The little shogger s-s-stabbed you," Gaston said. "Right … here."

Shader batted his hand away. "I know. I felt it, and then the demon rolled over me."

"Aye," Maldark said, "'Twas then I grabbed Gaston and fled, though I see it is to my shame."

"My spirit was parted from my body," Shader said. He couldn't blame any of them. They'd already shown more courage than he could imagine staying as long as they did. "I thought I was in Araboth, walking among the luminaries."

Ioana folded her arms and cocked her head. "You were dreaming?"

Shader sat on a beam and pulled his hat off, running a hand through his sweat-drenched hair. He flicked a look at Rhiannon. Her lips were working, her eyes moist, her fingers clenching and unclenching. He couldn't tell if she was relived, confused, or angry. It was easier just to look away and answer Ioana. "I wish I had been."

There was a hushed expectancy, as if nothing could surprise them anymore. Shader was starting to feel that his was the only world view to be turned on its head.

"The Statue of Eingana and the Sword of the Archon combined to drive off the creature. When it was cast back into the Abyss I fell with it."

He took a deep breath and hurried on, not wishing to dwell on the images of the luminaries warping and melting, twisting into creatures of nightmare.

Maldark was watching him through narrowed eyes. "I have passed through the Abyss," the dwarf said. "There are few who come out again. How didst thou manage it?"

"I had help," Shader said. "The Archon bought me some time…"

Ioana touched her forehead. "The Archon? But he's—"

"Real," Shader said. "As are so many of the myths. The sword really is his gift to Aeterna. I'd always thought it a fraud; a powerful one, but a fraud nonetheless. He couldn't free me, though. The Abyss seems inimical to him."

Ioana nodded, her focus far away. "It is the abode of his brother. The two are like oil and water, it is said. Light and darkness."

Shader became aware of the tightening of his stomach. He doubled over on his perch and grimaced. "Do you have any food? It feels like I've not eaten for days."

Cadris scurried about the attic as the others seated themselves in a semi-circle about Shader like children awaiting a ghost story.

Shader looked up and fixed his eyes on Rhiannon. "Sammy came for me," he said. "He brought me out of the Abyss."

She shook her head, her brow creased with strain. "Sammy? He's OK? How…?"

Cadris passed Shader a crust of stale bread and a cup of dirty water. Shader nodded his thanks, but kept his eyes locked to Rhiannon's.

"Huntsman still has him. I think he's changing the boy. He has new powers."

"Shog that!" Rhiannon stood, hands on her hips. The Liber fell to the floor in a heap of creased pages.

Velda pushed her spectacles back on the bridge of her nose and dropped to her knees. She scooped up the book as if it were a sickly child and clutched it to her breast. Ioana touched a hand to her shoulder and offered a weak smile.

"He also speaks with the Archon," Shader said. "The boy is special."

"I already know that," Rhiannon said. "But if you think I'm gonna let that bloody witch doctor take my Sammy…"

"What do you want to do about it?" Shader stormed, breadcrumbs spraying from his mouth. "We've all suffered, and there's bound to be a whole lot more suffering before this is over."

Rhiannon raised a fist, the knuckles scabby and raw.

Shader frowned. "What happened to you?" He took another bite of bread and did his best to ignore her rising anger.

"S-S-Shadrak's face," Gaston said. "She beat the living c-c-crap out of him."

"Now why doesn't that surprise me?" Shader said. "You don't want to mess with a Kwane."

Gaston laughed. "Shog, no. Those udder-pumping arms s-s-sure pack a wallop."

Rhiannon sniggered, her eyes glinting. Shader smiled, and for an instant the three were as they'd always been, utterly familiar and happy in each other's company. But then Rhiannon turned away, her arms wrapped tightly about her chest. Gaston lowered his head and moved to the back of the attic where he accepted some bread from Cadris.

"Where are the others?" Shader asked no one in particular. "Frater Hugues? Pater Limus?"

"Limus fell behind in the tunnels," Maldark said. "We tarried a while to look for him, but there was no sign. Hugues fled when the Dweller appeared. Ain knows where he is. Mayhap he is still at the templum."

"I saw no one when I left," Shader said, fearing the worst. "What about the White Order?"

Gaston looked up from the gloom at the rear of the attic, but said nothing.

"Barek led them to look for help," Rhiannon said over her shoulder. "There weren't enough of them to fight back, and they'd only have drawn attention to the rest of us. If they're lucky, they'll link up with the militia."

"Or the imperial troops outside the city," Gaston said.

Shader glared at him, but Gaston was looking at the floor, his shoulders bunched up about his ears. "They'll find no help there," Shader said. "Your attack won't have been forgotten. One other thing." He scanned the group. "The serpent statue given to me by Huntsman has been taken."

"Must've been Shadrak," Gaston said.

Rhiannon turned back to face Shader. "He came up from the crypt. We thought he'd come to help, though shog knows why. Guess we were too flaming scared to care at the time."

Shader's hand went to his back. The wound had healed, but he still felt the pain. "I'll find him." He narrowed his eyes and sucked in a long breath through his teeth. "But first things first. We have to get word to Barek and see if we can drum up some more support. We can't let the city fall to Cadman."

SERVILITY AND COMMAND

T HE SUN DIPPED below the distant towers of the city center, leaving streaks of pink and crimson across the darkening sky. Barek spat into a rag and rubbed at the basinet in his lap. He couldn't really see what he was doing, but that wasn't the point. He needed to keep busy.

The rest of the White Order knights were sitting around fires dotted about the hilltop at the center of Lesmallen, Sarum's easternmost suburb. It was a play area, judging by the wooden climbing frames and the knotted ropes hanging from the branches of trees encircling the camp. Further down the hill he could see the orange glow from the windows of the locals' cabins. Most had their own smallholdings and allotments; they were doing their best to live apart from the bustle of the city. Probably reckoned themselves among the lucky few now.

No one had approached the knights in the two days they'd been in Lesmallen. At best, they'd drawn suspicious glances, but mostly they'd been greeted by closed shutters and sullen silence. Lesmallen appeared to have escaped the worst of the plague, but clearly, its residents were taking no chances. It was Barek's guess that the locals thought the White Order was in the vanguard of trouble spreading out from Sarum's center like a cancer. Maybe they were right, he thought, but what choice had they had? They'd already lost four more men to the hordes of walking dead as they'd ridden clear of the chaos, and if they fled beyond the city walls, they'd have to answer for the attack on the imperial troops.

"That's my job, milord," Dave the Slave said, snatching the basinet from Barek.

The old hunchback had followed them up from Calphon where they'd passed him squatting in the gutter, clearing dead leaves from the drains. Barek shook his head and felt his face tightening in a wry smile as he realized he'd used the nickname the lads had given the bloke on account of his insistence that he do all the menial chores around camp. At first, they'd tried to send him away, but when he hung around they'd offered to pay him. Dave would accept nothing. He just kept groaning about penance and touching his brow in the Nousian manner.

"Sit yourself down, Dave," Barek said. "You've been on the go all day."

Dave stooped over him and twisted his neck to see better. He was mostly bald, but long strands of hair hung like twine over his shoulders. His forehead was a craggy overhang, the eyes beneath glinting with a feverish intelligence. His face reminded Barek of a horse's—long chin, flat nose, and lips that were thick and drooping, opening like a clam to reveal the stumps of yellow teeth. He was dressed in a sackcloth tunic and woolen trousers that stank like the furred-up pig shit Barek's dad used as compost.

"The Demiurgos loves an idler," Dave muttered, giving the basinet a polish with the hem of his tunic. "*Ora et labora*, I always says. It's hard work that paves the mountain path to Araboth. I'll bring your helmet back in the morning, polished clear as glass. Anything else I can do for you? Nice sizzling sausage? Hunk of crusty bread? How about

251

I groom your horse and pick the grit from her shoes?"

Barek raised a hand and forced a smile. "You've done more than enough, Dave. Get some rest. You'll need your strength in the morning."

Dave's eyes narrowed and his lips drew back in a snarl. He thrust the basinet under one arm, turned away from Barek and limped toward the camp.

"Can't please some people, eh, sir," Solomon said, stepping from the gloom like a ghost.

Barek suppressed a pang of irritation. The boy—Solomon had just turned sixteen— had shadowed him ever since the flight from the templum.

"I was about to grab some kip," Barek said, pointedly rolling out his blanket.

Solomon crouched down, eyes fixed on the thin strip of red that was fading from the horizon.

"Me too, sir. Just thought I'd see if there's anything you wanted me to do."

What was it about people wanting to do things for him? Barek gritted his teeth and forced himself to relax.

"Just get some sleep, Sol. There'll be plenty to do in the morning."

Solomon nodded, rocking on his haunches. "Sir..." He drew in a big gulp of air. "Back there at the templum..."

"You did good, Sol. We all did."

The lad pushed down on his thighs and stood. "I was scared, sir. I should've helped him—Master Shader."

Barek had been feeling the same way, but he knew there was nothing they could have done. No matter what ideals of bravery they held, they were only human after all. He shuddered at the recollection of the terror emanating from the demon.

"It takes more than swords to stand against some foes. Better to retreat and fight another day."

"That's what the others say, but Elgin, sir—excuse me for saying it— Elgin says if he was in charge he'd have made us stay."

Barek dropped his head. He'd been expecting this. What right did he have to lead the Order, just because Shader had left and Gaston was out of the way? Justin was the natural choice, but he'd last been seen out cold on the ground in front of the templum. Barek had assumed command because no one else had, but the challenge was bound to come sooner or later.

"Elgin has a right to speak his mind," Barek said. "Maybe in the morning we should elect a new master."

Solomon sucked in his lips. He opened his mouth to say something, but was arrested by a cry from one of the sentries.

"Someone's coming up."

Barek grabbed his sword and scabbard and ran toward the sound, Solomon close on his heels. He placed a hand on the sentry's shoulder— Gord Pelham from Broken Bridge.

"Who is it, Gord?"

"There, sir." Gord pointed into the darkness as a figure emerged from the tree line. "Blow me for a... I mean, bless my soul, it's Justin."

Barek's heart jumped and his mouth felt suddenly dry. "Justin," he called out. "You're OK."

Shadows flickered across Justin as he stopped to warm his hands above the outermost campfire.

"Shit would be a better way to describe how I feel." He turned to indicate the bloody tangle of hair at the back of his head. "Thanks for your help. Much appreciated."

Barek lowered his eyes and picked at his teeth with his thumbnail. "Justin, I'm sorry. Shader..." Barek tensed as Justin came toward him around the fire.

"Shader was right," Justin said, "and Gaston screwed up. Reckon I deserved it."

Barek looked up, mouth dropping open and no words coming out.

"I might be a hard bastard—" Justin slapped a hand on Barek's shoulder. "—but I'm not a total shogwit. OK, maybe I hoped we could take the good from Cadman and pass on the bad." He patted the pommel of his sword and rubbed the front of his chainmail hauberk. "And we already know I'm not your typical Nousian; but that business at the templum was too much. Shog, man, I got caught up in it at the time, but once the fighting died down I nearly crapped myself at what we'd done. How many we got left?"

"Thirty-five, including you," Barek said, scanning the camp.

Justin sniffed. "Got any food? I'm starving."

Dave hobbled over with a plate of sausages and a huge doorstop of bread. It gave Barek the creeps. Seemed like the hunchback knew exactly what was needed before anyone even realized there was a need. If Justin was concerned, he didn't show it. He snatched the food and began to wolf it down, speaking through mouthfuls.

"Thanks. And you are?"

Dave bowed so low his forehead nearly grazed the ground. "Dave, Master. Your humble servant."

Justin raised an eyebrow at Barek, who just shrugged. "Followed us from Calphon. He's been a great help."

Dave wrinkled his nose at that, spat, and shuffled off toward the next fire, collecting plates and mumbling something over and over in a low monotone.

"Cool," Justin said. "So, tell me, Barek, what's it like being boss now?" Justin wrapped an arm around Barek's neck and gave a big squeeze, leading him to the center of the circle of fires. The other knights stood, many of them drawing swords. Barek felt his chin quivering and couldn't keep the fear from his voice when he spoke.

"You're the leader, Justin. Always were, after Gaston, and Ain knows where he is now."

Justin released him and stood up tall, hands on hips. "The leader should be the strongest? Is that what you're saying?"

Barek grimaced. "Well, yes."

Justin drew his sword and held it high. "The strength of a man is measured by his sword, eh?" He spun round to take in the assembled knights, who must have seen something on his face as they began to laugh and put their weapons away.

Barek forced himself to look into Justin's eyes, which reflected the glow of the campfires, but may also have had a twinkle of their own.

"Come on, Barek. Why so serious? You're the boss now. The lads trust you, and just look at what you've already done."

Barek turned his palms up. "What?"

Justin raised his voice to make sure everyone could hear. "You brought the Order to safety. You made the big decision, man, and it was the right one."

"Bollocks!" Elgin said, stepping into the circle, his broad shoulders swallowing up his neck. He towered above Barek and Justin, his barrel chest making him seem almost as wide as he was tall.

"You're the boss, Justin, and that's final. Besides Gaston, no one else comes close with a sword. Don't get me wrong. Barek's a nice enough bloke, but he ain't got the balls to lead."

A few of the knights grumbled their agreement.

Justin's eyes were locked to Barek's, apparently awaiting his next move. Barek was about to say that he agreed with Elgin when Sol appeared at his side.

"I say Barek should lead. He's the one that got us out of the city. What we need now is a level head in charge."

Elgin snarled at him. "I'll level your shogging head if you don't shut it, wimp."

Sol stood his ground, despite the fact that his hands were shaking. "*In the absence of the appointed master—*" Sol was quoting Shader's rule verbatim. "*—a successor shall be elected by no less than a majority of seventy percent.*"

"Yeah? Well, I reckon I got about seventy percent right here," Elgin said, raising a club-like fist and stepping toward Sol. Without thinking, Barek got in between them, hand on the hilt of his sword, eyes narrowing.

"Back down, big man."

Elgin faltered, looked from Justin to Barek, and then bared his teeth. "You shogging little runt!" Elgin reached for his sword, but Justin's foot snapped out and caught him in the groin. Elgin deflated like an empty wineskin, clutched his balls, and sank to his knees. Justin lunged forward and cracked him on the chin with an uppercut that sent Elgin sprawling to the dirt.

"You got my vote, Barek," Justin said. "Don't let me down."

"Mine, too," Sol said, standing to attention and lifting his chin.

A chorus of agreement sounded from the watching knights, with the only dissent a feeble moan from Elgin. Barek caught sight of Dave the Slave looking up from the scrubbing of a pan, bottom lip sticking out, head cocked to one side and nodding slightly.

"That's settled, then," Justin said. "Barek's the new master."

Barek drew in a deep breath and rolled his shoulders to ease a bit of the tension. "What if Gaston comes back? Or Shader?"

"Shog them," Justin said. "Reckon they made their choices. Ain't that right, lads?"

A great shout of "Yeah" went up, and then, one by one, the knights knelt and bowed their heads.

A lump formed in Barek's throat and his eyes welled up. He waved his acknowledgement and then raised his voice.

"Dave," he called to the hunchback, who was standing just beyond the circle of knights. "Don't suppose you have any wine?"

Dave scurried forward still wiping at a pan. "I could ask about, Master." He nodded down the hill toward the houses. "I'd love it if you'd let me prepare a feast. Don't worry, Master, I'll do the clearing up."

"Did someone mention wine?" Gord hollered from his post. "What're you waiting for?"

As Dave hurried from the camp, Barek offered his hand to Justin. "I'll need you by my side, Justin."

"I know. So, what's the plan for the morning?"

Barek sighed. They didn't have enough men to retake the city, and yet they couldn't abandon the people.

"Don't see we have much choice," he said. "We are Nousians, after all."

Justin's mouth curled into a grim smile as he seated himself by a fire, gesturing for Barek to join him.

"Don't think I'm gonna like this," he said. "Maybe you'd better tell me once the wine starts flowing."

IN TOO DEEP

SOMETHING'S WRONG.

Cadman chewed anxiously at the tips of his chubby fingers. He peeked through the slats of the shutters onto the lamp-lit street outside Ambrook House. A cordon of corpses faced the building, red eyes glaring like jack-o'-lanterns. The broad plaza beyond was packed with rows of undead drawn up in a gigantic phalanx. The corpses were in varying states of decay and shrouded in soiled rags. They clutched an assortment of weapons—some martial, others janitorial. Nothing to be feared there. Outside, all was still. No one had dared approach his army, and the cadavers could do nothing unless Cadman commanded it: they were totally subservient to his will.

Cadman felt bone weary and would have yawned, only he'd forgotten how. He'd never raised so many corpses before, and yet he'd still only required a fraction of the statue's power. Maybe it was worth the risk, coming out of hiding to take center stage when the rewards were so high. The ever-present chill in his bones had turned to ice. He might have believed that had it not been for the memory of the look his driver had given him, the echoes of the mocking laughter. Oh, there'd been no repeat performance, not yet, at any rate, but he'd seen enough to rue the day he ignored his own advice.

Didn't Mama say never speak with strangers? I can't really see what else you'd call a mysterious man in black walking into the surgery demanding treatment for the rotting carcass of a cat. You're an oaf, Cadman, an imbecile. Never draw attention, never act, and never, ever trust a psychopathic dead-cat fetishist.

He fastened the buttons of his jacket over the mountain of his belly and thrust his hands into the pockets, where warmth still radiated from the eye and the fang.

Just tired, perhaps.

Cadman turned to the globe drinks cabinet he'd had brought up from Councilor Arkin's office the night before. He'd sold it to the councilor years ago and used the money to set up his surgery. Arkin had no further need of it. The old soak was out there in the phalanx, probably wielding a bottle of Scotch as a club. Cadman spun the globe around on its castors so he didn't have to look at Verusia then flipped up the top hemisphere and selected a Gallic brandy. He wished he could say it was good stuff— undoubtedly it was if Arkin's reputation was anything to go by—but it all tasted the same to him.

Someone screamed in the corridor outside. Cadman poured himself a double.

It was hard to tell if it was a woman or a man until the fellow started to plead. Cadman took a sip and swilled the tasteless fluid around his mouth. Councilor Willem, by the sound of it. Good show for the devious old scoundrel to hold out so long. No doubt caught on his way to the latrines. Poor chap had probably been holding it in for hours. *No mean feat with a prostate the size of a melon. Bravo, old chap. Bravo.*

As Willem's gurgling cries died away, Cadman flopped into his chair and glanced over the medical papers awaiting his attention. He picked up the first and read the patient's name.

"Dead." He scrunched it into a ball and dropped it on the floor.

"Dead." He did the same with the next. "Dead, dead, dead."

Tiring of the effort, he swept the entire stack into the bin and gave himself a refill.

"Shader still lives," said the whispering wind.

Cadman sprayed brandy all over the desk and leapt to his feet.

"Up here."

The ceiling bulged and sagged as a glob of blackness swelled into being. Cadman squinted and backed against the wall. A belly button popped out, followed by an avalanche of flab as the stomach dropped to the floor and quivered in a pool of lard. The black stuff parted and a face emerged, its features sliding about beneath the skin, swapping places so that eyes became ears, the chin a nose, and the cheeks great meaty lips. The continuous warping forced Cadman to look away out of fear for his sanity.

"You didn't say anything about the Sword of the Archon, coupled with which he had the body of the statue upon his person." The voice was sickly sweet, an innocent child who'd been led astray.

Sword of the Archon? What the deuce is that?

"How was I to know?" Cadman said, sidling back to the desk and pouring another drink with shaking hands. Most of the brandy splashed to the tabletop, but the rest he downed in one.

"Tut, tut, Doctor." The face took on a sterner aspect, older and drawn, the nose long and aquiline, gray hair slicked back and stained with yellow. Cadman dropped his glass and scrambled away, frantically trying to get to the door.

Blightey! For pity's sake, no!

"Just kidding," the Dweller said, its head morphing into that of a severe looking woman with a blue rinse.

Mama?

"Do you really think your old friend Blightey still looks like that? It's been how long since you left Verusia?"

Years. Centuries, even. "What is it you want?"

"Payment," the Dweller said. The black mass twisted into a column and sprouted limbs until it stood before Cadman sleek and androgynous, its face as featureless as the Void.

"I don't pay for failure." Cadman sounded braver than he felt. His fingers curled around the pieces of the Statue of Eingana in his pockets. The Dweller cocked its head, fingers twitching, wisps of dark smoke spilling from their tips.

"You'll pay Cadman. Everyone pays, sooner or later."

Cadman relaxed his hold on the eye and the fang. *Poker face, Cadman. Poker face. Best not to show my hand yet.* "What will you accept?"

The Dweller stalked toward him until its blank face was pressed close to Cadman's.

"Bring me Shader without his sword. Failing that, find me someone bound to him in love."

"And if I can't?" Cadman felt his illusion wavering; bones were starting to show through the translucent flesh of his fingers.

"Then I shall take your soul." The Dweller jabbed a black talon against Cadman's chest. "Three days, Cadman, and then I'll return."

The Dweller collapsed into a liquefied mush that seeped through the carpet, leaving a stain like an oily footprint.

Cadman reached into his breast pocket with tremulous fingers that were more bone than flesh. He plucked out his metal case, but fumbled it, spilling cigarettes to the floor.

"Butter fingers, butter fingers, butter fingers!" The chant rose to a wail as he dropped to his knees to gather them up. "Callixus!" He reached out with his mind and felt the sullen presence of the wraith. "Where the deuce are you? Do you have it yet?"

Flipping a cigarette into his mouth, Cadman patted his pockets in search of his lighter and at the same time attuned to Callixus' sight. He gazed through the wraith's eyes upon a murky interior—a warehouse by the look of it—lit by a single lantern. There were ropes and hooks hanging from wooden walls. A couple of bluff-looking men were gathered around a barrel, playing cards. One of them looked up as Callixus approached, dropped his cards, and gawped.

"I'm still making my enquiries," the wraith answered Cadman's question with a thought, "but I'm sure these gentlemen will prove most instructive." The last was spoken aloud as the gawping man's face came into close-up.

"Now we don't want no trouble," he spluttered.

The second man tried to make a run for it, but Callixus spun and Cadman saw his black blade slash down. The wraith turned back to the first man who was licking his lips, eyes darting left and right.

"I'm looking for a midget," Callixus hissed. "About this tall, and with skin as white as yours is now."

"Came by earlier," the man said so quickly the words were all jumbled together. "Looking for passage to the Anglesh Isles. Told him to go see Diaz, captain of the *Dolphin*. Reckon it'll take a lot of persuading to get anyone to go there, though."

"The *Dolphin*?"

Callixus' spectral hand came into view.

"That's it," the man said, his eyes locked to the fingers reaching for his chest.

"Thank you," the wraith said. "You've been very helpful."

The man went rigid and froth seeped from the edges of his mouth.

Cadman refocused his eyes on the office and lit his cigarette. "Don't take too long, Callixus. You might be needed back here." *In three days, most likely.*

The wraith's voice sounded like an echo from a drain as Cadman terminated their communication.

"I will find him. Abelard can deputize in my absence. He can be trusted."

Only because he has no choice, like the rest of you automatons. Which reminds me... "Abelard!"

The door creaked open and the death-knight entered, jaw hanging slack, and an eyeball swinging like a pendulum across his cheekbone.

"Time for another patrol," Cadman said, leading the way out into the corridor. "You can never be too careful."

This would be the seventh time they'd toured Arnbrook House, checking the locks on the windows and the bolts on the doors. Every possible way in was scrutinized for weaknesses, and Cadman never tired of familiarizing himself with all the escape routes. And then there was the matter of his prisoners. It would never do to leave them unattended for too long—they could get up to all sorts of mischief.

Abelard's hulking corpse scuffed along behind him without complaint. That was one good thing you could say about Callixus' second, Cadman thought: he had the patience of the dead.

THE LION'S DEN

EARLY NEXT MORNING Shader found himself a stray horse a few streets from the Templum of the Knot and rode through the barracks grounds that had recently housed the White Order. Finding nothing but a handful of sick knights who were starting to show signs of recovery, he sped south toward the river and then followed its banks eastward, seeking word of the Order.

By midmorning, he crested the hills of Lesmallen and was greeted by the smell of sausages and bacon. A lone sentry looked out over the city center, a thick cloak wrapped about his slender frame. Shader dismounted and shook his head, unable to keep the smile from his lips.

"Solomon Jonas. Still standing. Always said you had it in you."

Solomon didn't seem to know whether to draw his sword or prostrate himself. He opened his mouth to say something, but the blood drained from his face, and he started to tremble.

"What's going on?" someone called as heavy footfalls drew near. "Elgin," Shader said. "So you made it, too. Now that doesn't surprise me at all."

"Well shog me for a shogging shogger!" Elgin swore. He looked Shader up and down for a moment and then crushed him in an enormous bear hug. Elgin's breath reeked of stale wine, causing Shader to turn his head away.

"Where the Abyss you been?" Elgin asked. "We thought you were dead."

"Interesting choice of words," Shader said, wondering how much he should say. "But thank Ain I've found you. Is Barek in command?"

"Rode out earlier. Justin's his second," Solomon said, finally finding his voice.

"Justin?" Shader said. "Wonders never cease."

Elgin guided Shader through the camp where most of the knights were just waking, rubbing their heads, and groaning as an old hunchback hurried about with plates of food.

"Dave the Slave," Elgin said. "He's like the camp mascot. Says he saw a vision of a Nousian knight and when we rode by he took it as a sign from Ain. Complete nutter, but a bloody good cook. Polishes a mean boot too, and if you ever need wine, Dave's your man."

Dave stopped his scurrying and turned to face them. His twisted neck cracked and popped as he lifted his head to view Shader. He froze for a moment and then dropped to both knees.

"Holy Nous! Ineffable Ain! Blessed Archon!"

Elgin gave Shader a sideways look. Shader was both fascinated and disgusted as the hunchback started to crawl toward him, face in the dirt.

"Thank you, Ain, thank you," Dave cried as his fingers ran over Shader's boots. He lifted his eyes, mouth hanging slack and drool trickling down his chin. "I am your servant. I will do anything you ask. Anything. Thank you for coming. Thank you."

Justin sauntered over, wiping his greasy fingers on his surcoat and chewing a crust of bread.

"You're already pledged, Dave. A thousand times at least," he said. "Oh, my shogging…" Crumbs dropped from his mouth as he saw Shader. "I mean, Ain's bal… Holy Nous!"

Shader went down on one knee and bowed his head.

"It's a long story," he said, "and there's no time to tell it. Cadman holds the city. There are pockets of militia dotted around. We need to join up with them, and soon."

Justin crouched down and helped Shader to his feet.

"What are you doing?" he whispered. "You're our founder. I should be kneeling to you."

Shader looked him in the eye. "Not any more, Justin. I made my choice and I'll stick to it. You outrank me now."

"But I've done… I mean…"

Shader leaned in close so no one else could hear. "I know what you are, Justin. I'm doing this for the others."

Justin frowned and then nodded. His eyes flicked every which way, but never settled on Shader's. "Barek's already gone for help," he said. "I told him he was mad, but he's the boss."

"Where…?" But Shader knew the answer before he'd finished the question.

"There's a big camp of imperial troops a mile north of the city," Justin said. "More are pouring in each day. Once they know what's happened here, they'll listen to reason."

Shader turned and strode back toward his horse, Justin close on his heels. "Let's hope so, but after what Gaston did I doubt they'll be in a listening mood." Shader swung into the saddle and cast a look over the camp. "Get the lads ready, Justin. War is coming, and the time for hiding is past."

Dave the Slave hobbled up and took hold of Shader's boot. "Take me with you! Please!"

Shader dug his heels into the horse's flanks and galloped from the camp with the hunchback's cries in his ears.

"I must atone. I must atone!"

***

The pavilions of the imperial camp were visible from the suburbs, banners unfurling in the breeze and reminding Shader of the horrific battles he'd fought on the borders of Verusia. No one tried to stop him as he rode from the city. The troops had left their posts and Cadman's undead hadn't moved from the vicinity of Arnbrook House. He was waiting for something, but what it was Shader could only guess at.

He entered the camp with his hands raised, the horse slowing to a plod. A troop brandishing halberds immediately ran to intercept him. Someone grabbed his coat sleeve and dragged him from the saddle. He tried to speak, but his face was rammed into the ground. Rough hands took hold of his wrists and bent his arms behind his back. A knee pressed down hard on his spine and he heard the rasp of his swords being removed from their scabbards. Someone cursed, and the Sword of the Archon dropped to the ground beside Shader's head.

"The city has been taken," he spluttered through a mouthful of dirt. "I need to see your commander."

A boot slammed into his teeth and Shader tasted blood. His hands were trussed up behind him before he was hoisted upright and shoved in among the pavilions. A rough-hewn cross had been erected in the center of the camp. Nailed to it was the bloody body of Barek Thomas, his surcoat soiled and in tatters.

Shader gasped and whispered the youth's name under his breath. Barek struggled to pull himself upright upon lacerated arms and weakly raised his head. He stared at Shader with despairing eyes and then sagged, suspended only by loops of rope and the nails tearing across the skin of his palms.

The soldiers allowed Shader to pause long enough for the effect to sink in, and then he was ushered to a large pavilion outside of which stood the imperial standard and a ring of armored guards. With a soldier on either side firmly gripping his shoulders, Shader was forced through the awning and brought to stand before a translucent veil. Giant shadows moved across its surface, and raised voices came from the other side. There were two guards with halberds crossed in front of the veil, each heavily armored and cloaked in black. They snapped to attention, stepped to the sides, and then parted the veil to reveal the interior of the tent.

Half a dozen hanging lanterns shed their warm and dappled glow around the pavilion. There were four men inside, standing around a map table, engaged in fierce debate. Three were clearly high-ranking officers, judging by their polished armor and heavy velvet cloaks. The shortest—and the fattest—was tapping a baton against the map, red-faced and flustered. He had bushy whiskers and a drooping mustache of the kind that had been fashionable in Britannia when Shader was a child. Peering over his shoulder was a bluff looking soldier with a gaunt face and receding gray hair. The man opposite was ramrod straight, arms folded across his barrel chest. His eyes flitted from the map to the others as if he were assessing everyone in the tent. He was flanked by a lean man with red hair and a clipped goatee, who kept frowning and licking his lips.

The fourth figure was dressed in a black silk shirt, leather breeches, and buckskin boots. A simple band of gold held his great mane of gray-flecked dark hair in place. The face was angular, softened slightly by a close-cropped beard; the nose long and severe. Brilliant green eyes roved restlessly in deep-set sockets, and every so often the man would moisten his thin lips with a darting tongue.

"Unacceptable, *General* Starn. Utterly preposterous!" he roared at the fat man. "Are you a soldier or a milksop?"

The other two sniggered, but stopped when the man in black glared at them.

"If your courage was as great as your appetite, Starn, you'd stop whining and start fighting. Reputation, Starn, that's what this is about. Someone gives you a bloody nose and you damn well give them one back. If Templum knights want one of my cities they're going to get more than they bargained for."

Shader was forced to his knees in front of the group.

"Another one!" snapped the man in black. "If this continues we'll have defeated the lot of them without so much as a skirmish."

The others dutifully laughed and the man in black peered closer at Shader. "Name?" he demanded.

"Deacon Shader."

"Rings a bell. General Starn?"

"The liberator of Oakendale, my Lord Emperor," the fat man said, fiddling with his breastplate and scratching the armpit beneath.

Shader groaned inwardly. The Emperor Hagalle was notoriously intolerant of Nousians. He was reputed to be a cowering paranoiac, too frightened of his own shadow to set foot outside of Jorakum.

"The ringleader!" Hagalle said, and then stooped to stare Shader in the face. "You remind me of someone else." He leaned in closer, tilting his head from side to side. "Never mind," he said, straightening up. "Do we have another cross?"

"I was not involved," Shader said, feeling a pang of guilt, even though it was the truth.

"But you're with the Templum Elect, are you not?" asked the gaunt man with a smug grin.

"Not anymore," Shader said. "I've left the service of the Ipsissimus."

"Ha," Hagalle said. "You make it sound voluntary."

Shader met his gaze and winced as Hagalle raised his hand. The emperor's eyes narrowed and the hint of a smile tugged at the corner of his mouth. After an uncomfortable pause, he merely sniffed and wrinkled his brow.

"It's not the Templum you should be worrying about," Shader said. "The city has been taken from within."

"So the last one said," the barrel-chested man sneered, looking at his companions as if he'd resolved the issue and just wanted to get back to the previous discussion.

"Barek Thomas, the man you've crucified, is not your enemy."

Hagalle slammed a fist into his palm. "He damn well is. Broke my quarantine, assaulted my troops. Blast it, they even singled him out as one of the leaders."

Shader took a deep breath and fought to keep his voice calm. "He was following orders. You're right, Emperor; obedience in the Templum is not voluntary. They were under the command of a youth named Gaston Rayn. He was never elected, but used his strength and the uncertainty of the others to assume control."

Shader's face tightened with the effort of keeping focused on the outcome. It would do no good to point out that his own abandonment of the Order had led to Gaston's ascension. "Barek Thomas has been making efforts to put things right."

"Which is what he's doing," Hagalle said, laughing at his own joke. "Self-sacrifice is the Nousian path of atonement, is it not?"

Shader threw off the hands of his guards and surged to his feet. He smashed an elbow into one man's face and hit the other with a right hook. Both went down hard. General Starn's sword appeared in his hand so quickly that it seemed he'd used magic. Hagalle gently pushed it away and crossed his arms.

"That's better," he said, eyeing Shader. "I like a man to be direct. Can't stand pussyfooting around. Let's keep this honest, shall we? You think I'm an intolerant idiot and I despise your putrid sect."

The guards stood and dusted themselves down. One was holding his nose and cussing under his breath, the other rubbed at his chin and glowered.

"This isn't about religion," Shader said.

"It never was." Hagalle's voice was a low growl. "It's about empire building."

Shader bit his tongue before carrying on. "Have you heard of an artifact known as the Statue of Eingana?"

The man with the barrel chest guffawed but was silenced by a glare from Hagalle.

"Go on," the emperor said.

"After the Reckoning, the Dreamer Huntsman split the statue into five pieces and entrusted each to a guardian. One was in the keeping of the Gray Abbot of Pardes."

Hagalle made a fist, but remained attentive.

"Soon after my return from Aeterna, the abbey was attacked and the Gray Abbot's Monas symbol taken. It concealed a piece of the statue."

Hagalle turned to General Starn. "I ordered no such attack."

Starn shrugged. "Could it have been the Sicarii, Emperor?"

Hagalle sighed as if he couldn't believe how stupid his general was being.

"It was an army of corpses," Shader said.

"Oh, please!" the gaunt man protested to the accompaniment of a loud tut from barrel chest.

"That's enough!" stormed Hagalle. "Riken, Dalglish, out of my sight!"

The two bowed and backed out of the tent. Hagalle was chewing his lip, his face purple, eyes glinting dangerously.

Shader waited a moment before continuing. "The man responsible works for Governor Gen. He's some sort of medical advisor. Goes by the name of Cadman. He's the one now in control of your city."

Hagalle's eyes narrowed at the mention of the Governor. "I knew it. Backstabbing ponce. What did I tell you, Starn? Gen's been nothing but trouble, just like his arse-licking ancestors."

"I don't think the Governor's involved," Shader said. "This Cadman's not all he seems. He has power over the dead, and he possesses two pieces of the Statue of Eingana. He nearly got hold of a third." Shader's skin crawled as he once more felt the cold touch of the Dweller. "With the statue fully assembled he'll have the power of the Reckoning at his fingertips. My Lord Emperor, set aside your quarrel with Nousians. Let us help you."

"Fantastical nonsense," Hagalle said. "I would have heard, if this were true. I have eyes and ears everywhere. Everywhere!"

"The plague, my Lord Emperor," Starn said. "We have been effectively blinded to events in Sarum."

"And what of the plague now?" Hagalle asked.

"It's been dying down," Shader said. "It's my belief that the plague and Cadman are linked, but I can't understand why it should retreat as his power increases."

"Because the statue has now attuned to his necromancy," said a new voice, causing everyone to turn in astonishment.

"Please excuse my interruption," Aristodeus said, appearing out of nowhere, "but there is more at stake here than you can imagine. The time has come for you to play your part, Hagalle."

"Who are you to tell me what to do?" Hagalle took a step toward the philosopher.

Aristodeus raised a finger, his eyes locked on Hagalle's, icy and unwavering. "I'm the one who kept your pathetic empire together when you were too frightened to take a shit in case there were assassins down the latrine."

Hagalle's jaw dropped and Starn put his hands to his ears.

"If it weren't for me," the philosopher continued like a schoolmaster reprimanding an errant child, "the Eastern Lords would have crushed your so-called dynasty the day your father died; and even all his successes came from my hand. I don't have time to flatter imperial egos, Hagalle. I've watched over you since you were a boy, and you're still a boy now, as far as I'm concerned."

Shader watched his old mentor with the feeling that he'd never really known the man. All these years he'd been molding Hagalle, preparing him for whatever was unraveling. What did that say about Shader's own childhood, the years of lessons he'd had from Aristodeus? And more to the point, how had the philosopher been on opposite sides of the world at the same time?

"As Shader says, put aside your quarrel with Aeterna. You must join with her, if we are to survive the coming storm. All of us"—and here Aristodeus turned his eyes on Shader—"have our parts to play. The outcome is balanced on a knife's edge. Do not fail me now, Hagalle."

"I will never ally with Aeterna," Hagalle said. "But as for the matter of a ghoulish army in one of my cities, rest assured, it won't be there long."

"And Deacon Shader?" Aristodeus asked. "Don't forget I need him."

Shader looked at the philosopher, but saw nothing other than cold calculation in his gray-blue eyes.

"He will be kept here until I decide what action to take," Hagalle said.

Aristodeus nodded, seemingly satisfied.

"And Aristodeus," Hagalle said, his jaw set firm. "Next time I see you, I'll cut that bald head from your shoulders. Is that understood?"

A flash of anger crossed Aristodeus's face, but then the air around him shimmered, and he was gone.

Hagalle bunched his shoulders and stared at his feet. After what seemed an eternity, he spoke.

"Ready the troops, General."

Starn saluted and hurried from the pavilion, tripping on the flap as he went.

"So," Hagalle said, studying Shader, "you know the bald bastard, too. Funny that, because he's the one you remind me of. Something about the eyes. You related?"

Shader shook his head. A cold knotting had started in his stomach. Childhood memories drifted into mind and dispersed, drifted and dispersed. His mother and father; the Brinwood friars ... and then blackness. Where were all the others? His extended family? Just Jarl, Gralia, Frater Kelvin, and Aristodeus. Always Aristodeus...

"Got any Graecian in you?"

Shader swallowed and shifted his focus back to the interior of the tent. "Britannish, through and through."

"So, what's your role in all this?"

"No idea," Shader said, "but I'm getting the impression it's not going to be good."

Hagalle pursed his lips. The next instant he clapped his hands and nodded to the guards flanking Shader. They each seized an arm and bent them up high on Shader's back.

"What about Barek Thomas?" Shader asked.

Hagalle looked blank for a moment, scratched his beard, and then said to one of the guards, "Cut him down and chain him up with this one until I return from Sarum."

The emperor glared at the map he'd been studying when Shader arrived. Without warning, he smashed his fist into it, picked it up, and started ripping it to shreds. The guards hovered uncertainly for a moment and then bundled Shader out of the pavilion.

FENRIR FOREST

SHADER WAS DUMPED among a clump of grasstrees. His wrists and ankles were shackled with iron that pinched, cutting off the blood and numbing his fingers and toes. He felt a mixture of relief that Hagalle was going to investigate Sarum and hopelessness at his own situation. This Shadrak had taken the serpent statue, and he felt naked without it.

He felt even more vulnerable without the gladius. It had spared him from the Dweller and magically healed his body, but there was bound to be a price to pay. If anything, his cheating of death had somehow rendered life more precious. He'd always thought himself ready to meet his maker, but now he wasn't quite so certain. He allowed himself a sardonic smile. Hardly the self-surrender required of a Nousian.

Barek Thomas's broken and bloodied body was dragged beside him with no need for chains.

"Don't be *cross*," said one of the soldiers, a gap-toothed man with graying black hair swept back in a ponytail.

His balding companion punched him on the arm and groaned. "That's terrible, Pete."

Pete reached down and took hold of Shader's shackles. "Well, Anthony, I suggest you take your complaint up the *chain* of command."

"You stupid sod," Anthony said as they headed toward the tarpaulin shades on the edge of the grasstrees. "Hey, what d'you s'pose their favorite armor is?"

"Very good, Anthony, very good. Guess if we put them on work detail they'd be in the…"

Barek was pale from loss of blood. His hands were red and swollen where the nails had pierced him. He whimpered and mumbled something through dry and cracked lips.

"Try to rest Barek," Shader said, looking around for something the youth could drink. They'd been left no food or water, and little shelter from the sweltering sun. He called over to the guards, but they merely raised their canteens and drank appreciatively.

Shader felt his anger rising—it was directed more at himself than the soldiers. His rashness had put Barek's life at risk. The last thing you do with a lunatic like Hagalle is come to him with open arms. More Nousian idealism leading to yet another disaster. Shader shook his head. Maybe he was just chasing castles in the sky like his father used to say. Right now, he knew what Jarl would have done, and for once Shader was starting to agree with him.

Propping his back against the trunk of a grasstree, he scanned the area once more and saw the glint of something metallic reflecting the light of the sun. He squinted at it—a shining object skirting in and out of the stunted trees. As it drew closer he gasped, recognizing the Sword of the Archon racing through the air toward him. The gladius came to a halt in front of his face, a couple of feet above the ground. The blade shifted to Shader's wrists and touched the manacles. There was a flash of light, and the chains fell away. The sword did the same with the bindings around his ankles before settling itself snugly into his right hand, pulsing and purring to itself.

Shader looked to the guards' position some twenty yards away. They didn't seem to have noticed the sword's movement and continued their idle banter. The city of tents petered out to the west, the layout affording a straight avenue all the way to the edge of Fenrir Forest. The road from the north skirted the forest, bypassing its foreboding gloom.

The trees were clearly not indigenous, their leaves perennial and dark green. Fenrir sprawled all the way to the Western Ocean and for untold miles to the north. It was most likely the creation of the Ancients, with their penchant for introducing their own native flora and fauna into the barren soil of Sahul.

Their best option would be to head through the forest and make for the sea. Hagalle would find and confront Cadman, freeing Shader to go after Shadrak. He just hoped Rhiannon and the priests would be all right, and that Justin didn't go and do something stupid. Not that Shader could talk.

Barek groaned, his body going taut and then starting to spasm. Shader crawled to his side as the gladius began to glow. Casting a glance at the guards, he returned the blade to its scabbard. Heat passed into his thigh, rising along his spine and flowing to his arms and hands. Without thinking, Shader reached for Barek and gasped as light streamed from his fingers into the youth's flesh. Barek's tremors stilled and he shone like a luminary. The wounds made by the nails started to close, and the light dispersed. Barek's chest rose and fell like a bellows, his face ruddy and full of vigor.

"Master Shader," he said. We thought you were…"

Shader fell back, limp and spent, but the sword surged again, its heat passing through the scabbard to fill him with strength and euphoria.

One of the guards moved off, presumably to relieve himself, and the other was busy shoving food into his face.

Barek sat upright and tried to stand, but Shader put a restraining hand on his arm. The lad looked ready to burst with energy. He nodded and followed Shader's gaze toward the forest. They waited until the other guard returned, lacing his breeches. As soon as the soldiers recommenced their banter, Shader tapped Barek on the shoulder, and they scampered for the cover of the nearest tent. Checking to make sure they'd not been seen, they sprinted to the next one and then onto the bitumen avenue running down the center of the camp and leading to the forest.

A shout went up, but neither looked back. Shader ran with inhuman speed, and Barek kept up with him, a look of joy and wonder on his face.

Once within the forest's dark shelter, Shader looked behind. Scores of soldiers were hurrying from their tents and starting in pursuit.

Barek led the way deeper into the trees where no sunlight penetrated. Shader drew the gladius, letting its radiance light their way. The sudden brightness in the gloom was greeted by an angry sibilance.

They hurried on through thick foliage until the unnatural vitality left them. Once or twice, muffled screams sounded from somewhere behind, followed by the rustling of leaves. Eventually, their pursuers gave up the chase, and Shader beckoned for Barek to rest awhile in a small clearing, where a narrow shaft of sunlight broke through.

"Place gives me the creeps." Barek's voice was almost a whisper. "I came here once for a dare."

Shader raised an eyebrow.

"I was just a kid at the time. I skirted about on the edge of the woods for a bit and made out I'd gone inside."

Shader smiled. He'd done similar things back home, although the trees of Friston had always been more of a comfort than a fear. This place made the hairs on the back of his neck stand up. It reminded him more of Verusia, where the great firs loomed oppressively, and the feeling of being watched had proven devastatingly true.

"How'd you know where to find me?" Barek looked down at his perfectly healed hands.

"Justin told me what you were up to. I thought Gaston was the crazy one, but you're starting to come a close second."

Barek chuckled. "Hadn't bargained on the emperor being there. Even so, I thought he might've at least listened to reason."

"Probably did," Shader said. "But the reason of lunatics tends to run in tight circles."

They sat in stillness for a while, occasionally starting at the cracking of twigs or the sudden gusts of wind that ripped through the leaves. Finally, Barek broke the silence.

"What happened to you back at the templum?"

Shader thought about how best to answer. "A taste of death, I suppose." He stood and leaned against a gnarled trunk beneath branches thick with leaves that seemed to writhe in the darkness. "More than a taste. I can still feel the cold steel in my back, the acid touch of the demon." Shader suppressed a wave of nausea as the Dweller's stench once more filled his nostrils. It was like its presence had seeped into his skin, and now he'd never be rid of it.

"Even as it rolled over me, I knew I should already be dead. I was stabbed by an expert who was very precise with his aim. Part of me wishes this Shadrak had killed me before the Dweller..."

"Do you remember what happened next?" Barek asked.

"There was a burst of light and then I recall walking through a desert beneath an alien sky. I thought I was in Araboth with the luminaries." He gave a derisive laugh, which Barek seemed to miss.

"Araboth truly exists?"

"I never took you for a doubter, Barek."

The youth looked uncomfortable. "I'm not. It's just that faith is..."

"Difficult?" Shader said. "Tell me about it."

What the Archon had said about the Liber had been niggling away at the back of his mind. If he couldn't even trust the scriptures, then what could he trust? Was it all just smoke and mirrors?

"How do we even know if we're on the right path?" Barek said.

"I'm not the man to ask," Shader said more harshly than he intended. "Experience hasn't married well with my learning. You know, I used to look down on our priests. I sneered at their homilies, and yet when I follow my own path..." His thoughts drifted to Rhiannon—that day he'd carried her bloodied and half-naked to her home in Oakendale. His faith had been indestructible until that moment, and then he'd suddenly been pitted against an enemy he had no experience fighting. She'd tried to kiss him once, but he'd pushed her away, citing his vow of celibacy. When he'd finally worked out what to do, how to live a truly human life in the love of Ain, she'd done the same to him. It didn't matter that she'd been manipulated—that they both had. The moment had gone, and he was left with no choice but to follow blindly wherever Ain led him.

"Perhaps that was my mistake with the White Order," he said. "Maybe I overcompensated and grew too literal. Just look at the consequences for the Order, for you, for Gaston." He wanted to add Rhiannon, but couldn't quite say her name.

Barek's look showed he knew. Mercifully, he let it drop.

"Come on, Barek." Shader clapped the lad on the shoulder. "Let's put a bit more distance between us and the camp."

"Sounds like a plan," Barek said, standing and brushing himself down before giving Shader a hand up. "Which way?"

"Forward," Shader said with a shrug, and they headed deeper into the darkness of Fenrir.

SEER'S WEB

HAGALLE DREW REIN atop Carys Bridge above the shimmering waters of the Soulsong River and patted the neck of his gray gelding. He was regretting wearing his black doublet of stiffened leather for the heat was sweltering. He tightened the silk kerchief covering his mouth and nose. Shader might have been right about the plague's abatement, but you could never trust a Nousian.

Duke Farian rode up alongside, mopping the sweat from his brow. His usually immaculate beard was lank and matted. Hagalle suppressed a smile as he heard the galloping of horses behind.

"Majesty," puffed Farian, "there are hidden dangers everywhere. Let the scouts take the lead for we can't predict the flight of an assassin's arrow, or an ambush by this Cadman fellow."

"Sultan tells me the way is clear," Hagalle said, tensing against the possibility that he too was unreliable. "Sultan is a powerful seer, my Lord, and is right more often than not. However..."

Hagalle narrowed his eyes at the duke, wetted his lips, and then nodded. Wheeling the gelding, he cantered back across the bridge, the ranks of his bodyguard parting to admit him and closing as he passed.

The dark-skinned seer, Sultan, was swathed in heavy black robes and seemingly immune to the heat. He squatted over a splatter of blood that was beginning to pool from a cut to the palm of his hand. As Hagalle and Farian drew up, he looked at them askew.

"Truth Shader did speak, Great One," Sultan said in his thickly accented voice. The Sahulian tongue was apparently a challenge for his lipless mouth. "Plague no more." He stood to the accompaniment of cracking cartilage. "Plague never was."

Hagalle glared at the seer and then at Farian. "Speak clearly, man."

Sultan threw back his hood to reveal a black and crusted face, creased by untold years and the harsh aridity of the deserts of Makevar, where he'd served the headshrinkers before Ogalvy's occupation. He turned his sickly yellow eyes upon Hagalle and scrunched up his face in concentration, three broken stumps of teeth jutting from bleeding gums. "Poisoned the Dreaming is with bad magic. For the restless dead, Eingana has big tears."

Hagalle fought back his disgust at the seer's appearance. He hated having to rely on such vague prognostications, but his advisors had counseled that Sultan be brought along after he had prophesied about the dark magic being used in Sarum.

The seer threw him a haughty look, as if he considered Hagalle an imbecile. "Since the Reckoning, when Huntsman—" Sultan hawked and spat. "—made the dog-head's dreams destroy the Ancients, over the world has been stretched a web of power. Some read things there." He touched his clawed fingers to his chest. "Others its magic grasp for good or evil, and some drink from it so the mud will not take them."

Hagalle merely turned an astonished and slightly baffled look toward Farian.

267

"This Cadman," Sultan continued, "uses the Statue of Eingana to give strength to his death-magic. This not good. This makes plague in the web. You no catch it like a cough. Bad magic drawn to bad heart. Make body rot. These things have I seen." He glanced down at the pool of blood and began to apply pressure to the wound in his palm.

Farian snorted and leaned toward the seer. "Forgetting the mumbo-jumbo, Sultan, do we have anything to fear from this corruption?"

"Who can tell the ways of another's heart?" Sultan's eyes glinted.

Farian removed his kerchief, but Hagalle merely lifted a hand to his and then left it. One of the scouts galloped back across the bridge and pulled up before the Duke.

"There is a large force, Your Grace, surrounding the council offices at Arnbrook House. They're making no moves. The rest of the city is like a graveyard."

"Our foe seems to have committed his forces." Farian looked at Hagalle.

"Or he may wish us to think so," Hagalle said. "Where's that fat fool, Starn?"

Hagalle cringed as Starn stepped beside his horse and gave a polite cough.

"Good, General," Hagalle said. "Excellent. Did you hear all that?"

Starn slid the flats of his hands beneath his breastplate and drew in his stomach. His eyes crossed as he started to stammer a reply.

"Out with it man, we haven't got all day," Hagalle said. Balls of the gods, why had he been lumbered with such an incompetent oaf?

"What did you want me to hear, Emperor?"

"The enemy, Starn! The enemy. He's shown his hand."

Starn tugged down his breastplate and stood to attention. "Then with your permission, Emperor..."

Hagalle sighed and raised his hands to the sky. "Advance with the main army and let them see our strength, but under no circumstances attack without my say so. Do I make myself clear?"

Starn's face reddened, and he blinked repeatedly. "You want us to lay siege to the city, my Emperor?"

Hagalle rolled his eyes. "No, you buffoon. I want you to do as you've been told." He rapped his knuckles on the side of Starn's head. "Don't think. Obey."

Starn saluted, bowed, and nearly tripped over his own feet as he hurried off to comply with Hagalle's orders.

"A wise move, my Lord," Farian said. "See if we can lure them out into the open. Last thing we want is street-by-street fighting."

Hagalle bit down on his bottom lip. "But how long do we wait, eh, Farian? If this Cadman's got half a brain, he'll not give up the defensive advantage. Gods only know what's happening to my subjects in the meantime. Either they'll take the bait, or they'll split and run. If they do neither, we attack come morning."

Hagalle watched General Starn bumbling about relaying orders and wondered how on earth the once mighty armies of the west were now in the hands of such utter nincompoops. Once this was all over he'd be doing some serious restructuring. With the plans he had in mind for the empire, he'd need men of far greater caliber than Starn.

He caught Farian watching him out of the corner of his eye. And he was another one. Couple of prats, the both of them. Better off without them. If you wanted something doing...

THE DOME

THERE WAS A boy floating above his head.

"Ain's teeth!" Shader surged to his feet, but lost contact with the ground and spun skyward.

The boy's head whirled around him, laughing, fair hair plastered across his face. He reached out a hand and caught Shader's wrist to steady him.

"You're dreaming," he said.

"Sammy?"

"Huntsman sent me. They'll be glad you made it back OK." Sammy cast a look over his shoulder as if there were others watching. "Mamba's found the statue."

"Mamba?"

Sammy moved aside to admit the hulking black man with the serpent's head.

"It movesss wessst," Mamba hissed. "Towardss the docksss. Huntsssman thinksss it isss being taken to the Anglesssh Islesss."

The snake-man faded from sight, and Sammy was now no more than a swirling face.

"You must find it, Deacon," he said. "Find it."

Shader sat bolt upright and opened his eyes. He was surrounded by overhanging branches. Beside him, Barek slept on a bed of leaves.

"Come on." Shader shook the lad. "Time to go."

***

They walked for long hours, the humidity slowing their progress. With Barek's help, Shader removed his chainmail hauberk and dragged it along behind.

Barek stopped him and pointed through the trees at a vast dome thrusting from the earth, its black surface shimmering and flecked with green. They emerged into a circular clearing, approaching the dome with caution. It was coated with rock dust, the ground strewn with debris and uprooted trees.

"What is it?" Barek asked. "Something left by the Ancients?"

Shader crouched down to study the fresh earth around the base. "Looks like there's been recent movement. Forced its way through the earth."

"Earthquake?"

Shader shook his head. "Not in Sahul. At least, I've never heard of one."

They walked around the dome until they came to a broad metal ramp leading inside.

"Magic?" Barek asked, keeping his voice hushed.

"Think you were right first time," Shader said. "This has the feel of Ancient tech."

Barek stood at the foot of the ramp and squinted up at the dark interior. "It's like nothing else I've seen from that era," he said. "Sarum's towers are older than the Reckoning, and yet this is completely different. It reminds me of the tunnels beneath the templum. I don't like it. It's giving me goose bumps."

Shader felt it too, but wasn't about to add to the scaremongering. He'd seen enough of magic and demons to no longer doubt their existence, but this was something else. Clapping Barek on the shoulder he strode up the ramp. "'That which doesn't kill me, Barek...'"

He stopped at the top to wait for the lad, who was dragging his feet.

"Whisks me off to another world for a life of slavery?" Barek said with a grim set to his jaw. "Elias had this story about these little gnome-like creatures whizzing about in flying teapots or something. Said they were harvesting humans for experiments on another planet. Still, you never know with Elias. All depends on how much he's been smoking."

"You're rambling, Barek."

"Yes, sorry. Happens when I'm scared."

Shader slid the gladius from its scabbard. "I was quoting the Liber. 'That which doesn't kill me makes me stronger.'"

"Can't say I got on with that bit. Didn't seem to fit with the rest," Barek said. "Guess it's all part of the mystery."

The interior was a cavernous black metal chamber that gave off a greenish glow. A cloying mist hung in the air, smelling of age and decay.

"What the Abyss?" Barek said, dropping to one knee.

The floor had been chalked with strange markings—complicated sigils and words in a language Shader didn't recognize. A crude and massive triangle had been drawn upon the floor at a slight remove from the writing.

"What did I tell you?" Barek said, standing. "Magic."

A chill crept over Shader's flesh. He glimpsed movement out of the corner of his eye and pointed the gladius at a dark sheen on the wall. Keeping the blade before him, he advanced and started to discern the shadowy form of a man with a body of black mist. He could just about make out a cloak and armor, and a vaguely formed helm from which crimson eyes blazed. The figure was almost completely incorporeal and devoid of shade or color.

"Callixus?" Shader held up a hand to keep Barek back.

The gladius flared, igniting the blackness around it with a pure golden glow. The wraith-knight cowered before the blaze.

"Alas no," it said. "But praise Ain. I thought I'd never again see the surcoat of the Elect on a living being. Does the Order survive?"

"It still serves the Ipsissimus, although perhaps with less distinction than in your time." Shader lowered the sword. "What are you doing here? What is this place?"

"It is a tomb," the wraith said. "For those not permitted to die. Have you come to rot alongside me, to destroy me, or to help me?"

"Why aren't you with the others?" Shader re-sheathed the gladius. "You're known to my Order as the Lost, and yet clearly that's no longer the case. Callixus attacked Pardes, and I fought your comrades in Sarum. Why should we help you?"

"Because I am a deserter. I have broken my oath to the grand master."

"You disobeyed Callixus?"

Shader didn't know why he should be so shocked, after all, hadn't he defied the Ipsissimus?

"The grand master succumbed to despair, as did my brethren. I do not blame them. Our misery has been unimaginable, our desolation complete. Ain has not come to our aid during these lonely centuries. There is only so long hope can survive."

Barek stood beside Shader, pale-faced and trembling. "But you held out?"

The wraith turned its mournful eyes on the lad. "Ain is faithful, young man. He will come, in time. Maybe I'm deluded, like my brothers say, but I refuse to despair. Callixus should have punished me for my disobedience, but he did not. I saw hope in that. And now two brother Nousians stand before me with the blood of life pumping through their veins. Ain is good. Ain is merciful."

"What I don't understand," Barek said, "is why you don't leave. The door's open. We just walked in. What's stopping you?"

"Where would I go? What would I do? My life should have ended centuries ago. When Ain wants me, He will come."

"Maybe Ain's waiting for you to do something useful," Shader said.

The wraith's eyes flared.

"Your Order is an abomination," Shader said. "Even as we speak a battle is brewing and the Lost will be in the forefront of it. Maybe this is what Ain's been waiting for, a chance for you to stop being a victim. You're still a Nousian, aren't you? We're going to need all the help we can get."

The wraith let out a long hiss and drifted around the chamber. Black mist trailed behind it like cobwebs. "You know nothing of what we suffered. Nothing! Do you think I haven't thought of fighting back? We all have, but against this Cadman we are powerless."

Shader folded his arms across his chest. "Then why are you here and not doing his bidding along with the others? For Ain, all things are possible."

"Yes?" the wraith said. "Then why did he leave us? Why?" A sob escaped him, and he hunched over beside the wall. "Forgive me, Ain, forgive me. You are faithful. I trust in you."

Shader was about to make another retort when Barek silenced him with a finger to the lips. The lad approached the wraith and sat on the floor.

"You haven't told us your name," he said. "I'm Barek, and this is Deacon Shader."

The wraith looked up, the fierce glow in its eyes softening to a warm orange. "I was... I am called Osric."

"Osric," Barek repeated. "Tell us, Osric, what happened to your Order?"

Shader groaned. They hadn't the time for this.

Barek held up a hand. "Everything," he said. "Just as you remember."

Osric sank down to the floor and sat cross-legged, mirroring Barek. Shader bit back his frustration and joined them.

"The Ipsissimus ordered us to aid the Abbey of Pardes in the 432nd year of the Reckoning. The Gray Abbot had sent word of a mawgish incursion. There was no help from Sarum, but that was nothing new. The mawgs didn't make a direct assault, but the abbey was effectively under siege.

Our fleet arrived just as a massive invasion force set sail from the Anglesh Isles. We rode swiftly from Sarum's port, thinking we would have but a few days to raise sufficient defenses. There were three hundred of us, all Elect knights under the command of our grand master, Callixus. We were attacked from the rear by Sarum's militia and driven toward a large force of imperial troops who had been barracked at the city for this very purpose. Apparently, the emperor had heard news of our mission and suspected foul play."

"Nothing's changed there," Shader said.

Barek was rubbing at his palm with a thumb, tracing circles where the flesh had been pierced and then healed.

"We could easily have turned and crushed the militia without having to face the more heavily armed imperial troops. Callixus, however, had no wish to worsen the relationship between Sahul and Aeterna, and so sought to evade both forces. Just as we began to despair of so doing we were approached by an old Nousian, who offered to guide us. He showed us a route through the northern suburbs that led to Fenrir Forest. He said he would meet us there and show us a secret way to the abbey.

"We galloped beyond Sarum and entered the dark wood. It seemed odd that our guide waited amid the trees as we entered, for we had thought to have left him far behind in the city. Callixus found him trustworthy, and so we followed him deep into the forest. At last, we came to a clearing. A vast metallic dome rose up before us, a great edifice from a bygone age. The old man said it was the entrance to the tunnels that would take us to Pardes.

"We entered via a wide ramp and found ourselves in this very room. Our guide waited at the entrance, a look of smug satisfaction on his face; a look that has burned itself into my memory.

"Callixus must have sensed betrayal for he spurred his horse toward the villain. The old man cast something dark at the grand master, who fell writhing from his steed and began to decompose. We watched in dread as our lord was reduced to a seeping putrescence from which rose a shadowy form that drifted to the side of our erstwhile guide. I charged the old man but was struck down by the same magic.

"The villain laughed and then changed his appearance with some sort of illusion. There before us now stood a grotesquely fat man dressed in the scarlet robes of the governor of Sarum. He taunted the other knights and gloated about how easily deceived we'd been. He changed again, this time revealing his true form, brittle and skeletal, with filmy strips of dry skin clinging to the bone. Then he was gone, and the ramp rose up to seal us within this metal tomb. Here we suffered Ain knows how long until the air was exhausted. Callixus and I watched our brothers choking and gasping.

"They found no respite in death, however. The skeletal creature returned and employed a powerful necromancy, which raised them along with their steeds. Here we remained, entombed, but conscious throughout the centuries."

"This skeletal creature you describe..." Barek began.

"Now goes by the name of Cadman," Shader said.

Osric nodded.

"He was once governor of Sarum?" Barek asked.

"Probably not by design," Shader said. "Cadman's a liche, of that I'm certain. I've faced his kind before in Verusia. I expect he became too successful at whatever else he was doing and attracted unwanted attention. I can't imagine a less desirable position for a liche. They're cowardly wretches, always laying plans to ensure their own survival."

The creatures he'd fought in Verusia had largely been mindless minions. Their liche masters were rarely seen, and seldom stuck around in a fight. When cornered, though, they were deadly opponents. Shader had seen an entire company blasted apart by dark fire. The Seventh Horse had given chase, but found nothing other than shapes in the mist.

"But why would the Lost follow Cadman after what he's done to them?" Barek asked.

"Despair has robbed them of the strength to oppose his will. When faith in Ain dies—" Osric touched a spectral hand to his forehead. "—people will believe in anything: prophecies, powers, the influence of the stars. If they're desperate enough, they'll even believe lies."

"But not you," Shader said.

"My allegiance remains to Callixus, the man in possession of his own will, not the slavish automaton he's become. And while Ain is slow to answer my prayers, He grants me faith." Osric locked his eyes to Shader's. "But faith can be very dark."

Shader looked away and then stood. He walked to the entrance, staring out at the trees. "You still haven't told us what this dome is." He slapped a hand against the wall. A resounding clang echoed around the chamber.

Osric drifted to his side, following his gaze. "That I do not know," he said. "And I doubt Cadman really knows either. The world is full of mysteries, praise be to Ain. Do you intend to join this battle against my brothers?"

Shader thought for a moment before he replied. Sammy's voice was strong in his mind; that and the remembered pain of Shadrak's blade. "I don't think so."

"What?" Barek said. "But the White Order—"

"Are in good hands. Justin might be a terrible Nousian, but he's a capable knight with a good head on his shoulders." Shader grimaced, realizing he could just as well be talking about himself. "Hagalle may not take too kindly to our having escaped," he continued. "He has more than enough men to deal with Cadman. I'm going after Shadrak. I need to get back my piece of the statue."

"The Statue of Eingana?" Osric asked.

"You know of it?"

"There is a society within the Elect that ensures the Order remains true to its purpose. It is called the Saphra Society. Only a handful of knights are invited to join, mostly from the upper ranks. In my time, I rose as high as Marshall, so I was a member, as was Callixus. We preserve the secrets of the Order, the reason for its foundation."

Something else Shader had been kept in the dark about. What next? Some revelation about the Templum itself? Dark secrets concerning his parents? In this shifting world, he was beginning to wonder if he could even trust his memories, his sense of who he was. Shader fought to keep the bitterness from his voice. "Which is what?"

"The Elect were formed in response to the Blightey affair. When the Ipsissimus was murdered, his Monas was taken."

Shader knew all that. Blightey had eventually been cornered with the help of the Gray Abbot. "That's ancient knowledge." Shader suddenly thumped himself on the head. "Idiot," he said. "The Monas concealed a piece of the statue, just like the Gray Abbot's."

Osric nodded. "That's the *raison d'être* of our Order, Brother Shader. The Elect are trained with the sole purpose of protecting the artifact from those who would steal it. There have been many more attempts. Ipsissimi have been attacked by evil forces that have driven them insane or killed them. It is a function of the Saphra Society to ensure the artifact is safely passed on to the successor. You would have known all this if you'd not abandoned your duty as Keeper."

Shader spun to face the wraith. "What? How could you...?"

Osric pointed with a gaseous finger to the Sword of the Archon sheathed at Shader's hip. "The Ipsissimus would never permit the Archon's sword to leave Aeterna, and only the Keeper can wield it. There can be no doubt that you won the competition, for the sword follows your desires. I may have been blinded by its light when you entered the dome, but I am not blind to reason. If you had stayed in Aeterna, you would have known of the Saphra Society. The Keeper of the Sword of the Archon sits at its head."

Shader felt giddy. Aristodeus must have known all this. That night at the docks, he'd encouraged Shader to flee to Sahul. And the Gray Abbot—he'd been the one to suggest the tournament.

"This Society of yours," Shader's voice was hoarse. "Who founded it?"

"The Ipsissimus," Osric said, "but on the advice of the Gray Abbot and one other."

"Don't tell me," Shader said. "A bald man in white robes? Goes by the name of Aristodeus?"

Osric's eyes narrowed to glowing slits. "Yes, but how do you know this? He must have been dead for centuries."

The more Shader pieced together about his old mentor, the less he liked it. "There's obviously more to our beloved philosopher than meets the eye. What do you make of the fact that he knew I was planning to bring the sword to Sahul? In fact, he positively encouraged it."

The wraith's misty body rippled and his eyes flashed. "Ain preserve us," he whispered. "This is the time of Unweaving!" Osric floated away into the chamber and then turned back to face Shader. "Aristodeus said the time would come again, but I never thought I'd live to see it." He looked down at his ghostly arms and chuckled. "Now there's irony for you."

Shader looked blankly from the wraith to Barek.

"Does this have anything to do with the epic of the Reckoning?" the lad asked. "Only Elias said something about the Unweaving. Said it had begun before but had been stopped. Something to do with the Technocrat of the Ancients."

"Sektis Gandaw," Shader said. "The man who tried to un-create. Wasn't he betrayed by his own creatures?"

Barek was pacing, face furrowed with concentration. "The dwarves," he said. "They stole the statue and gave it to Huntsman's gods. You know, the spider, the toad, and the crocodile."

Osric's body was throwing off streams of black mist and his eyes were like flames. "Aristodeus told us he was there, that he would have failed completely had it not been for the dwarves."

Shader's head was pounding. He'd heard all that stuff about the dwarves and the gods before. Elias had wittered on about it incessantly back at Oakendale. Rhiannon had been his sounding board. Shader had spent more than one night drunk on scrumpy, listening to the bard's crazy histories. But Aristodeus's involvement in all this, that was news to him, and it made his skin crawl. There was something shouting at the bottom of his mind, clamoring for recognition, but every time he tried to focus in on it, he was met with emptiness.

"We must get the statue back," Shader said. "If Shadrak's taking it to the Anglesh Isles it can only mean one thing."

"Mawgs?" Barek said.

"Sektis Gandaw's creatures," Shader said. "Shadrak must be working for him."

"I will go with you," Osric said. "This must be the path Ain has prepared for me. This is the way of my redemption."

"I'm not sure," Shader said. "I need to think."

"If you have Osric with you, then maybe I should rejoin the White Order," Barek said. Shader shook his head to clear it. "But what about the emperor?"

Barek puffed out his cheeks. "If I run into him, I'll have to change his mind."

"You'll never sway him with words," Shader said.

Barek shrugged and merely offered Shader his hand. The two embraced and then Shader walked from the dome with Osric drifting alongside. He watched as Barek headed back through the forest in the direction of the city.

"What now?" Osric asked.

"Port Sarum," Shader said. "And if we're lucky, we'll find ourselves a ship bound for the Anglesh Isles."

"Water," Osric said with evident distaste. "I can hardly wait."

THE PRISONER OF ARNBROOK HOUSE

LALLIA PEEKED THROUGH the crack of the closet door. Cadman was passing along the corridor with a corpse-knight in tow, a huge shogger with its jaw hanging off and one eyeball swinging from a thread. It wore rusty chainmail with broken links and a once-white surcoat sporting the Nousian Monas. Maybe that would shut the bloody liberals up, she thought with some satisfaction. All that crap about the emperor being paranoid and intolerant of difference. She'd known from the word go the Nousians were shifty bastards. More than that, they were downright evil.

It all went wrong the day Zara Gen received that old tramp, Jarmin, and she'd been the one to greet him. She knew he was trouble from the minute she clapped eyes on him, but she'd assumed the Governor knew more about the situation than she did. Lallia clenched her teeth. Funny how you think you know someone, only to discover later that you got it completely wrong. She wouldn't be voting for him next election, that's for sure. That's assuming he wasn't dead along with the rest of the council.

Lallia began to wonder if she should have mentioned something about Cadman after she'd walked in on him. Maybe if she'd warned Governor Gen, the slaughter could have been averted.

Problem was, Cadman's dodgy pills had been good. More than good. And the perfume he'd given her in return for cleaning up his mess was still strong on her skin—even after all this time holed up in a closet with only a bucket to shit in and nothing to eat. At least he'd not been lying about that: it was potent stuff, and she'd not had a cold night since. Not until the death-knights had come, that is.

Cadman checked another window catch—three times as usual—and waddled along to the next. The death-knight watched the way they had come, red eyes taking in every inch of the corridor. Lallia ducked back behind the door as the skull turned in her direction. When she heard its shuffling footfalls move away she looked again. As she'd expected, Cadman was fiddling with the lock on Zara Gen's office door. Another death-knight stood guard outside, hands resting on the pommel of a broadsword.

Cadman stroked the end of his mustache, his ample frame quivering like jelly. With one thumb thrust into the pocket of his velvet waistcoat, he rapped on the door and entered, leaving the big death-knight and the guard outside. If there was anyone left alive in Arnbrook House, you could bet that's where they'd be. If it was the Governor, and if Lallia could find a way to get him out, who knows what the reward would be?

Lallia slid her back down the wall of the closet and wrapped her arms around her chest. It was a total bitch that Cadman had skeletons for guards. They never needed relieving, and so she'd had no opportunity to make a run for it.

Matted strands of chestnut hair hung over her eyes. If this went on much longer, she'd never pull again, no matter how good the perfume. Still, she thought, giving her bum a pat, it wouldn't do her figure any harm going without food for a few days.

She groaned as she realized she needed to pee. The stench from the bucket was getting unbearable, but what choice did she have? She swooned as she stood, steadying herself against the wall, and then pinched her nose shut as she moved to the back of the closet.

***

Elias reclined in the Governor's chair, tilting it onto its rear legs and putting his feet on the desk. Zara Gen glared at him from the seat opposite, his eyes saying what his lips could not. He'd been gagged and bound since he'd tried to nip out the door when the death-knights brought Elias in. He was lucky to be alive, Elias reckoned, as the skeleton on guard had grabbed him by the neck and raised its sword to strike. Zara Gen had broken free and scampered back inside the office, apologizing profusely, and the skeleton had remained outside. Within the hour, though, two more knights in rusty armor had come in and tied him to the chair. When he'd started to protest, they'd silenced him with the gag.

"Have I told you the one about the geezer from Britannia who slips through the gaps between worlds and ends up in some crazy afterlife where his bint's waiting for him?"

Zara Gen's eyes rolled into the back of his head.

"Funny ol' world, that one. You see, our protagonist is the only person not really dead, and he ends up with all these super powers. Strength of a titan, speed of a cat. He can even bound for yards at a time like some demonic kangaroo."

Zara Gen shuffled the chair away from Elias.

"Just passing the time. Nothing like a bit of confinement for reviewing stories and learning lyrics. What's up Guv, potty time?" Elias swung his feet off the table and sauntered over to the en suite latrine. "Don't know what you been eating, Guv, but it sure doesn't smell nice."

Zara Gen growled beneath the gag.

"No? Don't need the pan?"

Zara Gen was silent.

"Here's a gag for you, if you'll excuse the pun. What do you call a politician when he's always busy?"

More silence.

"No? Tied up. Next one: What do you call a politician who can't speak? A blessing. Sorry, not too good, that one. Don't blame you for not laughing—not that you could if you wanted to. Cheer up, Guv, ol' fat boy'll be back before you know it, and then the fun will really start."

Zara Gen remained a sullen presence.

"You are one tough audience. Sure you don't want a piss? No? OK. Don't mind if I nip in for a Jimmy? Only all this waiting for the big bad necromancer upsets my bladder."

A sharp rap at the door startled him.

"Quiet now, Guv." Elias rushed back behind the desk and seated himself. "Looks like playtime's over."

The enormous bulk of Dr. Cadman lumbered into the office. Elias caught a glimpse of the skeleton guard and a huge death-knight beside it before Cadman pulled the door shut and lowered himself onto the edge of the desk.

"I need you to tell me all you know about the Statue of Eingana," he said amiably, "and this Deacon Shader, who so rattled my dear friend Callixus."

Elias clamped his jaw shut. He'd shown enough indignity at the templum. It was obvious he wasn't going to get out of this alive, so he might as well put up a fight.

276

Cadman sighed. "I really don't have the time for this. There's a veritable ocean of imperial troops setting up camp outside the city, and I don't plan on sticking around to find out what they want."

With a slight gesture of his hand, the air about him shimmered, and the skin melted from his body. Fat withered into leathery strips that clung to mottled bones; the eyes sunk into empty cavities, and fleshy lips gave way to rotting teeth. Elias gagged and looked away from the decomposing corpse that now sat before him, but he could do nothing to dispel the pungent odor of decay and the cold unnatural terror seeping through his veins.

"There are many means of coercion, little man," Cadman rasped. "Trust me, I've seen more than anyone should of that sort of thing. But, out of all of them, I find the tortures of the soul the most efficacious. Do you have any idea what a liche can do to your humanity? And, of course, with the nature of my magic, the suffering doesn't have to stop at the point of death.

"You know, I learnt a good deal from my apprenticeship to Otto Blightey, not all of it pleasant, I'm sure you'll understand. I'll never forget his deftness at impaling; but it wasn't so much his ability with a stake that impressed me: it was what he did to the victims when they should already have been dead."

Elias began to blurt out everything he knew about the Statue of Eingana and then recounted the coming of Deacon Shader to Oakendale, his routing of the mawgs, and the founding of the White Order. Finally, he told the liche of Shader's love for Rhiannon.

Cadman nodded almost imperceptibly. "I have noticed," he said nonchalantly, "a presence, something shadowy and rather sinister attuned to power of Eingana." He cast a sideways look at the bard. "Do you think it's Sektis Gandaw?"

Elias frowned. "Difficult to say. The statue's always had its fair share of stalkers, not least of all Eingana's own brother, the Demiurgos."

Cadman stood and resumed his corpulence. He took his time siting his pince-nez on the bridge of his nose and then tapped his breast pocket three times. Plucking out a silver case, he flipped it open and selected a cigarette.

"One other thing," Cadman said, lighting up with a shiny Zippo Elias would have given his right arm for. "Did my old mentor, Otto Blightey, have any part in the statue's history?"

Elias gave a little cough and wished he had the guts to ask for a smoke. "That business with the Ipsissimal Monas a few decades after the Reckoning—Blightey found out it concealed an eye of the statue and stole it."

Cadman took three quick puffs on his cigarette and raised an eyebrow. "And you know this how?"

Elias tapped the side of his head. "Use of the ol' noddle, how else? Why'd you think they sent the Gray Abbot after him?"

"So," Cadman said, "the Gray Abbot's ingenious method of concealing his piece wasn't original after all. How disappointing."

Elias could see he was getting through to Cadman. If he continued to be useful, he might even get out of this with his life. "Something similar happened before, according to a tedious religious historian I once read…"

"Alphonse LaRoche?" Cadman said. "Believe me, I've read my fair share of him. You're referring to the burning, of course."

"Well, well, well, aren't you just the dark horse." Elias, wetted his lips, immediately regretting his choice of words. Cadman showed no reaction. If anything, he looked distracted. Elias redoubled his efforts. "On that occasion, long before the Templum rose from the ashes of the Reckoning, Blightey murdered some poor geezer named Hafran Thrall, a sort of forerunner of the Keeper of the Sword of the Archon."

"Yes, yes," Cadman snapped. "Your point?"

"Blightey used the sword to enhance his power."

Cadman's neck cracked as he nodded. "It was supposed to make him invulnerable, but he was hunted down and the ritual was interrupted. This is nothing new. It's all in LaRoche."

"Only part of him was strengthened," Elias said. "After the religious authorities burned Blightey at the stake, his skull survived, but it was locked in a casket and thrown into the Abyss by the Archon. Guess that's where everyone thought he belonged."

"Except Sektis Gandaw, who eventually rescued him," Cadman said. "But you're not answering my question." Cadman's eyes blazed at Elias, and dark mist spilled from his bony fingers. "Forget everything that happened before the Reckoning. What became of his piece of the statue?"

"It was returned to the Ipsissimus. Not the same Ipsissimus, mind, as Blightey managed to hang onto the eye for quite some time. I think it was Valens II to whom the Monas was restored. It's said he lived an unnaturally long life, but eventually went mad and threw himself from the roof of the basilica. The Monas has been passed down the line of succession ever since. That's where your friend Shader comes in. Well, not him personally, but his Order."

Cadman thrust his face toward Elias, the eyes suddenly black as the Void. "Go on."

"You won't find any of this in your standard histories," Elias said.

Cadman stood with his back against the door, a corona of cigarette smoke billowing about his head. He peered over the top of his pince-nez, waiting for Elias to resume. Elias didn't miss the tapping of fat fingers against his thigh. Apparently, Cadman didn't have all day. Elias, however, didn't want to see what happened next, once he'd finished his tale.

"The Blightey affair had shown the Templum to be vulnerable from within. Blightey was the principal architect of the new religion and had the ear of the Ipsissimus. In short, he was allowed too much access to the ruler of the Templum, and that's when things started to go wrong.

"Blightey just happened to leave Aeterna for the eremitical life after the Monas disappeared. He wasn't even suspected at first, and when he returned, having not aged a day, many years and a couple of Ipsissimi later, he resumed his position as counselor and spiritual director."

Cadman was nodding vigorously, a long trail of ash hanging from the end of his cigarette. "Blightey never mentioned this to me," he said. "Oh, he liked to gloat about the past; loved the effect of recounting his own twisted history to his agonized victims. I'll let you into a little secret."

Elias winced. He wasn't sure he wanted to hear this. If it was a particularly important secret, he doubted he'd be trusted with keeping it.

"It's what made me run from him in the end," Cadman said. "The endless lectures in front of the rack, or with some poor former student strapped to a chair…" Cadman's eyes wandered to where Zara Gen sat rigid and attentive. "…the Pear of Anguish forcing his jaws wide, teeth ripping through gums, breath gasping from a constricted airway. It was as if Blightey had to go on teaching others and then torturing them to death in order to generate some spark of pleasure in his life. Naturally, the more I learned, the more imperiled I became."

Thanks for sharing that. Elias licked his lips. *Makes me feel a whole lot better.*

"Please," Cadman said, dropping his smoking stub to the carpet and treading it underfoot. "Continue."

Elias wrung his sweating palms together. "Soon after Blightey's return to Aeterna, plague broke out. The Templum was largely unaffected, but as more and more citizens perished, suspicions were aroused. Blightey was summoned by the Templum Judiciary, but vanished before a hearing could begin. He left a trail of corpses in his wake. He was hunted for months, but no matter how close his pursuers came, he always managed to escape at the last minute.

"Finally, the Gray Abbot was called in. The official histories say he used the power of prayer to find Blightey, but it seems more likely he used his piece of the Statue of Eingana. Anyway, to cut a long story short, Blightey was captured and the Monas was taken from him. Before he was tried for his crimes, he was rescued by some sort of winged devil and went into hiding deep in the forests of Verusia."

Cadman wrinkled his nose.

Elias scrabbled about for something else to say. "What happens next is really interesting, particularly because it relates to Shader. There was some sort of high-powered meeting in Aeterna, and it was decided the Ipsissimus couldn't be trusted to keep the Monas safe—which is a laugh when you think how they consider him infallible."

Cadman puffed out his cheeks to the accompaniment of a sharp exhalation of air. Elias took the hint and went on.

"They set up this Order of fanatics known as the Elect to protect the statue. They selected the best soldiers in Nousia and ranked them by means of a tournament. They continue the practice today. The winner basically gets to play Hafran Thrall and become Keeper of the Sword of the Archon. It's supposed to be the same blade Blightey stole centuries before. The Templum believes it has power against the supernatural." Elias gave a little cough and did his best not to look at Cadman. "The Elect are ostensibly an elite fighting force answerable only to the Ipsissimus, but you can bet your life there's more to it than that."

"Such as?" Cadman asked.

"Well I don't know, I'm not a member. Even if I applied I expect they'd blackball me. But my point is that Shader's a knight of the Elect, and he won the tournament this year."

"I see," Cadman said. "Then that explains the sword and how he was able to wound Callixus." He flicked at his bottom lip with his finger. With a decisive nod, he clapped his hands together and turned to leave.

"Of course," Elias blustered, "there's a whole lot more I can tell you."

"Thank you. You've given me what I need." Cadman took hold of the door handle.

"But you need to hear about the skull." Elias was clutching at straws. "Remember the legend of how Blightey's skull escaped from the casket and made its way through the Abyss? His old pupil, Sektis Gandaw, built some contraption to bring him home—"

"We've finished," Cadman said.

"No." Elias was shaking now. "The skull resurfaces in the legend of Jaspar Paris. It lures Paris into the forest by assuming the form of a beautiful woman…"

Cadman was no longer listening. The door opened onto the armored cadavers outside.

"Jaspar Paris was saved only by the intervention of his spurned lover, Renna Cordelia," Elias said. "Don't you want to hear how it ends?"

Cadman paused for a moment, as if considering.

"The skull drank her soul." Elias said.

"And?"

"It rose into the air, flames spewing from its eye-sockets, and sucked her life force up! That's what it does!" Elias said. "He'll come for you!" Elias had no way of knowing that, but it never hurt to put the frighteners on a liche—or so he'd heard.

"I know." Cadman left the room, slamming the door behind him.

"But I can help you! There's so much more to tell! So much!"

There was no response. The office had taken on the feel of a tomb. Elias buried his head in his hands and emitted a loud sob.

He started as someone coughed.

Zara Gen's eyes were bulging, and he rocked the chair from side to side. Elias frowned, wiping the tears from his cheeks, but then he realized what the Governor wanted, and it definitely wasn't the pan this time. He set about untying Zara Gen with trembling fingers. No point being the obedient prisoner now. He'd told Cadman everything he knew, and it surely wouldn't be long before the liche realized keeping him alive was a risk he no longer needed to take.

***

Lallia watched as Cadman left the office with his hulking bodyguard and headed for the stairs. Pausing at the top, Cadman turned to the skeleton guard that remained outside Zara Gen's door.

"I think I'm finished with them," he said. "Best not leave wagging tongues behind." He waved a cigarette toward the door and then started down the stairs beside the big death-knight, chatting away amiably and completely unbothered by the lack of response.

The remaining skeleton lurched to attention, took hold of the doorknob, and stalked inside.

Lallia cast about from side to side until she spotted a broom. Snatching it up, she dashed across the corridor to Zara Gen's office. She slipped through the open door and gasped as the skeleton raised its sword and advanced upon a raggedy little man in a rabbit skin coat. There was a flash of red that caused Lallia to turn her head. Zara Gen barged past her and out into the corridor.

The skeleton turned at the noise, but Lallia leapt forward and clobbered it with the broom, sending it clattering and crashing into the desk. She threw down the broom and grabbed the scruffy man, dragging him out into the corridor and slamming the door.

"Typical bloody politician!" the scruffy man shouted at the back of the fleeing Governor.

"Shut it!" Lallia said. "This way!"

The skeleton's sword splintered the wood of the door and Lallia put her tail between her legs and scarpered.

"Elias, by the way," the raggedy man said. "Bard of Broken Bridge. And you are?"

"Shut your bleeding trap."

As Lallia reached the bottom of the stairwell, there was a loud crash from behind. The skeleton leapt into the corridor and ran at them with frightening speed.

"Quick!" Lallia said, taking the steps two at a time. She led the way through twisting passageways that were known to few, save the council's serving staff. As she reached another stairway, she cast a look over her shoulder and saw that the skeleton was gaining on them. "Out of the way!" She pushed a discarded tea trolley down the stairs. Elias jumped to the side, and the trolley hit the skeleton square in the ribs, slamming it to the floor below. "Keep running!"

She made for a metal ladder that led to a trap in the roof and chanced a look behind. The skeleton struggled up, ribcage smashed, one leg snapped. Its eye-sockets flared crimson, and then it continued to lurch toward them. Elias scrabbled up the ladder behind Lallia as she bashed at the trapdoor.

"Come on!" he said. The skeleton was already on the first rung.

Lallia threw her shoulder against the trap repeatedly until it gave. She climbed onto the roof, where the reddening sun was starting to dip below the horizon. Elias followed her out and slammed the trapdoor shut.

"How do we lock it?" he said.

"You could always sit on it." Lallia looked around for something heavy she could put on it instead, but already the skeleton was bashing at it from below.

"And get a sword up my jacksie? Sounds more like your sort of thing."

"Forget it," Lallia said. "Let's go."

They ran to the far side, looking in vain for somewhere to hide. Three stories down, Lallia could see hundreds of undead surrounding the building. "Shit! We're trapped."

The splintering of wood made them turn back to the trapdoor. The skeleton emerged onto the rooftop and limped toward them, the bone of its broken leg grating against the stone.

Lallia shoved Elias behind her and raised her fists. The skeleton lunged, and Elias screamed. He pushed past Lallia, caught the skeleton's sword arm, and heaved. The rotting ligaments held firm, and the skeleton fought back with shocking strength, forcing the bard to his knees. Lallia grabbed it from behind, wrenching at its neck. The skeleton struck her with the back of its hand and sent her reeling. She hit her head and came up groggy. She saw Elias snap off the skeleton's leg at the knee. It tottered about with its arms spread wide, and then Elias shoulder-charged it, sending it plummeting to the ground below.

Lallia peered over the edge of the building and saw the shattered remains scrabbling around like frenzied insects. A ripple passed through the horde of undead pressed around Arnbrook House.

"Look," Elias said, panting for breath.

The swell of corpses parted, and Cadman's black carriage clattered off to the east with a group of skeletal knights riding escort.

"What's happening?" Lallia asked.

"Buggered if I know," Elias said. "But for now I think we'll be safer up here."

Lallia nodded, flopped down on the parapet, and ran her fingers through the knots in her hair.

"End of the world," Elias chuckled, "but still time for personal grooming. My kind of girl."

Lallia slapped him playfully on the arm. She considered him for a moment, taking in the sharp angles of his face, the lank greasy hair, the eyes set so close together that he looked like a startled chicken.

"What?" Elias asked, mouth gaping with feigned shock and showing yellow teeth that hadn't seen a brush in days.

Lallia creased up with laughter. She might have been scared, tired, and desperate, but even she had her limits.

THE FATE OF THE *GHOST*

T HOUGHT YOU WERE in Gladelvi," Shader shouted above the din in the bar.

The Green Man was heaving with dockworkers celebrating the completion of a galleon—the first of many judging by the conversation. Nothing like an emperor's fears to bolster employment. Port Sarum had probably never had it so good.

Amidio Podesta's head slipped from his hand and crashed into his soup. He spluttered and cursed, came bolt upright, and wrung out his mustache.

"Cold." He wrinkled his nose, licking the broth from his lips and mopping his face with a sleeve. "What? Gladelvi? Bloody bastard wasn't there. Now I've a hold stuffed with Aeterna-tech and no one to sell it to."

"Where's the crew?" Shader seated himself opposite.

"Boozing and screwing, like they always do. A pox on the lot of them. A pox on Jarmin the Anchorite's radiant arse too. Don't even have the docking fees. Probably lose the ship now." Podesta sighed theatrically and picked up an empty glass. "Don't suppose you could stretch to a beer, eh?"

Shader slammed a purse of coins under his nose. "Half now, the rest when we get back." Podesta's eyes came into focus, and he straightened the tricorn on his head. "Where are we going?"

"The Anglesh Isles."

***

Dead man's money might not be the Nousian way of conducting business, but Ain would understand. After all, you can't take coin with you, and if he hadn't rifled the bodies on the plague carts, someone else would have. At least his purpose served the greater good, Shader told himself, and no harm had been done.

It was a remarkable thing how quickly a profligate crew of drunks and rakes could be assembled when the price was right. Shader drew in his lips, leaning on the rails of the aftcastle of the *Aura Placida*, watching the lights of Port Sarum recede until they resembled fallen stars.

"Hoist those squares and catch us some breeze!" yelled Podesta into the night air. "And give me some lateens on the mizzen, boys."

He took a swig of rum and hollered up at Shader. "Ain must love you, my friend. The tide's with us, and there's a west wind blowing."

Shader leapt down the steps two at a time and joined Podesta on the quarterdeck. He pulled off his hat and threw his head back, letting his hair billow out behind him. The salt spray on his face, the biting air in his lungs, quickened his pulse with more life than any sham resurrection. It felt good to be away from Sahul and back on the open sea.

"They can't have more than a couple of hours on us," Podesta said, offering Shader the bottle. "But no one knows these waters like I do. Can't imagine too many ships heading to the Anglesh Isles. Your pale-faced midget must be very rich, or very frightening, eh?"

Shader assumed it was the latter. He took a glug of rum and handed the bottle back. There were a hundred other ways a ship's crew could make money, all of them with a lot less risk. He looked at Podesta out of the corner of his eye. What would have happened if Shadrak had approached him first? Would the *Aura Placida* have taken the job?

Podesta saw him watching and stoppered the rum, a sudden look of sobriety falling over his ruddy face. "These are hard times, my friend. A man must take work where he finds it, eh?" He slapped Shader on the back and drew him into a hug. "But Ain is good to you, eh? And to me, I think. Just when I thought I was going to lose the *Placida* my good friend comes looking for a ship. Trust me, Shader, your money has bought you the best. Say one thing for Amidio Podesta: say he's favored by the gods."

Shader frowned at that and eased his way free of the embrace.

"Slip of the tongue," Podesta said. "But you know what I mean, eh? Ain loves us, my friend. Don't worry. We'll catch this Shadrak. They'll have to slow down when they reach the Makara Reef, and I've a little surprise for them."

Shader narrowed his eyes, but Podesta simply gave a gap-toothed smile.

"You'll see. When a customer doesn't turn up to claim his goods they become mine by default. That's why I love this business. There's always a silver lining, uh?"

Podesta made a beeline for the starboard rail and peered into the darkness. Shader joined him and saw a hazy yellow glow swaying in the wind.

"Here they come," Podesta said. "How do I look?"

He made a show of straightening his tricorn and fastening the buttons on his coat. Shader was spellbound by the approaching light, unable to work out what it was or why it swung from side to side. Podesta chuckled.

"Lantern on an imperial galleon," he said. "There is a blockade, you know. There's another up front, and I wouldn't be surprised if a third was taking a wide berth to our stern."

Shader stood back from the rail. This venture seemed about to end even before they'd gotten underway. "You don't exactly look worried," he said.

"I'm Amidio Podesta." The captain shrugged. "When you've wrestled with bull sharks, ridden waves as high as mountains, and emptied the wine cellars of Crown Prince Raoul of Quilonia right under his nose, worry seems to serve no purpose. Let's leave the worrying to lesser men, eh?"

Podesta strode to the mainmast and hollered up at the crow's nest. "Send the imperial signal, Elpidio."

"Aye Captain," the boy shouted back.

Shader peered up into the heights and a few minutes later saw a spark of light that winked on and off at different intervals. He'd seen something similar on campaign when they'd used a hooded lantern to send messages.

"Cleto," Podesta shouted. "Make sure our cargo's secure."

Shader tensed at mention of the name and then jumped as the swarthy sailor stepped out of the shadows.

"You mean the special cargo, Captain? Already taken care of. They won't find it 'less they rip the ship apart plank by plank."

"Good man," Podesta said as Cleto slunk back into the darkness. "Not in the moral sense," he offered as an aside to Shader, "but he's a handy old sea dog, no?"

The black hulk of a ship was now visible off the bow, and another was coming alongside. Shader ran back to the aftcastle and saw a third light trailing them at a distance. It seemed Podesta was fully conversant with imperial tactics.

"Sabas!" The captain's call was scattered by the wind.

Shader strolled back down to the quarterdeck with his fingers stroking the hilt of the gladius.

"Captain?" The black man's deep voice rolled up from the galley.

"Cheesy bread. All this excitement's making me hungry." Podesta gave Shader a half-smile. For all his bravado, the captain was clearly anxious.

Grapples were thrown from the starboard galleon, and after a few minutes of barked orders, the *Aura Placida* was boarded by a surly looking officer in a Sahulian bicorn, light breeches, and a heavily brocaded tailcoat. He was flanked by four troops in leather armor with cutlasses hanging from their belts. Behind them, Shader could see a long line of crossbows resting on the galleon's rail, lamplight glinting from the tips of quarrels.

Shader's eyes darted about in an attempt to locate the best cover. He shuffled in the direction of the mainmast. More lamps burst into light about the deck as the crew of the *Aura Placida* emerged to gauge the threat.

The officer swept off his bicorn and gave a formal bow. Podesta did the same, with an elaborate flourish of his tricorn. The officer lunged and Shader half-drew his gladius, but stopped himself when Podesta's arms opened wide, and he crushed the man in a huge bear hug.

"Benson, you old lubber! What are you doing aboard ship?"

Benson pulled back and held Podesta at arm's length.

"Amidio Podesta, you salty old scallywag. All this fresh sea air and you still smell like a cow's arse."

Podesta made a show of sniffing his armpits. "Well, my friend, you would be the expert on such things, eh?"

Podesta's hand moved behind his back and he made a twisting gesture with his wrist that could only have been intended for Shader. Suddenly getting his meaning, Shader buttoned his coat to conceal his Nousian surcoat.

"Bit late for setting sail," Benson said.

"Ah, my friend," Podesta put an arm around his shoulder and led him toward the galley, "this is why you're not a sailor. You don't understand these things. What did you do wrong for Hagalle to send you to sea?"

Benson chuckled. "If he builds any more ships I reckon we'll all be sailors. Someone needs to crew them."

The two passed from sight into the galley. Sabas's booming voice sounded in greeting. Clearly, Podesta wasn't the only one who knew the officer. Benson's guards visibly relaxed and the *Aura Placida*'s crew stepped forward to greet them. The crossbowmen stood down and muffled voices came from the galleon to mingle with the lapping of the waves.

***

Prayer was getting tough again.

Shader shut the Liber and threw it on top of his folded coat. His knees hurt from sitting cross-legged on the deck, and his eyes were sore from reading in the dim lamplight.

Podesta had worked his magic with Benson, and the *Aura Placida* was granted passage unhampered as she rode the waves toward the Anglesh Isles. It had taken Benson's men over an hour to load all the food, wine, and tobacco Podesta had gifted him. Shader shook his head and let the tiniest curl of a smile touch his lips. Podesta must have been playing both sides for years: smuggling for the Templum and supplying what the Sahulian navy lacked. It was a dangerous game; everybody apparently knew what was going on, but nobody cared. It reminded Shader of what they used to say in Gallia when he was on campaign: cheating on your wife was OK, providing you didn't get caught. He'd not seen the funny side at the time, but traveling with Podesta was giving him a whole new perspective.

Shader sighed and pulled the knotted prayer cord over his head. His own problem was fidelity to rules, not people. He wasn't so much concerned with others finding out; he was more worried about his own reaction. No matter how he justified it, he still couldn't quite see himself as holy unless he followed the Templum's moral code. Most of the other knights he'd known mitigated the Rule. It was common knowledge that even the priests took lovers, but Shader wasn't that kind of man. And that was a bloody nuisance as far as he was concerned.

It had been difficult seeing Rhiannon again at the templum. The white robes hadn't quite suited her. It was like covering a beautiful painting with an old sheet. He was sure it wouldn't last. Rhiannon was as much suited to the life of a priest as he was. The difference was that she already had a natural goodness, an easy way of being simply whatever it was Ain had made her. Shader knew he had to work at it, just as he'd had to work at everything else—all the philosophy with Aristodeus, the conduct becoming to an Elect knight, and especially unquestioning obedience to his superiors. The only thing that came naturally to him was killing, but that was perhaps to be expected, being raised by one of the hardest men in Britannia.

That was the only similarity between Shader and his father, though. If it hadn't been for their shared excellence with the sword, no one would have guessed they were related. Jarl was as straight as they came, an uncompromising man of action. In his way, he was as natural and earthy as Rhiannon. Shader, however, was too much of a thinker, a trait that often led to long spells of melancholy and self-doubt.

He stretched out his legs and tried to rub some feeling back into them. Taking up the prayer cord, he started working on the first knot while conjugating the Aeternam verb for "love"—*amare*. He'd simplified the practice from the endless litanies he'd been taught as a novice, whittled it down to one word that captured the essence of Ain. At least, it would if he could focus.

"Thought you could use a whiskey."

Shader was startled by the grating voice. He half expected to feel a knife at his throat, but instead Cleto crouched down beside him and held out a bottle. Shader took it without letting his eyes drop from the sailor's stubbly face. Cleto had clearly been in the wars and had probably survived his fair share of pestilence judging by the craters marking his skin.

"Peace offering," Cleto said. "For what I done last time. Got to thinking about it. Reckon it's about as low as a man can get, stealing from his shipmates."

Shader took the bottle and drank deeply. "You asking for forgiveness?" he said, passing the whiskey back to Cleto.

"Nah. Shog that Nousian shit, excuse my Gallic. What's done can't be undone. Just want you to know I got your back now. You're one of us."

Shader put the prayer cord back around his neck and blew the air through his lips. "Don't know about that, Cleto. I'm a passenger, not a crewman."

"Captain says otherwise, and I'm inclined to take what he says a wee bit seriously."

Shader nodded and looked down at the deck.

"You don't want to be sitting there too long," Cleto said. "You'll get piles."

With that he was gone, back into the darkness. Shader suspected he was always there, always watching and waiting for his moment. At least this time he might be watching for less nefarious reasons. Assuming his word was as good as his liquor.

***

The sun came up behind the *Aura Placida*, casting a red swath over the sea that set Shader thinking about the battle he'd left behind. The smell of bacon and strong coffee wafted up from the galley where Sabas was singing a sea shanty in a rumbling bass.

Shader ached all over from spending the night on the deck with only his coat for a pillow.

Elpidio passed him on his way to the crow's nest and stopped to hand him a tin mug full to the brim with black coffee. "Sabas said you'd need it," the lad said, with a wrinkling of his nose. "Can't see why people drink the stuff."

Shader smiled his thanks and took the cup, sipping the steaming contents.

"On lookout again?" he asked.

"Got the best eyes," Elpidio said, "and by the looks of it, Travid's fallen asleep." His eyes turned to the crow's nest where there was a decided lack of activity.

Elpidio hurried away and started to climb the mainmast as the others emerged on deck. Captain Podesta staggered past and stood at the rail to relieve himself. He shook off the drops and gave a shudder, then turned to Shader as he fastened his trousers.

"By the gods of the Great Green I need a coffee," he croaked before stumbling off toward the galley.

A slovenly looking youth came down from the mainmast like a sack of potatoes being lowered. It was a wonder he didn't fall, the way he swung from limp arms without any care for where he put his feet. Shader supposed this must be Travid, and judging by the gaping yawns he made no effort to suppress, it seemed unlikely that he'd seen anything during his watch besides his own dreams.

"Morning," he groaned as he passed Shader and stumbled in the direction of the cabins.

"Ship ahoy!" Elpidio hollered from the crow's nest.

Travid stopped in his tracks and raised his palms. "Weren't nothing there a moment ago. I swear."

The galley door swung open and Podesta strode out, fully alert, with a steaming cup of coffee in his hand.

"Captain," Elpidio called. "Two ships off the bow. One of them's a reaver."

Grim murmurs sounded among the crew and men swarmed to the prow to look out over the bowsprit. Podesta swilled his coffee overboard and handed the empty cup to Travid. As the lad took it, Podesta cuffed him on the ear, eliciting a loud squeal.

"You know what that's for, boy," the captain said, hopping to the base of the mainmast and pulling a spyglass from his jacket.

"That's a reaver all right. Looks like they've caught themselves a Sahulian merchantman." He handed Shader the spyglass. "Just there, to the right of the bowsprit. You see, eh?"

Shader squinted and then the ships came into focus. One was a caravel, not dissimilar to the *Dolphin*, but the markings were different, and it flew the Sahulian flag—a flightless bird set against the backdrop of a clenched fist.

"Reckon we've found our *Ghost*, eh?" Podesta said. "Back home in Sahulian waters. Seems some people will take any job."

The second ship was large—a galleon by the looks of it. The hull was dark as pitch and there were four masts, each rigged with billowing black sails.

"Good boy, Elpidio," Podesta called up to the crow's nest. "All hands on deck!"

Shader handed the spyglass back. "Is it mawgs?"

Podesta locked his eyes to Shader's. There was a grim set to his jaw. "Aye. And not a few of them either. Ship that size will be packed with hundreds of the shoggers. Every man grab a weapon!" he yelled.

Sailors ran for the cabins and came back with cutlasses, knives, and hatchets. A few had crossbows. None of it reassured Shader that they'd have a chance against a horde of mawgs. If they didn't turn about and flee back to Port Sarum, the mawgs would swarm over them like a plague of locusts, picking the bones of every crewman clean and disgorging the remains overboard for the sharks to finish.

"Are we running? Shader asked.

"That's exactly what they'd want. After finishing off the merchantman, they'd catch us in open water. The *Aura Placida*'s a good ship—" Podesta slapped the mast. "—but she's not as fast as a galleon."

"But if they board us…"

Podesta leaned in close, the blood draining from his face. "I know. You forget, I've seen what the bastards can do. But the crew doesn't need to know, eh?" Podesta raised the spyglass again. "They're pulling away from the other ship. They must think this is their lucky day, uh?"

Shader drew the gladius and ran his thumb along the edge of the blade. He'd neglected it somewhat, hadn't even taken a whetstone to it, but it never seemed to blunt.

"Someone's crossing over to the reaver," Elpidio shouted.

Podesta took a look through the spyglass and then passed it to Shader. "Fit the description?"

Shader could see a small figure in a hooded cloak swinging from the doomed merchantman to the deck of the galleon. He landed nimbly as a mass of mawgs rushed toward him. The little man's skin was pale, his short hair white. As the mawgs surrounded him, he held up an object, and they moved back. Without a doubt, it was the serpent statue.

"Shadrak," Shader said, handing the spyglass back to Podesta.

"They're coming about," someone called from the prow.

"Steady!" bellowed Podesta, drawing his cutlass. "Cleto!"

Cleto's head popped up through a trap in the deck. Nods passed between him and Podesta and then Cleto vanished back into the hold.

"Crossbows on the foredeck!" Podesta shouted. "The rest of you, defensive positions on the aftcastle. I want barricades up there—chests, tables, beds—anything you can find. You two!" He called over a couple of petrified sailors. "Bring up every last flask of oil. If they look like boarding, drench the quarterdeck and then join us on the aftcastle."

The sailors scurried off below. Shader frowned at Podesta.

"They're not eating my crew," the captain said. "Just a precaution. You can never have too many plans, eh?"

The *Aura Placida* continued to sail closer to the reaver and its victim. The merchantman was floundering and there was no sign of activity on deck. The galleon, however, began to turn its port side toward them. Podesta pushed his way to the front of the ship, Shader following him.

"What are they playing at?" the captain said. "They should be coming at us head on."

He had a point. Shader could now see that the prow of the galleon was fitted with a heavy metal ram. One hit from that and the *Aura Placida*'s hull would be breached. That would be the end of them. The two ships were now a few hundred yards apart, and Shader could see the massed furry bodies lining the rails of the reaver. A chilling roar went up from the mawgs, who began to jump and prowl about in barely suppressed frenzy.

"Look!" Shader said as slats on the side of the galleon's hull slid open and metal tubes popped out.

"What the Abyss?" Podesta said, leaning forward to get a better view.

He leapt backward as a wave of explosions sounded and smoke erupted from the bank of tubes. A shout of horror went up from the crew and then there was a series of splashes as heavy objects hit the water in front of the ship. Another roar went up from the mawgs as the *Aura Placida* continued to drift toward them.

"Bring us about!" Podesta shouted. He turned to Shader. "What was that?"

Shader had seen nothing like it before, but Aristodeus had once told him about thunderous weapons from a bygone era. "Aeterna-tech?" he wondered out loud.

"Perhaps," Podesta said. "But I think we can do better than that. Cleto!"

Cleto was there in an instant. Slung over his shoulder was a long cylinder made of a dull metal Shader didn't recognize. Cleto had hold of some kind of grip with one hand, and with the other he steadied the cylinder and rested his thumb above a red circular protrusion.

"Do you know what you're doing?" Podesta asked with a look of mild trepidation.

"Not a shogging clue," Cleto said. "But there were pictures in the box. I reckon it's a simple matter of pointing and pressing the trigger." He tapped his thumb against the button.

Podesta winced and gave him some room.

The bank of tubes on the galleon withdrew and then reappeared after a few moments.

"Whatever you've got planned," Shader said, "now would be a good time."

Cleto rested the cylinder on the forward rail and knelt down with his head beside it. He closed one eye, took aim, and pressed the button.

There was a deafening roar and Shader and Podesta hit the deck. Cleto was thrown back against the foremast as fire and smoke streaked from the strange weapon. Shader rolled to his feet in time to see something strike the mainsail of the galleon and erupt in flame. The top of the mast fell away and dropped toward the stunned mawgs beneath. The reaver banked and the tubes sticking from the hull drooped.

Shader ran to Cleto's side and helped him to stand. "You OK?"

"Shog, yeah!" Cleto said with a wide grin spreading across his pockmarked face. "Did I get 'em?"

"They lost a sail," Shader said, "but I think that's your only shot." He indicated the smoking cylinder that now had a split running down its length. "Unless you've got any more of those things down below."

Podesta called out over his shoulder. "Only one we had, eh, Cleto? Now answer me this." He shot a look at Shader. "What the shog did Jarmin the Anchorite of Gladelvi want with one of those, uh?"

Shader left Cleto to dust himself down and rejoined Podesta at the prow. "They're turning away," he said as the galleon increased the distance between them. "It's not like mawgs to run from a fight."

Podesta was biting hard on his knuckles. "Maybe they've got more important things to do, eh?" He pointed at the stern of the retreating ship where a white face was staring at them from beneath a black hood.

"We must give chase," Shader said. "We need to get the statue back."

Podesta's gaze switched to the floundering merchantman. "All in good time, my friend. Rules of the sea. Search for survivors first, eh?"

Shader opened his mouth to protest, but could see from the captain's face that he'd be wasting his time.

***

The waters were red around the merchantman as the longboat came alongside. Dorsal fins broke the surface, sending ripples through the blood, and here and there huge jaws burst above the waves to tear at the disgorged contents of mawgish stomachs. Shader kept as close to the center of the boat as possible, scarcely daring to move in case he was pitched into the water among the sharks.

"Hundreds of them," Podesta said, peering over the side. "No chance of survivors there."

Shader half expected a shark to leap from the water and drag the captain face-first overboard, but Podesta seemed unperturbed.

Cleto swung a grapple up top and the three climbed aboard.

The Sahulian flag snapped and fluttered above them, but other than that there was no sign of movement. The decks were slick with gore—half-eaten limbs and regurgitated bones. Shader stepped over the torso of a man whose hands still held fast to the railing, but whose legs had been ripped away at the hips. The three trod a path between chewed-up heads and strewn entrails, holding their noses against the stench of blood, piss, and excrement. Cleto retched and then bent double as his stomach emptied. He wiped the sick from his face with the back of his sleeve.

"Wait for us in the boat, my friend," Podesta said, to Cleto's obvious relief.

Shader pressed on to the quarterdeck, a discomforting feeling growing all the while. The ship certainly matched the description of the *Ghost* they'd been given in Rujala, but there was something about it that unsettled him.

He started as a hand clapped down on his shoulder.

"You feel it too, eh?" Podesta said, his breath heavy in Shader's ear. "Something very familiar about this ship. Look."

A corpse held onto the wheel in a death-grip, its clothes shredded, the flesh of one half of its body stripped to the bone. The head hung to one side, attached only by the slenderest thread of sinew. The eyes were white and frozen wide, the teeth bared in a silent scream that seemed to stretch to eternity.

"Ain," Shader muttered as he recognized what was left of the face. "Captain Diaz."

Podesta was ashen, a single tear rolling down his cheek. "The *Dolphin* was the *Ghost* all along." He fell to his knees and let his head drop.

It looked to Shader like a gesture of prayer. He'd always thought Diaz was Podesta's bitter enemy, but clearly the manner of Diaz's death had touched a nerve. Then Shader recalled the captain's story aboard the *Aura Placida* on their way to Sahul.

Shader knelt beside Podesta and put an arm around his shoulders. "Come, my friend," he said. "Time to leave."

Podesta shook him off and stood. "No!" he shouted, spittle flying from his mouth. "You're wrong. Go if you like, but I'm staying. Someone must have survived."

Shader felt his cheeks flush with shame. "You're right," he said. "I'm sorry."

Podesta held his gaze, the tears spilling freely now. He gave a curt nod, and then they both turned back to the blood-spattered decks and began their search. True to his word, Podesta left no stone unturned. He scoured every cabin, searched under tables, in cupboards, growing more frantic and enraged every step. Shader followed him, but kept his distance. They searched for over an hour, and Shader felt they could do no more when Podesta's eyes turned to a loose plank in the hold.

"Help me," he barked, drawing a dagger and using it to pry the board free.

Shader lifted it clear and started as something rushed past below. Podesta dropped to his front and reached into the gap.

"Got you," he cried.

There was an answering yelp and then Podesta drew a young boy to the opening. The child was biting and scratching, but the captain ignored the pain and uttered soothing words. Shader pulled the neighboring plank away and then reached down to help Podesta lift the boy up. He was a scrawny lad, no more than nine or ten. His face was streaked with dirt, his clothes soiled with dried blood. He started to shake as he looked from Shader to Podesta, his mouth opening and closing, but no words coming out. Podesta

289

drew the lad into an embrace and stroked the back of his head.

"There, there," he said, his voice thick with emotion. "You're safe now."

Podesta raised his eyes to Shader's. They were bloodshot and brimming with tears.

"Told you," he said with no sense of triumph. "Told you I'd find one."

THE BATTLE OF SARUM

THE STREETS WERE deserted, but if you looked close enough you could catch people peering through cracks in the curtains. Whatever might have befallen the center of Sarum, the suburbs had so far been spared.

General Starn pressed his back to the wall and stole a quick glance down the alleyway, holding up a hand to halt the men behind. The sun was high in the sky, and his blooming breastplate was growing more and more of a nuisance. He dug in between its bottom edge and his sore belly with the tips of his fingers. Sweat was streaming down his face and plastering his mustache over his lips. He blew to dislodge it before the tickling drove him stark raving mad. Once they were done and dusted here he'd have Mrs. Starn trim it for him and put him back on a diet of herrings and oatmeal. Shed a few pounds and the armor would fit as well as it had years ago, when he'd won it at the tournament in New Ithaka— back when Troy Jance was still on speaking terms with the emperor.

Starn was about to signal the company forward when he was barged out of the way, catching the side of his head on the wall. "Ooh, quite a knock that," he mumbled as the emperor strode past into the alley and stood there, hands on hips.

Indomitable, Starn thought. *Like a god of battle.* He felt a tad unworthy cowering by the wall. Not a good show to have the emperor take the lead. Not good at all.

The thirty men of the imperial bodyguard flowed past him, taking up their positions around Hagalle with seamless precision. Shields were raised in a defensive circle, but the emperor stood a good head above the tallest of the soldiers and suddenly looked vulnerable. A single arrow was all it would take. It didn't matter that the enemy thus far had been reported as walking corpses; a good general always had to plan for the worst.

The shield wall parted for Starn as he took up his place beside the emperor.

"Makes a change," Hagalle growled. "The scouts were right. Nothing. No movement in the northern suburbs. What would you say, General, press on to the central district and get a good look at the enemy ourselves?"

Starn scrunched his face up and tugged at his mustache. He'd have preferred a steady advance with the main army, but Duke Farian had been left to arrange that while Hagalle insisted on going ahead to make sure the scouts hadn't been lying. Starn had learnt long ago there was no point arguing with the emperor. He was a man of action, a brave man— whatever the slanderers might say. A man worthy to be followed.

"Lost your tongue again, Starn?" The emperor rolled his eyes, and Starn lowered his, feeling an utter disappointment.

"I was going to say…" he stammered, hating himself for his inability to speak in front of authority.

"What is it I pay you for, Starn?" Hagalle raised his voice, and the sniggers started among the soldiers. "Because I'm damned if I can remember. Wait here for Farian, if you like, but us men are pressing on. I want a good look at these ghouls for myself. You can never have too much reconnaissance, Starn. Never."

Starn looked up, straight into the mocking eyes of Dalglish. As Hagalle pushed through the encircling soldiers and headed toward the junction at the end of the alley, Dalglish pulled off his helmet to run his fingers through his slick red hair.

He opened his mouth to say something, a wicked curl twisting the edge of his lips, but Starn had had enough of that sort of thing.

"Attention, Captain Dalglish. Let's not forget our places, eh?"

Dalglish sneered, but put his helmet back on and clicked his heels together.

"Keep close to the emperor, Dalglish. This is a risky business. Every man at his best, what, what."

The troops had to jog to keep up with Hagalle, who stood at the crossroads with one hand resting on a twenty-foot tall iron post, atop which was a glass sphere. The way ahead broadened into an avenue flanked by rows of identical posts. Starn wished he could show them to Mrs. Starn. She'd always had a love of the Ancients, but there was little evidence of their civilization in Jorakum. Compared to Sarum, the Capital was something of a baby.

The streets to left and right of their position were sorry affairs, strewn with all manner of stinking waste. Black rats scampered about the refuse and occasionally raised their beady eyes to look at the company.

"Straight on," Hagalle said. "Can't see the enemy taking up positions down those shit holes. Place is a bloody disgrace. Makes you wonder what on earth Zara Gen has been doing all these years. I rather suspect Sarum will be having an election far sooner than he expects."

Dalglish flicked a look at Starn and then left and right along the streets. Starn guessed his meaning, put his fist to his mouth, and coughed.

"Not well, General?" Hagalle said, turning on him, arms folded across his chest.

"Um, no, Emperor. I mean, yes, I'm fine. It's just that, as Captain Dalglish has rightly pointed out..."

"Get on with it, man," Hagalle said, his shoulders bunching up around his ears.

Starn tugged down the front of his breastplate and stood to attention. "The area isn't secure, Emperor. If we continue on without..."

"Rubbish," Hagalle said. "Stay if you like, but I don't have the time for this."

"Permission to speak freely, Emperor?" Starn said in an unusually strident voice.

Hagalle glowered, but then raised an eyebrow and inclined his head. "General."

"We should wait here for Duke Farian to catch up, deploy a rear-guard to make sure our retreat isn't compromised, and send scouts east and west."

Hagalle gave him a slow handclap. "Tactically astute, as ever, General, but you are forgetting one thing: all the reports have been of a motley band of zombies who haven't moved from the front of Arnbrook House."

"With the exception of the black carriage," Dalglish whispered in Starn's ear.

"What?" Hagalle growled. "Speak up."

"The black carriage, Emperor," Dalglish said, his cheeks turning redder than his hair. "Scouts said it headed east across the city with an escort of cavalry."

"And that frightens you, does it?" Hagalle said.

Dalglish lowered his head.

"So," Hagalle said. "Unless anyone else has anything to add..."

The emperor's eyes scanned the troops, but no one dared meet them. "Good. Excellent. Then let's move it."

Hagalle turned on his heel and strode ahead, the rest of the troop scrabbling about him with shields raised and eyes darting everywhere. Dalglish shrugged, and Starn took a deep breath before following the others.

They'd gone no further than fifty yards when a loud clopping started up from a few blocks away. Hagalle halted, and the company once again surrounded him. The noise began to swell, rolling toward them like an approaching tidal wave. Starn was all too familiar with the sound.

"Cavalry!" he barked. "Orderly retreat. Let's get back to the alley."

Hagalle looked like he was going to protest, but was swept along by the soldiers following a direct order from their general. The main body of troops walked backward, facing the oncoming wall of noise, but Starn and Dalglish turned to take the lead. Starn's blood almost froze in his veins as dozens of shambling corpses spilled out from the rat-infested streets they'd just passed.

"What the Abyss?" Dalglish said, drawing his sword and banging it against his shield to alert the others."

Starn looked back the other way. A bank of fog roiled from the buildings edging the business district, and shadows were starting to take shape within it. The emperor was staring like a startled rabbit, his jaw hanging slack. The men were casting nervous glances about and looked ready to break.

"They're coming!" Dalglish called.

Starn spun. The corpses were shuffling toward them. Many were missing arms, and some had lost a leg. They crawled, hopped, and slid, drawn on by inhuman appetites Starn could only guess at. Some of the soldiers were shaking, and none besides Dalglish had drawn their swords.

"You men!" Starn found his parade ground voice and jabbed a finger at the twenty he wanted. "Two ranks deep, lock shields, and wait for my order."

"Sir!" they yelled in unison, drawing their weapons and lining up in front of Dalglish.

"Captain," bellowed Starn. "We're going to smash through and run. Understood?"

Dalglish licked his lips and nodded.

"Is that understood, Captain Dalglish?"

"Sir, yes, sir!"

"Soldiers," Starn indicated the remaining ten. "Orderly retreat. You will protect the emperor with your lives. Is that understood?"

"Sir, yes, sir!"

Hagalle was watching him. He nodded and drew his own broadsword, his eyes darkening, jaw setting. "Bloody good show, General."

Hagalle looked out front to where mounted knights were emerging from the mist. The horses were fleshless, their eyes blazing with red fire. The riders wore faded surcoats and ancient chainmail with broken links. They carried kite shields bearing the Nousian Monas, and blades nicked and brown with age.

"Must be about fifty," Starn estimated out loud.

"Not counting that lot," Hagalle said, as two more companies rode out from the side streets up ahead.

"A hundred and fifty, then," Starn said, straining to see how many corpses were milling behind. Another hundred, at least, he guessed, but he fancied their chances with them more than against the cavalry.

The undead horsemen formed up into tight wedges, making their intentions perfectly clear.

"Captain Dalglish," Starn yelled. "On my command hit them hard and keep going."

The mass of dead were so close Starn could see the lifeless whites of their eyes and the blackened stubs of teeth. The stench was overpowering—worse than the leg ulcers that had tormented his poor old mother.

"Steady," his voice rolled out. "Steady."

Dalglish cast a worried look over his shoulder. The corpses were almost upon them.

Starn's heart was pounding so loud he worried he might not be heard above its clamor.

Sucking in a deep breath, he roared at the top of his voice. "Charge!"

The shield wall surged forward and slammed into the undead. Bones splintered and rotting flesh pulped over the pavement. The soldiers in the back rank heaved, pressing against their colleagues with their shields. Those in front hacked and stabbed, carving through the first wave of corpses with ruthless efficiency.

A chilling screech sounded from behind, and Starn swung to see the cavalry sweep forward. They gathered speed, raised their swords, and charged.

***

"Hurry!" Gaston shouted as a window shattered and claws raked through, heedless of the jagged glass. "We need to leave now."

Maldark swung his war-hammer, crushing a hand. A head appeared above the windowsill, its lips cyanosed and eyes sunken, tongue black and bloated like a slug. Gaston rammed his sword down its throat and ripped it free. The creature's eyes swelled with blood and gore spewed from its mouth. Gaston winced at the pain in his ribs as he twisted to make sure the priests were clearing the room.

Maldark smashed another ghoul in the face, spilling brains. Two more pushed through the window. Gaston hacked the head from the first with a double-fisted blow, and Maldark used his hammer like a battering ram to send the other flailing to the street below.

Ioana ushered Cadris, Agna, and Rhiannon out of the attic and onto the stairs. Gaston backed toward them, weaving his sword through the air as three more slavering corpses dragged themselves into the room. Maldark spun, the hammer arcing viciously and crushing a kneecap. Gaston lunged, skewering an eye and backslashing across the throat of the next. Claws tore at his face and he fell back, raising an arm for protection. Maldark bellowed and threw his weight against the three, bowling them out of the window. Gaston ran to his side and peered out. Scores of ghouls were scuttling up the walls like grotesque spiders. The street below was teeming with undead. They were pulling people from their homes and ripping into their flesh. Screams mingled with growls, causing Gaston's heart to sink. His breaths came hard and fast; his arms were leaden and shaky.

"Always hope, boy," Maldark said, taking him by the shoulder and shoving him toward the door. "Keep moving. Protect the priests."

Maldark exited behind him and locked the door. Gaston squeezed past the priests on the stairwell and held up a hand for silence. He took the last few stairs to the ground floor on the balls of his feet, poking his head around the banister. Shadows passed across the shuttered windows, but the room was empty. Behind him, Agna was panting, her face gray and drawn. Fat Cadris was a quivering mess, eyes darting every which way. Rhiannon was tight-lipped, her pupils like saucers. For a moment, Gaston thought she was petrified, but then she met his gaze, and he saw her grim resolve. She was scared half to death, like they all were, but she wasn't ready to fold.

Gaston crept to the front door and peered outside. A mass of undead hissed and snarled from the alleyway to the left. They immediately stopped their frenzied feeding and began to lurch toward him. He stole a look to the right. The street was clear and there was a flash of red. He blinked and looked again. It was Governor Gen waving from an adjacent alley. Behind him, Gaston saw the glint of armor and swords.

"Quickly!" Zara Gen yelled. "We'll cover you."

A score of soldiers rushed from the alley and set up a line of shields across the street. Gaston recognized Captain Harding at their center barking commands, eyes rooted unflinchingly to the advancing corpses.

Gaston turned to the priests on the stairs. "To the door," he said. "Run to the right. The militia will buy us time."

Ioana went first, angling behind the shield wall. Rhiannon had to half push half shove Cadris, and it seemed to take forever for his waddling bulk to cover the distance. Agna was even slower. By the time she was halfway across, the undead slammed into the militiamen with such weight that the line began to sunder.

Maldark roared and charged into the throng, his hammer rising and falling with tireless regularity. The first ranks of undead fell before his onslaught, and Harding barked commands to his men. The shield wall began an orderly withdrawal back toward the alley. All the priests, bar Agna, had made it, and the retreating troops almost collided with her.

Gaston sheathed his sword and sprinted from the doorway to sweep Agna up. He dumped her in the arms of Zara Gen and then pushed his way through the militiamen. The undead pressed forward like an unstoppable mudslide, hundreds more pouring from the tributary streets.

The soldiers locked shields behind Gaston and Maldark, casting nervous glances at Harding. Gaston caught the Captain's gaze and shuddered. He could just as easily have been looking in a mirror.

"Go," Gaston said. "We'll hold them as long as we can. No point us all dying."

Harding was about to protest when Zara Gen called out to him.

"You heard the man, Harding. Follow me, and that's an order."

Maldark crashed his hammer against the ground, sending a shock wave through the first ranks of undead. Amber lightning sparked from the hammerhead and the air about it started to shimmer."

"You too, boy," the dwarf growled at Gaston. "You can do no more here. Look after Mater for me."

Maldark suddenly lunged at Gaston and bundled him into the alleyway. One of the soldiers caught his arm and dragged him after the others. A loathsome cry went up from the undead and they swept toward the dwarf.

Gaston sprinted to catch up with the priests, the militia taking the rear in case Maldark couldn't hold off the horde. Rhiannon was urging Cadris forward, and Zara Gen struggled on with Agna over his shoulder. Ioana led the way like a frantic mother hen. When Gaston reached her, she touched his arm with shaking fingers.

"There are too many of them," she said. "I could try to stop them—" She fingered her Monas. "—but my faith... I don't know if..."

"Keep moving, Mater," Gaston said. "Otherwise Maldark's efforts will be for nothing."

A cry from behind made him turn. Zara Gen lowered Agna to the ground, clutching his chest and breathing heavily.

"Can't go on," he panted. "Leave us here. I'll stay with her."

Gaston jogged toward them. "No way, Governor. You go. I'll stay—"

Something dark hurtled into him amid the sound of breaking glass. Shards tore into his skin, and hands gripped him around the throat, squeezing the breath from him. Zara Gen grabbed hold of the creature, but was struck across the face and sent flying into the wall. Gaston tried to pry the fingers from his neck, but they may as well have been made of steel. A rotting face pressed close, jagged teeth straining for his flesh. Gaston recoiled from the stench and kicked out with all his strength. His vision was starting to blur, his struggles growing weaker.

He saw a flash of movement behind the creature. Something white wrenched its head away. Gaston fell to his knees, panting for breath as Rhiannon slammed the ghoul into the ground and kicked it in the ribs, over and over. The creature shrieked and sprang up, grabbing her by the hair and dragging her into the side alley. Gaston forced himself to stand and staggered in pursuit. By the time he reached the alley, the ghoul's dismembered body was strewn all over the ground, but there was no sign of Rhiannon. He flopped against the wall, too exhausted to take another step.

***

Skeletal steeds pulverized the shield wall, their riders hacking left and right.

Inevitable, thought Starn, but ten brave men had bought them precious seconds.

Up ahead, Dalglish drove a corridor through the ghouls, his men bunching into a wedge, cutting and thrusting with desperate fury.

The emperor roared and spun to face the death-knights rolling over his men. A horse disintegrated from a double-fisted strike with his broadsword, the rider hurtling from the saddle, but immediately crawling back toward the fray. A score of riders wheeled to confront Hagalle, but he stood his ground, just as Starn knew he would. Hagalle bellowed his defiance and swung his sword in a wide arc, keeping them at bay.

Starn glanced back and saw that the last of Dalglish's men were through and running like the clappers as the undead closed ranks behind. With no time for thought, Starn grabbed Hagalle by the collar and dragged him toward the gap. The emperor swore, but then saw what was happening and charged into the opening, kicking a corpse out of his way and trampling it underfoot.

Two ghouls moved behind the emperor, but Starn was upon them, stabbing and slashing. He whirled as a death-knight reared up on its fleshless horse, grabbed a ghoul by the hair, and threw it in the rider's path. Hagalle smashed his way through to the far side and Starn dashed after. More ghouls lunged at him, claws gouging his breastplate. Starn dived, rolling and clattering his way beyond the undead. Hagalle stepped over him and swept his blade into the horde, spilling putrid entrails to the ground. He backed away, hacking wildly, giving Starn time to find his feet and run.

"I say, Starn," Hagalle yelled, pulling his sword from the belly of a cadaver and frowning at its blood-drenched yellow robes. "Wasn't that Duke Farian's man, Torpin? Bigger pain in the arse in death than he was in life."

The ghoul stumbled toward the emperor and spewed black vomit over his breastplate. Hagalle backslashed almost nonchalantly and the creature's head flew into the air. The body teetered, the hands still feeling about for someone to throttle. Hagalle lopped an arm off at the shoulder and booted what was left of Torpin into the mass of undead. The ghouls leapt upon the former herald, ripping away gray flesh with gore-spattered jaws.

Starn's breaths were sticking in his throat, his heart hammering in his chest. He couldn't think of anything to say.

Hagalle took the lead with long loping strides, but Starn only had short legs, and he was hardly in the best shape of his life. Mrs. Starn's apple pie was likely to be the death of him, he thought as he took a quick breather, leaning against a wall.

Dalglish stood at the mouth of the narrow alley, urging him on. Starn held up a hand and sucked in some deep rasping breaths. A sound like a hundred melons being pulped came from behind, and he looked back to see the death-knights riding over the ghouls and hacking them out of the way with rusted blades. The front two were almost through. Now or never, Starn told himself, and sprinted for the alley.

Dalglish and two others flowed back past him and locked shields. Hagalle grabbed him by the sleeve and tugged him after the retreating troops.

"Keep going, General. Don't want to lose you now."

The clash of blades on shields rang out behind as Starn struggled away from the melee. Two more soldiers ran to aid Dalglish and slow the advance of the death-knights. Good strategy, Starn thought. Dalglish had the knights bottlenecked. They could only come on two abreast, the shield wall giving ground one step at a time.

"More of them up ahead!" someone shouted down the line.

Hagalle was straining to see over their heads and cursed. "Where the Abyss are they coming from?"

Starn lacked the height to see. "How many?" he asked.

"Too damned many," Hagalle said.

"Over there," Starn said, spotting a passage between two houses and leading the way. The troop pounded after him until they reached an open square with an ornamental fountain at its center. A broad avenue led away to the east, and cobbled alleyways ran to the north and west.

"We can't keep running," Hagalle said. "The men are exhausted and our passage north is blocked."

Starn grimaced and then pointed to the broad base of the fountain that stood a couple of feet above the ground. "Form up there," he said. "Shield wall facing the avenue."

He was certain the death-knights would come that way, otherwise they'd lose the advantage of numbers.

Dalglish backed into the square with two bloodied men.

"Good show, Captain," Hagalle said. "Get those men behind the shield wall."

Dalglish took his place in the wall beside Starn. "Last stand time, eh?" He forced a grin that didn't extend to his eyes.

"We'll get out of this," Starn said, not knowing who he was trying to kid. "We have to. Told Mrs. Starn I'd be back for our anniversary."

Starn eyed the opening of the passageway they'd come through. As he'd expected, there was no sign of pursuit from the undead knights. Some of the men started to relax and lower their shields.

"Stay alert, lads," Starn said, pointing to the avenue with his sword. "They'll not give up so easily."

The rumble of hooves rolled toward them, funneling down the avenue and rising to a thunderous roar.

"Steady," Starn mumbled to himself. "Lock those shields!" His throat was raw from shouting. "Stand your ground, and let's see if we can break this wave."

He did a quick headcount as the knights came into view amid a swirl of dust. Sixteen men standing, two of them badly wounded. One fragile line against a cavalry charge at least a hundred strong.

"General," Dalglish spoke in his ear. "Don't want to add to the gloom, but back there, in the alleyway, the ones we cut down just got up again. They can't be killed."

Starn chewed on the edge of his mustache. So this was it, then. No more of Mrs. Starn's apple pie. No more lazy nights on the porch sipping wine. Still, best be grateful for the times he'd had. He almost wished he was like the Nousians; right now, he'd have loved a god to thank for Mrs. Starn. Wonderful woman. The best.

And then the knights hit.

The force was colossal, driving the shield wall back against the fountain. Men screamed, bones snapped, blades clashed. Starn felt like his face had been slammed into a wall. He was surrounded by a blurry confusion, his ears assaulted by the din. Someone fell, clutching his arm. He tried to grab the fellow and then saw the fingers were mere bones. He struck at the severed hand with the pommel of his sword as it started to crawl toward his shoulder. He managed to slip the blade underneath and flick the thing off. Someone pulled him back, and two soldiers stepped in front with shields raised. Starn shook his head, trying to restore his vision. The plinth had saved them, he was sure of it. The front horses must have tripped and those behind plowed into them.

There was furious fighting all around him. The man in front screamed as a sword punched through his back. Starn stabbed past his thrashing body, his blade grating against metal. To his left, Hagalle stood out above the others, his broadsword rising and falling with savage fury. But Dalglish had been right. No sooner had the death-knights been struck down than their bones crawled back together, and they returned to the fight.

Another soldier fell, blood spurting from his throat. Dalglish stood alone against two mounted foes. Starn forced himself forward and parried a blow from one as Dalglish hammered his sword into the other's horse, dislodging the rider. Starn jumped out of the way of a hoof and sliced the leg off at the knee. The horse tottered, and the rider fell forward straight into the path of Starn's backslash. The helmeted head clattered to the floor, righted itself, and glared at him with flaming eyes.

Dalglish staggered, blood spilling from a gash to his arm. Starn caught him and lashed out, denting a rusty shield. Four more riders pressed toward him, and he had to lower Dalglish to the ground to face them. Hagalle's sword still clove into the death-knights, but Starn could see no one else standing.

He turned the blade of one skeleton rider and grabbed the rim of its shield with his free hand, wrenching the arm out of its socket. The horse fell to its side, hampering the approach of the other three and affording Starn time to snatch up the shield. Another horse reared up, flailing about with its hooves. Starn stepped under them and slammed the shield into the beast. He met a vicious swing from a death-knight with his sword and punched the shield into its face. Another parry, a backward step, and he tripped on something, toppling onto Dalglish. A death-knight swung down, but Starn got behind his shield, his arm numbed by the force of the blow. He tried to stand, but his feet got caught up. The death-knight raised its sword again, then suddenly veered to the left, as if carried away by a tidal wave. White shapes flashed by amid the undead, bright steel scintillating in the sun. Starn keeled over and could see nothing but Dalglish's bloodless face staring wide-eyed up at the sky.

***

Maldark heaved against the living corpses piling on top of him, but knew it was hopeless. He felt the closeness of death and was relieved. If it was just about him, he'd have stopped struggling right then.

Throwing aside caution, he clung onto his hammer with a death-grip and narrowed his eyes. Heat coursed through the haft, singeing his fingers. Maldark gritted his teeth and hung on, the weight of the dead pressing him flat. He twisted his head to breathe, but his lungs refused to expand. A colossal roar burst forth from the hammer, accompanied by an explosion of golden light. The mountain of undead shuddered and then disintegrated, the ashes of the ghouls blasted into the air.

A new vigor flooded Maldark's body, and he surged to his feet brandishing the hammer that now shone with the intensity of the sun. More and more undead lurched from the buildings, jaws gaping and dripping gore. Maldark spun, searching for any sign of his companions. The dead had closed the path behind. He could see nothing but a great ring of putrid flesh tightening around him. Raising the hammer aloft, he bit down thoughts of unworthiness and let the words of the psalm pour from his lips.

"Why, O Lord, are they multiplied that afflict me? Many are they who rise up against me."

He swung the hammer in a wide circle, following its arc and spinning with increasing speed. As he whirled, thoughts of betrayal rose to torment him; the faces of dead friends, the broken bodies of the grandchildren of Eingana.

Beams of amber streamed from the hammerhead, driving back the hordes of undead.

"I will not fear thousands of the people surrounding me: arise, O Lord; save me, O my

God."

Unfaithfulness stabbed him like a rusted blade. He had no right to call upon the Lord. The only faith remaining to him was clutched firmly in his hands.

He continued to draw upon the puissance of his hammer, his veins swelling, his skin stretched to bursting. His eyes snapped wide, and a scream tore from his throat as golden light exploded with the brilliance of a million stars.

The undead wailed and then flew toward him, sucked by tremendous force. Wave after wave spun toward the hammerhead, vanishing into the air the instant they touched it. As the last of them passed from existence, Maldark collapsed to his knees, feeling as if he'd aged a century. His breath came in ragged gasps, his heart rattled against his ribs, but it didn't matter. He'd triumphed, and in some small way he'd started to atone.

The hammer sent a trickle of warmth up his arms, settling his breathing and granting him the strength to stand. The radiance faded from the head, and the haft grew cold as ice.

The chill extended to his spine, the nape of his neck. A shadow fell over his mind and Maldark clenched his teeth. There was always a price to pay. As he'd expected, his use of the power in his hammer hadn't gone unnoticed.

Perhaps there was still time. If he could just make it to a building…

Barely had he taken a step when a gigantic black hand materialized in the air before him. Maldark felt a sickening dread he'd not experienced for centuries; a naked vulnerability at the core of his being. He'd felt it before, back on Aethir. That was the day he'd betrayed Eingana.

***

Fleshless hands closed around Hagalle's neck. He rammed his elbow back, wincing as it struck bone. A skeletal rider flung itself from its horse, but he ran it through the ribs even as more hands pulled him from behind. He shifted his weight, twisted, and hurled his assailant over his head to crash into the nearest death-knights. A blade clanged off his breastplate and Hagalle chopped down, severing an arm. Something white flashed to his right. He spun, ready to strike.

"Climb up." A sandy-haired youth on a gray horse offered his hand.

Hagalle swung into the saddle behind him and gripped hard with his knees. The horse reared as two of the undead cavalry charged. The lad hacked the head from the first knight and the gray smashed its hooves into the other's horse, splintering bone and pitching the rider to the ground.

"Hold on," the youth called over his shoulder as they thundered toward a line of undead horsemen.

Hagalle toppled backward, but managed to catch hold of the lad's cloak. His sword arm trailed behind, and it was all he could do to keep his grip on the weapon. They hit the death-knights with a thunderous crack. Shards of bone shot all around them, but the lad leaned low against the horse's mane, and Hagalle buried his face in the cloak.

"We're through!" the lad cried as they hit the broad avenue and kept going.

Hagalle turned his head and saw a dozen or so white-garbed knights following them. The death-knights were in disarray, but they were already re-forming.

"Stop," he called out. "We must go back."

The youth slowed to a canter as the other knights drew alongside. "No way," he said. "That'd be suicide."

"Do you know who I am, boy?" Hagalle growled, and then he caught sight of the lad's face.

"Yes, Emperor, I know who you are, and you're too important to lose."

It was Barek Thomas, the lad he'd recently had crucified.

Hagalle shook his head. Curse his cowardly body; he'd started to tremble now he was out of the battle. "Why?"

Barek met his gaze. "Because that's what we were trained to do."

Hagalle rubbed at his temples. It made no sense. "My men," he muttered. "We can't leave them."

"They're dead," Barek said.

A red-haired knight rode alongside. "As we'll be, if we don't keep moving."

"Glad you made it, Justin," Barek said. "Elgin? Solomon?"

Justin pointed to a brawny youth and a skinny runt sharing a water-skin and casting nervous glances back toward the square.

Barek nodded, but there was no joy in his eyes. There were only twelve riders remaining.

"How many…?" Hagalle started to ask.

"Too many," Barek said, spurring the horse on as the death-knights drew up for another charge.

***

Maldark dropped his hammer as the black hand snatched him up and soared into the air high above the city. A chilling voice cut through his awareness.

"I know you."

The voice had a grating quality. It sounded clipped and artificial, but there was no denying who it belonged to.

"Sektis Gandaw." The name left Maldark's lips like a curse.

"Maldark the turncoat. How did you get here?"

The giant fingers tightened around his ribs.

"A swirling eye," Maldark said. "A stormy sea. The Lord cast me into Gehenna, and I passed through the Abyss. Next, I appeared upon a red mountain in the desert."

"Mystical nonsense," Gandaw said. "And to think I held such high hopes for the dwarves. That's what happens when you throw in rogue genes. I assume you know where the statue is. That is why you're here, isn't it?"

"Thou art the all-seeing one," Maldark said. "Why doest thou not tell me where it is?"

The hand released him, and Maldark plummeted toward the ground. He closed his eyes and steeled himself for death, but the impact never came. His head was wrenched back, and there was excruciating pain in his face and neck. He hung suspended by his beard, which was gripped by the thumb and forefinger of the giant hand.

"I'd rather hoped," said Gandaw's voice in his head, "your face would come away with the beard. You dwarves are too full of surprises. See how easy it is to kill you. You're nothing but an insect. You were at the center of a power surge, dwarf. Tell me, where is the statue? Do you have a piece?"

"What if I do? Doest thou forget, I've seen inside your mountain? Thy secrets are known to me. The black hand lacks the power to carry objects through the planes. Death holds no fear for me. Perhaps God will still be merciful. Drop me."

Maldark spasmed as sparks erupted around the hand.

"Nothing!" The hand shook him. "What have you done with it?"

The fingers started to blink in and out of existence and Maldark fell.

"I'll find it," Gandaw's voice echoed as the hand winked out of view.

Maldark dropped limply through the air. He held his arms wide and smiled. He hit something, bounced, and then tumbled down a rooftop. Instinctively, he clutched at the guttering as he rolled over the edge. Pain lanced through his shoulder and he let go, bouncing off a ledge and landing with a sickening thud on the ground.

He lay there for a minute and then gingerly started to test his limbs. Nothing broken, but he was going to hurt like hell on the morrow. He rolled to his knees and carefully stood. His skull felt like it was being pounded with a thousand sledgehammers, and he staggered and nearly collapsed. Shaking his head to clear it, he took a faltering step and tripped over the haft of his hammer. *Strange sort of luck*, Maldark grumbled internally as he lifted it. *Arnochian granite*. He patted the hammerhead. Must have kept Gandaw from detecting what was within. Whatever claims the Technocrat made about the creation of the dwarves, they had more tricks up their sleeves than he could account for.

Shouldering the weapon, he muttered a prayer for the others and stumbled in the direction of the river. He was sure he'd seen a tavern there. A drink or two to restore his soul, and then he'd summon his boat and return to the ocean. Sektis Gandaw had the scent of him now. There was no point imperiling the others.

***

What is that fearsome clatter?

"You drop something dear?" Starn mumbled into the dirt.

What on earth was he doing on the ground? Last thing he remembered was opening a bottle of Shiraz out on the porch. Can't have drunk that much, surely.

He covered his ears with his hands as a roaring tumult passed all around him. It sounded like a river bursting its banks, or the approach of a cyclone.

"Ethna? Ethna, are you all right?"

He had to get back to the house, shutter the windows. Oh, where was Mrs. Starn?

And then he remembered.

Starn sat up and watched the death-knights thunder past, pooling at the mouth of the southern alleyway and then filtering through two at a time.

Dalglish groaned beside him. "What's that racket?" he rasped.

Dalglish was lying in a puddle of blood, most of which seemed to be coming from his arm. Starn fumbled about in his pocket for his handkerchief and applied pressure the way the surgeons did. It was then that he noticed another wound—a bubbling slit beneath Dalglish's breastbone. Dalglish's eyes opened a little, and his cracked and dry lips parted.

"Shhh," Starn said. "They're going, Captain, though goodness knows why. Just you lie still."

Shouts went up from the eastern avenue and men began to stream into the square. Armored men. Familiar men. Men of the imperial army.

"Here!" Starn waved to get their attention. "Man down. We need help."

Hundreds of soldiers advanced, teams of them going to secure the entrances.

"Let them go!" Duke Farian shouted above the hubbub.

As the Duke stood surveying the carnage the emperor strode to his side. Farian said something and pointed at Starn. With that, Hagalle pushed his way through the ranks of soldiers and came to kneel at Starn's side.

"General," he said, voice thick with emotion. "Thank the gods you made it."

There were tears in the emperor's eyes, and for a moment Starn thought Hagalle was going to hug him.

"Dalglish is hurt," Starn said.

"A surgeon!" Hagalle bellowed into the mass of troops.

"What's happening?" Dalglish said in a reedy voice.

"Doctor's coming." Starn smiled down at him. "You'll be right as rain in a few days."

Dalglish's head rolled to the side, the barest of smiles touching his lips. "Think the emperor will send me home?"

Starn looked at Hagalle. The emperor's face was drawn, the tears falling freely. Starn stroked the hair away from Dalglish's face.

"Course he will, lad. Course he will. And when you get there, tell Mrs. Starn I said to make you some chicken soup."

Dalglish gave a rattling sigh.

"Tell her that from me, lad," Starn said. "Nice bowl of soup. Have you better in no time."

But Dalglish was no longer listening.

SEKTIS GANDAW'S SHAMAN

S A CHILD, Shadrak might've thought this latest turn of events was unfair. Against his better judgment, he'd led a posse of prats into the Maze, almost lost his life in the process, and then ended up enslaved by the Technocrat of the Ancients' world—a man who should have returned to the dust centuries ago. As if that weren't enough, once he'd fulfilled his task to assassinate Shader and steal the statue, he'd been chased by some kind of ghost and then set upon by the crazed son of Bovis Rayn. To add insult to injury, he'd not only lost some of his best weapons in the fight, but he'd picked up some nasty bruises from the black-haired bitch along the way. And to think she'd seemed no more than a sad drunk that night at the Griffin. That fateful bloody night.

If he hadn't been contracted to kill Bovis Rayn, he wouldn't have been shot with his own weapon. If he hadn't needed treatment from Cadman, he'd have never gone to the pub, never gotten involved in this Eingana business. If he hadn't run into mawgs in the Maze, and if Kadee's lingering influence hadn't made him inform the Sicarii, he'd not have been sent back with the journeymen. If he'd listened to his instincts and run when he'd had the chance, he wouldn't now be pressed in among a horde of mangy mawgs waiting to disembark.

The statue was bad news, he was certain of that. And there were things happening that were unnatural, to say the least. The shadowy presence of Sektis Gandaw, the dark wraith that had pursued him, and then, during the brief sea battle with the carrack, he'd seen the man he'd recently stabbed in the back staring at him across the waves. Shadrak dealt in certainties. His reputation had been built on careful planning, stealth, and making sure the odds were stacked decisively in his favor. Whatever was happening here, the child Shadrak would have definitely whined that it was unfair. But Shadrak was no longer a child, and if he'd learnt anything from adulthood, it was that life wasn't fair. You only had to look at Kadee's slow death to see that. You only had to look at the scorn he'd endured growing up. Sometimes his victims would beg for mercy, and when they realized it was in short demand, they'd sometimes cry about it not being fair. *Who says fair has anything to do with it?* he'd say. The strong and the cunning survive; the weak perish. That's just the way it is.

The mass of fur moved, and Shadrak was borne along with it. For once, he was cursing his strong sense of smell. "Shit" would have been doing the stench a disservice. It was far worse than that. Yellow eyes glared at him, hungry for his flesh, but the creatures displayed remarkable willpower. None of them touched him. Sektis Gandaw was clearly a master to be obeyed.

The throng parted at the foot of the gangplank, and Shadrak took his body through a series of stretches. The heat was oppressive, a hazy mist rising from the jungle floor and lending the trees a dreamlike quality. The tangled vines and creepers almost seemed to writhe, the moss upon the bark shifting into patterns that could have been faces.

303

Shadrak's cloak was already heavy with damp, but he refused to remove it. Best be prepared for anything, he told himself as he checked his remaining weapons: the stiletto he'd stabbed Shader with, the thunder-shot, and half a dozen razor stars. No more exploding vials. He frowned at that. As soon as he got back to Sahul, he'd need another trip to the hub of the Maze.

They'd stopped at a natural harbor, a widening of the estuary that was hemmed with roughly built jetties. One other boat was moored on the far side, a small fishing vessel by the looks of it. Shadrak squinted. There was a man sitting at the oars, casting nervous looks in their direction. A group of mawgs had noticed too and waded into the water.

A hulking brute lumbered toward him, rows of needle-like teeth protruding from black lips.

"Take statue to village," it growled. "Give to Krylyrd."

Shadrak held its predatory gaze. After a tense standoff, the mawg looked down. Shadrak noted the backward bend of its knees, the toughened leather of its torso. The limbs were protected by thick fur, the face as rigid as an old saddle. Points of weakness: eyes and armpits. If the jaws were open he'd fancy his chances with a blade through the roof of the mouth. Tough bastards, these mawgs. Always paid to know your enemy.

The mawg snarled and turned away, almost running on all fours as it rejoined the pack. There must have been a hundred or more entering the jungle, and at least as many still onboard the galleon. Barks and growls passed between the ship and those on the shore. Ropes were uncoiled and the gangplank was raised.

Shadrak was distracted by a chorus of yelps and the sound of splashing from the group who'd entered the water. They were swimming toward the fishing boat at an alarming speed. The oarsman half stood, teetered, and steadied himself on the side of his craft. He quickly set about untying the rope tethering him to the jetty. The instant he resumed his seat and lifted the oars, the mawgs capsized the boat and ripped into his flesh. Blood sprayed in a fountain, a dark stain spilling across the water.

When Shadrak looked back to the galleon, it was already underway, drifting back down the estuary toward the ocean. Presumably, a lift home wasn't part of the arrangement. Still, if the mawgs had been ordered to kill him, they'd have done so by now. Evidently, Sektis Gandaw had other tasks in mind for Shadrak.

He was about to start after the pack that had all but disappeared into the jungle when a dark shape flitted across his peripheral vision. Shadrak crouched down, pulling his cloak about him, but it was too late. He'd already been spotted.

Coal-fire eyes burned into him, and for an instant Shadrak froze. What could you do against an enemy that couldn't be killed? Cold dread sluiced through his veins, and his body grew weary and leaden.

What's the point of despair? Kadee's level voice commandeered his thoughts. *Eingana will break the sinew when she's ready, and there's not much you can do about it. But she does expect you to go down fighting.*

Shadrak clenched his jaw. That's what Kadee had done: gone down fighting against impossible odds. Unfair, perhaps, but she'd never complained about it.

He fought back the trembling as the wraith soared closer, its rusted chainmail and age-yellowed surcoat growing more substantial. A blade of black fire appeared in its hand.

Shadrak took a step toward the jetty where the fishing boat was moored, but the creature seemed to sense his intention and moved to intercept him. Plucking two razor stars from his baldric, he held them beneath his cloak and waited.

The wraith towered above him, a brooding shadow that shut out the sunlight. Its sword arm extended toward him, the black blade a hair's breadth from his throat.

"The statue you stole from the knight," the wraith hissed, holding out a spectral hand as if there were no choice but to comply.

Something gray sprang from the trees and the ebon sword swept down, slicing through fur and hide as if it were nothing but air. The mawg's severed torso fell to the jungle floor amid spurts of brackish blood.

Another mawg shoved Shadrak toward the tree-line and launched itself at the wraith, snarling and clawing. Shadrak hurtled through thick vegetation, the death cries of the mawg spurring him on. Thorns tore at his cloak and scratched his face. He hurdled a log, charged straight through a bramble bush, and swung across a patch of bubbling mud on a liana. Cold frost assailed his back, and it seemed as though a black cloud pursued him. Chill air swirled about his neck, and he felt the icy touch of a spectral hand. He threw himself to one side, flinging the razor stars one after the other. Both hit the mark, but passed through the wraith with no effect.

Scrabbling backward, Shadrak drew the thunder-shot and pulled the trigger. There was a faint click, but nothing more. That's why he always made such a fuss about being prepared. Should have gone back to the hub for more bullets before going after Shader.

The shadow-knight stalked toward him, making no attempt to defend itself. What would have been the point? The situation was hopeless. Nothing Shadrak could do would halt its progress. All his skill, all his training, and there was no chance. Life just wasn't fair.

He backed away and tripped over a fallen trunk. Terror sapped his strength, and despair flooded his heart. Shadrak reached into his pouch and withdrew the serpent statue. He held it out to the wraith, but the creature turned at a demonic screech from behind.

A ferocious looking mawg clad in crocodile hide and human bones snapped shut its jaws and shook a gourd in front of the wraith. A sharp rhythmic beat cut through the air, and the mawg began to hop and gesticulate. Its face was contorted into a grotesque leer, its body taut, fingers clutching. The wraith drifted toward the mawg but was halted by a violent thrust of the gourd and a bloodcurdling scream.

"No! You cannot stand against me! I am Callixus!" the wraith cried as it swirled into a black mist and was sucked forcefully into a vortex above its head.

"Ha!" The mawg clapped his hands with glee. "Gone to the Void!"

Shadrak climbed to his feet.

"I Krylyrd," it said. "Shaman of Sektis Gandaw. Come, you have what he wants. He be pleased with Krylyrd. You see."

305

THE VILLAGE

"SAIL HO!" ELPIDIO hollered from the crow's nest. Podesta jabbed his rum bottle in the direction of the black galleon skirting the coast of the archipelago and then took another swig. "Seems our reaver knows her business." He let out a burp. "Coastal reef must have taken a thousand ships at one time or another."

Shader clung to the forestays, swinging as the ship careened to starboard. They pitched into a deep trough and then righted, the bowsprit plowing into another colossal wave. If Podesta hadn't looked so blithe, Shader would have panicked and kept as close as he could to the longboat. On second thoughts, he'd have probably lashed himself to the mainmast and prayed. Maybe this once Ain would take pity on him.

Podesta could quite as easily have been strolling in a tranquil garden, the roiling waters affording about as much attention as a pleasing blossom or a passing butterfly. The finding of the boy aboard the *Dolphin* seemed to have settled him. It didn't matter that the child wasn't eating and had a raging fever. He'd hardly stopped coughing since they found him, and his skin was waxy and pale. It seemed he'd taken a few scratches, which had turned nasty. Sabas had been charged with caring for him. Podesta's job was apparently done.

"Don't worry about the reef, my friend," he said. "I'm given to exaggeration. Can't have been more than a hundred wrecked."

Shader took scant comfort from that.

The black sails of the reaver bulged like swollen stomachs as they caught the wind.

"Heading south into open water," Podesta said, squinting over the prow. "Not their usual hunting grounds."

The captain knitted his brows and gazed into his half-empty bottle. "Can't understand why we've not run into more of them."

Shader was well aware the captain had been expecting trouble from the mawgs. The crew had been practicing with more Aeterna-tech weapons—long slim barrels that blasted smoke and fired lead balls at frightening velocities. Cleto had been below decks pouring over the hand-written notes that had come with the shipment.

It seemed that the Templum archives had developed a leak, and it wouldn't have surprised Shader if it had come from within. There had been pressure on the Ipsissimus for years to return the knowledge of the Ancients to the world, not least of all from his likely successor, Exemptus Silvanus. Shader couldn't say he was too impressed with the weapons Podesta had procured. They took an age to load and sometimes exploded in your face. They also seemed ill-suited to fighting at sea. Cleto had made the discovery that the volatile powder responsible for producing the blast was rendered useless if exposed to damp. They'd have been better off with a couple more of the devastating weapons Cleto had used earlier; it might have only given them a single shot, but at least it had been a good one.

The *Aura Placida* sailed on past the archipelago and entered a strait between two larger islands. They tacked toward the northernmost shore and into a narrow estuary. All around the deck sailors scanned the shoreline while holding cutlasses, crossbows, and the Aeternam weapons.

The estuary broadened as they followed it inland until they entered a natural harbor fringed with mangroves. Jetties made from huge logs cut across the water. Podesta was frowning at them and tutting.

"Don't like this," he said. "Don't like it at all. Where are they, uh?"

Shader spotted an upturned boat bobbing beside a jetty off the starboard side. "Doesn't look mawgish," he said.

Podesta snapped open his spyglass and took a look. "It isn't. That's a Sahulian fishing boat, or I'm a teetotal landlubber. Now what the shog is that doing all the way out here, uh?"

"And where's the crew?" Shader said.

Podesta's face was grim as he looked to the helmsman. "Turn us into the wind, Mr. Dekker."

"Aye, Captain."

Podesta cupped his hands to his mouth and his voice boomed out. "Furl the sails! Ready the anchor!"

Shader gave him a questioning look.

"Don't want to be caught in the shallows, uh?" Podesta said. "We'll take the longboat. That way, if the reavers come, the ship still has a fighting chance."

The air grew still and humid the further they got from the ocean, leaving the sailors sweat-drenched and complaining as they went about their tasks. Shader removed his armor and unbuttoned his shirt. He borrowed a cutlass from Podesta to make up for the loss of his longsword. Sabas filled a backpack with provisions for him, and there was just about room enough to cram the Liber in on top.

Podesta left Dekker in charge and then climbed into the longboat beside Shader. The near-invisible Osric drifted at the bow, red eyes smoldering at the lapping waves. Cleto was next aboard, shouldering one of the Aeternam weapons, a cutlass swinging from his hip. Two more armed sailors followed him, stripping off their shirts and taking the oars.

The heat intensified as they took a tributary river into the mangroves. Here and there, the muddy banks were scarred with skid marks that led down to the water.

"Crocodile launch sites," Podesta said.

Shader's eyes were fixed on the water for any sign of movement.

"The crocs out here are big," Podesta said, seemingly unconcerned. "Seen them up to thirty foot. Tear a boat apart in seconds. Not much you can do about it if they attack, eh? Might as well not worry."

"Thanks for the reassurance," Shader said, fingering the pommel of his shortsword. "Thought we'd have seen more mawgs by now."

"Crocs probably got 'em," sniggered one of the rowers.

"That's been troubling me, too," Podesta said, wiping the sweat from his eyes and scanning the shoreline. "They should be snarling and throwing rocks at us by now."

"There they are," the other rower said, dropping oar momentarily to point at the left bank.

Half a dozen of the creatures were huddled together, watching them.

"Those are just children," Podesta said.

Cleto tugged one of the rowers away from his oar and took his place. "Go get me one," he said, a malign grin splitting his face.

"I ain't going near no crocs," the sailor said.

Cleto grabbed him by the collar and pulled him close. "You'll go, Rodders, 'cause you're the best swimmer."

"But..." Rodders looked to Podesta, but the captain seemed busy picking dirt from his fingernails.

"You'll go, Rodders, 'cause you know I'll do you far worse than any croc if you don't," Cleto said. "Get my meaning?"

Rodders swallowed and took a deep breath.

He entered the water on the side away from the mawg children and swam beneath the boat to surface amid a dense cluster of reeds. Shader frowned as he realized what Rodders was up to. One of the mawg children, a girl by the looks of it, came closer to the water's edge to study the boat. Rodders grabbed her and dragged her squealing into the water. The other mawg children shrieked and took off into the jungle as Rodders returned with his captive. Podesta helped haul the mawg to the deck and yelped as she sank her teeth into his forearm. He clouted her across the face, slamming her to the deck where she hissed and glared at him with yellow eyes.

"Cleto," Podesta said, clamping a hand over his bleeding forearm and looking daggers at the mawg child. "She's all yours. I want to know where the reavers are and where we can find this blasted Albino."

Cleto grinned, grabbed the child by the scruff of her neck, and dragged her to the back of the boat.

"Cleto speaks mawgish," Podesta said, rummaging through a pack and pulling out a bandage. "Main reason I let him join the crew. He's also an extremely persuasive fellow."

A shrill scream erupted from the child, causing Shader to reach for his sword.

Podesta placed a hand on his shoulder and whispered in his ear. "How important is this mission to you, uh? Sometimes tough measures are necessary for quick results. But all will be forgiven if the outcome is good, no?"

Shader shook his head, but relaxed his grip on the sword.

"Don't worry, mate," one of the sailors said. "They don't feel pain like we do."

There was a succession of thuds, a sickening gurgling noise, and then a sound like the ripping of cloth. Shader shut his eyes and hoped Ain had done the same.

There was a loud splash as Cleto dumped the body overboard and came to report his findings.

"Village is set back in the jungle." He pointed to the left. "But if we keep going down the watercourse we'll come up on the far side. It's gotta be safer. Could be all sorts of shit waiting for us in the trees."

Cleto twisted his neck at the sound of splashing. The body of the mawg girl was being thrashed about in the jaws of a colossal crocodile.

"Death roll." Cleto grinned as the monster began to turn over and over in the water, the mawg's corpse following limply like a rag doll.

"And Shadrak?" Shader asked, swallowing his rage. His nerves were on fire, muscles tense with the suppressed desire to ram a blade through Cleto's pockmarked face. It wasn't Cleto he should have been angry with, though. He should have felt shame for permitting it, but he already had more than enough of that.

"Last seen heading to the village on foot. Seems our reaver's gone to join the mawgish fleet."

"The mawgs have fleets now?" Podesta said.

"So she said." Cleto turned back to the blood spreading across the water. The crocodile went under, taking the child with it. Bubbles frothed madly on the surface, gradually petering out. "And this one's after some pretty big prey, if the child's to be believed."

The longboat continued through the swamp for another hour until it came to a vast inland lake. They grounded in the shallows, and Shader waded ashore. He pushed through slick foliage until he came to a cluster of dwellings crafted from bark and huge leaves bound together with twine. The bark had been sealed with a resin of some sort, presumably to render it waterproof. Podesta came puffing and panting up alongside Shader, mopping the perspiration from his face.

"Your ghostly friend seems to have vanished." He gestured with his thumb in the direction of the boat.

"He hates the sun even more than I do," Shader said, tilting his hat. "Loses substance in the light. He'll be somewhere nearby."

"I'll mind what I say then." Podesta glanced about nervously. "Looks like the mawg child was right. Looks like they packed up and took to the sea. Perhaps they got wind of our coming and fled before my fearsome reputation."

Shader blinked to clear the sweat from his eyes. The village extended deep into the jungle, the shelters packed closely together and radiating out from the center in tight symmetrical formations.

A slight chilling of the air alerted Shader to Osric's presence.

"There is something happening above the village," the wraith said. "I traveled to the foothills and heard drumming and chanting."

"Cleto, Ned, with us. Rodders, you stay with the boat," Podesta said.

"But…" Rodders started, and then raised his hands in surrender as Cleto scowled.

THE MESSAGE

HAIL HAGALLE!" ELIAS saluted a column of infantrymen snaking down Wharf Way. "Not cool," he muttered. Lallia seemed to think otherwise. Her eyes were glued to the uniformed arses and sparkling with more than reflected sunlight.

"Liberation and oppression: two sides of the same coin." Elias leaned in front to get her attention. "Walking corpses or marching..." He struggled to find the right word.

"Hunks?" Lallia said, licking her lips. "Bed warmers?"

Elias rubbed his fingers through his hair. "You really are a tart, aren't you?"

Lallia opened her mouth in feigned shock. "Just a healthy interest. It's not every day half the imperial army marches through your home town."

"Oh, I'll bet you'll be seeing a whole lot more of the army boys from now on. Don't expect ol' Hags to just up and leave. Cadman's given him all the excuse he needs to tighten the reins of power. You wait, there'll be flags on every rooftop and paid thugs roving the streets making sure we salute right. Before you know it there'll be taxes to pay for them, and you know what'll happen next, don't you?"

Lallia rolled her eyes.

"His imperial nutcase will start searching for the enemy within. Mark my words, Fanny-go-lightly, he'll be rounding up anyone a bit deviant, anyone who sticks out from the crowd. And you know who'll be first, don't you?" He turned the corner into the Domus Tyalae and made a wide sweep with his arm. "Your friendly neighborhood religious minority."

Elias's cart was still parked outside the templum. Hector was chewing nonchalantly on the hedgerows. The horse swung its huge head toward him as he approached, snorted, and let fall a steaming pile of dung.

"Sorry I left you, Hec." Elias patted the horse's flanks and scratched him behind the ear. "Let's see if there's some oats in the cart. Don't think those leaves are good for your digestion."

"I couldn't care less if Hagalle hangs the lot of them," Lallia said, glaring at the portico. "If it hadn't been for the Nousians none of this would have happened."

Elias grabbed her wrist and pulled her toward him. "Are your brains as loose as your knickers? The Nousians didn't start this, and in case you hadn't noticed, the chaps in the rusty armor with the flaming eyes were nothing more than zombies. I tell you, it's like landing a role in Dawn of the... Never mind. You're too young for that. My point is that the puppet-master's to blame, not the priests."

"Cadman?"

"Who else? Unless someone's pulling his strings. There's a whole lot of weird shit going down and I'm starting to feel like an itsy bitsy player in someone else's story. You know the sort—where it's all pre-ordained and the characters just get swept along by some fatalistic cosmic tide."

Frater Hugues appeared in the shattered remains of the doorway, his robes stained with various shades of brown and green. He was brushing what looked like potato peelings from his hair and mumbling to himself.

"Still here, then?" Elias said as he sauntered over to the porch. "You missed all the excitement."

"Holy Ain!" A big grin lit up Hugues's gnomic face, and he went to hug Elias.

The bard held up his hands and fanned his fingers beneath his nose.

"Sorry," Hugues said. "Been hiding in the compost. Mater sent me to get cleaned up." Hugues's face turned suddenly sullen, just the way Elias remembered him. "And I've had more than my fair share of excitement, thank you very much. Demons and walking corpses. It's enough to test your faith, that's a fact. The others are inside. Only got back a short while ago."

"Rhiannon?" Elias said, already stepping inside the templum.

"Not with them," Hugues said with a frown. "We've lost Limus too, and the dwarf."

Elias swayed, a wave of nausea washing over him. "What happened?"

Hugues narrowed his eyes and touched his forehead as Lallia approached. He pointedly kept his attention on Elias. "Best ask those who were there." He nodded inside, pressing his back to the wall as Lallia squeezed past.

She paused and held out a hand to him, as if she expected him to kiss it. Hugues stared at it like it was a moldy kipper washed in by the tide, his eyes wide and jaw clenched shut.

"Lallia, Frater Hugues," Elias said. "Hugues, this is Lallia. I think she likes you."

***

Soror Agna passed Elias a steaming mug of tea.

"Help yourself, dear." She gave a tight-lipped smile to Lallia before seating herself with the others at the refectory table.

The room was a mess—broken chairs, piles of glass that had been swept into a corner, patches of dried blood on the floor. The table itself had a couple of deep gouges out of the surface, and one of the legs had been hurriedly nailed into place.

Ioana had aged ten years, it seemed to Elias. She sat with her hands clasped at the head of the table. Elias wasn't sure whether to sip his tea or wait for a blessing. In the end, he decided on the former.

Cadris was cramming crumbling fruitcake into his gob as if he hadn't eaten for weeks. With a build like his, Elias thought, he'd have endured far longer than a few weeks without food. Cadris caught him staring and turned his nose up.

Gaston was seated opposite Elias. His face was a crisscross of claw marks, and his armor had been discarded in favor of bloodstained bandages wound tightly around his mid-section. His blond hair was lank and filthy, partially obscuring his downcast eyes. He looked nothing like the brash and arrogant youth Elias remembered from Oakendale. In fact, if he hadn't known better, Elias would have said he looked like a heroic veteran, battle-worn from an epic defense against all the odds.

Lallia brushed against the back of Gaston's chair as she went to pour herself some tea. She cast a disdainful look over the company and cocked an eyebrow at Elias.

"Well," Elias said. "This is cozy."

Ioana fixed him with baleful eyes. "Thank Ain you are safe," she said. "But we should spare a moment's prayer for those we have lost."

Like that's going to bring them back, Elias thought, slurping his tea. "Let me get this right," he said. "You misplaced Limus, left Maldark to do all the fighting, and abandoned Rhiannon. Am I missing something?"

311

"The dwarf gave us time to escape," Cadris said through a mouthful of cake. "Ain praise his courage. He is sure to be a luminary. A martyr even."

"We didn't know Limus was lost until we reached the tunnels beneath the templum," Agna said. "We've searched everywhere, but there's no sign of him."

Elias gave her his broadest smile. "It's only to be expected when one's preoccupied with self-preservation."

Agna's head bobbed above her teacup. "Quite. Quite. Such a shame, though."

Gaston placed his hands on the table and glared at Elias. "You weren't there. You've no r-r-right to judge."

There was a time Elias would have backed away from a confrontation with Gaston, but not today. "Oh, I've every right to judge you, Gaston, after what you did to Rhiannon. I'm all for forgiveness and atonement, but what did you do when you had the chance to make the slightest amends? Turned your back on her and left her behind, that's what."

Gaston looked down, his face drawn and shoulders slouched.

"That's enough," Ioana snapped. "Gaston did everything he could. Without him, we might all have been lost."

"Oh, bully for him." Elias gave a little clap.

Lallia shot him a warning glare as she pressed herself against the back of Gaston's chair and raised her cup to her lips.

"Well don't think you've had all the fun," Elias said. "If it wasn't for Lallia here—" He blew her a kiss. "—ol' fat-boy would have had my guts for garters. Did I tell you what happened when—?"

Agna's head hit the table with a thud. Cadris almost choked on his cake, and Ioana stared with wide eyes. Gaston was closest and shook Agna's shoulders. He recoiled as she came bolt upright, her eyes pools of white.

"Agna?" Ioana said. "Agna, are you all right?"

Agna's head swiveled toward her, drool trickling down her chin. "It's Limus," she said in a hushed voice. "Oh, Mater, it's Limus."

Elias put down his mug, scarcely daring to breathe. Lallia's face had drained of all color, and Gaston took his hands from Agna's shoulders as if they were on fire.

"Pain," Agna groaned. "Darkness."

"Oh, please," Elias said. "This is hardly the time for mystical bullshit."

"Shut it, Elias," Lallia said.

Elias sat back in his chair as if she'd slapped him. Agna's blank eyes continued to face Ioana.

"Cadman has him, Mater. His poor soul. He says he only has a moment; the effort is too great. He's falling, Mater. Falling into blackness."

Ioana sat as rigid as a statue. "Where is he? What can we do?"

"Dark. Dark everywhere beneath the trees. Limus says he is heading for Dead Man's torch," Agna said.

Gaston leaned forward. "The old beacon tower? I know how to get there."

"Too late for Limus." Agna's voice quavered, and her glasses slipped down her nose. "But Rhiannon is with him. Limus says he carried her from Sarum. He is taking her to Cadman. He says he must."

Limus carry someone? Elias doubted he had the strength to walk there unencumbered. "That doesn't seem very likely," he said.

Agna's eyes rolled, and the irises returned. "He is dead, Elias. Like the creatures in the city."

Elias put his hand to his mouth. *Poor Limus. Poor, poor Limus.*

"He was the best of us," Ioana said. "Who else would have had the strength to reach us?"

Gaston was shaking his head. "Ain was strong with him," he said, as if he'd had a great revelation. "Mater, I'll f-f-find a horse and go to the beacon. I might be able to b-b-bring Rhiannon back."

"No," Elias said, standing. "If Rhiannon's in trouble, the last thing she needs is to see you. I'm going."

"You?" Cadris said. "What can you do?"

Elias hadn't even considered that yet. Without the statue he was as useless as the rest of them, but he couldn't abandon Rhiannon. Not after what she'd been through. "I'll think of something. I'm not as helpless as I look. Actually," he said with a sudden flash of inspiration, "I've already got the inklings of an idea. Coming?" he said to Lallia.

Lallia looked at him as if he'd lost his mind. Maybe he had.

"Unless you're planning on converting," Elias said, indicating the priests.

***

The cart pulled up outside an immense warehouse on the edge of Calphon. Elias was sure this was the one, but it had been so many years. Decades even.

He jumped to the curb and patted Hector before tethering him to one of the towering lampposts. Lallia climbed down and stood with her hands on her hips.

"A warehouse?" She puffed out her cheeks. "Good plan."

"Just you wait and see," Elias said, heading inside.

It was as dark and musty as he remembered. Stacks of crates extended all the way to the far end with narrow passages between them. There were some rudimentary pulleys running across the ceiling, and an assortment of pallets and ladders.

An ancient man with a thick white beard and eyebrows like brushes, peered up from a ledger set on a slanted desktop. "Elias Wolf, the Bard of Broken Bridge," he said in a parched voice. "Thought you'd never come." He flicked through the crisp pages of the ledger until he found the right place. "You're thirty-five years in arrears," he said, looking up with rheumy eyes. "Have you come to settle up?"

Elias grimaced. "Stanley, my old mate," he said. "Gosh, how time flies. Look, I'm in something of a hurry. I need the ol' girl. Bit of a crisis."

Stanley shook his head and tutted.

"What if I leave the horse and cart as insurance?" Elias said, wondering how Hector would take that.

"I'm sorry, Elias," Stanley said.

"I've got instruments on board. And herbs." Elias raised his eyebrows.

Stanley drummed his fingers on the ledger. "That old pre-Reckoning guitar? The one you used to play at the Griffin?"

"Still do," Elias said, nodding enthusiastically, a terrible sinking feeling setting in.

"Deal," Stanley said, standing to shake his hand.

Elias's grip was limper than he normally liked, but needs must...

Stanley led them along the central aisle until they came to a particularly large crate standing by itself.

Elias stroked the wood and gave it a resounding slap. "Prepare to be amazed," he said to Lallia.

"I'm almost disappointed," Stanley said as he headed back to his desk. "I was hoping to keep it for myself."

Elias knocked out some bolts and flicked open the catches. Taking hold of the top of a panel, he pulled it away and let it fall to the floor.

"What the shog is that?" Lallia wrinkled her nose and peered inside.

"That, my dear," Elias said, beaming from ear to ear, "is a motorbike."

The chrome still shone the same as it had when he'd packed it away all those decades ago. The tank gleamed a vibrant red, its gilt star leading the eye to three letters he thought he'd never see side by side again.

"BSA Mark IV Spitfire. 1968." He gave the saddle a reverent pat. "End of the line, but what the hell, revolution was in the air."

Lallia gave him a blank look. Before her time. Before Elias's even, but for him it was a magical era; one year before the Summer of Love, the inspiration for the Golden Garden festival.

"Alloy wheel rims." He crouched to show what he was talking about. "Off-road tires, the ol' air-cooled 654 cc vertical twin, and enough horsepower to make Hector green with envy."

Lallia ran her palm over the leather saddle. "What's it for?"

"You of all people should know that," Elias said, brushing her hand out of the way. "You ride it." He reached behind the front wheel and located a steel canister. "Vacuum sealed." He tapped the side. "It'll keep forever in there."

"What?"

"Petrol, my dear. Probably the last drop on the planet." Elias unscrewed the petrol cap and emptied the canister into the tank. "A lot of people said I sold out when I bought the ol' girl." He removed his coat, wiped his fingers on it, and then slung it to the back of the crate. "But this baby's real technology—not that circuit board shit Gandaw was putting out. Pure craftsmanship."

Lallia sniffed. "If you say so."

Elias reached behind the back wheel this time and pulled out a black leather jacket replete with silver zips and a faded lightning bolt on the back. "Now let's go get Rhiannon," he said, slipping on the jacket and taking out a pair of sunglasses from the inside pocket. "How do I look?" he asked, tilting his chin and peering over the top of the frames.

"Ridiculous," Lallia said.

Elias flicked his hair back, kicked up the stand, and wheeled the bike out of the crate. He swung his leg over the saddle and beckoned for Lallia to get up behind him.

"What do I hold onto?" She glanced around nervously.

"Me," Elias said.

Lallia screamed as he fired the Spitfire up, opened the throttle, and roared down the aisle.

Stanley leapt up from his desk and shouted something, but Elias couldn't hear him above the thunder of the engine.

"What?"

"My guitar!" Stanley yelled.

"In the cart!"

Lallia's thighs pressed against his sides, her ankles crossing around his waist. Not quite the norm for riding pillion, but Elias could live with it.

"Hold on!" he called over his shoulder, and then they were speeding through the streets of Sarum like a bat out of hell.

A CONTRACT WITH THE ARCHON

THE MAWG CHILDREN stood upon the rough-hewn terraces of an earthen amphitheater. There were hundreds of them swaying and chanting in their guttural tongue. They crowded around an empty space below, which shimmered with cobalt light. A vibrant amber glow drew Shader's eyes to the creature at the center. The once black serpent statue was being held aloft by a cavorting male adorned with skulls and bones.

Shader crouched by the trunk of a yellow wattle and scanned the crowd for sign of the albino. Osric drifted alongside him, a barely visible outline, like something traced in the condensation on glass.

"We are too late, it seems. I suspect the thief has already departed."

"Is anyone going to tell me what's happening?" Podesta panted from a little way down the hillside.

Shader shushed him, his attention caught by movement in the air above the dancing shaman. The cobalt sheen began to coalesce into a sphere suspended over the shaman's head, its hue darkening as its density increased. The shaman screamed something at the assembled children and they responded with a cacophony of yapping and barking. He raised the amber statue skywards and let out a piercing shriek, the muscles in his arms and legs knotting, the veins ready to burst. The amber glow immediately dimmed. Turning in rage, the shaman pointed a long finger at one of the mawg children. The creature froze, its eyes wide with terror, and then it rose from its terrace and walked toward the shaman. As the child entered the space beneath the sphere, the shaman brought the statue down on its head with a sickening thud. The child crumpled to the ground, blood and brains spewing from its crushed skull. The shaman threw back its head and roared as the statue was wreathed in crimson flames, which licked at the sphere. The air shimmered, and the surface of the sphere cleared. Within, a gray-clad man seated on a dark metal throne came into focus.

Shader tensed. Everything about the man offended his senses. His black hair had an unnatural sheen and seemed too perfect. Shader doubted it would be ruffled by the fiercest wind. The complexion was bloodless, the clothes starched and somber.

The man reached out of the sphere and took the statue. He nodded once to the shaman, and then the sphere dissolved, and he was gone. The shaman collapsed to his knees and the children began to talk in hushed murmurs.

"There!" Podesta hissed, breaking Shader's rapture. "Heading into the trees."

Shader slid a little way down the hill and looked in the direction the captain had indicated. A small figure in black was moving toward the mangroves. Cleto tracked it with the slim barrel of his Aeterna-tech weapon.

Ned drew his cutlass and glared. "Must be that scutting Shadrak," he said. "Come on." He broke into a jog.

Cleto lowered his weapon. "Probably out o' range," he said, before setting off after

Ned.

"What about the statue?" Osric said.

"Too late," Shader said. "Our best bet is to catch Shadrak and find out what he knows."

***

Shader stopped at the banks of the lake. Podesta huffed and puffed behind him and stood with his fists pressed into his hips.

"Where the shog's Rodders?" he said in between breaths.

Shader pointed to the longboat drifting on the far side of the lake.

"Idiot's supposed to be guarding it," Podesta said. "And where the Abyss are Cleto and Ned?"

Footprints led into the trees on the left bank. Shader started to follow them and then drew up as he spotted a pair of boots sticking out of the undergrowth. Taking hold of them, he pulled the body out and stood back, wiping the back of his hand across his mouth.

"Poor old Rodders." Podesta removed his hat and stared at the corpse. The neck was twisted grotesquely to one side. "I'll make the stunted bastard pay, lad," he said. "You have my word. First, though," he said, cramming his tricorn back in place, "we need to get the boat."

He started toward the jetty, but Shader placed a restraining hand on his shoulder. About fifty yards distant something large slid down the mud and splashed into the water.

"Shog me for a stupid cretin," Podesta said. "Maybe you should go," he said to Osric. "Never been keen on crocs, myself. Especially not salties."

Osric floated to the end of the jetty and watched the rippling water in the wake of the crocodile. "I cannot cross water without a boat."

Podesta fished a long knife out of his boot and strained to see the salty. Patting the blade against his palm, he reached a decision. "If we head back toward the ship through the jungle the crew can pick us up in the other boat."

Shader shrugged and started toward the mangroves, following the trail of footprints. Podesta and Osric trailed behind. Ned was slumped against a trunk, bleeding out from a slit throat.

Podesta blanched, sweat dripping from his forehead, eyes darting from left to right. "Where the shog is Cleto?" he whispered.

Shader drew his cutlass and the Sword of the Archon and continued on a course parallel with the shore.

"At least if there are more crocs up here we'll stand a fighting chance, eh?" Podesta said, licking his lips. "Gods, I need a piss."

Shader held up a hand to silence him. There were three large salties basking at the edge of the mangroves.

"Inland a bit?" Podesta suggested.

The trio moved deeper into the jungle and found Cleto knocked senseless amid the foliage. He was missing his Aeterna-tech weapon and cutlass. He groaned and began to stir.

"What happened?" Shader asked.

"Bastard hit me from behind. Hit me hard," Cleto said, rubbing the back of his head. "Where's my shogging weapons?"

"You OK to continue?" Shader asked.

"Try to stop me." Cleto's eyes hardened as he pushed himself to his feet.

Shader hacked a path through the undergrowth. The thick canopy of leaves shut out the sun and rendered Osric more substantial, but it did nothing to reduce the sweltering humidity. Every few minutes Shader used his shirt to wipe the sweat from his eyes. Podesta shook the perspiration from his hair in a great shower and cursed Osric's indifference to the heat.

They cut inland for a few hundred yards and then headed west, following the course of the river. Fat black flies buzzed around them, flitting in and out of nostrils and eyes, and tenaciously returning to torment them no matter how many times they were swiped away.

They were halfway down a steep slope when there was a blast followed by a splash. Curses were shouted, and they heard the thrumming of arrows through the air, the phwat, phwat, phwat of them striking the water. Shader slipped and slid toward the noise, breaking through the mangroves into the rushes at the water's edge. Something dark and wet cannoned into him and tumbled away before he could react.

"That's him!" Podesta shouted, struggling back up the bank in pursuit.

"Wait!" Shader cried, regaining his feet and scanning the thick vegetation. Heedless, Podesta pressed on and was soon lost to sight.

"Ain't good for a captain to lose his head," Cleto said, rubbing his chin and squinting into the trees. "Reckon the little shit tried to board the Placida. Fired my sodding weapon."

A low gurgling sound, followed by a heavy thud, came from the mangroves.

Osric drifted alongside Shader. "This Shadrak is extremely skilful, it seems."

Shader's eyes narrowed. He handed the cutlass to Cleto.

The sailor looked nervous, his eyes darting all over the place. Sending him back up the slope would be testing his newfound loyalty to the limits.

"Stay here," Shader said. "Make sure he doesn't get behind us."

Cleto grunted, his knuckles whitening from the grip he had on the cutlass.

Shader started up into the trees, willing himself to relax. He let his peripheral vision do the looking.

"Let me go first," Osric said. "I doubt even he can slay the dead."

Shader nodded and glanced uneasily around as the wraith glided into the thicket. He sat cross-legged on the ground and rested the gladius across his lap. His heart was racing in anticipation of the fight, or of a swift and silent stab in the back. Fumbling with the straps on his pack, he pulled out his dog-eared Liber, thumbed through the pages, and then began to read from Aeternam in a soft rhythmic monotone. Years of discipline led him inwards where the stillness gave sway to other senses, finer and keener edged. He could feel the hot air playing over the hairs on the back of his hands, hear the whispers of the water, the gliding of the gulls on the thermals. His breathing stilled; his heart sounded like a ponderous drum in his ears. The gossamer net of his awareness crept through the jungle, caressing bark and stroking leaves.

He did not pause in his prayer as something cold and sharp touched his throat.

"Ordinarily I'd have stuck you without a word." Shader could feel the assassin's breath on his ear. "But you're already dead."

Shader smiled. "You've not noticed the blade a hair's-breadth from your groin?"

He'd heard the assassin's approach, felt the air bend around him. The gladius responded to his unformed thought instantly. If he'd wanted Shadrak dead, he would have been.

"Stalemate," the assassin said.

There was a sudden gasp from behind Shader, and the knife fell away from his throat.

"I beg to disagree," Osric hissed.

Shader turned and stood. The assassin was little more than three feet tall, pale-faced and with clipped, snow-white hair. His limbs were rigid and shaking, his pink eyes wide as they stared with horror at the ghostly hand protruding from his chest. Osric was

317

hovering behind Shadrak, his head slightly cocked.

"I wonder if it is unchivalrous," Osric withdrew his hand into Shadrak's ribcage, his eyes narrowing to fiery slits, "that my hand can pass through you unhindered, and yet..." Shadrak started to spasm. "...I can curl my fingers around your heart and squeeze it quite palpably."

Shadrak's shaking fingers edged toward one of the pouches on his belt.

"I wouldn't," Shader said, putting his Liber away. "I doubt you have the means of harming Osric here, and even if you did, I'd gut you before you could blink."

Shadrak ceased struggling and hung his head.

"My statue—" Shader began.

"Hardly yours," Shadrak said. "Unless you're calling yourself Eingana."

Shader drew in a deep breath and thumbed the edge of his sword. "What happened back there?"

Shadrak was quivering uncontrollably, his eyes fixed on his chest where Osric still had a grip on his heart.

"Didn't stay to find out. Did my bit and buggered off before they realized there was fresh meat hanging about."

Shader lifted the albino's chin and stared him in the eye. "How long have the Sicarii worked for Sektis Gandaw?"

"They don't," Shadrak said. "Just me, and not by choice. If I get my way, I'll not see that cold-blooded shogger again."

"Where can I find him?" Shader asked.

"Ask the mawgs—" Shadrak gasped as Osric's fingers emerged from his chest. "I don't know," he rasped. "Came to me with magic when the mawgs got me. Only saw the top half of him floating in a sphere. There were pictures behind him—flickering pictures, and dark metal walls. You'll be lucky to find him in Sahul, I reckon."

Shader turned away and grimaced. The trail had gone cold. Two pieces of the statue in Cadman's hands, and the body with Sektis Gandaw. Were they in league? If there really were five pieces of the statue, where were the other two? Maybe Huntsman would know—if he could be found. It had all started out so simply—retrieve the Gray Abbot's Monas. The longer this went on, the worse things got, the more acutely Shader felt his failure. Ain only knew what had happened to the Gray Abbot. If he was honest, that was the least of Shader's concerns. There were others he felt responsible for. Others he couldn't bear to lose.

"We need to head back," Shader said to Osric. "Go after Cadman."

The albino looked up at that. "Cadman?"

"You know him?" Shader said.

"He's the one who started all this. Sent me to Broken Bridge to find out all I could about the statue from some scruffy bard. After that we dragged in an old hermit and took a piece from him—a fang. Cadman wanted me to keep working for him, but the guild wouldn't have liked it. It was straight after the business with the hermit that mawgs started appearing under the city. Went with a bunch of amateurs to root them out and that's when I got into this mess with Gandaw."

"Does Cadman know about Gandaw?" Shader asked. "Are they working together?"

"No idea." Shadrak gasped and fell to his knees as Osric withdrew his hand and loomed over him.

"Let us hope not," the wraith said. "Three pieces of the statue is a lot of power."

"Big deal," Shadrak said, clutching his chest and taking long stuttering breaths.

"It will be," Shader said, "if Gandaw gets the other two. Even a self-centered bastard like you will have to stand up and take notice. Everything is threatened. Everything."

Shadrak stood and dusted himself down. "And I should care, why?" he said.

"Shogging world's screwed in any case, and before you suggest it, I don't take sides. Show me the money and I'll consider it, but otherwise take your best shot or let me go."

Shader's hand tightened on the hilt of the gladius. Osric's eyes simmered and he drifted so close to the assassin that Shadrak shivered.

"You got 'im?" Cleto called, trudging up the slope. "Hold 'im still and I'll bleed the little shogger."

Shadrak dropped into a crouch, eyes flicking dangerously, fingers brushing against his pouches. Shader pushed up close and touched the tip of the gladius to his throat.

"Am I going to see you again?" he said with ice in his voice.

"No one sees me," Shadrak said, "if I don't wanna be seen."

"You know what I meant." Shader pressed harder, breaking the skin.

"You won't get no trouble from me. Not without a contract, and I think the chances of that are pretty slim. Reckon your enemies might as well save their money. Cadman and Gandaw can sort you out."

Shader returned the gladius to its scabbard. "If Sektis Gandaw wins, he'll sort everyone out. Even you, Shadrak."

The albino touched his thumb to the trickle of blood running down his neck and then pressed it to his lips. "Guess I'll deal with that when it happens."

Shader nodded and flicked his gaze in the direction of the mangroves. Shadrak gave him a sideways look, patted each of his pouches, and scampered off.

Cleto took a step after him. "What, you gonna let him go?"

"Just did," Shader said. "You got a problem with that?"

Cleto's face creased in a silent snarl. "Oh, yeah, I got a problem, but like I said, you're with us now, so I guess my problem can wait."

Osric drifted alongside Shader as he watched the assassin enter the trees and disappear from sight. "Perhaps we should have killed him. Ain does not mind the shedding of evil blood."

Shader looked sternly at his companion and then shook his head. Maybe Cleto and Osric were right. Every muscle in Shader's body was stretched taut with the anticipation of cutting Shadrak down. What could you expect? After all, the assassin had stabbed him in the back. Shadrak would have had no compunction about slaying Shader, so why shouldn't he do the same? Ain, he told himself. Osric was wrong about that, same as Berdini had been. Ain would have minded, otherwise he wasn't worthy of worship. Shader grimaced. Even after all that had happened, he was still trying to be a Nousian. Not for the first time, he suspected it would be the death of him.

"Have to say I'm disappointed." Shader turned to the wraith. "Thought you'd have approved of my letting him go. Or have you lost faith in the goodness of Nous?"

"Nous has revealed Ain to us. We can be certain of his goodness."

Shader allowed himself a wry smile. "That's what I thought. Guess it comes down to how you interpret the revelations."

"A pox on your revelations," Podesta said, stumbling from the trees, trying to stem the bleeding from his throat. "Bastard missed the jugular, but if you two don't shut up, I'll end up theologized to death."

***

Shadrak stepped from the mangroves and slid down the bank toward the water's edge. The upturned fishing boat still bobbed at the end of the jetty. Perhaps he should have taken Shader's offer. At least that way he'd have had passage back to Sahul. An opportunity missed, he chastised himself. There would have been nothing stopping him ditching the agreement once he was home.

319

A column of mist was forming at the foot of the jetty. Shadrak watched, mesmerized, as it swirled and took on human shape. He backed away toward the trees, but something made him stop. This was no black wraith with burning eyes. He gasped as he recognized the creased dark skin, the beaded gray hair, and those eyes of sparkling green that could warm his soul no matter how far he fell.

Kadee.

Shadrak walked and then ran to the jetty, tears spilling down his cheeks, arms open wide. Kadee smiled, her whole face lighting up with that look that told him she loved him, no matter what. Just before he reached her, she held up her hands.

"You must not touch me, my baby fellah. I am here, and I am not."

Shadrak caught a glimpse of ghostly trees behind her, set against darkening alien skies.

"Kadee." He folded his arms across his chest and made no attempt to disguise the tears. "I've missed you."

"I know," she said.

"I've grown rotten without you. I've turned into everything you hate."

Kadee's eyes glistened with moisture, but her smile held firm. "I could never hate you, my son." She glanced over her shoulder at something Shadrak couldn't see. "I cannot stay," she said, "but there is someone I want you to meet. He can help you, Shadrak, just as he helped me."

A figure formed beside Kadee—a man, brown-robed and hooded. As Kadee began to dissolve back into the mist, the newcomer raised his head, and Shadrak shielded his eyes from the glare spilling from beneath the cowl.

"Kadee!" Shadrak held out a hand as if he could pull her back.

"She is safe," the man said in a voice that reminded Shadrak of a breeze rustling the leaves in a forest.

"She's dead," Shadrak said. "How much safer can you get?"

The man touched the tips of his bone-white fingers together. "The world is full of mysteries, Shadrak. Believe me, your mother will be much safer if you are prepared to act. You have been graced with favor, Shadrak. If not for the love of others you would have been slain at birth."

Shadrak felt the dark spaces of his mind welling up, clamoring for attention. He tried to frame a question, but the man waved him to silence.

"Now is not the time. Answers do not come so easily. You have to earn them. But first you have to trust."

Shadrak trusted no one. Not since Kadee had died, in any case. The hooded man seemed to read his thoughts.

"That's why I asked Kadee to introduce us. She trusted me, and now you must."

"Who are you? What do you want?"

The man threw back his hood and Shadrak fell to his knees, blinded by the blaze.

"I am the Archon, and I will not stand idly by and watch the worlds fall. You have aided the enemy, Shadrak. You had little choice, I grant you, but your actions have brought us one step closer to destruction. What we do from now on affects the lives of the three worlds, Shadrak: of Earth, and Aethir, and Thanatos, where the innocent dead are trapped. If you help me, you help Kadee. If you refuse, you will remain blind to what is going on, an ant in a game of giants."

The light faded as the Archon pulled his hood up. Shadrak blinked until his sight was restored and then climbed to his feet.

"Everyone wants something." Shadrak folded his arms over his chest. "The shogging masters, Cadman, Gandaw, and now you. Only you're worse than the rest of 'em, ain't you? Thought you could use Kadee to get to me."

"She understands," the Archon said. "You would do well to learn from her. Any woman who would take in a creature like you and give it the love of my sister Eingana should be listened to."

"Yeah, yeah, like you know her better than I do. Like you know the first thing about me."

"I know what you are."

Shadrak took a step closer, fingers curling around the handle of the thunder-shot. "Then shogging tell me."

"You think a pistol will harm me?" The Archon's voice rumbled like a gathering storm. "Even if it were loaded it would be useless. Nothing you could do would have the slightest effect. Frightening, isn't it?"

Shadrak started to tremble, in spite of himself. I'll find something, you shogger. Like it always did with him, the fear turned to anger. He opened his mouth to let it out, but the part of his mind that kept watch on his thoughts, words, and actions stepped in. He listened to it because it had served him well on so many occasions. *Bide your time, Shadrak. Bide your time.* "You're right. I'm sorry. Tell me what you want, and I'll do it for Kadee's sake."

The Archon swept his arm in wide arc, and behind him the air parted like a curtain to reveal a gleaming metal passageway. "This Maze of yours beneath the city of Sarum, do you have any idea what it is?"

Shadrak peered past the Archon, recognizing the corridor leading to the hub of the Maze.

"Must have been left by the Ancients," he said. "I've found stuff in there that don't belong in our day."

The Archon drifted closer, the hem of his robe inches above the ground. "It is a plane ship," he said. "Made from scarolite ore by the homunculi of Aethir. Is that a name you recognize? Homunculus?"

Shadrak's mind was opening up like an infinite void. There was something ... something he remembered, but it refused to come into focus. "It's what he said ... Cadman. When he took the bullet out ... He said..."

"Serve me well and all will be revealed. Come." The Archon stepped into the corridor. "I will show you how to work this ship, then you will be a far more effective player."

Shadrak followed him inside, gawping as the jungle vanished like a fleeting vision. The cold metallic surfaces felt like home. It was a relief to be away from the relentless heat of the Anglesh Isles.

"What d'you want me to do?"

"Nothing you're not used to. Wait. Observe. And when the time is right—" The Archon twitched his index finger. "—pull the trigger."

THE FALL

Aethir: Anno Domini 1980
(276 Years Before The Reckoning)

AMBER FIRE GUSHED from the maw of Eingana, engulfing the philosopher. The cavern floor split open beneath the old man, and smoky tentacles coiled about his burning body. The giant serpent hissed and thrashed, its tail smashing a row of kryeh from their seats. Wires ripped free of flesh, wings flapped, and screens died. Malevolent laughter rumbled from the depths, and then there was a thunderous crack as the floor sealed. There was no trace of Aristodeus.

Maldark shuddered. He noticed that Sektis Gandaw stood well out of range, despite his bravado.

"So much for philosophy. So much for causes. You see,"—the Technocrat sounded like an admonishing parent—"it is useless to deny the truth. Nothing can stand against pure science. Nothing! Not Eingana, not your meddling philosopher friend. Not even the fabric of the cosmos."

A thick chain choker cut into Eingana's neck the more she struggled.

"Look," Gandaw said. "See how easily she is harnessed like all the other forces in the universe. Aristodeus might have thought himself clever, but all his sophistry didn't save him from the fire. He nearly swayed you, Maldark, nearly won you over. But I designed you dwarves better than that. I would say you made the right choice, but everything was already written in your blood."

Maldark lowered his eyes as the homunculi began to drop down on cables, seeking purchase on the scales of Eingana's head. The great serpent snapped one up, crunched down, and spat blood. The others took the opportunity to land atop her head and hammer home their needles. Eingana screamed, her tail rippling and coiling like a corkscrew. The chief homunculus, Mephesch, waited until four needles were in place and lines were connected. As his colleagues jumped clear, Mephesch threw the switch.

Eingana stiffened.

A fierce pounding resounded about the chamber. Gandaw frowned and tapped a button on his vambrace, sending a sentroid hovering toward the metal doors. Maldark moved closer as the doors began to buckle. His Marshall, Dagar, followed.

"More hybrids?" he growled. "Thought we'd got them all."

Maldark wasn't so sure. He'd seen a few of them flee with the Great Spider when they'd finally realized their doom and the doom of their beloved Eingana.

The dwarf knights formed up in front of him, grim faces staring toward the door. Their surcoats were red with the blood of the hybrids and many had holes torn in the links of their armor. Maldark hefted his war-hammer and waited.

The sentroid surged forward as the door exploded inward. It fired a beam of light that bounced harmlessly off a huge chunk of scarolite being wielded as a shield. The black metal spun and hammered into the sentroid, sending it crashing into the wall. It dropped like a stone and split open on the floor—a steaming metal egg that continued to whir and click.

A gargantuan black man burst into the room, snake's head hissing, muscles swollen and thickly veined.

"Traitor!" Mamba spat at Maldark and charged.

The dwarves rushed forward to protect their grand master. Dagar's head was pulped by the snake-man's first blow. Fangs snapped down to tear the face from another. The dwarves pushed forward and rained blows down on Mamba. The shield caught most of them, but an axe found its mark, and the snake-man fell back.

"Betrayer!" he screamed, yellow eyes stabbing into Maldark like daggers.

Maldark caught Gandaw watching with cold indifference. He followed the Technocrat's gaze to Eingana where the giant snake was solidifying, her glistening scales fading to matt. Maldark gaped, the bile rising in his throat. Eingana's eyes flared with amber defiance even as she started to shrink.

"Sssee!" shouted Mamba.

The dwarves broke off and turned to watch the death of the serpent. A hushed awe settled around the cavernous chamber. How could they be sure this was God's will? Had she not fallen through the Void from His heart? What if she really was God's gift to them, as the dwarves had once believed, back before Gandaw had revealed her lies?

"Eingana," Maldark whispered, tears running down his cheeks. "What have I done?"

Gandaw seemed to sense the change. He tapped out some combinations on his vambrace and the metal panels surrounding the chamber started to rise, smoke curling from behind them.

"Help her," Mamba pleaded. "Pleassse!"

The dwarves were all watching Maldark, their eyes as damp as his own. He flicked his gaze around the room. The panels had opened a couple of feet and shimmering mist swirled beyond. He caught a glimpse of massive shapes in the alcoves.

"Don't be a fool, Maldark," Gandaw said, starting to rise toward the ceiling atop a metal disk. Mephesch was peering down from a balcony high above, his eyes narrowed, his mouth curling up at one corner.

Maldark flashed one last look at Mamba and then spun and hurled his hammer. There was a thunderous crash high up on the wall where Eingana was suspended from wires. The serpent was now no more than a small statue. Metal groaned and sparks flew. The hammer spun back through the air and landed snugly in Maldark's grip. The statue that had been Eingana fell.

"Flee!" Maldark shouted as the panels fully opened and four metallic behemoths rolled out into the room.

Sparks danced about their armored frames, which were conical like Gandaw's mountain. Tubes emerged from their bodies and spat fire at the dwarves.

Amid the screams and the smell of burnt flesh, Maldark lunged for the statue. One of the metal monsters swung toward him, but he grabbed Eingana and dived. The stream of flame singed his hair as it passed overhead. Without looking back, Maldark sprinted for the door. He skidded on the carpet of charred and liquefying dwarf flesh that was all that remained of his men, but strong hands caught him.

"Run!" hissed Mamba. "And keep on running."

IKRYS

CADMAN ENTERED THE tower alone, leaving a cordon of death-knights outside. The door creaked in protest, and he jumped out of his skin as a fist-sized spider scuttled away. Literally out of his skin, as the illusion of corpulence deserted him once more, and he couldn't be bothered to bring it back. Couldn't even be bothered to count anymore. He was bone weary and wanted nothing more than to shut himself up for a century and sleep. He slipped inside and pressed his back to the door.

The ground floor looked the same as he'd left it all those years ago: a circular chamber crawling with cobwebs, thick with dust, and coated with a growth of fluffy black mold that hung in strips like peeling wallpaper. The walls were six feet thick and reinforced by granite buttresses. The door was oak banded with iron and fitted with an incredibly intricate lock Cadman had brought from Verusia. The center of the room was stacked high with crates. For the life of him, Cadman couldn't recall what he'd packed inside them. A narrow stairwell wound its way upwards in a hazardous spiral with nothing to hold onto.

Braving the stairs to the first floor, he crunched his way across a carpet of dead cockroaches and lowered himself onto the scuffed and torn Chesterfield he'd shipped from Britannia. The leather was holding up rather well, considering the centuries he'd owned it.

Don't make them like they used to.

Cadman lay back and pretended he was still in Britannia; back with his mother in the thatched cottage, reclining on the Chesterfield and dreaming dreams of discovery.

Science had been his first passion, a vast unsullied canvass tugging at his natural curiosity. He'd had other dreams too—a place of his own in the country; a smallholding—oh, he'd have paid someone to manage it, but there was something altogether satisfying about self-sufficiency; a good woman to share it with—children even, if he'd had a lockable study where he could get away from them. But it was science that had really fired him up; science that had led him to Oxford, and science that had finally taken him to Verusia. Not pure science by then; more of a fusion of the arcane arts with rigorous methodology. The sort of thing that got you ridiculed by one community and reviled by another. It was a path with only one logical conclusion. A path followed in the footsteps of Dr. Otto Blightey, one-time fellow of Oxford himself, and now a mythical bogeyman who had proven all too real.

Cadman reached for a yellowish envelope speckled with insect droppings. He'd left it on the coffee table some considerable time ago. The address was smudged and almost illegible, but for the bottom line: *Verusia*. With a sinking feeling, Cadman slipped the letter out and scanned it. Oddly enough, he remembered sitting on this very sofa and agonizing over the wording. He'd written it shortly after his arrival in Sahul. An apology to Blightey for running out on him. An explanation; a plea for understanding, for forgiveness. It was the desperate hope of a desperate man appealing to reason, appealing for compassion. He'd not sent it. Cadman stuffed the letter back inside its envelope and dropped it back on the coffee table.

It had taken him centuries to work through the trauma left by Blightey, and now, with one scaremongering fairy tale, he was straight back to square one.

Damn that tatterdemalion ragamuffin! What's he have to go and put the frighteners on me for?

Jaspar Paris, Renna Cordelia, flying skulls that drank your spirit—all true. Cadman pushed himself up off the sofa. All too terribly true, and he only had himself to blame for raising the subject with the bard. No matter how far he ran, how much time passed, the threat of Blightey pursued him as inexorably as decay.

He took the stairs up to the second floor, noting with distaste that the canopy of his old four-poster was a sagging belly, the frame bowed, and the mattress a sodden heap with dense brown stains spreading across its surface. He made straight for the rusted ladder that led to a trap in the ceiling. His bony fingers rapped against the rungs as he ascended. The trap, warped by the centuries, refused to budge. Cadman directed his power at the stubborn wood until it crumbled into dust. He cried out as lesions cut into his bones. He could have used his pieces of the statue, probably should have, but something unsettled him each time he did. It was like the dip in temperature when a cloud covers the sun. At first, he'd thought it was Blightey, but now he wasn't so sure. Blightey had a distinctive presence, malignant and somewhat excitable, as if he couldn't wait to get his hands on you. Whatever it was that followed Cadman's use of the statue was almost detached, medical even—like a surgeon deciding where to make his first incision. It was deeply worrying. It could have been his own paranoia, he was well aware of that, but it never paid to take chances.

Clambering out onto the roof, he walked to the edge of the parapet and gazed at the waning moon. Even that looked like a spectral skull leering at him from the heavens.

He frowned at the driver sitting stoically down below in the driving seat of the carriage. Cadman felt a deepening of his familiar chill as he recalled the maniacal cackle, the eerie effect of the moonlight on the driver's back as they drove from the templum. It was the first time the man had shown any sign of life. Cadman shuddered. It had seemed like a veil had been ripped aside to reveal something beneath reality; something altogether more sinister and frightening than anything he'd ever imagined—and that was saying something. No sign of it now, though. The man was as lifeless as the zombies Cadman controlled. An empty vessel waiting for an animating intelligence. Numbers started bobbing up from the depths of Cadman's mind. He tried to let their patterns lead him from his worries, but a niggling thought slipped through the net: unless his own subconscious fears had somehow been reflected in the driver's uncharacteristic behavior, someone, or something else must have entered him. Either that, or the man had been acting dumb all along.

His fingers fell to the pieces of statue the same way his thoughts turned to counting. Pulling out the fang and the eye, he brought them together. Warm amber light wafted from them like stardust. Cadman was about to put them away when he glimpsed something pass across the face of the moon. The tatters of his heart thrashed about wildly in his ribcage. Had he just spied the presence that came whenever he used the statue?

He rubbed the pieces between his thumbs and forefingers. *Can't run forever, Cadman,* he told himself. He'd already come this far, taken so many risks. *In for a penny, in for a pound.*

He focused his thoughts through the glowing amber pieces. *Just a trickle of power. Maybe it won't be noticed.*

Cadman's mind called to whatever it was that had crossed the moon. He waited for the feeling of being watched, but there was nothing. Nothing but the chatter of his own disquieted mind.

And then he caught a scent, which struck him as odd as he'd smelled nothing for centuries. It was a sweet smell, fresh and deeply evocative. It was the smell of a pine forest. And then he heard laughter. Not heard exactly. It was as if his thoughts laughed with a mirth not quite their own.

The flapping of leathery wings startled him, and he looked up to see something spiraling down to the parapet. Some kind of creature, humanoid, in the loosest sense, but gray and gnarled like a gargoyle. Its head was angular and horned, the face a jutting beak edged with cruel fangs. The eyes were swirling pools of oil.

The creature lighted on the guttering and leered at him, a barbed tail rearing over its shoulder and swaying like a charmed snake.

"Are you following me?" Cadman said with as much command as he could muster.

"Not you exactly," the gargoyle said, fixing its eyes on the glowing pieces of amber.

Cadman thrust the fang and the eye into their respective pockets, but didn't uncurl his fingers from them. His mind sent out a dark thread and felt a reassuring compliance. Abelard was on his way up.

"You're not the first," Cadman said, drawing the illusion of fatness around him. "It seems everyone who's anyone is drawn to the statue." *Like flies to ordure.* He tightened his grasp on the pieces and sent Abelard a mental kick up the posterior.

The creature shifted its weight from foot to foot, its black eyes widening at Cadman's change of form.

"You have grown wary of using the statue," it said. "You have endured great pain rather than risk drawing attention."

"But you found me," Cadman said.

"I've been watching you for some time. I've also been watching the other watchers."

Cadman felt an icy thrill run through his bones. "Who?"

"I think you know." The gargoyle sat on the edge of the parapet and held its chin in its hands.

"Blightey?" The name fell from Cadman's mouth like a dread augury.

He half expected a comet to streak across the sky, or the skull of the moon to descend and devour him. He whirled around at a clamor from behind and then steadied himself with a string of counting. It was only Abelard emerging from the trapdoor.

The gargoyle rolled from its perch and stalked forward. At a click of Cadman's fingers, Abelard stood in its way and glowered through his one remaining eye, the other dangling uselessly over his cheek. The gargoyle cocked its head and grinned. Its tail whipped out, and the barb pierced Abelard's breastplate. Cadman gaped in horror as the death-knight stiffened and then fell to the floor in a shower of dust.

The gargoyle stepped up close to Cadman, bending its head toward his ear.

5, 4, 3, 2—Oh, crumbs!—1, 0, -1, -2—

"Shhh," the gargoyle hissed. "He might hear your thoughts."

Cadman took a step back, accepting the warmth of the pieces of statue, and glanced at the malevolent face of the moon.

"No, no." The creature wagged a taloned finger. "The other one might see."

"What other one?"

"The Technocrat of Aethir." The gargoyle gave a clacking chuckle. "Sektis Gandaw."

Cadman was starting to feel like a flightless bird cornered by feral cats. "Anyone else?"

"Besides the Dreamer shaman, the Archon, and a philosopher who thinks he can outwit fate, I think there is only one other, but you need not concern yourself with him yet. He is a patient player and has pursued Eingana for an eternity."

The more Cadman heard the more he wished he'd never become involved. Maybe he should just give the pieces to this creature and have done with it. After all, what was oblivion compared to the horrors of the Abyss?

"Not everyone means you harm," the gargoyle said. "Just those with more power. Think about it. If you find the rest of the statue, you'll be top of the heap. You'd be able to crush them on a whim. You'd even be able to destroy Blightey."

Now there was a thought. A world without Blightey. A world where Cadman didn't need to hide away in anonymity. A world without fear.

"But if I use the statue, they'll find me," he said.

"Only Sektis Gandaw draws near. Blightey has barely a whiff of Eingana, and he's not all that interested."

Probably bogged down with the day-job, torturing his way through the poor folk of Verusia in the hope of experiencing the tiniest spark of life.

"Sektis Gandaw is your greatest threat," the gargoyle said. "Like you, he was once a pupil of Blightey's, but he has far outgrown the master. You know what he plans for the statue? The Unweaving. It has always been his obsession—to unmake the cosmos and begin again. He seeks perfection; the sort of perfection that won't include you or me."

Cadman walked to the parapet and looked out across the dark forest. *What should I do? Back out now? Do I still have a choice?* "What are you?" He turned to the creature. "How do you know all this?"

"I am the slave of two masters. My name is Ikrys. I am a child of the Abyss."

Cadman stiffened.

"Not everything that comes from the Demiurgos is bad," Ikrys said. "And besides, I have not seen my home for centuries. "He has kept me here." Ikrys's voice dropped to a whisper. "The same one who haunts you. I am Blightey's unwilling servant. I must be seen to do his will; otherwise, you know better than most what fate I can expect."

Cadman nodded. "So tell me, what should I do?"

Ikrys folded his arms across his chest and stretched out his wings. "Gather the pieces. Make the statue whole. Take charge. I will help you, if you work quickly. Blightey will expect me back in a few weeks. You will need the full power of Eingana by then."

Cadman snatched off his pince-nez and squinted at the gargoyle. "What's in it for you?"

"I get to go home," Ikrys said. He shut his eyes and held up his hand for silence. "Armies are gathering," he said. "There will soon be a great battle for the statue. We must make ready. You must summon more dead."

"But I can't," Cadman said. "That would involve so much power from the statue that everyone from Aethir to Verusia would come."

"Use your necromancy. I will act as a channel. You will experience no more pain."

"You can do this?

Ikrys grimaced. "If I must."

Cadman felt a tug at his consciousness. He followed a black tendril of thought to the trees surrounding the tower. This cadaver was a strange one—something of a loose cannon. He felt its grudging obedience, but he could also sense its self-loathing, its desire to pass fully from life. Cadman probed deeper. It was the priest, Limus, whom he'd commanded to find someone close to Shader. Someone he could offer to the Dweller upon its return.

"Who have you got for me, Limus?" he asked silently with his mind.

"A friend." The priest was tormented, his thoughts almost strangled.

He was strong, this Limus, but still he had no choice. His corpse was Cadman's, nothing more than an automaton. The fact that he retained the flickering awareness of consciousness was more of a curse than a blessing.

Ikrys was watching Cadman attentively.

"This friend..." Cadman spoke the words aloud for the gargoyle's benefit. "Is it someone close to Shader?"

"Yes." Limus sobbed in Cadman's mind. "Her name is Rhiannon. She once loved him."

A HARMONICA IN THE NIGHT

THE RUMBLE OF distant thunder woke her. It was dank and cold, the air thick with must. Rhiannon winced at the thumping in her head that kept time to the regular drip-drip of water upon the hard stone floor. Her throat felt bruised and constricted. She coughed to ease it, gingerly touching the skin and wincing at the pain. Judging by the stiffness in her back and hips she had been there for some time. She forced herself into a sitting position and swept her hair out of her eyes.

The last thing she recalled was Pater Limus pulling her away from the ghoul. She'd been shocked at his strength, the easy way he ripped the creature limb from limb. She'd been frozen, rooted to the spot as he slung her over his shoulder and carried her off. She'd struggled against his cold, ungiving grip, the skin of his hands waxy and tinged with blue. He'd set her down so that he could throttle her with icy fingers, a single tear leaving its trail down his bloodless cheek. She'd tried to scream as her vision blurred and then darkness had taken her.

Her eyes adjusted to the gloom, and she saw that she was in a circular room with an uneven floor. Puddles of inky water collected in the depressions and damp climbed the windowless walls. A wooden ladder led to a trapdoor in the ceiling.

A muffled sound —was it a harmonica?—reached her from outside. She tilted her head at each successive note, recognizing the lilting melody of the wedding jig she'd been forced to learn as a child. The music stopped abruptly. There was a creak and a thud, footfalls from above. The trap in the ceiling rattled, and a crack appeared allowing dirty yellowish light to filter through. Whispers were exchanged and then the trap opened fully. A young woman backed down the ladder, her arse sticking out like it was on display. She turned and squinted at Rhiannon, a mass of chestnut hair framing a sultry face. She was dressed in a starchy white blouse and dowdy pleated skirt. Both were stained with sweat and dirt. An overpowering perfume wafted in with her.

A man clambered down behind her. He was wearing a black leather jacket with the faded emblem of a lightning bolt on the back. There was no mistaking the lank greasy hair, the spindly legs clad in patched denim.

"Elias!" Rhiannon rasped. Her throat felt like she'd swallowed glass.

The bard held a finger to his lips and squatted down beside her. "Ol' fatty's upstairs. I kid you not, every time he came to the window it was like an eclipse."

The woman with the chestnut hair was glancing from Rhiannon to the open trap. "Can she move? We need to go."

"Course I can move." Rhiannon forced the words out through the pain. She pushed herself to her feet and swooned. She would have fallen had Elias not caught her.

"What the clanging bell is that?" Elias peered at the back of her neck.

Rhiannon touched her fingers to an egg-sized swelling and winced. "Buggered if I know," she said. "Where the shog are we?"

"Dead Man's Torch."

"The old beacon tower? But that's miles from Sarum."

"Ah," Elias said, "but it's nothing when you have wheels, eh, Lallia?"

The woman winked at him and then sneered.

Rhiannon gave Elias a questioning look, but didn't bother pursuing it. She was too tired and in too much pain.

"That's a point," Lallia said. "How are we getting her back? There's only room for two."

"Strong girl like you," Elias said. "Walk back will do you good."

"Funny," Lallia said. She started up the ladder, but then stopped and craned her neck. "I heard something."

Elias pulled out a harmonica and gave a broad grin. "Still got the ol' magic," he said. "Even without the statue. Nothing like a bit of the ol' bardic charm to quieten the restless dead." He helped Rhiannon to the foot of the ladder and followed her up to a mildewed room stacked with crates. The iron-banded door was slightly ajar. "There's a bunch of those Nousian zombie-knights outside. And your mate Limus."

"Limus?" Rhiannon said, her heart lurching. "I thought he'd come to help me, but…"

"Sorry, love," Elias said. "Poor bastard's one of them now."

Rhiannon rubbed her throat and tossed off a quick prayer to Ain, for all it was worth.

As they left the tower Elias began to play a haunting lullaby on the harmonica. In the shadows of the courtyard, mounted shapes began to sway and then grew still. Rhiannon looked up at the tower. Something was perched on the roof, a hunched gargoyle with wings drawn up on its back.

"Hurry," Lallia called as she dashed into a thicket on the far side of the courtyard.

Elias continued to play his lullaby while nodding for Rhiannon to follow her.

Cadman appeared in the tower doorway, black vapors radiating from his fingertips to touch the mounted undead. Their limbs jerked, and red flared from their eyes.

"Follow Lallia," Elias said. "And just keep running. I'll draw them off."

Rhiannon stumbled into the undergrowth and was pulled roughly to the ground.

"Keep still," Lallia whispered. "Wait for Elias, and then we run. If you can't make it, that's your problem. Clear?"

Rhiannon was finding it hard to lift her head, never mind make a run for it. She fancied her chances better just curling up in the thicket and going to sleep.

"This way!" she heard Cadman shout. "Over here you ignorant bloody corp—"

The roar of thunder cut him off.

"Ready?" Lallia said, rolling to her knees.

The thunder came at them in a rising wall of noise. Rhiannon peeked out of the brush and saw Elias astride a red and silver two-wheeler speeding toward a clutch of skeletal horsemen. The din was incredible, the speed even more so. The death-knights raised their swords and charged. Elias skidded in a wide arc and sped away with half a dozen horsemen on his tail.

Rhiannon turned to Lallia for an explanation, but the woman was gone. She pushed her way through the brambles and stood. Her head rushed again, and she staggered before taking her first lumbering step toward the trees.

A flapping from behind caused Rhiannon to turn just in time to see the gargoyle from the parapet hurtle toward her on leathery wings. Talons gripped her shoulders, and a vicious barbed tail lashed out to stab her in the back of the neck.

***

"Come on, baby!"

Elias hunched over the petrol tank and let rip with the throttle. The wind tore at his hair as the Spitfire streaked across the clearing. He could see the undead riders in his mirror, feel the icy terror at his back, but he knew he could make it; knew the ol' girl wouldn't let him down.

Up ahead he could make out Cadman's grotesque bulk seeking to cut off his escape. No matter, Elias thought, he'd run the fat git over.

Something large fluttered down beside Cadman and dumped its load on the turf. As Elias sped closer he saw it was a body—Rhiannon's body—and that only made him madder. He pulled hard on the throttle and roared straight at Cadman.

Rather than run, as Elias had expected, Cadman stood his ground and raised his hands to the sky. The winged creature at his side pulsed with dark light, and a column of black fire erupted from Cadman's fingers. He threw down his arms, and the flame struck the earth. A split ran across the clearing and widened like an immense maw. Elias swung the bike around, but it careened and skidded toward the crevasse. With a last desperate scream, Elias plummeted into the chasm, the Spitfire tumbling after.

***

Cadman looked over the edge of the crack and allowed himself a satisfied grin. The dark magic was flowing once more, and this time without the pain, the terrible warping of his own body. He looked up to where Ikrys was depositing Rhiannon atop the tower. The creature hadn't lied about its abilities, but he still trusted it just about as far as he could throw it. *Too late for second thoughts, old chap,* one inner voice said.

I know, said the other, *but it never pays... You know what I'm going to say, don't you?*

Cadman thought he heard a sigh from somewhere between his ears.

He frowned into the crevasse as it shuddered and closed up like a flesh wound. No rumbling of the earth, no quake. It was more a case of darkness oozing across the breach and coagulating. A thick scar of charcoal running across the ground was the only indication anything untoward had happened.

Ikrys flapped down beside him. "Interesting."

"What did I just do?" Cadman asked, peering over the top of his pince-nez at the gargoyle.

Ikrys shook his wings and settled them on his back. "Does it matter? The girl is in our hands, and her would-be savior is dead. I told you I would help. Was not your power greater, even without the statue? Do you have any pain? Any warping of bone?"

Cadman patted his arms and chest. Nothing. Not even the slightest discomfort. Ikrys had channeled the dark energies as if they were his natural element. Perhaps they were.

"He was old. Older than anyone should be," Ikrys said, staring at the blackened earth. "The stench of Eingana has soaked into his flesh. Without life, though, there is no defense."

"Against what?"

"The one who raped her." Ikrys gave a sickly smile. "The Demiurgos will draw the corpse to the Abyss."

Cadman didn't like the sound of that. The last thing he needed was to arouse the attention of the Deceiver. He already had the eyes of the world on him, it seemed, not to mention the Dweller. That particular malevolence was evidence enough that he didn't want to mess with the Abyss, but he imagined the Dweller paled into insignificance compared with the being who'd spawned it.

"Well," he said with false bravado, "I bet your daddy's really pleased."

"Oh, yes," Ikrys said. "And he'll be even happier if you gather the pieces of the statue and free me from Blightey. Just think how he'll reward you if I can return home."

I'd rather not, Cadman thought, blowing out his cheeks and wishing he could bury himself in a deep hole a million miles away until this whole business blew over and was forgotten.

"Where's Lallia?" Cadman suddenly remembered. "The strumpet who was with the bard?"

Ikrys sighed and sat on the ground, holding his head in his hands. "Long gone," he said with a yawn. "And I'm too tired to care." The gargoyle curled up into a ball and closed his eyes.

"Up!" snapped Cadman. "That's the sort of sloppiness that will get us both killed. Up, and get after her, unless you want me to gift-wrap you and send you back to Verusia."

Ikrys lifted his head and whined. "I need to rest. Channeling is not as easy as it looks."

"Do it," Cadman said. "Or our agreement is at an end."

Ikrys clambered to his feet and unfurled his wings. "And I thought Blightey was bad," he said as he flapped into the air.

Cadman turned and started back toward the tower. For a moment, he desired nothing more than the security of its reinforced walls, but he quickly realized it was an illusory safety, no better than the blanket of fat he wore. The Dweller was coming for payment. If it didn't accept Rhiannon as a substitute for Shader, he was finished. He only hoped the old monk, Limus, had read the situation right. He'd said there was a bond between her and Shader. Perhaps it would be enough.

Actions beget yet more actions, he chastised himself as he entered the tower and made his way to the rooftop where Rhiannon lay prone beneath the clouds. Cadman peered over the crenellations at his servants, animated corpses, simply extensions of his own will. Among them, he could see the stooped and white-robed figure of Pater Limus. Somewhere in the depths of the cadaver's ravaged soul Cadman could sense a grief welling up into resistance. Most of his victims never showed such autonomy; their simple souls were either long gone or ousted at the moment of reanimation. This one was strong. Too strong. Cadman raised his hands and let loose a bolt of darkness that swiftly reduced the old monk's body to a bubbling putrescence.

"Shit, shit, shit!" Cadman bent double in agony as lesions tore through his fat flesh. The illusion vanished, but the cuts bit deep into his bones and frayed his ligaments.

He sensed Limus's soul fleeing the remains of his body, felt its fear and self-condemnation. Cadman didn't give a damn about the old priest's fate—whether his soul would languish in limbo or slowly dissolve into oblivion. The important thing was that, deprived of a body, it was unable to harm him, and that was an end to the matter.

THE TEMPLUM FLEET

THE WIND GUSTED, and Shader slapped down the page of the Liber. He tried once more to focus on the verse, but the salty ocean spray was spattering the paper and rendering it transparent. It would be all too easy to use that as an excuse to stop. He could equally well have used the frenetic activity of the *Aura Placida*'s crew as his reason to give up. There were teams of men in the rigging, and dozens more scuttling around the decks tying off ropes and securing anything that looked as if it could move.

The ship pitched violently, a torrent of water washing the planks and soaking Shader's breeches. He probably should have moved the minute the turbulence started; there hardly seemed any point now. He tugged down the brim of his sodden hat and stared at the page, but his attention was immediately arrested by movement out of the corner of his eye.

Captain Podesta strode the decks sporting a red polka-dot neckerchief that covered the gash he'd received from Shadrak. He'd been lucky; a hair's width to the right and he'd have bled out back in the jungle.

Shader blinked rapidly and tried to refocus on the verse. It was one of those oddities that were strewn throughout the Liber, passages that jarred with the reader and didn't quite seem to fit: "*Cessate et cognoscite quoniam ego sum Deus*"—"Be still and know that I am God."

Adeptus Ludo had pointed it out to him back at the seminary. It was the only passage in the entire Liber to use the word "*Deus*." Elsewhere, there was no mention of gods or God. The Templum considered the word a vulgar throwback to pagan times and outlawed its usage. Even in public readings, Ain's name was substituted for it, but the inexplicable blemish remained in every Liber produced. Scripture scholars argued interminably about its inclusion. Either it was one of the inscrutable mysteries of faith, or there had been an error in copying from the original—and now mysteriously lost—manuscripts, they said. Ain was simply "Ain" and Nous, the manifester of all things, was simply "Nous". Eingana was a ravished angel; the Archon was referred to as a "Radiant One", a being of light; and the Demiurgos was interchangeably called "the Father of Lies", "the Deceiver", and "the Smothered Radiance."

The Gray Abbot had told Shader that Frater Gardol referred to these peculiar passages as the "golden thread" running through the scriptures. Adeptus Ludo had lectured about something similar, before he'd been reprimanded by Exemptus Silvanus. Follow its course, he'd said repeatedly, and it will guide you through the labyrinth of obfuscation.

Be still and know...

"Cup of tea?" Elpidio crouched down beside Shader and thrust a steaming mug in his face. "Sabas said you looked like you needed one."

Shader closed his eyes, said a quick mental thanks to Ain, and then shut the Liber.

"Thanks, Elpidio, that was just the excuse I needed." An interruption from without. There was no sin in that. Shader took the scalding cup, quickly switching it to his other hand so he could grip the handle. "How's the boy from the *Dolphin*?"

"Been coughing blood. Sabas says he'll die if he don't eat something. Just been sitting with him, poor sod. Can't even tell us his name, so we've taken to calling him Little Amidio." Elpidio gave a quick look left and right. "Don't tell the captain."

"Knight's honor," Shader said.

"Eh? Oh, yeah. Good." Elpidio sat opposite Shader and copied his cross-legged posture. "What you doing, then? Praying?"

Shader set the cup down on the deck and thrust the Liber into his coat pocket.

"Kind of," he said, taking up the tea again and tasting it. "*Meditatio*, they call it in the Templum. Reading a verse over and over until the meaning sinks in and illumination follows."

"Oh," Elpidio sniffed. "Sorry I disturbed you."

Shader laughed at that. "Don't be. I've seen more illumination at the bottom of a deep well."

The ship banked, and half the tea sloshed onto the deck.

"So why do it?" Elpidio asked.

Shader shrugged and took another sip. It was a good question, the same one he'd been asking himself for years. Why, indeed? What was the point? Aristodeus would no doubt say it was all about self-regulation and fear of the unknown. Ludo thought it was a matter of love, of becoming more authentically human, selfless and self-giving. Those were ideals Shader admired, but they were also entirely alien to him. He supposed he was just hoping that if he followed the disciplines, he might suddenly be turned inside out, destroyed and rebuilt, like a lightning-struck tower.

"What's that for?" Elpidio pointed at the knotted prayer cord around Shader's neck.

Shader rubbed one of the knots between his thumb and forefinger. "It's an aid to *Contemplatio*," he said. "Helps to keep the mind busy while you sink into silence." *Be still and know that I am God.*

"Oh," Elpidio said. "My brain's always chattering. Seems nothing shuts it up, except maybe going up in the crow's nest. Don't know if it's the height or the wind whipping my face, but that's the only place I get any peace."

Shader nodded. He could only imagine what the boy had been through with the loss of his parents, the family business, and even his home. He was undoubtedly treated well on the *Aura Placida*. Podesta was like a father to him, and Sabas was as close as a hulking Numosian could get to being a doting mother. It could be a lot worse, he guessed. Probably was a whole lot worse for Rhiannon, after what she'd been through at the hands of Gaston.

"Where's your creepy friend?" Elpidio made a show of scanning the deck.

Shader nodded toward the forecastle. "Up there."

Osric was looking out over the bowsprit, his mist-like body virtually transparent, a grayish outline pearled with sea-spray.

Shader started as someone stepped from the shadows and headed toward the hold. "Ho, Cleto!" Shader raised a hand in greeting.

The sailor gave him a sullen nod and prowled off, muttering under his breath.

"What you do to him?" Elpidio said.

"Didn't let him kill the assassin back there in the jungle."

"Right," Elpidio said. "That was pretty dumb."

Shader gave him a wry smile. Maybe it was. Maybe he'd come to regret it, but it had certainly seemed like the Nousian thing to do at the time.

"As long as I don't get a knife in the back, I can live with Cleto's disapproval," he said.

Elpidio looked indignant. "He won't do nothing. Not now you're crew, more or less.

Captain says that's the way it is: no fighting among ourselves. We're all family here."

"And families don't fight?" Shader regretted the words the second they left his mouth.

Elpidio seemed to sense his discomfort and forced a smile. "Mine don't. Not anymore."

Shader held the boy's gaze. He saw the glistening of moisture around his eyes. Elpidio did nothing to disguise it.

"Mom used to say tears made you grow," he said. "Reckon I should be bigger than Sabas by now. Bigger than a giant, maybe."

"Tell me about you family," Shader said.

Elpidio looked away and wiped his eyes with the back of his hand. "Cleto says it don't matter. They were just gutted like pigs, and that's all there is to it."

"That all they were?" Shader kept his voice low and even. "The same as pigs?"

Elpidio sucked in a deep breath and faced Shader with bloodshot eyes. His cheeks were flushed, and freckles stood out on the bridge of his nose. "It's what we all are, ain't it? Shogging pigs. That's what Cleto says: we eat, shit, and die and no one gives a…"

"No one to mourn us? No one to remember?" Shader said, more to himself than to Elpidio. "Everything we do is insignificant? Everything we think is delusion?"

Elpidio frowned. "Eh? You saying it's all a load of bollocks? Nothing's worth it?"

Shader shook himself clear of that train of thought. He'd been down that path too often in the past. "Thought that's what you were saying, Elpidio. All this—" He swept out an arm to take in the ship. "—the great cities, music, art: all for nothing; all self-deception."

"You getting angry?" Elpidio pushed himself backward and uncrossed his legs.

"So what if I am?" Shader said. "None of it matters. We're all just mindless animals. Even your parents' carefully cultivated vineyard was really just a freak accident. If you wait long enough, perhaps a monkey will surpass them. Maybe this time next year we'll be drinking vintage Merlot produced by a herd of antelope."

Elpidio let out a blast of laughter and snot. "That's not even funny." He creased up, wiping his nose on his sleeve.

"Then why are you laughing?"

"I'm not shogging laughing." Elpidio let out another burst and was shaking from head to toe.

Shader laughed with him, but stopped abruptly when he noticed the tears streaming down the boy's face. "You miss them?"

Elpidio winced and then nodded. "Yeah," he croaked. "I miss them."

Shader held out his arms and let Elpidio bury his head in his chest, sobbing without restraint. Shader ran his fingers through the boy's hair and tried to find something to say that might bring even the slightest comfort.

***

Scores of black sails combed the waves like dorsal fins, sweeping ahead of the *Aura Placida* in a wide arc. Podesta passed Shader the spyglass.

"Looks like they have big quarry, eh?" he said, taking a swig from a bottle of rum.

Shader gasped as the scene came into focus. The reavers were bearing down upon a flotilla of white-sailed galleons. At this distance, and with the low cloud cover, it was difficult to be certain, but he could have sworn he saw the red Monas flapping from the masts of some of the ships.

"That's a Templum fleet," he said, almost not believing his own words.

"Aye," Podesta said. "Let's just hope the reason for their incursion into Sahulian waters doesn't join all the other unsolved mysteries on the seabed, eh? The reavers outnumber them two to one; with those thunder-weapons they used on us, your Nousian friends won't have a chance."

Shader focused in on the Templum flagship. The decks seemed to sparkle as sunlight glanced off of burnished helms and blades. It was hard to pick out any details at this range, but he was certain armored men were massing toward the aftcastle and swiftly forming up into disciplined ranks. He swung the spyglass and caught sight of a white-robed figure flanked by two men in black with splashes of crimson.

"The Ipsissimus." Shader's voice was hoarse.

"What?" Podesta took the spyglass. "Shog me for a salty seadog. What the Abyss would lure the old spider from his lair, eh?"

Podesta lowered the spyglass and pointed. "Two of the reavers are breaking away." He offered Shader the spyglass but there was no need. The black sails looked like rotten teeth at this distance, but Shader could clearly see them pulling back from the group and swinging toward the *Aura Placida*.

"Decisions, decisions, eh?" Podesta said.

Already there were murmurings among the crew, many of whom had stopped their work to gawp and gesture over the side.

The captain squinted out over the waves. "If we take a south-westerly course, we might just make it close enough to Sahul for the imperial fleet to get involved."

"Might?" Shader could see the two reavers growing steadily more visible as they closed the distance. "We still have quite a lead on them. Surely, we could—"

"Maybe. Maybe not," Podesta said, scratching his beard.

For a moment, he looked like the king of fools in his motley attire of garish colors, the tricorn crammed low on his head like a mockery of admiralty. The impression suddenly vanished, as if swept away by a gust of wind. Podesta drew himself upright, pulled back his shoulders, and hollered.

"Let go the mainsail! Hoist the lateens! Bring us about, Mr. Dekker! Prow to the enemy and make it snappy! Let's see if we can spear us a reaver with the bowsprit, eh?"

He gave Shader a mighty slap on the back and leaned out over the rail to observe the approaching ships. Cleto stepped out from behind the mast, gave Shader a sideways glance, and moved to Podesta's side.

"Want me to break out the rest of the cargo, Captain?"

"Good man, Cleto. Always like it when a sailor can read my mind. Ten men lining each rail to give the mawgs something to think about, the rest up on the aftcastle. That's where we'll make our stand if they board us. You know the drill. And don't forget the oil!"

"Captain," Cleto said as he hurried toward the hold.

"Oh, and Cleto, tell the men, no firing till they get my order. Understood?"

"Understood, Captain."

Podesta turned to Shader, a grim expression on his face. "Don't fancy our chances much," he said. "Best hope we have is to do the unexpected."

"Attack the two coming at us and then flee?" Shader asked, peering toward the main body of black vessels starting to surround the Templum fleet.

"No, no, no," Podesta said. "See, even you expected that, and a mawg's a much craftier creature than a knight or a priest, or whatever you are today. Straight down the center." Podesta pointed to the channel between the approaching reavers. "Right into the heart of the swarm."

"You're attacking the entire fleet?" Shader said. "That's suicide."

Podesta shrugged and stared down at the waves. "Sometimes we don't have all the choices we'd like," he said. "But if I'm going down to mawgs, it's not going to be because they ran faster than me. And besides, I thought a holy avenger like you might appreciate the opportunity to save your friends."

Shader didn't think that was very likely.

So this is where it was going to end. He'd never considered death at sea. Not quite the slow fading from life he'd envisioned at Pardes. But this is what he was trained for, as were the fighting men he'd seen on the Templum flagship. They were Elect knights, sworn to serve the Ipsissimus; sworn to die for him and to see it as an honor. Shader gripped the hilt of his sword and narrowed his eyes against the squall. This is where Ain had led him. So be it.

Cleto's barking voice ripped him from his thoughts and announced the commencement of the path they had chosen. Sailors who'd only minutes ago been coarse and carefree fanned out along the starboard rail with the same long-barreled weapons Cleto had taken to the jungle. The rest were massing on the aftcastle, many of them also brandishing the Aeterna-tech weapons, others with cutlasses and crossbows. Cleto strode the length of the deck, shouting commands in exactly the same tone as the Elect drill-sergeants had used. It was a marvel to watch: a line of scruffy seamen loading lead balls, tamping them down, and then raising the barrels to sight the enemy. Once he was satisfied, Cleto ordered them to lower their weapons and wait. He then ran to the aftcastle and went through the same routine.

Podesta was beside Dekker at the helm, gesticulating with sharp cutting motions of his hands and repeatedly uttering "uh?" and "eh?" to make sure he'd been understood. Dekker looked pale, rigid hands clutching the wheel as if it were holding him in existence.

A tortured howl came from the galley. Podesta's jaw dropped, and he turned to Shader, eyes wide and frightened, bottom lip trembling.

Sabas emerged from the galley with a hefty cleaver in each hand. He'd removed his apron and wore only breeches and a vest. He'd always looked a big man, but at that moment, Shader saw him as a giant, all bulging muscle, whereas in his usual attire he'd appeared stocky and not a little fat. He acknowledged Shader with a nod. The humor had left his eyes. They'd grown feral, and his lips were drawn back in a snarl. He came to stand before Podesta and lowered his gaze.

"The boy?" Podesta asked, his voice quavering.

Sabas shook his head. Podesta's hand went to his mouth, tears streaking his cheeks.

"Maybe it's good he don't have to go through this again," Sabas said in a low rumble.

Podesta nodded and wiped the snot from his nose. He sucked in a deep breath and drew his shoulders back. He flicked a look at Shader, but there was no sparkle in his eyes.

Sabas made his way up onto the aftcastle, the other sailors parting for him out of either fear or respect. Shader guessed they'd seen this side of Sabas before and knew what was coming.

Elpidio was leaning over the edge of the crow's nest to get a better look at the enemy. If the boy was scared, he was disguising it well. He noticed Shader watching him and waved.

"You might want to join the others up top," Podesta said, clapping a hand on Shader's shoulder. "They'll swarm the decks in no time. At least from the aftcastle we'll have a defensive advantage, eh?"

Shader indicated the men lining the rails. "What about them?"

"One volley and then they fall back. Dekker's the only one staying put. We need him to get us through and into the thick of it."

Dekker was visibly shaking as he clung to the wheel, his muscles taut as a dead man's, eyes fixed straight ahead, lips moving with silent words.

"I'll stay with him," Shader said.

"But…"

"If it's that important we break through, someone needs to keep Dekker alive."

"Point taken." Podesta held out his hand and Shader took it. "May Ain be with you, my friend."

"And with your spirit," Shader said as the captain turned and ran up the steps to the aftcastle.

"Here they come lads!" bellowed Cleto from up top. "Ready weapons!"

All around the deck, barrels were raised in perfect unison. The two reavers were almost upon them. Shader could see mawgs packed onto the decks like rats clinging to driftwood. The channel between the ships was narrowing as the mawgs realized what Podesta was trying to do, but fast as they were, it was still too late.

"I will stand with you," Osric whispered in Shader's ear.

Shader nodded his thanks, but took little comfort. His palms were slick with sweat, and his breaths came in ragged gasps. Once battle had commenced he knew he'd be fine. It was the anticipation he couldn't deal with.

The *Aura Placida* slipped between the reavers like she was threading the eye of a needle. The huge black barrels of thunder-weapons protruded from the sides of both galleons, but they dared not fire for fear of hitting each other. Dozens of mawgs leapt to the railings and started to fling themselves across to the *Aura Placida*.

"Fire!" Cleto roared.

There was a succession of thunder-cracks. Barrels smoked, and mawgs were punched back against their own hulls before plunging into the sea.

"Fall back!" Cleto yelled as another wave of mawgs prepared to leap from the galleon, jaws snapping, claws rending the air.

As the sailors scurried past on their way to the aftcastle, Shader drew the gladius and took up a position behind Dekker. The sailor was speaking audibly now, the same words over and over:

"I love you Mary, I love you Mary, I love you Mary…"

The prow of the *Aura Placida* was already through the gap and the mawgs howled their frustration. The main decks of both reavers were heaving masses of fur. Yellow eyes glared their hunger at Shader as they passed, and some of the larger mawgs reared up and beat their leathery chests with razor-sharp claws, gashing and gouging themselves. The spill of black blood whipped up a frenzy among the others.

Dozens more flung themselves across the waves. They were met with thunder and dropped like stones into the sea; all but two, whose claws found purchase in the carrack's hull. They hung there for a few seconds and then started to drag themselves upwards. As the first reached the top, Shader ran over and hacked away its arm. The mawg screeched and fell, but the other one made the deck and pounced. Shader twisted clear of a vicious sweep with a claw and backslashed across the mawg's throat. The thick fur saved the beast, and it barreled into him.

Parrying a bludgeoning blow as he stumbled backward, Shader managed to put the mainmast between him and the mawg. It came around the left-hand side, maw cavernously wide and filled to the gullet with thorny teeth. Shader thrust and the head pulled back behind the mast. It immediately reappeared the other side, and he jabbed at it again. This time, when it withdrew, he followed it. The mawg did as he'd expected and went back to the left. It roared its frustration when it found nothing but air, and then it screamed and thrashed as the point of Shader's gladius emerged from its chest.

Shader whipped the blade free and danced out of range as the enraged mawg thrashed about with blood pumping from its torso. He watched it for a moment, gauging the pattern of its movements, and then lunged with the gladius extended. The blade skewered an eye, and Shader pushed until he felt it grate against bone and hit something pulpy beyond. The mawg dropped like a sack of potatoes.

A cheer went up from the aftcastle, and Shader saw that they had cleared the two reavers. He wiped his blade on the mawg's fur and rejoined Dekker at the helm. Something shimmered behind the sailor causing Shader to start, but then he saw it was Osric's insubstantial image catching the sea spray. Shader was about to say something about the wraith not helping, but then realized Osric had been fulfilling their task to keep Dekker safe.

There was a succession of muffled booms, and clouds of smoke billowed up from the main mawg fleet. Shader's first thought was that it was a miracle, an act of Ain, but then he realized the smoke was coming from the thunder-weapons jutting from their hulls. Flames raced skyward along the masts of one of the lagging Templum ships. People were leaping overboard into the chopping waves as a black cloud rolled across the deck. The mainmast teetered, and the hull lurched dangerously.

The reavers had the Templum ships encircled, but it was getting difficult to see what was happening in the thick banks of smoke now spilling off the sinking ship. Shader's eyes were watering from the acrid fumes, and his stomach churned as the *Aura Placida* plunged into the troughs and rode the waves. They were coming up fast behind the nearest of the black ships. Shader blinked and squinted in an effort to gauge the numbers on both sides. There were about thirty reavers and fewer than fifteen Templum ships. Each of the reavers was packed with at least a hundred frenzied mawgs. Even if the Templum fleet avoided the thunder-weapons, it would be overwhelmed by sheer weight of numbers.

"They're coming about, Mr. Dekker!" Podesta shouted from the aft-castle. "Take us straight into the pack and keep running."

Shader looked back and saw the first two reavers turning in wide circles. The *Aura Placida* was caught between a rock and a hard place. Podesta's plan—if that's what you could call it—reeked of desperation. It struck Shader as the death wish of a man who'd never come to terms with what he'd witnessed at the hands of the mawgs as a child. Is that what this was, the result of the captain's obsession? Or was there really no other way? It was pointless worrying about it, Shader decided. The die was already cast. They were committed. All he had to worry about was keeping Dekker alive long enough to break through the reavers and scatter their formation. With any luck, it would afford the Templum fleet some room for a counterattack, although what they could do against the thunder-weapons, he couldn't imagine. No matter the source of Podesta's illegal Aeterna-tech, there was no way the Ipsissimus was going to have anything similar with his fleet. Not unless he was an utter hypocrite. Right now, Shader hoped that he was.

The aft of the closest reaver came looming into view, and for an instant, Shader thought Dekker was going to ram it. At the last minute, the *Aura Placida* swung to port and grazed the side of the mawg vessel. Timbers screeched, and the deck shuddered. Mawgs pitched overboard or tumbled on top of each other as volley upon volley of lead shot ripped into them from the *Aura Placida*'s aftcastle. Before the mawgs could muster any sort of attack, the carrack was through and speeding toward the Templum fleet at the center of the noose.

The reaver they'd struck swung around from the impact and headed straight for its neighbor. The Templum ships had given up running and were maneuvering into a defensive circle. The reavers saw they had them just where they wanted them and began to turn side on so that they could bring their thunder-weapons to bear.

"That one!" Podesta bellowed from the railing of the aftcastle. He was pointing with his cutlass toward the largest of the black galleons. "The flagship, Mr. Dekker. Ram her!"

The mawg flagship was halfway through its turn and presented them with a broad target. The *Aura Placida*'s bowsprit took on the aspect of a tremendous lance as it swung to the attack and the hunted became the hunter.

"Brace for impact!" Podesta shouted, and then there was a sickening crunch as planks splintered and the prow buried itself in the flank of the reaver. The flagship split and started to fold back around the remains of the bowsprit. Mawgs fell by the dozen into the water, but one—larger than the rest—levitated a foot above the deck and wheeled to face Dekker. Its face was pierced with human bones, and a chain of skulls dangled from its neck. The mawg extended two taloned hands, and fire spiraled from them. Dekker's jaw hung slack, but he seemed unable to release the wheel. Shader stepped in front of him with the gladius raised. The blade flared white, drawing the mawg's fire into itself and quenching it. The mawg snarled something at Shader and then gestured to its fellows. A great mass of fur bundled toward the *Aura Placida*'s foredeck howling like rabid wolves.

"Fly!" Shader screamed at Dekker. "Get up top."

Dekker tore his hands away from the wheel and sprinted for the aft-castle with Osric's ghostly outline close on his tail. Shader started to back away after him as the mawgs spilled to the quarterdeck and reached the mainmast. Two of them started to climb the mast by burying their claws deep into the wood. Shader looked up at the crow's nest and groaned. Elpidio was staring down, white-faced, eyes wide in panic.

Shader charged, but before he could reach the mast, the main swell of mawgs swarmed past it and fell upon him. There was a blur of fangs, claws, and fur. Talons glanced off his chainmail, shredded his coat. Shader stabbed and slashed with wild abandon, cleaving, cutting, impaling. He ducked and danced, always poised, always balanced. No thoughts, no regrets: raw movements born from hours of practice and years of bloody experience. His hat was torn from his head, and a claw raked the skin of his face, but Shader dropped low and gutted his assailant. He never stood still long enough for the mawgs to overwhelm him. His foot lashed out striking a mawg behind the calf and upturning it. Another grabbed him from behind, but Shader reversed his sword and rammed it through hide and flesh. He could see nothing but fur and fangs and blood, but he continued to whirl and slash like a devil. If he had to slay an army by himself, he would. There was no way they were getting Elpidio.

As if sharing his resolve, the gladius hummed and shone with white-hot brilliance. The mawgs raged at its blinding light, but still kept coming in an endless avalanche. Shader cut down another and backed against the mast. The two climbing mawgs were almost at the crow's nest, and he could hear Elpidio screaming. Jaws snapped an inch from Shader's face, causing him to duck round the other side of the mast. He jabbed forward, spitting an arm, ripped his blade free, and hacked down hard on top of a mawg's head. The beast crumpled into the path of the pack. For a second, Shader had a breathing space, and he took hold of the rigging draping from the mast. Before he could climb, the mawgs surged forward and he was forced to back away to the railings. Elpidio screamed again— a ghastly shrill shriek—and blood showered the decks.

"No!" Shader roared, charging back into the horde, cutting, stabbing, hacking, his limbs fuelled by rage and pain.

The mawgs closed around him, striking from all sides. A blow to the head turned his vision red and sent him reeling toward a wall of claws. Just before they struck him, there was a series of bangs and four of the mawgs fell forward with holes in their chests.

Strong arms grabbed Shader and pulled him through the gap.

"You're one crazy shogger," growled Cleto, dragging Shader toward the aftcastle as three other sailors covered them with the Aeternam weapons.

"Elpidio," Shader protested. "Elpidio!"

"Too late," Cleto said. "Now get your arse up there and kill some more o' the scuts."

Cleto shoved Shader toward the steps where other hands caught him and helped him up to the aftcastle. He turned as Cleto barked an order and the three sailors who'd covered their retreat fired again. Another mawg fell, but the pack continued to swell.

"Run!" Cleto yelled as the sailors tried desperately to reload their weapons.

Cleto bounded up the steps three at a time. Two of the others made it, but the third was snatched away into the pack. The sound of his flesh being ripped was unnaturally loud. His screams cut across the deck for longer than they should have, accompanied by rending, crunching, and disgorging. Finally, the big mawg they'd seen shooting fire from its fingers reared up with a hunk of dripping meat in each hand. It was hard to tell what body part it was, due to the gore, but thankfully, the screaming had stopped.

Podesta put his hand on Shader's shoulder and peered down at the mawgs.

"There's no end to them," he said in a hushed voice. "Shoggers must breed like rabbits."

He led Shader behind the two ranks of sailors armed with Aeternam weapons so that he could view the rest of the battle. Smoke billowed up in a wide circle making it hard to distinguish the Templum ships from the reavers.

"We must help them," Osric said. "It is our duty."

Shader felt it too, the pull of his Elect training, the sense of purpose the Order had instilled in him. For Osric, it must have been even worse: years of loyal service followed by an age of undeath, centuries in which to regret his failings. Shader had taken the easy route; he'd simply walked away from it all, reneged on his responsibilities. But now, faced with a real threat to the Ipsissimus, he wanted nothing more than to be at his side.

One galleon was ablaze, careening precariously. Fire erupted from the thunder-weapons of the reavers at intervals, sending up splashes of water or splintering through planks. The chorus of screams and explosions was muffled and eerily dreamlike. For an instant, the wind cleared the smoke, and Shader saw that the cordon of black sails was tightening about the remaining Templum ships. Clearly, the mawgs wanted to finish this with tooth and claw. As their weapons thundered again and the smoke screen returned, Shader thought he saw another vessel, much smaller than the rest, escaping the fight. Shader blinked and squinted, but then the little ship was lost to sight. He'd been mistaken: it hadn't been fleeing the battle; it was heading toward it.

"Steady." Cleto's voice brought Shader around.

The mawgs were now pressing onto the stairs, loping up cautiously. The entire quarterdeck behind them resembled a seething furry monster.

"Steady," Cleto called again. Shader thought he detected a slight quaver in the man's voice.

The lead mawgs were only a few steps from the top. The first line of defenders held their Aeterna-tech weapons to their eyes, the barrels wavering either from fear or the wind. The second rank looked like they would have run, if there had been anywhere to go. They clutched their own weapons in white-knuckled hands. Behind them stood the last line of defense: a huddle of grim-faced sailors brandishing cutlasses. Tough men, every one of them, but each betraying the hopelessness of their plight and the fear of what was to come. Sabas stood at the center, his black skin beaded with sweat, the two cleavers hanging loosely at his sides as if he had all the time in the world to bloody them.

"Fire!" Cleto roared.

There was a series of thunder-cracks. Blood sprayed; mawgs fell. One had a fist-sized hole through its chest; another lost half its face, yet still the horde pressed on, clambering over the bodies now clogging the steps. The front row of sailors knelt to reload as the rank behind took aim.

The mawgs howled and surged upward like frenzied wolves scenting injured prey. Another volley from the Aeterna-tech weapons decimated the first wave. The front rank of sailors stood and fired again as the men behind reloaded. There was time to get off one more volley before the mawgs reached the aftcastle and the sailors scattered to port and starboard.

Sabas roared and charged the horde's center, flanked by a score of men wielding cutlasses. The big man swung his cleavers in brutal arcs that sent up gouts of black blood. Shader went to follow him into the fray, but Podesta held him back.

"Wait, my friend. You've had your turn. Sabas will hold the steps for a while yet."

A rush of cold air told Shader that Osric had sped into the melee, and within moments blood was flying from the mawgs as if the air itself bore arms against them.

Sabas cut his way deeper into the pack, his arms swirling like the blades of a windmill. He reached the top of the steps where the mawgs could only come at him two at a time and hacked away with ruthless efficiency. The beasts never relented. It was almost as if they enjoyed the challenge, flinging themselves at this unyielding wall of death and trusting in their limitless numbers. Sabas would tire, they must have known that. It was only a matter of time.

It came sooner than Shader had expected. Sabas half hacked the head off of one mawg and then buried his second cleaver in the skull of another. The blade lodged there, but the creature didn't drop. It barreled on into Sabas, knocking him flat on his back. The big man let go of his blades and pounded his fists into the mawg's head as it snarled and snapped on top of him. Sailors pressed in and started to batter and stab the creature, but more mawgs were now surging up the steps and onto the aftcastle.

"That's our cue," Podesta said, charging in with his cutlass weaving a wicked arc and sending up sprays of black gore.

Shader leapt after him, cutting and stabbing with renewed ferocity. Between them, they drove the mawgs back to the steps and then took up a position either side, thrusting, blocking, and slashing. Osric must have been somewhere in front of them as mawgs were suddenly sliced open by an invisible blade. Panic spread through the closest creatures and they started to tear at each other in their desperation to get away.

Sabas was back up, but one of his arms was horribly mangled, and he had deep gashes across his chest and face. He clenched a cutlass in a meaty fist.

"Let me at them!" he bellowed, prowling toward the stairs.

"Stay where you are," Podesta called over his shoulder as he gutted another mawg. "You're too badly hurt."

"Don't have time to hurt," the black man growled. "But I'm gonna give them a whole load of hurt for what they did to my Elpidio."

He pushed past Shader and Podesta and cannoned into the mawgs. The cutlass swept down, and a head flew through the air. Sabas drove into the pack like a one-man phalanx, heaving and hacking with the fury of a titan. He cut a swath through the mawgs until he set foot on the quarterdeck. Shader ran down beside him, expecting the big man to stop there, but Sabas pressed on into the mass of mawgs still filling the deck. Within seconds, they surrounded him, and he went down amid spouts of crimson blood.

A passage of gore opened up in the scrum of mawgs who'd smothered Sabas. Limbs flew, oily blood sprayed, and the mawgs scattered from the big man's body. Osric was clearly visibly now—a translucent death-knight defined by the clinging black blood of his foes. The creatures backed away from him, and for a moment Shader thought the tide had turned. Then, the big mawg with the piercings and skulls stepped through their ranks with dark mist rolling from its claws. Osric gusted toward it, but the creature made a clutching, twisting gesture with its hands and a tiny black aperture appeared in the air before Osric. The wraith caught like a sail in a gale, stretching and fluttering toward the black hole. His sword arm was caught by some unimaginable force and corkscrewed into the opening, dragging the rest of him after it. Osric twisted his head, his crimson eyes flaring right at Shader. He held out his free arm as if Shader could catch hold of him and tug him clear, and then even that was gone. The mawg clapped its hands, and the black hole vanished along with Osric.

Shader's knees weakened, and he had to steady himself on the banister. He now stood alone at the foot of the steps. He glanced back up at the aftcastle to see Podesta ordering the survivors to take up crossbows and line the railing.

"Ready the oil, lads!" the captain bellowed.

A mawg leapt, and Shader stepped back as he impaled it. A thrill ran up his arm from the hilt of the gladius, which had once more started to hum and glow. Heat flooded his veins and cleared his head. It felt as if he'd rested for a week.

He met a vicious claw swipe with the blade and severed the mawg's arm at the elbow. Two more charged him at the same time, and he gave a little ground, retreating to the bottom step. The first mawg snapped its jaws at him, but Shader rammed the gladius through the top of its mouth and into its brain. The second lunged at his legs. Shader tripped on the next step as he slashed the mawg across the face and then kicked it back into the pack. He found his feet just in time to meet a clubbing blow from another mawg. Its hand flew over the rails into the sea and torrents of black blood spouted from the stump. Shader ducked under a strike from the remaining hand and buried the gladius in the mawg's belly. He ripped it clear and slashed across the creature's neck. Two more mawg's pounced, and Shader gave up another step.

The thrum of crossbows sounded from above and the mawgs fell, skewered with bolts. A couple more replaced them, and Shader retreated again, parrying claws desperately until he was once more on the aftcastle. Podesta joined him, and they resumed their position at the top of the steps, cutting down the mawgs in pairs. There was no let up, though. The mawgs just kept coming, and Shader was already starting to tire. Podesta looked like an animated corpse. His face had lost all color, and he was spattered with mawg blood. His eyes, though, burned with frenzy. Behind him, the sailors continued to fire into the mass below, but it was like spitting on a bushfire. One man leapt overboard, obviously thinking his chances were better with the sharks than with the mawgs. Another stood by a keg of oil, eyes tracking Podesta, but the captain showed no indication he was ready to make the ultimate sacrifice yet.

A snarling beast dived at Podesta's legs and bore him to the ground. Shader spun and stabbed it through the eye, but another came up behind him. He backslashed across its throat, but already others had made it to the aftcastle. Podesta scrambled to his feet, and they backed toward the stern. Shader glanced left and right.

"The oil, Captain?" he said. "If we're going to do it…"

"Not yet," Podesta said. "Not yet."

A dozen men on either side had thrown down their crossbows and taken up cutlasses. They looked finished, like dead men, but their jaws were set, and he knew there was no give in them. The mawgs roared their triumph and swarmed forward. The sailors leapt to meet them, screaming a chilling battle cry. Shader's blows were weakening as he cut and thrust, twisted and spun back into the wall of fur. A man's arm fell at Shader's feet, where the deck was already awash with red blood. He glimpsed Podesta whirling and hacking like a demon. Something struck Shader on the back, and he flew toward the gaping mouth of a mawg. He slashed wildly with the sword, missed, but managed to roll out of the way of a sweeping claw. He came up and rammed his blade into the groin of another mawg, wrenched it free and parried a clubbing forearm.

Shader felt a strange calmness. He moved with speed and efficiency, but it was as if everything had slowed down and taken on a dreamlike quality. This was it, his final moment on earth. This was how it was to end, and yet he fought on as if he didn't have a care in the world. It was a hazy game, a practice bout, maybe even someone else's nightmare, but part of him retained its grip on reality; part of him knew that this could only end one way. He risked a glance at the sailor by the oil keg.

Amber light flooded the deck, and Shader shielded his eyes from its brightness. The mawgs started screeching and thrashing the air. They lumbered about the aftcastle, some stumbling down the steps. A savage roar sounded from the quarterdeck. Shader peered over the rail to see the big mawg with the bone piercings pointing off the bow and gesturing for the pack to follow. As the mawgs started pouring down the steps, Shader squinted out to sea where the small ship he'd seen had taken up a position between the reavers and the Templum fleet. Someone stood before its single mast holding aloft a blazing amber object. Podesta handed Shader the spyglass, and once he'd got it focused, he gasped with recognition. It was Maldark the Fallen, armored in banded mail, gray hair and beard streaming in the gusting wind. He held his war-hammer aloft, its stone head shining with the radiance of the sun.

The mawgs started leaping into the sea and swimming toward the dwarf's boat. The same was happening on all the reavers: the mawgs were piling into the water, and soon the sea was a mass of dark shapes converging on Maldark.

"What the shog are they doing now?" Cleto growled.

Shader couldn't take his eyes off the scene. A remote part of his mind registered that Cleto was still alive, a fact that didn't surprise him in the slightest.

The mawgs streaked toward the little boat in a tide of slick fur. As the first claws raked against the hull, and mawgs started dragging themselves aboard, the blaze from Maldark's hammer burst across the waves. Flames scorched the swimming mawgs, who screeched and dived below the surface, but to no avail. The water may as well have been oil fueling the fire. Shader looked away, blinking against the flash-blindness. When he looked back, ash coated the sea around Maldark's boat. Hundreds of mawgs had simply been incinerated, but those at the rear were surrounded by a greenish glow emanating from the big mawg with the bone necklace. Under the shaman's protection, they were still battling the waves in a ragged semicircle.

The dwarf had his back to the mast and nearly fell. He took a step forward and tried to lift the hammer again, but he dropped to his knees with the effort. He looked up as the air above him ripped open. An icy thrill ran up Shader's spine as he recognized the cobalt skies he'd glimpsed during the mawg ritual on the Anglesh Isles. It seemed as if a blue veil had been rent to reveal a separate reality behind. Maldark's body sagged with what looked like resignation as a gigantic black hand pushed through the aperture and swooped toward him. Dark fingers curled around the dwarf, dragged him away from the hammer. Shader wanted to shout a warning as the mawgs closed in on the boat. He entertained vague ideas of stripping off his armor and flinging himself into the sea to go to Maldark's aid, but he did nothing. There was nothing he could do. Half a dozen mawgs dragged themselves dripping onto the boat. The shaman went for the hammer, while the others yelped as the giant fingers uncurled and offered the dwarf to their frenzy.

Do something! Shader urged. *Stand and fight!*

The shaman raised the hammer as cobalt swirls formed a sphere above. Amber scintillated from the head of the hammer for an instant, then sputtered and died. The shaman barked at the other mawgs who howled and tore into Maldark, smothering him beneath a mass of fur.

Shader couldn't even shut his eyes as the blood began to spray and the hammer burst into crimson flame. The sphere swelled into a vast rent in the sky, and the gray-clad figure appeared once more, reaching forward from his metal throne, fingers curling around the haft of Maldark's hammer.

THE GREAT WORK

SEKTIS GANDAW OPENED his eyes and allowed himself the barest of smiles at the war-hammer lying across his lap. Electrodes withdrew from his skull in quick succession, the wires retracting into the center of the array above the projection seat. He frowned, but only ever so slightly, as the skin punctures ringing his head like the marks of a thorny crown tightened and then sealed with a fresh dermal layer. He withdrew his hand from the black gauntlet and stood—a little too soon. Giddiness swamped him and he half fell, clutching the arm of the chair for support. A hundred needles pricked his skin, restoring equilibrium, and he sucked in a long, deep breath.

He flinched as something twitched in his peripheral vision. The sedatives calmed him even before he could berate himself; it was nothing but the holographic black hand upon its tray, extending and flexing its phalanges. He punched a sequence of buttons, and the hand flickered away.

The hammerhead was still warm from the transition, and Gandaw felt an uncharacteristic thrill as he caressed it. He was almost disappointed when chemicals flooded his arteries to return him to homeostasis. Curling his fingers around the haft, he felt the whir of circuits in his exoskeleton that enabled him to lift it as if it were a feather. He strode to a circular section of floor, which detached itself and bore him down to the ground level.

Mephesch was checking the connections on the body of the serpent statue. It was mounted upon a pedestal and wired into the nerve center of the symmetrical mountain. Microfilaments were attached to every inch of the statue, like the tendrils of a luminescent anemone.

"Not the piece I was after," Gandaw said, "but a fortunate find in any case. You were right about the Arnochian granite blocking our sensors. The recalibration worked perfectly. Now let's just hope we weren't deceived. These dwarves are as cunning as..." He wanted to say, "your lot," but thought better of it. Nevertheless, it was true. After all, had he not augmented his original dwarves with the genes of the homunculi?

He handed Mephesch the hammer. The homunculus staggered under the weight and then set it down at the foot of the pedestal.

"At least now we can now account for all five pieces," Gandaw said.

One was definitely among the Templum fleet that had set sail from Latia. The kryeh had detected its power, and with the acquisition of the body of the statue, Gandaw had been able to maintain a trace through his network of spies in the sky.

Mephesch rubbed his hands together and cocked his head.

"Is it ready?" Gandaw asked, stooping to inspect the panel displays around the base of the pedestal.

"We have limited control," Mephesch said. "If a piece of the statue really is concealed within the hammer it should reveal itself to the body."

Gandaw nodded, his eyes flicking from the hammer to the serpent statue's gaping mouth. "Proceed," he said, stepping back and stroking his chin.

Mephesch tapped the screen on his vambrace and then threw a switch set into the pedestal. There was a waft of ozone, followed by a low drone. The microfilaments surrounding Eingana's petrified body started to dance with multi-colored lights, and then the black stone of the statue began to shimmer. Amber radiance burned away the black until the statue shone with its brilliance. Gandaw's optics darkened against the glare, and he watched in satisfaction as Maldark's hammer began to pulse and glow in response. The top of the hammerhead rippled like water, and a shard of amber began to emerge. A ray of golden light shot from the mouth of the statue to connect with the shard, coaxing it free from concealment.

It was a fang, Gandaw observed. His second piece of the Statue of Eingana. It traveled along its beam of light until it hovered in the serpent's maw. The sinuous body writhed, and the mouth snapped closed. When it opened again, the fang was embedded in the upper gum. The serpent coiled and twisted, and then grew still as if suddenly fossilized. Mephesch flicked the switch, and the droning died down. The amber radiance around the statue pulsed a couple of times and then winked out, leaving dull black stone in its wake.

"Good," Gandaw said. "One step closer."

Mephesch lifted his black eyes to meet Gandaw's. His lips parted like a gash, curling upwards at the edges in a smile.

Gandaw didn't like that look; didn't trust it. But no matter, he thought, Mephesch was proving his usefulness, but it was a usefulness that would ultimately lead to his own demise, along with that of everything else in the imperfect universe.

"I'll be in my chambers," Gandaw said, instructing the floor disk to rise. "The slightest glimmer from the other pieces, call me."

Mephesch nodded as Gandaw was borne to the very top level of the mountain.

The disk set him down on a narrow walkway flanked by an army of sentroids. The spherical robots beeped and flashed as he passed them, scanning his vital signs and then standing down when they perceived no threat. They guarded the only way into his quarters, which were inaccessible from the outside. A thousand feet above ground level and shielded by fifty feet of scarolite. The only way into the mountain was from below, and even he wouldn't want to set foot in the passageways down there. If he wanted to get out, he could, but it would involve exterminating the aberrations he'd left roaming the lower levels. That would be a waste, though. Not only did the monsters he'd created over the centuries serve as a deterrent to would-be intruders, but there seemed little point eradicating them when he had no intention of venturing outside. It was utter chaos out there. At least in the mountain he had absolute control. Outside it was all so random, so many ungovernable factors that further evidenced the blindness of creation. Inside, Gandaw was the sole architect of everything that happened. There was no dissent. It was a microcosm of all he intended to create.

He paused outside the shimmering black door of his study and tapped in the code. The door slid open, and he stepped inside. Two sentroids descended, and he stood still as they scanned him. The door hissed shut, and the sentroids spun off to take up new positions either side of it.

He tapped out a sequence on his vambrace and a dazzling display of numbers and geometric shapes sprang into the air, whirling, dancing, gyrating. Arcs upon arcs, circles within circles; squares, lines, dots and digits, all held in perfect balance. It was a visual symphony of perfect harmony, the blueprint of the life to come, the promise of the future world.

A stool spiraled its way up from the floor, and Gandaw sat upon it with a satisfied sigh. One step closer. Even after all these centuries the desire burned strong. It was the only desire remaining to him, and that's as it should be, he reminded himself. Once you have everything, you have no need for anything else.

He was close. Closer than he'd been in centuries. The dwarf, Maldark, was out of the way, so there'd be no repeat of what happened the last time he'd harnessed the power of Eingana.

The idiot who had two of the other pieces of the statue had gone quiet. At first, their power had been used carelessly, and Gandaw had drawn near. The other piece was with the Templum fleet, on its way to Sahul. The mawgs had been decimated by Maldark's attack and would never be able to take it from so strong a force.

Think, he told himself. *Reason.* Three pieces so close together—so close he could almost touch them. Maybe he didn't have to do anything. After all, the wheels had already been set in motion. Armies were gathering in the vicinity of Sarum, presumably in response to the recent uses of the statue. War was coming, of that you could be certain. From what he had observed of Sahulian emperors, there was no way a Templum force was going to be tolerated on their soil. Conflict was bound to arise, and conflict leads to desperation.

Desperate men make mistakes, Gandaw reasoned, and he'd be watching, biding his time. He'd waited this long; he'd mastered the art of patience. Nothing good came quickly. He could wait as long as it took. After all, he was Sektis Gandaw, the Technocrat; the *Übermensch*, they'd called him during his rise to power on Earth. The *over-man*. They couldn't have been more right.

Man was nothing more than a beast, the biological bi-product of chemical reactions and random fluctuations. Nothing but an ape, and yet to most men, the idea was seldom entertained. To think of themselves as apes was preposterous; but no matter how much higher they considered themselves than primates, humans were always bound to their intrinsic flaws, their status as brutes.

The *Übermensch*, though, he was something more. He wasn't just a development of man, he was over and above him. Humanity was a pitiful laughing stock to him. The *Übermensch* was lord of his own destiny; he was self-made; there was nothing he couldn't do. They had known that and disapproved. Monkeys withholding their consent from a god.

For a moment, Gandaw was struck by the fact that he couldn't remember who "they" were. Machines had preserved his body all these centuries, enhanced his senses, and ensured his survival, but they'd failed to halt the erosion of his memories. Little pieces of his past crumbled away like melting icebergs year after year. He'd saved clusters of them, partitioned them away, sealed the organic memory nodules as best he could, but it was a patchy defense. Huge gaps of emptiness lay between the preserved recollections. If he concentrated hard enough, he could hop from one set of memories to the next as if they were stepping-stones above an abyss, but there was no continuity.

They. He focused on the thought. *Who were they?* And then it came to him with a sharp realization. "They" had been his rivals, all dutifully disposed of. "They" had been the wastrels behind the Global Garden Festival. "They" had been the alternative-lifers, who'd made their last stand in Sahul, or the ignorant Dreamers, who'd rejected his vision and brought about the Reckoning. There had always been a "they" dogging his movements, thwarting his progress, ever since he'd started on the path of perfection. Ever since he'd taken his first steps under the tutelage of Dr. Dee in London, when he'd learnt to scry upon the world of Aethir.

Gandaw stopped as a buried memory burst into consciousness. That was when it had all started, when he'd come to the conclusion that the world was a mess, that it needed fixing. There hadn't been a "they" until that moment. He hadn't been dissatisfied until the whisperings had started.

His head was pounding with the implications, but mercifully, the sedatives kicked in, and he could look at it more objectively.

Everything changed the day the voice had called to him. A voice from somewhere he no longer believed in; refused to accept. Somehow, his scrying activities had aroused the attention of a being trapped in a very dark place. He'd walled the memory off, he realized, beaten it back with the tools of his science.

More drugs surged through his veins, dampening down the rising feeling that he might have been mistaken, might not quite hold all the answers. There had been something back then that science couldn't account for. Not just the rudimentary science of the alchemists of his day, but the science he now worshiped at the altar of.

Another shot of tranquilizers entered his bloodstream. Memories are buried for a reason, he told himself. Especially childish memories of hell and bogeymen. Just part of the collective unconscious, he reminded himself, as his rational mind locked down the hatches against his flawed human nature. That's why everything has to be put right, why the Unweaving needed to happen. Then "they" would thank him for creating a universe that made sense. A universe without skeletons in the cupboard.

Gandaw almost allowed himself a smile. Almost, but not quite. Equanimity had been restored. He was back in control. The *Übermensch*.

But no matter how he tried to deny it, he could still feel the niggling presence of that dark memory haunting the shadows of his awareness. More of a sound than a presence; the muffled echo of the voice that had revealed the existence of the homunculi and opened up to him the possibilities of their technology. It was the voice of his erstwhile mentor, speaking to him from the Abyss. It was the voice of Otto Blightey, the Liche Lord of Verusia.

THE COMING CONFLICT

HADER WATCHED THE plumes of black smoke rolling off of Maldark's boat as flames consumed it, erasing the evidence of the dwarf's regurgitated remains. Tears streaked his scratched and bloodied face. Something about Maldark's ending had touched a nerve, but he couldn't quite put his finger on it. The minute flaming arrows had arced from the Templum flagship he'd gasped and stumbled as if they'd pierced his heart.

The archers had then turned their bows on the surviving mawgs as they'd fled the flames, howling and leaping into the sea. Not a single one had made it back to the reavers. At least that was something to be thankful for. Perhaps Maldark's attack hadn't been completely in vain. His intervention had saved the Templum fleet, but it had still been a failure.

Shader raised his eyes to the spot in the sky where the black hand had appeared and let out a long and anguished cry. The remnants of the *Aura Placida*'s crew turned their heads toward him, but he was beyond caring. Podesta was slumped beneath the mainmast knocking back a bottle of rum. Rivulets of blood ran down the wood, and as Shader watched, a fat glob dropped from the crow's nest to spatter the captain's hat.

"Ship ho!" someone called; someone who was not Elpidio.

Podesta tried to stand, but before he made it to his feet, Cleto tore himself away from the spectacle of flame and strode over to him, followed by the rest of the crew. Shader didn't like the way Cleto was standing with arms folded across his chest, nor the way Podesta had eyes only for the rum. He flicked a look to the sea where a longboat was bobbing toward the *Aura Placida*. He lifted his gaze to the Templum flagship and saw a white-robed figure peering through the smoke like a ghostly sentinel. Shader turned back to Podesta as Cleto barked angry words and a chorus of growled agreements passed through the crew. There were only a score of men left, all of them drawn and looking bloodless. Gutless, Shader thought as he realized what was happening. Sliding the gladius from its scabbard with a ringing scrape he advanced on the mob.

Cleto turned on him and scowled, raising the barrel of an Aeternam weapon and leveling it at Shader's chest. Shader had seen what the weapons could do, but he couldn't have cared less as he stalked toward Cleto. The sailors parted for him, eyes darting uncertainly.

"Stay out of this," Cleto said. "This is crew business and none o' yours."

"Funny that." Shader's voice was a parched whisper that split the air like the crack of a whip. "Seeing as it was you that said I was one of you now. Not just you," he added with a flick of his head toward the crow's nest, "but Elpidio too; and if there's one thing I've learned about you Quilonians, it's that you're—what's the word you use?—democratic. So, whatever business you have with the captain is my business, too."

Cleto tensed, his finger twitching over the weapon's trigger. Shader pressed on until the barrel was touching his chest, directly over his heart. He opened his mouth to yell at

Cleto, tell him to do it, but before a sound came out Podesta lurched to his feet and stumbled, steadying himself with one hand on the mast.

"Bravely done, my friend." He wagged the bottle in Shader's direction. Podesta's eyes were swollen and bloodshot. He forced his lips into a wide grin, but the rest of his face didn't comply. "Cleto's right," he said. "Captain's job is to protect his crew, not lead them into slaughter. I... I... caused this." He swept the bottle around to encompass the bloodstained decks. "My obsession. My fear."

Cleto lowered the barrel of his weapon and turned his eyes on the captain. Podesta met his gaze with a forlorn nod.

"I was just a kid," Podesta's voice quavered and tears fell freely down his cheeks. "Just a boy, like Elpidio, when they came. Blood in the water," his voice cracked. "Blood, blood, blood..."

Shader sheathed his blade and went to embrace him, but Podesta drew back.

"I failed you," Podesta said to the remnants of his crew. "And for that I will be forever sorry."

He removed his tricorn, rubbed at the spatter of blood, and handed it to Cleto.

"She's yours now." He slapped the mainmast. "Treat her well, Captain."

Cleto accepted the hat and wiped something from his eye as Podesta turned away and staggered toward the cabins.

"But what—?" Shader started to ask.

Cleto interrupted him. "Don't you worry about him. We'll see he's all right, won't we, lads?"

"Aye, Captain." The sailors saluted him.

Cleto fixed Shader with a narrow-eyed stare. "And what about you? What happens now?"

Shader was spared from answering by a shout of "Ho!" from behind.

The *Aura Placida*'s crew turned to look toward port where a head was poking above the rails. For an instant, Shader didn't register the clipped gray hair, the chiseled face, and the stiff deportment as the man climbed aboard. Chainmail sparkled in the resurgent sunlight, and the red Monas symbol seemed to have burst and spilled its own blood across the once white surcoat.

"The least you could do is salute, soldier," Ignatius Grymm, grand master of the Elect, said.

Shader's eyes filled with tears, but whether it was from the shock of seeing his old commander or from the losses he'd suffered, he could not say. He was awhirl with unnamable emotions and could only stare blankly back. Ignatius cocked his head, a look of concern passing across his blood-streaked face. Shader dropped to his knees and bowed his head. He could think of nothing else to do.

***

"His Divinity is very impressed with your actions," Ignatius said, leaning with his back to the rail as the Templum flagship rode the waves. "Personally, I thought it was suicidal."

Shader searched Ignatius' eyes for any hint of a reprimand, but all he saw was the sparkle of fondness. It did nothing to quell the conflict raging within him. If anything it just increased his guilt at deserting the Elect.

"I suppose it was in the spirit of the Order," Shader said. "Give no quarter and all that."

Ignatius clapped him on the back. "Oh, yes. I'm sure songs will be written about it. The lone knight taking on a hundred mawgs."

"More like a thousand," Shader said with a half-hearted chuckle.

"A million, then." Ignatius was watching him like a concerned parent. "Might as well save the poets the trouble of exaggerating the tale."

Shader dipped his head, grasping the rail and staring into the sea. "Only, I wasn't alone," he said as the faces of Sabas, Elpidio, and Osric flashed before his mind's eye. "And it wasn't even my idea to attack."

"Yes," Ignatius said, turning to join Shader's study of the waves. "What on earth possessed the captain to such an act of valor? Hardly the sort of behavior you'd expect from a smuggler."

"You know he smuggles for the Templum, don't you?" Shader said.

Ignatius chewed his top lip, his brows furrowing in thought. Finally, he pushed away from the rail and straightened his surcoat with a sharp tug. "A good man, nevertheless. Brave. Fearless."

Shader lifted his eyes to the horizon half expecting, half wishing to see the *Aura Placida* racing toward them. Ain only knew where Cleto would take the crew. Some port no doubt where they could make repairs. Shader had felt like he was watching the slow death of an old friend as the carrack limped away.

"He was terrified," Shader said. "The mawgs tore his crew apart when he was a kid. He was so scared he did the only thing he could: he faced his demons head on."

Ignatius was nodding his understanding.

"The only problem was," Shader continued, "he dragged the crew into his own nightmare. I don't suppose they'll ever forgive him." He couldn't see how they could; not with so many of their friends among the dead.

Shader winced as he pictured Elpidio's face again, and then his thoughts turned to Osric. Poor doomed Osric. Shader didn't know whether to be relieved that Osric's curse had been lifted, that he'd finally found the peace of death. He felt an icy knotting in his stomach, as if all his hopes, all his Nousian beliefs, were being sucked into a void at its center. Araboth. Shader shook his head with bitter recollection of his time in the illusory realm. That's where Osric should be now, but something about that last desperate look the wraith had given him told Shader there was no heavenly paradise waiting for him. It had been a look of utter horror, as if, at the last, Osric had glimpsed the madness of the Abyss, or worse still, the absolute emptiness of the Void.

He started at a tap on his shoulder and looked up into Ignatius' gray eyes.

"His Divinity is here," the grand master said, dropping to one knee.

Shader did the same as the Ipsissimus, accompanied by a black-clad exemptus in a red biretta, approached. The exemptus hobbled ahead, tapping the deck with a walking stick. His cheeks wobbled as he walked, and his paunch rippled beneath his robes. Shader recognized him from his consecration, and from that fateful day at the tournament.

"Deacon Shader, knight of the Elect," Exemptus Cane said through a spray of spittle. "Keeper of the Sword of the Archon." Cane looked pointedly at the gladius scabbarded at Shader's hip and then shuffled around to indicate the Ipsissimus.

Shader couldn't help staring. There was something different about the ruler of the Templum: he no longer had the pallor of death about him. His face shone with a vitality that matched the sparkle of his eyes, and he seemed taller somehow, less emaciated. The hair beneath his biretta was brown with a healthy sheen, whereas before it had been as gray as his bloodless face.

"Bend your knee and bow your head before His Divinity, the Infallible Ruler of the Nousian Theocracy, the Supreme…"

"They're already kneeling, Cane," the Ipsissimus said, "and their heads are bowed. I think we can safely say they know who I am, so please, let's not go through all that pomp and ceremony."

"But, but, but…" Cane's jowls shook, but he sealed his lips and dropped his chin to his chest at a withering look from the Ipsissimus.

"Please stand, Deacon Shader," the Ipsissimus said, holding out his hand.

Shader rose and planted a kiss on the Ipsissimus's golden ring. His eyes flicked to the gleaming Monas hanging above the white robe, its single amber eye glinting as if it held a miniature sun at its center.

"You have my thanks," the Ipsissimus said. "And my forgiveness. No one has ever left the Elect before, particularly with the Sword of the Archon, but your actions today have more than atoned for that little… blip."

The Ipsissimus threw an arm around Shader's shoulders as if they were old friends and led him away from Cane and Ignatius. They received some strange looks from the crew and the scores of battle-weary knights who stood to attention as they passed.

The Ipsissimus pulled open the door to a large cabin and gestured for Shader to enter. Shader cast a look back at Ignatius, but the grand master merely shrugged.

"It's quite all right," the Ipsissimus said. "I was going to offer you a drink."

Shader ducked inside the doorway. He was a little disoriented by the absence of gold and crystal, velvet drapery, and artistic masterpieces he'd come to expect from the highest echelons of the Templum. Instead, he was confronted with a low bed without a mattress, a single threadbare sheet, a chipped and scratched wooden chair that looked as if it would collapse if a cat leapt on it, and an upturned crate upon which stood a carved Monas, a burned-down candle, and a prayer cord. A string line had been tied across the back wall, and from this hung a couple of pristine white robes and a stained and patched nightshirt.

"Can't stand all the tawdry trappings that are supposed to go with the Office," the Ipsissimus said, easing past Shader and stooping to reach under the bed. "Have to go along with it in Aeterna, but here—" He stood with a bottle of wine and a couple of goblets clutched to his chest. "—here things are a little more as Ain prefers, don't you think?"

Shader stuck out his bottom lip and nodded.

"Oh, don't say anything," the Ipsissimus said, setting the bottle and glasses on the deck and feeling around under the bed until he located a corkscrew. "I know your type quite well; I know the sort of judgments you've secretly been making."

Shader opened his mouth to protest, but the Ipsissimus jabbed the corkscrew in his direction and continued.

"I've done it myself," he said. "Still do, as a matter of fact, Ain forgive me. Only the other day I made scurrilous remarks about dear old Exemptus Silvanus. Unforgivable comments, egocentrically critical and unbefitting a Nousian. Actually, since you've been kind enough to join me, would you be so good as to hear my confession?"

Shader took an involuntary step back and gave a little cough.

"But, Divinity, I'm not a priest."

"Ah, pshaw!" the Ipsissimus said. "You're a Nousian, aren't you? Nothing in the Liber that says you have to be a priest."

"But Templum Law, Divinity…"

"I'm Ipsissimus. Templum Law is whatever I say, isn't that so?"

Shader stiffened and swallowed. The Ipsissimus was watching him intently through narrowed eyes. A long silence ensued and then suddenly the Ipsissimus doubled up with laughter. Shader was too stunned to react, but the Ipsissimus's mirth continued, hands weakly slapping his thighs and head bobbing. His laughter grew shrill as he drew closer to the floor, his legs wobbling until he dropped to his knees. Tears rolled down his cheeks, and his breath came in stutters as if he were sobbing.

"Forgive me." He waved a hand at Shader. "I shouldn't have, but you looked so serious."

A high-pitched hoot escaped him, and Shader felt his cheeks tighten. The edges of his mouth curled, and then he could contain it no longer. He spluttered and sprayed spittle as a laugh burst forth, and then he was giggling with the Ipsissimus as he offered a hand and helped the old man up. Only, he wasn't old anymore. If he hadn't known better, and if it hadn't been for the eyes, Shader would have thought him a man in his thirties. The Ipsissimus must have seen the expression on his face.

"I succumbed," he said, touching the gilt Monas around his neck. Its amber eye glinted, and Shader felt a reciprocal purr from his gladius. "Such is the way of power." He looked momentarily older as his face creased with concern. "It disguises itself as a need or a means to an end. It has a strategy for all of us, and in my case, it convinced me that I was necessary in this coming war."

The Ipsissimus sighed and seated himself on the floor, gesturing for Shader to join him. He picked up the bottle and the corkscrew and flicked his eyes from the sheathed gladius to Shader's eyes.

"I know the names of every crewman on this ship," the Ipsissimus said, "and every Elect knight on board. It's no easy feat." The cork popped free, and the Ipsissimus poured a little wine into a glass and passed it to Shader. "I developed a system, a sort of memory game, where I think of something each person reminds me of and then store the image away in an imaginary castle up here." He tapped his temples. "It works pretty well up to a point, but it has finite capacity. Once I get above a certain number, I start to forget those I started with. How's the wine?"

"Excellent, Divinity, thank you." It was the truth, but even if it hadn't been, what else could he have said to the ruler of the Templum?

The Ipsissimus filled his own glass and then topped Shader up. "The crew." He raised his glass. "I remembered all their names, every single one of them, but then the mawgs attacked us, and now I can't recall the names of the dead. How do you explain that?"

"How many did you lose, Divinity?" Shader's mind was filled with the bloody faces of crewmen from the *Aura Placida* whose names he'd never known. He'd barely even acknowledged many of them. He sipped some wine and closed his eyes as his stomach knotted.

"Fifty-three on this ship." The Ipsissimus's voice was almost a whisper. They're still counting the survivors on the others, but with the sunken ships, we must have lost close to a thous…" The Ipsissimus took a long gulp of wine and gave a weak smile. "But you suffered losses too. Friends among them."

Shader's eyes brimmed with tears, but he didn't look away.

The Ipsissimus reached over and held his hand. "There is more suffering to come. Much more."

Shader nodded. How could it be otherwise? He could feel the walls of fate closing in around him, its cogs and wheels grinding inexorably, deaf to all appeals.

"I am sorry, Deacon Shader," the Ipsissimus said, "but you are at the center of what's happening. Don't ask me why, but Ain has placed you here for this very purpose."

Shader's eyes narrowed. "How do you know?" He didn't include the customary "Divinity", but the Ipsissimus showed no sign that he was bothered.

"Oh, there's no mystical explanation." The Ipsissimus released Shader's hand and took another sip of wine. "I was told some time ago, but I never paid it much notice. Now, however, after what I saw you achieve during the battle with the mawgs, I'm starting to realize they spoke the truth."

"Who?" Shader gripped his glass so tight that he half expected it to shatter.

"Aristodeus," the Ipsissimus said, "and…"

"And me," Huntsman said as his spirit shimmered into view.

The Dreamer had the look of a vulture about him as his leathery face craned toward

Shader on a spiny neck. At first, it seemed as if he'd sprouted wings and drawn them about his sinewy body, but then Shader realized it was the cloak of feathers. Huntsman's sharp eyes studied him, lids twitching, lips curling in the slightest hint of a sneer. Shader held his gaze, but had the uncomfortable feeling that, by doing so, he was giving far too much away. He felt the vein in his temple pulsating and pinched the bridge of his nose to relieve the tension building in his head.

Huntsman ruffled his feathers with a whiplash motion and swiveled his head to regard the Ipsissimus. Shader was on his feet in an instant, the gladius scraping and ringing as he drew it. Huntsman hissed and glared, a clawed hand emerging from beneath his cloak and making clutching movements in the air.

"Sit down, Shader," the Ipsissimus said. "Sit down. He's merely a spirit. And besides, he's a friend."

Shader obeyed without question, sliding the sword back into its scabbard and resuming his cross-legged position on the floor. His eyes remained fixed to the Dreamer's, though, and he fancied that he saw a glint of triumph in Huntsman's eyes. Huntsman's hand withdrew beneath the cloak of feathers, and he offered the Ipsissimus a thin-lipped smile.

This wasn't right, Shader told himself. The Ipsissimus of the Templum and a heathen sorcerer in the same room together. What if Huntsman had ill intentions? No one should come so close to the Ipsissimus. *Not even me*, he realized.

"Forgive him, my friend," the Ipsissimus said to Huntsman. "It's how they're trained."

Huntsman bowed his acceptance. "My people train dogs same way."

The Ipsissimus lowered his eyes and touched his fingertips together. "I have nothing but respect for my Elect," he said with careful clarity. "The sacrifice they make, the paradox they embody, allows the rest of us to live the ideal. Fighting for love is no simple matter of conditioning."

Huntsman's eyes widened with what might have been amusement, and then he dropped into a crouch opposite the Ipsissimus.

"You are wise my friend, but Sahul trembles; Eingana remembers. Once before, fate of all worlds was entrusted to such as he." Huntsman flicked his head in Shader's direction. "Fallen one, Maldark, was first to betray goddess. His actions are cursed throughout Dreaming. It is told that even his own people have withdrawn below ground out of shame.

I no longer trust this philosopher's plan. Much he does not tell us. His ways are not Sahul's ways. They cannot help Eingana."

Shader stiffened at the mention of Maldark. The dwarf had been afflicted with inconsolable guilt; whatever he'd done, he'd believed himself beyond redemption. Was that why he'd drawn the mawgs to himself? Had it been a despairing attempt at expiation? Shader couldn't accept that theory. There'd been something about Maldark's attack on the reavers, a purpose, a desperation to break through the mawg ships and to reach the Templum fleet. Whatever the motivation for Maldark's last battle, it certainly hadn't been suicide.

"Maldark was no fool," Shader said, staring at the deck.

"His actions in world of Dreaming were..." Huntsman's face contorted with the effort of finding the right word. "How do you say it?" He looked at the Ipsissimus. "Desecration. Yes, his actions were a desecration. Shall I tell you what he did?"

"Maldark was no fool," Shader repeated through clenched teeth.

The Ipsissimus touched the gilt Monas around his neck and looked from Shader to Huntsman. "Maldark?"

"Fallen," Huntsman spat. "Betrayer of gods; blight of Dreaming."

"My friend," Shader said. "And I will not listen to another disparaging word about

355

him. Understood?"

Huntsman glowered, but said no more. The Ipsissimus lifted his glass to his lips and took a sip of wine. "Tell me about him, Shader."

Shader reached for his own glass. He half-expected images to leap into mind, images of shared times, of camaraderie and laughter, but when he thought about Maldark, nothing came. The only recollections of the dwarf he had were of fighting: Maldark driving off the mawgs in the dilapidated house in Sarum; battling back to back against the undead knights of the Lost; standing shoulder to shoulder as the roiling horror of the Dweller burst into the Templum. Shader's mind replayed the bloody savagery of the reavers' attack and the moment of hope that had accompanied Maldark's arrival. He searched in vain for some other memory, something to match the fondness he felt for the dwarf, something to compensate for his loss. His only reward was the vision of a sea of swirling blood and carrion birds swooping down to peck at his friend's disgorged remains spilling out into the ocean.

"He was," Shader started, but couldn't find the words. "We were…" The realization struck him like lightning, leaving Shader with a feeling of nakedness so absolute he was certain the Ipsissimus and Huntsman could see into the deepest recesses of his soul; could expose him for the fraud he was. "We are the same."

"Hah!" Huntsman said with a sharp clap of his hands. "I told you so. Aristodeus cannot be trusted. His arrogance is bait for trap, and his ways are hateful to Sahul."

The Ipsissimus held up his hand for silence and studied Shader with eyes the blue of the winter sky over Latia. A dewy film coated them, dulled and deepened them, evoking the image of a glacial sea.

"This Maldark…" The Ipsissimus's voice was little more than the distant fracturing of ice. "He was the one in the boat that came to our aid?"

Shader nodded.

"He wore a white cloak like the Elect, but it bore a cross rather than a Monas," the Ipsissimus said. "Was he a Nousian?"

Shader shook his head. "I don't think so. I wanted to ask him about that, but there was never time. He mentioned—forgive me, Divinity— he mentioned God."

The Ipsissimus closed his eyes, his brow creasing. "He was clearly a warrior, and akin to our Elect. How can this be? The cross indicates he could not be one of them, and besides, he was… he was…"

"Too small?" Shader gulped down the last of his wine.

"Well, uh…" The Ipsissimus's head was bobbing as he struggled for the right thing to say.

"He was a dwarf of Dreaming," Huntsman said, as if that cleared things up.

Shader turned his eyes on the shaman. "How do you know this?"

Huntsman spread his arms and turned his palms upwards. "It is my business to know."

"It's a place." The Ipsissimus uncrossed his legs and rubbed his knee. "The Dreaming. Aristodeus refers to it as Aethir. I used to think it was a visionary thing, like inscape or… or…"

"A hallucination?" Huntsman gave a sour look. "My friend, we Dreamers know how you civilized folk regard us, but it is no matter. Your self-deception safeguards our knowledge and we are thankful for that. Dreaming is real, though it is not like this world. It is home of my gods, though they are exiled from it. It is also home to dwarves and all other creatures of Sektis Gandaw."

"The Dreaming is Sektis Gandaw's world?" Shader said.

Huntsman shook his head. "Sektis Gandaw is from this world. It is said he fled to Dreaming long before flowering of Ancients' civilization." Huntsman hawked and spat. "It is also said that he returned and made that accursed society. From his black mountain in Dead Lands of Dreaming, he sent out harvesters to bring back humans from Earth. He worked dark magic on them, joining them together, shaping them."

"To what end?" the Ipsissimus asked.

"My gods say he sought perfection. Each time he did not succeed, he cast out his failures and tried a new path. After much time, he gave up. Things of this world not good enough for him. He set about work of Unweaving instead, unmaking of all there is, so he could begin again. To do so, he needed power beyond any that comes from this world. He needed Eingana."

"A being of the Supernal Realm," the Ipsissimus said. "One of the three who fell through the Void."

"Mother of dog-head," Huntsman said. "He who made Dreaming. Father of my gods."

"But Maldark." Shader rubbed his forehead and frowned. "His cloak, the red cross, his God. How—?"

"Ain once had many names," the Ipsissimus said. "Just don't tell Exemptus Silvanus I said that. If Sektis Gandaw was bringing people from Earth, their knowledge, their culture would find a footing in the Dreaming. Perhaps you should tell us about these dwarves, Huntsman. It may help us to—"

The air beside Huntsman rippled, and a boy appeared. He was naked except for a loincloth. His skin was streaked with ochre, his fair hair wound into dusty dreadlocks.

"Sammy!" Shader rocked back on his haunches and stood.

The boy looked at him askance and then addressed Huntsman. "I can't find her. The ants say there's no sign."

Shader's heart flew to his throat. "Find who? Sammy, who are you talking about?"

The boy turned on him, tears streaking his begrimed face. "Rhiannon. I can't find Rhiannon."

Shader's hand covered his mouth, and he reeled. How could he have forgotten her? He glared at Huntsman, recalling that it was the shaman's machinations that had pulled them apart. His and Aristodeus'. "What's happened?" It was an accusation. "Where is she?"

Huntsman's joints cracked as he regained his feet. "There was a battle in Sarum. Terrible battle. Dead walked. Many were killed."

"No!" Sammy said. "She's not dead. I know it."

Huntsman placed a hand on the boy's head. "And I believe you. Trust your feelings."

"Then why can't I find her?" Sammy asked.

Huntsman's eyes flicked to Shader and then the Ipsissimus. "Some places Sahul cannot see. Blind spots. Things unnatural. Such was Sarum during plague. I return with you, Samuel. We look in web for empty spaces. Gain some knowledge."

"But…" Shader started.

Huntsman took Sammy's hand in his, and the air began to shimmer. He turned to the Ipsissimus as their bodies began to fade.

"Yours only piece not in enemy hands. It must not be lost. Our best hope is in unity. You must join with Hagalle and march to Homestead. With might of my gods it may be we can keep it from Sektis Gandaw and this necromancer."

The boy and the shaman vanished.

Shader spun to stare at the golden Monas hanging around the Ipsissimus's neck. Its single amber eye glinted, and Shader slapped himself on the forehead. He should have known. It was identical to the Gray Abbot's Monas—the one he'd failed to return.

"You," he said. "Maldark was coming to aid you, to protect the Monas from the mawgs."

The Ipsissimus held out a hand for Shader to help him up. "It does seem likely." He appeared to have aged again, his face now gray and haunted. "But enough speculation. We should make ready."

Shader wanted to ask what for, but he already knew. *You must be whole again*, the Archon had said. *The Ipsissimus is coming for the final battle, and he will need you.*

The Ipsissimus held the cabin door open. The salty spray from outside seemed suddenly like venom.

"Nice name, by the way," the Ipsissimus said as Shader slipped past him.

"Sorry?"

Ignatius Grymm was coming down the deck toward Shader, palms upturned to ask how it had gone. Shader's mind was a confusion of emotions. The Ipsissimus's bright eyes anchored him for an instant.

"Rhiannon."

The name struck Shader like a condemnation. His lips started to move in reply, but then the discipline of the confessional kicked in, and he said nothing.

The Ipsissimus gave the slightest of nods and started to pull the door to. "Speaking of nice names," he said, peeking through the crack, "did Investigator Shin catch up with you?"

Shader just looked at him, dumbfounded.

"Bardol Shin?" The Ipsissimus shook his head. "Of the Templum Judiciary? No? Never mind. Doubt you'd remember, even if he did, what with all this commotion. Ain be with you."

"And with your—"

But the door had already closed.

THE EMPEROR'S RULE

HAGALLE STOOD WITH his back to the wall as the other men in Zara Gen's office congregated around a globe drinks cabinet and pretended an interest in the map on its surface. Snippets of conversation reached his ears, but much of it was drowned out by the nagging voices within.

"—no idea how it got here," Zara Gen was saying. "I'm sure I saw one just like it in Councilor Arkin's office."

Duke Farian guffawed and clapped him on the back. "Very good, Governor," he said. "Very good."

"I'm sorry?" Zara Gen said.

"Worth a bloody fortune, you old scoundrel." Farian gave the Governor a jab with his elbow. "And that's without all the booze." The Duke stooped over the globe and ran his finger across the surface of a continent. "Do you know, I think this is an original Waldseemüller gore—either that or a bloody good copy. This would have been an antique for the Ancients. Look here—layers of printed paper, each meticulously prepared and pasted onto the sphere. Every gore," Farian droned on, "has a width of 30° of longitude—"

Master Frayn opened the lid and peered inside, eyes rolling like a glutted viper's. "So, gentlemen," he said, as if he were their equal. "What's your poison?"

Farian coughed and crossed his arms, rubbing his chin with his thumb and forefinger. "Must I remind you—?"

Hagalle knew they were glancing in his direction. His lips felt dry and cracked, and there was no saliva in his mouth. His heart was sending little shudders through his chest and rippling his shirt. He saw Frayn close the globe and perch on the edge of Zara Gen's desk. Farian whispered something in the Governor's ear, and Zara Gen nodded gravely. The Duke then pointedly moved the roll of maps he'd deposited on the desk away from Frayn's backside.

It's too darned hot in here, Hagalle thought, turning to open the curtain, and then thinking better of it. He fanned his face with his hand, all the while watching the recesses of the office out of the corner of his eye. *Too darned dark, too.* He shot Farian a look. The Duke caught it and muttered something to Zara Gen, who then stooped to speak in Frayn's ear.

The Sicarii slipped from his perch and crossed the room on the balls of his feet, treading as lightly as a dancer. Hagalle's eyes followed the glint of steel from the ball-pommel of the dagger sheathed at his hip. Frayn fiddled with the valve on the lantern hanging from its elaborate stand beside the door. The circle of its orange light brightened, but still didn't reach the corners.

Thump!

Hagalle started, his hand going to his chest.

Knock, knock.

He closed his eyes and took a deep breath. *About time, too*, he thought. *Let's get this over with and get these people out of my sight. By the gods, it's stuffy in here.*

Frayn got the door, standing behind it as it opened. General Starn bumbled his way into the office, puffing out his red cheeks. His eyes were bulging from his head as he made a show of wondering how the door had opened by itself. Frayn stepped into view when he shut the door and Starn raised a finger in mock admonition, grunting and coughing beneath his mustache.

Hagalle pushed away from the wall and Starn came to attention, clicking his boot heels and thumping his chest. He was as ramrod as he could be with such a curved spine and large gut. He looked like a comedy soldier, all stiff and starchy, but with a roly-poly edge to him. If he hadn't known better, Hagalle would have retired the man as an embarrassment.

Hardly the image to put the fear of the gods in the foe; but looks weren't everything. Starn had proven that at the Battle of Sarum.

"General Starn." Hagalle clasped his hands behind his back. He towered above the little man and found himself wishing Starn wouldn't keep lowering his eyes.

"Emperor!" Starn barked in a voice that sounded like he'd got mustache hair stuck in his throat.

"You know why you're here?"

Starn's cheeks grew redder. His eyes flicked up to the level of Hagalle's chest and then fell back to the floor. "I'll do better, my Emperor. You have my word on it."

Frayn resumed his lolling at the edge of the desk, and Zara Gen hovered behind his chair as if he wanted to sit, but didn't dare while Hagalle was standing. Farian loomed at Hagalle's shoulder, but was easily driven back by a glare.

"Better how?" Hagalle asked, taking a step toward Starn and glowering down at him.

"W-W-Well." Starn's jowls trembled. "Hrruh, hmm. I-I-I…"

"Careful, General," Hagalle said. "You're starting to sound egotistical." That was the word, wasn't it? Hagalle was sure that's what that bald sod Aristodeus had once called him.

To Hagalle's astonishment, Starn dropped to his knees and bowed his head further, as if he were intending to kiss Hagalle's boots.

"Forgive me, Emperor. I… Well… Mrs. Starn… I mean…"

Hagalle stooped and laid a hand on the general's shoulder. "No," he said. "You forgive me, General Starn. Forgive me for underestimating you; forgive me for ridiculing you. Your actions during the battle were…" Hagalle felt a lump in his throat and his eyes grew moist. He forced a cough and nodded to the drinks globe. "Master Frayn, would you do the honors?"

"Emperor," Frayn said as he dashed across the room and opened the globe.

"Whiskey," Hagalle said. "And you, General?"

Starn clambered to his feet, dusted himself down, and then tugged his uniform jacket straight.

"Well, uh, most kind, Emperor." He cast a look at Frayn. "Don't suppose you have a brown ale? No? Uhm, well, a stiff brandy then, what."

"Governor?" Frayn said. "Your Grace?"

Farian wandered over to look for himself, but Zara Gen waved away the offer of a drink. Hagalle studied him for a second and narrowed his eyes. *What's Gen up to? Trying to impress me with his austerity?* Hagalle scoffed and switched his attention back to Starn.

"When we return to Jorakum, General, I intend to have you properly honored."

Starn clasped his hands over his belly and gave a little bow.

"In the meantime, anything you want, anything at all, it's yours." Hagalle was regretting every bad word he'd said about Starn. He only wished he had more men like him; men you could rely on in a tight spot; men who'd never stab you in the back.

Frayn passed Hagalle his whiskey. Hagalle grimaced and set the glass to one side. Suddenly, he wasn't thirsty any more.

"Anything, Emperor?" Starn's eyes widened with hope or desire.

"Absolutely, General. You name it. A new horse, finer armor—you must admit you need a new breastplate!"

Starn laughed dutifully and accepted a glass from Frayn, taking an appreciative sip.

"What I would like, Emperor, more than anything…"

"Yes," Hagalle said. "Go on."

"…is to see my wife."

Hagalle stared at him open-mouthed. For a moment, his mind was blank.

Starn went on. "An early discharge, Emperor. I'm getting too old for this. I … I miss Mrs. Starn…"

"Out of the question," Hagalle snapped. "How dare you even suggest such a thing!" He turned and rolled his eyes at Farian, who tutted and shook his head. "This is hardly the time, General Starn. Hardly the time. With the news our scouts have just brought, you think my most senior general should be leaving?"

Starn fumbled his glass, spilling a little brandy on his jacket as he caught it. "Forgive me, Emperor."

Hagalle sighed and fixed his glare on Zara Gen. "Oh, sit down, Governor! You're making me nervous with your loitering."

Zara Gen lowered himself into his chair and twiddled his ponytail.

Hagalle ground his teeth and then addressed Farian. "Is the boy here?"

"Outside, Emperor," Farian said. "Shall I?"

Hagalle clicked his fingers, and Starn opened the door. The bumbling dolt poked his head outside and beckoned.

Barek Thomas shuffled into the room, his sandy hair recently washed and combed by the look of it. He still wore the white surcoat of his Order, but it was becoming threadbare, and he'd been unable to disguise the bloodstains. Hagalle's eyes flicked to Barek's empty scabbard and then to the youth's face. Something had altered—the tilt of the chin, the glint of the eyes in the lamp light. There was an altogether different air about the young knight from the nervous, pleading boy who'd shaken when he'd knelt before Hagalle asking for help. Hagalle fought to keep himself from sneering at the memory. Infernal impudence. As if he, the emperor of Sahul, needed some raggedy Nousian to rouse him to the defense of one of his own cities. Hagalle's eyes drank in the youth's poise: shoulders back, chest high, heels neatly pressed together. He raised an eyebrow and looked from Starn back to Barek. That's what had changed: the boy had bearing; he'd come to himself. He knew he'd done well at the battle. More than that, Hagalle bit his lip, the lad had saved his life and was bloody well expecting to be rewarded for it.

Barek started to say something, but was cut off by Starn putting fist to mouth and coughing. Hagalle caught himself scowling and swiftly manufactured a smile.

"Thank you, Mr. Thomas. Thank you for coming." His tone was measured and amiable, and he noted the lad relaxed in response. "Forgive me, Barek, but I'm not sure of your military title. Perhaps you could…" Hagalle made a winding gesture with his hand.

"Emperor." Barek dropped to one knee and bowed. "It is an honor. I am…"

Starn coughed again and put a hand on Barek's elbow to help him stand. The fat fool then whispered in Barek's ear.

"Sorry," Barek said, looking down at Hagalle's boots. "I am now Master of the White Order."

Hagalle inclined his head. "Master? Remind me, General Starn, do we have 'Masters' in the Sahulian army?"

"No, Emperor," Starn said. "Only one master, and that's your Imperial Highness. Other than that we have—"

"Thank you, General, that will do," Hagalle said, his cheeks starting to feel numb from all the smiling. "So, Master Barek, there are titular differences in our respective forces. Different worlds, different ways, don't you agree?"

"Oh, yes, Emperor," Barek started enthusiastically and then ran out of steam. He was glancing furtively from side to side.

"A man cannot serve two masters, Barek, surely you can see that." Hagalle took a step toward him and used his height to cow the lad. "Oh, I'm sure we could come up with a new title for the leader of the White Order, but what would be the point? The puppet-master would still remain." Hagalle smiled internally this time as Barek looked up with eyes as wide as saucers. Hagalle wagged his finger from side to side in a gesture of mock admonition. "You are either for the emperor of Sahul or for Nousia. You can't have it both ways."

"Emperor," Zara Gen said, standing. "Forgive my interruption, but did you not say this young man saved you during...?"

Hagalle held up a finger without even looking at the Governor. He waited until he heard the muffled thud of Zara Gen resuming his seat.

"Truly," Hagalle said, turning away from Barek and wandering over to the window, where he peered through the crack of the curtains. "I am grateful for your intervention. There's no doubt you are a brave man. Honorable even. But even the best of us can labor under deception."

"My Emperor," Barek said. "I am loyal to Sahul. My spiritual practices..."

"Are utterly incompatible with my will," Hagalle said in as nonchalant a tone as he could manage. "And besides—" He spun and glared at the knight. "—how do you account for the presence of a large Templum Fleet in Sahulian waters?"

"Emperor?" The lad's jaw hung slack and he glanced around the room for enlightenment or support.

Zara Gen was looking at his hands clasped atop the desk. General Starn seemed to have found something interesting on the carpet, and Master Frayn was positively statuesque.

"A coincidence?" Hagalle asked. "A new Order dressed like the Templum Elect rides to Sarum, butchers my soldiers, and then shows up at a key stage of the battle with a vast Templum force closing in from the sea. Oh, I have no doubt your presence helped turn the tide. General Starn here commended your intervention in his report, and I remain grateful for the ride away from the thick of it. In fact, that's why you're still alive. If I didn't owe you my gratitude, I'd have had the remnants of your Order burned at the stake as a warning to your Templum despot.

"I want to give you a chance, Barek. You're of Sahulian stock, so there's still hope for you. General Starn will have you escorted to the old militia barracks where you and your men will do some serious reflecting. I look forward to whatever decision you make in the next few days. Goodbye."

Starn ushered the lad outside, where Hagalle noted with satisfaction a contingent of imperial troops was ready to lock him in chains. The rest of the Order would have been arrested while they spoke.

"And now to the other matter." Hagalle clapped his hands and shot a broad grin at Zara Gen.

The Governor looked up and the color drained from his face. "The matter of the enemy within, Governor Gen?"

Zara Gen pushed himself upright and tugged at his ponytail. "My Emperor, I can assure you that I am utterly loyal. My family has served the Zaneish dynasty faithfully…"

"I know, I know, I know," Hagalle said. "Why does everyone take things so personally?"

Zara Gen lowered himself back into his chair, but his eyes never left Hagalle's.

"I was referring," Hagalle said, "to the Nousian menace that you have allowed to flourish in Sarum: the Templum of the Knot. Yes," he forestalled Zara Gen's unborn protest, "I know you think they were a boon during the plague, but do you not recall that saying of the Ancients, Governor? Wolves in sheep's clothing, I think it was. What better way of lulling us into a false sense of security while Daddy sets sail from Aeterna. What do you suppose their real function is, eh? To open the metaphorical gates while the city sleeps?"

"Emperor—" Zara Gen was back on his feet and leaning over the desk. The color had returned to his face, it was now as red as his robes. "—forgive me, but this is preposterous!"

"Really?" Hagalle said.

At that instant, Master Frayn's hand snaked out and grabbed Zara Gen by the neck. The Governor's eyes bulged, and he flapped his arms around uselessly. Frayn reached inside Zara Gen's robe with his free hand and withdrew a glittering silver Monas on a slender chain. With a sharp yank, he broke the chain and handed the symbol to Hagalle.

Frayn released Zara Gen, who sank into his chair with his head in his hands.

"I have eyes and ears everywhere, Governor Gen," Hagalle said. "Were you really so naive as to think your little visit from the most notorious Nousian in Sahul would go unnoticed? How long have we known, Master Frayn?"

"Riders were sent to Jorakum the instant Jarmin the Anchorite set foot in Arnbrook House, Emperor," the Sicarii said with a smirk. "We were just awaiting your order to take care of the priests."

Hagalle narrowed his eyes. The idiot wasn't supposed to have mentioned that in front of Zara Gen. Frayn licked his lips and started fiddling with his ridiculous oiled mustache.

"A good thing for you that our families have such a long history of mutual support, Zara Gen," Hagalle said. "I'm sure I don't have to say any more. Duke Farian will assume your duties. You are free to go—for now. Don't stray beyond the city limits. And, Zara Gen, we are watching."

Zara Gen slipped out of his office scarcely daring to breathe. The instant the door shut behind him, Farian sat behind his desk, and Hagalle turned his mind to the next problem.

"You may leave, Master Frayn. And in the future, be more careful with your choice of words."

"Emperor," Frayn said, before giving an ostentatious bow.

"Oh, and Master Frayn," Hagalle said. "Any news on Cadman?"

"Our best trackers are onto it, Emperor. Believe me, there's nowhere he can hide. He'll be dead by morning, along with those priests."

Hagalle nodded and waited for Frayn to leave the room. "So, Farian," he thumped the palm of his hand. "What are we going to do about this invasion?"

The instant the words left his mouth, Hagalle had a revelation. How could he have been so blind? The priests, the White Order, and the coming of the Templum fleet. Throughout all that had happened, there was one common denominator, a ringleader. How could he have dismissed all those reports of a Nousian knight showing up in the provinces and training the local youths? A man who'd apparently spent time at Pardes under the nefarious Gray Abbot; a man dressed in the attire of the Templum Elect and sworn to absolute obedience to the Ipsissimus.

"Farian," Hagalle said in a voice barely above a whisper. "I want men patrolling the streets, scouring the inns, walking the docks. Put the word out. I want this Deacon Shader brought to me. I don't care if he's dead or alive, but I want him. Is that understood?"

"Deacon Shader," Farian confirmed. "I'll alert the militia and reassign a troop of our own men. Should I inform the Sicarii?"

Hagalle thought about it for a moment. The assassins were becoming indispensable. Already they played a part in more of his plans than anyone else.

"No," he said. "I'm sure they have enough on their plate. Let's handle this one ourselves. Now, Farian, unroll the maps. I want to know exactly where these bloody Nousians are landing."

A RETURN TO UNDEATH

SOMETHING TUGGED RELENTLESSLY. A shudder passed through the Void, bringing with it an awareness of the absolute blackness; but awareness nonetheless. A groan escaped and was followed soon upon by a stark realization and the formation of a single thought.

"No!"

What remained of Callixus' soul rekindled its dark flame and protested against its unnatural perdurance. "Leave me here!" he screamed silently, for there was no sound in the Void.

The tugging increased, and Callixus felt his reawakened consciousness being sucked violently through the tiniest of apertures in the darkness until he re-emerged in the differentiated world of light and shapes.

One of the shapes detached itself from the others and came toward him. Callixus' vision was a kaleidoscope of gyring patterns that came into stark and corporeal focus upon a bulky figure in a velvet jacket.

"Welcome back, old chap," Cadman said with that air of false jollity that Callixus despised.

For an instant, he contorted with pain and wondered if he'd been brought back body and soul. Something wrenched at his gut, twisting and mangling. Callixus let out a long hissing groan and stared down at his gaseous hands. *Still a wraith*, he realized, and in the same moment, he knew that the pain had been nothing more than a manifestation of the hatred he held for Cadman, for what he'd made Callixus endure. For bringing him back.

A gray leathery creature dragged itself alongside Cadman and clung to his leg. It was sharp-faced and horned, with bat-like wings hanging limply behind. Callixus was reminded of the gargoyles that adorned the Ancients' templa back in Aeterna. The creature's black eyes swirled like ink in water, but hardened when they met his gaze.

"Allow me to introduce Ikrys." Cadman patted the gargoyle.

Ikrys winced and groaned, rolling to his back with arms and legs splayed. Callixus thought the creature was dying, so horribly warped were its limbs, but then Ikrys's body began to writhe and crack, bubble and straighten until, with a sigh, he hopped to his feet and snapped open his wings.

"Quite a resilient fellow, don't you agree?" Cadman said. "If only I'd met him sooner."

Ikrys cocked his head and leered at Callixus.

"He's been kind enough to channel the dark forces for me so that I don't suffer. More importantly," Cadman patted his pockets, "I don't have to use the statue."

"What you call the dark forces are my natural demesne," Ikrys said. "But the demands you make are great indeed. I would prefer to save myself for more useful tasks in the future."

Callixus drifted closer, his eyes surveying the courtyard outside the beacon tower.

"Why have you brought me back?"

"Besides your riveting company," Cadman said, clapping his hands together, "I need news. News about the body of the statue."

Callixus clutched at the fragmented memories that had been dragged from the Void with him. It was as if a fissure ran through his mind, and he needed to hop from recollection to recollection to make any sense of the scattered images.

"I had the albino." A ripple ran through his ghostly body as he recalled the shriek that had alerted him to the danger. "But a sorcerer aided him, and I was cast into the Void."

"What sorcerer?" Cadman asked. "Who could have such power over you?"

"A mawgish shaman. I do not know what happened to the statue."

"He has it, fool!" Ikrys snarled "And now he will reach for the other pieces, starting with yours." He pointed a long, taloned finger at Cadman.

Cadman's eyelid twitched, and for a split second, Callixus glimpsed a mottled skull beneath the illusion of flesh.

"Who is *he*?" Cadman demanded. "Sektis Gandaw?"

"Who else?" Ikrys said. "This incompetent has allowed another segment to fall into his hands. This changes matters greatly. His reach is lengthening. You will have to act swiftly before he locates your pieces and comes to claim them."

Callixus caught a sly look in Ikrys's eyes, but said nothing. Cadman fretted a moment longer and then seemed to grow fatter. It was like watching a child snuggle under the bedclothes. Ikrys winced and glared at the necromancer. Apparently, the enhancement of the illusion came at a cost. The gargoyle shook out his limbs, stretched his wings, and inhaled as if drinking invisible forces from the night air.

"I am not without power," Cadman said, adjusting his pince-nez on his nose. "I have my necromantic skills; I have two pieces of the Statue of Eingana; and I have you." He squinted at Ikrys.

Once more, a cunning look passed over Ikrys's taut and leathery face. Callixus wondered if it conveyed a secret amusement.

"Well," Ikrys said, "now that your grunt is back, it might be a good time to mention another threat I've detected."

Cadman clenched his fists and shut his eyes. "What threat?"

"The other woman, the one you said you knew—"

"The tart?" Cadman said.

Callixus looked at him for an explanation, but none was forthcoming.

"If you like," Ikrys said. "She proved extremely resourceful and had made it most of the way to Sarum when I caught up with her. She was intercepted by a group of black-clad men at the edge of the forest. They looked like they were about to do my work for me, but she spoke with one of them in private. He fondled her as he questioned her and then relayed what he learned to the others. After that, the man escorted her back to the city while the rest of the group altered their course."

"Altered it how? Where are they heading?" Cadman asked as he fumbled a cigarette into his mouth and struggled to light it.

"They are coming here," Ikrys said.

"Shit," Cadman said. "Shit, shit, shit. Black clothes you say?"

"As the night," Ikrys said with practiced innocence.

Callixus' hand went to the hilt of his sword. "Why have you kept this news until now, demon?"

Ikrys's tail arced through the air, its barbed tip stopping before Callixus' chest.

"Why, because I was waiting for you to deal with it. No point alarming the master until there's something we can do about it. So, be a good boy, and do whatever it is he pays you for."

Callixus half drew the black blade, but Cadman jabbed a cigarette between them.

"Cut that out, the pair of you. If these men are Sicarii, I'm finished. Do something, Callixus. You're supposed to be the strategist; and do it quickly before I send you back into the Void. No, on second thought, you'd probably like that, but I doubt you'd have such a peaceful time in the Abyss."

Callixus' vision blazed red. He released his grip on his sword and shut his eyes until he could once more feel the torment of his brethren, their despairing thoughts, their futile desire for revenge against Cadman. When he opened his eyes, he made sure to keep a neutral tone.

"The Lost have heard me," he said with a pang of pride tinged with loathing. "They are ready."

"Keep the assassins from the tower, Callixus. Do this for me and I may yet release you," Cadman said.

Callixus studied him for any sign that he was lying, but then realized there was no point. Cadman was the arch-liar; even his appearance was a distortion of the truth. If there were to be any end to this nightmarish existence, it wasn't going to come from an act of gratitude on Cadman's part.

"Come on, Ikrys." Cadman started walking back toward the tower. "We still have much to prepare. As if it's not enough having Sektis Gandaw hunting us from beyond the stars, and a bunch of trained killers at the door, we still have that blasted demon to deal with. The woman is secure on the roof? Good. Let's hope it's enough, eh? I trust you have some knowledge of the…"

Cadman's voice was cut off by the slamming of the door. The skeletal steeds of the Lost began to emerge from the darkness, the red eyes of the riders burning like embers. They would have all felt Callixus' despair as he once more looked upon his comrades. Without the need for speech, he conveyed his orders, and the former knights of the Elect took up their positions around the tower like nothing more than obedient guard dogs.

THE SLAUGHTER OF INNOCENTS

T HE HARD EARTH at the foot of the gangplank was as unfamiliar to Shader as the myriad realms he'd passed through on the flight from Araboth. His sea legs still wanted to sway, and a wave of nausea broke over him. Clutching the rail to steady himself, he glanced back at the ship, at the flashes of silver mail and white surcoats making ready to disembark. Ignatius Grymm was staring down at him like a disappointed father. He'd not said anything, but Shader knew the grand master had expected him to stay, to ride once more with the Elect.

The port of Dalantle was sleeping, save for a few fishing boats straggling in from the ocean. The Templum fleet spilled across the harbor, white sails furled, prows gently bobbing. One huge sitting duck, Shader shook his head, but the Ipsissimus must have known that. The imperial patrols had seen them—how could they not?—and alarms had pealed out across the bay while they were still in open water. Night had fallen rapidly, and the clamor had ended. Dalantle was already watchful, and messages had likely been sent.

Shader drew his coat tight against the chill air and headed toward the hazy lights of town. His chainmail felt so much heavier since he'd put it back on. Maybe he was just tired; maybe he'd get used to it again. He'd find an inn, see out the night, and then seek passage to Sarum in the morning. The stench of blood still filled his nostrils; it was as if it had seeped into his pores. Elpidio haunted every alleyway of his mind, one minute limned with misty luminescence, the next as a hunk of blue-dappled meat, stiff and waxen; neither true but both yelling for his attention, baying for comprehension, or grief, or vengeance. The swirl of emotions was as twisted as the knots on his prayer cord, which now hung from his belt like a flaccid serpent.

Shader left the harbor by a footpath that ran parallel to the main road. The way was lit by hanging lanterns that creaked in the breeze. The clopping of hooves sounded from somewhere ahead, and a dark shape came into view.

Shader's hand caressed the pommel of the gladius as he took to the shadows, waiting for the horse to pass. A hunched man walked before it, leading it by the reins, and muttering under his breath. The sound was rhythmic and sonorous, like a prayer chant, the words ill-formed but vaguely familiar. The man came into focus beneath the muggy light of a lantern, the chant sharpening at the same time into a litany of Aeternam. The horse came to a halt just beyond Shader's position, and the man turned to face him. Shader covered his nose and mouth against the stench and took a step back. He watched for the telltale smolder of red eyes, the cold presence of undeath, but saw only darkness under craggy brows. The man's face was both broad and long, his lips almost drooping. He'd seen this face before, he realized, at the White Order's camp above Lesmallen.

"Praise Ain! Praise Nous! Praise his holy Archon!"—Dave the Slave. "I knew you'd return. I waited. See, I waited. Oh, Nous be praised for giving me this chance to atone."

Shader's gut clenched with revulsion. He fought down the bile in his throat.

"What…?"

Dave shuffled forward and thrust the reins into Shader's free hand. He fumbled at his belt and removed a scabbarded longsword, which he handed over. Shader half drew it, instantly recognizing the blade.

"My father's sword? But how did—?"

"Nous revealed it to me. It was lost, but now it is found. Quickly, milord. Hurry. Nous's work must be done. Ride! Ride to Sarum! Evil besets the servants of Nous, and they have need of his champion."

Shader was jostled toward the horse and helped into the saddle. His mind felt heavy and numb. Questions half-formed and dissipated before he could voice them.

"How—?"

"Never you mind that," Dave said, guiding the horse in a circle by its bridle. "Make haste before they all perish. Ride for the Templum of the Knot."

The hunchback gave the horse's flank a sharp slap and Shader clung on as it cantered toward the town.

"Ride, I tell you! Ride!" Dave yelled. "The Sicarii are coming. Coming to kill the priests."

Ioana? Cadris? What about Rhiannon? Was she still with them? Sammy had said she was lost—

"Swiftly!" Dave flapped his hands and jigged from foot to foot.

Leaning low over the horse's neck, Shader dug his heels in and galloped for the Old Sarum Road.

* * *

Gaston muttered the Aeternam words softly as he fingered the knots on his prayer cord. He had remained in his pew as the priests returned to their rooms. His heart was swollen with gratitude and tears of relief rolled down his cheeks.

Mater Ioana was the last of the priests to leave the templum. She paused to rest a hand gently upon his shoulder. "Not ready for sleep?"

Gaston looked up through blurry eyes and smiled. "I should be exhausted, after all we've been through, but I feel…" He winced, trying to find a way to express the relief washing over him like a cleansing wave. More than relief, he realized: acceptance; belonging; the dim possibility of forgiveness.

"I know what it is you feel, Gaston." Ioana gave his shoulder a gentle squeeze. "We have all felt it at some time—me, Cadris, Agna, Velda. Even Hugues." Ioana shut her eyes for an instant, her face lit by a smile that seemed to radiate from within. "I think even Deacon Shader felt it once, although I could be mistaken. It is Nous accepting your burdens. You are where you're meant to be, Frater. You are home."

Ioana's fingers slipped from his shoulder and she headed out through the sacristy.

—*Frater.*

A shudder started in Gaston's chest and rippled throughout his frame.

—*Home.* Here in the templum, not among the knights of the White Order; not following in Shader's footsteps. Maybe that was the one good to come out of the evil he'd done to Rhiannon: it had forced the split from Shader. Ever since the founding of the White Order, even when Shader had abandoned them, Gaston had striven only to be like his mentor. He'd wanted nothing more than to serve Nous with heart and sword. Now, Gaston felt like scales had fallen from his eyes. It wasn't Nous he'd craved, it was Shader's approval; Shader's presence in his life. From the moment he'd fallen out with his dad, Gaston had felt like a hollowed-out skin, an empty carcass.

Shader had given him a glimpse of wholeness, but it hadn't been the truth. Maybe

369

they'd been too much alike, Gaston thought; too alike in their errors. For all his nobility and courage, Shader was not following Nous. He was a fighting man, a warrior of terrifying skill. In spite of his struggles with prayer and his attempt at the monastic life, Shader still resorted to the sword in his trials. Undoubtedly, he sought the good, but not in the way that Nous did. For Shader, morality was a matter of opposing evil and enforcing the greatest good. He believed the employment of pain, suffering, and even death was necessary if good were to prevail. The important issue was that good triumphed, whatever the means, whatever the cost.

As he worked his thumb and forefinger around the third knot on the prayer cord, feeling out its mysteries, Gaston heard a gentle thud on the roof. His senses flared to alertness, but he quickly quelled them with the thought that it must have been a possum. No sooner had he continued with the prayer than he heard another thud, this time followed by a slight scuffing sound. Rising to his feet he listened intently, but heard nothing else. Shaking his head at his own jumpiness, Gaston yawned and decided to call it a night. He put the prayer cord over his neck and strolled toward the sacristy and the adjoining door to the residences. As his fingers touched the handle, someone screamed.

Gaston ripped the door open and sprinted along the corridor past the priests' rooms. Pater Cadris and Frater Hugues emerged from the refectory, white-faced and trembling.

"That scream—?" Gaston said.

Hugues was transfixed by something outside the window.

Cadris stammered his reply. "I think it was Velda." He gazed fearfully down the corridor to her closed door.

"There are dark shapes outside," Hugues whispered.

Gaston headed toward Velda's door, but stopped when Ioana's burst open. She was panting, her eyes wide and fearful.

"Run, Gaston!" she commanded. "Run, all of you! The Sicarii—"

A black-garbed figure stepped out into the corridor from Velda's room. In his hand, he held a bloodstained dagger.

Without hesitating, Gaston bundled Ioana back into her room and followed her inside, dropping the catch.

"It's useless," Ioana said. "They're everywhere."

Another muffled scream came from a nearby room and then a door slammed. The sound of tramping feet filled the corridor outside, and a pounding started from the direction of the refectory. Gaston's heart matched the fierce beat as he cast about for some means of escape. Shadows passed across the window, and someone started rattling the door handle.

***

Shader rode through Calphon drawing looks from the whores arrayed along the pavements. A commotion broke out ahead as a couple of rogues set upon an old man who'd been foolish enough to walk home at night. The muggers scarpered as Shader's horse drew near, and he leaned from the saddle to offer the old man a hand up.

"Thank you, sir, thank you." The man dusted himself off and slapped a cap on his balding head. "I was just on my way—" He staggered back as if he'd seen a ghost and raised tremulous hands to his face.

"What is it?" Shader righted himself and looked around expecting to see the rogues coming back with reinforcements. The street was deserted.

"It's you!" The old man stumbled away and then started to run with bandy legs. "It's him!" he yelled into the night-blackened streets. "The one they're looking for! Guards! Guards!"

Faces appeared at windows and at the cracks of doors. Figures began to step from the shadows back where Shader had come from.

"I saw him first," the old man was protesting. "The money's mine."

Shader kicked the horse into a canter, but already a crowd was forming up ahead. Whistles sounded from somewhere in the distance, amid cries of "Make way! Make way!"

Springing from the saddle, Shader slapped the horse's rump and sent it galloping toward the crowd. He ducked into an alleyway and ran, cutting and weaving through a maze of byways until he was clear of the main thoroughfare.

He stopped to catch his breath by a battered fence that picketed a garden. How had the old man recognized him? The one they're looking for, he'd said. Who was looking for him? The Sicarii? Surely not—it was hardly their style to enlist the aid of the public; that'd do nothing for their reputation. Who, then?

He made his way through the underbelly of Calphon, threading a route back to the main road some way beyond the crowd. Keeping pressed to the wall, he peered around the corner, ducking back out of sight as a couple of soldiers jogged by. He sucked in a sharp breath. These were no mere militiamen; they were dressed in the livery of imperial regulars. He risked another look. The soldiers had stopped to consult with a large group of similarly garbed troops back down toward the crowd. After a brief exchange, they split off in pairs and scattered. Pulling his hat low and raising his coat collar, Shader hurried across the main road and continued toward the Mermaid. He reached the entrance to the tavern with footsteps close on his heels, but without waiting to see who it was, he slipped inside and shut the door.

The air was thick with smoke and the odor of stale beer and sweat. The place was heaving, all the tables taken and the spaces between packed with standing drinkers. Shader was hit by the wall of noise—raucous laughter, barking voices, the clink of coins and the chink of glasses.

He forced a passage to the window and peered out. Two imperial soldiers were passing from view up the street. They must have been right behind him. He waited a minute to make sure the way was clear and then made his way back to the entrance.

"Wait!" a woman called from the huddle.

Shader's hand went to the gladius, but he resisted the urge to draw it. He turned and looked up from beneath the brim of his hat.

A dirty-faced woman was squeezing through the crowd, her chestnut hair in greasy disarray as if she'd been dragged backward through a bush.

Her clothes were ripped and tatty—they may have once been some sort of servant's uniform. She met his gaze, ran her fingers through her hair, and plumped up her breasts.

Shader turned, a snarl half-formed on his face.

"Wait!" she repeated, touching his shoulder.

"Sorry, lady," Shader said. "I'm consecrated."

"What? No. How dare you!"

A waft of sickly perfume inflamed his nostrils. He backed into the entrance porch, dragging her with him. She opened her mouth to say something, but Shader took her jaw in one hand and pushed her against the wall.

"Out with it," he hissed. "Who are you?"

"A friend, you idiot!" She almost spat the words at him. "Or at least a friend of a friend."

Shader narrowed his eyes, willing her to explain.

"My name's Lallia." She extricated herself from his grip and straightened her top.

Shader's eyes flicked to the mountain of soft flesh threatening to burst free from its constraints and then met her cattish eyes.

"I know where your friend is," she said. "Rhiannon."

"What? How—?"

Lallia pressed herself against him and pulled his face close to hers. Shader struggled, but then her lips smothered his as the door opened.

"Make way in the name of the emperor."

A pair of soldiers pushed roughly past and entered the bar.

Shader's head reeled with Lallia's scent, and the warm wetness of her lips sent fire through his veins. She pulled away and whispered urgently.

"I went with Elias Wolf to rescue her, but we were attacked. She's being held at Dead Man's Torch. Dr. Cadman has her. I used to work with—"

"Cadman?" He had Rhiannon at the old beacon tower? Shader's head whirled with possibilities, but he couldn't focus. Other matters clamored for his attention.

"No time," he said. "I have to get to the Templum."

—*Rhiannon!*

"I'll come with you," Lallia said, running her hand down his arm.

"No." Shader shoved her aside. "It's too dangerous. Wait here."

She pouted and was about to say something, but he didn't wait to hear what it was.

"Shit," he said through clenched teeth as he sprinted back into the alleyways. He couldn't be in two places at once. The beacon was too far; he had to choose the templum. "Oh, Rhiannon," he groaned before shutting his mind to her plight and bitterly entrusting her fate to Nous.

***

Gaston reached under the bed and dragged out his sword.

"What are you doing?" Ioana asked.

"The Sicarii killed my dad," he said, drawing the blade. "They'll not do the same to my friends."

"But Gaston, you've made a choice. This is not our way."

Maybe it wouldn't have been his way, thought Gaston, if Shadrak the Unseen hadn't shown him the futility of peace. He winced, catching his train of thought: he was starting to sound like Shader—desiring all that Nous had to offer, but never quite able to release his grip on the sword. Now was not the time to worry about it. The choice, as he saw it, was simple: fight or be murdered. Much as he admired Ioana's faith, his own was still a frost-hardened seed in comparison. *Fallen at the first hurdle, Gaston.* He could almost hear his dad's condemnation from beyond the grave.

Gaston took hold of the door handle and pressed his ear to the wood.

Silence.

Waving Ioana back, he wrenched the door open and darted into the corridor. He swung his sword at a black shape to his left, but felt something sharp pierce his side. He slashed blindly behind him and heard a cry as his blade tore into soft flesh. Whirling, he met the stab of the first assassin and kicked out at the man's knee, snapping it backward and sending him screaming to the ground.

A lean man, cloaked and hooded, was kneeling mere feet away and bringing a hand crossbow to bear. Gaston dived as the bolt was released, rolled to his feet, and impaled the man on the tip of his sword.

Up ahead he could see more of the dark figures in the refectory. He heard Cadris crying for mercy and ran at the assassins. His first blow was parried by a shortsword as two Sicarii spun to face him while a third went for Hugues and Cadris.

Gaston turned a thrust from the shortsword and stepped back as the other Sicarii produced some sleek silver darts. The crash of Hugues upturning the refectory table distracted the dart-thrower, but the swordsman leapt to the attack with a ferocity that stunned Gaston. The man cut and stabbed with dazzling speed. It was all Gaston could do to block the blows; he had no chance of launching a counterattack.

As he backed down the corridor parrying desperately, he glimpsed Ioana's horrified—or was it disapproving?—face peering from behind the door to her room.

Cadris screamed from the refectory, and then something pierced the skin of Gaston's shoulder—the dart-thrower had got his focus back. Consumed suddenly by an old familiar fury, Gaston felt all uncertainty pass. He made a fierce parry that turned his assailant's sword, and in that moment struck the man with a thudding left hook. The assassin staggered and then found Gaston's blade skewering his belly. Another dart hit Gaston, this time in the thigh. He felt dampness around the wound to his side, and coldness where the first dart had struck him. He lunged toward the dart-thrower, but was hit twice more as the assassin skipped nimbly back. Giving up all hope of defending himself, Gaston ducked his head and charged, receiving another hit before he bowled the assassin over backward into the refectory.

Cadris was writhing on the ground, a deep cut to his abdomen, and Hugues was holding sternly to his assailant's wrists as the man sought a way to stab him.

Gaston hacked wildly at his own opponent, who was frantically seeking to regain his feet. More hooded figures appeared at the windows, and then the room was filled with the sound of breaking glass as they smashed their way inside. He risked a glance over his shoulder and saw an assassin kick down Ioana's door. It was over, and all Gaston could feel was the rage of despair. He delivered a vicious cut to the dart-thrower's head and followed it up with a thrust through the groin. The assassin screamed and spasmed, but then two of the newcomers pounced at him. He blocked a swing from the blade of the first, but the second caught him between the ribs. As the blood bubbled to his mouth, Gaston disemboweled the man with a blistering riposte.

He tried to turn in an attempt to reach Ioana, but something struck his lower back. Ioana was standing beside the wreck of her door, her attacker dead at her feet, and Deacon Shader was striding toward the refectory with two bloodied swords in his hands.

Gaston hacked feebly at his opponent, but the man easily blocked his blow and moved in for the kill. All sensation had seeped from Gaston's body, and he started to swoon, no longer caring about the blade about to strike. Shader yelled and hurled his gladius with such ferocity that it nearly tore the head from the assassin's shoulders. As Shader surged past him into the refectory, Gaston felt Ioana stroking his head and realized that he had fallen, and she was cradling him like a sick child.

Dimly, he saw Shader fighting with bewildering skill and speed, his longsword a glittering blur. There was panic on the faces of the Sicarii as they realized the deadly power of their opponent. Shader whirled to meet a desperate backstab and sliced through the assassin's wrist. The man fell on his arse and tried to scrabble away, but Shader's sword skewered him like a pig. Shader's eyes were like pools of ice as he dispatched the last of the assassins with a cut to the jugular. The monk Shader had given complete sway to a raw killer, heartless and unswayable. He turned a slow circle and then lowered his head as if disappointed there was no one left to kill.

Hugues retrieved Shader's gladius and offered it to him with either reverence or fear. Shader ignored him, dropped his longsword and fell to his knees at Gaston's side.

Shader appeared limned with silver, a specter of moonlight. A misty corona surrounded his head, warring with the deep shadows of his face. Another face came into sight behind Shader's shoulder—a woman, perhaps an angel with hair like flames. She was holding a lantern that blazed so harshly Gaston had to blink away tears. When he looked again, Shader had become a blur flickering in and out of existence.

"Mater—?" Gaston's voice rasped like a whetstone on a nicked blade. He coughed and dug deeper. "Did I—?"

Fingers brushed the hair away from his face—Ioana's?

"Oh, Gaston," someone said. He thought it was a woman.

Wetness touched his cheek. Was it raining?

Shader's mouth was moving, a smudge of twisting blackness.

"… fought well, Gaston … made … proud."

"Dad? Is that you?" Gaston's head sank deeper into the pillow and someone—Mom, most likely—pulled the covers over him. He tried to see, but his eyes were so heavy. *Look tomorrow,* he told himself. *I'll look tomorrow.*

Someone wailed.

It'll keep—

***

Shader reached out a hand to Ioana, but she pulled away, hugging Gaston to her breast and shuddering as she wept.

Soror Agna limped from her room, stooped and crooked as if she'd finally started to lose her battle with age. Hugues helped Cadris to his feet. The fat priest was bleeding from cuts to his face and arms, but he'd still managed to cover Gaston's body with a white sheet. Not a sheet, Shader realized as blood soaked through the material like the blossoming of a poppy—it was an altar cloth, though where had he—?

Sweet perfume wafted to his nostrils as the woman with the lantern crouched at his side. Shader stared blankly for a moment, his mind smothered by an obscuring pall. He looked from her to Gaston, to Ioana and back again. The woman from the tavern. He acknowledged her with a perfunctory nod. Lallia, the friend of Elias Wolf. She too was bloodied and shaken.

"You should have stayed behind." Shader said. He felt his lip curling, almost snarled. Isn't that what he'd told her to do? Wait at the Mermaid?

"Remember the three you killed on the way in?" Lallia asked, her head cocked to one side.

"Yes—"

"There were four." Lallia's cheeks puffed up as if she were going to be sick. She raised a blood-drenched kitchen knife in a shaking hand. "Had a crossbow pointed at your back. The blood's all his." Her grip failed, and the knife clattered to the floor.

Shader sucked in a deep breath, closed his eyes, and stood. Ioana watched him as if she expected him to do something, say something. She cradled Gaston as if her body warmth could revive him; held him toward Shader as if he had power over the dead. The cold touch of defeat crawled through his veins.

Agna somehow managed to kneel down beside Ioana, joints cracking like dry twigs underfoot. As she drew the cloth over Gaston's face, Shader's failure bubbled up to his throat, and he leaned against the wall, swallowing back bile.

He caught a flash of red out of the corner of his eye and craned his neck, expecting to be struck down by some new enemy.

"Mater," Zara Gen cried, stumbling down the corridor toward them, his crimson robes clinging like self-accusation. "Mater, I'm so sorry."

NOUS IS NOT NOUS

BOTH YOUR MOTHER and father are right, Deacon," Aristodeus said. "The world is like that: full of paradox."

Deacon lowered his sword. How could you marry peace with struggle? Service with power? Love with the sword? Silver streaked toward his face and, with an instinctive parry, he turned the philosopher's blade.

"Never drop your guard, my boy—even in the midst of debate. Your mind must be sharper than a razor, yet your awareness must be divided, concentric rings of widening focus rippling out from a still point. You must—"

Deacon's sword slipped between the words and touched the flesh of Aristodeus's neck. The philosopher's eyes bulged. It was the first time Deacon had seen him shocked. The old man's face tightened with suppressed rage, but then he smiled and gave that sagacious nod that said he'd planned for this all along.

"Excellent. Now you're getting it." Aristodeus pushed the edge of Deacon's sword away and thrust his own blade into the ground. "Killing for Nous," he returned to the former point. "It's why your father never joined the Elect; why he never embraced the faith like your mother did. It is the tension which defines you, makes you what you are."

"Confused?" Deacon said, ramming his sword back into its scabbard. "What's that got to do with the clear sight you say I need?"

Aristodeus sighed and put an arm around Deacon's shoulder. He reeked of sweat from their exertions, and wisps of white hair were plastered to his scalp. Deacon was as tall as his mentor; he figured he probably moved like him, too. Thought like him, even. The philosopher had molded him for so long now, Deacon could scarcely remember a time in his life when Aristodeus hadn't smothered him like an overprotective mother.

"Nous isn't what he seems, Deacon." Aristodeus leaned in close to whisper. "But don't tell anyone I said that—least of all your mother. Gods come and go, changing with the times and the needs of the people. Truth, however, truth remains constant."

Deacon stepped away from the philosopher. "Nous is not real?" Anger bubbled in his belly like magma.

Aristodeus rolled his head and chuckled. "Is that what I said?"

"Well—"

The philosopher tapped his temples. "Think, Deacon. Think! Please tell me I've not been pissing in the wind all these years. Head over heart, isn't that what I taught you?"

"Yes, but—"

Aristodeus opened his mouth to say something, but then rubbed his beard and shook his head.

"Some things you'll have to work out for yourself. Nous, my young friend, is most definitely real; but he is, as I have said, not what he seems."

Deacon felt like he was being mocked and didn't like it one bit.

"So, I've been duped. Is that what you're saying?"

"Not at all, Deacon. These things are mysteries—not because they can't be explained, but because they only come to us a bit at a time. Do exactly as you've been doing: keep to your devotions, as they may yet serve you well. Question constantly, but at the same time act as if it's all literally true, down to the very last Ipsissimal proclamation on the Archon's favorite tipple."

But Nous was supposed to be a person. Isn't that what Aristodeus had taught him from the start? A person of love? If that's the case, why did he require the use of a sword? Why did the Ipsissimus need an army? If Nous was so loving, then—

***

A footfall startled Shader awake. His back and neck ached from being hunched over on a pew. Ain, he was tired; more tired than he could ever remember being. He looked up to see Lallia, blood-smeared and wild-looking, like one of the Furies from Aristodeus's tales.

"The Mater says the lad who died was going to join the priests." Lallia spoke almost whimsically, as if her mind were somewhere else. She sat herself beside him, frowning at the altar.

Shader's muscles bunched under the onslaught of a molten stream. Whenever he tried to picture Gaston, he saw Rhiannon; saw what his protégé had done to her. His fingers clutched at the air as if it were Gaston's throat, and at the same time his eyes blurred with tears.

"Couldn't have seen him making it." Lallia brushed against him, placed a hand on his back. "Didn't look the sort to cower like the rest of them."

Shader nodded vigorously, his body shaking with unnamable emotions. "He knew how to fight."

"I'd say. You know what really pisses me off?" Lallia turned her face to look right into Shader's eyes. He was beyond caring about the exposure of his grief. His gaze never wavered from her verdant stare. "The way those priests mourn for him as if he were a disappointment. You know, the Mater even kicked his sword like it was some kind of des … desec… What's the bloody word?"

—Desecration.

"They'd sooner he did nothing?" Shader rasped through clenched teeth.

"You'd think," Lallia said, looping her arm in his. "Some people are just so up their own… You know what I mean."

Shader forced a smile. Lallia seemed to take some relief from it. Her lips parted, showing a flash of white teeth.

"You knew him, right?"

"I trained him," Shader said. "Made him what he was…"

"But?"

"It doesn't matter. He should be judged by what he did with his last breath." *—Not by what he did to Rhiannon.*

"Fair do," Lallia said. "Now, will you walk with me?"

"Why?" Shader was still half-dazed. Loss and grief had wedged themselves between the two sides of his nature, unweaving them, separating the strands into impossible allies.

—Mother and Father.

"I need to feel the night air," Lallia said, "and take some little pleasure in being alive. It's been hard, these past few days." Her look had turned to pleading, longing. "So much death."

Shader nodded and stood. As they left the templum, he felt only its utter emptiness.

She rested her head on his shoulder as they strolled in the direction of the Forest Walk.

They passed along broad avenues lit by the Ancients' lanterns atop their towering posts. The chill was restorative, cleansing; the warmth of Lallia against his side like a benison.

Shader burned with questions, but kept them to himself lest they marred the momentary calm. Finally, as they entered the arboretum, he could contain it no longer.

"Rhiannon—" He stopped and turned to face Lallia. "Is she…?"

Lallia's eyelids fluttered and she dropped her gaze. "I went with Elias." She shuddered with a suppressed sob. "We"—she waved her hands by her head—"had this message or something. One of the old priestesses went weird, said Rhiannon was at Dead Man's Torch."

"You told me Cadman had her? Why would he want Rhiannon?"

Lallia's face lost some of its color. "I wouldn't want to guess. I used to work with that fat shogger; only he's not fat—not really." She hugged herself and shuddered. "He's this … thing. Like a skeleton."

"A liche," Shader said. "Feeding on human life to sustain his own."

Only, why Rhiannon? Why her, specifically? Coincidence?

"We tried to save her." Lallia was whimpering like a child. She seemed suddenly less than she was—her assuredness had vanished, leaving her vulnerable, bashful even. "We freed her from the tower, but then creatures came; dead things and worse. I-I-I ran. I-I-I left them. Oh, poor Elias," she wailed. "I think something terrible…"

Shader embraced her, held her face to his chest, and let her tears soak into his surcoat. "I should go to her."

Lallia pulled back and made him look at her tear-streaked face. "It's too late," she sobbed. "I'm sorry. So, so sorry."

Shader's despair pooled in his gut. His knees buckled, but Lallia caught him. A groan left his lips of its own accord. Words too awful to utter sought to burst from his skin.

Lallia's cheek pressed against his, their tears mingling. The hot wetness of her mouth found his lips. Her scent fired his senses, excoriated his grief. He tried to break away, but Lallia held his head firm, forcing her mouth against his. Ashamed by his stiffness against her leg, he whimpered and managed to pry his face from hers. Lallia continued to suck at his lips, lick his cheeks.

"No—" Shader said, but without any real conviction.

Her hand felt his hardness, forced its way inside his breeches. Shader gasped, fire coursing up his spine. *Rhiannon.* He closed his eyes, struggled to see her. *Rhian—*

With a growl, he tore at Lallia's blouse, sending buttons pinging into the air. His fingers grasped the pliant warmth of a breast, kneaded it, thrilled at its wrongness.

Rhiannon had refused him. None of this would have happened if—

Lallia pulled his face to her breast and moaned as Shader's tongue found the nipple.

—She'd listened to Huntsman over him.

Lallia ground herself against his groin, at the same time seeking an opening in his armor, clawing and probing, scratching at the steel.

—All at Aristodeus's bidding. The philosopher had taken the choice from him. Always had.

With a snarl, he forced Lallia to arch away from him, her hair trailing toward the ground, her torso supported only by his hand on the small of her back. He ripped the remnants of her blouse aside and buried his face in her belly, sinking his teeth in, then running his tongue back up between her breasts. She cried out as he grabbed her hair and forced her back further until she lay upon the ground. She found a way beneath his chainmail and raked his back with her nails. Shader put his weight upon her, driving her head into the earth with fierce thrusts of his tongue.

She bent her knee and rolled him over so that she was astride his hips. She freed him from the constriction of his breeches and poised herself above him. He felt her hot wetness touch him, felt himself urging for her entrance.

"No!" he screamed, twisting away and dumping her to one side. She hit the ground hard and let out a rush of air.

Shader hurried to his feet, tugging up his breeches and stumbling away.

"What is it?" Lallia cried, hoarse and throaty.

"Keep back." Shader's hand gripped the hilt of his gladius. "What are you doing?"

Lallia sat up, her hands covering her breasts. Her allure had left her. To Shader, she now looked waxen and cold, like the Demiurgos frozen in ice at the heart of the Abyss.

"Whore!" Shader turned and ran through the trees back toward town.

"Shog you!" Lallia screamed after him. "You shogging hypocrite!"

Her words pierced his back like arrows. He raced on through the trees, snagging his surcoat on a low branch and cursing as he stopped to free it. His heart leapt to his mouth as something lurched from the shadows.

"Nous be praised!" Dave said, almost doubled up by the weight of the hump squatting like a malignancy on his back.

"What? How—?"

"Praise Nous! Praise Ain!" Dave shuffled toward him, eyes shrouded with darkness, mouth set in a grimace of condemnation. "Another moment..." The hunchback shook his head and let out a long hiss of air.

"How did you get here?" How had he covered the distance so quickly? Did he have another horse? Some other means of transport?

"Faith, master. The faith that moves mountains." The words cut like an accusation. "Fear not," Dave said, taking hold of Shader's hand and kissing it. "Nous is still with you. He will not let you fall. Not now. Not when there's so much at stake."

The gladius purred at Shader's hip, trickled warmth into his fingers.

—*Nous is not what he seems.*

Dave stiffened and cocked his head, almost as if he'd read Shader's thoughts.

"Nous is not Nous," he muttered, then headed away from the trees as if he expected Shader to follow him.

"What does that mean?" Shader hurried alongside.

Dave paused momentarily and looked up at the sky. "Don't rightly remember," he said before resuming his slow trudge toward the lamp-lit streets. "But I do know he needs fighters more than he needs those lily-livered friends of yours. Why'd you think you bear the Archon's sword?"

"How?" Shader shook with emotion. "How can Nous want killing? He's supposed to be a god of love."

"*The* God," Dave hissed through his teeth. "*The* God of love. But even a garden of love needs pruning. You are Nous's gardener, Keeper of the Sword, and there are deep-rooted weeds that require your attention."

"Nous wants me to kill? To go on killing? In the name of love?"

"There is a word for this kind of killing," Dave said, lifting his chin almost proudly. "It is a word from the oldest times; a word steeped in holy history. For where lies the harm in the slaying of evil? You would do well to remember it, master—"

But Shader was no longer listening. He already knew what the word was—he'd come across it often enough in the works of Berdini; heard it from the lips of Aristodeus.

Killing for Nous isn't murder, he used to say with a sardonic smirk. *Not homicide. When the sword of truth is used to root out corruption, the proper term is "malicide".*

"Stop following me," Shader said to Dave in a voice lacking authority.

Dave twisted his head to look up at him, silver starlight glittering in his eyes. His mouth hung slack, edged with drool.

"Just stop." Shader turned on his heel and ran for the templum.

DOOM OF THE SICARII

I T'S INSULTING," ALBERT muttered to himself in between puffs. His heart was bouncing about in his ribcage with such violence he half expected it to burst through his chest. His gut was jiggling like a bag of slops as his shoes pounded the earth in an effort to keep up with the other Sicarii. "What do they take me for, a bloody journeyman?"

It's not as if he was dressed for it. Running about in the wilds in the middle of the night was hardly Albert's thing, and he'd long-since abandoned the traditional cloak and dagger look for a smart dress suit he'd picked up during an overseas mission to Gallia. An assassin of his caliber didn't need to exert himself or sneak around in a mask. He was a professional, the consummate killer; not a throat-slitting hack like the rest of them. He paused to catch his breath and glare at his lithe companions darting through the trees like shadows. *Ham-fisted goons.* Good for nothing but second-rate thuggery.

"No slinking off this time, fatso." Master Frayn's whisper cut him like a knife.

Albert's heart almost exploded then, but he had the presence of mind not to show it. He even managed to act like he'd known Frayn was there all along.

"My particular skills call for discretion, darling," Albert said, tucking his thumbs into his jacket pockets and surveying the area. Not that he could see much—it was black as the Void. "As opposed to blundering headlong into danger without a clue what we're up against."

Frayn slipped in front of Albert, his face shrouded by the hood of his cloak. "So you were slinking off, then." It was a statement tinged with threat. "Maybe you've got somewhere else to be." Frayn pressed closer.

Albert had a thousand places he'd rather be. He thought he'd left this sort of activity behind when he'd earned his stripes with the guild, so to speak. For goodness' sake, had they already forgotten how the poisoning of half the council had saved them from being exposed and, in accordance with the written, if not the practiced, law, executed? The fact that the contract had been paid for by the other half of the council was by the by.

"If you're alluding to the spurious allegation about me undertaking private work with Shadrak, Master, may I remind you that the guild found no evidence of wrongdoing."

Frayn snorted and threw his hood back. He made a show of scanning the sky beyond Albert and then pinched the ends of his mustache straight. "Listen, Albert." Frayn checked to make sure no one was in earshot. "I don't like you, but at least I'm honest about that."

The feeling's mutual, Albert thought, but kept tight-lipped.

"But you're good at what you do. No, better than good. You're probably the best poisoner in Sahul."

Probably? Albert faked a smile.

"The guild is playing big tonight," Frayn said. "What with the attack on the templum and our mission."

—Ordered by the emperor, no less (unofficially, of course). Albert loved that kind of duplicity. Hagalle was a man he could respect.

"There may be..." Frayn wrung his hands as if he had a stain he couldn't get rid of. "...changes afoot, if you know what I mean."

Oh, absolutely. Frayn was so much up Hagalle's arse he'd need a lamp to see. "Changes? Whatever do you mean, Master." It never hurt to show idiots like Frayn a modicum of respect. The more important they felt, the more stupid they became.

Frayn cast a look behind and then draped an arm over Albert's shoulder. Albert forced himself not to wrinkle his nose.

"First I need to know who my friends are," Frayn said. "Understand?"

In your dreams, darling. Albert frowned in the direction of the other assassins. They'd all passed from sight into the cover of the trees. With their black cloaks, they were as good as invisible.

"Shouldn't we...?"

Frayn narrowed his eyes as if he could read Albert's thoughts. The reality was, he could probably barely read a book. The man was an arse, a laughing stock. He'd only made it this far in the guild because the other masters needed a fall guy. Master Rabalath had told Albert as much over dinner one night—boeuf bourguignon with chanterelles à la crème and a bottle of Quilonian Malbec. The bourguignon provided the perfect base for a dash of passionflower essence—not enough to induce sleep, but enough to loosen the old codger's tongue. If certain people on the council had their way and moved against the guild, they'd have the perfect target in Frayn, full of his own importance, kowtowing with all the nobles; he'd even said it himself: he was the face of the Sicarii. Oh, the chances were slim now, after Albert's success with eliminating the political idealists who objected to the use of assassins, but should the climate change, should Zara Gen rebuild his alliances, Frayn would be the first on the gallows, while the true masters, Rabalath and Paldane, would slip away like cockroaches through a crack in the floor. The guild would return to the realm of whispered rumors, while continuing to bring quiet death as inexorably as time.

"You're right," Frayn said, pulling his hood up. "We'll speak later, yes? And not a word to the others." He tapped the side of his nose and raced ahead.

Albert sighed and set off at a steady jog. His knees were burning, and his heart resumed its attempts to batter its way out of his ribcage. He snagged his trousers on a tangle of brambles, ripping the hem as he pulled his leg away. *Bugger!* There wasn't a tailor in Sahul he'd trust with stitching clothes of such quality. It could be years before he visited Gallia again. And the cost! It didn't bear thinking about. The shadows up ahead grew denser, revealing the presence of his comrades.

Albert started up a low mound in pursuit, but the thorny creeper clung on with the tenacity of a debt collector. He shook his leg and took a long stride, tripped on a root and pitched forward. With reflexes born of fear, his hands hit the ground first and jolts of pain shot through his arms and neck. But at least they'd taken the brunt of the impact. He knelt, accepting the knees of his trousers would be utterly ruined, and gingerly patted his jacket pockets. All still there. All intact. He held his breath a little longer and then blew it out through pursed lips. Occupational hazard, he thought wryly as he clambered to his feet. Many a poisoner had inadvertently died by his own hand.

One of the vials of toxin he carried in his jacket had been extracted from the notorious brown snake of the northern jungles and blended with extra-virgin olive oil. The oil slowed the rate of absorption, but the end result was as certain as syphilis in a Graecian bathhouse. Another was distilled from the Britannic death-cap mushroom and dried to a powder. The third was topical and extremely virulent. Get it on the skin and it was curtains for you. This Cadman they were after was no ordinary victim. Anyone who controlled an army of walking corpses was likely to prove difficult to kill.

Frayn apparently didn't think so. In his feeble mind, the reputation of the Sicarii alone was enough to put paid to ordinary mortals. He saw Cadman as his own man, his underworld doctor, his ears in the council; but Albert had been around long enough to know that Cadman was not simply going to lay down and die just because the guild was onto him. Frayn and the others could take their shot, and Albert hoped they were successful. But if not, he'd come fully prepared: a liquid for injection, a contact poison, and a powder for inhalation, all of which would kill anything living. The only potential flaw in the plan was that, judging by the company he kept, Cadman was not necessarily alive, at least not in the usual sense of the word.

The trees began to thin out as the ground grew uneven, rising and dipping in a succession of hillocks that protruded from the earth like tubercles.

"Over here," Frayn hissed in a stage whisper.

Albert trudged up a mound and hunkered down beside the master behind an immense gum tree. He could see the others now, all crouching at the bases of trees flanking the bumpy ground.

"There," Frayn said, pointing into the darkness. "Dead Man's Torch."

The tower was barely visible, a deepening of the blackness that rose like a pillar of shadow.

"There's a flicker from the upper level," Frayn pointed out. "Probably a candle. Not quite lights out, but I'd say we're expected."

A hooded Sicarii scampered over to them. "They have four guards around the base." He sounded like a boy—Carn Jenith, perhaps. "There's also a horse patrol, half a dozen of them."

"Undead?" Albert asked.

"Too far away to see," the lad said. "What are your orders, Master Frayn?"

Frayn gave a muted clap. "So there are ten of them and twenty of us—"

A tremor passed through the ground, and a murmur went up from the assassins.

"What—?" Frayn said, pinching his mustache.

Albert frowned and cast his eyes around the copse and back over the cluster of mounds. *Tumuli*, he thought. *Maybe one of the Dreamers' sacred burial grounds.* He wondered if he should mention anything to Frayn, but then the earth shook again.

"What is that?" Frayn strained a look toward the tower. "Horses? There'd have to be a hell of a lot of them. Earthquake?"

"In Sahul?" Albert said. Most unlikely. The funny thing was, the shaking seemed to have come from—

Someone screamed.

Yells filled the air; swords and knives were drawn, and the shadowy shapes of Sicarii could be seen hacking ferociously at the ground. Albert backed away from the tree. The earth where he'd been standing ruptured and a hand punched through, skeletal fingers clutching blindly. Another burst forth right beneath the young Sicarii and grabbed hold of his ankle. The lad yelped and fumbled for his dagger. Frayn looked aghast. He was shaking so much Albert thought he'd shit himself. When a third hand forced its way through the loamy ground, Frayn ran from the trees.

"Charge!" he yelled, waving his sword as he sprinted straight toward the tower guards.

A handful of others followed him, but most were caught by necrotic fingers. Albert turned and twisted, eyes scanning the ground before he set his feet down. He weaved a path through the questing hands that were emerging from the tumuli and the surrounding woodland. He saw an assassin pulled down, a dozen hands clawing at him as he thrashed about and screamed. Something touched Albert's shoe, and he stamped on bony fingers. He no longer felt the hammering of his heart. For all he knew, it had stopped. He was in the middle of a sea of writhing limbs fighting their way up from the grave. Another assassin went down, this time right beneath the earth as the skeletal arms forced the ground asunder, and bodies started to climb out. Skeletons, mud-caked and brittle, but with eyes the color of starlit rubies.

Albert huffed and puffed toward the tree line, hoping to join Frayn's desperate charge, but up ahead the assassins faltered as a figure, spectral and black, materialized before them, an ebon blade of wispy shadow held aloft. The wraith glowered with coal-fire eyes and emitted a terrible shriek.

Six riders trotted into view from behind the tower. They were heavily armored in visored helms and hauberks, their steeds skeletal, but with hellish eyes and flaming breath.

Frayn squealed and ran to the right, the five assassins with him following. Albert hesitated, checked behind, where scores of corpses were shambling from their graves and pressing in upon the surviving Sicarii. As Frayn's group reached the tree line to the east of the tower, more horsemen rode from the forest, fanning out to block their way. There were too many to count.

A light now shone from the upper window of Dead Man's Torch, and a bulky silhouette peered out. Something flapped down onto the parapet and watched like a vulture.

They hadn't seen him yet, Albert thought as he edged away to the left. Still hadn't seen him... Still hadn't—

The six original riders moved to cut off Frayn's group's retreat, and the corpses from the tumuli were now shambling out onto open ground. The wraith drifted to a position on the assassins' left flank.

Albert remained unnoticed. He sidestepped away, keeping as close to the tree line as he could, but watching all the while for limbs jutting from the ground. *One step... Two steps... Almost there...* Just another couple of steps and then he'd turn and flee. *Careful. Care—*

One of the six riders wheeled its mount and looked straight at Albert, its eyes red blazes through the visor of its helm.

"Shit!"

Albert spun and ran as fast as his legs would carry him. He leaped over a flailing hand, kicked an emerging head right off its neck, and sprinted through the trees. Branches tore at his face, snagged his clothing, but he hurtled on heedless. A chorus of screams rose behind him. Steel clashed with steel. Shouts. More screams, and a chilling wailing.

Albert flicked a look over his shoulder. The skeletal knight was weaving its mount through the trees in pursuit. Dipping his head, Albert ran on over a tumulus, dancing in and out of clutching hands, and down the other side. He stumbled, flapped his arms about for balance, but then stepped into a depression and wrenched his ankle.

"Shit!" he cried again. "Bloody rabbits! Shit, shog, bugger, damn!"

Half limping, half hopping, he forced his way through a thicket and out into the open. The skeletal steed was so close he could almost feel its fiery breath on the back of his neck. He reached into his pocket and grabbed the vials. It was useless, he knew, but he was damned if he was going down without a fight. He fumbled one and dropped it. The glass shattered, and dust puffed up into the air. Albert whipped out his handkerchief to cover his nose and mouth, hopping further into the clearing and trying to unstop one of the other vials. He didn't dare look back to see how close the rider was. His face was taut with anticipation of the death blow that could fall at any moment.

Giving up on the stoppers, Albert slung both vials over his shoulder and hopped even faster. The air shimmered in front of him and a beam of bright light cut across the ground ten paces ahead. The light grew upwards to the accompaniment of a rushing noise, and

Albert had to shield his eyes from the glare. The hoof beats behind him stopped, and he risked a quick look back.

The rider had drawn up to watch the light, seemingly as enthralled as Albert. He peered back at the glare through splayed fingers. It was now a rectangle of white radiance—like a doorway. In the entrance stood a silhouetted figure, humanoid—only much smaller. It held something in its hands—a staff? A tube?

"Get down!" the figure shouted as it pointed the staff at Albert.

Without needing to be told a twice, Albert flung himself face down in the dirt. There was a thunderous crack, a rush of air, and a resounding shatter. The figure stepped away from the light and held a hand out to him. Lifting his head, Albert looked into a face as pale as death and eyes like diluted blood.

"Shadrak! What are—?"

"No time," the albino said. "Come."

Shadrak slung the tube over his shoulder and helped Albert to his feet before starting back toward the light.

"New weapon, darling?"

"Later," Shadrak said beckoning him on.

Albert looked behind and saw the rider's headless body sitting bolt upright upon its skeletal steed. Its helm lay in two halves on the ground, fragments of bone scattered all around it.

They entered a metallic corridor lit by a ghostly blue glow. Albert blinked until his eyes adjusted as Shadrak tapped some buttons on the inside of the doorway, and a panel slid down.

"I was hoping for more of you," he said. "Seems I'm a bit late."

"That's an understatement, if ever I heard one," Albert said. "Is this the Maze? How come it's here? How did you know—?"

Shadrak touched a finger to his lips. "Orders from above. Now, you have a choice to make: either you go back out there and take your chances, or you come with me."

Some choice. Albert patted his jacket pockets but found them empty. He still had his cheese-cutter in his trouser pocket, but he doubted that'd do much good against skeletons wearing gorgets.

"Looks like it's your shout, darling," he said with a tight-lipped smile. "Where are we going?"

Shadrak turned on his heel and strode down the corridor. "The Homestead," he said.

"The what? The sacred site of the Dreamers? Why on earth would—?"

Shadrak tapped more buttons, and a section of the wall slid open. He turned to look back at Albert. "You in or out?"

"You're the one with all the cards," Albert said, ambling toward him. "Looks like the old team's back together."

Shadrak sniffed and passed through the doorway into a part of the Maze Albert had never seen before. Clearly, Shadrak had only revealed as much as he needed to. Albert couldn't blame him. He'd have done the same.

"Well call me Daisy!" Albert said, following him. "What the blue blazes?"

The corridor opened onto a spherical chamber dominated by a silver plinth that twinkled with lights. The top of the plinth mushroomed out to house dark mirrors with flashing symbols dancing across their surfaces. A background susurrus caused Albert's ears to pop, and deep in his bones he felt, rather than heard, a low droning.

Shadrak flicked some switches on the plinth, and two ovoid chairs rose from the floor. He gestured for Albert to sit, and as soon as he did, pliant restraints fastened across his lap and over his shoulders.

"What are you doing?" Albert yelped, suspecting he'd just stumbled into a trap.

Shadrak might have been a partner, when it suited him, but he was still an assassin.

Shadrak lowered himself into the other seat, and restraints rolled out to secure him. That calmed Albert somewhat, but he still didn't like it. There was a feel of magic about the place, a sense of wrongness. But Albert was no superstitious simpleton. He'd seen enough of the world to know there were secrets that had survived the Reckoning.

"This is Ancient tech," he said. "How—?"

"It's a little more than that," Shadrak said. "This, so I'm told, is the blending of science and lore: the combined knowledge of two worlds."

Albert glanced around at the glowing metal walls, the winking displays on the plinth; felt the giving steel of the restraints. Crazy as it sounded, he could quite well believe Shadrak.

"And we're going to the Homestead? In this?"

"Yup," Shadrak said, leaning back in his chair and closing his eyes.

Some unseen force yanked Albert's stomach through his shoes. It bounced back beyond the top of his head, and he vomited. The lights flickered, trees appeared in the walls and gave way to absolute blackness. The low drone became an insistent whine and then Albert felt all his weight dissipate as if he were a ghost.

NEMESIS

O NE HUNDRED AND twenty-six, one hundred and twenty-seven, one hundred and twenty-eight! Round four: one, two, three…"

Cadman's vision was starting to blur, the mortar between the bricks becoming indistinct and wavy, like the strands of a cobweb blowing in the wind.

"…six, seven, eight…"

Pinpricks behind his eyes; a pressure that threatened to pop them from his head as if veins of acid swelled up in their sockets.

"Soon, master, I will have it." A parched voice; the words clumsily formed as if the tongue were too large for the mouth. "Then I will have freedom? Yes?"

"…eleven, twelve—Will you stop that infernal chatter, I'm trying to concentrate!" *On counting bricks. Can't you see it's vitally important? Not like counting sheep, you know.*

Cadman sat up. Or rather, he tried to sit up, but his head barely raised a few inches and the rest of his body failed to comply.

"What? Where—?"

Flame coursed through the nerves of his neck where he'd cricked it. His head had been twisted to the left for as long as he'd been counting; it was easier to see the bricks that way. He tried to lift a hand to inspect the damage, but his arm was numb and apparently held fast above his head. His eyes were too sore to look. He strained his head from side to side, ignoring the impinged nerves sending fragments of glass through his scalp. A hint of dark movement in his peripheral vision caused him to strain his neck forward. Someone stooped over the end of his bed—it was a bed, right?—and grunted. There was a jolt and a squeak like a cog in need of oiling.

"Aaagh!" Cadman's arms were wrenched one way, his legs the other—just by a tiny increment, not enough to rip him apart, but enough to stretch the tendons and ligaments to their limits.

"Another turn and the ligaments will be permanently loose." A cold voice. It would have been clinical save for the hint of a thrill it conveyed.

Cadman tried to thrash about, but his hip joints popped and his arms felt like they were about to dislocate.

"Blightey!" *Oh my God, Blightey. I'm dreaming. Please tell me I'm dreaming. Wake up! Wake up!*

"What I most enjoy about the rack—" Otto Blightey seemed to be talking to someone else, as if elucidating torture for an interested student. "—is its inexorable tension. It is almost the perfect incarnation of nature's inherent cruelty; of the futility of life's struggle for continuance, the unrelenting march of time."

"It is as certain as the coming of the Dweller," said the first voice, as if it were chewing the words.

Cadman recognized it from somewhere. His mind threw up a tantalizing image of a winged gargoyle with eyes as black as pitch.

"Ikrys?"

Blightey turned the crank a notch and Cadman screamed as he'd never screamed before, a long drawn-out shriek of agony that echoed through eternity.

***

Cadman rolled out of bed and landed face first on the floor with a thud. He checked he could move his limbs, and breathed a shuddering sigh of relief that he was still fat and still unharmed.

Someone was murmuring, as if reciting a private litany. Cadman turned on his back and peered through the tiniest gap in his eyelids, dreading what he was going to see.

Thank God!

He was still in the tower—Dead Man's Torch. Still in his bedchamber. Still safe. Still alive.

The gargoyle, Ikrys, was hunched in the corner mumbling to himself over and over. The creature looked shriveled and grossly disfigured. Even he had surpassed his limits as far as channeling the dark forces was concerned. Scores and scores of the ancient dead had ripped their way from the earth at Cadman's bidding. Ikrys had said he was a creature of the Abyss, that the dark currents were his natural habitat. Nevertheless, he suffered as Cadman once had. Perhaps now the assassins had been dealt with they both could rest.

And then Cadman remembered. *Oh God*—that ejaculation again. When had he started using it? When had he stopped? God, it must have been centuries since he'd heard the expression. As far as he could remember, it had died with the world of the Ancients. The dream about Blightey must have been a warning from his unconscious, something to jolt him into action. The Dweller was going to return and would expect a suitable substitute for Shader. Cadman had to make ready, had to ensure that the woman was accepted.

"Come along, Ikrys, chop-chop," Cadman said, clambering to his feet. *That's another phrase I've not used in an age. What on earth's the matter with me?* "Can't have you moping about feeling sorry for yourself. We have a sacrifice to prepare, a demon to greet and…"

Ikrys shook his wings like a couple of limp dishcloths. He twisted his head at an impossible angle and gazed at Cadman through black slits beneath heavy lids that were so rough and gray they could have been carved from stone.

"And what?" The words came out like a blast of steam.

"Well," Cadman said, sounding much more amiable than he felt. "There are a lot of dead assassins outside. Can't have them idling away when they could be put to good use."

Ikrys groaned and curled into a ball.

"Come, come," Cadman said. "A big strong denizen of the Abyss like you. I thought you said the dark currents were your natural dwelling. Surely, you can help me raise a few more corpses."

Cadman was already reaching out with his mind, searching out the nascent corruption rising from the dead Sicarii like a clogging miasma. He sent out strands of black ichor to each silent heart and then placed a hand on the gargoyle's head, channeling the unnatural forces through him. Ikrys shuddered and retched, but almost instantly, the ethereal strands tautened and Cadman felt the wailing consciousness of twenty more recruits clamoring for his attention. With practiced ease, he dismissed their moaning to the periphery of his mind and headed up the ladder to the roof.

Rhiannon lay as still as death, back resting against one of the merlons that surrounded the parapet like rotting teeth. She looked pale and waxen, her lips slightly cyanosed.

Shit. Don't tell me she's snuffed it.

Cadman's black heart fluttered like the crushed wings of a butterfly. He hurried to her side and felt for a pulse. *Bradycardic, but regular.* He turned her head and felt the back of her neck. There was an oozing pustule where Ikrys had stung her. Maybe he'd been a bit overzealous with the venom. Still, at least she was in no state to cause any trouble.

Cadman peered over the parapet and gave a satisfied clack of his tongue as the dead Sicarii slipped into the shadows of the forest. The ancient corpses that had slaughtered them massed around the base of the tower and the Lost sat astride their skeletal steeds with the stoicism of granite.

A shimmering of the darkness alerted Cadman to Callixus' presence on the roof.

"Punctual as ever, eh?" Cadman said as the specter took on some semblance of solidity.

The former grand master of the Elect rested a hand upon the hilt of his black sword, red eyes flaring through the eye-slit of his helm.

"It is folly to meet this demon's demands," Callixus hissed. "It cannot harm you while my knights stand against it."

"Surely you're not suggesting I renege on an agreement?" Cadman said. "Have you begun to lose your Nousian morality at last?"

Callixus flinched, his eyes smoldering. "This Dweller was spawned in the Abyss…"

Cadman knew where this was going and really didn't have the time. "As was Ikrys. Are you going to deny how useful he's been?" He took Callixus' silence as affirmative. How could the wraith consider anything evil in comparison with his own unnatural perdurance? "Look at yourself, before you judge others," he said, and immediately regretted it.

"I see what I am, Doctor, perhaps more clearly than you see what you are. I judge myself with the eyes of Ain, even after all these centuries."

"You still loathe yourself? But I thought…"

The wraith floated toward Cadman as if he were about to strike. Cadman tightened his hold upon Callixus' will and the grand master came no closer.

"I despise what you have made me," Callixus said. "I am shamed by the weakness that allowed you to harness my soul. When Ain judges me, if ever you cede him the chance, I pray that he will be merciful, for I was given no choice."

Still angry? Still struggling? Callixus should have quieted by now. Most of the raised dead were acquiescent within weeks, but the grand master had been under Cadman's control for five hundred years. How could he still care? How could he remember anything else?

"Perhaps," Callixus continued, the words tumbling out as if they'd been pent up for decades, "Ain is still trying to teach me. The Elect are exemplary in all things but their pride. My impotence before your evil may be the means of my salvation."

Cadman shook his head, not quite believing what he was hearing. "Oh, Callixus, my old friend. You still cling to hope when all the evidence is against it. You really are remarkable—my absolute favorite. What would you have me do, release you?"

The glow of Callixus' eyes softened for a moment. "You would do that? Then why did you bring me back from the Void?"

Cadman wanted to touch him then, hug him even, but the gesture would have felt hollow. "I need you, Callixus. Right now I need you more than ever. I know you think I'm evil," —*and I'd be the first to agree with you*— "but give me a few more days. See this through to the end, not because I force you, but because I'm asking you." *Begging you.* "Hell, Callixus, I'm as lost as you are. Even more so, because I chose this path." As much as anyone could choose anything. What was it the Ancient World priests used to

387

say about seeds and stony ground, some getting smothered by weeds? If only Cadman hadn't been so assiduous in his studies. If only he hadn't looked down on those less capable than him. If only he hadn't met Blightey...

Too late for regret, Cadman. Way too late. He'd chosen his path and now he had to follow where it led. Oh, he could have hidden away in the shadows of Sarum for another century, more perhaps, but eventually he'd have had to face what he was. You could only put it off for so long, and Cadman had a nasty feeling his moment was coming. *Time to face the music, Ernst.*

An odd feeling was gnawing away at what remained of his innards. He struggled to decipher it, shook his head, and then looked up into Callixus' tormented eyes.

Compassion?

Surely not. He could almost hear Blightey laughing at the idea all the way from Verusia. "Too late for compassion, my dear Ernst," the Liche Lord would say. "You've stacked up too many tokens in the name of truth." Blightey's truth—uncompromising, cruel, unforgiving. One act of compassion won't make an iota's difference. What would be the point?

No point, Cadman realized. It would make no difference; there'd be no discernible gain.

Nevertheless...

"I release you." He clapped a hand on Callixus' ghostly shoulder. "But I ask you—I implore you—stay with me a few more days. Maybe Ain would want that." *Now that's stretching it!* "Maybe you could help me..."

Cadman turned away, his heart thudding like a ricocheting bullet. *Stop right there, Cadman, you cowardly, self-seeking, walking sack of rot! Fear, that's all this is. Just put up or shut up. Take the consequences of your actions.*

"I will stay," Callixus said, his voice thick with emotion he should not have felt. "I know how hard—"

"No," Cadman said, raising a hand for silence. "I don't need to hear that. The Dweller is coming and there's nothing I can do about it. It was my fault. I knew it was a risky gambit going after the statue, and now all the bad choices I've made are coming home to roost."

Cadman stooped over Rhiannon and started to drag her to the center of the roof. He paused for a moment, looked over his shoulder at the wraith, and felt he would have wept if he'd been capable. "Thank you," he said, and then tried to put the matter out of his mind with counting.

Rhiannon moaned and muttered something. For a moment, she looked exactly what she was: a sacrificial victim dressed in virginal white. *Well, I'm not sure about the latter.* The effect was ruined by the filth staining her robe, but it was enough to make Cadman pause and reflect. She could have been a pre-Raphaelite heroine, perhaps even a saint. He bent closer to hear, but then realized she was probably just talking in her dreams. Whatever venom Ikrys had in his tail, it would undoubtedly give Morpheus a run for his money. Cadman shook his head and sighed. Not that anyone in this topsy-turvy post-Reckoning nightmare would even know who Morpheus was anymore. Mythology had fallen during the time of the Ancients, and religion along with it. There had been no place for anything that lacked utility in Global Tech's world.

And to think, at one time, Cadman had trodden the path of science, a natural enough progression from his medical career. Odd that he didn't end up like the Technocrat himself, especially as they'd both shared the same mentor in Blightey. But Blightey had moved on since his tutoring of Sektis Gandaw. He'd told Cadman they'd fallen out, but if what Cadman had gleaned from history were true, that was an unmitigated understatement. There'd been a conflict of terrifying proportions, and Gandaw had emerged triumphant. Blightey had slithered away into obscurity, but he'd not been idle, and his threat certainly hadn't gone away. If the Liche Lord's millennia of existence had taught him anything, it was how to be patient. New protégés had come and gone—most of them had ended up on spikes outside Blightey's castle in Verusia—and by the time Cadman had come to the Liche Lord's attention, Blightey had immersed himself in practices far darker than science, far more primal and insidious.

"Doctor!" Callixus hissed.

Cadman's head snapped back, and his pince-nez flew from the bridge of his nose. Rhiannon's teeth were bared in a rictus grin, her fist raised for another blow. Before Cadman could react, Callixus smothered her like a vaporous pall, re-forming behind her with her wrists held in his spectral hands. She squirmed and cursed as Cadman fumbled around for his pince-nez. It was an automatic reaction, one he still cherished. He'd had no physical need of the eyeglasses for centuries, but that didn't mean he didn't *need* them. They were as necessary to him as Cognac and cigarettes. He twisted the frames back into shape and settled them on his nose. Rhiannon flinched, as if she expected him to hit her.

"Be still, my dear, be still," Cadman said, raising his palms. "Whatever I may be, I'm no brute."

She said nothing, but eyed him with undisguised malice.

Cadman couldn't really blame her. "If I could spare you, I would," he said with a gentleness that surprised himself. "Odd as it might strike you, I don't actually want anyone else to get hurt. Too much has happened already." *Too much that I didn't intend.* Or did he? Was he to blame for all the actions that had arisen from his initial action, his decision to seek out the statue? Was he culpable for accepting the path suggested by the Dweller, or was the demon to blame for tempting him?

"I am…" Cadman shut his eyes and tried to find the right words. *Why the hell am I explaining myself? What does any of this matter?* "I'm afraid." More than that: he was terrified. The longer you lived, the greater the fear of oblivion. He'd spent centuries running from death, outwitting mortality, sidestepping the big questions of his existence; but the Dweller made that impossible. Not only had it coaxed him from the shadows and back into the world of risks, but now it was on its way to exact payment for its services.

"Tell someone who cares," Rhiannon said, looking at him as if he were something she'd ordinarily scrape off her shoe. "You expect sympathy, after all the people you've killed? Shog, you're pathetic."

Cadman swallowed. He hadn't expected that. Didn't she know he had the power to kill her? Hell, he even had the power to raise her again and grant her an eternity of torment.

She continued to stare at him with fire in her eyes. Life.

"I didn't want to become like this." Cadman couldn't stop himself; he needed her to understand. "I just want to be left alone."

"Then crawl back under whatever stone you came from."

Callixus' eyes smoldered down at Rhiannon, but she paid no heed. She wore her anger, or her despair, like armor.

"Too late for that," Cadman said. "Far too late. Newton's First Law and all that." She'd have no idea what he was talking about, but Cadman wasn't really addressing her. He was speaking to himself. It's what he needed, what he should have done an age ago. "I know what the right thing to do would be." Just the acknowledgment sent icy fissures through his bones. "I know I'm being selfish." Self-preserving; self-absorbed. "But I can't do anything else. It's my fault—everything that's happened—but I'm too weak to make it right."

Some of the fierceness left Rhiannon's eyes. She studied Cadman just like his mother had done whenever he'd disappointed her.

"Then let me help you," she said.

She sounded sincere. *Impossible. She's just acting. She just wants to save her skin.* Her eye contact never wavered, and Cadman felt himself grimacing.

"But…" He wrung his hands. There was a tightness behind his eyes that extended through his cheekbones. It was as if the remains of his body remembered how to cry but lacked the tear ducts to do so. "How…? I mean, what…?"

Wind whipped through Rhiannon's hair, fanning it out behind her like a black halo. Callixus turned his head to scan the rooftop as the gust raced around them faster and faster, sucking dust and detritus into a funnel of air until Dead Man's Torch was the epicenter of a cyclone. Cadman staggered back, holding onto a merlon for support.

"Too late," said the voice of a child.

The wind dropped, leaving an ebon figure perched atop the crenellations. Its face was devoid of features, its body curved like a woman's, with jutting breasts and tapered hips; yet between its legs hung an appendage as huge as a horse's. A hazy miasma surrounded the androgyne, radiating a palpable malignancy as poignant as the plague that had ravaged Sarum. The head split down the center, revealing a man's face beneath, still black, as if carved from coal, yet unmistakable in its dour leanness.

"Deacon?" Rhiannon said, struggling, but still held firm by Callixus.

"Shader?" Cadman took a step back.

"Appropriate, don't you think?" the Dweller said. "After all, it was his soul you promised me."

Rhiannon turned her ire on Cadman. "You did what?" She looked from him to the black figure. "The thing from the templum? Is this…?"

Cadman nodded, his hand slipping inside his jacket pocket, fingers caressing the warm fragments within. "Lies and deception," he said. "That's all it is."

The Dweller laughed and hopped off the parapet, a leer spreading across Shader's face. "What would you expect? Like father, like son, don't they say? But I didn't force you into any bargain, Cadman. You did that of your own free will. I did as you asked: I killed the knight. You might at least have had the courtesy to tell me he carried the Sword of the Archon as well as the petrified body of Eingana. No, no, no." The Dweller wagged a finger to forestall Cadman's protests. "His soul, you said; either that, or a suitable substitute. Isn't that what we agreed? And if no substitute was forthcoming, then I could have you."

Cadman took another step back as a ripple ran through the Dweller's phallus, which began to stiffen.

The demon winked out of existence and appeared directly over Rhiannon, stroking itself to rigid attention. "So, lady,"—its voice was husky, urgent—"I assume you are here for me?" The Dweller looked to Cadman, who nodded. "I need to know—" It ran its hand up and down the length of its member. "—what are your feelings for Deacon Shader?"

"Shog him," Rhiannon said without hesitation.

The Dweller's hand stopped moving. "What, no love? No affection."

Cadman studied her face, searching for any sign she was lying. She was expressionless, utterly poker-faced. She may have been a hustler; she may have been bluffing. How would he know? How would the Dweller—?

"Shog him," Rhiannon said again. Her eyes dropped to the Dweller's appendage, and she sneered.

As if she'd uttered a word of power, the Dweller lost all cohesion, splashing to the floor in a liquefied pool. Cadman sighed with relief and was about to release the fragments when a bubble popped on the surface of the puddle. A rill of blackness oozed from the edge, twisting and coiling. The liquid began to simmer, tendrils sprouting, the central mass growing, roiling, churning. One after the other, heads burst forth from the rapidly solidifying bulk, drool trickling from their mouths, eyes rolling. Callixus dragged

Rhiannon back and released her so that he could draw his sword, but all the Dweller's eyes were on Cadman.

"Not good enough," one of the heads said.

A multitude of others leered at him, their eyes burning through his disguise, baring his true form; revealing him for the skeletal aberration he'd become.

"No," Cadman moaned. The black dread of annihilation he'd fled all his life boiled up from within. "No!"

"NOT GOOD ENOUGH!" all the heads yelled in unison.

Cadman screamed, his bony fingers fastening around the fragments of the statue, wringing force from the petrified remains of Eingana.

Fangs of lightning ripped through the night sky, flaring with amber radiance. The air withdrew with a hissing rush, and the scene atop the tower was suspended for an instant. Cadman stood outside of himself, looking down. The Dweller ceased its writhing and stood like a petrified insult to life, a mass of heads and tentacles, a glistening sculpture of malice. Rhiannon was held in mid-flight, halfway to the stairs, and Callixus—*oh, Callixus*—was frozen as his black blade arced toward the demon. Not only had the air withdrawn, but it seemed to Cadman that time had retreated like the waters before a tsunami. Pressure built—he fancied he could see shapes cordoning them, a ring of horrors from some unimaginable nightmare. The hiss was still present, but not in a true audible sense. No sound, just the feeling that his ears needed to pop, that something was about to blow.

Cadman plunged back into his skeleton. Callixus' sword resumed its swing, and the Dweller lashed out with flaccid tentacles. With the screech of a thousand banshees, the air rushed back, slamming into the demon and tearing it apart.

Cadman staggered and fell, but Callixus caught him.

"The woman—" Callixus said.

"Let her go." Cadman lay back in the wraith's ghostly embrace. He was tired. So tired. He thought about the undead outside. They would kill her. If he wasn't so tired he'd call them off. She didn't deserve this.

The pieces of amber in his hand flared and started to throb. Cadman struggled to sit up, opened his fingers, and stared in horror at the segments pulsing like a beacon. "Oh my God, oh my God—"

A fissure appeared in the sky, a jagged split of cobalt. Callixus turned to look up at it, at the same time helping Cadman to stand.

"What is happening?"

"Oh my God," Cadman said. "It's him. It's him!"

The fissure widened, permitting them the vision of a man upon a throne. The image zoomed closer and Cadman simply watched with paralyzing dread. It wasn't a throne, he realized: it was a metallic chair bedizened with crystals and lights, an array of leads dangling overhead, terminating in the scalp of the seated figure. The man himself was dressed in gray, his hair slick and unnatural, his face bloodless. Worst of all were the eyes. They were cold, sharp as scalpels. They examined Cadman as if he were nothing more than an ant, a specimen.

The eyes flared with argent, searching out the hidden spaces of Cadman's mind. He tried to pull away, but was held entranced. Suddenly, it seemed as if he were tugged toward the chair, but at the same time a spectral image of the man upon the throne shot toward him, hit him with the impact of a fist and sent him tumbling in on himself.

Cadman saw the chair and its figure withdraw, the fissure closing behind them, but the man's image—his doppelgänger—was within him. It was inside Cadman's body. No, he realized. It was inside his mind.

The man reared up like a giant, immense and powerful beyond all reckoning. Cadman squealed and ran, but where could he go? How could he run? He was in his own head.

"Do you know who I am?" the intruder asked in a voice devoid of expression.

"Yes!" Cadman wailed. "Yes!"

Cadman whimpered and crawled away—not in any physical sense, there was nothing physical here—but he backed into the shadows of his mind, covered himself with emptiness as if it were the soil of the grave.

"Say it!" the intruder's voice boomed through every cell and synapse, forcing Cadman to bury himself deeper and deeper in forgetfulness. "Say it!"

Cadman screamed as he plummeted into an abyss within himself. "Sektis Gandaw!" he cried, falling, gyring, and spinning.

He tried to slow himself with his arms, but when he extended them, there was nothing there—only wisps of blackness as wraith-like as Callixus.

Something sucked at him, tugged him to the side. He yelped as he hurtled forward, hit a hard surface, and bounced. No, not bounced: dispersed.

Cadman saw movement as if through glass. Wait—it was through glass. He was inside something made of glass. A tube. He was in a tube. Giant fingers closed around the tube as he fought to orientate himself. God, what was he? He lacked substance. He was roiling about in a test tube like trapped gas.

A gigantic eye peered in at him.

Let me out!

There was no sound.

The tube rocked, and images passed by in blurry succession. Finally, with a jolt, it settled. It seemed to be standing upright. There were other tubes beside it, each with their own gaseous contents swirling about.

Where am I? Cadman screamed silently.

Where am I?

***

Sektis Gandaw looked through Cadman's eyes and sought to synchronize the experience with his own body back inside the Perfect Peak. Bi-location took some getting used to. *Just a slight calibration...* His fingers on Aethir tapped out a sequence. The interior of the mountain shimmered and superimposed itself over the top of Cadman's vision. Mephesch was kneeling beside the projector seat checking connections.

"You have him?"

The words must have come out of both bodies simultaneously as the ghostly figure that had been atop the tower with Cadman inclined its head toward him.

"In a test tube with the others," Mephesch said. "No doubt to linger there forever, unless you come up with some use for him."

Unlikely, Gandaw thought. Not with the Unweaving so close now. Nevertheless, Cadman's memories might still prove useful in the meantime. He'd learnt long ago, from his conflict with Blightey's unnatural minions, that there were no organic memories to pilfer. Cadman had rotted away to little more than bone and cartilage. But the power that animated him, the strength that allowed him to endure, was eminently accessible, if you had the technology to process it.

"Sever the link with my own body, but not with Cadman's test tube," he told Mephesch. "Being in two places at one time is disorienting."

There was a faint click in his skull—Cadman's skull—and then the images from Aethir vanished.

Gandaw gazed at the amber fragments in his hand: an eye and a fang. The body of the serpent and the other fang were inside the Perfect Peak, ready for the work of

Unweaving. Just one more eye to locate. One more piece and Eingana would be whole.

The wraith insinuated its way into his vision. "Doctor?"

With an effort, Gandaw closed his eyes and drew upon the memories of Cadman's essence, stowed away beneath the Perfect Peak. Callixus. Yes, that was it. Cadman had bound the dead knight to his service and then released him. Gandaw could soon remedy that.

Cadman's control over his creations was strong, almost innate. With the merest thought, he shackled Callixus to his own will.

The wraith rippled, his eyes flaring with surprise or rage. "But you promised—"

"Be silent," Gandaw said, striding to the edge of the parapet and gripping it with skeletal fingers.

Dark shapes lumbered around the edge of the forest, every one of them connected to him by the merest thread of sentience. *Excellent. A readymade army.*

He drew upon more of Cadman's memories—a winged creature named Ikrys, flashes of stories, faces, hints, clues, speculations. Cadman must have been an imbecile, he thought as the words of an epic poem played across his mind, the story of the Dreamer Huntsman coming face to face with his so-called gods.

"Hybrids!" Gandaw almost felt anger. He moved his jaw from side to side, grinding his teeth. Speaking with this body could take some getting used to. He saw an image of a tabletop mountain in a sprawling red desert. "So that's where you fled to." The Dreamers had a name for it, that much he deduced from the poem... the Homestead. The place Huntsman had brought about the Reckoning.

He held up Cadman's pieces of the statue and concentrated. Nothing. Not the slightest link with the missing fifth piece. Either it was shielded, or Eingana was still finding ways to hide from him. Maybe it was Nous, he scoffed. After all, it had been with the Templum fleet.

Another of Cadman's memories insinuated its way into his consciousness. The bard had told Cadman the tale of Otto Blightey stealing the artifact from Aeterna. It had been concealed in the Ipsissimal Monas. What if that was still the case? What if the supreme ruler of the Templum was here in Sahul, a sort of last guardian of the statue?

With the power of the two pieces in his hands, and two more on Aethir, he knew he should have no trouble confronting the Templum force, especially with the backing of Cadman's undead army. But he was used to certainties, and the fact that he couldn't detect the last piece was evidence he'd been wrong, either about the statue or those who now held it. He hadn't had time to look at all the variables.

What if the Ipsissimus had some means of resisting him? He must have come all this way for a reason. Maybe Huntsman had a trick up his sleeve. Perhaps he'd underestimated them both. Gandaw didn't know the terrain, didn't know what forces could be arrayed against him. He was the one who should be calling the shots, not them. Maybe it was a mistake inhabiting Cadman's body. He could have waited on Aethir; played his usual patient game. Too late to worry about that now. *In for a penny, in for a pound.* Where had that come from? Perhaps if he stirred things up at the Homestead, Huntsman would be forced into a desperate act to protect his gods. He might even persuade the ruler of the Templum to come to their aid. At least that way Gandaw could choose the site of any battle and plan accordingly.

"Where is Ikrys?" he asked.

"Below," Callixus answered like a dutiful slave.

"Fetch him," Gandaw said. "Tell him I'm going to need a bigger army."

Much bigger, he thought. It never paid to take chances.

BREAKOUT

HADER'S ANGER TRAILED him like a cloak as he strode down the Domus Tyalae toward the templum. He wasn't even sure it was anger, and if it was, he wasn't clear who to direct it at. He kept telling himself he was furious with Lallia, but he knew that wasn't fair. Whatever she was, however she chose to lead her life, he knew he was just using her as a scapegoat. Was it Gaston? His death? What he'd done to Rhiannon? Was he angry with Rhiannon for listening to Huntsman and wrecking whatever chance of happiness they'd had?

He stepped over a black-clad body lying in a pool of its own blood just inside the narthex. He resisted an urge to kick it and carried on down the aisle toward the sacristy. He stopped at the door, wincing and clenching his fists. For a moment, he felt the shame of what had happened with Lallia and was overcome with self-loathing. Suddenly, he had perspective on his life, saw it for the sham it really was. His fingers brushed the hilt of the longsword Dave had mysteriously returned to him. He was definitely made from the same mold as his father, a man of violence, bred to be a killer. It didn't matter how hard he tried to hide that truth beneath a veneer of Nousian piety, the path of peace was beyond him. The monks at Pardes had known that all along, so why had they played along with the farce? Had they taken some sort of sick pleasure in watching him fail? Maybe Hagalle was right about Nousians. Maybe it was just some global cult of control…

Shader shook his head to put the thought from his mind. Nous wasn't to blame for his weakness. The Templum hadn't made him what he was. If anyone had shaped Shader, it was Aristodeus. But even the philosopher needed to be absolved as far as Shader was concerned. If the confessional had taught him one thing, it was that you left all your excuses, your blame of others, outside.

He pushed open the door and passed through to the corridor that was flanked by the priests' chambers. Frater Hugues was on his hands and knees scrubbing at the blood on the tiles. He seemed only to be diluting it, spreading stains of pink across the floor.

"Where—?" Shader started but stopped himself. His voice sounded too harsh.

Hugues looked up, his face set and hard.

"Agna's cleaning Velda's body in readiness for the funeral. Mater's doing the same for Gaston, and Dr. Stoofley's in with Cadris. He'll be lucky to make it, what with a cut like that." Hugues looked Shader up and down as if he knew where he'd been. "Thought you might have helped," he said. "Had to drag those dead assassins outside by myself. There's still one in the narthex, but he can wait."

"Have you alerted the militia?" Shader asked.

Hugues put his head down and started scrubbing again. "I might not be as educated as you," he said, "but I'm not totally stupid. Who do you think would've sent the Sicarii? They certainly wouldn't come here without a contract."

Shader hadn't had time to consider the matter. He'd just come because Dave had told him the priests were in danger. Nousians were always in danger throughout Sahul, but Sarum had been different…"

"Hagalle," Hugues completed his thinking for him. "That's who's in charge here. I bet the Sicarii were his cleanest option, but he's got control of the militia and the imperial troops. It won't be long before he sends them to finish the job."

Shader's cheek twitched. He set his jaw and narrowed his eyes. "Which room is Mater in?" He needed to see Gaston one last time. Needed to lay at least one ghost to rest.

Hugues stood and opened a door for him. Shader slipped inside and leaned with his back against the jamb.

Ioana was stooped over Gaston's naked body, wiping away blood with a damp cloth. Her robe was stained red, and she sobbed as she worked.

Shader kept still and watched her tenderly prepare Gaston for the grave. Ioana did not even show that she knew he had entered the room as she proceeded to dab the body dry like a mother with a baby. Finally, she retrieved Gaston's surcoat and covered his nakedness with it. It was stained with patches of pinkish dampness where she'd obviously tried to clean it. She was pulling it up to cover Gaston's face when Shader took a step away from the door.

"No," he said so softly she probably didn't hear him. "Mater, wait."

Ioana inclined her head toward him, her eyes moist and bloodshot. She forced a smile for his benefit, but it did nothing to assuage his guilt. He'd made Gaston what he was. He'd offered the lad a new life, a new sense of purpose, and then he'd abandoned him.

"What else could he have done?" Ioana said, stroking Gaston's hair. "He knew I disapproved and yet he fought to save us. Now I don't know who was right or wrong."

Shader moved to the bedside and rested his hand on Gaston's shoulder. It felt cold and unreal, as if the lad were made of wax. For an instant, Shader had the sense that the body was nothing more than a shell, that Gaston had gone somewhere else; that he was at peace. Delusion, he told himself. There was nothing peaceful about any of this. And yet the feeling didn't totally vanish.

"He did well," Shader said, looking directly at Gaston's face as if the lad could hear him. "Hugues says the emperor sent the assassins."

Ioana straightened up and felt behind her for a chair. She flopped into it and sighed. "Who else? Zara Gen would never do such a thing."

"Not judging by his reaction. What do you suppose that was all about?"

Ioana smiled at some private recollection. "He's one of us. Don't you see? That's why he's always let us be. He'd been impressed by Bovis Rayn when he preached in the city." She smiled weakly at Gaston's body. "We always wondered how Bovis got away with it, and why nobody objected to us being here. Then Zara Gen started meeting with me in secret, but he was finally accepted into the Templum by Jarmin the Anchorite."

Shader's jaw dropped. "And now he's no longer in charge?"

"The imperial troops have the run of the city," Ioana said, "and it looks like Hagalle's assumed direct control of Sarum. Either him, or one of his stooges—most likely Duke Farian. Sarum is no longer safe for Nousians."

"But Mater, the Ipsissimus is here in Sahul with an army. I arrived with them at Dalantle."

Ioana's eyes nearly popped out of her head. "His Divinity? Here? Oh my word! Hagalle's bound to know about it. He has enough troops in the area for a full-scale war."

Shader studied Gaston's face one last time, golden hair surrounding it like a halo. He pulled the surcoat up to cover it and made the sign of the knot above the body.

Hagalle had tried to kill the priests, and he was responsible for Gaston's death. There had been imperial troops searching for Shader out on the streets too. What of the others?

"Mater, have you heard anything about Barek and the White Order?"

Ioana stood. "Dr. Stoofley is here tending Cadris. He said the knights were being detained at the old imperial barracks. You should free them. I can't bring myself to trust Hagalle's justice."

"You would approve? If I get them out?"

Ioana looked up at him, dampness rimming her eyes. She nodded.

Shader turned on his heel and left.

***

The iron gates of the compound were flanked by a couple of militiamen. Behind them, through the bars, Shader could see squads of patrolling imperial soldiers. The walls surrounding the enclosure were too high to climb, and the gates were no doubt locked as well as guarded.

He ducked back inside the porch of the tailor's shop that stood opposite the barracks. Night hung heavy over the street, the stars wan and distant as if seen through a gauze. A few of the Ancients' tall lanterns flickered with orange light that sprang from some hidden source, casting long shadows, but providing just enough illumination to see by.

Shader took another look at the two guards on his side of the gate. He doubted either would have a key. Most likely, the troops on the inside were charged with letting people in and out. The militiamen were most likely there for show, to make it seem that Sarum still managed her own affairs. One of them wore captain's stripes; his face was thickly mustachioed, and he had the stiff bearing of a career soldier. The other was younger and looked utterly miserable, hugging his arms across his chest and shivering, in spite of the night being mild.

A direct assault would be useless. Shader would need to find some way over the wall to the rear of the compound, away from the light. Perhaps he'd be lucky and find something he could climb on. His hope diminishing, he stepped from the porch, but immediately pulled back as he saw a hunched figure approach the gates.

"Who goes there?" the captain challenged, drawing his sword. His young companion turned to call to the soldiers within the enclosure.

The hunchback walked right up to them and, with a sickening feeling, Shader realized who it was.

"Praise Nous for such a beautiful night, gentlemen. Praise his glorious name."

—Dave the Slave.

"Now look here," the captain said. "We don't want any trouble." He put a hand on Dave's shoulder and turned him away from the gate, then started as he clapped eyes on Shader.

"Ah, look," Dave said. "Nous's right hand has come to the aid of the righteous."

"Who are you?" the captain barked. "Show yourself."

Shader walked toward them, pushing his coat back to reveal his swords. "Deacon Shader," he said. "I've come for my friends."

The creak of old metal announced the opening of the gate. Half a dozen imperial soldiers spilled through onto the street, shields before them, spears raised.

"Captain Harding, City Militia. Look, there's no need for any trouble here. The emperor's holding your friends merely as a precaution. Now, I'm sure if we could—"

"That's him," a bearded soldier said, pointing his spear at Shader.

"Now wait a minute, gentlemen," Harding said, but already the soldiers were fanning out around Shader.

"This is my city," Harding said. "Back off until I give the order."

"Get lost, Harding," the bearded soldier said. "We can handle this. Go catch yourself a thief or something."

The young militiaman tried to draw his sword, but one of the soldiers pushed him in the back. As he tried to gain his balance, the soldier punched him in the face, and the lad went down. Harding went to draw his sword, but a spear point to the throat stopped him.

"Like I said," the bearded soldier growled. "Get lost."

Harding backed away shaking his head.

In that moment, Dave snarled and leapt. The bearded man screamed as Dave clawed at his face. Shader caught the fierce flash of the hunchback's eyes, the feral contortions of his face. The soldier toppled backward and Dave followed, landing on top of him and mauling his throat.

The other soldiers surged forward, but Shader stepped in among them, both blades leaping to his hands. He turned the thrust of a spear and gutted his attacker with the gladius. His longsword clanged against a shield, which he spun around and elbowed the man in the jaw. A rush of air from behind made Shader duck, a spear-tip grazing his cheek. He turned to face the attacker, but Captain Harding charged into the man's shield, bowling him over. Harding blocked another spear thrust and severed the soldier's hand at the wrist.

"Nous comes to liberate the just!" Dave cried out, slipping through the guards and rushing into the compound.

Shader could see more soldiers rushing to the gate from within, but Dave seemed oblivious. Just before the soldiers were upon him, he vanished.

Harding and Shader stood side by side as the remaining three soldiers in the street leveled their spears and pressed their shields together, advancing with caution.

"Run," Shader said. "This isn't your fight."

Harding shot him a look of disbelief, or disdain. "This is darn right unlawful," he barked loud enough for the imperial soldiers to hear. "I'll not stand for it."

The young militiaman groaned and sat up, rubbing his face. He found his feet and scarpered as a dozen more soldiers emerged from the compound and encircled Shader and Harding.

"This wasn't quite what I had in mind," Shader said.

"Battles never go as planned," Harding said, as if Shader were a rookie. "You watch my back, I'll watch yours."

"Thanks."

"Don't thank me," Harding said. "Once this is over, you're still under arrest. Orders is orders, but I'll be damned if these thugs from Jorakum are going to behave like this in my city."

The circle closed in, spears bristling. Shader's blades were a blur as he batted aside two thrusts, slipped inside and stabbed a soldier through the chest. He backslashed another across the face and skipped away to avoid being impaled by yet another. Harding was breathing heavily behind him, the clang of steel on steel deafening as he bashed at the wall of shields and hacked at spears. He groaned and fell against Shader, blood spurting from his shoulder, but he immediately lunged, skewering his attacker, ripping his sword free and swinging at another, who jumped back out of range.

"I'll be damned if these milksops are gonna take me," he growled. "In my day I'd have killed twenty by myself."

Another spear came for Shader's head. He swayed aside, hacked down on the haft, and broke it. The soldier barreled on behind his shield, but Shader spun out of the way and slit his throat. More soldiers spilled out from the compound and swelled the circle of attackers. Harding grunted as another spear took him in the side. Shader whirled, grabbed hold of the haft, and stabbed its wielder in the biceps. The man screamed and let go. A sound like an avalanche rose above the combat. Horses, Shader realized. It was all over then.

Harding staggered and pulled the spear out, blood gushing from the wound. He fell to his knees, panting. Miraculously, the wall of spears remained still.

"Would have taken them ten years ago," Harding gasped. "Must be getting old."

He sagged to the floor and Shader stood over him, swords poised to strike.

But no one moved.

Shader thought they were expecting him to surrender. Clearly, they knew nothing of the Elect. But then the circle split apart as the soldiers pulled back. Behind them, Dave the Slave walked before a line of mounted knights who rode out onto the street to surround the imperial soldiers.

"Barek!" Shader said, recognizing the sandy-haired youth in a mail hauberk and Nousian surcoat. He felt a rush of emotion swamp him. He didn't know whether to laugh or cry, but somewhere in among it all, he felt pride as he recognized some of the others: Gord, Solomon, Elgin, even Justin. Including Barek, there were only thirteen. How many had been lost along the way? These were the lads he'd trained, the lads he'd let down. In spite of his misgivings, in spite of his belief that they could be nothing without his lead, they came now to his aid when it was meant to be him rescuing them. He thought of Gaston, the most flawed and the most brilliant among them; thought of his waxy corpse looking more at peace than ever he'd been in life. Gaston, who'd done so much wrong, and yet at the last, even in the face of Ioana's disapproval, had vindicated everything Shader had ever fought for. Tears spilled down his cheeks as the imperial soldiers dropped their spears and were herded into the enclosure.

Barek dismounted and embraced him. "You came for us," he said. "I always knew you would."

Shader shook his head, feeling so inadequate. "A right mess I made of it, though," he said through the tears. "Barek, it's good to see you. Good to see you all."

"Any news of Gaston?" Barek asked. "Things weren't good between us last time we met."

Shader pulled back from the embrace and sheathed his swords. Without meeting Barek's eyes he said, "Gaston's dead."

Barek dropped his head.

"But he put us all to shame, Barek, at the last. He died saving the priests from Hagalle's assassins."

"Really?" Barek said. "He redeemed himself?"

Shader wanted to believe that; hoped it were true. But that was for Rhiannon to judge. If not her, then Ain.

"The Ipsissimus is here," Shader said, avoiding answering. "The Templum Fleet is at Dalantle."

"I heard," Barek said. "But Hagalle plans to attack them."

Shader nodded. He crouched down to feel for a pulse in Harding's neck. He'd lost a lot of blood, but his heart still beat, albeit faintly.

"The emperor's an idiot," Shader said. "Scared of his own shadow. He should be going after Cadman, who still has two pieces of the statue. The others are in the hands of Sektis Gandaw. Ain only knows what will happen if he gets hold of Cadman's."

"This all sounds so unreal," Barek said. "Like one of Elias's stories. Sektis Gandaw's a myth, like Otto Blightey. I still find it hard to accept this is happening."

"Me too," Shader said. "Me too."

"What should we do? There are so few of us left." Barek rubbed his horse behind the ear and then climbed back into the saddle. "Nevertheless, we are battle-hardened and yours to command, if that's what you wish."

"You have any spare horses?" Shader asked.

"Here," Dave the Slave said, leading the horse Shader had ridden from Dalantle. "Go,

Keeper of the Sword. Lead this holy Order. Ride to the aid of Nous's Vicar on Earth and bring death to the infidel, Hagalle."

"Thought I told you to leave me alone," Shader said. "And besides, what do you think fourteen knights could achieve against the thousands Hagalle commands? Why don't you do something useful? Take this man to the templum; see if Mater Ioana can do anything for him; or try Dr. Stoofley, if he's still there."

Shader was surprised that Dave did as he asked. The hunchback stooped and lifted Harding as if he weighed no more than a baby. Without a word, he trudged into the night and faded from view.

"There has to be another way," Shader said to Barek. "We have to make Hagalle see reason."

He mounted his horse and led the White Order northwards through Sarum's night-darkened streets. Reasoning with a madman was a task that didn't inspire much hope. Maybe the Ipsissimus would have more luck, if he could get close enough to parley. Failing that, the best they could do was pray and hope for some kind of miracle.

BROTHER OF MINE

RHIANNON DROPPED DOWN the last five feet of the ladder and twisted her ankle.
"Shit," she cried. "Shog, shit, and scut."

The room she'd entered was a bedchamber—presumably Cadman's.

The gargoyle-thing was curled up on the edge of the bed, breathing heavily. It appeared to be asleep. She glanced up at the trapdoor. There was no sign of pursuit, but it wouldn't be long till they noticed she'd gone. No time to hang about.

She tested her ankle and winced at the pain. She could walk if she didn't put too much weight on it. She took a step toward the gargoyle, intending to throttle it in its sleep, but then took hold of herself. Stupid to take risks now. She just had to get out of there.

The gargoyle snored, and Rhiannon held her breath. Once its breathing resumed its steady rhythm, she hobbled through the open door and limped downstairs.

The lower levels were unguarded, but the front door was secured from the inside. She drew back the heavy bolts one at a time, holding her breath whenever they squeaked. Taking hold of the handle, she cast a look over her shoulder to make sure she still wasn't being followed, and then pulled.

She slid through the merest of cracks and immediately saw movement out of the corner of her eye. Black shapes to either side of the door began to lumber toward her. Doing her best to ignore the pain in her ankle, she half ran, half hopped for the trees. More shapes emerged from the darkness to shamble in pursuit, but within a few strides, her ankle eased, and she was able to plant her weight on it. She tore into the undergrowth, veering to the left as a horde of groaning figures rose from a cluster of mounds.

"Ain," she whispered to herself, half in prayer, half in shock. "More shogging zombies."

She sprinted away from the main mass of undead, arms pumping furiously, breath coming in ragged gasps. The darks shapes from the tower still followed, spreading out like a dragnet. Ducking beneath overhanging branches, Rhiannon found herself on a woodland trail and picked up her speed. Something grabbed at her robe—it may have been a branch, but she didn't stop to find out—and then she slipped and tumbled down a bank. She hit the bottom with a thud that jarred her neck and sent a thumping pain through her skull. She crawled another pace before pulling herself up using a drooping branch.

Black figures lumbered through the darkness behind her, merging with the forest so that it seemed the trees themselves were moving, reaching out, coming for her. She pushed away from the branch and took a couple of steps, but then a hooded figure emerged from behind a eucalypt in front of her. A dozen or more black-cloaked figures slunk out to either side.

"Who the hell are you?" she found herself shouting in her panic.

The lead figure threw back its hood to reveal a sharp face dominated by a well-oiled mustache. The flesh was pale, the eyes red. Strips of meat clung to its teeth.

The others revealed their faces, each with the pallor of the grave and starting to putrefy.

Rhiannon whirled, looking for an opening, but the horde from the tower was closing in around her. She grabbed a branch and snapped it free from its trunk. It lacked weight, but she'd take whatever she could find. Crouching, she held the branch in both hands and dared the cloaked zombies to advance.

They drew daggers and came at her—lightly, on the balls of their feet, not at all like the shambling things behind. As they drew closer, Rhiannon saw that they all had grisly wounds—raked faces, gouged chests, ripped out throats.

Cracking twigs and rustling leaves startled her. She spun, still looking for some opening to slip through, but the noose had closed, and there was nowhere to run. A hundred pairs of hands reached toward her. She swooned and retched at the stench of decay, dropping the branch and falling to her knees. Cold fingers touched her—

Lightning flashed, its flicker making the movements of the dead appear stilted. A sizzling crack followed, and a thunderous blast rolled through the woods. Flesh charred, smoke plumed skywards, and bodies fell. Another explosion sent rotting carcasses hurtling into trees, and a passage opened through the horde. The cloaked zombies still came on, but the air in front of them swirled green like a vast shield of light. As they struck it, the corpses disappeared, as if they'd walked into the mouth of a cave.

Two figures ran through the corridor between the undead, one cloaked in feathers, the other much smaller and half naked. Recognition hit Rhiannon, and she knew she must have been dreaming; knew she must have been dead.

★★★

"Boy has heard it." —A man's voice, thick and awkward, as if the words were alien. "All of web shudders in warning. Sahul's children cry out."

"The ants." —A boy's voice, shrill and excited. "They tell me everything."

Rhiannon moaned and turned, trying to snuggle down away from the noise. The bed was too hard. Her arm felt numb beneath her. Something coarse ground into her face, and her lips were dry and dusty. She rolled onto her back and red heat seared through her eyelids. She covered her face with her hands, blinking rapidly.

"How many?" —Another man's voice, smoother, more refined, yet the accent wasn't Sahulian.

"As many as stars." —The first man again. She knew that voice. Huntsman. And the child—Ain, it had to be Sammy.

"Gently, my dear," the other man said. "Huntsman, a drink. I would do it myself, but in the spirit I lack the digits."

Rhiannon let her hands drop and risked looking into the blaze. She blinked again and realized she was facing the sun. She turned away and was startled to full alertness when she saw a rough pillar of rock—limestone—jutting toward the azure sky like a fossilized finger. She shook her head and focused. Not just one rock—hundreds of them. Pocked and twisted monoliths surrounded her like a petrified forest, or a city sprouting from the earth.

Huntsman crouched into her field of vision, a tight grin exposing the black stubs of his teeth. Sunlight glinted from the crystals beaded through his hair. He put something pulpy to her lips, and she sucked automatically, drawing sweet moisture into her mouth and gulping it down.

"Cactus," Huntsman said. "Keep you alive."

"Sammy?" Rhiannon pushed Huntsman's hand away. "Is he with you?"

"Here," the boy said.

He sounded so old.

Rhiannon rolled to her knees, and Sammy came to stand before her. He looked taller somehow, but she knew that was impossible. Then she realized it was due to his bearing. He stood straight and proud, like Huntsman. His fair hair was besmirched and twisted into stubby dreadlocks that reminded her of the trunks of grass trees. His cheeks were browned from exposure and daubed with ochre. He was naked apart from a soiled binding around his loins that may have been animal skin or some kind of treated leaf. Like Huntsman, he was barefoot, and his eyes—Sammy's sparkling playful eyes—were piercing pinpricks in the grime, distantly focused and utterly serious.

"What have you done?" she shrieked at Huntsman, surging to her feet and lunging for his face.

The old Dreamer swayed out of her reach. Before she could renew her assault, a white radiance stepped between them.

"He has preserved your brother, by all accounts."

The other man. His voice was strangely distant, dreamlike.

Rhiannon stepped back. "Oh my shogging— What are you?"

He was robed in white and wearing a biretta. His face seemed unnaturally young, although the eyes were those of an old man. Rhiannon could see right through him as if he were a ghost.

He frowned at her, ran his eyes up and down her filthy white robe. "Hardly the sort of language one would expect from a Nousian. Particularly a postulant."

Rhiannon's hand went to her mouth. "Oh my—" She bowed her head and wasn't sure whether or not to genuflect. "Oh, oh, oh." What was she supposed to say? How should she address him? "You're ... you're..."

"I am the servant of the servants of Nous, my dear, and you have been through a terrible ordeal."

"Ipsissimus," Rhiannon gasped. "The Ipsissimus? Here?"

"Not exactly here," the Ipsissimus indicated his see-through form, "but I am in Sahul. These are perilous times, my dear. I'm only sorry that you have been caught up in them."

Warm fingers curled around her hand. Sammy pressed in close, his dirty body complementing the stains on her robe. He looked so alien, so utterly unlike the little boy she knew and loved. Yet, when he pressed his head into her side, Rhiannon clutched it to her, ruffling his matted hair with her free hand.

"My friend," Huntsman said to the Ipsissimus. "This army of corpses, it marches now toward Homestead."

"Why would it do that?" the Ipsissimus asked. "Thought there was nothing there besides desert and the mountain itself?"

Huntsman's eyes widened in horror. "Gods of Dreaming."

"Even so—" the Ipsissimus started, but Huntsman cut him off.

"Cadman must think they know where rest of statue is."

"Do they?"

"No."

"Then we should stay out of it," the Ipsissimus said. "We can't risk the Monas."

"But we must go to them." Huntsman looked like he would have shaken the Ipsissimus if he had anything to grab onto. "He will kill them before he believes they do not know."

Rhiannon let go of Sammy's hand and stepped toward Huntsman. "It's not Cadman. Not anymore."

Huntsman looked at her as if she were crazy, but then realization crept across his face even before she explained herself.

"On the tower, on Dead Man's Torch," she said, 'something came for him: a man seated on a throne. The skies opened like someone had torn a curtain. This man—"

"Sektis Gandaw!" Huntsman seemed to visibly wilt as he said the name. The Ipsissimus merely closed his eyes.

"—he did something to Cadman," Rhiannon said. "Entered his body in some way. I think Cadman's gone—dead even, if that's possible."

"If Sektis Gandaw has the other four pieces—" the Ipsissimus said.

"He needs only one more," Huntsman finished. "To begin Unweaving: end of all things."

The Ipsissimus's spectral hand clutched the golden Monas around his neck. "Why hasn't he already come for it? With the other pieces, he could—"

"The Archon," Sammy said, his eyes rolling into the back of his head. "He wards it. The other pieces can no longer find it."

"Then Gandaw's barking up the wrong tree," Rhiannon said.

"No." Huntsman regained his poise and shook his head. "He wants revenge. My gods thwarted him once. He does not forget."

The Ipsissimus touched his fingertips together beneath his nose. "And you say they don't know about my Monas?"

"No," Huntsman said. "They never let me tell them."

"Then why—?" Rhiannon started.

"Sektis Gandaw doesn't know that. He will try to force knowledge from them, and they will be unable to answer," the Ipsissimus said.

"It is worse than that." Huntsman looked from Rhiannon to the Ipsissimus with panic in his eyes. "Sektis Gandaw hates my gods. He goes to slaughter them, just as he once slaughtered Barraiya People. My friend," he said to the Ipsissimus, "we must help them."

403

THE COMMON FOE

IPSISSIMUS THEODORE WATCHED his troops file past as he was borne along in a gilded lectica by four men. He loathed this mode of transport, but as Exemptus Cane was forever reminding him, it was what the people expected. An Ipsissimus had to be seen as more than human. Apparently, being carried on a cushion-strewn litter rendered one divine.

As columns of armored men marched past, seemingly oblivious to the heat, Theodore had an unquiet heart. He had never been comfortable with the use of force and yet his Templum had for thousands of years subscribed to a theory of just war. Theodore had always found this contrary to the example of Nous, who had embodied a strategy of non-violent resistance. In this case, though, when the future of Creation was at stake, he could see no alternative. And yet a quiet, nagging voice refused to grant him the peace that should accompany a decision made in good conscience; a voice that seemed to taunt him with the limitations of his own faith: *Trust in Ain. Be not afraid.*

Following the maps sent to Aeterna by the Jarmin in return for Aeterna-tech medicines and weapons, the column made its way south and east toward the Delling Ford. Theodore had been outmaneuvered on the armaments front. Exemptus Silvanus, more and more, was having his way in Templum affairs. And to think people believed the Ipsissimus wielded absolute power. The reality was closer to Quilonian democracy. It was no secret that Silvanus favored opening up the archives and releasing the knowledge of the Ancients. Some technology had already been made available—medical wisdom and such. It was a necessity. And then, during the Verusian campaign, strange armaments had started to appear, and transportation—most notably shipbuilding—had accelerated to rival the galleons of Sahul (which Hagalle had apparently modeled on a captured mawg reaver). Perhaps Silvanus was right. The Templum couldn't pretend the technology wasn't there, not when its rivals were rediscovering it by themselves. It was a perennial problem, but Theodore still believed with his whole heart that the sort of weapons they'd supplied to Jarmin didn't marry well with the way of Nous. It all reeked of power and hypocrisy, yet, even as Ipsissimus, he felt impotent against the tide.

The heat and dust forced the knights to remove their armor and walk their horses. Shade was minimal, at times non-existent, as they trudged across ruddy earth that seemed to foreshadow bloodshed. Scrubs of hard weeds and tufted grasstrees jutted from the desert, providing no respite from the scorching sun.

The scouts returned with news of an intercepting army to the south blocking the passage to the ford. General Binizo rode alongside the lectica to inform the Ipsissimus. He was your typical Latian, Theodore thought, careful not to be uncharitable—dark-eyed and swarthy, an impressive nose dominating his face. Binizo carried himself with a deportment that could have been construed as pompous if it were not the norm for one of his breeding.

"There are nearly four thousand men, Ipsissimus. No sooner had our scouts sighted them than a score of riders gave chase. They are highly skilled and were able to fire arrows from the saddle. They pursued our scouts for perhaps a mile before returning to the main force."

"Is it Hagalle?" the Ipsissimus asked.

"No banners were sighted, but I would assume so, Divinity."

Theodore nodded his agreement. "I had better get some rest. If the emperor is so ill-disposed toward us, I shall need to be prepared for a very long negotiation. If," he added, "we are granted the opportunity to talk. Oh, and General," Theodore said, stamping his foot so that the litter bearers would stop. "Find me a horse. I refuse to face the emperor of Sahul like some pampered Ancient world queen!"

Binizo wheeled his mount and touched his forehead.

"No," Theodore said. "On second thoughts, make it a mule." Hagalle already viewed him as an imperious conqueror. Maybe a touch of humility would help. "And inform Exemptus Cane that he may ride in the lectica." *Either that or break it up for firewood.*

***

"They have the high ground," Ignatius Grymm said, looking down on Theodore from his destrier.

"That is rather apparent," the Ipsissimus squinted up at the twin hills that rose in great natural steps either side of the valley. "Surely that can't be a natural feature." Theodore shifted his position on the mule to find a degree of comfort. The animal stank of musk and sweat, and he was sure it was infested with lice.

"Some sort of earthworks, maybe," the grand master said. "Either that, or canny fortifications. Sahul has seen its fair share of warfare. I was reading about the Zaneish rise to hegemony on the voyage from Aeterna."

Theodore gazed back over his own army deployed at the edge of Dour Wood, if the maps were anything to go by. A thin line of Britannic skirmishers provided a screen for the main force; hard men from the north, lightly armored in leather and equipped with slings and javelins for harrying the enemy, and long bladed knives for finishing the wounded. Behind them, to the left, just nudging out of the tree-line, were the Templum's shock troops: over a hundred knights of the Elect, heavily armored and perfectly disciplined. One coordinated charge from them was enough to decimate any army in Nousia. Theodore only hoped they'd enjoy the same success in Sahul, should it come to it.

The center was held by the heavy infantry units, nearly two hundred men in plate armor wielding fearsome glaive guisarmes twice the length of a spear and with hooks at the back of the blade for unseating riders. They had a contingent of the Ipsissimal Guard to their right and another to the rear—seasoned veterans in red cloaks with an embroidered white Monas. These men fought with short stabbing swords and rectangular shields. Theodore had seen them maneuvering in Latia and had been in awe of their ability to flawlessly change formation and to use their shields as a defensive wall. A long line of archers came next, each with Britannic long bows carved of yew. Bringing up the rear were the Elect Foot, Theodore's personal bodyguard, fighters of incomparable skill and loyalty. He imagined they were feeling a little forlorn back there with no one to protect—besides Exemptus Cane, who seemed quite at home in the Ipsissimal lectica.

"Are they a threat?" Theodore asked his grand master. It was so difficult to tell with these things. He'd never actually witnessed a battle, but he had endured years and years of endless parades with Ignatius wittering on in his ear about the pros and cons of every single unit.

"All enemies pose a threat, Divinity. The first rule of war is never to underestimate your opponent. Especially when he outnumbers you by at least two to one. See how Hagalle employs a screen like our own, only longer. He doesn't want to show his full strength. Those peltasts at the foot of the hill will split and run once the real fighting begins, making way for whatever he has behind. Those are light cavalry on the left hill, but too few to be more than a nuisance. I doubt he'll risk them against the Elect. Up there," Ignatius pointed to the top of the left hill and swung his finger over to take in the right, "he has twice our archers. If those are long bows, we lose the range advantage. Their heavy cavalry are on the right flank. He aims to use them against the Ipsissimal Guard, but if he does, we'll wheel away and let them face the guisarmes. What troubles me most is what he has guarding the mouth of the valley. Perhaps when we get closer we'll be able to see."

"If we get closer," Theodore said. "I have a feeling Hagalle is not going to want to parley. Nevertheless..." Theodore shook the reins and sent the mule plodding forward.

"You know my feelings on this, Divinity" Ignatius said, dismounting and handing the reins of his destrier to a young squire. The grand master took hold of the mule's bridle and walked beside it.

"You have surpassed yourself in letting me know," Theodore said with a smile. He knew how hard it had been for the grand master to speak his mind, even when asked. "But it is not with all this—" Theodore flicked his hand back at the Templum army. "—that we do Ain's work. We must reach out with humility and friendship. If Hagalle refuses us, then we shall have to think again."

If he didn't kill them. Theodore dreaded the thought. Such an incident would spark full-scale war between Sahul and the whole of Nousia. It was hardly the kind of legacy he was hoping to leave.

Ignatius led the mule out onto the dusty red plain between the forest and the hills. Sunlight glinted from the spears and armor of Hagalle's forces, making it difficult to see. Theodore wondered if perhaps he should have brought a white flag. Maybe his robes would suffice. In any case, even a total brute would be able to tell that two men and a mule hardly constituted an act of aggression.

The sun harried them every slow plodding step of the way, deadlier than a hail of arrows, more certain than a sword through the guts. Theodore wished he'd brought a waterskin. Now they were out of the limited shade of the eucalypts, they'd probably both shrivel and die before they came within talking distance of the imperial force, and even if they should make it, he'd probably be too parched to speak. If Ignatius was feeling the heat beneath his chainmail and cloak, he didn't show it. There was a sheen on his forehead beneath his iron-gray hair, but other than that the grand master was as stoic as ever.

Midway between the two armies, Ignatius brought the mule to a stop as the screening peltasts in front of the imperial force parted to either side of the valley mouth. Two staggered phalanxes guarded the pass between the hills. It was impossible to gauge their depth, but each was at least forty men wide and bristling with spears.

"Hoplites," Ignatius said, for once sounding surprised. "That's a throwback. I've studied them in Balzeal's *History of Conflict*, but this kind of warfare was obsolete by the time cataphracts and pikes were on the scene. Not to mention the longbow."

Theodore climbed down from the mule and shaded his eyes to get a better look. The hoplites must have really been suffering in the heat; they wore bronze breastplates and shouldered heavy, round shields.

"You think Hagalle's technology is expanding faster than his purse? Maybe he can't afford to upgrade his entire army," he said. "Does this give us more bargaining power?"

"I'm not sure, Divinity. Out in the open the Elect would smash through them, and head to head, our glaive guisarmes have the greater reach. But holed up there in the valley mouth, they may well prove an immovable object. I'd say Hagalle's plan is for a defensive battle. He seeks only to prevent us making further progress on Sahulian soil. He's hoping we'll turn tail and head back to Aeterna."

That wasn't really an option, not with the threat posed by the Statue of Eingana. And besides, Theodore had a feeling that his piece of the statue wasn't about to let him go anywhere but forward.

"If necessary, can we break through?" Theodore studied the grand master's face, but Ignatius was giving nothing away. His hesitation, however, caused Theodore to frown.

"There is an ancient story—" Ignatius stared out at the hoplites. "—of a few hundred men like these resisting an army of thousands—some say a million. If we get drawn into attacking their position, we may suffer heavy losses."

He didn't need to say any more. Theodore could already tell. They might even lose. "All the more need for diplomacy to succeed then," he said, abandoning the mule and walking toward the hills. Sweat soaked his robes and trickled in stinging rivulets down his legs and into his sandals.

"Divinity, wait," Ignatius said as a ripple passed through the massed troops on the right-hand hill. "They're coming down to meet us."

About thirty heavily armored troops, black-cloaked and bearing shields emblazoned with the Sahulian imperial Fist, made their way through the footmen fanned out along the slope. They marched in column around the front of the hoplites and then formed into a diamond about a central figure who towered over them.

"Hagalle?" Theodore watched as the clustered troops set out toward them.

"If it is, that's a brave move for an emperor."

More so than for an Ipsissimus? Theodore quashed the thought the instant it reared its head. Mind you, he'd heard Hagalle was fearful to the point of paranoia. If it was him, then either the rumors were false, or Hagalle was facing up to his fears. That might make him a very dangerous man.

Theodore looked back at his own troops some five hundred yards away. They were drawn up in disciplined ranks, and from this distance, there was no sign of the red dust that stained their cloaks. They looked pristine, immaculate; a professional army that would be very difficult to beat.

The mule was nuzzling the ground as if it were looking for something to eat. Theodore hoped it stayed put. The walk back in this heat suddenly seemed beyond him. He fingered the Monas around his neck and turned to face the approaching soldiers.

They stopped ten paces away and spread out in a semicircle. They were grim-looking men, each with a hand clutching the pommel of a scabbarded broadsword, each glaring with practiced intimidation. Theodore felt his hopes for a peaceful resolution slipping away. The tall man they'd been guarding stepped out in front and advanced alone. The soldiers looked from one to the other and started to follow, but the tall man held up a hand, and they stayed back.

Theodore knew at once he'd not been mistaken. Everything about the man's bearing screamed emperor. He had a leonine head with a sharp face. His gray-streaked black hair was drawn back in a ponytail, leaving the startling green eyes exposed above a distinguished nose. He wore a black enameled breastplate above black clothes, and a huge broadsword hung from his hip. If he was suffering from the heat, he showed no sign of it.

Ignatius stepped in his way before he could reach Theodore. Nervous looks passed between the emperor's troops, but they made no move.

"Get out of the way," the emperor said as if Ignatius were a truculent slave.

As Theodore expected, the grand master stood his ground. He folded his arms across his chest and met Hagalle with a level stare. Theodore put a hand on the grand master's shoulder and prompted him to step aside. He then lowered his head before the emperor and dropped to one knee.

"Divinity!" Ignatius sounded appalled.

"Very good," Hagalle said with a slow handclap. "And it might work in Nousia, but here in Sahul, we despise nothing more than false humility."

"Emperor Hagalle—" Theodore began, still averting his eyes.

"We also expect men to be men." Hagalle looked back at his bodyguards, who chuckled dutifully. "Not castrated milksops who dress like women."

Theodore saw movement from the side.

"No!" he said. "Stand down, Ignatius."

"But, Divinity—"

"I said, stand down."

Theodore climbed to his feet and did his best to smile as he met the Emperor's sardonic gaze. "Emperor, we have a common foe—"

"Shut it. Take your girlie army back to the ocean and sail on home to Aeterna."

Hagalle turned away, as if there were nothing else to be said.

"Emperor, I ask only—"

Hagalle spun, his fist coming straight at Theodore's face. The Ipsissimus tensed and blinked, but no impact came. Quicker than Theodore thought possible, Ignatius was in between them, his own hand clenched about Hagalle's fist.

"Ignatius, no!" Theodore said.

Hagalle's other fist came up, but the grand master pivoted and straightened Hagalle's arm behind him, forcing the emperor to the ground. The black-cloaks roared and drew their swords.

Ignatius jumped back, his own longsword rasping from its scabbard.

"Back, Divinity," he yelled. "I'll hold them."

"No, Ignatius. This isn't what I—"

Hagalle rolled to his feet and whipped out his broadsword, but the black-cloaks were upon Ignatius before the emperor could involve himself.

Two fell in a heartbeat, the grand master gliding in between them and weaving his sword through the air in a glittering sequence of thrusts, slices, and parries. He rolled around an attempted backstab and hacked his opponent across the hamstrings. The man screamed and fell amid spurting blood.

Theodore winced and flapped his hands around. How had he lost control of the situation? What had he done wrong?

The clash of steel cut through his thoughts as they formed, and he could do nothing except stare like a mesmerized beast. Ignatius hammered his sword against a shield and then kicked the man in the chest. He tried to back away, but the others had already started to outflank him. One of them charged at Theodore, but Ignatius still had the presence of mind to spot the peril to his Ipsissimus. He whirled through a vicious array of attacks, battering aside two men and dispatching the assailant at Theodore's feet.

A group of cavalry sped down the left hill and started out onto the plain. Theodore glanced behind, but his own army remained stationary, as he knew they would. Ignatius had given them a direct order not to interfere—no matter what happened.

A blade passed so close to Theodore's cheek, he felt the rush of air. Ignatius parried it and ran the man through. He spun to meet the onslaught of three others and was powerless to help Theodore as more soldiers cut him off and the Ipsissimus was surrounded.

The pounding of hooves rolled like thunder across the plain and Theodore forced his eyes shut, seeking out an instant's peace before the end. Grunts and cries came from the left where Ignatius was still battling, but then a trumpet cut across the din. The clash of blades stopped as everyone turned to the north.

Dust rose in plumes behind a wedge of horsemen thundering to intercept Hagalle's light cavalry. Theodore squinted as the imperial riders wheeled to meet the threat. The newcomers were in Nousian white, sunlight glinting from drawn swords. At the tip of the wedge rode a gaunt man in a pilgrim's hat and a black coat, the surcoat of the Elect billowing beneath.

They wouldn't dare, Theodore thought. The Elect would never disobey their grand master. But then he realized the Elect hadn't moved. These riders had come from nowhere. No—they came from the same direction as the imperial forces: they must have ridden from Sarum. And then he recognized the man in the pilgrim's hat: Deacon Shader.

The white knights smashed through the light cavalry like they were chaff, scattering them and continuing on through. Shader reined in before Hagalle's black-cloaks and leapt from the saddle. The others split, one group watching the black-cloaks, the other keeping an eye on the imperial army. Impossible, Theodore thought. Reckless. There were only a dozen or so of these white knights, and yet they stood against the foe with the same insolence that he'd come to expect from Ignatius.

Hagalle raised his sword and opened his mouth to bellow something, but Shader darted through the black-cloaks like a striking serpent and pressed the tip of the Sword of the Archon to the emperor's throat.

"Call off your grunts, Hagalle," Shader said through clenched teeth.

Hagalle tensed and snarled. Shader's sword pressed harder and drew blood.

"Last chance." Shader's voice was ice.

"Stand down," Hagalle said. "Do it, now!"

The black-cloaks sheathed their swords and bunched together, glowering.

"Now," Shader said. "You two have something to talk about."

Hagalle's face burned red. "I will not—"

"So talk."

***

"Ignatius Grymm, Barek Thomas," Shader said as Barek dismounted. "Ignatius here is grand master of the Elect. My former boss, if you like."

"Former?" Ignatius growled, although Shader saw the glint in his eye. "Vows are for life, Shader, or had you forgotten?"

Ignatius reached out to take Barek's hand, but the lad bowed his head and dropped to one knee.

"I see you've trained him well," Ignatius said. "But as for you not genuflecting before the Ipsissimus, Shader, I imagine the Judiciary will have a thing or two to say about that."

"Oh, they've got enough to beat me over the head with already," Shader said. "I shouldn't bother them with something so trivial."

Ignatius tapped Barek on the shoulder. "No need to kneel, lad. We're only joking."

Barek stood and did his best to smile. "Master Shader spoke of you often. I'm honored."

Shader inclined his head toward the Ipsissimus and the emperor who were engaged in a battle of words. At least, that's how it sounded. Hagalle was looming over the Ipsissimus, emphasizing every point with a thump of his fist into the palm of his hand. He shouted, rather than spoke, and seldom allowed the Ipsissimus to complete a sentence. The man was a bully and an idiot, Shader thought. If this went on much longer…

The black-cloaks were leaning on their shields, watching the argument with sullen expressions and occasionally whispering to one another. The White Order circled the gathering. Shader saw Solomon and Gord, Elgin and Justin, and smiled. Oh, they had their flaws, just as he did, but it was good to see them alive.

The Ipsissimus was speaking in a quiet voice, saying something about mawgs and holding out his Monas for Hagalle to see.

"Then it should be mine," Hagalle cut him off again. "It came from Sahul in the first place, and it's Sahul that's under threat, is it not?"

Ignatius' eyes narrowed, and his hand went to his sword hilt.

The air behind Hagalle shimmered and then swirled with green luminescence. Huntsman stepped out of the air followed by Sammy and Rhiannon.

Shader gasped and felt his heart thudding in his chest.

"This is bigger than Sahul, stupid white fellah," Huntsman said as the portal winked out of existence.

Sammy staggered and dropped to his knees. Rhiannon knelt beside him and cradled his head.

Huntsman's hands were curled into claws. He perched on one leg like a brolga and fixed Hagalle with venomous eyes.

"This boy has more sense than you." He indicated Sammy, who was pale and shivering, even in the heat. "He used all his strength to bring us here quick enough to stop your nonsense."

Hagalle roared and drew his sword. Huntsman made a grabbing motion with his fingers, and the emperor stumbled away clutching his throat.

"Kill him!" Hagalle gasped between pants.

The black-cloaks moved to obey, but Justin Salace nudged his horse closer and glared down at them.

Huntsman stalked toward the emperor, fingers splayed. "Aristodeus said you would be ready; said you weren't as stupid as you looked. I need your army, white fellah. I need it now."

"Huntsman, no," the Ipsissimus said, moving between the Dreamer and Hagalle. "This is not the way."

The intervention seemed to break the spell. Hagalle coughed and then lunged at Huntsman, barging the Ipsissimus out of the way as he did. Ignatius tackled him and landed atop Hagalle, fist raised to strike. The black-cloaks surged forward and the White Knights drew their swords.

"Cut it out, you flaming idiots!"

Everyone froze and looked back toward Rhiannon. She lay Sammy back on the ground and stood, dusting herself down. She then walked through the black-cloaks, who parted as if she were their queen. Shader took a step closer in case anyone tried to harm her.

"Back off, shoggers," Rhiannon said. "You too, knight-boy." She touched Ignatius on the shoulder, and he nodded, standing to resume his place beside the Ipsissimus.

"Excuse my language, Divinity," Rhiannon did her version of a curtsy, "but this needs to stop."

The Ipsissimus smiled and gestured for her to continue.

"Emperor—" Rhiannon offered Hagalle her hand and helped him to his feet. "I'm sorry; I know I'm out of my depth here—"

"At least you're a bloody Sahulian," Hagalle said. He leaned in closer and whispered something to her.

Rhiannon blushed and gave a polite chuckle. Shader had seen her do that before; knew she must be fuming, but playing along anyway.

"I'm also a Nousian," she said, straightening her robe.

Hagalle frowned at that, but said nothing. Like everyone else, he seemed to be waiting for her to go on.

"I've seen what we're up against," she said. "And I do mean us—all of us."

She took in the black-cloaks, the White Order, and then indicated the two armies drawn up on either side of the plain. "This Cadman captured me." She looked at Shader, but he couldn't read her expression. "Thought he could use me to repay a debt. When that didn't work out, there was a fight with a demon. You know the one I mean." She spoke directly to Shader this time and he shuddered at the memory. "Cadman won. Whatever else that statue is, it's bloody powerful, and he only had two pieces of it. But then something happened. The skies opened, and a man came through. He was seated on a throne or something. He... I don't know how to describe this. He went inside Cadman."

Huntsman nodded. "Sektis Gandaw. He has found a way back, but how, I do not know. He has never had the power. Not since my gods took last of his plane ships."

"He already had two pieces of the statue," Shader said. "Mine and Maldark's. Maybe that's how."

"Yeah, maybe," Rhiannon said. "But that means he's now got four."

The Ipsissimus fingered the Monas on its chain. "Then what should we do?"

"An army of corpses marches on Homestead," Huntsman said. "This is why we have come."

"More undead?" Hagalle said.

"Many more," Huntsman said. "Cadman—Sektis Gandaw—is ravaging sacred sites of my people. Ancient graves are being opened. Ants tell Sammy this army is more numerous than grains of sand in Great Desert."

"But they're heading to the Homestead," Hagalle said. "Why should we care? Even your people seldom go there these days. It's just a rock in the back of beyond."

Huntsman drew himself up and cocked his head. "It is home of my gods, last of their kind. They, it was, who rescued statue from Sektis Gandaw in Dreaming. We cannot let them die."

"Not convinced," Hagalle said. "I'm not sending Sahulian forces into the outback when there are cities to be defended."

"Against what Sektis Gandaw plans," Huntsman said, "there is no defense. First, he will slaughter my gods, and then he will come for you." He looked directly at the Ipsissimus. "Archon shields you for now, but Gandaw will find a way."

"Wouldn't it make more sense," Shader said, "for him to come for the Monas first, make the statue complete?"

"He is careful. Very patient," Huntsman said. "He must know last piece cannot be hidden from him for long, not now he has all others. But he will take no chances. My gods defeated him once before. He hates them beyond all imagining. He will not leave them unpunished."

Hagalle turned on his heel and strode away from the group. He stood with hands on hips, staring up at his army. Rhiannon followed him and spoke in his ear.

"Then we should go to the Homestead," the Ipsissimus said. "One final battle to decide the fate of the world."

"It is not just this world that is at stake," Huntsman said. "If Sektis Gandaw wins, he will start Unweaving. This world, Dreaming, even Abyss itself, will be unmade. All that exists will cease."

Hagalle nodded to Rhiannon and walked back to stand with the Ipsissimus and Huntsman. "You should make use of a lass like that," he said to the Ipsissimus. "She might well be infected with your disease, but she's still Sahulian, and she has the Sahulian gift of common sense. I'll go, if you will, but only on the understanding that you leave as soon as this is over."

"You have my word," the Ipsissimus said.

"Then I suppose that will have to do." Hagalle turned to Huntsman. "I take it you have some plan for marching thousands of troops across the center of Sahul without them dying of exposure and dehydration."

"Sammy," Huntsman said. "With rest and food he will regain his strength. Together, he and I will open a portal."

"Better hope you get your aim right," Hagalle said.

"We will." Huntsman nodded, gazing into the distance. "Homestead is most sacred site of my people. It will draw us."

ROGUE'S LAST STAND

ALBERT STEPPED OUT of the plane ship into a cathedral-like cavern. Natural phosphorescence bathed the walls in a greenish glow. The floor was a forest of twisted stalagmites, and stalactites hung from above, dripping with moisture. It was like standing in a dragon's jaws.

He turned back to the plane ship but saw only the rectangle of light from which he'd just emerged, and nothing but air and rock where the craft should have been. Judging by the immensity of the corridors he'd traversed with Shadrak, the craft was too large even for the cavern. Perhaps its peculiar nature allowed it to merge with the walls, or maybe it was somewhere else altogether.

Shadrak appeared in the light carrying a large metal box. He set it down before Albert.

"The globes explode when shattered," he said, opening the lid and lifting a glass orb for Albert to see. "These tubes spit fire in long gouts, and there are lengths of cable and pitons."

"Fascinating," Albert said. "I would thank you for your generosity, but I have no idea why you're giving them to me."

"You had a choice back there," Shadrak said, glaring at Albert with those unnerving pink eyes. "Stay and fight, or come with me and do what you're told."

"Yes," Albert said, rubbing his chin. "I must have missed that last bit."

Three shapes moved from the shadows surrounding a cluster of gigantic stalagmites. Albert took a step back, but Shadrak put a hand on the small of his back.

"I was told to expect this," he said.

"Told?" Albert said. "Told by whom?"

Albert flicked a look over his shoulder at the entrance to the plane ship. Perhaps if Shadrak was distracted, he'd be able to nip back inside. How difficult could it be to pilot the thing? If Shadrak could manage it then Albert was sure it would be a doddle for him.

The figures edged closer to the accompaniment of a sibilant hiss and deep throaty croaks. Albert's mouth hung open as he began to descry what they were.

The central figure had the body of a huge black man, thickly muscled and ridged with veins. His head, however, was serpentine, bobbing and swaying at the end of a sinuous neck. To his right loomed an even larger man, this one bronze-skinned and with the head of a crocodile. Its tawny eyes watched him the same way Albert would have eyed a crème brulée. The third figure was much smaller, a squat humanoid with the head of a toad and a tongue that flicked out as if tasting the air.

The three stopped a few paces from Albert and Shadrak. The albino placed the orb back inside the box and shut the lid.

"I am Mamba," said the black man with the snake's head.

"And I am Baru," Crocodile Head said.

Toad hopped closer and shot his tongue toward Albert. "Thindamura."

"Shadrak," the Albino said, "and this is Albert, your protector."

413

"Their what?" Albert said, inching back toward the rectangle of light.

A shadow passed overhead, and Albert looked up. He dropped into a crouch as it seemed the ceiling fell toward him, but then he realized that something was making a controlled descent. Something massive, with eight long legs dangling beneath it. Shadrak pulled him back to make way for a gigantic spider.

"The Archon said he would send aid," the spider said with a clacking of mandibles. "Yet he sends us only you."

"I don't know what he promised you," Shadrak said. "Just told me to bring help and that's what I've done. Albert's the best in the business, and he's got a box of tricks that's as good as a small army."

Protector? Box of tricks? Small army? What on earth was Shadrak playing at? Albert turned to ask him, but Shadrak had already slipped back into the rectangle of light. The door panel started to slide down.

"Good luck, Albert. I have to be some place else. Hold as long as you can, and we may yet get out of this alive."

"Get out of what? You can't just leave—"

But the rectangle of light had gone, leaving only rocks and air in its wake. There was a shimmer like a heat wave, a muffled drone, and then nothing.

The great spider shuffled toward Albert, watching him through rows of red eyes.

"I am Murgah Muggui. We are the last of our kind. If, indeed, you have the skills to aid us, we will be forever in your debt."

"Aid you? I'm a poisoner, for goodness' sake. I kill people for a living."

"I fear that is exactly the sort of help we will need," Murgah Muggui said. "An old enemy comes, and soon the last battle will be fought. Console yourself that you are laboring to preserve more than your own life. You are fighting for the survival of worlds."

"Then I think you've been sent the wrong man," Albert said. "I'm way too much of a cynic to give a damn about all that. A vintage Sauvignon and some mature cheddar is the only thing on my mind right now."

That and a million other things. Such as how he was going to repay Shadrak for this; how he was going to capitalize on the weakness of the Sicarii following their unprecedented losses at Dead Man's Torch; and—

A muffled boom shook the cave.

"What the—?"

"They are coming!" Thindamura hopped excitedly. "They are coming!"

"Who?" Albert said. "Who's coming?"

Baru turned his great head to look up at the ceiling toward the rear of the cavern. "The dead of Sahul," he said. "And creatures from Aethir."

Mamba flexed his bulging muscles and bared his fangs. "Sssektis Gandaw comesss. After all thisss time he hasss not forgotten."

Another boom, this one louder and more urgent. Rock clattered from the ceiling, and a crack raced across the rear wall of the cavern.

"We will be trapped down here," Murgah Muggui said. "Quickly! There is an old fault that runs all the way to the summit. If we go now we may yet evade them."

The three hybrid creatures ran from sight behind the stalagmites. Murgah Muggui rose into the air on a ropey strand of silk and scuttled across the ceiling.

Albert looked around helplessly, thoughts consumed with a thousand ways of killing Shadrak. Another explosion nearly threw him from his feet. Cursing under his breath, he stooped down, lifted the metal box, and ran.

He got no more than a dozen paces when the rear wall exploded. Rock spewed into the cavern, and a chunk struck Albert on the temple. He fell, cracking the back of his head against stone. He heard the metal box crash to the floor, and for a moment, feared it was about to detonate. The contents rattled and chinked, but did not break.

He rolled to his front and tried to rise, his head pounding and groggy. He couldn't quite focus on the ground beneath him—it seemed to pitch and roll as if he were at sea. Cold hands grabbed him and hauled him up. He probably should have screamed, but he was too disoriented to care. He grinned like an idiot as rotten teeth pressed toward him, red eyes glaring from a face that resembled off meat. Scores of corpses shambled about him clutching with cyanosed fingers. Albert retched, and his vision cleared. The stench of rot filled his nostrils, and screams bubbled up from his gut.

Suddenly, Baru was among the dead, ripping with his great jaws, pummeling with his fists. He tore Albert from his attacker and slung him into the arms of Mamba. The snake man passed him to the care of Thindamura and then leapt into the fray, bludgeoning the dead with his tree-trunk arms.

Toad led him toward a fissure in the cavern wall, but Albert pulled away and ran back for the box. Putrescence sprayed and limbs flew as Baru savaged the undead. A corpse lurched toward Albert, but Mamba clubbed it down. Hundreds more were still pouring through a cavity in the rear wall. Lifting the box, Albert struggled toward the fissure. Toad was hopping and gesticulating for him to hurry. Mamba and Baru fell back, flattening the dead with thunderous blows. They were both bleeding from dozens of cuts, but they seemed not to notice.

"Quickly," Thindamura croaked, flicking his tongue from side to side. "We must go up."

Albert ducked inside the fissure and set the box down.

"What are you doing?" Thindamura said.

"Buying us some time." Albert opened the box. "You hop along and I'll catch up."

Thindamura looked back at his fellow hybrids, saw the futility of helping them, and bounded up the slope before him.

Mamba backed into the opening, swinging his mighty arms and pulping rotten flesh. Baru fought for every inch of ground, snapping with his jaws and using his huge hands to break necks or batter limbs. The tide of undead continued to swell, and the two hybrids were forced to retreat.

Mamba almost stepped on Albert as the assassin snatched up three glass orbs and hurled them. Light flared amid a deafening crash and scores of corpses were blown apart. The smell of cooking meat wafted into the fissure. Albert shuffled up the slope a little way, pulling the box behind him. Mamba's bulk filled the opening; he was pounding and hissing as he fought to keep the mass of undead back.

Albert selected a couple of pitons and a mallet and proceeded to hammer one either side of the fissure. Mamba retreated before the horde as Albert pulled out a fluid-filled cylinder with a metal nozzle. He turned it around to get some sort of understanding of its mechanism. There was a trigger of sorts, like those he'd seen on crossbows. He wedged the body of the device into a crack, secured it with scree, and began to rig it to his tripwire. Mamba stepped over him, and Baru backed into the opening still clubbing left and right, but tiring visibly. He swung his head toward Albert.

"You need to go. Now!"

Albert made a few adjustments and then scrambled up the slope after Mamba. He looked back as Baru cried out. Bloodless hands grabbed the hybrid and dragged him down. Albert knew he should have gone back, but that really wasn't his style. He was about to resume his ascent when he saw a vast shadow descend upon the undead. Murgah Muggui ripped into them with her mandibles, pinned them down with her legs, and angled her bulbous body to bring her stinger to bear. Baru broke free and reached the fissure while the giant spider thrashed about, cutting a swath through the corpses. Her bulk backed toward the opening as she held off the throng of undead, but then something silver glinted in the cave. It was a sphere that sped through the air to the accompaniment of a shrill whirring whine. Murgah Muggui must have known what it was and tried to withdraw, but a beam of blinding light discharged from a nozzle in the sphere, and she screamed. For an instant, Albert saw her innards, as if she'd been struck by lightning, and then Murgah Muggui burst into flame. Her flesh roasted, giving off gouts of black smoke, and her limbs twitched and contracted.

"No!" Baru cried, stepping toward her.

"It's too late," Albert said. "You have to keep moving."

He scurried down, took hold of Baru by the shoulders, and turned him toward the slope. The hybrid let out a mournful cry and clambered upwards. Albert retrieved the box, stepped over his tripwire, and followed.

He'd gone only a few feet when he heard a high-pitched whir behind him. Instinctively, he hit the ground and light lanced over him, blasting a hole in the rock. He dragged the box around a bend, opened it, and fumbled around inside until he found another of the cylindrical weapons. He cradled it in his arms, located the trigger, and waited with his back pressed to the wall.

Baru turned and started back toward him.

"No," Albert hissed. "Get out of here."

The silver sphere rounded the corner, and Albert pressed the trigger. Flame gushed from the nozzle and struck the sphere, hurling it into the wall. It spun frantically, emitting a shrill scream and discharging beams of light in random directions. Albert kept firing as it turned first red and then white. The screaming rose to a crescendo, and the sphere crashed to the ground. Albert didn't release the trigger until the flames ran out.

The dead lurched through the fissure, jamming each other in the opening as they blindly sought out prey. Finally, one of them squeezed through and lumbered forward, right into Albert's trip wire. Flame shot across the passageway, melting flesh and filling the fissure with acrid smoke.

Albert nodded his satisfaction before setting off after the hybrids, dragging the box with him.

What the hell was he doing? He should never have been here. First Master Frayn's madcap scheme, and then Shadrak's double-edged rescue. This wasn't Albert's kind of work. He was a poisoner, not some desperado making a last stand just to save a bunch of freaks worshiped by savages.

Strong hands grabbed him and pulled him further up the slope.

"Give me the box," Baru said. "You must move quickly."

Already, the dead had passed through the flames and were closing inexorably.

"How far have we got to go?" Albert asked.

"A long way. We will tire before we reach the top, but these dead things will not."

"You go," Albert said. "I'll see if I can slow them down."

Baru glared at him and then nodded, clambering up into the darkness.

Albert carried the box around another bend and then scooped out the rest of the orbs. He'd used up all the fire cylinders and had no time to rig another trap. Instead, he placed all the orbs but one on the ground—fifteen of them. Holding the last orb, he backed away and waited.

Within moments, groping hands appeared, followed by a great swarm of cadavers lumbering toward him with frenzied eyes.

"Here we go," Albert told himself. "Trusting it all on one last throw of the die."

He hurled the sphere into the midst the others and threw himself around the corner. The passageway shook as a thunderous roar rolled along the fissure and a blast of heat scorched his back. Howls went up from the undead and the smell of burning flesh followed.

Albert waited for the heat to pass, found his feet, and ran as fast as his chunky legs would allow him.

The hybrids waited further up. Baru dropped behind to guard the rear while Thindamura kept the lead, hopping ahead and then crouching impatiently as the others caught up. At first, Albert thought he'd stopped the dead, but after half an hour of arduous climbing, he could hear shambling and groaning pursuing them up the fissure.

The hybrids seemed deflated by the death of Murgah Muggui, but still they kept moving upward, although Albert had the impression they did so purely for his sake. To his mind, they had given up.

Finally, Thindamura climbed some knobs in the passage wall and disappeared from sight. A moment later he reappeared.

"It is here," he said. "The opening to the summit."

The groaning of the dead echoed up behind them as first Mamba, and then Albert, followed Thindamura up the natural chimney. Baru brought up the rear.

"They are close," he said, his crocodile jaws clacking. "And they are many."

Daylight spilled through an aperture above them, and Thindamura leaned over the lip to offer Mamba a hand. The snake-man did the same for Albert, who emerged into blinding sunlight with Baru climbing out behind him.

Albert blinked and saw that they were on a vast rocky surface high above a sprawling red desert. The expanse of limestone was immense, like a giant's tabletop that ran for hundreds of yards in every direction. The clouds were so low it looked like he could step on them.

"Keep moving," Thindamura said, leading them away from the opening.

The first of the dead poked its head out and hissed, and soon corpses were spilling from the hole without end.

Albert was too exhausted to run, but he managed to stumble along behind the hybrids as they vainly sought a way to escape. They'd made it no more than a hundred yards when Thindamura stopped, his eyes goggling, tongue hanging flaccidly.

A figure had appeared upon a ridge at the far end of the Homestead. It was more bone than flesh, and wreathed in strips of mildewed fabric and dust-clogged cobwebs. Red eyes blazed at them across the distance.

A gray creature flapped down beside it on bat's wings, and a shadowy shape drifted to its side.

Mamba hissed, his tongue tasting the air.

"Is it him?" Baru asked.

"I think ssso," Mamba said.

Albert looked behind where the undead were still pouring from the hole. There were already hundreds of them, and yet still they came.

"Look," Thindamura said.

Albert turned back to the three figures. The skeleton held its hands high, amber light suffusing them. A jagged black crack rent the air before it, widening like a colossal maw. In the opening, armored riders appeared astride skeletal steeds. There must have been nearly two hundred of them, all in rusty chainmail and corroded helms. Flames flared from the horses' nostrils and an icy chill rolled out across the summit.

The skeleton then looked up at the sky, power pouring from its hands in pillars of amber fire. The heavens split like ripped fabric and admitted a cobalt wash. Black flecks filled alien skies, swooping nearer, until Albert saw they had the faces of feral women and broad leather wings. There were so many that the sky turned black.

The hybrids looked at each other, shoulders slumped in defeat.

"The kryeh," Mamba said, his voice flat and lifeless. "We are undone."

As scores of winged demons dived from the sky and a horde of undead closed in from behind, Albert could only watch in terror as the knights on fleshless horses charged.

THE BATTLE OF THE HOMESTEAD

GENERAL STARN FELT out of place, but that was nothing unusual. The emperor was issuing demands to General Binizo of the Templum army, and Binizo was politely, but doggedly, rebuffing him. The Ipsissimus stood back from the arguing, his attention focused on the antics of the Dreamer shaman and the boy. Huntsman was standing on one leg shaking a gourd while the boy scrabbled around on the ground and occasionally cast dirt into the air. Both seemed enraptured, their eyes almost pure white, their mouths frothing. The grand master of the Elect, Ignatius Grymm, looked on with barely suppressed disdain, and Deacon Shader was talking with a sandy-haired lad, his eyes all the while flicking toward a white-robed woman with long black hair.

Rulers, commanders, and heroes, by all accounts. And then there was Starn. Oh, he was officially a general, but titles meant nothing, not when you knew yourself as well as Starn did. He'd always worked hard, he granted himself that, but he was under no illusions about why he'd risen so high. The emperor considered him a bit of a dullard, a "yes man", and who was Starn to disagree with him? He'd masqueraded as someone important for too long. Once this battle was over, he was slipping off with Mrs. Starn somewhere the army couldn't find him. He'd saved enough money for a bit of land, and Mrs. Starn was as green-fingered as they came. A nice little smallholding outback where no one was likely to disturb them—

"Don't you agree, General Starn?" the emperor said.

Starn nodded automatically and puffed out his chest as he turned back to the strategic debate. So far, his only role had been to concur with the emperor. He'd missed whatever was under discussion, but his opinion didn't seem to carry much weight in any case.

General Binizo was watching him with one eyebrow raised. The man was as proud as a peacock and dressed immaculately in a red jacket and white breeches. His knee-length boots were polished so much, Starn could see his reflection in them. Now there was a real general, he thought to himself.

"You realize what you're agreeing to, General Starn?" Binizo asked.

"Uh, yes. Quite." Starn put on his best gruff voice.

"You'll be blind to whatever lies on the other side of this … this magical doorway our friends are conjuring." Binizo nodded at the Dreamer and the boy, both of whom were now chanting in some indecipherable tongue and making circular motions with their arms. "There's no telling what you might run into."

Oh. Starn hadn't thought of that. If only he'd been listening.

"Not a problem for the Heavy Foot, eh, Starn?" the emperor said, clapping him on the shoulder.

"The Foot, Emperor?"

"That's right, General. Haven't you heard a thing we've been saying? I need my best man in the vanguard. You take charge of the regiment, and I'll coordinate the bulk of the army."

Starn stroked his mustache and felt his cheeks reddening. "You're relieving me, Emperor?"

"Not at all. I'm entrusting you with the most crucial role."

Starn straightened up and saluted, all the while feeling like one of those canaries his father had told him about as a child—the one's Pop and his colleagues used to carry ahead into the mines to check for poison gas.

"I'll go ready the men, then," Starn said, bowing and leaving Binizo and the emperor to decide whose army was going to achieve the greatest glory. Starn dreaded what they'd be like once this was all over, once they had spoils to divide. Hopefully, the Ipsissimus would be as good as his word and the Templum army would just sail back to Aeterna. It didn't seem likely, though, not if all the things Starn had heard about Nousians were true. He was dreading telling Mrs. Starn about the campaign. He knew only too well what her thoughts would be on an alliance with Aeterna.

"General."

Starn stopped, took a deep breath, and wondered what he'd done wrong now.

"Yes?" He turned to see Deacon Shader walking toward him. The sandy-haired lad was on his way back to his Order, a group of a dozen or so knights attired in the manner of the Templum Elect.

"We have your back. No telling what you'll run into on the other side. I was hoping you'd have a minute to discuss how this is going to work."

"Good idea," Starn said. *I'm glad someone's taking this seriously.* "You have any experience of these portal things?"

"A little, although maybe not quite the same as this. Tell your men to expect a moment's disorientation. With any luck, we'll emerge in the open, but just in case we walk straight into conflict, it might be best if they adopt defensive positions."

"Thank you, yes, I had already thought of that. We'll be going in *testudo*. I believe the term's Aeternam in origin."

"Tortoise," Shader said. "Sounds like a good plan."

A flare of green drew Starn's gaze. Shader turned with him. The Dreamer and the boy now stood before a vast disk of swirling green light a hundred yards across. Starn strained his eyes, but could see nothing through the glare.

"This is it then," Shader said. "Good luck, General."

"Yes," Starn said. "You too. And, uh, Ain be with you." He winced inwardly as he said the words. He was definitely leaving that bit out of the tale he told Mrs. Starn.

***

Shader rode Gaston's mare like a talisman through the portal, Barek on his right and Justin on his left. Elgin was behind with Solomon and Gord, the lads at the rear forming the base of the wedge. Fourteen in all, including Shader. Not nearly enough.

They emerged into chaos—screams from up front, curses, and the sickening reek of decaying flesh. The line of infantry immediately before them was pushed back onto the horses as those up front tried to retreat. Someone was yelling above the din of battle, "Press on! Press on!"

Shader looked for Starn, but couldn't see him in the throng. The ranks up ahead began to buckle, the weight of some unseen enemy forcing them back. "Forward! Give no ground!" —It was Starn's voice, hoarse and insistent. The troops in the rear leaned into their shields in an attempt to drive their unit forward, but the front line sagged and terrible screams rent the air.

"Sound the charge, Barek," Shader said.

As soon as the first trumpet note blasted out, the foot soldiers parted down the center. Starn was bellowing, "Make way, make way!" and Shader thought he saw the general dragging a blood-soaked comrade to the right. As a channel opened, Shader drew his longsword and charged.

The White Knights stayed with him as he sped along the corridor between the footmen straight toward a surging tide of corpses. He hacked left and right, pulping rotting flesh like ripe fruit. The mare trampled corpses underfoot and carried on into the thick of the putrescence. Cold hands groped at Shader's boots, but his blade was a whir of flashing steel that bit through flesh, severing limbs. Barek's horse stumbled and nearly fell, the dead tugging it down into their writhing mass. Shader could do nothing, or else he'd lose momentum as he tore straight through the center with Justin on his left. He saw flashes of white out of the corner of his eye and risked a glance to see Elgin and Solomon in among Barek's attackers slashing their swords in murderous arcs, their horses kicking out and crushing ancient bones.

Inevitably, the charge faltered before the endless rows of the dead. The ones in front had their backs to Shader as if they engaged another foe, but then they wheeled cumbrously to face him. Gord forced his way alongside, and Justin trampled a cadaver to resume his place at Shader's left. Barek, Solomon, and Elgin had made it, too, and glimpses of white still moved among the corpses behind.

"There are too many," Barek said.

Shader stuck his sword through the mouth of a raving zombie. The mare was bucking and whinnying, trying to turn in a futile bid to escape. Elgin made two vicious cuts, felling a couple more corpses, and Solomon ripped a severed hand from his boot and cast it aside.

A great roar went up from the foot soldiers to the rear and rows of undead dropped like scythed wheat.

"Again!" bellowed Starn from somewhere in the phalanx.

The wall of shields heaved and swords rose and fell. Within moments, the undead capitulated and the infantry reached the last of Shader's riders just as a colossal wave of necrotic flesh was about to hit.

The Heavy Foot opened ranks to let the white knights through and then locked shields to meet the onslaught. The undead slammed into them, but the back ranks pushed with their shields and the line held. Shader weaved the mare through the troops with the other knights following. They emerged to the left of the conflict and for the first time, Shader saw the wispy clouds surrounding the summit of the Homestead. Beyond the army of the dead, he could see a man in a dark suit behind three unearthly figures with the bodies of men and the heads of animals. Facing them, a long line of cavalry was cantering toward a charge, and in the skies above hundreds of black shapes started to soar down.

***

Albert searched every pocket of his suit as the black shapes swooped. *Bugger all!* No poisons, no darts. He felt like an unprepared rookie. Damn that little runt, Shadrak. He should have allowed more time. A box of explosives was one thing, but for Albert, who was always so meticulous in his preparations, it was a one-shot wonder.

His fingers closed around his cheese-cutter. Fat lot of good it would do, but he readied it just the same. If nothing else, it had the familiarity of an old friend.

The hybrids paid no heed to the plummeting demons. All their focus was on the charge of the skeletal horses that was gathering speed with a cacophonous pounding of hooves on rock. Thindamura hopped from foot to foot; Baru growled and beat his chest, and Mamba thumped his fists together, his snake eyes glaring and venomous.

Albert rolled out of the way of a diving woman with bat's wings. He caught a glimpse of sickle-shaped eyes and fangs like daggers. He hit the ground and came up, wrapping the cheese-cutter around the creature's throat and pulling. He expected the others to crash into him at any moment, but he meant to take at least one of them with him.

Lightning arced through the sky, and flesh smoldered. As the demon thrashed out its last, Albert saw dozens more plunging to their deaths, trailing wisps of smoke. The others banked up and then swooped below the ridge of the mountain.

Just before the horses collided with the hybrids, Albert ran like the clappers, seeking the cover of rocks near the edge. A huge battle was raging back the way they'd come, the legions of undead fiercely engaged by heavily armored foot soldiers. He glimpsed a cluster of white-garbed knights skirting the edge of the melee, their leader in a broad-brimmed hat and long coat.

Albert skidded to a halt and flung himself behind a boulder, his eyes flicking all around in case the demons returned.

As the death-knights impacted with Mamba and Baru, toad-headed Thindamura bounded high into the air and came down upon a rider. With preternatural swiftness, he twisted the knight's head off and tossed it aside. He sprang onto the next horse and did the same to its rider.

Impossibly, Baru and Mamba met the charge with great clubbing sweeps of their arms and remained upright as the first horses disintegrated with the force of the collision. It was as if the hybrids were rooted to the rock of the Homestead; as if they were rock themselves. The riders encircled them—there must have been one … maybe two hundred—and began baiting the hybrids with bristling blades. Mamba and Baru fought back to back. The crocodile-man's jaws tore through helms while his fists pounded skeletal horses to dust. Mamba unleashed gouts of venom that ate through armor and bone like acid.

A sword pierced Baru's side, but he roared and crushed the rider's helm with a sledgehammer blow. Another blade took him in the hamstring, and he went down on one knee, twisted, and ripped off the horse's head with his jaws. Thindamura dived from horse to horse, wreaking havoc. His tongue whipped out, dragging a rider from the saddle, and then he somersaulted to avoid a scything blow that would have decapitated him.

A hoof took Baru in the head, and he swatted the horse aside. Another blade lanced into his shoulder, and he fell. Mamba stepped over him belching venom and clubbing riders and horses with bleeding fists.

Baru forced himself upright, hopping on his good leg, and Thindamura vaulted a horse to stand with his brothers.

The knights drew back, and for a moment, Albert thought the hybrids might prevail. But then he saw what was happening. The bones of the fallen were scuttling across the ground searching out their other members. With the patience of the dead, the knights waited for their colleagues to re-form.

Albert had seen enough. There was nothing he could do, and he couldn't say he even cared. This wasn't his fight, and his debt to Shadrak was more than repaid. As he slunk toward the edge of the tabletop mountain, he saw the man in the long coat charge to the aid of the hybrids with a handful of white knights in tow.

Good luck, my dears, Albert thought, as he started to climb down.

He could see the black demons spiraling away to the east, regrouping and preparing for another pass. At least they weren't in his way.

He found some good handholds and clambered down to a broad ledge that tapered at one end and wound around the top of the Homestead. He took a step toward the edge— and hit his head. He fell on his backside, more stunned than hurt. There was nothing there! How could he have—?

And then he realized. It had to be the plane ship.

***

Rhiannon stepped away from Huntsman as lightning danced around his skin. The Dreamer's hair stood on end like a crown of thorns as he discharged another bolt of sizzling energy into the sky. More black shapes fell smoking to the ground. The rest of the winged women rose higher and then swooped beyond the edges of the Homestead.

She strained to see Shader or Barek through the confusion of the battle. Swords rose and fell, blood spurted, and screams tore through the air. She saw the odd flash of white, the shimmer of steel, but could no longer tell if Shader was alive or dead. She saw no sign of Barek either, nor even Justin Salace.

General Starn's infantry had forced an opening, and the rest of the combined forces spilled through the portal. General Binizo relayed orders through trumpets and drums, the Templum troops seeking order amid the chaos. Hagalle rode a black destrier among his own soldiers, sword raised, yelling commands. Imperial archers formed disciplined lines and covered the skies, but so far the winged women stayed beyond their range.

Sammy held the portal open by himself, green light flaring from his fingertips. The last few soldiers stepped through and Sammy sagged, dropping his arms. The portal contracted, but just before it vanished a scruffy hunchback lumbered through flicking holy water from an aspergillum over the troops. He carried a bucket in his other hand, presumably containing water for his sprinkler.

Rhiannon caught Sammy before he fell, cradled him in her lap. The boy was ashen, a cold sweat beading his skin.

"You did it Sammy. You held the portal by yourself." Pride swelled in the pit of her stomach. She gazed with raw affection at his begrimed face, stroking his matted hair, and losing all sense of the battle that surrounded them.

"Ranny," he said. It was the first real acknowledgement he'd given her, the first indication that maybe he wasn't lost to her entirely. Rhiannon's eyes misted over.

"Yes, Sammy." *My sweet, sweet Sammy.* "It's me."

"Mom and Dad!" Sammy's eyes widened as if he'd awakened from a dream only to realize the nightmare was in the waking world. For an instant, he was utterly lucid, totally present, but as quickly as it had come the clarity sank back beneath the mire of forgetfulness.

Rhiannon clutched him tight, tears rolling down her cheeks and soaking into his hair. The roars of soldiers, the moans of the undead, retreated from her awareness like a haunting memory. Rhiannon rocked Sammy and cried. In that moment, nothing else mattered.

Sammy started and sat bolt upright. "Eingana!" he cried, looking out over the masses on the battlefield.

Rhiannon followed his gaze. On a ridge above a rocky outcrop on the far side of the Homestead, a trio of figures stood watching. It was impossible to make out features at this distance, but the one in the middle raised its arms to the sky and columns of amber flame spewed upwards. They met hundreds of feet above the battle, and where they touched, the sky began to part. Gray-blue light spilled through the rent, widening into a broad rupture through which thousands more dark shapes poured. At the same moment, another vast cloud of winged demons rose above the eastern ridge of the Homestead and soared toward the center of the conflict.

"Dreaming!" Huntsman cried. "He brings more aid from Dreaming."

Sammy stood and glared up at the cobalt heavens. "Look!"

Giant silver eggs were raining down in between the swarming demons. Rhiannon counted six of them plummeting toward the joined armies of the Templum and Sahul.

"Sammy," Huntsman said. "Can you—?"

"Yes," Sammy answered, raising his hands to the heavens.

Streaks of green light shot from his fingers and struck the aperture. Its edges shimmered and then the opening began to collapse in on itself. Sammy was shaking and dripping with sweat. His eyes rolled back into his head, and froth spilled from his mouth. As the tear began to knit, the silver eggs halted in their descent, altered course, and sped toward Sammy.

"Huntsman!" Rhiannon screamed, putting herself between Sammy and the eggs.

They thudded to the ground in quick succession, each bigger than a man. The Dreamer turned to face them, lightning rippling from the tips of his fingers. One by one, the eggs peeled open like metal flowers and enormous silver men pounded forth, creatures of living armor a head above the tallest men on the battlefield. Each had a single roving red eye with which they scanned the combatants until they picked out Sammy. In unison, they raised gleaming metal arms that terminated in wide barrels.

Rhiannon glimpsed the white robes of Ipsissimus Theodore among a unit of Elect foot soldiers. The Ipsissimus had seen the threat to Sammy and gesticulated wildly. A dozen men raced toward the metal beings, one of which broke away to face them. Smoke poured from its tubular arms and the ground exploded, flinging soldiers into the air.

The other five ran straight at Sammy, heavy feet sending up shards of rock where they struck. Huntsman unleashed a barrage of lightning, great forks that leapt from one to the other and sent them shuddering and crashing down. The remaining metal man spun round and fired— straight at Sammy. Huntsman screamed something and leapt in front, his body instantly swelling and changing into a gigantic spider. Rhiannon pulled Sammy down and covered his ears against the concussive blast.

Blood and flesh rained down upon them amid a shower of fine ash.

"Huntsman!" Sammy cried.

Rhiannon dragged him to his feet and pulled him along as the metal man swung its arms toward them, its terrible red eye running back and forth across its face. A storm of arrows clattered from its armor, forcing it to turn to face the new threat. Fire erupted through the ranks of Templum archers, and the metal man took a lumbering step toward the white-robed form of the Ipsissimus.

***

Shader and the surviving knights of the White Order slammed into the left flank of the Lost, shattering skeletal steeds and hacking down their riders.

Their horses crunched across a carpet of bones, all still rolling and clattering together as if some invisible model maker were reassembling his toys. A huge black man with a snake's head—Mamba, Sammy had called him—powered into the undead, pulverizing them with hammer blows from his fists. A smaller creature with the head of a toad leapt from horse to horse, snaring knights with its tongue or breaking their necks. Another lay prone on the ground, trampled beneath the hooves of undead steeds.

No sooner had they cut the death-knights down, though, than they began to re-form. The handful of white knights was quickly surrounded, and they backed their horses into a circle, defending for all they were worth. Mamba took a sword through the shoulder, and blood gushed from the wound to mingle with the scores of other cuts he had sustained.

Shader parried a rusty blade and drove his longsword through the visor of a helm to exit at the back in a spray of skull fragments. Barek was flailing around blindly, his blows lacking strength, his sword arm clearly numb. Justin's horse reared and crashed its hooves into the head of a skeletal steed. Solomon was hard pressed by a couple of death-knights, parrying for dear life and being battered into submission. Elgin dispatched his own attacker and swung to help Solomon, but fell from his horse with a sword in his side. Shader blocked another slash and took the rider's arm off at the elbow. On the ground below, limbs were still re-forming and grabbing at the legs of their horses. Solomon screamed and slumped in the saddle, blood gushing from a neck wound. Justin turned a blow meant for Barek's head and then groaned as a sword thrust into this back and exited through his chest.

Shader dropped from the saddle and drew his gladius, drawing energy from the Archon's blade. He struck a re-forming knight with the longsword and impaled another with the gladius.

The clamor of hundreds of hooves beating against the rock momentarily arrested the combatants. The death-knights looked about and then howled in rage—or perhaps it was shame—as a tidal wave of Templum Elect crashed into them.

Shader threw himself from the path of the charge, rolled and came up as the last of the Elect thundered past sweeping the dead before them. More fallen death-knights rose from the ground behind Barek's horse even as the lad sighed with relief at their salvation. Before Shader could react, a hunched shape was among them sprinkling water from an aspergillum.

"Yea though I walk through the valley of the shadow of death…" Dave chanted one of the oldest passages from the Liber, and where his water fell, the dead became dust.

The snake-man bashed his way to Shader's side as the death-knights crumbled all around them.

"Thank you—" he said, but then saw something at the edge of the main battle. "That man in white…"

"The Ipsissimus," Shader said.

"He holdsss the last piece of Eingana and one of Sssektisss Gandaw'sss metal men advancesss on him."

Shader grabbed the reins of his horse and swung into the saddle. Barek turned his mount to follow him.

"No, Barek, you've done enough. Stay with the Elect."

Shader sped back toward the main melee, knowing he'd never make it in time. The silver man stalked toward the frail figure of the Ipsissimus, blasting aside seasoned troops by the dozen. Shader rode like the wind, his heart sinking with the realization all was lost. Something bounced over him and, with a speed that should have been impossible, leapt from head to head of the combatants, gaining ground on the metal man.

***

Ipsissimus Theodore watched in horror as the silver colossus pounded toward him, bashing aside his surviving archers as if they were annoying insects. The Ipsissimal Guard swarmed around it, shoving with their shields, and striking useless blows with swords that may as well have been twigs. It pivoted, discharging two more missiles into their ranks. Smoke and flame gushed into the sky along with bits of bodies and the cries of the injured. Ignatius Grymm stepped in front of Theodore, shield held high, sword extended.

"Flee, Divinity!" he cried.

It was the first time Theodore had seen him panicked. Nevertheless, Ignatius stood rooted to the spot. Theodore looked all around—there was nowhere to flee to. There was fierce fighting everywhere, legions of walking dead wearing down the combined might of Aeterna and Sahul. *Oh, Ignatius, my old friend. My stalwart protector.*

The metal man swung its arms toward the grand master, but before it could fire, Ignatius sprang forward and rammed his shield into it. There was a concussive roar that shot Ignatius back over twenty yards until he struck boulders in a spray of blood. The metal man tottered away, desperately trying to right itself. Theodore wanted to pray, but couldn't take his eyes from the monster. He fingered the Monas on its chain and stared wide-eyed as the metal man steadied itself and came straight at him.

A squat shape bounded above the heads of the surviving Ipsissimal Guards who were regrouping and running toward Theodore. They would be too late, and even if they reached him in time, what could they do?

Long-barreled arms took aim at his chest, and Theodore experienced an almost disinterested calm. He even found himself wondering whether the blast would destroy the Monas. At least that would constitute some kind of victory. He became aware of a low whirring sound rising in cadence and snapped back to the moment, paralyzed by the realization of imminent death.

But then the squat shape bounded one last time and struck the metal man on the head with its feet before springing away. It was enough to topple the monster, which fell to its back discharging both barrels into the sky. The squat creature landed before Theodore, bulbous eyes rolling atop a toad-like head, its tongue flicking and retracting.

A dozen Ipsissimal Guards reached the metal man and began to pound it with their swords and shields. It thrashed about and then emitted a pulsing beep that began to accelerate.

Toad-head grabbed Theodore and leapt, carrying him over thirty feet and then covering him with its own body. A colossal explosion threw the Ipsissimal Guard hundreds of feet into the air amid a billowing black cloud shaped like a mushroom.

"Ain!" Theodore gasped as he struggled to his feet.

As the cloud started to disperse, he saw a lone shape winging its way toward him from the far side of the Homestead, and a shadow drifted through the combat with eyes like burning coals.

Toad-head lifted Theodore again and jumped further from the fray, but still the shadow came on as relentless as time. Its eyes flared, and it drew a black sword, which was wreathed with dark flames. A woman and a boy ran from the cover of some rocks. The boy stumbled and fell, but the woman raced on toward Theodore, a white robe flapping in the breeze. The woman who'd been with Huntsman...

Toad-head turned to face the approaching shadow, but suddenly arched his back and screeched as a barb punched through his chest.

Theodore fell back, gasping as the winged creature he'd seen in the sky whipped its tail back out, and Toad-head crumpled to the ground in a pool of blood.

**

"Hold tight!" Starn yelled, his voice muffled within the *testudo*.

The Heavy Foot bunched closer together, those in the middle of the square holding shields overhead to ward off the dive-bombing demons, and those on the edges guarding against the pounding undead. They shuffled blindly in what Starn hoped was the direction of the ridge where they'd seen the skeletal figure with the amber flames. The battle might be lost, but if they could get a crack at him—

The shield roof buckled as dozens of the demon-women hit. Starn thrust through a gap with his sword, but found only air. Someone screamed to his right, and the shield wall parted. It was only a momentary breach as a soldier skewered the invading corpse and plugged the gap.

They walked over a carpet of the dead, many of them in Nousian white. With the uneven ground and the relentless pounding, Starn knew it was only a matter of time before the *testudo* collapsed, and that would be the end of them.

Where were the reinforcements? Surely, the emperor was still alive? The hoplites had stood back from the melee, held in reserve. And where were the Templum's vaunted pike?

The *testudo* rocked again, and Starn tripped on a corpse. He looked down to find secure footing and saw the body he'd struck wore a red jacket and white breeches. *General Binizo. Poor old peacock.*

"Steady!" Starn shouted. He knew the men were already doing everything they could, everything he'd trained them for, but it wasn't going to be enough. It struck him as rather an apposite epitaph for his military career.

Demons struck the shield ceiling with a succession of thuds, and a number of men dropped beneath the weight. More screams came from the perimeter, and then a cheer went up. The demon-women were screeching and flapping furiously, and blood was showering down through the gaps in the shields. Starn made another thrust with his sword and then shifted his shield to peer out.

Massive polearms were ripping into the demons from beyond the edges of the *testudo* while squads of hoplites surrounded the undead on three sides, thrusting with murderous precision. Hagalle circled the fray on his destrier, sword waving in the air as he barked commands in a voice hoarse from shouting. The dead fell away from all but one side, but even there they were turning to assault the pike men.

"*Testudo!*" Starn bellowed, confident his unit would obey with absolute precision. "Phalanx to the left."

Shields were brought down, admitting the glare of the sun. With practiced discipline the soldiers pivoted until they faced the left in a square eight ranks deep.

"Heave!" Starn shouted, and the phalanx slammed into the backs of the dead, driving them onto the blades of the guisarmes.

***

Shader saw the shadow advancing on the Ipsissimus and bent low over the mare's neck as the wind flared his coat out behind him. One hand held the reins, the other gripped the hilt of the gladius, the only chance he'd have against Callixus. Soldiers threw themselves from his path, and undead were trampled as he closed the gap. Something swooped from the sky toward the Ipsissimus, and for a moment Shader took his eye off the wraith. The horse whinnied and reared, and Shader flew from its back, pitching heavily to the ground. Callixus must have turned and spooked the horse. He loomed over Shader with his black blade raised and red eyes glaring as the mare galloped away.

Shader shook his head and tried to clear it. Panic ensued when he realized he'd dropped the gladius. He tried to rise, but his legs were jelly. Out of the corner of his eye, he saw the glint of the shortsword, scrabbled about for its hilt, but when his fingers closed around it, Callixus had turned from him and was rushing toward the Ipsissimus.

A surge of energy from the sword drove away the fug from his mind. He rolled to his feet, new vitality coursing through his veins. The sword was purring as if it knew what was at stake.

Shader broke into a run, but something barged into his side. He lashed out with the gladius, striking rotting flesh. More cadavers lurched at him, and soon he was fighting for his life. Drawing his longsword, he fought with both weapons, weaving and cutting, thrusting and hacking, forcing a path. When he broke through, he was still fifty yards away. A gray creature with the wings of a bat and a tail like a scorpion's had cornered the Ipsissimus. And—Ain!—Rhiannon was tearing toward them like a crazy martyr willing to give her life for the Templum. He couldn't lose her. Not now. Not with so much left unspoken.

But all Shader could do was watch in despair as the creature grabbed at the Monas around the Ipsissimus's neck, and Callixus moved in for the kill.

***

"Ain, help me," Callixus prayed over and over again. "Ain, help me."

He rushed toward the Ipsissimus with the thoughts of Sektis Gandaw echoing through his mind. "Kill him! Bring me the Monas!"

Ikrys had got there first, but still Callixus was compelled. How could Ain forgive him for this? How could he atone for the slaying of the ruler of the Templum?

Ikrys ripped the Monas from the Ipsissimus's neck and raised his tail to strike.

"Ain, help me!"

"A cigarette, a cigarette, a cigarette…"

"Doctor? Is that you?"

"Callixus?" said the voice of Cadman. It sounded thin and wispy. "Gandaw must be distracted. Good gracious, I can see through your eyes! I thought I'd never see beyond this test tube."

"Doctor," Callixus said. "I need your help. Please!"

"I think he's noticed me! There's so little time. Find me, one day, if you can," Cadman pleaded. "It's dark here and I'm afraid. Once more, Callixus, I release you. Remember me…" Cadman's voice receded like a distant memory and suddenly Sektis Gandaw's resumed. Only, he didn't seem to have realized what Cadman had done.

Shackles fell away from the former grand master and he sped straight for Ikrys. As the creature's tail darted toward the Ipsissimus, Callixus' black sword swept down and severed its barb. Ikrys screamed and dropped the Monas. With savage fury, the gargoyle pounced at Callixus, talons cutting where no mortal weapon could harm the wraith. Callixus tried to make room to swing his sword, but Ikrys was too fast, too ferocious. The gargoyle grappled with him as if his body were flesh, bit into his neck with venomous fangs. Callixus screamed and his sword fell to the ground. Ikrys's hands fixed on either side of the wraith's helm and forced Callixus to gaze into swirling black eyes.

"No!" Callixus cried as a molten river appeared around him.

"Taste the Abyss, specter," Ikrys said. "For that is your new home."

Flames gushed from the magma, which squelched like quicksand, tugging at Callixus' spirit.

"No!" he screamed again.

But then the flames consumed him.

***

Rhiannon snatched up the black blade and swung with all her might. The gargoyle screeched and flapped into the air, gouts of black blood spilling from its side. The Ipsissimus stood petrified, his face the color of death. He merely stared at the gilt Monas lying at his feet. Rhiannon lunged for it, but the gargoyle was quicker, slapping her aside with its wings. She thrust with the sword, but it swayed away and raked her shoulder with its talons. Her arm went cold, and she switched the sword to her left hand. She couldn't let him take the Monas. Not now. Not after all the sacrifices.

The gargoyle made a play for it, but Rhiannon jabbed it back. Still, the Ipsissimus did nothing. Footsteps were pounding up from behind, but Rhiannon didn't dare to look. The gargoyle swiped at her face, she ducked, but then its other hand grabbed her sword arm and shook the blade from her grasp. She spun and aimed a punch at its head, but it twisted her wrist and threw her to the ground. With one hand it claimed the Monas, and with the other, it gripped her throat, forcing her to stare into its hellish eyes. Rhiannon twisted her head to the side, but it tightened its grip. She was choking. Choking—

Something cannoned into the gargoyle, knocking it to its back. Rhiannon rolled and

---

saw Shader atop the creature, trying to find a way through its flailing hands. It smothered Shader with its wings, knocking the gladius from his grasp. Shader threw a punch that snapped the gargoyle's head back, but the creature dislodged him with a whack from the stump of its tail. Rhiannon picked up the black sword again and took a swipe as the gargoyle flapped into the air. It tucked his legs out of the way of her blow and sped off toward the far end of the Homestead.

Shader was up in an instant and retrieved his gladius. With fury in his eyes, he turned on the Ipsissimus.

"You did nothing!" he raged. "Nothing!"

Rhiannon tried to touch him, tried to share in his despair, but Shader shrugged off her advance and ran toward the ridge where the liche that had once been Dr. Cadman awaited Ikrys with open arms wreathed in amber fire.

There were tears streaking the Ipsissimus's face, but Rhiannon couldn't go to him; couldn't risk another rejection of her touch.

Something tugged her robe from behind, and she turned to see Sammy gazing up at her, his face filthy, eyes blank and distant. He must have dragged his way to her even though he was exhausted to the point of death. She stroked his cheek and then pulled his face to her chest, running her fingers through his matted hair and hoping the end, when it came, would be swift.

**

Even the undead turned to face the figure on the ridge as the gargoyle landed and offered it the Monas.

Shader continued to run, weaving in and out of the stationary combatants strewn across the battlefield. The men looked too exhausted to move, too overcome with despair. The cadavers just seemed forgotten, and lacking volition of their own they simply stood there. A few surviving demons spiraled into the east, but all else appeared frozen in time.

Shader barged through a cluster of undead and sprinted for the slope leading up to the ridge.

Just before Sektis Gandaw's hands reached the Monas, the gargoyle drew it back. Amber flared from it, lancing skywards, searing a hole in the firmament. The skeleton that was Gandaw threw its arms up and then watched as the clouds were sucked toward the hole. They swirled and coalesced, forming a pattern like a gigantic skull.

Still Shader ran, knees burning as he fought his way up a scree bank.

"Blightey!" Gandaw cried out as the skull turned toward him, the eye cavities filling with a bloody hue. While he was distracted, the gargoyle sprang at him, reaching for the pieces of the statue that bathed his hands in amber light.

Shader reached the overhang leading to the ridge and had to sheathe his gladius to find hand holds. He swung a leg over the edge and then rolled to the top. Drawing the gladius once more, he dived straight at the gargoyle's back. The creature must have sensed the attack as it squawked and flapped a few feet into the air, carrying Gandaw with it, dangling by the wrists. Shader skidded beneath them, rolled, and came up with the sword ready.

The amber in Gandaw's hands flared, and the gargoyle released its grip. As Gandaw floated slowly down beside Shader, an aperture opened above him admitting cobalt skies that washed away the apparition of the skull. The gargoyle flapped its wings furiously as a gigantic black fist soared through the opening and struck it full in the face. The gargoyle went into a spin, dropping the Monas. Gandaw snatched it out of the air as the black hand gave the gargoyle an almighty slap, sending it into a tumbling spin. With more frantic flapping, it righted itself, but saw the hand racing in pursuit. With a screech of utter horror, it dived for the edge of the Homestead and disappeared. The black hand wavered for a moment, as if searching for its prey, and then retreated to the aperture.

"Kill him! Kill him now! Kill him for Nous!" Dave the Slave clambered over the lip of the ridge, eyes burning with zeal, lips drawn back in a feral snarl.

Shader raised the gladius to strike Gandaw's exposed back, glanced at Dave as the hunchback climbed to his feet, shaking his fists in anticipation—and hesitated.

Gandaw turned, amber fire snaking about his body and striking the ground. A shockwave rolled across the ridge, and Shader tumbled from the precipice. He clutched the edge with one hand and clung to the gladius with the other. Pain lanced through his shoulder, and his fingers began to slip. Dave threw himself to his belly and grabbed Shader's wrist.

"No!" he yelled. "No! You must not fail!"

The cobalt hole in the sky widened as a figure seated upon a throne came through. Shader looked into the frenzied eyes of Dave the Slave, watched the movement of his slavering jaws, and recoiled in horror.

"Hold on," Dave growled. "I am the voice of Nous. You must not fail!"

"No," Shader said. "No!"

He slipped through Dave's grip and tumbled down the scree bank with the hunchback's screams in his ears.

Shader's head cracked against stone, and he lay supine, gazing helplessly at the figure on the throne holding out the serpent's body of the Statue of Eingana with a single amber fang blazing like lightning. The liche that had once been Cadman accepted the statue even as Dave slid down the slope to Shader's side.

"Get up!" he cried. "Get up before it's too late."

It was already too late. Shader watched the liche slot the other fang inside the mouth of Eingana and then press home an eye. Too late for him, too late for the Earth, too late for Nous and all his damned creation. The liche clawed at the Ipsissimal Monas, pried the second eye free, and inserted it in the head of the serpent. It raised the Statue of Eingana above its head, amber bursting from it with scintillating luminosity. The man on the throne stretched out his arms, and the liche started to back toward him, the glare from the statue so intense the two figures were just silhouettes to Shader. The liche shook the statue in triumph and turned to face the throne, but then its skull shattered into a thousand pieces, and a thunder-crack shook the ridge. The liche fell, pitching the statue to the earth.

Shader tried to rise, but his head was pounding. A small figure holding a long smoking tube appeared above the far edge of the ridge. He dropped the weapon, vaulted to the surface, and sprinted for the statue with a black cloak billowing behind him.

Shadrak! Shader rolled to a sitting position and tried to screen out Dave's shouting.

The assassin dived for the statue as the man on the throne stood. The air rippled and some invisible force struck Shadrak, hurling him back across the ridge. The man stooped to pick up the statue and held it like a parent with a newborn child. The light faded enough for Shader to see he was dressed in a tunic and trousers of gray, with polished black shoes and perfect hair. The face was waxen and bloodless, the eyes cold and clinical. He caught Shader looking and glanced down at the remains of Cadman's skeletal body.

"A host body, no more, but it served its purpose."

"Gandaw." Shader struggled to stand, but slumped back down again. "You don't have to do this."

"Oh, but I do, you pathetic little insect. I've waited a long time for this."

Sektis Gandaw resumed his place on the throne and the aperture sealed, leaving only clear skies in its place.

"You have failed Nous!" Dave screamed. "You are cursed forever. You have doomed us!"

Shader's skull was a nest of stinging insects. Coppery blood was on his tongue, and his heart ricocheted around his ribcage, threatening to burst from his chest.

Voices. He could hear voices—Dave snarling, Barek telling him to back off. Someone was calling his name.

"Rhiannon, is that you?" His own words were a drowning mush. Their sloshing echo passed deeper and deeper into the heart of a black abyss, met with a rising stream of speech, coiled about it, became as one.

"Not good."

"Aristodeus?"

"Not good at all."

The story continues in
Shader: Book Three: *The Unweaving*...

D.P. PRIOR

"This author has mad talent
and will grip each new reader
and take them on a journey"
(Readers Favorite)

BOOK THREE

SHADER

THE UNWEAVING

SHADER

BOOK THREE
THE UNWEAVING
D.P. PRIOR

ACKNOWLEDGEMENTS

THANKS TO MY beta readers:

Ray Nicholson, for a great chapter by chapter breakdown, and for offering suggestions for that problematic scene.

Valmore Daniels, for a detailed and fearless critique, throwing in some much-needed early copy editing, advising on US English usage, and helping to improve the clarity of a few chapters.

Cover art and interior sketches:
Anton Kokarev (kanartist.ru)

Cover design &manuscript formatting:
Valmore Daniels (valmoredaniels.com)

Map of Aethir:
Jared Blando (theredepic.com)

Map of Sahul:
Theo Prior (dizeazedproductionz.blogspot.com)

Map of The Nousian Theocracy:
Mike Nash (mikenash.com)

Interior sketches:
Patrick Stacey (facebook.com/artof.pat)

Photo of the author:
Theo Prior (dizeazedproductionz.blogspot.com)

Conversion of italics from Pages to Word:
Paula Prior (flurriesofwords.blogspot.com)

Norga

Sarmatia

Verusia

Britannia

Gallia   Graecia

Latia

Quilonia

Ashanta

Numosia

Make

The Anglish Isles

Sahul

Rujala

The Nousian

According to the terms of Aeternam A

The Great West

evar

Nazca

New Ithaka

Theocracy

Agreement: Year of the Reckoning 24

W · E
S

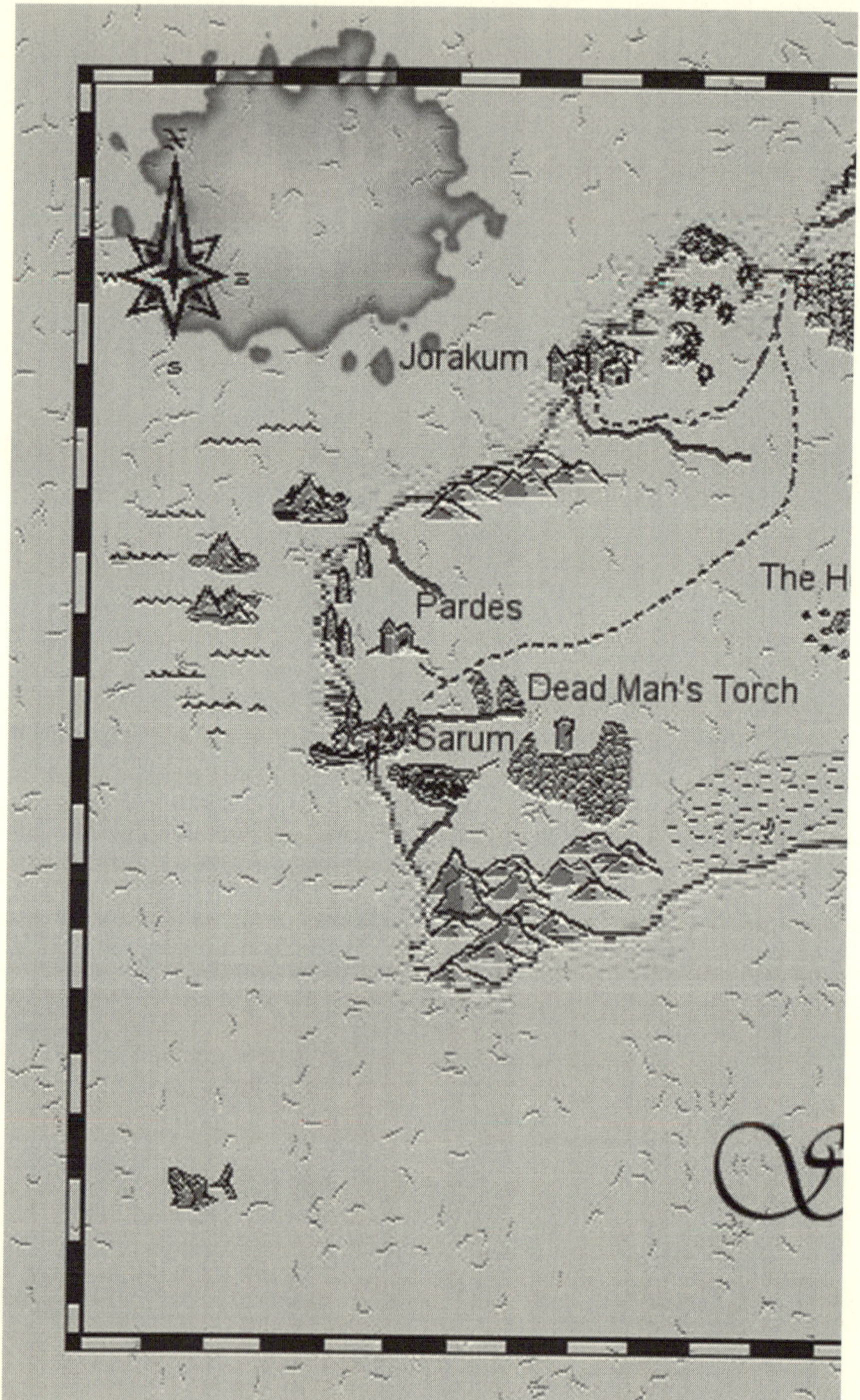

Jorakum
Pardes
Dead Man's Torch
Sarum

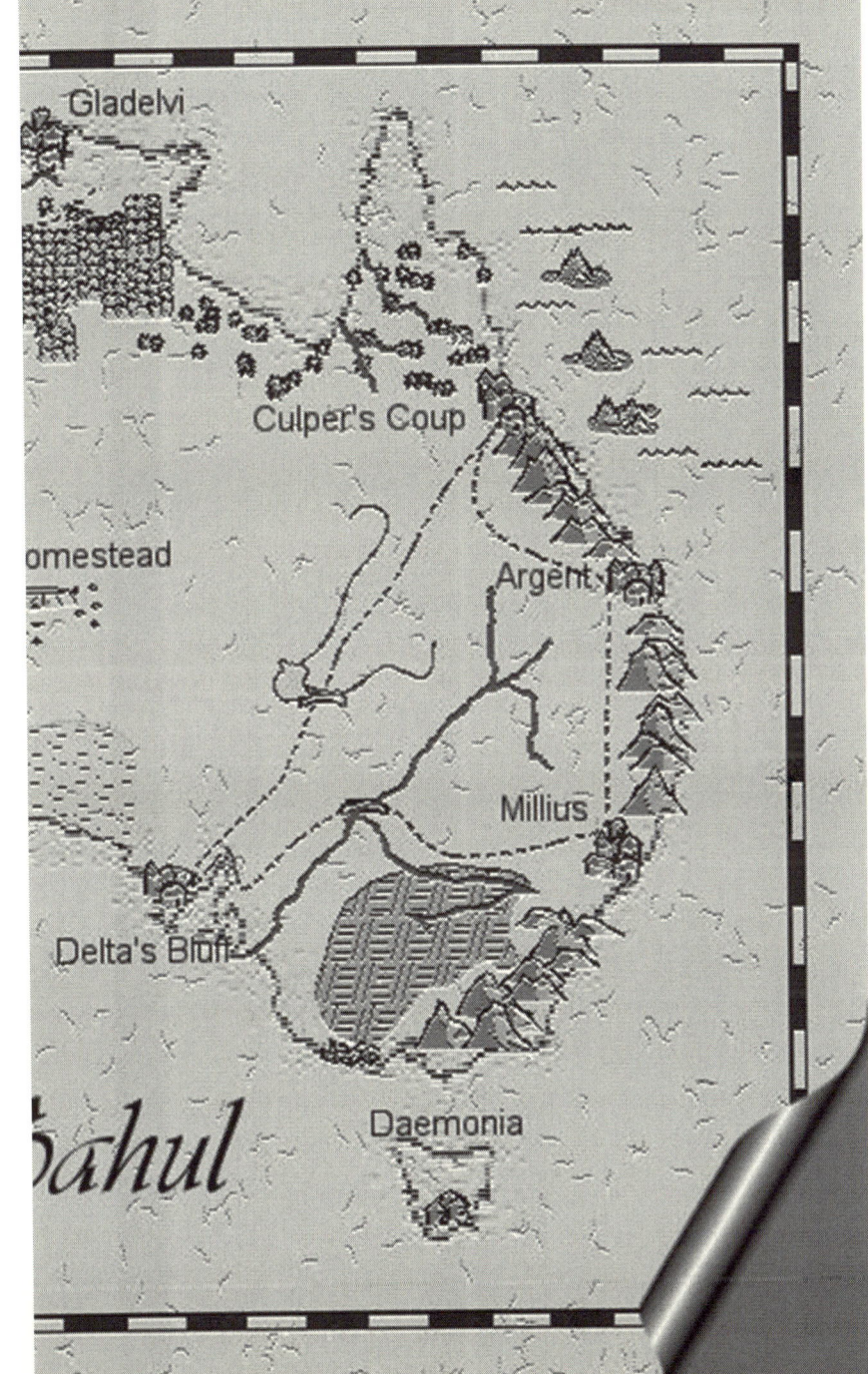

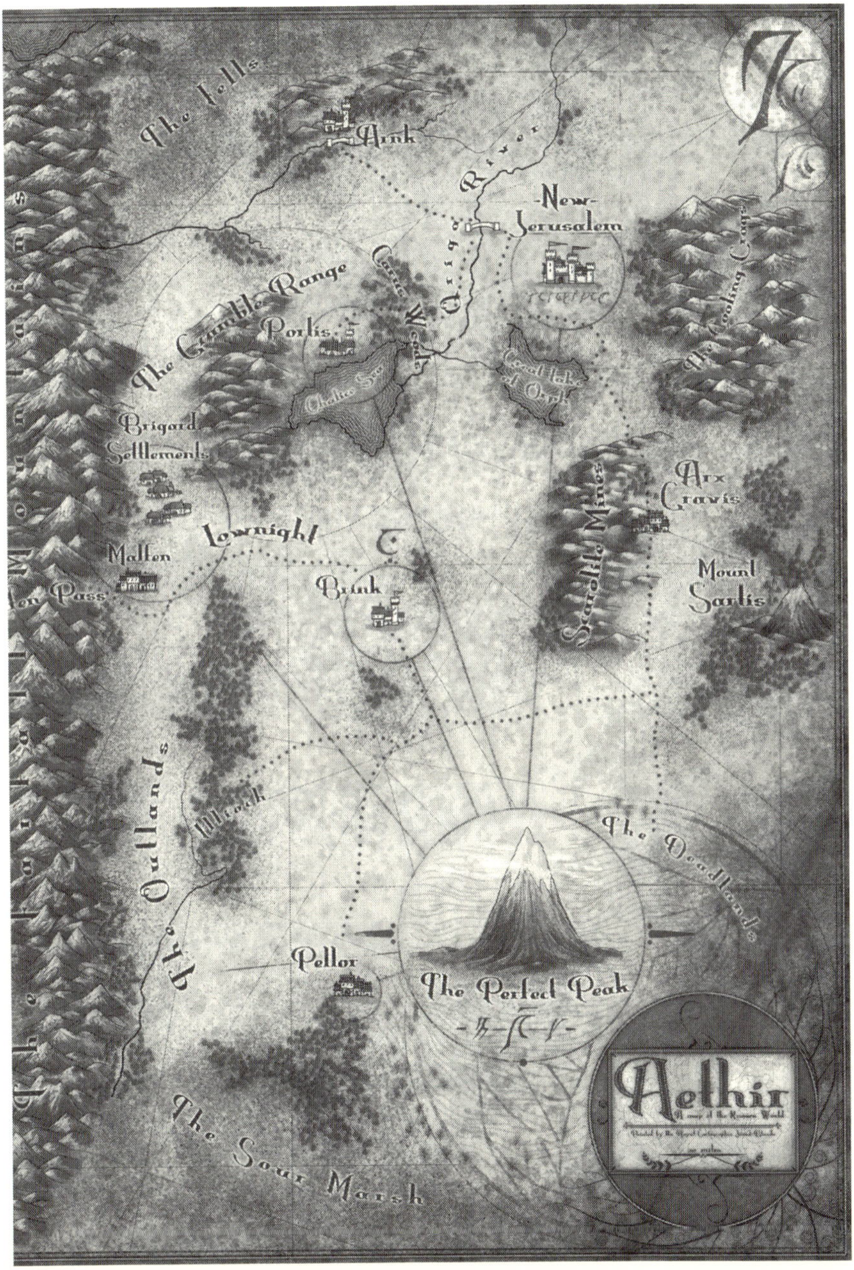
The Fells
Aink
River
-New-
Jerusalem
The Gamble Range
Porlis
Brigard
Settlements
Lownight
Malten
Brink
Arx
Cravis
Mount
Sartis
The Outlands
Pellor
The Perfect Peak
The Deadlands
The Sour Marsh
Aethir

A DWARF WITH NO NAME

Dwarven City of Arx Gravis, Aethir

One year before
The Battle of the Homestead

SO MUCH BLOOD.

Canals of it running through the streets of Arx Gravis. It dripped from the walkways and bridges like diseased rain, making the waters of Sanguis Terrae, the great lake at the foot of the ravine, a perfect match for its name. It even flowed along the corridors of power all the way to the Dodecagon, and though he knew the council chamber better than any other dwarf, knew the twelve stone doors were hermetically sealed, Thumil kept expecting the first trickle of red to seep through them, pool beneath the debating table, and rise till it drowned him and Cordy, that bald bastard Aristodeus, and … He looked at the once familiar dwarf twitching with nerves or damped down rage at the head of the table, scarcely dared take in the black axe clutched to his armored chest in white-knuckled hands. Looked and went blank. He couldn't say it. Couldn't say the name. It hardly seemed to fit anymore.

He straightened his blood-spattered robe. Hard to believe it had once been white. What must he have looked like now? Nothing like one of the Council of Twelve, that's for sure. Any illusions he might have had about status, about being untouchable in dwarven society, had scattered like rats before a mouser.

All he could focus on was those dead eyes that used to have the hue of walnut, at once sad but twinkling with good cheer. Now they were black as the Void and just as hungry. Hungry for more slaughter. Hungry for the murder of his own kind. They saw Thumil watching, narrowed when he squeezed Cordy's hand, wringing out what little strength was left in her. Then they flitted left to right, hunting out betrayal in the shadows beneath the amber glow-stones set into the lintel above each door. Used to be those lights gave the chamber a homey cheer, like the warm embers of the hearth in Kunaga's, where they'd grown drunk together, set the place heaving with bawdy songs and uproarious wit.

Thumil blinked back tears, met that tortured gaze that asked if he were friend or foe; read in that grimacing face the accusation of betrayal, the desperate need to trust. Those eyes had been ready to kill him, that much he knew. Didn't matter how close they once were, if it hadn't been for Cordy, he'd have been a head on a spike, along with all those other dwarves.

She'd always had the persuasion, Cordy. Only woman alive who could have got him to the altar, but even she'd nearly fallen victim to the black axe. Whatever trust their old friend still had in her was teetering on a knife's edge. There'd been no mercy in that demonic glare. None whatsoever.

The eyes were feverish now, fixed right on him, daring him, willing him, begging him. Shog, the poor bastard looked a mess, beard all matted and streaked with froth, face carved with frown lines like scars. But that's all it was now: a face. Thumil couldn't allow himself to give it a name. The mere thought that this butcher was once a person, once a friend, brought bile to his throat, sent spasms through his innards that made him double up.

Cordy let out a sob, gripped his hand tighter. Her palm was greased with sweat. Could have been gore, for all Thumil knew. Shog, she'd seen enough of it. The specks of crimson on her dress gave testimony to that, and there was a corona of roseate mist that swirled about her. Thumil blinked and it was gone. Must have been his eyes. Must have gotten blood in his eyes.

How he loved her at that moment, needed her, knew with all his heart it was the two of them against the world. He put his cheek to her beard, sought the comfort of its soft bristles, but it was lank, cold with the perspiration of fear, or perhaps the wetness of congealing blood. He couldn't bear to look, preferring instead the way his mind chose to picture her. How blessed he was to have her as his wife. How cursed in everything else. Maybe together they could keep the darkness at bay, forget what they'd seen, what they'd been forced to do; because it was a betrayal, however you looked at it, but it was the only choice they had. The only one they'd been given.

Aristodeus stepped behind the butcher, holding the black great helm aloft, flecks of green glimmering on its casing in the half-light. There was a collective intake of breath and then silence as the philosopher lowered the helm.

Thumil's heart lurched. He wanted so much to say no. What if the killing could be stopped some other way they'd missed? Council wasn't used to making emergency decisions. Trick him, was all the bald bastard offered—him and his homunculi friends. Trick him and kill him, or trick him and take his name, shame him like no other dwarf had been shamed, then shut him in the dungeons till a cure could be found. Thumil winced. There was no cure for evil like the black axe brought. Maybe killing would have been fairer to everyone.

He stretched out his hand, but Cordy put a restraining arm around his shoulders.

"No," he rasped, the word not passing his clenched teeth. He forced his lips open, groaned way back in his throat, felt his friend's name worming its way up from his guts, spilling into his mouth... and then it was gone as the helm covered the head and was sealed in place by a sparking theurgy from Aristodeus's fingertips. Locked tight, just like the shogger said it would be, never to be removed.

Aristodeus stepped back, rummaging in the pocket of his robe. "Well," he said, producing a pipe and wagging the stem at Thumil like he was making a clever point to a student, "that's that taken care of. You dwarves are safe as houses now, touch scarolite." He rapped his knuckles on the helm.

"Huh?" a muffled voice came from inside.

Two of Aristodeus's homunculi emerged from a wall, as if they'd been hiding inside the very stone. Thumil blinked and shook his head. Was it an illusion, like the concealer cloaks employed by the ravine city's assassins, or something more innate to their nature as spawn of the Abyss? One had hair like fleece, twisted into long gray ropes. The other's was a spray of slick black tendrils, surmounting an overhanging forehead and eyes like distant stars. They were carrying a rectangular block of crystal, which they set atop the table. With almost surgical care, one of them pried the butcher's fingers from the haft of the black axe, while the other lifted the cursed weapon free. The barest hint of a smile curled at the creature's gnomic face before it placed the axe on top of the crystal and gave a satisfied nod as it sank into the block, settling in the middle.

Cordy gave Thumil a look full of concern, but the best he could manage was a shrug.

Never liked dealing with homunculi. Never trusted them, but the philosopher had convinced the council there was no other way. Smug bastard probably thought he had them worked out, just like he did everyone else. Even now, he was tapping out the bowl of his pipe and refilling it, seemingly without a care in the world.

"See you again, Nameless Dwarf," said the homunculus with the dreadlocks, voice tinged with regret—or was it sarcasm?

"What's that?" the butcher asked, pivoting his head so he could get a better look through the narrow eye-slit of the great helm.

Thumil didn't like the way the others were already calling his old friend the Ravine Butcher, but 'Nameless Dwarf'? Is that all he was now, a dwarf with no name, a dwarf who, according to Aristodeus, never had one, not at any point in time?

Didn't make sense, as far as Thumil was concerned, but he couldn't deny the reality. One minute the name had been on the tip of his tongue, the next it was as if it had never been. How could he have known this dwarf all his life, known his father, Droom, and his mother, Yyalla, and yet not have a clue what to call him? How many years had they fought together? Drunk? Shog of all shogs, Thumil even knew his brother, Lucius. Had known, rather. Poor old Lucius had gone to the *seethers* for starting all this black axe business. Small price to pay, Councilor Grago had argued: one isolated action by the council to avert a major catastrophe. Old Moary had tried to prevaricate, as always, but Grago had scared them into action. First time in hundreds of years, and the taste of complicity was like vinegar to Thumil. Once was enough for him, and most of the other councilors had agreed. He wasn't about to make the same mistake again; wasn't about to watch his friend put to death. Grago wasn't happy about it, but what could he do without a majority vote?

"Nothing," Aristodeus replied to the helmed dwarf, holding something silver to his pipe and pressing with his thumb. Flame sprang up, and he swirled it around the bowl, sucking in air and smacking his lips. He returned the silver flame-maker to his robe and puffed out a couple of smoke rings. He gave a curt nod to the homunculi.

The little creatures picked up the crystal block containing the axe and carried it straight through the wall. Aristodeus winked at Thumil.

Thumil frowned after the dreadlocked homunculus, eyes boring into the stony surface that seemed to have swallowed him. There was something about how he'd uttered those words: 'Nameless Dwarf'. Thumil rubbed his beard. A shiver passed along his spine. It sounded oddly familiar, like it had always been there and had come home to roost from some ill-defined future. Cordy must've sensed his unease, gave his hand a reassuring squeeze. Was it a description or a name? Had the homunculus chosen it for him, or was it meant as a joke? Thumil caught himself nodding vigorously. A descriptor and a name, he decided. Had to be. Had to call him something. Wasn't a person otherwise.

"How are you feeling?" Aristodeus asked.

"In need of some mead or a flagon of ale," came the voice from within the helm. "A big bottomed lass and a stout drinking pal. We'll soak up the booze with a spit-roasted cow, and sing bawdy songs in the best bars in town…"

Thumil opened his mouth to join in the refrain then clamped it shut, tears streaming down his cheeks. Cordy hugged him so tight she nearly crushed the life out of him.

"Shogged out our brains," the Nameless Dwarf bellowed. "Nothing's the same as a brawl and some mead and a beer-drinking dame."

How many times had they sung those words together, terrorizing the taverns of Arx Gravis?

"Thumil?" said the voice from within the helm. "Thumil, is that you?" The eye-slit turned toward him. "Who's the lucky lassie?" He turned to Cordy. "Like the beard, gives me something to… Cordy? What's wrong with me? I didn't recognize… I mean, hang me for a shogger, you two were married last time I looked." His hand snaked out, took Cordy's. "There, see! A ring to match that golden hair of yours. Lassie, forgive me, I'm not myself. You too, Thumil. Am I forgiven?"

"Aye," Thumil said, sniffing back some snot and wiping the tear tracks from his face. "Course you are." He looked down at his feet, at the dark stains creeping up from the soles of his boots. His eyes followed the trail of bloody footprints to the door they'd entered by, now sealed like a sepulcher.

"No, wait. Something's wrong," the Nameless Dwarf said. "You've been here all along. Me, too. It's all a blur. Can't even remember my own name." He shook his helmed head from side to side, slapped at it with his palms. "Must've fallen out my ear." Bang, bang, bang. "Shog, it's lost. Help me get this thing off my head, will you? My name... I've lost my shogging name. Gods of Arnoch, do you know how stupid that sounds?"

Aristodeus stepped to the side of the chair, pipe clamped in the corner of his mouth. The eye-slit focused on him.

"Can you find it for me, laddie?"

"No," the philosopher said around the stem of his pipe. He glanced at Thumil, gave the impression of sighing. "No, I'm afraid it's gone."

Thumil closed his eyes, sought the narrowest crack in all the torment through which to slither away and once more know peace, but it was a hollow hope. None of them would ever know peace again after what they'd witnessed, after what this poor, cursed soul had done, Lord have mercy.

The Nameless Dwarf slumped forward in his chair, catching the face of his helm in his red-stained hands.

Aristodeus turned away, as if he had better things to do, casting casually over his shoulder, "Tell them it's safe to come in now, Councilor."

Thumil extricated his fingers from Cordy's one at a time. She must have been holding her breath, for she exhaled so sharply it sounded like air escaping from a corpse. He couldn't look at her right then, but he knew she'd manage. She was strong enough. Stronger than him. All that held him up was Aristodeus's command. He followed the bloody path to the door and slapped the stone with his palm.

"Thumil?" Old Moary's muffled voice came from outside. "That you?"

"It's all right to come in now," Thumil called, barely recognizing his own voice, it rasped so much.

There was a dull thud as the mechanism kicked in, and then the door clunked and ground its way up into the ceiling. It was a disconcerting thing, learning the Dodecagon could be locked from the outside. Normally, the councilors wanted to keep others out while they were debating. Made you wonder who'd instructed the engineers. Made you wonder even more what the original purpose of the chamber had been, back in the days of monarchy before Maldark the Fallen, before the Council of Twelve took over the reins of Arx Gravis.

"Is he held?" Throam Grago said, pushing his way into the chamber first. "Has the axe been removed?"

"The Council of Twelve?" the Nameless Dwarf said, sitting bolt upright and taking in the white-robed dwarves bustling through the doorway, then looking around the room as if for the first time. "The Dodecagon? Shog, this must be serious. What have I done, drunk the last bottle of Urbs Sapientii mead? Wait, no, Thumil, that would have been you, you sozzled old shogger."

Thumil dipped his head, clamping his eyes shut to hold in the tears.

"Yes, yes, Councilor Grago," Aristodeus snapped. "Just as I said it would be."

"Then we have him," Grago said. "To the *seethers*!"

"Oh, it is serious," the Nameless Dwarf said.

Aristodeus sighed and rolled his eyes. He crossed the chamber and made a show of inspecting the stonework, all the while puffing on his pipe.

"That's not what we—" Thumil started, but he sounded tired, defeated, even to himself.

"Pish," Grago said. "Never mind what was said. We are talking about the survival of our race. Risks, Councilor Thumil. The risks must not outweigh the benefits."

The rest of the councilors made their way into the Dodecagon, eyeing the butcher in the helm warily before gathering together in a tight clutch, as if they were afraid to sit at the same table as him.

"The ends justify the means," Tor Garnil said, as if it were a fact. "Councilor Grago is quite right; it's all a matter of proportionalism. If you take, for example, the paradigm of the—"

"My husband was speaking," Cordy said in a voice like a whiplash.

Thumil winced. They had her riled, and that was never a good thing.

"My dear lady," Garnil said, "your husband is an elected member of this council, whereas you are not."

"Look, you ignorant shogger," Cordy said, advancing on Garnil, fists clenched.

Garnil took a step back, right into Castail, who was in the middle of a hushed debate with Yuffie, couple of conniving backstabbers that they were.

"Wait, my dear," Thumil said, instantly regretting it.

"Don't you 'dear' me," Cordy said. "I've had a gutful of death already, and I won't let you stand for any more of it, Thumil, do you get it?"

Old Moary coughed into his fist, wiped the spittle from his gray beard. "Well, I don't know. I mean, what if—"

"No, Councilor," Grago said. "No more 'what ifs', no more prevarication. We are on the brink. On the brink, I tell you. The time for inaction is past. For too long have we cowered in the shadow of Maldark's sins, afraid to even take a shit without months of debate. We must—"

A long drawn-out groan reverberated from the Nameless Dwarf's helm. "Lucius?" The helm pivoted left then right. "Oh shog, Lucius went to the *seethers*. Poor old Lucius." The eye-slit came to rest on Thumil. "Thumil? Have I...? What have I...? Oh, no!" He went suddenly rigid, and his arms shook as he gripped the edge of the table. "Thumil, Cordy, was it me? Oh no, was it me?"

"Yes, it *was* you, you evil shogger," Grago said. "It was you all the way, cutting down decent dwarves, chopping them into pieces, sticking their heads on spikes. Why, had you forgotten? Wasn't it important enough to remember?"

"Thumil?" The voice was a shrill lament. "Say it isn't true. Say it isn't..."

Thumil forced himself to look at the Nameless Dwarf. His jaw hung slack and his eyes were transfixed. The black helm was overlaid with the phantom of his friend's face, a twinkle in those mournful eyes. But it was gone in a flash, replaced by dead eyes and a bloody visage, a visage that was better off encased in scarolite forever.

"I'm sorry," Thumil said. "Councilor Grago speaks the truth."

The helmed head slumped forward, those mighty shoulders shuddering. "Then kill me. Please, please kill me."

"See!" Grago said. "Even he agrees."

Aristodeus spun on his heel, face red with fury. "Remorse, you numbskull. Don't you recognize repentance when you hear it? Thought you dwarves read the Liber—no, wait, what was it Maldark called the scriptures? What did they used to be called on Earth?" He snapped his fingers and screwed his face up in concentration. "Damn. It's on the tip of my—"

"No," Grago said. "No, we don't read those scriptures. Not after what the Fallen did."

"Imbecile!" Aristodeus said. "Typical. Typical of you dwarves. Always throwing out the baby with the—"

"Isn't that what you did, philosopher?"—A voice like rustling leaves. "Weren't you once a man of faith, before you became too clever, even for the Supernal Father?"

A gale tore through the chamber, whipping up a vortex of sparks, flashes, tongues of flame. The whole coalesced into a cool conflagration then burst with the brilliance of a thousand suns.

Thumil's arm covered his eyes, and he instinctively dropped to his knees. Everything behind his eyelids was white, then red, then black as the Void and dotted with pinpricks of silver. He blinked over and over, shaking his head and slowly removing his arm. Where the vortex had exploded, now stood a man robed in brown, sunlight bleeding from beneath an all-enveloping cowl.

"So, here at last is our troublesome Nameless Dwarf. A time will come when the name that is not a name will be as cursed as the Ravine Butcher's, should we allow him to live. About time. About time the dwarves grew a backbone."

"Nothing is predetermined," Aristodeus said. "You know that as well as I, Archon."

It was like standing beneath the most awe-inspiring mountain, or gazing upon the endless ocean, such was the feeling of dread that rolled off the being. Thumil didn't know whether or not to throw himself to his knees and beg forgiveness for a life not always well-lived. In the end, he took his cue from Cordy, who merely snorted and glared daggers.

Grago must have done the same. He puffed up his chest and stuck his nose in the air. "Who the shog are you?"

"Silence!" There was thunder in the voice that time, and Grago dropped to his belly, along with half the council.

Aristodeus shook his head and held up a hand. "This, dear dwarves, is the Archon. If you still read the scriptures, you'd get some sort of idea of the manner of being he is."

Flames licked around the edge of the Archon's hood. "You grow too familiar, philosopher."

"Quite right," Aristodeus said. "And we can't have that, can we? We all know what familiarity breeds."

The Archon rose into the air and started to circle Aristodeus. "You have picked up the ways of your master, it seems. That doesn't bode well for you extricating yourself from his trap."

Aristodeus jabbed the stem of his pipe at the Archon, thought better of it and put it away. "Not my master, and you just watch. I'll pry open the jaws of his trap sooner or later. Have faith."

The Archon let out a laugh like a gust of wind. "Faith is something I have never lacked. I wish you could say the same. You are too proud, philosopher, just the way he likes them."

"Being right doesn't make one proud. Personally, I'd be more concerned about a Supernal Being who considers himself judge, jury, and executioner, wouldn't you, Thumil?"

Thumil groaned internally. What did Aristodeus have to go and include him for? He turned his palms up and shrugged. Cordy elbowed him in the back, and he probably deserved it.

"Now is not the time to lose your tongue, Councilor Thumil," Aristodeus said. "There was a vote, remember?"

Grago raised his head from the floor. "Technically, no."

"What, your fingers were crossed?" Cordy said.

It looked to Thumil like she was going to kick the prostate councilor for a moment.

"Uhm, I must just say," Old Moary said—Thumil was impressed to see he was still standing, a be-socked big toe curling from beneath his robe— "there was indeed a majority vote to stay execution. If you ask me—"

"Thank you, Councilor Moary," Aristodeus said. "Age and wisdom go hand in hand like—"

"You are the voice of this council?" the Archon said, drifting up close to the ancient councilor.

"Well, uh, no. I mean, not really. I've just been on the council longer than the rest, but our primary is Councilor Thumil."

Thumil's guts turned to mush, and his legs threatened to buckle. Cordy pinched his arse, which did the trick.

The Archon turned on him, ire suppurating from his cowl in fingers of fire. "Heed my words, Councilor Thumil. If this Nameless Dwarf lives, thousands will die. He is a pawn of the Demiurgos."

"Not if I keep him in stasis," Aristodeus said. "Nothing besides my own voice will be able to rouse him."

"You know this philosopher well?" the Archon said.

Thumil closed his eyes against the glare. He desperately wanted to see if the Archon had a face, but the brightness was blinding. "Not well," he said.

"And you would trust him?"

Thumil gave a sideways look at Aristodeus. "No."

"There…" the Archon said, turning on the philosopher.

"But no one's killing my friend."

Cordy gave his arm a squeeze. It didn't matter to Thumil that this god-like being could probably blast him from existence; with Cordy on his side, he'd always have a fighting chance.

Aristodeus coughed into his fist and gave a curt nod.

The Archon's hood shimmered with pent up flame but then settled back to a dull brown. "I cannot—will not—force compliance. Very well, but on your head be it. After all, it is your head to lose."

Fingers of ice ran their way over Thumil's flesh. Cordy tensed, her grip suddenly a vise that would never let go.

"With all due respect," Grago said, pushing himself up onto his knees, "Councilor Thumil does not speak for—"

But the Archon was gone, leaving only swirling dust motes in his wake, and then even they settled. The air grew heavy, and it felt to Thumil as though the ceiling were pressing down on him, causing his shoulders to stoop.

"Well," Grago said, making it all the way to his feet, "I still say we—"

"No," Thumil said, with more authority than he felt, and then he added more gently, "No."

Aristodeus caught his eye and nodded. "Come," he said to the Nameless Dwarf. "Time for your rest."

"Rest?" came the voice from within the helm. "Shouldn't there be a snifter of mead first?"

"Perhaps when you awaken."

Thumil thought Aristodeus was going to add, "If you awaken." After all, it was no ordinary rest he was talking about. If things didn't change, if Aristodeus couldn't—or wouldn't—find a way to eliminate the threat of the black axe, his old friend faced an eternity chained in a locked cell, unable to move a muscle; unable even to breathe.

The Nameless Dwarf shrugged. "Oh well. Can't say fairer than that." He let out an exaggerated yawn and stretched his thickly muscled arms above his head. "Don't suppose you fancy joining me, lassie?" he said to Cordy.

She chuckled, but her eyes were damp.

"Probably for the best," the Nameless Dwarf said as Aristodeus walked him from the chamber. "Don't want to set the bar too high for Thumil now, do we?"

"Goodbye, my friend," Thumil muttered into his beard.

The councilors were all up on their feet once more and clamoring for his attention. Their questions were like the cascading waters of the falls that fed the Sanguis Terrae in the depths of the ravine, forcing him in on himself, drowning him. Only Cordy's hand anchored him, gave him the strength to remain standing. She leaned in close to his ear, her breath warm on his cheek.

"I am with you, my love," she said. "Now and forever."

"I know, dear," he replied, even as a gulf of blackness opened up within his mind and threatened to swallow him. He patted Cordy's hand, shuddering as he sucked air through gritted teeth. "He was my friend, wasn't he?" He was starting to wonder. Was it possible that the past had vanished along with the name, and all that remained was the slaughter and the dwarf in the scarolite helm?

Cordy turned his face so that he had to look her in the eye. She was weeping openly now, and her lips quivered as she spoke. "Yes, my love, he was your friend. He was our friend."

She pulled him to her breast, shutting out the insistent councilors, cocooning him against the horrors he had witnessed.

—*on your head be it.*

The image of a baby, head dashed against the hard stone of Arx Gravis, sprang to life behind his eyes. Thumil groaned and tried to nestle further into Cordy's bosom.

After all, it is your head to lose.

THE END OF WORLDS

The Homestead, Earth

Year of the Reckoning: 908

ANDS GRIPPED SHADER'S arm and helped him to his feet. His vision swirled red and blue, slashed into ribbons by streaks of argent and gold. He blinked until his eyes regained their focus on the ruddy plateau of the Homestead beneath his feet, and above, the sapphire skies of Sahul. Silver glinted from the heads of pikes and spears, and the aureate sun glared down with a heat that seared its displeasure deep into his flesh.

"Barek," he said, shuddering as he faced the youth. "You made it."

Rhiannon was approaching, leading Sammy like the last walk of the damned and trailing Callixus's black sword.

A sea of troops looked toward him as if he might have some answer, might be able to tell them all was not lost. The Emperor Hagalle pushed to the front, glaring his unspoken accusations. General Starn was at his side, all stiff and proper, bleeding from a score of wounds and looking like he'd collapse if honor would let him. Behind them came the Ipsissimus, stooped and broken, like a man who no longer believed in salvation.

"So, it's over, then," Barek stated matter-of-factly. "This is the end of all things."

Dave the Slave hobbled into view, his hunchback a swollen malignancy full to the bursting with poison. He pointed at Shader and cried, "He has doomed us."

Shader's head was spinning from the concussion, his thoughts rising and breaking like waves on a reef. If only he'd struck Gandaw when he'd had the chance. If only he hadn't hesitated—

"Deacon?" Rhiannon said, releasing Sammy's hand and taking hold of Shader's face. "Deacon?"

Shader's eyes tracked Sammy's progress as the boy wandered away from his sister and went into the embrace of the huge snake man. At least one of the Hybrids had survived.

"I'm sorry, Rhiannon." *—For everything. For all you've suffered.*

"Is it true?" She pressed her face close to his, and all he could think of was the sweetness of her breath. "Have we lost?"

Shader pulled away, gestured to the sky where the throne had been. He was tired. Too tired to care about the end of Creation. But all eyes were on him, like he was the world's last hope. He had to say something, even if it was to confirm their greatest fears.

"Gandaw's beyond our reach now."

"You did this!" Dave inveighed. "You were given a chance—"

The hunchback dropped to his knees with a thud, and Shadrak the Unseen emerged from behind him.

"Kidney punch," the assassin said. "Which is mild, considering what I thought of doing."

Still alive, then, after he'd been flung across the ridge by some unseen force. Like a cockroach, Shader thought. Even if they were too late, and Creation fell, Shadrak would no doubt still be there, hunkered down in some nook or cranny in Gandaw's brave new world.

"Reckon I can find him," Shadrak said. "Sektis shogging Gandaw. But I don't know how much time we have."

And then Aristodeus was there, rubbing his beard like he always did when considering an interesting conundrum. He smiled at Shader, but there was no warmth in his eyes. If anything, he looked like a man tormented, a man who had staked his entire existence on one last throw of the die.

"You clearly don't understand the nature of the beast," he said. "Gandaw has planned this for millennia, and he's not about to mess it up by rushing. He has instruments that have mapped Creation one strand at a time, all so he can plug the data into his algorithms for the Unweaving. The only thing missing was an energy source big enough for the task."

"So it's over," Rhiannon said.

"If we do nothing." Aristodeus's words may have been meant for the Ipsissimus, but if they were, they were wasted. The Ipsissimus seemed lost in a world of his own, as absent as the Nous he was supposed to represent. "If you do nothing." Aristodeus spoke the words directly to Shader, and something was communicated between them: no more than a chill in Shader's spine, a knotting of his stomach, and the vague feeling that something like this had happened before.

Every frayed nerve in Shader's body screamed recognition, but his concussed mind just threw up blurs and rumors.

Aristodeus's eyes narrowed. They were bluer than the sky and glimmered like ice in the arctic sun. The philosopher's bald head was wrinkled with concern, but Shader had the sense it was not for his welfare. There was some secret, something Aristodeus wasn't saying, and Shader's whole being held the answer. But still his mind stalled, like a horse balking at a jump. Whatever it was, it was there, but on the far side of an unfathomable abyss.

The philosopher stepped away, and Shader's nerves quieted. His head was pounding from where he'd struck it when he tumbled down the ridge. The sun's scorching heat wasn't helping any. Ain, he was dry. When had he last had something to drink?

I think I can find him—Was it Shadrak who'd said that?

The albino was watching Aristodeus with a coolness that went deeper than mere curiosity at the philosopher's appearance out of nowhere, or the knowledge he claimed of the end of all things. Shadrak must have sensed Shader's gaze, for his pink eyes narrowed, demanding some kind of action. Shader looked at the others, as if their presence, their tangibility, might rub off on his thoughts.

Rhiannon had lost something—something as vague and indefinable as Shader's memories. She looked older somehow, face honed by conflict, eyes darker, tainted by what they'd seen. The color had drained from her lips, and her complexion had sallowed beyond its wan mystique, now appearing sickly, pallid like the dead of Sahul who first Cadman and then Gandaw had commanded against them. Walking corpses, necrotic ghouls. Maybe their undeath was contagious.

Barek looked numb from exhaustion and lucky to be alive. There was hardly any white left on his tabard, so drenched was it with his own blood and the putrid gore of the undead. His young eyes held the same dullness that had deadened the Ipsissimus's since the loss of his Monas and his failure to lift a finger to prevent it.

Shader's face tightened, and he sucked in air through clenched teeth. His anger hadn't passed, but he no longer knew if it was directed at the Ipsissimus, or at the deity who demanded pacifism at the point of a sword. Did he have the right to be angry at Nous, the son of Ain the Concealed, the one true Lord who was no-thing? But Nous *was* something. The more Shader trod the path of the Templum, the more he realized Nous was utterly human in his contradictions and paradoxes, in his broken promises and his ability to disappoint.

So, it's over, Rhiannon had said—for the worlds, Earth and Aethir. Ain's teeth, how many other worlds were threatened by Gandaw's Unweaving? And did it just involve the whole span of space, or would time be unpicked, too? All so that Sektis Gandaw could be his own origin, the still point of a perfect creation, a creation with no room for any of those left standing atop the Homestead, those who had given their lives defending the bedrock of existence. Those who expected something of Shader, something he didn't know how to give.

Worlds were going to fall. Creation itself was poised for oblivion.

If you do nothing, Aristodeus had said. But what could Shader do? Hadn't he already had his chance and failed just as completely as the Ipsissimus?

Dave the Slave remained on his knees. His mouth was still, but accusation burned in his eyes. Out of them all, the crazy prophet had expected the most from Shader. Ain only knew what he would do now that Shader had stayed his hand, refused to obey the 'Voice of Nous.' Shader couldn't hold onto Dave's eyes. They were the myopic eyes of a lunatic, a man whose faith was a dangerous obsession.

Looking away from Dave, Shader's gaze swept the battlefield, the tabletop summit of the Homestead, most sacred site of Sahul's Dreamers. The dead lay in piles that could have been spread out to cover a large field. Some were now twice dead, the remains of the disinterred automatons commanded by Sektis Gandaw. The others, mingled in bloody heaps, were sworn enemies driven together by desperation: the armies of Nousia and Sahul. Thousands dead, a fraction of that remaining, all waiting for Shader to act, to tell them there was still hope.

Finally, the giant snake-headed Hybrid spoke, all the while hugging the boy, Sammy, against his massive chest. Little Sammy Kwane, Rhiannon's brother, now weather-beaten and half-naked in the manner of the Dreamers.

"You have the Archon'sss sssword. Perhapsss there isss yet sssome hope."

Shader looked down at the gladius still snug in his grip, like it wanted to be there. The Sword of the Archon, won in the tournament in Aeterna. Isn't that what Aristodeus had prepared him for as a child?

Shader saw the philosopher watching him, nodding at Mamba's refusal of despair. Dave's glare seemed to say, "The sword you should have slain Gandaw with." —*You were given a chance.*

The snake-man turned to face Shadrak. "I will go with you, though my woundsss are many." He inclined his head, eyes widening in a manner that suggested familiarity, affection even. There was a deep gouge in his shoulder, and scores of gashes across his chest and legs. It looked as if he could hardly move his left arm. Sammy clung to him, as if he couldn't bare to let him go.

Shadrak held his gaze for a long while, as if he were appraising, or perhaps remembering. Finally he shook his head and looked away. "No, I have my instructions. Just me and Shader. No one else."

"Instructions?" Aristodeus said. "Who gave you instructions?"

"Not at liberty to say. Why, does that rain on your parade?"

Shadrak was following orders? Whose? Surely not the Sicarii: this was much bigger than them. Shader took some slight satisfaction from the fact that Aristodeus hadn't been expecting this. The philosopher bit down on his top lip, narrowed his eyes to slits. Green light swirled around him, and then he was gone, as if he'd never been there.

The Emperor Hagalle drew himself up to his considerable height, dwarfing the stocky General Starn even more than he normally did.

"And who goes for Sahul? This is far too important to entrust to a Nousian and whatever the hell you are." He shot a derisive look at Shadrak.

"I'm Sicarii, Emperor," Shadrak said, his tone genial, while the words implied threat, especially to one as paranoid as Hagalle.

Hagalle clenched his fists and glowered. If he'd proven anything to Shader in the last few hours, it was that he was a man who confronted his fears. The tension hung thickly between him and the tiny assassin, and then Rhiannon stepped forward.

"I'm from Oakendale," she said. "Place is a shithole, but I reckon it qualifies as Sahulian. I'll go."

She looked at Sammy, but he paid her no heed. His head was buried in the snake-man's chest. Something about the slump of Rhiannon's shoulders, the forced stoicism of her face, told Shader she already knew she'd lost her brother.

"No," Shader said, but his voice sounded thin and weak. He didn't want her clinging to him just because there was nothing for her here. Oh, she still had the Templum, but that couldn't be enough. Not for Rhiannon. Not the woman he knew. And besides, it had never been enough for Shader.

"He stabbed you, Deacon," Rhiannon said, jabbing a finger at Shadrak. "Or have you already forgotten that? No, don't tell me. You've forgiven him." She snorted her contempt.

The pain was still there, a dull ache in his lower back, in spite of the Archon's healing. It wasn't an idea Shader was comfortable with—traveling to an uncharted world with the man who'd killed him—quite literally—but what choice did he have? Without even asking him what he wanted, it seemed everyone had decided Shader was going on this madcap mission; after all, he was the Keeper of the Archon's Sword, wasn't he? But what could Rhiannon do? If Shadrak intended more harm, how could she prevent it?

"Yes," Rhiannon said. "I'm coming, and that's bloody final. I'll keep that little shit in his place." She glared at Shadrak. "And you know I can, don't you?"

Shadrak's hand went to his face, but he held her gaze with his unnerving eyes and snorted his contempt.

"Anyone else have anything to add?" Shadrak said, pulling up his hood, either to shield his head from the sun or to emphasize his profession. "Coz I'm keeping a list."

Hagalle looked at the Ipsissimus, but there was no response.

"I will accompany you, for that is the will of Nous," Dave said, lurching to Shader's side.

"Over my rotting corpse," Shadrak said.

"But Nous—"

"Can go shog himself." The assassin pushed roughly past him and strode for the edge of the mesa. Clusters of soldiers got out of his way and merely watched as he turned back and hollered, "You coming, or are we gonna sit on our asses and watch the shogging fireworks? Coz the end of the world's coming, Shader, and now's the only chance we have."

Rhiannon turned to her brother. "I... Sammy, I love..."

The boy's blank gaze seemed to freeze the words in her mouth. He took hold of the snake-man's hand and tugged it. The two turned away and walked back toward the massed troops and the bodies of the dead.

Shader took hold of Rhiannon by the shoulders. "You sure about this? Sammy—"

"Yeah, like he needs me," Rhiannon said, breaking free of him and storming after Shadrak.

I need you, Shader wanted to say, but a strange paralysis overcame his jaw, and the words remained unspoken. He set off after Rhiannon, lowering his eyes so he didn't have to look at the troops he passed. When he got to the edge of the tabletop, Rhiannon was already clambering down to a broad ledge that wound around the summit of the Homestead. He groaned, and already felt dizzy. He'd never liked heights. Not even as a child.

Shadrak looked up at him from the ledge. "Left my long-gun on the ridge. Shogged if I'm going back for it now. Ain't like it was gonna work, anyway, piece of crap. Not after I slung it down."

Rhiannon dropped the last couple of feet to stand beside the assassin. "Come on," she said to Shader. "What's the hold up."

Swallowing bile, Shader grimaced and lowered his feet over the edge. "No hold up," he said, twisting to face the rock wall. "Just wondering how falling and breaking our necks is going to help, that's all."

He looked back at the troops spread out across the mesa. They were moving among their fallen comrades, or collecting in groups, staring at him. He saw the Ipsissimus walking off by himself, a sorry-looking trio of Elect knights struggling to keep up, horses in tow. General Starn caught Shader's eye and saluted, then jumped as Hagalle barked something at him. What would they do now that the battle was over? What could they do, save wait and hope? He shook his head, and the weight of responsibility felt like the sky had dropped on him. Why him? Why did it all depend on him? Couldn't Aristodeus have found someone more worthy? Someone capable of at least taking the chances he was given?

He drew in a deep breath and held it, prodding the rock face with his boot until he found a good-sized niche. Then slowly, ever so carefully, he started to climb down.

The instant Shader reached the ledge, Shadrak turned and tapped the air with his fingers. Light flared in a horizontal beam before his feet and then swiftly grew upward to form a rectangular doorway.

"Well, don't just stand there gawping," Shadrak said, and stepped inside.

Shader could feel Dave's eyes on him, glaring down at the ledge. He pointedly averted his gaze. There was no need to look: the tingling running up and down his spine was evidence enough. But maybe the hunchback had been right. Maybe he should have finished the job. Why had he hesitated? Why had he not struck Gandaw in that fleeting moment of opportunity? It was a question that threw up a dozen more: Why had he left Aeterna for Sahul? Why had he left Pardes? Why had he almost given up all he was for Rhiannon? Why hadn't it been enough?

He clenched his fists, and acid ran through his veins. She was standing so close to him, he could smell her sweat. No doubt, she could smell his, too. It wasn't as if any of them had had time to wash these past few days.

Turning back to the doorway, he gestured for Rhiannon to go first. She screwed her face up and pressed it into the light.

"Oh my shogging—" She pulled back out again. "You have got to see this!"

She grabbed Shader's hand and dragged him through the doorway's effulgence behind her.

Shader's heart bounced up into his throat. It was enough to jolt him back to his senses He tensed and flicked his eyes around, searching for any hint of a threat. The gladius throbbed in his hand and eased the pain in his head, cleared his mind. It must have responded to the arousal caused by the transition, for where there had been rock and open sky, they were now standing at one end of a metallic corridor, burnished as smooth as glass and lit by an eerie blue luminescence from some invisible source.

Shadrak was striding ahead of them, completely at home.

It wasn't magic—at least not like any Shader had encountered. This had more the feel of Ancient tech about it, like the weapons he'd seen on Podesta's ship, or the sketches in the history books Aristodeus had made him read as a child. The closest thing that sprang to mind was the dome he and Barek had discovered in Fenrir. A wave of emotion rolled up his spine and made him shudder. With a quick prayer for the soul of Osric, who had endured centuries of torment only to give up his remaining half-life to protect those he owed nothing to, Shader touched his forehead and dragged his attention back to the task in hand.

The corridor went on so long it must have passed beyond the edge of the Homestead. Shadrak waited for them at a junction, above which were lintels inscribed with numerals. They followed him down the left-hand passageway, which was identical in every way to the entrance corridor, and paused before a slit partway along the wall. Shadrak pried open a silver panel and pressed a sequence of buttons. The wall slid open, revealing a rectangular cubicle, into which they stepped. The wall sealed behind them, and Shadrak tapped more buttons on the inside. The cubicle shuddered, and a low droning started up. Shader watched Rhiannon out of the corner of his eye, but she seemed more fascinated than scared.

Once the droning stopped, the wall parted, and Shadrak led them along another identical corridor. The wall opened to admit them to a spherical chamber dominated by a bedizened plinth flashing with pinpricks of multicoloured light and topped with black mirrors, across which symbols etched in light raced. A steady hiss like a gentle wind sounded in the background.

Rhiannon lingered in the corridor, staring at the floor. Shadrak had already moved to the plinth and was gazing at the mirrors while tapping buttons and twisting knobs. Rhiannon stooped to pick something up—a slender loop of wire that ran between two short wooden rods. She turned her face toward Shader and raised her eyebrows. Shader shrugged, and Rhiannon shook her head, pocketing the contraption. It looked like something you might slice cheese with.

"The plane ship is huge," Shadrak said as three ovoid stools twirled up from the floor and he gestured for them to be seated. "Way bigger than the summit of the Homestead. Goes right through it and beyond."

As soon as Shader lowered himself onto a stool, pliant silver straps wrapped around his waist and over his shoulders. Rhiannon stepped back, and Shadrak sighed.

"Safety precaution. When this thing moves, it gets a bit weird. Trust me, you're better off strapped in."

"Like I'm gonna trust you," Rhiannon said, but she sat down nonetheless, laying Callixus's sword across her lap.

Shadrak sat and let himself be strapped in, and the background hiss gave way to a sound like the droning of a thousand bees. Shader's stomach did a lazy flip-flop, and his body felt oddly weightless. When he looked at his arms, they lacked substance. He was as ethereal as Callixus had been.

"Don't suppose you're going to tell us how you came by this thing," Shader said, fighting back the urge to vomit.

"It was beneath Sarum for years. Found it by chance." Shadrak looked away pensively, as if replaying old memories. He shook his head and glanced at one of the black mirrors. "Never knew what it was till recently, and I ain't never done nothing like this."

"Like what?" Rhiannon asked.

Shadrak ignored her. He seemed rapt by whatever was in the mirror.

Shader saw what looked like a painting of a barren wasteland dominated by a lone mountain—no, it wasn't a mountain: it was too perfect, too symmetrical. More of a cone, formed from black rock—obsidian perhaps—and veined with what looked like malachite. The cone grew larger, and the angle of the image changed.

"That must be it," Shadrak said. "I'm just going on instructions, but that has got to be the Perfect Peak, Sektis Gandaw's scarolite mountain."

"Scarolite?" Rhiannon said.

"Yeah. Whatever that means," Shadrak said. "But this is where the shit's gonna kick off, apparently. When the Unweaving starts, this is where it'll spread out from."

"How do you know all this?" Shader asked. "Aristodeus?"

Shadrak frowned and shook his head. "Never you mind, mate. Just be grateful I got us here, right?"

The black mountain started to shimmer. The room pitched, and Shader found himself suspended above the plinth, held only by the restraints. Then he was falling to the left, the whole room rolling with him. An abrupt halt, as if they'd slammed into something, and he was upright again. And then the room began gyring at a giddying speed, Shadrak and Rhiannon broken blurs that were torn apart by invisible forces. Just as abruptly, the spinning stopped, and Rhiannon flopped forward against her straps.

"Shit!" Shadrak said.

Shader's stomach hit his mouth, and the plane ship plummeted.

THE SOUR MARSH

TELL ME THIS is supposed to happen," Rhiannon cried over the wail of klaxons.

Shader braced himself and gritted his teeth.

The plane ship fell and fell, the background susurrus now a torrent of raging water.

"Something hit us," Shadrak yelled. "Some kind of force from the mountain. That ain't s'posed to happen. This ship passes through walls."

"Gandaw?" Shader had to shout to be heard.

Silence.

They were no longer falling.

He forced his body to relax.

"I think we've crashed," Shadrak said as his restraints released him and he moved to the plinth.

Shader's straps retracted and he stood, but Rhiannon remained seated, wincing, her cheeks bulging, as if she were going to be sick.

"But there was no—" He was going to say impact.

"Plane ship," Shadrak said, as if that were answer enough. When Shader shrugged his incomprehension, the albino explained. "She merged with the sewers of Sarum, passed right through the rock of the Homestead. But to answer your other question, yes, it must've been Gandaw. I was told this is one of his ships."

"Told by whom?" Shader asked.

Shadrak pointedly ignored him. "Everything's still working." He peered into a mirror. "We're just not where we're s'posed to be."

"Was it a barrier of some sort?" Rhiannon finally stood and drew in a long breath. "Around the mountain?"

"Not as stupid as you look," Shadrak said.

Rhiannon bristled but bit her tongue. Shader sidled closer, but she had eyes only for Shadrak as she leaned on the black sword and glowered.

"Ain't the foggiest how this works." Shadrak slapped the side of a different mirror and waggled a lever. "But something tells me it's meant to show what's outside."

Shader stooped to look at the mirror. At first it seemed blank, as black as the Void, but then he discerned ripples of movement, bubbles and dark detritus that oozed across the surface.

"We'll have to do this the ol' fashioned way," Shadrak said, scurrying across the chamber and tapping a panel. A section of the wall slid open onto an endless corridor. "Stay here, if you like, but I'm going outside to see if it's started. I'm dying to see what the end of everything looks like."

"Oakendale," Rhiannon muttered, but Shadrak had already gone.

Or Britannia, Shader thought. At least that's what they would have said in Aeterna.

"Are you really going to use that?" Shader said, indicating the black sword.

"Too bloody right." Rhiannon shouldered the blade. "I'm not trusting my arse to Nous, if that's what you're thinking. Did that before, and look where it got me."

"Then you'll need something to keep it in," Shader said, "so you don't trip over it and lop your leg off." He unbuckled his belt and slid it through the loops of the scabbard holding his longsword. He removed the sword and propped it against the plinth, then handed the scabbard to Rhiannon. "Should fit."

"Don't I need a something to hang it from?" Rhiannon asked as Shader re-buckled the belt and adjusted the gladius's scabbard so that it hung just behind his hip.

"Here." He pressed close to her and reached for the knot of the rope that cinched her robe.

Rhiannon flinched and pulled back.

"Sorry," Shader said, raising his hands. "I wasn't thinking." Wasn't thinking about Gaston, and what he'd done to her.

Rhiannon shut her eyes and steepled her fingers over her lips. "No, it's OK. I just... You know."

Shader resumed his work on the knot, careful not to make any other contact.

"I should be good at this now," he said. "What with all those hours of meditating on the prayer cord."

Rhiannon scoffed. "You expect me to believe that?"

"See," Shader said with a little fanfare as the rope belt came away. "I'll be a luminary in no time."

Rhiannon gave a slow handclap. "Deacon Shader, raised to the altars. Just don't expect me to pray to you."

Shader threaded the rope through the back of the scabbard and then fastened it over Rhiannon's shoulder. She handed the black sword to him, and he recoiled. The air around the hilt was icy, and waves of darkness danced along the blade like a deathly miasma.

"You get used to it," Rhiannon said.

"Not sure I want to." Shader took the sword and hurriedly sheathed it on her back. "Might be a bit awkward, drawing it from behind, but it's the best I can do for now."

Rhiannon studied him for a moment and then dropped her eyes.

"Thanks," she said, before starting down the corridor.

Shadrak was on his way back as Shader followed her out the chamber.

"Lower level's submerged," he said. "Mud and slime. P'raps if we go up a floor or two..."

He located another panel, tapped out a sequence, and then led the way into a cubicle. After a moment's whirring and whining, the wall parted, and they emerged onto an identical passageway that terminated in a blank silver wall split down the middle. More button pressing, and this one slid open onto a vista so alien that Shader could only gawp.

An immense milky disk bathed the encroaching gloam with a consumptive pallor. At first, he thought it was an ailing sun, but once his eyes adjusted and he took in the surrounding darkness, he realized it was a moon—so close it seemed to sit on the horizon. Two more disks hung higher in the night sky, one as large as the moon back home, the other small and remote, seeming to trail its larger companion like the runt of the litter. They were set in deep cobalt skies that draped heavy above stooped mangroves and tangled briars. The ground squelched as he stepped from the plane ship, the loamy surface sucking greedily at his boot.

The sickly light of the closest moon washed the undergrowth with argent, granted it a sheen of unreality.

"Aethir," Shadrak muttered, pink eyes drinking it all in. "Feels weird... like a dream..."

"Isn't that what it is?" Rhiannon said. "The Cynocephalus's dream? That's what Elias used to say."

If she still grieved the bard's death, she didn't show it. She was too enraptured by the new surroundings.

"Not any dream, though," Shadrak said, as if Rhiannon hadn't spoken. "My dream. Like I've seen all this before." He hopped nimbly to a mound that protruded like an island amid the wetland.

Rhiannon gripped Shader's shoulder for support and lunged up beside the assassin.

Shader fought his boot free of the mire with a slurp of hungry mud and set it down on the firmer ground of the elevation.

"You think maybe Gandaw's hoping we'll get stuck in the bog?" Rhiannon said, wrinkling her nose.

Shadrak crouched and felt the grass atop the knoll. He scanned the tangled brush like a predator sniffing for prey.

Something pricked Shader's neck, and he slapped it away. He struck a pulpy body as large as a sparrow. Rhiannon squealed and whacked at her legs. Shadrak calmly pulled his hood up and all but vanished beneath his cloak.

"So, where to now?" Rhiannon swished her arm around to fend off more circling insects.

"Not sure." Shadrak's voice was low and uninflected beneath his hood. He may have been thinking. "I was directed to the mountain. Didn't say nothing about this."

Shader did up the buttons of his coat and pulled his hat low over his face. The stench of decaying vegetation rose from the ground like a contagion.

"Can you locate it on the mirrors in the plane ship?"

Shadrak stood. "No need. Assuming this place ain't completely screwed, the mountain's south from here. Maybe a little to the east."

"How can you tell?" Rhiannon's question was loaded with derision.

"I'm very observant," Shadrak said. It could have been a warning. "Look." He pointed into the murk. "The marsh there is studded with islands like this."

Shader followed the albino's finger but couldn't make anything out. The low ground was a black abyss to his eyes. As far as he knew, he could take a step in that direction and plunge into empty space. Shadrak's eyes were undoubtedly keener. Maybe that was a result of the kind of work he excelled at; either that or something more innate.

"Great," Rhiannon said. "Let's play stepping stones and see who goes under first."

"Just follow me." Shadrak leapt into the darkness, and it swallowed him whole.

"And how are we meant to do that?" Rhiannon called after him. "Can't see a bloody thing. And don't go giving me that crap about you being Shadrak the Unseen."

Fire flared and then settled into a controlled glow. It came from a stick of light in Shadrak's hand that revealed his flickering face. Without a word, Rhiannon jumped toward him. Shader drew the gladius and, as he'd hoped, the blade gave off a soft golden dweomer. Holding the sword aloft, he sprang after Rhiannon.

Something about the swamp muffled their footfalls and thickened the air with a pall of foreboding. Rhiannon followed Shadrak's thin light, gingerly finding her balance before each flurried leap, and Shader went next, the glow of the gladius picking out the white of her Nousian robe.

Shadrak waited for them at the foot of a bank that sloped sheerly above the mire. As Shader reached firm ground, he started. Something plopped in the sludge behind him. The head of a maggot-like creature tasted the air with its circular maw, which was ringed with jagged razors. It was as big as a man's forearm and segmented like a worm. Shader instinctively took a step back and bumped into Rhiannon, who was muttering and wringing out rank water that had soaked into the hem of her robe. She slipped, but he caught her arm, and when she steadied herself, her face wrinkled in revulsion at the thing squirming in the bog. The maggot emitted a hiss and then rolled languidly beneath the oozing surface.

More bubbles erupted across the mire, and the fetid grubs began to pop up in clusters, their writhing giving the impression that the swamp itself was alive and hungry.

"Ugly scuts, ain't they?" Shadrak said when he reached the top of the bank.

Shader jogged up the slope beside him, leaving Rhiannon hypnotized by the wriggling horrors and the staccato hisses they spat like sinister whispers.

The swamp spread endlessly away from the far side of the bank, an ocean of mire tufted with reeds and overhung with drooping boughs. Clouds of insects scoured the marsh in search of blood, and the ripples of the emerging maggots seemed to have no bounds.

"This ship of yours—" Shader started.

"Was set to go to the mountain," Shadrak said, rubbing his bearded chin. "No point trying again. Whatever force hit us last time is most likely still in place. Mind you, I might be able to hop the ship in a random direction. Anything's gotta be better than this."

"What's that?" Shader pointed at a hazy ball of golden light that winked into existence above a strip of dry land to their left. It hovered for a moment, and he had the sense it was watching them. It drifted away a few yards before returning.

"What is it, a dog playing fetch?" Shadrak said.

The sphere moved off again, a little farther this time, then swiftly returned.

"Don't like it," Shadrak said. "Marsh gas don't move like that, and my moth... Kadee," he corrected, "someone I'd trust with my life, told me stories about lights in swamps that lead people to their deaths. Let's get back to the ship."

"Agreed," Shader said.

They trudged back down the bank, and Shadrak led the way from one small island to the next. If it were possible, everyone was even more careful with their footing on the return journey.

"How come you can find the ship?" Rhiannon asked as Shadrak stood with hands on hips surveying the purplish haze. "All looks the same to me."

"Perfect memory," Shadrak said, tapping his temples. "And I'd swear this is where we exited."

"It is," Shader said, crouching down to study the footprints they'd left leaving the craft. They emerged from nowhere, which he supposed was where the entrance should be.

Shadrak walked ahead with his arms extended like a blind man's.

"He's shogging lost it," Rhiannon said. "I don't bloody believe it."

"It was here," Shadrak insisted, turning on her with his eyes narrowed to pinkish slits. "Something's happened."

"The swamp?" Shader said.

"Yeah, maybe it just swallowed it." Rhiannon hugged her arms tightly across her chest.

Shadrak chewed at his thumbnail, nodding to himself, as if he were running through all the possibilities one at a time.

"That don't make sense," he said. "The ship ain't solid, 'cept when it wants to be. Least that's how it looks to me."

"So what, then?" Rhiannon said.

"Must've left by itself," Shadrak said. "Unless it was taken."

Shader looked back across the bubbling mire and drew in a deep breath. "Leaves us with just one choice," he said, raising the gladius and leaping for the first island, not waiting to see if the others followed.

***

The maggots posed no threat—as long as they stayed out of the water. Shader mistimed a jump and landed knee-deep in the mire. One of the creatures immediately latched on to his boot, but in an instant he scraped it off with the gladius. It left a trail of putrid ichor on the blade, and there were puncture marks in the leather of his boot. After that, he never missed another jump.

The ground became firmer as they made their way south—at least, the way Shadrak said was south. The sphere of golden luminescence took a parallel course, always just behind, weaving in and out of the mangroves, pausing when they paused, resuming when they resumed. Shadrak barely took his eyes off it, and frequently hung back to check nothing else was following them. Finally, he drew his black cloak about him, buried his face in the hood, and slunk off into the brush, as if he planned to stalk the sphere.

Rhiannon walked with Shader, so close they could have been a couple. Once or twice, Shader thought she was going to take his hand, and even moved a little nearer, hoping that she would. There was something discomfiting about the marsh, he told himself, and Rhiannon's presence seemed to anchor him.

The largest of the three moons was sinking, the cobalt sky darkening almost to black as it crept beneath the horizon. The swamp, however, did not sleep. Insects buzzed, and things splashed and bubbled in the distance. Even the ground they now walked upon was slick with slime and writhed beneath their feet. Mosquitoes the size of rats bumped into them, drawn by their body heat.

They crested another rise and found themselves upon a stretch of grassland that was relatively dry. Shader cast around for tinder for a fire, while Rhiannon flopped to the ground with a weary sigh. Shadrak was nowhere to be seen. For all Shader knew, the assassin could be neck deep in a quagmire, led astray by the eerie glowing sphere. That would wreck any chance they had of getting back to Earth. Even if Shader could find the plane ship, he wouldn't have a clue how to pilot it. Still, it was a moot point if they couldn't stop Gandaw in time. Then there'd be no Earth to return to, no Aethir, no anything.

There was plenty of damp wood beneath the bent trees, but whenever Shader tried to break branches off, the trees swayed and lashed at him with barbed lianas. It seemed the flora was sentient, watching their progress, herding them, even, and defending against their intrusion.

Gathering what he could from the ground, Shader rummaged in his pockets for some matches. His fingers brushed against the bowl of the pipe Aristodeus had given him the day he'd left for Aeterna. It was a sort of joke: the philosopher had smoked frequently, particularly when laboring a point in one of his lectures. Shader had never used it, but right now he could feel the appeal. Maybe if they got back to Sahul, he'd search out some tobacco. Right now, the chances of that seemed pretty slim.

The wood took, but smoked and popped so much as to make them cough and move away from the little warmth the fire shed. Rhiannon shivered, her arms hugged about her, hair lank, and robe sodden.

"How's he know this is Aethir?" she asked.

"Shadrak? Doesn't he have some secret advisor? Besides, just look at the sky. You can't seriously believe we're still on Earth."

Rhiannon looked up at the unfamiliar stars, shaking her head ever so gently.

"Aethir's the Dreaming, isn't it?" She stared into the darkness for a while then lowered her gaze. "The spirit world of the Dreamers," she said to the ground. "Do you think this is what Sammy sees?"

"He's not gone, Rhiannon." *Not abandoned you.* "The boy's just hurting, like we all are. Your parents—"

"Not that it matters," Rhiannon said. Her tone was sullen, tinged with despair. "What's left to worry about, if Gandaw's going to end everything?"

Shader crouched beside her, touched her arm. "We don't know that," he said. "Maybe there's still a chance."

Rhiannon looked him in the eye. She needed someone to believe in, Shader could see that. She was assessing him, wondering if he was up to it. He stood and looked toward the horizon as the largest of the moons vanished, limning a range of distant mountains with pearly light.

"Where is the stunted shogger, anyway?" Rhiannon said.

"Ain knows. But if he's not back in the morning—assuming there is a morning here—we go on without him."

"Go on? Go on where?"

"South's what he said." Shader said it with more confidence than he felt.

"And which way's that?" Rhiannon asked.

Shader chose not to answer. What could he tell her? That he didn't have a clue? That they were lost without Shadrak, doomed to wander the marsh in circles till Gandaw put them out of their misery.

They sat in stony silence for a minute, and then Rhiannon turned her head toward him.

"Don't trust him, Deacon. Not after what he did."

Shader's hand went to his back. It was becoming an automatic reflex. "I know," he said. "But what choice do we have?"

"We're here. That's all we needed him for. We're better off without him."

Shader nodded to himself. She may have been right, but how could he tell? Whatever they were caught up in, whatever cosmic drama, it was too big to comprehend. If he allowed himself to think about it, he'd either go mad or be paralyzed by the enormity of any decisions he might make. One step at a time. That was all he could do. And if it wasn't enough—well, how could he be held accountable for the fate of worlds? If Nous wanted his service, then wasn't it about time he showed his hand?

He gave Rhiannon a wry smile. "I have no idea which way is south."

"Me neither."

Rhiannon settled down beside the smoking fire. She coughed and muttered something under her breath but stayed stubbornly facing the flames with her back to Shader.

Shader unwound his prayer cord from his belt and thumbed his way to the Gordian Knot. He sat cross-legged at a distance from Rhiannon and worked at the lines of the knot, which proved as ungiving as ever. His eyes swayed to Rhiannon's white-robed form, the graceful curve of her hips, the starkness of her black hair falling almost to her waist. Her breaths came heavily, her robe shuddering with each intake.

He opened his mouth to say something, but the words dissolved on his tongue. He longed to reach out and touch her, stroke away her pain, but he feared her rejection even more than he feared where such tenderness might lead. He shut his eyes and focused on the unsolvable problem of the knot, praying silently in his futility for Ain the Unknowable to reveal his will.

Shader knew that his dwindling faith was linked to his mounting disappointments; knew that he couldn't blame Ain for the loss of Rhiannon, the manipulations of Aristodeus and Huntsman. Even the Ipsissimus and his failure to act was no reason to impugn the faithfulness of Ain, and yet the knowledge alone was not enough to keep his heart from turning to ice. Ain was big enough to take it, Shader had no doubt about that; if not, then he wasn't the infinite deity the Templum claimed he was. But that was the problem—even more than the wedge that had been driven between Shader and Rhiannon; even more than Shader's shame at what Gaston had done: how could he trust anything the Templum said? The Gray Abbot had told him the Liber was a hotchpotch of philosophies and religions from the Ancients' world, sewn together for popular appeal by the Liche Lord, Otto Blightey. At the time, Blightey, in the guise of a friar, had been considered holy by the fledgling Templum, but even here they had been proven wrong. If the Templum was not infallible, what would possess someone to give their life to its teachings?

A cry sounded from the darkness. Shader's hand went to the gladius, and he stared into the gloom but could see nothing.

"That the midget?" Rhiannon said, rolling over and facing him.

The golden sphere—assuming it was the same one—appeared amid a clump of gorse, maybe fifty yards distant. It moved away a little and then returned to its starting point. A muffled scream punched through the murk, and Shader stood.

Rhiannon placed a hand on his leg. "What are you doing? You know this is a trap."

Shader sucked in a deep breath. She was right. It was too obvious, but at the same time, what if Shadrak was in trouble? What if they could reach him in time?

"You stay here. I want to take a look."

"You're kidding, right?" Rhiannon climbed to her feet. "If you're drowning in quicksand, I'm coming with you. There's no way I'm staying here on my own." Suddenly, she gripped his arm. "What the shog's that?"

Shader followed her finger and saw a figure drift through the undergrowth like a ghost. Within seconds it had vanished from sight.

"Shadrak?"

"Too tall," Rhiannon said.

Shader drew the gladius and strode in the direction the specter had gone. Rhiannon went with him, her fingers clamping about his free hand. Vines writhed above them, and a curling briar lashed at Shader's boot. The gladius swept down and severed it before it could coil around his leg.

As they pushed deeper into the thicket, the gladius's glow diminished, as if smothered by the malevolence of the swamp. Shader slowed, and Rhiannon's grip on his hand tightened. The way back was as black as pitch. Even the limning of the horizon had perished, and the two smaller moons were obscured by the undergrowth. Shader held the gladius before him like a torch. He could see the blade itself, but it shed no light on the way. He turned, seeking the route back to the fire, but thick tangles of creepers now blocked their passage. He could have sworn the mangroves had shifted to form a barrier behind them. Rhiannon pressed closer.

"What the shog is happening?"

Shader wheeled her to face the way the figure had headed. He could see nothing through the darkness. Feeling in front with the gladius, he led Rhiannon onward, testing the soft ground with every step. A low tremor passed beneath their feet, and from somewhere to the left, there came an answering slosh, like the lapping of viscous waves.

The golden sphere seemed to taunt them. It revolved around an invisible axis and then drifted slowly away.

"A light in the darkness," Shader said with wry humor, paraphrasing the passage from the Liber.

"Makes me feel a whole lot better." Rhiannon took a step toward it.

"Wait," Shader said, foreboding clawing its icy way up his spine. "Maybe Shadrak was right."

Rhiannon released his hand. "Don't see him coming up with any better ideas. Either we follow the light, or we stand here until morning. And we don't even know if that will ever come. I'm going. Do what you like."

With that, she strode after the sphere, heedless of the dangers that might lurk underfoot. Shader sighed and jogged to catch up with her, but no matter how much they quickened their pace, the sphere maintained the same distance ahead of them.

The undergrowth fell back like an invitation. Shader didn't like it one bit but could see no other choice. The best he could do was be prepared for the worst and pray he was strong enough to deal with the threat when it came.

The sphere set a zigzag course that seemed to follow a muddy track through the mire; only, when Shader looked back, the path had gone, covered over by dense vegetation. Up ahead, crepuscular light tinged the sky, revealing the jagged tops of distant mountains. Shader had no sense of direction other than that particular landmark. The dwindling stars were in unfamiliar constellations, and no sun had yet risen above the horizon. When the sphere gave an agitated wobble and fizzed off into the sky, Shader and Rhiannon were left stranded in the gray-blue half-light.

They entered a clearing surrounded by the silhouettes of twisted trees. The ground squelched underfoot, sometimes bursting like a blister to seep foul smelling fluid over Shader's boots. Rhiannon made no complaint, despite wearing only sandals. Her expression was stony, almost vacant, as if she despaired of ever getting out of there.

With a speed that should have been unnatural, the sun rose from its lair beneath the mountains, its golden glow brightening the sky into a canvass of pastel violet. Another sun rose behind it, smaller, and yet climbing higher, until the two settled like a pair of crooked eyes, and the sky turned to cobalt. As if taking their cue from the suns, or the departure of the sphere, hulking shapes began to lumber from the surrounding trees.

Shader stepped away from Rhiannon, forcing his body to relax, the gladius held loosely in his right hand. He heard the scrape of Rhiannon drawing the black sword. She was looking back the way they had come, where more of the creatures were stalking toward them. She flicked her hair out of her eyes and took a two-handed grip on the sword.

The creatures walked like men and carried weapons—clubs, stone axes, spears—but they were scaly, like lizards, and colored the greens and browns of the swamp. They had ridged foreheads and pinprick eyes ringed with yellow. Cavernous mouths revealed fangs like a serpent's and long flicking tongues. Most of them were naked, save for a few in tattered skins from some hairless beast.

One of the creatures, smaller than the rest, pushed to the front and held up a three-fingered hand to halt the others. This one was garbed in filthy gray trousers and the remains of a tunic. It wore a black gauntlet on its right hand, a glove almost comically large. Tongues of bluish flame raced about the fingers, of which there were four plus a thumb.

"Humans in Sour Marsh," it said with a slight lisp. "So rare, so rare. From Qlippoth, yes? Come to frighten Gandaw?"

"Qlippoth?" Shader said. "What's that?"

The lizard-man raised the gauntlet to indicate the mountains. "You know. Everyone knows."

Shader shook his head. "We're strangers here."

"Bah," the lizard-man said. "City folk, I say. Long way from home, but not strangers. Skeyr Magnus not stupid. Skeyr Magnus take power from Gandaw."

The lizard-man made a fist of the gauntlet, and the blue flames flared momentarily. A replica of the gauntlet appeared in the air and began to swell to an enormous size.

"Impressive," Shader said. "But I've seen that before."

Rhiannon drew back Callixus's sword, eyes tracking the giant hand—it was identical in every way to the one they'd seen Gandaw use above the Homestead. Shader did his best to remain relaxed, but he trusted his instincts to kick in at the first sign of attack.

"Long time ago, maybe," Skeyr Magnus said. "But now glove is mine. Gandaw weak without it. Skeyr Magnus new technocrat soon."

"You're sure about that?" Shader said. "Only, I saw an identical hand a few hours ago."

"Lies," Skeyr Magnus said, the giant fist shaking before him. "Only one glove. Skeyr Magnus steal it. Gandaw weak now."

"When did you steal it?" Rhiannon asked.

"Long time ago, me said. You stupid? Not listen to Skeyr Magnus?"

"But Sektis Gandaw made this glove?" Rhiannon said. Skeyr Magnus gave a curt nod, as if that proved his case. "Then what's to stop him making another?"

The lizard-man looked from the giant hand to the black gauntlet he wore, and a shudder rippled through his scales.

"Not possible. Gandaw weak. You will see. Skeyr Magnus new technocrat. You see. Gave own hand for glove. Much pain Skeyr Magnus felt. It burns onto bone. Much pain, but now much power. This, Gandaw fears."

Shader's eyes scanned the other lizard-men surrounding them. They were motionless, like heat-starved crocodiles in the Sahulian winter. If it hadn't been for the tracking of their eyes, they could have been mistaken for statues carved from the dried vegetation of the swamp.

"The mountains," Shader said. "Is Gandaw beyond them?"

"Stupid." Skeyr Magnus unclenched his gauntlet, and the giant black hand vanished. "That way Qlippoth. You must know. Everyone knows."

"Qlippoth?" Rhiannon asked. "What the shog's that?"

"Bad dreams. Nightmares. No one goes there. Even Gandaw scared of it."

Shader exchanged a glance with Rhiannon. "There was a light." He drew a circle in the air. "A golden sphere that was leading us toward the mountains."

"Wisp," Skeyr Magnus said. "Only fools follow wisps."

"So it wasn't yours?" Rhiannon said.

"No, not mine. Come to lure you across mountains. Take you to Qlippoth. You lucky Skeyr Magnus found you." The lizard-man waved his hand to take in the swamp. "Sour Marsh overflows from Qlippoth. Bad place. Evil. But Gandaw will not come here."

Rhiannon glanced at Shader then back at the lizard-man. "So, you're hiding from Gandaw?"

Skeyr Magnus puffed out his chest and glared, his yellow eyes darkening to amber. "Waiting only. Building army. One day take Perfect Peak."

Shader frowned. "Gandaw's mountain?"

"Many guards," Skeyr Magnus said. "But one day, Skeyr Magnus have big army."

"How soon?" Shader asked, sensing the possibility of an alliance. "You know Gandaw has started the Unweaving. There's not much time left."

"Bah," Skeyr Magnus said. "What Unweaving?" He looked around as if to emphasize the point that nothing had changed. "Lies to scare, make slaves of all. Skeyr Magnus no slave. He not scared."

"We are looking for the Perfect Peak," Shader said. "Can you help us get there?"

Skeyr Magnus thumped his hand into the palm of the gauntlet. The surrounding lizard-men shook their spears and advanced a pace.

"You not take science. Skeyr Magnus take it. Become stronger. Skeyr Magnus new technocrat. You see."

"We don't want the bloody science," Rhiannon said, but Skeyr Magnus thumped his hand again, and the lizard-men started to close the circle.

A thunder-crack blasted from the trees, and Skeyr Magnus yelped. Smoke billowed from his gauntlet, and blue flames crackled over its surface. He raised the gauntlet to his eyes and gaped at the hole that had been punched straight through it.

The lizard-men turned to the trees, seeking out the source of the attack. Skeyr Magnus shook with rage and clenched the glove into a fist. Sparks flew off, and then he began to spasm as they danced along his scales. Smoke effused from his limbs, and froth bubbled around his mouth.

The lizard-men turned back to him, as if awaiting his command. He shook violently and fell to the ground, body wracked with seizures.

"K–k–kill," he stammered.

Suddenly animated, the lizard-men surged toward Shader and Rhiannon. Another thunder-crack boomed, and a lizard-man dropped with a hole through its chest. Something was thrown, and a blinding flash of light erupted, scattering a group of the creatures and almost incinerating one.

Shader spun just in time to parry a spear thrust aimed at Rhiannon. He stepped inside and rammed the gladius into the lizard-man's eye. Rhiannon ducked beneath another blow and swung the black sword. Shader thought it lacked speed and power, but unnervingly, the blade sliced through a reptilian neck like butter, and the head rolled to the ground. Rhiannon looked momentarily stunned but then had to turn to block a savage axe blow. The haft of the axe shattered on contact, and the black sword followed through, spilling the creature's guts in ropes of steaming offal.

Shader whirled, skewering a lizard-man, spinning past a spear tip, and ducking beneath a club to eviscerate its wielder. Out of the corner of his eye, he saw Shadrak emerge from the trees, shrouded in black and flinging razor stars with deadly accuracy. Two lizard-men fell before they could reach him, and then the assassin tumbled in among a group, stabbing with two daggers, bobbing and weaving.

Rhiannon threw the black sword up to block a club, but the impact sent her sprawling into Shader.

Skeyr Magnus regained his feet and yelled something that was drowned out by the din of battle. The cordon of lizard-men pressed in, and Shadrak was lost from sight. Shader stabbed another, but the blade got caught between the creature's ribs. As he strove to pull it free, the lizard-men behind shoved, and the creature fell on top of him. Rhiannon drove the black sword through its head and swung to intercept an axe blow. Shader rolled to his knees, parried an overhead strike from a club and slashed his blade across the attacker's thighs.

Shadrak tumbled in beside them, sprang to his feet with a dagger in either hand, and jabbed left and right, each time finding his mark.

"What did you have to fire for?" Rhiannon yelled as she dodged an axe and hacked down, smashing through scales and bone.

Shadrak was too busy to answer, stepping and turning like a dancer, punching repeatedly with his daggers. Shader took a blow to the right shoulder, and his arm went numb. He switched the gladius to his left hand and slashed it across the creature's face.

A massive lizard-man reared up, swinging an axe with a two-handed grip. Shader turned to meet it, but an arrow ripped through its neck, and the giant toppled. Two more arrows cut into the lizard-men in rapid succession, and a tremor ran through the massed attackers. Another arrow struck, and then the lizard-men were running for the trees with Skeyr Magnus leading the way, his arms and legs pumping furiously, looking like nothing so much as a panicked chicken. Within moments, the clearing was still, and then a tall man stepped into view.

Shadrak drew his arm back to hurl a knife, but Shader caught hold of his wrist. Before anyone knew what was happening, the albino had slashed the back of his hand with his other dagger. Rhiannon punched him full in the face, and Shadrak stumbled backward.

"I'm sorry," he said to Shader. "I—"

"Heat of battle," Shader said. "Happens all the time."

He was about to apply pressure with his hand, when he felt warmth radiating from the hilt of the gladius.

"Not to me," Shadrak said, staring at the ground. "Won't happen again."

"Too bloody right it won't," Rhiannon said. "Want me to bandage that?"

"No need," Shader said. The bleeding had stopped, and new skin had already formed over the wound.

"What the shog?" Rhiannon said.

Shadrak looked up, and his eyes narrowed. If he was spooked by the healing, he was giving nothing away.

Shader sheathed the gladius, shook his head, and turned to face the newcomer.

The man was dressed in browns and greens that could have been woven from the undergrowth. A thick cloak hung to his ankles, its colors shifting to match the trees behind it. His face was angular, his complexion fair. The tips of pointed ears poked through shoulder-length golden hair, but it was the eyes that were his most arresting feature: like softly lit verdigris, unwavering and yet gentle, seeing more than Shader wished to reveal. A quiver of arrows poked over one of the man's shoulders, and he held a recurve bow in his left hand.

A half-grin curled one side of Rhiannon's mouth. "Don't tell me," she said. "You're an elf? Now I've seen everything."

The man raised an eyebrow. "If it can be dreamed, then it is likely to exist. Like a maiden with a black sword, a warrior with an enchanted blade, and a homunculus with a pistol."

Shadrak scraped his dagger blades against each other. "Homunculus? What's that s'posed to mean?"

"Pistol?" Rhiannon said. "You mean that piece of Aeterna-tech he keeps waving around like he's gotta compensate?"

"Shog off," Shadrak said. "And it ain't from Aeterna, so it can't be Aeterna-tech, got it?"

"Ancient-tech, then. Point about compensating's the same, though."

The elf gave a deep bow. "Forgive me. I make too many assumptions. Too much time alone in the Sour Marsh has robbed me of my manners. Please, allow me to start again. I am Gilbrum Eloha, an elf of Qlippoth."

Shader removed his hat and held it to his chest. He ran his fingers through the matted dampness of his hair. "The land of nightmares? Or was the lizard-man lying?"

"Skeyr Magnus?" Gilbrum said. "No, he speaks sooth, though he knows as little as his maker of the lands beyond the Farfall Mountains. Mayhap you Malkuthians know no more." He indicated the jagged peaks with a wave of his bow. "Ours is a world divided, like night and day. The side of the Farfalls you call Malkuth was a place of sweet dreams until the Technocrat came from Earth. There is still great goodness in Malkuth, but Gandaw's creations have wreaked much harm, and he has introduced life-forms alien to Aethir. Your kind, for example, the folk of New Jerusalem and its satellites."

"Jerusalem?" Rhiannon said with a glance at Shader. "Isn't that—?"

Shader silenced her with a hand. The mythical holy city mentioned in the Liber. It seemed that Earth and Aethir had certain things in common. This word, 'Qlippoth' he'd also seen in scripture. 'Malkuth' too, was a name dotted throughout the Liber, derived from an archaic language that only a few scholars in Aeterna understood. Adeptus Ludo, Shader's mentor in the seminary, was one such. Try as he might, Shader couldn't recall the meaning of either of them, but Jerusalem was a different matter: the City of the Luminaries. The place where Ain would be revealed in all his glory.

"You are not from New Jerusalem?" Gilbrum said.

"We're not from Aethir," Shader replied. "We came here from Earth in a…" He looked at Shadrak for help.

"Plane ship," the assassin hissed through clenched teeth.

Gilbrum narrowed his eyes and studied Shadrak for a moment. "Yes, I have heard of such things. Vessels of Sektis Gandaw. It was your people, was it not, who taught him the mysteries of travel between the worlds?"

"If you mean humans," Shadrak said, pointedly returning his blades to his baldric.

Gilbrum frowned but did not pursue the matter. "You two—" He indicated Shader and Rhiannon. "—wear the apparel of Maldark's dwarves, though the symbol is different."

"You knew Maldark?" Shader said.

"I know of his fall."

Shader sighed. There was more to the story the elf presumably hadn't heard, but now was not the time. "We are consecrated to Nous."

Rhiannon thrust the point of the black sword into the ground and tapped out a rhythm on the pommel, seemingly unaware she was doing it. The black flames dancing along the blade kept time.

"I know nothing of this Nous," Gilbrum said, eyeing Rhiannon warily. "Only what the Creator dreams. These things are mysteries to him, truths warped by the Liche Lord."

"Blightey?" Shader said. "You've heard of him here?"

Gilbrum shrugged. "Is there any place not darkened by his touch? Even the Creator's abode was not immune, and he still shudders at the memory. But Maldark's fall had another source, one even more corrosive. Gandaw may have duped him, but there is always a hidden root to deception."

"The Demiurgos?" Rhiannon said. "The Cynocephalus's father?"

"The Creator is thus afflicted," Gilbrum said. "But, yes, that is so. Maldark's dwarves held to the form of religion while denying its power to save. They professed faith, but relied on their own judgment, and in the end, it was hubris that allowed Gandaw to sway them."

Shader recalled Maldark speaking about how Gandaw had convinced the dwarves to betray the Hybrids and almost brought about the Unweaving once before.

"There is a home the Creator longs for," Gilbrum continued. "A realm beyond the Void, where gods are men, and the mysteries are ever more ineffable. But he has never seen it, and never will. He remains where he was sired, cocooned within Aethir, which he dreamed for his own protection."

Shader was about to ask what that meant, but Gilbrum's green eyes flicked to the left, and he took a firm grip on his bow.

"Gandaw's aberrations are returning—the lizard-men. Where are you heading? If you will permit it, I can lead you to the bounds of the marsh."

"The Perfect Peak," Shadrak said, thumbing in the direction they'd come from.

"The mountain of Sektis Gandaw? Then why are you traveling away from it?"

"Because he followed a glowing sphere." Rhiannon cocked her head at Shader.

Shadrak rolled his pinkish eyes. "What did I say?"

"More to the point," Rhiannon said, "where the shog were you?"

"Tracking your pursuers," Shadrak said. "This sort of thing always happens when I work with amateurs."

Gilbrum looked at Shader. "This sphere you saw, it was a wisp, a denizen of Qlippoth. Normally, no creatures from the nightmare realm can cross the Farfalls, but the pollution that has grown into the Sour Marsh has eroded a passage."

"Pollution?"

"Noxious rains from Qlippoth have seeped into the mountains. Over the centuries, they have formed a stream into Malkuth, spreading like mold, a cancer devouring the earth with calculated malice. The Sour Marsh is sentient, a unified whole."

"It's alive?" Rhiannon asked.

"One vast entity. An ocean of evil. Its entrance into Malkuth has brought others—parasites, like the creatures that inhabit the mire, and tempters like the wisps. It is a good thing the lizard-men stopped you, else you would have crossed the mountains and been lost."

"So, what about you?" Rhiannon asked, yanking the black sword from the ground and slipping the scabbard over her shoulder so she could sheathe it. "You said you're an elf from Qlippoth. Doesn't exactly inspire much trust."

Gilbrum swirled his cloak about him and vanished into the undergrowth. Shader's hand went to his gladius, and Rhiannon swore. Shadrak half-drew his pistol, but an instant later, the elf reappeared.

"We should go," he said. "Skeyr Magnus has brought more minions. Follow me."

THE STOWAWAY

STEALING SHADRAK'S PLANE ship seemed like the right thing to do—well, not right, exactly, but pragmatic. Opportune, even.

Albert hadn't wanted to get involved in this mess in the first place, but all along he'd been cajoled, bullied, forced against his will. First by Master Frayn on that ill-fated attack on Dead Man's Torch, and then by Shadrak, who'd rescued him from those skull-headed nightmares, only to thrust him headlong into a battle that was better off fought by those with the requisite training.

Watching Shadrak operate the controls en route to the Homestead had given him the idea, and finding the entrance to the plane ship on the ledge during the battle had been such a stroke of luck, Albert might have almost called it providential. Might, but not quite. Problem was, it had taken him forever to find the control room, and by the time he had, there were footsteps approaching. He hid in a shiny closet so immaculately clean it could conceivably have passed Mumsy's dust inspection. Not any longer, though. Not after the ship had lurched and juddered and tipped him upside down, and he'd spewed his guts all over those pristine surfaces. He endured an agony of waiting before he heard them leave—Shadrak and two others: a man and a woman. Wherever it was they'd chosen to come, it didn't sound exactly pleasant, judging by the snatches of conversation he picked up. Not his kind of thing at all.

He crept out of hiding and immediately set about finding a way to turn the situation to his advantage. Leaving Shadrak stranded would be just deserts for dumping him in the thick of things without so much as a by your leave.

A thing like the plane ship could take you anywhere, with a bit of practice. Anywhere but the Homestead would do just fine for starters, so long as it wasn't smack-bang in the middle of the mess Shadrak had rescued him from. Best of all, though, would be if he could get it to take him home to Sarum, so he could capitalize on the disaster that had befallen his brother Sicarii at Dead Man's Torch.

It looked simple enough to control; it was just a matter of moving around shapes on little black mirrors. When you'd worked through as many cook books as Albert had, when you'd digested everything there was to know about what the Ancients called chemical composition from every extant tome on the subject—and quite a few that weren't supposed to be extant—pressing and swiping glowing shapes in a certain sequence was a doddle—in theory, at least. With an eeny, meeny, miny, moe, he selected a flashing yellow triangle and tapped it. It grew larger and turned green. At the bottom of the mirror, a cross lit up, also green. Albert grinned and swiped the triangle down toward the cross; after all, what could be simpler than 'X' marks the spot?

The room tilted, and Albert cried out and clung to the control plinth.

Don't play with someone's else's toys, Mumsy used to say, and for once he was wishing he'd listened. His legs scissored in the air behind him, loose change cascading from his trouser pockets like hale on a tin roof. A klaxon blared briefly then shut off as the floor came level once more, and Albert heaved a sigh of relief. He could have used a shot of brandy, or something stronger, to settle his roiling guts. Once this was over—

"Nooo," Albert wailed as his feet flipped over his head, and he found his face pressed against the cold hard surface of one of the black mirrors. Lights zipped across his vision in a kaleidoscopic blur, and acid bile swilled into his mouth. "Stop it moving, stop it moving, stop it—" An obnoxiously pungent reflux interrupted his prayer before it led to rapture. Not that he was praying to anyone in particular, mind; it was more like a message in a bottle.

The room slammed down again, and Albert shot across the floor arse over head until his feet hit the wall. He couldn't quite situate the rest of his body: his stomach was practically smothering him, his chin was in his chest, and his trouser legs were cutting into his knees where they had run up his shins. Just his rotten luck if someone came in right now and caught sight of his lilly-white calves hanging like bloated sausages somewhere behind that infernal strip of black hair that was forever slipping toward the nape of his neck. Not the most practical position for breathing, perhaps, lying supine with your feet above your head, but at least it had gone still. Very still, in fact. Silent, even.

Before he dared move, Albert's hand crept into his jacket pocket in search of the reassurance his cheese-cutter always brought. It was an old friend, a faithful aid, equally at home in the kitchen as wrapped around a victim's throat. He inside-outed the pocket, scrunched at the fabric, did the same with the other pocket, and then, in a paroxysm of terror far greater than he'd just experienced following his experiment in flying the plane ship, he flopped to his side and flipped to his knees, all the better to pat himself down.

It was gone. Gone and most certainly gone. The pats turned to slaps, which turned to thumps, the last of which was aimed at his forehead. This was insufferable, intolerable, inconceivable. He never ceased fiddling with the cheese-cutter; it was always between his thumb and forefinger, like a Nousian's prayer cord, only infinitely more useful. The habit was so ingrained as to be unconscious. Perhaps it was so unconscious as to have been forgotten. Albert glanced around the chamber, dived in among his scattered coinage, and put his face to the ground like a bloodhound.

"Bloody shitting hell and shogging scu—" He clamped his mouth shut before he could say the unmentionable word. Even now, so many years after her unfortunate death, he winced at the slap Mumsy would have given him—right on the lughole, as she would have put it, sending shockwaves through his skull that would gradually ebb away to a persistent ringing. He was sure she dislodged a year's worth of memories with every clout. If nothing else, the recollection of the old bat gave him pause for thought and allowed him to reassert the rational over the primitive mind. It took a lot these days for Albert to lose control, and loss of control was a habit he couldn't afford to slip back into. Not in his line of work.

"Master poisoner," he reminded himself. "Deadly assassin." Not to mention consummate observer, reader of people, and devilishly devious criminal mastermind. If you say it enough, you'll believe it, Papa had always said; and if you believe it long enough, it will come true.

"Crowd out the negative." Albert gave a sharp clap as he stood. "Define yourself."

He stooped to roll down his trouser legs, tugging them smooth over the tops of his shoes. His heart still ricocheted from the loss of the cheese-cutter, but his mind was back where it belonged, firmly grasping the reins.

The lights on the control plinth had gone out, leaving the black mirrors blank as the Void. He gave one a sharp slap on the side of its casing, and it flickered to life, revealing an image of a desert studded with craggy rocks and what looked like enormous craters. He peered closer to get a better look, but the image broke up and disappeared. He gave it another slap, but nothing happened this time. He was about to kick the plinth, when it trumpeted an alarm that sent his hands over his ears.

"It wasn't me. I wasn't going to…"

Before he could complete the same automatic response he'd always blurted out as a child, silver fluid seeped from the base, bubbling and forming into beads that solidified and then started to roll up the plinth and across its surface. As they encountered buttons, switches, and mirrors, the beads dispersed. Lights came back on, the background hiss resumed, and the mirrors once more showed their pictures. Beads continued to form and go about their work like an army of termites.

Albert watched them, mesmerized, noting how they repaired and cleaned everything they touched. Some of them left the plinth and moved toward his shoes. He danced away from them, careful not to let them touch him. With a spin and a quick tap of numbers on the door panel—Shadrak hadn't exactly been discreet—he left the chamber and made his way down the interminable corridor until he reached the button on the wall. When he pressed it, the wall split open, and he entered a cubicle not dissimilar to the one in the Tower of Glass back in Sarum. He pressed another button, and the cubicle shuddered. Albert's guts felt a little queasy, but then the cubicle stilled and the doors opened onto another corridor, only slightly less interminable than the previous one. He half-jogged, half-walked toward the door he'd entered the plane ship by.

Judging by the terrain he'd seen in the mirror, his test run had been more than a little successful. He wasn't back atop the Homestead, that was for certain, but the desert told him he might be in the vicinity. Probably Barraiya lands. The mesa should be visible from miles away in every direction, so if he just nipped out and got his bearings, he'd be able to try moving the plane ship again. Either that, or he might run into a group of itinerant Dreamers and get them to guide him back to civilization in return for something nice and shiny.

Shadrak would likely kill him for this, but the little runt was no doubt miles away. Probably the best thing now, Albert thought as he entered the code and waited for the door to open, was to make his way back to Sarum and—

Well, bugger me senseless!

Two suns glared down at him from gray-blue skies. Ochre terrain spread as far as the eye could see, and here and there, outcrops of what looked like limestone stood as high as a man. There were craters dotted all over the place, reminding him of that perforated cheese he'd tasted in one of the provinces of Gallia.

He stepped out onto the desert sand and scanned the horizon. The plane ship had jumped quite a way, by the looks of it. Quite a way, indeed. Way off in the distance, he could just about make out the hazy peaks of a mountain range. Which distance, it was a little hard to say, what with there being two—

Oh, scu-scu-scu-crap.

Blinking did nothing to change the terrible truth. They were still there: twin orbs suspended in the heavens like duo Swords of Damocles. Not that they'd need to fall to wreak their havoc; Albert hadn't felt this crushed since Dana Woodrum had scoffed at the beautiful cupcakes he'd presented her with for her birthday and accused him of making them just so he could get into her knickers *(perish the thought; should have made the little trollop a tart instead).*

He shivered, shaking his head to stop the thoughts from cementing.

Yuk, yuk, yuk. All those humpy bits and her slimy, stinky grease-pot. Ugh.

He was imagining, of course, but he was sure he'd hit the nail on the head. How could it be otherwise?

Breathe, Albert, breathe.

He knew he'd nearly lost it, then, nearly shut the door on the outside world and locked himself into another endless spiral of slights and missed opportunities, embarrassment and regret. Fortunately, he'd played the Dana Woodrum scene out ad nauseam, and he had the perfect remedy: the very vivid recollection of her ever-reddening face and swelling lips, her hands clutching uselessly at her throat, and yellow drool dripping down her chin. How could he forget the stench of her shit as her organs collapsed and she slopped to the floor like a drowned invertebrate? *"Allergy, allergy!"* he'd screeched to her gobsmacked entourage. *"How terrible, how terrible!"* It had been a performance as sublime as Kenlith Brinsley's *Faerie King*. Oh, the gloating *satisfaction*. He'd observed her forever, haunted all the parties, endured the scathing remarks, but it had been worth it to know that she couldn't resist Sachertorte with a dollop of cream and chocolate sprinkles.

Albert became aware of his fingers questing through his jacket pockets. He could almost feel the wooden ends of his cheese-cutter and started to run his fingertip along the wire—but it wasn't there.

Two suns.

He could have a concussion, he supposed. Maybe it was a heat mirage. Maybe someone was playing a trick on him—Shadrak, most likely. *Pallid little midget doesn't want anyone messing with his toy, now, does he?*

He stared down at the ground, back up at the suns, the far off mountains. In the opposite direction, light shimmered and sparkled where the horizon became a faint strip of cobalt. Off to the left was—he thought it was another mountain at first—a city? Whatever it was, it was either very near, which he doubted, or very large. White walls—curtain walls, like he'd seen on the castles in Gallia—with tall towers and minarets poking their heads above. Now he knew the ship hadn't just hopped closer to Sarum; they didn't have architecture like that anywhere in Sahul. Even the gargantuan towers of the Ancients looked like rubble heaped up by cave dwellers compared to this.

He visored his eyes to squint across the stark landscape in the other direction and noticed plumes of dust swirling in the air. Was that a road? Black dots snaked out beneath the dust cloud, too far off for him to make out, but he'd have sworn on Mumsy's grave it was a caravan of some sort, and it was heading his way. Beyond the ant-like specks, he could see more mountains, or perhaps hills that weren't quite so distant, but other than that, he may as well have been on the moon.

He reached out behind and tapped the invisible hull of the plane ship, then crouched down and gathered some pebbles into the shape of a cross to mark the entrance. Brushing the dust from his palms, he straightened up and found his eyes drawn to one of the craters—or was it a blowhole? It was one of those things he knew he shouldn't do, but there were times his curiosity was irrepressible.

It'll be the death of you, Mumsy always used to say. Funny that, he thought as he set off for a butcher's at the hole, because her favorite saying had certainly rung true for her in the end.

Blasted thing was further off than it looked. Wasn't that always the way? Sweating like the proverbial pig, the fabric of his suit no doubt fading doubly quick in the collective sunshine, he scrabbled up a scree bank and saw that the hole was actually set into a gentle incline, where the ground had blistered into a low mound. Hole probably wasn't the best way to describe it. Cave mouth might have been better. Gaping maw was even closer to the mark. It was as wide as a house and the height of two grown men. The edges of the entrance glistened with what looked like dew, but when Albert stepped closer to examine it, he saw it was metallic.

Oh my gilded backside! Gold!

—All that glitters is not—

—Not in my experience. He quickly shut that train of thought down. He wouldn't be

who he was today if he gave in to that kind of negativity.

The moment he stepped across the threshold, the stench struck him like a fist in the face. His guts roiled, and he had to clench his arse cheeks to avoid an accident. The smell was a cross between putrefying compost and off-meat. He whipped out his handkerchief and held it over his nose and mouth. Blasted thing still stank of snuff. Washing seemed to have no effect, and yet he couldn't bring himself to throw it away. It was the only thing of Papa's left, so Mumsy had said. He took a couple of wary steps into the cave mouth, marveling at how the specks of gold continued to sparkle even out of the sunlight. When he went in deeper, it was like walking on stars that wound downward into the receding distance. Not a cave, then, Albert mused. A tunnel. And a big one at that. Hardly looked natural, either, the way the width remained uniform, the smoothness of the walls.

He pressed on until the light from outside was lost around a bend. The steady downward gradient became sheerer at that point, and he had to touch the left-hand wall for support. He'd gone no further than a few steps when he trod in something sticky. His foot came free, sock and all, and he had to balance on one leg and bend from the waist to try to retrieve his shoe. It came away from the ground trailing a thick rope of goo. He scraped off what he could against the wall and then dropped it so he could put his foot back down. He was still wiggling his toes and straining to get his heel in fully when a blast of wind rushed past him from the depths. Rotten wind, if such a thing existed, like a belch from a toothless crone with a mouthful of vomit. Not wind, then, he realized.

An exhalation.

The ground shook as something squelched and rustled down the tunnel to the accompaniment of an echoing hiss. The darkness ahead shifted and then got a whole lot darker as the specks of gold winked out, or were smothered.

Albert took a step back, crouching so he could use his finger as a shoehorn. Another wiggle of his toes, and he was backing up the tunnel. More of the gold flecks were swallowed by shadow, and another rush of fetid breath blasted him and sent Papa's handkerchief into a crazy spiral. He watched it like an enraptured child at a puppet show, reaching out a lazy hand to catch it. In that instant, a colossal maw ringed with serrated teeth opened right in front of his face. Albert whimpered, broke wind, and stumbled backward at the same time. The handkerchief hit the ground, the monstrosity roared, and Albert squealed his most high-pitched squeal and was running back up the tunnel as fast as his legs could carry him.

When he reached the cave mouth, he glanced back over his shoulder.

Papa's hanky—

A gargantuan flat head surged into the light, trailed by a purplish, segmented body. A dozen yellow eyes flickered open and locked onto Albert. He stumbled outside, not daring to take his gaze off the thing. Papa would understand. *Bye, bye, hanky.*

He watched, spellbound, as its sinuous body coiled into the cave and then undulated toward him, head swaying like a cobra's about to strike.

Albert had one thought: *Plane ship!* as he turned and ran, hell for leather. He half-slipped, half-rolled down the scree slope, leaping to his feet with the grace of a far more agile man. The monstrous worm roared from just above him, but Albert never stopped to look back. He scanned the ground for sign of the pebble cross he'd left, heart doing a tap dance against his ribcage, and a whole train of despairing thoughts ricocheting around his skull.

There! He spotted the cross and was about to sprint for it when the earth ahead ruptured, and another giant worm started to writhe forth.

Shit!

He turned and ran to the left, figuring he could cut a semicircle behind it, but a third wriggling body burst from the ground to block his way.

Shog!

Albert whirled and ran in the opposite direction, even as the first worm slithered down the scree slope in a cloud of dust and rubble. A fourth head split the earth ten yards in front of him.

Scutting, shogging, shit!

Dozens of the things were surfacing all over the place. Albert just kept moving, jiggling and wobbling this way and that, wincing and berating himself for uttering the word, screeching and whimpering every time a new worm emerged. He was done for, he knew it.

Curiosity will be the—

"Oh, shog off!"

Didn't I tell you? All that glitters—

"Shove it up your arse!"

He cut a zigzag course between the forest of writhing behemoths, and suddenly he was through and pelting along hard-packed earth toward the dust cloud following the caravan he'd spotted earlier. It didn't matter that he was fatter than a tub of lard; didn't matter he was as fit as a ten-day-dead corpse; he kept going and going. Even when the worms were just black lines in the distance. Even when the first wagons and carts were clearly visible, clattering their way along a road—*A road! A bloody civilized road!*—made from perfectly mortared flagstones.

"Help! Somebody! Help!" he yelled, waving his arms.

"Whoah," the driver of the lead wagon called out, snapping the reins and pulling the horses up sharp. "What's your bleedin' game, mate? Scared my ol' nag right proper, you did."

Curses sounded all the way along the caravan; horses nickered and snorted, and dozens of wheels ground to a halt. People jumped down, swigging from waterskins or heading in amongst the rocks, presumably to relieve themselves.

"Scared my bleedin' horse, I tell you. Ain't right. Ain't right at all."

He was a wiry whelp, ruddy from too much time beneath the suns, clothes caked in ochre dirt and looking a couple of sizes too big. *Lean times,* Albert thought. *Wolf at the top of the hill now scraping around for scraps like a hyena?* Either that, or he was wearing borrowed clothes. Stolen, even.

"My most heartfelt apologies, Mr...."

"Fargin. Buck Fargin. Surprised you don't know that."

Albert gave the cretin a bow, the most obsequious he could manage, given the circumstances. "Is this your caravan?"

"Not exactly."

"You hired it?"

"Not exactly."

Albert reached for his handkerchief to wipe the sweat from his eyes and then winced as he remembered what had happened to it. "Head guard?"

"Nope."

This is like getting blood from a stone. "Then I must beg your pardon, sir,"—*you asinine halfwit*—"but I am not from around these parts."

"I'd say." The man looked Albert up and down, hawked up a great gob of phlegm and spat. "Sorry. I get your shoe?"

Albert gave the offending matter a long stare before meeting the moron's gaze. He knew there would be no mistaking the look in his eyes, just as well as he knew this man was about as dangerous as a turkey among lions. "Your aim appears to be awry."

"A what?"

Albert wished he had his cheese-cutter. Now would be the moment to make a show of running his finger along the wire as nonchalantly as could be, while keeping eye contact and giving a sinister little half-smile. Still, intimidation could take many forms.

"I'm getting ahead of myself," he said, taking a step toward the wagon. The man visibly blanched and leaned away. Albert took another step. "I'm quite certain you almost spitting on my shoe was an accident. Perhaps you are unwell. I have some skill as an apothecary. Would you like me to—"

"What we stopped for, Fargin?" a deep voice rumbled from the back of the wagon. "There's less'n five hours till closing. You don't get me to Dougan's soon, I'll be shaking like a... like a... Oh, spew in a bucket, what the... Oh, shog it. Shogging forget it."

Buck rolled his eyes, looking relieved at the interruption. He craned his neck and hollered, "Just stay put. I got it under control." He gave Albert a conspiratorial nod. "Ain't that right."

"Indubitably."

"What?"

The wagon rocked as someone moved about inside.

"I'm coming down. Only thing you got control of is your pisser, and then only if no one says 'boo' to you."

Buck stood, still clutching the reins. "Don't you come down, you hear me. Just stay with the merchant's dice. Right?"

"Uh?"

"I said stay with—"

"What dice?"

Buck gave Albert a despairing look and dropped the reins so he could put his hands on his hips. "The stuff, you stumpy pillock. You know, the goods."

"Merchandise?" Albert offered.

"That's what I said."

A group of men from the other wagons had gathered halfway down the line. Your typical merchant types by the look of them. Heavy robes and gaudy jewellery, dandified hats that were no doubt all the rage in their obviously barbaric excuse for a culture. Mind you, the same could be said of Sahul, or indeed anywhere that wasn't Gallia. They were putting their heads together and then looking Albert's way, nodding and gesticulating.

"Never did," said the voice from the back of the wagon. "You said—"

"You want paying, or what?" Buck said, this time with venom in his voice, although it was more of a wasp's sting than a scorpion's. "Coz I can make sure you don't get no booze never again, right? Gaw, I ask you! Bloody thick twat. Never bleedin' heard of merchant's dice!"

Albert feigned a look of utter incomprehension. "Neither have I."

"You're joking, ain't you? Educated bloke like you. Merchant's dice. You know, it's a bleedin'—what do you call it?"

"Malapropism?"

Buck's eyebrows met above the bridge of his nose, like a particularly fat caterpillar. "Don't be a plonker. It's a, oh piss, it'll come to me... a... you know. When you buy something and sell it to someone else, you're taking a risk, like, ain't you? Like rolling a dice. Get it?"

"Die," Albert said. "Dice is plural."

"You trying to be funny? Coz if you are—"

"Not at all. I think I understand your meaning. You are a trader."

"Sort of," Buck said.

Ah, my favorite sort. "So what are you trading?"

Buck tapped the side of his nose with a finger and sat back down. "Mind your own. I ask, you answer. Got it?"

"Indeed."

"What I wanna know is, what's a ponced-up gentleman like you doing all the way out here? You from a rival guild?"

"Can't say a merchant's life has ever appealed to me."

"I didn't say merchant, now, did I?"

Albert narrowed his eyes and discreetly ran them over Buck's apparel. No recognizable insignia. Plain as a common laborer's.

"What other kind of guild could you mean? Agriculturalists'? Weavers'? Or perhaps you're referring to the archaeologists' guild; after all, there are some fascinating tunnels back the way I've just come. Riddled with gold."

"I reckon you know," Buck said. "See, I can tell. I call it my sixth sense. Who you with, the Scarfers? The Patterfeet?" He touched a brown-stained finger to his lips. "Nah, I'd say you're… Wait a minute. Gold? You ain't been messing around in no boreworm tunnels, have you?"

"If you mean by that, gigantic purple things with multiple eyes and lots of sharp teeth, then—"

Buck snorted and bent double, his mouth agape like an incoherent idiot's, which wasn't so far from the truth.

"That's fool's gold, you plonker."

"I know." (He knew now). "What do you take me for?" Though Albert had to admit, Buck had a point, and Mumsy would have no doubt agreed. *Reckless, Squidgy—Don't call me that!—Reckless to the point of stupidity.*

"Oh, that's ripe, that is," Buck said. "You hear that, Rugbeard? Geezer here's run into some boreworms."

Loud snores rolled up from the back of the wagon. Buck shook his head and took up the reins.

"Shogging dwarves. Bloody useless, if you ask me. Good for nothing, except maybe one thing."

"Oh?" Albert raised an inquiring eyebrow. "And what might that be?"

Buck shot a look over his shoulder at the congregating merchants then beckoned Albert closer. "Go on, then. Take a look in the back."

"But I thought you—"

"I'm a good judge of character, I am. Reckon I'm gonna throw you a line of trust and see what I can hook in return. Looks like you need me more than I need you, what with you being way out here in your nice suit and all. You can keep stum, I'd wager. Have a gander."

Albert went round the back of the wagon, lifted the canvas, and peered inside. The snoring was coming from a sack of filth with a greasy gray beard that must have hung below the owner's knees, if he were standing. Albert could see why Buck had called the fellow a dwarf. He couldn't have been taller than a child of six or seven, and he looked like he hadn't eaten for months. It was a wonder someone so frail-looking could make all that noise snoring. The dwarf's hand was resting on an odd-looking rectangle of black— Albert climbed up the step to get a closer look—stone? It was the size of a door, smooth, and with glinting flecks of some green mineral dotted about its surface. The wagon bounced as Buck came to look in behind Albert.

"Well?" he said, a self-satisfied grin on his face.

"You're selling tabletops?"

"Funny. Very funny. It's scarolite, silly. Rare as a pox-free pecker, and no chance of getting your hands on none without a nod and a wink to the dwarves. Mines outside Arx Gravis are fiercely guarded. Only ones not controlled by the Technocrat these days. See, we got connections with the miners. Well, a connection. This snoring pile of dung here used to work with them, till he got too pissed to swing a pickaxe. Other than that, no one sees hide nor hair of the dwarves. No one has for donkey's years. Big demand for scarolite in the city. You heard of Magwitch the Meddler?"

Albert climbed back down, and Buck joined him. The other merchants were returning to their wagons, muttering and gesturing impatiently.

"I'm not familiar with—"

"Crazy shogger, that one, but he pays good, if you know what I mean."

"And he's your guild—what's the term?—master?"

Buck laughed and clapped Albert on the back. "He's the client, stupid. No, my guildmast..." Buck wagged a finger in Albert's face. "Uh uh. Naughty, naughty. You won't get nothing out of me. Not till you spill the beans, that is."

"Beans?"

"What you're doing out here, dressed like that. Who you're working for. That kind of thing."

Albert wavered for a moment between making his excuses and going back to see if the boreworms had returned to their tunnels and ingratiating himself to this inarticulate nincompoop. Perhaps if he could find the plane ship, he'd be able to get it to move once more. It would have been helpful to know where he was. At least then he could have come up with a plausible story. He looked up at the twin suns glaring down from cobalt skies, and a light went on. He licked his lips and offered Buck his most congenial smile.

"I must admit, sir, that I am lost. Very, very lost. My companions have abandoned me, and I can only surmise that they were paid by a rival."

"What, a rival guild?"

"Restaurant. I have long been considered the finest chef in Sarum."

Buck frowned and rubbed his chin. "Sarum? Where's that, then? Never heard of it."

Albert turned around, making a show of thinking. "A long way off," he said, running a finger across the horizon.

"What, one of them Farfall communities?" Buck screwed his face up and curled the first two fingers of his left hand.

Albert nodded. "You never been there?"

"No. And don't plan on it, neither. Too near the bad shit over the mountains. You know, Qlippoth."

Albert adopted his best poker face. "Oh, it's not all that bad really. Not once you get used to it."

"Yeah, well you can keep it, far as I'm concerned. Reckon I'll stay put in NJ."

"NJ?"

Buck pointed along the road toward the white-walled city. "New Jerusalem. About the only real civilized place out here. Unless you count Arx Gravis, that is, and I'm inclined not to. Between you and me—" He cast a shifty look toward the back of the wagon. "—if it weren't for certain merchant's di... trade goods, we'd most probably leave the dwarves to rot. So," he said, rubbing his palms together, "you're a cook, are you? That's funny that, seeing as I work in a restaurant, too. Well, it's more of a simple eatery, I guess, but same thing. There's grub and booze and all. It's not my main job, like, you know, but it's kind of..." Buck gave Albert another of his conspiratorial looks.

"Your cover?" Albert pretended to look awed. "You don't mean to say—"

Buck leaned in close and whispered. "Keep it between us, eh? Our little secret. Like I said, I'm a good judge of character. Chef, my arse. You got a few stories to tell, ain't you, mate?"

Albert gave a delicate cough into his fist. "Well..."

"Go on with you," Buck said. "Can't shit a shitter, kiddy. You're a man of the trades. I could tell right off."

"You could?"

Buck drew himself up and puffed out his pigeon chest. "Look, mate—what you say your name was?"

"Albert."

Buck nodded knowingly. "OK, Albert, let's cut the crap. You're a professional; I can see it a mile off. You're also a long, long way from home, right?"

"Uh huh."

"And you ain't never been to NJ before."

Albert shook his head.

"Look," Buck said. "You hop in the back with Rugbeard there. I got contacts, if you know what I mean. I'll take care of things, fix you up with some work. You don't want to be going back to the shitty Farfalls, not if you can get on in NJ. We got stuff there you outlanders wouldn't believe. Heck, that's why everyone wants to come to NJ. If you're in the know, then you'll soon be in the money."

Albert cast another wavering look back in the direction of the plane ship. "What would you want in return?"

"Just that you remember. One day, not too far off, either, I'll need a favor back from you. You see, ol' Buck Fargin's going places, and when he does, he'll want all his pieces moving together."

How many times had Albert heard that sort of thing before? Cretinous petty thugs thinking they could make it big in the guilds. He was more than familiar with Buck Fargin's type. More than familiar with seeing their throats cut when they got too big for their boots, or watching their bloated water corpses bobbing about on the surface of the Soulsong.

"You'd do that for me?"

"Just remember, when the time comes…"

"Don't worry," Albert said with as much enthusiasm as he could muster. "You can count on me. I never forget a debt."

Heavy footsteps intruded upon the moment. Albert turned just as an immense man in a leather apron bore down on Buck. His head was completely shaven, the brow furrowed with deep grooves, face red with rage.

"Fargin, you little pillock. You gonna get this wagon rolling, or am I gonna shove it up your jacksy?"

All the blood fled Buck's face as he backed away toward the driver's seat. "Now hold on, Clive, I-I-I…"

The big man folded his arms across his chest and glowered until Buck was seated.

"And what the shog are you waiting for?" He turned his attention to Albert. "My boot on your arse? Get on with you."

Albert smarted at the shame of being spoken to so… so uncouthly. He pushed himself back onto the lip of the wagon bed, wary in case the oaf made good on his threat.

Clive growled, at the same time reaching into the pocket of his apron and pulling out a huge bread roll. "Cheese and pickle cob," he said, face tightening in a smile that was as false as Albert's show of helplessness. "And before you ask, fat boy, no, you can't shogging have none."

Clive turned on his heel and strode back toward the far end of the caravan.

Fat boy! It's just the cushion of good living. And in any case, what makes you think I'd want to imbibe your spittle, you muscle-bound primate?

Albert was about to duck inside when he risked another look at Clive's retreating back. By the time the big man reached his wagon, he'd already devoured the roll and was brushing the crumbs from his apron.

So, you like cheese and pickle, do you, my big brainless friend? Remind me to cook up some of my green tomato chutney. Goes down a treat with a slab of smelly blue vein and a hunk of soda bread.

He thumbed his nose and gave a smile full of shameless malignity, just at the very moment Buck cracked the reins and the wagon lurched forward. Albert landed flat on his back atop a very angry dwarf. Rugbeard shoved him off, rolled to his feet, and delivered a nose-crunching head-butt that brought tears to Albert's eyes.

"What the...? Who, what, where...? Oh, shog it," the dwarf said. He let out a rumbling snore while still on his feet. His eyes drooped shut, and he sank down on top of the slab of scarolite.

And you, mon ami, *are a drinker, if I'm not very much mistaken.* Albert made a mental note as he rubbed his swollen nose. He wouldn't forget. He never did. But first things first. He'd go along with Buck as far as it would take him, learn the ropes, make some contacts... He'd done it before, and he could do it again. He might be older now, a little thicker round the waist, but people didn't change all that much. They all still wanted the same things and made the same mistakes trying to acquire them. It was a game he'd played pretty much all his life, and he was already relishing the prospect of starting out somewhere new.

THE DEAD LANDS

THE ELF, GILBRUM, glided through the vegetation with long, easy strides. Vines and branches writhed around him and then recoiled, opening a path for the others to follow.

Out of the corner of his eye, Shader saw occasional flurries of movement—bulky shapes darting between clumps of sedges or hunkering down amid the roots of mangroves. If it was the lizard-men, they didn't appear keen on another confrontation. Maybe having their noses bloodied once was enough for them, or maybe they were just biding their time, waiting for a more opportune moment to strike.

In front of him, Shadrak shrouded himself in his cloak and trailed Gilbrum like a shadow. Rhiannon brought up the rear, sullen and listless, eyes locked on her muck-encrusted sandals. Mosquitoes dotted her robe, flitted in and out of her hair. She swiped at them halfheartedly, as if she'd come to realize the effort was futile.

Gilbrum wove a twisting path between the trees and then skirted a quagmire tufted with towering reeds. The mud made slurping, sucking noises as they passed, and something slithered across its surface.

The elf ran effortlessly up a steep bank and waited for them at the top. It was only when Shader trudged up beside him that he noticed Shadrak was no longer with them.

"He is close," Gilbrum said. "His preference is for stealth. It is the nature of his kind."

"What's that, scum?" Rhiannon said.

Gilbrum cocked his head, as if considering a reply, but then waved his hand to take in the sea of tall grass that rolled out ahead of them. "Follow in my footsteps. There are things in the grass that live for the taste of flesh. I know them well and can avoid them with ease."

The grass bent back as he approached, creating a narrow corridor for him to walk through. At its edges, countless snakes and scorpions slithered and skittered out of his path. What was visible of the ground was studded with milky-white pustules, within which hand-shaped shadows twitched and grasped. Gilbrum lithely stepped over them, or jumped when two or more were clustered together. When he stopped and turned back to beckon, Rhiannon gave Shader a worried look but then set off after the elf, careful to plant her sandals square in the middle of the footprints he'd left. Shader followed her, doing the same, but he drew the gladius just in case.

"So, this whole place is alive?" Rhiannon asked with a quaver in her voice.

Gilbrum held up his hand, eyes flicking left and right. "When you have been here a while, you can feel it breathe."

He continued in silence, the grass parting for him, until they emerged upon a muddy flat crawling with sausage-sized maggots. Gilbrum quickened his pace, slapping at them with his bow. Rhiannon hitched up her robe and danced across on tiptoe.

The rank stench of rotten eggs filled Shader's nostrils, and plumes of brownish gas hissed to the surface at the edges of the flat. Gilbrum paid no heed, but continued on as quickly as Rhiannon and Shader could follow. Up above, twin suns climbed into in the sky, blurred by a clogging miasma that rose from the marsh.

When they entered a copse of bowed trees surrounding a murky pond, Shadrak was waiting for them.

"Plane ship's definitely gone," he said.

Shader looked to Gilbrum for an explanation, but the elf merely shrugged and asked, "This is where you entered the marsh?"

"Close by," Shadrak said. "We were shunted off course by the Perfect Peak."

Gilbrum nodded. "The Technocrat has many defenses. The need must be dire indeed, if you would risk going there."

"You know of Gandaw's plans?" Shader asked.

"The Unweaving of all Creation? Who does not live in dread of this?"

"It has started," Shader said.

Gilbrum hung his head in silence, as if he were grieving or pondering a response. "And you will stop him?"

Shader shrugged. "Ain permitting."

Gilbrum sighed and cast his gaze around the marsh. "I would join you, only I am bound to this place. I have no freedom in Malkuth, save where the Sour Marsh has encroached."

"But can you lead us there?" Rhiannon asked.

Gilbrum nodded. "You can see the Perfect Peak from the edge of the Sour Marsh. A black moat encompasses it—another pollution, this time of Gandaw's making. The earth around the mountain has been dead for hundreds of years, devoid of all life. Yes, I will lead you there, but I would counsel against a direct assault. Metal orbs patrol the skies, and they spit fire that burns to the bone."

"What would you suggest?" Shader asked.

Gilbrum sighed again, and this time sat down cross-legged, gesturing for the others to do the same. When they complied, he reached beneath his cloak and drew out a small wooden box, which he placed on the ground. He opened the lid, and a ghostly fire spilled forth, casting a comforting warmth over them.

"The Unweaving was attempted once before," he said, "back when the Sour Marsh was a mere trickle at the foot of the Farfalls. It is not a swift process, this unmaking of worlds, and back then, Gandaw was thwarted by the dwarves. Their tale even reached their kin across the mountains, and thus made its way to us."

"Kin?" Shader said. "I knew a dwarf from Aethir. He was present at this first Unweaving. He told me the dwarves were creatures of Gandaw. How is it they have kin in Qlippoth?"

Gilbrum looked up at the sky and then focused on Shader. Moisture rimmed his verdant eyes. "Your friend was correct. Gandaw made the dwarves. He made them to mine the scarolite ore he had been led to by the homunculi."

Gilbrum's gaze flicked to Shadrak and then back to Shader. The assassin was rigid beneath his hooded cloak.

"Like so much that Gandaw made, the dwarves were not an original idea. Whatever has been dreamed, whatever has entered the minds of humans, was inspiration for his experiments. Long before Gandaw melded the races to form dwarves, the Creator had dreamed such beings for himself. Like my people, the elves, the dwarves were a remedy for the nightmares. We are the Creator's defense against madness." Gilbrum shook his head and looked off into the trees.

"If the Sour Marsh goes unchecked, the nightmares will encompass all of Malkuth. Aethir will be a living horror, and the Creator will be rendered insane."

Shader thought about something the Gray Abbot had told him. "Aethir is the Dreaming to the natives of Sahul—a country on our Earth."

Gilbrum was nodding. "The nightmares would seep through the portals between worlds. If the Sour Marsh spreads its evil throughout Malkuth, the Earth will be contaminated. For this reason, I cannot leave it untended. It is the task my people are charged with. One elf, for a span of one hundred years, must slow the progress of the marsh's malevolence. We can spare no more. Our people are few. The nightmares of Qlippoth are slowly killing us, just as they killed the dwarves."

"The dwarves of Qlippoth are dead?" Shader said.

Gilbrum picked up a fallen leaf and gave it his full attention. "The city of Arnoch was their mightiest structure. It enabled them to hold out for years against the worst horrors imaginable. The Creator dreams darkly, and his protectors ultimately fight a losing battle. Arnoch now lies beneath the sea, a lost testament to a good people. Gandaw's dwarves are a pale imitation, tainted with the blood of the homunculi, the spawn of the Deceiver."

"Spawn of the Deceiver," Rhiannon said with a sardonic smile at Shadrak. "Sounds about right, if you ask me."

Shadrak's eyes glowered red from beneath his hood, but he said nothing. Perhaps there was nothing he could say. Maybe he knew as little as Shader and Rhiannon.

"They have removed themselves from the life of Malkuth," Gilbrum continued. "They skulk in the sun-starved chambers of Arx Gravis at the foot of a deep ravine. But it is to them that you should go. Gandaw bred his dwarves for mining scarolite, and they know the tunnels that run beneath the Perfect Peak."

"What if we still want to take a look at this mountain for ourselves?" Shadrak said.

"I have said I will take you there." Gilbrum shut the lid of the wooden box, and its warmth gave way to the damp chill of the marsh.

Where the box had sat, the ground had dried, and tufts of virgin grass poked through the soil.

He stood and shouldered his bow. "Perhaps you have skills I am not familiar with. I know only that I can see no way to enter the Perfect Peak uninvited, apart from that I have described."

"It's a habit of mine to learn everything I can about an enemy before I make a move," Shadrak said. "Even if you're right, a quick reccy won't be wasted."

"Indeed," Gilbrum said. "I can see how such scrupulosity would make you a formidable foe; but what of you two?" He looked from Rhiannon to Shader. "What is your purpose in this? Forgive my asking, only your allegiance to this Nous of yours raises questions. The dwarves were deceived, and now they are impotent, afraid of where their actions might lead. Are you certain of what your Nous wants?"

Shader chewed his bottom lip and rubbed his thumb over the pommel of the gladius.

"As sure as I can be," Rhiannon said. "Way I see it, Gandaw wants to wreck everything, so if Nous is worth his salt, he's bound to want us to kick his—"

"What else can we do?" Shader asked. "If Nous wants us to permit the unmaking of the worlds, he has given no sign." Nor would he, Shader knew. The ways of Nous were always frustratingly vague, hence the years of moral theology just to comprehend what a just and loving deity might desire. "If we do nothing, when we have the power to act, we would be complicit in Gandaw's destruction of Creation."

"Like the dwarves," Gilbrum said.

"Like Nous, useless scut." Shadrak pulled out a knife and started to scrape beneath his thumbnail.

"What's that supposed to mean?" Rhiannon asked.

"Nous grants us free will," Shader said, more dismissively than he'd intended, his focus never wavering from Gilbrum. "He is lord of love." He is love. Adeptus Ludo had never tired of hammering that point home. "He would not desire the Unweaving."

"But what response would he make?" Gilbrum asked. "Would he want you to kill to prevent it?"

"What do you think?" There was vitriol in Rhiannon's tone.

Gilbrum offered her a hand up. "My people say the answer to fear is love, and yet we still have a use for arrows."

"I say we kill the shogger," Rhiannon said.

"Looks like we agree on something, then," Shadrak said, springing to his feet.

"Well, that's just... Not sure how I feel about that." Rhiannon shifted the sword on her back, ran a hand through her hair, and wandered away toward the undergrowth.

Shader tensed when he saw Shadrak follow her, but the two stopped and started speaking—or rather Shadrak did the talking, and Rhiannon just rolled her shoulders, making more eye contact with the buzzing insects than with the assassin.

Gilbrum crouched beside Shader, keeping his voice low. "There is love between you and the woman?"

Shader felt his face tighten. He fought the urge to glance at Rhiannon, and instead held Gilbrum's gaze. "Not like... Not the sort of..."

Gilbrum put a hand on his shoulder. His eyes rippled like emerald ponds. "This conflict is unnatural," he said. "Be careful, my friend, there is the taste of deception in all this."

In all what? Shader wanted to ask, but Gilbrum removed his hand and set off once more.

The elf led them at a brisk pace, the undergrowth recoiling wherever he set his feet, but creeping back as soon as the companions had passed.

Shader became aware of a pulse thrumming through the soles of his boots. Gilbrum explained this was the heart of the Sour Marsh. He halted the group and held up his hand. A faint susurrus rose from the boggy ground and whispered through the trees.

"Listen," Gilbrum said, holding his open palm above the earth. "The breath of the marsh. As I told you, it is a creature, all its parts extensions of one organic whole; and it is sentient, utterly evil."

Shader had the disquieting feeling the ground might suddenly shift beneath him, or open up to swallow him whole.

"That box of yours," Shadrak said. "Couldn't help noticing, but when the fire was burning, it reclaimed the land in some way."

"That is its purpose," Gilbrum said. "But the Sour Marsh is too vast, its infection too advanced. It smothers each new growth within hours. My task is futile, and yet I am sworn to keep trying. At best, I will slow the death of Aethir by a few hundred years, but in time, it will come."

"If Gandaw doesn't get there first," Rhiannon said.

"Yeah, but it's different with Gandaw," Shadrak said. "From what I've seen, he ain't no brainless wrecker."

"Really?" Rhiannon said. "And just what have you seen?"

Shadrak answered with a glare, the blades in his baldrics sparkling when he let his cloak fall open.

"You are right," Gilbrum said. "His evil is intolerance."

"Has my sympathy there," Rhiannon said.

"He can't abide imperfection," Shader said. "Apparently, Ain wasn't quite up to the task of creation."

"Got you," Rhiannon said. "Gandaw's going to straighten things out. Lucky old us."

"Maybe he has a point," Shadrak said. "If this crap spewing over the mountains is anything to go by."

"Oh, of course." Rhiannon applauded, a rictus grin revealing her teeth. "And don't forget the rest of the scum that infects Creation. You know, cheats, cowards, rapists; and let's not forget back-stabbing midgets."

"That's enough, Rhiannon," Shader said.

She turned on him, face reddening. "Don't you shogging tell me—"

"Shut it." Shader winced as he said the words.

Rhiannon spun away from him and punched a tree. "Shog!" she swore, rubbing her hand.

Gilbrum shook his head and set off once more. Shadrak was close on his tail, but Shader hung back a little way, making sure Rhiannon was still with them. Each time she nearly caught up, she stopped until Shader put more distance between them, and then she'd start walking again. Not once did she meet his gaze.

Shader's hand crept into his coat pocket, fingers stroking the cover of his Liber. He longed to open its pages in the hope of gleaning some inspiration, some wisdom, but right now, he viewed the scriptures with a cynicism that would have made Gandaw seem like a luminary. What kind of hope could he find in a book cobbled together by a creature as foul as the Liche Lord of Verusia? How could an entire religion have sprung from its pages? Out of all his Templum tutors, only Adeptus Ludo had raised the issue of inconsistencies in the Liber, disparate elements that made no sense unless interpreted from within the context of a 'golden thread' Ludo claimed ran through the scriptures, retaining some long-forgotten teaching. Creation might once have been a good; the Liber may have once been pure; but right now, it seemed to Shader both were irretrievably compromised. Maybe it was better if Gandaw had his way. Surely he couldn't make a worse job of it than Nous.

With a resolve he had to impose upon himself, he quickened his pace to catch up with Gilbrum. His concern for Rhiannon now vacillated between anger and indifference, both of which, he was all too aware, would dissolve like phantoms in the mist if he were to delve more than skin-deep.

"This Skeyr Magnus," he said. "What is it he wants?"

Gilbrum's eyes remained on the path ahead, and he spoke as if distracted. "To be a new Gandaw, perhaps. Power, like most. But his ambitions are born of fear. It is the way of all creatures. You know this, and you know the answer, but it is both too simple and too difficult."

"I don't know what you—"

"Love, my friend. It has always been about love. This Nous of yours obscures that truth, I think. The dwarves fell for the same reason."

"You blame Nous for the dwarves' betrayal of the Hybrids?"

"I do not," Gilbrum said. "For as I said before, I know nothing of Nous. But I do know about the Deceiver, the father of the Creator."

"The Demiurgos?"

Gilbrum nodded. "It was he who led Otto Blightey astray, and Gandaw was Blightey's pupil."

"What?" Shader said. "I thought they were in opposition. Blightey's a liche, a necromancer..."

"The antithesis of Gandaw's science?" Gilbrum said with a raised eyebrow. "It was Gandaw who found a way to bring Blightey back from the Abyss. The Archon had banished the Liche Lord's skull there, locked in a casket of scarolite. But even that was not strong enough to hold it. It broke free and drifted through the Abyss, finding its way to Gehenna at the heart of Aethir. There, it threatened the Creator. Blightey's skull has a terrible power, which even the gods fear. He secured a new body and stole the invulnerable armor the Cynocephalus had forged for his own warding. Thus protected, he waded through the acidic waters of the black river that spans the Abyss, until he discovered the means to reach out to Earth through the subtleties of dreams. This was how he himself had first been swayed by the demon known as the Dweller."

Shader stiffened, and fought down the memory of lashing tentacles, the despair as Shadrak's blade plunged into his back and the Dweller rolled over him.

"Blightey found what he was looking for in Sektis Gandaw: curiosity, ambition, a mind both ripe and receptive. He promised great things, persuaded the homunculi of Gehenna to instruct Gandaw until one day he would have the means to generate a corridor between Earth and the Abyss."

"But they later fought," Shader said, "and Blightey was driven back into Verusia." Where his evil still grew like a cancer, inexorably creeping toward the wider world, with only the Templum to drive it back, again and again.

Gilbrum gestured for them to stop before a knotted wall of mangroves. "My point is that the Liche Lord and the Technocrat were both deceived by the Abyss, one way or the other. Deception is insidious. It takes root where its presence is not suspected. The dwarves of Arx Gravis learnt this to their horror, and this is why they are afraid to act: they lost faith in their scriptures, and now they no longer trust their own judgment."

"So what can be done?" Shader asked. How could the truth in the Liber be separated from the lies? Was the task even possible anymore? How could his own reasoning be trusted, if it was founded upon Nousian morality?

"I cannot say," Gilbrum said. "But if this Nous of yours is anything like the god once worshipped by the dwarves, then you must act as he would act."

"And how is that?" Shader said.

"With love."

Shadrak was watching them from the shadows of a crooked tree, its limbs intertwined with its neighbor's to form a braided overhang.

"My mother would've liked you," he said without any warmth. "Simple truths for simple people; but those are the dangerous truths, the ones more complicated men will pay people like me to suppress. But you, Gilbrum, ain't exactly a simple man. Why is it you look at me every time you mention these homunculi?"

Gilbrum faced Shadrak's crimson stare. "The homunculi were begotten, not made. They are creatures formed of the substance of the Demiurgos himself."

"Figures," Rhiannon said, striding back to hover over them like she couldn't wait to get on.

Shadrak shot daggers at her but then turned back to Gilbrum. "And you connect me with them? Why? Coz I'm short? I was raised in Sahul, I tell you. I'm as human as they come."

Gilbrum stood absolutely still, his cloak a mélange of greens and browns that gave him the appearance of a lichen-covered trunk. "What about your parents?"

"None of your business."

"Did you even know them?"

Silver flashed from beneath Shadrak's cloak.

Shader's gladius batted the dagger aside before he'd even registered its flight.

Gilbrum remained impassive.

Shadrak was visibly stunned by the speed of Shader's reaction. He fumbled with a pouch but then stiffened as a black blade pressed against his throat.

"Touchy little shogger, aren't you?" Rhiannon said.

"Foster mother," Shadrak said softly. "I knew my…" He broke off and fixed his eyes on Gilbrum. "With all this talk of deception, we shouldn't lose sight of the fact that you're nothing but the dream of a mad god, the bastard son of the Demiurgos, by incest, if I heard it right from that scutting bard." He shot Rhiannon a look, and she tensed.

The elf stooped to pick up Shadrak's dagger, reversed it, and handed it back to him.

Shader nodded to Rhiannon, and she stepped away, thrusting the black sword into the ground and leaning on it.

Shadrak's expression was concealed by his hood, but he sheathed his dagger and crossed his arms.

Gilbrum scanned the trees, tilting his head back slightly to sniff the air. "They have left us. Skeyr Magnus and his lizard-men. It seems they fear to approach the Perfect Peak."

"We're close?" Shader asked.

"We've arrived." Gilbrum parted a tangle of vines between two mangroves and invited him to look.

The Sour Marsh gave way abruptly to bleached sand that spread into the distance, merging with the cobalt horizon. A oily river of sludge ran around the edge of the desert like a moat. Dark vapors effused from its surface, and for as far as Shader could see, malformed limbs splashed free of the goo and groped blindly before slipping from sight.

A mile or so from where they stood, a lone mountain jutted from the sand, perfectly symmetrical and black as coal, save for the veins of malachite picked out by the glare of the twin suns. A cloud of dirt covered the peak, and at intervals of a few seconds, jags of lightning flashed through the smog. Where they touched the sky, threads of discoloration spread like cracks in a mirror.

Glints of silver zipped and whirled around the base of the mountain, rising and swooping with astonishing speed.

Gilbrum's cloak whitened to match the desert. He crouched to scoop up some sand and let it run through his fingers. "The Dead Lands," he said. "Not sand, but bone."

"Bone?" Rhiannon wrinkled her nose.

Gilbrum stood and made a visor with his hand, peering at the black mountain. "Nothing lives here," he said. "Gandaw made sure of that before he built the Perfect Peak."

Shadrak's eyes tracked the movements of the silver objects flitting around the base. "They follow a set pattern," he said. "But I'll wager that'll change the moment we approach."

"We'll never know if we just stand here all day gawping," Rhiannon said. She stepped away from the border of the Sour Marsh toward the river of sludge.

Shader made to follow, but Gilbrum put a restraining hand on his shoulder. One of the silver shapes was speeding away from the mountain so quickly that, by the time Shader had blinked, he could see it clearly as a metallic sphere, spinning and reflecting sunlight from its surface.

Rhiannon froze where she stood.

The sphere came to a hover mere yards from her and began to circle her at head height. A slim metal tube emerged from its shell and pointed at her chest. In that instant, Gilbrum released an arrow. The tube twitched and spurted red flame, and the arrow turned to ash.

Shader lunged for Rhiannon, grabbed her wrist, and tugged her toward the marsh. The sphere sped past them and resumed its circling.

Shader drew the gladius without a thought, its blade meeting a second stream of fire and deflecting it into a tree. The trunk fizzed and blackened, then split down the middle. The nozzle swiveled in his direction, but a thunderous crack sounded, and the sphere spun backward before dumping itself in the dust.

"Get back," Shadrak said, pointing toward the mountain with his smoking pistol.

Two more spheres were racing straight for them.

Shader dragged Rhiannon back toward Gilbrum and the cover of the trees. Shadrak followed them, walking backward, with the little black weapon covering the spheres. Once they were all back within the the marsh, the spheres broke off and returned to their patrol of the mountain.

"Anyone got a plan to get past those things, now would be a good time," Rhiannon said, throwing herself to the ground like a sulking child.

"We go underground," Shadrak said. "If what Mr. Pointy Ears says is true, we pay these dwarves a visit."

"Then we need to find Arx Gravis," Shader said. "Let's just pray we have time."

"I'll leave the praying to you," Shadrak said.

Gilbrum's shoulders slumped, and his eyes grew dull. "I cannot lead you there. It is far beyond the bounds of the Sour Marsh. You must journey east, and yes, you must pray. The cloud and the lightning above the Perfect Peak were not there before. I fear you are right: the Unweaving has commenced."

"Do you have a map? Landmarks for us to look out for?" Shader asked.

"I am sorry," Gilbrum said.

"Then how——" Shader's words stuck in his throat as he saw they were being watched.

"Nous is merciful to sinners, Deacon Shader." Dave the Slave shuffled out of the undergrowth, his twisted frame the avatar of an angry god. "You are still his right hand, despite your failure to act."

Ice crept up Shader's spine. It wasn't the first time the hunchback had appeared out of nowhere. He should have been used to it, what with Aristodeus popping up all over the place, but in both cases, it had the feel of wrongness to it. Of course, it was possible, as the Voice of Nous, Dave had some divinely bestowed power. Possible, but not very likely.

Gilbrum's eyes widened, and he spoke in a low voice to Shader. "There is the taste of deception about this creature. I would not——"

"Nous has shown me the way to Arx Gravis," Dave said. "Come with me, if you would redeem yourself."

The hunchback limped away through the marsh, murmuring under his breath, but whether he was praying or cursing, Shader couldn't tell.

"Don't worry," Shadrak said. "I already got a dozen ways to kill the creep. I say we follow."

Gilbrum nodded. "Go, but be mindful that the dwarves are afraid to act. Even if they remember the tunnels, they may not grant you access."

"Doesn't anyone care that doomsday's underway?" Rhiannon said. "What is it with this place?"

"It's the Dreaming," Shader said. "Maybe death holds no fear here."

Gilbrum shook his head. "We share your fears, but we are bound by what we are. I am sorry I can do no more." With that, he slipped into the undergrowth and was lost from view.

Shader's eyes met Rhiannon's, but he could read nothing there. Her gaze was hard and empty.

Shadrak holstered his pistol and pulled his cloak about him, while up ahead, Dave the Slave beckoned with a curling finger.

With a prayer half-spoken in his mind, Shader stood aside to let Rhiannon walk in front of him, and they followed the hunchback deeper into the mire.

NOTHING'S PERFECT

FINALLY!

It was happening, after all these centuries. The Unweaving was well and truly underway.

Sektis Gandaw felt the resistance in his taut face relent. He'd grown so used to its mask-like rigor as to not notice, but now he felt a tug on his cheeks, the curling of his shriveled lips—the exoskeleton's built-in apothecary hydrated them as necessary, but there was only so much you could do. He imagined warmth suffusing his desiccated flesh like he was sure it once had. Useless sensation, useless emotional response. The sort of thing he had no time for. The sort of thing that would have no place in his universe. But he couldn't deny it; despite eons of discipline, millennia of damping down the slightest surge of passion, he was satisfied, content, a little elated, even. No doubt deserved, he acknowledged, even as he shut the feeling down with a mental command that triggered the release of equilibrating chemicals via a hundred pinpricks that barely registered, so scarred up and hardened were the injection sites.

"Finally," he said out loud this time, wholly approving of the detached monotone that emerged. It had begun. Endless series of meticulous calculations, hundreds of years of hunting for the pieces of Eingana that had been craftily hidden among the people of Earth. Only he could have done it. Only he had the patience, the fortitude, the scrupulous attention to detail that could deconstruct the entire chaotic cosmos, save for his mountain base. Sparing this island of imperfection irked him somewhat, but it was a necessary flaw that would be remedied once his creation had taken root. Once all else was stable, running smoothly, according to his own faultless laws, he planned to move beyond the Perfect Peak and watch as it was the last thing to be unwoven.

He steepled his fingers in front of his mouth, eyes glancing over the algorithms dancing across his desktop screen.

The numbers and symbols flickering before him were old friends, his children, his collaborators in dismantling and rebuilding. He knew each of them intimately. He'd pared them down, permutated them, checked and revised, checked and revised, every day, every week, every month, year after year after year. No one else could say they'd done that. No scientist, no writer, no artist could ever say that each and every single element of their creation was absolutely perfect, absolutely necessary and fit for purpose. Seeing the patterns of the Unweaving running like this, active and fulfilling their function, was as satisfying as it could get. The figures had moved beyond what they symbolized and now actualized what they stood for, all because he had unraveled the secrets of Eingana, worked out how to harness her power.

He tensed at the renewed attack of the nagging thought: He hadn't created the serpent goddess, so his cosmos wouldn't really be *creatio ex nihilo*, would it? Of course, he wouldn't be his own creation, either, would he?

He thumped down on the desk and then leaned back in his chair as equilibrium was restored. The patterns continued their procession across the screen. All perfect. So perfect.

Wait, is that an ellipsis out of place?

Couldn't be. Impossible. He'd scoured the algorithms with infinitesimal scrutiny, again and again and again. There was no error. Utterly impossible. That was the problem with smiling, with allowing the slightest shred of emotion: it opened a crack on imperfection, on self-doubt. This time, when he smiled, it was willed entirely, a sardonic smirk that put such human thinking back in its place.

Nevertheless, he had to see.

He knew the calculations so well that they played through his mind as he left the office and took the elevator down to the control center. Stepping through the sliding doors, he expected to see the glare of plasma screens winding their way up to the top of the conical chamber. His jaw may have actually dropped, and for an instant his mind went blank, scattering the numbers and symbols into confused streams of verbiage.

"Mephesch!" he yelled into the dark. "Put the screens on!"

His optics whirred into low-light mode, and he could pick out the motionless forms of the kryeh bent over their monitors, bat-wings clothing them like cloaks. The optics limned them with green, picked out the diminutive shapes of homunculi scurrying about the walkways.

A hum and a sparkle of amber drew his gaze to the apex, where, high above him, hung the serpent statue from the array of microfilaments that wired it into the heart of the Perfect Peak. There was a sound like a roaring wind, and the statue swelled to ten times its size, its eyes flaring amber, its fangs like lightning. Within moments, the wind dropped to a long drawn-out hiss, and the statue contracted to its normal dimensions, scarcely more than a foot in height. A crackle of amber burst along the filaments, and then all went dead.

"Bit glitchy, Technocrat." Mephesch sidled up beside him.

"What? Glitchy? What, what, what?" Gandaw gasped then winced as a thousand needles jabbed him to restore his euthymia.

"Nothing to worry about. Shall we?"

A transporter disk emerged from the floor, and they stepped onto it and let it take them up alongside Eingana.

Mephesch gave the serpent statue a slap, and its eyes flared once more as the microfilaments pulsed with amber light. Eingana remained petrified but seemingly defiant, festooned within the gossamer effulgence of the web supporting her. "Not quite perfect, but it'll do."

"Not quite what?" Gandaw said.

"What I mean is—"

"Then make it perfect! I haven't labored all these centuries to have some ignorant bloody homunculus botch my power source."

Mephesch grimaced and gave a little bow. "The network is perfect, the programming is faultless…"

"I know, I know," Gandaw muttered under his breath. "But? Come on, out with it?"

"I think she's putting up a fight."

"Impossible!"

The homunculus looked from Gandaw to the serpent statue. "I agree. Theoretically impossible, but sometimes things just can't be explained."

"Rubbish! If there's something awry, it's in the science, Mephesch. Understand? You merely ascribe to mystery that which you have not investigated thoroughly enough."

Mephesch nodded and cocked his head to one side. "You are right, Technocrat. It is a

491

failing of mine. Only, in this case, the science is your own."

"Which tells us what?" Gandaw asked.

Mephesch was dumb.

"It tells us—" Gandaw jabbed a finger at him. "—there has been an error in the application, an error that can only have been introduced by one of your people."

"But we followed your instructions to the—"

"Find it, Mephesch. Find it now."

Mephesch turned to look at the radiant statue. "Seems to be fine now, Technocrat. Maybe it was a bad connection."

Gandaw narrowed his optics, but he had to admit, it did seem to be working again. Did it really matter if there had been a mishap? Surely, if everything was working as it should now, it could still be perfect.

"What happened to the screens?" He switched his gaze to the walkways, where the kryeh stared at blackness. "Why aren't they working?"

"Not enough power," Mephesch said. "Virtually everything we have is being routed through the statue. We were certain you'd want to hit critical mass as soon as possible."

Gandaw let out a hissing sigh through clenched prosthetic teeth. "Is that what I said?"

"Well, uh—"

"You think it is acceptable to leave power for the elevators, for the lights in my office, indeed for everything but the screens? What is your rationale?"

The homunculus's shoulders rose to cover his ears, giving the impression his head was sinking into his torso. "I assumed the screens were now redundant, what with the algorithms being so infallible."

"Are you trying to be funny?"

"No, I merely thought that—"

"Switch them on, Mephesch. Now." Gandaw's fingers curled into fists but relaxed once the new infusion of drugs hit his veins.

"Even if we have to slow things down?"

"Even if," Gandaw said. "I've waited thousands of years, and I'm not about to rush things now. Come on, I want to see this."

The disk took them down to the ground floor once more. Mephesch crossed over to a console and flicked a series of switches. The amber net holding the statue flickered and then stabilized. Red emergency lights lazily blinked into being, bathing the kryeh in a hellish glow. The screen closest to Gandaw flashed on, tuning into a panoramic view of arctic wastes. The rest of the screens followed in rapid succession all around the circumference of the chamber, each showing a different landscape. The awakening continued on the next tier, each lightening screen chasing the next, the chain spiraling up through the levels until, finally, the single overhead screen 55 blinked to life and the Void yawned its terrible mysteries straight down at Gandaw. He looked away, feeling suddenly weak and foolish. When the pinpricks failed to activate, he asserted his will, ordered the chemicals to release. The exoskeleton emitted a whir and a sputter, but nothing happened.

Empty!

"I don't believe it!" Gandaw whined, spinning on his heels. He pulled open his coat, revealing the bandolier of empty vials crossing the front of his exoskeleton. "Piece of shit!"

He clenched his teeth, calmed himself with the thought that the drones would be right there, filling up his syringes. They should have already been there, actually. In fact, where were they? He caught Mephesch watching him, the flickering light from the monitors casting his eyes in shadow. Gandaw wanted to scream then, but he couldn't. Couldn't lose control. Not now, not when the Unweaving was so close; not after so many centuries of equilibrium.

It was the power, he realized. Mephesch needed to route more power to the drones, otherwise they'd lie dormant. A wave of panic rolled over him. For a moment, he thought his prosthetic heart was skipping beats, but that was ridiculous, wasn't it? He needed the chemicals. Needed them now. He had to have them.

"My drugs," he said to no one in particular.

Mephesch snapped his fingers, and one of his kin melded with the wall. "We'll have them for you in a moment, Technocrat."

Quick as a flash, the homunculus walked back through the wall clutching a box of refills. Gandaw spread his arms so that the creature could discard the old vials and fit the new. Within seconds, he felt the calming surge of tranquilizers. He was so relieved, he almost thanked the homunculus. Almost, but not quite.

"So, what's happening with the Null Sphere?" he asked. The algorithms and the statue should have produced a perfect sphere of nothing by now. His eyes tracked the screens until he located the view of the top of the mountain. It was hard to see anything. At first he thought the screen was dirty, but when he focused his optics, he saw that the summit was wreathed in filthy smoke. "That is meant to be the Null Sphere, is it not?"

He was dimly aware of Mephesch nodding slowly.

"Where is it? And what is this... this smog?"

The Null Sphere should have been plainly visible by now, a pool of oblivion hanging over the Perfect Peak, just like the Void peering down at him from screen 55.

"Well," Mephesch said, rubbing his chin. "Uhm..."

"Is it dispersing? It's meant to be compacting, increasing in mass. What is happening, Mephesch? It should be building toward critical. What is happening?"

"I'm sure it's nothing," the homunculus said.

"It's meant to be nothing, you imbecile!" Gandaw yelled at the screen. "A great ball of nothing getting denser and denser until it explodes with such infinite, perfect, omnipresent, cataclysmic, devastating, sublimely ordered... uggghhhhh!"

Mephesch gave a polite cough.

Gandaw's whole body was corpse-rigid until the exoskeleton made a pincushion of it and the muscles slackened.

"Yes?" he croaked, the tick-tock of his artificial heart deafeningly loud in his skull.

"Forgive me for thinking such a thing, Technocrat," Mephesch said. "But is there any possibility—I know how absurd this must sound—is there any possibility that an imperfection could have crept into the algorithms?"

The ellipsis!

The homunculus stepped back, as if he expected to be hit. Gandaw impressed himself, however, with how calm he remained. Of course, it was all down to the drugs, but he'd designed them, so he should take the credit.

"Route them back to my office, Mephesch. And shut the Unweaving down. There's no hurry." He was a patient man, the most patient who'd ever lived. His great work had been eons in the making. What cost could it possibly be to him if he were to labor a few more days?

"Re-route the algorithms?" Mephesch protested. "But that will take—"

"Seventy-six hours and thirty-nine seconds precisely." And then he'd need at least forty-eight hours to comb the data stream to make certain there wasn't more than one error. For he knew without a shadow of a doubt what the problem was, but he was no hack. With his knowledge of the algorithms, he could go straight to the offending symbol within seconds, but if one flaw had crept in to his tapestry of perfection, was there not just the tiniest possibility of another? What was so galling was that he'd missed it, right up until his triumphant review of the data stream when the process had already commenced. Wasn't that always the way? You could scrutinize something again and again from every conceivable angle, and then, at the point you put it into action, the gremlins appeared?

Mephesch pulled the main power lever, and the pulsing mesh around the statue shut down. A crackle ran around the chamber as the main lights blinked on. Gandaw clenched his jaw and zoomed in his optics so he could inspect every last detail of the statue. He'd done the same a thousand times before, but he had to be certain. He was about to break off and head for the elevator, when he thought he glimpsed movement—the slightest shift of its jawline, a glint in one of its eyes? He glared for an instant and then shook his head. He turned on Mephesch to see if he'd seen the same, but the homunculus started, as if he'd been caught daydreaming, the ghost of a grin melting away from his face.

Gandaw held his gaze for a long, uncomfortable while, but Mephesch had become as inscrutable as stone, his deep-set eyes twinkling in the strobing light from the screens. Finally, the homunculus gave a low bow and set about flicking the switches that would stream the data to Gandaw's office.

Not for the first time, Gandaw wondered about the origin of the homunculi. How come, of all the mysteries of the universe that had succumbed to the scalpel of his science, only the Abyss crossing the mouth of the Void and Mephesch's kin had continued to vex him? Everything had emerged from the same unified field, and so everything could be returned to it, and yet the Abyss, these crafty beings, and the gaping emptiness of the Void itself all seemed to say he'd got it wrong, that he'd missed something. Something very, very important.

With the steely resolve that the drugs provided, he shut out the voice of doubt. The theory was infallible. All that exists would cease to exist, save for the epicenter of the Unweaving, which was the Perfect Peak itself. That would have to include the Abyss, and if the Void really was nothing, then surely it would simply dissolve like a raindrop in the ocean of nothingness he was about to create. He emitted something like a sigh of relief. The theory still held good. These little disparities could easily be accounted for, squeezed into the perfect circle of his logic.

For an instant, his thoughts took on a life of their own, bubbling and echoing with laughter from a dark space he didn't recognize. He clamped down control in an instant. Had they been his thoughts, some kind of pseudo hallucination, or was it something else? He put the lid on that inquiry, too. He hadn't come this far to balk at the final hurdle. He was Sektis Gandaw, after all, Supreme Technocrat, perfectly rational, perfectly evolved, and perfectly in control. He did not entertain self-doubt, and he was certainly not prone to superstition. He couldn't help himself, though, from glancing up at screen 55 and frowning at the mist covering the mouth of the Void. As he peeled his optics away, he saw Mephesch watching him. It was of no matter. Gandaw had a nasty surprise for him and the other homunculi once this was all over: the same one he'd used on those thieving dwarves when they'd come to take the statue from him all those centuries ago. After that, he'd simply have to get rid of the aborted experiments in the roots of the mountain, and he'd have a blank canvas.

The smile that was curling up his lips of its own accord froze in place. His prosthetic heart thudded, and his skin was pierced by a dozen pinpricks. There was a shadow to his right.

A chill voice spoke inside his head. *"Technocrat."*

Gandaw suppressed a sigh of relief. He'd forgotten, though, and that was not acceptable. "Malach HaMavet."

The Thanatosian stepped back and gave a half-bow.

Gandaw's optics ran over him with a begrudging admiration. Not one of his creations, but fit almost perfectly for purpose: gangly limbs for speed and reach, obsidian skin as tough as boiled leather, padded feet for silent stalking, hollow bones and fibrous membranes between his arms and torso that allowed him to glide, and an ovoid cranium packed with senses so enhanced he could scent, hear, see his prey from miles away. And the speech—it was almost a masterstroke. Psionic induction that utilized the same pathways as an auditory hallucination in those it communicated with. The possibilities were endless. A private conversation in a crowded room; plotting, subterfuge, confusion of one's prey.

"Recovered, I trust?" Gandaw said. Only hours ago, the Thanatosian had been lying in pieces in a stasis tube.

HaMavet ran slender fingers down his body and inclined his featureless head. The blades that adorned his harness like splinted armor glistened, and one hand hovered above the handle of the pistol Gandaw had instructed the homunculi to give him.

"I am... better than before."

That would be the effect of the forced regeneration following vivisection. HaMavet was, after all, just another flawed organism of someone else's universe, and before Gandaw could find a use for him, he needed to know him inside out. He'd accomplished the latter with his usual scrupulosity. No fiber, no cuticle, no enzyme, no cell had gone unscrutinized, and while nothing's perfect, HaMavet's anatomy, not to mention his abilities, was a great improvement on anything Gandaw had found on Aethir or Earth. Thanatos, the homunculi had called the dark world they'd snatched him from, a planet of pure hostility. It hadn't figured on any of Gandaw's charts, but it was undeniably there, once he'd been shown where to look. He didn't like it. Didn't like it one little bit. There was about it something of the dread he got from the Void. Neither could be accounted for in his theories, but it was of no consequence. If he was right about the Unweaving, and he undoubtedly was, the slate would be wiped clean, and then there'd be no more nasty surprises.

He tapped out a sequence on his vambrace, and a projection beamed forth: Shader, the black-haired woman, and the albino, Shadrak. The memory of the homunculus's bullet shattering his borrowed skull threatened to break the surface and was swiftly quashed.

"These three were spotted by a sentroid in the Dead Lands. They must have followed me from Earth." Mephesch had reported an impact with the mountain's shields. It appeared one of the missing plane ships had been found after all this time. "There was another with them, a creature of the Sour Marsh." At the tap of a button, a second hologram sprang up showing a tall man with pointed ears. He wore an ever-shifting cloak that seemed to have been woven from foliage, and he carried a bow. Not one of Gandaw's, and not from Earth, which either meant he was something altogether unaccounted for, or one of the horrors from beyond the Farfalls.

"You told me yours is a planet of death," Gandaw said.

HaMavet was motionless. He had no eyes, but Gandaw knew he was drinking in every detail of the holograms. All living things were targets to the Thanatosian. Even Gandaw himself. The only difference was, he had something HaMavet wanted.

"You said you are harvesters. Your people live only to slaughter." No reaction. "Track them, and kill them." He was taking no chances. A lot could happen in seventy-six hours, and although nothing could penetrate the Perfect Peak's defenses, he'd learned long ago from Maldark and the dwarves never to underestimate his enemies. "Succeed, and I will return you to Thanatos."

HaMavet gave an almost indiscernible bow.

"Be cautious," Gandaw said. "The small one has a gun like the one you carry."

Faster than thought, HaMavet's pistol was out of its holster, and a blast reverberated around the chamber, ever diminishing until it was swallowed by the darkness of screen 55. There was a moment's silence, and then a kryeh on the second tier flopped backward and pitched over the railing.

HaMavet spun the gun on his finger and snapped it back into the holster.

Impressive. The weapon must have been totally unfamiliar, but already the speed, the accuracy… Gandaw nodded his approval and then glared at the blood pooling from the kryeh onto the burnished floor.

Mephesch clicked his fingers, and a team of homunculi came running.

384 WAYS TO KILL

SHADRAK HAD THOUGHT up far more than a dozen ways of killing the hunchback; he'd reached thirty-two and was still working on it. Blade to the balls, smother him with a cloak, throttle, drown, poison, garrote—if only he had Albert's cheese-cutter—bludgeon, shot to the head, shove him off a cliff, bury him alive... He'd come up with twelve variations on each, imaging three-hundred and eighty-four scenarios in all, each checked off with a finger. Didn't help his mood none there was dirt under the nails. Shog knew what germs were in among all the filth, but out here, in this cesspool of a swamp, there was sod all he could do about it.

Mud slurped at his boots, smothered his britches, and stuck to his cloak like a lead weight. The air beneath the mangroves grew even more stultifying than his thoughts, and the stench of rotten eggs steamed from the bogs. Twice, three wolfish heads burst to the surface, swaying atop sinuous necks. At first, he'd assumed there were three creatures, but on the second appearance, he spotted the hump of a scaly back, and it was clear all three heads belonged to the same beast.

It weren't just Dave had him riled, mind. It was also the elf. Those looks he'd given, like he knew some big shogging hilarious secret he didn't have the balls to share. It was bad enough putting up with the piss-taking as a kid—the dwarf jokes, and the "look like you've seen a ghost" crap. Yeah, he was different. Yeah, he was a freak, in most people's reckoning, but then to have some pointy-eared tree-hugger make out like he weren't even human... And he weren't the first, neither.

Then the bitch, Rhiannon, was constantly grumbling about food, but there was fat chance of finding any, far as Shadrak could see—least anything he'd want to shove down his gullet. The odd snake, brightly-crested lizards, and turtles with bony spines protruding from their shells didn't exactly work up no appetite.

What was most unsettling, though, was the course of the suns. They climbed and fell in the sky with no rhyme or reason. Soon as dawn came, midday sweltered, then cooled into dusk, which was immediately followed by a second rising. An hour later, midway through their arc, the suns dropped like falling apples, and the swamp was shrouded in night. Could've been the Sour Marsh screwing with things, or maybe that's just the way it was on this shogged-up world. Less than a day, and he'd already had enough of it.

Shadrak weren't no idiot; he knew what made him tick: he was a creature of routine and habit. How was that s'posed to work when there weren't no way of gauging time, when the suns didn't know their asses from their heads?

When they stopped to make camp, he slipped away by himself. He imagined the others thought he was scouting, making sure there was nothing creeping out of the dark, but truth be told, he was sick to death of the hunchback's ear-bashing of Shader and his 'scarlet woman'. One more word, and he'd have killed the shogger—all three-hundred and eighty-four ways. And he'd have taken his time about it, too.

Silver limned the tangled undergrowth as the enormous disk of one of the moons glided into the sky. The two smaller moons followed, washing the foliage with a

497

D.P. PRIOR

wavering half-light.

He could still hear Dave bollocking Shader for not acting when he had the chance, telling him his eyes should be on Nous, not on the flesh of his whore. He tensed, listening for Rhiannon to explode. The bitch was a hellcat; he had the cuts and bruises to prove it. But it was Shader's voice that shut the hunchback up. Pity Shadrak couldn't make out the words, but whatever they were, they'd done the trick. Probably the knight would have to beg his insipid god for forgiveness now, because it was doubtful Dave would have stopped for anything less than a cuss backed up by a threat. Shadrak knew men. Knew religious types, too. Only one who'd surprised him over the years was Bovis Rayn, and to be honest, the surprise hadn't worn off none, either. How could a man look so serene when you poisoned him then blew his brains out? Didn't make sense, if you asked him.

He felt a familiar warmth at the edges of his awareness, knew it was Kadee smiling and shaking her head. She understood, right enough. Least she thought she did. But Kadee was a child in her understanding. Shadrak loved her for it. Loved the peace it gave her, but when all's said and done, she was just another superstitious Dreamer.

The presence left him, and he instinctively drew his cloak about his shoulders. This weren't the time for ghosts from the past. Weren't the time for grieving, neither. The way Shadrak saw it, he had a couple of options. It's not like he was cut out for this saving the world kind of thing. That was best left to hero types, like Shader—or rather, what Shader most likely considered himself. The reality was, Nousians weren't no better than Dreamers. They were all just people hiding from the truth, praying to their imaginary friends. Didn't matter how complicated they made the bullshit, it was still bullshit, at the end of the day. Say one thing for killing folk, say it makes you honest. Everyone bleeds when you cut them, and most everyone shits themselves when they kick the bucket. No amount of dressing that up with fancy spiritual talk changed the cold hard facts.

"Don't forget, we have a contract."—The sound of the wind whispering in his ears.

Didn't quite account for the Archon, though. Weren't even certain he had veins, never mind blood flowing in them, and if he ever shit, you could bet it didn't stink. Weren't clear to Shadrak exactly what he was, and that was never a good thing. Know your enemy, he always said. Or rather, know your target. Till he did, best thing to do was play along and pick up what tidbits of information he could.

"Not showing yourself today? C'mon, don't be shy."

Warm air blasted Shadrak's back. He spun, pistol already in his hand.

The Archon hovered an inch above a pool of bubbling mud, hands tucked into the billowing brown sleeves of his habit. The cowl was like a cavern sheltering a bonfire.

"I need you to keep him alive."

"Shader?"

"He must reach Sektis Gandaw's mountain. You understand this?"

Shadrak twirled his pistol and holstered it. "Do it yourself, if it's so important."

"As I said, we have a contract."

"Sue me."

The Archon threw his hood back, and white fire burst forth.

Shadrak flung himself face-first on the ground. "All right, all right. Contract. I got you. Keep Shader alive."

"The Deceiver is near. He knows we are failing, that our last hope is weakening. Return to Shader and be vigilant." The Archon pulled his cowl back up.

Shadrak lifted his head, blinked to make sure he could still see, then climbed to his feet. "I ain't stupid. I know I'm out of my depth with this stuff. What I don't get is why you don't do something yourself."

"You are my hands and feet, Shadrak. You and certain others. I am of the world above. I dare not act directly, for justice would demand the same for my foe."

"Yeah, but what if I—"

But the Archon was gone.

He'd been about to ask, "What if I fail? What if I can't help stop this Unweaving?" Surely it was better to give the job to someone else. Someone who gave a damn. "Shogger."

"Takes one to know one," Rhiannon said. She strode straight past him without even a look.

"Guess that's why they call me 'the Unseen'," Shadrak muttered under his breath.

So, the Archon was from some other realm, and he was afraid of acting directly in case someone else did the same. Someone presumably as powerful as him, if not more so. Didn't take a lot to work out he was talking about the Demiurgos. Weren't exactly much, but it was a start.

He turned to watch Rhiannon disappear into the mangroves. He supposed she must have enjoyed the hunchback's company as much as he did. With any luck, she'd drown in quicksand, or get eaten by the three-headed bog beast. If he had an iota of Bovis Rayn's faith, it would've been tempting to pray for that.

Heading back toward the camp, he gritted his teeth as Dave started up again, about how it was grace that had brought him here, grace that sent him to show Shader the way.

"Grace, my ass," Shadrak muttered. He was about to add that it was more likely some capricious twist of fate, when a thought struck him. Grace didn't transport freaks like Dave between the worlds, but he damned well knew what did.

He slipped the pistol from its holster as he stormed into the clearing. The hunchback was squatting by a sputtering fire that was more smoke than flame.

Shader stood apart from him at the edge of the camp, peering into the brush. "Rhia... Shadrak, did you see—"

"That way." Shadrak cocked a thumb behind him. "Prob'ly yakking from too much *bullshit*." He tramped right across the fizzing kindling and stuck the barrel of his gun in Dave's face.

The hunchback's eyes bulged from their sockets, a sickly yellow creeping over the irises. Drool trickled from his twisted lips. He tried to stand, but Shadrak pressed harder, and he fell onto his back. Shadrak crouched over him, grabbed a handful of collar, and put pressure on the trigger. "One chance, shogger. How'd you get here?"

"Shadrak," Shader said. His footfalls drew close, and there was the unmistakable rasp of his sword being drawn.

"How'd you shogging get here?" Shadrak squeezed on the trigger. Just a fraction, but any more and it'd be too much.

Something sharp pricked at his back.

"Let him go," Shader said.

"Last time I'm gonna ask." Shadrak ignored the knight. Like the shogger had the balls to stab him in the back. If the roles had been reversed, would've been a different matter. He knew that from experience.

"Nous brought me," Dave slobbered, his tongue suddenly too big for his mouth. "I came by his grace."

"Bollocks!" Shadrak said, and to illustrate the point, kicked Dave where it hurt. Only, the hunchback didn't even wince.

"Shadrak!" Shader growled. "Don't make me—"

"What?" Shadrak yelled, slamming Dave's head into the ground and rounding on Shader. "The holy knight Deacon shogging Shader is gonna cut me down, is he? Had the chance before, and you didn't take it. Why should this time be any different?"

"Are you presuming upon my mercy?" Shader brought the gladius up to Shadrak's throat, but in the same breath, Shadrak had his pistol pointed at Shader's heart.

And then it was gone. The shortsword moved so fast, Shadrak didn't register until the pistol was at his feet and he was staring down the length of the blade, its tip a hair's breadth from his eyeball. His heart skipped a beat, and then his thoughts were racing—sway back, sideswipe; stamp on his toes, grab the wrist; razor star across the jugular; break a kneecap. Shader's cold eyes seemed to say he'd read each move and had it covered; whatever Shadrak did, he'd be dead before he drew breath. And so he took the only option remaining, for the time being. He did nothing.

"Mind telling me what that was about?" Shader asked without a trace of emotion.

"My plane ship," Shadrak said. "It didn't just disappear by itself, now, did it? Reckon we had ourselves a stowaway. How else do you think this shogger showed up like that?"

"Faith," Dave said, throwing his hands up in exasperation. "Plane ship, plane ship! What need has the servant of Nous for such devilry?"

"You asking me to believe in miracles?" Shader said, cocking his head and narrowing his eyes at the hunchback.

Shadrak thought about making his move then, but the glinting metal virtually caressing his eyeball convinced him otherwise.

"Everyone wants a sign," Dave countered. "Or are you too blind to see the graces Nous grants you?"

Shader's lip curled, and he looked like he was going to spit an angry retort, but instead he sheathed his sword.

"You don't believe that horse shit?" Shadrak said.

"No."

"So what, you want me to torture him?"

Dave steepled his fingers, and a hard look came over his face.

"Be like getting blood from a stone," Shader said. "I vote we work with what we've got. Let him lead us to these dwarves, at least until we come up with a better suggestion. Just have to keep an eye on him, that's all."

Dave snorted at that and set about poking the fire with a stick.

Shadrak picked up his pistol and wiped the dirt from it. He fished about in a pouch for a rag and proceeded to polish the barrel. "Oh, I'll keep an eye on him, all right. You can count on that."

Shader nodded and drew in a deep breath. "Good. Then that just leaves Rhiannon." He turned on his heel and slipped into the brush.

The skin on Shadrak's cheek pricked, the way it always did when someone was paying him too much attention. He looked up mid-polish and caught Dave's sickly eyes appraising him.

"What you looking at, freak?"

The hunchback sucked in his top lip and nodded ever so slightly before answering. "Nous is merciful, brother. He will forg—"

"Don't even think about it," Shadrak said. "Heard enough of that crap for a lifetime."

"Then surely you must—"

"How 'bout you shut the shog up and find something to roast on that sorry excuse for a fire. Least that way the bitch might stop grumbling when she gets back."

Dave got to his feet and craned his neck to look over his shoulder at a dense tangle of vines.

"I'm joking, turd-breath. Ain't nothing out there fit for eating."

"Nous will provide," Dave said.

Shadrak was about to cuss at that, but then the knotted vines shook, and trapped among their thorny strands was a white goat, bleating like it had no idea how it came to be there.

SALVE OF THE BLACK SWORD

T HE LARGEST OF the three moons bathed the swamp in silver, painting the drooping foliage with its sheen and lending it the cast of a dream.

More of a bloody nightmare.

Rhiannon plonked herself on a gnarled mangrove root just shy of a bubbling and spitting mire. Her sandaled feet trailed in the black sludge. No point worrying about it now, despite the fact it stank worse than shite and was probably crawling with leeches. Her calves were already caked from the day's slog through it, and the hem of her robe was a besmirched ruin.

The two smaller moons glared down at her like a pair of crooked eyes, coldly distant, the eyes of a sated predator too stuffed to pose a threat at the moment, but given long enough… Her skin crawled, and a tingle tripped along her spine. No way she was gonna chance sleeping on her own, but no way she was going back to the fire, either.

What she needed was a vigil, time to pray, get her soul back in synch with Nous. No, what she really needed was a drink, something to drown out the hunchback's voice still echoing around her skull, calling her a whore, blaming her for Shader's failings. Blaming her for everything. Hadn't she done all this for Shader's sake? Joined the Templum, dedicated her life to Nous, all so he wasn't diverted from the destiny Huntsman, or Aristodeus, or Nous Almighty himself had in store for him? Wasn't it enough to make the sacrifice without having Dave accuse her of doing the opposite? Wasn't it enough she could still feel Gaston between her legs, slipping about inside like some writhing slug? That shogging, twisted, hunchbacked, dribbling freak needed to watch his tongue, coz he had no idea what she'd been through. What she'd lost.

She squeezed her eyes tight against the faces of her folks, butchered on their own doorstep. She winced at the image of Sammy running off alone, and it felt like a rock had replaced her stomach when she thought of what the shaman had done to him, how her little Sammy had rejected her, left her with nothing. Nothing but Nous, and that amounted to pretty much the same thing.

She pulled the scabbard over her head and set it on the ground. The hilt of Callixus's sword rippled with black flame that defied the stark moonlight.

You have me, it seemed to whisper.

She scoffed and shook her head. That just about took the sodding biscuit. What, was she hearing voices now?

No.

She scrabbled back against the trunk of the tree, her hands walking up the bark till she was standing.

"Shog, I'm losing it," she muttered. The muscles throughout her body clenched, and she started to shake. Her breaths came in staccato gasps, and she began to swoon. A pint would settle her, or maybe a couple. Always did the trick in the past. Shog, a bottle of wine, even. Spirits. Anything. She looked from side to side, as if she expected to see a bar or a wine rack. Her mind's eye replayed her showing up at Gaston's with a bottle in either hand.

Only yourself to blame, whore.

She gagged and almost chucked up her guts.

The sword hilt pulsed and twitched, and her vision narrowed until that was all she could see. She fell to her knees, reached out with a shaking hand, and caressed the pommel. A sigh blew through her mind. Whether it was hers or someone else's, she couldn't tell. She curled her fingers around the handle and pulled the blade free. Acid coursed through her veins, and her heartbeat tripled, hammering out a dizzying tattoo that built and built till it threatened to explode from the top of her head. She turned the sword, brought its keen edge to the inside of her forearm. She gasped as the skin popped and hot blood seeped out. It stung at first, but she pressed deeper and then sliced, drawing the blade across her arm till oozing rivulets ran toward her wrist, pooled stickily in her palm, and dripped between her fingers. She shuddered and gasped. The sword hilt felt like a burning coal, and it sent tendrils of soothing heat deep into her muscles. Her shoulders dropped, her heart rate slowed, and she leaned back against the welcoming bark.

She started at a footfall in the undergrowth. A shadow loomed, and she dropped the blade, clutching her arm to her chest to keep it from being seen.

"Shit," she hissed as the front of her robe was soaked with hot wetness. She grimaced, shut her eyes tight, and clenched her jaw as Shader stepped out of the gloom and tilted the brim of his hat to cover his eyes. Nous all pissing mighty, she knew it was him coming. Why the shog couldn't he just leave her alone?

She turned her back to him, felt the tension rack up a notch. Perhaps, in the dark, he'd not seen.

"You all right?"

Rhiannon looked at him over her shoulder, forced a smile. "Yeah. Why wouldn't I be?"

"Dave. You shouldn't have to listen to that. Maybe I should have—"

"It's fine. Really." She smiled again, but her lips were drawn taut over her teeth. She wasn't fooling anyone.

Shader's eyes flicked to the sword on the ground. He took a step toward it.

"It's all right. Leave it," Rhiannon said. "I was just… You know."

"I'll wait for you back at camp."

Rhiannon nodded. "Yeah. Yeah, do that. I won't be much longer."

He turned, but before he'd taken a step, her heart leapt into her throat.

"Deacon."

He spun to face her. "Yes?"

"Do you trust him?"

"Dave or Shadrak?"

She gave a little laugh. "Either of them."

"Dave, I don't know. Either he's from Nous, or he's from the Demiurgos. Right now, I've no way of knowing. Shadrak, on the other hand, has something of a track record."

"So what are you going to do?"

Shader glanced at the black sword again, his eyes lingering too long for comfort. "Nothing."

"Sounds like a plan."

"Rhiannon." Shader stepped in close.

She tensed, wrapped her arms tighter about her chest.

"Rhiannon," he said again. "Is there something you want to talk about?"

She let out a shrill, hysterical laugh. Shog, she sounded like a loony. "You mean a confession?"

Shader's hand snaked out, gripped her by the shoulder. "I'm not a priest."

She gave up hiding what she'd done to herself, twisted round to face him, let him see her cut. "Well, you sure act like one."

He released her shoulder and cupped the back of her hand in his, gently lifting her arm. She watched him intently, bracing herself for the scolding.

"Rhiannon," he started, then clenched his teeth. With enforced softness, and without looking her in the eye, he said, "Need clean water."

"Got any booze?"

Shader shook his head. "Pity. That would have done it."

"For drinking, I mean."

Shader let go of her hand and drew his gladius.

Rhiannon winced and pulled back. She stared at the blade like it was a snake poised to strike. Her heart was racing again, and she was breathing ten to the dozen. On the ground, the black sword hissed, though whether out loud or in her mind, she couldn't tell.

Shader frowned and shook his head. "I was going to have it heal you," he explained. "Never mind." Instead, he cut a strip from the hem of his surcoat, re-sheathed the shortsword, and proceeded to bind her forearm.

Calm washed over her in cool waves that lapped at her burning nerves.

"What's going on, Rhiannon? Between you and Nous, I mean."

"Could ask you the same question." Her arm smarted from the cloth, and she tried to snatch it away, but Shader's grip was too strong.

"Grit your teeth. There, all done." Shader tucked the loose end in and sat down on the root. "I was skeptical about your calling, first off, but back there, at the Templum of the Knot, you seemed..." He struggled for the right word, chewed it over. "... happy."

Rhiannon snorted and lowered herself beside him. "Yeah, well a lot's happened since. Pain and suffering's meant to temper you, isn't it? Sort the wheat from the chaff."

"I don't know any longer." Shader cupped his chin in his hand, absently stroked his stubbled cheek with his fingertips.

"You might at least quote the Liber at me, chapter and verse. Soror Agna would have done, in any case."

Shader nodded, but he may as well have been a hundred miles away, talking with someone else. "Adeptus Ludo always used to lecture about the golden thread running through the Liber. I had this suspicion he was a bit of a crank, a heretic even. Stupid, really, because of all my teachers, he always spoke the most sense. The Gray Abbot said pretty much the same thing. He told me the scriptures we have now were cobbled together by the Liche Lord of Verusia posing as a pious friar. You see, somewhere in this tome—" He slapped the pocket of his long-coat. "—is an original teaching. It's still there, according to Ludo. At least, the essence of it is, just waiting to be teased out."

Rhiannon shifted to get comfortable. They'd not mentioned this at the templum. Soror Agna had always insisted on the literal truth of the Liber. For her, there were no inconsistencies that couldn't be surmounted with faith. The priests had all been the same, unquestioning in their obedience to the written word, and if a passage was unclear to them, they would defer to Mater Ioana.

"You know, I never thought of it before," Rhiannon said. "I'd always assumed it was the word of Nous or Ain or whatever. Never could get my head around that stuff. But sometimes the priests would argue about what a verse meant, and they'd go to Ioana for interpretation."

"She knew," Shader said. "At least, she had an inkling of the truth, I'm sure of it. My point is, how do we know what Nous wants if we don't even know which parts of the Liber are from him, and if we have no authoritative way of interpreting the golden thread, even if we could find it?"

"It's about love, any way you look at it, isn't it?"

Shader looked at her as if she'd just spoken in a foreign language. "I'm not sure what that means."

Rhiannon's eyes wandered to the black sword. She reached for it, started to wipe the bloodied blade on the tree root. "Me neither. Why don't you ask the freak? He seems pretty certain about everything. After all, he's the Voice of Nous, isn't he?"

"Maybe," Shader said, standing. "Maybe he is."

"What, so you think I'm a whore, too, do you? Thanks a bunch." She expected Shader to laugh, but he remained stony-faced.

"I need to be harder, Rhiannon," he said. "Harder. Come on, we're leaving."

"But it's still dark."

Shader's hand enclosed the pommel of the gladius, as he headed back into the undergrowth.

What if I don't want to leave? she wanted to yell at him. *What if you're better off without me?* Shog, she could have used some reassurance right about then; could have used him begging her to return to camp, but what did he go and do instead? Shogging turned his back on her; walked off, knowing all the while she'd have no choice but to follow like an obedient dog. She'd half a mind to stay put. Half a mind to shog off by herself. She cast a look at the shimmering face of the largest moon, glanced at its sisters staring down at her, playing their patient game.

"Shit," she said, whacking the black sword against the tree. "Shit, shit, shit." She struck the bark three more times and then stomped off after Shader.

A THING THRICE DEAD

GILBRUM'S FEET BARELY touched the marshland as he sped through the mangroves. Walking trees, he called them, their roots like giant spider's legs encroaching upon the brackish water.

Three sets of footprints shimmered like stars to his elvish vision. There should have been four. He'd known from the first there was something wrong about the hunchback. He should never have let them go with him. He'd seen no other choice, being duty bound not to leave the marsh himself. But then he'd realized, that made him the same as the dwarves, set in their ways, refusing to lift a finger to help the outside world. Theirs was a self-imposed exile, a penance, but his was a virtue no longer called for. What good would it do to restrain the Sour Marsh at the expense of all Creation?

He followed the tracks in between a cluster of bubbling pools, up a mud-slicked bank, and into the damp grasses skirting the entity he'd come to call home. Another step, and it was all over. Decades of service wiped out with a single act of disobedience. He lifted his foot... and set it down again. He couldn't do it. What if the reverse were true? What if it was a temptation, a trap? Perhaps the saving of Creation was a task for others. Was not reneging on one's responsibilities an act of pride, and wasn't that how the Demiurgos found his openings?

He closed his eyes, visualized Shader, Rhiannon, and Shadrak on their way to Arx Gravis. Could the hunchback really lead them there? Could he be trusted?

Accept it, Gilbrum—a voice from the past, long before he'd been assigned to the Sour Marsh. Dol Arium the prophet, speaking from the boughs of the Tree of Eingana, as he did to every child coming of age. *Accept what is not yours to change. A leaf fallen from the tree is a thing thrice dead: to self, the people, and to the law.*

"But what if everything ends?" he cried to the sky. "What does it matter then?"

But he knew what the prophet would say. Every elf did: *Be true or be nothing. Duty first, duty always.*

"Shader!" he called, not expecting to be heard. And then, more gently, he added, "Your god be with you."

The wind gusted, bringing with it the scent of lizard-men. He spun, nocking an arrow to his bow in one fluid motion.

There were two of them, face down in the grass, patiently stalking him like a pair of alligators. His arrow thrummed through the air and thudded into the loamy earth between them.

"Begone," he said. "I've no time for this."

But even as they scurried for the mangroves, a thought struck him.

"Wait!"

The brutes turned to face him.

"Skeyr Magnus," Gilbrum said. "Take me to him."

The lizard-men looked blankly at him.

"Skeyr Magnus. Your leader. Take me…" Gilbrum let out a sharp breath and rapped his fingertips against his head. "Leader," he repeated, and then made a fist and a crackling sound.

The lizard-men flung themselves to the ground and moaned.

"Yes," Gilbrum said, approaching. "Skeyr Magnus." He touched one on the shoulder, and it lifted its head, the glimmer of understanding in its amber eyes. "Take me—" Gilbrum tapped his chest. "—to Skeyr Magnus."

He followed them deep into the Sour Marsh, across bogs and thickets, coming at last to a basin littered with bones and loud with the croaking of frogs. Skeyr Magnus was crouched down, poking and prodding at the gauntlet attached to his arm with a thin-bladed tool. An open case of assorted tools was beside him on the ground. A dozen or so lizard-men lazed around the basin, but they sprang up when they saw Gilbrum, grabbing spears and clubs and forming a protective circle about their leader.

Skeyr Magnus bashed the gauntlet against the ground. There was a hiss and a shower of sparks, and then nothing but a plume of smoke.

"See what you do. This close!" Skeyr Magnus held up his thumb and forefinger to indicate. "This close to mending. Tell Skeyr Magnus, elf, why he no kill you."

Gilbrum smiled. "Because you've tried, and you know it is beyond you."

"One day," Skeyr Magnus said. "One day Skeyr Magnus catch you dozing. So close…" He blew smoke off the gauntlet. "Know-how, Skeyr Magnus has. Took it from Gandaw. Fix glove, then fix you, maybe."

Gilbrum seated himself cross-legged on the ground and rested his bow across his thighs.

Skeyr Magnus narrowed his eyes then shrugged and set about packing away his tools.

"What is it you plan to do?" Gilbrum said.

"Fix glove. Kill you."

"No, not about me. I mean, since you escaped the Perfect Peak, you've done nothing but skulk about the Sour Marsh. I've been watching you."

Skeyr Magnus rubbed his lower jaw and rolled his head. After a moment, he stood and picked up his tool case. "Skeyr Magnus patient. Fix glove, grow strong, then go back."

Gilbrum waved his hand in the direction of the Dead Lands. "To the Perfect Peak?"

"Kill Gandaw," Skeyr Magnus said. "Take science."

"Then what?"

Skeyr Magnus gave a low throaty laugh and spread his arms to encompass his lizard-men. "Who knows? Go to New Jerusalem, maybe." The lizard-men made a collective sound that could have been a gasp. "Live good life."

Gilbrum nodded slowly. He felt quite certain Skeyr Magnus didn't mean good in the moral sense.

Confirming his thoughts, the lizard-man said, "Good food, wine, women."

Gilbrum's stomach clenched at the thought, but he knew he shouldn't have been surprised. The lizard-men were only what Gandaw had made them, and the human part still desired human comforts. He gave Skeyr Magnus a sharp look. What if need of comfort wasn't the only human quality remaining to them?

"And if they won't give them to you?"

Skeyr Magnus made a fist of the gauntlet. "Then Skeyr Magnus take. Science too strong for humans."

"If that's your plan, you'll need to make a move soon," Gilbrum said as he stood. "Very soon."

"Not ready," Skeyr Magnus said. "Not stupid, Skeyr Magnus isn't. He wait. Fix gauntlet. Grow strong."

"You are wise," Gilbrum said, "but you may not have the time."

Skeyr Magnus glared at him, the muscles about his neck twitching. "Who say?"

"Sektis Gandaw has commenced the Unweaving of all things."

"Pah!" Skeyr Magnus said, turning on his heel and gesturing for his lizard-men to follow.

"If you don't believe me, look to the skies above the Perfect Peak. Already there is a cloud."

Skeyr Magnus whirled on him. "Skeyr Magnus come from mountain. If Unweaving start, he know. He see it. You lie. Want Skeyr Magnus to attack now when he weak. You too tired to hunt, elf? Want Gandaw to kill us for you?"

Gilbrum took a step toward him. "I do not lie. It has started. We must help each other, work together. Go to the edge of the Dead Lands. Watch the sky and see for your—"

One of the lizard-men grunted and fell like a stone, blood bubbling from his mouth. A silver dagger jutted from his ribs. From a treetop there came another flash of silver, then another, and two more lizard-men fell. Gilbrum shot a look at Skeyr Magnus, but the lizard-man was already bolting into the underbrush with the rest of his people in tow.

Something rustled the leaves. Gilbrum caught its scent, but it was nothing he recognized. He raised his bow and nocked an arrow. The treetop stilled, and for a couple of heartbeats there was no sound save the crashing of the lizard-men through the undergrowth. Then a voice sounded in his head, icy and as sharp as a blade.

"Too easy."

A shape of inky blackness emerged from the leaves and launched itself at Gilbrum. He fired, but the thing corkscrewed around the arrow. Silver glinted from its torso. Gilbrum flung himself aside, rolled to his feet, spun, and fired again. This time, the creature caught the arrow in slender fingers before tossing it to the ground. Its ovoid head tilted to one side, utterly sleek and featureless. On bird-like legs, it stalked toward him, as if it had all the time in the world. Gilbrum backed away, drawing another arrow and taking aim.

"Stay," he said, despising the quaver in his voice.

Another step, another arrow, and the creature lithely swayed out of its path.

It wore some sort of harness bedecked with gleaming blades, so many it seemed the thing was armored.

"One down," it said in his head as it delicately took a blade in each hand. *"Three to go."*

"Bit presumptuous, don't you think?" Gilbrum said, circling to the left and nocking another arrow. Three, it had said. Three to go. Shader, Shadrak, and Rhiannon. "Gandaw sent you?" he asked, playing for time.

The thing moved so fast, Gilbrum's arrow went awry. He ducked beneath a blade, grabbed a wrist, and tried to trip the creature as he spun it round. It rolled over his back and he felt a sharp pain in his shoulder blade. Without looking, Gilbrum swept out a leg, but the creature hopped over it, hanging in the air an instant on bat-like wings that spread beneath its armpits. As it landed, it flicked a blade at him. Gilbrum deflected it with his forearm, skipped back, and spun a scything kick at its head. He connected, but the creature rolled with the impact and slammed a blade into his hamstring.

Screaming, Gilbrum hit the ground hard and dragged himself toward a trunk. He used it to pull himself upright, taking his whole weight on one leg. On instinct, he swayed, and a blade thudded into the bark. He swung himself behind the tree and spotted Skeyr Magnus watching from a bank of reeds skirting the lip of the basin. He hopped toward him, hoping against hope the lizard-man would do something, but the second he realized he'd been seen, Skeyr Magnus lowered his head and vanished.

A shadow passed above Gilbrum, and he froze, perched on one leg as the creature descended with arms spread wide, leather membranes beneath them fluttering in the breeze. Swift as lightning, its hand went to a holster at its hip and came up blasting. A sound like thunder, a hammer blow to the ribs, and Gilbrum was on his back looking up at the overhanging foliage. Salty blood trickled from his lips. He tried to speak, beg for time. Time to warn this creature about the Unweaving. Nothing would be spared, not even it. The only sound that came out was a wheezing whimper.

Shader, he thought. *Must give him time.*

The creature loomed over him, a black blur in his failing vision. He was panting, gasping for every breath.

Shader, he thought again.

His fingers clutched at a tuft of grass, and he felt the familiar malevolence of the Sour Marsh tingle through them. His old enemy seemed like his closest friend at that moment. And then he realized: the marsh understood what was at stake. No matter its own incipient evil, it too clung to existence; it too was terrified of the end of all things.

"Help," Gilbrum rasped. He coughed up blood and tried again. "Help... me."

Tendrils lashed down around the creature, and creepers coiled about its legs. It slashed through one with a blade, but another took its place. Soon, the creature had holstered its pistol and was frantically cutting left and right with a blade in each hand. It no longer focused on Gilbrum; must have known he was going nowhere. Instead, it angled east, as if it already sensed which way Shader and the others had gone. One agonizing step at a time, it inched through the undergrowth that rose up against it with the full virulence the Sour Marsh.

Gilbrum's head lolled to one side.

Accept what is not yours to change. A leaf fallen from the tree is a thing thrice dead.

Had he fallen from the tree? Hadn't he done his duty, stayed within the Sour Marsh? And hadn't he done what was within his power and accepted what was beyond him? He'd failed to stop the creature, but he'd at least slowed it down, and perhaps kept hope alive a little bit longer. No, he wasn't a thing thrice dead, he was certain of that. He opened his mind to the vision of the Tree of Eingana, heard the sad lament of his people singing him home. He was dead only once...

FOR NOUS, ALL THINGS ARE POSSIBLE

SHADER STOPPED TO pick charred goat-flesh from his teeth. Dave hobbled to a standstill twenty yards in front and turned, waiting, as if they had all the time in the world.

A quick glance at the cobalt skies back the way they'd come gave the lie to that idea. Aethir's twin suns had risen in the time it took to skin and cook the goat. Now they scorched their ire upon the receding summit of the Perfect Peak looming above the distant smudge of the Sour Marsh. A corona of filth occupied the space between the suns, directly over the top of Sektis Gandaw's mountain.

"Ain't exactly impressive for the end of the world," Shadrak said, coming alongside and following Shader's gaze. "What happened to the flashes and all that?"

Rhiannon hung back behind, using the black sword as a walking stick, taking the odd swipe at the tufts of curling long grass scattered about the balding earth. She'd eaten nothing, hadn't even joined in the blessing when Dave had divided up the meat. Shadrak hadn't either, but that was hardly a surprise.

"How much time do you think we've got?" Shader asked.

"Buggered if I know, but if that's all it is, I'd say we'll all have kicked the bucket long before we get unwove, or whatever the word is."

Shader squinted at the dust cloud, trying to gauge any growth. Maybe Shadrak had a point. It could take weeks, months even, for the miasma to spread as far as the eye could see, and a sight longer to encompass the whole of Aethir. Then there was Earth, the other planets, and the stars. Wasn't the cosmos virtually infinite? At least that's what was implied in the lore of the Ancients the Templum had made available.

Dave lurched into motion and came shambling back toward them, gesticulating at the sky. "Come, come. To Arx Gravis. The Unweaving is near."

"Maybe that's not it," Rhiannon said, lopping the head off a lone thistle.

Everyone looked at her as if she were mad. She gave a nonchalant shrug and let her head fall to one side.

"From where I'm standing, it looks like someone needs to clean the chimney."

Shader rolled his eyes and turned back to the trail. Dave nodded and took the lead once more.

"All I'm saying is that I can't see anything being unwoven," Rhiannon said. "Maybe he's just stoking the furnace or whatever. Didn't anyone bother to find out how it's meant to happen?"

Aristodeus had said something about it not being too late; something about these things taking time. That was about it, as far as Shader could recall.

"Well?" Rhiannon said. "Don't you think we should have found out what it is we're supposed to be stopping. I mean, what if he's just smoking a bloody great pipe?"

Shadrak chuckled and shook his head at Shader. "You certainly pick 'em, mate."

Shader inclined his head. Couldn't argue with that, not when you considered his choice of traveling companions: a woman who was getting harder to understand at every juncture; a fanatical loony who claimed to be the avatar of Nous, and Shadrak himself, an assassin who'd once stabbed him in the back, quite literally. You had to wonder what it was that had brought the albino on this mission, what had brought on his apparent change of heart. Shader had seen enough of conversion experiences to know that Shadrak didn't fit the bill. Whatever he was about, he was a test, that's for sure. Shader had come that close to killing him back at the camp. It was only Nous that had held him back; only allegiance to what he imagined Nous would want. He shook his head. There it was again, the age-old dilemma. He'd been taught it was all right to kill for Nous under certain circumstances, but he'd never been comfortable with the explanation. Guess that came from his father. Jarl had seen the incompatibility from the off, which was why he'd always been a disappointment to Shader's mother. At least he was honest. At least he was clear about the kind of man he was. Not at all like his son.

I need to be harder, he'd told Rhiannon. Shader didn't even know what he meant by that. Harder how? More ruthless? More certain? More dogmatic? More like Dave?

He watched the hunchback forging ahead as if he had no doubts about where they were heading, as if he were in his own backyard. How he could maintain such a pace was beyond Shader. He rolled over the ground in long easy strides which belied his crippled frame. Shadrak, with his short legs, had to jog to keep up, but he seemed utterly tireless, almost pleased for the exercise. Rhiannon continued to lag behind, trailing them like a heavy penance.

He shouldn't have let her come—not that she'd given him much of a choice. She seemed to need it, need something to make up for Sammy. And it wasn't just her brother she'd lost, either. Her parents, her self-respect, her... he almost wanted to say honor, but that didn't sit right. What did her honor have to do with what Gaston had done to her? He was the one who'd acted dishonorably, and that was putting it mildly.

Poor Gaston; the thought crept in of its own accord. Had he made up for it in some small way back at the templum? Had his self-sacrifice for the priests been enough? Could anything ever be enough? Shader shuddered and closed down that avenue of thought. Maybe that's what he'd meant by harder: He needed to keep things simpler. More black and white. And yet the lure of the golden thread wouldn't quite release its grip. Ludo had always said with Nous things were never that straight forward. They were simple in a way—unimaginably so—but you had to know how to look. "Head to heart," he used to say to a classroom full of blank looks. He'd thump his chest, as if that made it clear. "Head to heart."

Was it all about love, like Rhiannon had said? Something about the way Dave spoke, the way he condemned, seemed to say not. If the hunchback was who he said he was, if he really was the Voice of Nous, where was the love? Could be that it was about something else entirely, like good and evil. That's what Shader had always believed: do the former and avoid the latter. Maybe that's what he meant by being harder. Maybe it wasn't just about avoiding evil; maybe it was about rooting it out and excising it wherever he found it. Isn't that what surgeons did to gangrenous limbs? Cut away the bad so that the good might live?

If only it were that easy. If only he could rip from the Liber all that Blightey had contaminated it with. The problem was, Blightey wasn't that crude. There were no obviously evil passages in the Liber. If there were, they'd have been removed centuries ago. What the Liche Lord had done was much more subtle. He'd woven together strands from various traditions and sown the seeds of confusion. The early Templum fathers had fallen for the wisdom he'd offered: the wisdom of popular appeal.

But how to sort one thread from another, that was the problem. If love was indeed the answer, what kind of love? Or was it even simpler? Everyone knew good from evil, didn't they? It was ingrained in the soul. That's what Exemptus Silvanus had taught: identify the disease and eradicate it. Maybe he had a point. Call a spade a spade, and stop making excuses. It was the kind of thinking that said Gaston was damned, and that's that. You touch fire, it burns you. You only have yourself to blame. Two standards: one for Nous, the other for the Demiurgos. One thing or the other. You couldn't make it any clearer than Trajinot, when the Seventh Horse had ridden against the undead hordes of Verusia. Simple, sure, decisive. Not like Shader's fatal delay atop the Homestead. Dave had a case to be answered: that indecision may just have condemned the worlds.

The hunchback craned his neck and peered back at Shader. He pursed his twisted lips and gave a nod that seemed to say, "That's better." Shader returned the look through narrowed eyes. Some of the luminaries were supposed to be able to read your soul, so it was entirely possible that Dave had been following his thoughts. He wasn't so sure, though. The chill pricking its way up his spine told a different story. When Dave broke off and continued on ahead, Shader was back to wondering how you could tell one way or the other. Was Nous trying to get him back on track, or was it something altogether more sinister? A third option was that he was imagining things, growing paranoid, like poor old Hagalle. A look over his shoulder at Rhiannon lunging and slicing with the black sword as she walked made the possibility seem that much more real.

They picked up a weather-beaten road, its pavestones cracked and riddled with mosses and lichen, and followed it mile after mile.

So much of Aethir reminded Shader of Earth. The tufted plains rolled on and on but gradually gave way to lush prairies and gently sloping downland. Purple thistles grew in clusters, standing up out of fields of dandelions and seas of daisies. It was all just a bit too beautiful, too good to be true. If it hadn't been for the twin suns skittering erratically in the gray-blue skies, he could have been persuaded he was in Britannia, hiking across the hills surrounding his father's Friston estate.

"So much for infinite variety," Rhiannon said, obviously noticing him looking. "You'd at least expect another world to have different plants."

Shader was inclined to agree, but then a thought struck him. The Dreamers of Sahul believed Aethir sprang from the mind of a dog-headed ape, the Cynocephalus, who was somehow cocooned at its center. Before Aethir, he had drifted alone in the cosmos, abandoned by his mother, terrified of his father. The two worlds were linked by dreams, they said, but perhaps the dreams flowed both ways, and the Cynocephalus's mind had only given birth to what was already in the minds of men.

They stopped above a deep valley veined with branching streams and carpeted with bottle-green grass. To their right, smoke billowed from the summit of a distant volcano that was skirted by a sprawling forest. Far, far ahead and to the left of the valley, the ground climbed toward craggy knolls and, beyond them, mist-shrouded mountains.

Dave began fussing around, laying tinder for a fire, rummaging through his pack. He unwrapped the remains of the goat, and the stench of rot hit Shader like a fist. He covered his nose and mouth and fought down bile. Rhiannon cursed and reeled away from the others. A few seconds later, Shader heard her spilling her guts. Shadrak simply buried himself in his hood and approached Dave in a wide semicircle. Shader didn't need to get closer; he could see the meat writhing from where he crouched. The carcass was riddled with maggots, and yet it had only been a few hours since they'd slaughtered the animal.

"Knew there was something rotten about this world," Rhiannon said, stumbling back and wiping drool from her chin with her sleeve. "Shog, that's rank."

"Maybe it ain't the place," Shadrak said, circling Dave like an uneasy shadow.

"Maybe it's him."

Dave hastily wrapped the goat-flesh and hurled it down into the valley. "Nous has given, and Nous has taken away."

"Well, tell Nous, thanks a bunch," Rhiannon said to the sky. "Now what are we supposed to eat?"

Shader opened his mouth to chastise her, but her hard eyes told him not to bother. His stomach grumbled, but he gritted his teeth and offered it up as a sacrifice. Did Nous not provide for his children? Did he not sometimes feed his luminaries with berries brought by ravens?

"No point stopping, then," Shadrak said, kicking away Dave's kindling. "Come on, let's get this over with."

Shader's feet were raw inside his boots. Given the choice, he'd have flopped to the ground and rested, taken his boots off and soaked his feet in cool water. Ain only knew how many miles they'd covered, and there was no indication of how far there was to go.

Dave eyed him curiously and then pointed to the distant mountains. "The scarolite mines, and nestled in the earth below them, Arx Gravis. Two more days, and we will be there."

"Two days!" Rhiannon said. "You gotta be kidding. What, we supposed to ask Sektis Gandaw to put the end of the world on hold while we're traveling?"

Shader instinctively looked back the way they'd come, but the Perfect Peak had passed from sight. There was a smudge in the sky, but it was hard to tell if it was rain coming or the effusion spilling from the mountaintop.

"There is time still," Dave said. "Nous sees all things. He is with us."

"However far we go this way," Shader said, "we still have to go back." It had been troubling him for hours. They needed to get inside the Perfect Peak, yet here they were getting farther and farther from it.

"Have faith in the Voice of Nous. Have faith." Dave shouldered his pack and turned back to the trail.

They followed the ancient road across the top of the valley until it entered a sea of man-high grass flowing around clusters of hillocks, which on closer inspection turned out to be heaps of slick vegetation. The whole region stank of cabbage, and the swaying of the grass sometimes gave the illusion of the hillocks breathing, shuddering, slithering. Here and there, the road was entirely obscured by thick growths of vines and dark leafy plants. Silence settled over the group, and Shader felt Rhiannon edging closer to him. Dave seemed oblivious, but Shadrak took the lead, drew his pistol, and motioned for them to stop.

The wind whistled momentarily, and then even that died. Shader held his breath, and his heartbeat thudded so loud in his head that he felt certain its clangor could be heard all the way to Arx Gravis.

Rhiannon lightly touched the back of his hand. He scarcely dared turn his head to look at her, and when he did, her eyes were wide and unblinking.

What was it? What had Shadrak—

A flutter of wings, a gobbling screech, and then bang!

Shadrak blew smoke from the barrel of his weapon and re-holstered it. Some kind of wild turkey scuttled in a tight circle with blood spurting from where its head had once been. Its wings spread wide, shuddered, and then the thing dropped dead.

"Shog Nous," Shadrak said. "Found that one my—"

A gurgling roar erupted from behind. Thorny tendrils burst through Dave's chest and ripped him apart in a bloody spray. Shadrak was swatted head over heels by a sinuous limb before he could react. Shader spun, just as a glutinous mass of vegetation loomed over him, creepers and barbed lianas whipping about the living hillock that formed its body. A vine lashed about his wrist before he could draw the gladius, yanked him straight toward a cavernous maw. He yelled and closed his eyes as breath like overripe compost washed over him, and then he hit the ground hard, rolled, and came up on one knee.

The limbs all went slack together, and the central mass quivered then sloughed away to both sides, revealing a corpse-gray human head with milky eyes and a toothless mouth that drooled greenish slime.

Rhiannon stepped away from the monster, fighting the black blade clear of its putrid flesh. A shiver passed through her, and she lifted her eyes skyward, raising the sword above her head. Her whole body tensed, and she gasped with what could only have been pleasure. Then she looked down at the thing she had slain, and the color drained from her cheeks.

Shadrak approached, brushing crud from his cloak and aiming his pistol at the decomposing mess.

Shader found his feet and fought to hold in the contents of his stomach as he made a slow circle of the thing. There was at least part of a human within the vegetable shell: the grotesque head, a flayed ribcage, the tail end of a spine, all fused with plant matter, and here and there banded with steel or braided with copper wire.

"What the shog is it?" Rhiannon said, stumbling back.

Shader licked his lips and shook his head, but he couldn't speak.

"Ain't natural, that's what," Shadrak said. "Reeks of tech."

"Ancient-tech?" Shader asked. "Here on Aethir?"

"Gandaw," Shadrak said. "What the shog's he done here?"

It hardly seemed to matter. Whatever vile experiments the Technocrat had conducted on Aethir, they would all cease to exist along with everything else once the Unweaving took place. How could anyone be so warped as to create something like this? And then to want to un-make everything? Gandaw was a lunatic at best. They had to get to the dwarves, had to find a way to put a stop to this. And then Shader's hope sank into his guts as he remembered. Dave had been cut to ribbons before any of them knew what was happening. Who was going to guide them now?

"Praise Nous," the hunchback said, climbing awkwardly to his feet.

There wasn't a mark on him. Had Shader imagined it? Imagined the limbs tearing through his chest?

"What the shog?" Shadrak said, taking aim at Dave's head.

"You're dead," Rhiannon said, advancing on him with the black sword. "I saw it kill you."

Shader narrowed his eyes. What devilry was this? How could Dave be standing there as if nothing had happened?

"For Nous, all things are possible," Dave said, and then he looked directly at Shader. "You of all people should know. He is merciful, Deacon Shader. Trust in him. Have the faith that can move mountains."

Shader felt Shadrak watching him. Rhiannon, too. There was nothing he could say. He was as dumbfounded as they were.

"What do we do now?" Rhiannon said.

"Keep going," Shader muttered; and then more loudly, "We press on."

What other choice did they have?

"You're the boss," Shadrak said in a voice dripping with venom. He rammed his pistol back in its holster. "But the turkey's coming with us."

Rhiannon struggled to re-sheathe her sword and sling it over her back. "Amen to that, but I'm not stopping to eat here, got it?"

"For once," Shadrak said, snatching up the dead bird by its legs, "I couldn't shogging agree more."

STARTING AT THE BOTTOM AGAIN

"HERE, CATCH," BUCK said, flinging something shiny across the kitchen. Albert caught it on instinct, turned it over in his hand. "A potato peeler. Why, thanks."

Smoke wafted up from the brazier atop the clay oven. Whatever was sautéing *(if one could stretch the meaning of the word)* in the cast iron pan was charred black on the outside and no doubt completely raw in the center. There was a steaming cauldron beside it, bubbling and spitting with far too much vigor for the sludge congealing inside. The stench was hard to discern—lamb, perhaps, but with more than a hint of tarragon *(not right at all)* and so much turmeric, the water had turned yellow and ponged like an Ashantan brothel *(speaking from hearsay, rather than experience)*.

He coughed into his sleeve, wincing at the memory of poor old Papa's hanky.

Twisting plumes of dirty smoke were winding their way up the crumbling brick flue, but much of it still wafted out into the kitchen, probably because the four-legged carcass turning on the spit obscured the opening.

Albert had to admit, though, it was a curious contraption. The spit was connected to a vertical shaft coming down the flue. Where spit met shaft, there was some kind of primitive gear. The shaft seemed to rotate of its own accord, and as it did, the spit turned, too.

"What makes it turn?" he said out loud, stepping closer and waving steam out of his face so he could crane his neck for a better look.

"Don't know and don't care," Buck said, thrusting his hand into a pail of carrots and proceeding to butcher them with ham-fisted chops of a blunt knife. Made you wonder at the quality of the cuisine if Buck was the best sous-chef they could come up with. "Spuds are behind you."

"Spuds?" Albert turned to look. "Oh, potatoes."

"Not much for peeling, eh? Look, I'll swap you. Come here, I'll show you how to chop."

Oh, please, will you?

Albert made a show of awed fascination as the cretin hacked away at the carrots like he was quarrying granite.

"See," Buck said, handing Albert the knife and relieving him of the potato peeler. "It's all in the wrist."

Yes, I'm sure it is.

Albert took up position in front of the chopping board, set the knife down like a surgical implement, shrugged off his jacket and handed it to Buck, then delicately took the knife back up again.

"Don't be shy, now," Buck said. "Bit firmer. That's it, show it who's—"

Albert held up a finger for silence. "Now, Master Fargin, wait, watch, and learn.

Handshake grip on the knife, index finger to the top and side of the blade, tip down, and rolling chop. Forward and down, forward and down."

Buck was looking at him as if he were mad. "But you ain't cut nothing yet. It ain't like we got all day for your poncy shenanigans."

"Stage two," Albert said. "Make a claw of your subordinate hand…"

"Eh?"

"Claw on carrot." He started to demonstrate as he spoke. "Slice down the middle; take one half, keep the blade rolling—forward and back—feed it the carrot, root at the top. Chop away from the root, always away. Chop, chop, chop chop chop, chopa-chopa-chop-chop. Aaaand the other half." He made short work of that one, too. "Rinse and repeat. Cut down the center, chop away from the root…"

He could tell Buck was gawping, even without looking at him. Years of practice, two years sous-chefing for the great Maurice Mouflet—Ain rest his soul—then a decade as the most acclaimed head chef in Western Sahul, until that business with the *boeuf à la mode*. Oh, the shame of it. The ignominy. Still, a quick shedding of Mouflet's borrowed name, a hasty relocation to Sarum, and no one was any the wiser.

"What's your game?" Buck said, a wary look coming over him. "You been shitting me?"

"Not at all," Albert said. "You so shrewdly discerned my talents when we met. It is no lie that I was once the finest chef in… well, it doesn't matter where. Don't suppose you'll have heard of it. Suffice it to say that I have many skills with which to serve your ambitions, Master Fargin."

Buck bit down on his top lip and nodded. "That's all right, then. Just like we agreed. You scratch my back…"

And I'll ram a knife in yours, you cretinous moron.

"And I will most definitely scratch yours," Albert finished for him.

"Good. I was hoping you'd say that. See, I knew you was gonna turn out a dab hand in the kitchen. Just wanted to see for myself. Thing is, I'm expecting someone: Magwitch the Meddler. Should be here any minute to pick up the scarolite, you know, from the back of the wagon."

"How could I forget?" A day's ride cooped up with that flatulent, snoring, hairy midget was going to be difficult to forget. Rugbeard had slept most of the way, only ever waking to relieve himself and bemoan the lack of booze. Even now, Albert couldn't shake off the stench of his stale beer belches. "Is the dwarf still…"

Buck nodded toward the restaurant—if you could call it such. Dougan's Diner was more of a soup kitchen crossed with a spit-and-sawdust tavern. "Propping up the bar, as usual. Place'd go down the crapper if it wasn't for ol' Rugbeard. Silly bleedin' plonker: gets a soddin' fortune for setting up trade between the guild and the scarolite mines, then hands all the dosh back to us in return for drink."

"So, the guild runs this… establishment?"

Buck put a finger to the side of his nose and winked. "So, my ol' mate, you handle the veg, and I'll hang about by the back door till Magwitch comes, all righty?" He set the peeler on the chopping board and went to peer out the dirty window at the rear of the kitchen.

Albert sliced up the veg with practiced ease. It had been a long time since he'd performed such menial tasks, but he was actually finding it quite relaxing. "What about the tomatoes? What's Chef want done with them?"

Before Buck could answer, the back door opened, and a boy of maybe twelve or thirteen stepped through. He had your typical peasant face, broad and flat, crooked lower teeth, thick eyebrows that nearly met above his stubby nose, and a shock of greasy hair that had probably never seen a brush. His cheeks were ruddy, and he was out of breath.

"What the shog are you doing here?" Buck rolled his eyes in Albert's direction and gave an exasperated shrug.

"Look, Dad, I got the bread, like you said." The boy produced a stale-looking loaf from his coat pocket. "And some plonk." He pulled a bottle of wine from the other side.

Buck clipped him round the ear. "Ain't I told you not to come here?" He raised his hand for a more substantial blow, and the boy ducked down, shielding his head with the bread and wine. Buck seemed to remember Albert was watching and turned it into a playful ruffle of the boy's hair. He gave one of those irritating false laughs and snatched the wine. "Good boy, Nils. Good boy. See that, Albert? Chip of the ol' block. We'll make a guildsman out of him yet, eh?"

The boy shoved the bread back in his pocket and puffed out his pigeon chest. "So, I did good, Dad?"

"Yeah, son, you did fine. Now sod off. I got a customer coming."

A huge grin cut the boy's face in two. He punched the air with delight and then slipped out the way he'd come. As the door slammed shut, the connecting door to the restaurant burst open, and a fat slob in a stained apron and lopsided chef's hat lumbered through. Greasy ringlets curled down from beneath the hat, and the man's face was a piebald of angry sores and scaly flakes.

"Fargin, you little shit, I got Senator Rollingfield in tonight, so you better get a shogging move on with my..." His rheumy eyes alighted on the perfectly cubed carrots on the chopping board, then lifted to stare Albert straight in the face. "... veg. Who the shog's this?"

Albert gave his most sheepish smile, but he was already trying to process what he'd just heard. Why on earth would a senator eat in a dump like this? Silly he should need to ask, he realized. The guild. It was a gratifying thought. Despite the two suns and three moons, this place he'd landed in was just the same as home: ladder-climbing crooks and bent politicians. He mentally rubbed his hands together. He was going to like it here, once he'd done a bit of ladder-climbing of his own, of course.

"His name's Albert, Chef," Buck said, tearing himself away from the door, but still straining to see out the window. "He's our new kitchen-hand."

"Oh, so you're doing the hiring now, are you?" The chef snatched up a pan and flung it at Buck with such force it would have brained him, if he'd not squealed and ducked out of the way. "And why ain't you diced my tomatoes? What the shog do I pay you for, you useless clump of dung?"

"There's a deal going down, Chef." Buck jabbed a finger toward the back door. "Big Jake set it up. Put me in charge. That's why I brought Albert in. Make sure everything got done right. Thought you'd be pleased."

The chef advanced on him a step then whirled on Albert. "You worked kitchens afore?"

"The finest in all Gallia."

"Shog's that?"

"Near the Farfalls," Buck said, opening the backdoor and stepping outside.

Chef turned his nose up. "Real kitchens, I meant. We got an important guest tonight. You do good, and you'll do all right by me. Shog things up, though, and you'll be floating down the shogging canal, got it? Now peel some spuds."

Albert forced a smile so false it nearly split his cheeks. As he set about the potatoes, the chef stirred the muck bubbling in his cauldron and dipped his finger in to taste it. "You wanna get on in the world, fat boy, then pay close attention to everything I do."

Oh, I will, Albert thought, feigning interest while the chef slurped the gruel off his fingertip and rubbed his chin, as if considering how to improve its near perfect flavor.

"Course I got it," Buck's voice came from outside. "Here, have a gander."

"Know what a terrine is, fat boy?" Chef asked.

Nothing like that stinking pot of diarrhea.

"I don't, Chef," Albert said. "Is that one?"

"Leave the spuds," Chef said. "Idiot boy can do them when he's finished his business."

Buck could still be heard talking with someone outside. Haggling, by the sound of it, and he seemed to be coming off worst.

"Chop them tomatoes and sling 'em in. See, we don't need no fancy recipes here. It's all about taste and experience. Punters love it."

Buck's muffled voice grew momentarily louder. "Take it or leave it! See if I care."

Chef frowned toward the back door and shook his head.

"Solanum lycopersicum," Albert said, picking up a string of tomatoes on the vine.

"What?"

Buck's voice cut across their conversation once more. "All right, all right, I didn't mean it. Take the sodding scarolite, but the guild ain't gonna be happy. Daylight bleedin' robbery is what it is."

"Tomatoes," Albert said. "From the nightshade family." *With stems and leaves that contain enough tomatine to keep you on the loo for a week, or even kill you if you boil enough of them up into a tisane.* "Curative," he muttered, stroking a stem. "Quite the miracle plant."

"Just get on with the chopping, right?"

"Certainly, Chef." Albert set about dicing the tomatoes with his usual efficiency.

Chef's mouth dropped open. "You know a thing or two about cooking?"

"I've picked up a little from some of the greats," Albert said. "But no one who'd hold a candle to you, Chef…"

"Dougan," Chef said. "Faryll Dougan."

"Provincial cooks, all of them," Albert went on. "Whereas the standards of a big city like this are somewhat more exacting. They cater for pigs at the trough, whereas your illustrious customers—" He nodded toward the restaurant door. "—are veritable gourmands."

Dougan nodded and narrowed his eyes. "Aye, that's right. Still, you can learn from anyone, I always say. "We'll have to talk, you know, share secrets."

"Sounds fabulous," Albert said, chopping away with abandon.

Dougan watched on, scratching at his face, flakes drifting down like snow and settling on top of his broth.

"Nasty sores you've got there."

"What's it to you?"

"I know a remedy that can sort that out, if you're interested." Albert held up the discarded leafy greens from the tomatoes. "My little gift to you."

"Oh, aye?"

"Tea of tomato leaves and stems," Albert said. "Tastes awful, but you'll have the skin of a sixteen year-old-virgin in no time at all."

"I will?"

"Change your life."

Dougan smiled, a big, brown, stub-toothed smile. "You and me are gonna get along just fine, fat—what did Fargin say your name was again?"

"Albert."

"Well, Albert, you scratch my back…"

"Indeed," Albert said.

"So what you waiting for?" Dougan snapped. "Let's be having it, then."

Albert gathered up all the greens and looked about for a pan to boil them in. "Trust me, Chef, after this, you'll never be the same again."

The back door opened, and Buck came in holding up a drawstring purse. "Now that's how to do business," he said with a grin. "Put him in his place, I did. Wanker."

"Oh," Albert said. "So, he paid up, did he?"

"Oh yeah," Buck said. "Too bloody right, he did. Fleeced the shogger good an' proper."

"Well, 'spose you won't be peeling my spuds now you're a made man," Dougan said.

Buck's mouth was working, but no sounds came out. Finally, he thrust the purse into his pocket and grabbed the peeler. "Don't worry, I'll do the spuds, Chef. I ain't proud or nothing. And anyhow, we got appearances to keep up, ain't we? Don't wanna blow our cover just coz I'm minted."

"You keep telling yourself that, Fargin," Dougan said. "But you don't get them spuds ready for Rollingfield's dinner, the only appearance you'll be keeping up is that of a bloated water-corpse, got it?"

"Yeah, right."

Chef grabbed a hefty iron pan, and Buck instinctively threw his hands up.

"All right, I got it. I got it. Shog's sake, don't get no respect in this dump. Just you wait an' see," he mumbled. "Buck Fargin's going places; then you'll learn to treat me right." He picked up a potato and pressed the blade to it. "Shog!" he yelled, putting his finger to his mouth and sucking on it. "Bleedin' cut myself!"

ARX GRAVIS

"NOUS HAS SHOWN us the way," Dave said. He spread his arms to encompass the length and breadth of the ravine that split the earth like a jagged wound. "Faith has led us here, I tell you. Faith and the will of Ain."

Shader came alongside Rhiannon at the edge of the drop. Her robe was soiled from two days' hard trek across terrain as barren as any you'd find in Sahúl. The skin of her face was raw from exposure to the twin suns, and her mood seemed rawer still. She acknowledged him with a roll of her eyes, which Shader took to be meant for Dave.

Shadrak slid up on his other side, cloaked and hooded against the heat, pinkish eyes calculating, scanning the depths.

The sheer walls of the crevasse dropped away into a bottomless abyss, which made Shader reel with vertigo. The albino steadied him with a pallid hand.

"Your faith's so strong," Shadrak said to Dave, "why don't I just throw you in, see if you can fly?"

The hunchback scowled but then lifted his face to the heavens in rapture. "I have such faith. Should I step from the edge, Nous would send his angels to hold me aloft. What of you?" He glared at Shadrak and then swiveled his gaze to Shader. "Is your faith that strong, Keeper of the Sword of the Archon?"

Shader bristled at the implied accusation. It was starting to wear a bit thin, Dave's relentless condemnation. For the Voice of Nous, he certainly didn't seem to place much stock in forgiveness. Or the grace of silence, for that matter. He put a hand on Shadrak's shoulder and stared into the ravine. Nothing. Just a yawning gash of blackness. He braved the edge as long as he dared and then stepped back.

"Just as I thought," Dave said.

"Shut the shog up," Rhiannon said. "Never thought I'd say it, but I'm starting to see eye to eye with the midget."

Shader's heart felt like it had filled with ballast as the hunchback stepped out over the brink and placed his foot on thin air. At least that's what it looked like, until he blinked and refocused. Dave was standing upon a narrow ledge that sloped gently downward. It vanished with the slightest movement of the eyes, making it seem he was gliding as he started to descend without concern.

"After you," Rhiannon said, licking her lips and swaying slightly—unless that was Shader's vision.

"No, no. You go—"

"For shog's sake," Shadrak said. "Let's just get on with it, shall we?"

Shader touched his forehead and then curled his fingers around the prayer cord hanging from his belt.

"You all right?" Rhiannon asked, shifting the black sword to a more comfortable position on her back.

"Fine." Shader tested the ledge with the tip of his boot.

"Want me to go first?"

"Said I'm fine." He stepped down onto the path, grimacing against the wave of dizziness that roiled up from his guts. He clutched a protruding knob of rock, first with one hand, then with both.

"What's the hold up?" Shadrak said.

"Shut it, stumpy." Rhiannon was right behind Shader, and she gripped his arm reassuringly.

Dave was twenty yards ahead, where the path ended abruptly. He jumped down to the level below.

Shader held on tight to the wall and craned his neck to see. The path made a zigzagging descent, each level a steep decline that ended in a drop to the top of the section below. His head started to swim, and the beckoning abyss ballooned up at him. He flung himself back against the rock face, heart thudding in his ears.

"Don't look—" Rhiannon started.

"I know," Shader said through a mouthful of bile. "Not planning on doing it again."

A slender rope snaked down past Shader's shoulder. He glanced up to see Shadrak lower himself over the edge, rope wrapped around his body and trailing beneath his feet. It was impossible to see what he'd anchored it to above, but it held good when he kicked himself away from the wall and paid out the rope through gloved hands. Within moments, he'd rappelled past Dave and dropped from the end of the rope to the next level. Shader wanted to call out to him, tell him to wait, but if he'd opened his mouth, he'd have vomited. With a swift glance up at them, Shadrak swirled his cloak about him and was swallowed by the darkness.

"Perhaps you should—" Rhiannon said, indicating the rope.

"No." Shader sidestepped along the ledge, back flat against the wall. "Definitely not."

Scarcely daring to breathe, he inched his way to the end of the first level and froze. It was only a drop of a few feet, but it may as well have been a hundred. He imagined himself missing the path below and plunging for an eternity before splattering on the floor of the ravine.

Dave was looking up at him, arms folded across his chest. "If you had faith the size of a grain of sand, you could do this." He turned to face the chasm and leapt.

Shader gasped.

Dave hung in midair, twirling, as if suspended on a string. He threw his arms wide, raised his face to the sky, and lay back. "Do not turn from Nous, and he will give you great power. Great power."

Shader's fingers fell to the pommel of his gladius, drew warmth from it. He felt the ice of his fear melting away and leaned out over the edge just enough to watch Dave cartwheeling down a few more levels.

"Deacon?" Rhiannon pressed close to his side, the warmth of her body eclipsing that of the Archon's sword. "Is that... is that the work of Nous? Soror Agna said—"

"If that's what Nous can do for you, then I must be sorely lacking in faith."

Steeling himself, he turned to the end of the ledge and jumped. He landed lightly in a crouch, straightened up and offered his arms to Rhiannon, but she waved him away and made the drop by herself. After that, it grew easier, and Shader picked up his pace, descending one slanting platform, jumping, and continuing down the opposing diagonal, deeper and deeper into the ravine. Dave nodded his approval and continued up ahead, but there was no sign of Shadrak.

Flecks of green sparkled from the deep like emerald stars. As they drew nearer, Shader saw there were veins of malachite in the walls, which had grown as black as coal. Even with his newfound confidence, he doubted he could have continued without the unearthly light. He looked back to see Rhiannon scraping her feet along the path with great care.

Her robe picked up the phosphorescence, giving her the appearance of a sickly ghost. She forced a smile as she reached his side, but her eyes were searching the levels below.

"Where's the creep?"

"Which one?" Shader said, eyeing Dave, who was once more waiting on a ledge, glaring up at them.

"You know, the little shogger with the pink eyes and the sunny complexion. The poison dwarf."

Shader chuckled, in spite of himself. "Living up to his reputation. Doubt we'll see him unless he wants us to."

"Yeah, right after he sticks another knife in your back."

Shader winced at the recollected pain. The thought had crossed his mind, too, but it made no sense. "Why come all this way, then? Why bring us here? Did you see what he did atop the Homestead? Almost took out Sektis Gandaw." Which was a damned sight more than Shader had done.

"Self-preservation," Rhiannon said. "If Gandaw wins, we all go."

"I don't know," Shader said. "There's something about him. Something—"

"Treacherous? It's there, plain as day. Don't trust him, Deacon. I'll watch your back, but what if he stabs you in the front next time, as a mate?"

They continued downward in silence, Dave leading them as if the dark paces beneath the earth were his home. Enormous bearded faces began to line their way, carved out of the black rock. Chiseled crowns sat atop their heads, each engraved with flowing script.

"Is that Aeternam?" Rhiannon asked. "The Templum's reach must be longer than I thought." She gave a nervous laugh and clutched her elbows. Her eyes were wide, the pupils inky pits drinking in the scant light.

"Aeternam's been around a lot longer than the Templum," Shader said, recalling what Ludo had taught him. But that didn't change the fact that it was odd seeing it here, all the way on distant Aethir, wherever that actually was.

A network of crisscrossing walkways loomed up from the depths, spanning the chasm like a spider's web. Where each walkway touched the walls, it ended in a stone door. Beneath the web, a vast edifice of jutting spires, fluted columns, arches, and crenellated towers began to appear in the gloomy light given off by the malachite. It was a citadel, built upon untold levels that dropped away without end.

Dave was waiting for them on a broad avenue that led out above the city, where it met a dozen other walkways at a central hub comprised of granite arches, one for each path. He glared at them, eyes bright with frenzy. "Come. We must hurry. The dwarves are slow in discerning, and we have already wasted much time getting here."

He turned and headed toward the junction, moving so fast, despite his lurching gait, that Shader had to jog to keep up with him. Rhiannon cursed, bringing up the rear. Dave approached the hub without slowing. It was unnerving how well he knew where he was going. If this were faith, it was like nothing Shader had experienced.

The instant the hunchback passed through their walkway's arch, brilliant red light flooded the avenue. Shader blinked and shielded his eyes in time to see lumps of rock detaching themselves from the ravine walls beside each of the doors. Blurry gray shapes stomped out onto the crisscrossing avenues and swarmed toward the center. As his eyes adjusted to the light, he saw that they were not rocks, but people, short and thickset, just like Maldark. They carried weapons—axes, spears, swords, and crossbows, and they were armored in heavy scales that looked to be made of slate. Thick beards smothered gnomic faces, hanging to waist level or below, and close-set pebbly eyes glinted from beneath outcropping brows.

Shader glanced behind, where more dwarves flowed toward them, as if the stone of the walkway itself were morphing. There must have been a dozen approaching from the rear, armed to the teeth and grim as death. Hard eyes glared at him, eyes as merciless as the rock that spawned them, but when they were within arm's reach, the dwarves stopped.

Shader turned a slow circle. Easily more than a hundred of the gray figures surrounded the central hub. Rhiannon's hand went to the hilt of the sword on her back, but Shader took hold of her wrist.

"Wait," he whispered.

She wrinkled her nose at that and snatched her arm away, but she made no further moves.

There was no give in those hard faces. Perhaps on normal ground, Shader could have taken a few of them, but on a walkway above a bottomless drop, he doubted he'd last more than a heartbeat.

The grinding of stone and the squeal of hinges drew his attention. One of the doors swung open, and through it processed a column of white-robed dwarves. An ancient graybeard led the way, hitching his robe as he walked. He wore tattered sandals and woolen socks with holes in them. Shader counted twelve in all, tight-lipped and solemn-looking, all very much focused on the light spilling from the arch, and on Dave, who was wreathed in crimson flames, but appeared not to have noticed.

The ancient dwarf worked his mouth thoughtfully and said, "Well, I don't know... I mean, what do you suppose—?"

"Deception!" snapped a surly-looking dwarf behind him. "The alarm does not lie."

A ripple passed through the white-robes as they conferred.

"But it's never been tested," someone said.

"How many Abyssal demons have you welcomed into Arx Gravis, Councilor Garnil?" Surly said. "And you, Councilor Moary?"

"Well, I'm not sure... I mean to say... What if...?" Graybeard said.

"The philosopher warned us," Surly said. "Warned us the day would come. Kill them, I say. Let's be done with it."

Graybeard's eyes nearly popped out of his head. "Now, Councilor Grago, that's a bit hasty, don't you think?"

Clearly, he didn't, the way his gaze swept the surrounding soldiers, gauging their readiness.

Rhiannon leaned in close to Shader. "You might have turned into a pansy, but I'm not going down without a fight."

Shader's hand curled around the hilt of the gladius, accepted its calming warmth. His eyes roved about, looking for Shadrak.

"Don't bother," Rhiannon said. "Probably halfway back to the swamp by now."

A white-robe made his way to the front of the group. Bald patches were spattered about his scalp and beard, as if someone had yanked out handfuls of hair. He pressed a finger to his lips, commanding the attention of the other white-robes effortlessly. He closed one eye, studying Dave with the other. "That one, I'll grant you, does seem a tad malefic, Grago, but I'd say you're doing the others a disservice."

"Malefic," Rhiannon said to Shader. "I like that. Shame old stumpy buggered off. I'd love to hear what they call him."

Dave whirled on her, red flames licking at his skin. Shader felt a wave of nausea wash through his guts. The hunchback's face was writhing, in a state of constant flux—lengthening, shortening, broadening, narrowing.

"See," the one called Grago cried. "It works! The beast reveals itself."

Hair sprouted from Dave's chin then retracted. His nose went from hooked to straight, to bulbous, then stubby. His eyes were smoldering like burning coals, and when he opened his mouth, it was lined with jagged teeth, and a forked tongue flicked out.

"Save me." Dave's voice was a parched croak. He advanced on Shader in tortured, lumbering steps. "Pray to Nous for my deliverance. They have cursed me. Have you no faith?"

Shader reeled. He stared uncomprehendingly at the warping hunchback, but it was the words that paralyzed him. Not their content, but something more visceral. They were enfleshed, tangible, ripping into his mind with the force of barbed arrows.

Rhiannon backed into him as she drew the black sword, trying to get away from whatever Dave was becoming, but there was nowhere to go.

Dave's arms cracked and lengthened; his feet burst free of his sandals, lengthening into talons, and his sackcloth tunic burnt away, the flesh beneath bubbling with tar that cooled into necrotic scales. "She has... killed your... faith!"

The words punctured Shader's galloping heart, made him stagger, and then Dave sprang at Rhiannon, claws like sickles slashing at her throat.

The black sword came up to deflect them, but tentacles snaked from the demon's back and wrapped around her arms and legs. Rhiannon gasped, the veins on her neck popping out as she fought for breath.

Killed... faith... Killed... faith. Sweat dripped from beneath Shader's hat, trickled down his nose, seeped across his vision. In sudden shock, he wiped his eyes and stared at the red staining his fingers. *Killed... faith.* She had done it, yes. She was the one who'd kept him from Nous. He tried to pull the gladius free from its scabbard, but it was stuck—as if it refused him. He was about to give up, batter her with his fists, when there was a succession of hisses and thuds, and the demon's body was peppered with quarrels.

The tentacles whipped clear of Rhiannon, and she stumbled back. Dave snarled and thrashed about, but the dwarves kept a safe distance, reloaded, and fired again. Dave recoiled this way and that, turned on the white-robes and prepared to spring.

"You don't touch me, shogger!" Rhiannon screamed. "No one does!" Before her words had settled, she stepped in and clove him in two with the black sword. Each half of the demon slid away to the side, still writhing, still gibbering. Both halves of the face cackled and drooled, and then fleshy tendrils lashed one to the other and drew them together. All the way down the demon's body, the mortal wound was knitting itself closed. A gasp went up from the dwarves, and armored troops took up defensive positions in front of the white-robes.

Dave laughed and turned his hellish eyes on Rhiannon as he started to sit up. "Stupid whore," he said. "You are damned, and you don't even know it. You think to slay me with a brother of the Abyss?"

Rhiannon flung Callixus's sword from her, hands shaking, lips trembling.

The scales fell from Shader's eyes, and certainty flooded him as he gripped the gladius. This time, it leapt from the scabbard. "I abjure you, Father of Lies!" he yelled, and flung the sword with all his might.

Dave screamed and jerked backward, the pommel jutting from his gaping mouth, the blade exiting the back of his head in a spray of putrid gore. His demonic frame shook and shuddered then was consumed in a burst of golden radiance.

When Shader stooped to pick up the gladius, it was as if Dave had never been there.

A hushed silence had fallen over the dwarves. The only sound was the slap of Rhiannon's sandals as she approached the black sword. She drew her foot back to kick it from the walkway but then went rigid. She craned her neck, as if listening to something, screwed her face up tight, and then sucked in a sharp breath between her teeth. She glanced at Shader like a frightened child, eyes moist and ringed with darkness. Finally, she picked up the sword and returned it to its scabbard on her back.

"What happened to you?" Rhiannon asked, narrowing her eyes, lips curling into a sneer.

Shader bowed his head in shame. "It was the words… What he said."

"He was a shogging demon, for Ain's sake. What do you expect?"

Shader sighed and shuddered. "The Demiurgos always traps us with truth." They weren't his words, they were Ludo's. How many times had he heard them and not understood? He'd come so close. So close to doing the enemy's work for him. If it hadn't been for the gladius being jammed in its scabbard…

"Take them!" Grago shouted.

Confused looks passed among the soldiers. Some of them advanced a step until an older dwarf in a red cloak and horned helm raised a hand to still them. He turned to the white-robes and shrugged.

Graybeard coughed into his fist and then said, "You get above yourself, Councilor Grago. We have yet to—"

"Discuss? Debate? Deliberate?" Grago said, playing to the crowd. "Haven't we seen enough? The philosopher's arch revealed the threat. What will it take, councilors, for you to actually do something?"

"A demon was unveiled, Grago, and it was dispatched. But of these others, we can say very little."

"She has a black sword, Garnil!" Grago fumed. "You heard the demon; it's an instrument of the Abyss."

"Yes, well," Graybeard said, "but what if—"

"No!" Grago yelled. "No, no, no, Councilor Moary. No more 'what ifs'. Arx Gravis came this close—" He held his hands up to illustrate. "—this close to allowing the enemy inside. Have you forgotten what happened last time exceptions were made? I bet you haven't, Councilor Thumil, for it was your friend, after all, who nearly destroyed us."

The dwarf with the bald patches in his hair and beard bit down on his lip. He looked furious—or distressed to the point of despair.

"And let's not forget how he did it," Grago continued, whirling to take in all the assembled dwarves. "With a demonic axe not so different to the sword this woman carries!"

"Nevertheless…" Thumil said in a quiet voice. All eyes were immediately on him, and when he continued to speak, not a word was missed by the white-robes and the soldiers. He had their rapt attention. "…we are a cautious people, Grago, and the Deceiver is prowling round like a roaring lion, looking for someone to eat."

There were grunts of agreement from the white-robes, although Shader noticed a couple of them leaned their heads together and whispered something. The soldier in the red cloak folded his arms across his chest and nodded, and a palpable calm settled over his men.

"We cannot afford rash action, not when we've seen today how close he is to our gates."

"But we never act at all!" Grago said. "Uggghh!" He threw his hands in the air and then slumped, shaking his head.

"I propose that we lock them up until we've had time to confer," Thumil said. "All those in favor say 'aye.'"

There was a chorus of assent from the white-robes, and then they all turned their eyes on Grago.

"Aye," he grumbled. "If we must."

"Good," Moary said, scratching his beard. "Captain Stolhok, would you mind terribly relieving our guests of their weapons?"

"Counfilor!" the red-cloak barked with a pronounced lisp. He approached Shader first and reached for the gladius.

Shader tried to warn him. "I'd take it—"

"Ouch!" the captain cried and flapped his hand about, blowing on it like he'd just stuck it in a blazing fire.

"—by the scabbard," Shader finished. He re-sheathed the gladius, unfastened his sword-belt, and handed it over.

"What'f thif?" Stolhok lisped, fiddling with the belt.

"Prayer cord," Shader said.

Stolhok looked to Moary, who looked to Thumil, who nodded. The captain handed it back, and Shader put it in his coat pocket.

Rhiannon sullenly pulled the black sword from its sheath and held it out, but the captain blanched and recoiled. He nodded for her to lay it on the walkway and then gestured for soldiers to take hold of her and Shader.

"We'll leave it where it is," the captain explained to Moary. "Better'n bringing it inside the city."

Moary looked to the other white-robes for approval, and they nodded, all the while eyeing the sword warily.

Stone manacles were snapped over Shader's wrists, and then Rhiannon's, and they were bundled away through the arch and onto a walkway leading across the chasm. The stone door at the end ground its way upward, and Shader was shoved into a dank and musty corridor that felt like it hadn't seen the light of day for a very long time. There was some kind of dim illumination, barely enough to see by, emanating from the stone walls themselves.

He cast a final glance over his shoulder, hoping against hope for some sign that Shadrak was still out there, but all he found was Rhiannon glaring at him like she wanted to scratch his eyes out and throw him from a great height.

He was almost relieved when they were separated. Rhiannon was dragged through an open doorway opposite the one they'd entered by, but Shader was taken down a winding staircase and along a series of low passages that forced him to stoop. At one stage, the soldiers up front walked straight through a wall. Shader tensed as he was thrust after them, then he was on the other side, as if the wall wasn't there. He looked back at it, and sure enough, it appeared to be solid. He lifted his manacled hands to touch it and encountered cold hard stone. Soldiers grabbed his elbows and set him moving once more.

They marched him along a sloping tunnel that bored deeper and deeper into the ravine. After an age, they stopped outside an iron door with a grille set into it at head height for a dwarf. Three bolts, each as thick as a forearm, reinforced a sturdy lock. A soldier unhooked a ring of keys from his belt and noisily matched one to the lock, while another wrestled with the bolts. The door squeaked open on rusty hinges, and Shader was thrust inside. His heart sank when it clanged shut behind him. The key was turned to a trio of answering clicks, and then the bolts clunked into place, one after the other.

A dim, greenish glow suffused the walls, lending its sheen to the draping cobwebs and spiraling motes of dust.

It was a circular cell, empty, save for a shadowy shape seated on a stone bench. As Shader's eyes adjusted to the low light, he could see it was a dwarf, powerfully muscled, wrists manacled to the bench. A black great helm covered his head, and chainmail hung down to his knees. His britches and boots were spattered with something dark that may have been blood, and he was coated with so much dust that he could have been mistaken for a statue. He was certainly as still as one, frozen in the rigidity of death.

The air was stale and musty, just like that in the domed tomb Shader and Barek had discovered in Fenrir Forest. His fingers automatically touched his forehead in memory of poor Osric, banished to the Void by a mawg shaman. Maybe this is what it had been like for him, all those centuries of captivity at the hands of Dr. Cadman. Shader fought to calm his pattering heart, told himself this was only temporary, until the dwarves had discussed what to do.

The brooding presence on the bench told another story, though. How long had he been left there before he finally died? And then the thought struck Shader: What if he wasn't dead? There was no stench, no sign of rot. A prickling sensation fanned out beneath his skin. What if this wasn't so different to what Osric said had happened to the Elect?

Shader edged nearer and reached out with a finger, gently touched an exposed forearm. Cold. Lifeless. He checked the fingernails for blueness, but there was none, leaned in close to the helm and listened for breathing, but all he heard was his own reflected back at him.

It had the feeling of wrongness, of some dark magic he couldn't explain.

He stepped back and stared at the eye-slit of the great helm. Green flecks glistened on the black casing, which appeared to be fused with the skin of the dwarf's neck. Was it for protection in battle, or part of his imprisonment? Why would they need to chain him in such an impregnable cell, particularly when he was virtually fossilized? Even in such a docile state, the dwarf radiated immense strength.

Shader took another step back. Maybe this was some kind of demon, even worse than Dave. Perhaps they hadn't been able to kill it and could only bind it and lock it away in the bowels of the city. That didn't bode well for Shader, though. What if they planned on doing the same with him, leaving him here for all eternity, or until the next victim was shoved in the cell and found his petrified body, or more than likely, his skeletal remains?

A great pit opened up in his stomach, and his hope plunged into it. He groaned and whirled about, vainly seeking a window, a vent, the merest crack. A desperate cry began to well up within him, and he opened his mouth to let it out but then slapped himself in the face. He couldn't give in to panic. One howl like that would be an admission of despair, and that would help no one.

He lowered himself to the cold floor and pulled the prayer cord from his pocket. As he picked away at the lesser mysteries, he sent up mental pleas to Nous. He ran through the litany of holy names in the vague hope that one of them might trigger a miracle, all the while knowing there was as much chance of Sektis Gandaw converting to religion and confessing his sins.

There wasn't the time for this. Shader bit down on his lip to stop from shouting out his frustration. Who was going to stop the Unweaving if he was shut up down here? Didn't the dwarves realize how close the end of all things was? Did they even care? He grimaced as he unraveled one of the knots and started on the next, steering his mind back to the litany: *Nous, glory of Ain, save your servant. Nous, light of the world, have mercy on me. Nous, eternal word, comfort me.* He was ripping at the threads on the prayer cord, whispering the words now against the back of his teeth. "Nous, scourge of demons, rescue me." His face was on fire with pent-up rage and frustration; his shoulders bunched up around his ears. "Nous, lord of the living,"—and then the dam burst—*"Hear my prayer!"*

The cry reverberated around the cell until it lost itself in the cobwebs, only to be replaced by the silence of the grave.

But then there was a clink, and Shader spun round to face the figure on the bench.

The dwarf's fingers splayed open and snapped shut into fists, and this time there was a fierce rattle as the chains clashed against the stone. A low growl echoed from within the great helm, and veins popped up along the swollen thews of his arms. He half-stood, chains pulled taut, his stocky frame shaking with effort. With a demented roar, he wrenched his arms together, and the bolts securing the chains to the bench sheared.

Shader gasped and edged away, but the black helm swiveled in his direction. Thrashing from side to side, chains whipping about him in a clashing fury, the dwarf bellowed a bloodcurdling battle cry and lumbered toward him.

NOT A GOD

BLOODY AMATEURS, SHADRAK thought, clinging like a sloth from one of the struts underpinning the walkway. How the Abyss were they planning to save the world by handing themselves over to a bunch of stunty, beardy… He stopped himself; felt the sting of old wounds. Bit close for comfort, that. How often had he been called the same, or worse?

Hooking his legs through one of the crossbeams, he let go with his hands and eased himself back until he was hanging upside down.

The city below was arranged in descending tiers, like badly stacked plates. Broad, spiraling avenues and corkscrewing steps spanned the spaces between levels all the way down to a glimmering lake in the bed of the chasm. Ant-like figures shuffled along roads and cobbled pavements, and here and there laden carts trundled behind beasts that may have been goats. An intricate system of canals carved up the lower city into perfect geometric shapes, while above, stone barges drifted along aqueducts that served the loading bays of squat warehouses. On the fringes, colonnaded arcades merged seamlessly with the ravine walls, linked to the central sprawl of buildings by granite viaducts and bridges suspended from cables of wound steel. Smoke puffed from chimneys, wafting toward the sides of the ravine, where it was sucked into vents hungry as a pituri smoker's lungs. An immense tower rose through the center of the city's layers like the hub of a wheel. It had countless archways, and windows of stained glass, and its patinated bronze cap rose to within a hundred feet of Shadrak's upended head.

He hung lazily, lapping up the topsy-turvy view, enjoying the calm that washed over him. That was the way it was with heights for him; always had been. Prob'ly why he'd made such a good cat burglar in his youth. All good experience that had transferred well into the killing trade. Always made him laugh how the rich bastards, secure at the top of their impregnable towers, crapped their britches when they woke up to find him at the foot of their beds. Most of 'em blustered or denied what was happening, right up until their brains were splattered across the headboard. He almost smiled at the memories. There was a time when he'd loved the job. Except on the rare occasions the guild stuck its nose in, he worked alone, and that meant he could do things his way. The right way. There was something extremely satisfying about a murder well done. And then that whole thing with Bovis Rayn had happened, and Kadee had worked her way through the fault lines cracking open the husk of his conscience. He didn't like it one bit. Didn't like the confusion. Now, more than ever, he needed certainty. Everything else was just a distraction that would likely get him killed.

But what to do next, that was the issue. If he'd been his own man, like he'd been back in Sarum, he'd have lowered himself to the central tower and shuftied around for sellable pickings, coz you could bet your bottom copper people who could build a city like Arx Gravis had stuff worth nicking.

Problem was, he weren't his own man no more, not since his pact with the Archon. Granted, he'd had no choice, not if he'd wanted to live, and not if Kadee had anything to do with it. Then there was the small matter of a lack of rope; what he'd brought with him was still staked to the hard earth above the ravine, and while he might've had a love of heights, he weren't stupid enough to chance the jump.

No, best thing for it was to get going. He swung his torso up and took hold of the struts so he could crawl back to the central hub and the archway that had exposed Dave for what he was. It had been amusing at the time. Left to his own devices, Shadrak would've watched the fun and then buggered off and abandoned Shader and the bitch to their fates, but a nagging voice at the back of his mind kept warning him not to piss the Archon off again.

The whole thing was starting to grate. Hadn't he done his part by bringing Shader to Aethir? He couldn't be expected to babysit him as well. It weren't like it was his fault the moron had gone and got himself caught. That was it, far as Shadrak was concerned. Quest over, and it weren't him that'd screwed up. If the Archon didn't like it, he could go shog himself.

He chinned up to the edge of the walkway, and when he was sure it was clear, clambered onto it.

The archway that had burned red when Dave enter it was dull and lifeless now, and Shadrak hunkered down beneath it, wrapping his cloak about him like a shadow in case there were still dwarves watching, concealed against the walls. He caught sight of Rhiannon's black sword lying on the stone. Thing like that would fetch a shitload of denarii in certain parts of Sarum. He started toward it, but then light exploded inside his skull, and he reeled away. He bit his lip to keep from screaming. Felt like a crown of jagged glass had been forced down tight over his head.

"All right, all right," Shadrak yelled, then clamped his jaw shut and whispered through gritted teeth. "Shog's sake, what am I s'posed to do? Weren't my bloody idea to come here. If you ask me, you'd be better off using your hocus-pocus to get me inside Gandaw's mountain. Then we'll see how almighty he really is."

He could feel a presence before him, but the white fire behind his eyes made it impossible to see.

"You lack the purity of heart," the Archon said.

"Yeah, right, and Shader has it?"

The light faded, and Shadrak blinked the Archon into focus. He was ghost-like, translucent, as if he were midway between worlds.

"I am beginning to wish I hadn't agreed to this approach," the Archon said. "But it is too late to find another way."

"Your choice, your problem," Shadrak said.

The Archon studied his face for a long while and then said, "Shader was not my choice."

"Oh?"

Smoke plumed from beneath the Archon's cowl, and when he raised his ivory hands, the heat of a furnace rolled off them. "I do not enjoy inflicting pain, Shadrak, but time is not with us."

Shadrak's hand went to his pistol grip, for all the good it would do. "What I don't get is this purity shit. I don't need to be shogging holy to put a bullet through Gandaw's skull. Like I said, get me to the mountain, and I'll take care of the rest."

The Archon shook his head. "If it were just the Technocrat, then I might agree with you, but he has harnessed the power of..." He paused, as if what he was saying pained him.

Shadrak grew suddenly alert, watching for any sign of weakness.

"He has harnessed the power of my sister. You cannot stand against her."

"Family, eh? And you're leaving this to a loser like Shader?"

"I can only—"

"Yeah, yeah, act through idiots like me who are stupid enough to do your dirty work for you. What the shog's up with you god types?"

"I am a servant, not a god."

Well that was good to hear. Gods couldn't be killed. At least that's the way Kadee's people told it. Them and the bloody Nousians, who said their god was put to death only to come back to life again. Shadrak had an answer for that: steady supply of bullets, and he'd keep the shogger dying and resurrecting all day. Sooner or later, Nous'd grow tired of it and stay shogging dead.

"So, let me get this straight," Shadrak said. "You're the servant of Nous All Bleedin' Mighty, the Lord of Shogging Love, and yet you're gonna fry my brains if I don't do what you say, right?"

Light flickered at the edges of the Archon's hood. "Nous is not who you think. Indeed, even the name is a fabrication of the Liche Lord's. He is as far above me as I am you."

Shadrak scoffed. "You got a problem with my height?"

The sun burning within the Archon's cowl flared red, and Shadrak backed away from its scorching heat.

"OK, I'm going," he said. "Rescue Shader, then what? Ask the dwarves nicely to let us use their tunnels? Maybe they'll spare a bite to eat, while they're at it. And if I'm honest, I could use a trip to the crapper."

"They will take no part in this," the Archon said. "Bad advice brought you here."

"And you didn't think to say something?" Shadrak knew that pointy-eared elf couldn't be trusted, nor the sodding hunchback.

"You must find a way, Shadrak. Either to persuade the dwarves, or to find some other means to take the mountain."

"Give us a second and I'll rustle up an army," Shadrak said, half-expecting a backlash for the sarcasm.

"That might work. Keep it in mind. Now hurry."

Dust motes circled the Archon's feet, wound their way toward his cowled head, spiraling faster and faster until he was consumed by a sparkling tornado, which then puffed out of existence.

Shadrak sprinted along the walkway, almost wishing someone would spot him so he could do to them what he couldn't to the Archon.

The door the dwarves had taken Shader and Rhiannon through was hermetically sealed, only a hairline crack revealing its existence. He ran his hands over the surface, looking for hidden panels, some sort of mechanism to open the thing. Nothing. Not even a chip or a crack.

"Great," he muttered up at the twin suns. "What am I s'posed to do now, knock? Hello? A little divine intervention, if it ain't too much to ask." His only answer was the fleeting shadows of buzzards circling overhead.

He unrolled his tool pack, selected the thinnest pick he had, and ran it around the crack of the door. It struck something about halfway up on the left-hand side, but whatever it was had no give in it and felt far too large to be the sort of mechanism he could trip. He put his eye to the crack but couldn't see a thing. Perhaps with a match or a lantern—but of course he had neither. He drummed his fingers against the door while he chewed the problem over. A hammer and chisel might've done the trick, if he'd had them, but then again, the noise would've brought every dwarf in the city running. Same with explosives. He fiddled with a globe in one of his belt pouches, considered it anyway, but then decided it wouldn't do nothing 'cept char the stone. Rate he was going, it'd be quicker to wait for a thousand years of rainfall to whittle away the door one drop at a time. True to bloody form, though, there weren't a single sodding cloud in the sky.

He rolled up the pack and put it away. They must've done something to open it: a signal, a password, a combination of knocks. If only he'd paid more attention. That had certainly been his intention, but then his focus had shifted onto Shader, expecting him to do something, put up some semblance of a fight, rather than being led meekly away.

"Shog it." Shadrak snapped, thumping the door and wincing at the pain. "That's it," he told the heavens. "Hit me with your best shot, coz I've had it about up to—"

There was a loud clunk, followed by the grinding of stone upon stone as the crack at the bottom widened, and the door started to slide upward. Shadrak whirled out of the way just in time, flattening his back against the wall.

A dwarf stepped out—or rather, parts of a dwarf did. Shadrak blinked and looked again. He could see the profile of a nose and beard, forearms and hands, and hints of legs terminating in leather boots. What was it, some kind of wraith, like Callixus? And then he noticed the air around the bits of the dwarf he could see rippling ever so slightly, and he realized what it was. The dwarf was wearing a hooded cloak that merged perfectly with the surroundings—first the darkness of the interior, but as he emerged onto the walkway, his cloak blended with the ocher of the ravine wall.

Shadrak slipped a dagger free from his baldric and waited half a dozen heartbeats, but there was no sound from within. Chances were, this dwarf was alone, but what was he about? After standing with hands on hips, taking in the view—or perhaps he was scanning for more intruders—the dwarf turned back to face the doorway, at the same time holding up two rectangular pieces of stone the length of a finger and snapping them together. The door started to descend, and the dwarf gasped as Shadrak sprang and slit his throat from ear to ear. The dwarf's hands flew to his neck, and his lips trembled. Blood ran through his fingers, pattered on the walkway, and then his knees buckled, and he fell over backwards, smacking his head on the stone.

Shadrak wiped the blade on the dwarf's tunic and was about to unfasten the cloak when he remembered the door. *Shog*, it was six inches from closing. He cursed and gritted his teeth, but then his eyes fell on the length of stone the dwarf held in his white knuckled-hand. Snatching it up, he pulled the two segments apart, and the door started to rise again. He then quickly removed his cloak and swapped it for the dwarf's. Pulling the camouflaging material around him and tugging down the hood.

He took a step toward the doorway, but a niggling thread tugged at his conscience, made him stoop to cover the corpse with his discarded cloak. He sighed and shook his head.

"Oh, Kadee," he muttered under his breath. "Kadee, Kadee, what are you doing to me?" She was more trouble in death than in life, and yet, was she truly dead, if she could stand alongside the Archon and speak with him? He'd never been one to believe in the afterlife and all that, but facts was facts. He couldn't deny her presence, unless, of course, he was losing it. Maybe if she was some other place, somewhere better, he could... He shut the thought down; cursed himself for a prat. No point living in false hope. That sort of thing'd get him killed sooner than he'd like. If there was any truth to it, he'd know when the time came, when they put him six feet under. Only thing he had to say on the matter was she'd better be all right, coz if she weren't, he might just have to make a premature visit, set things straight.

He slipped inside the entrance then snapped the stones together and waited for the door to grind shut.

There was a corridor bearing left and right, and an open doorway straight ahead. It was mostly dark, but the walls were splashed with wan light that seemed to come from the stone itself.

Old habits die hard, and so even with the protection of the cloak, Shadrak stuck to the shadows and moved silently on the balls of his feet through the open doorway. He flattened himself against a wall as he heard muffled footfalls and the low rumble of voices approaching. Four red-cloaked dwarves passed him by without a glance, deep in conversation about demons, the Demiurgos, and the sins of the Fallen.

"Bringing 'em into the city'll curse us, I tell you," one in a bronze helm and scaled armor said. "Should've killed 'em when we had the chance, like we should've done with you know who."

A scrawny ginger-beard with an awkward gait made a show of mock horror. "Oh, you mean the Nameless Dwarf."

"Not funny, Gline. Not shogging funny at all," said an older dwarf, whose face was crisscrossed with scars.

"Yeah, show some respect, Gline," Bronze Helm said. "Lot of people died to that bastard."

"Stupid shogging name, anyway," Gline said.

"Ain't a name, if you ask me," Scar-Face said. "But that's about what he deserves."

"Way I heard it, Thumil gave it to him," Bronze Helm said.

"S'right, Kal," the fourth said between wheezes and puffs. He was as wide as he was tall, purple-faced, and with a nose so bulbous it looked set to burst like an overripe melon. "Way them two was up each other's arses, wouldn't surprise me if he was in on it."

"Nah," said Scar-Face. "Not Thumil, he's too bloody holy."

"Ah, shog it all." Fatso gave a long drawn-out sigh. "Shog it all to hell. No point fretting when there ain't a thing to be done 'cept wait on the council to work things out, and we all know how long that'll take. C'mon, let's pay it no more heed. A beer and a bun'll see us right, lads."

Gline clapped him on the back. "Couldn't agree more, Trogweed. Couldn't agree more."

Shadrak tensed, expecting them to exit through the door to the walkway and discover the body he'd left under his cloak. Much to his relief, the door never opened, and the dwarves' footfalls grew steadily more distant, their voices more muffled, until all he could hear was the sound of his own breathing.

This was not how he liked to work. Not at all. Too much left to chance, and it was only due to the luck of finding the camouflage cloak he'd gone undetected. The Shadrak the Unseen who was so feared in Sarum employed a raft of tricks in order to pass unnoticed—distraction, misdirection, hunkering down in places too small for a regular assassin; but now he truly was unseen, even when he was right under the noses of his enemies. He almost wished he had someone to thank for that—providence or whatever the Nousians credited their coincidences to. He scoffed at the idea and then shrugged. Why not? Maybe someone was watching over him. Maybe Kadee. After all, this is what she would have wanted: to see him doing the will of the Archon, for no doubt it aided the Archon's beleaguered sister, Eingana, the supreme goddess of the Dreamers.

Shadrak took a razor star from his baldric and continued in the direction the dwarves had just come from. The passageway dropped down three stone steps after twenty feet and did the same after the next twenty. He passed a number of tributary corridors but kept to the main artery. Gradually, the illumination from the walls increased, until up ahead it was as bright as day. A lone dwarf stood guard outside an iron door on the right, and opposite him there was a metal panel set head-height for Shadrak, and eye-level for a dwarf.

Shadrak slowed to a creep on the tips of his toes, drawing his arms inside the cloak and ducking his head so that the hood obscured his face.

The dwarf remained stock-still, but his eyes began to flick this way and that. Shadrak paused, wondering if he'd been seen, but then the dwarf bent down and tugged a flask from his boot, took a swig, and replaced it.

Shadrak closed the gap between them, quiet as a mouse, and when he was within touching distance, he let the razor star clatter to the floor. The dwarf started and then bent to get a good look at it, and in that instant, Shadrak grabbed him by the head and gave a short, sharp twist. There was an answering crack, and then he lowered the body to a sitting position beside the door. He scooped up the razor star and took a closer look at the panel.

It seemed to be a cupboard of sorts, and much to his satisfaction, it had a keyhole. He unfurled his tool pack and selected a curved pick, fiddled about in the lock until it clicked, then pried the panel open.

"Well that was easy," he muttered, grinning that he'd struck gold first time.

Shader's gladius lay within, which told him the iron door opposite must be the cell they were holding him in. He reached out and took hold of the pommel, and he yelped, snatching back his hand as if he'd touched a hot stove. "Shit, shog, and bollocks!" he said, skipping back and almost tripping over the dead dwarf.

He approached the sword again, this time with more caution, and took hold of it by the scabbard. Breathing a sigh of relief that he didn't receive a second scorching, he slung the sword-belt over his shoulder and turned his attention to the iron door.

It was your typical cell door: narrow observation grate and a huge rusty lock. Predictably, the guard had the key on his belt, and the door gave a resounding clunk when he inserted it and turned.

"You can thank me when we get out of here," he said, throwing back his cloak and slipping into the cell, pulling the door shut behind him. "Oh, shog, it's you."

"Miracles never cease," Rhiannon said. She was seated on a stone bench, manacled hands hanging between her knees. "Thought you'd be halfway back to the marsh by now, looking for your plane ship."

"Chance'd be a fine thing," Shadrak said, kneeling so he could examine the manacles. Stone, which was different. Lock looked pretty simple, though. He took a needle from his tool pack and inserted it into the tiny keyhole. A wiggle and a click, and it snapped open. "I was hoping to find Shader." He made short work of the second manacle, and Rhiannon let them drop to the floor, rubbing her wrists.

"Me too," she said, "rather than the milksop wearing his clothes."

"I was gonna ask about that," Shadrak said.

"Yeah, well don't." She wiped her face, flicked the sweat from her fingers.

Shadrak frowned at her as he stood. She was drenched, beads of moisture standing out on her forehead like a circlet of diamonds. He stepped away.

"Don't worry, it's not catching," Rhiannon said. Her eyes fell on Shader's gladius hanging from Shadrak's shoulder. "Where's mine?" She surged to her feet. "You got it, didn't you?"

"Still on the walkway," Shadrak said. "I got distracted."

"You got what? What are you, a shogging imbecile?" Rhiannon started for the door.

"It ain't going nowhere," Shadrak said. "The dwarves are scared shitless of it. First, we get Shader, then we get the sword."

"Wrong," Rhiannon said. "Sword first, then Shader."

"Shader."

"Sword, you stunted shogger, or do I have to beat the crap out of you again?"

That was it. Shadrak had had enough of the bitch. He whipped out two knives and stepped in fast. Rhiannon gasped and backed up against the door.

"What was that?" she asked, pressing her ear to the door and holding up a hand.

"Shog off," Shadrak said. "Think that's gonna work on me?"

"Quiet," she said. "I can hear footsteps."

Shadrak listened. She was right. Someone was coming down the corridor.

"Hey, Grik," a voice said. "Grik, wake up. I've got you some nosh. Drosa from Pigs in Pastry sends her regards. Got you some ale, too. Well, it's Ironbelly's, but it's better'n nothing."

Shadrak slipped his daggers back in the baldric and ushered Rhiannon away from the door. He pushed it open a crack. A scraggly-haired red-cloak was leaning over the dead dwarf, proffering a pie and a frothing flagon.

"Grik? Come on, mate, no sleeping on the job. Grik? Oh, my shogging—"

Shadrak darted through the opening and yanked him inside the cell by his beard. The flagon clattered to the floor, and the bread landed in the dead dwarf's lap.

"Shut the door," he told Rhiannon.

"Don't hurt me, don't hurt me," the dwarf squealed. "I ain't done nothing. I was just bringing grub for... Poor ol' Grik." He started to sob.

Shadrak slammed him up against the door and wedged an elbow into his windpipe. "The other prisoner—the man with the hat and the long coat—where'd you take him?"

"I didn't take him nowhere. Honest, I didn't."

"Then let me rephrase," Shadrak said, taking out a punch dagger and holding the tip a hair's breadth from the dwarf's eyeball. "Tell me where he is."

"Your guess is as good as mine," the dwarf stammered. "I just got here."

"But you know this place, know where prisoners are held?"

"Yeah, but—"

Shadrak rammed his knee into the dwarf's groin, causing him to double up and spit his eye on the blade. His scream was so shrill it made Shadrak want to smack him in the teeth next. Blood streamed from the dwarf's skewered eye, drenching his beard.

"Stop it," Rhiannon said.

"You wanna find lover boy?"

"Shog you. Leave him alone. He doesn't know anything."

The dwarf whimpered and fell to his knees, clutching at his ruined eye. "Please. Please!"

Was it the dwarf whining, or Kadee? Shadrak shook his head. Right now, he couldn't give a shog who it was. She weren't gonna do this to him, no matter how much he missed her. He was an assassin, not a Dreamer. Eingana's scaly hide, she'd make him a shogging Nousian next.

"Tell me where they took him," Shadrak insisted. His blood was up more'n it should've been. Had been ever since the Archon stopped him leaving, but he'd kept a lid on it till now. Sooner they got Shader out, sooner they could get this shogging Gandaw business sorted, and then he was off.

"I don't know!" the dwarf cried.

Shadrak kicked him in the head, and the dwarf toppled over sideways.

"Then guess."

He hunted about in his tool pack for a scalpel and held it up as he crouched down beside his shaking victim.

"Go on. I'll give you three chances, and I'll know if you're making it up."

THE NAMELESS DWARF

SHADER SWAYED OUT of the way of a clumsy haymaker and circled behind the dwarf. A grunt echoed from within the black helm, which swiveled side to side, hunting for him. If he'd had a weapon, he knew he'd be wise to strike now. The dwarf seemed drowsy, rusty from so much time chained to the bench. Given a few more moments, though, he might well warm up, and then there was no telling what he could do. The problem was, Shader had nothing, save for the chain linking his wrists together, but he could hardly strangle an enemy whose head and neck were encased in metal—if indeed it was metal; it had more the texture of stone. And then, of course, there was the morality of striking from behi—

The dwarf shuffled round to face him, inclining the helm to one side, gauging his every move. Boulder-like shoulders rolled backward, then he brought his hands together in a thunderous clap, while stomping his boots on the stone floor. He shook his helmed head vigorously, grunted, growled… then sighed and squatted down.

Shader retreated, weaving to the right, trying to remove himself from the helm's narrow field of vision. This time, however, the dwarf tracked him with ease, rising from his squat to stand lightly on the balls of his feet.

Shader darted back the other way, but the dwarf exploded after him with unimaginable speed. He turned his head away just in time, and the dwarf's fist struck the wall. Blood sprayed from ruptured knuckles, but he didn't seem to notice. Shader twisted aside from an uppercut that would have shattered his jaw and stumbled toward the door. The dwarf closed down the space between them like a seasoned boxer, and there was nowhere left to run. Without a sword, Shader knew he didn't stand a chance. He'd never faced anyone so fast—save maybe for Bardol Shin en route to Pardes; but Shin hadn't had the dwarf's prodigious strength to back up his speed. Shader was fast himself, and he could probably duck and dive a few more blows, but sooner or later he'd tire, which was something he couldn't imagine happening to the stocky powerhouse glaring up at him through the narrowest of slits.

Glaring, but not attacking.

"Do I know you, laddie?" the dwarf asked.

"I—"

"Thought you were that shogging philosopher, but he's a crusty bald bastard, and you must be half his age with ten times his hair. Funny thing, that. Could've sworn I heard his voice. Must've been dreaming."

Shader tried to will his body to relax, but his eyes roved of their own accord to the dwarf's blood-speckled arms. "I am Deacon Shader, a knight from—"

"Never heard of him. Gods of Arnoch if I can remember the name of the bloke I was swinging for, but I'm sorry I mistook you for him. Can't see shog out of this helm, and what with that and the daze of sleep, dwarf's bound to make mistakes. Am I forgiven, laddie?"

"Of course," Shader said, hoping he didn't sound as relieved as he felt. "This philosopher you mentioned, his name wouldn't happen to be Aristodeus, now, would it?"

The dwarf rattled the chains dangling from his wrists. "Aye, that's the shogger. Tricked me, he did. Tricked me and trapped me." His hands went to the sides of the great helm. "Feel different, though, since waking up. I feel... less angry. Less scared."

Shader couldn't imagine him being scared of anything, and if this was him being less angry, he'd hate to see what he was like before. He supposed the blood spatters on his hauberk, boots, and arms offered some indication.

"It was Aristodeus who put you here?" Shader asked.

"Aye. Him and the council. Shoggers would've killed me if they'd had their way. Can't say I blame them, either. After what I'd done..." He lowered his head, and his voice choked away.

So, Aristodeus had a foothold on Aethir. Was there nowhere free from his influence? "I know him," Shader said.

The dwarf looked up, his eyes invisible, inscrutable, through the blackness of the helm's slit.

"I once considered him a friend and mentor, but now I'm not so sure."

"Ah, he means well, laddie. He might be a lying, cheating, flatulent windbag, but his heart's in the right place. Least Thumil thinks so, and that's good enough for... Oh, my shogging nugget-sack! Thumil and Cordy—they were in the Dodecagon when I was trapped." He rapped the helm with his knuckles and then raised his bloodied hand to the eye-slit. "Ouch, that smarts. Must've cut myself." He shrugged and carried on. "They stood up for me, even after everything. Shog, I wanted to die, wanted to die so much, but they still cared." He went silent, his massive shoulders bunching up around the sides of the helm.

"Thumil?" Shader prompted. That had been the name of one of the white-robes outside, the one with patchy hair.

"Councilor. The best of 'em," the dwarf said. "Though I would say that, because I served under him when he was Marshal of the Ravine Guard, and because he is... was my friend."

"Sounds to me like he still is," Shader said.

The great helm pivoted left and right. "Loyal to a fault, ol' Thumil, but he knows. He knows."

"Knows what?" Shader asked.

"More'n I do, that's a fact. It's like my memory's a book telling the story of my life, but someone's taken an inkwell and splattered every page with black splotches. Some of it's still there, but other bits are missing. I see snippets—most of 'em bad—but I can't piece it all together."

Shader nodded then made his way to sit on the bench. "Well, it's not as if we're going anywhere soon. Why don't you tell me about yourself? It could help." He wanted to believe he made the suggestion out of compassion, love of neighbor in the Nousian sense, but he knew himself better than that. If he was going to get out of here, he needed help, and what better ally than this monstrous dwarf? Clearly, he was a force to be reckoned with, and chances are he knew his way around the city. If he could get Shader to the council, maybe they'd listen. Once they knew of the threat, it was inconceivable they'd not get involved. And if all else failed, he might at least know a way into the tunnels Gilbrum had spoken of.

The dwarf sauntered over and sat beside him. "I'm not sure. I'm thinking there's things in my noddle I don't really want to know."

"Then start with just what's necessary. Tell me your name."

The dwarf chuckled. "Ah, you got me there, laddie. Got me good 'n' proper."

Shader shrugged his incomprehension, but before the dwarf could explain, the grille on the door slid open. Muffled voices came from outside, followed by a metallic scratching and a resounding clunk. A few more words were exchanged, and then the door opened a crack, and the balding, white-robed dwarf from the walkway backed inside. At his nod, the door was shut behind him and the key turned in the lock, then he faced Shader, gave a lopsided smile and held his palms up apologetically.

"Precautions. I'm sure you understand."

After what had happened with Dave, Shader could see why the dwarves were being less than hospitable.

"We had no idea—Thumil, isn't it? About our companion, I mean."

That wasn't strictly true. There had been plenty of warning signs, but need had blinded him. Need and a faith that was little better than a patchwork cloak, more holes than tattered fabric. What was it Ludo had said about a snow-covered dunghill? That about summed it up.

Thumil pursed his lips and raised an eyebrow. "Kind of played into the hands of the traditionalists. Those of us with a more progressive leaning have been espousing the merits of opening our doors to the world for quite some time, but your friend has probably made sure they are fitted with bigger bolts and reinforced with steel. It's a rare thing, folk visiting Arx Gravis. Rarer still to have them brought inside."

"He was a trap," Shader said, stomach tightening at the memory of what Dave had become, what he'd willfully failed to see. "A deception of the Demiurgos."

"That's precisely what we've been afraid of all these centuries."

Shader frowned and looked at his cellmate for an explanation. The dwarf was stony-still, back to being a brooding presence masked by the great helm.

"I see you've met," Thumil said. He scratched at his beard, and a clump of hair came away in his hand. "Tried talking to him?"

"Yes, but—"

"Me too. Used to come daily, when he was first brought here. Then days turned to weeks and weeks to months. I don't know, I guess I just hoped he'd..." He stopped and stared at the sheared bolts on the floor beneath the bench, his eyes tracking to the loose lengths of chain dangling from the dwarf's wrists. The color drained from his face, and he backed toward the door. "What have you done?"

"Hoped he'd what?" The helmed dwarf pushed himself up from the bench.

Thumil yelped, and his knees buckled. His eyes nearly bulged from their sockets, and he couldn't take them from the black helm. He scrabbled weakly against the iron of the door, as if he had the vain hope of passing straight through it.

"Hoped I'd say something?" The dwarf took a step toward him. "I would've, if I'd known you'd been here. Weeks, you say? Months? How long has it been? Forgive me, Thumil, I feel I've been dead, and this is my tomb."

Thumil's teeth chattered, and spittle sprayed from his mouth when he spoke. "It's not possible. How can you be awake? Aristodeus said only he could... Oh, never mind. Are you... Are you...?"

"Cured? Well, I don't feel like you're all trying to kill me, if that's what you mean. Not that you were—not you and Cordy. Least not all the time. What I mean is, I think I'm myself. The rage has gone."

"Yourself?" Thumil said. "You remember who you are?"

"Some. Not all. Not a lot, actually. I was just saying to what's his name here—"

"Shader," Shader said, rising from the bench so he could offer Thumil a hand up.

"I know, laddie, I know. Just a bit slow on the recall, is all, but once the cobwebs are out of my nonce, I'll be right as... right as... You know, Thumil. What's the expression?

Right as mead! Or was it ale?"

Thumil gripped Shader's wrist, pushed his back into the door, and got his feet beneath him. "You remember your name?"

"That's where I thought you could help." He gave the helm a sharp rap. "It's in here somewhere, I'm sure of it, but it won't show itself."

Thumil sighed and lowered his head. "I'm sorry, old friend."

"But you remember it, surely?" Shader said. "Tell him what it is."

Thumil looked up, eyes glistening with unshed tears. "I can't."

"What do you mean you can't?" Shader said. "Don't you want to—"

"It's gone."

A groan rumbled up from within the great helm.

"What do you mean it's gone?" Shader said. "Surely—"

"Gone for all time. Gone from all time, as if it never existed. As if he—"

The dwarf flopped heavily onto the bench and cradled his helmed head in his hands. "Should've killed me, Thumil. You should've let them send me to the *seethers*."

"I couldn't," Thumil said, the tears running freely now. "You were... you are..."

"Not after what I've done, Thumil. Not after what I've done."

Thumil took Shader by the arm and walked him across the cell.

"They call him the Nameless Dwarf now," he said. "Well, I started it, but it wasn't me, if you know what I mean."

Shader didn't and shook his head.

"It struck me, so clear, so forcefully. It was like an echo back through time, and then this being, this Archon, came and—"

Shader gripped him by the shoulders. "The Archon was here?"

Thumil nodded. "Last year, though it seems a lifetime ago. He and the philosopher argued. He wanted to kill..." He indicated the Nameless Dwarf with a nod. "Said one day it would be a cursed name."

"Is now," the Nameless Dwarf said. "That's the point of it. A dwarf with no name is a dwarf most shamed, isn't that what the Annals say?"

Thumil grimaced. "The worst punishment a dwarf can receive." He looked up at Shader. "We are a people steeped in tradition, in history. Names are very important to us. They are memorized by our families, all the way back to the founders. One gap in the roll of names brings dishonor to the whole lineage. Our laws allow for the striking of a dwarf's name from the family roll, but only for the most heinous crimes. It's a shame few would want to bear. In fact, none have. All others so condemned have preferred death, and their wish has been granted."

"There's still time," the Nameless Dwarf said. "Grab a spear and come straight back. I'm not going anywhere."

"That's enough!" Thumil barked like a drill sergeant.

Shader tensed, expecting an eruption, but the Nameless Dwarf simply gave a mock salute and lay back on the bench.

Thumil let out a low sigh and raised his eyes in what looked like silent prayer. "This is worse," he said. "His name hasn't just been struck out, it's been plucked from existence, taken from time. It's the only way Aristodeus could reassure the council, the only way we could start to forget what he did."

"Aristodeus can do that?" Shader said. "He can erase a name from history?"

"Obliterate it," Thumil said. "I don't know how, or where his knowledge comes from, but it seemed better than the alternative. The council wanted blood, Shader. I've never known them to be so... decisive."

"Except with Lucius," the Nameless Dwarf mumbled from his bench before rolling onto his side with his back to them.

Thumil leaned in close and kept his voice low. "Lucius was his brother. Bit of an egghead, if you know what I mean. Pupil of Aristodeus." He touched his forehead in the Nousian manner, but then proceeded to touch his chest and each shoulder. "Why we made an exception for that bald bastard I'll never know. Had the run of the city at times, it seemed. Certainly has the gift of the gab, that one. Silver-tongued shogger."

"Aye," the Nameless Dwarf mumbled, then smacked his lips and yawned deep within the great helm.

"He has a brother?" Shader said. "Maybe he could—"

"Dead," Thumil said. "Defied the council. Defied all our traditions when he pored over the most ancient of the Annals in search of relics from the lost city of Arnoch. What he found wasn't left by our mythical ancestors, though. It was a snare of the enemy, who had inserted clues to its existence in our sacred histories. Lucius was so convinced he'd found the resting place of the Axe of the Dwarf Lords. When we warned him against pursuing his mad quest, he set off anyway into the bowels of the earth. The whole thing reeked of deception to us. For once, the whole council was unanimous, and a decision was reached in a day. See, we spurn action. Have done ever since Maldark, but when one of our own acts, and puts the city at risk, then we'll make an exception. Our assassins caught up with him before he went too far, sent him to the *seethers*."

Shader opened his mouth—wanted to know if it was his Maldark—but Thumil must have thought he was asking about these *seethers*.

"You don't want to know. Deep down is where you'll find them, though I wouldn't advise you to go looking. Spawn of the Abyss, most likely, but they make their nests in the dark spaces of Gehenna."

"Gehenna?" That struck a chord. Shader fished out his Liber and started riffling through its pages. "The cursed valley outside the holy city?"

"Jerusalem," Thumil said.

"You know of it?" Shader said. "How—?"

Thumil frowned. "Here, give me that." He took the book and scanned a page at random, furrowing his brow and muttering. "What's this?" he said, handing the book back. "What've you done to it?"

"What do you mean?"

Thumil took a step closer and fixed him with a stern look. "Profaning the sacred, is what I call it. Hardly anyone reads the scriptures these days, not since Maldark's Fall, but I do. It's something of a passion, and that—" He wagged a finger at the Liber. "—is traducement."

"If I knew what that was…" Shader said.

"Lies. Calumny. Heresy. It's been falsified. Whole passages are missing. I can tell that at a glance. And there are things in their place that are just plain wrong." He waved his hands and looked away.

"You're right, it was altered," Shader said, "but I'm told there is a golden thread running through it that retains the original truths."

"Bah," Thumil said. "Golden thread, my gonads. And what's with this outfit you're wearing? It's like a parody of Maldark's order. Who are you, Shader? Where do you come from, and more importantly, who do you serve?"

"I knew Maldark," Shader said. "Considered him a friend."

"Rubbish. That'd make you old enough to be my great, great, great, great—"

"There isn't the time for this," Shader said. "I am a knight from a far away place. I am pledged to the Ipsissimus, ruler of the Templum—"

"Templum? So you know Latin?" Thumil said, whirling on him. "Go on. You are some kind of holy knight, part of a temple."

"It's a bit bigger than that," Shader said. "Our Templum is the bride of Nous, son of the All-Father, Ain."

Thumil shook his head. "Sounds oddly familiar, though the words are screwed up. Listen, Shader, you sure you know what you're about?"

That was the question to trump all questions. Shader's mouth hung open like an imbecile's. He had no way of answering.

A loud snore reverberated from within the great helm, and Thumil turned his gaze on the Nameless Dwarf.

"Look, nothing happens quickly here. By the time the council is ready to see you, it'll likely be the Feast of Arios. Takes us weeks to agree an agenda. I'll root about in my study, bring you some things to read. Maybe that'll give us something to discuss."

"Maldark was helping me," Shader said. "Helping me to avert a cataclysm that will come to pass long before your bloody feast day." His fingers flew to his forehead in acknowledgment of his swearing.

Thumil raised an eyebrow.

"Listen to me. Have you heard of Sektis Gandaw?"

"Who hasn't?" Thumil said. "According to history, he's the reason we shut ourselves away down here in the first place. Him and that tricky bastard toasting his toes in the Abyss."

"Well, he's still alive," Shader said.

"I know that," Thumil said with a shrug. "Out of sight, out of mind, is our way. We're no threat to Gandaw and his experiments, and from what I hear, he keeps himself to himself for the most part."

"And what does your history tell you about Maldark? About his Fall?"

Thumil scoffed. "Nearly brought about the Unweaving, that's what. If it hadn't been for that shogger betraying the so-called goddess—"

"Careful," Shader said, heat flooding his face. "I watched him die trying to atone for the past. There's no one braver, no one more honorable."

Thumil sighed and wrapped his arms about his chest. "Forgive me. Even in our legends, Maldark made amends, but it is said he never forgave himself for delivering Eingana to the Technocrat. When Gandaw reduced her to a statue and commenced the Unweaving, it was Maldark who saved her from him. He handed her over to her grandchildren, the Hybrids, the offspring of the Cynocephalus, and then set himself adrift on the black river that runs from the depths of Gehenna through the heart of the Abyss. The statue of Eingana vanished from Aethir. To this day, no one—Gandaw included—has a clue where the Hybrids hid it."

"They took it to Earth," Shader said. "My world. The world Gandaw hails from. He's found it, Thumil. Found the pieces of the statue and assembled them. The time of the Unweaving is upon us."

Thumil staggered, as if he'd been struck with a sledgehammer. He stood gawping for a moment, the silence between them filled only by the rhythmic snoring coming from the bench. Finally, he shook his head and carried on as if Shader hadn't just mentioned the end of the world. "Earth? What do you take me for? Earth's no more real than Arnoch. I don't know what your game is, Shader, but the idea of Gandaw finding the statue on Earth is as believable as me finding a cask of mead at the end of a rainbow."

"I'm not joking," Shader said. "Earth is very real."

"In the stories, maybe. It's their way of explaining where someone as evil as Gandaw comes from. Some go so far as to say he sent his minions back to Earth to kidnap people to experiment on. There's even stuff about it in our Annals, how the dwarves are just modified Earth folk. I wouldn't place too much stock in it, if I were... You're serious, aren't you? Even if you're deluded, you believe what you're saying."

"I can assure you, I'm not deluded, Thumil."

"Well, you would say that, wouldn't you. It's what defines delusion. Listen, if Gandaw really had the statue, how come we're all still here? Don't you think he'd have started the Unweaving by now?"

"I think he has started. When we left the Sour Marsh, there was a brown cloud above the Perfect Peak."

Thumil's jaw dropped. "You've been to the Sour Marsh? All the way up to the Dead Lands? Then why didn't you put a stop to it, rather than bring your problems here?"

Shader inhaled sharply through clenched teeth. He offered up a mental prayer for calm. This was it, his one and only chance, and he didn't need to blow it now by becoming exasperated. "The mountain is guarded by silver spheres that spit fire. The only way we're going to get inside is through the tunnels you dwarves used for—"

"The scarolite mines?" Thumil said. "You want to use the tunnels that run from the mines to the Perfect Peak? But they've been closed for years."

"But you can get us into them?"

Something was different. Shader frowned, trying to work out what it was. And then he realized. The Nameless Dwarf had stopped snoring.

Thumil rubbed at his beard, frowning as strands came away in his fingers. "They could be unblocked, I suppose, but shog knows what you'd find inside. According to the Annals, back when we were mining for him, Gandaw had the tunnels infested with giant ants to keep the scarolite from being stolen. The only reason our boys weren't eaten is because he made an ant-man to control them. Horrible thing, by all accounts, and I pity the poor bastard he took and melded into it."

"I'll deal with that hurdle if we cross it," Shader said. "The question is, will you help us?"

Thumil puffed his cheeks up and blew out a big breath. "That's putting the cart before the horse, I'd say. Council still needs to meet to decide what to do with you after that business outside. Then, and only if they reach a decision, which is by no means certain, I could propose admission to the tunnels, but the problem there is that it would constitute an action that may have ramifications in the outside world. Last thing the council wants is to be implicated in anything that might come to Gandaw's attention. You see, everything we might do is fraught with peril. One action leads to another, and before you know it—"

"That's just ridiculous," Shader said. "You can't hide away from the world."

Thumil shrugged. "For some, Arx Gravis is all there is."

"But you'll stagnate," Shader said. "Grow sick as a society."

Thumil chuckled. "That's what I've been saying for years, but the council moves slowly, and always with caution."

"Then convince them they need to get a move on," Shader said. "Tell them about the Unweaving."

"You've yet to convince me," Thumil said, "and I can assure you, the council will take a lot more persuading."

Shader raised his arms, turned in a circle, as if he could find more sense in the walls of his cell. "Forget the council, then. If they'd rather debate while the worlds return to nothing, let's bypass them. You could get us into the tunnels."

Thumil looked horrified. "That's the sort of attitude that leads to dictatorship." He pointed at the sleeping Nameless Dwarf. "That's what happened with him, when he came back from Gehenna with the black axe. So decisive, so sure, and yet all he left behind him was blood and destruction. I'll not do it. No dwarf would." He turned round and raised his fist to knock on the door.

"I would."

Thumil froze and then slowly faced the bench.

The Nameless Dwarf stretched and yawned inside his helm, then swung his feet to the floor and stood. "Seeing as you won't kill me, and seeing as I could get very, very bored holed up down here now I'm awake, I might as well make myself useful."

"No," Thumil said. "No, that won't help at all."

The Nameless Dwarf folded his arms over his chest, the eye-slit of the great helm focused squarely on Thumil. He radiated menace, and Thumil must have sensed the change in the atmosphere, because he turned back to the door, muttering as he knocked.

"I'll speak with the council, tell them of the urgency, but don't get your hopes up. They are fatalistic, at best, Shader, and they don't want to be blamed for anything."

"Lucius used to say it's been more than a thousand years since Maldark's folly," the Nameless Dwarf said. "Surely we can start to take baby steps into the world once more."

"And look where it got him," Thumil said as the door swung open and spears bristled across the threshold.

"Everything all right, Councilor," a gruff voice said from the corridor outside.

Thumil didn't even bother to answer. He just stepped between the spear tips, which started to withdraw, until someone yelled, "Shog, he's awake! The butcher's awake!"

Two red-cloaked dwarves surged into the cell, spears leveled. Their resolve ebbed the instant the great helm turned on them, and both took a step back. Three more dwarves filtered through the doorway, outflanking the Nameless Dwarf and paying Shader no heed.

Outside, voices were raised with agitation, and above them, Thumil could be heard saying, "It's all right, Captain. He's all right. No, that won't be necessary. Did you hear me? I said no."

A burly dwarf with a salt and pepper beard and a horned helm pushed his way inside, a double-bladed battle axe over one shoulder. Shader recognized him from the walkway, and it looked like the recognition was mutual, the way the dwarf scowled at him, no doubt remembering the shock he'd got from the gladius.

The other dwarves watched him for instructions, spear tips trembling in hands slick with sweat.

"Captain Stolhok!" Thumil yelled, but the newcomer slammed the door, and the sound from the corridor died in an instant.

The Nameless Dwarf turned his back on Stolhok, shaking his helmed head.

"What'f up, fogger," Stolhok said, "fcared to fafe someone who ain't fcared of you?" Spittle accompanied his every word and clung like ale-froth to his mustache.

Shader almost laughed, but immediately battened down the hatches on that particular sin.

"You might consider substituting 'frightened' for 'scared', laddie," the Nameless Dwarf said, "and 'fight' for 'face'."

"What?" Stolhok looked to his men, who all shrugged. Then the penny dropped. "Why, you fogging piefe of fit!"

Stolhok swung his axe in a vicious arc. Shader stepped in, went for his wrists, but before he could blink, the Nameless Dwarf spun on his heel, crashing an elbow into Stolhok's nose and following through with a skull-jolting punch with his other hand. Stolhok's knees buckled, and he dropped like a stone, a fountain of blood spurting from his ruined nose. The Nameless Dwarf's hand snaked out to snatch the axe before it hit the ground. He held it for a moment, turning it over and over. The semicircle of spears shook, and worried looks passed between the dwarves.

"Now look here," one of them said. "We don't want no trouble now, do we lads?"

"That's right," said another. "Just put the axe down and move to the bench, and no one needs to get hurt."

Reversing the axe, the Nameless Dwarf clanged its head against the floor and leaned his weight on the haft.

The dwarves skittered back against the walls, spear tips wavering.

"Don't know about you, laddie," the Nameless Dwarf said to Shader, "but I'm parched as a parrot and stiff as a morning glory. Quick flagon down at the Queen's Beard, then I'll take you over to the scarolite mines. How's that sound?"

He strode toward the door, but before he could lay a hand on it, a guard darted in and took a jab at him. The axe swept down so fast that Shader only realized what had happened when the spear tip clattered to the floor, and the dumbfounded guard was left staring at the splintered end of his shaft.

The others shuffled forward, but Shader raised a hand and they stayed where they were.

"Bugger," the Nameless Dwarf said, pounding the side of the great helm with his fist. "How'm I gonna drink in this bucket?" He turned on the guards. "Any of you lads know a good blacksmith?"

They all exchanged looks.

"Won't help, my friend," Shader said. "It's fused to your skin."

The Nameless Dwarf ran his fingers along the seam connecting the helm to the base of his neck. "Bloody shogging shogger," he grumbled, shoving the door open and stepping out into the corridor. "Where's that bastard philosoph... Oops."

A dozen spear tips came at him at once. He twisted past two, batted a third aside with his axe, and hacked down. Someone screamed, and a hand splashed to the floor, fingers still wriggling. A spear glanced off his chainmail, and another grazed his shoulder. He roared and swung the axe like a scythe. The spearmen scurried back, but the Nameless Dwarf was relentless, stepping in close and bashing away with the flat of his blades.

"My hand!" a pale-faced dwarf screeched. "He lopped off my shogging hand!"

Someone started blowing short, desperate blasts on a trumpet.

The dwarves in the cell crept toward the Nameless Dwarf's back, but Shader stepped in front of them.

"Out of the way," one of them snarled, "or we'll gut you like a pig."

The clash of axe on armor was deafening. Shader risked a glance over his shoulder. Four guards were down, and the Nameless Dwarf was bleeding from a score of cuts. He caught sight of a white robe, but then a rustle of movement forced him to turn back. He sidestepped a spear thrust and wrapped his chains around his assailant's neck. The others poked at him, but he kept the sputtering dwarf between himself and their spear tips.

Another clang came from behind, followed by a dull thud.

"Don't hurt him," Thumil cried. "He's using the flat."

"Not on my shogging wrist, he didn't!"

"Don't hurt him? What about us?"

Shader dragged his captive to the doorway then shoved him back into the cell, pulled the door shut, and slid a bolt across.

Heavy footfalls were pounding down the corridor to the left, and that seemed to give the guards renewed courage.

"C'mon, lads, we can take him," one yelled, and lunged with his spear. It struck the Nameless Dwarf in the guts, snapping a link on his hauberk.

"Laddie," the Nameless Dwarf growled, "I'm trying to give you a chance." He took hold of the spear haft and yanked, pulling the wielder into a crunching headbutt with the great helm.

"Stop!" Thumil cried, waving his arms and stepping between the Nameless Dwarf and the dozen standing spearmen. "Please stop!"

"You'll do no such thing!" yelled Grago, just coming into view at the head of a column of heavily armed red-cloaks. "Kill him and anyone who gets in the way."

The Nameless Dwarf backed up against the door beside Shader. "Crouch down and put your hands on the ground."

He raised the axe and Shader understood. The blades came down, sending up stone chips and dust, and shearing straight through Shader's chains. He went to snatch up a spear from an unconscious dwarf, saw he had a dagger in his belt, and grabbed that instead.

"Ready?" the Nameless Dwarf said, stepping away from the door and twirling his axe like a baton.

The spearmen parted to admit the newcomers. Banded armor creaked, swords glinted in the unnatural light, and hard eyes glared from visored helms. They were packed into the corridor, four abreast with shields locked, and Nous only knew how many ranks deep.

Thumil stepped in front of them. "Stop, in the name of the council."

A couple of spearmen grabbed him and pulled him aside.

"Ready." Shader said, licking his lips and turning the dagger over and over in his hand.

The shield wall advanced, inexorable as the tide.

"One." The Nameless Dwarf rolled his shoulders.

The red-cloaks picked up pace, hammering their swords against their shields.

"Two."

A shout went up from the phalanx, and they started to jog.

"Thr—"

Thunder boomed, light flashed, and smoke billowed, flooding the corridor.

Hands gripped Shader's arm. He raised the dagger, then his jaw dropped.

"Come on," Rhiannon said, "let's go."

Shadrak strode through the roiling smoke, blasting away with his pistol. He was like a ghost, part in, part out of reality. All Shader could see were his hands and face, his blood-colored eyes. Screams went up from the red-cloaks, and then they were panicking, bumping into each other in their hurry to retreat.

"Friends," Shader explained to the Nameless Dwarf. "Quickly, come with us."

The great helm swiveled between Rhiannon, Shadrak, and the routed red-cloaks.

"Ah, shog," the Nameless Dwarf said. "I could've had them."

Thumil staggered from one side of the corridor to the other like a blind man. A cluster of guards crawled about looking for their spears, and from somewhere deep in the scattered phalanx, orders were barked.

"What the shog're you waiting for?" Shadrak said, backing toward Shader. He whipped a piece from the handle of his pistol and snapped another into place. "Move!"

They tore along the passageway, which sloped deeper and deeper into the ravine.

"Other way," the Nameless Dwarf panted. "Only fifty of 'em, give or take. I tell you, I could've—"

"Someone shut scuttle-head up," Shadrak hissed. "I'm trying to concentrate." He ran his hands over the left-hand wall, muttering and cursing. "It was here. I shogging know it was here."

"After them!" Grago's voice rolled down the corridor behind them, and the tramping of boots on stone sounded every bit like an approaching avalanche.

"Sure that's only fifty?" Rhiannon asked, casting a worried look over her shoulder.

"Give or take, I said." The Nameless Dwarf walked past Shadrak and stepped right through the wall, as if it wasn't there. An instant later, his helmed head popped back through. "I take it you were looking for this, laddie. You have to have the knack, see, because they shift."

"How the shog—?" Shadrak started.

"Old miner's trick. My pa was... Ah, never mind. Coming?"

Rhiannon went next, as if she did this sort of thing all the time.

"After you," Shader said to Shadrak.

The assassin's cloak merged seamlessly with the passageway. His eyes flicked past Shader as the first of the dwarves came into view up the incline. He unfastened a belt and handed it to Shader along with the scabbarded gladius. "Guess you might be needing this."

Shader buckled it on, and they stepped through the wall, emerging at an intersection. For habit's sake, he pulled the prayer cord from his pocket and hurriedly tied it to the belt.

"Pub's this way," the Nameless Dwarf said.

"Yeah, well the walkway ain't," Shadrak said, heading in the opposite direction.

"After a drink, laddie."

Shadrak whirled round, gesturing with his pistol for Shader and Rhiannon to follow him. "You do what you like, pan-head, but we're getting out of here."

The dwarf growled, and Shader approached him with hands raised.

"You can't drink in that thing, remember?"

"I'll get a reed. A long twisty one to poke through the eye slit."

Rhiannon sniggered. It was the first good humor Shader had heard from her in a long time. He gave an answering laugh of his own, but her eyes immediately hardened, and she turned to follow Shadrak.

At that moment, a sword poked through the wall, followed by a bearded head encased in a visored helm. The red-cloak's eyes widened, and he started to yell something as he stepped into the corridor... right into the Nameless Dwarf's fist.

"Ah, shog it, laddie," the Nameless Dwarf said to Shadrak. "Have it your way, but you owe me a pint."

"Whatever," Shadrak said, raising his pistol as another dwarf started to separate from the wall.

"No!" the Nameless Dwarf said. "No killing. These are my—"

Shader stepped in and brained the emerging red-cloak with the pommel of his gladius.

"Come on!" Rhiannon said, setting off down the corridor.

"You lot go on ahead," Shadrak said. He produced a glass sphere from a belt pouch. "This'll hold 'em." He caught the eye slit of the great helm watching him. "Don't worry. No one'll get hurt. Trust me."

"Hmmm," the Nameless Dwarf grunted, but he started after Rhiannon anyway.

Another head peeked through the masonry. Shadrak launched himself into the air and delivered a jaw-cracking kick, and stone formed back over where the head had been.

"Best get going," he said to Shader before lobbing his globe through the wall. There was an answering muffled boom, and then he tore off after the Nameless Dwarf, his cloak merging with the tunnel, making it seem the stonework itself was rippling.

Shader touched his forehead and shut his eyes for a second, and then he followed the others with long, loping strides.

Rhiannon led them through a maze of twists and turns along a gentle incline. Once or twice, she faltered, but Shadrak prompted her with hissed, impatient commands. When they arrived at the door they'd first entered by, they were confronted by half a dozen red-cloaks.

"Look what we got," one of them said, running his thumb along the edge of his sword.

"Nice one, Storz. Reckon we'll be up for promotio... Oh, shog my shogging shog-stick."

The Nameless Dwarf strode toward them whistling a jaunty tune.

The red-cloaks clustered together, brandishing shaking swords and bringing their shields so high their eyes were barely visible peeking over the rim.

"Now, just calm down, son," Storz said. "Don't make me shog you up."

A deep, rumbling laugh rolled up from the great helm.

"I'm serious. Don't come any closer. We can settle this without—"

"Meat for the dwarf lords of Arnoch," the Nameless Dwarf sang in a booming bass.

Cries of "Oh, shog," went up from the red-cloaks, and they started to jostle each other for the place at the back.

"Bones to be ground for their bread," the song continued.

"I'm warning you," one of the red-cloaks said.

"Hold down a bloke with a headlock; gouge both the eyes from his head!"

The Nameless Dwarf roared and charged right at them, but the red-cloaks scattered and went tearing off down the corridor. He checked his charge and turned back to the others, letting out a loud hoot, bending over double, and snorting with laughter.

"Glad you're having fun," Shadrak said, producing a sliver of stone and breaking it into two halves.

The door began to grind its way upward, letting in a blast of fresh air from the walkway.

The Nameless Dwarf sobered in an instant. "Where'd you get that?"

Shadrak ducked into the widening gap and stepped over a black bundle as the others followed him outside. It was a cloak, Shader realized. Shadrak's old cloak, by the looks of it, and it was covering something.

"Is that...?" The Nameless Dwarf reached down and pulled away an edge of the fabric. Dead eyes stared up at him from a bearded face. Black blood crusted the corners of the mouth, and the beard was drenched in crimson.

Shader knelt for a closer look, moved a clump of beard aside, and revealed a gash across the throat.

"Nice," Rhiannon said. "That your handiwork, midget?"

Shadrak scowled, and his pink eyes narrowed to slits when the Nameless Dwarf straightened up and turned on him.

"Well, laddie?"

The assassin's cloak whipped up behind him in the gusting wind, taking on the blue of the sky, the ocher of the ravine wall. Sunlight glinted from the blades nestled in his baldric, and a pallid hand crept toward one. "So what if it is? It's what I do. You got a problem with that?"

"As a matter of fact, I have."

"Yeah?"

"Yes." The Nameless Dwarf set his axe-head on the walkway and folded his hands atop the haft. "Can't blame you for not knowing, laddie, but this city's seen too much blood. Way too much."

"Look, mate," Shadrak said, "no one asked you to come along. If you don't like it—"

"I asked him," Shader said. "He can help us get into the tunnels."

The Nameless Dwarf swung his axe up onto his shoulder. "That I can, laddie, but only on condition that your little friend here doesn't kill anymore of my people."

"Who the shog are you to tell me what to do?" Shadrak said. "And besides, my ma told me never to trust a bloke with a bucket on his head."

"I'm with the midget there," Rhiannon said. "It's not like we know anything about him. Last thing we need is another Dave."

Shader cast a quick look back at the entranceway. "You planning on closing that?"

"Oh shit," Shadrak said. He fumbled his two pieces of stone back together and the door started to come down.

"Thanks." Shader held up his arms, letting the broken chains dangle from the manacles. "You any good with these?"

Shadrak sighed and put away his pistol and the door-stone so he could bring out a rolled leather pack. He found a thin pick and set to work.

"Look," Shader said, as the first clasp clicked open. "This is… Well, he doesn't have a name anymore."

The great helm dipped toward the walkway.

"They call him the Nameless Dwarf now."

Shadrak wasted no time with the second manacle and held his pick up to the dwarf. The great helm nodded.

"There a reason for that?" Rhiannon said. "I mean, it doesn't sound good."

"Aye, there's a reason, lassie," the Nameless Dwarf said, holding his arms out.

Shadrak scoffed as he fiddled about with his pick. "Sounds like the sort of stupid monikers the journeymen are always coming up with. Twats." The comment was punctuated by the clangor of a chain dropping to the walkway. The Nameless Dwarf rubbed his wrist before Shadrak set about the other one.

"It's no worse than Shadrak the Unseen," Rhiannon said.

"Yeah, well that weren't me. It's a reputation, ain't it?"

"I could think of something better," Rhiannon mumbled.

"Won't catch me using it," Shadrak said. "No offense, mate. It's just a bit wanky, if you ask me. Reckon I'll just call you Nameless, if it's all the same to you." The other manacle snapped open, and he slung it from the walkway, the chain snaking in its wake.

The great helm tracked its descent. "Careful, laddie. There's people down there."

"Oops," Shadrak said.

The door had barely thunked into place when it began to rise again. "We need to move," Shader said. "Which way… uh, Nameless?"

The dwarf pointed toward the archway they'd entered by. "Past the bald bastard, out of the ravine."

"Bald bastard?" Shader said.

All eyes turned to look where Nameless was pointing.

—Aristodeus!

A CHANGE OF PLAN

THE PHILOSOPHER STOOD on the far side of the arch, toga flapping in the wind, a leather satchel on one shoulder. He was turning Callixus's black sword over and over in his hands.

Shader glanced back at the door in the ravine wall. It was starting to rise, and dozens of boots could be seen in the growing gap at the bottom.

Nameless started toward the philosopher with Rhiannon in tow. Shadrak pulled his cloak tight, until only his hands and eyes were visible.

A red-cloak, keener than the rest, rolled beneath the rising door, and Shader took that as his cue to leave.

"Now this I wasn't expecting," Aristodeus said, upending the sword and leaning on the hilt. His gaze was fixed on Nameless. "You weren't meant to awaken without... ah!" His eyes flitted to Shader. "Of course." He chuckled and shook his head. "Well, they said there was trouble."

He nodded behind them at the red-cloaks gathering in front of the now fully open door as he fished a black rectangle from his satchel and pressed his thumb to it. It beeped and flashed. He gave a little shrug and put it away again.

"But how to turn this to our advantage?" He pursed his lips, inclined his head, and then clicked his fingers. "Could work in our favor, I suppose. A moment, please!" he yelled over their heads.

Shader turned to see Grago emerge at the front of the soldiers. Thumil pushed through beside him.

More doors were opening around the ravine walls, and from one came a group of white-robed councilors. A blonde-haired and bearded dwarf in a sky-blue dress broke away from them and ran across her walkway toward the central hub. She was flicking looks at Nameless, and at the same time waving to Thumil, who hurried along his own walkway to meet her.

"What do you mean, 'of course'?" Shader said. "He wasn't meant to awaken without what?" *What have I got to do with it?* At every twist and turn, Aristodeus seemed to show up. What was this, just a game to him? Shader's childhood mentor may as well have formed the same blistering carapace as Dave, for all he really knew him. Who was this man who'd had such an influence over his formative years, who'd steered him on the course to the Templum? Was there any corner of Shader's life he hadn't crept into?

"His voice," Thumil said, approaching them, hand in hand with the bearded woman. "Only his voice could break the spell."

"Must be the accent. No other explanation for it," the philosopher said. "Dear ol' Britannia. Starting to miss her yet?"

Accent, my foot, Shader thought. Aristodeus did a good job of sounding Britannic, but he'd never shaken off his Graecian roots.

547

"Accent or no accent," Nameless said, "I've a bone to pick with you, laddie."

He took a step toward Aristodeus, but Rhiannon barged past him, sweat beading her forehead, drenching her robe.

"Give it to me," she demanded. "Now."

Aristodeus narrowed his eyes, an enigmatic smile tugging at the corner of his mouth.

Rhiannon's fists clenched, and her body shook with restraint.

Shader tensed, readied himself to pull her back.

Aristodeus noticed and let out a chuckle. He reversed the sword and handed it to Rhiannon. As it passed beneath the arch, red flames flared along its blade.

Aristodeus worked his jaw and gave a slight shrug. "Not a pleasant weapon, but then are any?" He cocked a look at Nameless.

Rhiannon caressed the sword but started when she caught Shader watching her. With a sullen scowl, she maneuvered it into the scabbard on her back and folded her arms across her chest.

"Laddie," Nameless said, tapping the side of his helm, "I understand the need for trickery, but it's taking things too far when I can't get the shogging thing off, even for a pint."

"I'm sorry," Aristodeus said, popping his pipe in his mouth and rummaging in his pocket for some tobacco. It was an action Shader had seen a thousand times. It meant the matter was closed. "Too dangerous."

"But the black axe…" Nameless said.

"Safe place." Aristodeus tamped down the pipe and patted his robe. "Anyone have a light? Mine's out of gas. No, of course not." He sighed and thrust the pipe away. "At least, safe while you wear the helm. The link must not be re-established." He cast a look at the assembled dwarves. "They'd never allow it, in any case."

"Then destroy it," Nameless said. He didn't sound convinced.

"Can't be done," Aristodeus said. "Least not yet. Give me time, and I'll work it out."

Nameless hefted his axe to his shoulder. The philosopher flinched and took a step back.

"What about grub?" Nameless said. "I've come up with a beer-drinking plan, but a dwarf needs meat and bread and great steaming bowls of salty broth. It's not like I've got any spare." He patted his belly. "If you don't get a move on, I'll be a bag of bones in no time." He dropped his head to his chest. "Course, maybe that's for the best."

Aristodeus held up his hands. "I'll come up with something. I hadn't expected you to wake from stasi… sleep. I suppose I could…" He scratched his beard. "Yes, that would work."

"What, laddie? What would work?"

Prickles of ire simmered beneath Shader's skin. A thousand questions jostled for first place on his tongue, and finally one slipped the restraints of Nousian humility, made him impatient for his turn. "You knew about Dave, didn't you?"

Aristodeus frowned, but it was more a frown of perplexion than of disapproval. "Dave?"

Nameless gave a double cough, but Shader ignored it.

"The hunchback. That demon. Was he part of your meddling as well?"

"I assure you," Aristodeus said, "I do not meddle. I strategize, maneuver, prognosticate, even, but never meddle."

"Could've bloody well fooled me," Rhiannon said.

A blur of movement out of the corner of his eye told Shader Shadrak was circling behind Aristodeus. His first instinct was to warn the philosopher, but then he thought why should he? Maybe it was time for some answers.

"Needs must when the Demiurgos defecates on my doorstep," Aristodeus said. "We all have to make sacrifices, my dear. Even you."

"Tell me about it," Nameless said. "Or rather, tell my rumbling tummy."

Shader pressed forward, eyes refusing to let the philosopher go. One blink and the bastard would vanish again, like he always did. "Dave," he said.

Aristodeus actually looked flummoxed.

Ordinarily, Shader would have paid to see that, but right now his humor had seeped away along with his tact. "Don't play dumb, you—"

"The demon that triggered the arch," Thumil said.

Shader spun to face him. He'd forgotten he was there. Forgotten the white-robes and the hundreds of soldiers still filing out onto the walkways all the way around the ravine. A quick glance below told him the dwarves had cut off every avenue of retreat. If things turned nasty now, it didn't look good.

Thumil looked drawn and haggard, and in the stark light of the two suns glaring down at them, his patchy scalp was starting to rival Aristodeus's for sparseness. The golden-bearded woman squeezed Thumil's hand, and he immediately straightened up, as if drawing strength from her.

Shader turned with deliberate slowness back to the philosopher. "Don't tell me you didn't know."

"All I *know* is that the alarm was triggered, and my presence here was required." Aristodeus pursed his lips and shrugged at Thumil.

Thumil nodded. "Thought it was best, particularly with…" He nodded to Nameless.

"So, this weird hunchback just materializes out of thin air," Rhiannon said, "leads us here, and you had nothing to do with it?"

Steel glinted behind Aristodeus. Shader caught a glimpse of pale skin, a pinkish eye. He gave the slightest shake of his head, raised his fingers. Hopefully, that would be enough to stay Shadrak's hand.

"No idea who or what you are talking about," Aristodeus said. He seemed to forget he had no light as he thrust his pipe back in his mouth, chewed the stem, muttered something, and put it away again. "I can't be expected to be everywhere, know everything."

"You hear that?" Rhiannon said, sidling up to Shader. "Was that an admission of fallibility?"

Shader ignored her. "He was a crazy, a zealot. I found him with the White Order, waiting on them hand and foot."

"Bet Barek loved that," Rhiannon said. "Elgin, too."

Aristodeus seemed to be holding his breath. It was the first time Shader had commanded his full attention. Ever. If Shadrak had wanted to strike, Aristodeus would have had as much chance as… as Shader had in the Templum of the Knot, right when the Dweller surged over him.

"It was a demon, right enough," Grago yelled, storming toward them.

Aristodeus hissed at him and held up a finger. Grago stopped dead in his tracks, his face flushed and ready to burst like an overripe tomato. The other councilors shuffled around him, straining to catch the conversation.

"He was there, waiting, when I got back from the Anglesh Isles," Shader said, "and then he was here, in the Sour Marsh."

Murmurs sounded from the white-robes, and Thumil made that gesture again, touching his forehead, chest, and both shoulders. The golden-bearded woman tutted, but whether at mention of the Sour Marsh or Thumil's gesture, it was hard to say.

"I'll admit it does smack of my style," Aristodeus said, stroking his beard. His voice remained even, but the blood had drained from his face. His eyes seemed darker, somehow, and he was blinking furiously. "But I have…"

His jaw dropped, and for a second Shader thought Shadrak might have stabbed him, but then he realized he'd seen that look before—during one of their daily chess matches back in Britannia. Aristodeus had been wittering on flippantly, barely looking at the board, he was so used to winning. Shader had spent the night before reading everything he could on strategy, determined to find a way through his mentor's impregnable defenses. Apparently, he'd found it, in a book on the innovations of the masters: a gambit written by none other than the philosopher himself. And there it was again, that same look: eyes aghast, mouth agape, a pulsing tic high on one cheek.

"... no knowledge of him," Aristodeus finished in the hushed tone of a man just starting to realize he'd been had. Air rushed from his lungs like the last breath leaving a corpse. "I am such a fool. It won't happen again. The enemy is cunning, more so than I could have imagined." He smacked his lips and narrowed his eyes. "But I am better."

"Boo!"

Aristodeus shrieked and then clutched his hands to his heart and cursed.

Shadrak threw off his hood and stepped from behind him, sauntering back through the arch. "Don't get too cocky, now, mate."

Nameless clapped the assassin on the back. "Laddie, you might be a runty, bloodthirsty little pipsqueak, but I think I'm warming up to you."

"Wish I could say the same," Rhiannon said.

Grago and the rest of the councilors edged nearer, flanked by a contingent of red-cloaks. All around the ravine, slate-armored troops formed up into disciplined phalanxes that left no exit uncovered.

Shader licked his lips and kept track of Aristodeus's eyes. If they were going to get out of this, a lot would depend on what the philosopher said and did. Him and Thumil, who appeared to have the ears of most of his colleagues; and judging from the talk in the cell, he had a grasp of the looming peril, even if he was yet to be persuaded of the necessity of action.

Aristodeus, however, looked ghastly, in spite of his bravado. Motionless as he stood, his eyes were frenetic and still reflected the hellish fire of the archway, even though it had abated the moment Rhiannon sheathed her sword.

"Ah, lassie," Nameless said. "I'll grant you he's a wee bit prickly, but I've a feeling in the bristles of my beard we're all going to be great friends."

Shadrak rolled his red eyes, and Rhiannon dug her fists into her hips, thrusting her chin out like an enraged bird of prey.

"Yes? Well, you thought that poor bastard with his throat slit was bad enough, but that was nothing compared to what your new buddy did in the cell."

The great helm panned toward Shadrak. "Laddie?"

"How do you think we found you?" Shadrak said. "Bit of pragmatism, is all. The bitch should count herself lucky I had a distraction."

"You killed someone else?" Nameless stiffened.

"More than killed," Rhiannon said.

"No, no, no," Nameless said. "No more killing. These are my—"

Shadrak circled him. "You mean to tell me you ain't never killed?"

Grago took that as his cue and strode up. "Oh, he's killed right enough. Butchered, more like. And you, sir—" He jabbed a finger at Aristodeus. "—have some answering to do."

Aristodeus blinked, and his eyes came sharply back into focus. "Is that so, Councilor Grago?"

"It most certainly—"

"It was me that persuaded them." Thumil released the woman's hand and approached Aristodeus.

Grago ceded him ground and looked back at his fellow councilors, raising an eyebrow.

"You told me there was a way to end the terror," Thumil said, "and I believed you."

"And I was right," Aristodeus said.

Thumil pressed his chin into his chest and lowered his eyes. When he raised his head, it was to Nameless he looked. "I lied to you. Betrayed you to save the people."

Nameless was rigid.

"Do you remember what you did?" Thumil asked, cocking his head and taking in the black helm, moisture rimming his eyes.

"Some," Nameless answered, voice a hundred miles away.

"But not all?" Thumil said. "That's good. I wouldn't wish that burden on you, old friend. But it wasn't just you I betrayed. My god... you know, the scriptures, Maldark's faith..."

"Oh please!" Grago said. "Haven't you given up on that nonsense yet? Fat lot of good it did Maldark and his kin."

The golden-haired woman glared and raised her fist, and Grago stepped back, muttering to himself.

"Cordana, please," Thumil said, gently gripping her shoulder. "Cordy."

She rested her hand atop his and gave the barest of nods.

"My point is," Thumil said, "that I was desperate." He turned back to Aristodeus. "Desperate enough to believe you."

"The killing stopped," Aristodeus said, steel in his voice. "If that involved a little white lie to your imaginary friend in the sky, then so what? It's the lesser of two evils."

"I don't know," Thumil said. "I don't—"

"You were my friend, Thumil," Nameless said. "Even with the madness upon me, some tiny part of me still recognized that, trusted you enough to let ol' baldilocks here put the helm on me. I think I knew deep down. Knew that it wouldn't increase my power, like you said, protect me from mortal blows. I even think..." He paused and looked down at his boots. "I think, somewhere in this daft nonce of mine, I didn't want it to. I wanted to be stopped. Killed even."

"And so you damned well should be," Grago said.

All around the ravine, weapons clashed against shields in affirmation.

"Yeah, well whatever he's done," Rhiannon said, "it's nothing compared to what I saw in the cell. You want Nameless dead? Fine. But fair's fair; you'll have to kill the poison gnome, too."

Grago nodded at his fellow councilors. Moary conferred with the others, and they all looked flustered. Grago beckoned to a red-cloak, and within moments a knot of soldiers was advancing.

Shadrak raised his pistol in the air. There was a crack of thunder, and smoke plumed from the barrel. The soldiers stopped dead in their tracks.

Aristodeus rubbed his brow and sighed. "No one is going to be killed. At least not here. Not today. But," he said to the councilors, "if you take no action, right here, right now, the worlds will be unmade, and if there is anyone left to tell the tale, which I sincerely doubt, your names will be cursed unto all eternity for doing nothing."

"That, sir, is heresy, and you know it," Moary said. "It was acting that nearly brought us to the brink of doom before. That is why we can do nothing. Every step we take into the affairs of the world may be a snare of the Demiurgos."

"Yes, yes, yes," said Aristodeus. "So you don't even ask someone to pass the mustard in case it's a trap. I knew dwarves were thick-skulled, but this is getting ridiculous. I'd tear my hair out, if I had any. I thought Lucius was getting through to you, but you went and had him killed."

"It was his action that led to the finding of the black axe," Grago said.

"Yes, well," Aristodeus said. "I didn't foresee that."

"And what else haven't you foreseen?" Shader said. "You claim you knew nothing about Dave, too, and yet you continue to interfere and manipulate. This is just a game to you, isn't it? A game you're not even certain of winning."

Aristodeus's eyes hardened. "It is no game, Shader. And if it were, the stakes are higher for me than for anyone else alive."

"Because you're so bloody important?" Rhiannon said. "Remind me to genuflect next time I see you."

Nameless lurched into motion, and when he did, every dwarf in the ravine seemed to flinch. "Way I see it, Baldy here gave my brother the taste for action. Lucius found mention of the black axe in the Annals—"

"I had no idea about that," Aristodeus said. "It shouldn't have been there."

"Which is why we have the code of non-action," Moary said. "Even our histories cannot be trusted. I mean, well, what if the Demiurgos planted reference to the axe, hoping that someone would be foolish enough to go looking for it?"

"Lucius was no fool," Nameless said. "His sin was to hope. To hope that the axe was a link to a glorious past, something we could take pride in. Surely it's better to fall trying than never to try at all."

"Tell that to the families of those you slaughtered, Butcher," Grago said. "I think we can all see where this is leading."

"I haven't finished!" Nameless said.

Grago paled and stood rigid, mouth agape.

"Lucius only sought the black axe, but you—" Nameless took in the councilors. "—actually *did* something. You sent assassins and had him fed to the *seethers*. He didn't get to act. You got there first. If you hadn't killed my brother, I'd never have completed his work for him. There's no telling how different things would have worked out then. For all his faults, Lucius was no warrior, so I doubt he'd have made much of a butcher. My point is, you were prepared to act then, but what are you prepared to do now?"

Thumil's face lit up, and he spread his hands. "He's right. If we do nothing, then we are complicit in the end of all things."

"How do you know?" an extremely fat councilor said.

Moary scratched his head. "Well, I don't know. I mean, what if..."

"Oh, we need to start acting all right," Grago said, "but in accord with our own reasoning. Our own agenda. I've been saying this for years, and yet it's fallen on deaf ears. Certainty of purpose, a clear vision of who we are and what we want is—"

"Save it, Grago," Cordana said. "We are not replacing the Demiurgos's will with yours."

"You have no right," Grago said. "Just because you are the wife of a councilor—"

Aristodeus took his pipe back out and rapped the bowl against the stone of the archway until he had everyone's attention. "None of us has the luxury to indulge your circular arguments. Whether you accept it or not, Sektis Gandaw has in his possession the Statue of Eingana. Even as we speak, he is commencing the Unweaving."

All eyes looked to the sky. Besides a few soaring buzzards, there was nothing but an expanse of cobalt-blue and the glaring orbs of Aethir's suns.

"Well, that's all very well for you to say, but what if... What I mean is, what evidence do you have?" Moary asked.

"There was a brownish smog above the Perfect Peak," Shader said. "That's all we've seen."

Hushed conversations echoed around the walls of the ravine.

"Then why are we still here?" Grago asked. "What's taking so long?"

"It is not a fast process," Aristodeus said, "unpicking every thread of Creation. And besides, I am reliably informed Gandaw's plans have been set back."

"Set back how?" Grago demanded.

Aristodeus held up a hand to silence him. "Be that as it may, we do not have unlimited time. A few days, a week at most, and then a great big nothing. When the lights come back on, assuming they do, Gandaw will be at the center of his own creation, and I doubt very much any of us will be perfect enough to feature in it."

"So what are we expected to do?" Moary said. "Trust you again, even after Lucius? Even after you told us the Ravine Butcher could only be awakened by your voice, and yet here he stands?"

"Do nothing," Shader said, sensing his chance.

"What?" Aristodeus said.

It seemed an obvious ploy. The dwarves were afraid to act, and yet here they were preventing anyone from leaving.

"Stand aside," Shader said. "Keep out of our way. Is it not action to prevent our going?"

The white-robes turned to each other, clearly confounded.

"We only need to enter the mines," Shader said, "so that we can travel to the roots of Gandaw's mountain. All action will be ours, not yours."

Aristodeus was grinning from ear to ear. He gave Shader a knowing wink.

Grago took a stranglehold on his beard and shook his head. "Clever. Very clever. But, is it not the case that willful non-action is itself still an action, albeit a negative one? No, my brother councilors, we cannot let them go, for in doing so, we may still be found culpable."

"That's illogical, incoherent, and idiotic, Grago," Aristodeus said, "and you know it."

"You're wasting your breath, laddie," Nameless said.

"I agree with Councilor Grago," the fat dwarf said. "But it's more than a case of—what was it you said, Grago?—'willful non-action'. If we allow these people to enter the mines, we are, in effect, opening the mines to them. We need no more complicated argument. We are prohibited, by our own laws, from granting outsiders admittance, are we not?"

"Balderdash!" Aristodeus fumed.

Thumil shrugged. "An excellent point, Councilor Bley, which leaves us with only one solution."

Expectant eyes were upon him, and Thumil seemed to grow in stature, as if he were a professor lecturing a class of awed undergraduates. The funny thing was, they seemed to swallow it.

"If we prevent them from leaving, we are guilty of the act of preventing."

Begrudging nods of agreement.

"If we admit them to the mines, we are guilty of the act of admittance."

More vigorous nodding this time.

"So, what are you going to do if we ignore you and enter the mines anyway?" Shadrak said, a wicked smirk on his face.

"Then you would be forcing us to act in preservation of the law," Thumil said. "And if we are forced, we cannot be held culpable. Marshal Vayn."

"Councilor?" A hardened old red-cloak stepped forward and saluted.

"Take a legion and see no one enters the scarolite mines."

Shader shook his head as the marshal barked a few commands and a ripple of troop movement ran across the walkways. "And I thought you were—"

Thumil held up a finger. "You are free to go, so long as you steer clear of the mines."

"Are you an imbecile, Thumil?" Aristodeus said. "Don't you care about the Unweaving?"

"Shog him," Shadrak said. "Let's go it alone, if these scuts are too stupid to do anything."

"How?" Shader said. "You saw those things around Gandaw's mountain. How are we going to get inside?"

Shadrak shut his eyes, as if thinking. When he opened them, he shrugged. "Shogged if I know. Raise an army?"

"Twat," Rhiannon said.

Aristodeus growled something.

"Could always try New Jerusalem," Nameless said. "The senate's got a fair few legions."

"Actually," Aristodeus said, instantly brightening, "that's not such a bad idea. Do you have influence with the senate?"

Nameless shook his helmed head. "Never even been there, but you hear things. My pa used to say there were always folk from New Jerusalem showing up at the mines, wanting to buy scarolite on the sly."

"And did they?" Grago asked.

"Not for me to say. Point is, they have an army that would dwarf ours, excuse the pun. Sounds like the best bet we've got, if you ask me."

Shader turned to Aristodeus. "It's quicker if you go ahead. Magic yourself there, or whatever you do."

Aristodeus shook his head. "Can't do that. I need to prepare for other contingencies, and besides, the senate and I don't exactly see eye to eye."

"What contingencies?" Rhiannon said. "Way I see it, we're running out of options."

"There are always options, my dear," Aristodeus said. "And believe me, this business goes deeper—much deeper—than our current threat from Mr. Gandaw. We must stay one step ahead of the enemy at all times."

"You're sure about the mines?" Shader said to Thumil.

"I'm sorry, Shader. We are dwarves. I don't expect you to understand."

Shader sucked in a breath through clenched teeth, but he nodded all the same. "All right," he said, "how far to New Jerusalem?"

"Couple of days, at a guess," Nameless said.

Thumil grunted in agreement.

"Two days?" Shader said. "We'll need food. Water."

He might as well have appealed to the rock walls of the ravine for all the acknowledgment he got from the dwarves.

Aristodeus rolled his eyes as if this were just one more problem he had to sort out, but before he could say anything, Shadrak whipped out his pistol, spun it on his finger, and re-holstered it.

"Leave it to me. Bagged us that turkey, didn't I?"

It wasn't encouraging. Besides that, and the goat, they hadn't exactly seen much else out there to eat.

Nameless must have sensed his uncertainty, and patted him on the shoulder. "I'll flush out some squirrels for you, laddie, and the little fellow can shoot them. Boil them up over a campfire, and you'll not tell them from chicken. Well, you will, but you can always pretend."

Shader caught Rhiannon's eye. "Best get a move on, then."

She held his gaze for a long while before she spoke. "I'm not coming."

"What?"

"Not if he's going with you." She glared at Shadrak. "Not after what he did to that poor sod in the cell. He's a shogging psycho, Deacon, and don't forget what he did to you in the templum."

"We all go," Shader said. "There's too much at stake." He'd seen enough of what Shadrak could do to know that things might very well hinge on him. It was the assassin who'd got them out after he and Rhiannon had messed up. You didn't have to approve of Shadrak to know how useful he could be in a tight scrape.

"Him or me," Rhiannon said. "Your choice."

Fire rose to Shader's cheeks, and his temples began to throb. What was it about Rhiannon? Why did she have to be so bloody difficult?

"Why don't you come with me?" Aristodeus said.

"You?" Rhiannon said.

"If our nameless friend here is traveling to New Jerusalem, he's going to have to be fed. I could use some help gathering my apparatus and taking them on ahead to the city."

"I am not—"

Aristodeus waved away her response before she gave it birth. "And there are matters I would discuss with you—these contingencies I mentioned before. Would you at least allow me the chance?"

Rhiannon's eyes narrowed to slits. She snaked a look at Shader, all venom, as if he'd done something she'd never forgive. As if he were Gaston Rayn, or worse.

"Fine," she said. "Anything's got to be better than this."

Aristodeus held out his arm, and she took it. "When you get to New Jerusalem," he said to Nameless, "go to the Academy. Ask for Master Arecagen."

"Arecagen?"

Aristodeus grimaced, as if he could no longer take the frustration of making himself understood. "Just ask for him. I'll meet you there and make sure you don't starve. Mark my words," he said loud enough for the councilors to hear. "The day is coming when you will thank me for preserving this kinsman of yours. He's special, this one, and if I can only set him on the right track, he could yet prove our greatest weapon."

"Never been called a weapon before," Nameless said. "Except maybe once, but she was a feral lassie from the wharfs. All hips and melons. You know the sort I mean?"

Before anyone could respond, green light swirled about Aristodeus and Rhiannon, and they vanished. One minute they were there, the next they were gone.

As quickly as that, Shader had lost her again, only this time he wasn't quite so sure how he felt. Jealous, maybe, but if he were, it was barely noticeable. Angry, resentful, disappointed? An overwhelming confusion of emotions fought for his attention, leaving him blank and bewildered. Truth be told, he was probably relieved, he thought, but that wasn't right, wasn't what Nous expected. But there lay the second problem. He was suddenly aware he didn't care all that much for what Nous wanted anymore.

All along the walkway they'd approached from, the red-cloaks were falling back.

Thumil gestured toward the top of the ravine. "Go. Now. Before they come up with another objection."

Shader offered his hand and then remembered something Thumil had said back in the cell. "Those books you mentioned, the scriptures."

Thumil slapped himself on the forehead. "I'm sorry, with all that's happened it completely slipped my mind." He cast a look behind at the stony faces of the councilors. Some of them were muttering among themselves, and there was a palpable tension seeping into the soldiers. "You should leave. Maybe when all this is over, maybe there'll be a few changes here, and if there are, you would be most welcome. I'm literally dying to have someone to discuss my reading with. Religion isn't something we dwarves like to talk about, not since Maldark."

Cordana pressed up close to Thumil and took his hand. "You said you'd ask, remember?"

"Ah, yes, my dear, of course." He coughed and gave Shader a sheepish look. "My wife does not share my spiritual views..."

Cordana wrinkled her nose at him but then softened it with a smile.

"But she does... I mean, she..." He suddenly looked flustered, waving his hand around as if trying to pluck the words from the air.

Cordana touched her belly and sighed. "We are trying for a baby, but the doctors say I'm barren. Either that, or Thumil's too old."

Thumil nudged her with his elbow. "Most likely it's my illness." He indicated the bald patches on his scalp and beard.

"Anyway," Cordana continued, "we were hoping you'd give us your blessing, what with you being a holy man and all."

The idea cut Shader like a blade. Him, holy? After all he'd done, all he'd failed to do? He didn't even know if you could call him Nousian anymore, not after the things he'd discovered about the Liber. All his training, all his prayer, and he was as uncertain of his faith as... as... He caught sight of Nameless watching him through the slit of the great helm. He chewed his lip and nodded. "Of course. But Nous... I mean—"

Thumil patted him on the shoulder. "I've seen enough of the way you carry yourself, and enough of that book of yours to know we're praying to the same god. Just because the words have been twisted, doesn't mean your prayers aren't heard. Have faith, son. Surrender yourself to this Nous of yours, and let him carry you through the trials that lie before you."

Shader didn't know about that. Didn't know if he could, but he made a mental note to pray on it. He took the Liber from his pocket and thumbed through it until he found the appropriate passage.

"Benedicta tu, Nous, qui conlocat sterilem in domo matrem filiorum laetantem..." The words never seemed to leave his skull; his voice sounded muffled and dead to him, but he could see from Thumil and Cordana's faces they were listening with rapt attention, clutching each other's hands tightly.

When he finished, he closed the Liber, feeling numb. The couple smiled their thanks and embraced each other. At least it appeared to have done them some good, but as far as Shader could tell, it was all smoke and mirrors. His faith wasn't just wavering. Right then, it was dead and buried. But he had nowhere else to go. It was all he'd ever known, all his mother had taught him. Strangely, Aristodeus had always encouraged it, too. The philosopher had always had such strong ties with Aeterna, even to the Ipsissimus himself, and yet, judging by comments he made, the faith was nothing more to him than an child's plaything, or a means to an end.

"Nameless, laddie?" Nameless was saying to Shadrak. "I think I like it. You have a way with oxymorons."

"Eh?" Shadrak said. "What's that, a stupid cow? Think she just left with ol' baldy."

Shader chuckled. It was a chink in the dark clouds smothering his spirit, but at least it was something. A pang of guilt sent his hand to his forehead. What was he doing? It was pure reflex after years of habitual practice, but ridiculous as it seemed, worrying about the displeasure of a deity he barely believed in, he still made the sign. This time, when he laughed, there was real mirth in it, as if something within had been set free. What it was, though, Shader couldn't yet say.

"You should do it more often, laddie," Nameless said.

"Do what?"

"Laugh, laddie. Laugh. It's good for the soul. Come on now, time waits for no one."

Nameless trudged on down the walkway without a look back at the city that had been his home.

The black cloud closed up around Shader, and he doubted he could have laughed again if he'd wanted to. Even the memory of laughter seemed impossibly distant as he watched the dwarf's massive shoulders bunched up about the great helm, the powerful gait, the axe clutched in both hands. It was like a bas-relief from those ancient templa in Aeterna, the ones that depicted tortured souls condemned to rove the Abyss for all eternity.

"I reckon he's all right, that one," Shadrak said, following Shader's gaze.

Shader certainly hoped so. He turned back to Thumil and his wife, but they were deep in conversation. The faces of the councilors behind them were inscrutable. If they were going to miss the Nameless Dwarf, they certainly didn't show it. More than likely, they were relieved to see him go. They could hardly be blamed for that after what Thumil said had happened. Maybe they were still considering what they could and couldn't do. And then it occurred to Shader, as he and Shadrak set off after the black-helmed pariah waiting for them at the foot of the climb: They were scared. Scared of what they'd unwittingly unleashed on the outside world, and suddenly he could no longer see the good humor effortlessly flowing from Nameless. Instead, all he felt was a great foreboding, a trepidation at some horror that was yet to come.

GOING PLACES

T HE CLANGOR OF a kitchen at full tilt, the odor of hard labor, the aroma of cooking! It was enough to bring tears to Albert's eyes. Yes, the sous-chef was more suited to bricklaying, the washer-upper needed a rough mama to scrub behind his ears, and the waiter was... well, the waiter was the greasiest toe-rag of the lot.

Right on cue, Buck shouldered his way through the swinging doors, plates and bowls stacked high in his hands, held steady by his chin.

"All pucker out there," he said, depositing the crockery on the side. "Ol' Rollypolly's slurping it up like there's no tomorrow."

"Rollingfield," Albert said, wiping his hands on his apron. "Senator Rollingfield. So, he likes my terrine?"

"Your terrine?" Buck said. "Chef Dougan's, you mean."

Albert didn't know how to break it to him, but what they'd served the senator was as far removed from Dougan's rancid concoction as a lace hanky from a snot rag.

"After taking my tisane, Chef went for a little lie down, and during the hiatus, I took it upon myself to—"

"Farryl!" a booming voice sounded from the restaurant. "Farryl Dougan, you steaming offal of a man." The doors swung open, and in flounced the senator, capacious toga speckled with tomato sauce. "I don't know how you've done it, but you've excelled yourself."

His gelatinous jowls wobbled as he turned his piggy eyes on Albert. When he tilted his head so he could peer down his nose, it was hard to focus on anything but the crusted cavities of his hairy nostrils. Funny that, seeing as the manner of the man got right up Albert's nose. He couldn't help but think that the haughty chin tilt exposed a throat eminently suitable for his cheese-cutter, if ever he found it again.

"Where's that arse Dougan?" Rollingfield asked.

"Having a lie down, Senator," Buck said with a nauseatingly obsequious bow.

"Tell him he deserves it," the senator said. "Sterling meal, what. Can't believe it's the same chef."

Albert coughed delicately into his fist. "I'm afraid it was more than a lie down, Senator. Chef Dougan was taken unexpectedly ill."

Buck took on the semblance of a startled hare. "But you said—"

Albert threw an arm around his head, pulled him into a fierce hug. "I wanted to tell you, Buck, truly I did, but I knew how devastated you would be."

Rollingfield's shoulders slumped, and all the pomposity went out of him. "Is he going to be all right?"

"Alas, no, Senator. He has gone ahead of us on the road to eternity. So sad. So very sad."

Buck tried to say something, but Albert squeezed him tighter.

"Dead?" Rollingfield looked genuinely shocked.

"Which is why I had to complete the meal with my own humble hands. My tribute to an unsurpassable god of the kitchen. I trust it was tolerable."

Rollingfield looked at him closely out of one eye. It was a calculating look, shrewd. The look of a man who'd played the game of politics for a very long time and could read you like a menu. When his other eye opened, there was a glint of recognition in it.

"More than tolerable, uh…"

"Albert, Senator."

"Albert. It's a rare talent you have there."

Something told Albert the senator wasn't just talking about the terrine.

"Join me at my table, Albert. We should talk. Just you, mind. And waiter," he said to Buck, "another carafe of red."

Albert watched the senator's cumbrous buttocks roll beneath his toga as he lolloped back through to the restaurant.

"Shog," Buck said, extricating himself from Albert's embrace, "you're in there."

"Yes," Albert said, "I believe I am."

"But you're dead meat, all the same."

"I am?"

Buck leaned himself against the counter and puffed out his cheeks. "Chef was well liked by the guild. Right up Dozier's arse, he was."

"Dozier?"

"Guildmaster of the Night Hawks. Top dogs around here, 'cept maybe for the Dybbuks, and they don't play by the rules."

Albert chuckled at that. *What a concept!* "No honor among thieves, eh?"

Buck scoffed. "They ain't thieves. They're more like merchants, only they ain't exactly got the blessing of the senate."

"With one or two exceptions, no doubt. Like our friend Rollingfield?"

"I don't know all the ins and outs of it," Buck said, "but they dine together, him and Dozier. Reckon they talk more'n they eat. That's the thing of it. They always moan about Chef's cooking, but they keep coming back."

Albert put a hand on Buck's shoulder and injected as much sincerity as he could into his voice. "You're a shrewd man, Buck Fargin. Thank goodness I ran into you when I did." He started toward the swinging doors and cast over his shoulder, "Time for a few changes around here, don't you think?" When Buck frowned, Albert added, "Just remember, anything that happens, anything you see me doing is for our mutual benefit. I haven't forgotten I owe you a back-scratching. When it comes to maneuvering, I've a lifetime of practice. Keep your wits about you, be patient, and question nothing. Do that, and in a few short months, there'll be a new king on the throne."

"King? Throne?"

"You, Buck. How do you think this Dozier rose to become guildmaster? Hard work and fair play?"

Before Buck could answer, Albert pushed through the doors into the restaurant.

Rugbeard was still there, propping up the bar. Actually, he seemed to be sleeping, drool soaking into his beard, a half-empty flagon clutched in a limp hand.

The dining area was half-full but growing emptier by the second as a handful of soldiers muscled the clientele outside. The soldiers were somewhat classical in style: leather kilts, bronze cuirasses, greaves and vambraces. They each had a shortsword hanging from a belt with a golden eagle buckle.

Complaints about unfinished meals fell on deaf ears, and Albert couldn't help feeling aggrieved his cooking was being discarded in the name of this thuggery. Worse still, considering his plans to run the establishment, these were patrons who were unlikely to come back.

Rollingfield was eyeing him above the rim of a wine glass.

"Forgive my legionaries," he said, running his wine-stained tongue around his plump lips. "They are somewhat unimaginative in carrying out my orders. I thought it best, however, that we talked alone." He gestured for Albert to take the seat opposite.

A soldier tapped Rugbeard on the shoulder, eliciting a loud snore.

"Leave him," Rollingfield said. "Even if he heard anything over his own din, his booze-sozzled brain would forget it in an instant." He rolled his eyes at Albert. "Odious heap of dung. Still, he has his uses. Puts the fear of the plague in the punters, what."

The last of the customers was slung unceremoniously out into the street, and the soldiers locked the doors and closed the blinds. Albert's hand strayed to his pocket, seeking the reassurance of his cheese-cutter and finding only fluff.

Rollingfield guzzled down the dregs of his wine and slid the glass onto the table. He plumped up his belly and wriggled back into the chair, one eyelid drooping shut, the other hanging half-open like a sagging curtain. The exposed bloodshot eye roved around the tomato-smeared bread crusts he'd obviously used to mop up the sauce on the plate. Of the terrine, there was nothing left, which Albert took as a compliment.

"And what about me, Albert?" the senator said, languidly peering up at him. "Are they going to find me face down on the table covered in my own vomit?" He shook his head and gave a low, gurgling chuckle.

"Senator?"

Rollingfield's eyes snapped fully open, and a thin smile slashed through his puffed pillow-cheeks. "Don't worry, my friend, I feel quite safe with you. Quite safe. At least for the time being." He leaned forward, nudging the table with his belly. "I've been in this game a long time, Albert. Long time. And I'm sure you have, too. These kinds of meetings, between people such as you and I, are not uncommon now, are they?"

Straight to the point, then. Well, if that's how he wanted to play it. Albert interlaced his fingers and pursed his lips. "No, Senator. No, they are not."

"I knew it!" Rollingfield clapped his pudgy hands. "Good man, Albert. Good man. No mincing,"—he raised an eyebrow at that, and Albert felt someone had just bathed him in sewage—"no beating around the bush."

"Perish the thought, Senator."

"So, what is it, then?" Rollingfield asked. "The Dybbuks? The Catterwauls? No, no, let me guess. Man with your culinary skills, your bearing, your evident education... has to be with..."

"The Veneficis, senator," one of the soldiers ventured.

"I was about to say that, Corporal." Rollingfield sighed and narrowed his eyes. "Well, Albert?"

"Sicarii, Senator. You've probably never heard of them. Not from New Jerusalem. Long way off."

"I see. Brink? Portis? Surely not Malfen?"

Albert relaxed back in his chair and gave a sheepish smile.

Rollingfield tapped the side of his nose. "Say no more, my friend. Now, no one can blame you for not knowing, seeing as you're from out of town, but Dwan Dozier is not going to be happy about this. You see, Albert, the Night Hawks have their territory, as do the Dybbuks and the smaller guilds. Chef Dougan might have been a turgid little fart serving swill to clients who wouldn't know a ratatouille from a rat's arse, but he paid his dues."

"Protection?"

Rollingfield refilled his wine glass and proffered the carafe to Albert. Albert hesitated for a second then took it.

"It's the way of the world," Rollingfield said. "You know that. Dougan paid the Night Hawks to keep the Dybbuks away. Nasty crew, the Dybbuks, not the sort you'd want to be dealing with. Leader's some kind of sorcerer, and his second's a shapeshifting bitch who's a devil in a knife fight. Dozier liked this place for meetings, too. Probably because no one of any note would be seen dead here."

"Surely not?" Albert said.

"It wouldn't be good for me to be observed meeting with the guilds," Rollingfield said, "so what better place to come? Anonymity is everything in the subtler aspects of my profession."

"Quite so, Senator. Quite so."

"Every profession has its subtler regions, Albert. Am I right?"

Albert said nothing, happy to let the senator lay it all out for him.

"I, for one, would rather this establishment served decent food, if I'm to be forced to meet here. I'm something of a gastronome." He jiggled his gut for emphasis. "And I know talent when I see it. But let's come clean, Albert, shall we? I've exposed myself to you,"—that eyebrow raise again, accompanied by the feeling of falling into a nest of cockroaches—"now you do the same for me. Let me make it easy for you. You dabble in herbs and the like."

"It's more than that, Senator."

"Yes, yes. You have, shall we say, expertise in the pharmaceutical arts."

"Poisons, Senator. It's something of a passion."

Rollingfield's smile was broad, wet, and full of unsavory promise. "Excellent. You are exactly the man I'd hoped you were, Albert. You'll appreciate, in my trade, from time to time it is necessary for truculent politicians to take a turn for the worse."

"It's the way of the world, Senator."

Rollingfield's laugh was coupled with a release of gas that caused him to shift his weight onto one buttock. "Pardon me. Must have been the terrine."

"My apologies, Senator."

"The way I see it, Albert," Rollingfield said, "meetings at Dougan's Diner would be far more bearable if the food was edible. You pick up here, and I'll see to it that the guild leaves you alone. I'll have my legal man switch the deeds. I don't think Dougan had any living relatives, and even if he did, leave it to me. We'll take care of that. For your part, just keep paying Dozier and you'll have no trouble. Play your cards right, and keep serving this quality of food, and I'll consider moving my offices here. Just joshing, of course, but you get my meaning. And from time to time, I may have special work for you. How does that sound?"

Like a dream come true.

"Can I change the name?"

"Please do." Rollingfield stood and dusted the crumbs from his toga. "How's the weather now?"

The corporal peeked through the blinds. "Sky's turned mauve, Senator. Must be a storm coming. Twister, I'd say."

"Maybe," Rollingfield said. "All the same, best be off. I'll be seeing you, Albert. Oh, and congratulations on becoming the new owner of... what are you going to call it?"

"Queenie's, Senator. After my dear old mama."

"Queenie's? Like it. Very good."

A soldier unlocked the door and held it open for Rollingfield to squeeze through, and the others filed out after him.

Buck slid out from the kitchen, absently wiping at a glass with a dish towel. "That seemed to go well."

Eavesdropping little dog turd. "Ah, Buck. Glad you were listening in. This Dozier you mentioned, can you set up a meeting?"

"Uh, well…"

"Thought you were a big man in the guild. Shouldn't be too much trouble for you."

Buck's face took on the semblance of a constipated donkey. "Well, you see, I'm kind of freelance. I do a bit of this, bit of that."

"You're a dogsbody?" *Thought as much.* "You don't really know Dozier, do you?"

"Yeah, I do. I see him when he comes in here."

"But you don't actually know him."

Buck dropped his chin to his chest and shook his head.

"You might at least recall what he likes to eat."

"Pie and chips, but he never eats more'n a bite. Says it tastes like shite."

"Well," Albert said, surveying his new acquisition and already planning the wall coverings, "that's all about to change."

THE TOWER OF IVORY

"**B**IT CRAMPED, ISN'T it?" Rhiannon turned her nose up at the white-walled room—although white would have been stretching it. It had more the look of yellow-stained teeth about it, or old bones. "There's not enough room to swing a cat in here."

Aristodeus riffled through some papers on a desk, scribbled a note on one of them, and reached for a chain hanging from the ceiling.

"Then it's a good job I don't have a cat." When he pulled the chain, a trap opened, and a ladder extended in sections.

It was a cat Rhiannon likened him to, though, when he lithely bounded up the rungs. For an old codger, he certainly was agile.

"And besides," Aristodeus called from above, "what it lacks in length and breadth, it more than makes up for in height."

"That's what they all say."

Rhiannon heard him stomp around upstairs, dragging things across the floor, cursing and muttering. She took hold of the ladder and peered up, half-inclined to go see for herself what he was up to, but something about the stark light lancing down the opening unsettled her. It didn't seem quite natural.

Same as how they'd arrived here, quick as a flash. No bells and smells, no nothing, save for a green glow and a gut-curdling feeling of wrongness. The mere recollection made her retch, and she fell back against the ladder in a swoon.

"I'll be right with you," Aristodeus said. "Soon as I find the... Ah, there it is!"

Rhiannon pushed herself away from the ladder, blinking to clear her head as she took in the room. It must've been ten, maybe twelve feet square, and most of that was taken up with clutter: stacks of ancient-looking books on the floor, wooden crates, a scatter of boxes. The desk was intricately fashioned from what looked like walnut, its top inlaid with leather and gold leaf. It was piled high with notebooks and loose sheets of paper, but she couldn't make head nor tail of what was written on them. Looked like Aeternam, but her Aeternam was about as good as useless. Not much better than her knowledge of Nousianism, despite the hours of painstaking catechesis at the hands of Soror Agna. Bit of a joke, really, if you asked her. Rhiannon Kwane, a consecrated religious! Sad thing was, she'd really believed it was possible, really thought she'd had a vocation. Right up until she watched Mom and Dad murdered by those... those... Nous all bloody mighty, they were her friends once, even Gaston.

She shook the memories out of her head, and her eyes alighted on a wall chart. It depicted four interlocking circles, one atop the other, and within each was a diagram. She edged closer to see better: ten smaller circles arranged in a pattern of three columns, and there were connecting lines between them. Cursive lettering crowned the larger circles, and there were blockish symbols inside the smaller ones. Just looking at them made her head hurt, and she turned away, spotting a door on the adjacent wall. It was the same off-white as the walls, ceiling and floor, yet it had a gleaming brass doorknob that just begged to be turned.

She reached for it and drew back, feeling suddenly guilty, like the sisters and brothers at the Templum of the Knot had just seen her innermost thoughts, witnessed her depravity for themselves. She extended her hand again. This time, her fingers tingled, and she could swear there was heat—intense heat—coming from the other side of the door. She licked her lips, and a ripple ran up her spine to her neck. It seemed to come from Callixus's sword. Her mind flashed back to Soror Agna telling her the story of Jose and Carmella, their disobedience of Ain when they'd opened the Box of All Ways. She had to know what was beyond the door. Had to—

"No! Don't touch that!"

Rhiannon's heart bounced into her throat and she whirled round.

Aristodeus slung a knotted mess of tubes to the floor and clambered down the ladder with dozens of clear packets tucked under his arm.

"I'm feeling sick," she said. It wasn't exactly a lie. "Just needed to get some air."

"Nothing wrong with the air in here," Aristodeus said as he shot back up the ladder to grab a crate. It rattled as he once more descended. Catching her look, he set the crate down and squinted at some print on one of the slats. "Nutrition. Marvelous stuff, and keeps forever. Now, where did I put the cannulae?" He rummaged around in some boxes beneath his desk. "Or would you say cannulas? It's so easy to forget who I'm speaking to."

Rhiannon didn't have a clue what he was talking about and really didn't care. The air felt stifling, and she could've sworn the walls were closing in. "Don't you have a window or something? I can't breathe."

"Ah, here they are!" Aristodeus held up a see-through packet backed with white.

Rhiannon's vision blurred, and a wave of nausea washed over her. She put out a hand to steady herself on the desk. "Door," she gasped. "Open the door."

Aristodeus set the packet down. He touched a palm to her forehead then pressed two fingers to her neck. "Febrile and fibrillating. Here, sit down." He pulled out the chair for her, and she collapsed into it. Callixus's scabbarded sword caught on the backrest. She cursed and shifted it over to one side.

"I'm fine. I just need some air, is all." Rhiannon put her head in her hands and leaned her elbows on the desk.

"Not pregnant, are you?"

"What?" Surely not. Her guts churned as her mind flashed back to Gaston's grunting and thrusting. She sat bolt upright, hands finding their way to her belly. "No! What do you think I am?" She couldn't be anyway, she told herself. She'd had the menses since, hadn't she? Yes, at the Templum of the Knot, so she couldn't be. She let out a long breath and shook her head.

Aristodeus patted her on the shoulder, gave a gentle squeeze. "It's the effect of the transition. Don't worry, it'll wear off."

"Wear off a bloody sight sooner if I could just get some air, take a walk. Or am I a prisoner?" She cocked her head and narrowed her eyes. She could almost feel the black sword pulsating on her back, eager for the fight, thirsty for blood. A thrill coursed through her veins, and she shuddered, suddenly sickened by what she'd just felt.

"You wouldn't want to open that door," Aristodeus said. "Believe me."

"Why not? Where the Abyss are we?"

He gave a tight smile and rolled his eyes. "It's just not ready yet. I have a hard enough time maintaining the vertical, never mind the horizontal."

Rhiannon followed his gaze to the ceiling and the open trapdoor. "How many stories?

How high's it go?"

"Last time I counted, seventy-two, but it's never enough. Now listen. I don't expect you to understand, but I do need you to obey a few simple rules. Go nowhere, touch nothing, without my express permission. Understood?"

Rhiannon wrinkled her nose at him. "How long you planning on staying? Thought we were just grabbing some junk and heading for this New Jerusalem before the dwarf starves to death."

"We are, Rhiannon. We are. But first things first. There are matters I want to discuss with you."

"Let me guess. Shader?"

Aristodeus frowned and perched on the edge of the desk. "He's not quite what I'd hoped for."

"Tell me about it." She knew she was being unfair, that she expected too much from Shader, but if he didn't grow some balls soon, work out who and what he was, she'd... Well, she didn't know what she'd do. It wasn't like they were an item. Huntsman had seen to that, and he was only acting on the advice of Aristodeus, in any case. She ground her teeth and felt a rush of heat beneath her skin. "What are you up to? What have you done to him?"

Aristodeus sighed and began to kick at invisible objects. "My relationship with Shader is rather complex. Suffice it to say, I had a vision for him that is not coming to fruition, and if things don't change very soon, the enemy will..." He licked his lips and sat perfectly still. Rhiannon could almost hear the cogs of his mind turning. "He will win."

"Gandaw?"

"Gandaw's the immediate threat, the first wave, if you like. Mind you, if he pulls off the Unweaving, it's game over. He almost succeeded before. I tried to stop him, but things... things didn't go to plan."

"Seems to happen to you a lot."

Aristodeus tutted and stood. "When you consider the infinitude of permutations, the sheer magnitude of the battlefield, the cunning of the adversary, I'd say I've been thwarted very few times. Very few indeed."

"Good on you. So it's a long game, but you've got all the cards, right?"

"This is no game, girl!" A fire came into Aristodeus's eyes, and for a moment Rhiannon felt she'd blown the lid off a volcano. She shrank back in her chair.

"Shouldn't we... Shouldn't we get going?"

Aristodeus held up a hand, and his face softened. "Time has no meaning here. We can take as long as we like, get acquainted, discuss strategy, and still get there before Shader and the others."

"Strategy? Right. Like I know a lot about that. What is it with you? I thought you were meant to be some all-bloody-knowing philosopher. Hello! I'm from Oakendale. You know, farmer's daughter and all that."

Aristodeus leaned in close. Too close. "You sell yourself short, Rhiannon. It's not how Elias saw you."

Rhiannon's insides clenched at mention of the bard. Ain, how she missed him, but when had she had a chance to grieve? It wasn't like she'd had a minute to come to terms with what had happened to Mom and Dad, or Sammy. Just the thought of the change that had come over her little brother made her fists bunch so tight she thought the knuckles would split. Sammy. Her Sammy siding with that snake-headed bastard over her, the sister who'd virtually raised him.

"And it's not how Shader sees you, either. His faith, his vocation wasn't so shallow he'd toss it away for just anyone. He sensed something in you, Rhiannon, just as I do now."

Bullshit. She wasn't falling for that. Shader had liked her well enough, but not for the high-sounding reasons Aristodeus was hinting at. If she hadn't stood firm, whatever shreds of holiness still clung to him would have been burned up in the heat of his passion. Maybe she should have given him what he wanted, what she wanted, too, back then. Least that way none of this other shit would've happened. Or would it?

"Now, I have a proposal for you."

Aristodeus reached for her breast.

What the...? Rhiannon swung for him, but he caught her wrist in an iron grip that hurt right down to the bone. Her heart pounded in her ears. *No! Never again.* She reached for the sword on her back with her free hand. Aristodeus released her, stepped aside.

"Calm yourself, girl. What's the matter with you?"

"What's the matter with me? Shog you, you pervert. That what you had in mind all this while? Bring me back to your squalid little shit hole for a quick grope and a romp?"

The color drained from his face. His lips worked silently for a moment before he said, "I was going for your shoulder."

"Never heard them called that before."

Aristodeus sighed, and the color came back to his cheeks, red and fiery. "I said proposal, not proposition. For goodness' sake, if I wanted to cavort, I would already have done so."

"Over my dead body. Oh, don't tell me, that's the way you like it."

Aristodeus clutched at the air above his head. "If there is a God, now would be a good time. Grant me patience!" He closed his eyes and took a long, slow breath. When he opened them again, he seemed tired, maybe a little... smaller. The wind had gone right out of his sails. "I was merely trying to... Oh, never mind." He whirled away from her, slinging out his arm, as if he were throwing an invisible hat. The wall shimmered and vanished, and beyond it stood another room, this one lit by the orange glow of a crackling fire. Beside the fireplace were a couple of barrel chairs and a side table, atop which were two glasses and two bottles.

Aristodeus winced, and sweat beaded upon his forehead. "Have you always been strung so taut?" he said, leading her into the room and standing behind one of the chairs, indicating she should sit there.

"You said 'God'." She removed the scabbard from her back, leaned it against the hearth, and lowered herself into the soft-cushioned chair. Soror Agna would've had a fit if anyone had said that in her presence. Some of the oldies used it, back in Oakendale, but no one rightly knew what it meant. All she knew was that the word offended Ain, so they'd told her.

"It's an old name," he said, "from an ancient time. Don't let it trouble you. Always someone telling us what not to say or think."

She felt the philosopher's fingers on her shoulders, his thumbs kneading the knots in her upper back. At first she flinched, then she stiffened, and finally, when he persisted, tears spilled onto her cheeks and she shook.

"Let it all out, Rhiannon. You are quite safe here. Let it all out."

He moved away to the table, popped the cork on one of the bottles, and poured a golden liquid into both glasses. It fizzed and sparkled as he passed her one.

"Hiedsieck 1907 Diamant Bleu cuvée. A woman of your appetites—" He gave her a knowing look that nearly bought him a smack in the face. "—should appreciate this. Just remember, sip, don't glug."

Scowling at him, Rhiannon took the glass and ran it under her nose. "1907?"

"Different calendar," Aristodeus said. "Before the Reckoning. A long time."

"Is it drinkable?"

Aristodeus took a quaff and smacked his lips. "Extremely. It was part of a consignment en route to Tsar Nicho… a powerful ruler, when the freight ship was sunk. There was a war going on at the time. Big war. The war to end all wars, they said."

"So how'd—"

Aristodeus waved her to silence. "The bottles were brought to the surface some eighty years after the ship sank, but don't worry, I've not been hoarding my stock for centuries. I doubt even Diamant Bleu would be quite so vibrant after so long a time. Mine comes, you could say, fresh from the wreck." He tapped the side of his nose and gave a look of mock surprise before seating himself in the other chair. Setting his glass down, he took out his pipe, tapped the bowl on the edge of the table, and proceeded to fill it.

The champagne was bitter-sweet, with tangs of overripe pear and citrus, maybe a hint of musk. It had only the ghost of bubbles, but what could you expect after so many years? She took another sip, then drained the glass. Aristodeus looked up, shook his head, and took a taper from beside the fire to light his pipe.

"Impressions?" he asked.

"Too early to say." She held out her glass for a refill, and Aristodeus obliged.

"Tell me," he said, taking a puff on his pipe, "what happened?"

She took another swig, spilling some down the front of her robe. Aristodeus raised an eyebrow, then made a show of smoking nonchalantly.

"To my parents, you mean?" Or did he mean with Gaston? How much did he know? Anything?

"Wherever you want to start. There is plenty of time, and I am a good listener."

She opened her mouth to start, but he popped the pipe from his mouth and gestured with the stem. "Tell me anything, everything, but only if you wish it."

She looked into his glinting blue eyes, seeing in them an easy familiarity she'd not noticed before. There was something about the shape of his face, too, the nose, his cheekbones. The barest hint of a smile curled one corner of his mouth, and he stroked his beard, watching her watching him. When he gave the subtlest of nods, she couldn't help herself; it all came pouring out, the tears, the self-hatred, Gaston, her parents, Sammy. As she bled herself dry, Aristodeus topped up her glass, barely touching his own drink. He chewed on his pipe stem, grunted attentively, occasionally asked her to clarify something.

"Life can be so… disempowering," he said when she ran out of things to say.

Ain, she'd never told anyone so much about herself, not even Elias, and he'd known her since birth. She'd let a few things slip to Shader, but since Gaston, she'd closed in on herself, spoken to him in fits and starts, and most of that venom. Did she blame Shader for Gaston? It made no sense, but it sure had changed how she thought of him, how she thought of anyone with a cock and fruits. She looked up, aware she hadn't responded to Aristodeus's comment. His head bobbed, a new warmth exuding from his face. He was right; he was a good listener, and best of all, he hadn't judged her, least not in any way she could tell.

"Events like those you describe can make you despair. It all seems so unfair. You burn for vengeance, or at the very least for justice, and yet Nous demands that you forgive, offer your sufferings as a sacrifice."

Yes, that was it. That was how it felt. All that anger, that natural rage, but she couldn't let it out, not in any way that would make things right.

"There is wisdom in what the Templum teaches," Aristodeus said, "but it is a hard path, a narrow gate through which few pass. I struggled with it myself, once upon a time, but I am, shall we say, too proud for such a life. Too self-reliant. Shader is different. He inherited his mother's piety."

Rhiannon leaned forward at that. She knew a little of Shader's past, but only what he'd told her.

"His father was an altogether different influence." Aristodeus leaned back in his chair and took a long pull on his pipe. "A good man, by all counts, a strategist, an organizer, a leader. They complemented each other, Jarl and Gralia. Could have been the perfect match, if only they'd shared the same faith. Jarl was too much the pragmatist, and far too honest to accept the Nousian way. You see, killing was in his blood, and he knew it. It's a rare thing for a military man to lay down arms and take up the life of a lamb."

"But Shader is both," Rhiannon said. "His father and mother."

"Aren't we all, those of us who knew both parents? But with Shader, it is more complex. Most of us are thrust haphazardly into the care of those that sired us, and it's blind luck whether or not they are suitable."

True enough. Would she have chosen differently, if she'd had the choice? Would things have turned out better if she'd not grown up in the arse-end of Sahul with parents as common as muck? Part of her cried yes, but in the main she'd been happy, hadn't she? Mom and Dad had been good sorts, done the best they could.

"In Shader's case, a little more thought went into the parents—or rather, the foster parents."

Rhiannon spluttered out some champagne she'd not even been aware she was drinking. "What?"

"Please don't tell him, but our friend is not from Britannia, as he believes. Oh, he was raised there, but he and I share a common homeland: Graecia, nestled in between Latia and Verusia. It's an arid country, these days, steeped in history. The cradle of philosophy; the godfather of culture—at least what I consider to be the best in culture. My point is that Shader was not simply the product of place or biology. He was plucked from Graecia and planted in the somewhat less salubrious soil of Britannia."

Rhiannon took a careful sip. "But why?"

"*Pietatis et belli*. Piety and war. Gralia and Jarl were the perfect exemplars of what I hoped to achieve."

"You? You did this? You took Shader from his real parents? Did they agree? Does he have any idea?"

Aristodeus rapped his pipe against the side of the hearth, spilling burnt tobacco to the flames. "They did not notice, and he must never know."

"Didn't notice? How—?"

"We are getting too far from the point. You do not have to remain as you are, bitter, angry, repressed, and powerless. If you wish it, I can offer you what I gave to Shader, albeit somewhat belatedly."

She shook her head absently, not really knowing what she was rejecting, what he was offering. "I'm already taken."

Aristodeus's eyes widened.

"By Nous."

He scoffed at that. "Rhiannon, Rhiannon, what I have heard today gives the lie to that vocation. You know as much yourself. Why stubbornly cling to what you know is not your true calling?"

"Shog you."

He spread his hands. "I rest my case. Look." He leaned sharply forward, penetrating her with those startling eyes. "That sword you have—" He nodded to Callixus's black sword propped beside the fire, absorbing the light from the flames. "—I can teach you how to use it."

Now it was her turn to scoff. Hadn't she been the one to cleave that half-plant, half-man in two? Hadn't she done what Shader and the midget had failed to do? "I can already use it, thanks."

"Anyone can hack like a butcher. Oh, I'm quite sure you have the fire for combat, but what about the grace, the skill, the speed of hand and eye? You've seen Shader in action?"

She nodded.

"I trained him," Aristodeus said, "and it is a rare pupil who outgrows his master."

Rhiannon studied him with a new respect. "You're a swordsman? Aren't you a bit too bookish for that?"

"I am many things, my dear, and I have lived long enough to excel in more than one discipline."

She eyed the black sword, imagining what she could've done if she'd had such a weapon before and known how to use it. Her parents might still be alive for one; and Gaston... She cut off the thought of what she would've done to him; it didn't sit right with her, not now he was dead.

"You can make me as good as Shader?"

"Maybe better."

She leaned forward, curled her hands around the sword hilt, lifted it to her lap. "Why?"

Aristodeus tucked his pipe away and steepled his fingers. "Because Shader is failing. He lacks both the purity of his mother and the ruthlessness of his father."

"That surprises you?" What did he expect? Taking two opposites and blending them in one individual? It was no wonder Shader was so screwed up.

"Maybe not with hindsight. The problem is, both qualities are needed. He has just enough holiness to wield the Sword of the Archon, but not an iota of that needed to unleash its full might. And as for decisiveness in striking the killing blow..." He left it unspoken, but she knew he was referring to the Homestead, and Shader's balking at the final hurdle. He had a point. If Shader had struck true, this could all have been ended right there and then.

"That's been your plan all along? Have Shader kill Gandaw with a magic sword?"

Aristodeus gave a tight smile. "The sword is more than magical. It is intimately linked with the Archon himself. You could say it's a part of him. But it's not Gandaw we need it for. If it had just been Gandaw we had to worry about, the Unweaving would not even be a possibility, and I would have ended this centuries ago." He closed his eyes, and a tic started up beneath one of them.

"Gandaw has the Archon's sister and has found a way to harness her power against her will. This makes him, you might say, god-like."

"The statue? Eingana? The sword is for her?"

Aristodeus opened an eye and pursed his lips. "Seems logical, don't you think? Her might is beyond any we can muster. Only her siblings can rival her. The Demiurgos is no doubt loving every minute of this, and even if he could free himself from the Abyss, he'd be more likely to ravish her than kill her. And the Archon will not act directly for fear of ceding to the Demiurgos the same liberty. It seems the Aeonic Triad are bound by a rather compelling form of justice." He shook his head, leaned back, and studied Rhiannon. "You'll never be accepted by the Archon's sword, but we must nevertheless plan for every eventuality. If Shader fails, nothing we do will matter, for there'll be nothing left. If by some miracle he succeeds, the war will not end there, and we must be ready for the next phase. Maybe the enemy can be fed a dose of his own medicine." He reached over and tapped Callixus's sword, winced, and sat back.

"What... what can I do? I'm no Shader, and this sword... I'm not sure if—"

Aristodeus squeezed her knee, and she didn't even flinch. A warm tingle thrilled its way up her spine.

"Let us enjoy another bottle." He grabbed the second and popped the cork. "We should talk some more, get to know each other better. There's no hurry. We'll begin slowly, then take the feeding apparatus to New Jerusalem and go from there. How does that sound?"

Rhiannon's eyes were rooted to her glass as Aristodeus refilled it.

"Something to eat?" he said. "I have some excellent brie, if only I can find a knife to cut it."

With a start, Rhiannon remembered entering the plane ship atop the Homestead with Shader and the midget. She felt about in her robe pocket and brought out the wire between two sticks she'd found on the floor.

"This any good?"

"What's that, a garrote? No, a cheese-cutter. Perfect," Aristodeus said. "Like the company."

He shuffled his chair closer to hers so they could chink glasses.

Rhiannon laughed, feeling a rush of heat through her veins that burned away the tension and left her more at peace than she could remember.

NEW JERUSALEM

DAWN LIGHT BLED atop the city's battlements as one sun crested the horizon. The scale of the walls reminded Shader of the Homestead. They must have been close to five hundred feet tall, and they extended for miles without end. The sections stretching between the scores of cylindrical towers were heavily buttressed, and embrasured on dozens of levels. Lanterns ghosted in between the merlons, and cones of stark light roved the ground before the walls. The architecture was of a magnitude Shader had never before witnessed. Not even Sarum could hold a candle to New Jerusalem, and the city's defenses dwarfed those at Trajinot entrusted with keeping out the hordes of the Liche Lord. A cluster of bronze-capped minarets peeked above the walls, and way off to their left, the top of a ramshackle tower billowed smoke that swirled into a dirty canopy of smog.

Boggy ground squelched beneath their boots as the trio trudged toward the city. The second sun rose to join its twin, and they both climbed with unnatural swiftness, setting the domes of the minarets aflame and limning the smog with gold.

Shader glanced back the way they'd come, where the sky was stained with a patch of mauve. It must have been way past Arx Gravis, perhaps as far as the Sour Marsh.

"Reckon it's started?" Shadrak said, following Shader's gaze.

It was hard to tell from here, but the discoloration could have been spilling from the Perfect Peak. "Either that, or there's a storm coming."

"You get twisters here, mate?" Shadrak asked the dwarf.

Nameless stopped to take a look, grunting something that might have been an answer. He appeared indestructible, with his mail and muscles, and the great helm denied him any hint of expression, any suggestion that beneath its dark casing there was still a living, breathing person.

Nameless' mood had dipped the further they got from Arx Gravis. It could have been the lack of food and drink, or homesickness. Or maybe it was grisly memories rising to the surface now he'd left the scene of his crimes. He'd done little more than huff and grumble since they'd left the ravine. His shoulders seemed permanently stooped, as if the helm were too heavy for his head. If he hadn't kept on moving, one cumbrous step at a time, he might have sunk beneath its weight, down through the earth to whatever infernal realm lay at the heart of Aethir.

Lightning flashed in the distance, forking and branching across the patch of mauve like cracks in a mirror.

"Storm it is, then." Shadrak shrunk into his new cloak, merging with the browns and greens of the fens that were beginning to cede ground to the freshly plowed fields skirting the city.

"Nah, laddie." Nameless' voice was a distant rumble. "Not a storm."

A cloying dread gripped Shader's innards. Something was odd about the lightning, something about the way it… And then he realized. The flashes had traveled upward, and now he could see tiny spots of blackness left in their wake, like the dead flesh of an infected wound. Nameless was right; this was no storm.

"We need to hurry," Shader said. "There's no telling how much time we have."

From what Aristodeus had said, it could have been days. But what if he was wrong? That business with Dave had already shown the philosopher wasn't as omniscient as he liked to think. For all Shader knew, they could have mere minutes remaining. Seconds, even. It was best not to think about it.

The shadow cast by the walls fell over two or three acres of farmland. It smothered the blaze of the twin suns and sent a chill into Shader's bones. He tugged his coat tight about him and pressed on, not checking to see if Shadrak and Nameless were following.

He'd known this was coming, but seeing the start of the Unweaving up close was more than a little unsettling. It brought everything he'd been wrestling with his whole life starkly into focus and left it teetering on a knife's edge. So many choices never fully made: Nous and the sword; the way of a pious mother, or that of a battle-hardened father. Please one, disappoint the other. Aristodeus had told him this from the start and had then proceeded to blend the best of both, so he said. Clearly, it hadn't been about keeping his parents happy; that much was obvious now. Aristodeus had had a purpose. Always had a purpose, and now it was coming to a head. Deacon Shader—neither one thing nor the other. A holy idiot or a brutal killer. The two didn't mix, no matter what Aristodeus said. You couldn't kill for Nous. Shader had always known that, argued against the theology that permitted it, but he'd never decisively chosen.

He'd almost found a third way, he realized, thinking back to the day he'd told Rhiannon how he felt. He'd been so convinced she wanted it, too, felt the anticipation bursting through his pores, and then she'd rejected him. Oh, she'd dressed it up to save his stupid pride, but he'd seen right through it. She was about as interested in his purity as she was her own. And that was all a sham, her joining the Templum of the Knot, just like his own attempts at holiness. Who was he kidding? Lallia had shown him just how difficult chastity was. He'd kept it intact on that occasion, but only just. He could still smell her scent, musky and heady. Whatever she used, it had fired his blood like a witch's potion. And it wasn't prayer that had protected him, either: it was violent rage. Maybe he'd made a choice long ago without even knowing it. You only needed to look at his track record to see he was his father's man through and through.

Is that what Aristodeus needed, a killer to get the job done? If that was the case, why not use someone like Shadrak? Or did he need a luminary? Shader shook his head. There were far better choices in that respect. Mother Ioana, for one.

"What we gonna do, knock?" Shadrak said.

Shader brought his attention to bear on the monstrous barbican thrusting out from the curtain wall between two towers. It was big enough to be a castle in its own right, and in place of gates, it had huge double-doors of stone etched with cursive script. He barely glanced at the writing but saw enough to know it was Aeternam, or whatever it was Thumil had called it.

Nameless walked right up to them, the great helm pivoting as he scanned the letters. "Something from the time of Maldark," he said. "Latin's not too good. No call for it, except for scholars, and Thumil, of course. Dead language, if you ask me."

"Maldark?" Shader squinted where Nameless pointed. He started to translate out loud: "The last act of the dwarves of Malkuth, a gift for the first of the free." He turned to Nameless for an explanation.

"Malkuth's everything this side of the Farfalls, laddie. The first of the free, though… I can only guess that's the colonists. Legend has it they were brought to Aethir by Gandaw in magical ships that crossed the stars."

Shader glanced at Shadrak, who merely narrowed his eyes and gave an almost indiscernible shrug.

"Brought from where?" Shader asked. "Earth?"

Nameless nodded. "Says something about it in the Annals of Arx Gravis, those that go back before the fall of Maldark, but can't say I ever read them. Lucius was the brains of the family. I was…" He flexed a bicep and gave it a good squeeze. "…a big dumb ox, by comparison."

Shader found that hard to believe. "And Latin," he said. "I've been meaning to ask, how come you dwarves have Latin? It's virtually the same as what we call Aeternam." Not only that, but how come the dwarves of Aethir—Maldark among them—and even the elf, Gilbrum, spoke the lingua vulgaris, the common tongue used universally on Earth since the time of the Ancients?

Nameless coughed to clear his throat. "We don't, these days. Not most of us. Latin came with the scriptures, but no one follows them anymore."

"Except Thumil."

The great helm bobbed in agreement. "He's a special case. Well, he's another sort of case, too, but yes, he has a passion for all things historical. Says he rooted out the scriptures when he was researching Maldark. Thing is, they changed him." He went quiet for a moment and then added, "For the better, I'd say, but others will tell you they made him soft."

Shader knew exactly what he was talking about: self-regulation; self-sacrifice. Sure, that could make you look weak. Maybe that's why he struggled with it so much.

"What's the rest say?" Nameless asked.

"May this city vouchsafe the protection of these, our brothers, our fellow victims; and may it serve as an acceptable penance for our sins."

"That'll be about Maldark's betrayal," Nameless said. "From then on, my people mistrusted themselves so much they withdrew from the world above. It's why we have the council, bunch of procrastinating codgers that they are. They scrutinize every choice facing Arx Gravis in the most minute detail, so that the errors of the past aren't repeated. The Demiurgos, they say, has eyes and ears everywhere and is always baiting us. Thing is, the council reckons every act carries its own risks, so it's always safer to do nothing, and in any case, by the time they've finished debating an issue to death, they've forgotten what it was in the first place, so there's no need to do anything about it."

"Think they've noticed we're here yet?" Shadrak looked up at the crenellations atop the barbican, where there appeared to be a change of guard taking place. "Want me to climb the walls, slit a few throats, and open them doors from the inside?"

"Can't been done, laddie," Nameless said. "Dwarf stonework. Mortar's thinner than a gnat's hair. Even with fingers as dainty as yours, you'll find no purchase."

Shadrak gave a tight-lipped smile and patted one of his belt pouches. "Then you don't know much about my line of work."

"Don't know much about anything since I woke up," Nameless said, rapping his knuckles on the great helm. "Noddle's numb as a leper's knackers."

Shader shook his head as he looked at the walls. Each stone was the size of a house. It boggled the mind as to how anyone could have lifted them into place. "Must've had some skill to build this. Your people, I mean."

"Aye, laddie. Aye, that they did. You'll not find stonework like that even in Arx Gravis. They call these the Cyclopean Walls. I heard it said a race of one-eyed giants lifted the blocks into place."

Shader chuckled.

"I'm serious, laddie. Mind you, there's more than one version of the tale. Some say Gandaw made the cyclopes from the raw stuff of humans brought from Earth, same as he did with my peop…" He tailed off. "Gandaw did a lot of experimenting here in Malkuth. When he'd exhausted his line of work with a species, he exterminated it, and that's what they say happened with the cyclopes."

"Doubt he was chuffed them helping out with the walls," Shadrak said. "Not if they were s'posed to keep the colonists safe. I take it you mean safe from him?"

"Aye, you're not wrong there. Course, there's another legend that says the cyclopes were natives of Qlippoth on the other side of the Farfalls, but no one believes that anymore. Nothing crosses the mountains."

"Save the Sour Marsh," Shader said.

Nameless turned to look at him through the eye-slit. "Good point. I hadn't thought of that."

A trumpet blast sounded from the barbican, and a soldier peered down at them through a crenel. His face was framed by a bronze helm with a white horsehair crest.

"A galea?" Shader said, more to himself than anyone else. He'd seen such a helm on display in the Aeternam Museum. It had been dated to a few thousand years before the Reckoning, at a time even the Ancients would have considered ancient.

"Eh?" Nameless said, craning his neck so he could see.

"His helmet. It seems out of place."

The soldier made a funnel of his hand and threw his voice. "Salvete, amici. Quo vadis?"

"Shog's he say?" Shadrak said, hand slipping to his pistol.

"Latin, at a guess," Nameless said.

Shader ran a quick translation through his mind. The pronunciation was a bit off, but essentially it was the same as Templum Aeternam. He called back, "Ave, amicus. Quaeramus Academiae. Nos intrare?"

"Hold on, hold on," the soldier said. "Not so fast, mate. All I know's the greeting, and that's only coz the bloody senate'd have me job if I didn't learn it right. Say again."

"We're heading for the Academy," Shader said. "May we enter?"

The soldier frowned and made a claw of his forefinger and pinkie. "What's your business there?"

"Our business," Shadrak said.

"Right. I see. Well…" The soldier took his helm off and scratched his sweat-slicked hair. "Doors don't normally open till zenith, and then only for a few shakes of a rattler's tail."

"Looks of the suns, laddie," Nameless said, "can't be far from zenith now."

"Uh, one moment." The soldier disappeared for a few seconds and then popped back into view. "We'll make an exception, seeing as there's a storm brewing, by the looks of it. Give us a second."

A heavy clunk sounded from inside the barbican, followed by squeaking and groaning as the stone doors opened outward.

Shadrak started forward, but Nameless put a restraining hand on his shoulder. The assassin's eyes flashed dangerously, and his hand slipped inside his cloak.

"Might want to take that off," Nameless said.

"Yeah? And why's that, then?"

"Folks see you blending with the surroundings, and they'll assume you're up to no good. Don't need to get off to a bad start now, do we?"

Shadrak gave a curt nod and removed the cloak, bundling it under his arm. It looked like he was carrying a boulder the same color as the city walls.

"Give it here, laddie," Nameless said. He took the bundle and stuffed it up the front of his hauberk. The effect was comical—a pronounced bulge that he patted affectionately. "They'll either think I'm up the duff or a bit too friendly with the beer. Don't worry," he said as Shadrak gritted his teeth and shook his head. Nameless produced a drawstring purse and shook it so that it clinked. "Big city like this, bound to be a rogue's outfitters. I'll buy you a new one. All I ask in return is a pint in the nearest watering hole."

"Just give it back when we leave," Shadrak said, starting through the doors. "After you've washed the dwarf sweat off it."

"How about you, laddie?" Nameless said, walking beside Shader into the mouth of the barbican. "A half, even. Something to wet the whistle."

"You can't drink, remember?"

The dwarf stopped for a moment and rubbed the top of his great helm. "Oh, shog, I completely forgot. Silly really, seeing as that's why we're heading to the Acad…"

Nameless dried up as they entered a long hallway lit by softly glowing crystals set into the vaulted ceiling. Corinthian pillars, similar to those favored in Aeterna, ran in three evenly spaced rows, and polished wooden doors flanked both sides of the hall. Switchback railings formed a maze-like channel down the center, presumably for queuing people entering and leaving the city.

A bleary-eyed guard stood yawning inside the entrance. He wore a galea like the soldier on the walls, only this one had a red plume instead of white. The rest of the uniform was exactly what Shader had seen in the museum: a bronze breastplate over a red tunic, a leather kilt, and sandals with crisscross straps. A gladius hung from a narrow girdle around his waist, and he half-leaned on a rectangular shield edged with gold.

"Follow the railing all the way to the far end," he said, cocking a thumb over his shoulder. "State your business at the desk, do as the clerk tells you, then be on your way swift, like, so's you don't hold up the line."

"What line?" Shadrak said. "Ain't no one else here."

"Don't get lippy, son," the guard said. "Boy yours?" he asked Nameless.

Shadrak tensed, his eyes narrowing to bloody slits.

The dwarf clutched his padded belly and laughed. "Did you not notice, laddie, he has a wee wisp of a beard?"

The guard peered closer at Shadrak. "Oh, yeah. Sorry, mate." He waved a hand about. "It's the light in here. Damn wizard globes. Give me a good lantern any day."

Shadrak gave a tight smile, his eyes hard as nails and calculating as a snake's. He turned and started to head across the room, ignoring the labyrinth of railings.

"Excuse me, sir," the guard said, fingers curling round the hilt of his sword. "Keep to the line."

"What?" Shadrak said without looking back. "You having a laugh?"

"Sir!" the guard barked as Shadrak continued across the hall. He raised a whistle to his lips. "Sir, I demand—"

"You don't want to do that," Nameless said, stepping in close.

The guard froze, his jaw hanging slack, the whistle held in trembling fingers. Shader felt it, too: the waves of menace rolling off of Nameless, yet the dwarf's voice was almost amiable.

"You don't want to upset the little'n," he said. "Gets a bit uppity at times. Between you and me, he's got a vile temper and bites like a bitch in heat." Nameless clapped a hand on the guard's shoulder, eliciting a wince and a whimper. "Leave him be, laddie."

The guard nodded mutely and lowered his whistle.

"Good boy," Nameless said. "Good boy. Now, to show our appreciation for your consideration, we'll follow the line, won't we, my friend?"

Shader looked from the guard to Shadrak, who was already on the far side of the hall, speaking to someone at a desk. "Uh, yes, if you insist."

"That I do, laddie. That I do."

They left the guard wide-eyed and shaking as they followed the twists and turns of the passage between the railings. Shader bristled with frustration as they walked back and forth for an eternity, rather than taking the direct route like Shadrak had done. Nameless had got it into his head they were following the rules, and there was an air about him that brooked no argument. When they reached the other side, the assassin was already pacing, clearly raring to go.

A middle-aged woman sat behind the desk riffling through loose leafs of paper. She was dressed in a drab black robe, her graying hair pulled into a bun. Every now and then, she'd lick her thumb and give a double cough in the back of her throat. After a long while of being ignored, Shader gave a polite cough of his own. When that elicited no response, Nameless hacked and wheezed and hawked up what sounded like enough phlegm to drown a rabbit. The woman glared up at him, but Nameless turned the eye slit on Shader. When he spoke, it sounded like he was chewing on gristle.

"No… where… to spit." He followed up with some gurgling, gulping sounds, and gave a satisfied belch. "Shog, tastes like a witch's septic discharge."

The clerk wrinkled her nose and turned her attention back to her paperwork, stamping with renewed vigor.

"Know what that tastes like, do you?" Shadrak said.

"No idea, to be honest, but I'm sure the lassie here could help us out."

"Shhh," she said. "I'm trying to concentrate. Just wait your turn, and I'll be right with you."

Nameless pivoted the great helm left and right then shrugged. "This is our turn."

The clerk sighed and tutted, stamped another piece of paper, and looked up. A change instantly came over her face, as if she'd just pulled on a mask. Suddenly, she was bright-eyed and giving them a broad, white smile. "Gentlemen," she said, "are you visiting or returning home?"

"Visiting," Shader said. "We have business—"

"Welcome to New Jerusalem. Please remove your weapons and place them on the desk for cataloguing, and I'll need you to empty your pockets."

She raised an eyebrow at Shader's Liber when he pulled it out, checked the title page, and sniffed. "Just the one sword, sir?"

"Just the one."

"And you, sir," she said to Nameless. "Just the axe?"

"Only weapon I'd care to show in public, lassie."

She shook her head, as if she heard that one all the time.

"What's this?"

"Prayer cord," Shader said, starting to untie it from his belt.

"Might want to keep that hidden, sir."

Shader looked to her for an explanation as he removed it and stuffed it in a pocket, but none was forthcoming.

"Doors are open dawn, zenith, and dusk, unless you're with the guilds or the senate, which I think we can assume you're not. Any questions?"

"So, we ain't free to come and go as we please?" Shadrak asked.

"Price we pay for our freedom," the woman said.

"Freedom from what?" Shader asked.

The woman glanced to the right, where scores of guards were filing in and taking up posts around the hall. One of the soldiers caught her eye and started toward them but stopped when she held up a hand.

"In our city, you follow our rules, understood?" She shook her head, rolled her eyes, and muttered something under her breath.

"Right you are, lassie," Nameless said, snatching up his axe. "Now, will you want to see my weapon on the way out?"

She didn't even bat an eyelid. "It's what you bring in that concerns me."

"Aye," Nameless said, hefting his axe to his shoulder. "Big'n like this is bound to be a concern."

Past the desk, the hall was dark and devoid of furnishings. The ceiling crystals cast no light, and heavy cobwebs hung like drapes. Four signs marked the exits: 'Visitors', 'Residents', 'Guilds', and 'Private'. A guard stepped from the shadows to usher them into a featureless gray corridor that took them to a squat chamber. Barred windows looked out onto a gloomy street. A couple of soldiers with crossbows watched from each. Between the windows, a massive oak door was fastened shut by three thick bolts. A man in a wrinkled toga stood to the side of it next to a waist-high table, upon which were stacks of booklets and papers.

"Welcome, friends. Welcome to New Jerusalem, bastion of the free and first city of Malkuth. My name is Lawson, your greeter today. Is this your first visit? Good, well, then you'll need one of our exquisite street maps and a guide book, which details places of interest such as the Capitol, the Old Mint, our incomparable restaurant strip, the…"

Shader was distracted by Shadrak sidling up to the table behind the man and pocketing a map.

"… Cotze's Foundry, the Raymark Brewery—"

"Let me see," Nameless said, snatching the map from the greeter's hand. "How much?"

"We have a special discount this week only. A denarius for the book, half that for the map; but if you take both, we'll work something out."

"Denarius?" Shader said. They had denarii here? After the Aeternam—Latin—he shouldn't have been surprised.

"A lot of time and preparation went into the design, sir. I hardly think it's too much to—"

Nameless withdrew his purse and fished out a couple of silvers. "Just the map, laddie."

Shadrak rolled his eyes and shook his head.

"Two sistercii," Lawson said. "That'll do nicely. Thank you, sir. Have a great day. Uh, guards, would you be so kind…"

One of the soldiers sighed and set about pulling back the bolts so that he could open the door.

"Once again, welcome to our city," Lawson said.

Outside in the street, it could have been night, so dark were the shadows thrown by the Cyclopean Walls. Glowing crystals suspended from tall posts shed dirty yellow light in swaths upon market stalls bustling with activity. The bitter aroma of freshly brewed coffee hung heavy in the air, and a brief gust of wind brought a whiff of pipe smoke to Shader's nostrils. It made him think of Aristodeus, and that led to thoughts of Rhiannon. He was surprised, and not a little guilty, to realize he was relieved at her absence. Whatever changes had come over her since Gaston, since Sammy, didn't sit well with him. But that wasn't all. Something wasn't right about Callixus's black sword, and the way she clung to it like a drug.

Shadrak slipped in among the crowd and disappeared.

"There he goes again," Nameless said. "Slippery little shogger, that one."

Something tugged at Shader's coat. Quick as a thought, he slapped a hand down over his pocket.

"Sorry, guv," a stoat-faced man said. He stank of piss, and his clothes were threadbare and stained. "Missed my footing."

Nameless took a step toward him, and the man slunk back into the throng.

"Just like the Sanguis Terrae wharfs," he said. "Pickpockets, waghalters, and rutterkins galore. The gnome should be in his element."

"Gnome?" Isn't that what Rhiannon called Shadrak? The poison gnome? She'd been joking, but with Nameless, it was hard to tell.

"Yes, you know, our shifty little homunculus. Miners call them deep gnomes, though you wouldn't want to say that to their face. Did I mention my pa was a min… Well, shog me, I remember his name. Droom. Droom and Yyalla—that's my ma. Only…"

"What?" Shader said. "Only what?"

Nameless shook the great helm from side to side. "Family name's missing, like they never had it. It's gotta be in here somewhere." He slapped the helm. "I don't mind them taking my name, but not my family's. Just wait till I get my hands on that shogging philosopher."

"Have a look at that map you bought," Shader said, "then you'll get your opportunity a whole lot faster."

Nameless unfolded the map and tried scanning it through the eye-slit before giving up and handing it to Shader. "Canny old goat, that Aristodeus. Knows full well I need him to feed me, so there's no chance I'll get to wring his scrawny neck anytime soon."

"That's Aristodeus for you," Shader said. "Always one step ahead."

"Least if there's a turd on the ground, he'll be the first to tread in it. Shog, that'd do me the world of good."

The map divided the city into dozens of squares, each of which was intersected by straight roads forming a perfect grid. These were the main thoroughfares, as far as Shader could see, but in reality there were countless other tributaries, cul-de-sacs and blind alleys they passed that the map didn't show. The Academy was on the cusp of a quadrant north-east of their current location. Shader glanced up, catching sight of the smoking tower they'd seen from outside. He looked back at the map and found it marked Cotze's Foundry, and it appeared to be only a couple of blocks from their destination.

They set out onto the high street and followed it north through the shaded market stalls, making their way around the scattered pavement tables and chairs in front of a bewildering array of eateries. The smell of roasted meat and garlic set Shader's stomach grumbling. Nameless muttered something and picked up the pace. Poor dwarf hadn't had anything to eat or drink since they'd left Arx Gravis, and Ain only knew when he'd eaten before that. Mind you, the squirrels Shadrak had shot hadn't exactly sated Shader's appetite. He'd have given his right arm for a hot stew and a hunk of fresh-cooked bread.

He trailed Nameless east down a side street labeled EW 41st. They must have been at the rear of yet more restaurants. Crates were stacked outside weatherbeaten doors, and here and there refuse spilled from overturned cans. There was something reassuringly familiar about the rats scampering through the waste. For all its size and grandeur, New Jerusalem was just the same as any other large city.

They turned north onto NS 20th and left the shadows cast by the Cyclopean Walls. Shader had to blink against the dazzling sunlight reflecting from the flagstones. The temperature went from cool and refreshing to a mugginess like that of Sarum, and suddenly the stench of rotting food became overbearing. The further they went, the scarcer the people became, until they were walking through a ghost town with only their echoing footfalls for company.

In his hurry to get out of the sweltering heat and the rank smell, Shader chanced a right turn into a narrow alley. Iron staircases ran down the backs of tall, dilapidated houses. These clearly hadn't been built by the dwarves. If anything, they were of more recent construction, but it seemed likely they'd crumble into dust long before the dwarven stonework that formed much of the rest of the city. The shade was welcome, though, and light at the far end of the alley showed it connected to another main street. They'd gone barely twenty yards when three dark figures stepped from an alcove. One of them snapped his fingers, producing a tongue of flame, which he used to light a cigarette.

The other two raised crossbows.

"Oh good," Nameless said. "This is what I get up in the morning for."

In spite of his words, the dwarf remained still and relaxed, his axe slung casually over his shoulder.

Shader's hand hovered above the hilt of his gladius. It would do no good from this distance. In the time it took to cross the thirty or so feet between them, he'd be staring blankly up at the sky with a quarrel jutting from his chest.

"Let me guess," the smoking man said. "You got lost and just happened to wander into our territory? No, don't tell me: You're a pair of those underground holies come looking for converts. Am I close? No? Hows about you're a couple of Night Hawks wanting to jump ship now there's a new king on the dung-pile? See, thing is, no one comes down here less they's really stupid or they got business with—"

In one smooth motion, a shadow dropped down behind the trio, rolled left, lunged right, and the two crossbowmen crumpled into heaps.

"Thing is," Shadrak said, ramming a punch dagger into the smoking man's kidney, "you got a big gob that's just about starting to piss me off."

The man screamed, and his cigarette dropped to the ground. Shadrak kicked him in the back of the legs, sending him sliding off the dagger onto his knees.

"Stop!" the man cried through a mouthful of bubbling blood. "Wait!"

Shadrak whirled in front of him and rammed his elbow into his nose. There was a sickening crunch and a cry like a squealing pig.

Nameless turned the great helm on Shader. "Give the gnome his due, he's a tough little runt. Got the makings of a featherweight circle fighter, if you ask me."

"That's enough, Shadrak," Shader said.

Shadrak picked up the still-burning cigarette. "Nothing's enough for these types." He jabbed the cigarette in the man's eye, and this time the scream was even more shrill and terrible. "Show 'em one jot of mercy, and they'll take it as weakness." He burned the other eye and stood back to watch the man thrashing and whimpering on the ground.

Shader knew he should do something but couldn't move. Partly, it was disbelief, not only that Shadrak had dispatched the three so easily, but that it was possible for someone to delight in such cruelty. Nameless was rooted to the spot, but he still seemed relaxed. Maybe he was enjoying the spectacle as much as the assassin.

The thrashing subsided, and the man curled himself into a fetal ball. Shadrak bent over him and punched the dagger repeatedly into his skull. There was a grunt, a few twitches, and then nothing.

"Shogging journeymen," Shadrak said. "Hate the scuts." He wiped his dagger on the man's clothes and straightened up. "Place ain't so bad," he said. He threw Shader a paper-wrapped package. "Good food, lame city watch, and now what sounds like rival guilds ripe for the picking. Makes me want to set up shop."

The package contained a hunk of fresh bread and a slab of cheese. Shader glanced guiltily at Nameless and then tore into it.

"Sorry, mate," Shadrak said to the dwarf. "Had a haunch of lamb earmarked for you, and a bottle of wine, but then I remembered…"

Nameless growled.

By the time they reached the main street, Shader had wolfed down his bread and cheese and was feeling better for it. He shielded his eyes against the glare of the suns as they emerged from the alleyway into a bustling shopping district, loud with the clatter of carts and the clip-clop of horses. There seemed to be an unwritten rule that the shabbily dressed and grimy lacklusters stuck to the gutters, while the center of the street was taken over by those clearly with a purpose of one sort or another: merchants, well-dressed ladies, toga-clad officials, and patrols of soldiers in the kilts, breastplates, and galeas they'd seen at the barbican.

They tagged along behind a man in a wide-brimmed hat and drab gray robe. He was handing out slips of paper to anyone who'd meet his eyes, weaving his way in and out of the central throng. As they passed a pavement restaurant sheltered by an awning, the man went from table to table leaving his slips for the diners. Some pocketed them surreptitiously, but others shook their heads or snapped their fingers at the waiters.

When they came out the other side of the awning, the man was waiting. He looked through narrowed eyes at Shadrak and Nameless then clasped Shader's hand and gave a half-smile. He turned away and entered the open door of a three-storey house nestled between two shops. A balding man peered around the jamb, checked the street both ways, then shut the door.

Shader held the slip of paper he'd been left between his thumb and forefinger. There was a drawing on one side of a bird stabbing itself in the breast with its beak. On the reverse was written, *O Oriens, splendor lucis aeternae, et sol iustitiae: veni et illumina sedentes in tenebris, et umbra mortis.*

"What's that he gave you?" Nameless said.

Shader passed it to him, but Nameless shook his head and handed it back.

The language, the imagery, reminded Shader of certain passages in the Liber. "O Dayspring," he translated for Nameless. "Brightness of the everlasting light, Sun of Justice, come to give light to them that sit in darkness and in the shadow of death." Sun of Justice was one of the titles the Templum gave to Nous. Was it possible the Nousian Theocracy's influence was felt even on distant Aethir? Or was this something else?

"Sort of thing Thumil used to spout," Nameless said, "when he was drowning in his own vomit in Rud Cairy's mead hall."

"Scripture?" Shader asked.

"You don't want to hear what I call it," Nameless said.

Shader eyed the door, half-inclined to go and knock, half-aware he had other more important matters to attend to. He flicked a look to the skies to satisfy himself the mauve wasn't getting any closer. He looked back at the house and stepped toward it. Surely it wouldn't make much diff—

"Tavern!" Nameless cried, setting off at a staggered run. He pulled up sharp and slapped the side of his helm. "Shog, shog, and double shog. I forgot again!"

Shadrak was on him like a shadow. "Outfitters," he said, pointing at the clothes store opposite. "My cloak, remember?"

"Ah, laddie," Nameless said. "You've a fine memory on you. Here, hold this." He handed Shadrak his axe, ambled over to the store, and went inside.

Shader's gaze returned to the townhouse, but the moment had passed. Maybe the distraction was Nous's way of telling him to get on with what they'd come here to do, before it was too late.

Nameless returned a few minutes later with a sky-blue cape trimmed with gold, and a hessian knapsack.

"You're having a laugh," Shadrak said, snatching the cape from him.

"Thought it was rather fetching, laddie. It has a hood. All we need now's a tinkling bell and you'd earn a pretty penny as a prancing pixie."

Shadrak stormed into the shop with the cape. Nameless chuckled and pulled out the concealer cloak so he could stuff it into the knapsack. Shadrak eventually came out, his pale cheeks flushed scarlet. He was fastening a black cloak around his neck as he approached.

"Now why was that so hard?" he said, accepting the knapsack from Nameless.

"Well, I just thought—"

"Well don't."

"It'll draw the heat," Nameless muttered at Shadrak's retreating back. "And you still owe me a pint. Two, if you count the bag. I'm keeping a tally."

Shadrak held up his middle finger and kept walking.

The street opened onto a crowded plaza, which was dominated by a three-tiered fountain sending up sparkling arcs of crystal-clear water. Sunshades had been set up all around the perimeter, where market stalls were bustling with trade and thick with the smells of fish, roasting meat, and ale.

Nameless turned the great helm to face a beer tent jostling with raucous patrons clutching frothing tankards as big as buckets.

"Oh, look," Shadrak said, an impish grin crossing his face. "I'm right parched, I am. Reckon I might grab myself one of those."

"You do that, laddie," Nameless said. "I would join you, but I never touch the stuff these days."

Shader studied the map and lifted his eyes to the broad avenue leaving the plaza on the far side. "Come on. It's just off that road."

"Look," Shadrak said. "Another one of them weirdoes handing out slips."

"More than one," Nameless said, pointing out a hooded man weaving in and out of the customers gathered round a stall that sold cheese and olives.

The one Shadrak had spotted wouldn't have stood out from the crowd at all, if not for the way he went from person to person offering pieces of paper. Maybe there was still time, Shader thought, checking on the sky. Wispy fingers of mauve seemed to be clawing their way toward the city walls, but when he blinked, he realized it was a matter of perspective. The discoloration was still some way off.

An old woman noticed him looking, touched her forehead and breast, grimaced, and lowered her hand.

"Don't look good, mister. Enjoy the sun whiles it lasts, I say."

Shader nodded, forced a smile. "Those men going through the crowd, who—"

An earsplitting boom rocked the plaza. Shader instinctively ducked and clapped his hands to his ears. All about him people were running and screaming. He spun a circle, trying to locate the source of the blast, but there was nothing to be seen.

Shadrak was staring up at the sky. "Just a clap of thunder. Don't know what all the—"

There was a second boom, and this time the assassin swore and covered his ears. "What the shog is it?"

Out of nowhere, rain sheeted across the plaza. Shader sprinted for the shelter of a doorway at the edge of the square. Shadrak was close on his tail, but Nameless merely ambled after them at his own pace, seemingly oblivious to the rain pinging from his helm. Stalls were swiftly covered, and within minutes the square was empty.

"Funny thing about this rain," Nameless said catching up with them.

"What?" Shadrak grumbled from beneath his hood. "It's shogging wet?"

"It's falling sideways."

Lightning flashed, and a second or two later there was another thunderclap. A dust devil stirred up the center of the plaza, swirling to the height of a man before spinning into a covered stall and dispersing.

Leaving the shelter of the doorway, Shader led the way down the avenue. Fierce winds were gusting, and it was all but impossible to look at the map. Dust got blown in his eye, and he blinked it clear. Up ahead, above the rooftops, he caught a glimpse of the smoke-billowing tower they'd spotted earlier.

"Cotze's Foundry." He pointed it out to the others. "Must be near."

"Want my advice?" Shadrak said. "Follow the geezer in the hat."

A man in a long gray coat and a chimney-stack hat was picking his way along the sidewalk, completely unfazed by the weather. It was like he was in a bubble of sunshine and calm.

"That a wizard?" Nameless asked. "Don't see their kind in Arx Gravis, but I don't mind telling you, this codger has put a creep in my crotch."

"Let's follow," Shader said. Besides Dr. Cadman and the Liche Lord's lieutenants at Verusia, he'd no experience of wizards, either. They weren't exactly common on Earth. About the only other magic he'd witnessed was from Huntsman and Sammy, and he still wasn't sure that was magic. Then there was Elias and his music, of course. Poor old Elias.

They followed the man down a series of backstreets. The architecture started to change in subtle ways the further they got from the plaza, but after a while the difference was startling. Twisty narrow buildings leaned precariously over cobbled streets. Flying buttresses and arched walkways crossed overhead, and many of the buildings had burnished turrets atop which flew flags of various designs: horse heads, skulls, green garlands, frogs, snakes, geometric shapes, pyramids of numbers. They passed a crooked house with a corrugated-roofed verandah. Two old men sat outside on rockers, absorbed in a game of cards. In front of another, an old woman leaned on a broom, scowling at the sky. She nodded as they passed, one eye roving other them, the other shut tight.

"The Academy?" Shader asked.

She cocked her head toward the far end of the street. "Left down Lovers' Lane. Can't miss it. Big bloody pile o' bricks. All bleedin' pillars and marble. Say, you watch yourself in there, boys. I mean, I tell you, her next door, she had a thing going with one of them student—"

"Thank you," Shader said, not wanting to linger.

"Yeah, well, like I said, there was this student once. Nice to look at, if you know what I mean, but right sickly, he was. Anyhows, ol' Mrs. Covey—"

"Madam," Nameless said with a bow. He clapped Shader on the shoulder and led him on down the street, Shadrak muttering under his breath behind them.

The old woman waved her broom at them. "I was only trying to say—"

"Anyone ever tell you, you stink of piss, lady?" Shadrak called back at her.

"Why, you uncouth little runt. I've a good mind to—"

"Hag," Shadrak yelled. "Gap-toothed crone. Shogging frog-eating—"

"That's enough," Shader said.

"It's enough when I say it is. Witch!"

Nameless turned to face him. "Are you going to behave yourself when we get there, laddie, or do I have to leave you outside?"

"Scu—" Shadrak started, but then thought better of it.

The man in the tall hat was down the far end of Lovers' Lane when they entered it. Shader redoubled his pace, but Nameless didn't keep up with him.

"What is it?" Shader cast over his shoulder.

"Nothing, laddie." Nameless waved him on. "I won't be far behind." His voice had dropped to a low monotone, each word chewed over and spat out with agonizing slowness.

Shadrak glided off into the shadows beside the dwarf. He'd do his own thing, no doubt. Shader had given up worrying about where he was.

He continued to the end of the lane, grimacing against the stench rising from the cobblestones. Rats scampered out of his way, burying themselves in moldering piles of refuse, or splashing through the dank water spilling from the gutters. Made you wonder what kind of lovers used this place. Maybe they should've heard the old woman out, after all.

The lane ended at a wrought iron gate flowing with intricate whorls and vinework. It stood ajar, and the hinges moaned as Shader pushed through. The cobbles of the lane gave way to a mosaic pathway between banks of trellises interwoven with ivy and dotted with violet petals. After a stretch, the pathway opened onto an ornamental garden skirting a towering edifice. Harmonious pairings of rockeries and fountains, flowerbeds and herb gardens did their best to soften the looming gray facade of the Academy.

Undeterred, Shader made his way to the broad stone steps leading to a colonnaded portico. Flying buttresses splayed from the sides of the building, like the legs of an enormous spider. Each story—there were seven in all—was surrounded by a stone balustrade, upon which sat gargoyles in various lewd poses. The windows were of stained glass, depicting men with the heads of beasts, retorts, crucibles, patterns of fire, water, air, and earth. Passing beneath the shade of the portico's vaulted ceiling, he approached twin doors of polished oak, which stood open like an invitation.

Shader frowned back at Nameless, who was trudging through the garden, great helm dipped toward his feet. A cloud seemed to have settled over the dwarf, and all his movements were heavy and dull. Shadrak slipped into view behind him, turning this way and that, pink eyes glittering scarlet in the sunlight. And that's when it struck Shader: The storm still raged beyond the garden, but here, all was tranquil and calm as a perfect summer's day.

Inside, he was greeted by the smell of must and sulfur. To the right, the antechamber opened onto an enormous circular room with balconied levels rising all the way to the roof. Each was crammed with bookshelves, and the floor space of the lower level accommodated dozens of desks. Shining crystal globes were suspended from silver chains hanging down from the distant ceiling. There were people browsing the book cases, and still more bent over the desks, with stacks of books and papers before them. The man with the tall hat was leaning on a counter sharing a joke with the librarian. He looked round briefly, but Shader was already turning away.

On the opposite side of the antechamber, there was an impossibly vast hall dominated by displays of skeletons, some human, but most of giant beasts. Some were four-legged, with long sinuous necks, while others stood upright and had cavernous maws lined with sword-like teeth.

The antechamber continued past both rooms to a reception area. A young girl with pigtails looked up from the desk and studied Shader with doleful eyes.

"Master Are..." Who was it Aristodeus had told Nameless to ask for?

"Straight ahead, second door on the left," she said. "They're expecting you."

Nameless' footsteps echoed up behind. "I can hardly wait," he grumbled.

"Good," Shadrak said. "Pleased to hear it. Sooner we get this over with, sooner we can stick that bastard Gandaw and go home."

The girl's eyes widened for an instant but then resumed their scrutiny of the three.

"Thank you," Shader said, and led the way along a carpeted corridor where raised voices spilled from an open door.

"... you're missing the point," Aristodeus was saying, every word punctuated by a dull thump.

"No, it is you who are missing the point: the point of your swollen-headed hubris!" The second voice was a lilting bass, stressing the consonants like a declaiming actor.

"That the door, you reckon?" Shadrak said with a thin smile.

"Have you no logic?"—Aristodeus's voice again. "If your so-called magic is drawn from the dreams of the Cyn..." He trailed off as Shader moved to the doorway. "Oh, you're here." The philosopher shook his head and turned away "Nothing like taking your time when everyone's depending on you."

"It's your game," Shader said, edging into the room so that Nameless and Shadrak could enter. "I'm just the pawn, remember?"

The other man in the room laughed. "Aren't we all? In his inflated mind, at least."

He was half a head taller than Shader, broad-shouldered and barrel-chested. Salt and pepper hair crowned his head in twisted spikes, and his beard was a braided trident. He threw out an arm in an expansive gesture, spreading his crimson cloak like the wings of a bat. The air about his fingers shimmered, and a staff appeared in his grip.

"In case you haven't noticed—" Aristodeus clicked his fingers three times before letting out a long breath and going to stare out of the window. "—the very worlds are being unwoven. You think that's a natural storm coming in from the Perfect Peak? You think it's magical?" He sneered the last word and peered over his shoulder at Shader. "Master Arecagen here thinks a bit of psychic self-defense will see it off!"

"That is not what—"

"Uh, uh, uh," Aristodeus cut him off, wagging his finger.

Arecagen tensed, his knuckles whitening around the staff.

"Call it a semantic issue, if you like," Aristodeus said, "but it makes no difference. You draw power from the Cynocephalus, from the raw material of his dreams, yes?"

The wizard sighed through clenched teeth.

"Well, let me tell you—" Aristodeus strolled back over, taking in Shadrak and Nameless with his sparkling eyes before coming face to face with Arecagen. "—Gandaw's Unweaving will pull the rug out from under you. Everything will be undone, Arecagen. Everything. No Cynocephalus, no magic. *Simplex sigillum veri*, my friend. The logic of the position is mine."

Simplicity is the sign of truth. Shader had heard the phrase a hundred times from the philosopher's lips, but it struck him this time like a slap in the face. Isn't that what he should be doing with the spiritual life, paring back all that wasn't essential and getting to the heart of the matter?

"... and where's your evidence?" Arecagen was saying, punctuating the words by rapping the heel of his staff against the polished floorboards.

Shader tuned him out, struggled to finish his thought. Isn't it what Ludo had meant by moving from the head to the heart? Didn't Nous demand simplicity, like that of a child? It was complexity that had stayed his hand atop the Homestead, a refusal to see things in black and white. Good and evil was what it came down to, and by failing to act, had he colluded with the latter? It was a revelation, hearing the Aeternam phrase here, but whether it was from Nous, the Demiurgos, or his own mind, he couldn't say. In any case, the message was clear. He needed to be more decisive, more inflexible in doing the right thing. But how you could discern—"

"Deacon? Come back to us, boy," Aristodeus was saying.

Shader blinked his eyes back into focus.

"Look, Arecagen," Aristodeus said, "why not turn your magic on the Perfect Peak? At least it might create a distraction and keep eyes off of Shader."

"Impeccable logic," Arecagen said with a shake of his head. "Even if we could penetrate the scarolite, which we could not, Gandaw has harnessed the power of Eingana, if you are to be believed. What chance do you think magic drawn from the Cynocephalus would have against his mother? No, defense is our best chance."

"Balderdash!" Aristodeus said. He was red in the face and clearly not used to being argued with in this way.

Arecagen raised a placating hand. "We must agree to disagree. I'll not hinder your efforts, and you, I trust, will allow me mine."

"The enemy of my enemy..." Nameless said. There was no inflection in his voice, none of his usual exuberance. He sounded defeated to Shader, half asleep.

"If I must," Aristodeus said. "I'd prefer it if we sang from the same hymn sheet—" He shot Shader a fake smile. "—but needs must. I take it you will honor our agreement, in spite of our disagreement?"

"How long will it take?" Arecagen cast a wary eye over the tubes and packages heaped on the desk.

"An hour at most. I would have said once a month, but things being as they are, we may not make it to a second feeding."

"Just today," Aristodeus said, "and then you can find somewhere else. Clear my desk, and shut the door on your way out. Gentlemen." He gave a stiff bow and left.

"Typical," Aristodeus muttered as he pushed the door to. "They plan to expand the Academy's magical shielding over the entire city, as if that will do a damned thing. The senate's just as bad. This idea of yours," he said to Nameless, "getting the senate to send their legions against the Perfect Peak—they're going to take some persuading. They're convinced they've appeased Gandaw over the years by suppressing religion, just as he did on Earth. What they fail to realize is that he's way beyond that now. They're just assuming he's going to do the same as he did in the Global Tech days. And the idea that he'd save their city and wipe out all else is too absurd for words. Just think, nothing left in existence save the Perfect Peak and New Jerusalem drifting in the void of all voids until Gandaw gets round to his megalomaniac fiat. And even if he doesn't spare the city, as far as they're concerned, nothing can get past the Cyclopean Walls. Why is it so difficult to understand that there won't be any walls if everything's unwoven?"

Shader glanced at Nameless. The dwarf stood still as a statue.

"Deluded bunch of Romanophiles," Aristodeus said.

"What's that, boy love?" Shadrak said, starting to poke about the room, looking in drawers and cupboards. "You old robey types are all the same."

"Pretentious, is what it is," Aristodeus said. "If I thought it would do any good, I'd have gone to them myself, but I have more than enough on my plate with that bloody woman of yours."

"Rhiannon?" Shader said. "She's her own woman, not mine. Where is she?"

"You're right there," Aristodeus said. He closed his eyes and drew in a long, slow breath. "Left her propping up a bar. She certainly knows how to drink."

He wasn't wrong there, Shader thought. "Which bar? Where?"

"Place called Dougan's Diner, a roach-infested cesspit on 71st, north-south, not east-west."

Shader started for the door.

"No, Deacon." Aristodeus laid a hand on his shoulder. "You must try the senate. I've never had good relations with them; there's a lot of history between us, but you may have a chance. Go to them, tell them what you've seen, what's coming. If they resist, reason with them. Please don't let all those endless lessons I gave you be for nothing."

"Don't sweat on it, mate," Shadrak said. "I'll get her. Even the mother of all bitches has got to be better than listening to anymore of this shit, and I don't reckon my presence at this shogging senate is gonna do us any favors." Before anyone could stop him, the assassin was out the door.

"Whatever you do," Aristodeus called after him, "don't eat the food."

"But Nameless?" Shader said. The dwarf still hadn't moved since they'd set foot in the room.

"Leave him with me," Aristodeus said. "I'll tube-feed him, and he'll be... I was going to say back to normal. The stuff in those packets is something of an Ancient world miracle. He'll be fueled up and ready to go for a couple of days or so. After that, I'll look into a more long-term formula. Map," he demanded, holding out a hand.

Shader gave it to him, and Aristodeus scanned it before jabbing it with a finger. "Senate building, plumb in the center of the spider's web. All roads lead to Rome, as they used to say before the Reckoning. Now hurry." He thrust the map back in Shader's hand and ushered him through the door. "And keep your coat fastened. Last thing we need is for them to see your surcoat and assume the Monas is some variation on the Cross."

Shader opened his mouth to ask what he meant, but Aristodeus slammed the door in his face.

HUNTED

FIST-SIZED HAIL hammered against the rooftop, and sleet spewed across the purple stain spreading above New Jerusalem. Reminded Shadrak of the rotting flesh of Councilor Milhard back in Sarum. Scut had been stupid enough to wear the silk shirt that arrived in a package outside his door. Must've itched like the Abyss, but by the time he'd ripped it off, the mottling covered his entire upper body. Albert had treated it with enough poison to wipe out a small village. It was chilling how the poisoner watched like an excited kid through the window and patted himself on the back for a job well done. Chilling, but kind of satisfying. Even for a politician, Milhard was a jumped up little twat with a thing for the boys.

Shadrak pressed his back into the chimney breast, making a tent of his cloak so that he could study the map he'd taken when they entered the city.

New Jerusalem was designed along a simple grid, all carved up neat into roads and intersections going north-south or east-west. Didn't take no genius to find 71st. Soon as he did, Shadrak scrunched up the map and threw it to the street below. No need for it now; he only had to look at something once to have its image burned into his head. After navigating the Maze—the plane ship—New Jerusalem was gonna be a doddle.

His face tightened at the thought of the plane ship, and his eyes narrowed as he ran through the possibilities for the thousandth time. He couldn't have just lost it, not with his memory. Either the Sour Marsh took it, or someone had found it. He wouldn't have put it past the shogging Archon to have hidden it, to make sure the job got done.

A flash erupted in the sky, way back the way they'd come. Shadrak stood, holding onto the chimney so's the gusting winds didn't fling him after the map. Where the light had flared, the purple smudge was speckled with black. Impossible to tell how big the spots were from so far, but whatever was happening over the Perfect Peak, it weren't good.

He slid to the edge of the roof on his ass and was reaching for the drainpipe when he saw a dark shape out of the corner of his eye. It was on an adjacent rooftop, standing, no thought for the storm.

Shadrak rolled from the roof, caught hold of the guttering, and shimmied along till he'd put the building between him and whatever it was watching him. Coz it was watching—so much for the the camouflage cloak he'd taken from the dwarf!—he was sure of that. Heaviness worked its way into his arms, and his fingers felt numb. His heart was slinging around in his chest, and an icy prickle crept up his neck. He hadn't felt that way since... since he was a kid, when he'd stumbled across them ghouls picking over the corpse of a streetwalker and run for his life. The day he'd found the Maze. Stuff like that didn't happen to him now. He was Shadrak the Unseen. He watched others; they didn't watch him.

He dropped to a window ledge, found fingerholds in the wall beside it, and climbed down.

The street was deserted. Water spilled from overflowing gutters, and swirls of wind sent leaves and dust dancing into the air.

Something leapt from the rooftop and glided down to the pavement further along the street. It was black—all black, save for the shimmer of silver on its torso—with slender limbs and a long head. Shadrak caught himself staring, momentarily frozen. It had no eyes, no facial features at all. Quick as a flash, its hand went to its hip and came up firing.

Shadrak dived and rolled and ran. Air whistled past his ear, and then he flung himself headfirst at a window. His arm came up at the last instant, and glass shattered. He tumbled out of the fall, ignoring the stinging cuts crying out all over his body.

Scanning the room, he took the stairs up two at a time, barged through a door, and ran across a bed. A woman screamed, and a man swore. Whole place stank of sweat and other stuff, but Shadrak went straight for the sash window, lifted it, and climbed out onto the sill.

He saw everything larger than life, slow and easy, like he always did when his blood was up. Without a thought, he jumped for the drainpipe and made the roof.

More screams from below, and two thunder-cracks.

It's got a gun. He shut the thought down before it paralyzed him, but it refused to stay buried. *A scutting gun. What the shog?*

He sprinted and threw himself to the next roof and kept running without breaking stride. He kept on leaping from rooftop to rooftop until he was sure nothing could have kept up with him. Collapsing against an ornate balustrade, he focused on slowing his ragged breaths. He'd panicked, he knew that, but he also knew that if he hadn't panicked, he'd most likely be back to the dirt. Whatever that thing was, it was fast. Faster than should have been possible. Question was, why had it come after him? Chance? Bad luck? Or was it something else?

He looked up at the roiling skies, half-expecting the Archon to appear and tell him what the shog was going on. A few more deep breaths, and his heart stopped its flapping. He checked his pistol, replaced the cartridge with a full one. Saving the near-empty cartridge in a pouch, he re-holstered the pistol and stood, looking around warily. He was seeing shadows everywhere, but that only told him he was still creeped out.

Settle down, Shadrak, he told himself. *Cool head, calm hands, or you're dead meat.*

He made a couple of practice draws, spinning the pistol before holstering it each time. He couldn't get over how fast that thing was, how close it had come to hitting him, despite his frantic efforts to get away. With one last look around, he decided there weren't nothing more he could do. Death, when it came, was as swift and as sudden as a knife in the back, in his experience. Shog all you could do about that, save be sharp and honed, and ready to do whatever it takes. He'd been cheating death most his life; no reason this should be any different.

He made his way to 71st calmer than he should've. If the shogger came for him, weren't a whole lot he could do, save kill or be killed. Worrying about it was just gonna achieve the latter. Didn't stop him studying the shadows and listening keenly, all the while treading so soft he wouldn't miss the slightest rustle, the barest scuff, the most whispering breath.

Besides the odd patrol of bedraggled and miserable-looking guards, he didn't see nothing.

He found his way to the diner with his nose. The sign above the door used to read 'Dougan's Diner', but some scut had half-painted it out and put 'Queenie's' there instead. Can't have been long ago, neither, coz the paint was still running from the base of the letters. Whatever Aristodeus had said about the food, it sure smelled good from outside, and it set his stomach rumbling. Garlic, if he weren't mistaken, and the yeasty smell of fresh-baked bread.

Bells tinkled as he pushed through the door. Looked like they'd come out the other side of a busy patch, what with the tables being stacked with smeared plates and half-empty glasses. Only other entrance was louvered swing doors at the far end, from beyond which came the clatter of pots and pans, and a tuneless whistle that sounded kind of familiar.

The waiter was over by the bar, between a short, bearded punter with mottled cheeks and Rhiannon, who was out cold, a pint of beer clutched in her hand. The waiter jumped, like he'd just stuck his hand in boiling water. Shadrak narrowed his eyes. Bloke was a weedy looking beggar in outsized clothes. The only thing that set him out as staff was the neat black pinny tied round his waist. What he was doing up so close to the bitch was anyone's guess, but Shadrak reckoned she'd be more'n a little pissed when she came to.

"We're closed," the whelp said. "Can't you read?"

Shadrak stepped closer, eyes pointedly moving to Rhiannon and back.

"I was checking her pulse," the waiter said. "Too much to drink, silly cow."

"Strange place to look," Shadrak said.

"Yeah, well I ain't no doctor, now, am I? And who do you think you are anyway, telling me my business?" His eyes widened, and he guffawed. "What the shog are you, a dwarf to a dwarf?" He patted the bearded man on the back. "Eh, Rugbeard? You didn't tell me you had a kid."

The bearded man seemed oblivious. He downed his drink, belched, and then tugged Rhiannon's tankard out of her grasp. Must've been roughly the same height as Nameless, though skinny and knotted up with arthritis, by the looks of him.

"Spirit of a dwarf," he said to no one in particular, "but not the stomach." He took a long pull on Rhiannon's drink and then fell forward, his head smacking against the bar. Within moments, he was snoring.

"Get me a bucket of water," Shadrak said.

"Bucket?" the waiter said. "Don't you mean glass? Mind, little geezer like you might be better off with a wooden cup, so's you don't cut yourself."

Shadrak growled and whipped out a knife. "Cut you, you shogging scut, if you don't shut your trap and do as you're told."

"Yeah?"

"Yes." Shadrak advanced on him, pressed the tip of his blade against the idiot's nuts.

The waiter's lips trembled, and a tic started up under his eye. He gulped and tried to back away, but Shadrak went with him.

"Water, you cretin. In a bucket. Understand?"

The waiter nodded and cocked a thumb over his shoulder toward the kitchen. Shadrak turned him around and booted him up the ass, sending him sprawling through the louvered doors. Someone yelled, and the waiter started blubbing.

Shadrak lifted Rhiannon's head by the hair. Her face was smeared with puke, the sight of it making him nearly gag. He dumped her head back down with a thud. Was gonna take more than a bucket of water to rouse her, that was for sure.

The kitchen doors flew open. "Knife or no knife, I'm not having that kind of carry on in my... oh, my scutting... I mean, shag the Ipsissimus! Shadrak!"

"Think I'll leave that to you, Albert."

Same as ever, the poisoner was dressed in one of his Gallian suits, but he wore a stained white apron over the top. His bald head was covered by a chef's toque, which he removed and clutched to his breast.

"I..." Albert started, chewing his bottom lip. "I suppose you're wondering how I came to—"

"Where's my shogging plane ship?" It didn't take no genius to make the connection.

He should've known. *Bloody Sour Marsh ate it, my gonads!* "I should've left you to those corpse things back at Dead Man's Torch."

Albert waved his hat around, the same way he used to flap his hanky when he was nervous. "No, no you shouldn't have, Shadrak. I can explain about the ship, but just look around. Me coming here has done us both an enormous favor."

"Where is it?"

Albert gave a delicate cough. "Safe. It's safe. I crash… set down a little way from the city. Hitched myself a lift here."

The waiter peered out from behind one of the kitchen doors. "Safe, my ass. Picked him up near some boreworm holes, I did. Stupid sod nearly got himself ate."

"Eaten," Albert said. "And you're exaggerating. Haven't you got something useful to do, like fetch that bucket of water?"

"But you said—"

Albert slammed the door on him.

"Ah, my fingers! You squashed my fingers!"

Albert rolled his eyes and shook his head.

"Twat," Shadrak said.

"That, old friend, is Buck Fargin, soon to be guildmaster of the Night Hawks."

"What's that, flower arrangers' guild?"

"Entrepreneurs, Shadrak."

"Thieves, then."

"And assassins. This city, Shadrak, is incredible. It makes Sarum look like a village. I've already made a contact in the senate, and plans are afoot to raise our friend here—"

Buck shouldered his way through the doors, sloshing water from a bucket all over the floor. He swore and set the bucket down.

"Mop, cretin. Mop," Albert said.

"I know, I know!"

"You're going to use him to front up the guild, which, naturally, you'll control behind the scenes?"

"I could use some help."

Shadrak looked around at the diner. He could see what Albert was up to. He'd seen it all before. "You got a nice place here, Albert. Didn't exactly waste much time."

"None at all. The owner was on oaf, more suited to bricklaying than cooking. He fell ill, and so I stepped into his shoes, with the blessing of my senator friend, I might add. Come on, Shadrak, what do you say? You and me, taking over the guilds one by one. You always used to talk about that in Sarum."

Shadrak smiled and shook his head. It was tempting, but what good would it do if the worlds were gonna end?

"I can't, Albert. Not right now. You seen the storm outside?"

"So?"

"It's the Unweaving, Albert. It's started. If we don't find a way to stop Gandaw, there won't be no guilds for us to run."

"We? Surely you're not suggesting—"

"There's three of us—" Shadrak picked up the bucket. "—and her." With a heave, he upended it over Rhiannon's head.

"Shog!" Rhiannon shot upright, as if she'd been struck by lightning. "Shog, shog, shog." She tried to stand, but the stool tipped over, and she fell sprawling to the floor.

Shadrak toed her in the ribs, but she just grunted and rolled onto her side. Within moments, she was snoring as loudly as the dwarf.

"This is gonna be harder than I thought," Shadrak said.

"What the shog?" Buck said, bashing his way through the doors with a mop. "All I spilt's a little trickle. What you have to go flood the place for?" He tried to hand Shadrak the mop. "You clean it up."

"Careful, Buck," Albert said. "This is Shadrak the Unseen, probably the nastiest bastard I've had the pleasure of working with. He must be in a rare good mood. The way you've been carrying on, you should be floating down the sewers by now."

"Still time for that," Shadrak said.

Buck paled and set about mopping up the water with vigor.

"Don't worry about her," Albert said, stepping over Rhiannon on his way back to the kitchen. "I have the perfect remedy for drunkenness. She'll be right as rain in a couple of hours. Well, not quite right, but she'll be conscious."

"Thanks," Shadrak muttered under his breath. "I can hardly wait. And Albert..."

The poisoner paused in the doorway. "Dearest?"

"I haven't forgotten about the plane ship."

APPEASEMENT

HADER'S EYES DRANK in the view, but he couldn't believe what he was seeing. The avenue opened up onto a vast piazza flanked by colonnaded walkways that formed two halves of a broken circle. A slender obelisk stood at the hub, and at the far end, broad steps led up to the portico of a domed basilica—Luminary Trajen's Basilica, down to the last detail. Only the Monas was missing from the top of the dome. In its place was a cross, just like the ones from his dreams, the ones he'd seen as a child, smothered in the undergrowth of Friston. Just like the cross on Maldark's surcoat. Poor, lost Maldark, torn and bloodied, defiant to the end. Even the gigantic statues atop the colonnades looked the same as those in Aeterna. If not for the Cyclopean Walls in the distance, and the red-plumed and kilted soldiers stationed at intervals all the way to the basilica, he'd have thought he was back in Latia, and all that had happened had been a waking nightmare.

The darkening skies swirled above the city, a maelstrom of purple clouds fractured by jags of unnatural lightning. Far to the west, the black spots had coalesced into a pool of inky blackness that looked for all the world like a dead or dying sun.

Tugging down his hat against the sheeting rain, he cut a path across the center of the piazza. Soldiers sheltering beneath pillars glanced at him, but for the most part their eyes were on the sky. He splashed through the puddles threatening to flood the mosaic floor and took a moment's shelter at the base of the obelisk. The basilica dome loomed above him like the head of a curious god, just the same as in Aeterna, and the curving colonnades created the impression of all-embracing arms.

When he reached the steps, a soldier moved to intercept him.

"Business?" The man looked miserable, water cascading from his bronze helm, running in rivulets down his spear shaft, spattering his shield.

"I need to speak with the senate."

"Don't we all?"

"It's urgent."

The guard puffed out his cheeks, eyes focused beyond Shader's shoulder on the chaotic skies. "Always is, sir. Always is. Desk on the left as you go in."

What should have been the narthex was a reception area with a long counter closing off the entrance to the nave. Behind it were a pair of ornate doors and a couple of guards with crossed spears. A sign hanging by chains from the ceiling marked it as the 'Senate Chamber'. In front of the counter, smaller signs pointed to a dozen or so doorways, each with its own guard. A rope railing sectioned off the right side of the chamber, beyond which men in white togas mingled. Just inside the entrance, a drenched crowd had gathered, looking out at the rain, mumbling and pointing.

To the left, there was a disinterested soldier behind a leather-topped desk. His galea sat atop a stack of papers, and a scabbarded sword hung from the back of his chair.

"Swords, axes, spears, daggers on the table," he said, without looking up from the book he was reading. "You can hold on to bows, but I'll have the arrows."

"I need to—"

"Don't worry, I'll keep them safe." He gestured with his thumb to a pile weapons of the floor.

Getting anything back from that pile would be like finding the proverbial needle in a haystack, but Shader knew it wouldn't be a problem as far as the gladius was concerned. Hadn't it come to free him from Hagalle's chains? It had flown through the air as if held by an invisible hand. He drew it from its scabbard and placed it on the desk.

"Name?" the soldier said, shutting his book and taking up a quill. He dipped it in an inkwell and looked up expectantly.

"Shader. Deacon Shader. I need to—"

"Keep hold of this." The soldier scrawled on a slip of paper, tore it in half, and gave one piece to Shader. "You'll need it on the way out. No slip, no sword." He eyed the gladius hungrily and then fixed a broad smile on his face. "Make your way to the main counter, and they'll be only too glad to help. Good day, sir."

Shader was halfway to the counter when he heard the soldier cry out. He turned round to see the man flapping his hand about like he'd stuck it in a fire.

"Static," Shader said. "Happens all the time."

The queue at the counter was short but slow-moving. Those being seen to asked the most inane questions, and the clerk listened with practiced interest before hunting through drawers of paperwork, as if there were some kind of virtue in being slow. Shader tapped on the Liber in one pocket, fiddled with his prayer cord in the other, all the while raising himself on tiptoe to see what the hold up was. Last time he'd been in line for any length of time was for confession, and Nous alone knew how long ago that was.

The thought occurred to him, that was what his problem was: a soul like a drain badly in need of unclogging. So many thoughts, words, actions heaping sin upon sin, and yet here he was carrying on like the last great hope of all Creation and putting Nous to one side to be picked up when he'd set the cosmos to rights. Not him, he realized: Aristodeus. Was that where his allegiance lay? With the philosopher, rather than the creator of all things? He squeezed the prayer cord so tight one of the knots dug into his palm. He lifted his hand to look at the red mark it had left, and his mind threw up an image of Barek nailed to the tree.

What would the lad be doing now? What could he do, save wait for the darkness to fall? Pray, maybe. Shader scoffed at that. For all he knew, prayers to Nous could be answered by the Demiurgos, considering the hand Otto Blightey had in organizing the Liber.

He stepped to the side of the queue so he could get a better look at what the clerk was doing. His eyes were drawn to a patch of wall, where the paint was lighter, as if something had once hung there but then been removed. It was in the shape of a cross, just like the one adorning the dome of the basilica.

"Is there problem, sir?"

Shader started. A soldier stood at his shoulder, peering at him through narrowed eyes.

"I need to speak with the senate." He indicated the line in front of him. "It's urgent."

The guard gave a slow nod. "I'm sure they won't be much longer."

"Look," Shader said. "You've noticed the weather? Is that normal?"

The soldier puffed his cheeks out and looked about till he caught the attention of one of his colleagues, who stepped toward them. "Keep your voice down, sir. No need to start a panic."

"I know what it is," Shader said. "If I don't see someone soon, there'll be no one left to panic. There'll be nothing left at all."

The other soldier took hold of him by the arm. "Step this way, please."

Shader complied and, with a soldier on either side, was escorted to a door. The guard on the door let them into a waiting room.

A woman with the same long black hair as Rhiannon looked up from a row of chairs. She was scantily clad in the most gaudy colors, and her face was rouged and streaked with tear tracks.

"Won't be long, darling," one of the soldiers said. "Then you can be on your way."

She rolled her eyes and sighed. "What you done?" she asked Shader.

"Done?"

But before she could respond, Shader was whisked off down a corridor and into a windowless room with a desk and two chairs.

"Wait here, sir. Someone will be with you shortly."

The guards left, shutting the door with a clang, which was when Shader noticed it was iron. Then he saw the reddish stains on the whitewashed walls. The desktop was dappled with dark splotches.

Surely not, he thought, recalling the cell he'd been dumped in at Arx Gravis. *Surely not again.*

To his relief, the door opened almost immediately, and a hawkish man in a gray tunic came in with both guards in tow. With a curt nod to Shader, he seated himself at the desk and gestured for Shader to take the chair opposite.

"I am Darylius Mesqui, clerk to the Senatorial Prefecture for Civic Rectitude. I will take some details and ask some questions, after which you will have the opportunity to ask questions of your own." He held out a hand, and one of the guards passed him a clipboard. The other set an inkwell and quill on the desk, and then both retreated to the door and stood in front of it, arms folded across their chests.

Shader leaned toward Mesqui. "Are you a senator?"

"No, which is why I introduced myself as a clerk."

"Then you're wasting my—"

Mesqui held up a finger. "Details, my questions, then yours." He dipped the quill in the inkwell and scratched away at the paper on the clipboard.

"This is urgent," Shader said. "I must—"

"Name?" Mesqui said without looking up.

"I gave it to the guard on my way in. Can we just—?"

Mesqui sighed and scratched his forehead. "Must I repeat the question?"

Shader gritted his teeth. "Look, there isn't time for this. It's a senator I need, not a clerk." He started to stand, but strong hands pressed down on his shoulders.

"Make it easy on yourself, sir," the guard said. "Just answer the questions."

Shader narrowed his eyes, and the guard stiffened and gave an almost imperceptible nod, as if to say, "Come on, then." With a sword, Shader would have cut the grunt down to size, but without one, he wasn't so sure. He shouldn't have left the gladius at the front desk. If he'd insisted on bringing it, they'd have had a hard time stopping him. Fighting back the urge to say something he might regret, he lowered his eyes and decided to do this the other way. The Nousian way. He almost sneered at the idea, but then looked at Mesqui with what he hoped was contrition. The problem was, humility hurt, just as much as biting his tongue.

"Shader," he said. "Deacon Shader, as I already told the guard on the desk. Don't you people talk?"

Mesqui rolled his eyes. "May I continue, or would you like to tell me how to do my job?"

"Get on with it," Shader said. He sucked in a breath between gritted teeth. Who was he kidding? Deacon Shader, humble? The harder he tried, the more he wanted to grab

Mesqui by the throat and throttle him till he got someone in authority, someone who could make decisions. Someone who might just recognize the urgency of the situation and do something about it.

Mesqui appraised him with practiced indifference, waiting, as if for a truculent child to quell its tantrum. Finally, with the raise of an eyebrow, he resumed.

"From?"

Shader let out a trickle of breath and willed his shoulders to relax. "Friston. South East Britannia."

"Outlander, eh?" Mesqui scribbled away on the clipboard. "Where's that, near Illioch? Pellor?"

"Malfen way, I reckon," one of the guards said.

"Oh." Mesqui peered down his nose at Shader. "You don't look like a brigand."

"Merc, I'd say," the other guard said. "Fighting man, whatever. I could tell that first I saw him. It's all in the walk."

"Mercenary," Mesqui said out loud as he wrote. "Good."

"No," Shader said. "That's not—"

"Now, Mr. Shader," Mesqui said, "empty your pockets onto the table."

A rustle of movement from behind made Shader glance over his shoulder. Both guards had their fingers hovering above the pommels of their shortswords.

With a shake of his head, Shader tugged the Liber from his pocket and slid it onto the table.

Mesqui leaned over it and squinted at the title. "Liber?" His eyes widened, and he looked past Shader to the guards.

"Yes," Shader said. "It means 'book'."

"I'm not an imbecile, Mr. Shader," Mesqui said. "I can read Latin." He then muttered, almost to himself, "But this looks..." He riffled through the pages, pausing now and then to skim over a passage, all the time shaking his head. "This is yours? You read it? You pray?"

Shader sat back and looked up at the ceiling. What could he do? He couldn't lie. No matter how tenuous his faith in Nous had become, he couldn't deny him.

"Yes."

Mesqui sat perfectly still for a long moment, eyelids drooping almost shut. Finally, he pinched the bridge of his nose and sucked in a whistling breath through his teeth. "I think it's best you see the prefect."

Shader took back the Liber and slipped it in his pocket. "Is he a senator?"

Mesqui stood and picked up the inkwell, balancing it on his clipboard. "Yes. Yes, he's a senator. Thank you for your time."

Shader rose from the table and made to follow him to the door, but Mesqui held up a hand.

"The prefect will be with you presently."

The guards parted for Mesqui to exit then shut the door and stood either side of it, one tapping out a rhythm on the pommel of his sword, the other clenching and unclenching his fists.

Shader instinctively reached for the comfort of his gladius, even as he recalled it was probably somewhere in that heaped pile at the front desk. The chances of him getting past the guards, should it come to it, were slim to nothing without a weapon. If he could snatch a sword from one of them, backslash, thrust, elbow to the face... He rehearsed the moves in his mind. It might work, but then again...

He sat back down and decided instead to offer it up to Nous. No matter what Aristodeus said about the senate's hostility to religion, surely that paled into insignificance against the coming cataclysm.

595

He didn't have long to wait. The door was slung open, and a pot-bellied man in a white toga flounced in.

"Mr. Shader." He held out a hand, eyes twinkling, a perfect smile cutting a white line across his box beard. "Senator Whittler. I'm the prefect here at the Civi-Rec. Mr. Mesqui has given me the bare essentials, but you'll have to fill in the blanks." He came round the table and grunted as he lowered himself into the chair Mesqui had used. "I'm so, so sorry you've had all this trouble getting to see me." He threw up his hands and rolled his eyes. "That's bureaucracy for you. Now, how can I be of help?"

Shader was too taken aback to speak. No mention of the Liber, no grilling about religion; just an offer to listen. "Uh…"

Whittler leaned his elbows on the table and nodded encouragingly.

"Sektis Gandaw," Shader said.

Whittler's eyes darkened, but his smile remained fixed in place. He stuck out his bottom lip, prompting Shader to go on.

"I need to speak to you about Sektis Gandaw."

Whittler spread his arms. "What's to tell? Gandaw's not troubled us for decades. Why, we've heard nary a peep from him since the revolution." He thumped his chest three times and then cocked his head. "The Harrowing of the Holy?"

Shader shook his head dumbly.

"The Triumph of Reason? You mean you don't know? Don't they teach history these days?" Whittler raised his eyes to the ceiling.

"I'm not from around these parts," Shader said.

"So Mr. Mesqui tells me. Malfen, he says." Whittler wrinkled his nose. "But surely, even there, the candle of history still burns, albeit faintly. I assumed that's why you'd come, a representative of the dispossessed, returning to Old Mother New Jerusalem with a message of repentance. Tell me I'm right. In amongst that den of thieves, there's a thriving—what do you call it?—church?"

"I'm sorry, Senator," Shader said. "I have no idea where this Malfen is."

"Probably best you keep it that way," Whittler said. "So, I'm an ignorant buffoon who needs to stop jumping to assumptions. Hardly news to my ears. I hear it from the wife all the time. So, you're not a prophet on a mission, which is something of a relief. Do you know how many I've hung out to dry since taking up this post?" He held Shader's gaze for a long while and then broke away with a broad smile. "Forgive me the gallows humor. It's an unappetizing task, but someone has to do it. Do you know, I have an easier time licking my own balls than keeping the fish down."

Shader swallowed a lump. "I'm sorry, I don't know—"

"Oh, you do. The religious nuts who prowl round the markets handing out their nauseating little slips of paper. We got wise to the fish symbol and banned it, but the name stuck. Probably come up with something else by now, but they'll always be fish to me—slippery, and if you don't get them off the streets, they start to stink like the Abyss." Whittler chuckled at his own joke and leaned back in the chair, clasping his hands over his belly. "So, what is it about Sektis Gandaw you want to tell me?"

Shader took a deep breath. "This storm—"

"Oh!" Whittler exclaimed. "A little inclement weather and everyone's talking about the end of the world. Let me ask you something, Mr. Shader. Why would Sektis Gandaw leave us in peace all these years and then decide to wipe us out without a word of warning? It's a storm—an unusual one, I'll grant you—but a storm nonetheless."

"It's the start of the Unweaving," Shader said.

"Naturally," Whittler said. "Or the Demiurgos ate some spicy food and let rip with an almighty fart. Reason, Mr. Shader, reason. That's what has lain at the heart of our city since the revolution. Up till then, it was all superstition and nonsense. You only have to look at the statues outside the basilica to see the kind of thing our illustrious first settlers bequeathed us. If I had my way, they'd all be pulled down, but apparently it would be a crime against art and culture. It's the price we have to pay for democracy. Reason demands evidence, Mr. Shader. Evidence. Have you been to the Perfect Peak, spoken with Gandaw yourself?"

Shader nodded. "Believe me, it has started. You're no fool, Senator. You know what's going on."

Whittler's eyes flicked between the two guards before he leaned across the desk and spoke in a whisper. "It makes no sense. We eradicated all that Gandaw despised on Earth. We are a city devoted to reason, have been for decades. He has no cause to turn on us."

"It's not about you, Senator," Shader said. "It's about everything. Gandaw sees all of Creation as imperfect. He wants to start again."

"No," Whittler said. "He is unhappy about the fish, that's all. They've grown bolder again. Scarcely a day goes past without them scouring the markets for converts and meeting in secret to eat the flesh of their so-called god. But we're dealing with that, and Gandaw would know. He sees everything. This is just a warning. A warning, I tell you. And besides, we have the Cyclopean Walls. What harm could possibly befall us?"

"They'll be uncreated along with everything else," Shader said.

"And you've seen it, you say? Seen what's happening at the Perfect Peak?"

"Inverted lightning, a smog cloud, and now these weather patterns. But more than that: I've seen Gandaw, fought against him on Earth."

"Earth?" The color drained from Whittler's face. "You've been to Earth?"

"It's where I'm from."

Whittler stroked his beard and scoffed. "According to the myth, we're all from Earth, Mr. Shader, if you go back enough generations."

"No," Shader said. "I've just come from Earth. Sektis Gandaw has once more harnessed the power of Eingana. He has commenced the Unweaving."

Whittler's eyes roved back and forth for a while. He smacked his lips and tutted. It was hard to tell if he thought Shader was mad or lying. With a brisk wave of his hand, he moved on. "But we are fellows of reason. Gandaw would not destroy us, if it weren't for the fish." He stared Shader in the face, eyes wide and feverous. "The book. Mesqui said you had a book. Show me."

Shader passed him the Liber, and Whittler flicked through the pages, muttering to himself. Finally, he handed it back and gave a resolved nod.

"It's close enough. Different in parts, but it's the same jumbled verbiage. What's that beneath your coat?"

Shader's hand flew to his collar, where the white of his surcoat was plainly visible.

"Remove it."

The guards stepped in close, giving Shader no choice but to take off his coat.

Whittler peered at the red Monas symbol on the surcoat. "Explain."

"It is the Nousian Monas, Senator," Shader said. There seemed no point holding back now.

"This city was built by dwarves," Whittler said, "on the orders of Maldark the Fallen, the great betrayer, and a devotee of the slave religion."

"I know who he was," Shader said, a hint of steel entering his voice. "Your point?"

"Your clothing is the same, save for this… this Monas. Maldark wore a cross, like that thing on the dome outside. How many of you are there?"

"On Aethir?" Shader said. "Just me." Rhiannon sprang to mind, but what good could come of mentioning her? And Shadrak, well, Whittler seemed to be asking about wearers of the Monas; keeping the assassin secret wasn't exactly a lie, more a sin of omission.

"Just you," Whittler said. "And your arrival coincides with the storms coming from the Perfect Peak. Coincidence? I think not. You know, Mr. Shader, I have a theory—more of a hypothesis, really—and I propose to put it to the test. You said that you fought Gandaw on Earth. That didn't go too well, I'm guessing, otherwise you wouldn't have come here." He flashed a look at Shader. "How did you come here, by the way?"

Shader pressed his lips together and narrowed his eyes.

"It's immaterial," Whittler said. "Do you want to know what my hypothesis is? I think Sektis Gandaw is angry that you've followed him here. I think this storm is a warning to those foolish enough to harbor you. In the best tradition of his scientific method, we need to put my theory to the test." Whittler stood and loomed over Shader. "I trust I made it clear earlier how we treat fish?"

Shader started to protest, but Whittler held up a hand for silence.

"Oh, you might be a fish with a different symbol, but you're a fish all the same. You see, I think Gandaw will be very pleased with us, if we deal with this problem for him. I have a hunch he'll be placated."

"That's where you're wrong," Shader said. "It's not me he's after. He wants everything to end. Everything."

"No," Whittler said. "No, you're the one who's wrong. It's deviation he wants to eradicate. If we appease him, he'll spare us; he'll find a place for New Jerusalem in his future world."

Whittler headed for the door but turned back to Shader as a guard opened it for him. "Prepare yourself. There are a few formalities we need to go through—a trial of sorts." He flashed a smile. "The demands of bureaucracy! But by the morning, the crisis should have passed, and you'll have made the ultimate sacrifice, for which we'll be eternally grateful. Gentlemen," he said to the soldiers. "You know what to do. Same as you do with all fish."

"Senator," they said in unison.

The door slammed shut behind Whittler, and the guards turned to face Shader. One of them took off his studded belt and wound it around his fist. Shader cursed and lunged at him. The rasp of the other guard drawing his sword made him turn—straight into a skull-jolting punch to the jaw. The sword pommel hammered into his temple, and his knees buckled. Metal studs exploded against his lips in a spray of blood. He tried to rise, but blow after blow pummeled him into the ground. He curled his legs up to his chest and covered his head with his arms. They began to stomp on him, and he rolled desperately from side to side, but it did no good. They had him, sandaled feet thudding into him with unerring precision. His mind cried out for the Archon's sword. It had come for him once before, freed him from his chains; if it came again—

He screamed as a rib cracked.

If it came, he'd—

One of the soldiers grunted as he crouched over Shader, reached for his face, and pressed thumbs into his eyes. Shader cursed and tried to bite, but the hands moved to his hair and yanked him into a snarling face.

—kill them. He'd kill the whole shogging lot of—

The soldier slammed his head into the floor.

THE ART OF PERSUASION

MY, *A SENATOR in my bed. Aren't I the lucky one!*
Except it was Chef Dougan's bed—he'd not be needing it anymore—and the senator was Rollingfield, drugged to the eyeballs and corpulently naked. His discarded toga was a sorry heap on the floor. It didn't seem possible it could fit Rollingfield's lily-white mountains of blubber.

Albert screwed his face up as he touched two fingers to the senator's throat and raised an eyebrow at the half-empty cocktail glass on the nightstand. Just the memory of Rollingfield tonguing the cherry and guzzling the advocaat was enough to give him a case of the shivery jingles. He shuddered and shook his cheeks. *Oh, the idea! Mammaries as pendulous as Mama's, and peccadilloes that'd make even her turn in her grave. Well, river. Estuary, even.*

Albert let out a hissing sigh of relief. Rollingfield's pulse was down to a trickle, which is just where he needed it.

"You may enter," he called out as he stepped back from the bed and straightened his shirt.

The door opened a crack, and Shadrak slipped in. "Well?" His pink eyes widened at the semi-conscious whale on the mattress. "Ugh."

The color would have undoubtedly drained from his face, if it had been there in the first place.

"Lovely, isn't it?" Albert said, sweeping up his jacket from the back of the chair and shrugging it on.

"Shog, Albert," Shadrak said. "Tell me you didn't…"

Albert rolled his eyes. "I think we can safely say there was never any risk of that." Mind you, given the senator's immense bulk, there might not have been much choice, if he'd been the domineering type. It's times like these when pharmaceutical genius was a man's best friend. "Don't worry, darling, you're still my favorite."

"Just get on with it," Shadrak said, "'less you want me to shove your head in lard-boy's crotch till he pops."

Albert made a face and risked a look. Mercifully, whatever horrors might have dangled there were buried beneath rolls of fat. "Thank you, but I've already eaten." Just thinking about it made him feel sick. Best not to even go there. What people saw in all that messy business was beyond him. Just give him a good book and a steaming mug of cocoa any time. "Right, well, he's docile as a doting damsel. I'd say we have a good five minutes before he's completely comatose."

Buck burst into the room just as Albert was situating himself on the edge of the bed once more. Wasn't the cretin supposed to be out bending the ears of the underworld's finest? Surely he hadn't succeeded? That would be too much to hope for, but it would relieve them of the unsavory task of questioning Rollingfield…

"Girly's after your balls, Chef. Don't know what you gave her, but it sure stinks out the crapper."

"Girly?"

"Bitch," Shadrak said.

"Her that was slumped at the bar," Buck said. "You know, long black hair and that."

Albert pinched the bridge of his nose. The cretin had to tell him this, why?

"So, what's your shogging point?" Shadrak said. "Ain't you got any word on Shader yet?"

Buck puffed out his chest and gave a frowning shake of his head. "Nothing. Not a word on the streets. But we'll find him, if this don't work." He gave an uncertain look at the senator sprawled atop the bed. "I got my best man on the job."

Albert scoffed at that. *As predicted, the toe-rag hasn't spoken to a single guild contact, presumably because he carries as much weight with them as a latrine scrubber with His Holiness, the Supreme Ipsissimus of the Nousian Theocracy.* Best man, my foot. "Are you saying there's been some kind of miracle, and your boy's not inherited a single one of your defining traits?"

"Eh?" Buck said.

Before Albert could answer, the sound of dry-heaving interspersed with cursing and a bowel-splitting blast of flatulence came from downstairs.

"Oh, how awful," Albert said. "Poor dear. What did you say here name was again?"

"Bitch," Shadrak said.

Albert sighed. "Real name."

"Rhiannon."

"Thank you."

"But I prefer bitch."

"Must have given her too big a dose. Oh, well, accidents happen. Shall we?" Albert leaned over Rollingfield and pried open an eyelid. *Dead as a doornail.* He gave the senator a resounding slap in the face. Well, not quite dead, which was as it should be.

Rollingfield smacked his chops and muttered something incomprehensible. His liver-spotted hand groped around the blubber burying his crotch. "Oooh, where is it, my boy. Find it for Papa."

Albert held either side of Rollingfield's face. "Look into my eyes, Senator."

"Oh, yes!" Rollingfield's chins quivered, and his tongue darted between his lips. "What else? Anything, anything at all."

"Good, Senator. Now listen."

"I'm listening, dear boy. I'm all ears for you. Tell me you like what you see. Go on, tell me."

He jiggled his belly fat and tried to roll over, but Albert kept him pinned on his back. Last thing he wanted was to be confronted with an arse-crack like a canyon and a vile podex all puckered up and pleading... *Don't even think about it. Do not go there!*

Despite his best efforts, "Urgh," slipped out involuntarily.

Behind him, Shadrak sniggered.

"Think I'm gonna throw," Buck said.

The door opened and closed, and Buck's footfalls sounded like a herd of cattle stampeding down the stairs—not that Albert had ever experienced stampeding cattle, but one heard about such things from butchers and rustlers, or whoever happened to be offering the primest cuts at the time.

"Future guildmaster, you say?" Shadrak said.

"It's how you like them, Shadrak. Be honest. Now, can we get this over and done with?"

"My way's better." Shadrak patted the knives in his baldric.

"I didn't cultivate"—Albert clamped his hands over Rollingfield's ears and hissed—"such a high-up political ally just to have you send him bobbing down the river."

"Not in Sarum now, Albert. Mind you, he'd keep the fish in food for months, if we could get his fat ass out of here."

Albert sighed and did his best to tune Shadrak out. He removed his hands from the senator's ears, eliciting a jowl-wobbling, overly moist smile.

"Ooh, you are naughty," Rollingfield said. "But I like it. Whispering your salacious secrets, and not letting me hear because I'm such a bad boy." He rolled onto his side and slapped himself repeatedly on the buttock. "Bad Grayum. Bad, bad, bad Grayum."

Albert looked at Shadrak, who merely shrugged and mouthed, "Should've given him more."

Indeed. I wanted him suggestible, not suggestive.

"Senator," Albert said above the spanking. "Senator!"

Rollingfield flopped onto his back and lifted the apron of flab that had been covering his nethers.

Oh, Mother!

Albert shifted his gaze to the senator's glazed eyes. "Before we... Before we get down to business, uh... Grayum—"

"Gray-Gray. Call me Gray-Gray."

"Before we get down to business, Gray-Gray, I wanted to ask you to do something for me."

Rollingfield propped himself up on one elbow. His face was flushed, and his wrist was making brisk rhythmic motions that Albert didn't want to think about. "Anything you like, dear boy. Absolutely anything."

"It's about the senate."

"Oh, no, not now. Rut first, politics later."

"But you said anything, Gray-Gray, remember?"

Rollingfield sighed and fell back on the bed. "One of those, are you? A little tease. Very well, what is it you want to know? Be quick now."

"A friend of a friend went to the senate building earlier today, and he's not been seen since."

"Tall fellow in a brown hat and a white thingymawhatsit?"

"Surcoat, Senator?"

"If that's a tunic-y thingy with a red embroidery-doobry."

"Yes, Senator. Do you know—?"

Shadrak's breath was hot on Albert's ear as he whispered, "That's him. Ask where he is."

"Yes, yes, thank you," Albert hissed back, swatting the midget away. *Because I obviously wouldn't have thought of that myself.*

Rollingfield pushed himself into a sitting position and peered at Shadrak. "Who's the little fellow? Not that it matters." He patted the mattress. "Come on, sonny, don't be shy."

Shadrak growled and stalked over to the far side of the room.

"Senator," Albert said, "I need to know what happened to this man. His name is—"

"Shader," Rollingfield said. "He told us at the trial. Well, we call them trials, but it's merely a formality, all over in a jiffy. Only way to deal with these religious types. Good looking fellow. Such a waste, come morning."

"Waste? What do you mean?"

"Enough," Rollingfield said. "I don't know what was in that cocktail, but I'm going to explode if I don't have you right this instant, and then I mean to have your little friend, too. Oooh, I've not felt so vigorous in years."

"A moment more, Senator." Albert frowned at the glass on the nightstand. For whatever reason, the powder seemed to be having a paradoxical effect. He could only assume it was down to the absorbency of the blubber. "He's going to be executed? Tomorrow? Do you know where he is now?"

"Well, the prison, of course. Now do be a good chap and suck—"

"Prison?" Albert's heart lurched at what he thought Rollingfield was suggesting, and he swallowed a mouthful of bile.

"Small one," Rollingfield said, glancing at Shadrak. "Just like you. A teensy-weensy, prisony wisony. Do you know—"

Shadrak strode over to the bed. "Tell me where, and if it's a prick you want, I got one right here." He palmed a dagger as he spoke.

"Oh, yes," Rollingfield gasped. "Yes, yes, yes." He rolled onto his hands and knees.

"Street," Shadrak said. "What street's it in?"

Rollingfield twisted his neck to look at Shadrak, a thick rope of slobber running from the corner of his mouth. "Ooh, I feel... sleepy." He flopped over onto his side.

"Street!" Shadrak said, raising his dagger.

Albert grabbed his wrist and held up a staying finger. It was finally working, thank the great pie-maker in the sky. But another second, and it would have all been for nothing.

"The prison, Senator. We could all go together, and there the four of us could do such things. You said you liked the look of Shader, remember?"

"Ooooooh, yessssss," Rollingfield said. "101st... Arse-end of the basilica buildingy-thingy... sena... senate build..."

Rollingfield's mouth hung open, and drool trickled down his chin onto the sheets. Within moments, he was snoring like a pig with a bad cold.

"I do hope I didn't accidentally overdose him," Albert said. "Could be catastrophic for his liver."

"He'll live," Shadrak said. "You never make mistakes in that department, Albert."

Albert smiled internally. "No. No, I suppose I don't. Come on, let's leave him to his beauty sleep." *He certainly needs it.*

"How you gonna explain him waking up here?" Shadrak said.

"That's Fargin's job. Now, do you have any idea where this senate building is? What was it he said, 101st Street?"

Shadrak tapped the side of his head. "All in here, Albert. All in here." His eyes narrowed to bloody slits as he looked at the snoring senator. "I was gonna ask him about that thing that attacked me."

"Bit late for that now," Albert said as he opened the door and gestured for Shadrak to go first.

Buck was loitering on the stairwell, arms folded across his chest.

"Thought you were coughing your guts up," Albert said.

"Yeah, well, would've done if I could get a turn in the crapper."

"Then how...?"

Buck gave a sheepish grin.

"You swallowed it, didn't you?"

Buck hawked up a great wad of phlegm and looked like he was about to spit it out until he caught Albert's glare. Made you wonder about the kind of male-bonding activities he got up to, not to mention the company he kept. He gulped it down and did his best to look serious. "So'd he spill?"

"What on earth are you... oh, the beans, you mean. Did he talk? Indeed, he did."

"Are we gonna stand about on the stairs all day, or do I have to sling you down them head first?" Shadrak said as he pushed past Buck. "With any luck, you'll break your bleedin' neck."

"Oi," Buck said.

Albert put a warning hand on his shoulder. "Come on, don't upset the poison pixie."

They followed Shadrak into the restaurant. He pulled out a chair from a table, reversed it, and sat down.

"This prison on 101st Street," Shadrak said to Buck. "What do you know about it?"

"No way," Buck said, taking the chair opposite. "No shogging way. That's only the most heavily guarded place in New Jerusalem. No one gets in or out. Not never."

Albert paused, halfway to the kitchen. It sounded to his ears very much like a challenge. He was about to go back and join them, but then he remembered what Shadrak was like. The albino would leave no stone unturned. He'd eke out of Buck every last detail he knew about the place, and then he'd plan for every possible scenario. If they'd had the time, he would have probably staked the prison out for a week or two until he was absolutely certain about what needed to be done.

Shadrak looked up from the table and caught Albert watching him. A look of understanding passed between them, and Albert started to turn toward the kitchen, but then Shadrak said, "Don't think you're staying out of this, Albert. I'm gonna need your expertise."

"You have a plan? Already?" The cretin hadn't even filled them in on what little he probably knew yet.

"Let me put it another way," Shadrak said. "I ain't letting you outta my sight till I get my plane ship back. Got it?"

Just then, Rhiannon came stumbling out of the latrine. "I'm coming with you. To get Shader, I mean." She promptly doubled up, vomited, and went back in.

Albert winced and looked away.

"No," Shadrak said. "You are most definitely staying here."

"Yeah," Buck said, like he was suddenly someone important.

"You, too," Shadrak said. "No offense. You might shit the locals, but I know a pillock when I see one."

Buck's mouth was working silently, but he clearly couldn't think of a retort.

Shadrak steepled his hands on the table and fixed him with a stare. "Now," he said, "impress me with your knowledge of the prison."

"Impregnated, it is," Buck said. "There's no way you'll get your mate out."

Albert slapped a palm to his forehead as he joined them at the table.

"What?" Buck said. "I ain't kidding."

"I know," Albert said. "That's what worries me, but the word you're looking for is 'impregnable'."

"That's what I said."

"Of course you did."

Shadrak clicked his fingers. "You two finished? Good. So, what makes it impregnable? Locks? Traps? The number of guards?"

Buck shrugged at each suggestion.

"All of the above?" Shadrak said.

Another shrug.

"So, tell me if I'm wrong, you don't know shog all about it, and you've never been there, right?"

Buck grimaced and drew in a deep breath. "I hear things."

"Who from?" Shadrak slid off his chair and came round the table toward him.

If he'd had the height, Albert thought, Shadrak would have been pretty intimidating, but even without it, Buck was fidgeting like a virgin on her wedding night—*if indeed there are still such things as virgins of marrying age, yours truly excepted.*

"Well, people say things—"

"The guilds?" Shadrak said.

"Maybe."

Shadrak grabbed him by the collar. "Maybe? What the shog do you mean, 'maybe'? Do you or do you not know anything other than bullshit about the prison?"

Buck shook his head, his eyes welling up. "Only what I told you. I don't know nothing more'n that."

Shadrak wrenched him from his chair and bundled him toward the door. "Then shog off, and don't waste my time."

The door swung open, and a tall, bald man with a gray box beard came in. Albert's heart leapt into his mouth at the sight of the white toga. Surely the senate hadn't worked out what had happened to Rollingfield and come for him so soon.

Before anyone could speak, Shadrak booted Buck up the rear and sent him tumbling into the street. At the same time, an armored man in a black great helm entered. He was short—not as short as Shadrak, but about the same height as Rugbeard, who was still snoring away at the bar.

"Nameless," Shadrak said. "About shogging time. What kept you?"

"I kept him," the bald man said.

"Nameless?" Albert said. "What kind of a—?"

The latrine door slapped open, and Rhiannon staggered out once more. She looked green as a corpse, her eyes bloodshot and sunken. "Oh, great," she growled. "What the shog do you want?"

The bald man looked down his nose at her. "From you, nothing more at this juncture. When you are… recovered, we should talk."

"Nothing to say to you," she said, propping herself on a stool next to Rugbeard and reaching for a bottle.

"I wouldn't," Albert said. "The stuff I gave you doesn't mix well with alcohol."

Rhiannon groaned and held her head in her hands.

"Thought you'd found a way to get that thing off your head," Shadrak said to Nameless. "Got a belly full of booze and gone to sleep it off."

"The feeding takes time," the bald man said. "And there were other matters."

"Such as?" Shadrak said.

"Other matters."

"It's all right, laddie," Nameless said, clapping a hand on his shoulder. "Just making sure I'm safe—" He rapped the side of his great helm. "—after what happened."

"I ain't got a shogging clue what you're talking about," Shadrak said, "but right now, I couldn't give a stuff. We got problems of our own. Shader—"

"He's not back from the senate?" the bald man said.

"Yeah, like you didn't know," Rhiannon said.

"I didn't, but perhaps I should have."

"So, what are you going to do about it?" Rhiannon said.

"Me? Nothing. There's nothing I can do." For an instant, the bald man looked haunted, and something fiery flashed across his eyes. He regained his composure in an instant, though. "I am… I am already overstretched, and some actions are just a little too—"

"What, you mean you can't be bothered?" Rhiannon said. "Or is the great Aristodeus a coward as well as a creep?"

"You wouldn't understand if I told you!" he thundered. A hush settled over the restaurant, as if lightning had just struck.

It was Nameless who finally broke the silence. "Way I see it, laddie, if you won't or can't do anything, you should go pour yourself a drink and let the grown-ups do the thinking."

"Did I hear right?" Albert said. "Aristodeus, is it? Come, let me get you something to eat." It never hurt to know a person's gastronomic preferences. One day, the knowledge could prove invaluable.

"No." Aristodeus waved away the offer. "But you are right," he said to Nameless. "This is something you could do. Think of it as reparation." The last was said with a cruel grin, but Nameless seemed to just shrug it off.

Aristodeus went to hover over Rhiannon at the bar. "Perhaps we should make use of the time, have our talk, after all."

"If we must," Rhiannon said. "Unless you've got something better to do?"

Rugbeard sputtered and shook, turned his head the other way, and resumed his snoring.

Shadrak went back to the table and sat down. Nameless and Albert followed suit.

"Look," Shadrak said, "all we know is Shader's in a cell somewhere on 101st Street."

Nameless started fumbling in his pockets, but Shadrak put a restraining hand on him.

"No need for a map, mate. I've got it all memorized. Now, usually, I'd stake it out, see all the comings and goings, work out the locks and all that, but we don't have the time. Way I see it, if we can't prepare for the specifics, we prepare for everything. That's why I need you, you devious old bastard," he said to Albert, "and you, my friend," he said to Nameless, "are there for if it goes tits up."

"Stealth and hammer, laddie," Nameless said. "Sounds like a plan to me."

Albert was scratching his head, wondering how on earth his skills could be of any use when they knew so little about the target. If it was a matter of killing a few guards by poisoning their grub, then he was the man for the job, but when they had no idea how many or what they liked to eat... What was it Shadrak had said? Prepare for everything? What they needed was a one-fit solution, and with a flash of inspiration, he thought he knew what it was. They could always sort the wheat from the chaff afterward.

He was halfway to the door before Shadrak said, "What? What is it?"

Albert threw the door open and hollered out into the street. "Buck! Buck, you cretinous oaf!"

Buck came skulking from the alley at the side of the diner, having no doubt been eavesdropping.

"Changed you minds? Need me, after all?"

"How could we ever do without you, Buck? Now, where's the nearest blacksmith's?"

Buck opened his mouth to answer, but Albert carried on.

"I need a bellows and a—shit, where are we going to get some tubing?"

Someone coughed behind him, and he turned to see Nameless standing up and lifting the front of his chainmail hauberk. There was a coil of clear tubing taped to his belly, one end terminating in a blue cap, the other penetrating the skin.

"Feeding tube," Nameless said with a nod to Aristodeus. "I'm sure old baldilocks has plenty more where this came from." With a grunt, he yanked it out and stemmed the flow of blood with his free hand.

"Yes," Albert said, coming back inside and taking the tube between his thumb and forefinger. "Yes, that will do nicely."

THE GIFT

DRIP, DRIP, DRIP.

Shader groaned and opened an eye a slit. It would open no further, and warm fluid seeped from the eyelid, blurring what little sight he had. Waves of nausea rolled up from his guts and swamped his waking mind. He was itching all over, as if tiny ants were crawling across every inch of his skin. He tried to move, but it felt like a mountain had fallen on him. His mouth was rank, and when he ran his tongue across his teeth and gums, it was met with the coppery taste of blood. Slowly, he crept a hand up to his face, wincing as it passed his misshapen jaw. His fingers traced his swollen eyelids and a fist-sized knot on his forehead. Biting his lip, he pushed himself upright. The surface beneath him was soft—a mattress—and what he took to be a bed-frame creaked as he shifted his weight. He coughed up bile, and a shard of ice lanced through his chest. He clutched his hand there, taking in short, sharp breaths that whistled and rattled.

Orange light wavered at the foot of the bed, and he blinked it into focus. The first gasps of dawn dimly lit a barred window. He gingerly swung his feet over the edge of the cot and rolled forward to stand. His head thumped against the frame of the bunk above, and he swore, immediately grimacing in response. Someone moaned, and then he heard it again, the sound he had awoken to: drip, drip, drip—the monotonous splatter of water on the floor beside his cot.

He was in a whitewashed room no bigger than his cell at Pardes. Besides the window and the bunk, and the dark smears across the walls and floor, the only other feature was a solid iron door. Dust motes swirled up from the crack where it met the floor.

His thoughts were a fuzzy jumble, and flashbacks of snarling faces and striking fists cut across them. He dimly recalled being dragged a fair distance. Then there was a court of some sort, where the questions had been accusations he'd been too dazed to answer. He must have blacked out there, for he remembered no more.

From outside the window, he heard coarse voices, a peal of bawdy laughter. Minding his head, he used the bed-frame to hoist himself to his feet and shuffled over to take a look. The silhouettes of half a dozen men moved about a platform across the street. They were working on a wooden frame with two vertical beams and something at the top between them that glinted red in the burgeoning light of the rising suns. He pressed his face up against the bars and strained with his squinted eyes. It was a blade—a broad sheet of metal between the two uprights. A pulley line ran from it down the side of one of the posts. A workman took hold of the line and gave it a sharp yank. The blade streaked down and thudded into the base block. The other workers laughed and grunted and muttered approvingly as the blade was hoisted back into place and the line was tied off.

A cloying chill seeped through Shader's blood. He'd seen such devices during the Gallic uprising, when he'd led the Seventh Horse against the insurgents—lunatics who'd

606

seen Gandaw's technocracy as some sort of enlightened ideal. By the time the Elect had retaken the rebel towns, thousands of Nousians had been dragged to the guillotine.

This one was for him, without a doubt. Him and whoever else was being kept in this slaughterhouse.

A cough sounded from the bunk, drawing Shader back to see who he shared the cell with. As he reached the head of the bed, he slipped and had to catch himself on the frame. What he'd assumed was water was thicker and sticky. In the low light, it was visible only as dark splotches on the floor, but it was obvious what it was.

An arm flopped over the side of the top bunk, trailing a long rope of blood. A wrinkled face followed, staring down at him with nothing but cavities for eyes.

Shader took a step back, heart pounding fiercely, racing breaths like glass shards in his lungs.

"Peez," the old man rasped.

The reddish glow coming through the window gave his skin a hellish hue, but that was nothing compared with the gashes that crisscrossed his monstrously swollen face. In place of crow's feet, bloody streaks surrounded the empty eye-sockets, and dark tears tracked all the way to his lopsided chin.

"Peeez... Peesh... bee," he said in a voice like the scuffing of leather on stone.

The old man shuddered and then rolled over the edge of the bed. Shader lunged and caught him, crying out at the angry stabs that shot through his joints. The man was a dead weight, but thankfully so emaciated Shader could cradle him against his chest. He hung there limply, mouth working at words that would not come.

Shader turned a slow circle, numb as to what he should do. Finally, he settled on lowering the man onto the bottom bunk. The mattress he'd so recently been lying on was a ripped and stained mess, crawling with dark specks. Still, it had to be better than the stone floor.

A wide gash opened across the wizened face, but then Shader realized the old man was smiling—a weak, toothless smile full of resignation.

"Peees," he said again. "Bruvver."

"Peace?" Shader said.

The man's smile broadened, and he rocked his head from side to side. He slid a twisted, claw-like hand to his forehead. Shader thought he was making the Nousian sign and did the same, but then the man let his hand fall to his chest. He splayed his thumb toward his right shoulder and then dragged the fingers over to the left—just like Thumil had done.

The action seemed to give him strength. He grabbed Shader's wrist and drew him close, moistening his cracked lips with his tongue. Shader pressed his ear close.

"Goh ees we ya." The battered head fell to one side, and the man let out a long sigh before he tried again. "Goh...d... God ees wi... wiv you."

"God?" Shader said, frowning even as he pronounced the word. "You mean Nous? You are Nousian?"

The smile flattened into a line, and the old man's brow creased. He made a guttural noise in the back of his throat and broke into a coughing fit. Shader drew back until he'd finished. The man tried again, and this time the choking sound became a 'K'.

"K," Shader said with a nod. "Go on."

"Kri... Kriz..." He groaned and shook his fists. He made one more attempt, and then all the tension left his body, and he lay still.

Shader pressed two fingers to his throat. He still had a pulse, but it was weak and thready.

A gnarled hand came up and brushed him off. The old man's arthritic fingers scrabbled around at the collar of his tunic, and he pulled out a pendant on a chain. He shook it and held it out to Shader, taut against the chain.

"What is it?" Shader asked. "I can't see clearly."

He shook it harder.

"You want me to take it?"

A nod.

Shader reached behind the old man's neck and unclasped the chain. He brought the pendant close to his face and squinted at it through his slitty eyes. It was pewter, or perhaps tarnished silver. On one side there was the image of a woman in a hooded shawl or mantle, her hands clasped over her heart, and on the other there was an inscription: *Causa Salutis*—Cause of Our Salvation.

"I don't understand," Shader said, rubbing the pendant between his thumb and forefinger.

The old man reached up and fumbled about until he found Shader's hand, and then he closed Shader's fingers around the pendant. With that, he let his arm flop back onto the bed, and the smile returned to his face.

Shader pressed his fist to his lips, letting the chain brush against his forearm. Something stirred within him, sent a tingle coursing through his veins. Unfathomable emotions churned around in his guts and surged upward, spilling from his eyes in waves of stinging tears.

"Peace," the man on the bed whispered in perfect clarity. "Do not fear. Peace." He let out a rattling breath and stilled.

Shader bit down on his trembling fist, wishing he could have spoken with the man, found out who he was, what he was about. He leaned over and laid his hand across where the man's eyes should have been, uttering a prayer to Nous for the repose of his soul. The voice of his own doubt rolled about at the back of his mind. Would Nous do anything for this man, who so obviously had never heard of him? He tried to cut off the train of thought, but it had already insinuated itself into being. Would Nous do anything for anyone? Was there even a Nous at all?

The voices from outside grew louder momentarily, and Shader could have sworn he heard the clinking of glasses. He was about to go and look, when he caught the scent of something rotten. He cast about the cell, expecting to find a decomposing rat that he'd somehow failed to notice before, but then his eyes fell upon tendrils of smoke curling up from beneath the door. He took a step closer, tugging the collar of his surcoat over his mouth and nose. He swooned and stumbled, then spun away toward the window. The room lurched, like he was at sea aboard the *Aura Placida* once more, and then he dropped to his knees. The last thought that struck him as he pitched to the floor was, why would they go to all the trouble of building a guillotine if they were simply going to gas him to death?

LADY LUCK

THE SUNS ROSE bloody, and as they climbed higher, they lit up the sickness roiling in from Gandaw's mountain. The brightening sky was all smudges of greens, grays, and browns, like some shog-wit artist had mixed a palette with the muck that ran through the sewers beneath Sarum. Made Shadrak think of the plane ship. Made him think on what he was gonna do to that fat scut Albert if he didn't get it back.

Shadrak settled into a crouch atop the roof of the blockish building that ran adjacent to the basilica. It was half as tall as the Ancients' towers in Sarum but looked even older, if that were possible. Gave him the overview he wanted, though: a hundred feet above the cobbles and a bird's-eye on the evil-looking contraption on the wooden platform. Blade on the thing looked like it could slice through stone, but it was plain enough that weren't its purpose.

The prison Buck had made so much of looked of newish build and weren't exactly the impregnable fortress he'd made it sound. It was a squat brick and mortar construction with just the one way in and out—an iron-bound hardwood door that wouldn't have looked out of place on a dungeon, or one of them bankers' strongholds back home. The soft glow of lantern light spilled over from the far side, where workmen had been hard at it since he arrived. Heavy bars lined a broad window on the wall facing him, ten yards back from the door.

He'd checked the place out an hour earlier. On the other side, at the back, there was another barred opening, this once much smaller. He hadn't got close enough to see inside, but it figured that had to be the cell. Whole thing weren't much bigger'n Kadee's shack, and that weren't much more'n a sheepcote, if you was realistic, so there can't have been more'n one cell. The space at the front was prob'ly the guards' room. There hadn't been any coming and going in the time Shadrak had been watching, but occasionally a dark shape would pass across the bars of the window. To his reckoning, there was at least three inside, and no more'n five. Then there was the geezer on the door, a gormless looking grunt in a leather kilt and cuirass, but he'd already nodded off a couple of times, leaning on his spear. Course, if there was a change of guard, they was buggered, but there weren't much he could do about that. Dawn was well and truly here, and if Rollingfield was to be believed, that meant Shader had scant time left.

Albert was already in position, kneeling beneath the nearside window and running the tubing Nameless had yanked from his guts up through the bars. The other end was attached to the hand bellows Buck had come back with, and that was connected to the bell-jar containing the stinking gassy crap the poisoner had concocted. Stuff had killed the kitchen rat faster'n a bullet. Albert reckoned it'd knock a bloke cold in the same amount of time. Soon as the guards accused each other of cutting the cheese, the whole bunch of 'em would be sleeping like babes. Prisoners, too, if a whiff of the stuff got through to the cell. Shader might be pissed off, but he'd be alive. Only good thing about that was getting the show back on the road. Sooner Gandaw had his shogging throat slit, sooner they could all go back to what they was doing before Cadman's madcap scheming had lit a fuse under all their asses.

Nameless staggered on past Albert under the weight of a beer keg he'd lugged all the way from Dougan's Diner—or Queenie's or whatever Albert had changed the name to. He had a bag full of tankards slung over his shoulder, and its clanking had told Shadrak he was approaching even before he was visible.

The guard on the door started awake as Nameless set the barrel down at the front of the prison. Before the bloke could say anything, Nameless cried out in a booming voice, "Beer for the workers! Come and get it, lads!"

A chorus of exclamations erupted from the far side, and a big geezer came into view. He said something to Nameless and the guard, but when Nameless simply tapped the barrel and filled one of the tankards, the man was hollering to his mates, and pretty soon the dwarf was at the center of an impromptu piss up. The guard clearly had no idea what to do about it and in the end accepted a beer himself.

By that time, Albert was pumping furiously on the bellows, and the job was as good as done.

Shadrak cast a look over the rooftops. He'd been doing so pretty much since he'd arrived, but thank shog there'd been no sign of the thing that had attacked him on his way to the diner. What he did see, though, was a group of soldiers heading along one of the backstreets toward the prison. He cursed and started back down the drainpipe he'd come up. That was the problem with these last minute plans: left too much to chance, and Lady shogging Luck was a bitch who took a mile every time he gave her an inch.

He dropped the last ten feet to the road and rolled to his feet. A split second before the group emerged onto 101st, he found the shadows and slid out a couple o' blades.

There was four of 'em, all in padded jerkins—poor man's breastplate—which kinda told you the caliber of prison guards the senate was willing to pay for. Only weapons they had was shortswords in battered scabbards they prob'ly grave-robbed, or got handed down from granddads who were real soldiers. They was whispering and sniggering—something about a whore named Harmony—and one of them coughed up some phlegm and stopped for a riddle in the gutter. The others left him to it, and so Shadrak crept up behind and hissed. The soldier spun round, dick in hand, and got a dagger across his throat. Geezer tried to scream, but all that came out was a gurgling choke, and then he crumpled to the ground in a puddle of his still-steaming piss.

"C'mon, Tor, you gormless twat!" one of the other soldiers called without looking back. "Stop playing with yourself and keep up."

Shadrak glided along in their wake, padding on the balls of his feet. Got so close he could smell the sweat on the straggler's jerkin. Bloke must've had a sixth sense, coz he turned at the last instant. Only difference was, he got a knife in the guts 'stead of his kidney. Squealed like a pig, though, and that got his mates interested.

"Oi!" The bigger of the two remaining soldiers, a mackeral-backed swad, whipped out his sword.

Shadrak tumbled under a windmilling slash and stuck him in the gonads. In the same movement, he took a swipe at the other one, but the runt skipped out of the way and tripped over his own feet. Gonad-boy staggered back, white as a sheet and clutching his knackers.

"Oi, what?" Shadrak said, kicking out at his knee and getting that satisfying crack in response.

The big bloke went down screaming, but Shadrak shut him up with a deft cut across the jugular.

"What's up, cockleburr?" Shadrak advanced on the runt, who was scrabbling back on his ass, mouth trembling and nothing coming out but spittle. Poor bastard hadn't even thought to draw his sword, he was so scared. "Lost your swagger now your mates are shogged?"

He stepped in close and rammed a dagger through the bloke's thigh. The scream was shrill as a girl-child's, but what was really pathetic was that there was still pleading in his eyes. You got this sort all the time: those who thought they'd never die. If only they begged enough or promised riches beyond your wildest imaginings, they'd get off the hook. Problem is, Shadrak liked the begging, and as far as the second were concerned, guards like this lot didn't get paid enough to exactly make a big difference in his life. He grabbed a fistful of hair and yanked the bloke's head closer.

"W-W-Wait! I can pay—"

Stab, stab, stab in the face. "No, you can't." Shadrak let go, and the soldier slumped to the ground.

As he retrieved his dagger from the man's thigh, a familiar presence tugged at the back of his mind, but he wouldn't let it in.

"Not now, Kadee," he muttered. "Can't you see I'm working?"

When he reached the prison, a clutch of workmen were unconscious at Nameless' feet. The dwarf was perched on the edge of the barrel, holding a tankard up before his great helm and staring at it through the eye-slit. The guard had his sword out and was stumbling toward Albert, who was reeling in the tubing with a smug grin on his fat face. Albert hadn't seen the danger, and he bent down to disconnect the tubing from the bellows. The guard raised his sword and half-tripped, half-ran in a swaying zigzag toward him. Shadrak ran, too, but he was too far off to use a dagger. He stopped for a moment to sheathe one of the knives and grab a razor star. A booming laugh from behind made him turn. Nameless had the tankard raised in a toast, and the great helm was looking straight past Shadrak at Albert. Something clanged to the pavement.

Spinning round, Shadrak let out the breath he hadn't realized he'd been holding. The guard was facing him, arched back at an unnatural angle, arms thrashing, legs twitching. His sword was at his feet. Albert had something wrapped around his neck and was grinning like the cat that got the cream. A couple more shakes and shudders, and the guard flopped to the pavement. As Shadrak drew close, Albert unwound a garrote from the bloke's ruined neck.

"Credit where credit's due, eh, Shadrak?" Albert said, straightening up and picking bits of flesh from the wire. "Chef Dougan might have been a terrible cook, but his cheese-cutter works a treat—much nicer than the one I lost." He stuffed it in his jacket pocket and adjusted his rumpled collar.

"Good job, Albert," Shadrak said. "That all of 'em?"

"Unless there's a change of guard on the way."

"There was," Shadrak said, slipping the razor star back in his baldric and wiping his dagger clean on his cloak. "But not no more. Any sign of a key?"

Albert rifled through the guard's pockets, checked his belt, and came up shrugging. "It's all yours, then." He gestured toward the door.

Shadrak slipped out his tool-pack and unrolled it. He hadn't had chance to analyze the lock when he'd scouted the place out, but it can't have been that tricky, by the looks of it. He put a hook pick between his teeth till he needed it and took out the torsion wrench. The lock was at eye-level for him; anyone else would've had to bend down. Without looking, he wagged his fingers over his shoulder. "Light," he hissed. "Bring me some light."

Nameless came up behind him with one of the workmen's lanterns. "Poison or no, I'd have a swig of ale, if not for this shogging helm, even if it killed me."

Shadrak's face tightened with irritation, and he gave the dwarf a narrow-eyed look.

Nameless tossed the tankard over his shoulder and held the lantern close to the lock.

"What you need is a hammer and chisel," he said. "Lock like this isn't sturdy, not like the ones in Arx Gravis. One good whack—"

"What I need is peace and quiet," Shadrak said. "Do I tell you how to lop heads off with that axe o' yours?"

He placed the torsion wrench in the lower part of the keyhole and applied torque to the cylinder, turning it the merest fraction of an inch. Taking the pick from his teeth, he poked it into the upper part of the keyhole and felt around for the farthest pin. He pushed up on it, maintaining the torque on the cylinder, until he felt it set. The lock was simpler than he'd expected, similar to those used on most of the houses in Sarum, which were based on the Ancient-world locks that could still be found in the towers that had survived the Reckoning.

"My way's quicker," Nameless said.

Shadrak bit his lip to stifle a reply. The dwarf was prob'ly right, but that ain't how Shadrak worked. No noise, no mess, no sign he'd ever been there. It might've been a habit, but it was one that'd served him well. He popped the remaining pins and turned the cylinder with the wrench. The lock clicked, and he pushed with his shoulder—but the door didn't budge.

"Crap," he muttered, and then, "shogging, scutting bollocks."

"Oh, don't tell me…" Albert said, breathing down Shadrak's neck. He stank of garlic, but that was nothing unusual.

"Yep," Shadrak said, stepping back from the door and giving it a kick. "Barred from the shogging inside."

"Well, that's… sensible, I suppose," Nameless said.

"This is why I don't like rushing," Shadrak said. "Everything needs to be planned out in advance."

"In my experience, laddie," Nameless said, "life's not like that."

Shadrak sucked in a breath through gritted teeth. He scratched at his beard and shook his head.

"Here," Albert said, handing him the pick and wrench. "Can't say we didn't try."

"Stand back," Nameless said, passing Albert the lantern and hefting his axe. "I'll have a crack at it."

"No," Shadrak said a little more harshly than he'd intended. Didn't matter how strong the dwarf was, it'd take forever to hack through the wood, and in that time the place would be swarming with militia. "We'll use this."

He took his last remaining globe from his pouch. He'd been saving it in case the creature that had attacked him came back. See, even when he had a plan, it came to shite like everything else on this poxy mission. That's why he worked alone. Worst shogging thing when you wanted to get a job done was relying on others, or having to dig them out of the messes they got themselves into.

He moved away from the door, gesturing for the others to follow. He gave the globe a good shake, in the hopes of making whatever made it bang a bit more excitable, and then he threw it at the center of the door. A thunderous boom threw them from their feet and sent clouds of black smoke billowing away on the wind. Shadrak propped himself up on one elbow, coughing and waving the smoke out of his face.

Albert groaned as he sat up and clamped a hand over his mouth and nose, but Nameless lay flat on his back, a deep laugh bubbling around inside his great helm.

"That'll do it, laddie," the dwarf said, kicking his stumpy legs in the air. "Just can't wait for the part where the militia come running and I get to crack a few skulls."

"Such a pity we don't have more time," Albert said with a tight smile, as he stood and brushed himself down.

Shadrak rolled to his feet. "Stay here and keep watch," he said to Nameless. "Albert, with me."

"Anything for you, laddie," Nameless said, grabbing his axe and using it to push himself upright.

Shadrak headed through the wreckage of the doorway. There was a door with a grille opposite, and off to one side there was a heavy wooden chest. Two guards were slumped over a table, greenish drool oozing from their mouths.

Albert lifted one's head and used his thumb to raise an eyelid. "Oops," he said. "A bit over-zealous with the mixture, I fear." He let the head drop with a thud onto the table.

"But Shader—" Shadrak said, starting toward the cell door.

"Oh, he'll be fine. I dare say only a trickle made it through to the cell. Here—" Albert unclipped some keys from a guard's belt and flung them to Shadrak.

Shadrak rattled through them till he found the one that fit the lock. There was a healthy clunk as he turned it, and he pushed the door open.

Shader was face down on the floor. His hair was matted and caked with filth, and his surcoat was a shredded mess, soaked in red. A pair of bunks was the only furniture in the whitewashed room. Bloodstained sheets draped down from the top one, and on the bottom lay a scrawny corpse with a face so bruised and bloodied it didn't seem human.

Albert stooped over Shader and turned him onto his back. Taken a right pummeling, by the looks of him: split lip, puffy black eyes, streaks of dried blood from dozens of cuts.

"He's breathing," Albert said.

"Yeah, but look at the state of him. Game to Sektis Gandaw, I'd say."

"Really?" Albert said, stepping away from Shader. "You believe all that stuff?"

Shadrak shrugged. He didn't know what to believe anymore. He'd seen some crazy shit lately and got himself mixed up with the Archon's machinations. But he still remembered the emotionless face of Sektis Gandaw, the cold confidence he exuded.

"Yeah, I believe it, though what the shog we're supposed to do about it now hero boy's down is anyone's guess."

"Help me," Shader mumbled from the floor. "Help me up."

Albert looked at Shadrak and stuck out his bottom lip. Together, they supported Shader as he stood, coughing and wincing, clutching his side.

"Where's it hurt?" Shadrak said.

Shader looked at him through slitted eyes. "Everywhere." He shrugged off their help and lurched toward the bunk-bed. His fist was tightly closed about something that trailed a silver chain.

"Dead," Shadrak said, glancing over his shoulder at the open door.

"I know." With agonized slowness, Shader lowered himself to one knee beside the bed. Grunting, he set the other knee down, too, and bowed his head.

"Ain't like you knew him," Shadrak said. He wanted to add, "So get a shogging move on," but something about Shader warned him not to. In spite of his injuries—and they looked severe—he was tight as a spring, and tension rolled off him in murderous waves.

Albert gave a delicate cough and nodded that they should go. Shadrak grimaced and cocked a thumb in Shader's direction. Albert's shrug didn't exactly help the situation none.

For shog's sake! Shadrak stepped toward the bed, for once wishing Kadee's face would pop into his head and tell him what to do. He'd never been good at the softly, softly stuff. That had always been her department.

"Look, mate... Shader..."

Shader pulled a bloodstained sheet over the corpse's face. He knelt there like some crazed ecstatic; like some heartbroken teen that'd been dumped; like Shadrak had knelt the day Kadee had gone back to the dirt.

"We need to…" Shadrak said.

Shader pulled himself up using the bed-frame. A single drop of blood fell from the fist around the chain and spattered on the floor. He opened his fingers and looked at what he'd been holding so tight it had cut him—some kind of necklace, far as Shadrak could see. Shader fastened it around his neck, tucked it beneath his tattered surcoat. He look a lurching step and staggered as his leading knee buckled. Shadrak caught him by the elbow, and Albert scurried over to take the other side like an overprotective nursemaid. Shadrak shook his head at that. Seems you never really knew people.

"Don't hurry or anything, laddies," Nameless hollered from outside, "but there's a whole bunch of soldiers coming our way."

"How many?" Shadrak called back.

"How would I know?" Nameless cried, a hint of effort in his voice, like he was on the move. "I'm just a grunt. Can't count that high."

"Oh, shit, shitty, shit, and shit," Albert muttered, eyes darting all over the place.

"Move," Shadrak said, heading through the door, dragging on Shader's arm.

Soon as they entered the guard room, the clangor of steel on steel and barked orders broke like a thunderstorm.

Shader snapped his head round to glare at the chest. He pulled free from Albert and Shadrak and took a tottering step toward it.

"Bugger this," Albert said, pressing himself against the wall beside the wrecked main door and glancing outside. "Ooh, that must have hurt."

There was a muffled thud from the road and a grunt that turned into a whimper.

Shader shuffled to the chest, leaned over it. "Locked," he muttered.

"Here." Shadrak threw him the keys.

A roar went up from the street, but it rolled on into a booming song:

"I once had a terrible ooze, from my dwarfhood down to my shoes…"

"That Nameless?" Shadrak asked, backing away toward the entrance.

Albert nodded, eyes riveted to the scene outside. "By Mama's moldy… By my word, he's good. He's practically dancing."

"If I'd known so before," Nameless sang, "she's a pox-ridden whore…"

Crash, clang, thud.

"Three down—" Albert said.

"How many to go?" Shadrak risked a peek through the debris of the door.

Must've been two dozen of the kilted soldiers, all of 'em with tall rectangle shields and shortswords. The three on the ground had lost their helms, and their shields was mangled beyond repair. One of them was clutching the stump of his arm, blood spraying from it like a fountain.

"… I'd have saved up my coin for some booze." Nameless insinuated his way between two shields with bewildering footwork and rammed his axe haft into one soldier's nose, spinning even as he did and scything the blade at the other's midriff. The soldier swung his shield in the way just in time and hurtled back into a group of his comrades.

"Good show, laddie," Nameless said, as if he'd intended it all along. "Nice reflexes."

The rest of the soldiers backed off, forming up into a tight shield wall.

"Pikes," someone yelled. "And crossbows. Now!"

A soldier at the back broke off and ran down the street.

Shader stumbled to the doorway, shrugging on his coat and tugging his hat down low over his face. Must've been in the chest. He adjusted his scabbard so it sat behind his hip. Only thing was, it was empty.

"Sword?" Shadrak asked.

Shader nodded in the direction of the basilica. "In there."

"Oh, for shog's sake," Shadrak said. "If you think I'm going—"

Shader staggered past him, out into the street.

"Good lad," Nameless said. "Nothing like a bit of rough and tumble to get the blood flowing, eh? You'll be right as rain in a jiffy."

Shadrak exchanged a look with Albert. In a minute the place would be swarming with more soldiers, and if they did bring crossbows, they was shogged. He slipped the pistol from its holster and indicated with his eyes that he and Albert should make a run for it down the side-street Nameless had lugged the barrel along. Albert was sweating like a pig, but he nodded all the same. Weren't no surprise. He was the last person Shadrak would expect to make a stand of it.

Shader was limping toward the basilica, hand stretched out before him like a blind man's.

"Laddie?" Nameless called after him. "The fight's this way."

Trumpets blasted in the distance, and bells started clanging.

"Go!" Shadrak said. He rolled round the doorway and sprinted for the side-street.

Albert half-jogged, half-skipped behind him, puffing and wheezing.

"Shog!" Shadrak said. A mass of pikemen was coming straight at them. He veered across the street to the mouth of a narrow alleyway, and Albert bundled in beside him.

"Now what?" he said.

Shadrak held up a hand. "Look."

Nameless was goading the cordon of soldiers, running up and slapping his axe against the shield wall and dancing clear before they could jab at him. But it wasn't him Shadrak was interested in.

Shader's splayed fingers shook with tension as he faced the overshadowing basilica. His eyes were closed, his whole body taut.

"What on earth—?" Albert started, but he was cut off by a yell from inside the basilica, followed by a series of screams.

Nameless whirled to see what was going on, and the soldiers he'd been taunting did the same. There was a tense moment, punctuated by the thump, thump, thump of footfalls as the pike unit bore down upon them. Then came a sharp thwat, a glint of metal, and a resounding clang. Nameless staggered back as a crossbow bolt ricocheted from his great helm and clattered to the ground. Before he could react, one of the basilica windows shattered outward, and Shader's sword streaked through the air amid a shower of glass and slapped itself into his palm. Golden light erupted around his body, and Shadrak had to shield his eyes against the glare with his arm. There was more footsteps: faster, moving away from him. He blinked until he could see Albert legging it down the alley.

The pikemen had slowed to a stunned walk, and the shield wall was more of a scattering of gaping idiots. Shutters were thrown open on a couple o' buildings overlooking the street, and crossbows poked from the windows.

Shader held the sword aloft as the blaze spiraled back up into the blade. The stiffness seemed to have left him. He was standing poised on the balls of his feet, and there was no sign of the cuts and bruises that had marred his face. He glanced at Shadrak and nodded, as if to say everything was under control now; that Shadrak could go. Then he spun on his heel and strode straight toward the shield wall. The soldiers tried to reset, but Shader was upon them, and unlike Nameless, there was nothing playful in the way he cut and thrust with the precision of a surgeon.

The pikemen rushed forward, but Shadrak wheeled back out into the street and let off a couple o' shots with his pistol. One soldier went down with a hole in his head, and the rest scattered for the scant cover of the buildings.

"Shader," he called. "Nameless."

All he could see of Shader was the flashing blur of his sword as it rose and fell. Blood sprayed, men screamed, and even when they tried to encircle him, he swayed and struck like a serpent.

Nameless charged them from the rear, and soon it was a rout. If he hadn't seen it with his own eyes, Shadrak wouldn't have believed it. There was something unnatural about the two of them—the way they fought. The soldiers broke off and ran, but Shader didn't stop. Rather than taking the opportunity to get out of there, he went after them, cutting them down from behind.

Nameless turned the great helm on Shadrak. "Go, laddie. I'll bring him back."

The pikemen were moving again. Shadrak fired, and they ducked back into cover. He cast a quick look at the rooftops, in case his shots had drawn any more attention. Last thing they needed right now was that scutting creature to show up. With a nod to Nameless, he pulled his hood up and sprinted down the alley.

FALL FROM GRACE

SCREAMS.

More screams.

The tramp of feet.

A blur of bodies, running, turning. Men, open-mouthed, pleading.

The spray of blood, hot on his hand, spattering his face.

The purity. The purpose.

The soldier at the back whirled, slashed wildly with his shortsword. Shader swayed and lunged, and the man went down. Two more broke away from the pack. One barreled at Shader behind his shield, chopping the air with his sword like a crazed butcher. The gladius tore through the shield as if it were made of paper, sliced guts, and sent a string of crimson arcing to the road. The other threw down his shield and raised his arms in surrender. With a half-turn, Shader back-slashed, already picturing the gore spewing from a ripped throat, but a hand caught his wrist, gripped it like a vise.

"No, laddie," Nameless said. "I won't allow it."

The soldier stumbled back, then turned and fled.

With a flash of movement, Shader snatched the gladius with his other hand and hacked down at the great helm. Nameless smacked it aside with his axe-haft and slammed the flat into Shader's shoulder, knocking him from his feet. Shader hit the ground hard, rolled, and came up swiping for the dwarf's midriff. The axe was a blur as it turned aside the sword, and the haft hit Shader between the eyes. With a crack, the back of his head hit the ground, and he dropped the gladius. He blinked up at the dwarf standing astride him, axe slung carelessly over his shoulder.

"… won't allow it," he was saying. "Won't let you do what I did."

Shader rubbed his forehead. It smarted, and already a knot was forming. The ravine. Nameless was talking about the massacre at the ravine. "You remember?" he said. Nous, his hands hurt—the palms—both of them. Felt like they were on fire.

"Aye, laddie, I remember. Not everything, but more than I'd like."

Shader shook his head, tried to find the right words. This wasn't the same, though, was it? He hadn't… Nous Almighty, he hadn't—

"Enough!" Nameless bellowed.

Shader pushed himself up onto an elbow. The dwarf wasn't talking to him.

The soldiers were regrouping further down the street, locking shields and eyeing each other, as if to say, "Who's going first?"

Shader looked at one palm, then the other. The skin was chafed, raw. No, more than chafed: it was blistered.

A movement out of the corner of his eye made him look up. There was a dark shape on one of the rooftops—sleek and black. He could have sworn it was studying Nameless. It looked like a man, only… He blinked, and in that instant it was gone.

"I said, enough!" Nameless roared.

The shield wall buckled and retreated a couple of steps.

The clatter of arms made Shader look back toward the prison. A ragged pike unit was closing in, drawing confidence with each step. There were at least six bodies in the intervening space: soldiers, bleeding out on the ground; men Shader had cut down in his rage.

Someone fired a crossbow from an upper window; the bolt glanced off Nameless' hauberk and clattered to the ground. The dwarf swung round, and for a moment, Shader thought he was going to charge at the building, maybe even wade into the pikemen, but then Nameless reached down and tugged him to his feet.

"Come on, laddie, let's get you back. No sense in any more killing."

Shader stooped to pick up the gladius. "Back whe—Ouch!" He recoiled, sucking at his scalded fingers. It was like touching a boiling pan. Was it… Was it because…? His mind, his heart, his faith sunk like a stone down to his guts. What had he done? Sweet Nous, what had he—?

"Now, laddie!"

The shield wall shuffled forward a step, and the pike unit leveled its weapons and came on with purpose. Another crossbow bolt fizzed through the air and kicked up dust from the road a few feet short of them.

Shader withdrew his hand into the sleeve of his coat and used it like an oven glove to retrieve the gladius. He fumbled the blade back into its scabbard, just as a cry went up from the shield wall, and it surged forward.

Nameless grabbed Shader's arm and dragged him into the mouth of an alley. The pikemen veered as one, someone yelled a command, and then they charged.

Nameless slapped Shader on the buttocks with the flat of his axe.

"Go on, laddie," he said as he turned to face the onslaught. "I'll catch you up."

***

"What do you mean you can't use it?"

Aristodeus's face was red as blood, and spittle flew as he raged; but there was more to it than anger. Shader had never seen the philosopher's eyes so wide, so bloodshot, so… haunted.

Thunder rolled outside the window, and lightning sheeted upward into the sky, its flash reflecting in Aristodeus's sclera, fleetingly giving him the look of the damned.

"Well?" he said, stabbing a finger at the gladius sheathed at Shader's hip.

Shader felt his cheek twitching; felt the muscles of his neck stiffen, bunch up. Despite the fire in the philosopher's tone, he looked away. What could he say? He needed to think; needed to think about what he'd done…

Nameless was over at the bar, seated beside another dwarf, who was red-faced for a different reason, a frothing flagon of ale tipped just beneath his bulbous nose. Shader only had a dim recollection of Nameless catching up with him, guiding him along street after street until they reached the comparative safety of the diner.

Rhiannon hovered by the latrine door, looking green as grass. When he met her glare, she turned away. She sneered at Aristodeus, flicked her eyes over to the bar, and then looked down at her feet. But Shader could still feel her glancing between him and the philosopher. Something was going on; he knew her well enough to see that; but what?

"So, we're shogged, is what you're saying?" Shadrak said. He was leaning back in his chair, feet crossed on a table. He eyed the crust he'd been nibbling, snorted, and tossed it over his shoulder.

The kitchen doors swung open, and the podgy man in the Ancient-world suit—Albert, they'd called him—backed through them carrying a steaming dish in each hand.

"Best I could do at such short notice," he said, turning to see who was listening.

Silence.

Shader realized they were all watching him, waiting for a reply. He sought out Nameless, but he found no support in the great helm's empty eye-slit.

Aristodeus sucked in a long breath through his teeth. "What have you done?"

"Nothing I haven't done," Nameless said. "Nor most of the people in this room, if I'm right."

Aristodeus shot him an irritated glare and then fixed his eyes on Shader once more.

"I killed them," Shader said, barely recognizing his own voice.

"So shogging what?" Shadrak said. "Scuts had it coming. Would've done it myself if—"

"It was more than that," Aristodeus said, taking a step closer. "You've killed before, and the sword didn't reject you."

Shader closed his eyes, tried to think of a way to admit his shame. His faith was a sham. He was no better than his father—no, it was worse than that: Jarl Shader would never have cut down a fleeing foe; would never have tried to kill a man who surrendered. He looked up, drawn once more to Nameless. If the dwarf hadn't stopped him…

"It was the rage," Nameless said. "Same as with me."

"No," Shader said. "Not the same."

The dwarf stood. "What's that supposed to mean, laddie?"

"This is the Sword of the Archon, not some demon-possessed axe."

"Meaning?" Nameless crossed his arms.

Albert gave a delicate cough. "I take it no one's hungry, then. Such a waste of good chowder."

The dwarf at the bar raised a shaky hand. "Bring it here, sonny, and grab me another beer, while you're at it."

"Meaning, the sin is all mine," Shader said.

Rhiannon scoffed. "Here we go again."

Shader flashed a look at her, and she instantly lowered her eyes and pulled up a seat at the bar on one side of the drunken dwarf. Nameless returned to his stool on the other side, and Shader was dimly aware of Albert plonking down the food and complaining as he filled a tankard from a keg.

"Me, too," Rhiannon said, rubbing her stomach and wincing. "Sooner chance it than listen to any more of this shite."

"And me," Nameless said. "Not that I can drink in this thing—" He rapped the side of the great helm then delivered an almighty slap to the other dwarf's back. "—but it's yours if you'll lighten the mood with a story. The taller, the better."

"There is only so long I will be ignored," Aristodeus said.

"Face it, Baldy," Shadrak said, "your scutting master plan is shogged. Don't know why you didn't send an expert in the first place." He drew his pistol and made a show of polishing it with a napkin.

"Years and years and years," Aristodeus said, thrusting his face into Shader's. "Do you think I wanted to train you? Wanted to keep coming back to that stinking little hovel in the armpit of Nousia?"

Shader focused in on that; it was like a fissure closing up, a lacuna of hidden motives, long-since suspected, but always ambiguous, now coming into perfect clarity.

"That was it all along, wasn't it?" he said, locking eyes with the philosopher. "I always knew you wanted something from me; something very specific; but you played me so well, got me thinking you were a friend, family, even."

Aristodeus turned away. "Oh, I was far more than that to you."

"Yes? And what might that have been?"

Aristodeus flicked his fingers dismissively over his shoulder. "Time is not on our side. Whatever you may think about my motives, it is imperative that you wield the Sword of the Archon. Believe me, nothing else will suffice."

"Who says?" Shadrak stood and holstered his weapon. His pink eyes were narrowed to slits.

Aristodeus threw his hands in the air. "Are you all complete bloody morons?" He whirled on each one of them, eyes blazing with indignation, or maybe desperation.

"The little fellow has a point," Nameless said. "You have all the answers, then maybe you'd better start sharing them with the rest of us."

Aristodeus tensed, and for a moment it looked like he was going to strike the dwarf. Nameless turned on his stool to face him, the empty eye-slit of the great helm a portent of menace. The philosopher sighed, and his shoulders slumped.

"All I can say—and I mean that quite literally—is that I tried once before to stop Gandaw. I..." He grimaced and licked his lips. "I failed. I didn't factor in the power of Eingana, which he had somehow harnessed. If it weren't for the dwarves—for Maldark—"

"The Fallen?" Shader said. "What—?"

Rhiannon cut across him. "So, your plan's to neutralize the statue with the Archon's sword. You want to pit sister against brother."

Aristodeus rolled his head and looked around, his eyes eventually settling on a chair at Shadrak's table. He pulled it out and sat down. "Not quite, but almost." He flashed her a smile that said, *Go to the top of the class.* "The statue really is Eingana: her fossilized essence. That was Gandaw's genius: to harness the power of a god."

"Eingana's no god," Shader said. "Not in the true sense of the word. Neither's the Archon, for that matter."

"You're right there," Shadrak said. He gave a curt nod to himself.

"Semantics!" Aristodeus said. "The point is, the Aeonic Triad have incomparable power," and then he added, "at least in this cosmos. What Gandaw threatens—the end of all things—is madness. He wants to unmake what does not come from him, so that he can make all things anew, with himself as the one and only creator."

Albert insinuated his way into the conversation by starting to stack the plates on the table. "Isn't that what we all want, ultimately?"

"Weirdo," Rhiannon said.

Aristodeus snatched an olive from one of the plates and popped it into his mouth. He chewed noisily and licked his lips.

Albert cocked his head and watched the philosopher, then said, "What I mean is, it's natural to want to control." He proffered Aristodeus the last olive, which was accepted with relish.

"Which is why you're such a obsessive, conniving bastard, Albert," Shadrak said.

"Look who's talking," Albert said. "How many times was it you followed Councilor Hordred home till you were absolutely certain of his every habit? Seven? Eight?"

Shadrak gave a little cough and spoke behind his hand. "Twelve."

"My point is," Aristodeus said, "that Gandaw's—"

"A nut job?" Rhiannon said.

Shader glared at her. He was about to say this was hardly the time for her childish nonsense, but then it hit him like a fist in the face. "Deceived."

Aristodeus jabbed a finger at him. "Exactly. Gandaw thinks he's in control; thinks he's fathomed everything there is to fathom; thinks he has the perfect plan to unweave the old and create the new, but he forgets what he is. He's no god. He's human, and as flawed as the creation he judges so harshly. But more than that, he's blinded by his own hubris.

Yes, he can control Eingana, but does he know what she really is, where she comes from? Do any of us?"

"Huntsman—" Rhiannon started to say.

"Huntsman was an ignorant savage," Aristodeus said, "wise in his way, and somewhat powerful, but give him an artichoke and he'd have worshiped it as a god." He nodded approvingly at Shader. "Maybe all that training wasn't completely wasted. Deception is what underlies this whole bloody mess. Self-deception, yes, but a whole other layer of deception beneath that."

"The Father of Lies," Shader said. "The Demiurgos."

"Eureka!" Aristodeus said. A look of relief came over him, and he dabbed at an eye with his finger. He may have been wiping away a tear.

"Laddies, laddies, laddies," Nameless said. "Much as I'd love to listen to your theologizing all day, this peeling away the layers of the onion doesn't solve our immediate problem, now, does it?"

Shadrak gave a slow handclap. "Thank shog for that. At least someone's got his head out of his arse."

"Yes," Albert said. "I was rather wondering how analyzing Gandaw's obvious megalomania is going to put an end to what he's up to."

As if to punctuate his point, another crash of thunder shook the windows, and in its wake, the diner was noticeably darker.

"So, what you're saying," Shadrak said, "is Shader's the only one who can handle Gandaw." He shook his head, as if at some private joke. "But to succeed, he needs the sword."

"If it were a simple matter of fighting prowess," Aristodeus said, "I'd have finished Gandaw when I had the chance."

"Yeah, well maybe you ain't as good as you think," Shadrak said. "Maybe I should have a crack at him."

Aristodeus slapped a palm to his forehead and pressed his lips tightly together. "Eingana is our problem. How many times do I have to—?"

"But only the righteous can wield the Sword of the Archon!" Rhiannon said, as if a light had suddenly gone on. "That's why..." She looked Shader directly in the eye. "That's why this creep sent Huntsman to warn me off you."

"So I'd remain holy," Shader said, shaking his head as memories bobbed to the surface of his mind like bloated carcasses: a father who lived to fight; a mother who was a virtual luminary; Nous and the sword—always Nous and the sword, the paradox that had ever defined him. "Ain's teeth, Aristodeus, were they even my real parents?"

The philosopher waved away the question. "The important thing is—"

"And Rhiannon?" Shader asked. "You think you had the right?"

Aristodeus pushed himself to his feet and drew himself up to his full height. "This isn't about you, Deacon," he said in a voice full of weariness. "We are talking about the end of all things. Sacrifice. If there's one thing I hoped you'd take from all that Nousian balderdash, it's sacrifice. The needs of the other..."

He was quoting the Liber. Shader finished for him: "... outweigh the needs of the suffering servant."

"Oh, please," Rhiannon said. "That's just about love; you know, self-giving love. Least that's what Soror Agna said. Not quite the same as you shogging around with people's lives and expecting them to take it."

"You," Aristodeus said, turning his finger on her and fixing her with a glare, "need to keep quiet." He raised an eyebrow, and something was communicated between them. Whatever it was, Rhiannon sighed and backed away to the bar.

"The homunculus is right," Aristodeus said, indicating Shadrak.

"Shog off," Shadrak said, his fingers curling around a blade in his baldric.

"Forgive me. The assassin? The albino?"

"Darling," Albert said, "you really are asking for it. I'd try Shadrak, if I were you."

"Very well," Aristodeus said. "Shadrak is right. We need to deal with the immediate crisis. What happens after that—if there is an after that—is a battle for another day. You are the only one remotely close to being able to wield the Archon's sword," he said to Shader. "I've already tried once." He brushed his palms together. "And these two"—he took in Albert and Shadrak—"have a trade that's hardly compatible with holiness. Rhiannon is... well, she's Rhiannon." Already, she was knocking back a glass of something at the bar. "And Nameless..."

"Why not just spit it out, laddie?" Nameless said. "A murderer? A maniac? What's the word for someone who attempts to butcher his entire race?"

"I was going to say," Aristodeus said, "that you might have been the perfect choice, had you not had your own brush with the Demiurgos. I'm sorry, Nameless, but the black axe wounded you far more deeply than it did your people."

The sound of thumping footsteps passing the windows drew everyone's attention. There was a collective intake of breath, but when the footfalls faded away, the tension left the room. Then the door burst open, and a grubby-looking man in clothes that looked a size too big came in, dripping puddles on the floor.

"It's all right; wasn't looking for you. They was on fire duty," he said.

"Last place they'd look is a shithole like this," Shadrak said.

"Do you mind?" Albert said. "If you'd seen what it was like under Chef Dougan, you'd be singing my praises."

The grubby man took in everyone in the diner, puffed out his chest, and bobbed his head from side to side. His eyes alighted on Shader. "Buck Fargin," he said, offering a grimy hand. "With the Night Haw—"

"They didn't follow us for more than a few streets," Nameless said. "When the lightning started up again, they fled."

"Whatever," Aristodeus said before turning to Shader. "Right now, what you need—and I never thought I'd hear myself saying this—is confession."

"Buck," Albert said, "aren't you still keeping watch?"

"Nah, reckon you're safe for the time be—"

Shadrak cocked a finger at him, and Buck rolled his eyes and went back out into the rain, slamming the door behind him.

"Can't," Rhiannon said. "There's no priest."

"Poppycock," Aristodeus said. "A good outpouring of the heart to your beloved Nous is all it takes. Trust me, the rest is all smoke and mirrors."

"Rhiannon's right," Shader said. "There needs to be a priest."

"Well, what do you expect me to do?" Aristodeus said. "Rustle one up out of thin air?"

Rhiannon emptied her glass and nodded. "Isn't that what you do? Seems to work well enough with champagne."

"There simply is not the time."

Another boom rocked the diner, this one much closer. Somewhere in the distance, glass shattered, and a gusting howl ripped through the street.

"That the Unweaving?" Shadrak said.

"Side effects, maybe," Aristodeus said, "but when it really gets underway, expect to see distortions, and then pockets of nothingness. If I'm right—and I only have Gandaw's early theories to go on—emptiness will coalesce above the Perfect Peak until it goes critical. Once it does, everything that exists will be snuffed out faster than you can blink."

"What I don't get," Shadrak said, "is why the bleeding Archon don't just sort Gandaw out. I mean, surely he can handle his sister. Way I heard it, the Demiurgos handled her good and proper."

Aristodeus gritted his teeth. "The Archon is a law unto himself. I cannot answer for—"

"If Gandaw captured Eingana," Rhiannon said into her drink, "couldn't he do the same to her brother?" She looked round as if it were obvious. "Couldn't Gandaw do the same to the Archon as he did to her?"

Aristodeus's mouth dropped open, and his focus turned inward. He hadn't even considered that, Shader realized. The great Aristodeus, master thinker, and he hadn't even considered why the Archon took no direct action.

"Perhaps," Aristodeus said after a moment. "But there's more to it: a Supernal concept of justice. The Archon must tread carefully. Each action he takes grants a similar permission to his brother, the Demiurgos. The greater the action, the greater the chance the Demiurgos will be released from his trap."

"Then we shouldn't linger any longer," Shader said. "Sword or no sword, it's down to us to do something. Judging by the state of things out there, I doubt we have enough time to trek back to the mountain. Can you get us there?"

"You must confess first!"

"Can you, or can't you?"

"My freedom is not as total as it might look," Aristodeus said.

"You manage to get around right enough when it suits you," Rhiannon said. "It'll be a damned sight quicker if you do that magic trick you did with me."

"The Perfect Peak is made of scarolite, understand?" Aristodeus said. "It shields Gandaw from such 'magic', as you call it." He sighed and turned to Shader. "If you won't do as I ask, then you have failed, Deacon. Failed. You leave me no choice. Desperate times call for desperate measures. Come!" He held out a hand to Rhiannon.

She looked up blearily from the bar. "You're joking."

"And bring that with you." Aristodeus pointed at Callixus's sword, which was propped up in the corner.

"But—" Rhiannon started.

Aristodeus turned back to Shader. "Do what you can, but it's wasted effort without the Sword of the Archon. Just remember, on your head be it!"

Rhiannon sauntered over with the black sword clutched in both hands. Aristodeus grabbed her in a rough embrace, green light swirled, and they vanished.

"What, now he's gonna use her to save the world?" Shadrak said. "You gotta be having a laugh."

Albert gave a dry chuckle, but then he picked up the stacked plates and headed to the kitchen. Shader heard him mutter as he passed, "So, our bald friend likes olives, does he?"

"I can get you there," the drunken dwarf said from the bar.

All eyes turned to him.

"I can get you to the mountain, and I can get you there real quick."

"How, Rugbeard?" Nameless said. "We've already tried Arx Gravis—"

"—And there's no way in above ground," Shadrak added.

"Old miner's secret." Rugbeard tapped the side of his nose and winked at Nameless. "Kept since afore you was a twinkle in your daddy's eye."

THE ANT-HILL

T HEY LEFT THE city in a covered wagon. Shader rode in the back with Shadrak and Albert. He'd suggested they hid in empty crates, in case they were stopped at the gates, but Rugbeard said there'd be no need. It was a guild wagon on loan to Buck Fargin, and the guards didn't question guild business; after all, Rugbeard said, it was the guilds that supplemented their wages and gave them gifts for their families on all the major feast days.

Once they left the shelter of the Cyclopean Walls, unnatural winds buffeted the wagon, and the air about them shrieked, as if it were a beast being torn asunder. Lightning flashed through the canvas, and every now and again, the horse pulling them would balk and whinny.

Shadrak seemed to take it all in his stride, and passed the time meticulously cleaning each and every one of the daggers and razor stars in his baldrics. When he'd finished that, he unholstered his pistol, took a rectangular segment out of the handle, shook it, and then replaced it with another from a belt pouch. He looked down the barrel, blew dust from its end, spun it on his finger, and re-holstered it. Even then, he didn't stop checking his pockets and pouches.

Albert looked completely out of place in his suit. Sweat beaded on his bald pate, and at one point he reached into his breast pocket for something that was no longer there, rolled his eyes, and wiped his brow with the back of his hand. After that, he sat staring down at a cheese-cutter, the wire held taut between his hands, for all the world looking like a Nousian praying the prayer cord.

Nameless sat upfront with Rugbeard, who insisted on driving, despite being too drunk to walk in a straight line. When the canvas flapped, Shader caught glimpses of them: Nameless like some brooding metal statue in his great helm and mail, Rugbeard a mass of gray hair and beard tousled by the wind. The two of them kept up an amiable banter, and once or twice they broke into song.

Shader stumbled to the front, arms out to steady himself as the wagon rocked and juddered. He pushed through the canvas and gripped Nameless' shoulder to steady himself.

"… name of yours," Rugbeard was saying. "Ain't none of my business, but whatever it was, must've been serious."

Nameless nodded. "Aye, that it was."

"And your pa was Droom, you say? I didn't know him well, but I worked a few veins of scarolite with him way back. Same team as Targ, your pa. Bloody good explosives man, ol' Targ." Rugbeard swallowed thickly and rubbed his eye. "He was good to me, Targ, when I left the mines."

Shader felt he was intruding and would have gone back inside, but up ahead a whirling vortex of black—he could only call it light—crossed the road and went spinning through a field, carving its own path and leaving bizarre patterns in the crops. A shadow passed across the face of one of the suns, and its twin started to strobe, making their progress appear stilted, staccato.

"I remember Droom's lads, too," Rugbeard said. "Lucius was the elder, but for the life of me, I can't remember your real name, and you say you can't, neither?"

"Gone," Nameless said, staring straight ahead. "Like I never had it."

The dwarves grew silent, but Rugbeard's eyes kept flicking to Nameless, as if he couldn't comprehend the magnitude of the suffering being unnamed caused him. Or perhaps he was wondering about the guilt, or the extent of the atrocities that warranted such a punishment.

Shader could relate to that. It was easy for Aristodeus to tell him he needed to confess, but it wasn't that simple. Not only did it require a priest, but he also needed contrition, and right now, that's the last thing he felt. Something had snapped when the old man in the cell had died. He was sure there was more to it than that—all the losses, the perpetual struggle to follow Nous, only to keep fighting and killing, fighting and killing. It was Rhiannon, Aristodeus and all his scheming; it was Sektis bloody Gandaw and his madness; but more than any of that, it was his own vileness; his continual failures. And then, of course, there was the rage, or rather his outraged sense of justice when he'd been imprisoned, beaten, and condemned to death, all for trying to avert the end of all things. Nous wouldn't have reacted as he had, he was certain; and yet, the longer this went on—this impossible struggle against the odds—the more conspicuous Nous became by his absence. He did nothing, offered nothing. It was all pious words and platitudes, but at the end of the day, what proof was there that it was worth it? Yes, faith was a struggle. He could almost hear Adeptus Ludo telling him with a heartfelt sigh and a gentle nod of his head, but it was a struggle that had grown too heavy to bear. The corrosion had set in the minute the Gray Abbot had told him about the Liche Lord's perversion of the Liber. All that was left was some tenuous golden thread that he no longer had the strength to look for.

Idly, he held the old man's pendant between his thumb and forefinger, twiddled with the chain around his neck. There'd been a connection, he was certain of it. There'd been something communicated between him and the dying man in the prison. If only the old man could have talked. Ain's teeth, if only Thumil had remembered those books back at Arx Gravis, or if Shader had had the time to speak with him at length. There was mystery here on Aethir. Deep mystery, and a part of him wanted to believe it contained truth, the sort of truth that had bled from his Nousian soul since this whole business with the Statue of Eingana had started.

Rugbeard broke him out of his ruminations.

"Heard things was bad at Arx Gravis last year." He was talking to Nameless.

"Aye. Pretty bad."

Rugbeard eyed him warily. "They says the streets was running with blood; that even the waters of Sanguis Terrae was tainted with it. They says it was a black axe that caused it. They says it was a deception of the Demiurgos."

"Aye, that's what they say."

"Pity the poor bugger that did it, I say."

"Pity those he murdered," Nameless said. "Pity their families."

"Them, too," Rugbeard said, "but you gotta wonder after that poor bastard, eh?" He stared long and hard at the great helm, but Nameless would say no more.

"What's this plan of yours?" Shader asked, thinking it best to break the awkwardness between the dwarves. "You said it was a miner's secret."

The wagon lurched as a tremor ran through the road. Off in the distance, a greenish brume roiled above some hills, which were stretching, contorting, as if they were putty in invisible hands.

"Got to know the mines better'n most after I gave up teaching." Rugbeard looked over his shoulder at Shader, watery eyes checking to see he was being heard. "Had my uses once, you know."

"You were a teacher?"

"Taught the Annals, till no one cared a shog about the past. The council didn't exactly encourage history. It was too dark in places, and there was things in them records most folk simply didn't want to know."

Nameless turned to watch him then.

"Aye, you know what I'm talking about, sonny. See," Rugbeard said to Shader, "there was life on Aethir long afore the Technocrat came. Oh, it was all dreamed, they say; dreamed by the Cynocephalus; but they was powerful dreams, and they shaped all this." He made an expansive gesture. "There was creatures, too, and races, just like us; just like you. But when Sektis Gandaw came and started his experiments, the indigenous life was either wiped out or altered.

"It's said even the Cynocephalus was scared of Gandaw and what he was doing, and he was terrified enough already. With a father like his, you can hardly blame him. The Cynocephalus's screams caused the earth to groan, and the Farfall Mountains was thrown up, a dividing line right down the middle of our world. Them races that Gandaw hadn't already warped or killed fled over the mountains into Qlippoth."

Rugbeard rummaged around under his bench and produced a costrel. He proffered it to Nameless, who merely shook the great helm, and then held it over his shoulder to Shader. It was tempting, but that would have been another step on the slippery slope to despair. Shader already felt he had one foot in the Abyss, the way he was going. No need to make it any easier for the Demiurgos. He waved the costrel away. Rugbeard shrugged, took the reins in one hand so he could work the stopper free, and then poured the contents down his throat. He growled, shuddered, and slung the costrel from the wagon. After he'd wiped his mouth on his sleeve, he took the reins in both hands again and cocked his head toward Nameless.

"You believe in the Lords of Arnoch, son?"

A body of water glimmered some way off to the left, and a low range of mountains could just be made out to the right. Shader thought he recognized the route they'd taken on the way to New Jerusalem.

"Aren't we heading toward Arx Gravis?" he asked.

"Them's the Cooling Crags, sonny." Rugbeard nodded toward the mountain range. "Arx Gravis lies straight ahead, but we'll be stopping a long ways afore that. Once we're by the Great Lake of Orph—" He looked over toward the ever-nearing water, which was reflecting the turmoil of the skies and sending up a shimmering haze. "—we'll pull up short of the mines proper."

"But we've been denied access to the mines," Shader said.

"By the council," Nameless added.

Rugbeard chuckled. "What those ol' codgers don't know can't hurt 'em. You see, there's more'n one way to the old mines."

Nameless swiveled on the bench to face him. "There's just the one tunnel, straight as an arrow between Arx Gravis and the Perfect Peak. Had to be that way, else it would've been too hard to guard the scarolite."

"Ah," Rugbeard said, "but what else did Gandaw do to ensure no one else got their hands on the ore till he was done with it?"

"That was just a legend," Nameless said. "And besides, I don't see how that can help us, do you?"

"You will, sonny," Rugbeard said. "Just you hold on. You will. But you never answered my question. You believe in the Lords of Arnoch?"

Nameless sighed. "Another legend. False history. False hope."

"Yes, yes," Rugbeard said. "An alternative to the truth that Gandaw made us; made us from Earth humans and something else."

"Is that true?" Shader asked. "Gandaw altered humans to make the dwarves?"

Nameless looked off into the distance.

Rugbeard fished around for another costrel and took a deep swig. "They say the Lords of Arnoch once killed a dragon."

Nameless let out a low, rumbling laugh and slapped him on the back. "Go on, then, laddie. You know you want to. I only wish I could join you in a dram to warm my cockles."

"You have dragons here?" Shader said. Then he recalled the Gray Abbot's painting of the Reckoning, depicting fire-breathing dragons wreaking havoc upon the cities of the Ancients' world. If there was any truth to the belief that Huntsman unleashed the power of the Dreaming on the Earth, then it stood to reason the dragons must have come from Aethir.

"If we still do," Rugbeard said, "they must be wary of crossing the Farfalls. I've heard no tale of dragons in Malkuth, and don't expect to, neither. But my point is—" He looked sharply at Nameless. "—legends ain't the same as lies, and I wouldn't believe everything the Annals say, nor the council, neither, for that matter."

"The Annals spoke about the black axe," Nameless said. "My brother found a reference to the *Pax Nanorum* that—"

"Nothing about no *Pax Nanorum* in the Annals," Rugbeard said. "Not when I was teaching."

"That's what ol' baldilocks said. Then how—?"

"Sounds like tampering, if you ask me. The *Pax Nanorum's* in the legends about Arnoch, sure enough." For Shader's benefit he added, "The Axe of the Dwarf Lords, only theirs was gold, not black."

Shader gnawed on a knuckle. So, it wasn't just the Liber. Were there no reliable truths?

"But we was talking about the dragon," Rugbeard said. "The one that was brought down by the Lords of Arnoch. You see, a big ol' red wyrm was terrorizing the shores of the sea the great city stood watch over. Didn't matter how many folk it fried, how many it chomped up and ground into dust, it kept coming back. Course, that's the way of the Cynocephalus's nightmares: they don't ever stop, lest someone faces up to 'em and puts 'em in their place.

"Anyhow, Arnoch was like an island of hope in the face of the worst dreams of the Cynocephalus. If the dwarf lords hadn't stood against the tide of horror, it would've overflowed and infected all of Aethir. Worse than that, the dreamer himself would've gone stark-raving mad, maybe even perished at his own hands. Don't need me to tell you what'd happen to the world of dreams if there was no one to dream it."

Shader looked out at the boiling waters of the lake as they finally passed along its shore. It wasn't just a haze he'd seen earlier; it was steam, and the heat stung his face like the sun on a scorching Sahulian day.

"That normal?" he asked.

Rugbeard sucked in his lips and made a popping sound. "Nope. Can't say that it is."

"Are we there yet?" Albert called from inside. "I need to micturate."

"There's a bucket in the back," Rugbeard called over his shoulder. "Either that, or tie a knot in it. Won't be long now. Anyways," he said, scanning the way ahead and giving the reins a gentle flick, "the Lords of Arnoch kept watch over the sea, but they also patrolled the skies using baskets hung from enormous balloons. They was filled with gas that was lighter than air, but they wasn't exactly safe. A single lick o' flame, and that gas'd go up—boom!

"One day, the dragon was razing the fishing villages along the coast, but then he gets all purposeful and comes at Arnoch itself. Flames charred the city walls, hundreds was killed, and just when all hope seemed lost, and the city was making ready to sink beneath the waves, as it was designed to do in the worst of all perils, Lord Kennick Barg asked permission of the king to go out after the beast on his own. The king agreed, seeing as there was nothing to lose, and brave Lord Kennick goes up in a ballon, hollering insults at the dragon for all he was worth. The wyrm grew mightily pissed, turned its ire on him and him alone. It soars right at the ballon and unleashes a searing torrent of flame, and kabooooom! No more dragon. No more Lord Kennick, neither."

Rugbeard turned his gaze on Nameless. "That's our model; what we were supposed to be like. Don't believe all this Gandaw shite. Where's the proof? In the Annals? Pah, you've seen just how much they can lie. In the council, bunch of prevaricating old sods that they are? Too ready to despair, ever since Maldark, I say. Too ready to see everything as doom and gloom, and themselves as no more than botched experiments. We're better than that, my nameless friend, and someone needs to ram an axe-haft up the council's asses to tell 'em so. Now, have a look under your end of the bench; see if I got any more grog down there."

They rattled along in relative silence, while above them, both suns flared briefly and then began to flicker like guttering candles. In the far distance ahead, what looked like a third sun—black as the Void—sent dark fractures through the surrounding sky. Shader couldn't be sure, but each time he looked, it seemed the black sun had grown larger. His back ached from hovering at Nameless' shoulder for so long, and he desperately needed to stretch his legs. Nameless seemed to notice and gave up his seat, squeezing past Shader to get to the wagon bed. Within moments, he was bantering away boisterously from beneath the canopy, as if he hadn't a care in the world—as if the worlds and all they contained weren't about to end. Stranger than that, though, was that Shadrak laughed out loud, and it was a far cry from his usual sarcastic sneering; it could almost have been described as good-natured. Shader shrugged. He'd felt it, too, from time to time. Whatever it was about Nameless, it seemed to be contagious.

He plonked himself on the bench beside Rugbeard. The gladius's scabbard banged against the wood, and he instinctively reached out to adjust it on his hip, thought better of it, and shifted his own position instead.

Rugbeard flicked him a look. "What you gonna do, sonny? Way I heard it, you'll need that sword, but here you are scared to even touch it."

Shader's hand found the pendant beneath his surcoat. He raised it up to his eyes, studied the image of the woman, the inscription on the other side.

Peace, the old man had said with his dying breath. *Do not fear. Peace.* And if he'd been afraid of dying, he hadn't shown it. Even mutilated as he was, and in incalculable pain, he'd been resigned to his fate; serene, even. What was it that brought him such calm? Shader closed his hand around the pendant. Was it just relief from suffering? Was it the despairing acceptance of a man who couldn't take any more? Or was it something else? He tucked the pendant back beneath his surcoat.

Right now, Shader just wished he could pray. Wished he had someone to pray to. His faith had been like the guttering suns since the Gray Abbot had planted the seeds of doubt, but in all honesty, it had never been strong; not like Gralia's—simple, childlike, even. Aristodeus again. He'd no doubt set it up like that, introduced the paradox by way of Jarl Shader. Ensured Shader was holy, but not too holy to fight. Well, he'd miscalculated, if that was his plan. All he'd done was introduce a fault line that just needed the knowledge of Blightey's tampering with the Liber to bring the whole edifice of belief crashing down like a house of cards.

But the Gray Abbot hadn't despaired, had he? Even with the knowledge of what the Liche Lord had done, he'd clung to the faith; to the golden thread. Hadn't he? The same with Ludo, and he was no fool. It's like the adeptus knew the value of the social side of Nousianism, the cohesion it brought, and was willing to put up with it for the sake of a deeper truth. But what was that truth? He started to reach for his Liber, but then shook his head and sighed. What would be the point? Even if there really was a golden thread, he had no idea how to weed it out from all the chaff Blightey had surrounded it with.

Rugbeard was watching him, waiting for an answer, but what answer could he give, save the truth?

"No idea what I'm going to do. No idea, at all."

"Well, sonny," Rugbeard said, "in that case, you'd better fish out another costrel from under the bench. If the end of the world is nigh, I don't want to face it sober."

They drove along the shoreline for an hour or so, and then Rugbeard pointed out a barren hill set back a couple of hundred yards from the lake.

"There it is. That's where we're heading."

Shader could see a range of mountains rolling away beyond it.

"That be the scarolite mines outside Arx Gravis," Rugbeard said. He steered a course for the hill. "But this is the secret I was telling you about."

As they drew nearer, Shader could see the hill was made of packed earth, as if it had been piled there during some mammoth dig. Holes pocked its surface, many of them big enough to drive the wagon through. They pulled up close, and Shader climbed down. Albert was straight out the back and rushed into the cover of some scrub. Shadrak leapt lithely from the wagon, fingers still checking his pouches and weapons. Nameless steadied himself with a hand on one of the bows that provided a frame for the canvas before jumping off and landing amid a puff of dry earth. Rugbeard busied himself hammering an iron spike into the ground and tethering the horse to it.

"Is that—?" Shadrak started.

"An ant-hill," Nameless said. "So, it wasn't just the drink talking, Rugbeard."

The old dwarf chuckled as he slung his mallet into the back of the wagon and took down a hooded lantern from inside. "Like I said, there's an ocean of difference between legends and lies."

"So, those are tunnels," Shader said. "Big ants."

"Giant," Rugbeard said. "More of Gandaw's creatures. It's said they had no queen, just a controller, part ant, part human. They say they never aged, neither, not the ants, nor the ant-man."

"And you want us to go in there?" Albert said, traipsing back over, doing up his trousers.

"Hill's deserted nowadays," Rugbeard said. "Last I heard, the ant-man and his pets was out Malfen way. Probably trying to cross the Farfalls to be with all the other monsters."

A muffled boom rolled across the sky, and the ground shook beneath their feet. Dirt cascaded down the side of the ant-hill, and something dark and sleek poked from one of the holes and then disappeared.

Shader was already moving toward it, heart pounding. He'd only caught a glimpse, but he'd have sworn it was the thing that had been watching Nameless from the rooftop during the fight with the soldiers.

"Was that an ant?" Albert said.

"It was standing upright," Nameless said.

Shader scrabbled up a bank of dirt until he reached the opening. There were footprints leading away down the tunnel, and a smudge of similar markings around the entrance.

But they weren't ordinary footprints; they were long and slender, the impressions left by the toes splayed wide.

"Looks like it was hanging round the entrance for some time," Shadrak said, coming up alongside him. "Waiting."

"You think it's the ant-man?" Albert asked.

Rugbeard was next up, shaking his head, eyes wide and bulging. "But they was in Malfen. That's what folk say. Surely—"

"That weren't no ant, and it weren't no shogging ant-man, neither," Shadrak said, drawing his pistol and slipping into the tunnel. "Wait for me here."

Nameless and Albert struggled up the bank, and the four of them stood staring out to the south, where the black sun was wobbling, expanding, and its fractures were thrashing about like tentacles. And then, as if the dreaming god of Aethir blinked, everything was plunged into darkness. Albert screamed; Rugbeard groaned; Nameless muttered, "Shog," and Shader gasped. Was that it? Were they too late?

The next instant, the darkness lifted, but there was no sunlight now, only a crepuscular gray that turned the surrounding landscape dull and lifeless.

Shadrak came back down the tunnel. "Gone," he said. "Scut sure does move quick."

"You know what it was?" Shader asked.

"Thing that attacked me in the city," Shadrak said. "Certain of it." He unfastened his cloak and slung it down the hill, and then took the concealer cloak from his knapsack and put it on.

"It was outside the prison," Shader said with a glance at Nameless. "Watching from the rooftops. Staring at Nameless."

Shadrak's pink eyes blazed. "So why'd it do nothing? Thing like that could—"

"Must've got a look at these," Nameless said, flexing his biceps. "Thought better of it."

"My advice," Shadrak said, "is stay alert. Anything moves in there, hit first, worry about what it was later."

Rugbeard struck flint to steel and got his lantern burning.

"You said it had a…" Albert pointed at Shadrak's pistol.

"Gun? Yeah, it did, and it's shogging fast."

"Come on," Nameless said, sauntering into the tunnel. "No point worrying about things we have no control over."

Rugbeard ran up alongside him, holding his lantern aloft and sending long shadows across the floor and walls.

They moved through a maze of winding tunnels bored out of the earth. At first, Shader was tense—the same as he'd been when chasing Shadrak through the mangroves on the Anglesh Isles, never knowing when the dagger was going to strike. Shadrak was almost invisible in the cloak, no more than a shifting blur beside the tunnel wall. Albert brought up the rear, fiddling nervously with his cheese-cutter.

At one point, Shadrak took the lantern from Rugbeard and scanned the ground. "Tracks have gone," he said, raising the light to inspect the ceiling and walls. Finally, he handed it back to Rugbeard. He muttered something to himself and pulled the concealer cloak tight, merging with the tunnel once more.

"He's not used to it," Albert whispered in Shader's ear. "He's the one that's supposed to be unseen."

Rugbeard brought them to a steep decline, which they had to descend on their backsides, before they emerged into a mine tunnel. It was lit by a soft, greenish glow that emanated from veins in the otherwise black rock. The green flecks in Nameless' great helm picked up the light and sparkled like emerald stars in response. Struts and supports lined the walls and ceiling. They were not wooden, as Shader would have expected, but appeared to be cast from a smooth gray material that was as hard as granite. Iron rails with stone sleepers threaded down the center of the tunnel.

Rugbeard led the way to a long mine cart, the likes of which Shader had never seen before. The undercarriage was of rusted iron, but the main body was a sleek silver capsule, caked in rock dust. Rugbeard wiped a patch of grime away with his hand, revealing a row of five buttons. He pressed each in turn, and the side of the cart slid open to admit them. There were three rows of seats inside, each upholstered with padded leather, and at the front was an array of levers and knobs. Rugbeard toggled a switch, and a panel lit up. The smell of ozone wafted through the tunnel, accompanied by a low, pulsating hum.

"Hop in," Rugbeard said with evident relish. "I ain't used one of these for donkey's years."

BIRTH OF THE UNWEAVING

O NE THING CENTURIES of experimentation had taught Sektis Gandaw was never to rely on readouts.

He stepped onto the transporter disk and allowed the sedatives to do their work as it plunged to the roots of the Perfect Peak.

Not that the Unweaving could be classified as an experiment—it had been too meticulously planned for that and was better thought of as an actuation; and not that the monitoring instruments were unreliable—they were perfect in every way; after all, he'd made them himself. It was just that you could never be one-hundred percent certain something was working as you'd predicted until you saw it with your own eyes.

Gandaw allowed himself a wry chuckle at that, and at the same instant, the disk touched down, reoriented itself, and skimmed along one of the horizontal tubes that splayed out beneath the mountain. They weren't exactly his eyes; those had rotted away eons ago. Granted, most of the stem cells he'd grown a new pair from were his, but they'd been augmented with just about everything nature had to offer and capped with the most intricate nano-technology he'd invented. Well, maybe not invented. A taunting voice in his head reminded him he owed a debt to the homunculi for introducing him to their otherworldly science, but he closed the lid on that particular intrusion with a quick influx of neurotransmitters.

The disk slowed to a stop beneath a vertical tube and then rose. As it neared the surface, an iris valve began to open above.

The inner voice had returned mere days ago, like a cockroach creeping up from the bubbling abyss that lay beneath his rational mind. It was Blightey, he was sure of it. Just a ghost, a memory that refused to die. He'd told himself time and again not to worry; after all, hadn't he defeated the Liche Lord after bringing him back from the Abyss? It wasn't so much the threat Blightey presented that disturbed him; it was the lingering sense of mockery. As if he'd forgotten something—which was ridiculous—or as if he had somehow been led astray…

The disk wobbled as it passed through the valve; it wasn't meant to do that. Gandaw stepped off, onto the bleached dust of the Dead Lands. Wind buffeted him and sent strands of his plastinated hair across his vision. He swept it out of his face with a surge of irritation. The hair wasn't meant to do that, either. Even now, centuries after making the humiliating adverts that had launched Global Tech into the stratosphere, he could still hear the promise he made to his customers:

New from Global Tech: the plastination revolution! Hair you can style with just a thought. No more brushes, no more bad hair days. Permanently perfect hair, because you deserve it!

Only it wasn't perfect, clearly. He ceased trying to pat it down and let the wind muss it up. He wondered when it had lost its hold. It had never occurred to him to monitor it, not in the unchanging environment of the Perfect Peak. The consumers would have all turned back into dust by now, in any case—dust surmounted by an imperishable wig. He wanted to tell himself it had been good enough, one of a string of products that had generated the capital to take Global Tech to world domination, but 'good enough' was one step down from perfection, and it was an infinite step, at that.

Three silver spheres shot toward him from the mountain. *Tardy.* Even the sentroids were no longer living up to his expectations. They stopped abruptly and then began to circle him, each in its own orbit.

Anything could have happened in the seconds he'd been left unguarded.

With a thought, he flexed the limbs of his exoskeleton. At least that was working correctly. Servos whined, and a shudder passed beneath his coat sleeves. Before his legs could extend, he stood down the system from defense mode.

It was hard to recall what the Dead Lands had looked like last time he'd been outside. He was fairly certain the sky had been some shade of blue—cobalt, most likely—and the suns had been golden, maybe even amber. Now, though, the sky was a like London's smog all those centuries ago, and the bone-dust that formed an island around the Perfect Peak was shifting, morphing into jagged monoliths that crashed and reformed like waves. Even the vegetative border of the Sour Marsh was in upheaval, a writhing, undulating mass. The scarolite mountain itself was the only stationary point, an anchor amid the chaos, just as it should be. And, of course, it wasn't really chaos if it was planned for, was it? These were expected side effects, the grumblings of nature as it prepared to be unwoven.

High above the Perfect Peak, the Null Sphere glistened blackly, gyring and pulsing as it aspired toward critical mass. Every every iota of matter stretching back to the point of origin billions of years ago, pared back to its constituent elements, codified and oriented to the meta-algorithm of Unweaving. The whole matrix of Creation uploaded bit by bit into a negative energy sphere powered by the Statue of Eingana. The epitome of perfection. Some fool had once said that man with his rational mind repeatedly tried to cram the universe into his head, but his head invariably split. Idiot! Had Gandaw not achieved this? Had he not contained the algorithms of everything that existed in his eons-old mind and worked out a way to unmake them? No stone had been left unturned. Nothing—not even the tiniest microbe—had escaped his processing.

Screen 55—That mocking thought again.

Gandaw sent a mental signal to the transporter disk. He'd seen enough. Everything was going to plan. He really didn't need to waste his time and energy worrying about—

What about the Void? How do you account for that?

He started to descend, patting down his errant hair as the tube shielded him from the wind.

And the Abyss... You know it exists... You brought Blightey back from it, and yet you have studiously ignored it.

He wanted to retort that the Abyss was an absurdity, someone else's fantasy. Wanted to say that the Void was just absence, not a thing in itself, and so no part of his equations. Blightey had been trapped; no one was denying that, and Gandaw had brought him back by converting the largest particle accelerator in the Great West, but there was never any question of the Liche Lord being trapped in the infernal realm. An alternate plane of existence, maybe. That made much more sense; and if it were such, then it also lay outside the scope of the Unweaving. No, the Abyss was just the same old superstitious nonsense that he'd finally put paid to before the Reckoning, when the ignorant hoped for an eternity of bliss, and feared one of never-ending torment; back in the days when the masses were controlled by a persistent delusion about God.

But—the seditious thought started.

Gandaw severed it at its source with a thought of his own, sharp as a scalpel. Intracranial lasers followed his direction, excised the responsible memory nodes from the preserved organic core of his consciousness.

Ah, you can run, but you can't hide!

He started. Surely it couldn't have survived... And then he realized: this thought *was* his own.

You can't unlearn something and pretend that it doesn't exist.

There were things in his calculations he'd not accounted for. The horror of the realization would have undone him, were it not for a massive influx of chemicals from his exoskeleton.

He'd known it all along. Known he was afraid of the Void and all it implied; known he couldn't accept the reality of the Abyss. And now it was too late. Even if he could stop the Unweaving at this late stage, how could he study emptiness itself? How could he research the abode of a being reputedly formed from the very stuff of lies?

As the drugs took effect, Gandaw's rational mind reasserted itself. It was nerves, that was all; another indictment of a flawed creation. He was succumbing to phantasms, to irrational fears. It was only natural—much as he despised that term—but there was no excuse to indulge such primitive nonsense.

Without even noticing the intervening journey, Gandaw found himself back in the control room at the heart of the mountain.

Mephesch greeted him with glittery eyes and flicked a look at the chronometer on his vambrace.

"One hour, thirty-five minutes and twenty-two seconds to go, Technocrat."

Gandaw wanted to say, "Good", or "Excellent," but all he could manage was a nod.

He strode past the homunculus and craned his neck to look up at screen 55 and the inky image of the Void. Gaseous strands crisscrossed its face like a taunt. He was about to turn away, when a flicker of flame limned the entire web. He glanced at Mephesch, who merely shrugged blankly, and when he looked once more at the screen, the flames had gone.

"Problem, Technocrat?" Mephesch said.

No, Gandaw silently told himself. *No. No. No.* He fixed Mephesch with what he hoped was a confident stare. "No. Nothing. No problem."

Mephesch stuck out his bottom lip and nodded, then he turned his attention to the tiers of screens.

The kryeh remained hunched over their terminals, each one poised to cry out the instant their respective screen went blank; when there was nothing left in that region of space for the satellites to convey. When the satellites themselves had ceased to exist.

All going to plan. All going perfectly to plan.

If he repeated the mantra enough, he'd believe it to be true. Had it really come to this? Endless eons of rigorous planning only to rely at the last on self-deception. Maybe it would work in spite of the omissions. Probably it would. How much difference could it make, leaving out two things that couldn't possibly fit with the pattern of the rest of creation? But there it was again, that gulf between 'good enough' and perfection. Only, he was starting to get the inkling this was about more than being blind-sided by irrational fear; more than a simple case of negligence. He was starting to feel like he'd been duped.

WHERE TIME HAS NO MEANING

"**K**EEP YOUR GUARD up!" Aristodeus yelled.

Rhiannon couldn't. Her arms were leaden, the black sword a ponderous weight. "Can't you at least open the shogging door? It's bloody stifling in here."

The white-washed walls of the philosopher's tower seemed to be closing in on her, and the ceiling threatened to crush her to the ground. There was no room for maneuver, and that meant the swordplay was relentless; no retreat, just stand your ground, parry, thrust, block, slice; either that, or receive a sharp slap with the flat of a blade.

"We've been going at it for hours," she said. "Shouldn't the world have ended by now? What's the point of all this, if we don't even take a pop at Gandaw?"

Aristodeus sighed and lowered his sword. "As I've said a thousand times, it would not be wise to leave the tower, nor open the door—even a crack."

"Why? What's out there? Where the shog—?"

He held up a hand to cut her off. "And as for the Unweaving, consider it on hold. It's more complex than that, but let's just say time has no meaning here. We could train for days, years even, and still emerge before the end of all things. Call it a gift. Call it a blessing, if you like. Call it a responsibility."

He lunged at her and she batted his blade away with ease.

"Good. It's paying off. Still a poor substitute for Shader, though. If you're to have any chance, we'll need to go in together. You must be fast, very fast, and you'll need the element of surprise. Without Shader's sword, our chances are virtually nil, but I refuse to sit back and do nothing. If Gandaw doesn't see us coming, and if that evil-looking sword of yours can penetrate his exoskeleton, who knows, maybe we won't need to deal with Eingana."

"So, what, you just magic us in and hope he's looking the other way?"

Aristodeus shook his head and adopted a defensive stance. "I can't get us through the scarolite. The mountain's shielded against anything I can muster."

"What, then?"

Aristodeus looked up at the ceiling and sucked in his top lip. "I fought Gandaw once before, and he used Eingana's power to send me here. I have a theory—a desperate one, nonetheless—I might be able make the return trip, follow the fault-line of his own making. This tower is, shall we say, a construct of my will. It's all that wards us from what's outside. It is not, however, altogether stationary. It can be relocated, moved, propelled, even. You've already seen what I can accomplish with my will, else how else would I have brought you here? No, just wait and see. I think I can get us to Sektis Gandaw. Now, fight!"

He launched a blistering series of attacks. Rhiannon parried frantically until he backed her up against the door. He pressed in close, the whiskers of his beard scratching her face.

His breath stank of garlic and wine, same as before, when he'd... when she'd drunk too much champagne. She tried to knee him in the groin, but he saw it coming, blocked her with the hilt of his sword.

"My first choice would be for Shader to get back on track," he said, and then his tongue darted out and poked at her tightly closed lips. "Maybe that dwarf will knock some sense into him, but I can't count on it. Which is where you come in. And don't think the game stops with the Unweaving. What's happening is far bigger than Sektis Gandaw. Yes, it's all over if Gandaw wins, but if not, there's a much bigger problem lurking in the shadows."

He pushed himself away from her.

"You lack strength, speed, and stamina. We'll work on all three. But first, if you've had enough for today—and don't forget, we'll be doing this day in, day out, until you're ready, no matter how long it takes—there's something we must do, sober, this time."

Rhiannon screamed and swung the black sword with all her might. Aristodeus was quicker, though, and he grabbed her wrist and stayed the blow.

"We must plan for the endgame, should we ever reach that stage. Now, look at me. Look at my eyes. Are you telling me it was just the champagne last time, or do you see something there, something familiar?"

She saw something right enough. She saw the same leering hunger Gaston shogging Rayn had when he raped her. Never again, she had sworn, and yet she'd already let it happen, let him ply her with booze.

"Yeah, I see something familiar right enough," she said, but before she could tell him exactly what it was, she was riveted to the ice-blue of his eyes, the way they darkened at the edges like a gathering storm. How could she have not noticed before? Had it been the drink? "Shader," she said. "You have Shader's eyes."

"What else?" he demanded. "Imagine there's no beard."

He was right. The angles of his face, the jawline...

"You're related? But how—?"

"More than that. Much more. I'm a planner, my dear. Always have been, always will be. If we can stop Gandaw, and it's a big 'if' right now, there's something I'm going to need from you. Something very important. Hear me out. I'll explain everything, and when I've finished, I have no doubt you'll give it to me."

OUTCLASSED

SHADRAK'S EARS POPPED as the mine cart raced along an unending tunnel. Green blurs streaked past the windows, but other than that, the walls outside were black as pitch, broken only by evenly-spaced gray struts. He craned his neck to look behind, same as he'd been doing since they'd left. Nothing but darkness. He turned back with a sigh. Shog, when had he gotten so jittery? The answer to that was never far from his mind: Ever since that scutting thing had come at him in the city. He'd never felt so slow, so clumsy, so... outclassed.

First off, he'd thought it had just been bad luck, that he'd been in the wrong place at the wrong time. Then he'd thought it'd been after him specifically—though what the shog for, he had no idea; it weren't like he'd had time to make enemies on Aethir. But then Shader said it'd been watching Nameless from a rooftop, which told a different story. Chances are, it was after all of them, in which case, why hadn't it killed them already? It had the ability, of that he had no doubt. But then, couldn't he say the same of himself? No matter how easy the job, no matter how good he knew he was, didn't he always stalk his prey first, observe its ways, test out its strengths and weaknesses? Instinctively, he pulled the concealer cloak tight about his body and let its cavernous hood swallow his face.

Albert was beside Shader on the seat in front. Shadrak could tell he was nervous by the way he kept reaching into his breast pocket for his absent handkerchief.

Shader was rigid, looking straight ahead, hat tugged low over his eyes. He'd not been right since they broke him out. A pall of defeat hung over him—same as with Kadee in the last stages of her wasting. If Aristodeus had put all his eggs in that partic'lar basket, things was well and truly shogged. And if whisking Rhiannon away was his fallback plan, then things was doubly shogged. Weren't nothing that bitch could do that Shadrak couldn't achieve with a sharp knife or a gun.

Nameless sat next to Rugbeard up front. The old dwarf was harping on about the good ol' days or some shite, but Nameless might as well have been asleep, for all the reaction he gave.

Without warning, the tunnel walls bulged and contracted.

"Ain't right," Rugbeard yelled over his shoulder.

The tunnel began to twist and turn, like they was passing through the insides of a writhing serpent.

Rugbeard raised his hands. "Ain't right, I tell you. These here tracks run straight as the crow flies."

The undulations stopped as quickly as they'd started, and the cart picked up speed, hurtling through the darkness like a bullet. Shadrak's head was slammed back by the pressure, the skin of his cheeks pulled taut. Albert and Shader were bent like bows, but the two dwarves sat as solid as stone. Shadrak's skull felt like it was gonna cave in, but then they began to slow.

"Hold on!" Rugbeard called out. "Some shogger's left a cart on the track!"

The undercarriage screeched, and the cart juddered. Shadrak was flung head-first into Albert's back. There was a girlish scream and the smell of garlic mingled with stale sweat. Albert pitched forward, but Shader caught hold of his jacket and steadied him. A few more jolts, and the cart came to a halt. Rugbeard hit a switch, and the sides slid back, revealing a stone platform lit from above by flickering strips of crystal.

Shadrak wasted no time exiting onto a stone platform. In front of them was an identical cart. They'd missed it by a hair's breadth.

Rugbeard was next out, gesturing at the other cart and complaining. "Driver would've been fired back in the day! Ain't nothing short of dangerous, is what it is."

"You telling me this tunnel's still in use?" Shadrak said.

Nameless lumbered out beside him. "No, laddie. My folk haven't come to the Perfect Peak in a very long time."

"So," Albert said, gingerly stepping onto the platform, as if it might sprout teeth and bite his legs off, "some irresponsible dwarf miner abandoned the thing years ago, did he? If you ask me, you should take a belt to his hairy little behind."

"No, sonny," Rugbeard said. "That ain't what I'm saying. See—" He stroked the iron of the undercarriage. "Still warm."

Shader walked straight past them and stood before a huge circular portal that must have been thirty-feet in diameter. Its center was a swirl of steel petals surrounding a central aperture no bigger than a coin.

"Iris valve, sonny," Rugbeard said. "Only, we don't have the code." He wandered over to it and slapped a panel on the wall.

"This is the way?" Shader turned and asked him.

"Right into the roots of the Perfect Peak," Rugbeard said. "Far as I ever been. Even back in the day, the ore would've been dropped off here, and Gandaw's creatures would take it into the mountain."

A tingle ran up and down Shadrak's spine. He pushed past Rugbeard and glared at the panel. Glowing geometric shapes winked at him from behind a rectangle of dark glass. Weren't that different from the panels on board the plane ship, but there was more to it than that—something familiar; but when he tried to probe his memories, they wafted away like pituri smoke.

"It'll take more than lock picks for that," Albert said. "Suppose you could blast it, if you had any more of those blasty things left. And, in any case, you'd need a wagon-load of them to even dent—"

Shadrak placed his fingertips on the glass, each one touching a glowing shape. When he traced his fingers along the surface, the shapes moved with them, just like the ones on the plane ship. With a quick succession of swipes, he rearranged the patterns, and they started to flash green. There was a sharp rush of air, and the petals of the iris valve retracted until the aperture filled its circular frame. He stepped away from the panel, his mind blank.

"Laddie?" Nameless said.

Shadrak waved him away. He shut his eyes and pinched the bridge of his nose. He had no idea how he'd done that. None at all. Same as with the plane ship; he'd adapted to its weird technology like a duck to...

He caught the stench of rotting vegetation, heard the slosh, slosh, slosh of water, the sharp release of sibilant breath. In his mind's eye, he looked up into the face of a snake. Huge arms cradled him—human arms, black and thickly muscled. He gasped and snapped his eyes open.

Nameless was watching him closely, the great helm tilted to one side.

Shadrak sucked in air and shook his head. He'd seen that snake-man before, atop the Homestead. Although, even then, there had been something familiar about the creature. So, that explained the snake-man; and the smell, the water… prob'ly just the Sour Marsh. Scutting mind must've been playing tricks on him. Shog, when was the last time he'd slept? Really slept, in a bed, and for more than a few snatched hours?

"Come on," he said, "let's get this ove—"

Shader pushed past him and stepped through the iris valve. The instant he crossed the threshold, a red light started to wink on the panel. Before Shadrak could say anything, Rugbeard had gone after Shader.

"So much for caution," Albert said. "What's the red light?"

"How the shog should I—?"

There was a crackle from beyond the iris valve, a burst of light, and a scream.

"Rugbeard!" Nameless cried as he ran through the aperture.

Albert rolled his eyes at Shadrak, and then they were off after the dwarf.

Shadrak was met with the impression of a vast space and the stench of roasting meat. Something silver flashed above him. Nameless roared and flung his axe. Metal struck metal, and sparks flew. The axe clanged to the floor, and the silver sphere it had struck whirred and gyred away in a spray of sparks. It flew in a wide arc, steadied itself, and then dived toward the dwarf. Shadrak's hand came up with scarcely a thought, and the pistol bucked in his grip. There was a blinding flash, and silver rained down in a thousand pieces that clattered to the floor.

Shadrak threw himself into a roll and came up beside a pile of black ore. Pistol held in both hands, he scanned for any more of the things.

The others were grouped together around the charred and smoldering body of Rugbeard. Nameless dropped to one knee and let out a long, keening, moan. Albert glowered at the corpse, and Shadrak knew him well enough to realize it weren't because the dwarf had been struck down; it was because the poisoner had been thwarted in some way. Had Rugbeard done something to offend him, something to draw his ire? Albert had a long memory, that's for sure. He weren't someone to get on the wrong side of. Shader just stood there, dumb, as if he'd barely even noticed.

Nothing. No movement. Shadrak made his way around the ore stack, trusting the cloak would keep him more-or-less invisible. They were in a chamber so massive he could barely see the far wall, and the entire floor space was littered with piles of black and green ore as tall as houses. A metallic rasp turned his head, and he swore as the iris valve snapped shut. High above, red lights blinked like evil stars, and smoke began to rise through grills set into the floor.

"What's happening?" Albert said.

Shadrak looked to the others for an answer, but Shader was staring at the smoke coiling about his boots like a man consigned to the Abyss and despairing that anything could be done about it. Nameless was cradling Rugbeard and rocking back and forth. Smoke engulfed his great helm, as though a fire burned within. Sweat was streaming down Albert's face.

"We have to get out," Shadrak said, sprinting for the iris valve. There was a panel on the inside, but when he tried to move the symbols, they remained frozen. He stepped back and fired the pistol. Sparks flew, black smoke plumed from the panel, and the symbols died. The iris valve remained stubbornly shut.

"Now what?" Albert said.

It was hot. Too hot, and the soles of Shadrak's feet were blistering through his boots. He shuffled from foot to foot and then started to run in a wide circle, just to break the contact with the floor. Albert followed suit, hopping and squawking like a deranged folk dancer.

"To the scarolite!" Nameless bellowed, setting Rugbeard down and barreling for an ore stack. He jumped onto its base and beckoned for the others to join him.

Albert made a beeline for the stack, but Shadrak veered toward Shader, grabbed his coat sleeve, and dragged him over to Nameless. The knight offered no resistance, but neither did he seem to appreciate the danger he was in. Shogging useless scut, far as Shadrak were concerned, but if keeping him alive would get the Archon off his back, get this whole farce over and done with, then he didn't see he had much choice.

The instant he set foot on the scarolite, Shadrak breathed a sigh of relief.

"Best insulator there is," Nameless said, by way of explanation.

It was a brief respite. The heat continued to rise, and the air grew thinner. High above, another silver sphere swooped into view and began to circle the ore stack. Shadrak fired, but the pistol only clicked in response. That can't have been right. No way he could've been out. Unless... When he'd fled the creature in New Jerusalem, he'd switched cartridges so's he wouldn't run out of bullets. When he'd reloaded again in the back of the wagon, he must have put the near-empty one back by mistake. Cursing, he fumbled in his belt pouch for another. A nozzle emerged from the sphere, and fire crackled from it. With blinding speed, Nameless swept up his axe and deflected the beam, then yelped and dropped the weapon. The axe head was glowing red.

The sphere circled them and then soared toward Albert.

Shadrak snapped a fresh cartridge in place and let rip with three shots. The first two ricocheted from the outer casing, but the third sent the sphere whirling and shrieking to the far side of the stack.

"Bugger," Albert said, pointing at the far wall.

Brownish-yellow gas was cascading down from vents and rolling out across the floor.

"If that's what I think it is—"

"What, Albert?" Shadrak demanded. "What is it?"

"If you get a whiff of horseradish, ask me again. Although, if the concentration's high enough, you might not get the chance."

Shadrak cast his eyes around frantically. There weren't no way out he could see; no exit save for the iris valve, and that was a dead end.

A whining, droning sound reached his ears, and the silver sphere spun into view. It dropped a few feet, righted itself, and then started to rise in fits and starts.

A carpet of dirty gas was inching its way across the chamber, and more of the stuff was flooding out from the far wall.

Albert was scurrying up the ore stack toward its summit some twenty feet above the floor. "Once there's enough volume, it'll start to rise," he said.

Shader curled his fingers around the hilt of his gladius. He winced and gritted his teeth. He tried to draw the sword but finally let go, nursing his blistered palm.

Nameless climbed up after Albert, sure-footed as a mountain goat. Shadrak saw no choice but to follow him. Far as he was concerned, Shader could do what the shog he liked. Situations like this, it was every man for himself.

At the top, he leaned back to look up. The ceiling was maybe fifty feet above, crisscrossed with girders, and there was a circular opening just shy of the ore stack, toward which the silver sphere was heading. On instinct, Shadrak holstered his gun and leapt from the summit. He caught hold of the sphere, and it spat fire at him, singeing the hood of his cloak. Grabbing the nozzle, he ripped it from its socket amid a spray of sparks. The sphere emitted a shrill cry and shot upward. Shadrak clung on by the tips of his fingers.

As it cleared the opening, Shadrak glimpsed a dark shape crouched by the edge, looking down, a gun clutched in one slender hand. Its featureless black head lifted, but it seemed confused, unsure of where to focus. In that instant, Shadrak let go of the sphere.

As he fell, he reached for his holster. The pistol came up and kicked in his hand. At the same moment, a hammer blow struck him in the shoulder. He missed his tumble and smacked face first into the floor, the gun scooting away from him.

Blood pounded in his ears, and he struggled to breathe. Hot wetness soaked through his shirt, drenching the concealer cloak. He rolled over, drawing a dagger as he scrabbled into a sitting position.

The creature lay on its back, its chest rising and falling to the accompaniment of gurgling, sloshing breaths. Its gun was a couple of feet from its twitching fingers.

"Laddie?" Nameless called from below.

"Shadrak!" Albert cried. "The gas is rising!"

Pain tore through Shadrak's shoulder as he crawled toward the creature. There was a hole punched clean through its chest, but even as he watched, the wound was starting to close up. With a desperate lunge, he fell on the thing and stabbed it in the head over and over and over and over. Then, taking no chances, he hacked repeatedly at its neck until the head came away, and he tossed it to the chamber below.

"Lovely!' Albert called up. "Now get us out of here!"

Numbness seeped from Shadrak's shoulder into his arm. Gasping for every breath, he crawled over to his pistol and holstered it, but when he went to pick up the creature's weapon, it burst into flame and was instantly reduced to a pile of dust.

"Shadrak!" Albert's voice was shrill.

"Laddie?"

"Hang on," Shadrak muttered under his breath. He didn't have the strength to call back.

He turned a slow circle on his knees until he located a glowing panel on a plinth beside the lip of the opening. A red light blinked above the main display. He used the plinth to pull himself upright with his good arm. His fingers flicked over the symbols of their own accord, turning them green, and there was a droning sound from above. Looking up, he saw another opening in the ceiling, through which a metal disk descended. As it passed down to the chamber below, his jaw dropped. There was nothing attached to the disk—no cable, no rope; the thing was just floating on air.

"Get on!" he yelled, voice hoarse and grating.

"It's below the level of the gas," Albert called back. "What do we—"

Shadrak wanted to shout, "Shog off and die," but instead he clung to the plinth as his knees buckled. His breaths came in ragged gasps. If the bleeding could be stopped, he'd recover; he knew that. He'd had worse before and lived to tell the tale.

He could hear Albert's protests from below, and then Nameless barked, "Get the shog on! All right, laddie, bring us up!"

How? How could he... But already his fingers were working the symbols, as if he'd done this all his life. He heard the whine of the disk coming back up, then he made a few more swipes. The blinking red light went out, and Shadrak slid down the plinth to lie limply on the floor. Coldness spread through his limbs, and he retreated into the warmth behind his eyelids. Kadee's smiling face was there waiting for him.

"No, Shadrak," she said. "Not now, little fellah. Not now."

Something rocked him.

"Shadrak?" It was Albert.

"Laddie? Laddie, are you all right?"

Someone knelt beside his head. He opened an eye a crack—all he could manage. Shader, opening a book, starting to read from it.

"Oh, no," Shadrak rasped. "No you shogging don't."

He tried to move, but Albert leaned in close and restrained him. "I can stem the flow of blood. Just keep still."

Albert unclasped Shadrak's concealer cloak and took a knife from his baldric to cut up the fabric. Shadrak didn't even have the energy to complain, and there weren't no point asking why Albert hadn't cut a swath from his own fancy suit.

"That the thing that attacked you in the city?" Nameless asked.

Shadrak grunted that it was and tried to focus his eyes on the headless body. He half-expected it to sprout a new head, but thankfully it looked as dead as a decapitated shogger should look.

"Best leave me here when you're done," he said.

"Oh no," Albert said. "You're coming with us. No one else knows how to use these panels."

"Too weak, Albert. You need to find Gandaw, stop the Unweaving."

Nameless walked over to the opening and peered down. "Gas has cleared," he said. Then he was on his belly for a better look. "And the iris valve's open. Was that you?"

Shadrak nodded. "Just don't ask me how."

Shader stood and put his book away. "Can you send this disk down again?"

"If someone holds me up long enough to work the panel. Why?"

"Albert," Shader said. "Think you can drive that mine cart?"

Albert scoffed. "If a drunken sot like…" He glanced at Nameless, who was climbing back to his feet, thought better of it, and concluded, "I think so."

"Take Shadrak back to city. There's nothing more he can do here."

"And I'm a useless waste of space?" Albert said, finishing packing Shadrak's wound and starting to wrap strips of concealer cloak about it. "Is that what you're implying?"

Nameless stepped up close to him. "It's for the best, laddie. You'll see. Saving the world is dwarf's work."

"And what about Shader?" Albert said. "What about the sword he can no longer use?"

"We'll cross that bridge, when we come to it," Nameless said.

Once Albert had finished tying off the improvised bandages, Nameless helped Shadrak to stand over the panel.

"When we're on the disk," Shadrak said to Shader, "slide these two symbols together; they should turn green, which means you're good to go, then swipe them toward the bottom of the glass like this." He demonstrated without actually moving the symbols.

Shader nodded that he understood, and then Albert helped Shadrak onto the disk.

It was a shogging embarrassment, limping from the fray and dependent upon a homicidal chef for your survival, but at the end of the day, when you're done, you're done. Still, despite the world being about to end and Shadrak not being able to do a thing about it, he felt a smile tugging at the corner of his mouth as the disk started to descend. Least he'd taken down that shogger. It had been fast. Faster than he could have imagined, but when push came to shove, he'd been better, and that's the way he liked it.

ROOTS OF THE MOUNTAIN

SHADER KNEW HE had to focus, had to find the fire to go on, but at his core there was a mire sucking him in on himself.

He was dimly aware of Nameless stomping ahead, and the clangor of their footfalls on the cold steel floor. They passed through shimmering halls that loomed at the edges of his perception, and along passageways straight from nightmare that seemed to lead nowhere.

The roots of Gandaw's mountain were a warren, though it was a warren with design. The halls were the hubs, with the corridors the spokes, uniformly gray and flanked by an endless succession of sliding doors like those in Shadrak's plane ship. Soft light bled from glowing panels, and strips of crystal glared starkly overhead. Ribbed tubing of some sleek material ran the length of the ceilings, and at every intersection, a silver globe hung down from a sinuous stalk, each with a winking red light that reminded Shader of the coal-fire eyes of Callixus and the knights of the Lost. It set him on a train of thought that he, too, was lost, and in his case, the gravity of guilt was that much greater. The Lost, after all, had been compelled.

As a peripheral part of his consciousness monitored their passage, he relived the beating he'd taken at Sarum all those years ago, felt every blow and the even graver injury of failure. He'd wanted to take the punishment in atonement for his sins, wanted so badly to imitate his beloved Nous. Only, it had been a self-willed delusion. He'd had no real faith; just the desire for what he'd seen in others, men like Ludo, the Gray Abbot, even the grandmaster, Ignatius Grymm. His blood boiled as he once more soaked in the icy fire of vengeance that had never been fully extinguished, even after he'd gone back and given far worse than he'd got.

But what he'd done to the wharfies back then paled in comparison with what he'd done to the soldiers outside the jail. Had experience taught him nothing? And what hurt most, more than the humiliation of being helpless beneath the pummeling fists of the guards, was the fact that, for all his theology, all his acts of heroic virtue, he was the same enraged boy who'd wanted nothing more than to bash Brent Carvin's head to a pulp for killing his dog. Ain's teeth, he could have foregone all the discipline, all the forced piety, and still ended up just the same. It was in the blood, and nothing was going to change it. He wanted to say he was Jarl's boy through and through, but that would have been doing his father a disservice.

And Gralia... There was no need to guess what his mother would have thought. He started to picture himself before her, and the shame sent a single tear beading down his cheek.

Ludo's voice insinuated its way into the turmoil; it was the voice of the gentle confessor, the ever-understanding spirit of Nous. It pointed out the losses, made them an excuse for his anger: Osric, Maldark, the knights of the White Order—lads he'd been responsible for and then abandoned.

"Not your fault," Ludo would have said, but Shader begged to differ.

No wonder Rhiannon had rejected him. It didn't matter that Huntsman and Aristodeus were behind it; give her time, and she'd have done it anyway. You can only fool people for so long, and if anyone could see through his charade of holiness, it was Rhiannon. But that still didn't explain why she'd pallied up with the philosopher; why she'd agreed to go off with him. The pang of jealousy that twisted up Shader's guts was just ludicrous. What was more important was what Aristodeus was up to. Had he given up on Shader? Was Rhiannon part of some new and desperate plan? There was no doubt she was the better choice. Shader knew he'd been a disappointment, knew he'd gone from one failure to the next, so that now he couldn't even wield the sword he'd been nurtured for, right when he needed it the most.

What galled him more than anything, though, was that he knew he was despairing and could do nothing to shake himself out of it. Its numbing strands were almost palpable, wrapping themselves around his limbs like creepers smothering a tree. With a burst of anger, he might have thrown them off, but the only rage he could muster was aimed at himself. Even stronger was the impulse to simply lie down and let whatever was about to happen go ahead without him. He was too tired. Tired of being tasked, whichever way he turned; tired of being Aristodeus's puppet; tired of the very contradictions that seemed to define him. Nous, he was starting to sound like the dwarves of Arx Gravis, apathetic, afraid to act out of fear of deception.

You're hardly to blame for that, Ludo's voice rolled across his thoughts, full of cloying empathy and an even bigger dose of naiveté.

Yes, he was to blame. Shader willed his legs to go on, all the while telling himself he was succumbing to the wiles of the Demiurgos, and at the same time not believing a word of it. The torment had to stop, one way or the other, and right now he didn't care how.

Nameless held him back with an arm across the chest. Up ahead, a tiny man no bigger than Shadrak came through an open door pushing a metal trolley. He was dressed head-to-foot in gray. A white mask covered his mouth and nose, and his eyes were enclosed in clear goggles. Surgical instruments lay atop the trolley, and on the shelf beneath, Shader caught sight of pink-stained tubing and a glass bell jar smeared with blood. There was something red and misshapen within, but before he could get a good look, the man wheeled the trolley down an adjacent corridor.

"Homunculus," Nameless said. "Had my fill of them in Gehenna. Shifty little shoggers. Still, he's left the door open. Fancy a butcher's?"

The instant he crossed the threshold into the vast room, Shader was freezing. Frost caked the walls, and set into the ceiling there were blue crystal globes and vents that gusted down chill air. The floor formed a walkway around a domed cage made from the same green-flecked black as Nameless' helm. Within the cage, a red-scaled and winged reptile, easily the size of a wagon, lay curled up and unmoving. One plate-sized eye was half-open, the sclera yellow, slit down the middle by a purplish pupil. Fangs like scimitars protruded from either side of its crocodile-snout.

"It's alive," Nameless said. There was awe in his voice. "Listen."

Low, rumbling breaths sent faint shudders through its scales, and plumes of steam rose from its cavernous nostrils.

"Poor ol' Rugbeard was right," Nameless said. "Seems there were dragons, after all. Just never thought I'd see one in such a state. Have to wonder, though…"

He pressed up close to the bars, and Shader did the same.

"About what?" Shader said.

"If there really was a Lord Kennick Barg to blow that dragon up with his balloon. If there really was an Arnoch." Nameless snorted and then shut the door on that idea by jabbing a finger through the bars at the dragon.

Lacerations crisscrossed its thorax, and a fresh incision that had been stitched with thick twine weeped blood and pus. Its forelegs had been hobbled, and its frost-dusted wings hung limply, pierced with sparking rings. Gossamer threads pulsing with beads of light trailed down from the top of the cage and attached to the rings.

Shader moved around the walkway to the other side and instantly shut his eyes against the horror there. Half the dragon's skull had been removed, replaced with glass, and within, glowing metallic worms burrowed in and out of its exposed brain.

He started as Nameless clamped a hand on his shoulder.

"Come on, laddie. I've seen enough."

Leaving in silence that felt almost reverent, they continued past row upon row of sealed doors. Muffled noises came from behind some of them—chirps and growls, moans and gurgles. A few of the doors had windows, and through them they could see all manner of aberrations: tentacled things with the heads of women; giant clams that scuttled in frantic circles, snapping voraciously at invisible food; four-legged fish with cloven hooves; spiders with wings. In one cell-like chamber, there was an enormous mawg with a glass bowl for a head, within which the brain had been divided into segments connected by copper wire. Its eyes were set on stalks that protruded from the bowl, and one of its arms had been replaced by a pincer harvested from some gigantic insect.

When they reached a stairwell, Nameless led them up a floor to a sprawling hall, where dozens of the floating disks they'd ridden out of the poison gas carried homunculi up and down. If the creatures spotted them, they didn't show it, and Nameless didn't let Shader linger long enough to find out. They were immediately off into yet more labyrinthine corridors, until they reached another stairwell leading up to the next level.

Shader's knees ached, and his calves were burning by the time they reached the top and emerged into a diamond-shaped room with a door set into one of its walls. It was open, and a sparkling silver trolley stood right outside. There were a number of steel implements on it—forceps, tweezers, a miniature saw—and a yellow sack of some glossy material hung from a hook at the top.

"Either there's a way through here," Nameless said, "or we backtrack; though these ol' stumpy legs of mine might have a thing or two to say about that."

Shader couldn't care less either way. If the dwarf had jumped off a cliff right then, he'd have followed.

Nameless stepped through the doorway and immediately backed straight out, retching and groaning.

"What?" Shader said, grabbing his shoulder. "What is it?"

Nameless waved him away and bent double, clutching his stomach. "I will not throw up in this shogging helm. Understand? I refuse."

Shader was sure he was talking to himself.

Nameless straightened up, and his chest rose and fell like a bellows. After a moment, he let out a long sigh. "Laddie, you don't want to go in—"

But Shader was already at the doorway. "Nous preserve us," he whispered, covering his mouth and nose against the stench—rot, decay, death, with something astringent that made his eyes water. Even breathing in short sniffs of air through his fingers, he had to fight the impulse to gag, but at the same time, he didn't retreat. Couldn't.

Inch by inch, he crept into the room, taking in the grisly scene with an unblinking sweep. Tiny bodies hung from meat hooks—human bodies. Babies. More were laid out atop burnished steel tables, and still others had been crammed into jars filled with greenish liquid. The lid of a long metal chest was partially open, with an infant's foot sticking out of it.

Shader gasped, and instantly a wave of nausea washed over him. He looked back at the doorway. Nameless was standing there, cradling his axe. The eye-slit of the great helm panned slowly across the room, drinking in the abomination. Was this what Sektis Gandaw saw as work? Was this how he wiled away the centuries?

Shader turned back to the tables. There was something about the bodies lying upon them; their necks were arched at unnatural angles. He stepped in close and touched his fingers to a stone-cold cheek so he could move the head. He flicked a look at Nameless, as if communicating his revulsion could somehow lessen it. The baby's spinal cord had been snipped just below the base of the skull. Same with the others. And they were all so tiny, smaller than any newborn he'd seen.

He felt Nameless hovering at his shoulder, turned to him.

"Are they—?"

"No, laddie. No, I don't think so." Nameless lifted a baby's waxen arm and examined it. "Proportions are wrong for a dwarf. They're human."

Shader started to protest that they were too small—too small to have come to term—but then he noticed the corpse had no hands, just bloody stumps with protruding nubs of jagged bone. The feet were missing, too, as if they'd been crudely hacked off.

Using the table to steady himself, he edged toward the chest and lifted the lid. The foot that had wedged it open dropped to the floor with a dull thud. There were hundreds more inside, frozen in ice that had a pinkish tinge from the blood. He lowered the lid and slid to his knees. His head dropped, and his hands automatically clasped together, as if he were going to pray. Only, he had no words; nothing but a silent scream that welled up from his guts to his ribcage. He tried to breathe, but that just forced the torrent upward into his skull, where it bubbled and seethed and pressed for an exit. But when the dam burst, it was with a whimper. He barely noticed the tickle of tears rolling down his cheeks.

"Why?" he muttered in the voice of the boy who'd lost his dog to an act of violence so casual it seemed almost banal. "Why take their feet?"

He didn't expect an answer; didn't even expect the dwarf to hear him, but Nameless let out howl full of despair. Shader pulled himself up using the chest, turned round in time to see the dwarf raise his axe overhead and roar. The sound reverberated through the room, but as it petered out, Nameless sagged against the edge of a table.

"This is..." He turned the eye-slit on Shader. "Even I... with the black axe... I mean, I couldn't have done such... Wouldn't!" He let go his axe, and it clattered to the floor as he made his way over to Shader and grabbed him by the hand.

"I killed them—my own people; hundreds of them, but not children. Not babies."

"It was the axe, not you," Shader said. "Never forget that."

Nameless shook his head. "I should have been stronger. But no matter how weak I was, it couldn't have made me do this." He released Shader and held out an arm as he turned to take in the room. "Not even the *Pax Nanorum* could have made me kill a child... Could it?"

Shader didn't know. How could he? He'd not been there, never even clapped eyes on the black axe. He wanted so much to believe Nameless had the strength of will to resist the power of the Abyss, but he'd succumbed before. Why should the Demiurgos's will be any less potent when it came to killing children?

He reached out, laid a hand on Nameless' shoulder. "No, my friend. You would have beaten it. It could never have made you do something like this."

The great helm dipped in what Shader took as a nod.

"Never," Nameless mumbled. "I could never hurt a child."

Suddenly, he stiffened and pressed up close. "Pray for me."

Shader took a step back. He swept off his hat, ran his fingers through his hair. "I—"

"Thumil used to, so he said. Must've worked, too, when you think about it. I got this helm." He rapped his knuckles on it. "Shogs up any chance of a flagon of ale, but it freed me from the axe. Thumil always said his god worked through people, and I reckon even ol' baldilocks qualifies."

Aristodeus as a conduit for the actions of a god? Shader doubted he'd want to hear that; the mere thought would have challenged his sense of omnipotence.

He started to reach for his Liber, but instead touched the pendant the old man in the cell had given him. He held it up and stared long and hard at the image of the lady on its front. Closing his eyes, he silently asked her to help him—help him to pray, to whatever was true and right and holy; whatever it was that had been there before Otto Blightey sowed his seeds of confusion throughout the Liber.

Nothing happened, but then, he hadn't expected it to. Not sure what else he could do, he placed a hand on top of Nameless' great helm and made a show of moving his lips. After a moment or two, he turned away and put on his hat, tugging it low over his eyes.

"Thanks, laddie," Nameless said from behind him. "Now you."

"What?" Shader said.

"Pray for yourself."

Shader scoffed at that, but Nameless grabbed him by the arm and spun him round.

"It's what's needed, laddie, if we're to put a stop to this madness. Pray. For forgiveness, if that's what you need. Pray that you break free of this stupor that's followed you since the prison; but most of all, pray that you see this evil for what it is and have the courage to destroy it, all the way down to the roots." He stepped back and pointed a finger at the gladius hanging from Shader's belt. "With the tools you've been given."

Shader felt the heat rise to his face. His muscles clenched, and he narrowed his eyes. "Oh, I'll fight evil, all right, with my bare hands if I have to; but prayer... Even if I knew there was anyone listening, I wouldn't hold my breath for an answer. And as for forgiveness!"

"So, what you did to those soldiers back at the jail," Nameless said, "the ones who ran away..."

Shader smarted at the memory. He opened his mouth to say something, to shout, but Nameless' words rolled right on over him.

"... You saying there's no forgiveness for that, for what you did?"

Shader sneered and let his eyes rove around the room, drinking in the senseless death, as if it somehow affirmed him in his guilt. "How could there be?"

"So what about me?" Nameless said.

"What about—?" But Shader could already see where this was going.

Nameless thrust the great helm up close to Shader's face. "What about me? If you're beyond redemption for losing control, where does that leave me? You only killed a handful. I murdered hundreds. Hundreds!"

"It's not a numbers game!" Shader said. "It doesn't matter how many you killed; how many I killed—"

"Matters to me," Nameless said. "Matters a whole lot."

Shader gritted his teeth and tried to calm himself. "What I mean is, I acted from within. It's who I am, and all this... this..." He fumbled the Liber out of his pocket and held it up. "This bullshit is just to keep me reined in, get it? Only, back at the jail, I was smarting so much, it would've taken a damn sight more than doctored scriptures to restrain me."

"No," Nameless said, walking away to the far side of the room and facing the babies impaled on meat hooks. "There's more to it than that. Has to be." He moved a couple of bodies to one side, and peered behind them. He pointed at the closed door he'd uncovered.

Shader nodded that he'd seen.

"Thumil's no fool," Nameless went on. "He'd not waste years of his life studying and praying if that's all it was about."

"And he's right," Shader said, slipping the Liber back into his pocket. "But it's beyond me right now. I don't even know who I'm praying to anymore."

Nameless gave a last lingering look at the bodies then turned back. "Maybe you don't need to know. Just pray, laddie. Head to the heart, Thumil used to say." He bent down to pick up his axe, spat on the blade, and gave it a quick polish. "To be honest, I thought he was just drunk and rambling most of the time, but I'm starting to see the sense of it. Keep it simple."

Without warning, he swept the axe up and brought it down hard on a table. It left a huge dent in the surface.

"This," Nameless said, stroking the head of one of the babies, "is evil. That's enough to tell me we're on the right side, far as I'm concerned. You sorry for what you did to those soldiers? Really sorry?"

It was more than that. There was a knot of feelings—rage, despair, sorrow, shame—but Shader couldn't unravel them. What he'd done was wrong, no doubt about that, but there wasn't anything that was going to restore his honor, or his piety, for that matter. He gave the dwarf a long hard look. Nothing would bring back the dwarves Nameless had slaughtered, either.

"I'll take that as a yes," Nameless said.

Shader's head was reeling. This was insane. A dwarf red to the elbows in the blood of his own people lecturing him on prayer and forgiveness! He made a fist around the pendant, offered up a silent plea for help, for guidance. He didn't know who the woman was supposed to be, but that wasn't such a big change, considering his disillusionment with Nous and Ain. Something about the way the old man had given him the pendant, something about his serenity in the face of suffering made Shader want to believe it was a step away from confusion. Though where it would lead was anyone's guess: a dead end, a false trail? Or maybe it was a strand of the golden thread, a hint of what lay beneath the doctrines of the Templum. That would be too much to hope for.

But one thing Nameless had said resonated with him. *With the tools you've been given.* Perhaps that didn't just refer to the sword.

Nameless made way for him as Shader leaned over the baby, touched two fingers to its forehead, and muttered the prayer for the dead. Maybe it didn't matter if Blightey had messed up the words. If Thumil was right—if the old man's serenity was a witness—and there was a god worth praying to, then surely the intention was enough, whatever name you used, whether it be Nous or Ain or anything else under the sun. A true god, an omniscient god, a loving god would understand.

"Ready, laddie?" Nameless asked as Shader finished the prayer.

"Ready." He clapped the dwarf on the back. "Now let's go smite some evil."

He still felt hollow; and he was acutely aware of why Aristodeus had lost belief in him; he'd lost belief in himself. But something had changed. What it was, was hard to say. He felt unburdened, somehow. Maybe it didn't matter what Blightey had put in the Liber. Maybe it didn't matter if he grasped all the mysteries of the Templum. Whatever had changed had started in the prison cell. There had been something fatalistic about the old man's endurance. No, it was more than that: he'd been resigned, yet trusting, and the pendant was the key to that trust, Shader was certain.

A tingle ran through his hip, and his fingers strayed to the hilt of the gladius. When it didn't burn, he grasped it tightly and felt it purr.

As Nameless pushed through the hanging corpses, he asked, "Why do you suppose these ones have hands and feet?"

Shader had no idea. He shook his head at the memory of the chest filled with feet. How come he'd found no sign of the missing hands?

"Makes you wonder why Gandaw chopped them off in the first place," Nameless said. "It's not like they were going to run away. And as for the hands, maybe he was worried they'd come back to life and throttle him for what he'd done to them."

"Perhaps they need us to be their hands and feet," Shader said, clenching his jaw. "Maybe we need to do to Gandaw what they can't."

"I'm with you there, laddie." Nameless hunched over the door panel, trying to get a good look through the eye-slit of his helm.

"Let me," Shader said.

It was similar to the panel Shadrak had shown him how to use to control the disk. At first glance, the glowing symbols were a confused jumble, but Shader willed himself to focus. How hard could it be to get the door to open? As if in response, a green shape drew his eye—a circle atop a triangle. A keyhole?

When he pressed it, the image expanded, and the door slid back.

"I would have had it in another second or two," Nameless said.

The room beyond pulsed with a soft amber glow. Some kind of elliptical track ran round the center of the ceiling. Dozens of women were hung spread-eagled from it by metallic cords around their wrists, and others that inserted into a similar track on the floor. Their eyes were completely white, their mouths gaping. They each had the pallor of death, and yet their bellies were grossly distended, as if they were heavily pregnant.

The track carried them forward a few feet and clunked to a halt. Snaking tubes rose from the floor and inserted into their abdomens, delivering a brownish fluid before retracting. The track moved them on another few feet, and the same thing happened again.

"Let's not linger here," Nameless said, indicating a door on the far side.

This one slid open as they approached. Shader gave the dwarf a quizzical look, but Nameless simply shrugged and walked through.

Shader followed him into a hall that was at least twice as large as the inside of Luminary Trajen's Basilica; maybe even bigger, because he couldn't even see the far side. All around the walls at ground level there were frosted oval windows. Each was as tall as a man, and behind them, shadowy forms were moving.

"Not sure I like the look of this, laddie," Nameless said. "Ready to put up with some stumpy-leg grumbling?"

Shader couldn't take his eyes from the windows. "What was that?"

"Back the way we came?"

"Agreed."

The instant Shader turned round, the door slid shut. He raced to the panel beside it, but the display was blank. He pressed the dark glass, gave it a slap, but nothing happened.

"Uh, laddie…" Nameless said.

Shader whirled back to face the hall. The frosting was melting away from the windows, and in some cases the glass—or whatever it was—was starting to bulge where hands pressed against it.

Nameless seemed to take it all in his stride. "Can't go back, so that only leaves us one choice," he said as he casually slung his axe over his shoulder and headed out across the center of the hall.

Shader's hand crept to the hilt of the gladius. It thrummed lightly, and he took that as further confirmation of its acceptance. He wished he found it reassuring; wished it confirmed that his contrition had been enough; but the Sword was the Archon's, and that didn't necessarily mean that Nous agreed. Didn't tell him anything about whether or not there was a Nous, either, or some hidden god that Blightey had obscured with the name.

An arm burst through a window, pale fingers twitching at the air. There was no shattering of glass, just the tearing of some kind of clear membrane. The head was next out, stretching the membrane until it split. The face was human, though bloodless, and white eyes roved sightlessly back and forth. Where there should have been hair, wires were bundled up around the cranium, and a single red light was nestled in among them. The second arm punched through, this one an articulated silver tube that ended in a metal hand. Enough of the membrane had fallen away to reveal a shallow alcove behind it.

Shader picked up his pace till he came alongside Nameless. The dwarf may as well have been out for a gentle stroll.

"That sword of yours behaving, laddie?"

Shader half-drew the gladius.

The great helm bobbed. "Good," Nameless said. "Limber up. Way that door shut behind us, I doubt there's going to be a big, gaping exit."

Shader drew the gladius fully, as all about the room more limbs and faces pressed and ripped their way free of confinement. He made a few practice strokes and rolled his shoulders.

"You ready?" he asked.

Nameless tapped the head of his axe. "Can't wait, laddie. Can't wait."

Shader glanced back at the door they'd entered by. They must have been fifty paces from it, and yet there was still no sign of the opposite wall, and creatures were starting to step from their alcoves as far into the distance as he could see. Those either side were a good twenty feet off, lumbering, shuffling, lurching toward them. Their legs were braced with metal struts, and they wore what looked like steel sandals that whirred and clicked as they walked.

Nameless sauntered on ahead, whistling a jaunty tune. Shader followed more cautiously, flicking looks over his shoulder, where the creatures were closing in, cutting off any thought of retreat, even if there had been a way through the door.

"Reminds me of the circle fights back home," Nameless said, as more creatures moved to block any further progress forward. "Fancy a wager?"

It reminded Shader of the undead raging through Pardes, and the mawgs swarming the *Aura Placida*. He could still see vividly what they'd done to Maldark, the flood of red within his boat gushing into the sea. He'd had energy then, both times, but even so, he'd soon reached his limit. There were only so many times you could swing a sword before your arm turned to lead.

Still they came, lumbering from the far reaches of the room, too many to count, and swelling the ranks making up the circle until it was at least ten deep. The noose narrowed as the creatures in the front drew closer, almost close enough to touch. The smell of bad meat was thick in the air and brought bile to Shader's mouth.

"All right, that's far enough," Nameless said.

With deft footwork, he pivoted and swung his axe in a murderous arc. The blades sparked across metal and threw up shreds of gray flesh that didn't bleed. The creatures merely stumbled then continued to press forward.

"Shog," Nameless said. "That doesn't bode well."

Shader hacked at an arm, and the gladius sliced through dead flesh and metal with no resistance. The limb fell twitching and grasping to the floor. A slash across the neck sent the head flying, and the body crumpled, the metal braces on its legs still whirring and clicking.

Nameless brought his axe down with all his weight behind it, ripping through a shoulder and sending a metal arm skimming across the floor. He rammed the butt of the haft into the creature's nose, reversed his grip, and powered the blade right through its jaw. Shader saw it fall, but already Nameless was swinging for the next one.

A blur of movement caught Shader's eye. He threw his sword up in time to block a silver hand that was reaching for his throat. He cut left and right in quick succession, felling half a dozen of the things before they could advance a pace. Nameless, though, was struggling. He was bellowing some bawdy song and chopping with all his prodigious strength, but the effort was taking its toll. Already, his blows were weakening.

Driving forward with each kill, Shader started to cut a path through the circle.

Nameless backed in behind him, bashing away furiously and panting with every breath. A metal arm clubbed against the great helm and sent him reeling into Shader. Nameless roared and sent a thunderous hack into the creature's midriff, shearing through steel and flesh. He followed up with a sweep to the neck, and then kicked the headless body away from him.

The press was stifling, and the stench of rot threatened to overpower Shader. He struck to his right, but a fleshy fist caught him on the left temple. He stumbled, reversed his sword, and stabbed back into pliant flesh. Spinning, he ripped the blade up through the creature's torso and split it in two all the way to the head.

Nameless went down beneath a barrage of blows, his axe clattering to the floor. He grabbed two of the creatures round the ankles and surged upright, flipping them into the throng. Retrieving his axe, he staggered backward, flailing about wildly, but with no real conviction.

A fist came at Shader's face, but he swayed aside and rammed the gladius through a gaping mouth.

The ranks were thinning in front, and he redoubled his efforts. If he could just break through, get his back to the wall—

He felt Nameless fall into him from behind. Shader rolled past him, slashing wildly at the bulging wall of creatures. The dwarf seemed dazed, barely managing to bat away grasping limbs with the flat of his axe. Shader hesitated, drew back, and then barged into him with all his might, sending Nameless headlong out of the circle.

Rather than doing as Shader had hoped, Nameless turned round and hacked a creature's legs out from under it.

"Run," Shader yelled. "To the wall."

"You run," Nameless said, swaying on his feet. "I'll hold them."

"For all of two seconds," Shader wanted to call back, but something hit him in the base of the skull. He spun and delivered a scything cut to a neck.

With a flurry of chops and slashes, he backed into the channel left by Nameless, but already it was closing over. Cold hands fastened on his arms, held him firm. Shader ripped one off, sliced through another. More limbs came at him from either side, and the bulk of the circle surged to engulf him. His knees buckled, and he started to go down, but a strong hand grabbed him by the collar of his coat and pulled him clear.

"Got you!" Nameless cried, shoving Shader behind him and batting an arm away as he fell back.

Together, they fought a determined but ailing rearguard all the way to the wall. A narrow channel had opened up along that side of the hall, and they edged along it, battling for every step.

A glimmer of movement drew Shader's eyes to the ceiling. Fifty or so yards ahead, a disk was coming down, a lone homunculus standing on it and watching them intently.

Come to gloat? Shader thought, but as the disk touched down, the homunculus jumped off and tapped at a vambrace on his wrist. The mass of creatures fell back from the disk, until it was surrounded by an island of open space, and the horde pressing Shader and Nameless from the front parted, creating a corridor that led to it.

Shader saw the opportunity first and practically flung Nameless ahead of him into he opening.

"Go!"

This time, the dwarf obeyed.

Shader leapt into the fray, the gladius a whirlwind before him. The instant he'd done enough to create a breathing space, he turned and set off after Nameless. Already, the channel was closing up, and he had to duck and dodge grasping fingers and clubbing blows.

The homunculus stepped away from the disk and weaved his way into the mass of bodies until he was lost from sight.

Nameless was slowing, but he was seconds from the disk, when a huge creature stepped from an alcove and raised a metal arm with a barbed spear tip in place of a hand. With a sound like the crack of a whip, the spear flew at him, trailing a length of chain. Nameless twisted at the last possible instant, but the tip tore through his side in a spray of blood and the clatter of broken links from his armor. The creature yanked on the chain and reeled him in like a fish. Nameless stumbled onto his knees and slid toward it, one hand clasping the base of the spear jutting from his side. Just as the creature reached out to grab him, he swung his axe with the other hand, hitting it in the guts with unbelievable force. It bent double, and bones punctured its skin in half a dozen places. The chain slackened, and with a sickening roar, Nameless tried to pull the spear tip out. The barb must have caught, and his roar turned into a scream as he slumped to the floor.

Shader got there ahead of the lumbering crowd and decapitated the creature. He knelt beside Nameless and took in the damage. Beneath the break in his chainmail, there was a fist-sized hole through the side of his torso. Thankfully, there were no exposed entrails, and it didn't look like any major organs had been hit. With a quick look back at the advancing horde, he said, "Grit your teeth."

Nameless grunted, and Shader pushed the spike out through his back. When the barb emerged, he swept down with the gladius and sheared it away. Sheathing the sword, he placed one hand on Nameless' shoulder, and with the other pulled the chain out through the front. Nameless bucked and shuddered, and when the chain came clear and snaked to the floor with a clatter, he bellowed, "Shog, shog, shog!" The bellows turned to coughs, and then he managed to croak, "That hurt."

"I can heal you," Shader said, starting to draw the gladius again, but Nameless put a hand over his.

"No, laddie. No magic. Not from that thing. I saw how it sliced through those shoggers like they weren't even solid. Has the feel of the black axe about it."

Shader hooked an arm under Nameless' shoulder and helped him to stand. "But you'll bleed to death."

"Come on, laddie," Nameless said, scooping up his axe and limping toward the disk. "Help me get my boot off, and I'll plug the wound with a sock. Should be a needle and thread in my pack."

Shader supported him on one side, casting wary looks at the creatures, who were lumbering in from all sides and closing up the gap the homunculus had made. "You don't have a pack." The dwarf must have been delirious from loss of blood.

"I don't? Used to, back in the day. Wonder where it is. Oh, well, guess that's me shogged, then. Unless I use two socks."

"The same socks you've been wearing since I met you? How long were you cooped up in that cell? And it's not just about stopping the bleeding. What about the risk of infection?"

"Laddie, I'm a dwarf. We don't do infection."

The instant they made the disk, the horde grew frantic. Those in the front ranks parted to admit three more of the huge creatures. They each raised metal arms and launched spears trailing chains. Shader threw Nameless to the platform and dropped on top of him.

There was a succession of dull thuds as the spears struck some invisible barrier, and the chains clunked heavily to the ground.

The homunculus appeared off to the right. He gave a single nod and tapped at his vambrace. With a whir and a shudder, the disk lifted into the air. As it passed through a hole in the ceiling, it gathered pace, shooting up through level after level. Shader's ears popped, and Nameless moaned as he was rocked from side to side. He had one hand vainly trying to staunch the flow of blood, the other draped over the haft of his axe. After what seemed an age, the disk entered a metal shaft, shook violently, and came to a halt.

THE UNWEAVING

THE DISK HAD come to rest in some kind of silver-walled cubicle, where it fit seamlessly into the floor. One of the walls had a hairline crack down its center, and there was a panel adjacent to it. Shader could hear someone running about outside. There was a clang of metal, a searing hiss, and beneath it all, a sound like the roar of flames.

He placed a hand on the wall. It radiated heat, and through the crack he could see a flickering orange glow. Stepping away, he bent to examine the panel's black mirror. The same keyhole symbol he'd used before loomed larger than the others around it and winked repeatedly. Above it, the Aeternam word 'Signum' stood out. It was followed by a colon and a series of geometric shapes, all of them flashing green. 'Signum' meant 'sign' or 'signal', but in Aeterna it was also used as a challenge, a kind of 'Who goes there?' The response was typically a password. But if the same held true here, and if green meant 'good to go', like Shadrak had said, then someone had already entered it.

"Boot, laddie," Nameless rasped. He was lying on his back in a pool of blood, holding a leg out. The hand clamped over the front of his wound looked flayed, it was so red.

Shader took hold of the boot, but before he could pull, he heard a man say something from beyond the cubicle, not loud enough for him to make out the words, but the timbre of the voice was somehow familiar.

"That ol' baldilocks?" Nameless said.

Aristodeus? Yes, he was right. But what was the philosopher doing here? How did he—?

Another man spoke, the sound clipped and toneless. Shader had heard the voice before, atop the Homestead.

"Think we've arrived," he said. "That's Sektis Gan—"

There was a cry and a clash, then a boom rocked the cubicle. Shader ducked instinctively. Nameless tried to roll onto his side, let out a gasp, and lay back. His chest fluttered as it rose and fell, and rattling breaths came from within the great helm.

"Think I'll take the magic, after all," he said. "If you don't mind, laddie."

Moving aside Nameless' blood-soaked hand, Shader touched the gladius to his wound. Golden light flowed down the blade, and Nameless cried out as his back arched. Searing heat cauterized the flesh, and muscle knitted together. Nameless hummed something—a few notes of a song, perhaps—and then sagged back against the floor when Shader withdrew the sword. His breathing was steadier now, and besides the broken links of his chainmail, and the red smears and spatters, there was no sign of the injury. Shader only hoped it wasn't too late. The floor was slick with blood, the air heavy with its cloying stench.

"Thank you, laddie," Nameless said in a voice full of slumber. "Just thirty winks and I'll be right as—"

A woman screamed.

Shader whirled toward the crack in the wall, shot a glance at the panel. Aristodeus... Aristodeus was in there. Surely he'd not brought—

Another scream, and this time, he had no doubt.

"Rhiannon!"

Nameless struggled to rise but slumped back down. "Go, laddie. I'll follow... when... I..." His words trailed off, and he was still.

Shader spared him a look to make sure he was still breathing, then he clenched his jaw and pressed the keyhole symbol. Heat flooded the cubicle as the crack in he wall split open with a hiss. The instant he stepped through, his eyes watered from the smoke.

The chamber he entered was like the inside of an enormous cone. Tiers of walkways, each with banks of flickering screens, wound all the way up to the apex. Winged creatures were hunched over the screens—kryeh, like the ones that had terrorized the troops at the Homestead.

Shader's boots were sticky with Nameless' blood, and he tracked red across the floor as he stepped warily away from the cubicle with the gladius held before him.

A flame-filled chasm rent the chamber in two, and from within its maw, the top of a slender tower poked, its ivory walls blackened with soot. Aristodeus was staring wide-eyed from an open sash window just below the tower's turreted roof, and Shader followed his gaze to where Rhiannon was suspended in midair. A silver sphere hovered above her, bathing her in blue light. Even more shocking, though, was how different she looked. She was armored in dark leather, with black boots all the way up to her knees. Her hair was pulled back in a braided tail, and where her arms were exposed, they looked harder, more defined. Her eyes glared defiance, and not a little frenzy. Callixus's black sword was directly beneath her feet, lodged in the fizzing and sparking shell of a metal crab the size of a pony. More of the crab-things were heaped around the room in smoking piles.

Shader's eyes flicked to Aristodeus. What had he done to her? How was it even possible in so short a time?

"Clever," came Sektis Gandaw's voice from high above. It carried effortlessly, as if by magic, a dispassionate, inhuman monotone. "A two-pronged attack. Though when an action is futile, it begs the question: Why waste effort by making it doubly so?"

Shader craned his neck. At first, all he saw was an inky cloud belching waves of blackness near the cone's truncated ceiling. It looked and felt alive, and each time it breathed, a tinge of nausea crept beneath his skin. Then, within the miasma, he could make out the form of a serpent with glowing amber eyes and fangs like jags of lightning—the Statue of Eingana. Atop its head, a crown of pulsing filaments sent a constant ring of sparks up through the ceiling. At the center of the circle they formed, a single mirror glared down, showing nothing but a black hole that seemed to beckon and tug.

A disk drifted out from behind the statue and made an arcing descent, until it hovered twenty feet above Shader. Sektis Gandaw stepped to its edge and inclined his head to look down with eyes of incandescent blue. His face appeared gray, mask-like, beneath pitch black hair that glistened like oil. He wore a billowing brown coat, beneath which Shader glimpsed dark metal greaves and bands of thigh armor. One hand was gloved in black; the other looked desiccated, and ribbed tubing ran from the knuckles up under the coat sleeve.

"The password," Gandaw said. "How did you work it out?" As he spoke, he lifted his wrist, tapped at a vambrace, and gave a slow, satisfied nod.

Shader threw a look at Aristodeus, who shrugged and turned his palms up. A ripple passed through the philosopher's body, and for an instant he flickered. If Aristodeus noticed, he didn't show it.

Gandaw, however, seemed impressed. "Bilocation? I thought only I'd mastered that. It's been quite a day of discoveries. First—" He gestured toward the smoking chasm. "—tangible evidence that the Abyss may well constitute an empirical fact, after all, and now a philosopher who can be in two places at the same time."

"What are you talking about, Sektis?" Aristodeus said. "Has one of your memory nodes ruptured and corrupted what's left of your brain?"

Gandaw surveyed him for a long moment and then replied, "Simply an observation. Where there is a certain density of shielding—in the case of this mountain, scarolite—bilocated simulacra have been known to flicker, whereas the originals, generally, do not."

Aristodeus glanced at his hands. "What flicker? Maybe you need your optics tested." His voice had risen in pitch, and a tic had started up on his cheek.

"Stolen technology, no doubt," Gandaw said, as if he didn't really care. "Leftovers from Global Tech, or did it come from here?" He let his disconcerting eyes rove the chamber, and when he didn't find what he was looking for, visibly stiffened. A fine tremor ran through his coat, his shoulders dropped, and he drew in a long, shuddering breath. He lifted his arm and spoke into his vambrace. "Mephesch?" The next words came out slow and deliberate: "Where are you?"

"On my way, Technocrat," a crackling voice answered.

Shader's eyes strayed to Rhiannon hanging beneath the sphere. She hadn't moved since he'd entered the chamber. Was she even breathing?

"Thank you for reminding me," Gandaw said, following his gaze. "Though, why the sentroid hasn't killed her already—"

"No technology," Aristodeus said quickly.

Gandaw's head pivoted sharply in his direction. "What?"

"I didn't use technology to bring us here." He tapped the side of his head.

"Oh, please," Gandaw said. "I've dissected and analyzed every last strand of human DNA, scrutinized every possible permutation of the genome, and rigorously tested the whole pathetic organism *ad nauseam*. There is no hidden power of the mind that allows you to teleport, let alone move an entire tower. I don't care how old you are and how inflated your ego is, you are either lying or deluded. No, wait, I hadn't factored in the new data to hand. What can we extrapolate from the empirical evidence for the reality of the Abyss? Must we not now hypothesize the existence of its reputed creator?

"You see, Aristodeus, last time you tried to thwart the Unweaving all those hundreds of years ago, that very same chasm opened up and swallowed you. All I did was unleash the power of Eingana. What happened next was as unexpected to me as I'm sure it was to you. I confess, I should have investigated the phenomenon, and it's been niggling away at the back of my mind ever since. But I recently had something of an epiphany. It doesn't matter that there are two imponderables in this miserable universe that I've not set my scalpel to. I thought it mattered, thought I knew all there was to know, but then I realized I'd been deceiving myself. The Abyss, and that—" He jabbed a finger toward the lone mirror at the top of the chamber.

Its hungry emptiness hit Shader with sudden clarity. Somehow, Sektis Gandaw had a mirror showing something that shouldn't be seen—couldn't. He realized with a primal dread that he was gazing directly into the Void.

"—didn't fit into my grand hypothesis, and so I left them out. I deceived myself. Maybe you've done the same; or maybe someone's deceiving you. Could it be that you are bilocating without even realizing it? That your essence is elsewhere, kept by a master who allows you a long leash?" He looked at Shader. "You holy types invented the myths. What do you think? Is it possible that the impeccable mind of Aristodeus has fallen prey to the deceptions of the Demiurgos?"

A haunted look passed across Aristodeus's eyes, and for a moment, his mouth hung open. Then he clamped it shut, and his face grew as stoic and mask-like as Gandaw's.

"You don't believe that, Sektis. All this speculation is hardly your style. What are you up to? Stalling?"

The patter of feet alerted Shader to someone behind him. It was the homunculus from the disk, the one that had saved him and Nameless. He glanced at the open door of the cubicle he'd entered by, expecting to see a tiny set of crimson footprints alongside his own, but there was nothing. Nothing save Nameless' blood-drenched body on the floor. How had the homunculus entered, if not from the cubicle? It was as if he'd simply stepped through the wall.

"Ah, Mephesch," Gandaw said. "Re-route enough of Eingana's power to close that rift, would you?"

When the homunculus looked at him blankly, Gandaw said, "She opened the exact same chasm in 1980, when this upstart philosopher plunged to what should have been his death."

"One thousand one hundred and eighty-four years ago, Technocrat," Mephesch said. "Two hundred and seventy-six years before the event known as—"

"Yes, yes, the so-called Reckoning. Your point?"

Mephesch glanced at Aristodeus and grinned. "He doesn't look a day above seventy."

Aristodeus frowned at that, but he was as rapt as everyone else.

"My point, Gandaw said, is that if Aristodeus has found a way to re-open the rift Eingana created and subsequently closed, it stands to reason, does it not, that she can seal it again?"

"But the Null Sphere, Technocrat…"

"A minute's delay, at most," Gandaw said. "Just do it; it'll save worrying about the clean-up later."

Aristodeus started to protest as the homunculus leaned over the shoulder of a kryeh and slowly tapped at its mirror, all the while flicking glances between Gandaw and the tower poking up above the chasm. Symbols sprang to life, where before the mirror had shown the image of a snow-capped mountain range. A brilliant burst of amber lanced down from Eingana's eyes.

"No!" Aristodeus cried. "Shader! Shaaaderrrrrrr!"

He was flung back from the window. With a shake and a rumble, the white tower sank slowly beneath the flames, and the chasm closed over it. When the tremors had subsided, the floor looked as good as new, as if the tower had never been there.

"Every action has an equal and opposite reaction," Gandaw said. "Somewhat predictable, but what do you expect from such a pedestrian creation?" He turned his eyes on Shader. "Sorry to see him go? Indifferent? Glad to fill his place in the pecking order?"

"He's dead?" Shader said, but Gandaw merely stared at the floor where the chasm had been.

Shader wasn't really sure how he should feel. If he lingered long enough on childhood memories, on the endless hours of lectures, the grueling training regimens, he'd miss the philosopher, wouldn't he? But there were too many dangers in the present to allow him the luxury of nostalgia, too many questions Aristodeus would no longer be able to answer before he could feel one way or the other. That's if he was dead. He'd survived the chasm before, hadn't he, if what Gandaw said were true? Hundreds of years ago… he'd plunged into the Abyss.

"You knew each other?" he finally asked. It was a lame question, but he didn't know what else to do. He'd never felt so out of his depth; never felt so useless. It made him realize that, if he didn't exactly miss Aristodeus, at that moment, he needed him. Needed someone to tell him what to do.

Gandaw turned back to face him. "Aristodeus liked to think we did. I can only assume it was an ego thing, what with me being the supreme Technocrat, back then, and him being, in his own estimation, at any rate, the greatest mind of the age. The truth is, I met him only once—well, twice, if you count his ill-fated attempt to stop the Unweaving last time round. He was sent to see me in London—on Earth—before my exile, at the behest of some obnoxious hippy-inspired bioethics commission or other. I forget what they were called—one of the curses of longevity for an imperfect organism. They had grown concerned at my success with melding." When Shader raised an eyebrow, he explained: "Fish with beast, plant with man, that kind of thing. It was early days and inestimably crude, but we all have to start somewhere. The strategy was that a face-to-face meeting would render me vulnerable to Aristodeus's silver tongue. Find out what your opponent wants, he believed, and you can talk your way into a compromise agreement. I imagine he underestimated my goal, and the bioethics commission overestimated his capacity to reject a bribe."

Shader's eyes flicked around the chamber, looking for something—anything—a clue for what to do next. There was no telling how long they had left until everything ended, but if he couldn't keep Gandaw distracted, it was all over for him, Rhiannon, and Nameless right here, right now. In the absence of a better plan, he had no choice but to keep Gandaw talking. The problem was, he didn't think he was the only one playing for time.

"You bought him off?"

Gandaw shrugged. "Secondhand knowledge, a limited immunity from Global Tech controls. But enough of him. You, Mr. Shader, have been quite the nuisance. Tell me, why didn't you end this at the Homestead when you had the chance? No, hold your answer." He pointed at Rhiannon. "Mephesch, the woman next. I don't know how many times I've told you, the sentroids should be set to kill; we don't have the energy to waste on stasis beams."

"Sorry, Technocrat," Mephesch said, rapidly tapping at his vambrace and raising it to his mouth.

"Rhiannon?" Shader said. "You're going to kill—?"

"Won't feel a thing," Gandaw said. "And besides, in a few more minutes, everything she's ever known will cease to exist. Think of it as a mercy killing."

A nozzle emerged from the silver sphere holding Rhiannon aloft.

"No," Shader muttered. By the time he thought to draw the gladius, he knew it was too late, and his 'no' became a scream.

There was a grunt of effort from behind him. Silver streaked past his head and struck the sphere with such force it exploded in a shower of sparks. Metal debris clattered down, and Nameless' axe fell with it, clanging as it struck the floor, and skittering off till it came to rest against a wall.

Rhiannon seemed to hang in midair for a second, then she dropped like a stone. Shader lurched toward her, but she was too far away. She tucked her knees in, rolled as she hit, and came up smoothly. Shader could only watch in astonishment. She moved like a cat, and the veins along her biceps stood out in ridges as she took hold of Callixus's sword and wrenched it free of the crab-thing.

"That the shogger?" Nameless said, stumbling into the chamber and pointing up at Gandaw. "Doesn't look like much to me."

The fabric of Gandaw's coat ripped as he suddenly grew from within. His entire frame shuddered, and then he swelled again. The coat and the gray tunic beneath disintegrated, swirling about him in a cloud of dust. Where his chest should have been, there was now a black breastplate, flecked with green. His legs and arms were encased in scarolite, too, and the air around his head grew denser, solidifying into a clear, crystal dome.

659

"Ah," Nameless said. "Lassie, pass us my axe, would you?"

Rhiannon backed away to the wall, black sword held tightly in white-knuckled hands. Without taking her eyes from Gandaw, she used her foot to shunt Nameless' axe across the floor to him.

As Mephesch ran for cover, Gandaw raised his gloved hand and extended the palm. The glove smoldered and fell away to reveal metallic fingers, each tipped with fiercely sparking crystals. Lightning arced between them, and the hand glowed white-hot. With quick stabbing movements, he aimed first at Rhiannon and then at Nameless. Balls of fire streaked toward them both. Rhiannon dived, but the blast drove her head first into a console. Nameless could barely walk, never mind run, but he ducked like he'd somehow seen it coming, and the fireball sped over his head to explode against the ground.

Gandaw spun toward Shader and unleashed a barrage of missiles. The first was wide, but the explosion was deafening.

Ears ringing, Shader sprinted for a console and hunkered down behind a seated kryeh as the second fireball struck where he'd been standing a split second before. He braced for the scorching pain of the blast, but instead, all he felt was the throbbing of the gladius in his grasp as it drank in the flames.

He emerged from cover and held the sword in front of him. This time, when the third fireball hit, the gladius threw the full brunt of the blast straight back at Gandaw. It exploded against the edge of his disk and sent him plummeting toward the floor. Grapnels shot out from his armor and snagged a railing, and then reeled him in. Effortlessly, he took hold of the rail and vaulted over it, landing with a resonant clang on the walkway.

"Rather attached to her, aren't you?" Gandaw nodded down toward where Rhiannon was slumped over the console. "Not quite the same disinterest you showed for the philosopher. So, you see, already I have more data on you. And your sword—a weapon that can both nullify and redirect energy. More stolen technology?"

"Don't answer, laddie," Nameless said. "He's stalling for some reason. I say we get up there and see how well he talks when I cut him a second mouth with my axe."

Gandaw stepped back from the railing and cast his eyes back and forth. For a moment, he took on the appearance of a cornered rat. Within seconds, though, he resumed an air of calm confidence. With the ghost of a smile, he said, "Mephesch, the kryeh, if you please. Release them."

The homunculus popped up from behind a console and ran his fingers over the mirror. Shader was stunned at first. He'd thought Mephesch was helping them. Was he frightened of disobeying a direct order, or was this something else? Wasn't it the nature of the homunculi to deceive? If he'd betrayed Gandaw, why wouldn't he do the same to others? Shader started to run at him but knew he'd be too late. With a half-formed prayer, he flung the gladius like a javelin. Mephesch ducked behind the console, and the sword flew overhead.

The kryeh all about the chamber jerked and unfurled their wings. As the homunculus got up and ran, the sword turned in a wide arc and shot toward him. Mephesch dived— and passed straight through the wall, as if it weren't there. The gladius drew up sharp and then reversed direction until it slapped back into Shader's palm.

The kryeh flapped furiously a couple of feet above their chairs and let out ululating screams as the wires that connected them to their consoles ripped free in sprays of blood.

Nameless' voice tore Shader away from the gruesome sight. "Gandaw, laddie. Your sword!"

This time, he simply slackened his grip, and the Sword of the Archon launched itself at Gandaw like a comet. Gandaw threw up both hands and instinctively ducked, but even before the blade reached him, it struck something solid and rebounded. For a brief moment, a sphere of blue light flickered around Gandaw and then vanished.

Shader snatched the returning gladius from the air as the kryeh on the lower levels screeched and flew at Gandaw. More of the creatures flocked overhead, gathering into a tightly packed wedge and diving. Gandaw scattered them with a fireball, and the few that pressed their attack squawked as they struck his invisible barrier. In a great cacophony of beating wings and cawing cries, they spiraled about the chamber in a frenzy, crashing into walls and bumping off the apex, as if all they wanted was to break out.

"I should have seen that coming," Gandaw said through gritted teeth. "Just need to teach them who's master, that's all."

He exploded a fireball against the ceiling, obliterating the lone mirror that hung there. Half a dozen kryeh dropped, smoldering and lifeless, hitting railings, bouncing, and ending up crumpled on the floor. The rest descended like a murder of crows onto the ground floor consoles. Their caws turned into mournful wails, and they started to rip out tufts of their own hair with hands that were utterly human, save for the long-taloned fingers. Many scratched at their breasts, leaving trails of crimson streaking down their feminine torsos. The legs, though, were anything but human; they were articulated like a bird's, with three claws at the front and one at the back.

Shader spun round as Gandaw detonated another fireball, this one above and behind the kryeh. They let out a collective squawk and took to the air once more. They wheeled as one toward Gandaw, then shied away. They circled Shader, passed over Nameless, and looked like they were starting to regroup for a concerted attack when the squawking took on a different sound: less frenetic; more triumphant. And then, in a mass of beating wings, they swooped toward Rhiannon's unmoving body.

Nameless had already seen it, and he was closer. Even as Shader started to run, the dwarf was in the thick of the kryeh, bellowing a song at the top of his voice, and scything about with his axe. Each swing drove the kryeh back a few paces, but they instantly flapped closer again. Most switched their attack to Nameless, but a few bypassed him and alighted on the console Rhiannon was draped over.

Shader hurled the gladius, shearing the head clean off a kryeh. As the sword returned to his hand, he reached Rhiannon and dragged her back from the console, letting her slump to the floor at his feet.

Nameless burst through the cloud of wings threatening to smother him, whirled back to face it, shook his axe like a madman, and roared. The kryeh dispersed, but then they flew behind him in an arc and came at Shader.

"Sorry, laddie," Nameless yelled above the din. "Unintentional."

The gladius was a dazzling blur as Shader cut and chopped, hacked and slashed in every direction. He ducked, wheeled, spun, and kicked, eyes taking in every move the kryeh made, predicting every attack. The sword fed golden fire into his limbs, making them faster than thought and tireless. It felt featherlight in his hand, yet each blow he delivered was brutal, solid, and utterly devastating. For an instant, he almost stopped in awe at what he was doing, but then resumed his impeccable focus with a series of thrusts and cuts that sent two more kryeh to the pile of bodies atop Rhiannon.

Nameless' axe rose and fell with grunts of effort. Mostly, he was just hitting air as the kryeh flapped and fluttered away from his strikes, but then he found his timing and started to aim a little ahead of, a little behind the target, and soon, he was adding his own kills to the pile.

Above, on the next tier, Gandaw hurried along the walkway toward a metal staircase that led up to the next level. Before Shader could react, a kryeh raked its claws across his coat collar, narrowly missing his throat. He backhanded it away, and as it gathered for a renewed attack, he plunged the gladius between its breasts.

"Gandaw!" he cried toward Nameless. "Stop him. I'll hold them!"

"Got you, laddie!" Nameless shouted back. Clutching his axe to his chest, he ducked down and charged through the kryeh. One of them followed him, clawing from behind, but Nameless twisted, turned, and swung for it with almost casual grace. The kryeh fell to the floor in two pieces, and Nameless reached the steps and started upward.

The kryeh surrounding Shader rose into the air. At first he thought they were going after the dwarf, but then they began to circle overhead, cawing mournfully at the mass of dead bodies heaped on the floor.

Shader took the opportunity to extricate Rhiannon from the bodies that had fallen on her. She moaned when he dragged her out of the pile. He brought the gladius toward her, directed a stream of golden light into her chest. The instant it touched, Rhiannon screamed, and the front of her leather corset started to smolder. She whipped her arm up, grip still tight upon Callixus's unearthly sword. Black flames licked about the blade, hissing and spitting. Her eyes flared, and she swung the sword at Shader. He caught her wrist, pressed her down against the floor. She gasped, and the fierceness left her as quickly as it had come.

"Deacon? What... Oh, my shog!"

She pushed him off and got to her feet. Her eyes fixed on Nameless, who was pounding across the walkway above. Gandaw was halfway up the steps to the next level, and he seemed not to have noticed the dwarf hot on his heels.

Rhiannon lurched forward and stumbled. Shader steadied her by the elbow and then shoved her toward the steps as the kryeh dived once more. He hacked one out of the air as it sped at Rhiannon, but another made it past. He called out a warning, but she was already in mid-swing, and the black blade sliced into human flesh, exiting through the leathery membrane of a bat-like wing.

Shader backed up the steps behind her, fighting a furious defense. A talon grazed his cheek, then another cut him above the eye and sent a stream of blood across his vision. He willed the gladius to heal him, but nothing happened. It felt heavier in his grasp—more like a normal sword. Even as he blocked another claw and hacked down through a skull, he wondered what he'd done, how he'd lost the sword's favor again. But he can't have done, he realized; he was still holding it, wasn't he? And there was no burning sensation in his hand. Perhaps it had limits. Perhaps it was conserving its power for something more, for something he couldn't do by himself.

Rhiannon reached the walkway and set off at a run. A trio of kryeh moved to block her, but she bashed one aside without breaking her step, and dropped to the floor, sliding beneath the others on her knees. When she reached the end of her slide, she flowed back to her feet, whirled, and delivered two powerful blows that put an end to the pursuit.

Shader tripped over the last step and fell back onto the walkway. Immediately, the kryeh swarmed over him, biting, scratching, clubbing with their fists. He dropped the gladius and covered his face with his hands, tucking in his elbows to protect his sides. He drew his knees in and tried to roll clear. The skin of his face, legs, and arms stung in a dozen places. Desperate, he rolled onto his front and, keeping his head down, splayed out his fingers in search of the gladius. A kryeh landed on his back, knocking the wind out of him. He slumped, still clawing the cold metal floor for the sword. He heard Rhiannon call to him; heard her footfalls coming nearer, and then a reverberating clunk sounded from above, and the room was plunged into shadow.

The kryeh squawked and flew toward the ceiling. Shader pushed himself to his knees and caught a glimpse of the homunculus—Mephesch—who'd both helped and betrayed them. He was standing over a console on the level below. He looked up, directly at Shader, gave an enigmatic smile, and then turned his eyes toward the conical chamber's apex. Shader followed his gaze, passing over Nameless on the second tier, gaining on Gandaw. The Technocrat was oblivious, staring up at the ceiling with a look of horror on his usually impassive face.

"No!" he cried. "Mephesch! Mephesch, what is happening? We are not shielded. I am not shielded!"

A hole had opened up, and the walls at the top of the cone were slowly receding into the level below. A fierce wind blew down the funnel, buffeting the kryeh as they swarmed through the aperture and out into the black. Because that was all Shader could see: a sphere of absolute darkness hanging above the Perfect Peak, pulsing, beating like a gigantic, malevolent heart. With every beat, it swelled and grew denser. Its oppressive weight was almost tangible, and a sickening wave of wrongness rolled through Shader, sending him reeling back against the railing.

Rhiannon stumbled and clutched her stomach as she gazed up at the burgeoning dark. Steadying himself, Shader picked up the gladius, strode over to her, and led her by the hand toward the next flight of steps up.

The walls of the cone continued to retract. As they passed beneath Shader's level, he saw just how dense they were, each level sitting within that below in concentric circles, each with its own rooms and passageways sandwiched between twin walls of scarolite at least ten feet thick. Down and down they went, level by level, until the heart of the chamber, with its tiered walkways and flickering screens, was little more than a skeletal framework, completely exposed to the raging elements.

Shader looked down over the railing and felt himself swaying like he was on the crow's nest of the *Aura Placida*. Not that he'd braved those heights, but Elpidio had, and the wind whistling in from above seemed to echo the boy's screams when the mawgs ripped him to pieces.

They were hundreds of feet up, atop what was now the truncated summit of the Perfect Peak. Far, far below, the white sands of the Dead Lands swirled and formed into tortuous vortices that spun wildly in every direction. The mangroves at the edge of the Sour Marsh were stretched to impossible heights and bowed beyond breaking point. The gloaming skies were fractured, like broken glass, and way off in the distance, a cordon of shimmering fog whirled dizzyingly up into the heights, ever expanding to engulf more and more of the hazy, unreal landscape.

Nameless' roar focused Shader back on the walkways. Up above, the dwarf charged and swept his axe down on Gandaw with awesome power. The same sphere of brilliant blue flashed and sparked all around Gandaw as the axe head lodged within it. Nameless hung on with both hands and pushed his boots against the sphere in an effort to free it.

Gandaw swung his metal hand toward Nameless, lightning crackling between crystal-tipped fingers.

Shader cried out and started to run. Somewhere at the back of his mind, he heard Rhiannon curse, knew she was following.

He drew the gladius back in a last desperate effort, even though he knew it would be futile.

Flame swelled upon Gandaw's palm, and Nameless' helm jerked up as he realized the danger.

Something huge and dark smashed into Gandaw from above. His protective sphere spat blue sparks, buckled, and fizzed out. At the same instant, Nameless yelped and fell on his rear, still clutching his axe.

Gandaw was momentarily stricken, gawping wide-eyed at the massive black fist that had struck him. It was the same as the one that had caused such carnage at the Homestead, disembodied and the size of a cart. Down below, a fearsome clamor arose as hundreds of lizard-men swarmed into the chamber from the top of the truncated mountain. They must have been there all along, Shader realized, clinging to the outer casing until the walls were lowered. More of Mephesch's scheming? More duplicity? He recognized Skeyr Magnus among them, making a fist with a smoking gauntlet. He must have fixed it after their fight in the Sour Marsh, although only just, by the looks of it.

Skeyr Magnus made a jabbing motion with the gauntlet, and the giant fist responded by hammering into Gandaw. The Technocrat crashed through the railing but managed to cling on with his desiccated hand. From the other, he discharged a barrage of fireballs that sent the black hand spinning away.

Nameless leapt to his feet and ran at Gandaw, swinging the axe down at the hand holding onto the railing. A coil snaked out of Gandaw's armor and wrapped around Nameless' ankles, tripping him and whipping him into the air. Nameless hacked through the coil and fell, landing heavily. Gandaw used both hands to pull himself up and back onto the walkway.

Shader pulled Rhiannon into him as the tide of lizard-men rolled past them on their way to the next level. They ran, leapt, and bounded, some of them scaling the railings in their frenzy to get at Gandaw. It was easier to go with the flow than fight against it, and so Shader held on tight to Rhiannon and let them be swept along by the horde until they reached the steps and climbed up.

The black hand righted itself and soared back toward Gandaw. This time, he blasted it almost casually and then tapped out a sequence on his vambrace as the hand was repulsed once more.

The first of the lizard-men to reach him, he backhanded with such force it ripped the creature's head clean off. He kicked another straight through the railing and out above the Dead Lands, where it flailed and screamed as it plummeted toward the ground hundreds of feet below. Just as the main tide threatened to hit him, though, Gandaw took a step back, let off another fireball, and then ran for the steps to the next level.

A trio of silver spheres rose out of the Dead Lands and tore into the lizard-men with sizzling bursts of lightning. Clouds of smoke plumed up, carrying the stench of roasted flesh and ozone. Some lizard-men panicked and scattered, seeking the cover of consoles, chairs, the bodies of the fallen, but the spheres pursued them relentlessly, cutting them down in their tracks.

As Shader and Rhiannon made it to Nameless and helped him to stand, Gandaw joined in the massacre, blasting down into the lizard-men, and then he sent a devastating volley straight at Skeyr Magnus, who was still on the ground floor, no doubt letting his people take the bulk of the risks for him. Skeyr Magnus threw his gauntlet up to cover his face, and the black hand instantly appeared in front of him, fingers splayed, palm facing the onslaught. The fireballs exploded against it, and for a moment, it looked like the lizard-man would survive, but then his gauntlet burst into flame and sent sparks shooting across his skin. With a howl and a scream, he was slammed into the floor and lay there smoldering. The black hand winked out of existence.

Rhiannon was already halfway up the steps before Shader realized she was no longer holding his hand. Nameless was right behind her. By the time Shader reached the steps and climbed up, she was yelling at Gandaw and charging with the black sword held high. Gandaw hadn't seen her coming, but he still managed to get off a shot. Rhiannon must have predicted it, for she rolled beneath it and swung. A coil snapped out of Gandaw's armor and caught her wrist, locking the sword in mid-swing. Gandaw brought his metal arm round till it was directly in Rhiannon's face. Shader's heart leapt into his throat, and his legs felt leaden as he pounded toward them. Nameless saw the opening, though, and threw himself at Gandaw, swinging his axe for all he was worth. It struck the scarolite armor like a thunderclap—and shattered.

"Oh, shog," Nameless said, as Gandaw aimed his metal hand at him instead.

Fire blasted from the palm, and there was no missing this time. Nameless must have known, for he ducked into it and took the full brunt of the explosion on his great helm.

There was a muffled boom, and flames flared briefly, but then fizzled out as if they'd struck water. Nameless fell like a plank, his black helm clanging against the metal of the walkway.

Rhiannon kicked out at Gandaw. He swung his aim back to her, but before he could fire, Shader was there. He slammed the gladius into Gandaw's transparent helm with every ounce of strength he could muster. The crystal—or whatever it was—cracked, and Gandaw gasped. The second blow sheared right through the metal hand, and Gandaw screamed.

Shader expected a shower of blood; what he got, though, was sparking wires and a glimpse of moving cylinders in place of bones. He drew back the gladius for a thrust, but the coil holding Rhiannon reeled her in and smacked her against Gandaw's breastplate. Another coil sprang out and wrapped around her neck, tightening, constricting, making her gasp and choke for every breath.

Gandaw took a few steps back. His blue eyes blazed fiercely with either fear or rage; Shader couldn't tell which, but within moments, they dulled. A halo of soft light irradiated the glass helm, and the crack Shader had made melted over until there was no sign of it.

Gandaw raised his remaining hand. At first, Shader thought he was surrendering, but then he saw the flashing red light on his vambrace.

One of the sentroids massacring the lizard-men broke off and soared to a position above Gandaw's head. A beam of blue light shot from it and bathed Gandaw and Rhiannon, lifting them high into the air and bearing them toward the Statue of Eingana. The black sword fell from Rhiannon's grasp and drifted like a feather all the way to the bottom.

Shader cursed and started for the steps, when the other two sentroids sped straight at him and unleashed searing streams of fire. He threw up the gladius, and it answered with a surge of aureate brilliance that sent the beams back on themselves. The sentroids erupted in flame and crashed to the floor below.

Shader quickly scanned the room as he raced to the steps. At least now the lizard-men would have a chance. But it wasn't the chance he'd hoped for. Skeyr Magnus was back on his feet and barking commands. His scaly hide was charred and blistered, and smoke still rolled off of him. The few lizard-men that remained bounded over the edges of the walkways and escaped down the side of the mountain. Magnus gave Shader a last look, full of desperation, full of despair, and then he clambered down, out of sight.

Futile, Shader thought, even as he climbed the steps. *Utterly stupid.* What did they hope to achieve by fleeing? He glanced up at the pendulous black sphere gyring above the Perfect Peak. They had only minutes—moments, even—before it ruptured, or exploded, or perhaps imploded to unmake everything there was; everything that had ever been.

Lightning arced upward into the sky, illuminating the Dead Lands with its stark flash. In its wake, a purplish vortex materialized and spun along the fringe of the Sour Marsh, tearing up grotesquely distorted mangroves and flinging them far and wide.

Giddiness washed over Shader, and he clutched the bannister. His eyes were drawn to the ground floor, as if he could find his anchor there, but instead the whole structure swayed, and he forced himself to look up.

The sentroid carried Gandaw into the inky cloud beneath the the black sphere and brought him alongside the serpent statue. Questing filaments sprouted from his armor like hair and inserted themselves all over Eingana's petrified body. In response, light exploded along the blade of Shader's gladius like a sunburst, and it was all he could do to hold on as the sword carried him into the air.

Gandaw looked up as Shader reached his height, hanging with both hands from the blazing gladius. He immediately returned his focus to Eingana, eyes half-closed in concentration. Rhiannon twitched against his chest. Her face was bloodless, her lips tinged with blue. If Shader didn't do something... But what could he do? He was barely able to cling on. How was he supposed to fight?

Light pulsed along Gandaw's filaments, and Eingana's fangs flared amber. Flame gushed from her maw and struck the bottom of the chamber. The mountain shook, and with a succession of tortured cracks, a fracture worked its way across the floor, until it yawned into another gaping chasm—the same chasm that had swallowed Aristodeus. Only, this time there was no white tower. This time, gigantic ribbons of shadow quested forth like avaricious fingers. Shader felt himself tugged in their direction by an unseen force, but the gladius increased its upward pull and held him in place.

Gandaw noticed, and annoyance flashed in his eyes. Then, the coils holding Rhiannon released her and she fell. Shader let go of the gladius with one hand, reaching for her on instinct, but it was no good. She was already plunging toward the rift. Ice rose from his guts, coursed through his veins, froze the scream in his throat. He felt his fingers slipping on the hilt; felt himself about to drop, and no longer cared. No longer cared about anything.

A hand shot out from the edge of a walkway and grabbed Rhiannon by the wrist. Shader gasped, not believing what he saw as Nameless, lying on his belly, held onto her, the muscles in his arm bulging, veins sticking out like they were going to burst. His other hand gripped the railing, anchoring him against the infernal force tugging them down. He arched his back and pulled, and inch by inch brought Rhiannon up onto the walkway.

The gladius jerked sideways, twisting itself in Shader's grip until it aimed like a spear at the sentroid holding Gandaw. With a sudden surge of movement, it shot forward with Shader clinging on, legs swinging crazily, and embedded itself in the silver sphere. The sentroid shook and sparked and burst into flame—and Gandaw fell, his filaments ripping free of the statue and flailing around him as they retracted into his armor. Grapnels snagged a railing and reeled him to the safety of a walkway. Down below, the chasm trembled and then snapped shut like the jaws of a monstrous beast.

Almost immediately, Gandaw turned to a console and made a series of swipes and taps on its mirror. The Statue of Eingana was slowly lowered toward him, the crown atop its head still ablaze with sparks that stretched into strings of fire that fed into the base of the black sphere.

The gladius matched Eingana's descent, and Shader reached out to grab her. Pain jolted through his fingers and up his arm. He cried out and could only watch helplessly as Gandaw plucked the statue from the air.

"Seconds to go!" he raved. "Seconds!"

Amber light blasted from Eingana's maw. The gladius came up to meet it with a wall of golden radiance. Where the two forces collided, a keening wail arose. At first, Shader thought it was coming from the gladius, but then he realized there were two cries. Brother and sister. Eingana and the Sword of the Archon, forced to fight, and both of them screaming.

Above them, the black sphere ballooned and shuddered.

The filaments reemerged from Gandaw's armor and penetrated the statue. Instantly, it was awash with amber, and then it burst forth like a small sun. Shader was thrown back, but golden effulgence exploded from the gladius and met Eingana's assault force for force. Where the two powers collided, flames erupted, burgeoning into a conflagration that consumed Shader and Gandaw but burned neither. The metal of the walkway, however, was white hot and smoldering, and Shader glimpsed Nameless and Rhiannon sheltering at the edge of the flames. There was nothing they could do. It was his fight alone now. His and Gandaw's.

"Deadlocked," Gandaw said, face rapt with concentration. "Stay like this and you'll perish in the Unweaving." He glanced up at the black sphere shaking violently and growing denser by the second. "Let me raise the walls, shield us. Otherwise we'll all die."

"Isn't that what you want?" Shader said.

"Not me," Gandaw wailed. "Not me!"

Shader willed the gladius to do more, willed it from defense to attack. It bucked in his grip, shrieked, and it was all he could do to hang on.

"Please," Gandaw cried. "Lay down the sword!"

"Don't do it, laddie!" Nameless yelled from beyond the conflagration. All Shader could see of him was a blur in the haze.

"No, Deacon," Rhiannon said, a wavering form beside the dwarf. "Don't stop!"

A low drone came from the black sphere, growing in volume. The sound reverberated through Shader's bones, pressed on his skull, threatening to crush it.

Seconds remaining... Seconds, and he wasn't ready; wasn't ready for oblivion.

"You're a man of faith," Gandaw said, barely visible through the blaze coming off the statue in his grasp. "If you can't trust me, place your faith in your god. Lower the sword."

Shader felt himself inching the blade down, felt the gladius slackening off its resistance to Eingana's onslaught.

"No!" Rhiannon cried.

"Fight, laddie. Fight!"

But it was fighting that had given the lie to what he was, wasn't it? Fighting he'd always been too scared to give up, in case it put him at the mercy of others. In case he suffered the pain of humiliation. In case he lost control.

"Do nothing and we all die," Gandaw said.

Was that so bad? What benefit was it for a few to survive when all the worlds were going to perish? He remembered the old man in the cell, and the calm he radiated as he went to his god. Felt the old man's hope as he passed on what he most treasured.

Shader's fingers went to the pendant around his neck. What was it Thumil had said back at Arx Gravis? *Surrender yourself to this Nous of yours... let him carry you.*

He shut his eyes and prayed for the strength to let go, the courage to abandon himself. But it wasn't to Nous that he prayed, nor to Ain the Unknowable. It was to the lady on the pendant.

He released the gladius, and it clanged to the floor.

Its light died instantly. Eingana's attack petered out as Gandaw whirled around to the console and swiped across its mirror. With a rattling hum, the walls of the chamber began to rise, and when Gandaw made a few more passes across the mirror, they raced upward and closed the chamber tight against the Unweaving.

The instant the ceiling snapped shut, obliterating sight of the black mass that was about to end all things, Gandaw turned back in triumph—and sent a wall of amber flame straight at Shader.

The gladius shot up of its own accord, whirling, spinning, drawing the fire into itself, wrapping itself in the flames. A sound like a gasp came from the statue, and for a moment, Eingana's attack faltered.

"Finish him!" Gandaw yelled.

The hum from beyond the apex rose to the roar of a thousand waterfalls. The walls of the chamber warped and buckled, and time seemed to stand still.

Gandaw's mouth opened and closed with macabre slowness.

"Yeeeessss!" slewed from his lips in an endless stream.

Wrong! Shader heard Aristodeus's voice in his head, laced with the same criticism as during all those years of lessons. Never satisfied. Nothing was ever good enough. *Wrong decision!*

But all he felt was disappointment pitting in his stomach, the disillusionment of misplaced faith.

The sword stopped spinning and aligned itself, tip facing Gandaw.

Faster than everything else in the room, as if it were immune to the new constraints on time, it shot forward.

Gandaw cried out and ponderously raised his arms, but the sword wasn't aiming for him.

With a thunderous crack, it embedded itself in the heart of the statue.

Eingana shuddered, and the glare of her eyes and fangs went out. Tendrils of golden light wrapped her in their embrace, and amber feelers of her own came out to intertwine with them. The serpent's body began to swell. Stony scales cracked and sloughed off; long-fossilized jaws closed, and a forked tongue flicked between them.

"No! What have you done?" Gandaw cried.

Eingana grew and grew and grew until her monstrous head swayed high above Gandaw. She dashed the sparking crown against the ceiling, crushing the filaments linking her to the black sphere, and then, with a second blow, the crown shattered. The chamber stilled, and from outside came nothing but a deathly silence.

The Archon's sword jutting from Eingana's body sank deeper, until black scales closed over it.

Gandaw took a step back, but Eingana's tail whipped around his legs and held him fast. Coil upon coil, she wrapped around his body, until all that was visible was his head, aghast beneath its crystal helm. His lips moved fast now, and a babbling stream of pleas left them, and then Eingana's jaws opened and her head snapped down. Gandaw screamed, and greenish fluids sprayed as she crunched down on him and swallowed him whole.

Shader watched in fascinated horror as a bulge passed down the serpent's throat, deeper and deeper through her sinuous body. Amber eyes turned toward him, and he braced himself for a similar fate. The serpent's head bobbed atop its neck, and it seemed to Shader that she nodded. Then, with a flick of her tail, she vanished, taking the Sword of the Archon with her.

Shader sank slowly to his knees. Numbness spread from his mind to his limbs, and he hung his head in exhaustion. His hands were shaking, and the rims of his eyes burned with the need to shed tears.

Rhiannon's hand on his shoulder made him look up. She let out a long sigh and managed a tight smile.

Nameless kept his distance, a morose figure encased in his black helm, his squat bulk hanging languid.

"Why didn't you tell us?" Rhiannon said, her voice so soft Shader wasn't certain he'd heard her right. Her fingers stiffened on his shoulder, and she let go. "Thought you'd given in. You should have bloody told us."

Mephesch's head poked above the walkway, and then he rose into view atop a floating disk. He was beaming from ear to ear, but after catching Shader's eye, his expression turned sober, and he stepped off the disk and set about swiping symbols on the console mirror Gandaw had so recently been using. With a clunk and a hum, the ceiling snapped open a crack, and then the walls began to sink once more toward the floor.

Shader shielded his eyes against the brilliance from above, but then peeked through the gaps in his fingers. The black sphere was gone, and instead, a ray of sunlight lanced down through the opening, dust mites dancing along its length all the way to the floor of the chamber.

"Least you did it," Rhiannon said. It sounded begrudging at first, but then she said,

"Deacon, you did it." She wouldn't meet his gaze, though, and instead craned her neck to look upward, where the receding walls gave way to skies of brilliant cobalt dotted with gossamer wisps of cloud. High above the Perfect Peak, the twin suns blazed with newfound health and vitality.

As the walls retracted fully, exposing the stark expanse of the Dead Lands, Mephesch hopped back on his disk and descended all the way through the ground floor and down into the roots of the mountain.

Shader forced himself to his feet as greenish light flared out on the open plain. A portal swirled into existence, and a figure stepped out of it. Shader blinked against the glare, seeing little more than a silhouette, but Rhiannon tutted and went to lean out over a railing to watch the figure approaching. Even without seeing him clearly, Shader knew who it was. It was starting to seem that nothing—not even the gaping maw of the Abyss—could stop Aristodeus from returning like a fly to a pile of dung.

Way back past Aristodeus, at the edge of the Sour Marsh, a line of lizard-men spread out, staring up at the pristine sky. One at the front raised an arm toward the mountain, in what Shader took to be a salute. From this distance, the hand looked overly large, and once or twice it sparked. Skeyr Magnus, then, still standing after everything.

Shader waved in acknowledgment. What had brought the lizard-men to the fight, and at such a critical moment? He fingered the old man's pendant, and then wondered if he'd received his answer as a circle opened in the bleached dust of the Dead Lands and Mephesch emerged on his disk. Aristodeus opened his arms and quickened his pace, and the homunculus ran to him. As the two of them walked back to the disk, Rhiannon shouldered her sword and strode past Shader, heading to the steps and climbing down.

Shader was about to follow, when he caught sight of Nameless still standing there. He hadn't moved an inch, and looked every bit like a statue, a memorial to gloom and despair.

"Nameless?" Shader said, walking over to him. He'd taken the full force of one of Gandaw's fireballs to the head. Maybe he was—

Nameless jerked and then shook himself. "Laddie? By the Lords of Arnoch, laddie, you did it!"

Shader hesitated for a moment, and then gripped the dwarf by the wrist and clapped him on the shoulder. "I did nothing." It was the truth. Nameless and Rhiannon had fought tooth and nail and had both nearly been killed in the process; Skeyr Magnus and his lizard-men, too. But when it had come down to it, in the heat of the moment, Shader had frozen. If it hadn't been for the sword…

"I was watching, laddie. I saw just what you did. Shog me for a shogging shogger, but if you'd listened to this stupid old dwarf, we'd have lost everything."

"Listened to you?" Shader said. He had no idea what Nameless was talking about.

"I told you to fight, remember. It's what I'd have done, what I always do. But if you'd gone on fighting, there'd have been no one to break the deadlock, and the worlds would have ended. I see it now, but at the time, I thought you'd failed us. Failed everyone."

Shader had thought the same himself, thought he'd played into Gandaw's hands.

"How did you know?" Nameless said.

Why didn't you tell us? Rhiannon had asked.

Shader looked away, down into the open chamber, where she stood leaning on Callixus's black sword as Aristodeus and Mephesch came up through the floor on the floating disk.

Truth was, he hadn't known. If anything, he'd despaired, or been close to it.

Do nothing, and we all die.

Fight on, same conclusion.

What other choice had there been? It had been purely pragmatic, hadn't it? Selfish, even. At least by complying, by putting the sword down, there had been a slim chance of survival—for himself, Rhiannon, and Nameless, but not for anyone else. Or was it more than that? Had it been Thumil's words that had swayed him? The old man's faith, the image of the lady? It was all such a blur. There was no clarity to what he'd done.

"Thumil told me something before we left Arx Gravis," he said. Maybe he couldn't be sure why he'd acted as he had, but one possibility stemmed from despair and blind luck, whereas the other held the promise of hope; hope that there were other forces at play, that he wasn't the one holding all the cards.

"Only good advice I had from Thumil was to steer clear of Ironbelly's ale," Nameless said.

"He spoke about surrender."

"What?" Nameless spat the word, as if it were an affront.

"Not in battle."

"Ah, well, that's all right, then, laddie. Least I think it is."

"He meant not always needing to be in control. Surrender to Nous, or whoever it is he prayed to. Giving yourself over to a higher power."

Nameless snorted and shook the great helm. "Sounds like a bad idea to me. That's the kind of thing that led to my…" His voice choked off, and he crossed his arms over his chest. After a moment's silence, he said, "The black axe was like that. Don't see myself surrendering to any higher power after what it made me do."

"This is different," Shader said. "A willing surrender, not a…" He didn't know how to say it. Possession? Nameless made it unnecessary, though.

"Old baldilocks was right." He cocked a thumb down below, where Aristodeus was looking up at them expectantly. "This was beyond me. Have to say, laddie, I don't get what you're talking about. The whole thing stinks of madness and deception, but proof's in the pudding, I guess."

"What's that supposed to mean?" Shader asked.

"You were right. I just have a hard time seeing how. Guess that's why you're the savior of the worlds, and I'm just a butcher with too much blood on his hands."

Shader took hold of Nameless' shoulders and looked straight into the eye-slit of the great helm. He intended to show confidence, to offer words of consolation, but the dark eyes that stared back at him were so full of sorrow, so haunted, he wavered and looked away.

"No, my friend," he managed. "If it hadn't been for you"—and Rhiannon—"I'd have never gotten close enough." If it hadn't been for so many others—Shadrak, Albert… And then the full magnitude of it hit him: all the people who'd given so much, first to stop Dr. Cadman, and then the Unweaving: Barek, Huntsman, General Starn, Captain Podesta, Maldark the Fallen… There were too many to name. Even poor, flawed Gaston had ultimately given all he had. Shader only hoped it had been enough.

For a moment, it was clear to him. It wasn't all on his shoulders. Never had been. But more than that, he was filled with the pervading sense that all was well; everything was as it should be; that there was a guiding hand steering the course of the worlds, whether or not he could discern it.

If only it could have stayed like that. If only these revelations didn't flicker away to nothing like an oxygen-starved flame. He clung to the feeling while he could, but even as Nameless clapped him on the back and led the way down the steps toward Aristodeus, Rhiannon, and Mephesch, Shader knew his insight wasn't complete.

THE PARTING OF WAYS

THE WAGON PULLED up just shy of a crater-pocked plain that stretched away from the road.

"This it?" Shadrak said. "This where you left it?" He scratched inside the sling holding his injured arm tight to his chest. Shogging thing was infested with lice, he was sure of it. Either that, or Albert had cut it from Fargin's shite-encrusted loin cloth. Amounted to about the same thing, though, he reckoned.

Buck looked over his shoulder from the driver's seat. "It's where I found him."

Albert didn't look so sure, sat in the back with Shadrak, a half-eaten pastry clutched in his pudgy hand. He stood and turned a slow circle, using his spare hand as a visor. "They all look the same to me," he said.

"Yeah," Buck said. "Once you've seen one boreworm hole, you've seen 'em all."

Shadrak grunted as he rolled forward from the crate he'd been using as a chair and found his feet. Pain lanced down his arm, all the way to the fingers. He bit his lip and grimaced. Shog, he hated being injured. Once he'd stubbed his toe kicking in some shogger's door. Blasted thing had swollen the size of a sausage and made him hobble for weeks. Hadn't done the target no good, though. He'd still got a bullet through the back of the skull; waste of a bullet, but there weren't no way he was gonna hop after him. Injury like that to his dignity weren't the kind that would ever heal.

"Find it," he said to Albert.

"You find it," Albert said, taking a bite of pastry and making more noise than a cow chewing the cud.

Shadrak knew it was the pain, knew it was the annoyance of being hurt and all, but he was right out of patience. A couple of day's practice, and he was as good with the left hand as the right. He drew his pistol, twirled it once on his finger, and took aim.

Albert got the message clear as mud, without another word spoken. Shadrak gave a satisfied nod; reckoned he was a dab hand at non-verbal communication.

Cramming the rest of the pastry in his gob, Albert shuffled to the end of the wagon bed and sat on his arse so he could get down. The wagon bucked when he dropped off the end, the horse nickered, and Fargin cursed. Then Albert was trudging off over the plain like a chastised kid, waving his arms and swinging his hips. He blundered first one way, then the next, without a shogging clue where to look. Suddenly, he stopped and waved excitedly, then squealed and ran off toward a hole. Shadrak could just about make out a brown-stained piece of cloth fluttering in the breeze that Albert dashed toward and snatched out of the air. Another one of Fargin's?

"Yes!" Albert cried back at him. "Papa's hanky! Now I know we're in the right place."

He skipped ahead like the other sort of kid—the one who's just got what he wanted for his birthday—and rebounded as if he'd hit a wall, landing flat on his back.

"What the shog?" Buck said, looking up from attaching a feedbag to the horse's nose.

"Reckon he found it," Shadrak said.

"Year but what? I don't see nothing."

"Make sure you keep it that way," Shadrak said, pointing the gun at him before holstering it.

"I'm looking the other way," Buck said, "even if there ain't nothing to be seen."

Shadrak leapt from the wagon and winced at the jolt of pain from his shoulder. He trudged over to Albert and started feeling in front of him with his fingers splayed out.

"Thanks for helping me up," Albert mumbled as he stood and brushed himself down.

"Bad arm," Shadrak said, without pausing in his search.

"Only one," Albert said. "Nothing wrong with the other. Unless you're telling me it's numb from too much—"

"Got it!" Shadrak said, finding the invisible recess and pressing the button.

The door slid open to reveal a rectangle of stark light hanging in midair.

Before he could step across the threshold into the plane ship, a voice spoke in his head—a voice like the rustle of dry leaves.

"I need you here, Shadrak."

"Shog you," Shadrak replied. "I done my part. You got no hold on me now."

"What's that?" Albert said. "What did you say?"

Shadrak glared at him then turned away and whispered, "I'm finished with you, understand?"

"You're finished when I release you," the Archon replied in his mind. "The first threat has been eliminated, but there is a bigger plan, and a great deal of… work for one such as you. You are contracted, Shadrak. Your life is owed to me."

Why didn't the shogger show himself? He might've been powerful, but he weren't no god, not if what the bald bastard said was right, not to mention what the Archon had said himself. Shot to the head might do for him, and even if it didn't, it would be worth the try just to piss him off.

"Do not fret," the Archon continued. "I will grant you some leeway."

"Suppose you're leaving, then," Albert said from behind. "I can't persuade you to—"

Shadrak held up a hand for quiet. "Leeway?" he muttered. "What's that s'posed to mean?"

"Stay here. Stay in New Jerusalem. I will call upon your talents from time to time, but other than that, do as you please."

"And the plane ship?"

"Use it to re-stock, but no more than that. Try to flee, and there will be grave consequences. Very grave."

"Yeah? Such as?"

"Kadee," the Archon said. "Death is not the end it once was. You know that, don't you, from the Anglesh Isles, when I permitted you to speak with her?"

"Where is she, then?" Shadrak hissed. "Harm her, and I'll shogging kill you."

"You lack the means."

Much as it was tempting to put him to the test, that wasn't Shadrak's way. He didn't know enough about the Archon yet; he still needed to watch and learn. That pretty much made his mind up for him.

"Leaving?" he said, turning back to Albert. "You must be joking. Thought you had a proposition for me?"

Albert stared dumbly at him for an instant, and then his eyes lit up. "Taking over the guilds?" he said. "You're in?"

"Wait here," Shadrak said as he ducked into the rectangle of light. "I need some supplies. With any luck, I'll find another of those long-gun things, like the one I shogging dropped atop the Homestead. And Albert…"

"Yes?"

"Not a word to Fargin."

Scut like that couldn't be trusted to keep his mouth shut, but when the time was right, he'd make the perfect kingpin: easy as shog to put the frighteners on, and thick as two short planks.

***

There should have been a sense of triumph, of jubilation, but for two days Shader had prayed and prayed and prayed, and he'd met with nothing but aridity. Had he really expected a response from the woman on the pendant? Had he really expected some deeper insight from the Liber—maybe even the faintest glimmer of the fabled golden thread?

His eyes were sore from poring over the text with only the flickering light of an overhead strip of crystal to read by, but at least he'd found something to go on: Causa Salutis, the inscription on the pendant, appeared in one of the more obscure passages in the Second Book of Unveilings, toward the end of the Liber.

That particular book had always struck him as a confusion of mythological images that had no authoritative interpretation. It was seldom, if ever, read at public worship, and yet Ludo had studied it assiduously, as if that's where he hoped to pick up the first strands of the golden thread. "The cause of our salvation will be," is how the passage translated from the Aeternam, "the Immaculata"—the immaculate one—"who crushes the deceiver beneath her heel." It was a good start to assume the passage referred to the woman on the pendant, but if Shader hoped to find out more than that, he was bitterly frustrated. If there were a hermeneutic that could shed light on the passage, it was beyond him. As an Elect knight, he'd been grounded in theology, but not enough to wrestle with the deeper mysteries. He wasn't even sure if the Adepti and Exempti had the knowledge he sought. If only Ludo had been there to ask.

Mephesch had set them up with rooms on the level beneath Gandaw's control center. Shader's was spartan, purely functional—a steel-walled square with a chrome wash basin and a shelf made from some malleable gray material that served as a bed. It molded itself to his shape when he lay upon it, and though his sleep wasn't restful, it was at least comfortable.

He'd given up trying to speak with Nameless. The dwarf had grown sullen and withdrawn, and for the most part stayed behind the locked door of his chamber. Rhiannon was little better. Whatever relief she'd shown at the thwarting of the Unweaving had quickly evaporated into a simmering silence. She could barely bring herself to look at Shader, never mind talk. Given the choice, Shader would have gone straight home, only that was in Aristodeus's hands, and he didn't appear to be in any hurry.

Coupled with which, Shader no longer knew where home was. He'd not had the breathing space to give it much thought. He could hardly go back to Oakendale after abandoning the White Order, and the brothers at Pardes made no bones about not wanting him back. What did that leave him? Britannia? With Jarl dead and Gralia cloistered with the sisters on the Isle of Vectisin, there was nothing for him there. That really only left Aeterna, but after absconding with the Sword of the Archon, even if it had worked out for the greater good, would the Templum still want him? And with the shattered state of his faith, would he even want to go back, return to the life of the Elect? There was always the priesthood, he supposed, but it was for Nous to give vocations, or at the very least, it was a decision of the Templum. Was it possible to be a priest and not share the staunch faith of the luminaries? Mind you, unless Tajen, Narcus, and the others he'd met in the Abyss were all simply parts of Shader's deception, they'd not exactly ended up rewarded for their faith.

But in spite of his doubts, in spite of his failures with prayer, he knew of no other way. If he dug deep enough, if he joined Ludo's quest for the golden thread, maybe he'd find something worth looking for. The alternative was too dispiriting to consider, a darkness too absolute to bear.

When he was there, Aristodeus seemed to spend all his time in Gandaw's chambers, rooting through his personal laboratories, and making himself at home as the new lord of the Perfect Peak. But he still continued to come and go like he always had, never lingering in one place for more than a few hours. It had been the story of his life since Shader first met him, always breaking off mid-lesson and leaving no sign as to where he'd gone. Shader had grown to expect it, but after what Gandaw had said before sending the white tower back into the jaws of the chasm, he was starting to suspect a more sinister reason for the disappearances. Was the philosopher really in the grip of the Demiurgos, trapped in the Abyss, yet somehow managing to escape for short periods? A projected image, yet at the same time solid and capable of delivering stinging blows with a practice sword, as Shader had experienced as a child? It was something Shader meant to ask him about, if ever he got the opportunity. Aristodeus had been scathing about Gandaw's theory, but he'd also looked uncomfortable. Had he been deceived all along, or was he as in control of the situation as he always seemed to be?

And Gandaw himself... Why did Shader feel no satisfaction that he'd finally been defeated? At the end, the Technocrat had cut such a pathetic figure, desperately pleading for an alliance so that he didn't perish in his own Unweaving. And the deception, the betrayals by the homunculus, Mephesch... did that make Gandaw just another victim of the Demiurgos? Did that go any way toward mitigating his guilt? Maybe Shader would never know. Gandaw's was a long and complicated history, riddled and infected with influences from the homunculi and even the Liche Lord of Verusia, Otto Blightey himself. It wasn't just pity Shader felt, or even misplaced empathy; it was more a sense of foreboding, like they had been stripping away layer upon layer of evil—first Cadman, then Gandaw—only to find a denser, more insidious malevolence beneath it. Peel away enough layers, and there was little doubt as to what you'd find at the core: the Demiurgos, waiting, watching, manipulating from the very heart of the Abyss.

When the knock came at his door, Shader thought it might be Nameless, then both hoped and feared it was Rhiannon. He rolled off of the shelf-bed and pressed the keyhole symbol on the panel.

As the door slid open, Mephesch looked up at him, a curious twinkle in his pebbly eyes.

"Aristodeus would like to see you."

The homunculus turned on his heel and walked away, as if Shader had no choice but to follow. Given the likelihood Aristodeus was the only one with the power to return him to Earth, Shader thought that was probably right. Without Shadrak's plane ship, there was unlikely to be any other way back, and much as Aethir intrigued him, he didn't feel like he belonged here. He could almost feel the weight of the Earth tugging at him, and the more he thought about it, Aeterna was where he needed to be.

They took a disk up toward the top of the cone that had been Gandaw's control room. Mephesch led Shader out onto a walkway and through a concealed door into a scarolite-lined vestibule. The door opposite was made of the same green-flecked black, and there was no panel beside it.

Mephesch spoke into his vambrace: "We're here."

The door slid open, and they entered an octagonal chamber with desks and screens set against every wall. Nameless was reclining on a padded black chair in the center of the room. His hauberk was up around his waist, and a tube ran into his stomach from a clear bag on a metal stand. Green liquid passed from the bag along the tube with a steady drip, drip, drip.

Rhiannon had her feet up on a desk and her arms crossed under her breasts, in a way that plumped them up, made them look swollen. Shader averted his gaze the instant he realized it had been drawn.

Aristodeus was seated at a desk on the other side of the room from her, rattling through some glass tubes in a case, occasionally taking one out to look at more closely. Directly above him, suspended in midair, was a long crystal case, from within which Shader could just about make out the dark form of an axe.

Aristodeus spun round on his chair. He held up a test tube to the light glaring down from an overhead crystal. Its contents were inky and vaporous, one moment coalescing around the top of the tube, the next striking out for the bottom or dashing against the glass of the sides.

"Cadman?" Aristodeus said.

Mephesch nodded. "And the others contain—"

"Later, Mephesch, later. Fascinating as all this may be, there are rather more pressing matters." He carefully put the tube back in the case and dismissed Mephesch with a flick of his fingers.

"Now, Shader," he said as the door slid shut behind the homunculus, "I expect you're wondering what I've been up to these past two days."

Rhiannon snorted, causing Aristodeus to shoot her a glare.

"Not really. I'm more interested in getting back."

Rhiannon stiffened slightly. She brushed her hair out of her face and looked at him casually, disinterestedly, almost.

"To Earth?" Aristodeus said. "Figured as much, which is why I've been working with the homunculi to find a way."

"You've not had any trouble popping up here, there, and everywhere before," Shader said. "Why now?"

"I travel from A to B," Aristodeus said, "and the effort is prodigious. More so when there are passengers." He cocked a thumb at Rhiannon. "Given that we are currently at B, it would be necessary to return to A prior to predicating a new B."

Rhiannon dropped her boots from the desktop and stood. The hilt of Callixus's black sword hung from a new scabbard at her hip. "What he's saying is that he'd have to take you to his poxy white tower first and give you the bull about not stepping outside."

"Because A's the Abyss?" Shader said. "You travel back and forth from the Abyss?"

Aristodeus closed his eyes and took a deep breath. "Don't you worry about that. That is a problem for minds far older and wiser than yours. It's an ages-long campaign, Shader, a battle of wills, but given our progress here, I'd say I have the upper hand."

"Can I get up now?" Nameless asked in a dull voice.

Aristodeus went over to the stand and squeezed the bottom of the bag. "A few more dregs and you'll be good to go."

"I would have taken you back by now," Aristodeus said to Shader, "only there was a slight problem."

"He can take me there," Rhiannon said, "but not you."

"Why?" Shader said. "I've been to the Abyss before and lived to tell the tale. Why not now?"

"Because you are my anchor," Aristodeus said. He took out his pipe and started to fill it. "Last time you were there, it was nearly my undoing. If the boy hadn't gotten you out—"

"Sammy?" Rhiannon said.

Aristodeus gave her a tight-lipped smile, and a confusion of emotions played across her face as he went on. "There was distance, if you can call it that, between us on that occasion, but both of us so close together in my tower..." He popped the pipe in his mouth and spoke around the stem. "Game over."

"Why? Why not with Rhiannon?"

Aristodeus fumbled about in his robe pockets and raised his eyebrows hopefully before cursing and putting the pipe away. "Why is it no one ever has a light?"

Shader's fingers touched the box of matches in his pocket, but he chose to say nothing. Why should he lift a finger to help the bald bastard, after all he'd put them through?

"Well?" Rhiannon said. "You gonna tell him? How come I can go with you, and he can't?"

Something was communicated between them. Shader had no idea what it was, but it made him edgy, and something else. He fixed Aristodeus with a hard stare and chewed his bottom lip. It was ridiculous, he knew, but he felt the pinch of jealousy.

"Too risky," Aristodeus said. "Which is why I've had to come up with another way." He turned to Shader. "What I mean is, it's too risky you and I being in the same space within the Abyss at once. Think of it like chess. I am the king—"

"And Shader's your queen?" Rhiannon said.

"Lassie," Nameless said from his reclining chair. "Behave."

"That is not what I was trying to say," Aristodeus said. "My point is, I cannot place all my eggs in one basket. I might have the advantage at the moment, but the slightest miscalculation, the smallest error—"

Rhiannon sneered.

"Right now," Shader said, "I couldn't give a damn if you win or lose. Just get me home, and then find yourself some new pawns."

"Yeah," Rhiannon said, "I'm sick of it, too. Maybe you can drop us both off in Sahul."

Aristodeus whirled on her but then instantly softened, speaking in a cloying tone. "I would prefer it if you stayed here, at least until..."

Rhiannon's eyes dropped to the floor, and for a long moment an uncomfortable silence hung over the chamber.

"All right," Aristodeus finally said, "I suppose I could countenance that, if it's to Oakendale you return, and if you stay out of trouble."

"What's it to you?" Shader asked. "She'll go wherever she wants, whether you like it or not."

Red flooded Aristodeus's face, and he clenched his fists. "This is not about megalomania, Shader! Can't you see that? Did I waste all those years trying to educate you, teaching you to think? Gandaw was the control freak, not me. Do you think I want to fight this battle? Do you? Have you any idea how long it's gone on for, how many centuries? I am pivotal, Shader. Understand? Pivotal. And I am getting close."

Shader narrowed his eyes and kept his voice low, full of threat. "Close to what?"

"Freedom, of course. And after that, turning the tables on the Demiurgos and sending him back where he came from."

"The weight of the universe on your shoulders, eh, laddie?" Nameless said. "Felt like that myself once."

"This is not the same!" Aristodeus said. He wrenched the tube out of the bag and rapidly coiled it up and lay it on Nameless' belly. "Tape," he muttered. "Tape, tape, bloody tape." He located what he was looking for on a desk and began to tear off strips from a spool, which he used to stick the coiled tube to Nameless' skin. "There, you can go now. Just remember, once a month—"

"Yes, yes, laddie, back here for dinner. How could I ever forget?" Nameless jumped up from the chair and tugged down his hauberk. "Well, with your permission—" He turned the great helm on Aristodeus. "—think I'll see what Pellor has to offer. Heard it's a festering backwater and a den of thieves, but that just tells me I won't get bored. Who knows, if it doesn't work out, might even head back to New Jerusalem, maybe even catch up with the little fellow."

"Shadrak?" Rhiannon asked. She looked at Aristodeus. "Please don't tell me you're sending that scutting shogger back with us."

"Not one of mine," Aristodeus said. "I couldn't care less what he does."

"Speak for yourself," Shader said. "If it hadn't been for Shadrak, you'd not be standing here. Neither would the rest of us."

Nameless offered his hand, and Shader took it. "Glad we see eye to eye on that, laddie. Credit where credit's due, eh? And don't forget what you did, either. Makes this old dwarf proud to have been there with you."

Shader's instant reaction was to withdraw, to deny he'd done anything save look on as the gladius put an end to Gandaw's enslavement of Eingana, but Nameless tightened his grip and drew him into a hug.

"You did good, laddie, and if anyone tells you otherwise, they'll have my axe to... Shog, the blasted thing broke." He turned the eye-slit of his great helm up to where the black axe lay encased in crystal. "Don't suppose..."

"No!" Aristodeus said, rushing over and ushering him toward the door.

"Just joshing," Nameless said, tapping the side of his helm. "The ol' bucket's still working."

"Even so," Aristodeus said, "it's not a matter to joke about."

The door slid open, and Nameless stood there for a moment, head bowed. "No, laddie, you're right there. No joking matter." He suddenly looked up. "You have a lead, though? So we can destroy the axe and get this thing off my head. I thought you said—"

"Yes," Aristodeus said, "but you'll have to be patient. There are a million and one other things to do, but I'm already working on it."

"Till we meet for dinner, then," Nameless said. He waved at Rhiannon and gave Shader a nod of respect as he stepped outside, and then the scarolite door slid shut behind him.

"Right," Aristodeus said. "Work to do, and time, as they say, waits for no one. Well, that's not strictly true, is it, my dear?"

Rhiannon rolled her eyes.

Time? Was that it? Was that why Rhiannon had changed so much in a matter of hours? "You've been training her, haven't you? In the Abyss." He said it like an accusation.

"It's called turning adversity to one's advantage," Aristodeus said. "Gandaw—or rather Eingana—might have put me into the Demiurgos's clutches, but there is no time in the Abyss, what with it being across the mouth of the Void. You can hardly blame me for making the most of it."

"How long?" Shader looked to Rhiannon for an answer, but she merely shrugged. "How long have you been training?" When she ignored his question, he turned back to Aristodeus. "What do you want her for?"

"Insurance, in case you screwed up."

"Fat lot of good that did," Rhiannon said. "I killed a few metal crabs and then got snatched by that silver sphere."

"Yes, well, thankfully Shader did what I hoped he would, so the effort wasn't entirely wasted. You may have bought him some time."

"More than that," Shader said. "If it hadn't been for Rhiannon and Nameless, I'd never have gotten anywhere near Gandaw."

"Bollocks," Rhiannon said. "But don't get sidelined. He hasn't told you everything yet."

"Nor shall I," Aristodeus said. "Suffice it to say that I always have a fallback plan, and in this case, given that you somehow managed to lose the Sword of the Archon, I'm glad to have two more irons in the fire."

"Nameless?" Shader said. "He's one of them, right?"

"Maybe," Aristodeus said, "but Rhiannon will play the greater part. Don't take that as being let off the hook, though. You are still my weapon of choice. Once I find the sword, you'll be hearing from me."

"Well, let's just hope you don't find it," Shader said.

Aristodeus glowered for an instant but then masked his irritation with a smug grin. "With or without it, you may still prove useful. I'll have to see. In the meantime, Mephesch is outside. He'll take you to the particle chamb... the portal room. They've worked hard, the little beggars, modifying technology Gandaw used to to retrieve the statue from the Homestead. Just tell him your destination, and he'll plot a course. One good thing about Gandaw, he left us eyes and ears everywhere."

"Good," Rhiannon said. "So, even a shithole like Oakendale should be easy to find, right?" She cocked her head at Shader, and for the first time in a long while, she smiled. "Fancy a beer at the Griffin?"

Shader stared blankly at her for a second. Beer? That would be good. Or maybe something stronger, after all he'd been through. But the Griffin? Oakendale? He tried to read her, but in her eyes there was nothing but pain and something else... anguish, maybe. Possibly even fear.

"I'd love to," he managed, "but I'm not going to Oakendale."

She shrugged and did her best to look nonchalant. "Where, then? Sarum? Or you heading back to Pardes for another go?"

He shook his head and gave her a wry smile. "Aeterna," he said.

Rhiannon gasped, and her hand went to to her stomach, as if she were going to be sick.

"I will see you again," he put in hurriedly, but she waved his words away.

"Why? Why Aeterna?" She drew in a deep breath and ran her hand over her head.

"You all right?" Aristodeus asked, moving to hover over her like an over-protective father.

"Fine," she said.

"There are things I need to find out," Shader said. "And there's something I should have done a long time ago."

"I may still have need of you," Aristodeus said. "Don't lose sight of that. Just need to find that blasted sword or something else to get the job done."

"Forget it," Shader said, fingering the pendant beneath his tattered surcoat. "I've made my decision. No more fighting. Not for you, not for anyone." He held up a hand when the philosopher tried to protest. "No more words, Aristodeus. I'm done with you. I'm off to Aeterna, and that's final. And who knows, if they can forgive me for running off with the sword in the first place, and if Adeptus Ludo can set me straight about one or two things, I might even—"

"No," Aristodeus muttered, as if he'd finally been taken by surprise. "You can't. You're not cut out to be a priest. You're a fighter, Shader. You know that. You always have been."

"Yes, well, you made sure of that, didn't you?" Shader said.

Rhiannon was staring at him open-mouthed, and her eyes had darkened to wells of emptiness that, even if he relented and went back to Sahul with her, he knew he could never fill. They'd both come so far since he'd almost given up the consecrated life for her; they'd changed so much. She'd rebuffed his advances for the sake of his soul, so she'd said, but in reality it was Aristodeus again, manipulating behind the scenes. So much suffering, so much heartache, and all so the philosopher could gain an advantage in a centuries-long struggle with the Demiurgos.

He reached out a hand to touch her cheek, wiped away a single tear with his thumb. Her lips were trembling, but he couldn't do anything to comfort her. He was no longer even sure if he wanted to. Damaged goods is what they were now, and no one but Aristodeus was to blame.

"Come on," Shader said, placing a hand on Rhiannon's shoulder. He half-expected her to swipe it off, but she left it there and let him guide her to the door. "We can talk on the way to this portal room."

Now it was Aristodeus's turn to look jealous, and he took a step toward them, but then stopped in his tracks to wipe a bead of sweat from his glistening pate.

The door slid open, and they stepped into the vestibule. Mephesch was waiting for them, an enigmatic smile playing across his face. Shader didn't trust the homunculus as far as he could throw him, but that wasn't his concern. That was a problem for minds older and wiser than his, he thought with bile.

"Do what you must," Aristodeus said, "but when the time is right, I'll call upon you."

"And the answer will still be no," Shader said as the door closed behind them.

Here ends the First Shader Trilogy:
Against the Unweaving

The story picks up in the second trilogy:
Against the Abyss

starting with Shader: Book Four:
The Archon's Assassin…

ABOUT THE AUTHOR

D.P. Prior is the bestselling fantasy author of the Nameless Dwarf and Shader series.

Raised on a diet of old school Sword and Sorcery, and later influenced by the Heroic Fantasy of David Gemmell, the literary epics of Stephen R. Donaldson, and the "grimdark" offerings of Joe Abercrombie, Prior combines the imaginative daring of the old with the realism, tight point of view, and gallows humor of the new.

As well as being a prolific author, D.P.Prior is also an experienced fiction editor with an impressive portfolio of clients (http://homunculuseditingservices.blogspot.com).

He has also worked as a personal trainer, and is a competing member of the US All-Round Weightlifting Association.

Website: http://dpprior.blogspot.com

Twitter: @NamelessDwarf

Facebook: https://www.facebook.com/dpprior

Email D.P. Prior with comments, feedback, questions, and donations of wine: derekprior@yahoo.co.uk

For freebies, special offers, and notification of new releases from D.P. Prior, please subscribe to the New Release Mailing List: http://on.fb.me/1bDEBXz

ALSO BY D.P. PRIOR

The Nameless Dwarf

The Ant-Man Of Malfen
The Axe Of The Dwarf Lords
The Scout And The Serpent
The Ebon Staff
Bane Of The Liche Lord

The Nameless Dwarf: The Complete Chronicles

Shader

Sword Of The Archon
Best Laid Plans
The Unweaving
The Archon's Assassin
Rise Of The Nameless Dwarf *(forthcoming)*
Saphra *(forthcoming)*

Against The Unweaving: Shader: The Entire First Trilogy

Legends Of The Nameless Dwarf

Book 1: Return Of The Dwarf Lords *(forthcoming)*
Book 2: King Of Arnoch *(forthcoming)*

Carnifex *(forthcoming)*

The Memoires of Harry Chesterton

Thanatos Rising

Printed in Great Britain
by Amazon.co.uk, Ltd.,
Marston Gate.